5
9
10
14
15
S.A.S
975
A A I

THE ILLUSTRATED BOOK OF GUNS

THE ILLUSTRATED BOOK OF GUNS

An illustrated directory of over 1,000 military, sporting, and antique firearms

EDITED BY DAVID MILLER

PUBLISHED BY
SALAMANDER BOOKS LIMITED
LONDON

A SALAMANDER BOOK

Published by
Salamander Books Ltd.
8 Blenheim Court
Brewery Road
London N7 9NY
United Kingdom

A member of the Chrysalis Group plc

ISBN 1 84065 172 5

THE EDITOR

David Miller is a former officer in the British armed forces and has seen service in the Falkland Islands, the Far East, and Europe. He is a noted military historian who has written more than 40 books on weapons and warfare, ancient and modern, and has contributed to many specialist and historical military magazines. For some years after leaving the services he was a staff writer on the *International Defense Review* journal, and an Editor with the Jane's Group of military directory publishers, and is now a full-time defense journalist and commentator.

CREDITS

Project Manager: Ray Bonds
Designer: Megra Mitchell, Mitchell Strange Design
Typeset by SX Composing DTP
Color separation by Studio Tec
Printed and bound in China by Metroprint Ltd

ACKNOWLEDGMENTS

The publishers are grateful for the use of photographs supplied by Terry Gander, Ian V. Hogg, and various manufacturers, including in particular Accuracy International Ltd; Heckler & Koch GmbH; Parker-Hale Ltd; Sturm, Ruger & Co Inc; Steyr-Mannlicher GmbH. The pubishers also acknowledge the assistance provided by the management and staff of various museums at which many of the photographs were taken, including the Buffalo Bill Historical Center, the Civil War Museum, Gene Autry Western Heritage Museum, and Weapons Museum (School of Infantry, Warminster, UK).

ADDITIONAL CAPTIONS

ENDPAPERS: 1, Browning 125 over-and-under 12-gauge shotgun. 2, Italian reproduction of Kentucky flintlock rifle. 3, US 0.30in caliber M1A1 carbine with shoulder stock in folded position. 4, US Browning Model 1919A4 light machine gun. 5, Belgian Galand Velo-Dog revolver. 6, US Ruger Blackhawk revolver set up for All Comers' category competition by Andy Wooldridge of British Shield Gunmakers. 7, German Walther P38 9mm pistol. 8, Italian Franchi SPAS 12 12-gauge shotgun. 9, British Tranter revolver, second model. 10, British Tranter revolver, third model. 11, Lanchester Mark I, a British World War II submachine gun based very closely on the German MP 28. 12, German Bergmann 1897 (No 5) pistol. 13, One of a pair of French LePage holster pistols once owned by Emperor Napoleon. 14, Czechoslovakian Vz 61 Skorpion submachine gun, with butt extended. 15, German Walther TPH self-loading pistol.

PAGE 1: British Webley & Scott 0.38in (9.6mm) Mark IV revolver.
PAGES 2-3: 1, Enfield 7.62mm L1A1 rifle, first British version of the Belgian FAL. 2, German Sauer 7.65mm Model 38R pistol. 3, Russian Makarov 9mm PM pistol. 4, Bayonet for the British L1A1 rifle (picture 1). 5, Colt 0.32in Model 1903 pocket pistol. 6, Armalite 5.56mm AR-15, civilian forerunner of the US military M16 and M16A1 rifles. 7, Spanish Star 9mm self-loading pistol. 8, Kalashnikov 7.62mm AKM folding-butt version of Russian AK-47 rifle. 9, German Walther 7.65mm Model PP pistol. 10, US Remington 0.45in M1911 self-loading pistol, a copy of the Colt M1911. 11, Brazilian Taurus 0.357in Magnum revolver with (12) special tool for stripping and reassembly.
PAGES 4-5: Examples of weapons produced by The Volcanic Repeating Arms Co., a subsidiary of the Smith & Wesson company which produced a variety of carbines and pistols in the United States in the 1350s. All were marketed under the name "Volcanic" except those indicated. 1, 0.38in caliber 30-shot carbine. 2, 0.38in caliber 20-shot carbine. 3, 0.30in caliber 6-shot pistol. 4, 0.30in caliber 6-shot pistol. 5, 0.38in caliber 10-shot pistol. 6, 0.30in caliber 10-shot target pistol. 7, 0.38in caliber 26-shot carbine. 8, S&W 0.38in caliber 10-shot pistol. 9, 0.38in caliber 10-shot pistol. 10, 0.38in caliber 10-shot pistol, with its detachable stock which transformed it into a carbine. 11, 0.38in caliber 10-shot pistol. 12, S&W 0.30in caliber 6-shot pistol. 13, 0.38in caliber 8-shot pistol.

Contents

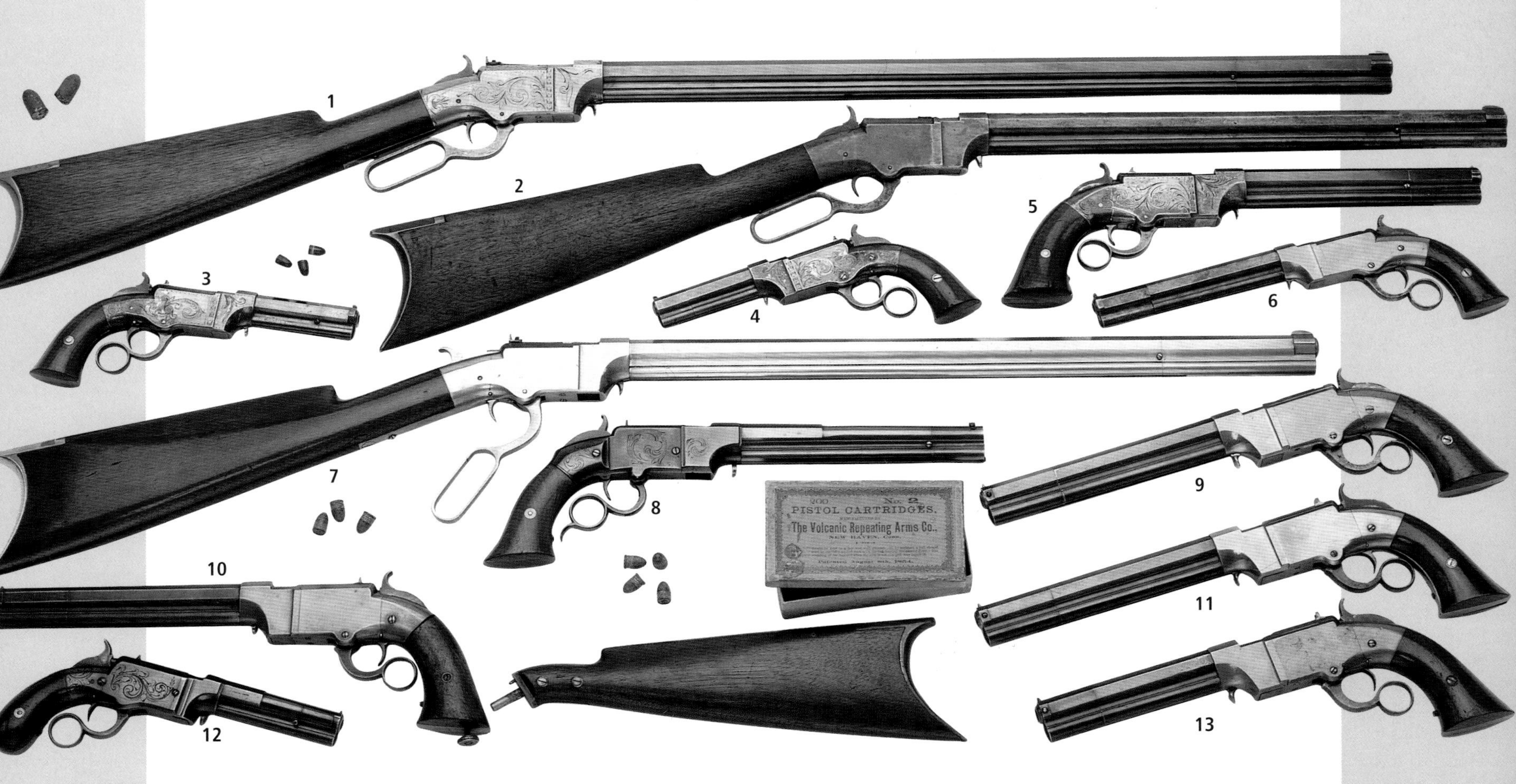

1
2
3
4
5
6
7
8
9
10
11
12
13
200
No. 2
PISTOL CARTRIDGES.
The Volcanic Repeating Arms Co.,
NEW HAVEN, Conn.

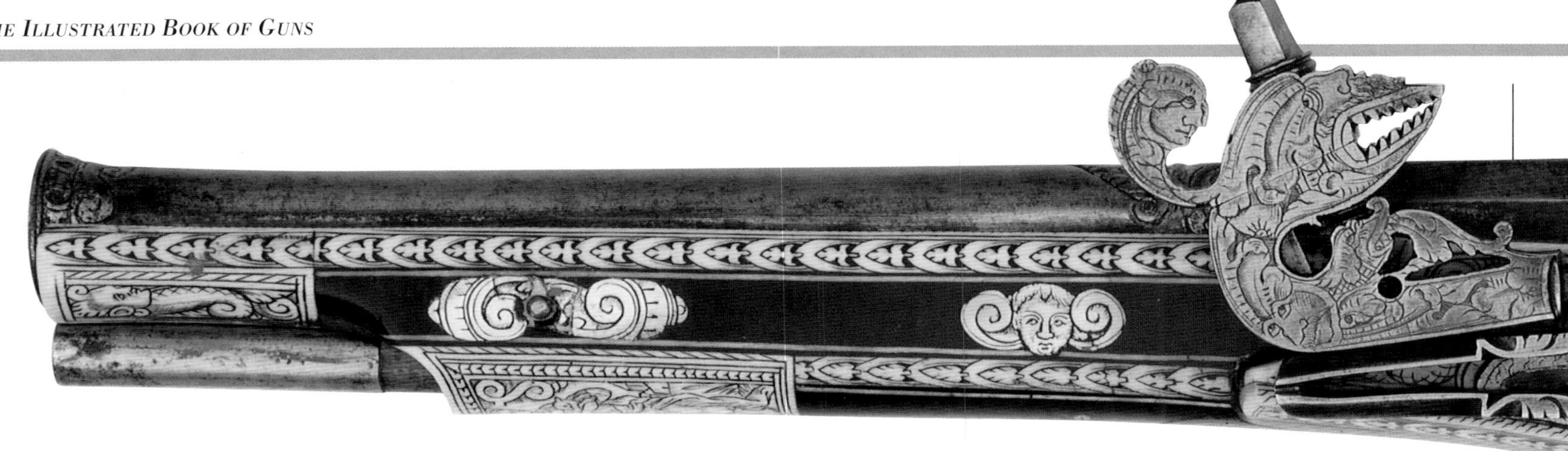

INTRODUCTION

No matter how sophisticated modern weapons systems may be, war – and, not infrequently, so-called peacekeeping as well – usually becomes a combat between small groups of men, fighting each other at very short range, using machine guns, rifles or pistols. Thus, not surprisingly, many people are interested in the weapons which infantry soldiers, para-militaries or policemen may use, but the ever-increasing necessity for security prevents most of them from seeing such small arms close-to. This book seeks to overcome this by enabling readers to study the capabilities, appearance and history of a selection of over one thousand of the most significant small arms, whose origins date from the 16th to the 21st Centuries.

Since sporting and competitive shooting is a source of pleasure to hundreds of thousands of people around the world, a wide selection of important small arms devoted to sporting activities – such as hunting, "black powder" competitions, skeet, and clay pigeon shooting – are included. Of course, many of the arms developed for one use cross-over to other disciplines, examples being competitive precision target shooting and military or para-military sniping.

Firearms have also long held fascination for collectors, the worksmanship, effectiveness, and sheer aesthetic qualities of small arms being subjects for discussion whenever collectors meet. Guns have an attraction that is often coupled with an intrinsic value that will not normally decline, since they are produced in finite numbers when compared with other militaria. This book is bound to be of great interest to collectors as well as enthusiasts, but quite properly there are restrictions on ownership and trading with firearms (and ammunition); these are often severe, may apply even to deactivated weapons, and they vary from country to country, and even from state to state within a country. Collectors, then, who are attracted to the many fine weapons included in this book are advised to check on their national and local firearms laws before attempting to obtain a firearms certificate and acquiring weapons for display or use.

LEFT: An elaborate 16th Century wheel-lock pistol. In these weapons a vice gripping a piece of iron pyrites was lowered until it made contact with a wheel. The wheel was on a spring which was wound and then locked by a sear (latch). Pulling the trigger released the wheel which started to spin, scraping against the iron pyrite stone and generating sparks, using exactly the same principle as in a modern cigarette lighter. In this case, the sparks reached the priming, thus igniting the charge which then drove the bullet up the barrel.

BELOW: From the early 1700s onwards, many weapons designers sought to perfect an automatic weapon which would bring a new dimension of firepower to the battlefield. The breakthrough eventually came with Hiram Maxim's machine gun and an early example is seen here in the hands of a Boer soldier in about 1900. This gas-operated Maxim had an air-cooled barrel and was controlled by means of a single pistol grip, but both water-cooling and the much more effective double spade grips were introduced in the decade following this picture. The Maxim achieved success in the small wars of the late 19th and early 20th Centuries, but its true effect on the battlefield was not realized until the outbreak of World War I when it became one of the most feared of all weapons.

BELOW LEFT: In the United States' Civil War marksmen began to come into their own, one of the most famous units being 1st Regiment of United States Sharpshooters, which was also known as Berdan's Sharpshooters after its commanding officer, Colonel Hiram Berdan. The majority of men were armed with the Sharps 0.52in caliber rifle, as is the man seen here, Private Truman Head, whose nickname was "California Joe." They wore green hats and coats and although their trousers were originally sky-blue (as in the rest of the Union Army) these were later changed to green, as well.

ORDER OF ENTRIES

The weapons have been divided into five categories: pistols and revolvers; rifles and shotguns; submachine guns; light machine guns; and heavy machine guns. In the pistols and revolvers category the entries have been arranged by country (listed alphabetically), then by company and then by approximate date of entry within the company. In the other four categories, the weapons are arranged by country (again listed alphabetically), and then by approximate date of entry into service.

In most cases the category into which a weapon fits is self-evident, but in some cases it is not; for example, some automatic pistols can be fitted with a butt which makes them virtually indistinguishable from a submachine gun. In such cases the weapon is placed in the category to which the basic version belongs.

Many weapons were, or are, produced in a wide number of versions with only the most minor differences between them. Where this is so, every effort had been made to give the specifications and pictures of the most common version, with the various versions described in the text.

Some notes about data are necessary, and the reader is advised also to consult the glossary for explanations of specific terms. Measurements for weapons manufactured before about 1870, particularly caliber, are approximate and even after that date minor variations in dimensions may be found in the various reference books, depending upon who took the measurements and the method used.

- **LENGTH** is overall and, in the case of weapons with folding butts, is the length with butt extended.
- **BARREL LENGTH** is measured from the forward end of the chamber to the muzzle.
- **WEIGHT** is the total weight of the weapon, plus (where applicable) one empty magazine, but less bayonet (if fitted), and without ammunition. In the case of heavy machine guns the weight with tripod is given separately.
- **CALIBER** is as given by the makers. It should be noted that calibers originally given in inches are not always converted to metric measurement.
- **RIFLING** if known or appropriate is given in the specifications list of many entries.
- **OPERATION** is also given in the specifications list of many entries, or described in the text of the entry in other instances.
- **CYCLIC RATE** of fire is the rate at which an automatic weapon would fire if it had a continuous supply of ammunition in unlimited quantities, expressed in rounds per minute (rpm). This is essentially a theoretical figure, since weapons are very rarely required to fire continuously, and, in any case, there are inevitable pauses for reloading, clearing stoppages, and over-heating.
- **MUZZLE VELOCITY** (abbreviated to "Muz vel") is as given by makers and, except with the most modern weapons, is an approximate figure.
- **RANGE** is given only for heavy machine guns which could be fired from a fixed mount – eg, a tripod. In all other weapons the range is not given since it depends to such a large extent on the firer's skill and expertise, the circumstances in which he/she is firing (ie, in the calm on a range or in the face of imminent attack from an approaching enemy). It should also be noted that in the case of weapons being fired on "automatic" the accuracy decreases rapidly with the length of the burst.

TOP: A United States infantryman using his 7.62mm M60 in the light machine gun role, firing from behind a fallen tree "somewhere in Vietnam." The array of ammunition belts are testimony to the weapon's high rate of fire, excellent in its effect on the enemy but which makes keeping such weapons supplied a major problem for the infantry squad.

LEFT: Quite apart from their role in war, rifles and pistols are also widely used for sport, both for target shooting and, as in this example, for trap shooting. All firearms are inherently dangerous, particularly so in the wrong hands, but when properly used and under careful control they can be safe and can give considerable pleasure.

Above: A United States Marine Corps member of Second Reconnaissance Company undergoing parachute training in 1961. His weapon is the 0.45in M3A1 submachine gun, popularly known as the "Grease Gun." Like the British Sten, the M3A1 was designed in a rush at the start of World War II and was intended to be manufactured quickly and easily from readily available materials. Also like the Sten, it was a great success and served with front-line troops well into the 1960s, and with second-line troops and guerrillas right up to the end of the 20th Century.

Left: A British soldier fires his 5.56mm L85A1 rifle, using the bipod for sustained, semi-automatic fire. This was one of a number of rifles introduced in the 1980s and 1990s to use the new NATO standard 5.56 x 45mm round. Also known as the "Small Arms for the 1980s" (SA80) program, the L85A1 has demonstrated that even with modern technology and procurement processes total success in weapons design cannot be guaranteed and it has suffered from a number of well-publicized shortcomings.

Right: The very latest in submachine gun design, the Parker-Hale Personal Defence Weapon (PDW) fires 9mm ammunition and was introduced in 1999. A traditional problem with submachine guns has been "weapon climb" when firing on automatic, but the PDW is claimed to have completely eliminated this, using a new, patented technique. In the configuration seen here it weighs 5.25lb (2.4kg) and the magazine holds 32 rounds.

Pistols & Revolvers

Pistols and revolvers are very close range weapons, intended for either offensive or defensive use by military, para-military, and police forces, but are also popular among sportsmen for competitions and, in some cases, for game shooting. They are designed to be carried in a holster and fired using one hand only, although, obviously, the other hand can be used to steady the weapon, if required.

As the following pages show, the pistol has a history going back to the 16th Century and vast numbers of different designs have been produced to meet a seemingly insatiable demand. For many years, a pistol was, by definition, a single-shot weapon, but designers spent much effort in devising methods of increasing this, initially by fitting two or more barrels. Then gunmakers decided to use a single barrel and to place several bullets (usually six) in a rotating cylinder, thus giving birth to the revolver, which took several decades to perfect, but led to such excellent and reliable weapons as the products of Colt and Smith & Wesson in the United States, and Webley in the United Kingdom.

An alternative approach came with the self-loading automatic pistol, which, as with the machine gun, used the recoil of one bullet to load the next, with the rounds being contained in a magazine which fitted either into the underside of the weapon or into the butt. Some pistols and revolvers were fitted with detachable butts, thus producing weapons which were virtually SMGs.

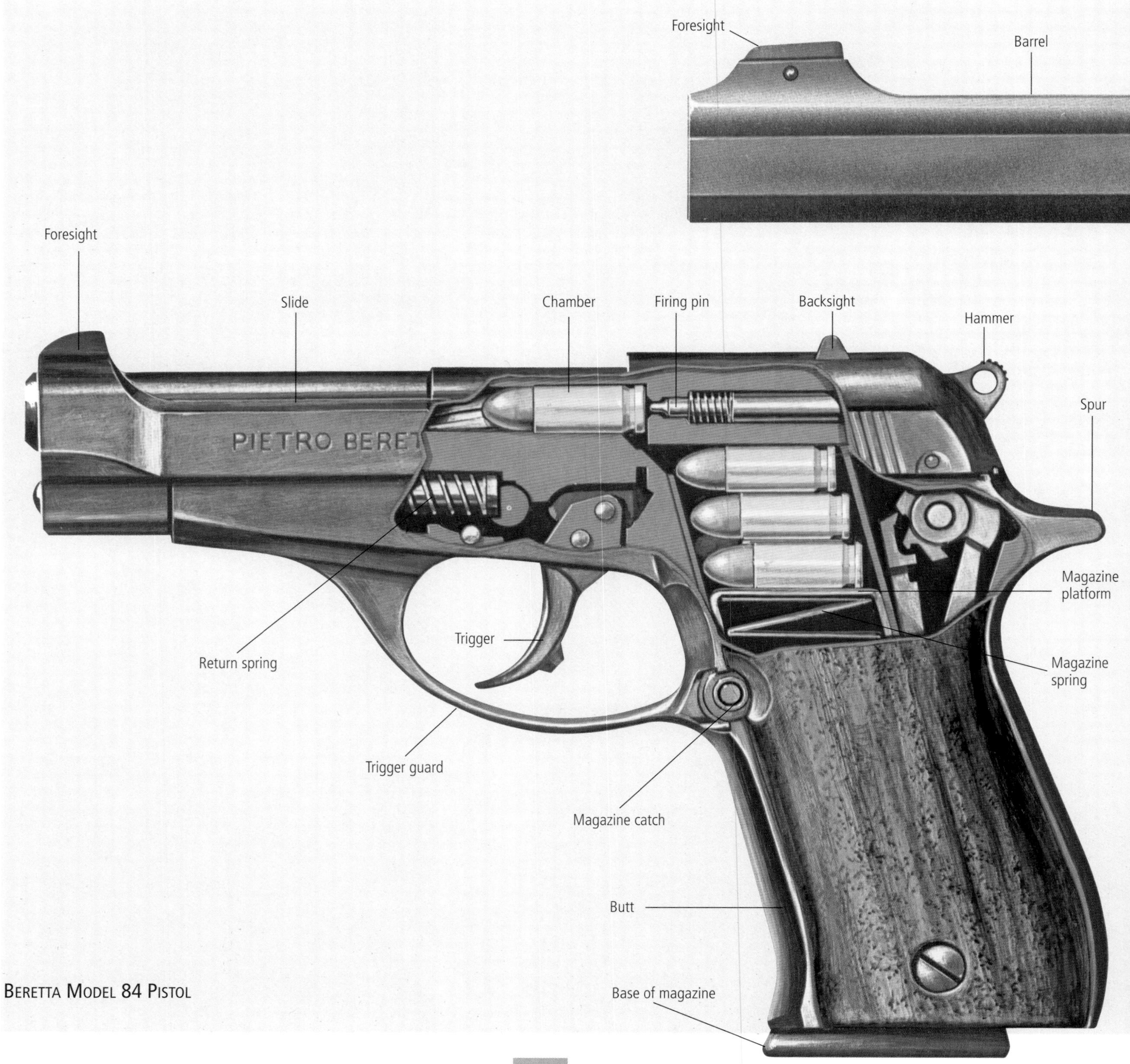

Beretta Model 84 Pistol

Beretta Model 84 Pistol

The Model 84 was chambered to fire the internationally standardized 9mm Short cartridge, and since this round is relatively low-powered, the weapon worked on the simple blowback principle, without any requirement for breech-locking. The firer pulled the slide to the rear by hand, which cocked the hammer, and then released the slide which was driven forward by the spring to chamber a round. To fire a round the trigger was pulled to the rear and the hammer struck the rear of the firing-pin which then hit the cartridge and fired the round. As the round traveled down the barrel the recoil thrust the slide to the rear, compressing the recoil spring as it did so, ejecting the spent case and chambering the next round, and the firing cycle continued. There was a manual safety which could be operated by either left or right hand. The Model 84 had a double-column magazine, but without the long grooves which characterized the magazine of the Model 81. This weapon had an anodized aluminum frame and was considered to be both safe and very reliable mechanically.

Webley and Scott Mark VI Revolver

Almost certainly the most common and best known of the many Webley and Scott revolver designs was the Mark VI, first introduced in 1915 and remaining in service until well into the 1930s. It was issued to the British Army and was also used extensively by various Commonwealth forces and also occasionally by the police.

In operation, pressure on the trigger depressed the cylinder stop and allowed the cylinder to rotate and bring the next chamber in line. Continuing steady pressure on the trigger caused the hammer to fall so that its nose struck the cap of the cartridge. At this stage the cylinder was prevented from rotating by the stop. The hammer could also be first drawn back manually to the cocked position, which decreased the amount of pressure required, and so aided accurate shooting. The sequence was repeated either at double or single action until all the rounds were fired. The empty cases were then ejected.

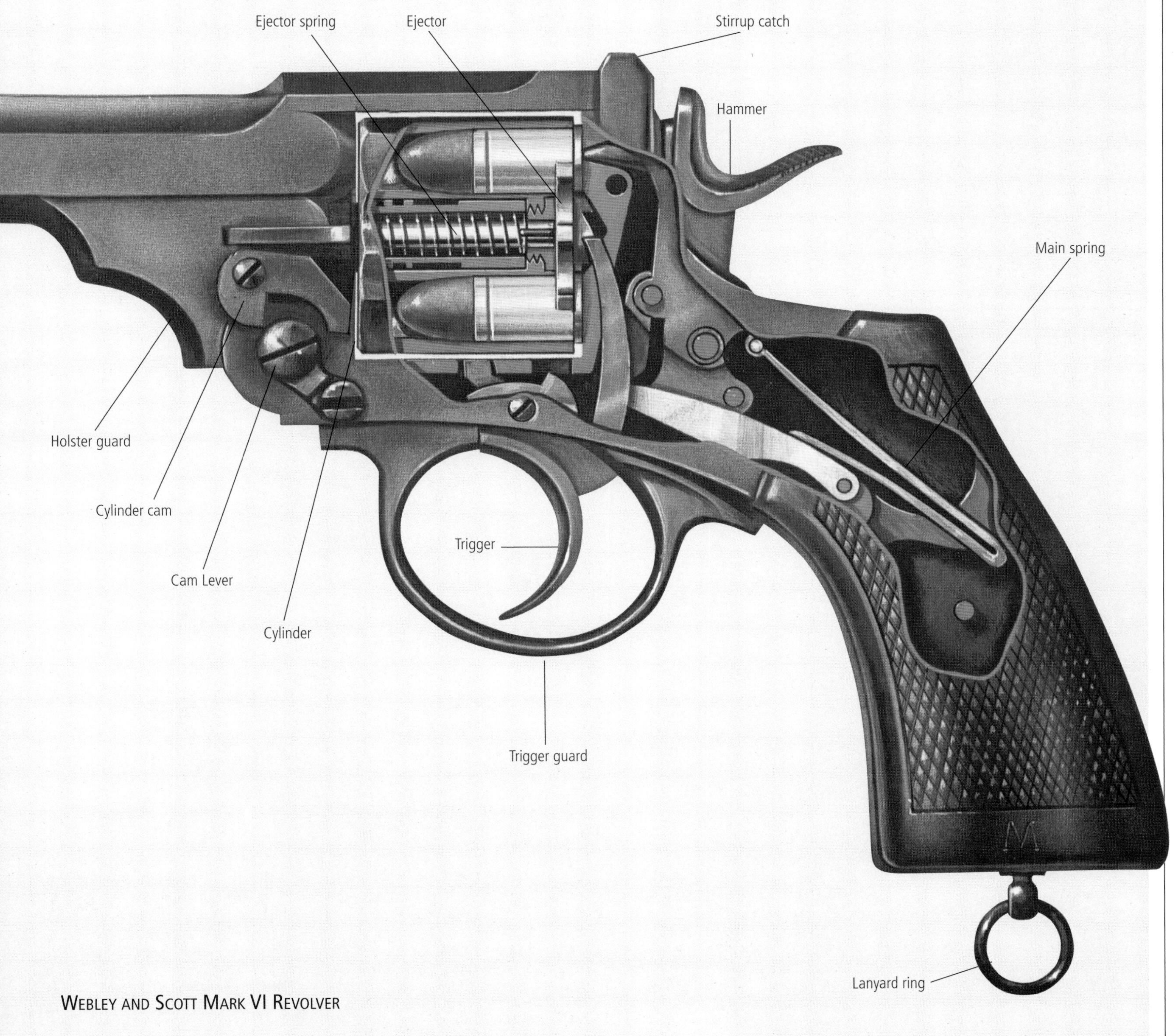

Webley and Scott Mark VI Revolver

Gasser Revolver — Austria

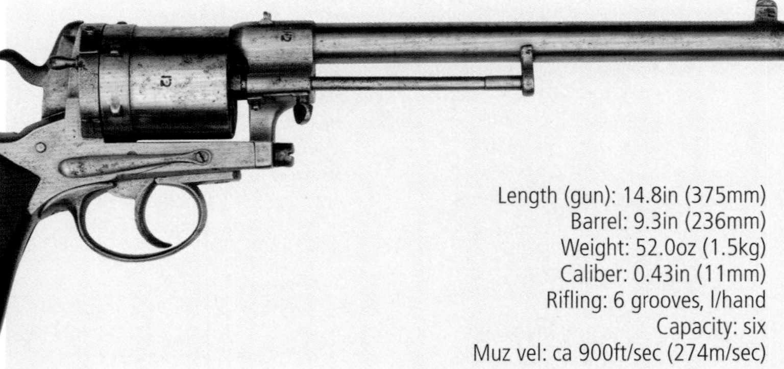

Length (gun): 14.8in (375mm)
Barrel: 9.3in (236mm)
Weight: 52.0oz (1.5kg)
Caliber: 0.43in (11mm)
Rifling: 6 grooves, l/hand
Capacity: six
Muz vel: ca 900ft/sec (274m/sec)

The great Austrian firm of Gasser was founded in 1862 by Leopold Gasser, who patented this revolver in 1870. He died in 1871 and was succeeded by his son, Johann, who continued to manufacture large numbers of revolvers of this and similar types almost until the end of the 19th Century. Gasser revolvers were used by the Austro-Hungarian Army and were sold extensively as civilian arms in Austria-Hungary and throughout the Balkans. In common with all original Gasser revolvers, this weapon is an open-frame model with no top strap. Its basic construction is fairly similar to that of the early Colt, except that there is a threaded hole below the barrel, which screws on to the front end of the axis pin instead of on to the wedge. It has a bottom-hinged loading gate and a sliding ejector rod on the right-hand side; the front end of the rod is cut into an arc of similar diameter to the barrel and fits firmly against it. The lock is of double-action type and is fitted with a safety device in the form of the flat bar above the trigger-guard. Internal pins attached to the bar's rear end held the hammer at half-cock and could only be released by pressure on the trigger. The arm is extensively marked: it bears the inscription "GASSER PATENT, GUSS-STAHL"; an Austrian eagle; and an emblem showing an arrow transfixing an apple, with the words "SCHUTZ MARK." It is a massive weapon, chambered to fire the cartridge originally developed for the Werndl carbine, and was really only suitable for use by mounted men. Even so, it would be hard to use without a detachable butt, which was not fitted.

Mannlicher Model 1901 Pistol — Austria-Hungary

Length (gun): 9.4in (239mm)
Barrel: 6.5in (165mm)
Weight: 33.0oz (0.9kg)
Caliber: 7.63mm
Rifling: 4 grooves, r/hand
Capacity: eight
Muz vel: 1,025ft/sec (312m/sec)

The Steyr factory first made self-loading pistols in 1894, when it produced some made to the design of Ferdinand, Ritter von Mannlicher, a German living in Austria, who is perhaps now best remembered for his excellent military rifles. Several models were made over the next few years; the arm illustrated here is the Model 1901. As is to be expected from a factory with the high reputation of Steyr, the weapon was very well made and finished. It was basically of blowback design, but of the type usually known as retarded blowback. There was no positive locked-breech system: the rearward movement of the slide was mechanically retarded for a very brief period to ensure that the gas pressure in the barrel fell to a safe level. This system also incidentally permitted the use of a relatively light slide without engendering excessive recoil. Although the magazine was located in the butt – in the style familiar on modern arms – it was not, in fact, a detachable box but an integral part of the arm; and it was loaded from the top by means of a charger. If the user desired to empty the magazine, the slide was drawn back and pressure was put on the small milled catch (visible in the photograph) above the right butt-plate; this allowed the magazine spring to force out the unexpended rounds.

Montenegrin Gasser Revolver — Austria-Hungary

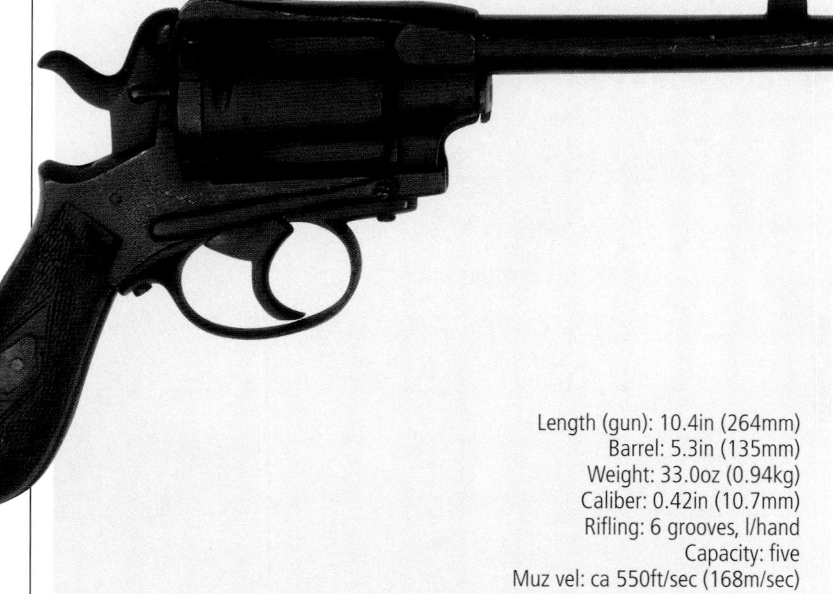

Length (gun): 10.4in (264mm)
Barrel: 5.3in (135mm)
Weight: 33.0oz (0.94kg)
Caliber: 0.42in (10.7mm)
Rifling: 6 grooves, l/hand
Capacity: five
Muz vel: ca 550ft/sec (168m/sec)

The term Montenegrin Gasser is used to describe a fairly broad category rather than a particular arm. The revolver illustrated here has a solid frame, but is otherwise generally similar in principle to the Gasser arm (qv). In particular, it has the same flat safety bar which acted against the hammer until the trigger was pressed. Some Montenegrin Gassers are of breakdown type, with a circular pierced extractor plate at the rear of the cylinder; others have open frames; and some were made with single-action locks. They are often highly decorated. The story is told that in the late 19th Century King Nicholas of Montenegro had a considerable financial interest in the factory and, in order to maintain his income, insisted that every adult male in his kingdom should possess one of these revolvers. The story may well be apocryphal – but it has an authentic Ruritanian flavor! Although an example of this arm is well worth inclusion here, the specimen photographed is in very poor condition and it is impossible to find any of the usual identification marks upon it.

Mannlicher Model 1903 Pistol — Austria-Hungary

Length (gun): 10.5in (267mm)
Barrel: 4.5in (114mm)
Weight: 35.0oz (1.0kg)
Caliber: 7.65mm
Rifling: 5 grooves, r/hand
Capacity: six
Muz vel: ca 1,090ft/sec (332m/sec)

Like most other firms concerned with self-loading arms, Mannlicher realized that the future of such weapons lay in the military sphere; thus, development had to be concerned with weapons firing powerful cartridges from locked-breech systems. The Mannlicher Model 1903, seen here, was of that type. It was cocked for the first shot by drawing back the bolt by means of the milled knob visible on top of the frame. When released, the bolt went forward, stripping a cartridge from the magazine and chambering it. When the bolt was fully forward, a bolt-stop rose from the frame and supported it while the round was fired. Then barrel and bolt recoiled for about 0.2in (5mm), after which the bolt-stop fell. The barrel now stopped, but the bolt continued backward to complete the recocking and reloading cycle in readiness for the next shot. The pistol had an internal hammer which acted on the firing pin; it also had an external cocking device in the form of the curved lever visible above the trigger. The magazine was of box type and could be removed by pressing in a small catch on the front of the trigger-guard, which allowed it to drop down. The small milled catch at the back of the frame was the safety. Perhaps the most remarkable aspect of this weapon is that although it fired a cartridge of the same dimensions as the Mauser, the actual charge was less: thus, the Mannlicher was not considered safe to fire the 7.65mm round used in the Mauser self-loading pistol.

Rast-Gasser Model 1898 Revolver — Austria-Hungary

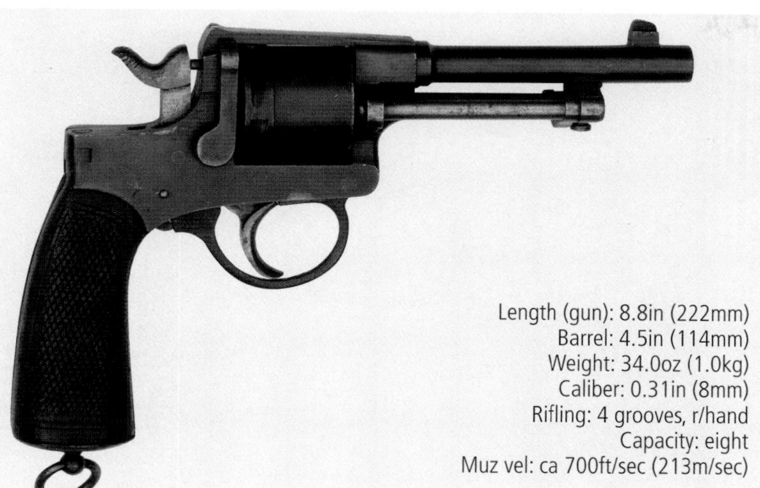

Length (gun): 8.8in (222mm)
Barrel: 4.5in (114mm)
Weight: 34.0oz (1.0kg)
Caliber: 0.31in (8mm)
Rifling: 4 grooves, r/hand
Capacity: eight
Muz vel: ca 700ft/sec (213m/sec)

Leopold Gasser produced revolvers on a very large scale during the last quarter of the 19th Century. His factories were in Austria, and his revolvers were widely used by the armed forces of many Balkan states. The revolver seen here is an example of the Rast-Gasser Model 1898 Service revolver. It is of solid-frame type, with a round barrel screwed in; its eight-chambered cylinder is plain, except for slots for the stop. The revolver was loaded through a bottom-hinged loading gate, the inside of which is fitted with a small projection which engaged the frame and prevented it from being drawn farther back than the horizontal. When the loading gate was open, the hammer was disconnected, but the cylinder could still be rotated by the action of the trigger, which speeded up loading. The usual groove was provided on the frame to ensure that the cartridges were not obstructed on their way in. The ejector rod is hollow and worked over a rod which was connected to the projection below the barrel; this projection also housed the front end of the axis pin. When it was not in use, the handle of the ejector rod fitted round the axis pin. The lock is of double action type and there is a separate firing-pin on the frame. Access to the mechanism was by means of a hinged cover which extended over almost the entire left side of the frame (the rear hinge is visible, just above the butt). The revolver is of old-fashioned appearance and it was best fired with the arm slightly bent; it was, however, very well made, although the cartridge it fired was too lacking in power to be of very much use for service purposes.

Roth-Steyr Model 1907 Pistol — Austria-Hungary

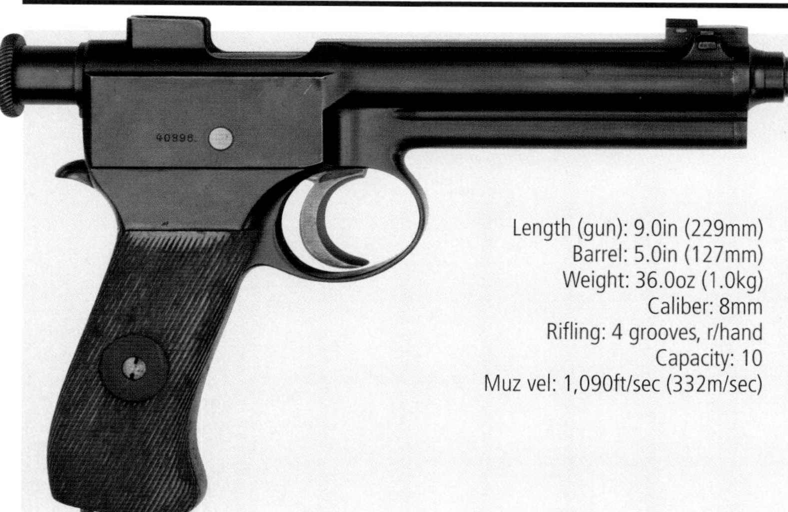

Length (gun): 9.0in (229mm)
Barrel: 5.0in (127mm)
Weight: 36.0oz (1.0kg)
Caliber: 8mm
Rifling: 4 grooves, r/hand
Capacity: 10
Muz vel: 1,090ft/sec (332m/sec)

This pistol first went into full production in 1907, when it was taken into service by the Austro-Hungarian Army, mainly for use as a cavalry arm. This was the first occasion on which any major power adopted a self-loading pistol in place of a revolver. The Roth-Steyr pistol fired from a locked breech – and this mechanism was of a very unusual type. The bolt was very long: its rear end was solid, except for a sleeve for the striker, but its front part was hollow and was of sufficient diameter to fit closely over the barrel. The interior of the bolt had cam grooves cut into it, and the barrel had studs of appropriate size to fit the grooves. When the pistol was fired, the barrel and bolt recoiled together within the hollow receiver for about 0.5in (12.7mm). During this operation, the grooves in the bolt caused the barrel to turn through 90 degrees, after which it was held while the bolt continued to the rear, cocking the action as it did so. On its forward journey, the bolt picked up a cartridge through a slot on its lower surface and chambered it, while the action of the studs in the grooves turned the barrel back to its locked position. The magazine, which was in the butt, was an integral part of the weapon and was loaded from a clip.

Steyr Model 1912 Pistol — Austria-Hungary

Length (gun): 8.5in (216mm)
Barrel: 5.1in (130mm)
Weight: 35.0oz (1.0kg)
Caliber: 0.357in (9mm)
Rifling: 4 grooves, r/hand
Capacity: eight
Muz vel: ca 1,100ft/sec (335m/sec)

As far as hand guns were concerned, Steyr's chief endeavor in the early years of the 20th Century appears to have been to produce an acceptable self-loading pistol of military type. This the firm accomplished with the appearance of the Model 1912 pistol illustrated here. It is a solid, square looking arm with some external resemblance to the famous Colt self-loader of the previous year. It has the same heavy slide, with the barrel inside it, which covers the whole of the frame. When the action was in the forward position, two lugs on the top of the barrel engaged in two corresponding slots in the slide. When the slide was drawn back for initial loading, the barrel moved with it for a short distance and was rotated sufficiently to disengage it from the slots. The barrel then stopped, but the slide continued to the rear and cocked the hammer. It then moved forward, driven by the recoil spring, stripping a round from the magazine and chambering it. During this forward movement, the barrel rotated back into the locked position in readiness for the next shot. The magazine was in the butt and was loaded by a clip from the top of the frame, with the slide to the rear. This pistol was in Austro-Hungarian service during World War I, until 1918.

Steyr 9mm Special Purpose Pistol — Austria

Length (gun): 12.7in (322mm)
Barrel: 5.1in (130mm)
Weight: 45.0oz (1.3kg)
Caliber: 9mm
Rifling: 6 grooves, r/hand
Capacity: 15-/30-round box magazine
Muz vel: ca 1,214ft/sec (370m/sec)

The Steyr 9mm Special Purpose Pistol (SPP) is generally similar to the Steyr Tactical Machine Pistol (TMP) (qv), but whereas the latter, despite its name, is properly categorized as a submachine gun, the SPP is most definitely a pistol. The SPP's frame and top cover are made of a synthetic fiber material, and the weapon does not have the forward grip of the TMP, although there is a small extension of the fore-end of the body, which is intended to keep the firer's fingers away from the muzzle. The SPP fires the 9 x 19mm Parabellum round in the semi-automatic mode only. The cocking-handle is at the rear of the weapon and the weapon is recoil-operated, the breech being locked by a rotating barrel. The box magazine is housed in the pistol grip and there are two sizes: for 15 and 30 rounds, respectively.

TOMISKA LITTLE TOM PISTOL — AUSTRIA-HUNGARY

Length (gun): 4.7in (119mm)
Barrel: 2.3in (59mm)
Weight: 15.0oz (0.4kg)
Caliber: 6.35mm
Rifling: 6 grooves, r/hand
Capacity: six
Muz vel: ca 800ft/sec (244m/sec)

Alois Tomiska, a Viennese gunsmith, designed a self-loading pistol which he patented in 1908 as the Little Tom. It had a fixed barrel and an open-topped slide; the recoil spring was contained in a sleeve below the barrel. It had a double-action lock; thus, its external hammer could be cocked either by the rearward movement of the slide or by direct pressure on the trigger. The greater part of the hammer lay within a recess at the rear of the frame, but enough of its milled comb protruded to make thumb-cocking possible. When the slide was removed, it was possible to gain access to the lock by pushing up the right butt-plate. Pistols of this type appear to have been made by several European factories after the end of World War I, when Tomiska himself worked for Jihoceská Zbrojovka (later Ceská Zbrojovka) in Czechoslovakia. Tomiska's long career did not end until 1946.

BROWNING MODEL 1900 ("OLD MODEL") PISTOL — BELGIUM

Length (gun): 6.4in (163mm)
Barrel: 4.0in (102mm)
Weight: 22.0oz (0.6kg)
Caliber: 7.65mm
Rifling: 5 grooves, r/hand
Capacity: seven
Muz vel: ca 850ft/sec (259m/sec)

John Moses Browning's first successful venture was a machine gun made by the Colt company and adopted by the US Navy in 1898. Two years later he produced a self-loading pistol, of the type shown here. However, after a disagreement with Winchester, with whom he had worked for some years, Browning came to the conclusion that more interest might be shown in his self-loading pistol in Europe than in the United States – where the revolver was almost universally predominant. In this he was right: the great Belgian firm of Fabrique Nationale (FN), Liège, showed immediate interest, and the weapon was soon in production in great quantity. It is robust, reliable and mechanically simple; and although it has not been made since 1912, many are still to be found. The barrel is fastened to the frame; above it is a moving slide which contains the recoil spring. The slide had, of course, to be operated manually to load the first round. When this was fired, gas pressure forced the empty case backward, taking with it the breechblock and slide and compressing the recoil spring, which also operated the striker. The spring then took over and forced the whole assembly forward, stripping a cartridge from the box magazine in the butt and chambering it in preparation for the next shot.

BROWNING MODEL 1900 PISTOL — BELGIUM

Length (gun): 6.8in (171mm)
Barrel: 4.0in (102mm)
Weight: 22.0oz (0.6kg)
Caliber: 7.65mm
Rifling: 6 grooves, r/hand
Capacity: seven
Muz vel: ca 940ft/sec (287m/sec)

This example has some slight variations from the "Old Model" and since something is also known of its personal history it is worthy of inclusion. This model was the first of a long series of self-loading pistols to be made by Fabrique Nationale of Belgium to the designs of the famous American John M. Browning, and it is frequently referred to as the "Old Model." It fired a cartridge originally specially designed by Browning for use in this particular model; the same round is now widely used in numerous other self-loading pistols. The magazine fitted into the butt. The pistol is numbered (not dated) "1948" and thus must be from one of the very earliest batches produced. After 10,000 of these arms had been made, subsequent examples had a lanyard ring fitted to the frame. The original design on the butt-plate incorporated a replica of the weapon and the words "F.N." On later examples the pistol was omitted. This particular specimen has been fitted at some time with non-regulation aluminum grips. It is known to have been carried as a private weapon by a French infantry officer during the Algerian Insurrection of 1954-62. A pistol of this type was used by the student Gavrilo Princip, who assassinated the Archduke Ferdinand and his wife at Sarajevo in June, 1914.

BROWNING 7.65 MODEL 1910 PISTOL — BELGIUM

Length (gun): 6.0in (152mm)
Barrel: 3.5in (89mm)
Weight: 21.0oz (0.6kg)
Caliber: 7.65mm
Rifling: 6 grooves, r/hand
Capacity: 7-round box magazine
Muz vel: 925ft/sec (282m/sec)

Following their acquisition of John M. Browning's patents, Fabrique Nationale (FN) developed the design, leading to the Model 1910, which was first produced to take the 7.65 x 17mm Browning round, although it was later also available in 9 x 17mm Short caliber. The weapon was blowback operated and the fore-end was tubular in shape because the recoil spring was mounted around the barrel and held in place by a nosecap with a bayonet fastening, resulting in an unusual and easily identifiable profile. It had a grip safety. The Model 1910 had only limited military success, although some were taken into German service during World War I, but it was widely used by police forces and sold well commercially.

Browning 7.65mm Model 1910/22 Pistol — Belgium

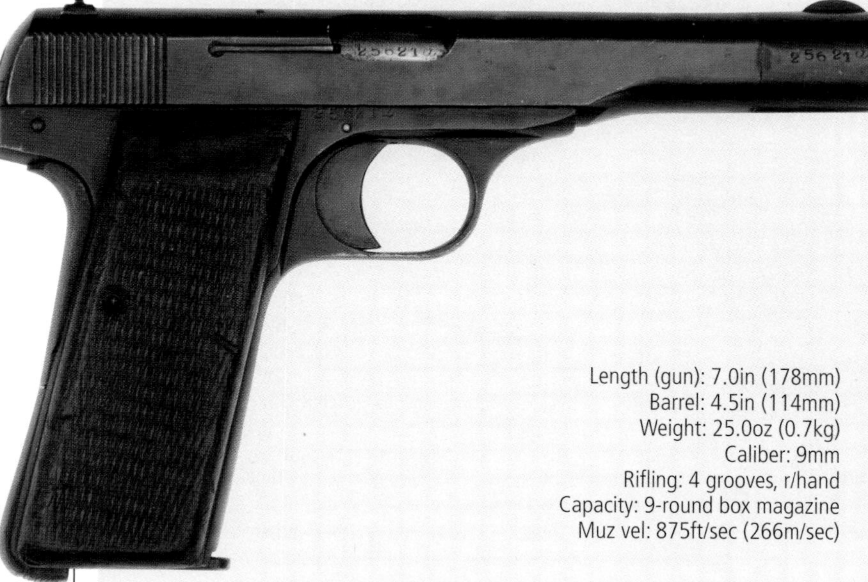

Length (gun): 7.0in (178mm)
Barrel: 4.5in (114mm)
Weight: 25.0oz (0.7kg)
Caliber: 9mm
Rifling: 4 grooves, r/hand
Capacity: 9-round box magazine
Muz vel: 875ft/sec (266m/sec)

In 1922 the FN designers produced a modified version of the M1910, known as the M1910/22. In the modified weapon, the barrel was lengthened to improve accuracy, which, in order to avoid lengthening the existing slide, was achieved by adding an extension to the nosepiece. The butt was also extended to accommodate a larger magazine. The M1910/22 was originally produced in 7.65mm, but was later also produced in 9 x 17mm Short, this being the maximum caliber considered safe for a blowback weapon. This weapon was adopted by the Belgian, French, Greek, Netherlands, Turkish, and Yugoslavian armies in the 1920s and by the German Luftwaffe in World War II, to which it was known as Pistole 626(b).

Fabrique Nationale/Browning 9mm "Fast Action" Pistol — Belgium

Length (gun): 7.5in (191mm)
Barrel: 4.8in (121mm)
Weight: 35.0oz (1.0kg)
Caliber: 9mm
Rifling: 4 grooves, r/hand
Capacity: 14-round box magazine
Muz vel: n.k.

This was one of several attempts by Fabrique Nationale to produce a successor to the Browning GP35. One such attempt was the Browning Double-Action 9 (BDA-9), which used the same action as the GP35, but had a double-action trigger, a decocking lever, and a larger trigger guard to enable the weapon to be fired either with two hands or with one hand with a glove. There was also another version, known as the Browning Double-Action Only (BDAO), which had a slightly different trigger mechanism, and was developed especially for the police market. Neither of these were developed beyond the prototype stage and another attempt was the Browning Fast Action, of which some 12 prototypes were built. This version was intended to afford the safety in carry of a double-action arm, but preserving the speed and accuracy on the first and second shots of a cocked-and-locked single action. In brief, the hammer was mounted round a large hub which carried the sear engagement. The hammer was pushed forward over a latch for the carry; the first pressure on the trigger released it to spring back round the hub before the sear was released to fire. As a result, trigger pressure was light and easy for each shot, rather than being rough and heavy for the first shot with a drastic change of system for the second shot, which is the case with most double-action pistols.

Fabrique Nationale/Browning 9mm GP35 "High Power" Pistol — Belgium

Length (gun): 7.8in (197mm)
Barrel: 4.7in (118mm)
Weight: 35.0oz (1.0kg)
Caliber: 9mm
Rifling: 4 grooves, r/hand
Capacity: 13-round box magazine
Muz vel: ca 1,100ft/sec (335m/sec)

This was the last of John Browning's pistol designs, which he worked on from 1914 until his death in 1926, and is, in essence, a logical development of the weapon he had designed when he was with Colt, and which they had produced as the M1911 (qv). His work was then continued within the FN factory and, after several modifications, it was introduced in 1935, when it was adopted by numerous armies. It was made in various versions, including one with an adjustable sight and a combined holster/stock of the type found on the original Mausers. When the Germans occupied Belgium in 1940 they continued the production of these weapons for the Wehrmacht as the Pistole 640(b), although it is said that various Belgian sabotage operations lowered the quality, sometimes to the point where the weapons were actually dangerous to use. Meanwhile, a number of FN engineers had escaped to Britain, taking the drawings with them, and in 1942 they were sent to Canada where the John Inglis factory undertook production for the Allies. After the war manufacture reverted to the FN factory at Liège and the weapon was also put on the civil market as the "High Power." The weapon was adopted by the British Army in 1954 as the "Pistol, 9mm, Browning, Mk1*" and has served with over 50 armies since. It is, undoubtedly, one of the greatest pistol designs.

Fabrique Nationale 5.7mm Five-seveN© Pistol Belgium

Length (gun): 8.2in (208mm)
Barrel: 4.8in (123mm)
Weight: 22.0oz (0.6kg)
Caliber: 5.7mm
Rifling: 6 grooves, r/hand
Capacity: 20-round box magazine
Muz vel: 2,133 ft/sec (650m/sec)

The Five-seveN© pistol has been developed by FN as the hand-held element of the company's P90 personal defense weapon system. Much of the Five-seveN© is made from synthetic materials, including the outer casing of the slide and it uses a new type of delayed blow-back developed by FN specifically for this application, in which the slide is briefly held by cams until the barrel has withdrawn some 0.12in (3mm), whereupon they unlock. There is provision for mounting a laser target designator (LTD) or a small light in front of the trigger.

Galand Velo-Dog Revolver — Belgium

Length (gun): 4.7in (119mm)
Barrel: 1.2in (30mm)
Weight: 10.5oz (0.3kg)
Caliber: 0.216in (5.5mm)
Rifling: 4 grooves, r/hand
Capacity: six
Muz vel: ca 600ft/sec (183m/sec)

The term "Velo-Dog" is used to describe a group of cheap pocket revolvers which were made in very considerable numbers at the end of the 19th Century. They were made in quantity in Belgium, France, Germany, Italy, and Spain; the last-named country was particularly prolific. The Velo-Dog was invented by Charles François Galand, whose name is mentioned elsewhere in connection with self-extracting revolvers. Galand's first model was of open-frame type, with an orthodox trigger and guard, as on the arm seen here; but later models, wherever produced, tended to have solid frames, completely enclosed hammers and folding triggers. The earliest Velo-Dogs fired a long 5.5mm cartridge with a light bullet; later they were designed to fire 0.22in (5.6mm), 6mm and 8mm Lebel rimmed cartridges, and even 6.35mm and 7.65mm rimless rounds. The name is believed to stem from a combination of "Velocipede" (the early term for a bicycle) and "Dog," although this seems an odd linguistic mixture. There is, however, little doubt that these revolvers were designed principally for the use of pioneer cyclists, who appear to have been much troubled by fierce dogs. Special deterrent, but less lethal, cartridges, loaded with salt, pepper or dust shot, were also supplied. Even so, it seems by modern standards an extreme way of dealing with a nuisance. Arms of this type were still advertised in European makers' catalogs after World War I.

Galand & Sommerville Revolver — Belgium

Length (gun): 10.0in (254mm)
Barrel: 5.0in (127mm)
Weight: 35.0oz (1.0kg)
Caliber: 0.45in (11.4mm)
Rifling: 5 grooves, r/hand
Capacity: six
Muz vel: ca 600ft/sec (183m/sec)

Charles François Galand of Liège in Belgium and Sommerville, a partner in a Birmingham firm, took out a joint patent in 1868 for a self-extracting cartridge revolver of the general type illustrated. The arm was made in Birmingham and on the continent. It does not appear ever to have become popular in Britain, but a good many revolvers on this principle were made in Europe. This particular specimen is well made but is unnamed, although it carries the name "Wm POWELL of BIRMINGHAM," who was probably the retailer. It bears Birmingham proof marks, and somewhat unusually an Enfield Small Arms mark of crossed lances with a "B" beneath them. The revolver was opened by gripping the milled studs at the bottom of the frame and drawing them forward. This activated a plunger below the barrel (very like the ram on a percussion revolver) and forced both barrel and cylinder forward, leaving the empty cases held by their rims on the extractor. The partial return of the cylinder to the extractor allowed fresh rounds to be loaded.

Mariette Pepperbox Pistol — Belgium

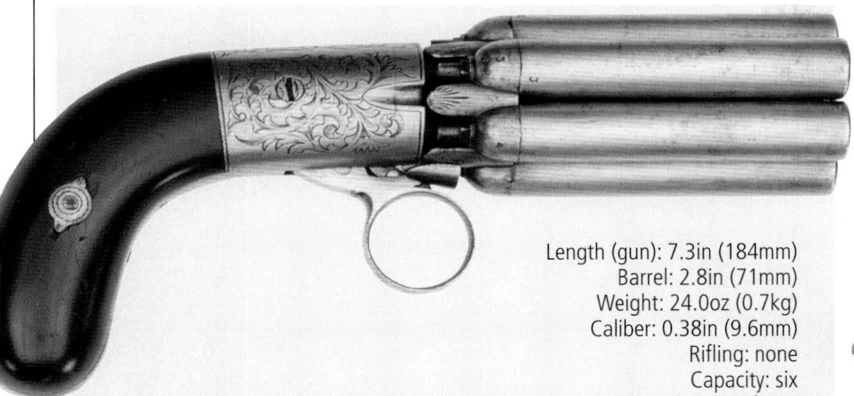

Length (gun): 7.3in (184mm)
Barrel: 2.8in (71mm)
Weight: 24.0oz (0.7kg)
Caliber: 0.38in (9.6mm)
Rifling: none
Capacity: six
Muz vel: ca 500ft/sec

This Mariette-type pistol, made to a design patented in Belgium in 1837, is of Belgian manufacture and bears the Liège proofmarks. It is of the orthodox design of the type, in that its barrels, instead of being bored from a single block, are screwed separately onto six chambers, into which the nipples are fixed. Each barrel has four rectangular slots at 90 degree intervals round the muzzle to facilitate its removal with a special key, and each barrel is also numbered, as is each chamber. The cluster of barrels is screwed to a spindle on the standing breech, access to which was gained by way of the central space left in the cluster of barrels. As may be seen, the nipples are in the same axis as the barrels; this reduced the chances of a misfire and made the arm neat and compact. Pressure on the ring-trigger caused the barrels to rotate, bringing each in turn into line, and also drew back and released the internal hammer, which struck the nipple on the lowest barrel. There are partitions between the nipples, and in addition a further shield rose as the hammer fell to guard completely the nipple being fired. Re-capping was achieved by pressing the trigger sufficiently to allow the barrels to be manually rotated: a small slot was exposed in the right-hand side of the frame, allowing the caps to be slid into place. The butt is of ebonised plates, on a strap inscribed "MARIETTE BREVETTE."

Double-barreled Pocket Pistol — Belgium

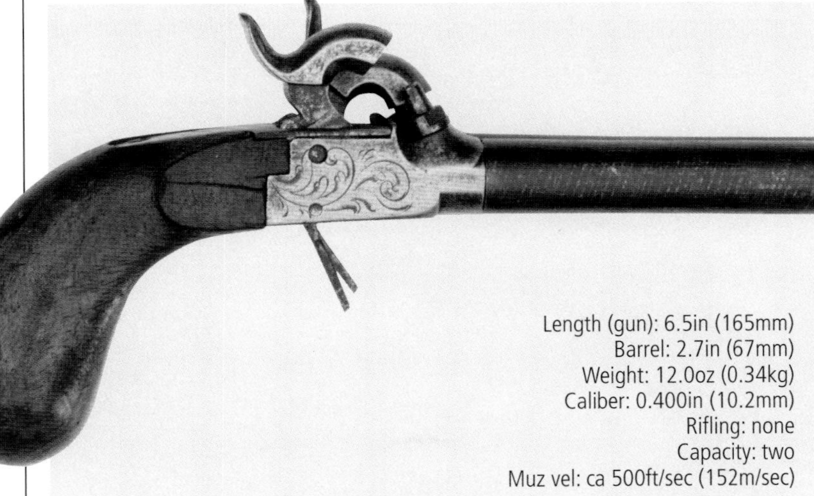

Length (gun): 6.5in (165mm)
Barrel: 2.7in (67mm)
Weight: 12.0oz (0.34kg)
Caliber: 0.400in (10.2mm)
Rifling: none
Capacity: two
Muz vel: ca 500ft/sec (152m/sec)

Muzzle-loaded pistols were, of course, far too slow to reload in action, so double-barreled arms were popular, because they allowed the user a second and perhaps vital shot at an adversary. This particular specimen, which is of medium quality, is fairly typical of the small pocket pistols turned out by the thousand by a variety of Belgian makers in the first half of the 19th Century. The barrels are of the screw-off variety and fit over male screws of about 0.3in (7.6mm) diameter, containing the chambers. The muzzles each have four deep notches, equally spaced round the circumference, which at first sight appear to be rifling but which are, in fact, intended to take a key. The barrels have a very marked damascus-type spiral figure; but this was probably etched on with acid to improve their appearance, for they are, in fact, solid metal tubes. The two locks have folding triggers which were extruded only when the hammers were placed at half-cock, a common device which made it possible to dispense with the somewhat bulky trigger-guard, while still avoiding the risk of the triggers catching in the lining of a pocket when the weapon was drawn. The butt is of common bag shape without a cap, and the width of the double breech makes it rather wide and clumsy. Pistols of this kind were commonly sold very cheaply and a good many are still to be found.

Copy of Adams Revolver — Belgium

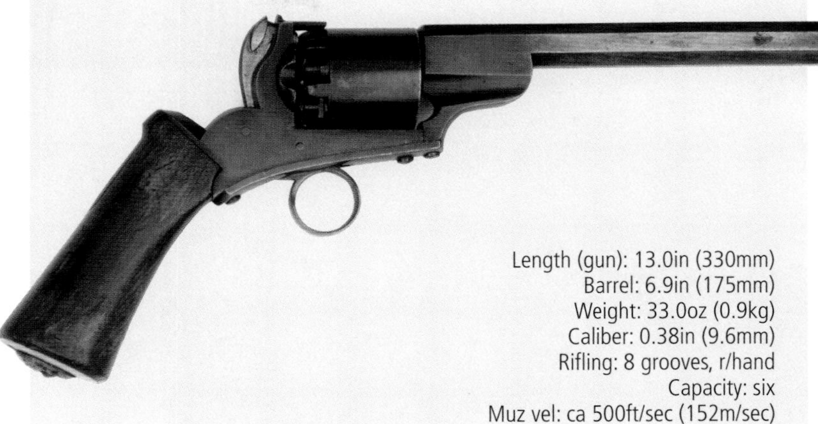

Length (gun): 13.0in (330mm)
Barrel: 6.9in (175mm)
Weight: 33.0oz (0.9kg)
Caliber: 0.38in (9.6mm)
Rifling: 8 grooves, r/hand
Capacity: six
Muz vel: ca 500ft/sec (152m/sec)

Although Adams revolvers were made under license in Belgium, the name on this pistol – "DAVID H, BREVETTE" – is not that of a licensee. The arm resembles those made by D. Herman of Liège and is probably a pirated copy. The frame is made separately from the octagonal barrel, which is attached to it Colt-fashion by means of a robust cylinder pin and a lump screwed to the lower part of the frame. A rammer, essentially similar to the type used on Beaumont-Adams revolvers, is attached to the left-hand flat of the barrel. The cylinder is of the normal Adams type and bears Liège proofmarks. The lock, too, is of the Adams self-cocking type; on the left-hand side is fitted a spring safety-bolt to hold the hammer clear of the nipples. A flat plate protrudes far enough forward from the top of the frame to cover completely the nipple under the hammer; this was presumably intended to remove any risk of fragments of the copper cap blowing back into the face of the firer. The trigger is of the ring type often found on earlier pepperbox pistols. The one-piece butt, which is held between two tangs, is fitted with a butt-cap of German silver. It contains a percussion cap compartment, with a lid made in the form of a grotesque mask.

Continental Pinfire Revolver — Belgium

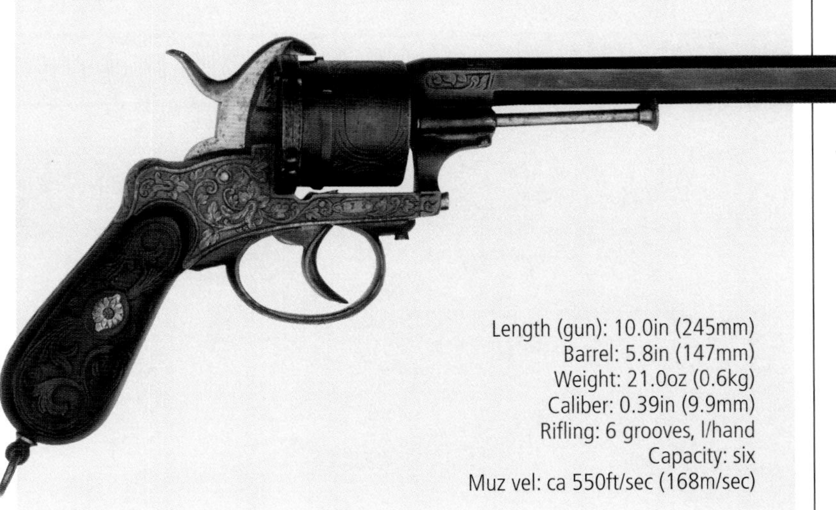

Length (gun): 10.0in (245mm)
Barrel: 5.8in (147mm)
Weight: 21.0oz (0.6kg)
Caliber: 0.39in (9.9mm)
Rifling: 6 grooves, l/hand
Capacity: six
Muz vel: ca 550ft/sec (168m/sec)

This is a medium-quality pinfire revolver of quite large caliber. Like many of its kind, it is strictly anonymous, bearing no name or markings other than a number and Belgian proof-marks on the cylinder. It has an octagonal barrel with a very high and somewhat flimsy foresight; the backsight is a simple notch on the top of the hammer nose. The cylinder has long, machined projections, the higher parts being almost level with the pin apertures. These were engaged by a cylinder stop which rose from the lower frame when the trigger was pressed, locking the cylinder when the appropriate chamber was in line with the barrel. The lock is of somewhat later type than on most weapons of this kind, and the hammer could be manually cocked if required. The revolver is fitted with the usual ejector rod – with an additional refinement: it was held by the tension of a small, flat spring which prevented it being pushed into a chamber accidentally and so interfering with the revolution of the cylinder. The arm is blued, with the exception of the hammer, trigger, and ejector rod, and is covered with rather crude engraving. The butt plates are of some black composition, bearing an elaborate pattern, and the weapon is fitted with a lanyard ring, suggesting that it may have been intended for military or paramilitary use.

MINIATURE REVOLVER — BELGIUM

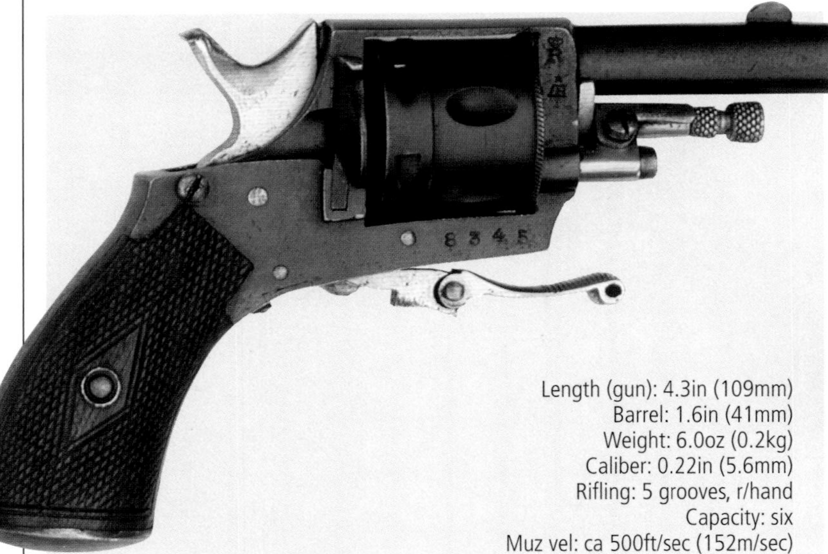

Length (gun): 4.3in (109mm)
Barrel: 1.6in (41mm)
Weight: 6.0oz (0.2kg)
Caliber: 0.22in (5.6mm)
Rifling: 5 grooves, r/hand
Capacity: six
Muz vel: ca 500ft/sec (152m/sec)

Until the later 19th Century, few provisions for the control of firearms existed in most countries; any law-abiding citizen could purchase and own firearms almost without restriction; although this freedom was, of course, balanced by heavy penalties in the event of the arms being used for criminal purposes. The tiny pistol seen here is a cheap but well-finished and reliable revolver of the type produced in Belgium in the 19th Century. It has a solid frame with integral round barrel, complete with foresight. Its cylinder is chambered to take six, short, copper-cased, rimfire cartridges. It was loaded through a bottom-hinged loading gate, the insertion of the cartridges being facilitated by a groove in the frame; and the chambers are recessed to accommodate the cartridge rims. The ejector rod is housed in the hollow axis pin and could be drawn forward and then swiveled in order to bring it in line with the chamber opposite the loading gate. The double-action lock was activated by a folding trigger. Rather unusually, there is a safety lever on the left side of the frame; when this was pressed down, it prevented the hammer from rising. Apart from the hammer, trigger, ejector, and safety, the weapon is blued and bears the appropriate proof marks and the number "8345." At about 1900 revolvers like this could be bought in England very cheaply, and they were particularly recommended to cyclists!

BULLDOG PISTOL (COPY) — BELGIUM

Length (gun): 5.5in (140mm)
Barrel: 1.9in (48mm)
Weight: 12.0oz (0.3kg)
Caliber: 0.32in (8.1mm)
Rifling: 5 grooves, r/hand
Capacity: six
Muz vel: ca 550ft/sec (168m/sec)

In 1878 the British firm of P. Webley and Sons (which had by then begun to establish its excellent reputation for revolvers) introduced a group of weapons under the general title of "British Bulldog." They were solid-frame, five-chambered arms of 0.44in (11.2mm) and 0.45in (11.4mm) caliber, and were intended primarily as civilian arms. Britain was then a well-settled and generally law-abiding country, but many people liked to keep a pistol handy in the house for protection against aggressive vagrants or burglars. There was also a considerable demand from civilians going out to work in the more remote parts of the British Empire. These reliable Bulldog weapons soon became popular; they were quickly copied in France, Belgium, German, Spain – and even in the United States. The weapon illustrated is a Belgian copy of poor quality, with a folding trigger

ADAMS CENTER-FIRE REVOLVER (COPY) — BELGIUM

Length (gun): 11.0in (279mm)
Barrel: 6.0in (152mm)
Weight: 35.0oz (0.99kg)
Caliber: 0.42in (10.7mm)
Rifling: 6 grooves, r/hand
Capacity: six
Muz vel: ca 600ft/sec (183m/sec)

By 1868, John Adams, brother of Robert and managing director of the Adams Patent Small Arms Company, had patented and produced a center-fire cartridge revolver based on the original percussion revolvers produced by Beaumont-Adams a dozen years earlier. The conversion involved a new bored-through cylinder; a loading gate; and a sliding ejector rod fastened to the right front of the frame, so that it was permanently in line with the chamber opposite the loading gate. A deep groove had to be cut into the frame behind the gate to allow the cartridges free entry. No corresponding addition to the frame was needed on the left side because none of the chambers was fully exposed; therefore, the cartridges could not fall out. The new Adams was very quickly copied by Belgian makers – and the weapon seen here is one such copy. Although at first sight it appears to have a solid frame, it is in reality in two parts: there are screws at the bottom front of the frame and by the hammer nose – the construction is, in fact, similar, to that of the Deane-Harding percussion revolver (qv). The plain cylinder with its top-hinged gate and cartridge groove is, for all practical purposes, identical to that of the original Adams from which it is copied. The only real difference lies in the provision of a Webley-type swivel ejector rod instead of the fixed, sliding model brazed to the original Adams frame. The rod, which was normally housed in the hollow axis pin, pulled forward and swiveled. To remove the cylinder, the ejector rod was withdrawn and the small stud visible on the front frame was depressed. Then the milled end of the axis pin was drawn forward.

COPY OF R.I.C. REVOLVER — BELGIUM

Length (gun): 8.8in (222mm)
Barrel: 4.0in (102mm)
Weight: 24.0oz (0.7kg)
Caliber: 0.45in (11.4mm)
Rifling: 7 grooves, l/hand
Capacity: six
Muz vel: ca 650ft/sec (198m/sec)

The original Royal Irish Constabulary revolver was first put on the market by P. Webley and Son of Birmingham in 1867 and proved an immediate success. The force from which its title was derived adopted it in 1868, as did many other colonial forces, both military and police; it also proved extremely popular as an arm for civilian use. The revolver inevitably went through a number of changes in its long history, but its essential characteristics were never really changed. Inevitably, such a popular arm was very widely copied in the United Kingdom, in continental Europe, and even occasionally in the United States. The quality and reliability of these pirated versions varied considerably. The weapon illustrated here is characteristic of the type: it is a copy of the Webley Model of 1880. It has a solid frame with an octagonal barrel screwed into it; the cylinder is unusual in having elliptical fluting. The lock is of double-action type with a wide hammer comb. The ejector rod is housed in the hollow axis pin. This appears to be one of the better copies, for it is well made and finished, but it bears no marks other than a crown over the letter "R." This is the normal Belgian mark for black-powder revolver barrels which have been tested with a charge 30 percent above the intended norm.

Double-Barreled Revolver — Belgium

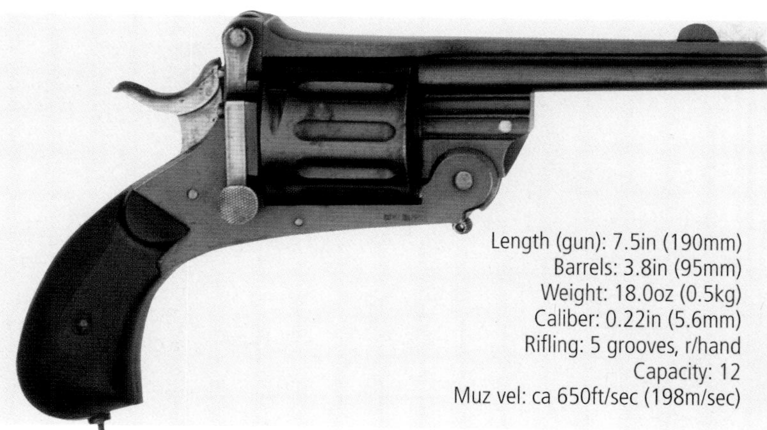

Length (gun): 7.5in (190mm)
Barrels: 3.8in (95mm)
Weight: 18.0oz (0.5kg)
Caliber: 0.22in (5.6mm)
Rifling: 5 grooves, r/hand
Capacity: 12
Muz vel: ca 650ft/sec (198m/sec)

This late 19th Century side-by-side, double-barreled revolver fired both barrels simultaneously. The barrels, which are round, appear to have been machined out of a single piece of metal and the top rib then attached. The frame is of bottom-hinged type; the locking device being of the Pryse type, involving the use of two centrally-hinged vertical arms. Each arm has a stud at the top of its inner side; the studs were forced inwards under the pressure of a spring, so that they passed through holes at the top of the standing breech and engaged a rearward extension of the top rib. The lock is of double-action type, with a folding trigger which made the arm convenient for the pocket. The hammer nose is flat and acted on a pair of firing pins mounted in the rear of the standing breech. The fluted cylinder, which is, of necessity, large in relation to the overall dimensions of the weapon, is hollow in the center to reduce weight. It is fitted with a star-shaped extractor which automatically threw out the rounds or empty cases when the revolver was opened smartly. The butt is of bird-beak type with wooden side plates. The top rib bears Belgian inspection marks and the frame is stamped with a rampant lion with the letters "RV" beneath it. Overall, the weapon appears to be of good quality and is well finished. It is not, however, very clear what it was meant to achieve – except to hit its victim twice at each discharge. This presumably increased the stopping power of the weapon considerably, but it is likely that a normal six-chambered revolver in 0.32in (8.1mm) caliber would have done the job as well.

Copy of Smith & Wesson Model No 3 Revolver — Belgium

Length (gun): 8.0in (203mm)
Barrel: 4.0in (102mm)
Weight: 22.0oz (0.6kg)
Caliber: 0.38in (9.6mm)
Rifling: 5 grooves, l/hand
Capacity: six
Muz vel: ca 740ft/sec (226m/sec)

The Smith & Wesson double-action, break-open, pocket revolvers in 0.38in (9.6mm) caliber were useful weapons, combining compact dimensions with a cartridge possessing considerable stopping-power. They soon became popular in the United States and elsewhere, which inevitably led to the pirating of the design, particularly in Belgium, where the revolver seen here originated. The 19th Century saw a considerable degree of industrialization in that country: in particular, Belgium's capacity to produce small arms of all kinds increased very rapidly as the century progressed. Although there were large factories, a very considerable part of the Belgian output came from small, anonymous back-street workshops, usually family concerns. The people employed in such workshops were often skilled as well as hard-working; and although some cheap and unreliable arms were produced, most were adequate – and certainly as good as could be expected at the low price charged. The revolver seen here is a close copy of the Smith & Wesson third model, produced from 1884 until 1895, and is of as good a quality as might reasonably be expected, considering its origins. It has a round barrel with a top rib and a round, brass foresight; the backsight is a notch cut in the front of the barrel catch, which is of the usual T-shape. The lock mechanism is of the orthodox double-action type. The weapon is blued and is fitted with either pearl or imitation-pearl butt-plates. It bears Belgian proof marks.

Copy of Smith & Wesson Russian Model — Belgium

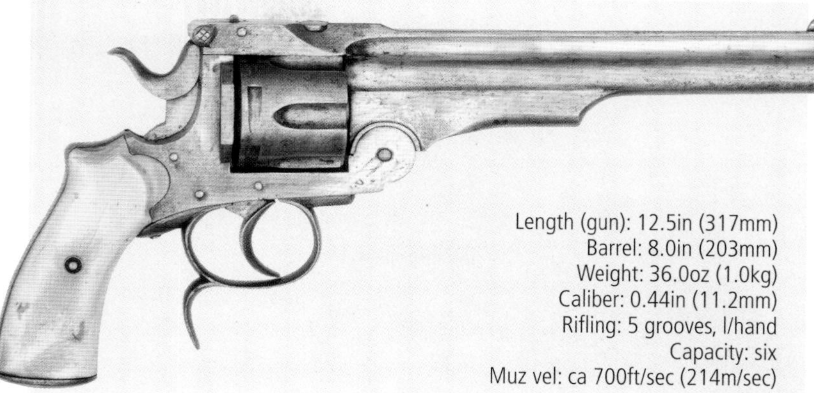

Length (gun): 12.5in (317mm)
Barrel: 8.0in (203mm)
Weight: 36.0oz (1.0kg)
Caliber: 0.44in (11.2mm)
Rifling: 5 grooves, l/hand
Capacity: six
Muz vel: ca 700ft/sec (214m/sec)

Smith & Wesson's Russian models (qv) were fine weapons of their type, and thus they were inevitably copied. As has already been explained elsewhere, various European countries, and Belgium in particular, were quick to turn out their own versions of any popular arm. These were usually made in small, family workshops, where they could be produced a good deal more cheaply than their more reputable prototypes. Of course, the copies were of varying quality: at best, they never attained the quality of the originals; at worst, they were positively dangerous. The revolver illustrated here, which is based on the various Smith & Wesson Russian models, is of relatively poor quality. Certainly, some corners were cut in its manufacture. Although it is not possible to assess the quality of the metal, the workmanship and general finish are crude. In particular, it lacks the groove across the top of the hammer which engaged a flange on the barrel catch – which was a feature always to be found on the genuine article. The lock is of double-action type; it did not rebound, but was fitted with a manual half-cock. The butt-plates are of bone or ivory, probably the former, and the arm was originally fitted with a lanyard ring, now missing. The barrel is spuriously inscribed "SMITH AND WESSON" and there are Belgian proof marks on the cylinder, enabling its true origin to be established.

Galand-Type Revolver — Belgium

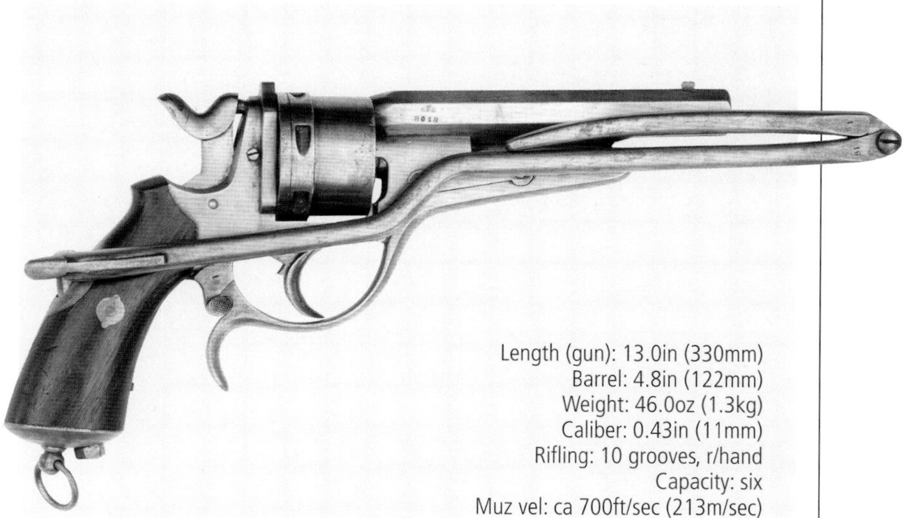

Length (gun): 13.0in (330mm)
Barrel: 4.8in (122mm)
Weight: 46.0oz (1.3kg)
Caliber: 0.43in (11mm)
Rifling: 10 grooves, r/hand
Capacity: six
Muz vel: ca 700ft/sec (213m/sec)

Charles François Galand was a well-known Belgian gunmaker during the second half of the 19th Century, and he invented and patented a number of improvements to the revolver. He was, perhaps, best known for an improved method of extracting cartridges from the cylinder. Although Galand made a number of these arms in conjunction with the British maker Sommerville of Birmingham, it is generally true to say that the type was more popular on the continent than in Britain; and it was very rarely found in the United States. The system of operation was fairly simple. The spur on the trigger-guard formed the rear extremity of a long lever hinged to a very long front extension of the cylinder axis pin. When the milled catch at the rear of the trigger-guard was pulled backwards, the whole lever could be drawn down to the vertical position. This action drew forward the barrel and cylinder along the axis pin. During the last part of its travel, the rear plate of the cylinder, which is pierced with holes for the cartridges, stopped, while the main cylinder went on for a further 0.5in (13mm), leaving the empty cases behind it on the plate, whence they could be shaken clear. The lock is of double-action type and the weapon is fitted with a folding, skeleton stock (seen here in the folded position), a feature which contributed little, if anything, to the steadiness of the aim taken. The weapon is of plain but robust construction; its weakest point was undoubtedly the very flimsy skeleton stock which made it difficult to grip the butt properly.

R.I.C. Pocket Type Revolver — Belgium

Length (gun): 8.0in (203mm)
Barrel: 3.0in (76mm)
Weight: 28.0oz (0.8kg)
Caliber: 0.45in (11.4mm)
Rifling: 7 grooves, r/hand
Capacity: five
Muz vel: ca 600ft/sec (183m/sec)

The Royal Irish Constabulary (R.I.C.) revolver first appeared in 1867, establishing the reputation of its manufacturer, P. Webley and Son of Birmingham. As might be expected, such a successful arm was widely copied: it is probable that imitation R.I.C. revolvers greatly outnumbered the originals. Civilian purchasers of weapons were not always very selective; and although a soldier, policeman or traveler, any one of whom might have to depend on his revolver for the preservation of his life, would choose carefully, this was not the case with all users. If a revolver looked effective, and was cheaply priced, this was enough for most civilians. Nor was their trust always misplaced, for many of the R.I.C. copies were perfectly adequate weapons for household defense. Some were worse than others – and some were very popular indeed. The example illustrated here stands at the lower end of the scale: it was hardly worth the little money it sold for. In general appearance it resembles the earliest version of the original Webley, with a plain cylinder and the distinctive hump in the top strap just in front of the trigger. It has the usual round, stubby barrel cast integrally with the frame, and it was so badly made that the right barrel wall is appreciably thicker than the left. Although it bears Birmingham proof marks and the barrel is stamped "TRULOCK & HARRIS, 9 DAWSON ST DUBLIN" its origin is obviously uncertain, and it could have been made by one of many back-street Belgian workshops which made copies of several weapons, and spuriously stamped.

Saloon Pistol — Belgium

Length (gun): 14.5in (368mm)
Barrel: 10.1in (257mm)
Weight: 28.0oz (0.8kg)
Caliber: 0.22in (5.6mm)
Rifling: 7 grooves, r/hand
Capacity: one
Muz vel: ca 750ft/sec (229m/sec)

Pistols of this kind were popular for target practice in Europe in the late 19th Century. Duels were by then still quite common in continental Europe, where young men of fashion considered it prudent to keep in practice in case of a challenge. Small-bore weapons firing bulleted caps were adequate for this kind of exercise; their relative lack of noise and smoke made them eminently suitable for practice in an indoor saloon, hence their name. Although this particular specimen, which is of Belgian origin, bears no maker's name, it was well made and finished. The barrel was hinged and was broken by pressing forward the catch protruding from the frame in front of the trigger-guard. It was provided with an extractor.

Miniature Pistol — Belgium

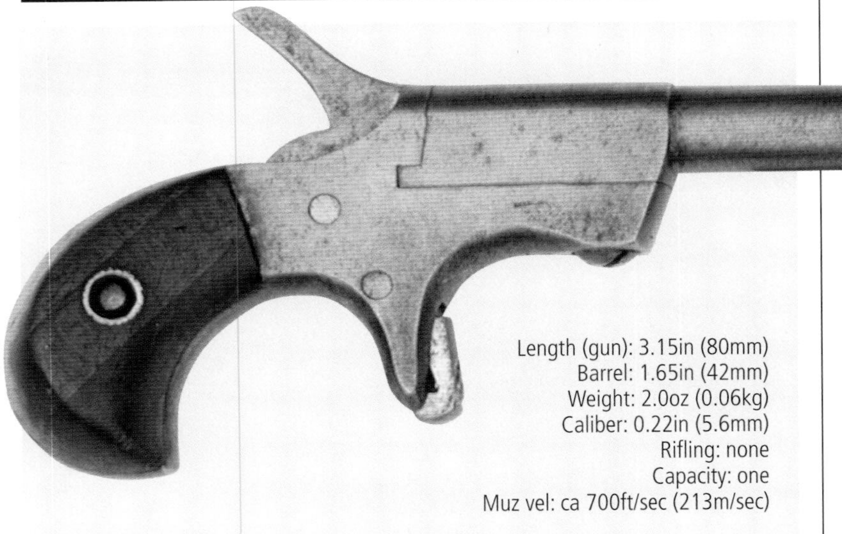

Length (gun): 3.15in (80mm)
Barrel: 1.65in (42mm)
Weight: 2.0oz (0.06kg)
Caliber: 0.22in (5.6mm)
Rifling: none
Capacity: one
Muz vel: ca 700ft/sec (213m/sec)

The process of miniaturization has always fascinated designers in many fields, so it is hardly to be expected that the designers of weapons should be exempt from it. The products of this branch of the trade fall into two main categories. In the first place there are so-called apprentice pieces, made by young men in the gunmakers' workshops to demonstrate their skills. These are often small works of art in themselves. Secondly, we find normal production-line weapons which have simply been made on a reduced scale, but which will fire commercially available cartridges. The little pistol illustrated was a weapon of the latter type; it was made in Belgium, probably at the end of the 19th Century. It was of very simple construction, with a single-action hammer and a sheathed trigger. The barrel was mounted on a horizontal pivot, the head of the screw being just visible in the photograph, in the bulge of the front of the frame. In order to load, the hammer was cocked and the breech swiveled to the right to allow a cartridge to be inserted. As the hammer fell, its nose entered a slot cut in the barrel just above the chamber: this prevented any risk of the barrel turning at the moment of firing. The pistol was smooth-bored and was designed for a bulleted cap, but would chamber a 0.22in short cartridge.

Chamelot-Delvigne Service-Type Revolver — Belgium

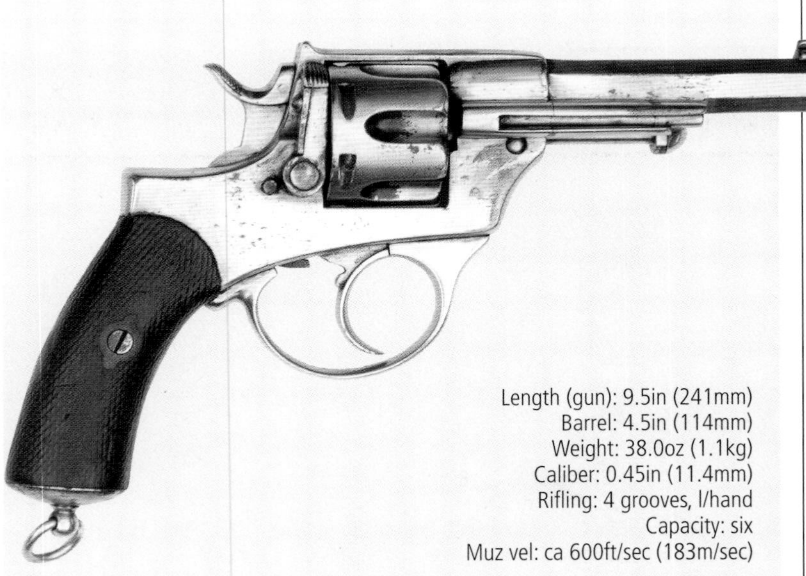

Length (gun): 9.5in (241mm)
Barrel: 4.5in (114mm)
Weight: 38.0oz (1.1kg)
Caliber: 0.45in (11.4mm)
Rifling: 4 grooves, l/hand
Capacity: six
Muz vel: ca 600ft/sec (183m/sec)

The first firm to patent and manufacture the Chamelot-Delvigne double-action lock for revolvers was Pirlot Frères of Liège, Belgium. Although little is known of the lock's origins, it proved to be strong, simple, and reliable, which made it highly suitable for use on military arms. It was used by a number of countries – notably Belgium, France, Italy, and Switzerland – in the last 30 years of the 19th Century. The weapon illustrated is probably fairly typical, although its origin is obscure: it has no visible markings other than a crown with, apparently, the initials "G.A." beneath it, and it is probably of Belgian make. It has an octagonal barrel, screwed into a solid frame. The foresight was laterally adjustable and the backsight is a V-notch at the rear of the top strap. There is a bottom-hinged loading gate which opened to the rear; a small stop projected from the frame to prevent it from dropping too far. The ejector rod worked in a sleeve, the head of the rod being turned inward when not in use to fit over the long forward extension of the axis pin. The latter is held in place by a spring-loaded stud on the left side of the frame.

Taurus Magnum Model 86 Revolver — Brazil

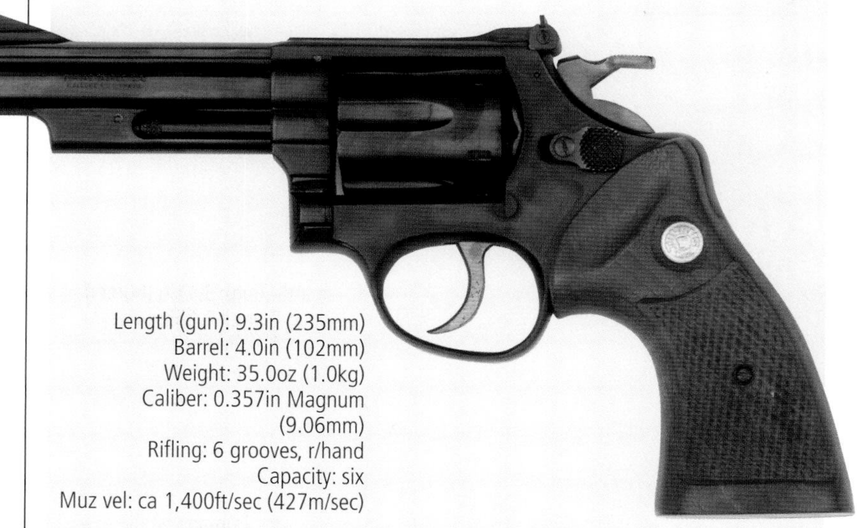

Length (gun): 9.3in (235mm)
Barrel: 4.0in (102mm)
Weight: 35.0oz (1.0kg)
Caliber: 0.357in Magnum (9.06mm)
Rifling: 6 grooves, r/hand
Capacity: six
Muz vel: ca 1,400ft/sec (427m/sec)

The 0.357in (9.06mm) Magnum revolver was originally introduced by Smith & Wesson in 1935, the cartridge being designed in co-operation with Winchester. The Magnum cartridge is about 0.1in (2.54mm) longer in the case than the 0.38in (9.6mm) Special cartridge, and it may be safely fired only in revolvers specially designed for it. It is popular in the United States, particularly perhaps for game shooting, because of its power and flat trajectory, and it is sometimes used as a rifle cartridge. The weapon illustrated was manufactured by Taurus of Brazil, who began to make revolvers of this caliber in 1975. These arms sell well in the United States and are reputed to be of good quality; certainly, the workmanship and finish of the specimen illustrated leaves little to be desired. It is of solid-frame type and has a round barrel with a very wide top rib; the foresight is of ramp type and the arm is fitted with a micrometer backsight, the whole sighting plane being milled to reduce reflection. The cylinder holds six cartridges, the ends of the chambers being recessed to enclose the cartridge heads, and it swings out to the left on its own separate yoke. It has the usual pin-operated extractor; the pin is located in a housing beneath the barrel when the cylinder is in position. There is a separate firing-pin in the standing breech, and the hammer has a wide, flat comb for ease of cocking. The large checkered butt is of two-piece construction and no metal work is visible, except at the back. Small, white-metal medallions in the butt are marked "Taurus Brasil," with a bull's head in the center.

Inglis Browning 0.455in No1 Mk1 (Browning GP35) Pistol — Canada

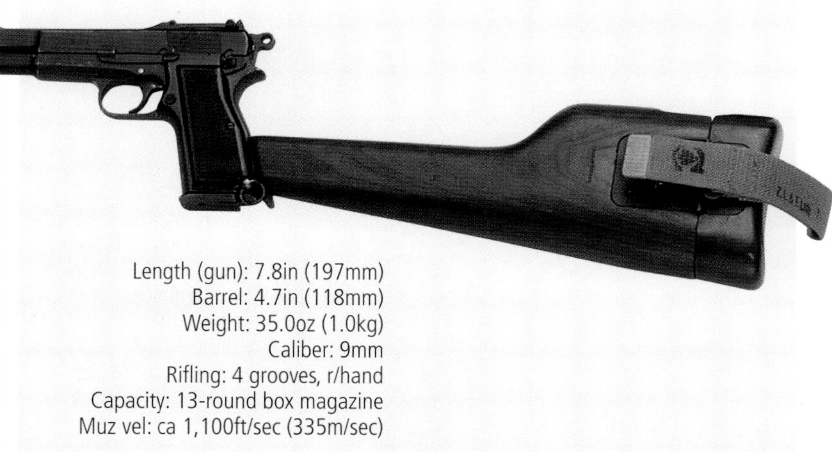

Length (gun): 7.8in (197mm)
Barrel: 4.7in (118mm)
Weight: 35.0oz (1.0kg)
Caliber: 9mm
Rifling: 4 grooves, r/hand
Capacity: 13-round box magazine
Muz vel: ca 1,100ft/sec (335m/sec)

A team of Belgian engineers from the Fabrique Nationale escaped to Britain in 1940, taking with them a number of designs, including those for the Browning GP35 (qv). In 1942 they were sent across the Atlantic, where they helped to establish a production line for the Browning GP35, which was designated the Pistol, Canadian, No1 Mk1 and rechambered to take the British 0.455in round. This picture shows an Inglis-produced Browning together with, rather unusually, a wooden holster-cum-stock.

Ceská Zbrojovka Model 1924 Pistol — Czech Republic

Length (gun): 6.3in (160mm)
Barrel: 3.5in (90mm)
Weight: 24.0oz (0.7kg)
Caliber: 7.65mm
Rifling: 6 grooves, r/hand
Capacity: 8-round box magazine
Muz vel: ca 800ft/sec (244m/sec)

The design of this pistol originated in Germany with an engineer named Nickl, who worked for Mauser. In the early 1920s the company sent Nickl to Czechoslovakia to help establish a Mauser rifle production line and when he learnt that the Czechoslovak Army was looking for a pistol he recast his design to take the 9mm Short round and the weapon went into production at Brno in 1922, as the Vz-22. This had a slightly complicated method of operation: at the moment of firing the barrel and slide were locked to each other and as the slide moved to the rear it caused the barrel to rotate slightly and to unlock itself, following which the reloading cycle carried on in the usual way. It had an external hammer and a safety catch was fitted on the left side of the frame, which was released by pressing the circular stud immediately below it. In 1926 the production line moved to a new factory and the opportunity was taken to simplify the pistol, the only visible evidence of which was that hard rubber grips replaced the previous wooden ones. This new weapon was designated the Vz-24 and remained in production until the mid-1930s.

Ceská Zbrojovka CZ27 Pistol — Czech Republic

Length (gun): 6.3in (159mm)
Barrel: 4.0in (102mm)
Weight: 25.5oz (0.7kg)
Caliber: 9mm
Rifling: 6 grooves, r/hand
Capacity: eight
Muz vel: ca 900ft/sec (274m/sec)

Following the introduction of the CZ 24, the designer decided that the locking system was unnecessary for such a relatively low-powered round, and redesigned the pistol to eliminate this feature and simplify the design. The result was the CZ 27. Externally it appears to be almost identical to the 1924 model, the main apparent difference being that the finger-grooves at the rear of the slide were vertical rather than diagonal. The pistol worked on straight blowback, with its recoil spring mounted around a rod situated below and parallel with the barrel. It had an external hammer and there was a magazine safety on the left-hand side of the frame, just above the magazine release stud. In pistols made before 1939, the milled top rib was marked "CESKA ZBROJOVKA AS v PRAZE," together with the serial number. When the Germans occupied Czechoslovakia, manufacture was continued on a considerable scale: weapons made during that period are recognizable by the fact that the inscription reads "BOHMISCH WAFFEN FABRIK AG IN PRAG." The left side of the slide on this specimen is also marked "PISTOLE MODELL 27 KAL 7.65." Manufacture of this model continued until 1951.

CESKÁ ZBROJOVKA MODEL 39 PISTOL — CZECH REPUBLIC

Length (gun): 8.1in (206mm)
Barrel: 4.7in (118mm)
Weight: 33.0oz (0.9kg)
Caliber: 9mm
Rifling: 6 grooves, r/hand
Capacity: eight
Muz vel: ca 950ft/sec (290m/sec)

An arms manufactory was established at Pilsen in Czechoslovakia, then a newly-founded country, in 1919, and moved to Strakonitz in 1921. It made a wide variety of weapons and accessories for the Czechoslovak Army. After World War II, the Ceská Zbrojovka (CZ) company, like Czechoslovakia itself, came under Communist control; its weapons production was then greatly reduced in favor of other items. Between the two World Wars, however, the company made a whole series of pistols, both small-calibered pocket types for sale commercially and arms of somewhat heavier calibers for military use. The earliest of these fired from a locked breech, but as the short cartridge employed hardly warranted the use of this system, subsequent models reverted to simple blowback. The Ceská Zbrojovka Model 39 pistol illustrated here is very well made and finished, but it was not a success as a military arm. In spite of its weight and bulk, it fired only a low-powered round, and its exposed hammer could not be cocked: the arm had to be fired by a quite heavy pull on the trigger, and this, of course, hardly contributed to its accuracy. It was very easy to strip: forward pressure on a milled catch on the left of the frame allowed the slide and barrel to be raised on a rear hinge.

CESKÁ ZBROJOVKA CZ 1950 PISTOL — CZECH REPUBLIC

Length (gun): 8.2in (208mm)
Barrel: 4.7in (119mm)
Weight: 34.0oz (1.0kg)
Caliber: 7.62mm
Rifling: 4 grooves, r/hand
Capacity: eight
Muz vel: ca 1,000ft/sec (305m/sec)

This self-loading pistol had its origins after the end of the World War II, when the Czech Army decided that it needed a new pistol. The new weapon was in production by 1950. It was basically similar to the German Walther PP (qv) although there were some manufacturing differences. It was a reasonably effective pistol but, like many European service arms, its caliber lacked the essential stopping power for service use; therefore, within a very short period, it had been replaced as a military arm, although it continued in use for police purposes. It was replaced by the Ceská Zbrojovka CZ 1952 (qv) which, although of the same caliber, fired a much more powerful round from a locked breech, working by means of a roller device similar to that on the German MG 42 machine gun. This pistol was, in its turn, replaced by the Russian Makarov (qv).

CESKÁ ZBROJOVKA 0.38IN ZKR-551 REVOLVER — CZECH REPUBLIC

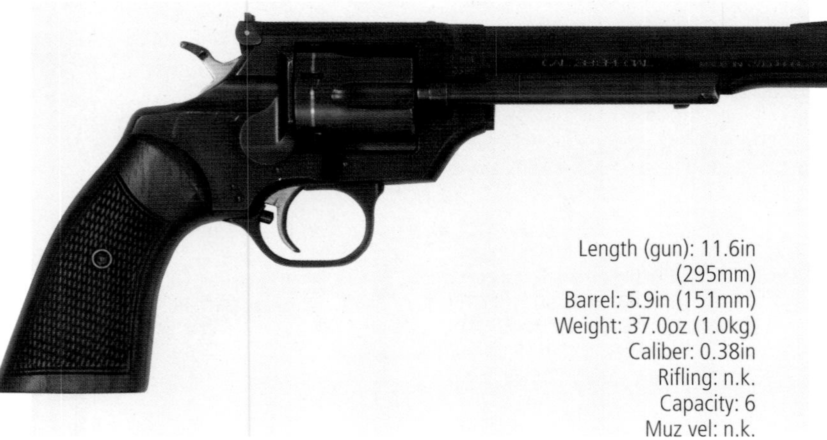

Length (gun): 11.6in (295mm)
Barrel: 5.9in (151mm)
Weight: 37.0oz (1.0kg)
Caliber: 0.38in
Rifling: n.k.
Capacity: 6
Muz vel: n.k.

The Czechoslovak ZKR-551 was introduced in 1957 and was a six-shot, target revolver, chambered for 0.38in Special caliber. A competition weapon, it was, in fact, intended for just one event, the UIT Centerfire, which involves one shot per exposure of the target. It was an elegant and impeccably built weapon, distinguished by a low bore line and a fast lock time, with no serious vices. It has a solid frame with gate loading, using a gate to the right of the frame which rocks rearward, locking the action and freeing the cylinder to rotate clockwise. The cases are manually ejected by a sprung-rod ejector mounted offset to the right under the barrel, as in the 1873 Colt.

DANSK SCHOUBOE MODEL 1907 PISTOL — DENMARK

Length (gun): 8.8in (224mm)
Barrel: 5.0in (127mm)
Weight: 42.0oz (1.2kg)
Caliber: 11.35mm
Rifling: 6 grooves, r/hand
Capacity: six
Muz vel: ca 1,600ft/sec (488m/sec)

Lieutenant Jens Torring Schouboe was an officer in the Danish Army and also, apparently, a director of the Dansk Rekylriffel Syndikat; he was closely involved with the development of the famous Madsen light machine gun. In 1903, Schouboe patented a self-loading pistol, but although it was well made and reliable, it failed to sell. He therefore decided that what was needed was a heavier arm of the same general type but of service caliber, the result being the weapon illustrated here. Like his earlier arms, this was of simple blowback design, without any breech-locking mechanism – but while this type of action was easy enough to incorporate into small pocket pistols firing low-powered cartridges, it was very hard to do so in a service-type arm without making it extremely heavy. Schouboe's answer to this problem was to produce a cartridge firing an extremely lightweight bullet which, he reasoned, would not only reduce recoil but would also leave the barrel faster, thus reducing the period of maximum pressure. The bullet was basically a wooden round with a thin metal jacket. Schouboe's solution worked: the weapon was very satisfactory from the purely mechanical point of view – but it had two serious defects as a military arm. The first was that the bullet was too light to have very much stopping power; the second was that it lost accuracy very quickly, presumably for the same reason. Although Schouboe produced improved versions, it was never popular and manufacture ceased in 1917.

Longspur-Type Revolver — Europe

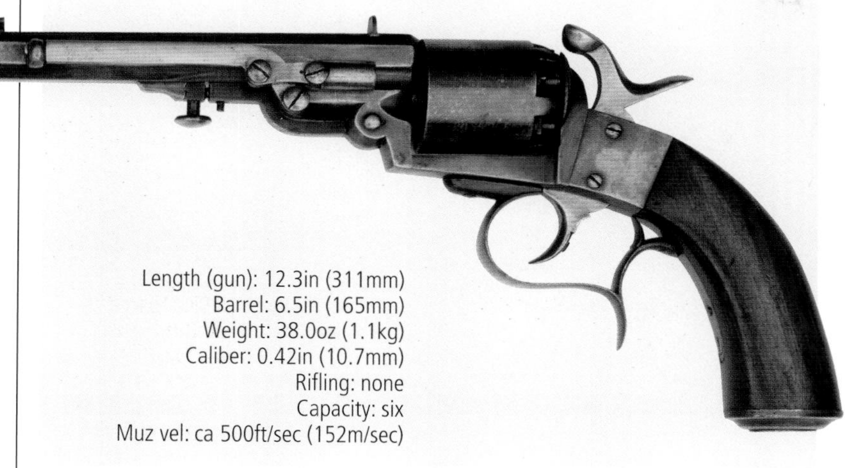

Length (gun): 12.3in (311mm)
Barrel: 6.5in (165mm)
Weight: 38.0oz (1.1kg)
Caliber: 0.42in (10.7mm)
Rifling: none
Capacity: six
Muz vel: ca 500ft/sec (152m/sec)

The origins of the weapon illustrated here are obscure. There are no proof marks or inscriptions of any kind upon it; but the affinity of its general style with the Webley Longspur revolver (qv) suggests that it is a Western Europe copy of that arm. The frame is made in one piece, without a top strap, and with a short upper tang and a long lower tang into which is screwed the one-piece walnut butt, with its metal butt-cap. The octagonal barrel is a separate component and is fitted to the frame in a somewhat complex way: a cylindrical hole in the lump below the breech end fits over a very long axis pin; the bottom of the lump is also braced against the lower frame to make a very rigid joint. To remove the barrel it would have been necessary first to slide back the mushroom-shaped stud below it and then to draw down the lever behind it to the vertical. This disengaged a half-round locking pin from it corresponding recess on the axis pin, allowing the entire barrel to be drawn forward and clear. The lever of the rammer, which is of Kerr's type, locked into a hook on the left-hand side of the barrel. When the lever was raised vertically, the ram, which has a conical hole in its nose, was forced into the appropriate chamber. The cylinder is plain, with nipple partitions, and the lock is of double-action type. There is no special cylinder stop: the nose of the hammer is so shaped that it fits exactly between two nipple partitions, preventing any rotation of the cylinder. The revolver is plainly constructed, strong, and robust.

Continental Tip-Up Revolver — Europe

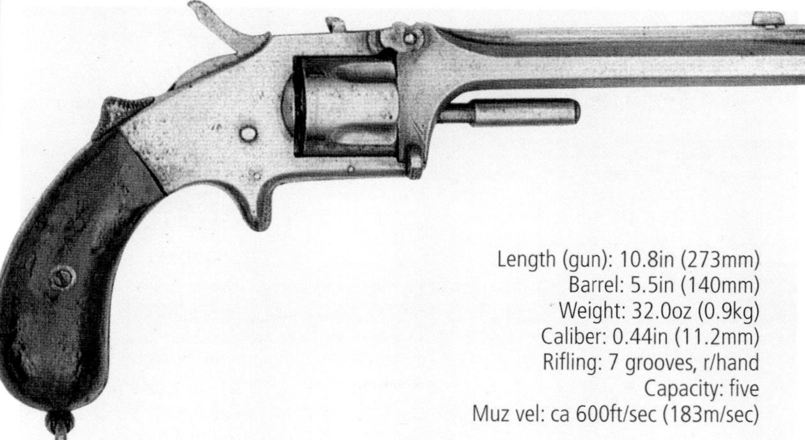

Length (gun): 10.8in (273mm)
Barrel: 5.5in (140mm)
Weight: 32.0oz (0.9kg)
Caliber: 0.44in (11.2mm)
Rifling: 7 grooves, r/hand
Capacity: five
Muz vel: ca 600ft/sec (183m/sec)

The centerfire cartridge quickly became more popular than the pinfire and Smith & Wesson patented a 0.22in (5.6mm) cartridge of this type in the United States in 1855-56. It was subsequently produced also in 0.32in (8.1mm) caliber. One of the difficulties of Smith & Wesson's patent for a bored-through cylinder was that it was valid only in the United States. Thus, although the patent gave them an American monopoly, the firm had no protection against the cylinder being copied in Europe or elsewhere; as a result, pirated copies soon began to appear. It is generally thought that the firm of Webley was producing such unlicensed copies in the early 1860s; but as these were, of course, unmarked, it is impossible to be certain. The weapon illustrated here is something of a mystery: although obviously of Smith & Wesson type, it bears no name or mark other than the date, 1874, on the left-hand side of the barrel frame, and one or two manufacturing numbers on the cylinder. The major differences (apart from size) from the genuine arm are the provision of a backsight on the top frame; the fact that the cylinder stop rose from the bottom; and that the weapon is of centerfire rather than rimfire type and is fitted with a sliding safety behind the hammer. The weapon appears to be well made, although it lacks the finish of a real Smith & Wesson. Its size, and the provision of a lanyard ring, suggest that it was intended for use as a military or perhaps paramilitary weapon.

Lahti L/35 Pistol — Finland

Length (gun): 9.4in (239mm)
Barrel: 4.7in (119mm)
Weight: 44.0oz (1.3kg)
Caliber: 9mm
Rifling: 6 grooves, r/hand
Capacity: eight
Muz vel: ca 1,100ft/sec (335m/sec)

This pistol was invented by Aimo Lahti of Finland and was produced by Valtion, the Finnish state factory. It was originally intended to be made in two calibers, 7.65mm and 9mm Parabellum, but the former never got beyond the prototype stage. The arm was adopted as the official pistol of the Finnish armed forces in 1935; it gave good service in the Finnish campaign against the Russians in the early part of World War II, when it was found to be particularly reliable in very low temperatures. Although, as may be seen, it bore a general resemblance to the Luger, this is fortuitous: the two were quite different mechanically. The Lahti fired from a closed breech the bolt being unlocked after a brief rearward travel and going on to complete the usual cycle. The mechanism incorporated a bolt accelerator – a curved arm which was so designed that it increased the rearward velocity of the bolt. A version of the Lahti was also used by the Swedish forces, by whom it was called the M/40. The Swedes had originally settled for the German Walther P38 (qv) but when war intervened they turned instead to Finland. The Finns supplied some, but later they were made under license by the Swedish firm of Husqvarna Vapenfabrik. Although the Swedes make excellent weapons, their M/40 was generally considered inferior to its Finnish prototype.

Châtellerault Gendarmerie Pistol — France

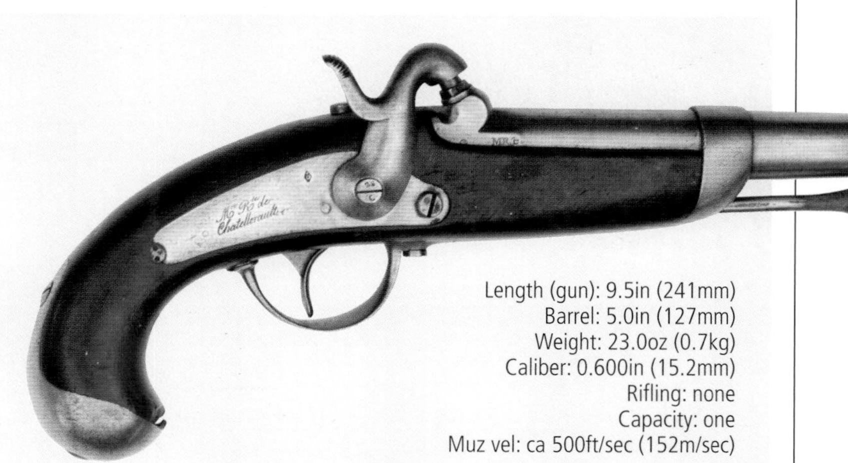

Length (gun): 9.5in (241mm)
Barrel: 5.0in (127mm)
Weight: 23.0oz (0.7kg)
Caliber: 0.600in (15.2mm)
Rifling: none
Capacity: one
Muz vel: ca 500ft/sec (152m/sec)

This pistol was made at the great Royal Factory at Châtellerault in 1845, three years after this model was first produced in response to the need for change to the new percussion system – a process then being carried out by all major military powers of the world. The pistol has a short stubby barrel, about 1in (25.4mm) of which is octagonal at the breech end, and the nipple stands somewhat higher than is usual on comparable British weapons. It is possible that the barrel is, in fact, a conversion from the earlier flintlock variety. There are the usual tang screws, the front end of the barrel being secured to the stock by a steel collar with its long lower tang inset into the woodwork, where its rear end meets the front end of the trigger-guard. The hammer, which is of characteristic shape, is mounted on a back-action lock neatly in-let into the stock, where it is retained by a screw with its lower end sited in a small plate. The tail of the lock is held in position by a second small screw, the head of which hooks over it. The stock, which appears to be of walnut, has a steel cap, and the trigger-guard is made of the same metal (there is, in fact, a complete absence of brass on this weapon). The ramrod, the front end of which is badly corroded and blackened in this example, passes through the collar and into a hole in the stock. This is a very neat and compact arm, suitable for service use, but portable in a pocket if necessary.

CHÂTELLERAULT SERVICE PISTOL — FRANCE

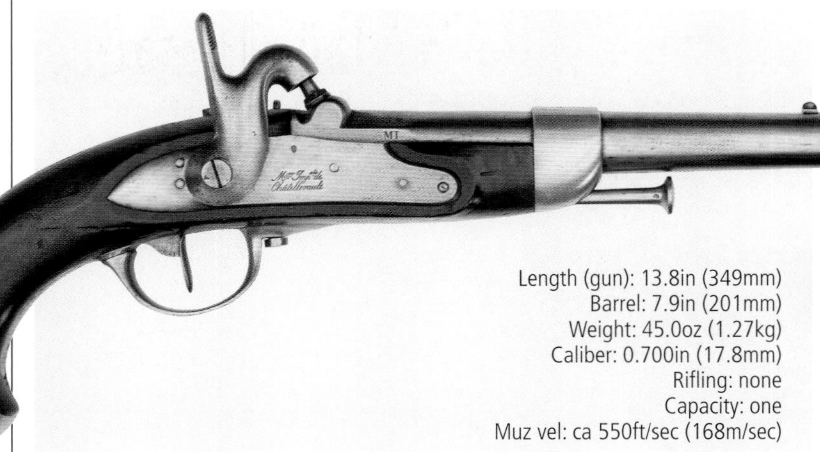

Length (gun): 13.8in (349mm)
Barrel: 7.9in (201mm)
Weight: 45.0oz (1.27kg)
Caliber: 0.700in (17.8mm)
Rifling: none
Capacity: one
Muz vel: ca 550ft/sec (168m/sec)

French arms developed certain easily recognizable characteristics which make the origins of arms like the pistol seen here quite clear. This pistol is plainly made and of sound and robust construction, well-suited to service use. The slightly tapered barrel – which is, of course, smooth-bored – has both fixed foresight and backsight. The tang is marked "Mle (ie, "Model") 1842" and bears the date "1855," and the letters "MI" may be seen just in front of the nipple lump. There are further markings on the left-hand side of the breech. The lockplate, which is severely plain, bears the (abbreviated) inscription "Manufacture Imperiale de Châtellerault," marking its origin in one of the great French factories. The hammer, with its near-vertical checkered comb and its massive, in-turned nose is at once recognizable as French. The solid brass cap holding the barrel to the front of the stock has a rearward projection on the left side with a retaining screw, and connects up to the sideplate on which the heads of the lock screws rest. The steel ramrod is retained in a recess running through the brass cap and into the stock. The stock is of walnut, the top and bottom of the butt being reinforced with steel strips: the top strip just touches the massive brass butt-cap with its swivel lanyard ring.

LAGRESE REVOLVER — FRANCE

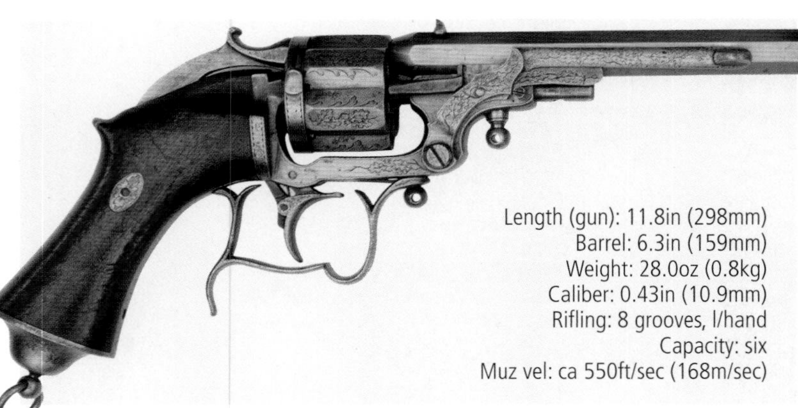

Length (gun): 11.8in (298mm)
Barrel: 6.3in (159mm)
Weight: 28.0oz (0.8kg)
Caliber: 0.43in (10.9mm)
Rifling: 8 grooves, l/hand
Capacity: six
Muz vel: ca 550ft/sec (168m/sec)

This revolver, made by Lagrese of Paris in about 1866, is well made and finished, but is of somewhat ornate appearance and extreme complexity. The frame, including the butt, is made in one piece without any top strap; the octagonal barrel is screwed to the front end of the frame, through which also passes the cylinder axis pin. This appears to make a rigid joint and there is no play apparent – although the permanent gap between the barrel and the cylinder is about 0.05in (1.3mm), which must have led to a considerable loss of gases. The arrangement of the cylinder is also strange. It is fitted with a separate back plate which incorporates a loading gate. Conical apertures were pierced through the back plate to allow the nose of the hammer to reach the cartridges. In order to load, it was necessary first to put the nose of the hammer into a safety hole in the plate. This held the plate rigid but allowed the gate to be opened and the cylinder to be rotated clockwise. A groove on the right side of the butt allowed the rounds to be slid in. The ejection was of percussion rammer type, in which an upward pull of the lever forced the ram backwards into the chamber. The lock is of the self-cocking variety, but there is a basic comb on the hammer which allowed it to be drawn back slightly and then lowered into the safety hole mentioned earlier. The arm is lightly engraved but there are no traces of any finish: it is difficult to know whether it was originally bright or has been over-cleaned. The barrel is inscribed "Lagrese Bte a Paris." All in all, this is a truly remarkable weapon.

DEVISME REVOLVER — FRANCE

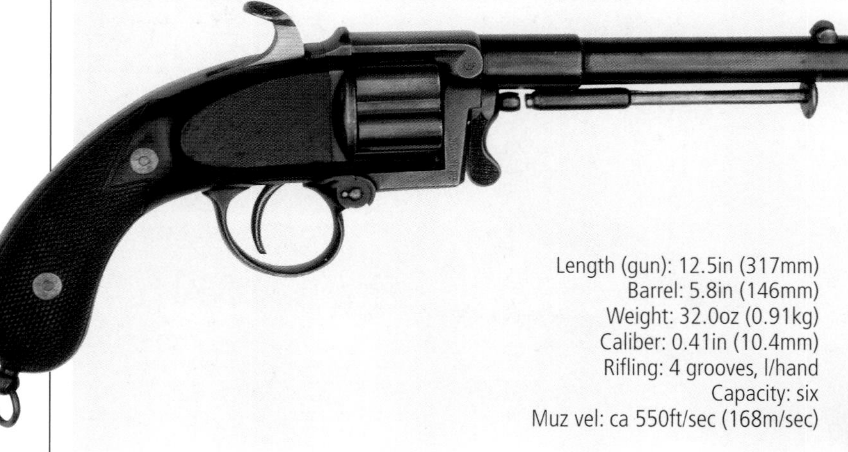

Length (gun): 12.5in (317mm)
Barrel: 5.8in (146mm)
Weight: 32.0oz (0.91kg)
Caliber: 0.41in (10.4mm)
Rifling: 4 grooves, l/hand
Capacity: six
Muz vel: ca 550ft/sec (168m/sec)

The manufacturer of this weapon was F. P. Devisme, a Parisian gunmaker of considerable repute, who had produced a self-cocking percussion revolver in limited quantity before 1830. He was also an early experimenter with centerfire cartridges. The revolver seen here is of the type first shown at the Paris Exhibition of 1867, and it is fairly closely based on an earlier percussion revolver by the same maker. It has a cylindrical steel barrel screwed into a frame which is, in turn, hinged at the bottom of the standing breech, just in front of the trigger-guard. Pressure on the vertical milled lever in front of the frame allowed the barrel to drop down to an angle of about 45 degrees, giving access to the cylinder. The locking device is somewhat unusual, for it is based on the cylinder axis pin. The front end of the pin passes through the frame and is attached to the opening lever. The rear end has on it a rectangular stud which entered a corresponding socket on the standing breech when the arm was closed. Returning the opening lever to its normal, vertical position caused the stud to turn in the socket and locked it firmly. The extractor pin sleeve is attached to another sleeve round the barrel: the movement of the lever activated a simple rack-and-pinion device which swung the extractor pin out to the right, in readiness to knock out the empty cases one at a time. The lock is of single-action type and is fitted with a half-cock to hold the hammer nose clear of the rounds in the chambers. The weapon is of excellent quality and finish, with barrel and cylinder blued and the remainder case-hardened. The top of the barrel is inscribed "DEVISME a PARIS," and the frame marked "DEVISME BTE."

LEFAUCHEUX PINFIRE REVOLVER — FRANCE

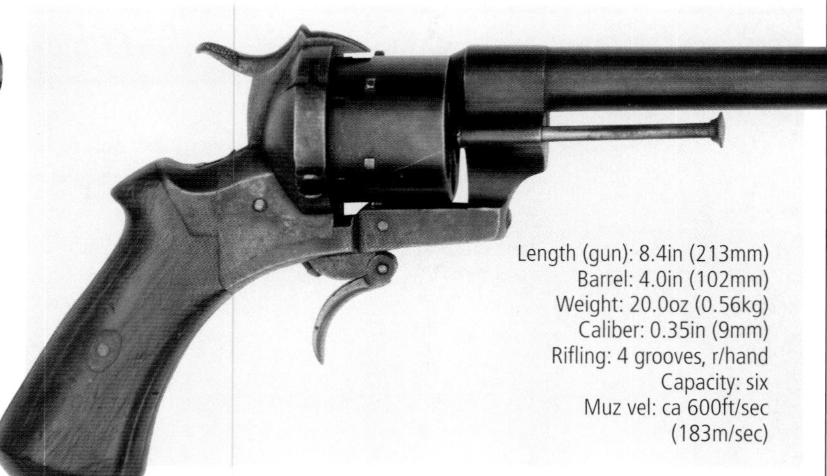

Length (gun): 8.4in (213mm)
Barrel: 4.0in (102mm)
Weight: 20.0oz (0.56kg)
Caliber: 0.35in (9mm)
Rifling: 4 grooves, r/hand
Capacity: six
Muz vel: ca 600ft/sec (183m/sec)

As soon as the percussion system made it possible to produce fire by means of a remote blow, the major problem for firearms was very largely solved – although, of course, a good deal more experiment was necessary before a reliable system could be perfected. In particular, there remained the difficulty of obtaining perfect obturation – ie, the prevention of burning gases escaping from the breech at the moment of firing – without making the breech mechanism so complex that it offered little or no advantage over the existing muzzle-loaders. The pinfire cartridge was invented by a Frenchman named Casimir Lefaucheux as early as 1828, and was in quite extensive use, mainly in Europe, before 1840. However, it does not seem to have aroused much interest in Britain until its appearance at the Great Exhibition held in London in 1851, when it was shown in conjunction with an arm of the pepperbox type. A more modern type of arm was then developed by Casimir's son Eugène, who patented it in Great Britain in 1854. The general style of this weapon is clear. It is plain and of robust construction: the octagonal barrel is attached to the axis pin (as in Colt arms) and is further braced against the lower part of the frame, making a reasonably rigid joint. The heavy standing breech is fitted with a top-hinged loading gate with a spring catch, and a simple sliding rod is provided for knocking out the empty cases. The small, square studs on the otherwise plain cylinder engaged with the cylinder stop and held the cylinder rigid at the moment of firing. The weapon has no trigger-guard, and the trigger folded forward, thus making it less bulky for carriage in a pocket.

Lefaucheux Fist Pistol — France

Length (gun): 4.8in (122mm)
Barrel: 1.9in (48mm)
Weight: 11.0oz (0.3kg)
Caliber: 0.275in (7mm)
Rifling: none
Capacity: six
Muz vel: ca 450ft/sec (137m/sec)

This type of pistol is called coup de poing in France, where it originated, and the translation "fist pistol" seems to be as appropriate as any. It is in many ways a rather ugly little weapon. Its long, fluted, pepperbox cylinder is made from a single piece of metal, and the front end of the cylinder axis pin is supported by a bracket screwed to the front end of the lower frame. The standing breech consists of a flat, circular plate: a semi-circular portion is cut out on the right-hand side so that the weapon could be loaded from the breech end. This loading aperture is filled by a bottom-hinged gate fitted with a small stud to give purchase; and its bottom end bore on the small, horizontal, L-shaped spring screwed below it on the frame. There is a further shallow depression, into which the hammer fitted, on top of the standing breech. The lock is of self-cocking type and could be fired only by steady pressure on the trigger, which is of the forward-hinged variety and is thus without a trigger-guard. The cylinder was normally free to rotate, but when the trigger was pressed a cylinder-stop rose from the lower frame and engaged one of the studs which can be seen on the cylinder. When loaded, the cylinder could be positioned so that there was a pin on each side of the hammer head, thus making it relatively safe to carry the loaded weapon in a pocket. Once the rounds had been fired, the empty cases could be pushed out through the open loading gate by means of a separate extractor pin. Arms of this kind sometimes incorporated a knuckle-duster and dagger, and are known as "Apache pistols," a reference to the denizens of the underworld of 19th Century Paris.

Lefaucheux Pinfire Naval Revolver — France

Length (gun): 11.3in (286mm)
Barrel: 5.3in (133mm)
Weight: 34.0oz (1.0kg)
Caliber: 0.43in (11mm)
Rifling: 4 grooves, l/hand
Capacity: six
Muz vel: ca 650ft/sec (198m/sec)

Casimir Lefaucheux and his son Eugène were closely concerned in the development of the pinfire cartridge. The pinfire revolver never really received anything approaching complete acceptance in Britain; but matters were very much otherwise in continental Europe, where it was quite widely used. The French Government carried out extensive trials with pinfire weapons in the course of the Crimean War (the other arms concerned were the American Colt and the British Beaumont-Adams; both, of course, percussion arms), and as a result a Lefaucheux pinfire revolver was selected in 1856 for use by the French Navy. It is in every respect a well-made and reliable weapon: plain, solid, well-balanced, and worthy of being distinguished as a service arm. It has a round barrel with a lump fitting over the cylinder axis pin and fastened also to the lower frame, to which it is both slotted and screwed to make a rigid joint. It has the usual solid standing breech with a loading gate on the right-hand side. The cylinder revolved freely except at full cock, when a stop protruded horizontally from the lower part of the standing breech and locked the cylinder by acting on the rectangular blocks between the pin apertures. This arm was also adopted by the Italian Navy in 1858.

Le Mat Revolver — France

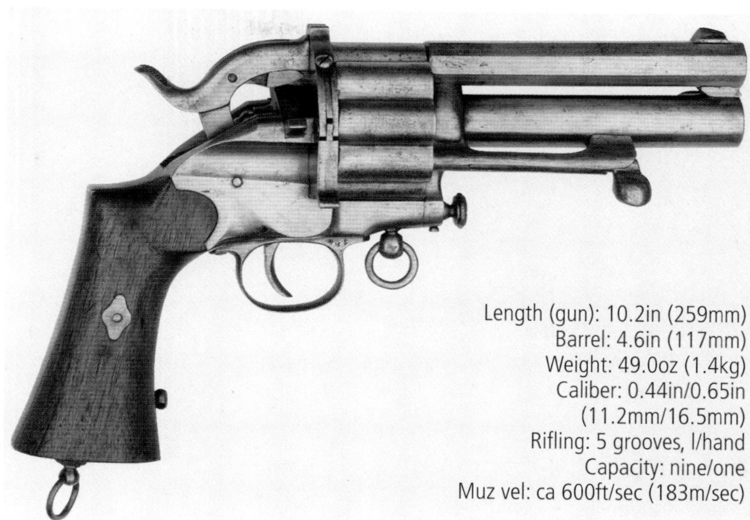

Length (gun): 10.2in (259mm)
Barrel: 4.6in (117mm)
Weight: 49.0oz (1.4kg)
Caliber: 0.44in/0.65in (11.2mm/16.5mm)
Rifling: 5 grooves, l/hand
Capacity: nine/one
Muz vel: ca 600ft/sec (183m/sec)

This revolver is a cartridge version of the earlier percussion Le Mat; it was made in France, probably in about 1868. It is of a somewhat complex, built-up construction, being based on its lower, shot barrel, which was firmly seated in the standing breech and acted also as an axis pin for the revolver cylinder. The lower frame of the upper barrel has a sleeve which fits over the lower barrel; an extension from this is screwed firmly to the lower frame, making what appears to be a good, rigid joint. The upper barrel and cylinder (which has nine chambers) allowed the arm to be used as an orthodox single-action cartridge revolver, with a loading gate and a sliding ejector rod of Colt type. To load the lower shot barrel, it was necessary first to cock the weapon and then open the side-hinged breechblock by manipulating the catch visible behind the cylinder The breechblock has its own firing pin; to ensure that this was struck, a hinged block on the underside of the hammer was first turned downward. The action of opening the breechblock also activated a semi-circular extractor which engaged under the rim of the cartridge case and pushed it clear. This powerful arm was used in French penal colonies in the second half of the 19th Century, but it does not appear to have been used for military purposes.

Lepage Napoleon Pistol — France

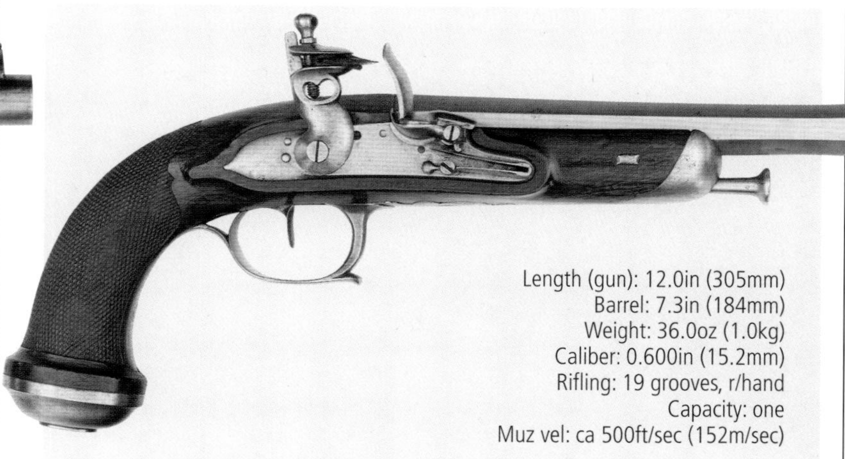

Length (gun): 12.0in (305mm)
Barrel: 7.3in (184mm)
Weight: 36.0oz (1.0kg)
Caliber: 0.600in (15.2mm)
Rifling: 19 grooves, r/hand
Capacity: one
Muz vel: ca 500ft/sec (152m/sec)

In June 1815, the allied armies of Great Britain and Prussia fought a brief but bloody campaign against the French Army under Napoleon. The campaign ended with the great allied victory of Waterloo, and a few days later the French Emperor surrendered himself to the British. Soon afterwards he was sent into exile on the remote island of St Helena, some 47 square miles (122sq km) of bleak volcanic rock rising from the South Atlantic. Although he was not imprisoned in the strict sense of the word, the island was strongly garrisoned by British troops and the seas around it patrolled by British warships. At some stage towards the end of Napoleon's life, Dr Arnott, medical officer of the 20th Regiment (later the Lancashire Fusiliers), which then formed part of the garrison, was called in to treat him, effecting at least a temporary cure. Napoleon was grateful and gave Arnott a number of presents, including a gold snuff-box on which he had scratched the single initial "N" – and a fine pair of holster pistols, one of which is seen here. This is a handsome weapon, very characteristic of its maker, Lepage of Paris, whose name is engraved on the top flat of its octagonal barrel. It is, of course, a flintlock, and somewhat unusual in that it has multi-grooved rifling, which would have conferred the capacity to throw a ball of about 0.8oz (23gm) to a considerable distance with great accuracy. The pistol is a strictly service arm, plain and unadorned, but well worthy to have been carried by one of the world's greatest soldiers.

MAB MODEL D PISTOL — FRANCE

Length (gun): 5.8in (147mm)
Barrel: 3.2in (81mm)
Weight: 26.0oz (0.7kg)
Caliber: 7.65mm
Rifling: 7 grooves, r/hand
Capacity: nine
Muz vel: ca 800ft/sec (244m/sec)

The initials MAB stand for the Manufacture d'Armes de Bayonne, a company which, since 1921, was chiefly concerned with the manufacture of self-loading pistols of pocket type. The company's products were well made, but most of them were based on the designs of others: the weapon illustrated here, for example, bears a considerable resemblance to the Browning. It was first put on the market in 1933 as the Model C but, enlarged and with a better-shaped butt, reappeared as the Model D – under which designation it was still in production up to 1988. It is of simple blowback design: when the cartridge is fired, the slide and block are forced to the rear, compressing the coil spring which is located round the barrel. The subsequent forward movement strips a round from the magazine and chambers it ready for the next shot. Access to the recoil spring is obtained by pressing up the rear end of the small bar visible under the muzzle: the nose cap can then be turned and removed, taking the spring with it.

MANURHIN MR-32 "MATCH" REVOLVER — FRANCE

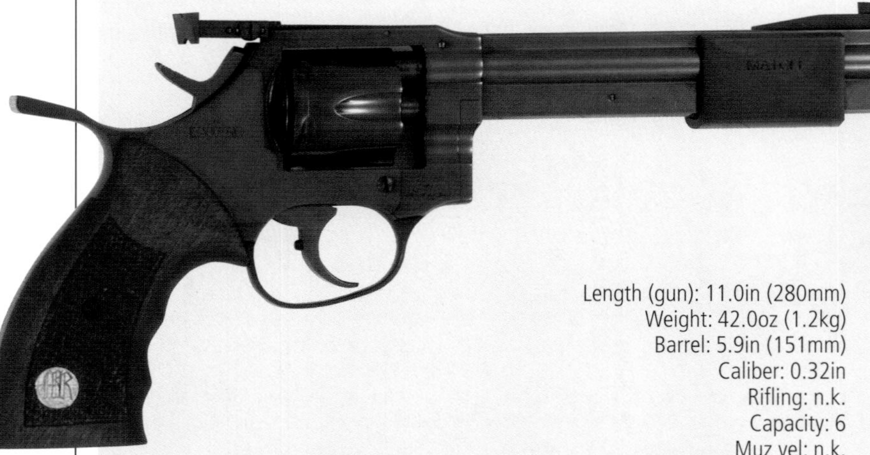

Length (gun): 11.0in (280mm)
Weight: 42.0oz (1.2kg)
Barrel: 5.9in (151mm)
Caliber: 0.32in
Rifling: n.k.
Capacity: 6
Muz vel: n.k.

Manurhin (Manufacture des Machines du Haut-Rhin) was a French company, which produced a range of very high quality pistols for both service and target use. The MR-32 "Match" was designed specifically for UIT Centerfire match competitions and was based on the Manurhin MR-73, which was produced in both 0.357in Magnum and 0.38in Special versions. The MR-32 fires 0.32 Smith & Wesson Long cartridges and is single action only, with a distinctive tang, which is designed to enable the firer to place his or her hand very precisely on the backstrap, a major problem with target revolvers. The crane-mounted cylinder swings to the left and the Smith & Wesson-type thumblatch clears locks at the rear of the cylinder and at the ejector rod tip. There is a square notch rear-sight, adjustable for windage and elevation, and a changeable square post foresight. The pistol-making facility at Manurhin was purchased by the Belgian Fabrique Nationale in the early 1990s.

MARIETTE FOUR-BARRELED PEPPERBOX — FRANCE

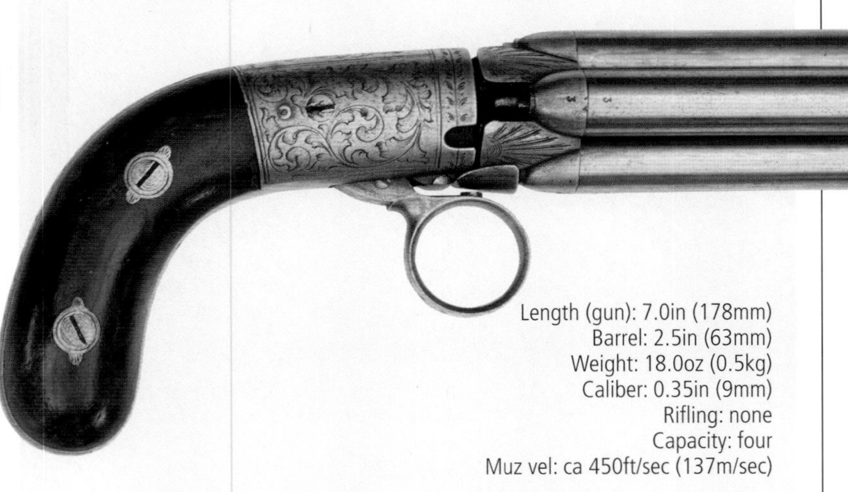

Length (gun): 7.0in (178mm)
Barrel: 2.5in (63mm)
Weight: 18.0oz (0.5kg)
Caliber: 0.35in (9mm)
Rifling: none
Capacity: four
Muz vel: ca 450ft/sec (137m/sec)

The arm seen here is another of the continental Mariette pepperbox pistols. This particular arm, which has four barrels, is one of the immediate successors to the four-barreled, double-locked, turn-over pistols but with additional refinements peculiar to pepperbox arms. It has a rotating breech with four chambers: a separate barrel is screwed onto each chamber, and each barrel is numbered to correspond with its own chamber. The rotating breech is screwed onto a spindle in the standing breech, to which access could be gained – with some difficulty – by way of the narrow space between the barrels, which very nearly touch each other. The barrels could be removed individually by means of a squared key, which fitted into four slots equally spaced around the muzzle; these slots may give the quite incorrect impression that the barrels are rifled. The nipples, which are set in shallow depressions, are in prolongation of the axis of the barrels; they could be capped by way of the U-shaped aperture seen on the right-hand side of the frame. The ring-trigger rotated the barrels and activated the hammer, and also incorporated the usual hood which masked completely the nipple which was actually being fired.

ST ETIENNE MODÈLE 1777 — FRANCE

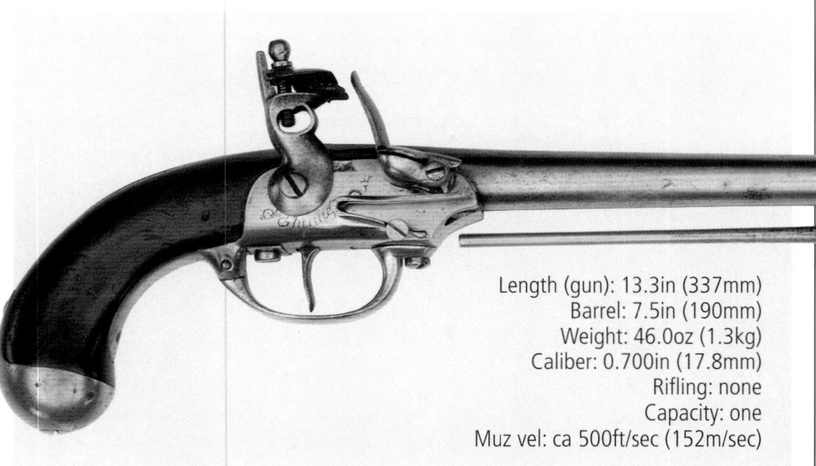

Length (gun): 13.3in (337mm)
Barrel: 7.5in (190mm)
Weight: 46.0oz (1.3kg)
Caliber: 0.700in (17.8mm)
Rifling: none
Capacity: one
Muz vel: ca 500ft/sec (152m/sec)

This is one of the last of the new weapons that equipped the French royalist army before the country was overwhelmed by revolution in 1789. It was made at St Etienne, and is a plain, robust weapon, well-suited to service use and quite capable of being used as a club without sustaining significant damage. As may be seen, it is built on a solid brass frame and is fitted with a walnut butt with a heavy brass butt-cap, the top strap being of iron. The cock is of the common ring-necked type which, although perhaps less elegant than the swan-necked variety, gave much greater strength at the point where a fracture was most likely to occur. The tapered barrel, firing a ball about 1oz (28.35gm) in weight, has no sight of any kind. The complete lack of any stock in front of the trigger-guard necessitated special arrangements for the ramrod (which is shown here at full length below the arm). It was normally housed in a hole in the front of the frame, which is just visible in the photograph. This hole is angled slightly, so that when the ramrod is in position its front end just touches the underside of the barrel. This arrangement presumably was necessary to reduce the risk of the ramrod catching on the edge of a holster. This pistol is of particular interest in that it was the pattern for one of the earliest military pistols to be made in the United States. France supplied many arms to the American colonists in the War of Independence, and in 1799 and 1800 Simon North, a famous American maker, received contracts to make very similar pistols in partnership with his brother-in-law, Cheny. Such arms are rare.

St Etienne Dueling Pistol — France

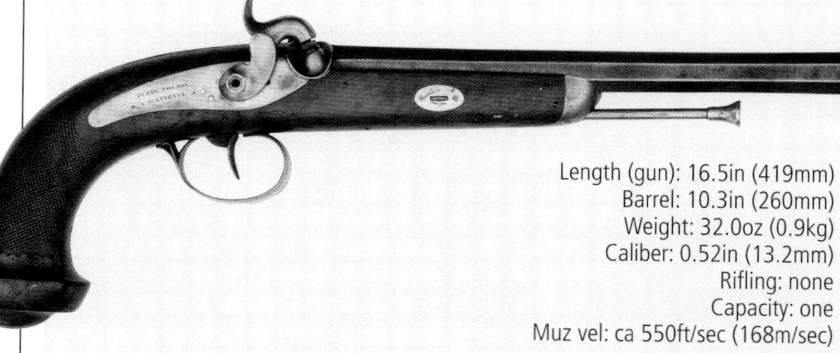

Length (gun): 16.5in (419mm)
Barrel: 10.3in (260mm)
Weight: 32.0oz (0.9kg)
Caliber: 0.52in (13.2mm)
Rifling: none
Capacity: one
Muz vel: ca 550ft/sec (168m/sec)

This is a plain but well-made weapon manufactured at St Etienne, probably in about 1835. Although described as a dueling pistol, it may rather have been intended for general target use. The barrel, which is smooth-bored, is of damascus type, but appears to have been made with single twist only, so that the attractive figure usually found on fine-quality guns is absent. The appreciable swamping, or thickening, at the muzzle end is clearly visible in the photograph. The pistol has a patent breech, the nipple being inset into a fence, and is fitted with a bead foresight and a simple V backsight, both fixed. The barrel is held on to the stock, which appears to be of walnut, by a very long top tang which reaches almost to the bulbous butt, together with a second, lower, tang incorporating the trigger guard; the two are connected by a screw running through the butt. In addition, a single flat key passes through a loop below the barrel; its end, in its protective oval plate of German silver, can be seen in the photograph. The lock is of the type known as back-action, in which the mainspring is behind the hammer. This allowed the lockplate to be set farther back towards the butt and helped to keep the breech narrow. The ramrod, which passes through a hole in the steel nosecap and into a recess in the stock, is of steel with a brass end. The pistol is well balanced and its large checkered butt provided a firm grip; the large knob, with its steel cap, appears to be somewhat superfluous, although it may perhaps have helped to balance the weapon and thus make an important contribution to accurate shooting.

St Etienne Service Revolver Model 1873 — France

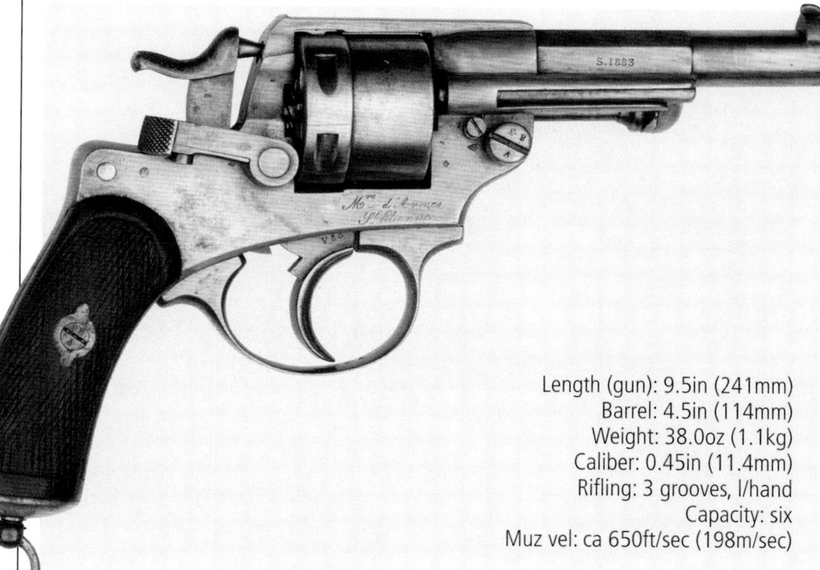

Length (gun): 9.5in (241mm)
Barrel: 4.5in (114mm)
Weight: 38.0oz (1.1kg)
Caliber: 0.45in (11.4mm)
Rifling: 3 grooves, l/hand
Capacity: six
Muz vel: ca 650ft/sec (198m/sec)

This was the first centerfire revolver to be adopted by the French Army and was made at the great factory of St Etienne. It has a solid frame and is very heavy and robust. Its barrel, which is half round and half octagonal, is marked "Mdle 1873" on the top flat; the upper left flat bears the number "H99683" and the upper right flat is inscribed "S1883." The revolver has a Colt-type extractor rod, working in a sleeve. When it was not in use, the front end of the rod was turned under the barrel, where it was held against the end of the cylinder axis rod by light spring pressure. To remove the cylinder, it was therefore necessary first to turn down the rod, then loosen the large-headed screw just beneath it, and then draw the axis pin forward. The loading gate is hinged at the bottom and was opened by being drawn backward – as may be seen in the photograph. The lock is of orthodox double-action Chamelot-Delvigne type (so called, although little or nothing is known of its originators). The hammer of the specimen shown here is set at half-cock, with the hammer head held safely clear of the rounds in the chambers. A large, irregularly shaped inspection plate on the left-hand side of the frame is held by two pins and a screw; the end of the latter is visible at the rear end of the frame, above the butt-plate. The revolver is numbered "H99683" on its main components and "V83" on the minor ones.

St Etienne 8mm Modèle 1892 (Lebel) — France

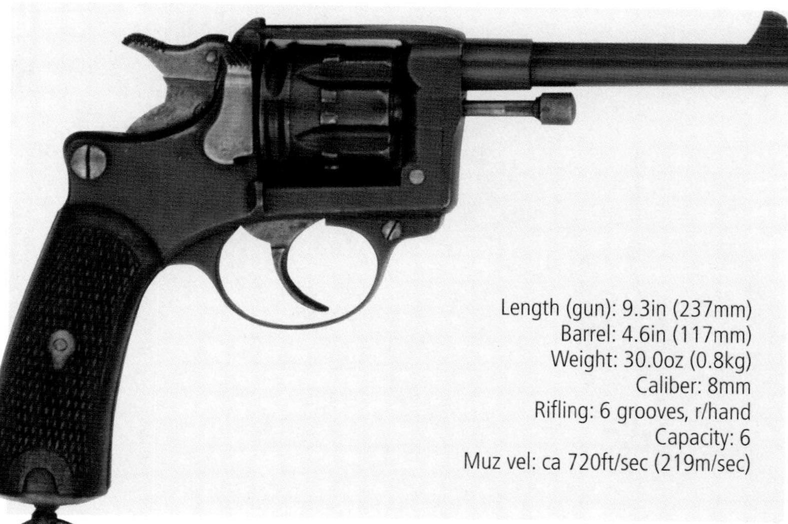

Length (gun): 9.3in (237mm)
Barrel: 4.6in (117mm)
Weight: 30.0oz (0.8kg)
Caliber: 8mm
Rifling: 6 grooves, r/hand
Capacity: 6
Muz vel: ca 720ft/sec (219m/sec)

This revolver was a development of the Mle 1873 (qv) and was fielded in 1893, remaining in service with the French Army until World War I and with the French police for some years after, as well. Its official designation was the Revolveur 8mm Modèle d'Ordonnance M1892, although it was more usually known simple as the "Lebel" after a colonel of that name, who was deeply involved with military weapons at the time of its design. It was developed by and produced at the government arsenal at St Etienne. It was a solid frame pistol with a cylinder on a separate frame, which, somewhat unusually, swung out to the right for loading and unloading. When closed the cylinder was held in place by a large, hinged lever on the right-hand side of the frame, while the mechanism could be inspected by removing a plate on the left-hand side. The revolver was reliable but its cartridge – the 8 x 27mm Lebel – was generally considered to be somewhat underpowered. The Mle 1892 was also produced in Belgium and Spain, and there were some minor variations over the years; for example, some have round barrels, while others have hexagonal.

St Etienne Model 28 Pistol — France

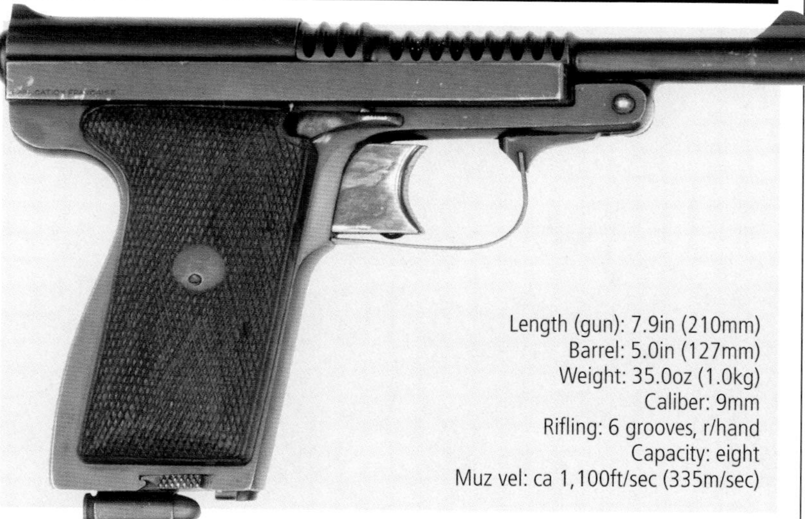

Length (gun): 7.9in (210mm)
Barrel: 5.0in (127mm)
Weight: 35.0oz (1.0kg)
Caliber: 9mm
Rifling: 6 grooves, r/hand
Capacity: eight
Muz vel: ca 1,100ft/sec (335m/sec)

The Manufacture Française d'Armes et Cycles de St Etienne began to make self-loading pistols just before the outbreak of World War I. These arms were all of similar design and of broadly similar type; being small-caliber, pocket arms. In 1928, however, the firm produced its Military Model, a specimen of which is illustrated here. Like all the manufacturer's later pistols, the arm was of a very distinctive type. The barrel was hinged at the front end and when a catch on the frame was pressed, the breech end rose clear of the slide, almost like a modern shotgun. Another strange feature was that the magazine carried an extra round in its base. When the magazine had been pushed home, this extra round was withdrawn and placed in the breech; then the barrel was closed and the pistol was ready to fire. When the magazine was withdrawn, the breech rose automatically. It was possible to withdraw it partially and then load and fire single rounds, leaving the magazine's contents as a reserve. No extractor was fitted: the empty cases were blown clear by the residual gas pressure in the barrel after the shot had been fired. There was no locking system, the pistol functioning by blowback only – and it was probably this factor which doomed it, for the system meant that it had to fire a cartridge too weak for service use. It could also happen that a misfired cartridge – admittedly a rare occurrence with modern ammunition – could not be extracted without the use of some improvized tool.

ST ETIENNE MODEL 1950 PISTOL — FRANCE

Length (gun): 7.6in (193mm)
Barrel: 4.3in (109mm)
Weight: 34.0oz (1.0kg)
Caliber: 9mm
Rifling: 4 grooves, l/hand
Capacity: nine
Muz vel: ca 1,100ft/sec (335m/sec)

The revolvers originally used by the French armed forces all suffered from the defect of firing weak cartridges. After the end of World War I, therefore, France decided to follow the example of virtually every other country on the European continent and change to a self-loading pistol. There followed a period of sporadic and somewhat leisurely experiment – at a time when another war was unthinkable – and it was not until 1935 that a self-loader was adopted. This, the MAS Model 1935, was a very sound and well-made weapon of basic Browning type – but it suffered from the same defect as the French revolvers: its 7.65mm round lacked stopping power. After 1945, when France embarked on a major rearmament program, one of the requirements was for a new pistol. The arm chosen was a re-designed Model 1935, capable of firing the standard 9mm Parabellum cartridge. This was a success and at last placed a good pistol into the hands of French servicemen. It is still in use, some produced at Châtellerault, as well as Saint Etienne.

TURBIAUX PALM-SQUEEZER PISTOL — FRANCE

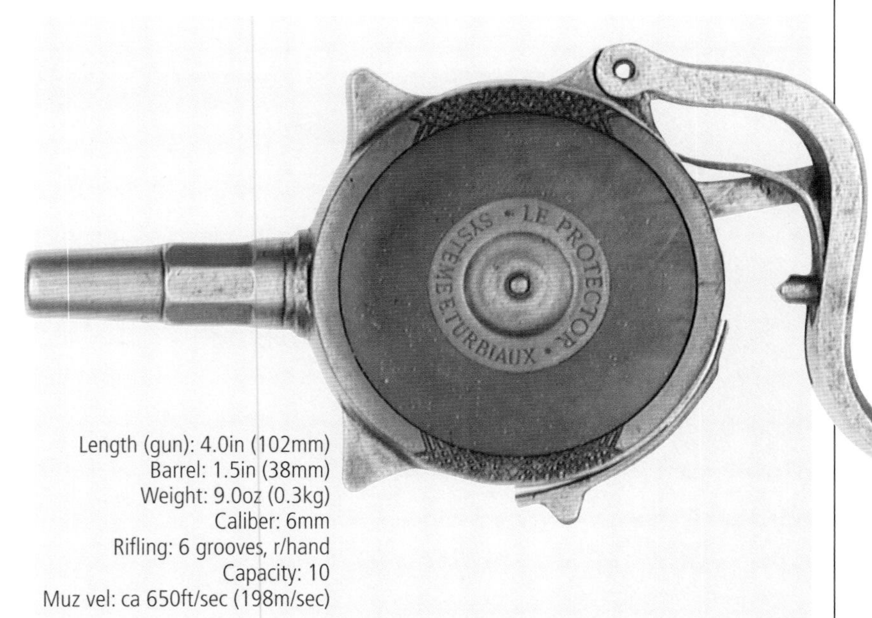

Length (gun): 4.0in (102mm)
Barrel: 1.5in (38mm)
Weight: 9.0oz (0.3kg)
Caliber: 6mm
Rifling: 6 grooves, r/hand
Capacity: 10
Muz vel: ca 650ft/sec (198m/sec)

This was a most unorthodox type of pistol: it was held in the palm of the hand, with the barrel protruding between the fingers, and fired by squeezing in a trigger device. It was invented by Jaques Turbiaux, a Parisian, who patented it in 1882. These pistols were briefly popular in Europe; some were made in the United States, but failed to sell. In order to load, it was necessary to remove the top cover and insert the cartridges into the body of the pistol, where they lay radially, bullets outward. The specimen illustrated here was of French origin; American versions had a ring on each side of the barrel for the user's first and second fingers, and a safety.

ST ETIENNE (MAS) 7.65MM MODÈLE 1935A/1935S PISTOL — FRANCE

Length (gun): 7.5in (190mm)
Barrel: 4.3in (110mm)
Weight: 25.7oz (0.7kg)
Caliber: 7.65mm
Rifling: 4 grooves, r/hand
Capacity: 8-round box magazine
Muz vel: 1,000ft/sec (305 m/sec)

The French state factory, Manufacture d'Armes de St Etienne (MAS), worked for some years on an automatic pistol following World War I, eventually selecting a design from the Societé Alsacienne de Construction Mécanique (SACM). This bore some similarities to the Colt M1911, but there were differences, principally that the weapon was chambered for the French Army's 7.65 x 19.5mm Longue round, which was not particularly powerful and used only by French forces. The new pistol had a magazine safety, a safety catch on the slide and a revised firing lock. The original production version was the Modèle 1935A, which was produced only by SACM, and can be recognized by the curved lines of its butt and the fact that the muzzle is flush with the front of the slide (left picture). In 1938, with war looming, it was decided to simplify the weapon to make it easier to manufacture, which resulted in a revised barrel-locking system; it can be recognised by its straight-sided butt, the muzzle sticking out slightly from the front of the slide, and a generally lower standard of finish. This version, Modèle 1935S (right picture), was produced at four factories in France.

Pinfire Revolver — France

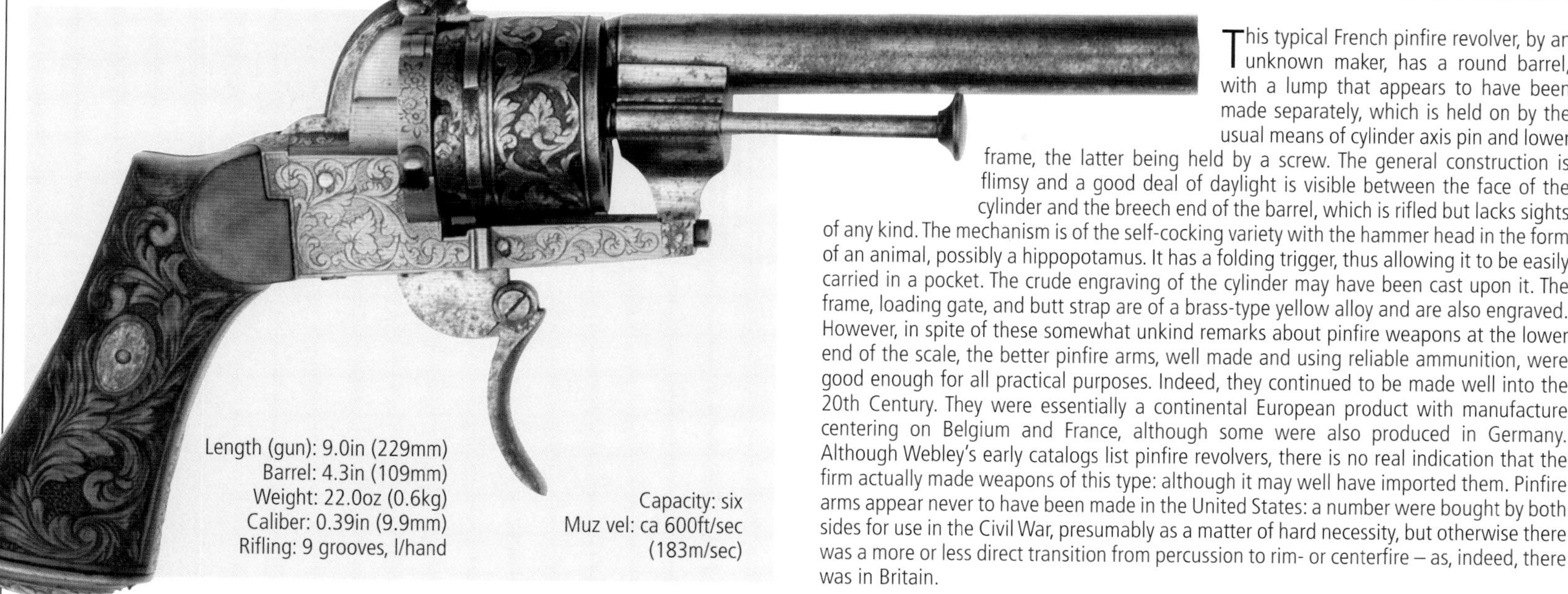

Length (gun): 9.0in (229mm)
Barrel: 4.3in (109mm)
Weight: 22.0oz (0.6kg)
Caliber: 0.39in (9.9mm)
Rifling: 9 grooves, l/hand
Capacity: six
Muz vel: ca 600ft/sec (183m/sec)

This typical French pinfire revolver, by an unknown maker, has a round barrel, with a lump that appears to have been made separately, which is held on by the usual means of cylinder axis pin and lower frame, the latter being held by a screw. The general construction is flimsy and a good deal of daylight is visible between the face of the cylinder and the breech end of the barrel, which is rifled but lacks sights of any kind. The mechanism is of the self-cocking variety with the hammer head in the form of an animal, possibly a hippopotamus. It has a folding trigger, thus allowing it to be easily carried in a pocket. The crude engraving of the cylinder may have been cast upon it. The frame, loading gate, and butt strap are of a brass-type yellow alloy and are also engraved. However, in spite of these somewhat unkind remarks about pinfire weapons at the lower end of the scale, the better pinfire arms, well made and using reliable ammunition, were good enough for all practical purposes. Indeed, they continued to be made well into the 20th Century. They were essentially a continental European product with manufacture centering on Belgium and France, although some were also produced in Germany. Although Webley's early catalogs list pinfire revolvers, there is no real indication that the firm actually made weapons of this type: although it may well have imported them. Pinfire arms appear never to have been made in the United States: a number were bought by both sides for use in the Civil War, presumably as a matter of hard necessity, but otherwise there was a more or less direct transition from percussion to rim- or centerfire – as, indeed, there was in Britain.

Single-Shot Pistol — France

Length (gun): 5.5in (140mm)
Barrel: 4.0in (102mm)
Weight: 3.0oz (0.08kg)
Caliber: 0.22in (5.6mm)
Rifling: none
Capacity: one
Muz vel: ca 450ft/sec (137m/sec)

This tiny pistol can be only marginally described as a weapon: it should, strictly, be classified as a dangerous toy! Nevertheless, it was a firearm by definition and has been included accordingly. Although it is thought to be of French origin, the marks on it are so faint that it is impossible to be sure. However, it was probably made towards the end of the 19th Century, when it could have been purchased for a few cents in a gunsmiths or hardware store without any kind of formality – together with a supply of bulleted caps for which it was designed. These consisted of a short, rimfire case, containing fulminate compound but no powder, with a spherical lead ball as projectile. The round probably equaled the pellet from a modern air-rifle in terms of hitting power.

Bergmann-Bayard Self-Loading Pistol — Germany

Length: 9.9in (251mm)
Barrel: 4.0in (102mm)
Weight: 35.5oz (1.0kg)
Caliber: 9mm
Rifling: 6 grooves, l/hand
Capacity: six
Muz vel: ca 1,000ft/sec

The Bergmann-Bayard pistol seen here was designed specifically as a military arm, originally under the trade-name "Mars," and was the first European pistol of its kind to fire a 9mm cartridge, which was a very powerful round. The Spanish Army put in a considerable order, but Bergmann had trouble with contractors and few, if any, pistols were ever actually supplied by him. He eventually sold the rights to Pieper of Liège, who completed the order and also sold some of these arms to the Greek and Danish Armies. Once these orders were completed, Pieper put an improved version on the market as the Bergmann-Bayard. The pistol worked on a system of short recoil. The barrel and bolt recoiled together for about 0.25in (6mm); the barrel stopped; and the bolt was unlocked by being forced downward and continued to the rear, extracting the empty case (if any) and compressing the return spring which was contained within it, coiled round the long striker. On its forward movement, the bolt stripped a cartridge from the magazine in front of the trigger-guard and chambered it in readiness for the next shot. The pistol was considered to be clumsy in use, and recoil from its powerful cartridge was considerable. Military models were often fitted with a detachable holster stock of hard leather, to improve long-range accuracy.

BERGMANN 1896 (NO 3) PISTOL — GERMANY

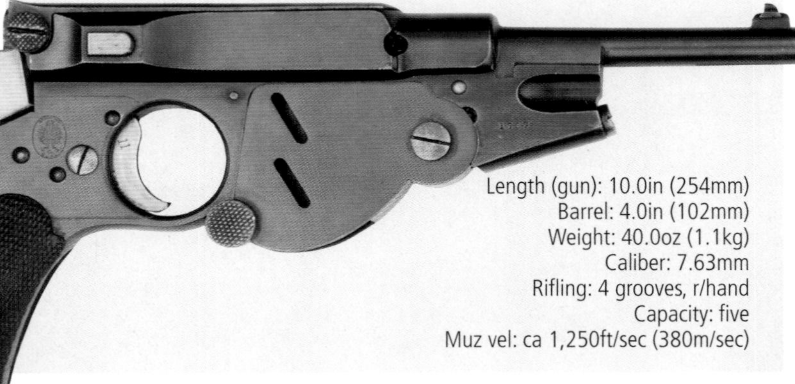

Length (gun): 10.0in (254mm)
Barrel: 4.0in (102mm)
Weight: 40.0oz (1.1kg)
Caliber: 7.63mm
Rifling: 4 grooves, r/hand
Capacity: five
Muz vel: ca 1,250ft/sec (380m/sec)

By 1894, Theodor Bergmann had developed a reasonably successful self-loading pistol, of which an improved version appeared in 1896: this is the weapon illustrated here. It was a well-made arm of simple blowback type; perhaps its main point of interest (in the early versions) was its complete lack of any mechanical system of extraction or ejection. In fact the action was so designed that the bolt opened while there was still sufficient gas available to blow the cartridge case out backwards. The case then struck the next round in the magazine and, in theory at least, bounced clear – although in practice this process was somewhat unpredictable. A gas escape port in the chamber served as a safety device should the case have ruptured under pressure. The early cartridges had no rim of any kind and were quite sharply tapered to avoid any risk of sticking. However, the system was not considered to be reliable, and later versions were fitted with mechanical extractors, necessitating the use of cartridges with grooved rims. The pistol was loaded by pulling down and forward on the milled grip by the trigger-guard, which opened the magazine cover. A five-round clip was inserted and the cover was closed. A lifter spring pushed the rounds up under the bolt one by one and the empty clip was finally ejected downwards. Rounds could be loaded without the clip, but the feed system was by no means reliable in this case, since the rounds were liable to become displaced.

BERGMANN SIMPLEX PISTOL — GERMANY

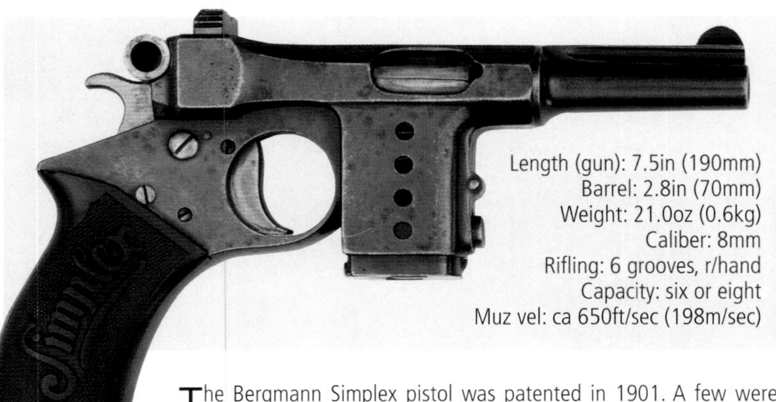

Length (gun): 7.5in (190mm)
Barrel: 2.8in (70mm)
Weight: 21.0oz (0.6kg)
Caliber: 8mm
Rifling: 6 grooves, r/hand
Capacity: six or eight
Muz vel: ca 650ft/sec (198m/sec)

The Bergmann Simplex pistol was patented in 1901. A few were made in Austria, but in 1904 the design was licensed to a company in Belgium, which thereafter turned the arm out in quite large numbers until 1914, when production finally ceased. Although the general shape of this weapon characterizes it as being obviously of Bergmann origin, its scale is much smaller than that of the designer's other weapons: the Simplex was originated strictly as a pocket arm. It fired a specially-designed cartridge (which is no longer available) and, because it was of low power, it was possible to design the weapon on the blowback principle, with no need for a locked breech. The pistol was cocked by pulling back the bolt by means of the cylindrical cocking-piece, visible just in front of the hammer. When released, the bolt went forward under its recoil spring, stripped a round from the magazine and chambered it ready to fire; after the first shot the process was repeated automatically. The lock was a simple single-action revolver type. The weapon had a detachable box magazine in front of the trigger in the orthodox arrangement: it was removed by pressing the small stud on the front of the magazine housing, which allowed it to drop downward. On Belgian-made examples, the barrel was screwed into the frame, whereas the original Austrian arms had their barrels forged integrally. The Bergmann was simple and reliable: it sold well as a pocket pistol, although the fact that it required a special cartridge must have been to some extent a limiting factor.

BERGMANN 1897 (NO 5) PISTOL — GERMANY

Length (gun): 10.5in (267mm)
Barrel: 4.4in (112mm)
Weight: 26.5oz (0.8kg)
Caliber: 7.63mm
Rifling: 4 grooves, r/hand
Capacity: five
Muz vel: ca 1,100ft/sec (335m/sec)

Although the Bergmann 1896 model worked fairly well, it did not achieve real popularity, principally because it was less effective than the Mauser which went on to the market at about the same time. Apart from small, pocket arms, it was by then clear that the main requirement for self-loading pistols would be for military versions – and as these were always required to fire a powerful cartridge, it was necessary that they should fire with the breech locked. If this was not done, the cartridge case would be pushed out of the chamber when the gas pressure was still high and, unsupported by the walls of the chamber, it was likely to rupture. In 1897, therefore, Bergmann patented a pistol of the type seen here. In this design the barrel and bolt were locked together at the instant of firing and remained so during the first 0.24in (6mm) of recoil. A cam in the frame then forced the bolt slightly sideways and unlocked it from the barrel, which then stopped. The bolt continued to the rear, to cock the hammer, and then came forward, stripped a round from the magazine, chambered it, locked on to the barrel, and forced it back to its forward firing position. The magazine was of detachable box type, incorporating its own platform and spring. The pistol could, however, also be loaded through the top of the frame by means of a charger. Much to Bergmann's disappointment, no country adopted this arm, although several experimented with it.

Borchardt Self-Loading Pistol — Germany

Length (gun): 13.8in (349mm)
Barrel: 6.5in (165mm)
Weight: 46.0oz (1.3kg)
Caliber: 7.65mm
Rifling: 4 grooves, r/hand
Capacity: eight
Muz vel: 1,100ft/sec (335m/sec)

This weapon, which appeared in 1894, may be classed as having been only moderately successful in the commercial sense. It made use of the principle, firstly clearly defined by Maxim, of harnessing the backward thrust of a fired cartridge to reload and recock the weapon. It fired from a locked breech – a system later made famous by Luger – which worked roughly on the principle of the human knee-joint. When it was straight and locked, it was virtually immovable, but as soon as the joint was pushed upward it opened easily and smoothly. When the cartridge was fired, the recoil drove back the barrel and bolt until lugs on the receiver caused the joint to rise, thus allowing it to break. The barrel then stopped, but the bolt continued to rear against a spring. When the bolt's rearward impetus was exhausted, the compressed spring drove it forward again, stripping a round from the box magazine in the butt and chambering it ready for the next shot. This was the first time such a principle had been applied to a pistol; it worked well, but the weapon was expensive to make, since it called for fine workmanship and the use of steel of very high quality, especially for the manufacture of the joint pins. The arm was also very bulky, and thus was practically impossible to fire with one hand. To surmount this difficulty, it was provided with a strong and well-fitting stock (which, as may be seen, incorporated a holster): in fact, it seems to have been generally regarded more as a light carbine than as a pistol.

Commission Reichs-Revolver M1883 — Germany

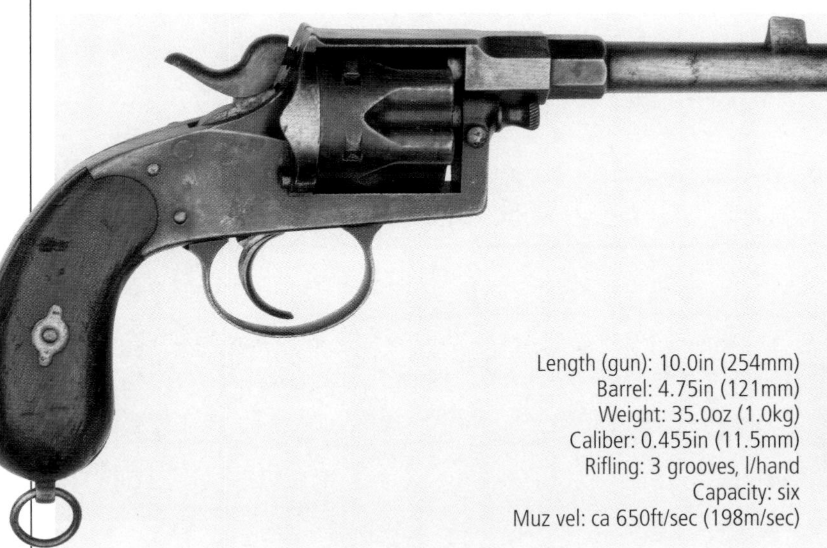

Length (gun): 10.0in (254mm)
Barrel: 4.75in (121mm)
Weight: 35.0oz (1.0kg)
Caliber: 0.455in (11.5mm)
Rifling: 3 grooves, l/hand
Capacity: six
Muz vel: ca 650ft/sec (198m/sec)

In 1879 several commissions were set up to supervize the re-equipment of the German Army with modern weapons. This revolver, which is sometimes called the Reichs-revolver, was one of the results. There were two models, one of 1879 and one of 1883; the arm illustrated is of the latter type. It has a solid frame with a short stem into which the barrel is screwed. The six-chambered cylinder was removed by pressing in the spring stud on the front of the frame, pulling the axis pin forward, and opening the loading gate. Rather surprisingly, there was no integral system for ejecting rounds or cases; this had to be done either with the axis pin or with some improvized implement of suitable dimensions – which must have made it a slow process in action. The breech-ends of the chambers are recessed so that the heads of the cartridges were fully supported – a sensible precaution with most of the earlier metallic cartridges. The lock is of single-action type with a half-cock, and, somewhat unusually in a revolver, there is a safety catch on the left side of the frame. This particular specimen was made at Erfurt in 1894; since this was after the passing of the German Proof Act, the revolver bears a number of proof marks. All major parts are numbered "9775," but the minor components are marked with the last two digits only. The butt-strap is also stamped "30.A.1.53," probably the mark of an artillery unit.

Coster Pinfire Revolver — Germany

Length (gun): 10.4in (264mm)
Barrel: 5.4in (137mm)
Weight: 26.0oz (0.7kg)
Caliber: 0.35in (9mm)
Rifling: 6 grooves, r/hand
Capacity: six
Muz vel: ca 550ft/sec (168m/sec)

This is an attractive arm, strong and well-made, as one would expect of a German weapon, and of unusually good quality and finish. It has a one-piece frame with a top strap and an octagonal barrel, on which the top flat is narrowed to form a distinct rib. It has an unusually high (and thus, perhaps, slightly vulnerable) foresight, while the backsight is a V-shaped notch on the rear of the top strap. The cylinder is unfluted and has long and elegantly-formed projections: these engaged against the cylinder stop, which rose from the lower frame when the trigger was pressed. It was fitted with the usual loading gate, with a thumb piece and a spring catch projecting below it. This held the gate firmly in position, yet allowed it to be opened with quite light thumb pressure. The cylinder was removed by pulling forward the axis pin, and on the left-hand side of the frame is a vertical spring and stud which prevented accidental removal. The lock is of double-action type: the arm could be fired either by simple trigger pressure, or by preliminary cocking of the hammer, according to circumstances. There is an upward bulge at the rear end of the top strap and this prevented the protruding pins from fouling it when the cylinder rotated, and there is a corresponding notch on the bottom of the frame. The pistol is well blued and engraved, with the exception of the hammer, trigger, foresight, and ejector rod, which are of bright steel. The one-piece butt – its shape typical of German arms – is held by two tangs. The top strap bears the inscription "J A COSTER IN HANAU," and there is a gold monogram (apparently C.T.) on the top tang.

Erma Conversion Unit — Germany

Length (gun): 11.9in (302mm)
Barrel: 7.7in (196mm)
Weight: 36.5oz (1.0kg)
Caliber: 0.22in (5.6mm)
Rifling: 6 grooves, r/hand
Capacity: five
Muz vel: ca 1,100ft/sec (335m/sec)

When Germany began to rearm in the 1930s, it was decided that there was a requirement for a means of converting the then standard Luger service pistol to fire 0.22in ammunition, for the purpose of small-range practice. The concept was not, of course, a new one: it had earlier been applied to revolvers – but whereas this end can be accomplished in a revolver by no more than an easily removed barrel liner and an alternative cylinder, a self-loading pistol, with its very different method of functioning, necessarily requires a more sophisticated arrangement. The solution was provided by the Ermawerke company of Erfurt, which produced a conversion kit. This included an insert barrel; a light breechblock containing its own mainspring; a toggle unit; and a magazine of the appropriate size. The kit had been invented by an Ermawerke employee named Kulisch and patented as early as 1927, so there were few delays in putting it into production. The Erma conversion unit was highly effective in transforming a locked-breech arm into a blowback type: the 0.22in rifle cartridge was powerful enough to compress the special spring, and the cartridge rims did not, apparently, cause many feed problems. The arm proved very accurate: grouping well up to 55yd (50m).

Heckler & Koch VP-70 — Germany

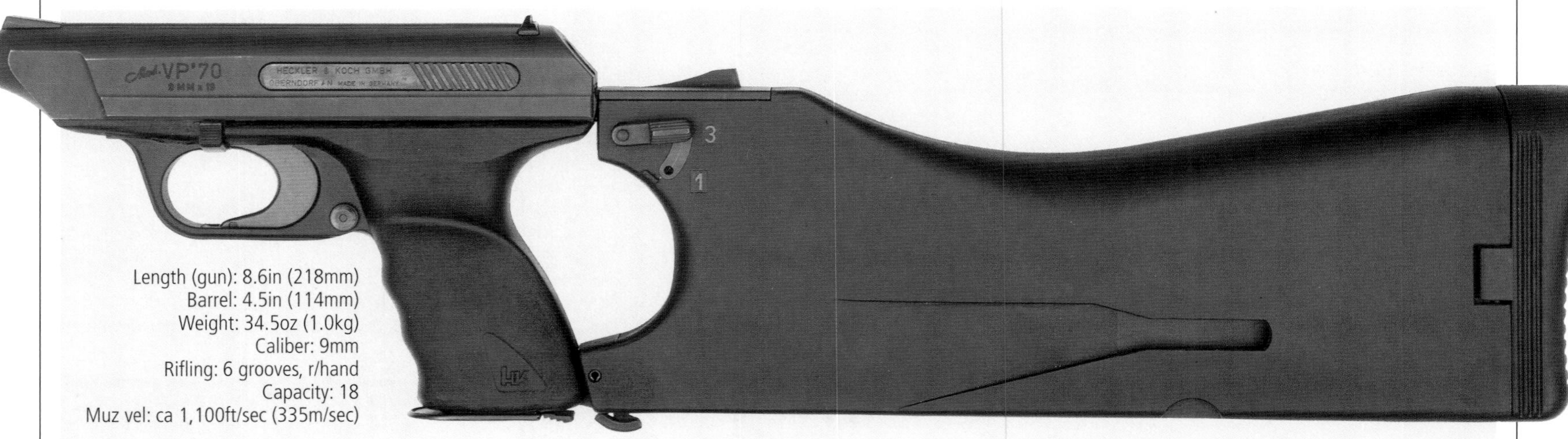

Length (gun): 8.6in (218mm)
Barrel: 4.5in (114mm)
Weight: 34.5oz (1.0kg)
Caliber: 9mm
Rifling: 6 grooves, r/hand
Capacity: 18
Muz vel: ca 1,100ft/sec (335m/sec)

The West German firm of Heckler & Koch was established at Oberndorf-Neckar as soon as the manufacture of arms was again permitted in Germany after World War II. It quickly established a reputation for military firearms, and is particularly noted for its famous automatic rifle, but also makes service-type pistols. The arm illustrated is the VP-70, a blowback weapon, which fires a 9mm Parabellum cartridge of considerable power. The lock is of double-action pattern only, but in order to facilitate deliberate shooting it is fitted with a type of hesitation lock. This allows a pause between a fairly heavy first-pressure cocking and a much lighter second pressure on the trigger for actual firing. This system makes it safe to carry the pistol with a round in the chamber: a safety catch is not normally fitted. The weapon is fitted with a detachable holster-stock; when this is attached, the weapon can be used either for single shots or three-round bursts. The merit of this system is that the bullets are clear of the barrel before the muzzle has a chance to rise, thus removing the basic disadvantage of the so-called machine pistol. The VP-70 magazine accommodates 18 rounds, and although this can only be achieved by staggering the rounds, it does not make the butt unduly bulky.

Heckler & Koch 9mm P7 Series — Germany

Heckler & Koch's P7 series has its origin in a police requirement for a pistol that would be completely safe to carry when loaded, but which could be brought into action very fast when needed. The result is a neat weapon using a gas-retarded, blowback-operating mechanism based on that used in the World War II German Volksturmgewehr (VG-51), in which a proportion of the gas from a fired cartridge is bled through a port immediately ahead of the chamber into an expansion chamber beneath the barrel, where it acts against a piston attached to the nose of the slide, thus retarding the slide's rearward movement. As soon as the bullet leaves the muzzle, the pressure inside the barrel drops and the gas in the cylinder seeps back into the barrel, enabling the slide to continue its rearward journey unimpeded, ejecting the used cartridge case and then loading the next round. Cocking is achieved by squeezing the lever, which runs the length of the forward face of the butt: squeezing the lever cocks the striker for the first shot and recocking is then automatic for as long as the lever remains depressed; releasing it decocks the piece. No separate safety lever is required. Sights are square format with three-dot low-light system and both are mounted in lateral dovetails. There are five weapons in the P7 series, the two basic members being the P7M8 and P7M13 which differ only in their magazines: the P7M8 carrying eight rounds and the P7M13, 13. The P7K3 is the smallest in the P7 series and has a straightforward blowback action without the gas-delay system, but retains the cocking lever. The P7K3 fires the 9mm Parabellum round, but can be converted to fire 0.22in LR or 0.32in (7.65mm) ACP rounds. The P7M10 fires the 0.40in Smith & Wesson round and is generally identical to the P7M13 apart from a heavier slide; it carries 12 rounds. The P7M7 fires the 0.45in ACP round and employs a unique oil-buffered delay system. The picture shows the P7M8 with the slide held open by an empty magazine; the cocking lever in the forepart of the butt can be clearly seen.

Length (gun): 6.8in (171mm)
Barrel: 4.2in (105mm)
Weight: 27.0oz (0.8kg)
Caliber: 9mm
Rifling: 4 grooves, r/hand
Capacity: See text
Muz vel: 1,155ft/sec (350m/sec)

Heckler & Koch 9mm P9/P9S Pistol — Germany

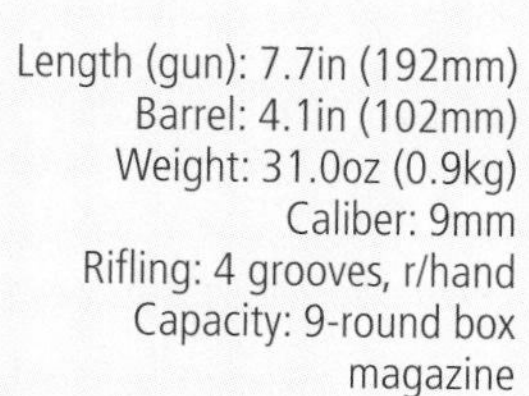

Length (gun): 7.7in (192mm)
Barrel: 4.1in (102mm)
Weight: 31.0oz (0.9kg)
Caliber: 9mm
Rifling: 4 grooves, r/hand
Capacity: 9-round box magazine
Muz vel: 386ft/sec (351m/sec)

In the late 1960s, Heckler & Koch undertook a major re-examination of current pistol design, which resulted in the 1972 announcement of the company's P9S, which adapted the roller-locked bolt of its G3 rifle and MP submachine gun to the configuration of a reliable delayed blow-back system of operation. The P9S has a concealed double-action hammer, with an indicator pin which protrudes when the hammer is cocked, and a decocking lever in the right front of the butt group. The P9S pistol has polygonal rifling, which – it is claimed – helps reduce the deformation of the bullet, thus increasing the muzzle velocity, while the absence of corners at the bottom of the grooves means less accumulation of fouling, and an improvement in both accuracy and ease of maintenance. The P9S was adopted by the Bundesgrenzschutzpolizei (German Border Police) and numerous other police and para-military forces, and while production has ended in Germany it continues under license in Greece. The basic model was the double-action lock P9S in 9mm (see specifications), as described, but another version, the P9 had single-action firing only. A few were made chambered for the 7.65mm Parabellum round, while the export version, intended primarily for the United States, was chambered for the 0.45in round, in which case the magazine held only seven rounds and the muzzle velocity was reduced to 286ft/sec (260m/sec).

Heckler & Koch Universal Self-Loading Pistol — Germany

Length (gun): 7.9in (200mm)
Barrel: 4.4in (112mm)
Weight: 29.6oz (0.8kg)
Caliber: 0.45in
Rifling: 4 grooves, r/hand
Capacity: 10-round box magazine
Muz vel: 885ft/sec (270m/sec)

Introduced in 1993, the Heckler & Koch USP (Universal Self-Loading Pistol) was intended to meet contemporary military, police and para-military requirements. It was initially designed around the 0.40in S&W round, but was then adapted to the 9mm Parabellum round, and then to the 0.45in ACP (see specifications), in which latter case the weapon is marginally larger and heavier. It uses a locked-breech double-action, with a Browning cam lock and a recoil buffering device, but a modular approach to the design has resulted in great flexibility, with customers being able to choose between as many as nine alternative action and safety combinations. Mounting grooves are already fitted for scopes, night sights, and laser spot projectors. Another version, the USP Compact, is identical in all mechanical and operating respects to the USP but is dimensionally smaller; the 0.45in version, for example, is 7.1in (180mm) long, weighs 28oz (0.79kg) and takes only eight rounds. Like the larger USP, the Compact is also available in 0.40in S&W and 9mm Parabellum versions. The Mk23 Mod 0, a variant of the USP to meet a US Special Operations Forces requirement is described on the following page.

HECKLER & KOCH 0.45IN MK 23 (SOCOM) PISTOL — GERMANY

Length (gun): 9.7in (245mm)
Barrel: 5.9in (150mm)
Weight: 42.0oz (1.2kg)
Caliber: 0.45in
Rifling: Polygonal; r/hand
Capacity: 12-round box magazine
Muz vel: 850ft/sec (260m/sec)

In 1990 US Special Forces Command (SOCOM) issued a new operational requirement for an Offensive Handgun Weapon System consisting of three elements: a handgun; a laser-aiming module (LAM); and a sound/flash suppressor. A number of very demanding criteria were announced publicly and any arms manufacturer in the world was allowed to enter, although, in the event, just two did so: Colt, with a Knight's suppressor; and Heckler & Koch with one of their own company's suppressors. Each company produced 30 Phase I prototypes, the eventual winners being the Heckler & Koch pistol, but with the Knight's suppressor, even though it was most unusual for a component from a losing entry to be selected. The LAM was made by Insight Technology of Londonderry, New Hampshire. The pistol was a development of H&K's 0.45in version of the USP, but with a longer slide, a slight extension of the barrel for the screw attachment for the suppressor, and mountings for the LAM. It was accepted for service as the "Pistol, Caliber .45, Mark 23 Mod 0" (but is usually known, simply, as the "SOCOM Pistol") and deliveries started in May 1996. The LAM is attached to the underside of the pistol ahead of the trigger guard and projects a red spot onto the target, enabling the weapon to be sighted with great accuracy. The suppressor screws on to the muzzle and provides a substantial reduction in both flash and noise, the latter being aided by the fact that the bullet is just sub-sonic, thus avoiding the characteristic "crack" of a supersonic bullet. Specifications relate to the weapon without suppressor.

KUFAHL'S NEEDLE-FIRE REVOLVER — GERMANY

Length (gun): 9.6in (244mm)
Barrel: 3.2in (81mm)
Weight: 22.0oz (0.6kg)
Caliber: 0.300in (7.62mm)
Rifling: 5 grooves, l/hand
Capacity: six
Muz vel: ca 500ft/sec (152m/sec)

Kufahl's revolver has a barrel and frame made out of a single piece of iron, although the top strap, across the cylinder, has been welded on separately. The octagonal barrel is rifled and has a noticeably swamped muzzle. It is fitted with a laterally adjustable foresight; the backsight consists of a V-notch in the raised part at the rear of the top strap. The butt is a single piece of wood, partially checkered, and is held in place by a screw through the lower tang. The rear trigger-guard is also hooked into this tang, with its front end held in place by a screw. The cylinder is not bored through: instead, there is a small hole at the rear of each chamber to allow the needle to reach the front-loaded consumable cartridge. The cylinder axis pin could be removed by turning it through 90 degrees and drawing it out from the front; a small spring stud on the left side of the frame held it in place to avoid this process being carried out accidentally. Steady pressure on the trigger first forced the bolt forward and rotated and locked the cylinder; then it allowed the needle-holder and needle to go forward and fire the cartridge. Once the trigger was released, the needle and holder were automatically retracted, thus allowing the cylinder to rotate in readiness for the next shot. The pistol, which is well made and finished, bears the inscription, "Fv. V. Dreyse Sommerda" on the top strap. It is numbered "12620" on the left side of the frame; the right side bears the inscription "Cal 0.30.", suggesting that this arm was made for the British or American markets.

Lignose Einhand Model 3A Pistol — Germany

Length (gun): 4.6in (117mm)
Barrel: 2.1in (53mm)
Weight: 18.0oz (0.5kg)
Caliber: 6.35mm
Rifling: 6 grooves, r/hand
Capacity: nine
Muz vel: ca 800ft/sec (244m/sec)

This pistol was originally manufactured by the Bergmann company in about 1917, but the rights were then sold to the Lignose company, under whose name it is better known. A notable problem of the days before self-loading pistols were provided with double-action locks and other refinements was that it was dangerous to carry such a pistol with a round in the chamber – but, at the same time, it was a relatively slow, two-handed business to prepare it for action. Lignose sought to overcome this problem, and the word Einhand (one hand) suggests the method. The front end of the trigger-guard of this weapon was very far forward because the brass section was attached to the slide, which thus could be drawn back by the pressure of the first finger. The finger could then be swiftly moved back to the trigger, to fire.

Luger Parabellum Model 1908 (P08) Pistol — Germany

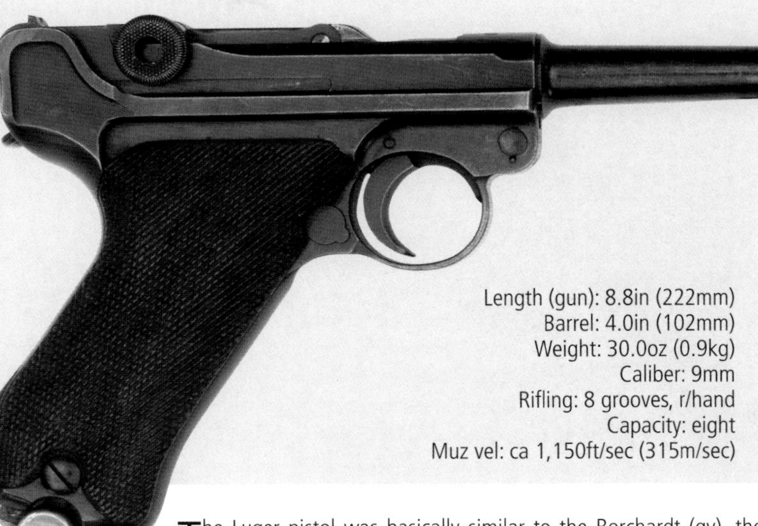

Length (gun): 8.8in (222mm)
Barrel: 4.0in (102mm)
Weight: 30.0oz (0.9kg)
Caliber: 9mm
Rifling: 8 grooves, r/hand
Capacity: eight
Muz vel: ca 1,150ft/sec (315m/sec)

The Luger pistol was basically similar to the Borchardt (qv), the design having been modified and improved by Georg Luger, and was put on to the market at the very end of the 19th Century, manufactured by Deutsche Waffen und Munitions-fabrik (DWM) of Berlin. After several earlier models, there appeared the pistol illustrated here. It was put into production in 1908 and was almost immediately adopted by the German Army, which was then seeking a new self-loader to replace its earlier revolver. Of course, this assured the arm's success, as many smaller countries followed Germany's lead and purchased large numbers of Lugers for their armed forces. It served the Germans well during World War I and, like the Mauser, became something of a household word, establishing a popular reputation which is, perhaps, greater than its real merit. After World War I, its manufacture was taken over by Mauser, who continued to make both military and civilian models. This example is one of those made by Mauser and is dated "1940." In 1938 the German Army adopted the Walther P38 but Lugers were in production until 1943.

Luger Artillery Model 1917 Self-Loading Pistol — Germany

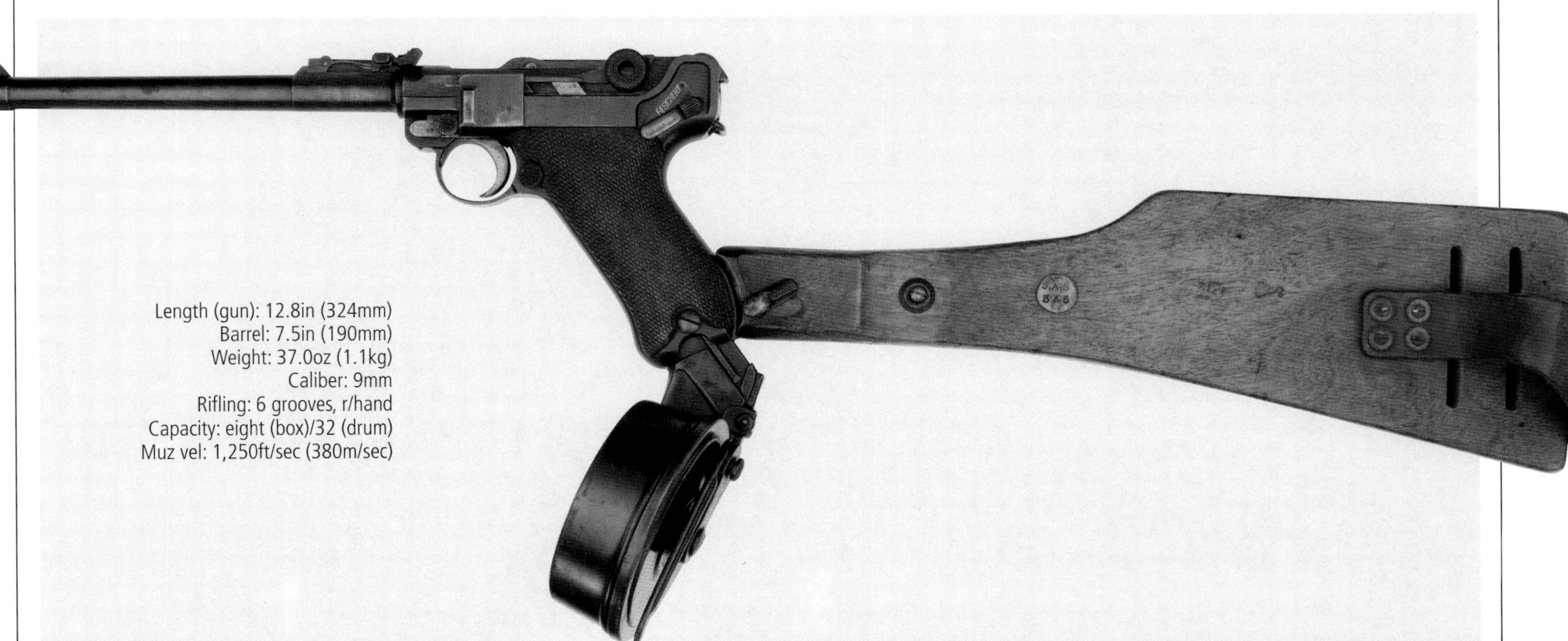

Length (gun): 12.8in (324mm)
Barrel: 7.5in (190mm)
Weight: 37.0oz (1.1kg)
Caliber: 9mm
Rifling: 6 grooves, r/hand
Capacity: eight (box)/32 (drum)
Muz vel: 1,250ft/sec (380m/sec)

The Luger Parabellum self-loading pistol was adopted by the German Army in 1908, and its subsequent record in World War I made it a household name. In 1917, this was followed in its turn by the Artillery Model, illustrated here. The Luger worked on a system of short recoil, during which the barrel and bolt remained locked together. The toggle joint then passed over curved ramps and opened upward, detaching itself from the barrel. When the bolt had reached its rearmost position, it was forced forward again by a return spring, stripping a cartridge from the magazine and forcing it into the chamber en route. It then locked, and could be fired again in the normal way. The standard Luger had a box magazine in the butt, but the example seen here is fitted with an extension type, the so-called "snail drum" magazine with a capacity of 32 rounds. A special tool was needed to load this magazine, which tended to jam: this was cured by replacing the original round-nosed bullet with a pointed one. As may be seen, the Luger also had a detachable stock, which converted it into a carbine and made it a very light and handy weapon for local defense. It was originally issued to machine gun detachments and artillery observers in exposed forward positions. As stocks of the arm increased, it was also issued to non-commissioned officers of forward infantry units, where, like the Mauser, it was found to be a very handy arm for such work as night raids.

LUGER 08/20 PISTOL — GERMANY

Length (gun): 8.8in (222mm)
Barrel: 3.8in (95mm)
Weight: 30.0oz (0.9kg)
Caliber: 7.65mm
Rifling: 8 grooves, r/hand
Capacity: eight
Muz vel: ca 1,150ft/sec (351m/sec)

The aftermath of World War I saw Germany largely disarmed; only a few troops and police were retained for internal security and border patrol duties. Severe restrictions were also imposed on Germany's production of firearms and military equipment of all kinds. However, some degree of manufacture for export was later permitted, and since vast stocks of components were still hidden away in various places a good deal of cannibalization went on, while many salvaged weapons were also reconditioned and found their way on to the world markets. The original title of "Parabellum" for DWM's Model 1908 had by then largely given way to that of "Luger," while the suffix "/20" indicated post-war manufacture. The demand for this arm was considerable – partly for use and partly because it was a popular souvenir. The pistol illustrated here appears to be one of the post-1918 arms put together by DWM, whose monogram appears on the toggle joint. One way of circumventing the restrictions imposed by the Treaty of Versailles, which laid down that all weapons made must be of less than 9mm caliber, was to bore 9mm barrel blanks for smaller-caliber rounds. Another was to make the barrels marginally shorter than the imposed maximum of 4.0in (102mm). Both are used here.

MAUSER ZIG-ZAG REVOLVER — GERMANY

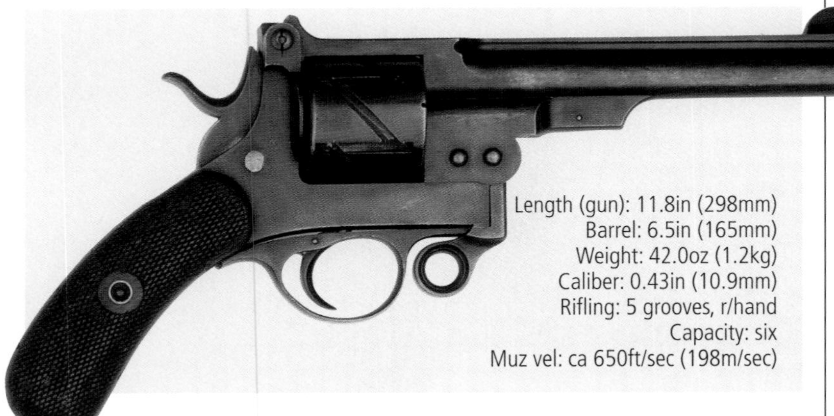

Length (gun): 11.8in (298mm)
Barrel: 6.5in (165mm)
Weight: 42.0oz (1.2kg)
Caliber: 0.43in (10.9mm)
Rifling: 5 grooves, r/hand
Capacity: six
Muz vel: ca 650ft/sec (198m/sec)

This proposed German service revolver was designed by Peter Paul Mauser, a very famous name indeed in the history of gunmaking, although he was better known for rifles than for pistols. The revolver produced in 1878 is top-hinged. When a lever on the left-hand side of the frame was pushed upward, it allowed the ring in front of the trigger to be pulled downward. This freed the catch and allowed the entire barrel and cylinder to be raised just past the vertical, where it locked. Increased pressure on the ring operated a cam which forced a star ejector out of the rear face of the cylinder, throwing the cartridges or empty cases from the chambers. The extractor was then returned to its normal position and the revolver reloaded and closed. Some care had to be taken to ensure that the rounds did not slip out of their chambers during the process of reloading. Perhaps the most interesting feature of the weapon is its unusual method of cylinder rotation. When the trigger was pressed, a rod with a stud on its upper surface was forced forward so that its front end protruded through the barrel catch, ensuring that it could not be opened by accident. At the same time, the stud engaged one of the diagonal slots on the cylinder and thus caused the cylinder to rotate through one-sixth of its circumference. When the trigger was released, the rod was retracted: during this stage, the stud simply rode back along one of the straight grooves of the cylinder. The revolver was never adopted for service use in Germany, since it was considered by the authorities to be too complex.

MAUSER MODEL 1896 SELF-LOADING PISTOL — GERMANY

Length (gun): 11.0in (280mm)
Barrel: 5.5in (140mm)
Weight: 40.0oz (1.1kg)
Caliber: 7.63mm
Rifling: 4 grooves, r/hand
Capacity: 10-round box magazine
Muz vel: 1,400ft/sec (427m/sec)

The name of Mauser is among the most famous in the world where firearms are concerned, the first gunsmith of the family to achieve fame being Peter Paul Mauser, who was responsible for the famous German Model 1871 rifle, which replaced the needle-gun after the Franco-Prussian War. This was followed by a series of progressively better rifles, culminating in the Model 1898 rifle. The company first became interested in pistols in the 1870s and it is probable that the Model 1878 "Zig-Zag" (qv) was the company's first successful handgun. By the 1890s Hiram Maxim's idea that the recoil of one cartridge could drive the mechanism that loaded the next had been universally accepted and it may have been the appearance of the Borchardt pistol (qv) that inspired the Mauser company to try its hand at a similar, self-loading weapon. The outcome was the Model 1896, which achieved considerable success, but was succeeded very quickly by the improved Model 1898 (see next entry).

Mauser Model 1898 Self-Loading Pistol

Germany

Length (gun): 11.8in (298mm)
Barrel: 5.5in (140mm)
Weight: 40.0oz (1.1kg)
Caliber: 7.63mm
Rifling: 4 grooves, r/hand
Capacity: 10
Muz vel: 1,400ft/sec (427m/sec)

The first Mauser self-loading model appeared in 1896 and, with relatively minor improvements, it developed into the Model 1898 pistol seen here. It operated on the short recoil system: the barrel and bolt recoil locked together for a short distance, after which the bolt was unlocked and continued its rearward movement, while the barrel stopped. The return spring, which is inside the bolt, was compressed during this rearward travel, which also cocked the hammer. As the force of recoil died, the compressed spring took over and drove the bolt forward, picking up a cartridge from the magazine and chambering it on the way. The closure of the bolt locked it to the barrel as it drove it forward – and the pistol was then ready to fire its next round. The hammer (shown cocked in the photograph) struck an inertia firing-pin in the bolt, which fired the cartridge. Initial cocking was, of course, necessary before the first shot: this was achieved by pulling back the milled ears visible at the rear of the frame. The rounds were fed from a box magazine in front of the trigger-guard, which was initially loaded from a 10-round clip. When the last round had been fired, the magazine platform held the bolt open and thus indicated the need for more ammunition. The Mauser pistol was the first to feature this system. Unlike its predecessor, the Model 1898 was designed to take a stock, which acted also as a holster. It also had an adjustable leaf backsight, which on the weapon seen here is graduated to 492yd (450m), although the scale on some weapons goes up to 766yd (700m).

Mauser Model 1912 Self-Loading Pistol

Germany

Length (gun): 11.8in (298mm)
Barrel: 5.5in (140mm)
Weight: 44.0oz (1.25kg)
Caliber: 7.63mm
Rifling: 6 grooves, r/hand
Capacity: 10
Muz vel: 1,400ft/sec (427m/sec)

The Model 1912, illustrated here, did not differ significantly from its predecessor of 14 years before. Weapons of this type were, of course, made by the thousand for use in World War I. In 1916 the German Army had a requirement for Mauser pistols to fire the straight-sided 9mm Parabellum cartridge, and it was quickly realized that conversion of the standard Model 1912 would be relatively simple. The arms thus altered were all distinguished by a large figure "9," cut into the butt-grips and painted red. The Mauser pistol was widely used in World War I because, unlike many earlier 20th Century campaigns, it involved a good deal of close-quarter fighting. The emphasis as far as the infantry was concerned was, of course, on the rifle, light machine gun and medium machine gun; nevertheless, it was found that a Mauser pistol with its shoulder-stock attached was a handy weapon for raids, clearing trenches, and similar operations. It was used in very similar fashion to the sub-machine gun which the Germans finally adopted in 1918. A Mauser-type pistol with a capability for automatic fire was, in fact, made in Spain in the 1930s. However, the combination of a light bolt traveling over a very short distance and a powerful cartridge was not successful, and the arm's rate of fire made it impossible to shoot with very much accuracy.

Mauser 7.65mm Model HSc Self-Loading Pistol

Germany

The HSc (Hahnlos, Selbstladung Model c = Hammerless, Self-Loading Model c) was developed by Mauser in the late 1930s for the civilian market, but with the outbreak of war it was quickly taken into military use. It was of modern appearance, but was not actually "hammerless," since the hammer was virtually out of sight in the slide with a small spur protruding which enabled the firer to cock the weapon with his thumb. The Mauser Hsc was mainly produced in 7.65 x 17mm caliber, but some examples in 9mm Short and 0.22in were also manufactured. Following the end of the war production continued in France and was later re-started by Mauser, until they licensed production to an Italian company in the 1970s.

Length (gun): 6.0in (152m)
Barrel: 3.4in (86mm)
Weight: 21.0oz (0.6kg)
Caliber: 7.65mm
Rifling: 6 grooves, r/hand
Capacity: 8-round box magazine
Muz vel: 960ft/sec (290m/sec)

PETERS-STAHL PISTOLE 07 MULTI-CALIBER TARGET PISTOL — GERMANY

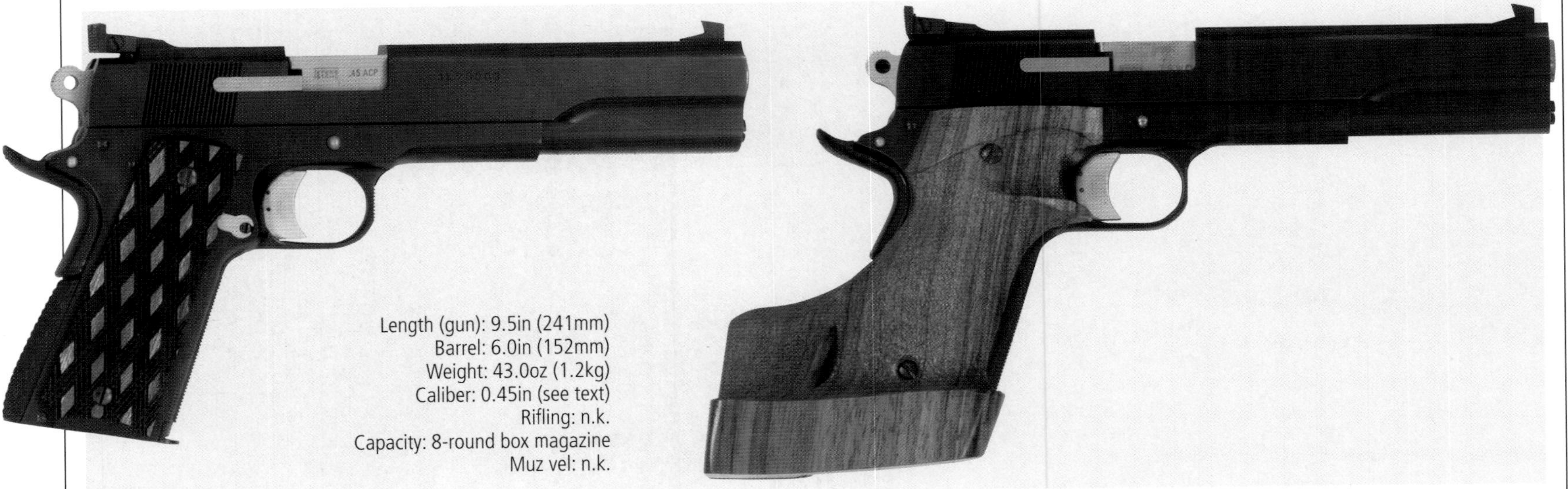

Length (gun): 9.5in (241mm)
Barrel: 6.0in (152mm)
Weight: 43.0oz (1.2kg)
Caliber: 0.45in (see text)
Rifling: n.k.
Capacity: 8-round box magazine
Muz vel: n.k.

This competition handgun was introduced in 1986 and incorporates a number of interesting features. The Pistole 07 uses a Caspian Arms 1911 receiver, but the upper structure is a new design manufactured by Peters-Stahl, which replaces the Colt's link unlocking system with cams. The weapon is of all steel construction, with a hammer-forged barrel with polygonal form rifling. The trigger has been finely tuned and the long slide shifts the center of balance forward, helping the gun hold more solidly on target and dampening the recoil of light loads. The extension of the tang should also be noted. As is to be expected on a competition weapon, the backsight is click adjustable in small increments for windage and elevation, and the undercut, interchangeable post foresight gives a dead black Partridge picture. Perhaps the most interesting feature, however, is that the Pistole 07 can be converted quickly from one caliber to another simply by replacing the barrel and magazine, while the same breechblock, recoil spring, and all other elements are retained unchanged. The calibers covered are: 0.45in ACP; 9mm Parabellum; 0.38in Super; and 0.38in Special Wadcutter. In 0.45in and 9mm caliber the weapon operates with a locked breech, but in 0.38in caliber it operates as a blowback weapon and the magazine capacity is reduced to five rounds. The pictures show a 0.45in version (left) and the 0.38in Special Wadcutter version with special wooden butt plates (right).

RHEINMETALL 7.65MM DREYSE PISTOL — GERMANY

Length (gun): 6.3in (159mm)
Barrel: 3.7in (93mm)
Weight: 25.0oz (0.7kg)
Caliber: 7.65mm
Rifling: 4 grooves, r/hand
Capacity: seven
Muz vel: ca 850ft/sec (259m/sec)

The Rheinmetall company of Sommerda, Germany, has been in business (although not under its present title) since 1889. In 1901 it took over Waffenfabrik von Dreyse, the company which had been founded in 1841 to manufacture the famous Prussian needle-rifles and also needle-revolvers. The pistol seen here is of a type designed by Louis Schmeisser and was placed on the market in 1907; it was named Dreyse, although Nikolaus von Dreyse himself had by that time been dead for many years. The pistol was of slightly unusual design. The slide was positioned above the barrel, which lay in a trough in the main frame. At the back of the frame, above the butt, were two parallel rectangular plates, joined at the rear to provide a backsight, but otherwise open to allow the slide to pass between them. The top of the breechblock, which was integral with the slide (but lower, so as to align with the chamber), could be seen between these plates when the slide was forward. When the slide was drawn back to cock the weapon and chamber a round, the breechblock protruded through the rear of the frame; when the slide went forward, the end of the striker protruded slightly as an indication that the arm was cocked. In order to strip the weapon it was necessary to push in a small catch at the rear of the frame, allowing the whole upper part to be pivoted forward on a pin in front of the trigger.

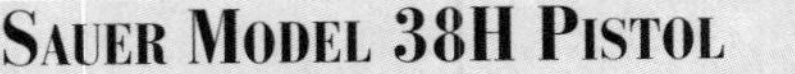

SAUER MODEL 38H PISTOL — GERMANY

Length (gun): 6.8in (171mm)
Barrel: 3.3in (83mm)
Weight: 25.0oz (0.7kg)
Caliber: 7.65mm
Rifling: 4 grooves, r/hand
Capacity: eight
Muz vel: ca 900ft/sec (274m/sec)

The German firm of J. P. Sauer & Sohn is an old one, with a reputation for producing high-quality weapons. At first, its products were mainly sporting guns and rifles, but the company began to make self-loading pistols in 1913 and continued to do so until after World War II, when it turned to revolvers. The weapon illustrated here is one of Sauer's best products. It was first put on the market in 1938 (hence its Model number), but the outbreak of war soon afterwards restricted its use to German forces – and for some reason manufacture was not resumed afterwards. It worked on the blowback principle, having a fixed barrel and an overall slide with the breechblock inside it. It had an internal hammer (hence the "H" – for Hahn, hammer – in the Model designation). The first round was chambered in the usual way by the manual operation of the slide, which also cocked the hammer, but thereafter there were various options. If required, the hammer could be lowered by pressing the trigger, with the thumb on the milled catch behind it, and allowing the catch to rise slowly. To fire after this procedure, the pistol could either be cocked by depressing the catch with the thumb, or fired double-action by pressing the trigger.

Schuler "Reform" Pistol — Germany

Length (gun): 5.3in (133mm)
Barrel: 3.0in (76mm)
Weight: 12.0oz (0.3kg)
Caliber: 6mm
Rifling: 7 grooves, r/hand
Capacity: four
Muz vel: ca 780ft/sec

In the early days of cartridge weapons, before the self-loading arm had been invented, many ingenious attempts were made to solve the problem of the physical bulk of revolvers. The weapon illustrated here was a Belgian copy of a design by August Schuler of Suhl, Germany. The basic lock mechanism was that of a normal double-action revolver, in which the hammer acted on a firing pin in the frame. The forward end of the frame consisted of a pair of parallel side-plates, between which fitted a set of four vertically-stacked barrels. These were first loaded and then pressed down like a clip between the plates, where they were held in place by a small spring-loaded stud. The top round was fired first; then, pressure on the trigger raised the block of barrels so that the second cartridge was in line, ready for the next shot. The three lower barrels had small holes drilled on their upper sides to connect each to the barrel immediately above; thus, when the second and subsequent barrels were fired, enough gas passed upwards to blow out the empty case in the barrel above. The comb of the hammer was shaped in such a way as to deflect these ejected cases away from the direction of the firer's face.

Schwarzlose Model 1908 Pistol — Germany

Length (gun): 9.2in (234mm)
Barrel: 4.8in (121mm)
Weight: 32.0oz (0.91kg)
Caliber: 9mm
Rifling: 4 grooves, r/hand
Capacity: six
Muz vel: ca 1,000ft/sec (305m/sec)

Andreas Schwarzlose, a German from Charlottenburg, is perhaps best remembered as the inventor of a medium machine gun with a simple but effective blowback action but his real interest was in self-loading pistols, and from 1892 onward he produced a variety of ingenious mechanisms. Perhaps unfortunately for Schwarzlose, the Mauser was fairly well established by the time that his arms appeared, and thus they never really had the success they deserved. However, he persevered, and by 1908 he had produced yet another model, of the type illustrated above. It is, in many ways, a remarkable arm: perhaps its most interesting feature is that the usual blowback system has been replaced by a blow-forward mechanism. The breechblock is an integral part of the frame, but the barrel is mounted on ribs and was therefore free to be forced forward by the explosion of the charge; this left the empty case held in an ejector, which threw it clear mechanically. On its forward movement, the barrel stretched a heavy recoil spring; when its forward impetus was exhausted, the spring drew it backward, scooping the next round from the magazine and also cocking the hammer. The metal arm in front of the butt is a grip safety: it had to be firmly gripped, in the proper firing position, or the trigger would not function. There is, however, a stud on the left side of the butt which allowed the safety to be locked in, if necessary.

Walther Model 9 Pocket Pistol — Germany

Length (gun): 4.0in (102mm)
Barrel: 2.0in (51mm)
Weight: 9.5oz (0.3kg)
Caliber: 6.35mm
Rifling: 6 grooves, r/hand
Capacity: six
Muz vel: ca 800ft/sec (244m/sec)

Carl Walther Waffenfabrik has produced numerous self-loading pistols since 1908 and this was the ninth in the series, the last before the introduction of the famous PP (qv). It was one of the smallest and neatest self-loading pistols ever made, well-suited for concealment in a waistcoat pocket or in a lady's handbag. It had a fixed barrel with an open-topped slide and was of simple blowback type. The slide was retained on the frame by a dumbbell-shaped catch at the rear, which was held in place by a small spring catch. When this was raised, the entire assembly was forced out to the rear under the pressure of the striker spring. When the weapon was cocked, the rear end of the striker protruded slightly through a hole in the upper circle of the catch to indicate that the arm was ready for action. The slide is marked "WALTHER PATENT MODEL 9," with details of the company.

Walther PP Pistol — Germany

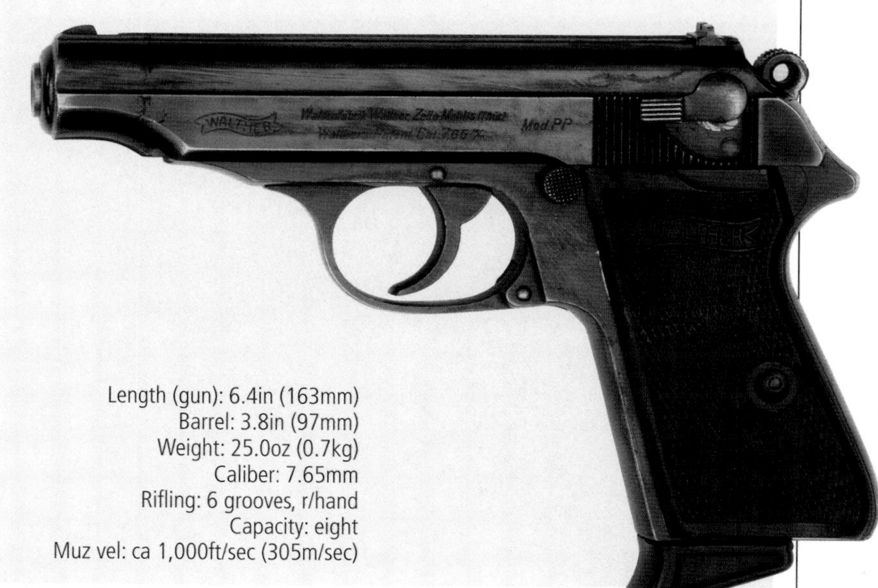

Length (gun): 6.4in (163mm)
Barrel: 3.8in (97mm)
Weight: 25.0oz (0.7kg)
Caliber: 7.65mm
Rifling: 6 grooves, r/hand
Capacity: eight
Muz vel: ca 1,000ft/sec (305m/sec)

The Carl Walther Waffenfabrik (weapons factory) was established in 1886, but did not begin to make self-loading pistols until 1908. Its first nine models were numbered, but in 1929 it produced a tenth model designed specifically for police work, and this was designated the Polizei Pistole or "PP." It was of a new and, to some extent, revolutionary design, and rapidly achieved popularity after its appearance in 1929. It was very soon adopted as a holster arm by several European police forces, and later also became the standard pistol of the German Luftwaffe. Its main feature was its double-action lock, which was basically of revolver type and which involved the use of an external hammer. A considerable risk was involved in carrying hammerless self-loaders – and even, to a lesser extent, many earlier hammer versions – with a round in the chamber. However, when a round had been loaded into the chamber of a Walther and the safety catch applied, the fall of the trigger could be disconcerting, but was completely safe, for the action of the safety placed a steel guard between the hammer and the firing pin. The pistol was easily stripped by pulling down the trigger-guard and pushing very slightly to the left, after which the slide was eased off.

WALTHER PPK PISTOL — GERMANY

Length (gun): 5.8in (147mm)
Barrel: 3.2in (80mm)
Weight: 20.0oz (0.6kg)
Caliber: 7.65mm
Rifling: 6 grooves, r/hand
Capacity: seven
Muz vel: ca 1,000ft/sec (305m/sec)

The Walther PP was immediately popular, and two years later a smaller version was made for concealed use. It was intended for plain-clothes police work and was known as the "PPK" (the "K" standing, it is said, for Kriminappolizei (criminal police)). The Walther PPK pistol was of blowback type and it had several interesting and important features. The most notable, perhaps, is that it was provided with an external hammer activated by a double-action lock; this allowed the pistol to be carried safely with a round in the chamber and the hammer down. Thus, all that was necessary to bring it into action was to push off the safety catch and press the trigger. It also had an indicator pin which protruded through the top of the slide when there was a cartridge in the chamber – a very useful feature in any self-loading pistol, where the rounds cannot be seen as they can in a revolver. The earliest versions of this pistol had complete butt-frames with a pair of grips, but later examples had a front strap only, with a one-piece, molded wrap-around, plastic grip. Most also had a plastic extension on the bottom of the magazine, to increase the area of grip.

WALTHER 0.25IN TPH POCKET PISTOL — GERMANY

Length (gun): 5.5in (140mm)
Barrel: 2.8in (70mm)
Weight: 11.0oz (o.3kg)
Caliber: 0.25in
Rifling: n.k.
Capacity: 7-round box magazine
Muz vel: n.k.

The Walther Taschenpistole mit Hahn (= pocket pistol with hammer), introduced in 1969, is a short, stubby pistol of the traditional "vest pocket" variety, but built to very modern standards. It is normally chambered for the 0.25in ACP round, although 0.22in LR is also available. It has a fixed barrel and is blowback operated without any provision for "cocked-and-locked" carry. There is an outside hammer, with a hammer trip safety on the left-hand side. Sights are square post foresight; square notch backsight. Both foresight and backsights have white dots for low-light use and the weapon is remarkably accurate at ranges up to 100yd (91m).

WALTHER P38 PISTOL — GERMANY

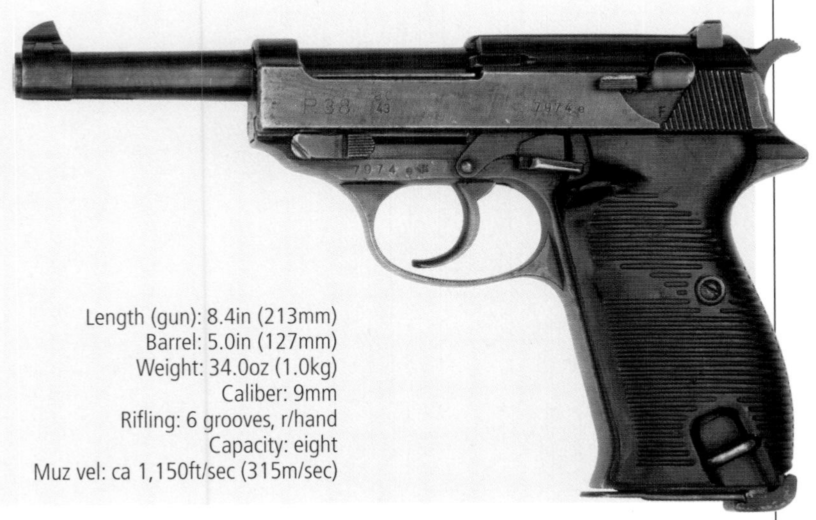

Length (gun): 8.4in (213mm)
Barrel: 5.0in (127mm)
Weight: 34.0oz (1.0kg)
Caliber: 9mm
Rifling: 6 grooves, r/hand
Capacity: eight
Muz vel: ca 1,150ft/sec (315m/sec)

In the early 1930s, the Carl Walther Waffenfabrik developed two prototype military self-loading pistols, the Model AP (= Armee Pistole [Army Pistol]) and HP (= Heeres Pistole [Army Pistol]). The AP was of hammerless type and the HP had an external hammer; and since the latter arrangement was considered preferable by the German military authorities, the final model was thus equipped. The new arm, the P38, was easier to manufacture than the Luger P08 (qv) and by 1943 it had largely superseded the older weapon – although the Luger continued in use to the end of World War II. The type of cartridge used in the P38 made it necessary to employ a locked breech. The lower part of the barrel incorporated a separate locking block, the lugs of which engaged in recesses in the slide when the pistol was ready to be fired. When a cartridge was fired, the barrel and slide recoiled briefly together, until the lugs were carried out of the slide; then the barrel stopped, allowing the slide to continue to the rear to cock the hammer. The slide then traveled forward under the pressure of the recoil spring, to continue the cycle by pushing another cartridge into the chamber. The only actions necessary to fire the loaded pistol, therefore, were to push up the safety catch with the thumb to the "fire" position (the position which is shown in the photograph) and then press the trigger.

Walther 0.32in GSP-C Target Pistol — Germany

Length (gun): 11.5in (292mm)
Barrel: 4.3in (108mm)
Weight: 45.5oz (1.3kg)
Caliber: 0.32in
Rifling: n.k.
Capacity: 5-round box magazine
Muz vel: n.k.

The Walther GSP is a highly specialized target competition weapon, and is generally considered to be a brilliant design in every respect; it has certainly proved very successful in competition shooting. The weapon has a die-cast aluminum frame and the forward mounting of the magazine gives it a distinctive profile and solved a lot of design problems, but nothing is ever gained without penalty and this made overall length a critical dimension. Thus, in order for the Walther GSP to comply with the rules by fitting inside the referee's box magazine and still to have a barrel of sufficient length to reassure shooters (who expect to see a long barrel on a target pistol) the heel support has been cut short, thus sacrificing some stability of hold. Sights are interchangeable post foresight; square notch backsight. The GSP is available as a three-caliber kit, with conversions to 0.22in LR or 0.22in Short for Standard Pistol, Standard Handgun, Ladies Match, and Rapid Fire Pistol events.

Snaphance Pistol — Germany

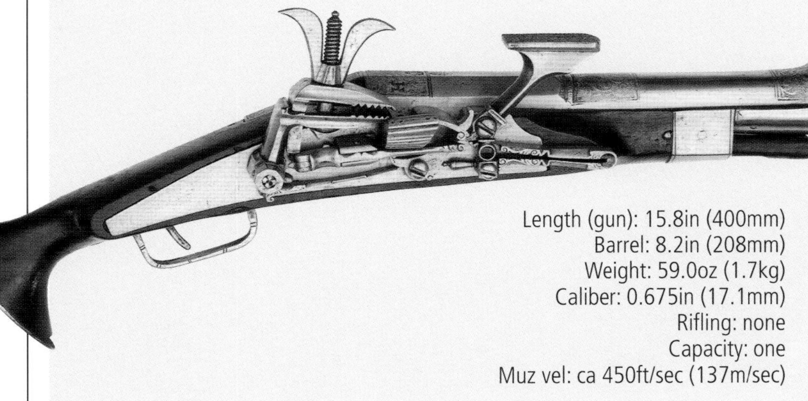

Length (gun): 15.8in (400mm)
Barrel: 8.2in (208mm)
Weight: 59.0oz (1.7kg)
Caliber: 0.675in (17.1mm)
Rifling: none
Capacity: one
Muz vel: ca 450ft/sec (137m/sec)

In terms of development the snaphance (or snaphaunce) pistol seen here fell between the wheel-lock and the flintlock. Although the name given to this arm is of Dutch derivation, there is no evidence that the type originated in the Low Countries, and the lock on this example appears to be of Franco-German origin. The pistol, which was made in about 1575, has some gold damascening on the barrel but is otherwise plain, although well made. Soon after the invention of the wheel-lock, many European gunmakers began to seek ways of incorporating the principle of flint and steel – then the only practical way of ignition known – into a weapon better suited to the primitive manufacturing facilities then available. Instead of a complex wheel mechanism, this pistol had a "cock" which "pecked" forward when the trigger was pressed. The piece of flint held in its jaws struck a steel plate positioned over the shallow priming pan, from which the touch hole led into the breech. The steel was situated at the end of a pivoted arm, which could be held either safely forward (as in the photograph), or backward, over the pan. The steel was usually linked to a sliding pan cover, which thus opened automatically when the steel was pulled back preparatory to firing. The cock had a short throw, so a strong spring was fitted to give it sufficient impetus to strike a shower of good hot sparks. The long wing-nut on the jaw screw, holding the flint firmly in position, therefore had the secondary function of allowing a good grip to be taken to cock the arm.

Rifled Cavalry Pistol — Germany

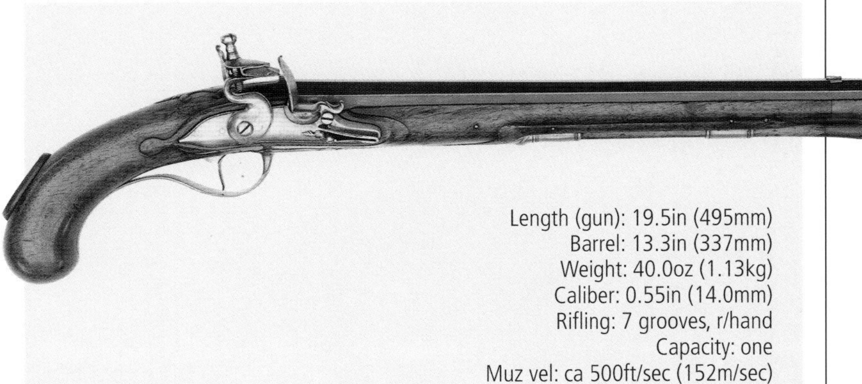

Length (gun): 19.5in (495mm)
Barrel: 13.3in (337mm)
Weight: 40.0oz (1.13kg)
Caliber: 0.55in (14.0mm)
Rifling: 7 grooves, r/hand
Capacity: one
Muz vel: ca 500ft/sec (152m/sec)

This pistol was probably made in Germany in about 1715, at a time when the cavalry had largely reverted to shock action. Even so, pistols were usually carried, and in some European countries it was the custom to arm a few men of each troop with weapons of superior precision, so that they could in some degree hold their own with enemy skirmishers. Although severely plain (apart from a little shallow engraving on the trigger-guard), as befits a service arm, it is of excellent quality. The lock is of standard type, with the slight down-droop at the rear characteristic of the period, and it is well stocked in some hardwood which is not immediately identifiable. Its ramrod, also wooden, has a horn tip and is held in position by one pipe and a tail-pipe. The octagonal barrel is very sturdy, which is not surprising in view of the fact that it is rifled with seven rounded grooves. Rifled barrels necessitated tight-fitting bullets, and these, in turn, led to increased pressures at the breech. The pistol's foresight is square in section, while the backsight (which is just visible behind the steel) has a shallow V-notch. The flat metal plate which is seen at the back of the butt incorporates a keyhole: it was clearly intended to serve as the attachment point for a further butt (unfortunately missing in this case) which would convert the arm into a carbine. When used in this way, with a carefully-measured charge and a well-cast ball wrapped in an oiled patch, it is probable that it would have shot fairly well up to about 150 yards (137mm), a range well outside the accurate capacity of a smoothbore musket.

Pinfire Revolver — Germany

Length (gun): 11.0in (279mm)
Barrel: 6.0in (152mm)
Weight: 27.0oz (0.8kg)
Caliber: 0.43in (11mm)
Rifling: 5 grooves, l/hand
Capacity: six
Muz vel: ca 600ft/sec (183m/sec)

The pinfire cartridge consisted of a rimless, cylindrical, brass case containing the charge; a bullet; and, most important of all, an internal percussion cap inserted into a small compartment in the cartridge's base. The inner end of the small brass-wire pin which gave the cartridge its name rested on this cap. When it was driven inwards by the blow of the hammer, it set off the cap and thus fired the charge. The most interesting aspects of this weapon (by an unknown German) are the apertures running from the chambers to the rear edge of the cylinder, several of which are clearly visible. To load the revolver, it was necessary to open the top-hinged loading gate, place the hammer at half-cock, and insert the cartridges into the chambers in such a way that the pins protruded from the apertures. The hammer was so shaped that when it fell it struck the outer end of the pin and thus fired the cartridge. The thin brass case expanded at this instant and prevented any rearward escape of burning gases. Then the metal's natural elasticity caused it to contract, so that it could be easily removed by the sliding rod below the barrel. Copper was also used for cases, although it was somewhat less elastic.

Fegyvergyar Frommer Baby — Hungary

Length (gun): 4.8in (121mm)
Barrel: 2.3in (57mm)
Weight: 14.0oz (0.4kg)
Caliber: 6.35mm
Rifling: 4 grooves, r/hand
Capacity: six
Muz vel: ca 800ft/sec (244m/sec)

Rudolf Frommer was one of Fegyvergyar's designers and engineers and was with the firm from 1896 until 1935. This "Baby" of 1912 was basically a smaller type of Frommer "Stop" service pistol of the same year. It worked on the system known as long recoil, in which the barrel recoiled almost its full length before returning, leaving the breechblock to come forward after it, stripping a cartridge from the magazine and chambering it. This independent movement of barrel and breechblock made it necessary to have two separate springs, both of which were housed in the separate cylindrical tunnel, visible above the barrel.

Fegyvergyar Pisztoly 12M/19M (Frommer stop) Pistol — Hungary

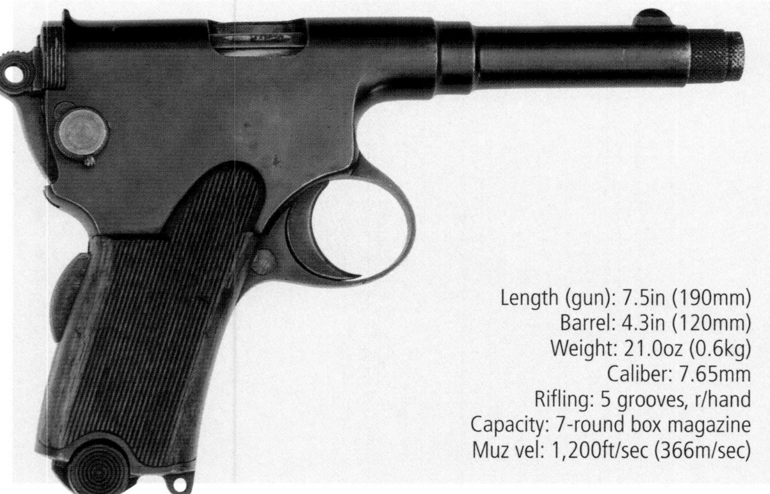

Length (gun): 7.5in (190mm)
Barrel: 4.3in (120mm)
Weight: 21.0oz (0.6kg)
Caliber: 7.65mm
Rifling: 5 grooves, r/hand
Capacity: 7-round box magazine
Muz vel: 1,200ft/sec (366m/sec)

In the Austro-Hungarian Empire, which was broken up in 1918, the various elements of the Imperial Army tended to be armed in different ways. As far as the Hungarian element – Honved – was concerned its standard pistol was the Pistol 12M, made at the Royal Hungarian Arsenal at Fegyvergyar and designed by a team led by Rudolf Frommer. This pistol, which was a simplified version of a design which had appeared in 1903, was also known as the "Frommer Stop" and was of an unusual type, since it worked on the long recoil principle in which, following firing, the barrel and bolt remained locked together as they traveled rearwards or a distance marginally greater than the length of the cartridge. The two were then unlocked and the barrel returned to its forward position, extracting and ejecting the empty case as it did so, while the bolt remained locked. On completion of its travel the barrel tripped the bolt stop, thus releasing the bolt which then traveled forwards, stripping the top round from the magazine and chambering it as it did so. Among other complications, this involved the use of two return springs; one to draw the barrel forward and a second to make the breechblock follow it. The initial pistol to this design was the Model 12M, fielded in 1912, followed by the virtually identical Model 19M, which remained in production until at least 1930. The large circular stud just forward of the hammer is the inspection cover release catch, which allowed the shooter to examine the mechanism. Note also the grip safety which was fitted on both models. This was a complicated system for a weapon as small as this, but, nevertheless, the system worked and both Models 12M and 19M enjoyed a good reputation.

Fegvergyar Model 1937M/Pistole 37 (U) Pistol — Hungary

Length (gun): 7.2in (183mm)
Barrel: 4.3in (110mm)
Weight: 27.0oz (0.8kg)
Caliber: 9mm
Rifling: 6 grooves, r/hand
Capacity: 7-round box magazine
Muz vel: ca 900ft/sec (274m/sec)

The Hungarian firm of Fegyvergyar (Fegyver es Gepygar Reszvenytarsasag) was established in the 19th Century and soon had a reputation for producing good quality, well-designed, if somewhat complicated, weapons. Its first self-loading pistol appeared in 1903 and this was followed by a number of improved models, including one which was adopted by the Hungarian Army during World War I as the Model 12M (also known after its designer as the "Frommer Stop" (qv). The Model 37M, was the last in the series and was a simple a blowback weapon with a fixed barrel and an overall slide, with the recoil spring situated on a rod beneath the barrel. The first round was chambered in the normal way by the manual operation of the slide, which also cocked the external hammer. There was a prominent spur on the magazine to extend the butt length and improve the firer's grip. This version fired a 9mm Short cartridge suitable for a blowback design and its only safety device was its grip safety. In 1941 the German Wehrmacht placed a contract for a 7.65mm version, which, apart from the first few, were all fitted with a safety catch of orthodox type on the left-hand side of the frame and did not have the spur. These were used mainly, but not exclusively, by the Luftwaffe, and were designated "Pistole 37 (U)" (U = Ungarisch [Hungarian]) by the Germans; the slide was marked "P MOD 37 Kal 7.65" together with the manufacturer's code "j.h.v." and the last two digits of the year of manufacture. It was used almost exclusively on the Eastern Front and is now rather rare, making the weapon much sought-after by weapons collectors.

Fegyvergyar FEG P9R — Hungary

Length (gun): 7.8in (197mm)
Barrel: 4.8in (121mm)
Weight: 37.0oz (1.1kg)
Caliber: 9mm
Rifling: 6 grooves, r/hand
Capacity: 15-round box magazine
Muz vel: ca 1,110ft/sec (335m/sec)

The Hungarian State Arsenal carried out an exercise in "reverse engineering" in the 1970s, as a result of which they started producing copies of Fabrique Nationale's 9mm GP35 (Browning "High Power") (qv) under the designation FEG 9; indeed, the copies were so precise that many of the parts were inter-changeable. This was offered to but rejected by the Hungarian Army, as a result of which the FEG 9 was offered for sale commercially in both Eastern and Western Europe. This was followed by the FEG 9R, which was essentially the same pistol, but with a number of significant modifications designed by FEG engineers. This involved deleting the GP25's transverse cam bar, camming the barrel into lockup with the back of the recoil spring guide rod, which is secured in place by the slide latch crosspin. The P9R has a steel frame, while the otherwise identical P9RA has a light alloy frame, making it some 6.3oz (180g) lighter. The Model P9RK has a shorter barrel, while there is also a special left-handed version which is an exact mirror-image. The latest version is the Model B9R which appears to be similar to the P9R, but has a number of minor changes.

IMI Desert Eagle Pistol — Israel

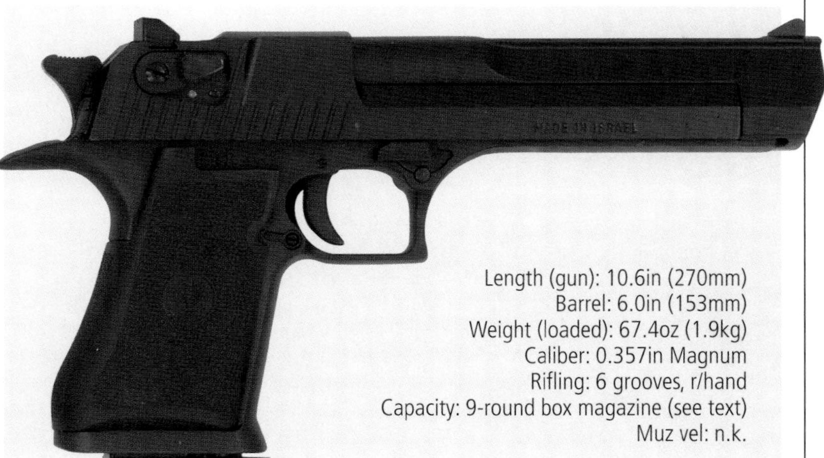

Length (gun): 10.6in (270mm)
Barrel: 6.0in (153mm)
Weight (loaded): 67.4oz (1.9kg)
Caliber: 0.357in Magnum
Rifling: 6 grooves, r/hand
Capacity: 9-round box magazine (see text)
Muz vel: n.k.

The Israeli Military Industries (IMI) Desert Eagle was originally developed as a sporting weapon and has since been offered on the military market as well. The Desert Eagle has a fixed barrel, and on firing a proportion of the gases is diverted through a gas port just in front of the chamber into a duct, which channels the gas forward to a point just beneath the muzzle where it is turned through 180 degrees downwards into a gas-cylinder containing a short-stroke piston. The gas drives the piston to the rear, which, in its turn, drives the slide, whose first action is to rotate and thus unlock the bolt, which then withdraws, extracting and ejecting the empty case as it does so. The slide is then pushed forwards by the return-spring rod, strips off and chambers a round, and rotates the bolt into the locked position ready for firing. The standard version of the Desert Eagle is chambered for 0.357in Magnum, but three calibers are available, each having different capacity magazines: 0.357in Magnum (9 rounds); 0.44in Magnum (8 rounds); and 0.50in Action Express (7 rounds). Standard barrel length is 6.0in (153mm), but lengths of 10.0in (254mm) and 14.0in (355.6mm) are also available. The weapon is normally provided with a blade foresight and a U-notch backsight. However, a backsight adjustable for elevation and windage is also available and the receiver is grooved to accept telescope mounts. Specifications relate to the 0.357in Magnum (standard) version.

ARMI SAN MARCO COLT MODEL 1860 0.44IN — ITALY

Length (gun): 13.8in (350mm)
Barrel: 8.0in (203mm)
Weight: 44.0oz (1.2kg)
Caliber: 0.44in
Rifling: 7 grooves, l/hand
Capacity: 6
Muz vel: ca 600ft/sec (183m/sec)

In 1981 the MLAIC decided to allow replica classes for all shooting disciplines under its jurisdiction and manufacturers were quick to produce a range of very high quality weapons to meet the resulting demand. This beautifully made and finished reproduction Colt Model 1860, made by Armi San Marco, together with the Uberti Remington New Model Army (qv), are among the most popular in this category.

BERETTA MODEL 1934 PISTOL — ITALY

Length (gun): 6.0in (152mm)
Barrel: 3.8in (95mm)
Weight: 23.0oz (0.7kg)
Caliber: 9mm
Rifling: 4 grooves, r/hand
Capacity: nine
Muz vel: ca 750ft/sec

The first Beretta self-loading pistol, the Model 1915, was of wartime quality and was designed to take a 7.65mm cartridge; this was soon replaced by a version in 9mm caliber, which was considered more suitable for service use. Development continued after World War I, with a steady improvement in design until 1934, when this weapon appeared. Like its predecessors, the Model 1934 worked by simple blowback action: thus, although it was of 9mm caliber, it fired a short cartridge in order to keep the gas pressure within safe limits. As may be seen, it had an external hammer: this could be cocked either by the rearward movement of the slide, or manually, and it had a half-cock position. Most examples were fitted with a curved lower extension to the magazine to ensure a firm grip for a user with a large hand, but some (like the example seen here) were fitted with plain magazines. This arm became the standard Italian service pistol in 1935: this particular example is marked with the letters "RE" surmounted by a crown, indicating that it is a military model. During the course of World War II, many British officers acquired Beretta pistols of this model in the expectation that they would be able to fire standard 9mm Parabellum Sten-gun ammunition through them, but they found that this ammunition would not fit.

BERETTA MODEL 1935 PISTOL — ITALY

The Model 1935 was very similar in all essentials to the earlier Model 1934 but was of the smaller caliber of 7.65mm. The specimen illustrated is fitted with a spur-shaped extension below the magazine to offer added support for the little finger of the firer's hand. Like the Model 1934, the Model 1935 had a safety catch on the left side of the frame and was usually fitted with a loop for a lanyard on the lower part of the butt. It was extensively issued to the Italian Navy and Air Force and was also used by the Italian police. The specimen illustrated bears the initials "PS" (Publica Sicurreza), indicating that it is a police weapon. Like most Berettas of the period, this arm bears details of the caliber on the left side of the slide, which is also dated "1941." The date is followed by the Roman numerals "XIX," its date in the Fascist Calendar of 1922.

Length (gun): 6.0in (152mm)
Barrel: 3.8in (95mm)
Weight: 23.0oz (0.7kg)
Caliber: 7.65mm
Rifling: 4 grooves, r/hand
Capacity: seven
Muz vel: ca 800ft/sec (244m/sec)

BERETTA MODEL 81 7.65MM PISTOL — ITALY

Length (gun): 6.8in (171mm)
Barrel: 3.8in (95mm)
Weight: 24.0oz (0.7kg)
Caliber: 7.65mm
Rifling: 6 grooves, r/hand
Capacity: 12-round box magazine
Muz vel: 985ft/sec (300m/sec)

In 1976 Beretta put no fewer than three new pistols into production: Model 81, Model 84, and Model 92. The Model 81 fires the 7.65mm cartridge and operates on the straight-forward blowback principle. The slide is pulled to the rear manually, which cocks the hammer and on release the slide is driven forward by the recoil spring, chambering a round as it moves. The recoil from the fired case thrusts the slide to the rear, compressing the recoil spring as it does so, and allows the firing cycle to continue. When the slide is forward and the pistol ready to fire, the extractor protrudes slightly from the side in order to give the firer a visual indication of the weapon's readiness to fire. There is also a manual safety which can be operated by either left or right hand. The pistol has a double-column magazine, which holds 12 rounds and is virtually identical with that of the Model 84, except that it has long deep grooves along each side to hold the smaller rounds.

BERETTA MODEL 84 9MM PISTOL — ITALY

The second in this series of Beretta pistols, the Model 84 is chambered to fire the 9mm Short cartridge and, since this is a relatively low-powered round, the weapon works on the simple blowback principle, without any requirement for breech-locking. Manual retraction of the slide cocks the hammer and chambers a round on its forward motion. The recoil from the fired case thrusts the slide to the rear, compressing the recoil spring as it does so, and allows the firing cycle to continue. When the slide is forward and the pistol is ready to fire, the extractor protrudes slightly from the side in order to give the firer a visual indication of the weapon's readiness to fire. There is also a manual safety which can be operated by either left or right hand. The pistol has a double-column magazine, but without the long grooves which characterize the magazine of the Model 81. Both Models 81 and 84 have anodized aluminum frames, and are very reliable mechanically.

Length (gun): 6.8in (171mm)
Barrel: 3.8in (95mm)
Weight: 22.0oz (0.6kg)
Caliber: 9mm
Rifling: 6 grooves, r/hand
Capacity: 13-round box magazine
Muz vel: 920ft/sec (280m/sec)

Beretta Model 92/92S 9mm Pistol — Italy

Length (gun): 8.5in (217mm)
Barrel: 4.9in (125mm)
Weight: 35.0oz (1.0kg)
Caliber: 9mm
Rifling: 6 grooves, r/hand
Capacity: 15-round box magazine
Muz vel: ca 1,280ft/sec (390m/sec)

In the 1970s Beretta updated their Model 1951 to produce the Model 92; first fielded in 1976, this was taken into service by various armies and was also sold commercially under the trade name of "Brigadier." The Model 92 differed from the Model 1951 in having a double-action trigger and magazine capacity was increased from 8 to 13, thus necessitating a somewhat bulkier butt. Otherwise, there was little change, the Model 92 being initially loaded in the orthodox way by inserting the magazine and pulling the slide back by hand, which cocked the hammer and chambered the first round. As it fired the powerful 9mm Parabellum round the Model 92 necessarily used a locked breech mechanism, in which the rearward pressure of the fired case drove back the barrel and slide, which were locked together by a block. Having traveled about 0.3in (8mm) the locking block pivoted downwards to disengage from the slide, whereupon the barrel stopped but the slide continued to the rear to complete the reloading cycle. Next to appear was the Model 92S which was identical with the Model 92 apart from changes to the safety catch, which was situated on the slide instead of the frame and which could also be used as a de-cocking lever. Both the Model 92 and 92S were sold to numerous military and police users and remained in production until the mid-1980s.

Beretta US Army M9 (Model 92SB/92F) 9mm — Italy

Length (gun): 8.5in (217mm)
Barrel: 4.9in (125mm)
Weight: 32.0oz (1.0kg)
Caliber: 9mm
Rifling: 6 grooves, r/hand
Capacity: 15-round box magazine
Muz vel: ca 1,100ft/sec (335m/sec)

When the US Army announced a competition to replace the venerable, but greatly respected, Colt M1911A1, which had served the US armed forces for some 80 years, Beretta modified their Model 92 to meet the new requirement. The resulting weapon, the Beretta 92SB, was the clear winner and, following some further changes to meet US Army requirements, the new weapon entered service as the Pistol M9 in 1985, with initial orders for some 500,000 weapons. (The M9 has the company designation, Beretta 92F.) The M9 pistol is entirely coated in a Teflon-derived material and the barrel is chrome-plated, while its action uses the locked-wedge design pioneered in the Walther P38. The weapon is loaded in the orthodox manner by inserting the charged magazine into the butt, following which the slide grip is used to pull the action to the rear, cocking the hammer, and then released to chamber a round. On firing, gas pressure drives the barrel and slide to the rear, locked together by a wedge, but, having traveled some 0.3in (8mm), the locking wedge pivots downwards, disengaging from the slide; the barrel immediately stops but the slide continues rearwards to complete the reloading cycle. Unlike many automatic pistols, these Berettas are of an open slide design – ie, the greater part of the barrel is exposed and not covered by the slide. The changes required by the US Army were virtually all concerned with the grip and included an enlarged trigger guard to enable the firer to use a two-handed grip, an extension to the base of the magazine and a slight curve to the foot of the front edge of the butt. The Beretta M9/92F is now the standard pistol in the US, Italian, and many other armed forces and para-military forces such as the French Gendarmerie Nationale.

Beretta Model 93R 9mm Pistol — Italy

Length (gun): 9.5in (240mm)
Barrel: 6.1in (156mm)
Weight: 39.5oz (1,120g)
Caliber: 9mm
Rifling: 6 grooves, r/hand
Capacity: 15- or 20-round box magazine
Muz vel: 1,230ft/sec (375m/sec)

The Beretta Model 1951R was developed in the 1970s for use by the Carabinieri, special forces, and, in particular, government close-protection squads, and was a modified version of the company's Model 1951 pistol. Firing 9mm Parabellum rounds, it had a large, wooden foregrip at the front of the slide, and could fire single rounds or fully automatic; it did not have a butt-stock. The Model 1951R had only a short production run and a replacement did not appear until the Model 93R which is designed to meet a similar operational requirement and is, in effect, a machine-pistol. The mechanism of the Model 93R is virtually identical to that of the Model 92 pistol, but with a modification to enable it to fire three-round bursts, as well as single rounds. It also has some additional fitments, including a muzzle brake, a folding-down, metal forestock, an enlarged trigger guard, and a folding, steel, skeleton butt stock (not shown here), which clips on to the heel of the butt grip. Thus, particularly when firing three-round bursts, the shooter brings the stock into his or her shoulder and with the right hand on the butt grip and finger on the trigger, and places the left thumb through the front of the over-sized trigger guard and the fingers around the fold-down foregrip. The 93R has been taken into service by Italian and other national special forces.

Bernardelli P018-9 9mm Pistol — Italy

Length (gun): 8.4in (213mm)
Barrel: 4.8in (122mm)
Weight: 36.0oz (1.0kg)
Caliber: 9mm
Rifling: 6 grooves, r/hand
Capacity: 14-round box magazine
Muz vel: 1,150ft/sec (350m/sec)

Introduced in 1984, the Bernardelli is an all-steel automatic pistol, with major components machined from forgings. It is recoil-operated, using a locked breech, with cam unlocking. Ribs on top of the barrel at the breech end seat in the roof slide. It has a post foresight and a square-notch backsight, laterally dovetailed, which can be adjusted for windage using an Allen key. It has selective double action. In its standard form it is chambered for the 9mm Parabellum round, but is also available for 7.65mm Luger. There is a compact version of the P018/9, which is also available in both 9mm and 7.65mm calibers.

Bodeo Model 1889 Service Revolver — Italy

Length (gun): 10.5in (267mm)
Barrel: 4.5in (114mm)
Weight: 32.0oz (0.9kg)
Caliber: 0.41in (10.4mm)
Rifling: 4 grooves, r/hand
Capacity: six
Muz vel: ca 650ft/sec (198m/sec)

The Bodeo revolver took its name from the head of the Italian commission which recommended its adoption in 1889. This recommendation being approved, the Bodeo was put into production; by 1891 it had become the standard Italian service revolver, remaining in service for at least 50 years. The Model 1889 was made in two distinct types: a round-barreled version, with a trigger-guard; and an octagonal-barreled version, with a folding trigger. The revolver seen here is of the latter type. Although not an arm of particular distinction, the Bodeo was simple and robust – which is presumably why it lasted so long. The barrel is screwed into the frame, and the cylinder was loaded through a bottom-hinged gate which was drawn backwards to open it. Ejection was by means of a rod which was normally housed in the hollow axis pin. As in the Rast-Gasser revolver (qv), the loading gate was connected to the hammer in such a way that, when it was opened, the hammer would not function, although the action of the trigger still turned the cylinder. This arrangement, which is known as the "Abadie" system, was frequently found on European weapons. Revolvers of this type were made in a variety of Italian factories, and during World War I a number were also manufactured in Spain for use by the Italian Army.

Fabbrica Armi Sportive (FAS) Model 601 Competition Pistol — Italy

Length (gun): 11.3in (287mm)
Barrel: 6.0in (152mm)
Weight: 40.0oz (1.1kg)
Caliber: 0.22in
Rifling: n.k.
Capacity: 5-round box magazine
Muz vel: n.k.

This weapon was originally marketed in the early 1970s as the IGI Domino, but was subsequently modified and renamed the Fabbrica Armi Sportive (FAS) Model 601. It is a very sophisticated weapon and when it appeared it was one of the first of the new generation of low bore axis competition pistols. The designer's aim was to produce a weapon which combined optimum performance with reasonable price, although early examples were plagued by parts breakages and it took several years fully to debug the design; thereafter, however, it became a top-level competition gun. The Model 601 is a semi-automatic, blowback-operated competition pistol chambered for the 0.22in Short cartridge. Notable developments compared to the IGI Domino include significantly greater hand support, a more steeply raked grip and, most importantly, a much lower bore line, which significantly reduces muzzle torque on recoil. It also dispenses with the muzzle brake fitted on the earlier model, but introduces large ports running the length of the barrel, with the venting adjustable by plug screws. The Model 601 makes interesting comparison with the Walther GSP (qv), which was designed to meet approximately the same requirement. The Model 601 uses gas pressure in the bore to act on the cartridge case and use it as a piston to drive slide rearward. The weapon has a square post foresight and a square notch backsight click adjustable for elevation and windage. The five-round magazine is inserted from the top of the gun through the ejection port.

Glisenti Chamelot-Delvigne-Pattern Italian Service Revolver — Italy

Length (gun): 11.2in (284mm)
Barrel: 6.3in (159mm)
Weight: 40.0oz (1.1kg)
Caliber: 0.41in (10.4mm)
Rifling: 5 grooves, r/hand
Capacity: six
Muz vel: ca 625ft/sec (190m/sec)

The revolver seen here is the Italian version of the Chamelot-Delvigne et Schmidt Model 1872 (Schmidt was a Swiss officer who made some changes in design). There was also a version with a folding trigger – and, therefore, of course, no trigger-guard. The arm is of solid-frame type, with an octagonal barrel which is screwed into the main frame. The foresight is slotted in and the backsight is a U-notch on the lump (visible just in front of the hammer), the top straps also being grooved. The six-chambered cylinder is grooved and has rear notches for the cylinder stop. The ejector rod worked in a sleeve; when it was not in use, its head was turned in under the barrel, where it fitted over the front end of the cylinder axis pin. To remove the cylinder, it was first necessary to turn down the head of the ejector rod and press in a stud on the left front of the frame; this allowed the pin to be drawn forward. The spring loading gate is hinged at the bottom and was opened by drawing it to the rear. There is a small stop on the frame, against which the gate rested when in the open position. The lock is of double-action type; very slight pressure on the trigger lifted the hammer to the half-cock position, which allowed the cylinder to be rotated for loading. The butt has uncheckered side plates and a swivel ring for a lanyard. These revolvers were made in various Italian factories; this one carries the name of the Royal Manufactory of Glisenti, Brescia, on the left of the frame. Versions of the arm were in production until 1930.

Glisente 9mm Model 1910 Pistol — Italy

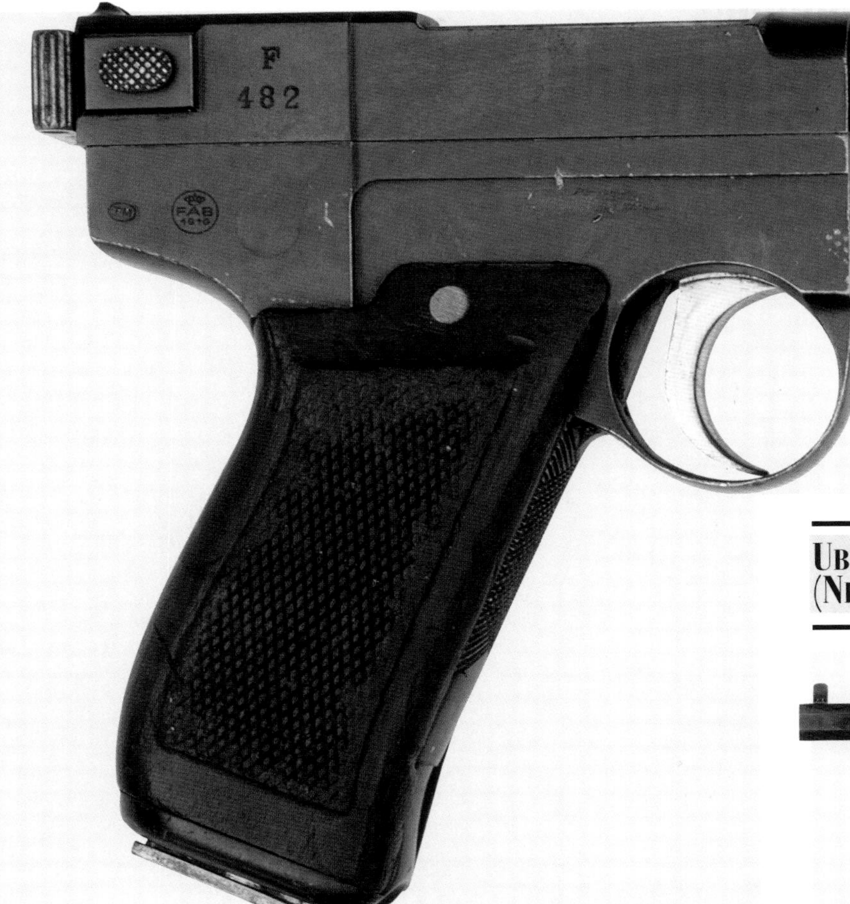

Length (gun): 8.3in (210mm)
Barrel: 3.9in (99mm)
Weight: 29.0oz (0.8kg)
Caliber: 9mm
Rifling: 6 grooves, r/hand
Capacity: seven
Muz vel: ca 1,000ft/sec (305m/sec)

The Italian company Real Fabbricca d'Armi Glisenti (later Siderurgica Glisenti) began its operations in about 1889. After some earlier experiments with self-loading pistols, the weapon illustrated here was put into production in 1910 and was adopted by the Italian Army. The pistol fired from a locked breech. When the first shot was fired, barrel and bolt recoiled briefly together. The barrel then stopped in its rearward position, while the bolt, having unlocked itself, continued to travel. As it came forward, it stripped and chambered the next round and drove the barrel forward. As it did so, a wedge rose from the frame and locked the whole into position. The system was complex and not very strong; thus, the cartridge fired was less powerful than the Parabellum of comparable caliber. The pistol's trigger mechanism was peculiar: the striker was not cocked by the moving parts, but by a projection on the trigger; the striker was forced backwards against a spring until it tripped and then came forward to fire the round. This made the trigger-pull very long. The milled screw at the front of the frame held in position a plate covering much of the left side; its removal gave access to the working parts. Although it became obsolete in 1934, some were in service in World War II.

Uberti Reproduction Remington Model 1863 (New Model Army) Percussion Revolver — Italy

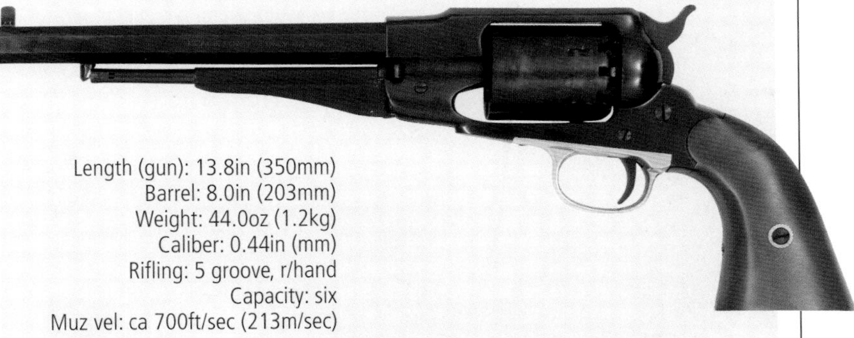

Length (gun): 13.8in (350mm)
Barrel: 8.0in (203mm)
Weight: 44.0oz (1.2kg)
Caliber: 0.44in (mm)
Rifling: 5 groove, r/hand
Capacity: six
Muz vel: ca 700ft/sec (213m/sec)

This is a replica of one of the strongest and most reliable service revolvers used in the American Civil War, made by the Italian company, Uberti. Like the original Remington Model 1863 (qv), it is a percussion weapon, using rammer-loading from the front of the cylinder, usually aided by ready-prepared paper cartridges.

Pedersoli Reproduction Le Page Target Pistol — Italy

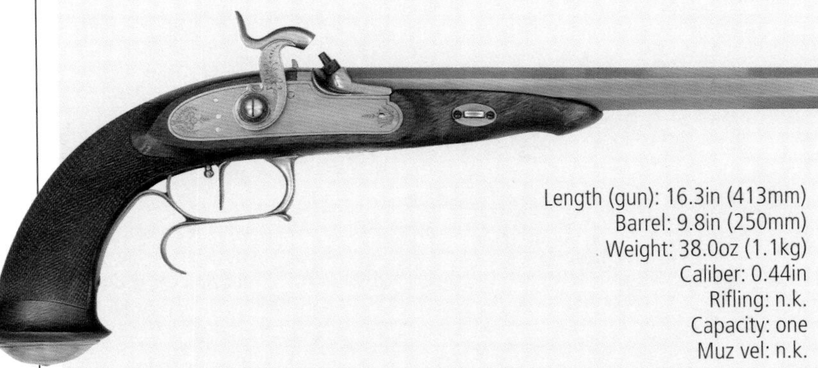

Length (gun): 16.3in (413mm)
Barrel: 9.8in (250mm)
Weight: 38.0oz (1.1kg)
Caliber: 0.44in
Rifling: n.k.
Capacity: one
Muz vel: n.k.

Le Page was one of the foremost Parisian gunmakers operating in the period 1830-1870, and this is a modern reproduction of one of his typical products, made by Pedersoli of Italy. It is a muzzle-loading, percussion pistol, firing a 0.44in bullet.

Uberti Reproduction Murdoch Scottish Flintlock Pistol — Italy

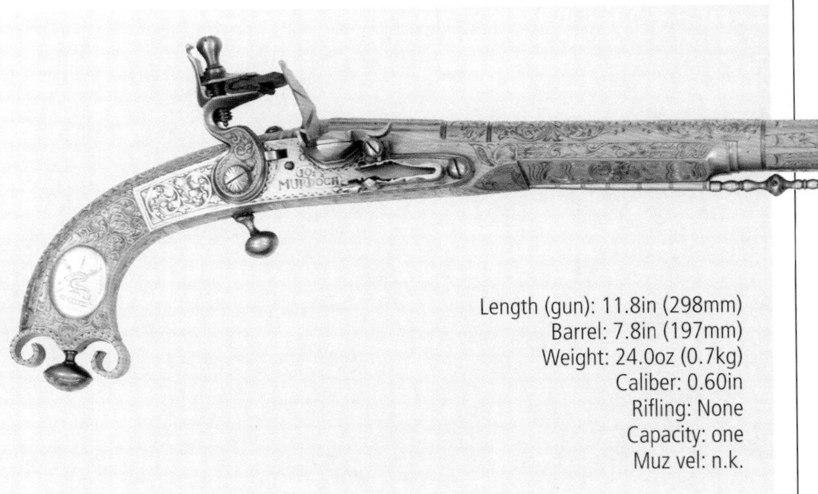

Length (gun): 11.8in (298mm)
Barrel: 7.8in (197mm)
Weight: 24.0oz (0.7kg)
Caliber: 0.60in
Rifling: None
Capacity: one
Muz vel: n.k.

Made by Italian company, Uberti, this is a modern reproduction of a Scottish, all-steel pistol made by John Murdoch of Doune, near Stirling, Scotland, in about 1770. These attractive-looking weapons were intended for use as part of Highland full dress, although they were fully functioning weapons and perfectly capable of being fired, if the need arose. The modern reproductions are also capable of firing, but very few collectors would choose to do so, preferring instead to use these exceptionally attractive examples of the gunsmith's art for display purposes only.

WHEEL-LOCK PISTOL — ITALY

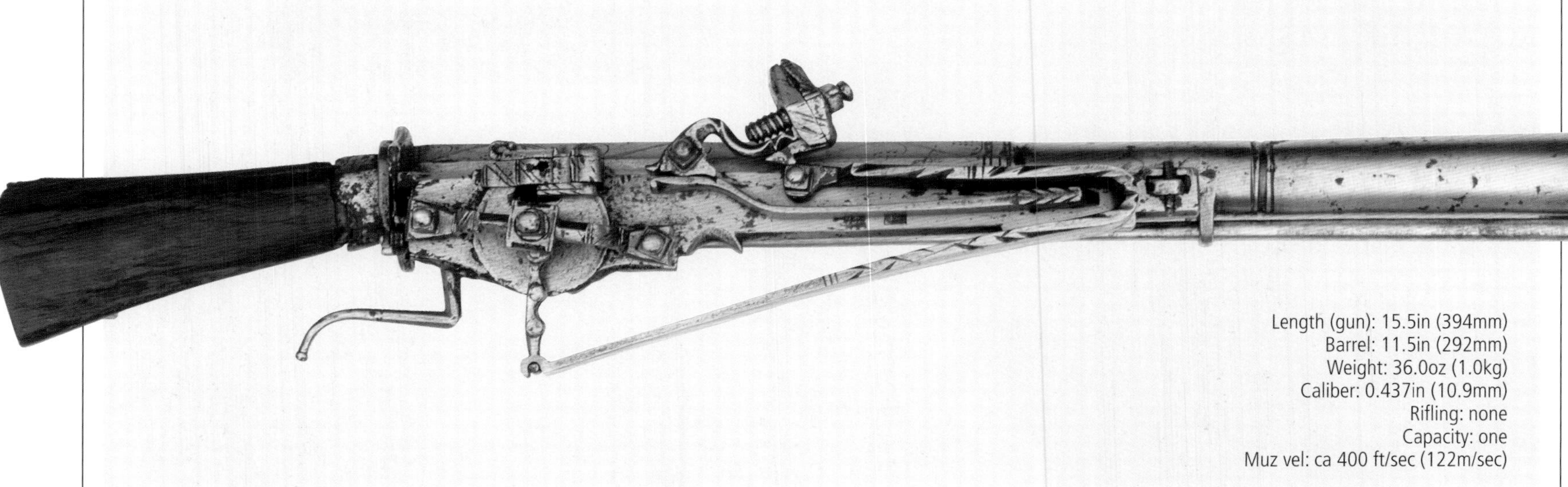

Length (gun): 15.5in (394mm)
Barrel: 11.5in (292mm)
Weight: 36.0oz (1.0kg)
Caliber: 0.437in (10.9mm)
Rifling: none
Capacity: one
Muz vel: ca 400 ft/sec (122m/sec)

The general principle on which the wheel-lock worked was quite simple in theory, although remarkably difficult to put into practice. The wheel, which gave the lock its name, was spun mechanically by a spring, so that its roughened edge rubbed briskly against a piece of pyrites and caused sparks. The upper part of the wheel protruded through a close-fitting slot in the pan, which was connected to the barrel by a touch hole. Once the arm was loaded and the pan primed, it was necessary to wind the wheel (usually about three-quarters of a turn) by means of a key, open the pan (unless this was also done by mechanical means), and pull down the hinged jaws holding the piece of pyrites until it was held firmly against the wheel. Pressure on the trigger then allowed the wheel to spin against the pyrites, thus striking sparks and igniting the priming. This mechanism, when well made, was reasonably reliable in dry weather, although the relatively poor quality of temper of the springs made it advisable not to leave it wound (or "spanned," as it was often referred to) for longer than was necessary. The arm illustrated was made in Italy in about 1530, and was a plain but well-made weapon, apparently intended for use rather than ornament. Note in particular the straight grip, presumably a legacy of the mace. This certainly gave a good hold on the arm but must have made it virtually impossible to direct the ball with any real degree of accuracy, except in action at very close quarters.

NAMBU MEIJI 26TH YEAR SERVICE REVOLVER — JAPAN

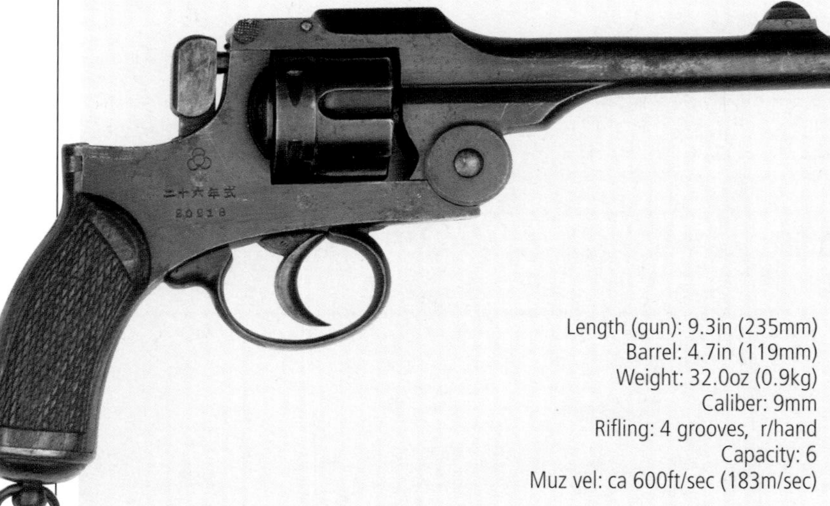

Length (gun): 9.3in (235mm)
Barrel: 4.7in (119mm)
Weight: 32.0oz (0.9kg)
Caliber: 9mm
Rifling: 4 grooves, r/hand
Capacity: 6
Muz vel: ca 600ft/sec (183m/sec)

Most Japanese military equipment was dated by the year in which it was introduced to service, based on the regnal year of the current emperor. Thus, this weapon, the first Japanese-made revolver, entered service in 26th year of the reign of the Emperor Meiji, which equates to 1893 in the Western calendar. At that time Japan was emerging from many centuries of medieval seclusion and was learning as much as it could – and as rapidly as possible – from the West. Thus, there is nothing original about this weapon, which is an amalgam of ideas culled from a careful study of contemporary European and American weapons. The Imperial Japanese Navy had earlier purchased a quantity of Smith & Wesson No 3 Models, which had been found satisfactory, so it is not surprising that the S&W formed the basis for this Japanese revolver, but there were also ideas gained from the Galand (Belgium), Nagant (Russia) and others. It had an octagonal barrel with a foresight bed into which the blade was pinned, while the backsight was incorporated into the top frame. The weapon was opened by lifting the top latch, after which the barrel was swung downwards, activating the automatic ejector. The lock was of the self-cocking type and as the mechanism was slow to respond, accurate shooting was virtually impossible. Access to the mechanism was gained through a large side plate, similar to that found in the Austro-Hungarian Rast & Gasser Model 1898 (qv). This was a good effort, bearing in mind the fairly primitive state of Japanese industry at the time, but this cannot have been a very effective weapon in combat.

NAMBU 4TH YEAR 8MM TYPE A SELF-LOADING PISTOL — JAPAN

Length (gun): 9.0in (229mm)
Barrel: 4.7in (122mm)
Weight: 31.0oz (0.9kg)
Caliber: 8mm
Rifling: 6 grooves, r/hand
Capacity: 8-round box magazine
Muz vel: 1,100ft/sec (335m/sec)

This was the first Japanese attempt at a semi-automatic pistol and was designed by a retired army officer, Colonel Kirijo Nambu. The Model 04 (also known as the Nambu Type A) was initially intended for sale to civilian customers and to army officers, who at that time had to buy their own weapons (a custom learnt from the British). It was a locked breech weapon, with the breech being locked by a floating locking block attached to the barrel extension. As the barrel moved forwards the this block was lifted as it rode across the frame, thus forcing a lug upwards to engage and lock into a recess in the bolt. The weapon had a grip safety but no holding-open lock, so that when the last round in a magazine had been fired the bolt was held open by the magazine lips, but when the mag was removed (seldom an easy matter) the bolt then closed, needing to be recocked after the new magazine had been fitted. Sights were: fixed post foresight; ramped notch backsight. Early models had a wooden holster stock which attached to the butt, but this was abandoned in 1912. The Model 04 was adopted by the Imperial Japanese Navy in 1909 and by the Thai Army in the early 1920s, but was never formally adopted by the Japanese Army, although many officers bought one privately.

Nambu 7mm Type B (Nambu "Baby") Pistol — Japan

Length (gun): 6.7in (171mm)
Barrel: 3.3in (83mm)
Weight: 21.0oz (0.6kg)
Caliber: 7mm
Rifling: 6 grooves, r/hand
Capacity: 7-round box magazine
Muz vel: 950ft/sec (290m/sec)

As explained previously, Japanese officers had to buy their service revolvers out of their own pocket and when the Type 4 failed to sell in sufficient numbers Colonel Nambu was forced to re-examine the product. As a result, he discovered that most officers considered the Type 4 to be too large and cumbersome, so he designed a smaller, neater weapon, chambered for a 7 x 19.5mm round, which he designed specifically for this weapon. The result was the Nambu "Baby," a short recoil weapon, which appeared in 1909 and was, in effect, simply a scaled-down Model 04. Despite all this, the "Baby" had no advantages to offer over contemporary European and American pistols and was much more expensive, so it never achieved much success; it remained in low-volume production until the early 1930s, when it was phased out.

Nambu Type 94 8mm Pistol — Japan

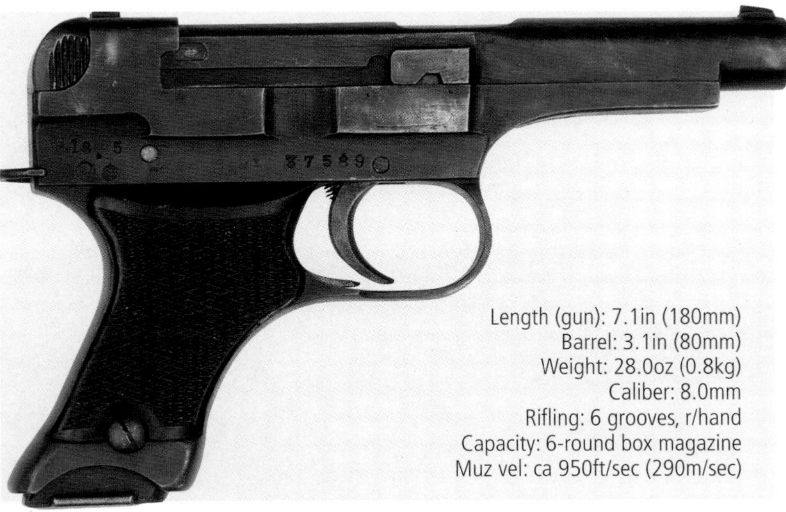

Length (gun): 7.1in (180mm)
Barrel: 3.1in (80mm)
Weight: 28.0oz (0.8kg)
Caliber: 8.0mm
Rifling: 6 grooves, r/hand
Capacity: 6-round box magazine
Muz vel: ca 950ft/sec (290m/sec)

This weapon holds the unusual distinction of being universally accepted as one of the worst pistols ever made. The design originated with a retired army officer turned gun designer, Colonel Kirijo Nambu, who had already produced a number of pistol designs, but, although reasonably effective, they had been both bulky and expensive and, since Japanese officers had to buy their own weapons, his wares had achieved little commercial success. So, in 1929 he set out to produce a simpler and cheaper self-loading pistol and the Army Ordnance Department showed considerable interest in the prototypes. Unfortunately, the department then assumed that this gave it the right to interfere in the design and the result, as always when committees become too powerful, was disastrous. The slide covered the entire top of the frame and barrel and the weapon was cocked by pulling this back by means of the milled ears at the rear, but unfortunately this also exposed the sear bar which was situated on the left-hand side of the frame, so that it protruded slightly, making it possible to discharge the weapon accidentally by a blow. The trigger mechanism was particularly unreliable and it was also possible to fire the pistol prematurely, before the breech was locked. These problems were inherent in the design, but all were exacerbated by the increasingly poor standard of workmanship as the war continued, those manufactured in 1944-45 being especially bad. On top of all this the original intention had been to produce a pistol which was cheaper than its predecessors, but the actual weapon proved to be even more expensive.

Nambu 14th Year 8mm Pistol — Japan

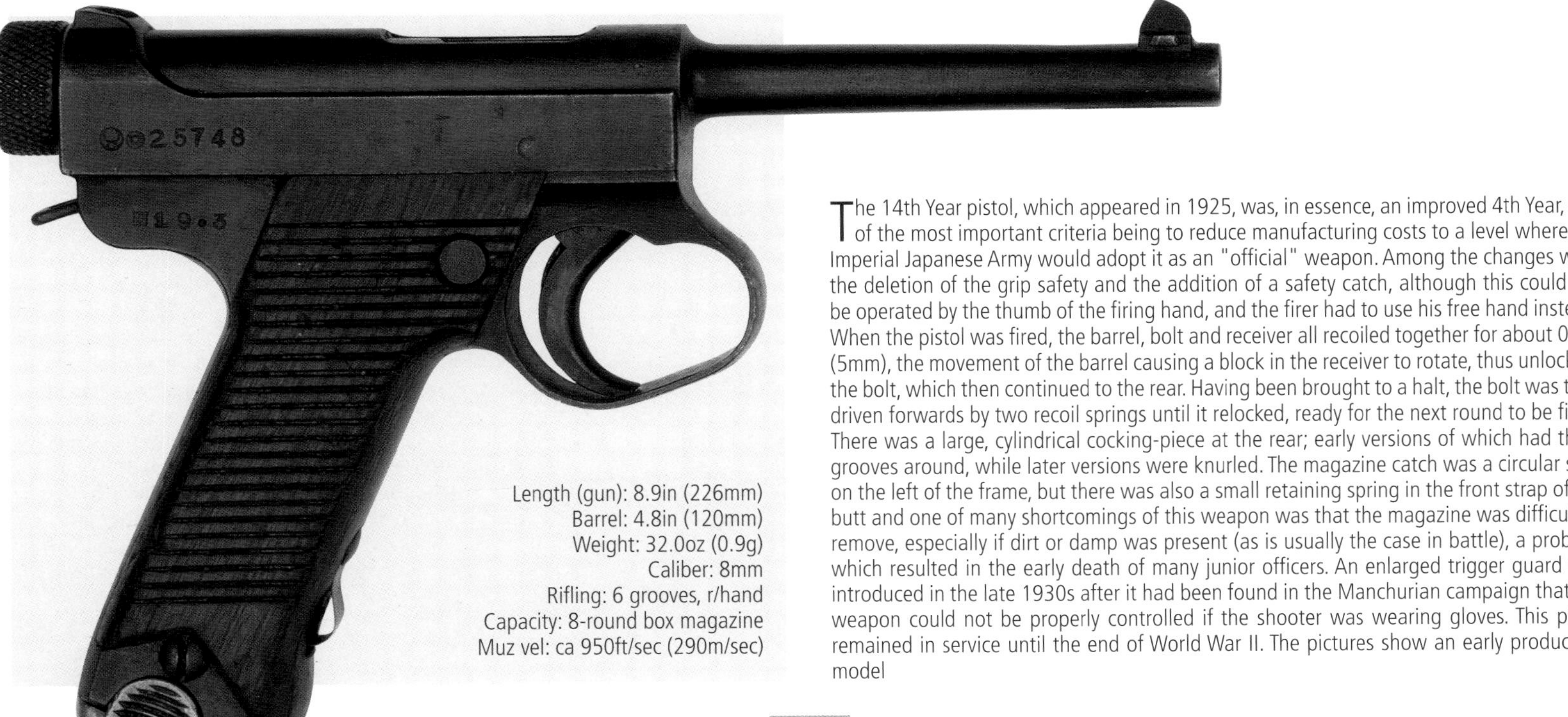

Length (gun): 8.9in (226mm)
Barrel: 4.8in (120mm)
Weight: 32.0oz (0.9g)
Caliber: 8mm
Rifling: 6 grooves, r/hand
Capacity: 8-round box magazine
Muz vel: ca 950ft/sec (290m/sec)

The 14th Year pistol, which appeared in 1925, was, in essence, an improved 4th Year, one of the most important criteria being to reduce manufacturing costs to a level where the Imperial Japanese Army would adopt it as an "official" weapon. Among the changes were the deletion of the grip safety and the addition of a safety catch, although this could not be operated by the thumb of the firing hand, and the firer had to use his free hand instead. When the pistol was fired, the barrel, bolt and receiver all recoiled together for about 0.2in (5mm), the movement of the barrel causing a block in the receiver to rotate, thus unlocking the bolt, which then continued to the rear. Having been brought to a halt, the bolt was then driven forwards by two recoil springs until it relocked, ready for the next round to be fired. There was a large, cylindrical cocking-piece at the rear; early versions of which had three grooves around, while later versions were knurled. The magazine catch was a circular stud on the left of the frame, but there was also a small retaining spring in the front strap of the butt and one of many shortcomings of this weapon was that the magazine was difficult to remove, especially if dirt or damp was present (as is usually the case in battle), a problem which resulted in the early death of many junior officers. An enlarged trigger guard was introduced in the late 1930s after it had been found in the Manchurian campaign that the weapon could not be properly controlled if the shooter was wearing gloves. This pistol remained in service until the end of World War II. The pictures show an early production model

NAMBU 14TH YEAR 8MM PISTOL/SWORD COMBINATION — JAPAN

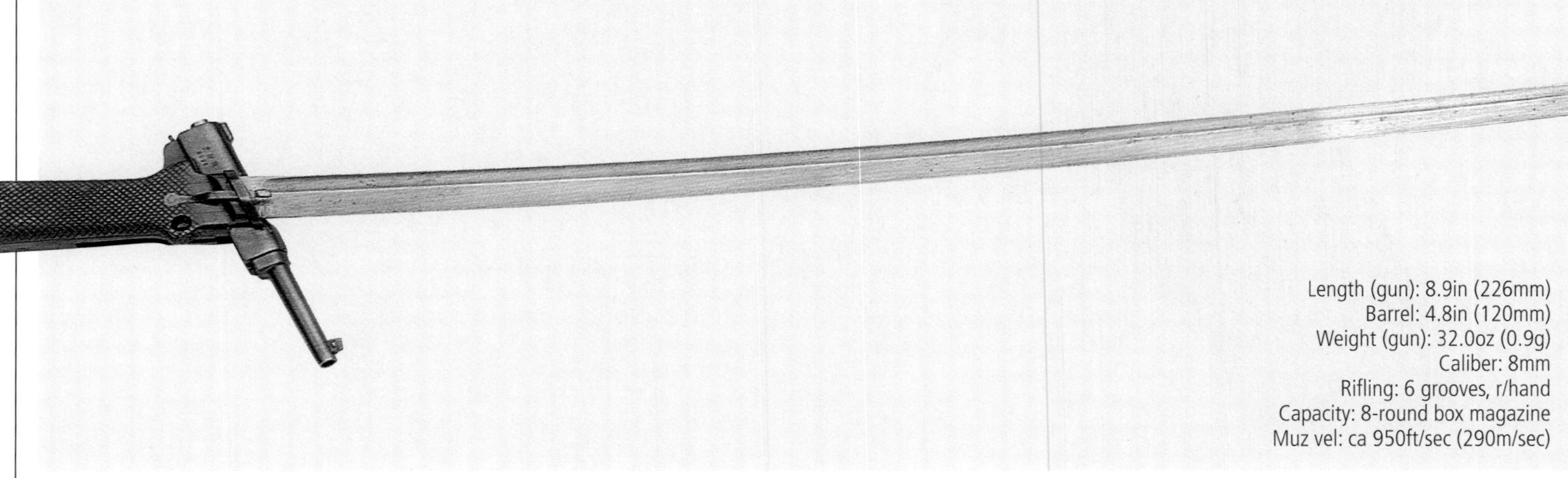

Length (gun): 8.9in (226mm)
Barrel: 4.8in (120mm)
Weight (gun): 32.0oz (0.9g)
Caliber: 8mm
Rifling: 6 grooves, r/hand
Capacity: 8-round box magazine
Muz vel: ca 950ft/sec (290m/sec)

This amazing "combination" weapon is included for its curiosity value, since, although there are examples of pistols being fitted with short bayonets or dagger blades, this is the only known example of a combined automatic pistol and sword. The pistol was a Nambu 14th Year (qv) and it should be noted that in the picture the trigger group and magazine are both missing. The sword blade was some 29.0in (744mm) long and the scabbard was modified slightly to accommodate the pistol. In normal sword construction there is an extension, known as a "tang," around which the handgrip is constructed, but whether or not in this case the tang extended down the side of the pistol into the stock is not apparent. This was probably a "one-off" constructed to satisfy the whim of a traditionally minded officer, but it would seem that the sword blade would have made firing the pistol rather difficult, while the weight and size of the pistol would have made the use of the sword problematical as well. Like most combinations, it would have been most unsatisfactory and its tactical value must have been minimal.

SUGIURA 7.65MM SEMI-AUTOMATIC PISTOL — JAPAN

This very rare pistol was manufactured in a Japanese Army arsenal in Manchuria during the Japanese occupation of that country in the 1930s and early 1940s. A 7.65mm caliber weapon, its design appears to have been based upon that of the Colt Model 1903, which was in service with both Chinese and Japanese armies at that time. The fact that its design and production was undertaken at all exhibits a degree of dissatisfaction and distrust of the Imperial authorities in the home country, and of their procurement policies. Apart from its caliber no details of this weapon are known with any degree of certainty.

RADOM WZ MODEL 1935 9MM PISTOL — POLAND

Length (gun): 8.3in (211mm)
Barrel: 4.5in (114mm)
Weight: 37.0oz (1.1kg)
Caliber: 9mm
Rifling: 6 grooves, r/hand
Capacity: eight
Muz vel: ca 1,150ft/sec (351m/sec)

An arms factory was set up soon after the end of World War I, in the town of Radom, Poland, intended principally for the production of military rifles. Soon after 1930 it was decided that the Polish Army required a self-loading pistol. After the consideration of various designs, an indigenous model was finally adopted, and by 1935 the Wz-35 was in extensive production. Like most later self-loading pistols, it was based on the designs of the American John M. Browning, with some relatively minor changes either for ease of manufacture or in the shape of actual improvements incorporated in the light of experience. The pistol worked in the orthodox way: lugs on the upper surface of the barrel engaged corresponding slots in the slide when it was locked; the barrel recoiled briefly and then dropped to disengage when the slide was either drawn to the rear manually or blown back by the gases produced by the explosion of the cartridge. As may be seen, the weapon had a grip safety at the rear of the butt. No manual safety as such was fitted, but the arm incorporated a device for retracting the firing pin, and this allowed it to be carried safely with a round in the chamber and the hammer down. This device was activated by the lever below the back-sight; the action of cocking the hammer manually returned the firing pin to its proper position.

Nagant Model 1895 Revolver — Russia

Length (gun): 9.1in (230mm)
Barrel: 4.4in (110mm)
Weight: 28.0oz (0.8kg)
Caliber: 7.62mm
Rifling: 4 grooves, r/hand
Capacity: seven
Muz vel: 1,000ft/sec (305m/sec)

The Belgian brothers, Emil and Leon Nagant, cooperated with the Russian S.I. Mosin to design and produce the Mosin-Nagant Model 1891 rifle, and they went on to design this revolver which was adopted by the Imperial Russian Army in 1895. This weapon was chambered for the 7.62 x 38R Nagant round and, although appearing at first glance to be a conventional revolver, it incorporated one unusual feature. Virtually all revolvers have a small gap between the rear end of the barrel and the front face of the chamber, through which a small proportion of the propellant gases escape, thus (at least in theory) reducing the efficiency of the weapon. All designers were aware of this problem and most kept this gap to a minimum by a combination of good design and precision in manufacture, but a few have tried to overcome it altogether and the Model 1895 is one of the very few weapons (perhaps, even the only one) in which this has been successfully achieved. This involved two features, the first of which was a specially designed cartridge with a narrowed neck which fitted snugly into the rear of the barrel and expanded on firing to create a gas-tight seal. Second was a mechanism which not only rotated the cylinder but also pressed it home on aligning a new chamber and later withdrew it slightly before rotating for the next round, thus, again enhancing the integrity of the seal. The Model 1895 was initially produced in the Nagant factory at Liège, Belgium, but the Imperial Russian Government then bought the patent and moved production to Russia. One curious feature was that there were two versions, one using single-action for soldiers and non-commissioned officers, and a double-action version for officers.

Tula-Tokarev TT-30/TT-33 Automatic Pistol — Russia

Length (gun): 7.7in (196mm)
Barrel: 4.6in (117mm)
Weight: 29.0oz (0.8kg)
Caliber: 7.62mm
Rifling: 4 grooves, l/hand
Capacity: 8-round box magazine
Muz vel: ca 1,350ft/sec (411m/sec)

The designation of these two pistols takes the first part – Tula – from the name of the State Arsenal where they were manufactured and the second part – Tokarev – from the name of the designer, Feodor Tokarev, a well-known Russian weapons designer from the 1920s onwards. The recoil-operated, single-action TT-30 (see specifications) was mechanically a copy of various Colt-Browning types, chambered for the Russian 7.62 x 25mm pistol round. Tokarev incorporated one or two minor modifications to simplify manufacture and a few other details, which actually improved the design. In 1933 a new version appeared – the TT-33 – which incorporated even more improvements, and was again simplified in order to speed up production. In the TT-30, for example, the barrel locking lugs were machined onto the barrel's upper surface, but in the TT-33 these were replaced by bands which went completely round the barrel; this involved no mechanical changes, but cut out a time-consuming milling process during manufacture. Another improvement in the TT-33 was that the entire lock mechanism could be easily removed, greatly facilitating maintenance. Neither version had a safety catch, but the hammer could be placed at half-cock. At first sight the weapons appear to be of the hammerless type, but much of the hammer was concealed, with only the cogwheel-type hammer comb visible, just behind the backsight. The TT-33 was marginally longer and heavier than the TT-30, but to users they were virtually identical.

Makarov 9mm Pistol — Russia

Length (gun): 6.4in (161mm)
Barrel: 3.8in (97mm)
Weight: 25.0oz (0.7kg)
Caliber: 9mm
Rifling: 4 grooves, r/hand
Capacity: eight
Muz vel: ca 1,075ft/sec (328m/sec)

The Makarov pistol dates from the early 1950s and became the standard pistol for both the Soviet forces and the Warsaw Pact. Externally it was in almost every respect a copy of the German Walther PP. However, there were some mechanical differences: by far the most important of these is the fact that the weapon had no locking system but fired on a simple blowback action. It was loaded in the orthodox way by inserting a magazine and operating the slide manually to chamber a round and cock the action. On firing, the slide was blown back by the rearward movement of the case. To avoid excessively stiff springs and heavy slides or breechblocks, the cartridge used was an intermediate one in terms of power, although apparently adequate. The pistol had an external hammer with a double-action lock; this meant that it could be carried safely with a round in the chamber and the hammer down. When the pistol had been loaded, the movement of the safety catch – situated on the left rear of the slide, above the buttplate – to the "safe" position allowed the hammer to drop safely and also locked the slide. When the last round in the magazine had been fired, the magazine follower rose to such a level that it pushed up the slide stop and held the slide to the rear, indicating that replenishment was required. To strip the weapon, the magazine was removed and it was ensured that there was no round in the chamber. The front of the trigger-guard was then pulled down and twisted slightly so as to bear on the frame; the slide could now be removed to the rear.

MARGOLIN "VOSTOK" MTs 0.22IN SELF-LOADING TARGET PISTOL — RUSSIA

Length (gun): 10.9in (276mm)
Barrel: 7.4in (187mm)
Weight: 37.0oz (1.0kg)
Caliber: 0.22in
Rifling: n.k.
Capacity: 6-round box magazine
Muz vel: n.k.

In the 1960s and 1970s, top level competition pistol shooters generally used self-loading pistols made in the United States or Europe, but as such weapons became ever more sophisticated and expensive, club-level shooters, particularly in Britain, turned to less expensive weapons. One of the most highly regarded of these was the Russian MTs pistol, which was not only relatively cheap but also of very high quality, the standard of workmanship being especially noteworthy. In those Cold War days even the place of manufacture of a target pistol was highly classified by the Soviet authorities, but British shooters believed that the MTs was at the State Armaments factory at Tula; what they did know was that the MTs was designed by a blind man, Mikhail Margolin, a remarkable achievement. The MTs was blowback-operated using an unlocked breech, and had an external hammer. The sights consisted of a square foresight blade, which was click adjustable for elevation, and a U-notch backsight, which was click adjustable for windage. As sold, the MTs came complete with an additional barrel and muzzle weights. Its only defects were its rather light overall weight (though muzzle weights helped) and a general air of mechanical complexity, but it was a good gun and gave good service.

CAUCASIAN FLINTLOCK PISTOL — RUSSIA

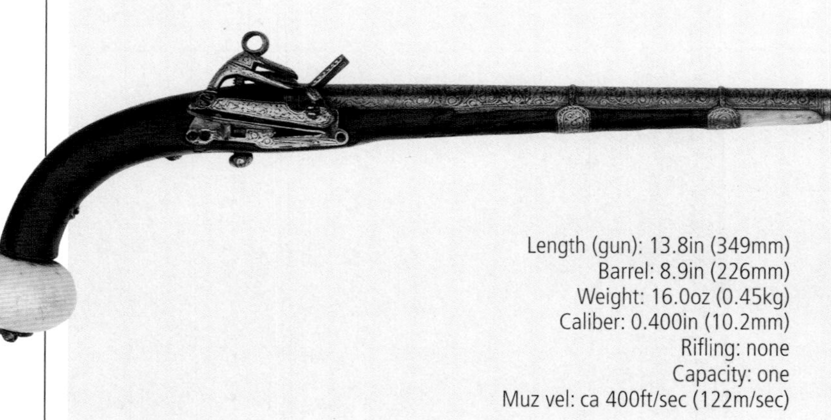

Length (gun): 13.8in (349mm)
Barrel: 8.9in (226mm)
Weight: 16.0oz (0.45kg)
Caliber: 0.400in (10.2mm)
Rifling: none
Capacity: one
Muz vel: ca 400ft/sec (122m/sec)

These arms take their name from the fact that they were made and carried in the general area of the Caucasus mountains (now called Bol'shoy Kavkaz), a range extending from the Black Sea to the Caspian, and are sometimes also known as "Cossack pistols." They were probably assembled by local craftsmen, although the locks and barrels were frequently imported from Spain, Italy, and elsewhere. The barrel of this specimen is decorated with an elaborate pattern of silver inlaid with black, in the Italianate style known as niello. The lock is of characteristic miquelet type, a form which originated in the Spanish province of Catalonia. In this type the sear projected horizontally from the lockplate and acted directly on the projection at the bottom of the cock, the jaws of which have a distinctly reptilian appearance. The sear can be seen just above the button trigger, which is practically universal on pistols of this kind. The pan cover and steel are combined and the face of the steel is scored with eight vertical grooves to ensure a good spark. The entire lock – and, indeed, all the metal parts except the barrel and lanyard ring – are damascened in gold. The stock is of the orthodox slim design and has a thin covering of black leather with an ivory tip and a large, ivory, ball-butt, designed to prevent the weapon from slipping from a greasy hand. Ramrods for these arms were carried separately, often on a cord or ribbon around the user's neck. In spite of their regional title, weapons of this kind were made, or at least used, over much of Russia.

ARANZABAL EIBAR 11MM REVOLVER — SPAIN

Length (gun): 11.0in (280mm)
Barrel: 5.0in (127mm)
Weight: 36.0oz (1.0kg)
Caliber: 11mm
Rifling: 7 grooves, r/hand
Capacity: six
Muz vel: 700ft/sec (213m/sec)

In the 19th Century the Spaniards, like the Belgians, were producing large quantities of handguns, most of which were no better than medium quality. They were, however, cheap and therefore popular, particularly in South American countries, which provided obvious markets for Spanish arms of all types. In spite of the extent of their manufacture, it is probable that most Spanish service weapons were imported at that time, and it is equaly clear that many of these were later copied. The weapon shown, which was made by Aranzabal, is a break-down self-ejector. It is a heavy and apparently robust weapon, although the lockwork is relatively poor, and bore a general resemblance to the products of Smith & Wesson.

ARRIABAN PINFIRE REVOLVER — SPAIN

Length (gun): 11.5in (292mm)
Barrel: 6.4in (163mm)
Weight: 34.0oz (1.0kg)
Caliber: 0.43in (11mm)
Rifling: 4 grooves, l/hand
Capacity: six
Muz vel: ca 650ft/sec (198m/sec)

This weapon is very closely based on the Lefaucheux Pinfire Naval revolver (qv). Of course, armies also needed the revolver, and here the pinfire achieved considerable popularity: it was adopted in one form or another by Norway, Sweden, and Spain, as an arm for officers and certain categories of mounted troops. The weapon illustrated here was made by Arriaban and Company of Eibar, probably in the mid-1860s, when Spain first adopted the arm. The Spaniards had a long and honorable history of gunmaking. Spanish gunsmiths were particularly noted for their barrels, for the manufacture of which they had considerable deposits of high-grade iron ore in the Biscayan area. Although they were never able to compete in the highly industrialized areas of Northern Europe, they maintained a considerable export trade with their erstwhile colonies in South America, where cheapness was much more important than high quality. Although little is known of the history of the pinfire revolver in South America, it is possible that it was quite widely used. The weapon seen here is of solid construction, with a round barrel fastened to the axis pin and the lower frame. A rearward extension to the barrel lump slides over the lower extension of the frame (to which it is screwed) and fits into a slot in the lower part of the standing breech. The lock is of single-action type and there is a lower spur on the trigger-guard to give added grip for the firer's fingers.

Bernedo 6.35mm Pocket Pistol — Spain

Length (gun): 4.5in (114mm)
Barrel: 2.0in (51mm)
Weight: 15.0oz (0.4kg)
Caliber: 6.35mm
Rifling: 6 grooves, r/hand
Capacity: six
Muz vel: ca 800ft/sec (244m/sec)

Vincenzo Bernedo y Cia of Eibar was one of the many small Spanish firms to produce cheap self-loading pistols. During World War I, the company was involved in the manufacture of Ruby pistols (qv), but after the war had ended Bernedo developed a new design, a specimen of which is illustrated here. The weapon was of pocket type and of the usual blowback design. The barrel was almost fully exposed, with the slide to the rear of it. A small catch was situated just below the barrel; when the cylindrical part of this was lifted, it could be pushed out through a loop on the lower part of the barrel, and the barrel could then be drawn forward. This was facilitated by the fact that the lower part of the loop had flanges which fitted into grooves in the frame of the weapon. This weapon's slide bears many Eibar proofmarks, and the butt-grips are marked "V BERNEDO."

Echeverria Star Model B 9mm Pistol — Spain

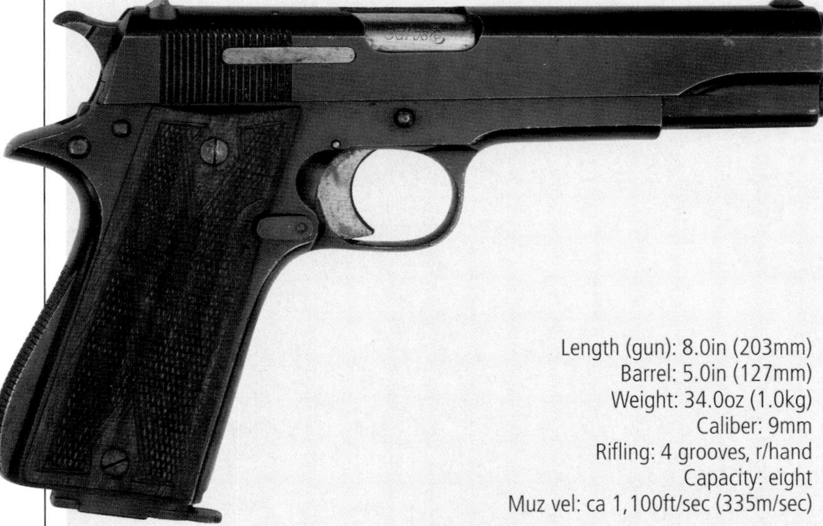

Length (gun): 8.0in (203mm)
Barrel: 5.0in (127mm)
Weight: 34.0oz (1.0kg)
Caliber: 9mm
Rifling: 4 grooves, r/hand
Capacity: eight
Muz vel: ca 1,100ft/sec (335m/sec)

This arm is another of the Spanish self-loading pistols based more or less closely on the Colt Model 1911 and its variants. The firm of Echeverria came into existence in about 1908 in Eibar, and has been making self-loading pistols of one kind or another ever since. The trade name of "Star" was adopted in 1919 and has been in use ever since on a quite bewildering variety of pistols of various types, sizes, calibers, and systems of numbering and classification. The pistol illustrated here is a Star Model B, introduced in about 1928. It was fairly closely based on the Colt, but lacked the grip safety peculiar to that arm. It was a robust and well-made weapon, and since it was chambered for the powerful 9mm Parabellum cartridge it necessarily fired from a locked breech. This worked on the well-known Browning principle: after a brief period of recoil, the rear end of the barrel dropped, thus unlocking itself from the interior of the slide, which continued to the rear and cocked the hammer. Having done so, it came forward, chambered the next cartridge, and relocked the breech in readiness for the next shot. This model pistol was still used by the Spanish armed forces into the 1980s.

Echeverria Model DK (Starfire) Pistol — Spain

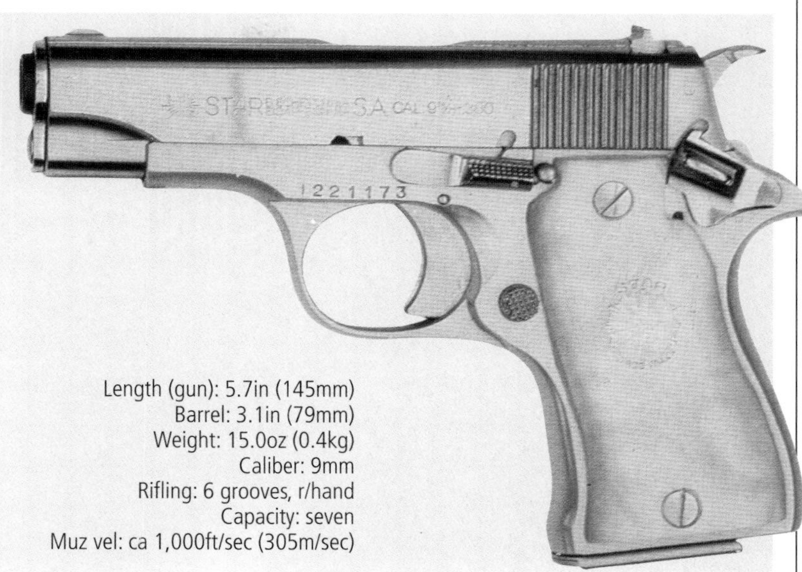

Length (gun): 5.7in (145mm)
Barrel: 3.1in (79mm)
Weight: 15.0oz (0.4kg)
Caliber: 9mm
Rifling: 6 grooves, r/hand
Capacity: seven
Muz vel: ca 1,000ft/sec (305m/sec)

This pistol is based on the company's Model D of about 1930 – although the design has been considerably modernized – and appeared in 1958 under the designation of DK. It is of fairly orthodox type, firing from a locked breech of Browning type, the barrel and slide being fixed at the moment of firing. They recoil briefly together until the rear end of the barrel drops, disengages and stops; the slide continues rearward to cock the hammer. It is forced forward again under the influence of the recoil spring (which is located beneath, and parallel to, the barrel), stripping and chambering a cartridge and relocking the breech in readiness for the next shot. The weapon is quite well made; the butt is comfortably shaped, although inevitably on the short side for even quite a small hand. The frame is of some light alloy with a satin finish and the steelwork is bright. This particular specimen, which is known as the Starfire in the United States market, is supplied in a case with a spare magazine and cleaning rod. It is an attractive enough arm of its kind, and may be said to justify Echeverria's modern reputation for reliability.

Gabilondo Ruby Pistol — Spain

Length (gun): 6.0in (152mm)
Barrel: 3.4in (86mm)
Weight: 30.0oz (0.9kg)
Caliber: 7.65mm
Rifling: 7 grooves, r/hand
Capacity: nine
Muz vel: ca 800ft/sec (244m/sec)

The Spanish firm of Gabilondo began to manufacture a pistol of the type shown here in 1914 under the trade name of "Ruby." It was not a particularly distinguished weapon in any sense of the word, but it appeared on the market at a time when many countries urgently needed arms; thus, a contract for a large number was soon placed by the French Government. The demand was, in fact, so large that Gabilondo was soon forced to put the manufacture of these arms out to subcontractors. The model was discontinued in 1919, although a smaller version in 6.35mm caliber continued in production under the same name for several years.

GABILONDO LLAMA 9MM PISTOL — SPAIN

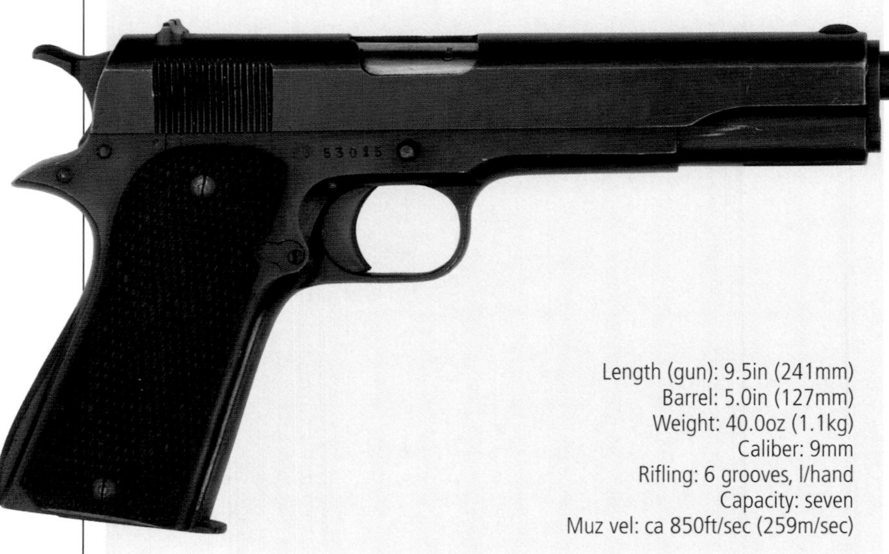

Length (gun): 9.5in (241mm)
Barrel: 5.0in (127mm)
Weight: 40.0oz (1.1kg)
Caliber: 9mm
Rifling: 6 grooves, l/hand
Capacity: seven
Muz vel: ca 850ft/sec (259m/sec)

The great success and wide acceptance of the Colt Model 1911 (qv) self-loading pistol and its successive variations made it inevitable that the arm should become the subject of extensive copying. In this field, Spanish manufacturers were particularly active. In 1931 the Spanish firm of Gabilondo y Cia began to manufacture a new range of Colt-type pistols under the general trade name of "Llama," and these arms have continued in production until the present day. They are, in general, very well-made and reliable weapons and sell in considerable quantities. They have been produced in a wide variety of models and calibers – some of blowback type, some with locked breeches, and yet others with grip safeties – so that individual models are not always easy to identify. The pistol illustrated here appears to be a model produced in ca 1939. Its general style, which very closely resembles that of the Colt, is clear from the photograph. It was designed to fire the 0.38in Colt Super cartridge – a very powerful round, and one which, of course, necessitates a locked breech. This pistol has no grip safety but is fitted with an orthodox safety catch on the left, below the hammer.

UNCETA MODEL 1911 VICTORIA PISTOL — SPAIN

Length (gun): 5.8in (146mm)
Barrel: 3.2in (81mm)
Weight: 20.0oz (0.6kg)
Caliber: 7.65mm
Rifling: 7 grooves, r/hand
Capacity: seven
Muz vel: ca 750ft/sec (229m/sec)

The firm of Unceta Y Esperanza was first set up in Eibar in 1908 with the intention of turning out pistols which, although reasonably inexpensive, were to be of good quality – a condition which was achieved very consistently. This particular specimen is an example of the first pistol of the type made by the firm under the trade name "Victoria" or 1911 Model; a virtually identical type was also produced in 6.35mm caliber. It is a close copy of the 1903 Browning and worked on simple blowback, the recoil spring being housed round a rod below the barrel. When the safety catch, located on the left-side of the frame, was set at "safe," it engaged a notch almost in the exact center of the frame. If the slide was drawn to the rear with the catch still at "safe," a second notch about 1.2in (30mm) farther forward engaged the safety and held the slide to the rear; the barrel could then be removed by rotating it and drawing it forward. The pistol gained wide acceptance and the company went from strength to strength. It adopted the trade name "Astra" in 1914, but it also made a variety of other names. Between the two World Wars, Unceta was one of the companies which took advantage of the serious restrictions imposed on German armaments firms to manufacture a close copy of the Mauser Model 1896; the Spanish arm sold quite well in South America and elsewhere.

TROCAOLA BRITISH ARMY REVOLVER — SPAIN

Length (gun): 10.0in (254mm)
Barrel: 5.0in (127mm)
Weight: 40.0oz (1.1kg)
Caliber: 0.455in (11.5mm)
Rifling: 8 grooves, r/hand
Capacity: six
Muz vel: ca 650ft/sec (198m/sec)

The revolver illustrated here was made by "TROCAOLA, ARANZABAL y CIA, EIBAR, ESPANA," and is so marked along the top rib of the barrel. This firm is believed to have started making revolvers soon after 1900, and almost all its arms were close copies of other manufacturers' designs – principally Colt and Smith & Wesson. In the early days the company's products were of good quality and finish, and in 1915 a quantity of Trocaola arms were bought for use by the British Army, which always insisted on a high standard. These revolvers, of which the one shown is an example, were given the British designation of "Pistol OP, 5inch Barrel, No 2 Mark 1." The revolver shown is a close copy of a Smith & Wesson. It has a round barrel with a foresight pinned into a slot on the top rib. The backsight is a notch in the barrel catch, which is of standard T-shape and was opened by upward thumb-pressure on the milled studs above the hammer. When the arm was opened and the barrel pushed smartly downward, the extractor came into action automatically and threw out the cases. The revolver is blued, except for the case-hardened lock mechanism, and appears to be of sound construction. It is numbered "1389" and the left side of the barrel is stamped with an Enfield inspector's mark of crossed flags. Trocaola's trade mark, visible on the frame below the hammer, was very closely modeled on that of Smith & Wesson – and could easily be mistaken for it at a glance. This, it may be supposed, was the maker's intention.

Unceta Astra 400 Pistol — Spain

Length (gun): 9.3in (235mm)
Barrel: 5.5in (140mm)
Weight: 38.0oz (1.1kg)
Caliber: 9mm
Rifling: 6 grooves, r/hand
Capacity: eight
Muz vel: ca 1,100ft/sec (335m/sec)

The Spanish company of Unceta y Cia of Eibar and Guernica made self-loading pistols almost from the beginning of the 20th Century. The firm's early products were mostly pocket pistols, but in 1921 it produced a heavier, service-type pistol of a different design. This was the Astra 400, a specimen of which is illustrated here; it was adopted by the Spanish Army in the same year as it appeared. The pistol had a stepped slide of tubular form: its front end enveloped the barrel, while its rear end acted as breechblock. The recoil spring was positioned around the barrel and inside the slide, and was held in place by the bush visible at the muzzle. The pistol had an internal hammer and a grip safety. Probably the main point of interest is that although it fired a cartridge of considerable power, it worked on straight blowback, without any form of breech-locking device. This was made possible by the use of a heavy slide and an unusually strong recoil spring, which between them reduced the backward action to within safe limits. This made the pistol rather heavy and, in spite of the grooved finger-grips on its slide, it was quite hard to cock.

Flintlock Pistol 16th Century — Spain

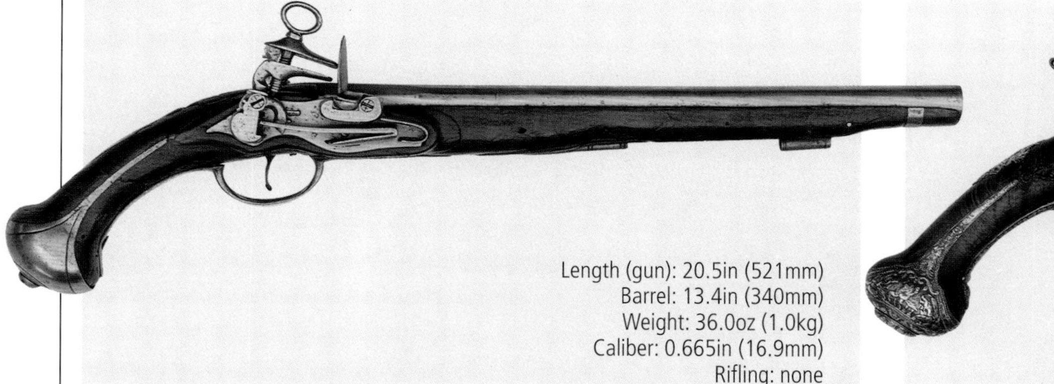

Length (gun): 20.5in (521mm)
Barrel: 13.4in (340mm)
Weight: 36.0oz (1.0kg)
Caliber: 0.665in (16.9mm)
Rifling: none
Capacity: one
Muz vel: ca 400ft/sec (122m/sec)

In the Spanish pistol seen here, the barrel was round, except for about 2in (51mm) of rounded octagonal at the breech end, and was slightly swamped (ie, opened out) at the muzzle end. The lock was of the pattern now usually known as miquelet (or miguelet), a type which is believed to have originated in the Spanish province of Catalonia some time early in the 16th Century. When the trigger was pressed, the sear was withdrawn and the cock fell, the flint in its jaws striking the vertical steel and knocking it forward; taking forward also the horizontal pan cover – an integral part of the steel. This allowed the sparks from the blow to ignite the priming and fire the charge. The mainspring was necessarily a very strong one; and for this reason a top ring was fitted to the cock to provide a firm grip. The trigger and trigger-guard were of orthodox type, the tip of the trigger being turned back on itself; and the butt had a steel cap with long spurs reaching almost the whole way up the butt. The ramrod (missing in this case) was held in a groove on the underside of the stock by a brass loop and tailpipe. The style of this weapon, particularly its trigger and the long "ears" of the butt-cap, indicate that it was probably made quite early in the 18th Century. It was designed to be carried by a mounted soldier in a holster on the saddle and was in every respect a plain, robust arm, well suited to cavalry service.

Flintlock Pistol 1720 — Spain

Length (gun): 21.3in (540mm)
Barrel: 14.1in (358mm)
Weight: 49.0oz (1.4kg)
Caliber: 0.625in (15.9mm)
Rifling: none
Capacity: one
Muz vel: ca 500ft/sec (152m/sec)

The very fine pistol illustrated was made by Juan Fernandez, a famous maker who worked in Madrid from 1717 until 1739. This was at the height of French influence and fashion, so it is not surprising that Fernandez, like most other makers, should have abandoned the indigenous miquelet lock and made instead arms of the type shown. The barrel, which is well blued and heavily decorated with gold inlay, is round for two-thirds of its length, the breech end being octagonal. This was considered to give a much stronger breech. The lock is of the usual French type and the lock-plate, the tail of which droops slightly to the rear, is beautifully ornamented with battle scenes in gold and silver damascene. The cock is of the graceful type known, for obvious reasons, as "swan-necked." The flint is seated in a small patch of leather; this was considered desirable not only to hold the flint rigid but also to cushion it against the repeated shock of striking the steel. The combined steel and pan-cover (later often known as frizzens) are decorated with rearing horses; these appear to be mainly ornamental, although they also prevented the pans from opening too far by exerting pressure on the frizzen springs. The trigger has a curled-back end and there are long spurs on the highly ornamented butt-cap, which, together with the shape of the lockplate, indicates a date of manufacture not later than about 1720. The stock is of a wood not immediately identifiable – walnut, cherry, and pine were all in use at the time – and is elaborately carved, with a cap at the muzzle matching the end of the ramrod. This beautiful pistol was probably made either for royalty or for some rich nobleman.

HÄMMERLI MODEL 207 OLYMPIA TARGET PISTOL — SWITZERLAND

Length (gun): 12.9in (328mm)
Barrel: 7.1in (180mm)
Weight: 39.0oz (1.1kg)
Caliber: 0.22in
Rifling: n.k.
Capacity: 8-round internal magazine
Muz vel: n.k.

The Hämmerli 200-series owed its origins to the Walther Olympia pistol, which was used by the German team in the 1936 Berlin Olympics, and which was used as the start-point for the Hämmerli Model 200 which was introduced in 1952. This led to progressively improved models, through the Model 205 of 1960 to this Model 207 which appeared in 1964. Such was the excellence of this design that for many years the gun to use in the UIT Rapid Fire competition was one or other of the Hämmerli 200-series. The Model 207 is semi-automatic, using the propellant gases to drive the spent cartridge case rearwards, and is fitted with a square post foresight and a square notch backsight, which is click adjustable for elevation and windage. The design objective in all Rapid Fire pistols is to minimize muzzle lift, caused by recoil forces, on discharge, in order that the sight picture presented to the shooter remains as undisturbed as possible. One way of achieving this is to carry a barrel weight and the Hämmerli Model 207 carries quite a heavy one. In addition to that, however, there is a series of ports drilled through the top of the barrel down into the bore, through which peak pressure gases are vented upwards as the bullet travels down the bore, with, finally, a large, upward-venting muzzle brake, intended to give the muzzle a final downwards vector.

HÄMMERLI MODEL 208 TARGET PISTOL — SWITZERLAND

Length (gun): 10.0in (254mm)
Barrel: 6.0in (152mm)
Weight: 35.0oz (1.0kg)
Caliber: 0.22in
Rifling: n.k.
Capacity: 8-round internal magazine
Muz vel: n.k.

The successor to the Model 207, Hämmerli's Model 208 was introduced in 1958. It was a semi-automatic weapon, blowback operated, using an unlocked breech. It was of all steel construction, being machined from a solid block, and was chambered for the 0.22in Long Rifle cartridge. This was the mandatory round for the Standard Pistol event, which involved firing five rounds in 10 seconds at a range of 27.3yd (25m) at the international precision target, and required very tight grouping for a good score. Sights consisted of a square post foresight and a square notch backsight, which was click adjustable for elevation and windage. The Model 208 was very successful, although it was constantly being challenged by the FAS Model 601 and Britarms Model 2000 (qqv).

SIG 9MM P-210 (MODEL 1949) PISTOL — SWITERLAND

Length (gun): 8.5in (215mm)
Barrel: 4.7in (120mm)
Weight: 32.0oz (0.9kg)
Caliber: 9mm
Rifling: 6 grooves, r/hand
Capacity: 8-round box magazine
Muz vel: 1,100ft/sec (335m/sec)

The French Army's Model 1935A 7.65mm semi-automatic pistol was designed by the French company, SACM, based on patents held by a Swiss named Petter. These patentrights were then purchased by the armaments company, Schweizerisches Industrie Gesellschaft (Swiss Industrial Company [SIG]), for use in a potential design for the civilian market and when, in 1946, the Swiss Army stated a requirement for a new pistol SIG had a design ready. This was accepted into service as the Swiss Army's Model 1949, but although fairly expensive it was also sold abroad in large numbers. The great majority of semi-automatic pistols have a slide which moves along rails machined outside the frame, but in the P-210 these rails are inside the frame, giving much improved support to the slide and being credited with a large contribution to this weapon's famed accuracy and smoothness of operation. The P-210 uses the Browning locking system, with a lug underneath the breech which moves the barrel out of engagement with the slide. Models within the P-201 range included the P-210-1 (polished finish, wooden grips); P-210-2 (matt finish, plastic grips); P-210-4 (special version for the German Bundesgrenzschutzpolizei [border police]); P-210-5 (target pistol with 6in/150mm barrel); P-210-6 (target version with 4.7in/120mm barrel). Models P-210-1, -2, and -6 can be converted between 7.65mm to 9mm Parabellum simply by changing the barrel and return spring; a 0.22in conversion is also available. There is a regular requirement for small caliber pistol which will emulate the appearance and performance of a service pistol, but without the accompanying noise and recoil. Some weapons have been designed in 0.22in caliber from the start, but others use conversions, one of the simplest and most elegant being that for the SIG P-210-1. This simply involves removing the 9mm slide assembly and barrel and replacing it with a similarly self-contained assembly in 0.22in caliber. The only other replacements are for the magazine and the firing pin, but the whole process takes a minute or so and requires no technical expertise whatsoever. This picture shows the P-210-1 with the 0.22in assembly fitted. In the 0.22in assembly, the barrel is, of course, of 0.22in caliber, but the operation is changed to blowback, there is a lighter spring, and the slide has been made as light as possible, one step being to machine a "saddle" between the backsight and ejection slot, simply to remove excess metal.

Sig-Sauer 9mm P-220 (Model 1975) Pistol — Switzerland

Length (gun): 8.1in (206mm)
Barrel: 4.3in (109mm)
Weight: 30.0oz (0.8kg)
Caliber: 9mm
Rifling: 6 grooves, r/hand
Capacity: 9-round box magazine
Muz vel: 1,132ft/sec (345m/sec)

The SIG-Sauer P-220 is an improved version of the P-210 (qv), re-engineered to render it simpler and cheaper to manufacture, and also to incorporate some police-generated safety requirements. The P-220 is built on a rugged aluminum frame and uses a heavy-gauge, stamped slide with a welded nosepiece. The breechblock is a separate machined part that is keyed into the slide and retained by a rollpin. The P-220 is available in a variety of calibers, including: 9 x 19mm Parabellum (see specifications); 7.65mm Parabellum; 0.45in ACP and 0.38in Super, and all models have the magazine catch on the heel of the butt, except for the 0.45in version, which uses a push-button on the side of the frame. There are three controls on the left of the frame, which (from rear to front) are the slide latch; the decocking lever (see below); and the disassembly lever. The P-200 series, which includes the compact P-225 and large capacity P-226, conforms to a requirement stated by the West German Police in 1975 for a self-loading pistol with the reactive qualities of a revolver – ie, it could be carried with complete safety, but then drawn and fired without having to disengage a manual safety. This is achieved by placing a magazine in the butt and pulling the slide to the rear and releasing it, which chambers a round and cocks the action. The shooter then presses down on the decocking lever, which raises the sear out of engagement with the hammer, which then rotates under pressure from a spring until the sear engages in the safety notch, thus holding the hammer clear of the firing pin. To further enhance safety, the firing pin is itself immobilized by a locking-pin which is pushed through by a spring. In this configuration the pistol will not fire even if dropped to the ground. To bring the pistol into action, a long pull on the trigger will fire it in the double-action mode, or the hammer can be cocked manually and the weapon fired in the single action mode, using a lighter, shorter trigger pull. The P-220 was adopted by the Swiss Army as the Model 1975 and is also used by the Japanese Self-Defense Forces (JSDF), by various special operations forces, and by police forces; the number in service is approaching 200,000.

Sig-Sauer 9mm P-225 Pistol — Switzerland

Length (gun): 7.1in (180mm)
Barrel: 3.9in (99mm)
Weight: 29.0oz (0.8kg)
Caliber: 9mm
Rifling: 6 grooves, r/hand
Capacity: 8-round box magazine
Muz vel: 1,115ft/sec (340m/sec)

The P-225 is a foreshortened and redesigned version of the P-220, which arose in the first place from a West German police requirement. In the competition to meet that requirement the SIG P-225 competed against weapons from Mauser, Walther, and Heckler & Koch and was the only one to pass the 10,000 round test. It was then ordered by the West German police (to whom it is known as the P6) and set the pattern for the new generation of pistols. It is almost totaly safe to carry with a round in the chamber, but can be used instantly, without having to disengage latches, and requires only pressure on the trigger to shoot. The controls on the left of the receiver are the slide hold-open (rearmost), then the decocking lever that lets the hammer down safely, and beneath that the push-button magazine release, while in the center of the weapon is the stripping (takedown) lever. The single-stack eight-round magazine permits the shooter to be offered a very comfortable and compact grip, which is a most desirable characteristic.

Sig-Sauer 9mm P-226 Pistol — Switzerland

Length (gun): 7.7in (196mm)
Barrel: 4.4in (112mm)
Weight: 26.40z (0.7kg)
Caliber: 9mm
Rifling: 6 grooves, r/hand
Capacity: 15-round box magazine
Muz vel: 1,148ft/sec (350m/sec)

When the US Army, acting as agent for all US armed forces, issued its requirement for a new pistol to replace the Colt M1911A1 (qv), SIG-Sauer entered the competition with their P-226, with many of the parts being taken from the existing P-220 and P-225 designs. It is chambered for the standard NATO 9 x 19mm Parabellum round and is fitted with a detachable box magazine housing 15 rounds. Mechanically, the P-226 is virtually identical to the P-220, from which it differs basically in having a wider butt to house a 15-round magazine and in the magazine catch which can be operated by either left- or right-handed shooters. The weapon lost out in the finals of the competition to the Beretta 92SB (M9) (qv) but, despite this, large numbers have been sold to, among others, the US Coast Guard, British Ministry of Defence, and the New Zealand armed forces. In addition, a sporting model has been developed, which has a stainless steel slide and is available with either the standard 4.4in (112mm) barrel or with a longer, 5.0in (126mm), barrel. The P-226 is available chambered either for the 9mm Parabellum or 0.357SIG rounds.

Sig-Sauer 9mm P-228/P-229 Pistol — Switzerland

Length (gun): 7.1in (180mm)
Barrel: 3.9in (96mm)
Weight: 29.0oz (0.8kg)
Caliber: 9mm
Rifling: 6 grooves, r/hand
Capacity: 13-round box magazine
Muz vel: 1,115ft/sec (340m/sec)

These two pistols are virtually identical, except that the SIG-Sauer P-228 (see specifications) fires the 9mm Parabellum round, while the P-229 fires the 0.40S&W or 0.357in SIG round. They are, in essence, a P-225 (qv) with a larger magazine and there is a substantial commonality of parts between the three weapons. The P-228 has been purchased by many United States' government agencies, including the US Army (9mm Compact Pistol M11), the Federal Bureau of Investigation (FBI), and the Drug Enforcement Agency (DEA), and by the British Ministry of Defence. The P-229 is chambered for 0.40in S&W or 0.357in SIG rounds, all that is required to change from one to the other being a change of barrel. For both of these calibers the magazine holds 12 rounds. It uses a machined, stainless steel slide which is manufactured in the United States, with an aluminum alloy frame manufactured in Germany. There are three control levers, all on the left side of the weapon. Nearest the muzzle is the release lever for stripping; the middle lever, just below the slide, is the decocking lever; the rearmost lever is the slide latch. Like all SIG pistols, the P-229 has an automatic firing-pin safety, operating without a traditional safety control lever, with the first shot when the hammer is at half-cock requiring a longer trigger pull. Both the P-228 and P-229 are fitted with high contrast Stavenhagen sights, but a tritium-enhanced foresight and luminous rearsights can also be fitted.

SIG-SAUER 9MM P239 PISTOL — SWITZERLAND

Length (gun): 6.8in (172mm)
Barrel: 3.6in (92mm)
Weight: 23.0oz (0.8kg)
Caliber: 9mm (see text)
Rifling: 6 grooves, r/hand
Capacity: 7-round box magazine
Muz vel: 1,115ft/sec (340m/sec)

The SIG-Sauer P-239 was specifically designed with female users in mind, to meet the increasing requirement created by female shooters in armed forces, law enforcement agencies, and para-military organizations. Company research established that because most women's hands are smaller than men's, they needed a pistol which packed the same performance, but in a physically smaller package. The smaller size also makes the pistol easier to conceal, whether the shooters are women or men. This size reduction has been achieved by restricting the number of rounds in the magazine to eight in the 9mm version (seven in 0.40S&W and 0.357SIG versions) in order to eliminate the double-stacking of rounds and thus produce a smaller butt. A 10-round magazine is, however, available as an optional extra. The P-239 is a mechanically locked, recoil-operated, auto-loading weapon. The sights are adjustable, the rear sight having six notches, while five different foresight posts are available. As with earlier SIG pistols, the P-239 has a machined, stainless steel slide with a light alloy frame and is black anodized. Three versions are available, firing NATO standard 9mm Parabellum, the American 0.40 Smith & Wesson, or SIG's own, newly developed 0.357in round, which is more powerful and with a higher muzzle velocity than earlier rounds.

SPHINX 9MM AT-2000S PISTOL — SWITZERLAND

Length (gun): 8.0in (204mm)
Barrel: 4.5in (115mm)
Weight: 36.3oz (1.0kg)
Caliber: 9mm
Rifling: 6 grooves, r/hand
Capacity: 15-round box magazine
Muz vel: 1,155ft/sec (352m/sec)

Sphinx Engineering SA of Porrentruy in Switzerland originally manufactured the Czech CZ Model 75 pistol under license, but then developed so many improvements to that design that the outcome was an entirely new design, designated the AT-88S. This pistol was successful and attracted orders from numerous police forces. Further minor improvements then led to the AT-2000, of which there are many minor variants. The AT 2000S is a recoil-operated, semi-automatic, double-action pistol, using Browning cam locking, and is available in either 9 x 19mm Parabellum (see specifications) or 0.40in S&W calibers. The various versions include: AT 2000P (shorter, lighter); AT2000H (compact version); AT2000SDA/PDA/HDA (identical to -S, -P and -H versions above, but double- rather than single-action, together with a new Sphinx-developed safety system); AT 2000PS (police special, with 16-round magazine).

TURKISH BLUNDERBUSS PISTOL — EASTERN EUROPE

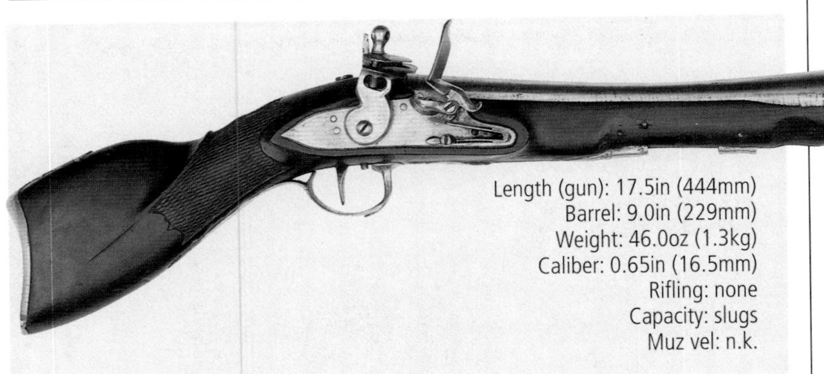

Length (gun): 17.5in (444mm)
Barrel: 9.0in (229mm)
Weight: 46.0oz (1.3kg)
Caliber: 0.65in (16.5mm)
Rifling: none
Capacity: slugs
Muz vel: n.k.

The pistol seen here is a plain, crude, and in many ways ugly little arm. Parts of it, or perhaps the entire weapon, were probably made in Europe in the first quarter of the 19th Century, for export to the Middle East. The lock is plain, with a brass pan, and the cock is of the ring-necked type commonly found on European military arms of the period. The furniture is of plain cast brass without ornament of any kind, while the stock, with its characteristic checkered, dwarf butt, is of walnut. A rectangular brass loop is attached to the side-plate on the left-hand side of the stock, indicating that it was intended to be carried on a crossbelt by a mounted man. By far the most interesting part of the weapon is the barrel, which is narrowest at its mid-point. Its external diameters are: breech 1.2in (30.5mm); center: 0.95in (24mm); and muzzle 1.5in (38mm). There are distinct signs that the barrel was originally of octagonal section and that the muzzle was then beaten out to its present circular, bell form. Somewhat unusually, it is fitted with a ramrod. This may be a further indication of its European origins, for many weapons of indigenous manufacture were used with a separate rod, carried slung around the neck. Blunderbuss arms tend to be the subject of many mis-apprehensions. They were originally used mainly as naval weapons, sometimes of large bore, and when equipped with swivel mountings must have had an obvious value for repelling boarders.

ADAMS POCKET REVOLVER — UK

Length (gun): 9.0in (229mm)
Barrel: 4.5in (114mm)
Weight: 20.0oz (0.6kg)
Caliber: 0.32in (8.1mm)
Rifling: 3 grooves, r/hand
Capacity: five
Muz vel: ca 550ft/sec (168m/sec)

This was essentially a pocket pistol, lacking the stopping-power considered necessary for service use. It has the usual solid frame and octagonal barrel, and the system of mounting the cylinder was also the same as other Adams' designs; the axis pin (or arbor, as it is often called) was drawn forward to remove it, and a spring pin on the right-hand side of the frame prevented it slipping out accidentally. The lock is of the self-cocking pattern and the spring safety-plunger can be seen on the left-hand side of the frame. This held the hammer nose clear of the nipple and allowed the pistol to be carried loaded; it had the advantage that it released itself automatically as soon as the trigger was pulled. The most distinctive feature of this weapon is probably the patent Brazier rammer attached to the left-hand flat of the barrel. Joseph Brazier, who patented it in 1855, was a well-known Birmingham gunmaker whose firm was one of those which made Adams revolvers under license. A number of other licensees, in Britain, in continental Europe, and in the United States, also made revolvers on the Adams pattern, and the weapon illustrated may be the product of one of these firms. Unfortunately, the revolver has been so heavily over-cleaned that it is really almost impossible to speculate on its origin: the cylinder bears London proof marks, but that is all the evidence there is to consider. Revolvers of this type and caliber were neat and compact and very soon became popular as pocket arms for self-defense. The self-cocking lock did not make for long-range accuracy, but this would hardly have been a serious disadvantage in a pocket arm.

ADAMS SELF-COCKING REVOLVER — UK

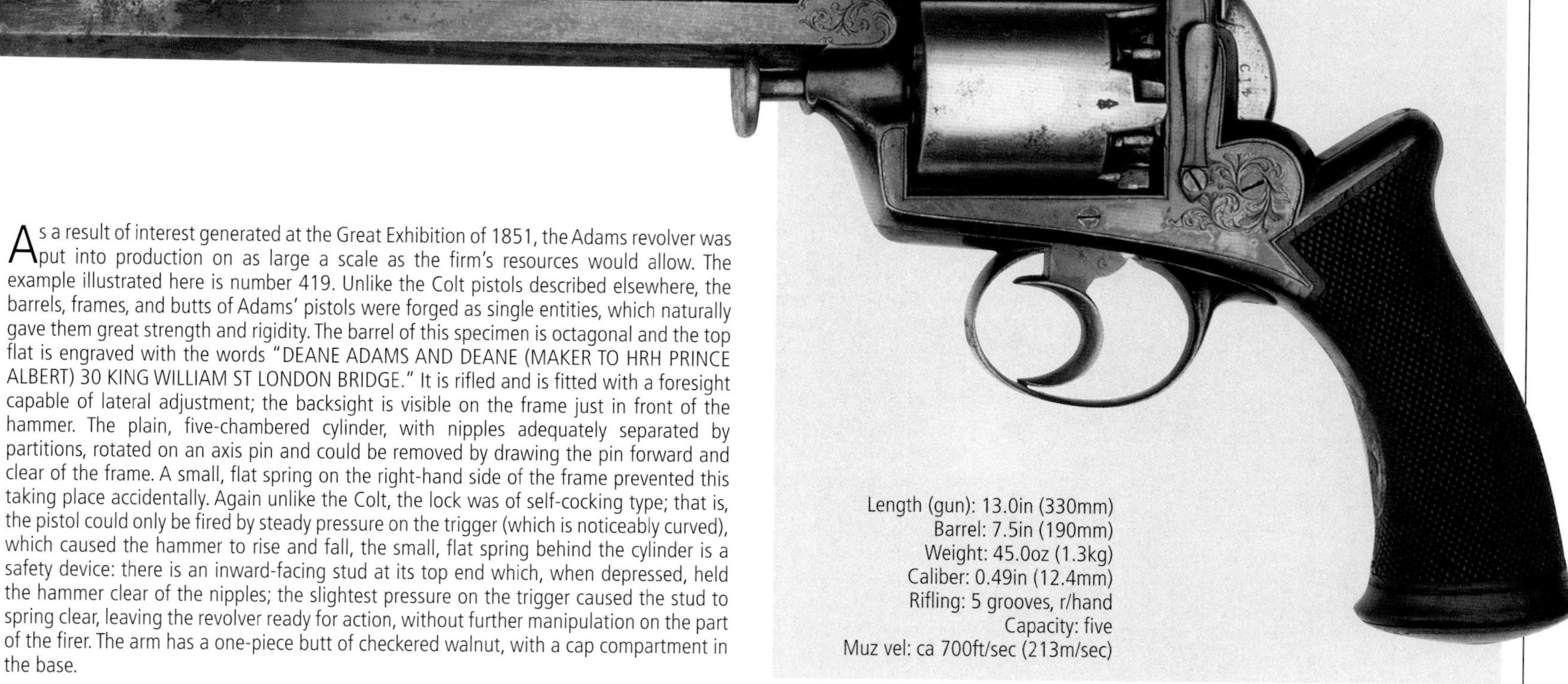

Length (gun): 13.0in (330mm)
Barrel: 7.5in (190mm)
Weight: 45.0oz (1.3kg)
Caliber: 0.49in (12.4mm)
Rifling: 5 grooves, r/hand
Capacity: five
Muz vel: ca 700ft/sec (213m/sec)

As a result of interest generated at the Great Exhibition of 1851, the Adams revolver was put into production on as large a scale as the firm's resources would allow. The example illustrated here is number 419. Unlike the Colt pistols described elsewhere, the barrels, frames, and butts of Adams' pistols were forged as single entities, which naturally gave them great strength and rigidity. The barrel of this specimen is octagonal and the top flat is engraved with the words "DEANE ADAMS AND DEANE (MAKER TO HRH PRINCE ALBERT) 30 KING WILLIAM ST LONDON BRIDGE." It is rifled and is fitted with a foresight capable of lateral adjustment; the backsight is visible on the frame just in front of the hammer. The plain, five-chambered cylinder, with nipples adequately separated by partitions, rotated on an axis pin and could be removed by drawing the pin forward and clear of the frame. A small, flat spring on the right-hand side of the frame prevented this taking place accidentally. Again unlike the Colt, the lock was of self-cocking type; that is, the pistol could only be fired by steady pressure on the trigger (which is noticeably curved), which caused the hammer to rise and fall, the small, flat spring behind the cylinder is a safety device: there is an inward-facing stud at its top end which, when depressed, held the hammer clear of the nipples; the slightest pressure on the trigger caused the stud to spring clear, leaving the revolver ready for action, without further manipulation on the part of the firer. The arm has a one-piece butt of checkered walnut, with a cap compartment in the base.

ADAMS 0.44IN SELF-COCKING REVOLVER — UK

Length (gun): 11.5in (292mm)
Barrel: 6.5in (165mm)
Weight: 30.0oz (0.9kg)
Caliber: 0.44in (11.2mm)
Rifling: 3 grooves, r/hand
Capacity: five
Muz vel: ca 550ft/sec (168m/sec)

The original massive Adams "Dragoon" type, 38-bore revolver was a bulky arm and, although suitable for mounted men, was rather too heavy for a man on foot. The revolver shown here is of the next size down and was of nominal 54-bore (about 0.44in/11.2mm caliber). The word "nominal" is used deliberately, because some of the earliest models were, in fact, 56-bore and bear the small number "56" on the front of the frame: the weapon here is one such. It is of the usual strong, one-piece construction and its octagonal barrel is, of course, rifled. It bears the inscription "DEANE ADAMS AND DEANE, 30 KING WILLIAM STT, LONDON BRIDGE," and has London proofmarks. The cylinder, which is bright, has the usual five chambers and horizontal nipples separated by partitions; it bears the usual London proofmarks. It is slightly unusual, in that it rotated in an anti-clockwise direction. The cylinder could be removed by first withdrawing the small plug on the upper end of the vertical spring on the front of the frame, and then drawing the axis pin forward. The lock is of self-cocking type and a safety device to hold the hammer clear of the nipples is located on the left-hand side of the frame. Comparison with the Beaumont-Adams 0.44in revolver will show that the cylinder is appreciably shorter in this specimen. No rammer is fitted; the bullets had oversized felt wads attached to their bases and were only thumb-tight in the chambers – this made for fast loading.

ADAMS REVOLVER CONVERSION — UK

Length (gun): 11.5in (292mm)
Barrel: 6.5in (165mm)
Weight: 33.0oz (0.9kg)
Caliber: 0.44in (11.2mm)
Rifling: 3 grooves, r/hand
Capacity: five
Muz vel: ca 550ft/sec (168m/sec)

The revolver seen here was originally an Adams self-cocking, percussion arm, which has been converted to a breechloader to take centerfire cartridges. The weapon has been fitted with a bored-through, five-chambered cylinder: this, in turn, necessitated the fitting of a loading gate, which can be seen on the right-hand side. The gate is hinged at the bottom and opened backwards. Its bottom end was supported on a flat spring screwed to the lower part of the frame; the pressure of the spring held the gate firmly open or closed, as required. A piece of metal of the required shape has been screwed to the left-hand side of the frame to prevent the cartridges slipping out, and has been carefully fitted in front of the spring safety which holds the hammer clear of the rounds. The only other addition is a simple ejector rod working in a sleeve, which has been brazed on to the frame. No change has been made to the lock, which remains on the self-cocking principle. The lower flat of the barrel is engraved "P.W. ADAIR COLDSTREAM GUARDS." An upper flat is engraved "CRIMEA, SEBASTOPOL" – a campaign in which Captain Adair served and in which, presumably, he carried this revolver. He was later in his career appointed Colonel-Commandant of the 4th (Militia) Battalion of the Somerset Light Infantry.

Annely Flintlock Revolver UK

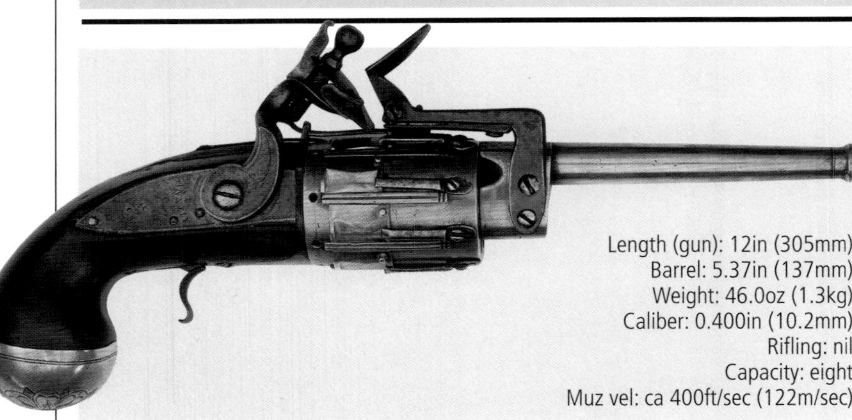

Length (gun): 12in (305mm)
Barrel: 5.37in (137mm)
Weight: 46.0oz (1.3kg)
Caliber: 0.400in (10.2mm)
Rifling: nil
Capacity: eight
Muz vel: ca 400ft/sec (122m/sec)

The development of the snaphance lock made some sort of repeating arm a practical proposition, and by the early years of the 17th Century a number had been produced. The system of having a cylinder pierced with chambers which might be successively aligned with a barrel had already been tried on carbines, so this offered a starting point for further experiment. Most of this took place in continental Europe, mainly in Holland and France; there is no evidence that revolvers were made in Britain before about 1650. The flintlock revolver seen here was made by T. Annely; and although it dates from the earliest years of the 18th Century it may be taken as being reasonably typical of its kind. It has a round, cannon-type barrel of brass (most of the remaining metal is of the same material), which is fastened to the frame by means of the cylinder axis pin. The brass cylinder has eight chambers, each with its own pan and touch hole normally covered by a sliding pan cover. The hinged steel is mounted on an arm which is attached to the barrel lump, and the neck of the cock is therefore bent over so that the flint will strike it. The lock is of back-action type, and its plate (which may not be the original one) is engraved with the maker's name. The action of cocking the lock caused the cylinder to rotate by means of a pawl and ratchet; when the cock fell, a lever attached to it pushed open the cover of the pan in line with the barrel. The butt has a rounded plate bearing a Tudor rose. The weapon has no trigger-guard. Weapons of this type were reasonably efficient, but they were very difficult to make; the drilling of the chambers presented a particular problem.

Baker Transitional Revolver UK

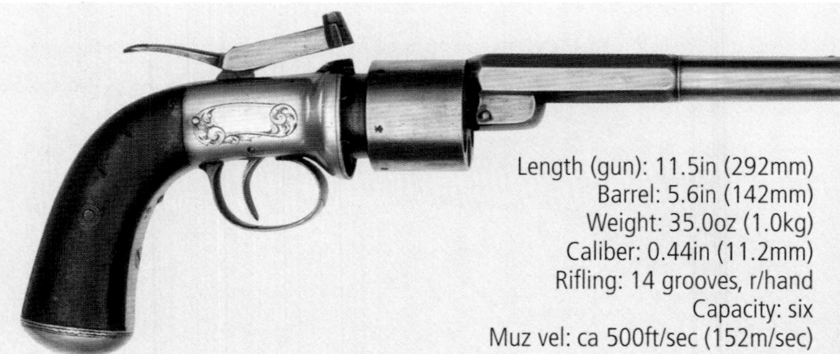

Length (gun): 11.5in (292mm)
Barrel: 5.6in (142mm)
Weight: 35.0oz (1.0kg)
Caliber: 0.44in (11.2mm)
Rifling: 14 grooves, r/hand
Capacity: six
Muz vel: ca 500ft/sec (152m/sec)

This revolver was made by T. K. Baker of London and it has been cleaned bright at some time. A somewhat old-fashioned look is given to the rifled barrel by the fact that it is octagonal for just over half its length. The cylinder is deeply rebated at the rear to give a seating for the nipples which, in orthodox pepperbox fashion, have no partitions between them; a factor increasing the risk of a chain-fire discharge. The rear face of the cylinder is cut to form a ratchet, with a further, outer row of six slots for the cylinder stops. The hammer, although similar in some respects to the bar-type hammers encountered on some of the earlier pepperbox pistols, is in fact of single-action type and had to be cocked for each shot; hence the provision of the long hammer spur. The action of placing the hammer at half-cock caused the cylinder to make a very slight rotation in an anti-clockwise direction; pulling the hammer back to full cock brought the next chamber into line and also locked the cylinder in such a position that the top chamber was in line with the barrel. Although positioned so as to strike centrally on top of the frame, the hammer was slightly angled, so that when the arm was cocked the foresight could be aligned with a shallow V backsight on the hammer itself. The frame is of German silver and incorporates nipple shields; the butt-plate, which is held by a single screw, is of walnut. Arms of this type had three basic weaknesses as compared with the later percussion revolvers: the nipples are placed at right-angles instead of straight into the charge, which increased the chance of misfires; there are no shields between the nipples; and the method by which the barrel is held in place, screwed to the axis pin without any secondary brace to the frame, was unsatisfactory. In the latter case, although the pin is robust and is firmly seated at the breech end, there must have been a tendency for the barrel to work loose, which would lead to loss of power, to inaccuracy and, possibly, to real danger to the firer if the chamber and barrel were actually out of alignment at the moment of firing.

Baker Gas-Seal Revolver UK

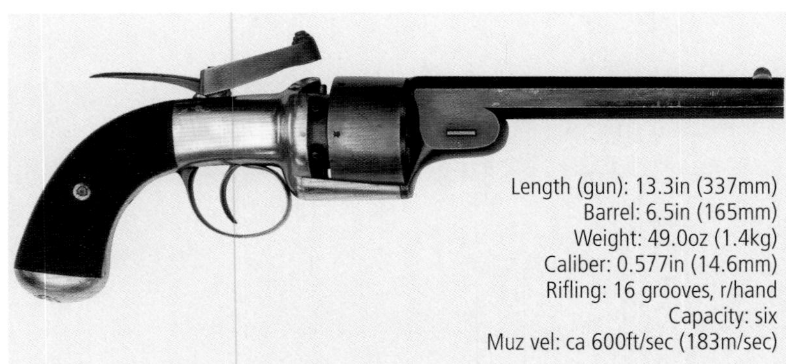

Length (gun): 13.3in (337mm)
Barrel: 6.5in (165mm)
Weight: 49.0oz (1.4kg)
Caliber: 0.577in (14.6mm)
Rifling: 16 grooves, r/hand
Capacity: six
Muz vel: ca 600ft/sec (183m/sec)

This pistol is of the type known as gas-seal, in which the cylinder reciprocated so that each chamber was locked securely to the barrel at the time of firing. Most British gas-seal revolvers bear a strong resemblance to each other (compare, for example, this weapon with the Beattie on the facing page and the Lang gas-seal revolver on page 69). It is now generally agreed that most arms of this type were not developed until after the Great Exhibition in London in 1851, which gave a considerable impetus to revolving arms of all kinds. This is a heavy, service-type weapon, made by T. K. Baker of 88 Fleet Street, London. The design was registered on April 24 1852, nearly one year after the Great Exhibition had made the revolvers of Colt and Adams well known in England. This arm has an octagonal, blued barrel with multi-grooved rifling. The barrel is held rigidly to the weapon by the combination of a key through the axis pin and a lower extension locking on to the bottom of the frame. The short cylinder, which is case-hardened, is rebated at the rear in order to provide a seating for the nipples, which are at right-angles to the barrel axis and without partitions. The hammer is of the bar variety but it is of single-action type, with a long, rearward spur for cocking; it is slightly angled, so that the fixed sights could be aligned when it was cocked, and is fitted with a sliding safety. The frame is of German silver, with butt-plates of some hard, black composition, and the strap bears the number "2151."

Barbar Pocket Screw-Off Pistol UK

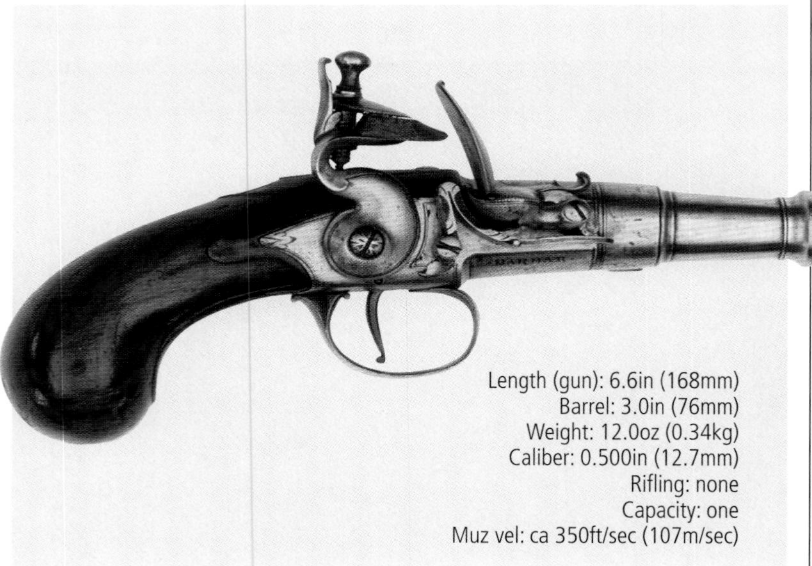

Length (gun): 6.6in (168mm)
Barrel: 3.0in (76mm)
Weight: 12.0oz (0.34kg)
Caliber: 0.500in (12.7mm)
Rifling: none
Capacity: one
Muz vel: ca 350ft/sec (107m/sec)

This weapon was made by the well-known London gunsmith Barbar in about 1740. During the 18th Century, the streets of London were dangerous places at night; although most gentlemen then habitually carried swords, many liked to have a pair of pistols handy also. These were usually carried in the capacious flapped pockets of the long waistcoats then worn, where they were available for instant use. The weapon seen here (which was originally one of a pair) is a good example of the type. It is a strictly fundamental piece, without ornamentation of any kind, but its quality is excellent – as is only to be expected from a maker of Barbar's repute. Because it has a screw-off barrel, it could be loaded with a tight ball which would stay in place. A common enough problem with muzzle-loaders was that the ball, unless held in position by an over-wad, would move forward if the arm was jolted. The very short barrel would, of course, reduce the pistol's power at anything more than point-blank range – but this would constitute no disadvantage in the sort of close-quarter brawl for which the weapon was designed.

Bentley Revolver — UK

Length (gun): 12.0in (305mm)
Barrel: 7.0in (178mm)
Weight: 33.0oz (0.9kg)
Caliber: 0.44in (11.2mm)
Rifling: 14 grooves, r/hand
Capacity: five
Muz vel: ca 600ft/sec (183m/sec)

The earliest Webley-Bentley revolvers appeared in about 1853, and various modifications were made thereafter to the original design. The arm illustrated here was probably made in about 1857 to a design that remained popular for some years. The frame and butt are forged from a single piece of iron; but the barrel, which is hexagonal, is a separate component. It is fastened to the axis pin by a wedge; the bottom of the lump, which has a small aperture on its inner side, is braced against a corresponding peg in the lower part of the frame. This was an innovation, apparently based on Colt's system, since in earlier models the barrels were screwed to the axis pin and further braced by a thumbscrew; this method, a Bentley invention, was also used on the Longspur revolver (qv). The cylinder has wide arc-shaped partitions between the nipples and the bullets were forced into its five chambers by means of a Colt-type rammer. The lock is of self-cocking type and incorporates a safety device, also a Bentley invention, upon the hammer head: if the trigger was pressed sufficiently to bring the nose of the hammer clear of the frame, the flat stud visible at the back of the hammer could be depressed, causing the hammer's front end to rise so that it fouled the upper edge of the frame and thus was held clear of the nipples. Because this catch was spring-loaded, only a slight pressure on the trigger was required to release the front end and let it drop back flush. The revolver, of only moderate quality, is marked "J. PARKINSON, MACCLESFIELD," presumably the retailer.

Beattie Gas-Seal Revolver — UK

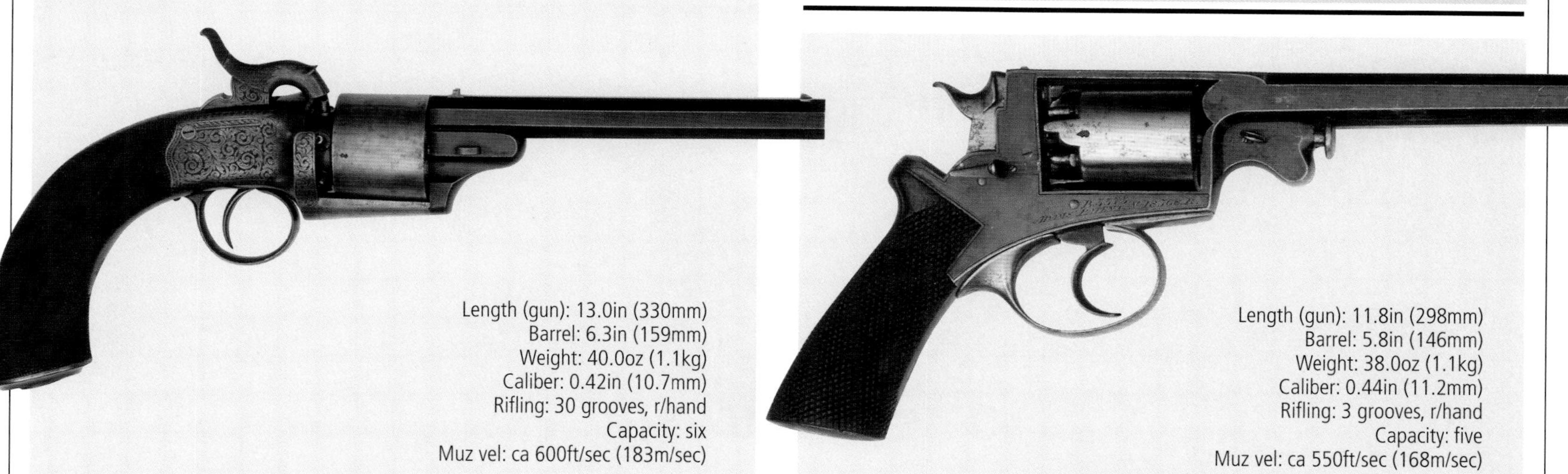

Length (gun): 13.0in (330mm)
Barrel: 6.3in (159mm)
Weight: 40.0oz (1.1kg)
Caliber: 0.42in (10.7mm)
Rifling: 30 grooves, r/hand
Capacity: six
Muz vel: ca 600ft/sec (183m/sec)

This gas-seal revolver was made by Beattie of London in the mid-1850s. The browned barrel is octagonal and has multi-grooved rifling. The rear end of its case-hardened cylinder is rebated in the orthodox way in order to provide a seating for the nipples, which are, as usual, at right-angles to the axis of the chambers and are not separated by partitions. Each chamber bears a proof mark. The barrel is securely wedged to the axis pin by means of a flat, sliding key with a retaining screw; it also has an extension which engaged with the lower part of the frame to give a secure, rigid join. The hammer is of single-action type; thus, it was necessary to re-cock it for each shot, an action which also rotated the cylinder by means of a pawl and ratchet. Early percussion revolvers had no rammer, which meant that the bullets could be no more than finger-tight in the cylinders. In consequence, that part of the burning gases which was inevitably deflected downwards, into the gap between the face of the cylinder and the end of the barrel was sometimes liable to flash past the bullets in the neighboring chambers and ignite their charges. Gas-seal revolvers overcame this by having the rear ends of their barrels slightly coned and the front ends of their chambers correspondingly opened out, so that the one fitted closely over the other; a reciprocating device was essential, to impart the necessary backward and forward movement to the cylinder in addition to its normal rotation.

Beaumont-Adams 0.49in Dragoon Revolver — UK

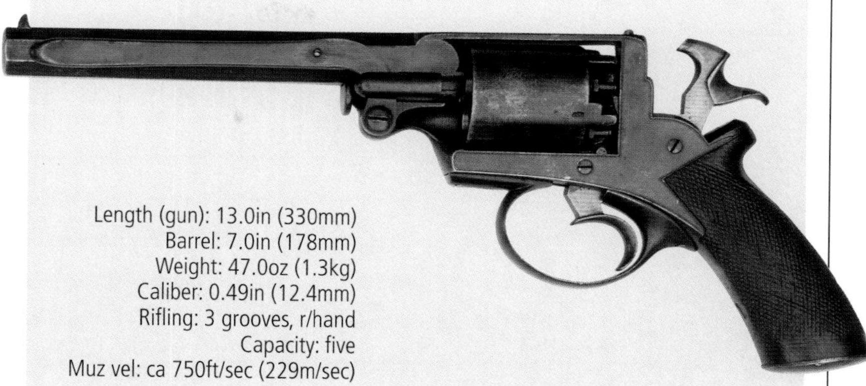

Length (gun): 13.0in (330mm)
Barrel: 7.0in (178mm)
Weight: 47.0oz (1.3kg)
Caliber: 0.49in (12.4mm)
Rifling: 3 grooves, r/hand
Capacity: five
Muz vel: ca 750ft/sec (229m/sec)

One great improvement over previous Adams revolvers, which is at once obvious on the revolver seen here, was the addition of a double-action lock, the invention of Lt F. Beaumont of the Royal Engineers. British officers liked fast-shooting arms for use at close quarters, but their heavy trigger pull naturally affected their accuracy at longer ranges. The new lock overcame this disadvantage by giving the firer a choice of single-action or self-cocking, according to the circumstances in which he found himself. The Beaumont-Adams revolver illustrated here has the solid frame and octagonal barrel of the earlier Adams, but the shape of the butt is of more modern appearance and the curve in the trigger is less pronounced. The new mechanism made it possible to place the hammer at half-cock; thus, the spring plug was no longer necessary, but there is a sliding safety on the right-hand side of the frame. This intervened between a nipple and a partition, thus preventing the cylinder from rotating and making it impossible to draw the hammer back to full-cock. Another very interesting addition was a rammer. The first Adams was loaded with wadded, finger-tight bullets in slightly over-sized chambers; but although this speeded reloading, there was a risk of a bullet slipping forward and jamming the cylinder. A tight bullet also gave better shooting and a good, water-tight seal, so Adams followed Colt's example and fitted a rammer. The lever of the rammer was held against the barrel by light spring pressure against a stud, and when the lever was drawn upwards, the rammer itself was thrust backward with considerable force.

Beaumont-Adams 0.44in Revolver — UK

Length (gun): 11.8in (298mm)
Barrel: 5.8in (146mm)
Weight: 38.0oz (1.1kg)
Caliber: 0.44in (11.2mm)
Rifling: 3 grooves, r/hand
Capacity: five
Muz vel: ca 550ft/sec (168m/sec)

The original Adams revolvers of 1851 were self-cockers and thus could only be fired by quite heavy pressure on the trigger; this made them fast to use but somewhat inaccurate, except at close range. This deficiency was remedied in 1855 by the adoption of a double-action lock, the invention of Lieutenant F. Beaumont of the Royal Engineers. This allowed preliminary cocking for deliberate shooting, without affecting the rate of fire, and immediately became popular. It appears that only two calibers were made: the massive "Dragoon" arm (qv) and the smaller 54-bore (about 0.44in/11.2mm caliber) shown here. This weapon, while still having adequate stopping power, was of more manageable dimensions than the Dragoon, and was thus particularly favored by unmounted officers, who had to carry their own revolvers. Like all Adams' weapons, the revolver is of strong construction. It has the usual one-piece frame with integral octagonal barrel, which is rifled and bears the foresight; the backsight is a simple notch on the frame above the standing breech. The plain cylinder, with its horizontal nipples separated by partitions, is somewhat longer than those of the original Adams, to allow for a heavier charge, and bears London proofmarks. There is a Kerr-type rammer on the left-hand side of the barrel. The lower frame is marked "B14886" and "Adams Patent No 30550 R," and carries an "L.A.C." (London Armoury Company) stamp near the axis pin.

BEAUMONT-ADAMS 0.32IN REVOLVER UK

Length (gun): 8.5in (216mm)
Barrel: 4.5in (114mm)
Weight: 24.0oz (0.7kg)
Caliber: 0.32in
Rifling: 3 grooves, r/hand
Capacity: five
Muz vel: ca 450ft/sec (137m/sec)

This is a very ornate example of a Beaumont-Adams revolver, which was made by the London Armoury Company in about 1861. It is well blued and inlaid with gold, with a crew on the butt. It is of 12-bore (0.32in) which was about the smallest caliber considered to be adequate to have adequate stopping power. These weapons could be fired either by simple pressure on the trigger or by the preliminary manual cocking of the hammer, which, in effect, combined the best locking features of the Colts and the original Adams in a somewhat more orthodox manner than that of Tranter (qv).

BIRMINGHAM BOX-LOCK PISTOL UK

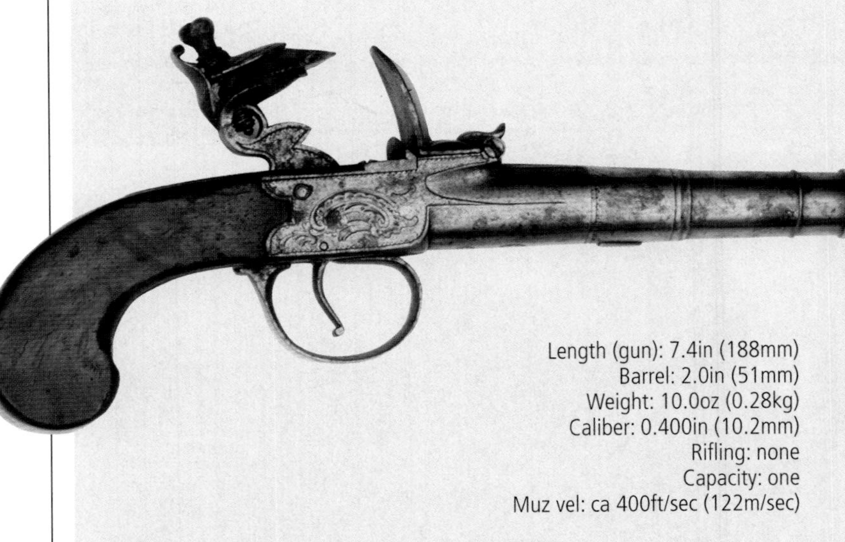

Length (gun): 7.4in (188mm)
Barrel: 2.0in (51mm)
Weight: 10.0oz (0.28kg)
Caliber: 0.400in (10.2mm)
Rifling: none
Capacity: one
Muz vel: ca 400ft/sec (122m/sec)

The weapon seen here is fitted with what is known as a box-lock. This type of lock was probably introduced in the late 17th Century, but only became popular in the mid-18th Century, mainly because it was a somewhat more compact lock for pocket arms than the orthodox side lock. As may be seen from the photograph, the breech is made with two parallel side-plates, between which the cock is mounted centrally, with its own separate, flat, plate cover incorporating a rear tang for fixing the butt. The trigger has a similar plate, incorporating the butt tang. No tumbler is fitted in this type, since the bottom of the cock itself is notched to hold the sear. The arrangement necessitates the placing of the pan on top of the breech, with a flat frizzen spring inset into the breech in front of it. The butt is of the flat or slab-sided variety, having been cut from a plank and its edges chamfered off. The screw-off mechanism is similar to those shown earlier, and a key would have been used to remove the barrel. Specimens are sometimes found with a hinged key permanently attached below the barrel, but these are relatively rare. The pistol is lightly engraved and bears private Birmingham proof marks, indicating that it was made before the establishment of the official proof house at Birmingham in 1813; the likely date of manufacture is about 1800. The left side-plate is marked "E Taylor," which could be a retailer's name: the weapon is of fair quality and is typical of the numerous arms of this type turned out by small makers in Birmingham and elsewhere in the earliest years of the 19th Century.

BIRMINGHAM POCKET PERCUSSION PISTOL UK

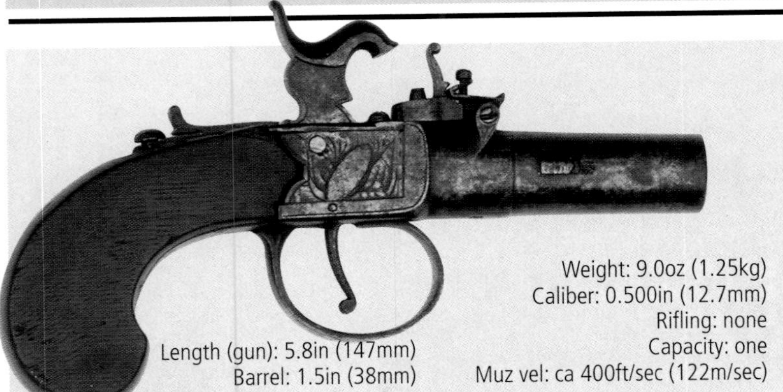

Length (gun): 5.8in (147mm)
Barrel: 1.5in (38mm)
Weight: 9.0oz (1.25kg)
Caliber: 0.500in (12.7mm)
Rifling: none
Capacity: one
Muz vel: ca 400ft/sec (122m/sec)

This is another example of the kind of small pocket pistol turned out by the thousand by makers of all grades, from the great names of the London trade down to the anonymous makers in small back-street factories in Birmingham. Until the late 19th Century, the streets of most cities were considered dangerous places, particularly at night, and many respectable citizens considered it prudent to go armed: the rich in their coaches with armed retainers, the less wealthy on foot, with a stout stick and the comforting weight of a pair of pistols in their overcoat pockets. The pistol illustrated is fairly typical of its kind, small and compact but of man-stopping caliber if used at close quarters and probably adequate to deter the average footpad. It is of the common box-lock pattern, with the mechanism retained between two rear projections from the side of the breech and enclosed by top and bottom plates. This weapon has a sliding safety; when the pistol was at half-cock, the safety could be pushed forward until it engaged a notch at the rear of the hammer, thus holding it immovable until the safety was withdrawn. There is no pop-out trigger in this case, the weapon being fitted with a trigger-guard of orthodox pattern. Probably the most interesting feature of this particular specimen is the provision of a device to prevent the percussion cap from falling off the nipple while the arm was in the user's pocket. There is a spring-loaded ring round the nipple: once the hammer had been placed at half-cock, this ring was raised by forward pressure on the vertical lever against a small spring, which allowed a cap to be placed in position. The ring was then lowered again, and held the cap firmly in place without in any way interfering with it being struck by the falling hammer.

BLANCH PERCUSSION PISTOL UK

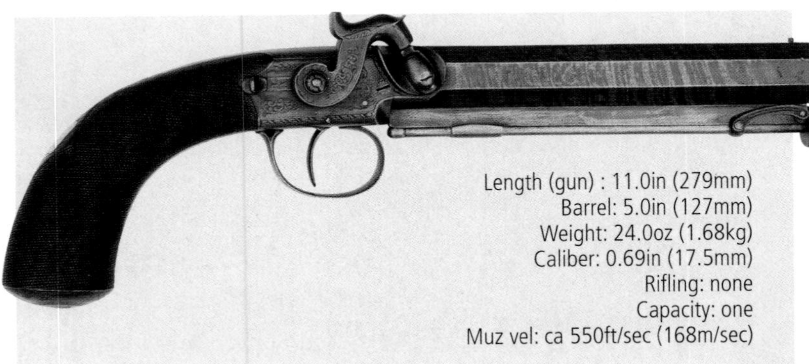

Length (gun) : 11.0in (279mm)
Barrel: 5.0in (127mm)
Weight: 24.0oz (1.68kg)
Caliber: 0.69in (17.5mm)
Rifling: none
Capacity: one
Muz vel: ca 550ft/sec (168m/sec)

By about 1830, the perfection of the percussion system had made it possible to streamline pistols very considerably, and this specimen provides a good example. It is an arm of excellent quality, made by J. Blanch and Son of Gracechurch Street, London, a well-known manufacturer of pistols and revolvers during the 19th Century, whose name appears on the top flat of the barrel. The octagonal barrel is of damascus type, in which previously twisted threads of iron and steel have been flattened into a ribbon, twisted spirally round a mandrel, and welded into a tube, before being finished and filed to shape. The barrel was then often treated with acid to bring out the figuring, which is clearly visible on this arm. It is fitted with a patent breech of the type originally developed by Joseph Manton, with a rear fence to protect the eye of the firer from flying fragments of the copper cap. The flat hammer has a deep recess in the nose with a slot at its forward end. Unfortunately, the comb of the hammer has been broken off, a not infrequent casualty in arms produced in the days when metallurgy was still not far advanced. The butt, which is well shaped and fits comfortably into the hand, is finely checkered overall, except for an ornamental, diamond-shaped portion at the rear with an inset rectangular escutcheon plate. The butt-cap incorporates a small compartment for carrying percussion caps; this has a close-fitting lid, which is held in place by a spring and could be opened with a thumbnail. In the absence of any stock in front of the lock, the swivel ramrod lies against a metal rib attached to the lower flat of the barrel. Swivel ramrods were especially useful on service pistols, when speed in reloading was important, since the ramrods could not be dropped accidentally. This gun is essentially a service weapon, well-sighted and firing a heavy ball of musket bore with a reasonably large charge of powder, and was probably one of a pair.

Blanch Four-Barreled Pistol — UK

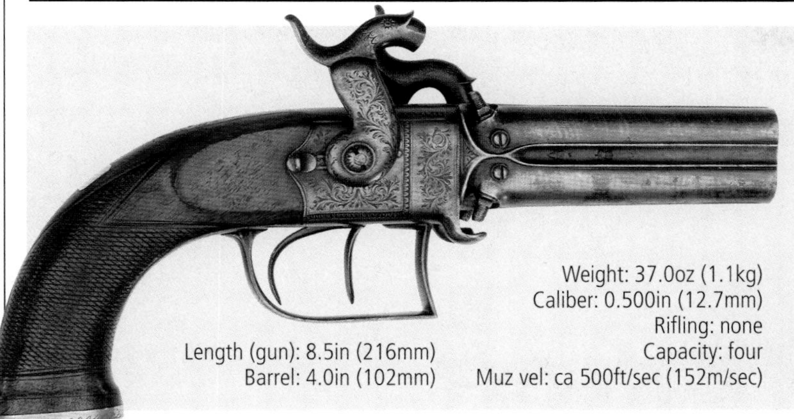

Length (gun): 8.5in (216mm)
Barrel: 4.0in (102mm)
Weight: 37.0oz (1.1kg)
Caliber: 0.500in (12.7mm)
Rifling: none
Capacity: four
Muz vel: ca 500ft/sec (152m/sec)

Almost from the discovery of gunpowder, men had desired firearms which would produce as many shots as possible without reloading. This was considered to be particularly desirable in the case of pistols, which were essentially weapons for use at close quarters, when there was no time to go through the complex process of reloading. Multi-barreled arms went some way towards solving this problem. This weapon was made by Blanch of London and bears the maker's name on the left-hand side of the breech, below the hammer. The barrels have been bored out of a solid piece of metal, and the damascus-type figuring on them must therefore be a later ornament, etched on with acid. Each has its own nipple with a screw plug beneath it to facilitate cleaning. The barrels were held in position by a spring catch; when it was desired to rotate them, it was first necessary to release this catch by pressing back the squared front of the trigger-guard – hence its somewhat unusual shape. There are two hook-like projections on the lower part of the frame to hold the lower pair of percussion caps in position. The hammers are gracefully shaped and have deep hoods which completely enclose the nipples. The latter, rather unusually, are lightly threaded, presumably to help keep the caps in position. The pistol has sliding safety catches which held the hammers securely at half-cock. The checkered walnut butt is of essentially modern shape, looking forward to the revolver rather than back to the pistol. The ramrod below the weapon was normally screwed upwards into the butt. All in all, this is a most elegant pistol, although rather bulky.

Booth Pocket Percussion Pistol — UK

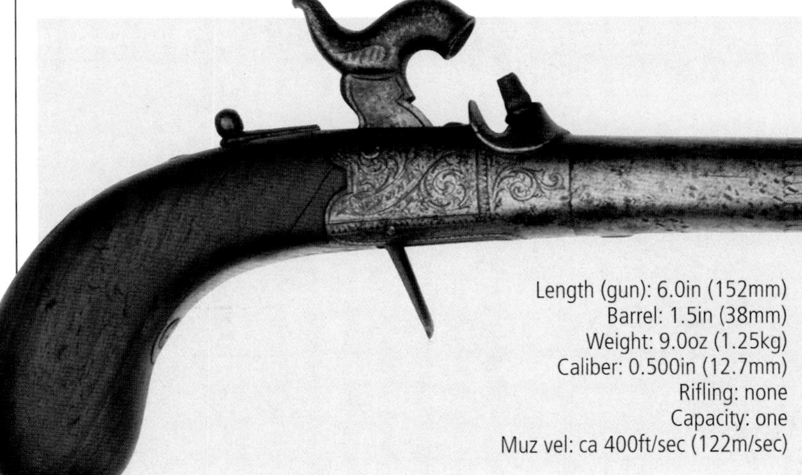

Length (gun): 6.0in (152mm)
Barrel: 1.5in (38mm)
Weight: 9.0oz (1.25kg)
Caliber: 0.500in (12.7mm)
Rifling: none
Capacity: one
Muz vel: ca 400ft/sec (122m/sec)

Pocket pistols were introduced as soon as the early gunsmiths had learnt to make weapons small enough for the purpose, and they retained their popularity in Britain into the 20th Century. The advent of the percussion system in the early years of the 19th Century made it simpler to produce compact weapons suitable for the pocket, for it then became possible to do away with the bulky cock, pan, and frizzen, and substitute a simple hammer and nipple. The specimen illustrated probably dates from about 1835. It is of the box-lock type, in which the hammer and trigger mechanism are fitted centrally behind the barrel in a box-like compartment. Its short, stubby barrel is of the screw-off variety and is of large enough caliber to take a lethal ball, although the pistol's small charge would make it ineffective at anything above the point-blank range for which it was designed. There is a fence behind the nipple to deflect any fragments of copper that might fly from the cap; the nose of the hammer is deeply recessed for the same purpose. The hammer is fitted with a sliding safety, of which the flat bar and knob are visible behind the hammer in the photograph. The mechanism was so designed that when the hammer was down, the trigger folded forward into a recess in the bottom of the breech: cocking the action caused it to pop out in readiness for firing. The characteristic rounded butt, often referred to as "bag-shaped," has a small silver escutcheon plate let into it. The curved scroll visible on the breech bears the word "SUNDERLAND," while a similar scroll on the other side is inscribed "R. D. BOOTH."

Britarms Model 2000 Pistol — UK

Length (gun): 11.0in (280mm)
Weight: 42.0oz (1.2kg)
Barrel: 5.9in (150mm)
Caliber: 0.22in
Rifling: n.k.
Capacity: 5-round box magazine
Muz vel: n.k.

The Britarms Model 2000 was designed by Chris Valentine in the early 1970s as a state-of-the-art Standard Pistol and may be broadly be described as an upmarket equivalent of the Fabrica Armi Sportive Model 601 (FAS) (qv). The Model 2000 is a sophisticated design, rendered in the finest steels, and is highly regarded, although the firm was plagued for over a decade by changes of ownership and low volume production, as a result of which it took longer than usual to work the "bugs" out of this fascinating design. It is a semi-automatic, blow-back weapon, firing from an unlocked breech, using gas pressure in the bore to act on the cartridge case, which then acts as a piston to drive the slide to the rear. It is of all steel construction, machined from the solid. Sights are: square post foresight, square notch backsight.

Bumford Screw-Off Flintlock Pistol — UK

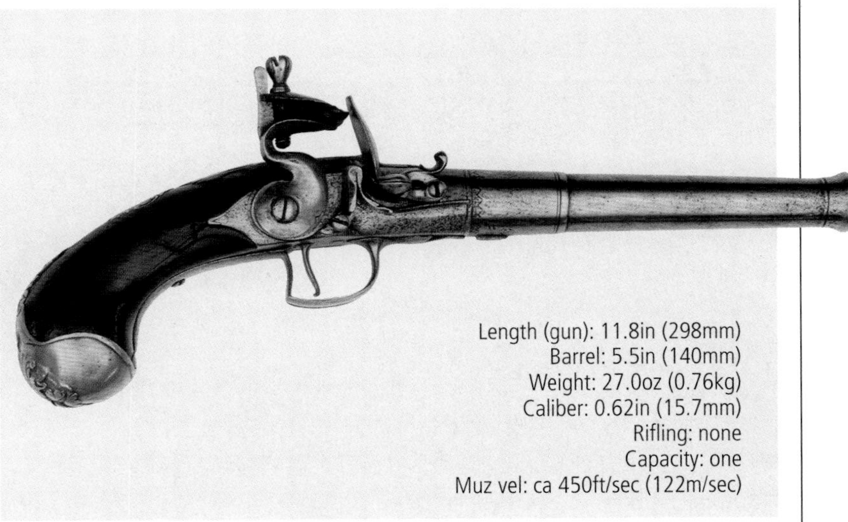

Length (gun): 11.8in (298mm)
Barrel: 5.5in (140mm)
Weight: 27.0oz (0.76kg)
Caliber: 0.62in (15.7mm)
Rifling: none
Capacity: one
Muz vel: ca 450ft/sec (122m/sec)

This is a cannon-barreled pistol with a removable barrel, and thus could be loaded from the breech end. In order to remove the barrel, a circular key was slipped over it and locked near the breech end by means of a stud (visible in the photograph), which fitted a corresponding notch cut into the inner circumference of the key. This enabled the barrel to be made a good, gas-tight fit with the breech. The somewhat abrupt swell at the bottom of the butt is characteristic of the general type, as is the cast-brass butt-cap with its simple design of foliage and the brass escutcheon plate just visible above it. Screw-off barrels, which originated a few years before the so-called Queen Anne type, made possible the use of a carefully measured charge and a tight-fitting ball. In this weapon, the powder chamber is contained within the male screw and has a concave top. The chamber was loaded vertically, the ball was balanced on the top, and the barrel was then screwed on again with the key. This sytem was a slow process, but it eliminated the need for ramming and was particularly useful in rifled barrels. This specimen, which was made by the London gunsmith Bumford in about 1755, is of medium quality. Many of the finest specimens had elaborate silver furniture and ornament; such features, being hall-marked, are of considerable help in dating these arms.

COGSWELL PEPPERBOX PISTOL — UK

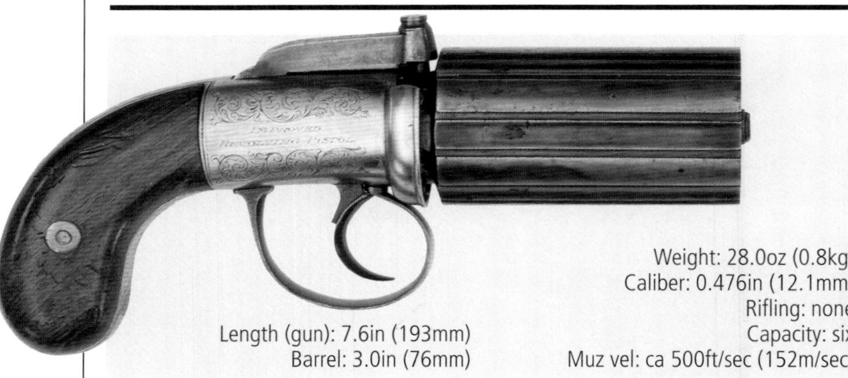

Length (gun): 7.6in (193mm)
Barrel: 3.0in (76mm)
Weight: 28.0oz (0.8kg)
Caliber: 0.476in (12.1mm)
Rifling: none
Capacity: six
Muz vel: ca 500ft/sec (152m/sec)

This pistol may be considered representative of arms of its type made in London for the upper end of the market. It was made, probably in about 1850, by B. Cogswell, a well-known London gunmaker, and is a well-finished arm of good quality. Its six smooth-bored barrels have been drilled out of a single steel cylinder, with the intervals between the barrels machined out into plain but elegant grooves. Unusually – and perhaps somewhat unnecessarily – each barrel is neatly numbered at the breech end, while the grooves are stamped alternately with view marks and proof marks. The chambers are in a cylinder of somewhat smaller diameter than the barrel cluster, and the nipples are screwed into the chambers at right-angles to the axis of the barrels. There are no partitions between the nipples, and this must have increased the great risk of multiple discharge; a risk made greater by the fact that such pistols usually employed especially sensitive caps to compensate for the relatively weak blow struck by the type of hammer fitted. Unlike a revolver cylinder, there was, of course, no obstruction in front of any of the muzzles; thus, multiple fire exposed the user to no danger – except, perhaps, the shock of a massive discharge. The breech mechanism is of German silver and is discreetly engraved in the English style. The left-hand side bears the inscription "B. COGSWELL, 224 STRAND, LONDON," while on the right-hand side are the words "IMPROVED REVOLVING PISTOL." The breech includes a nipple shield: the advantages and disadvantages of such a provision roughly balance out, for the protection afforded to the caps was offset by the increased risk of several barrels going off together. The butt consists of a continuous strap of German silver, with walnut plates held in position by a screw.

COLLIER FLINTLOCK REVOLVER — UK

Length (gun): 14.3in (362mm)
Barrel: 6.25in (159mm)
Weight: 35.0oz (0.99kg)
Caliber: 0.473in (12mm)
Rifling: none
Capacity: five
Muz vel: ca 550ft/sec (168m/sec)

In 1818, Elisha Collier, an American citizen living in London, took out a patent for the flintlock revolver seen here. This ingeniously designed weapon has an octagonal, smooth-bore barrel attached to the frame by a top strap and by the axis pin on which the five-chambered cylinder revolved. The problem of priming the pan for successive shots was very cleverly overcome. The rear end of the cylinder is surrounded by a close-fitting gun-metal sleeve surmounted by a pan. Each chamber vent could be aligned in succession with an opening at the bottom of the pan. The combined pan cover and steel, attached to the top strap, incorporated a small magazine so designed that the act of closing the cover caused the correct amount of priming to be deposited in the pan. When the trigger was pressed, the flint acted against the steel in the normal way, and the flash from the priming passed through the aligned vent and fired the charge. It was then necessary to re-cock, re-close the pan and cover, and rotate the cylinder manually in order to bring the next loaded chamber into position for the next shot. The breech end of the barrel was coned, the mouths of the cylinders being counter-sunk to fit over it, so that when rotating the cylinder it was necessary to draw it back a little against a spring to disengage it. The forward action of the cock thrust a steel wedge against the rear end of the cylinder, to hold it rigidly in position while the shot was fired. This device not only ensured that the barrel and chamber were aligned at the critical moment, but also helped to prevent the escaping gases from accidentally igniting the charges in the adjacent chambers.

COOPER PEPPERBOX PISTOL — UK

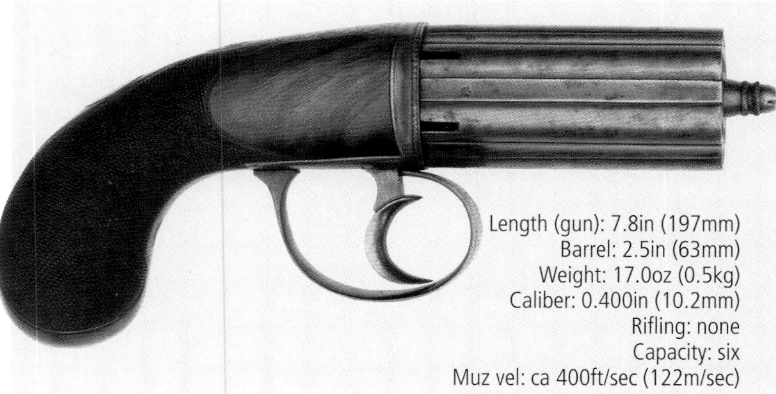

Length (gun): 7.8in (197mm)
Barrel: 2.5in (63mm)
Weight: 17.0oz (0.5kg)
Caliber: 0.400in (10.2mm)
Rifling: none
Capacity: six
Muz vel: ca 400ft/sec (122m/sec)

This weapon was made by the British gunsmith J. R. Cooper, who produced a large number of pepperbox pistols in the period 1840-50. Many of them were closely based on an arm of similar type patented in Belgium in 1837 and made thereafter both there and in France, under the name of Mariette. This example, however, is of more distinctly British type. The top tang of the frame bears the inscription "J R COOPER, PATENTEE," although it is not known if it was, in fact, ever patented in England. The weapon is well, if plainly, made: its six barrels have been bored out of a solid block of metal and the grooves between the barrêls bear Birmingham proof marks. The firing mechanism is internal and is of double-action only; thus, considerable pressure would have had to be exerted on the trigger to fire the arm. Naturally enough, this requirement did not make for accuracy at anything above point-blank range. The barrels could be loaded while attached to the weapon (a separate ram-rod being provided in the case, which is not shown here), but in order to cap the nipples it was necessary to unscrew the front cap and remove the cylinder from the pistol. The nipples, which are placed in line with the axis of the barrels, are set in deep, circular recesses, in order to reduce the risk of a multiple discharge; the slots visible at the breech end of the barrels were mainly to allow for the escape of gases. As the strike came forward to fire the top barrel a cylinder-stop also emerged from the bottom of the standing breech and engaged in the lowest slot, thus preventing any rotation of the cylinder at the moment of firing.

COOPER PEPPERBOX PISTOL — UK

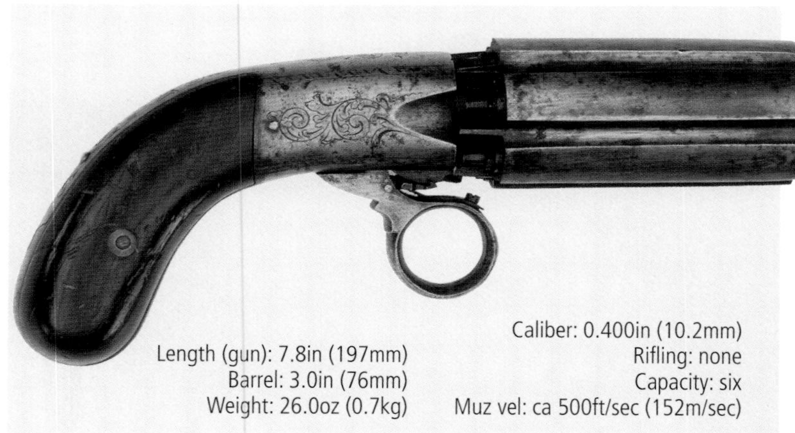

Length (gun): 7.8in (197mm)
Barrel: 3.0in (76mm)
Weight: 26.0oz (0.7kg)
Caliber: 0.400in (10.2mm)
Rifling: none
Capacity: six
Muz vel: ca 500ft/sec (152m/sec)

This is another pepperbox pistol by J. R. Cooper who was well known for the production of arms of this type; but although he seems to have produced a number of good-quality arms of his own design, with adequate triggers and guards and often handsomely cased, most of his pistols were more or less closely based on the design of the Mariette range of arms, patented in Belgium in 1837 and widely manufactured thereafter both in that country and in France. In the arm seen here, the left-hand side of the breech bears a scroll containing the inscription "J R COOPER, PATENT," although it is not certain that it was, in fact, so patented. The barrels are bored out of a solid cylinder of steel, with shallow grooves between each; each groove bears a Birmingham proof mark. The nipples are in the same axis as that of the barrels and have flat, rectangular shields between them to reduce the risk of multiple fire. A V-shaped groove on the right-hand side of the frame allowed the caps to be placed in position. Pressure on the ring-trigger drew back an under-hammer – basically similar to a normal hammer, but combless and working upside down – and a spring on the trigger released the hammer at the right moment, allowing it to strike the cap on the lowest nipple. The butt consists of a continuous strap, with a pair of side plates held in position by a single screw. The weapon is lightly engraved. This pistol may be said to be reasonably typical of most of Cooper's Mariette-type arms: there is little elegance about it and the finish may fairly be described as rough.

Daw Revolver — UK

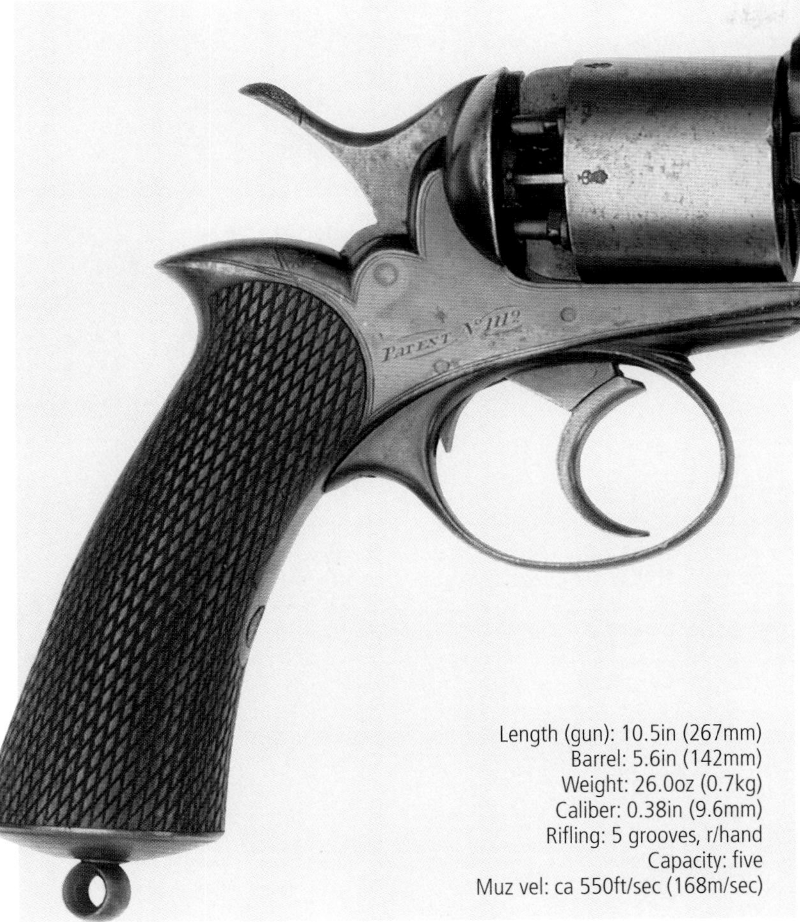

Length (gun): 10.5in (267mm)
Barrel: 5.6in (142mm)
Weight: 26.0oz (0.7kg)
Caliber: 0.38in (9.6mm)
Rifling: 5 grooves, r/hand
Capacity: five
Muz vel: ca 550ft/sec (168m/sec)

G. H. Daw was a well-known figure in the London gun trade in the mid-19th Century. He was in partnership with D. W. Witton until 1860, but thereafter traded alone as George H. Daw. In his earlier days he was extensively involved in the design and manufacture of gas-seal revolvers. In 1855, the experienced firm of Pryse and Cashmore patented a double-action lock which Daw took up with enthusiasm. His revolver can be compared to the Colt: the barrel is wedged to the axis pin and is further braced against the lower frame, and it is fitted with a compound rammer of Colt type. The barrel is basically cylindrical but with a top and bottom flat, the former bearing the inscription "GEORGE H DAW, 57 THREADNEEDLE ST LONDON, PATENT NO 112." The double-action lock is unusual in that it is of the type known as a "hesitation" lock: by slowly pressing the trigger, the hammer was brought to full-cock, whence a further slight pressure fired it. It could also be cocked manually, and when faster shooting was needed a somewhat stronger pressure on the trigger caused the arm to fire double-action. The standing breech has a large U-shaped cutaway at the top, allowing ample room for re-capping, and the hammer-head is made with a hood which fitted it exactly when lowered, thus preventing the blowback of cap fragments. Each nipple partition has a small stud which corresponds with a recess in the bottom of the hammer-nose. This allowed the hammer to be left down on a partition when a fully capped and loaded revolver was carried, without any risk of accident. Although well made and mechanically sound, the Daw weapon seems somewhat fragile for military use.

Deane-Harding Revolver — UK

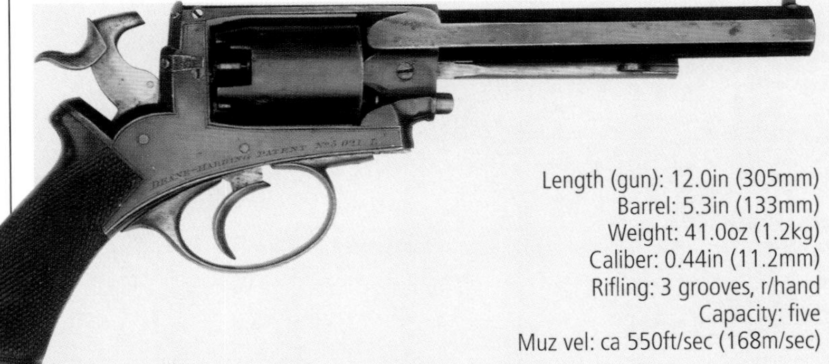

Length (gun): 12.0in (305mm)
Barrel: 5.3in (133mm)
Weight: 41.0oz (1.2kg)
Caliber: 0.44in (11.2mm)
Rifling: 3 grooves, r/hand
Capacity: five
Muz vel: ca 550ft/sec (168m/sec)

The Deane of the title of this arm is the older of Adams's two original partners. After severing the partnership, Deane continued to trade in firearms, and in 1858 he began the manufacture of a new revolver patented in that year by William Harding. The weapon shown is of the popular 54-bore service caliber. Perhaps its main point of interest is the manner of its construction: the barrel, barrel lump and upper strap constitute a completely separate component from the frame. In order to strip the weapon, it was necessary first to remove the pin from the hole visible in front of the hammer nose. The barrel was thus pushed downwards to an angle of 45 degrees, which was sufficient to disengage a hook at the bottom of the lump from a corresponding socket in the lower frame. Various types of locking-pin were employed; in this specimen, the pin was replaced by a screw, but this was a non-standard modification. The barrel group incorporates a rammer, which was also patented by Harding. When the lever below the barrel was released, by means of a spring, and pulled downward, a hook (concealed in the lump) drew the ram into the bottom chamber until the lever was vertically downwards. This method was efficient but is said to have been rather flimsy for service use. The lock is of double-action type, and the whole arm is broadly comparable to the Beaumont-Adams – to which it was clearly intended to be a rival. It is known that the Deane-Adams breakup caused some ill-feeling: Deane, in his Manual of Firearms published in 1858, suggested that the addition of the Beaumont lock to Adams' original revolver made it over-complex and liable to derangement; although there seems to have been little truth in this charge. It is difficult to assess the real value of the Deane-Harding revolver in practical use. Some contemporaries felt it could always be relied upon to malfunction at a critical moment. Certainly, it never became popular.

Edgecumb Arms Combat Ten Revolver — UK

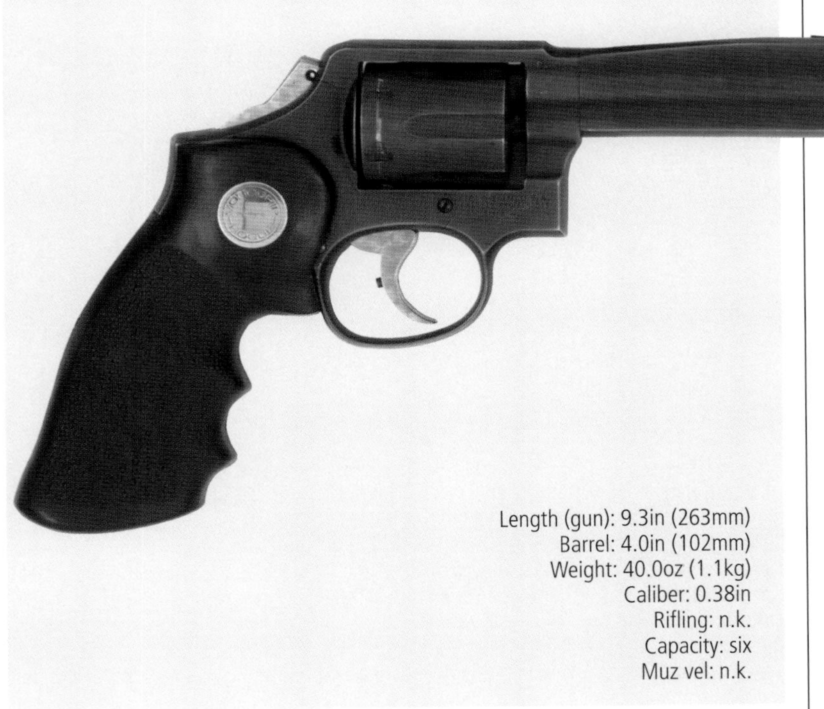

Length (gun): 9.3in (263mm)
Barrel: 4.0in (102mm)
Weight: 40.0oz (1.1kg)
Caliber: 0.38in
Rifling: n.k.
Capacity: six
Muz vel: n.k.

One of a number of "police" revolvers to appear in the 1960s for the newly established competition shooting, the Edgcumbe Combat Ten was built on a Smith & Wesson Model 10 frame, with a Douglas barrel. The crane-mounted cylinder swung out of frame to the left for hand loading and unloading. There was a standard square notch backsight, while the square ramp foresight was integrally milled into the barrel between integral protective ribs. Early products had an Edgcumbe roller bearing action, but this was subsequently replaced by a reworked standard action. Hogue grips were fitted as standard.

ENFIELD MARK II SERVICE REVOLVER — UK

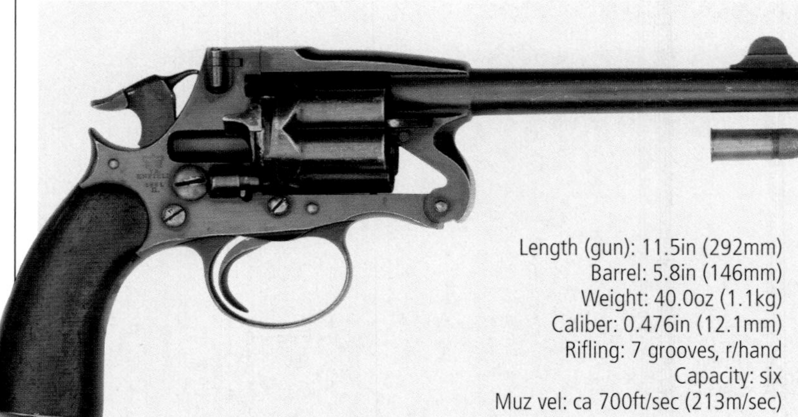

Length (gun): 11.5in (292mm)
Barrel: 5.8in (146mm)
Weight: 40.0oz (1.1kg)
Caliber: 0.476in (12.1mm)
Rifling: 7 grooves, r/hand
Capacity: six
Muz vel: ca 700ft/sec (213m/sec)

In the late 1870s, the British Government decided to develop a new and more powerful service revolver. Various colonial campaigns during the previous years had shown that the bullet of the standard Adams 0.45in (11.4mm) could not always be relied upon to stop a charging fanatic; thus, a new and more powerful round of 0.476in (12.1mm) caliber was developed. Because there were doubts, mistaken as it turned out, as to whether a top-break revolver of Webley type could handle such rounds safely, a completely new arm was developed. The designer mainly concerned was a Philadelphian inventor with the very Welsh name of Owen Jones; his revolver was finally approved for service in 1880. As may be seen in the specimen illustrated (which is, in fact, a Mark II), the barrel is hinged to the front of the frame and fastened with a spring catch just in front of the hammer. However, when the revolver was opened and the barrel forced downward, the cylinder remained in the same axis and was simply drawn forward along its pin. This left the cases held by their rims in a star-shaped extractor on the standing breech, whence they could be shaken clear. The need for the cylinder to be drawn well forward accounts for the rather ugly bulge below the barrel. The Enfield Mark II was adopted in 1882. Its main points of difference from the Mark I were the provision of a device in the loading gate which prevented the action from working if the gate was open, and vice-versa, and the fitting of a safety catch on the left side of the frame.

ENFIELD 0.38IN NO 2 MK I* REVOLVER — UK

Length (gun): 10.0in (254mm)
Barrel: 5.0in (127mm)
Weight: 27.0oz (0.8kg)
Caliber: 0.38in (9.6mm)
Rifling: 7 grooves, r/hand
Capacity: six
Muz vel: ca 700ft/sec (213m/sec)

The new Enfield No 2 Mk I revolver issued in 1932 proved generally popular with the British Army. However, complaints were received from the Royal Tank Regiment (whose personnel carried their revolvers in open-topped holsters) that the hammer spur of the Enfield tended to catch on various fittings in the tanks while they were mounting or dismounting. In 1938, therefore, the Mark I*, seen here, was introduced. The two revolvers were essentially similar; the main functional difference being that the new model had no comb on the hammer. It could thus only be fired by pressure on the trigger, a rather odd reversion to the original Adams revolvers of 1851. As a contribution towards accuracy, the weight of the mainspring was lightened to reduce the trigger pull to about 12.0lb (5.4kg), a reduction of 2.0lb (0.9kg) from the earlier model. Also, the butt-plates were modified by the addition of thumb-grooves to give a better grip, which were identical on each side, so that the revolver could be used either right- or left-handed. The end of the screw holding the grips in position fitted into a circular brass disc of 0.75in (19mm) diameter, which was sunk into the right grip. The disc was presumably originally intended to bear unit marks and numbers, but these are rarely to be found on extant examples. The self-cocking concept was not popular – imported American revolvers were much preferred – but in spite of this, most of the Mark Is with the original hammers were gradually called into the workshops and modified to the new system.

ENFIELD NO 2 MK I REVOLVER — UK

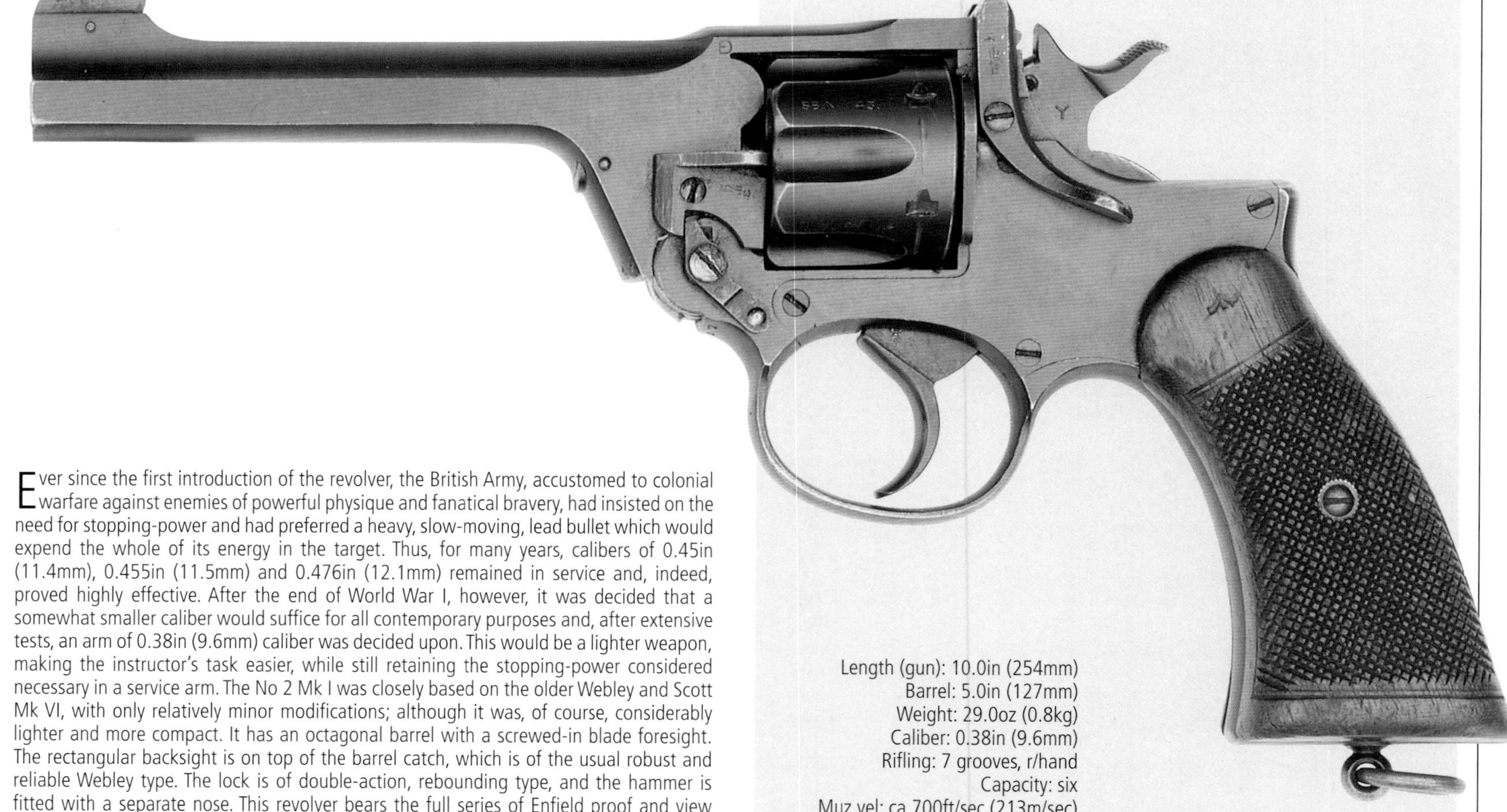

Length (gun): 10.0in (254mm)
Barrel: 5.0in (127mm)
Weight: 29.0oz (0.8kg)
Caliber: 0.38in (9.6mm)
Rifling: 7 grooves, r/hand
Capacity: six
Muz vel: ca 700ft/sec (213m/sec)

Ever since the first introduction of the revolver, the British Army, accustomed to colonial warfare against enemies of powerful physique and fanatical bravery, had insisted on the need for stopping-power and had preferred a heavy, slow-moving, lead bullet which would expend the whole of its energy in the target. Thus, for many years, calibers of 0.45in (11.4mm), 0.455in (11.5mm) and 0.476in (12.1mm) remained in service and, indeed, proved highly effective. After the end of World War I, however, it was decided that a somewhat smaller caliber would suffice for all contemporary purposes and, after extensive tests, an arm of 0.38in (9.6mm) caliber was decided upon. This would be a lighter weapon, making the instructor's task easier, while still retaining the stopping-power considered necessary in a service arm. The No 2 Mk I was closely based on the older Webley and Scott Mk VI, with only relatively minor modifications; although it was, of course, considerably lighter and more compact. It has an octagonal barrel with a screwed-in blade foresight. The rectangular backsight is on top of the barrel catch, which is of the usual robust and reliable Webley type. The lock is of double-action, rebounding type, and the hammer is fitted with a separate nose. This revolver bears the full series of Enfield proof and view marks, date "1932" and number "B4447."

Hill's Self-Extracting Revolver — UK

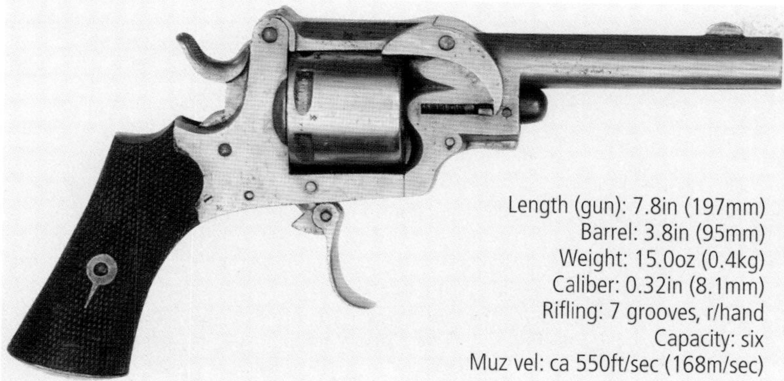

Length (gun): 7.8in (197mm)
Barrel: 3.8in (95mm)
Weight: 15.0oz (0.4kg)
Caliber: 0.32in (8.1mm)
Rifling: 7 grooves, r/hand
Capacity: six
Muz vel: ca 550ft/sec (168m/sec)

Although the metallic cartridge was a valuable innovation, the system of reloading the earliest types of cartridge revolver was slow. It was necessary first to put the hammer at half-cock, open the loading gate, swing out the pin (if it was not already in alignment), and push out the empty cases one by one before loading fresh rounds. There were many attempts to speed up this process. The revolver seen here is of "tip-up" type, dating from around 1880, but it is more complex than other "tip-ups" because no special manual operation was necessary to eject the empty cases. There are two hinges: one where the top frame is attached to the standing breech, and a second where the barrel joins the frame. The pivot pin of the latter is also visible in the crescent-shaped lever, although the joint itself is concealed behind it. To open the weapon, it was necessary first to press the flat lever (just visible) on the lower front corner of the frame and raise the barrel. At this stage, the front hinge remained rigid and only the rear one opened. When the barrel was vertical, the limit of the rear hinge was reached and the crescent-shaped lever also locked. Continued pressure on the barrel caused the front hinge to come into play, allowing the barrel to continue backwards beyond the vertical. Then the small stud which protrudes from the front of the frame, and is attached to the extractor rod, bore on the front end of the crescent and was thrust downward, so pushing out the star extractor and the empty case.

Kerr Revolver (No 27) — UK

Length (gun) : 11.0in (279mm)
Barrel: 5.8in (146mm)
Weight: 42.0oz (1.2kg)
Caliber: 0.44in (11.2mm)
Rifling: 5 grooves, l/hand
Capacity: five
Muz vel: ca 550ft/sec (168m/sec)

When the partnership of Deane, Adams and Deane was dissolved in 1856, it was replaced by the London Armoury Company, which was able to provide capital for the large-scale manufacture of Adams revolvers to meet military contracts. One of the shareholders was the company superintendent, James Kerr, inventor of the rammer used on the Beaumont-Adams revolver (qv). In 1858, Kerr patented a percussion revolver of his own design (of which this, No. 27, is an early example). Kerr's idea, a very sensible one, was that, however robust a revolver, there was always the risk of breaking a spring. Although this was not necessarily a serious accident in a civilized country where a competent gunsmith might easily be found, it was a grave matter in more remote parts of the world. Kerr therefore designed his new revolver with a detachable lock, which could be removed by two screws, on the assumption that even a primitive blacksmith might be able to replace a spring to which he had easy access. The idea was successful: Kerr's revolvers proved popular in the various British colonies and also as service arms with the Confederate forces in the American Civil War. The locks of the early models were of single-action type, but double-action locks were sometimes fitted later. This specimen, which is cased, was presumably a presentation model and is well-engraved, but most were plain.

Kerr Revolver (Later Model) — UK

Length (gun) : 10.6in (269mm)
Barrel: 5.5in (140mm)
Weight: 34.0in (1.0kg)
Caliber: 0.44in (11.2mm)
Rifling: 5 grooves, l/hand
Capacity: five
Muz vel: ca 550ft/sec (168m/sec)

So as not to contravene Adams's patent for a solid frame, Kerr's revolvers had the barrel and top strap forged as a separate component and then fastened to the frame by two screws: one just below the aperture for the hammer nose; the other at the front lower end of the frame. The fit is so accurate that at first sight the revolver could be taken to have a solid frame. This revolver, like all the arms in the series, is fitted with a new type of rammer, also the invention of Kerr. It is centrally placed below the barrel: when not in use, the lever was held between two lugs on the lower side of the barrel by means of a spring catch. Drawing the lever downwards forced the ram (which is concealed in the barrel lump) into the lowest chamber. The central position of the rammer made it difficult to arrange for the cylinder axis to be inserted from the front; thus, in this revolver, it was inserted from the rear, the end of it being visible behind the hammer. There is a small spring catch on the left-hand side of the frame to prevent it slipping out accidentally. The main point of interest is, of course, the detachable lock, and in this example it has been removed from the revolver and reversed so as to show its internal mechanism. It has a sliding safety on the lockplate; when pushed forward, it engaged a slot at the rear of the hammer and prevented it from being drawn back. A number of Kerr revolvers were bought and used by the Confederate States during the American Civil War: these examples are now particularly sought after by collectors, but they are extremely hard to identify.

Kynoch Revolver — UK

Length (gun): 11.5in (292mm)
Barrel: 6.0in (152mm)
Weight: 42.0oz (1.19kg)
Caliber: 0.455in (11.5mm)
Rifling: 7 grooves, r/hand
Capacity: six
Muz vel: ca 650ft/sec (198m/sec)

In 1880 the British Government adopted the Enfield revolver but further trials, and combat use, showed that it was not good enough, and a number of makers developed models they hoped might replace it. One such arm was the Kynoch revolver, illustrated here. It appears to have been originally patented by a British inventor named H. Schlund in 1885 and 1886, and it was subsequently manufactured in a wide variety of calibers by George Kynoch in his gun factory at Aston Cross, Birmingham. The Kynoch revolver was a heavy arm of service caliber, of the type which the maker presumably hoped would be at least in contention as a replacement for the unpopular Enfield. It has an octagonal barrel with a top rib and an integral, half-round foresight. It is of hinged-frame construction, and was opened by pushing forward the catch which can be seen at the rear of the frame. When the weapon was opened thus, the automatic extractor was brought into play. By far the most interesting aspect of the arm, however, is its lock, which is based closely on the type originally invented by William Tranter (qv). Pressure on the lower trigger – which is, in effect, a cocking lever – brought the concealed hammer to full-cock; subsequently, a very light touch on the trigger was sufficient to fire it. A later Kynoch version was made with a much shorter double-trigger, entirely contained within the trigger-guard, but the type never achieved popularity.

LANCASTER FOUR-BARRELED 0.476IN PISTOL — UK

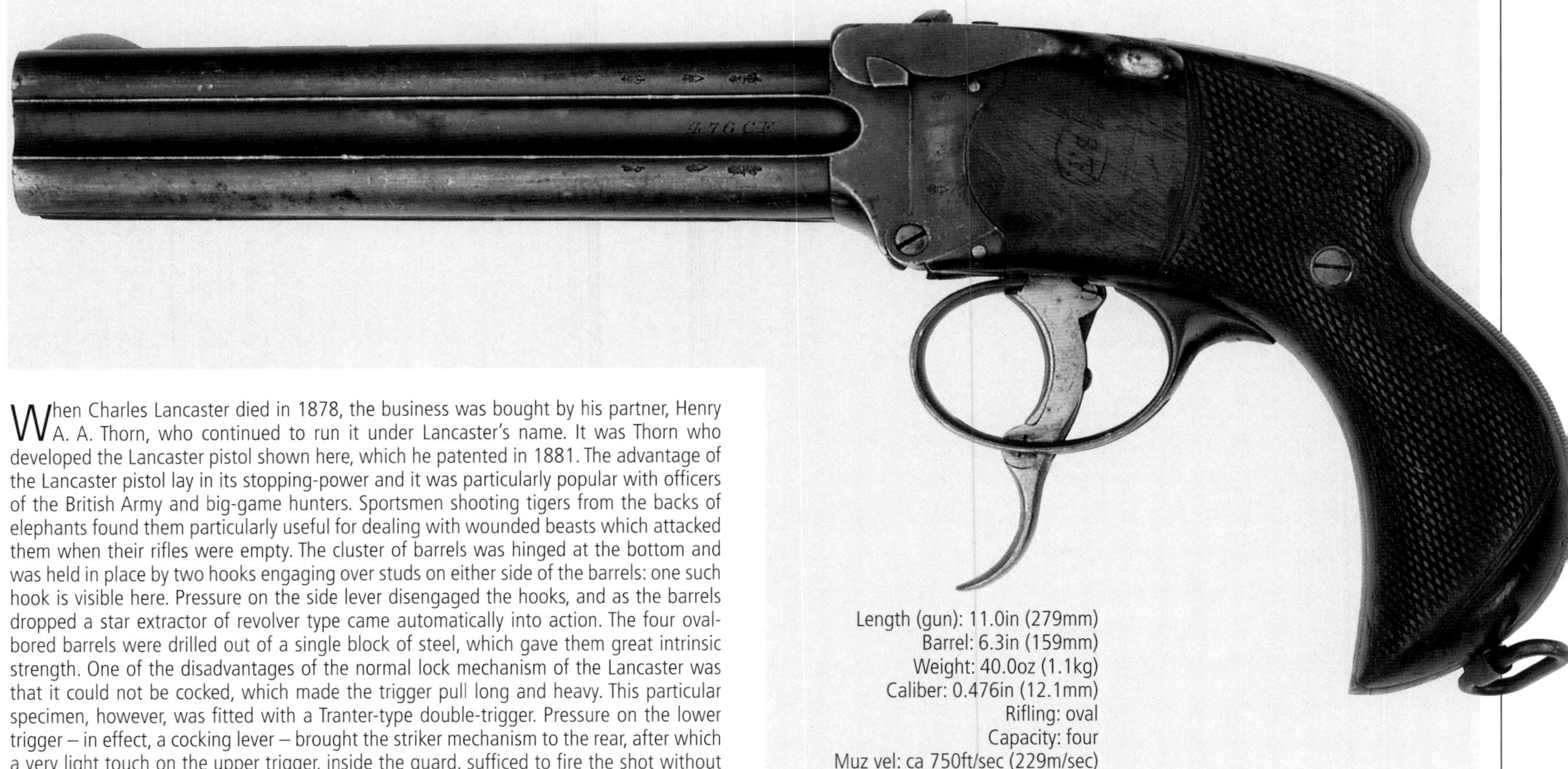

When Charles Lancaster died in 1878, the business was bought by his partner, Henry A. A. Thorn, who continued to run it under Lancaster's name. It was Thorn who developed the Lancaster pistol shown here, which he patented in 1881. The advantage of the Lancaster pistol lay in its stopping-power and it was particularly popular with officers of the British Army and big-game hunters. Sportsmen shooting tigers from the backs of elephants found them particularly useful for dealing with wounded beasts which attacked them when their rifles were empty. The cluster of barrels was hinged at the bottom and was held in place by two hooks engaging over studs on either side of the barrels: one such hook is visible here. Pressure on the side lever disengaged the hooks, and as the barrels dropped a star extractor of revolver type came automatically into action. The four oval-bored barrels were drilled out of a single block of steel, which gave them great intrinsic strength. One of the disadvantages of the normal lock mechanism of the Lancaster was that it could not be cocked, which made the trigger pull long and heavy. This particular specimen, however, was fitted with a Tranter-type double-trigger. Pressure on the lower trigger – in effect, a cocking lever – brought the striker mechanism to the rear, after which a very light touch on the upper trigger, inside the guard, sufficed to fire the shot without disturbing the aim.

Length (gun): 11.0in (279mm)
Barrel: 6.3in (159mm)
Weight: 40.0oz (1.1kg)
Caliber: 0.476in (12.1mm)
Rifling: oval
Capacity: four
Muz vel: ca 750ft/sec (229m/sec)

LANCASTER FOUR-BARRELED 0.38IN PISTOL — UK

Length (gun): 8.5in (216mm)
Barrel: 4.3in (108mm)
Weight: 27.0oz (0.8kg)
Caliber: 0.380in (9.6mm)
Rifling: oval
Capacity: four
Muz vel: ca 625ft/sec (190m/sec)

Most Lancasters were purchased strictly for their stopping power and the most common calibers were undoubtedly either 0.476in (12.1mm) or 0.45in (11.4mm). Some were, however, made in other calibers to special order, the arm shown here being one such. Unlike the 0.476in pistol, it was fitted with a single trigger only. On this particular specimen, the butt-plates have been removed in order to show the lock mechanism. Pressure on the trigger caused the vertical hammer-like lever to move to the rear, taking with it the grooved cylinder, which was fitted with a fixed striker on its forward circumference. The cylinder slid along a fixed horizontal rod, the rear end of which can be seen. In the course of its rearward movement, the cylinder was turned through 90 degrees by the action of the guide in one of the transverse grooves. When this cycle was complete, the mechanism tripped, allowing the cylinder to go forward under the impetus of the mainspring. During this forward movement, the guide was engaged in one of the slots parallel to the axis, so that there was no resistance. The striker fired the cartridge and was then revolved through a further 90 degrees by the next pressure on the trigger, thus bringing it into line with the next live cartridge. The ejector was worked by a transverse arm. The lower end of the arm protruded slightly below the lower pair of barrels: when the barrels were open, this lower end bore on a corresponding projection on the front of the frame, thus lifting the extractor.

LANCASTER DOUBLE-BARRELED PISTOL — UK

Length (gun): 11.0in (279mm)
Barrel: 6.5in (165mm)
Weight: 26.5oz (0.8kg)
Caliber: 0.476in (12.1mm)
Rifling: oval
Capacity: two
Muz vel: ca 750ft/sec (229m/sec)

Although similar in general principle to the four-bareled weapons, this Lancaster double-barreled pistol differed somewhat in detail. The barrels were hinged at the bottom in the same way. The locking system – two hooks engaging over studs on the sides of the upper barrel, controlled by a thumb-lever on the left side of the weapon – was identical; but there was no double-barreled arm of the small pin on the frame, intended to stop the movement of the lever at the proper position. The difference lay in the system of extraction. In the double-barreled Lancaster, when the barrels were opened the vertical lever at their breech end initially moved with them, until its lower end caught the horizontal projection just above the trigger. When this happened the lever stopped, but as the barrels continued to move, the extractor was drawn out by means of a protruding pin which engaged in a slot at the upper end of the lever. This particular extractor was not spring-operated: when the barrels were closed, it was pushed back into place by the face of the standing breech, on which it bore. This double-barreled pistol was, of course, lighter and better balanced than the four-barreled version. Like most Lancaster pistols, it was fitted with a foresight and a shallow V-backsight. However, the trigger pull was so long and heavy that accurate shooting would have been difficult, except at close quarters – but since these pistols were, in fact, specifically designed for close action, this was not, perhaps, an important defect.

LANG DOUBLE-BARRELED HOLSTER PISTOL — UK

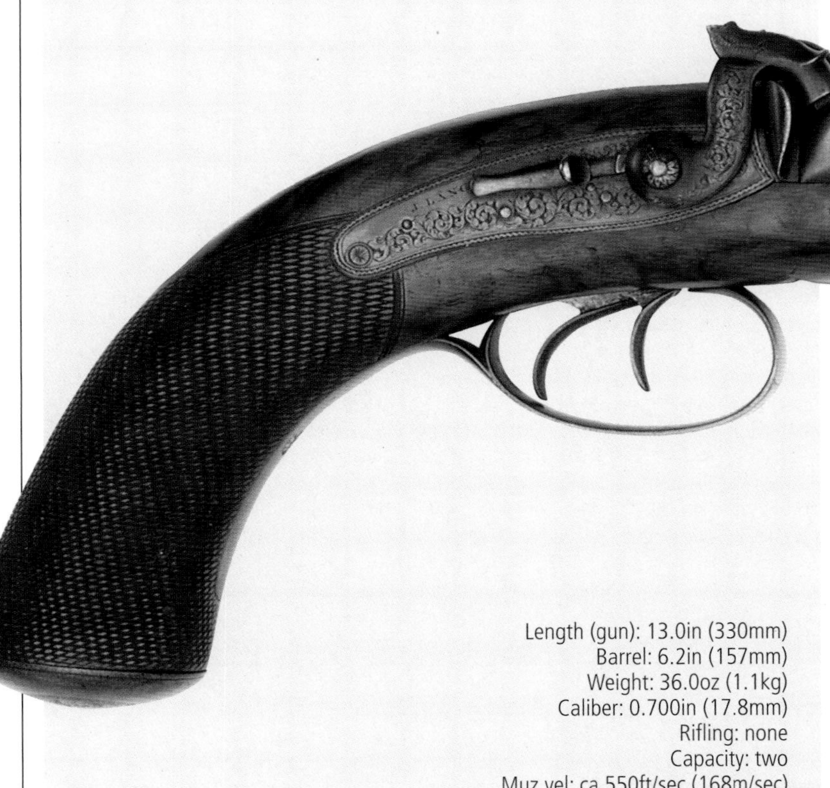

Length (gun): 13.0in (330mm)
Barrel: 6.2in (157mm)
Weight: 36.0oz (1.1kg)
Caliber: 0.700in (17.8mm)
Rifling: none
Capacity: two
Muz vel: ca 550ft/sec (168m/sec)

This pistol (one of a pair) was intended for use by generals and staff officers and was made by Joseph Lang, 7 Haymarket, London, a famous maker of the time. The pistol is doubled-barreled, an improvement much facilitated by the introduction of the percussion system; although double-barreled flintlock pistols were made, the need for two bulky flintlocks made them somewhat clumsy. The smooth-bored barrels are of damascus type with a most attractive figure, and are of a caliber to take a musket ball, making them formidable weapons. It has a bead foresight mounted on the top rib between the barrels; the backsight consists of a shallow V-groove on the standing breech. Both sights are fixed. The chambers are also equipped with platinum plugs which would have blown out if the arm was seriously overloaded, thus preventing damage to the barrel. The nipples are on top of the breeches and have shields to protect the eyes of the firer from flying fragments. The locks are of back-action type and fit neatly on to each side of the carefully tapered stock, so that the hammers do not protrude beyond the outside line of the barrels; this ensures that the pistols are reasonably narrow across the breech. The locks are equipped with sliding safeties, which engaged in slots in the hammers when the latter were in half-cock position. The barrels are held to the stock by a hook at the breech end and by a single flat key. The pistol has an ingenious swivel ramrod; both barrels could thus be loaded without running any risk of dropping the ramrod, an important consideration for a mounted man attempting to re-load on the move.

LANG FOUR-BARRELED TURN-OVER PISTOL — UK

Length (gun): 9.0in (229mm)
Barrel: 4.0in (102mm)
Weight: 37.0oz (1.1kg)
Caliber: 0.500in (12.7mm)
Rifling: none
Capacity: four
Muz vel: ca 550ft/sec (168m/sec)

This very fine weapon by Joseph Lang is intermediate between the double-barreled type and the early "pepperbox" revolvers. The four barrels of this weapon are bored out of a solid block of steel and the attractive damascus effect has been etched on later with acid. Each barrel has its own nipple and shield, and each is equipped with a platinum safety plug to reduce the risk of damage from either an overcharge of powder or an unnecessarily powerful percussion cap. The two hook-like projections on the standing breech were intended to prevent the caps on the lower nipples from being blown off when the upper barrels were discharged. Each pair of barrels has a small, fixed bead foresight on the rib between them, the ramrod being carried in two pipes in the third rib, while the fourth rib bears the proof marks. The butt is finely checkered and has the usual butt-cap, with a compartment for carrying spare caps. The hammers are gracefully shaped; both have deeply-hooded heads with front slots and both are fitted with sliding safeties to lock them at half-cock. The system of firing the pistol was simple. Once the top pair of barrels had been discharged and the hammers re-cocked, the cluster of barrels was turned clockwise (from the firer's point of view) through 180 degrees on its central spindle, thus bringing the second pair into position. The barrels are held by a simple spring catch in order to prevent any accidental movement.

LANG GAS-SEAL REVOLVER — UK

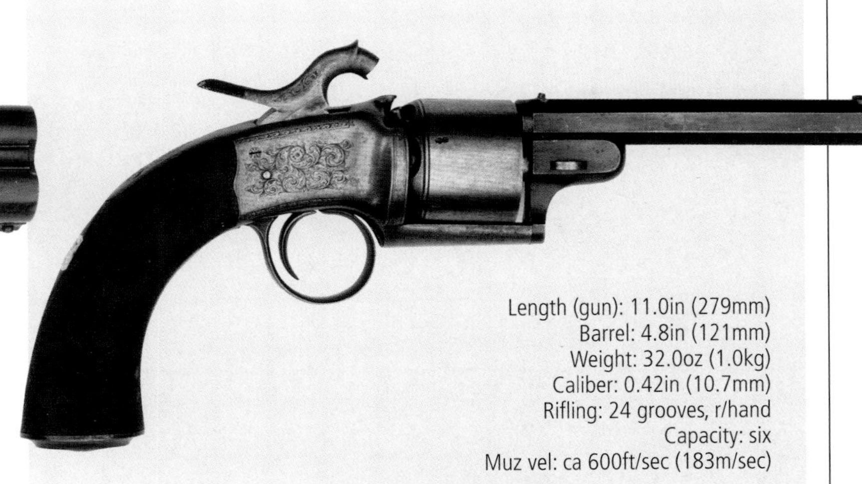

Length (gun): 11.0in (279mm)
Barrel: 4.8in (121mm)
Weight: 32.0oz (1.0kg)
Caliber: 0.42in (10.7mm)
Rifling: 24 grooves, r/hand
Capacity: six
Muz vel: ca 600ft/sec (183m/sec)

This revolver has an octagonal, blued, multi-grooved barrel, bearing the inscription "J LANG 22 COCKSPUR ST, LONDON," and is fitted with laterally adjustable sights, the hammer being offset a little to the right in order to facilitate taking aim. The barrel is keyed to the axis pin and has the usual projection engaging with the lower edge of the frame, which made a good and rigid joint. The cylinder is rebated at the rear, the different diameters being joined by a coned section containing circular depressions for the nipples, which are inclined slightly backwards from the vertical. The frame is of case-hardened iron and is lightly engraved; it has two tangs to hold the finely checkered butt with the usual cap compartment in the base. The hammer, which is without a safety catch, is slightly unusual in that it had only two rearward positions instead of three: the usual first position, which held the nose just clear of the caps, was omitted. Drawing the hammer back to half-cock allowed an internal spring to force the cylinder back sufficiently for the top chamber to clear the barrel cone, while drawing the hammer back to full-cock rotated the cylinder by the necessary amount to bring the next chamber into line. As the trigger fell, a cylindrical metal ram was thrust forward to hold the cylinder securely locked to the barrel at the moment of firing. As in many gas-seal weapons, the chambers were larger in caliber than the bore. This ensured that a ball which loaded easily into the chamber was still a good and gas-tight fit in the barrel, giving a considerable improvement to both the range and velocity of the weapon.

Manton Dueling Pistol — UK

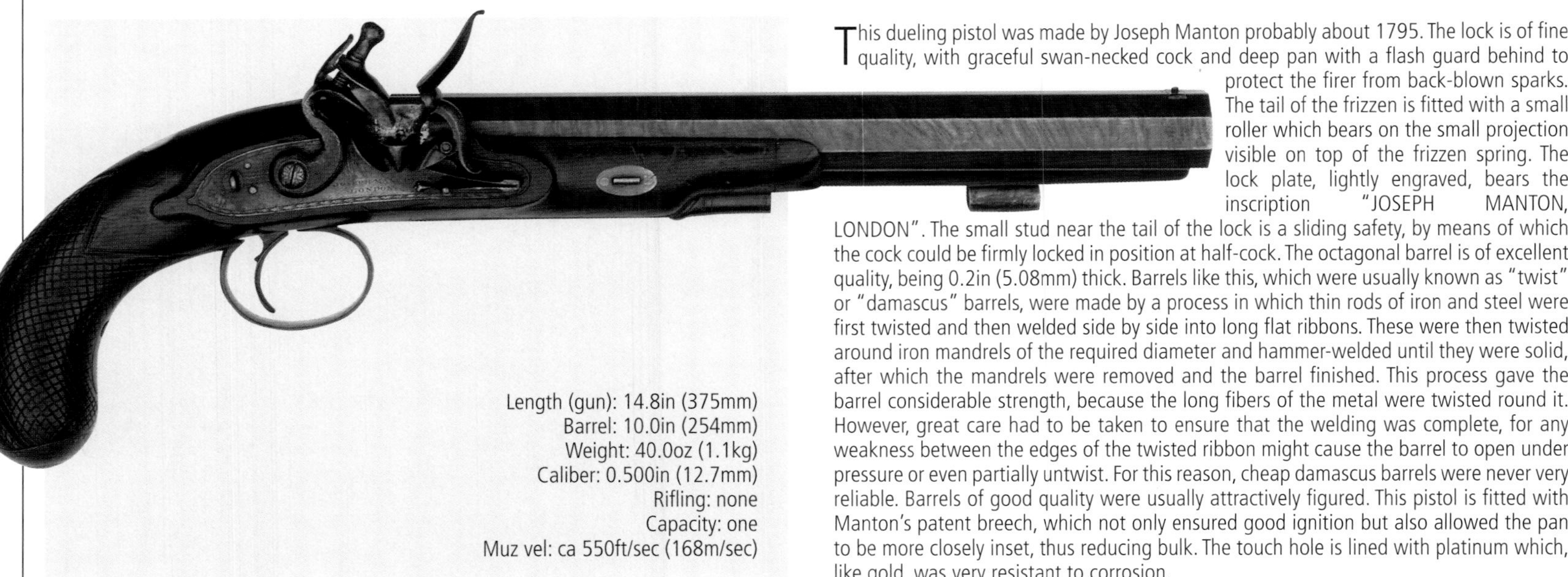

Length (gun): 14.8in (375mm)
Barrel: 10.0in (254mm)
Weight: 40.0oz (1.1kg)
Caliber: 0.500in (12.7mm)
Rifling: none
Capacity: one
Muz vel: ca 550ft/sec (168m/sec)

This dueling pistol was made by Joseph Manton probably about 1795. The lock is of fine quality, with graceful swan-necked cock and deep pan with a flash guard behind to protect the firer from back-blown sparks. The tail of the frizzen is fitted with a small roller which bears on the small projection visible on top of the frizzen spring. The lock plate, lightly engraved, bears the inscription "JOSEPH MANTON, LONDON". The small stud near the tail of the lock is a sliding safety, by means of which the cock could be firmly locked in position at half-cock. The octagonal barrel is of excellent quality, being 0.2in (5.08mm) thick. Barrels like this, which were usually known as "twist" or "damascus" barrels, were made by a process in which thin rods of iron and steel were first twisted and then welded side by side into long flat ribbons. These were then twisted around iron mandrels of the required diameter and hammer-welded until they were solid, after which the mandrels were removed and the barrel finished. This process gave the barrel considerable strength, because the long fibers of the metal were twisted round it. However, great care had to be taken to ensure that the welding was complete, for any weakness between the edges of the twisted ribbon might cause the barrel to open under pressure or even partially untwist. For this reason, cheap damascus barrels were never very reliable. Barrels of good quality were usually attractively figured. This pistol is fitted with Manton's patent breech, which not only ensured good ignition but also allowed the pan to be more closely inset, thus reducing bulk. The touch hole is lined with platinum which, like gold, was very resistant to corrosion.

Manton Percussion Dueling Pistol — UK

Length (gun): 14.8in (375mm)
Barrel: 9.3in (235mm)
Weight: 38.0oz (1.1kg)
Caliber: 0.42in (10.7mm)
Rifling: 30 grooves, r/hand
Capacity: one
Muz vel: ca 600ft/sec (183m/sec)

This pistol was produced by John Manton in about 1823, and has an octagonal twist barrel with unusually thick walls – the top flat being engraved: "JOHN MANTON AND SON, DOVER STREET, LONDON" – and although clearly a dueling pistol it is somewhat unusual in being lightly rifled. This was not generally considered to be a sporting practice in the case of such arms; but it may be that the owner was not too particular in this respect. The barrel is screwed into a breech plug about 0.7in (17.8mm) long, and is fitted with hooks which lock into recesses in the standing breeches. The top flat of the breech plug is inset with rectangular gold plates (each bearing a crown and the words "MANTON, LONDON") and the nipple bolster is fitted with a circular platinum safety plug, intended to blow out if the internal pressure was too high, to prevent the bursting of barrels. The half-stock is of fine walnut with horn tip, the butt being finely checkered to give a secure grip, and the barrel is held to it with a single flat key (and by the hook already described). As the pistol is half-stocked, the lower flat of the barrel is fitted with half ribs, equipped with a single pipe, to hold the ramrod (not shown) which was of ebony with brass tip and ferrule. The trigger-guard has the almost universal pineapple finial, together with a long rear tang let into the butt. This is a beautiful weapon, plain and austere as befitted its role but of unmistakeable quality, and almost certainly extremely accurate at the short ranges at which duels were normally fought.

Memory Holster Pistol — UK

Length (gun): 14.8in (375mm)
Barrel: 8.5in (216mm)
Weight: 32.0oz (0.91kg)
Caliber: 0.62in (15.7mm)
Rifling: none
Capacity: one
Muz vel: ca 500ft/sec (152m/sec)

This fine pistol was made in 1780 by a gunmaker named Memory, who worked in Southwark, London, in the last quarter of the 18th Century. Although he is not generally regarded as having been among the really top-ranked English pistol makers, it will be clear from the illustration that Memory's products were of very high quality and finish. The barrel is of brass, the front two-thirds being round and the breech end octagonal, a most favored style during the period. The breech end is highly ornamented, while the muzzle, although by no means to be described as a blunderbuss, is slightly swamped. The barrel is held to the stocks by a flat key passing through a loop on its underside. In later years it became customary to inset a small plate round these keys, so that they could be tapped out without any risk of bruising the stock. The lock is of typical English type, the plate being beautifully engraved and bearing the name "MEMORY" within a small ornamental scroll. The cock, also decorated, is of swan-necked type, the angle of the edge of the flint to the steel being carefully calculated to ensure the combination of a good shower of hot sparks with the fastest possible opening time for the pan, rapid ignition being an essential requirement for accurate shooting. The pan speed naturally depended also on the frizzen spring; and it will be noted that the frizzen spring on this pistol has a small semicircular projection on its upper surface. When the pan is closed, the tail of the pan cover is forward of the projection and snaps down on the other side, thus helping to accelerate opening time. The stock is of fine walnut and the butt-cap, which has long spurs, is finely chiselled and gilded.

Mortimer Repeating Pistol

UK

The diarist Samuel Pepys recorded seeing a repeater, probably made by John Dafte or Harman Barne(s) of London, in 1664; but although the theory of making such weapons was sound enough at that time, the technical problems of producing accurately fitting parts with crude hand-tools were so considerable that very few were made. By the end of the 18th Century, however, manufacturing techniques had improved considerably and one or two London makers again turned their attention to repeating weapons. Among them was H. W. Mortimer, who produced the arm seen here. This pistol has at its breech-end a horizontally revolving block into which two recesses are cut, one for powder and one for a ball; and there are two corresponding tubular magazines in its butt. In order to load the weapon, it was held muzzle downward and the loading lever was pushed forward. This brought the recesses in the block into line with the magazine, and one ball and one charge were fed into them by gravity. The action of pulling the lever backward caused the block to counter-rotate. As the recess holding the ball passed the breech, the ball rolled in; the recess holding the charge then moved into position behind it to act as a temporary chamber. This second motion of the lever also cocked and primed the arm. Although most ingenious, such arms never became popular, mainly because of the problems of obturation – ie, the escape of burning gases. Any minor discrepancy in fitting the various parts could lead to the explosion of the powder in the magazine – with disastrous results to the firer.

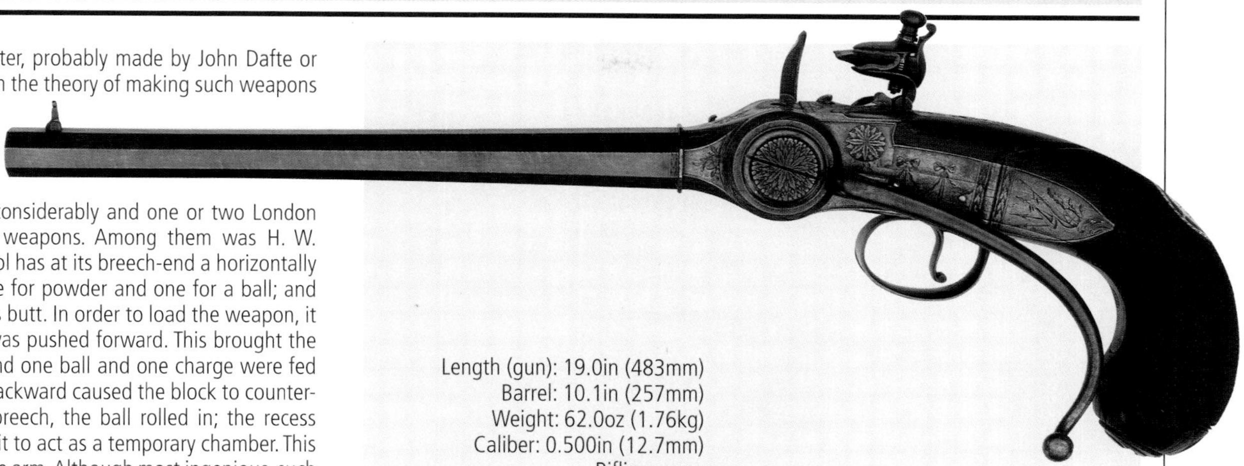

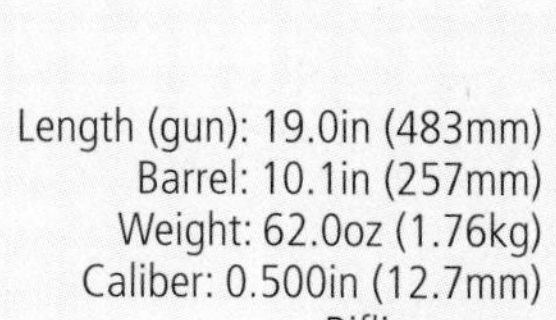

Length (gun): 19.0in (483mm)
Barrel: 10.1in (257mm)
Weight: 62.0oz (1.76kg)
Caliber: 0.500in (12.7mm)
Rifling: none
Capacity: seven
Muz vel: ca 450ft/sec (137m/sec)

Mortimer Dueling Pistol

UK

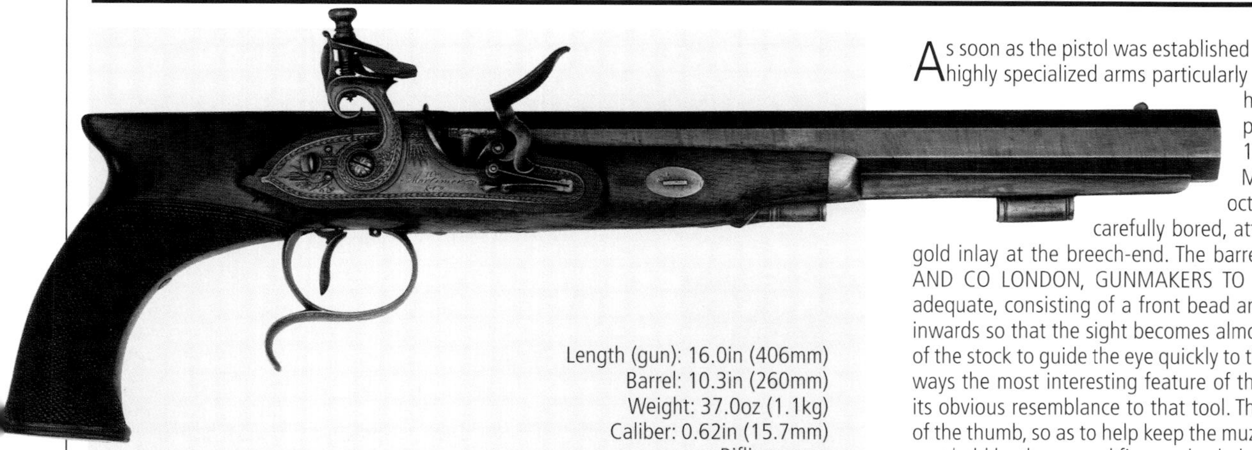

Length (gun): 16.0in (406mm)
Barrel: 10.3in (260mm)
Weight: 37.0oz (1.1kg)
Caliber: 0.62in (15.7mm)
Rifling: none
Capacity: one
Muz vel: ca 550ft/sec (168m/sec)

As soon as the pistol was established as a dueling weapon, gunsmiths began to develop highly specialized arms particularly for dueling, almost invariably in pairs, and usually handsomely cased with a variety of accessories. The pistol seen here was one of a pair made soon after 1800 by the well-known London maker H. W. Mortimer of the highest quality. The heavy, octagonal, damascus twist barrel is extremely carefully bored, attractively figured, and discreetly ornamented with gold inlay at the breech-end. The barrel bears the proud inscription: "H. W. MORTIMER AND CO LONDON, GUNMAKERS TO HIS MAJESTY." The fixed sights are simple but adequate, consisting of a front bead and a deep U-backsight, with top ears which curve inwards so that the sight becomes almost an aperture. A long groove is cut along the top of the stock to guide the eye quickly to the line of sight. The stock is of fine walnut, in many ways the most interesting feature of the weapon, being known as "saw-handled," from its obvious resemblance to that tool. The back spur is designed to fit neatly over the fork of the thumb, so as to help keep the muzzle down. The spur below the trigger-guard, which was held by the second finger, also helped to achieve this important end, as did the heavy barrel. As the pistol is half-stocked, the front part of the barrel has lower ribs along which the ramrod lay (not shown), made of wood with horn tips. Dueling had virtually ended in Britain by 1830, but many fine pairs of pistols survive.

Muley Blunderbuss Pistol

UK

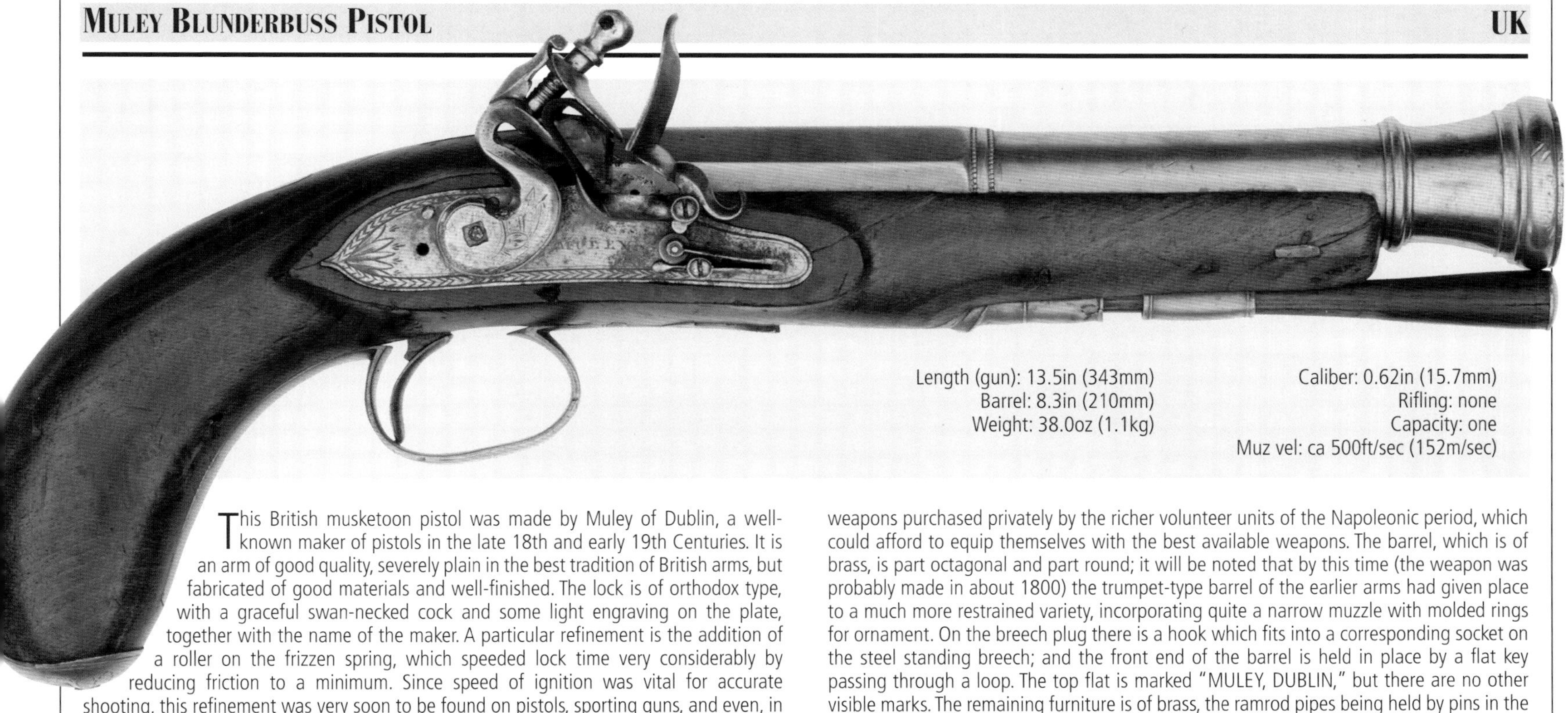

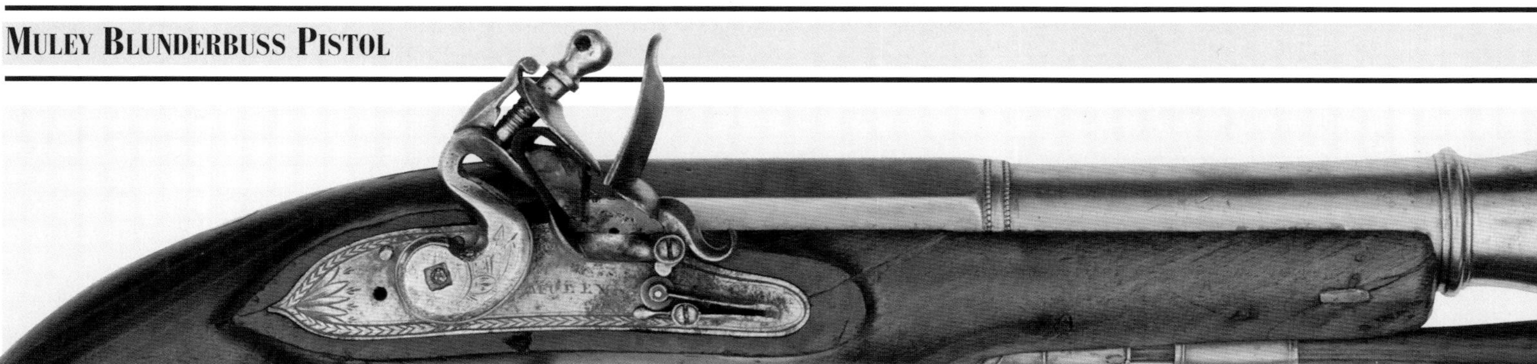

Length (gun): 13.5in (343mm)
Barrel: 8.3in (210mm)
Weight: 38.0oz (1.1kg)
Caliber: 0.62in (15.7mm)
Rifling: none
Capacity: one
Muz vel: ca 500ft/sec (152m/sec)

This British musketoon pistol was made by Muley of Dublin, a well-known maker of pistols in the late 18th and early 19th Centuries. It is an arm of good quality, severely plain in the best tradition of British arms, but fabricated of good materials and well-finished. The lock is of orthodox type, with a graceful swan-necked cock and some light engraving on the plate, together with the name of the maker. A particular refinement is the addition of a roller on the frizzen spring, which speeded lock time very considerably by reducing friction to a minimum. Since speed of ignition was vital for accurate shooting, this refinement was very soon to be found on pistols, sporting guns, and even, in some cases, on military muskets – although in the latter case it was usually limited to those weapons purchased privately by the richer volunteer units of the Napoleonic period, which could afford to equip themselves with the best available weapons. The barrel, which is of brass, is part octagonal and part round; it will be noted that by this time (the weapon was probably made in about 1800) the trumpet-type barrel of the earlier arms had given place to a much more restrained variety, incorporating quite a narrow muzzle with molded rings for ornament. On the breech plug there is a hook which fits into a corresponding socket on the steel standing breech; and the front end of the barrel is held in place by a flat key passing through a loop. The top flat is marked "MULEY, DUBLIN," but there are no other visible marks. The remaining furniture is of brass, the ramrod pipes being held by pins in the usual way. The ramrod (which may not be the original one) is of wood with a brass tip.

Murdoch Scottish All-Steel Pistol — UK

Length (gun): 12.0in (305mm)
Barrel: 7.4in (188mm)
Weight: 22.0oz (0.62kg)
Caliber: 0.556in (14.1mm)
Rifling: none
Capacity: one
Muz vel: ca 500ft/sec (152m/sec)

This pistol was made about 1770 by Murdoch of Doune, a small town near Stirling, Scotland, which was a noted center for manufacture of pistols. It has a round steel barrel, with slight flares at the muzzle, and an elegant lock. The butt terminates in the incurved horns which gave the type its particular name. The small knob between the horn is the handle of a pricker, which could be unscrewed from the butt and used to remove fouling from the touch hole. The trigger is of the universal button type (which changed slightly in shape but never in principle) and there is no trigger-guard, a characteristic which may also be regarded as universal in the type. Almost every part of the weapon is covered with fine engraving. When the Royal Highland Regiment was first raised in the middle of the 18th Century, every one of its soldiers carried a musket, bayonet, broad-sword, and Highland pistol, the latter being worn in an arrangement of straps, not unlike a modern shoulder holster, under the left arm. It was soon found, however, that the pistol was of no military value to an infantryman, so these arms became purely ornamental. Frugal colonels, anxious to save money, then bought cheap Birmingham-made versions, usually from the maker Isaac Bissell, until pistols ceased to be worn by the rank and file in 1776. Although officers continued to carry pistols, this marked the beginning of the decline of the Highland pistol, except as an item of ornament. The weapons experienced a brief resurgence in the first half of the 19th Century, when Scotland had a period of romantic popularity.

Parker Field Gas-Seal Revolver — UK

Length (gun): 12.5in (317mm)
Barrel: 6.0in (152mm)
Weight: 38.0oz (1.1kg)
Caliber: 0.42in (10.7mm)
Rifling: 24 grooves, r/hand
Capacity: six
Muz vel: ca 600ft/sec (183m/sec)

This gas-seal revolver bears the maker's inscription of "PARKER FIELD AND SONS, 233 HIGH HOLBORN, LONDON," a firm well known for the production of weapons of this type. As might be expected, it is a very well-made and finished arm, the usual multi-grooved, blued barrel firmly wedged to the lower edge of the frame and fitted with laterally adjustable sights. The case-hardened cylinder is, however, fluted, giving the weapon a distinctive appearance, and there are flat shields between the nipples to eliminate the risk of multiple discharge. The hammer had the customary three rearward positions, with a safety which locked it securely in the first; the system of rotation and reciprocation was the same as that of the Beattie revolver. The major point of interest in this arm is the existence of a compound rammer below the barrel: when the long arm was pulled down, a horizontal rammer housed in the cylinder below the axis key exerted powerful pressure on the bullet and ensured that it was seated very securely in the chamber. This refinement went some way toward making the application of the gas-seal principle unnecessary.

Pinches Turn-Over Pistol — UK

Length (gun): 5.9in (150mm)
Barrel: 1.6in (41mm)
Weight: 11.0oz (1.31kg)
Caliber: 0.31in (8mm)
Rifling: none
Capacity: two
Muz vel: ca 450ft/sec

This is a small, pocket percussion pistol, sometimes known as an "over-and-under" because of the relative position of its barrels. It is of good quality and was made by Pinches of London in about 1830. The barrels are of screw-off type: their muzzles have deep, star-shaped indentations to take a key of similar section, so that they could be removed. Such indentations are often found on weapons of this kind, and may give an initial but quite erroneous impression that they are rifled. The barrels are screwed into a standing breech and, like those of many pocket pistols, are chambered. The pistol has a single hammer with a pop-out trigger and a strongly made sliding safety, the front end of which engaged over a projection on the back of the hammer when the latter was set at half-cock. The top barrel was fired first; the pistol was then placed at half-cock and the barrels rotated manually through 180 degrees so as to bring the second barrel uppermost. The standing breech was provided with a simple spring device to prevent any accidental rotation. The hook-shaped device in front of the trigger was intended to ensure that the cap did not slip off the lower nipple when the pistol was drawn. The finely checkered, bag-shaped butt has a butt-cap, apparently made of German silver; but there is no cap compartment within it. This pistol is an elegant little weapon: the arrangement of the barrels makes it flat and compact, and thus most suitable to be carried inconspicuously in a waistcoat pocket, or even in a lady's bag or muff – a useful companion, in fact, for any traveler in the lawless world of a century and a half ago, without effective police.

Podsenkowsky MCEM 2 Pistol UK

Length (gun): 14.0in (356mm)
Barrel: 9.0in (229mm)
Weight: 88.0oz (2.5kg)
Caliber: 0.35in (9mm)
Rifling: 6 grooves, r/hand
Capacity: 18
Muz vel: 1,200ft/sec (366m/sec)

Once World War II had ended, the British Government decided that, although the cheap, mass-produced Sten gun (qv) had given good service, something better was needed for the post-war Army. All potential successors were given the overall title of Machine Carbine Experimental Model (MCEM) with a serial number to distinguish them from each other. The MCEM No 1 was the work of H. J. Turpin, who had been closely concerned with the original Sten, but the No 2, which is illustrated here, was designed by a Polish officer, Lieutenant Podsenkowsky, who, like thousands of his compatriots, had offered his services to Great Britain. The weapon illustrated was less than 15.0in (380mm) long and its magazine fitted into the butt, making it more a pistol than a sub-machinegun. The bolt was made to what was then an advanced design and consisted of a half-cylinder 8.5in (216mm) long; the striker was at the rear, so that at the moment of firing almost the entire barrel was inside the bolt. There was no cocking handle: the bolt was drawn to the rear by hooking a finger through a slot above the muzzle. Because of the weapon's light weight and rate of fire, vibration was considerable, and eventually a light, rigid-canvas butt was provided; this finally converted it to a true sub-machinegun. Even so, it was never adopted for service use.

Pryse 0.577in (Bland-Pryse) Revolver UK

Length (gun): 11.5in (292mm)
Barrel: 6.3in (160mm)
Weight: 46.0oz (1.3kg)
Caliber: 0.577in (14.6mm)
Rifling: 5 grooves, r/hand
Capacity: six
Muz vel: ca 650ft/sec (198m/sec)

In 1877, Webley began to make a new type of break-open revolver patented by C. Pryse. However, since other makers also appear to have produced similar arms, Webley was clearly not the only patentee. Although the specimen shown here bears no identification marks of any kind, there is every reason to suppose that it is indeed an arm marketed by a firm named Bland. The major point of interest is its massive 0.577in (14.6mm) caliber, a true "man-stopping" round, which would have halted any assailant in mid-stride. Indeed, the size and weight of the revolver, coupled to the very hefty recoil, must have posed a considerable challenge to the shooter and it is worth noting that the marginally smaller, modern 0.5in (12.7mm) Browning round is considered a heavyweight when fired from a rifle. The 0.577in round was adopted as the British Army's rifle round in the late 1860s and the War Office then approved a revolver round of the same caliber. Webley produced their No 1 Revolver (qv), while Bland-Pryse produced this as a competitor.

Pryse 0.455in Service Revolver (Unknown Maker) UK

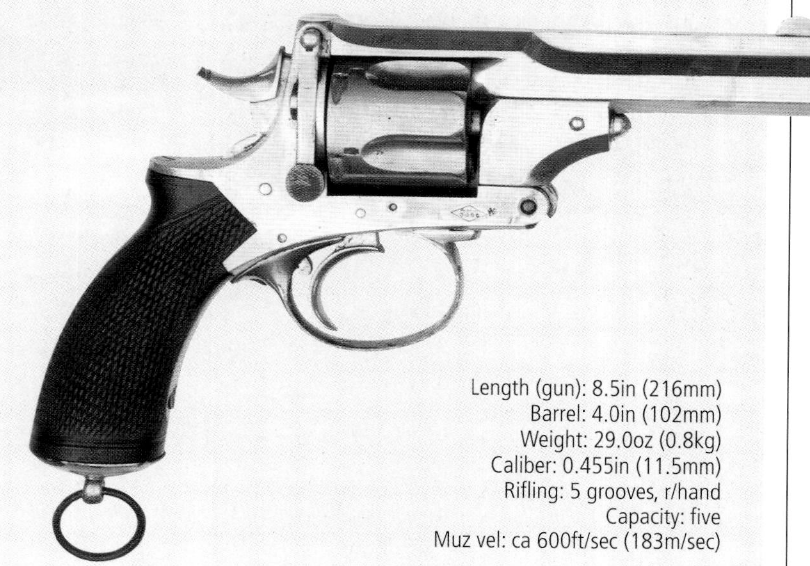

Length (gun): 8.5in (216mm)
Barrel: 4.0in (102mm)
Weight: 29.0oz (0.8kg)
Caliber: 0.455in (11.5mm)
Rifling: 5 grooves, r/hand
Capacity: five
Muz vel: ca 600ft/sec (183m/sec)

Another variation on the Pryse theme is this British Army revolver, with Birmingham proof marks. The right side of the frame is marked "Patent 3096" and the left bears the legend "First Quality." Pryse revolvers were popular for many years in the British Army and one of the greatest generals of the late Victorian era, Field Marshal Lord Roberts of Kandahar, is known to have carried one made by Thomas Horley of Doncaster. One of numerous good ideas in the gun was that the end of the topstrap fitted into a slot in the top of the standing breech, where it was secured by a cylindrical lug entering from either side. This was a strong and successful feature, although, curiously, it was not mentioned in the patent document. The characteristic feature of Pryse revolvers is that they are of break-open type, with a star-shaped ejector at the rear of the cylinder. The action of opening the revolver to the full brought this automatically into play, driving it backwards with some force and thus throwing out the empty cases. After completing this action, it snapped back into position under the pressure of a spring.

Pryse 0.45in Constabulary Revolver (Rigby-Pryse) UK

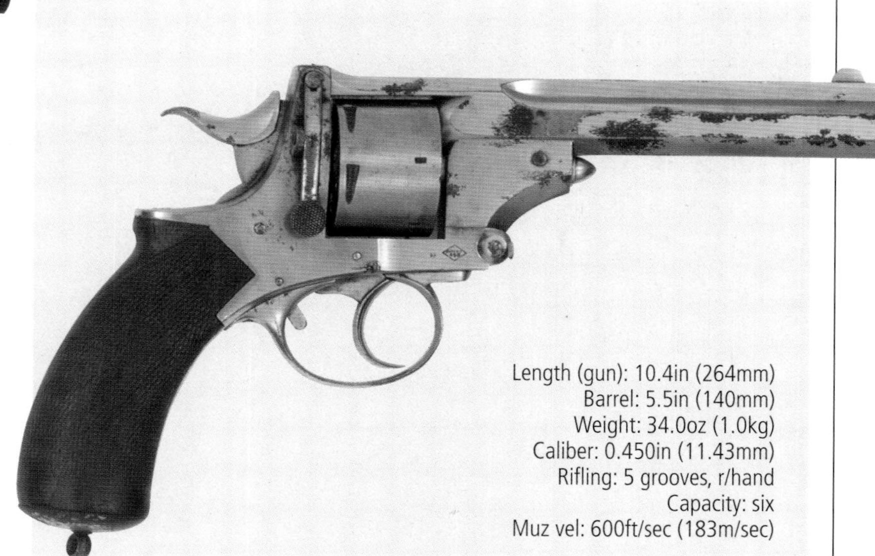

Length (gun): 10.4in (264mm)
Barrel: 5.5in (140mm)
Weight: 34.0oz (1.0kg)
Caliber: 0.450in (11.43mm)
Rifling: 5 grooves, r/hand
Capacity: six
Muz vel: 600ft/sec (183m/sec)

Yet another version of the Pryse revolver, this was intended for police use. One feature of the Pryse design not yet covered is that it had a "rebounding hammer." In this system, after a shot has been fired, the hammer is taken back about 0.125in (3.2mm) to half-cock, where it is locked rigidly and even a violent blow directly upon it will not drive it forward, thus greatly reducing the risk of an accidental discharge.

RIGBY OVERCOAT POCKET PISTOL UK

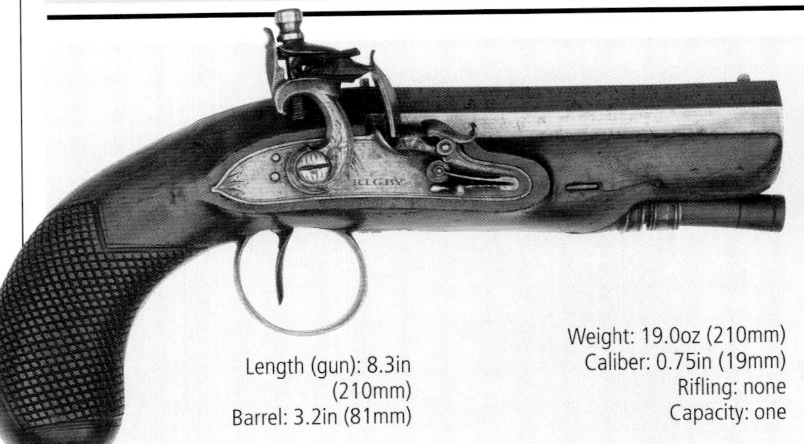

Length (gun): 8.3in (210mm)
Barrel: 3.2in (81mm)
Weight: 19.0oz (210mm)
Caliber: 0.75in (19mm)
Rifling: none
Capacity: one

Flintlock pistols tended to fall into two broad categories: belt or holster pistols, which were bulky and were often carried on the front arch of a saddle; and pocket pistols. The latter were again often sub-divided into very small waistcoat-pocket arms, and heavier types designed to be carried conveniently by a traveler in his overcoat pocket. In the early years of the 19th Century, many English highways – particularly, perhaps, those in the vicinity of London – were much troubled by footpads and highwaymen; so anyone who carried valuables usually provided himself with some means of self-protection. Stage coaches always had armed guards, but many individuals also liked to have a personal weapon as well, and as the sword had gone out of fashion this was usually a pistol. The example shown here is by John Rigby of Dublin, Ireland, and was probably made in the first quarter of the 19th Century. Like most British arms of the period, it is severely plain, with no more than a trifle of engraving on cock and trigger guard – but well-made arms had little need of ornament to point up their quality. It has a horn-tipped, wooden ramrod and is fully stocked, with a neatly checkered butt. The elegant lock is of the type often found on dueling pistols. Perhaps its main characteristic is its stubby, octagonal twist barrel, the yawning muzzle of which might prove a deterrent to would-be robbers. It fired a lead ball of 12-bore – ie, 12 bullets aggregated one pound (0.45kg) of lead – and would have been a most formidable arm at close quarters. It is fitted with both foresight and backsight; but these would hardly have been necessary at the range at which it was most likely to be used.

SHIELD 0.357IN MAGNUM LONG-RANGE FREE PISTOL UK

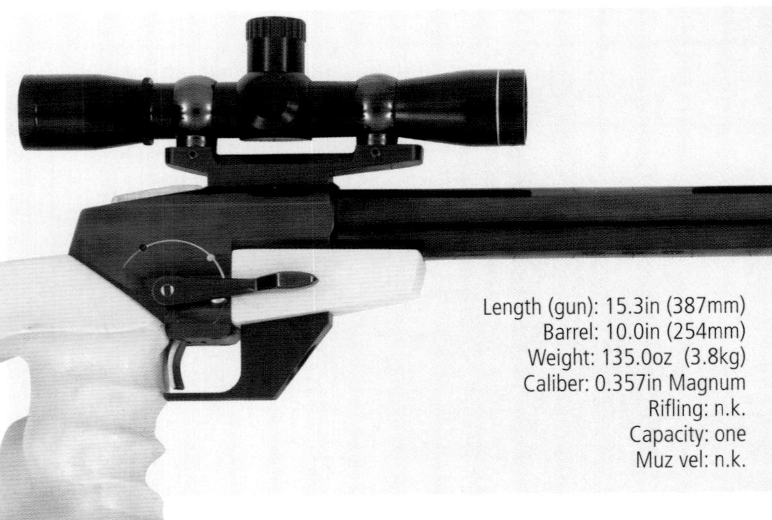

Length (gun): 15.3in (387mm)
Barrel: 10.0in (254mm)
Weight: 135.0oz (3.8kg)
Caliber: 0.357in Magnum
Rifling: n.k.
Capacity: one
Muz vel: n.k.

This unusual looking pistol was designed specifically for the International Long-Range Pistol Shooter's Association (ILRPSA) Free Pistol "B" competition, and was designed and built by Andy Wooldridge of the British company, Shield Gunmakers. The pistol is chambered for 0.357in Magnum, loaded to maximum allowable length-overall with 180-grain Speer 0.358 rifle bullets ahead of 16.5 grains of H4227 with CCI Bench rest primers. It will hold a 4.5in (114mm) group at 219yd (200m). It is sidelever operated and is fired by an internal hammer operating over a 47-degree arc. The trigger engages a free-floating sear, and is adjustable between 16.0-32.0oz (0.45-0.9kg) let-off weight, but the rules admit any safe trigger weight, and most shooters seem to prefer releases in the region of 16.0oz (0.45kg). A maximum barrel length (measured from the breech face to muzzle) of 12.0in (305mm) is permitted, although this pistol comes in at 10.0in (254mm). The ILRSPA rules lay down that the maximum permitted grip circumference is 10.0in rule, measured with a wire loop and that only the butt of the pistol may contact the rest; as a result all British Long-Range pistols such as this have a perfectly flat butt of precisely 10in circumference. Sights are Leopold M8 4x scope.

SHIELD MODIFIED 0.357IN RUGER BLACKHAWK TARGET REVOLVER UK

Length (gun): 15.0in (380mm)
Barrel: 9.0in (230mm)
Weight: 88.0oz (2.5kg)
Caliber: 0.357in (9.1mm)
Rifling: n.k.
Capacity: six
Muz vel: n.k.

This weapon is designed for the All Comers category competition which is shot in three stages, starting at 109yd (100m) where two sets of five shots are shot in thirty seconds, followed by two identical stages at 219yd (200m) and 328yd (300m), each consisting of 12 shots in 12 minutes, with two sighters permitted prior to each stage. The gun is a Ruger Blackhawk (qv), rechambered from 0.30in M1 carbine and re-barreled with a Douglas premium 1.25in (3.2cm) outside diameter blank, machined square, of 0.357in (9.1mm) bore diameter with a 1-in-10 twist. Specialization extends to the ammunition, as well, with slightly different rounds for each of the three ranges. The foresight is a 0.14in (3.6mm) blade in a Parker-Hale tunnel, with a custom adapter block and extended sunshade. The Beeman backsight is mounted on a 3.5in (88.9mm) extension, with a custom backplate and 3.32in x 0.085in (84.3 x 2.2mm) notch.

SHIELD 7.62MM LONG-RANGE FREE PISTOL UK

Length (gun): 20.3in (54mm)
Barrel: 12.0in (30.5mm)
Weight: 165.0oz (4.7kg)
Caliber: 7.62mm
Rifling: n.k.
Capacity: one
Muz vel: n.k.

This dramatic looking pistol was designed for ILRSPA Free Pistol "A" competition shooting. Very unusually for a pistol, it has a Mauser bolt action and is chambered to fire the NATO 7.62mm round. Sights are Burns 7x telescope in custom mount.

SHIELD 0.45IN NEW SERVICE LONG-RANGE FREE PISTOL UK

This curious weapon started life as a Colt New Service revolver (qv), which the builder found discarded in a bin in a gunsmith's workshop. The builder used this as the basis of a weapon designed to produce a weapon for the ILRSPA "Pocket Pistol" competition which calls for two sighters followed by two sets of five shots in 30 seconds at 109yd (100m). It has a barrel 3.6in (90mm) long with a grip of maximum 10.0in (254mm) circumference, with no wrist support. The gun operates on selective double-action and the retracting thumb latch on the left of the frame frees the crane-mounted cylinder to swing out for loading or unloading. The 0.45in (11.4mm) barrel is machined from a Douglas blank and has 1-in-16in (406mm) rifling, with its massive underlug giving some forward inertia to the resist recoil, but, it has to be said, more in the interest of recovery than of comfort. In the case of the sights the rules state that they may not overhang either the muzzle or the wrist-joint and the pistol complies – just – as the picture shows. The foresight is a 0.14in (3.6mm) post in a short Parker-Hale tunnel, with a custom adapter block, while the Beeman backsight is mounted on a short extension, with a custom backplate and 1.2in (30.5mm) notch.

Length (gun): 9.5in (241mm)
Barrel: 3.6in (90mm)
Weight: 71.0oz (2.0kg)
Caliber: 0.45in (11.43mm)
Rifling: n.k.
Capacity: 6-round box magazine
Muz vel: n.k.

Sterling 9mm Mk VII Pistol — UK

Length (gun): 14.8in (375mm)
Barrel: 4.0in (102mm)
Weight: 88.0oz (2.5kg)
Caliber: 9mm
Rifling: 6 grooves, r/hand
Capacity: 10-round box magazine (see text)
Muz vel: 984ft/sec (300m/sec)

This weapon was developed from the Sterling submachine gun (qv), the essential differences being a much shorter barrel (4.0in/102mm compared to 7.8in/198mm) and the lack of a butt-stock. The Mk VII fired the 9mm Parabellum round and, as issued, it had a 10-round magazine, although the housing accepted the usual 20- and 34-round magazines as well. The Mk VII fired from a closed bolt and was recoil operated. The Mk VII had many shortcomings as a pistol and offered no advantages over the submachine gun version. The sights are the same as on the submachine gun, consisting of a square post foresight and a flip-over aperture backsight.

Thomas Revolver — UK

Length (gun): 10.8in (273mm)
Barrel: 5.8in (146mm)
Weight: 31.0oz (0.9kg)
Caliber: 0.45in (11.43mm)
Rifling: 7 grooves, l/hand
Capacity: five
Muz vel: ca 600ft/sec (183m/sec)

Loading early cartridge revolvers was a slow process and it was not long before people started trying to improve it. In 1869 J. Thomas, a Birmingham gunmaker, patented this revolver. The weapon is of cast steel with a heavy octagonal barrel, its main features being its very long cylinder aperture and the knob beneath its barrel (lower photo). The revolver was loaded in the normal way, through the loading gate behind the right-hand end of the cylinder, and it discharged by means of its double-action lock. The real point of interest is the system by which the empty cases were ejected. Pressure on the end of a small spring on the front of the frame released the barrel catch and allowed the barrel to be rotated until the knob (which was there simply to give a firm hold to a hot or oily hand) was uppermost (upper photo). Then the barrel was drawn forward, taking the cylinder with it to the front of the aperture. A star-shaped extractor was attached to the standing breech, which held the cases firmly by their rims until they were fully out of the chambers. Then they were thrown clear by a flick of the wrist, the barrel and cylinder were turned back, and the revolver was reloaded in the usual way. There is also a flange on the barrel which worked in a slot on the frame. This flange was set at a slight angle to the circumference of the barrel: when the latter was turned it exerted a powerful camming action and drew the cylinder very slightly forward, thus loosening the tightest of cases. The system was effective but was soon overtaken by better ones: thus, revolvers on this system were made in relatively small numbers and are now rare.

Tower Sea Service Pistol — UK

This weapon is broadly representative of British martial pistols in the period 1740-1840. It was made in about 1790 and differs from earlier models chiefly in the fact that it has a somewhat shorter barrel and lacks the long ears on the butt-cap. It is of very plain and robust construction, fully stocked in walnut with a very heavy cast brass butt-cap which would have been more than capable of cracking a skull – a use to which it may occasionally have been put in the days when hand-to-hand fighting was a common feature of warfare. The lock-plate is of the usual type and bears a crown with "GR" beneath it and the word "TOWER" across the tail. This indicates that the weapon was assembled in the great armory at the Tower of London; although its parts would almost certainly have been manufactured elsewhere by various government contractors. The small crown and arrow below the pan is a lock-viewer's mark. The cock is of the ring-necked type, popular in military weapons because it added greatly to the strength of what had formerly been their most fragile part. The bottom end of the screw holding the top jaw can be seen protruding into the aperture. The barrel, which is of course smoothbored, and is without sights of any kind, also bears proof and view marks at the breech end. The ramrod (not shown) was of plain steel with the usual slightly domed head. The weapon is also equipped with a belt-hook, which consists basically of a flat spring, the rear end of which is screwed firmly through the brass side-plate and into the stock, the spring itself lying along the stock.

Length (gun): 16.3in (413mm)
Barrel: 8.0in (203mm)
Weight: 49.0oz (1.39kg)
Caliber: 0.58in (14.7mm)
Rifling: none
Capacity: one
Muz vel: ca 500ft/sec (152m/sec)

TOWER PERCUSSION PISTOL CONVERSION UK

Length (gun): 15.0in (381mm)
Barrel: 9.0in (229mm)
Weight: 36.0oz (1.1kg)
Caliber: 0.700in (17.8mm)
Rifling: none
Capacity: one
Muz vel: ca 500ft/sec (152m/sec)

The weapon seen here was made, or at least assembled, at the Tower of London in about 1796, for use by the Light Dragoons. It is in rather poor condition, but a good example of one of the methods used in the early 19th Century to convert flintlock arms to the new percussion system. The advantages of the new system were considerable: it made no difference to accuracy and very little to power, but it gave reliable ignition, particularly in bad weather when there was little or no chance of persuading a flintlock to produce a spark – and even less of damp priming actually igniting. It also made the arm less bulky by doing away with the relatively clumsy cock and pan. The method used in the case of the pistol shown here was simple. A hollow metal tube, closed at one end, was screwed into the touch hole. This tube, usually known as the drum, was threaded on its upper side to receive a screw-in percussion nipple on to which the cap fitted. The old flint cock was replaced by a simple hooded hammer, and the conversion was then complete. The pan and frizzen were, of course, removed: the plugged screw holes are clearly visible on the lock-plate. The simplicity of this method made it both quick and cheap and it was very widely used by civilian gunsmiths. In general, however, it was not employed in military conversions, where the favored method was to weld or braze a nipple lump into the required position and then drill it for a military nipple – unless, indeed, the whole barrel was replaced. The new nipple lumps were usually shaped in such a way as to fit into the hollow left by the pan.

TOWER CAVALRY PISTOL 1720 UK

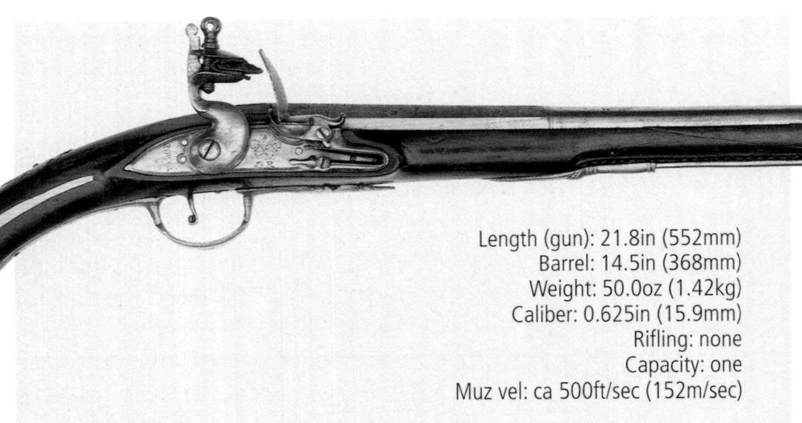

Length (gun): 21.8in (552mm)
Barrel: 14.5in (368mm)
Weight: 50.0oz (1.42kg)
Caliber: 0.625in (15.9mm)
Rifling: none
Capacity: one
Muz vel: ca 500ft/sec (152m/sec)

The weapon seen here is a pistol of the type carried by British heavy cavalry regiments. Although it is not dated, the cypher "GR" indicates that it must have been made after the death of Queen Anne in 1714; and its general style – notably its length; the back-curled tip of the trigger; and the long ears on the brass butt-cap – indicates that it was probably made very soon afterwards, perhaps in about 1720. The lock, with its swan-necked cock, is of typical Tower type, and it will be noted that the tail of the frizzen rests upon a very different type of spring from those found on many other cannon-barreled weapons. Just over one-third of the breech-end of the barrel is octagonal, such a configuration then being considered likely to produce a breech more robust than a cylindrical one. The caliber of the weapon means that it could fire spherical lead balls weighing about 0.8oz (23gm) each: this, in conjunction with its long barrel, which allowed a fair-sized charge to be consumed before the ball was clear, gave it a reasonable initial velocity. Cavalrymen then wore heavy clothing and sometimes even a light breast-plate, so that a fair degree of penetrative power was desirable. A loose-fitting bullet bouncing down a smooth-bored barrel would, of course, lose both its velocity and accuracy very quickly – but that factor was not considered to be of much importance: the principal arm of the cavalryman was the sword, and the pistol was usually only resorted to in a mêlée, when the first impact of a charge had been dissipated.

TOWER CAVALRY PISTOL 1842 UK

Length (gun): 15.5in (394mm)
Barrel: 9.0in (229mm)
Weight: 52.0oz (1.5kg)
Caliber: 0.75in (19mm)
Rifling: none
Capacity: one
Muz vel: ca 500ft/sec (152m/sec)

By 1838 the pistol had been abolished as a general issue to British cavalry regiments. There were, however, certain exceptions: Lancer regiments were allowed to retain one pistol per trooper, and all sergeant-majors and trumpeters also continued to be armed with them. The weapon illustrated is the Model 1842, designed by George Lovell who was then Inspector of Small Arms and well known for his work on percussion weapons. Lovell was a great believer in the virtues of strength and simplicity in military arms, and he also introduced a common caliber to facilitate the supply of ammunition in the field. This is a very solid, robust arm with a rather short butt, which detracts somewhat from its general appearance. It has a smooth-bored barrel of full musket bore, held on the stock by a long screw and one flat key. Its swivel ramrod is retained by a combined nose-cap and pipe of cast brass. The lock is unusually large, being of the standard type used in the Pattern 1842 musket, and is held in position by two screws, the heads of which rest on small brass cups. The full stock is walnut; the butt-cap and trigger-guard are brass. Instead of the usual ring in the butt, a steel sling swivel is screwed into the front of the trigger-guard.

TOWER SEA SERVICE PERCUSSION PISTOL UK

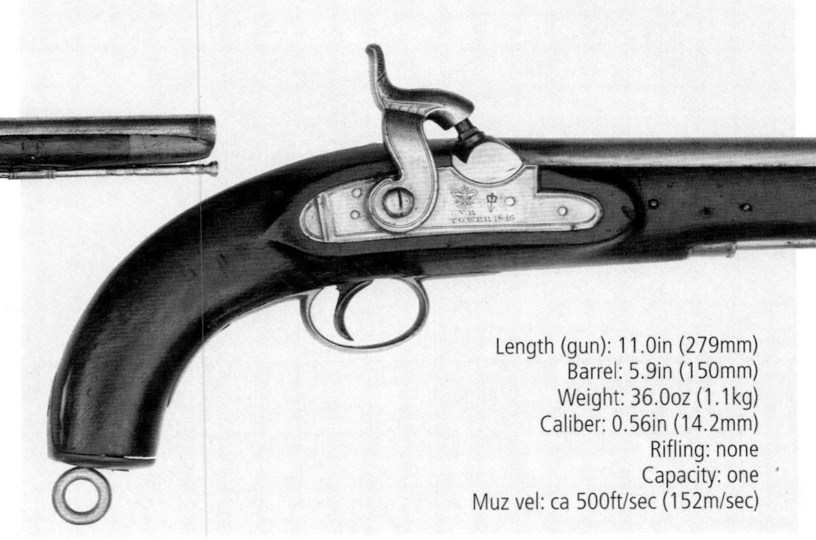

Length (gun): 11.0in (279mm)
Barrel: 5.9in (150mm)
Weight: 36.0oz (1.1kg)
Caliber: 0.56in (14.2mm)
Rifling: none
Capacity: one
Muz vel: ca 500ft/sec (152m/sec)

This is another of the new range of percussion pistols produced by George Lovell in 1842. It has a smooth-bored barrel profusely marked with proof and inspection stamps and, being a sea-service arm, is of smaller caliber than musket-bore. The barrel, which has no sights, is held to the butt by a long screw and a single pin passing through a loop about 3in (76mm) from the muzzle. Like many of the new percussion pistols, this one was made up from the large stocks of flintlock parts remaining in store. This practice, although highly desirable from the point of view of the Treasury, imposed some limitations on design. The fact that this arm is a conversion is obvious from the shape of the upper edge of the lockplate: it has an arc-shaped depression, originally intended for the pan but now filled by the nipple lump, which appears to have been welded on to an original flintlock barrel. The hammer is of basic Lovell type, although the neck is flat rather than rounded. The swivel ramrod is held in a single tail-pipe. The butt-cap and trigger-guard are of cast brass, the former having a steel lanyard ring. As this arm was for naval and coastguard use, it is fitted with a long belt-hook, screwed to the left-hand side of the stock. Thus it could be carried ready for use on the cutlass belt, leaving both hands free. This was of considerable advantage to men scrambling about on pitching vessels.

Tranter Revolver, First Model

UK

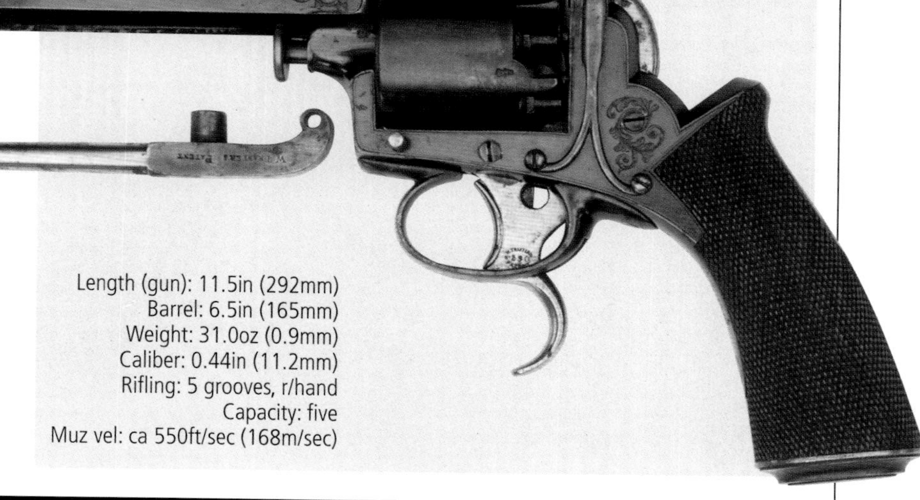

William Tranter was a Birmingham gunmaker of the highest repute, who realized that although self-cocking revolvers were excellent for fast shooting, their heavy trigger pull had an adverse effect on accuracy beyond point-blank range. He therefore set to work on a double-action lock and by 1853 had patented the weapon seen here – thus forestalling Beaumont. Pressure on the lower trigger (which is, in effect, a cocking lever) cocked the combless hammer; a very light pressure on the upper trigger was then sufficient to fire the shot. When speed was more important than accuracy, both triggers were pulled together, thus giving the fast shooting needed in a close-quarter mêlée. Tranter's revolvers were all fitted with rammers, and it is by the variations in these that the different models are identified. However, the numbering of the models does not necessarily relate to the strict chronological order of their appearance. The weapon seen here is the first model; it is equipped with a detachable rammer, an example of which is shown below the arm. In order to use the rammer, it was necessary to put the ring on its end over a peg (visible) on the bottom of the frame and then raise the lever so that the ram bore on the bullet and forced it into the chamber. Round the base of each bullet was a cannelure, or groove, which contained a bees-wax mixture: the expansion of the bullet on firing forced bees-wax out into the bore, helping to reduce hard fouling and facilitating cleaning.

Length (gun): 11.5in (292mm)
Barrel: 6.5in (165mm)
Weight: 31.0oz (0.9mm)
Caliber: 0.44in (11.2mm)
Rifling: 5 grooves, r/hand
Capacity: five
Muz vel: ca 550ft/sec (168m/sec)

Tranter Revolver, Second Model

UK

Tranter's revolvers are usually classified by type of rammer. The rammer on the second model, seen here, represented a compromise: it was so designed that it could be easily enough removed by aligning the recess on its ring with the pin protruding from its anchor peg, on the frame, and lifting it off. On the other hand, the fit was so good that the rammer could be left in position on the revolver without any risk of it falling off. In order to carry the loaded revolver in safety, it was, of course, necessary to keep the nose of the hammer clear of the caps on the nipples – and since the system precluded any use of the normal half-cock, some other device was needed. Tranter's solution was most ingenious: it consisted of a spring in the shape of an inverted Y, which can be seen here on the left-hand side of the frame, behind the cylinder. When the hammer was slightly raised, a stud on the inside of the upper arm was interposed between the hammer and the nipples; it remained in position until pressure on the lower trigger brought the hammer back to full-cock, when it automatically disengaged. This was a simple and effective device which, unlike the similar safety on the Adams, called for no conscious effort on the part of the firer to remove it before beginning to shoot – and it was much preferred to the detachable version. Tranter's revolvers soon became popular with service officers, because they were both mechanically sound and well made. It is true that there were initially some criticisms of Tranter's system; but in practice it proved both fast and simple in operation, and thus remained in service for a long time.

Length (gun): 11.5in (292mm)
Barrel: 6.5in (165mm)
Weight: 29.0oz (0.8kg)
Caliber: 0.44in (11.2mm)
Rifling: 5 grooves, r/hand
Capacity: five
Muz vel: ca 550ft/sec (168m/sec)

Tranter Revolver, Third Model

UK

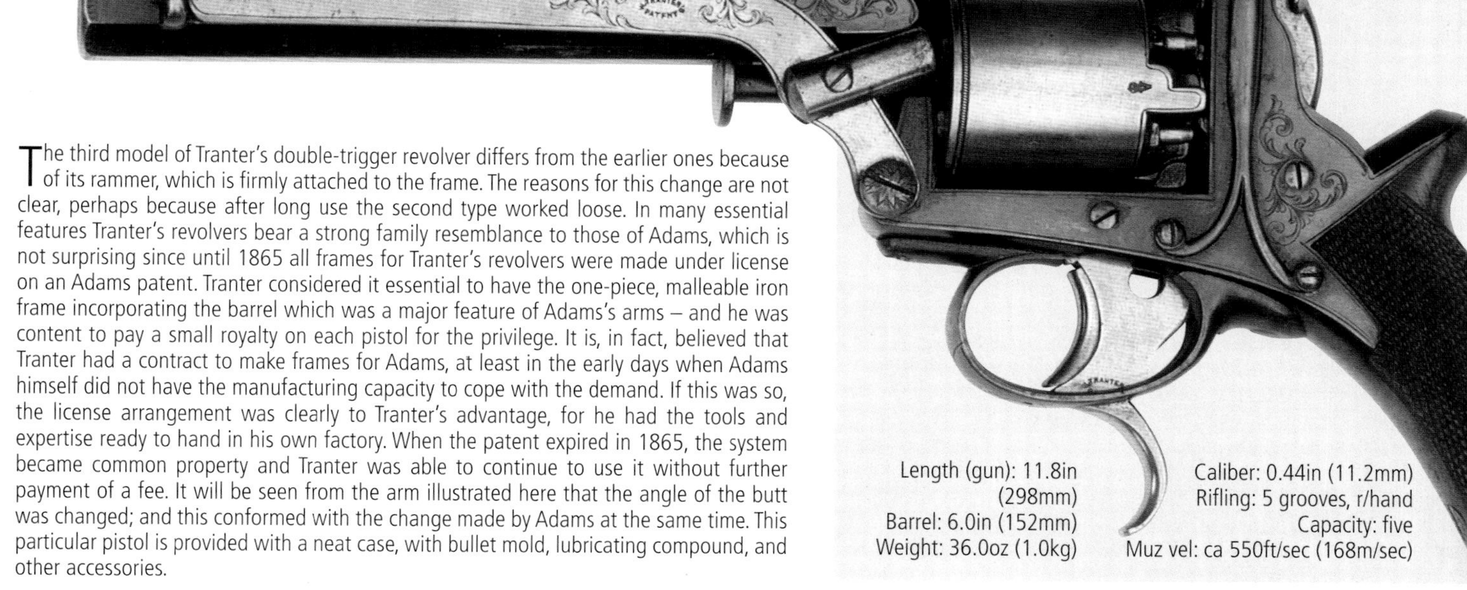

The third model of Tranter's double-trigger revolver differs from the earlier ones because of its rammer, which is firmly attached to the frame. The reasons for this change are not clear, perhaps because after long use the second type worked loose. In many essential features Tranter's revolvers bear a strong family resemblance to those of Adams, which is not surprising since until 1865 all frames for Tranter's revolvers were made under license on an Adams patent. Tranter considered it essential to have the one-piece, malleable iron frame incorporating the barrel which was a major feature of Adams's arms – and he was content to pay a small royalty on each pistol for the privilege. It is, in fact, believed that Tranter had a contract to make frames for Adams, at least in the early days when Adams himself did not have the manufacturing capacity to cope with the demand. If this was so, the license arrangement was clearly to Tranter's advantage, for he had the tools and expertise ready to hand in his own factory. When the patent expired in 1865, the system became common property and Tranter was able to continue to use it without further payment of a fee. It will be seen from the arm illustrated here that the angle of the butt was changed; and this conformed with the change made by Adams at the same time. This particular pistol is provided with a neat case, with bullet mold, lubricating compound, and other accessories.

Length (gun): 11.8in (298mm)
Barrel: 6.0in (152mm)
Weight: 36.0oz (1.0kg)
Caliber: 0.44in (11.2mm)
Rifling: 5 grooves, r/hand
Capacity: five
Muz vel: ca 550ft/sec (168m/sec)

TRANTER REVOLVER, POCKET MODEL — UK

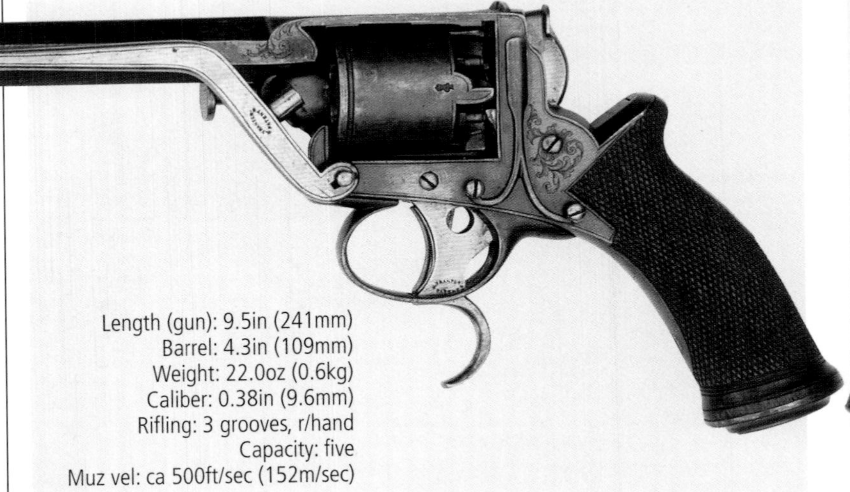

Length (gun): 9.5in (241mm)
Barrel: 4.3in (109mm)
Weight: 22.0oz (0.6kg)
Caliber: 0.38in (9.6mm)
Rifling: 3 grooves, r/hand
Capacity: five
Muz vel: ca 500ft/sec (152m/sec)

Tranter's revolvers were made in a considerable variety of calibers to suit all needs. The first model was produced in 38-bore (0.500in/12.7mm), 50-bore (0.45in/11.4mm), 54-bore (0.44in/11.2mm), 80-bore (0.38in/9.6mm), 90-bore (0.36in/9.1mm), and 120-bore (0.32in/8.1mm). (The calibers in inches and millimeters are rounded off to their modern equivalents.) The second and third models appear to have been reduced to the three basic calibers; ie, 38-, 54- and 120-bore. The pistol illustrated here is of 80-bore (0.38in/9.6mm), and it will be seen that it is the second model, with detachable rammer. Like all Tranter's revolvers in this series, it conformed closely to the standard design and was fitted with the patent safety device and the usual cylinder axis retaining spring on the right-hand side. Like all Tranter's arms, it bears the inscription "W. TRANTER PATENT" on the upper trigger, just above the guard, and on the rammer, opposite the ram itself. The frame is of the later pattern, with raked-back butt; as it does not bear the words "Adams Patent," it must be presumed to have been made after the patent's expiry in 1865. It bears the usual light engraving on the sides of the frame and at the breech end of the barrel, the top flat of which is engraved "GASQUOINE AND DYSON, MARKET PLACE, MANCHESTER," this being the name of the retailer. This is in every respect a neat and compact weapon and, although a pocket pistol, it is of sufficient caliber to give it very reasonable stopping-power.

TRANTER RIMFIRE REVOLVER — UK

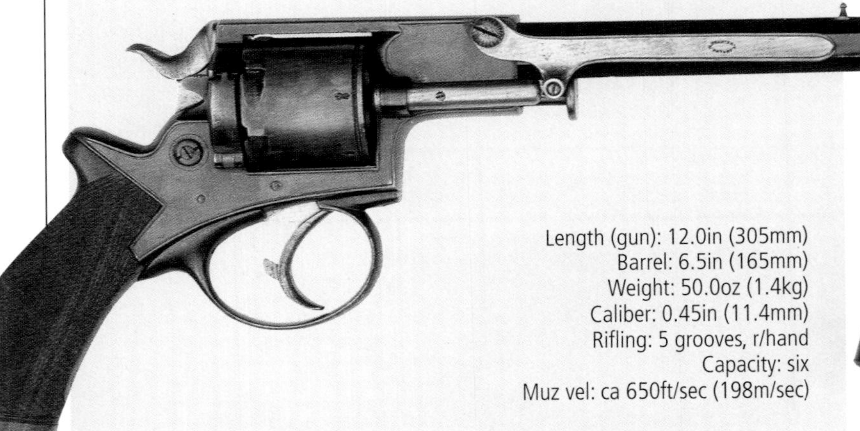

Length (gun): 12.0in (305mm)
Barrel: 6.5in (165mm)
Weight: 50.0oz (1.4kg)
Caliber: 0.45in (11.4mm)
Rifling: 5 grooves, r/hand
Capacity: six
Muz vel: ca 650ft/sec (198m/sec)

The name of Tranter has already been mentioned several times in this book but always in connection with the early double-trigger percussion revolvers. Apart from these, Tranter also produced a good many double-action percussion revolvers, in a variety of sizes, in order to compete with Beaumont-Adams arms (qv), especially military arms in service calibers. Once the popularity of the new Smith and Wesson breechloading revolvers was assured, Tranter, a competent and enterprising individual, wasted little time: by 1863 he had placed on the market the rimfire revolver seen here. This was the first of its type to be produced (or, it might be safer to say, acknowledged) by a British maker. Tranter had used the Adams frame, under license, for his revolvers and the cylinder (which is, of course, bored through) has six chambers instead of the five customary in Tranter's earlier models; and the rear ends of the chambers are recessed to accommodate the rims of the cartridges. There is a bottom-hinged loading gate on the right-hand side of the standing breech. The rammer lever, which is inscribed "TRANTERS PATENT," acted downwards, forcing the ram into the chamber through a sleeve. It was a close fit, in order to push out the cases by their forward edges. This meant that chamber and ram had to be most carefully aligned.

TRANTER POCKET REVOLVER — UK

Length (gun): 8.0in (203mm)
Barrel: 3.5in (89mm)
Weight: 19.0oz (0.5kg)
Caliber: 0.32in (8.1mm)
Rifling: 5 grooves, r/hand
Capacity: seven
Muz vel: ca 550ft/sec (168m/sec)

When trade fell off after the end of the American Civil War in 1865, Tranter increased his production of revolvers and the weapon illustrated is typical of his arms. It has a solid and robust frame, into which the barrel is screwed, and a plain, seven-shot cylinder with recesses to accommodate the cartridge rims. The cylinder was rotated by a pawl, worked by the hammer, acting on a ratchet; the latter was cut out of the actual cylinder instead of attached to it. The cylinder stop rose from the bottom of the frame and engaged the rectangular slots towards the front of the cylinder. The cylinder pin was retained by a small, vertical spring: pressure on the bottom end of the spring allowed the pin to be withdrawn. The weapon has a bottom-hinged loading gate on the right-hand side of the frame, into which a groove has been machined to allow the copper rimfire cartridges to be inserted. No ejector is fitted: to unload, it was necessary either to use the cylinder pin or to lever the cases out by inserting a knife-point or small screwdriver into the wide slots around the rear edge of the cylinder. This was a somewhat slow method; but presumably it was felt that seven rounds in the cylinder would usually be ample for self-defense. The lock, which is of single-action type, is fitted with a half-cock and was operated by the sheathed trigger usual on pocket arms. The weapon is marked "TRANTERS PATENT" on the frame and is numbered "10719" on the butt cap. The top flat is inscribed with the name of the retailer: "PARKER FIELD AND SONS, HIGH HOLBORN, LONDON."

TRANTER CENTERFIRE REVOLVER — UK

Length (gun): 10.5in (267mm)
Barrel: 5.0in (127mm)
Weight: 35.0oz (1.0kg)
Caliber: 0.45in (11.4mm)
Rifling: 5 grooves, r/hand
Capacity: six
Muz vel: ca 650ft/sec (198m/sec)

The adoption by the British Army of a breechloading rifle firing a centerfire cartridge in 1866 soon led to a considerable interest in this type of round – and eventually to the supersession of the rimfire type for service use, although it was still used in pocket pistols. William Tranter was an early entrant in the field of cartridge revolvers: by 1868 he had produced an up-dated version for use with the new Boxer cartridges. The general appearance of the Tranter revolver illustrated here is familiar, for it is still broadly based on the Adams frame which Tranter had used so successfully in his earlier weapons. The frame is still solid, with an integral, octagonal barrel, and the six-chambered cylinder is plain, except for the slots cut for the cylinder stop. The loading gate has a rearward spring catch; light downward pressure was required to operate it. The lock is of the double-action type. An innovation is the provision of a built-in firing pin on the standing breech; the end of the pin was struck by the hammer. The extractor pin is attached to a swivel mount which allowed it to be swung out into line with the right-hand chamber. A small spring catch, visible in the photograph, held the pin safely in position but allowed it to be removed for cleaning. An irregularly-shaped plate on the left side of the frame allowed access to the lock mechanism. The frame and ejector pin mount are marked "TRANTERS PATENT" and the revolver is numbered "13061."

Tranter Revolver Conversion UK

Length (gun): 10.3in (260mm)
Barrel: 6.0in (152mm)
Weight: 26.0oz (0.7kg)
Caliber: 0.38in (9.6mm)
Rifling: 5 grooves, r/hand
Capacity: five
Muz vel: ca 600ft/sec (183m/sec)

Although he is, perhaps, best known for his double-trigger arms, William Tranter also made a number of single-trigger, double-action revolvers from 1856 until 1863 and this weapon was originally of that type, although it subsequently underwent conversion. The perfection of the metallic rimfire cartridge naturally led to a demand for revolvers to fire it, and many existing arms were converted to meet this demand. In this Tranter conversion, the main change was the provision of a new, bored-through cylinder, with the addition of a loading gate on the right-hand side of the frame and a shield on the left to prevent the cartridges from slipping out. A new hammer, suitable for the firing of rimfire rounds, was added. There is no integral ejector, but the empty cases could be pushed out through the loading gate by means of a rod, which screwed into the butt when not in use.

Tranter "Army" Revolver UK

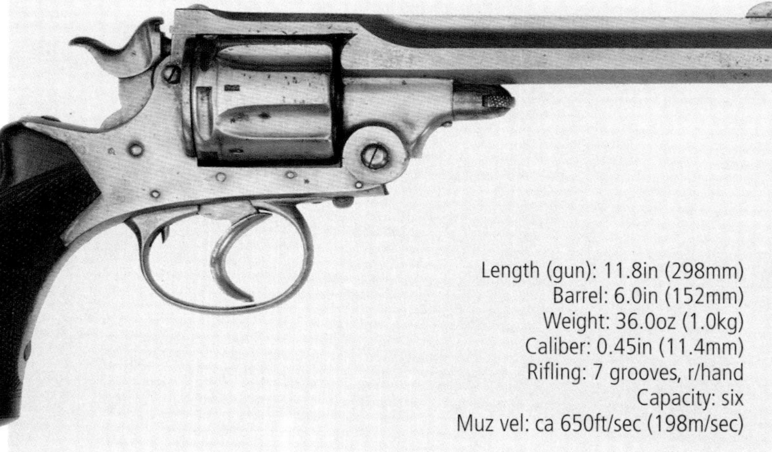

Length (gun): 11.8in (298mm)
Barrel: 6.0in (152mm)
Weight: 36.0oz (1.0kg)
Caliber: 0.45in (11.4mm)
Rifling: 7 grooves, r/hand
Capacity: six
Muz vel: ca 650ft/sec (198m/sec)

William Tranter made some well-known double-trigger revolvers and was also one of the earliest, if not the earliest, makers of metallic-cartridge revolvers in Britain. The obvious advantage of the hinged-frame or break-open revolver – particularly as regards speed of ejection or reloading – were quickly seen by Tranter, who, by 1879, had patented and put into production his own revolver of this type, one of which is illustrated here. It has an octagonal barrel with a raised top rib and a round foresight (the backsight being a groove on the back end of the top strap), and a six-chambered fluted cylinder with an automatic ejector. The cylinder could be removed by first opening the revolver and then pressing the milled catch visible below the barrel; the cylinder could then be lifted off its axis pin. The lock is of double-action type and has a rebounding hammer. The locking system consists of a rear extension to the top strap, with a rectangular aperture which fits over a shaped projection on top of the standing breech. The long, pivoted hook on the left of the frame is basically similar to that on the Webley, but fits over a projection on the top frame. An additional safety device is provided by a slot in the hammer (clearly visible in the photograph) which, when the hammer was fully down in the firing position, engaged a corresponding flange on the revolver's strap.

Turner Pepperbox Pistol UK

Length (gun): 9.3in (235mm)
Barrel: 3.5in (89mm)
Weight: 32.0oz (0.9kg)
Caliber: 0.476in (12.1mm)
Rifling: none
Capacity: six
Muz vel: ca 500ft/sec (152m/sec)

This weapon was made by Thomas Turner of Reading, a well-known provincial gunmaker of the 19th Century, and is of excellent construction. Its six smooth-bored barrels are drilled from a single block of steel in the usual manner; but somewhat unusually, each is numbered at the breech end, the ribs between them being stamped alternately with either a view mark or a proof mark. The nipples are at right angles to the axis of the barrels and, as may be seen, there are no partitions between them. This must have increased the risk of the barrels chain-firing, an event likely to be disconcerting to the firer – and even more so to his proposed victim. The breech also incorporates a nipple shield to prevent the percussion caps from being brushed or shaken off; however, by canalizing the flash from the cap, this must also have contributed to the risk of more than one barrel firing from a single cap. The bar hammer is of standard double-action type and required considerable pressure on the trigger to operate it. The trigger action also activated a pawl and ratchet to rotate the barrels. These rotated on an axis pin screwed into the standing breech; they are held in place on the pin by an engraved brass-headed screw which fits flush with the muzzles. Access to the nipples was gained through an aperture in the flash shield just to the right of the hammer, and slight pressure on the trigger raised the hammer nose from the nipples sufficiently to rotate the barrels manually in anti-clockwise direction. The hammer and frame are both lightly engraved, with the inscription "THOMAS TURNER, READING" in an oval on the left-hand side.

Webley Longspur Revolver UK

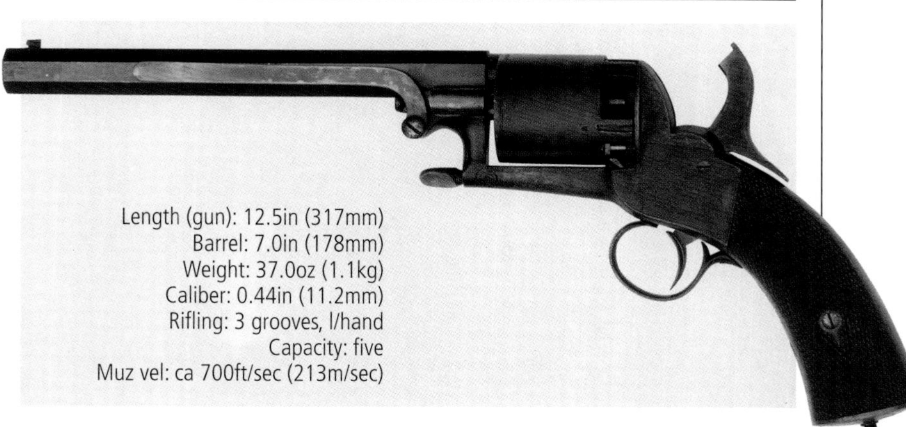

Length (gun): 12.5in (317mm)
Barrel: 7.0in (178mm)
Weight: 37.0oz (1.1kg)
Caliber: 0.44in (11.2mm)
Rifling: 3 grooves, l/hand
Capacity: five
Muz vel: ca 700ft/sec (213m/sec)

This revolver, known as the "Longspur" from the length of its hammer spur, was patented in 1853; there were various models, of which the one seen here is the third. The frame of the weapon is of malleable iron; the octagonal barrel is a separate component and is attached to the axis pin by means of a threaded sleeve in the lump at the rear end of the barrel; the lower part of this lump butts on to the lower projection of the frame and is attached to it by a thumbscrew. The cylinder, which is case-hardened, has five chambers with horizontal nipples separated from each other by partitions. The first model had a detachable rammer; the second had a simple swivel rammer pivoted back horizontally across the frame below the cylinder. In this weapon an integral spring held the lever flush against a small stud on the left-hand barrel flat when it was not required for use. Raising the lever thrust the hollow-nosed rammer into the chamber with sufficient force to allow the use of tight-fitting bullets. The lock is of single-action type and is equipped with a half-cock to hold the hammer nose just clear of the nipples. The trigger is rather small, as is its almost circular guard. The weapon has a finely checkered, two-piece butt held by a single screw. The inspection plate on the left-hand side of the frame is visible in the photograph. A foresight and a backsight are provided, the latter being a notch on the top of the hammer. The pistol is blued and lightly engraved, and bears several inscriptions: the inspection plate is marked "WEBLEY'S PATENT." On the strap is "BY HER MAJESTY'S ROYAL LETTERS PATENT."

WEBLEY DOUBLE-ACTION REVOLVER UK

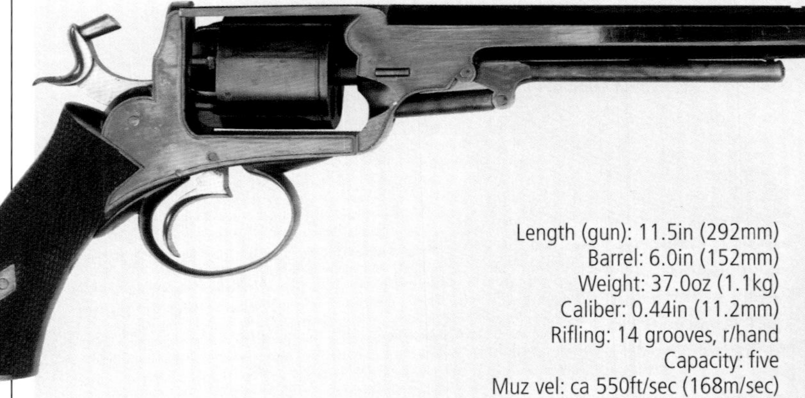

Length (gun): 11.5in (292mm)
Barrel: 6.0in (152mm)
Weight: 37.0oz (1.1kg)
Caliber: 0.44in (11.2mm)
Rifling: 14 grooves, r/hand
Capacity: five
Muz vel: ca 550ft/sec (168m/sec)

After the Webley Longspur (qv) the firm of Webley produced a series of self-cocking percussion revolvers. These were followed by two types of double-action pistol: one with a solid frame, with a barrel screwed in; the other, shown here, of two-piece construction. The octagonal, multi-grooved barrel is made with a top strap and a lump. The rear end of the strap fits into a slot cut across the top of the standing breech above the nose of the hammer; a hole in the lump fits over the front end of the axis pin; and a small stud projects from the lower frame to fit a corresponding hole at the bottom of the lump – thus giving a rigid, three-way locking system. The whole is held firmly together by a Colt-type wedge driven in from the left-hand side and retained by a small grub screw. The cylinder is of the usual Webley type, each chamber being numbered serially from one to five in an anti-clockwise direction. The lock is of double-action type, with a half-cock but no safety catch. The revolver is fitted with a rammer of Colt-type: the lever is held in place below the barrel by a spring catch fastening over a pin on the lower flat. The butt has a cap integral with the tang, and the butt-plates are finely checkered. The entire weapon is well-blued, except for the hammer and trigger, which are bright, and the rammer, which is case-hardened. The top strap is marked "P WEBLEY AND SON, LONDON," which suggests that the firm may have had its own retail outlet in the capital at that time.

WEBLEY NO 1 REVOLVER UK

Length (gun): 9.5in (241mm)
Barrel: 5.0in (127mm)
Weight: 42.0oz (1.2kg)
Caliber: 0.577in (14.6mm)
Rifling: 7 grooves, r/hand
Capacity: six
Muz vel: ca 600ft/sec (183m/sec)

The Webley No 1 Revolver was of 0.577in (14.6mm) caliber, exactly the same as that of the service rifle. Although it is, perhaps, difficult to appreciate the fact from a photograph, one's first reaction on seeing the arm is to wonder at its massive construction. The revolver is built on a robust, solid frame with integral barrel. As in many Webley products of the period, the barrel (although in this example octagonal) is noticeably higher from bottom to top than from side to side. This is particularly true of the muzzle-end; even in a short barrel the taper is quite obvious. The cylinder is fully fluted and the lock is of double-action type. One of the problems connected with the early Boxer cartridge was a marked tendency for the primer to bulge backwards under the force of the explosion. In some forms of breech mechanism, this was not particularly important; but in a revolver of orthodox type – ie, one in which the bas of the cartridge was forced back against a robust standing breech – there was always the risk that a bulged primer would prevent the cylinder from rotating. Obviously, if this should happen at a critical moment it might have very serious results for the user. The Webley No 1 was therefore fitted with a detachable backplate which rotated with the cylinder; it was pierced with holes to accommodate the hammer nose, into which the primers might expand, if necessary, without fouling the mechanism. This was reliable, if slow. The earliest cartridges fired lead balls, but later marks were loaded with elongated bullets with hollow, plugged bases to assist expansion into the rifling. This method had been used successfully in the percussion Enfield rifle and its Snider conversion.

WEBLEY R.I.C. REVOLVER NO 1 UK

Length (gun): 9.3in (235mm)
Barrel: 14.5in (114mm)
Weight: 30.0oz (0.9kg)
Caliber: 0.45in (11.4mm)
Rifling: 5 grooves, r/hand
Capacity: six
Muz vel: ca 650ft/sec (198m/sec)

The arm illustrated here is the No 1 Model, but as the manufacture of all varieties of this revolver seems to have overlapped a good deal, it is not possible to date it very accurately. It has a basically round barrel which is, however, slightly raised on its upper side, on which a flat rib has been machined. The foresight is slotted in, and the backsight, as usual, consists of a long groove on the top strap. The barrel is screwed into a solid frame. The six-chambered cylinder is plain, except for recesses for the cylinder stop at the rear end. Plain cylinders, it should be noted, are usually indicative of earlier models: on later models the cylinders are fluted to achieve a small reduction in weight. The extractor is of the usual type, although its knob is acorn-shaped. The loading gate is standard. The revolver has a double-action lock, with a half-cock which held the nose of the hammer well clear of the cartridges in the chambers. The checkered walnut butt is of one-piece type and is held by two vertical screws; one downward from the back of the frame and one upward from the butt-cap. These revolvers were made in a variety of calibers, none smaller than 0.410in (10.4mm), and they were widely used all over the British Empire. They were also very extensively copied in various European countries.

WEBLEY R.I.C. REVOLVER NO 2 UK

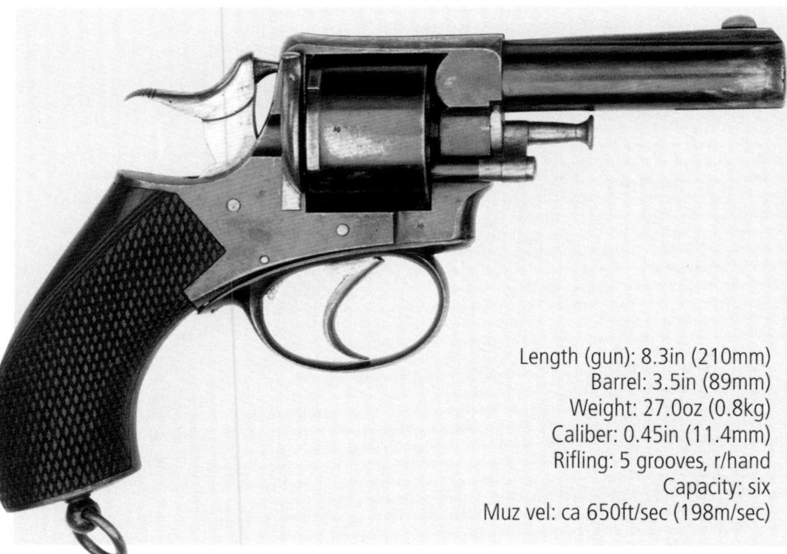

Length (gun): 8.3in (210mm)
Barrel: 3.5in (89mm)
Weight: 27.0oz (0.8kg)
Caliber: 0.45in (11.4mm)
Rifling: 5 grooves, r/hand
Capacity: six
Muz vel: ca 650ft/sec (198m/sec)

The first R.I.C. arm adopted was the Webley revolver, which was known thereafter as the Royal Irish Constabulary revolver. The specimen illustrated here is the No 2 Model and was probably made in about 1876. The barrel is round, although the shape of the top rib gives a distinct impression of taper, and is screwed into the frame. It has a semi-round foresight, slotted in; the backsight is a long, V-shaped groove along the top strap. The six-chambered cylinder is plain except for raised flanges at the rear; the ends of these are held by the cylinder stop, which rose from the lower frame when the trigger was pressed. The extractor pin was housed in the hollow cylinder axis pin when not in use, but it could be withdrawn on a swivel in order to align it with the appropriate chamber. Once the pin was drawn, the cylinder could be removed by drawing the axis pin forward by means of its flat, milled head (visible in the photograph). Access to the chamber was by means of a loading gate which is hinged at the bottom and opened sideways against a flat spring. The lock is of double-action type. This particular revolver was carried by Major Webb of the Bengal Cavalry in the Second Afghan War of 1878-88; it is marked "MANTON & CO, LONDON & CALCUTTA" on the strap and was, presumably, purchased in India. The left side of the frame is stamped "WEBLEYS RIC NO 2 .450 CF," with the flying bullet trademark, and it also bears the arm's serial number, which is "10974."

Webley Bulldog Revolver UK

Length (gun): 5.5in (140mm)
Barrel: 2.1in (53mm)
Weight: 11.0oz (0.3kg)
Caliber: 0.32in (8.1mm)
Rifling: 5 grooves, r/hand
Capacity: five
Muz vel: ca 500ft/sec (152m/sec)

In 1878, P. Webley and Son began to manufacture and sell a range of revolvers under the general name of "British Bulldog." These were primarily designed for civilian use (although some were used for service purposes) and were plain, robust, reliable arms. The first of the series was a heavy, centerfire arm in 0.442in (11.2mm) caliber, followed by others, including 0.45in (11.4mm) caliber to appeal to as wide a market as possible, and then by revolvers in smaller calibers better suited for use as pocket arms. The revolver seen here is the smallest of these pocket types and is classed as the second model, which appeared in about 1880. It is constructed on a solid frame with an integral barrel. The vertical dimension of the barrel at the muzzle is appreciably greater than it is at the breech-end; this gives a markedly tapered effect, even in a very short barrel. As was the universal practice in these early Webley revolvers, the cylinder is plain – except for the slots at its rear end to accommodate the cylinder stop, which rose from the bottom of the frame when the action was cocked. It was originally fitted with a bottom-hinged loading gate. The ejector pin was normally housed in the hollow cylinder axis pin, whence it could be withdrawn and swiveled for use. Once this had been done, the cylinder axis pin could also be withdrawn, if required, by means of its flat, milled head; thus, the cylinder could be removed. The mechanism is of double-action type and the arm was designed to take centerfire cartridges. Rimfire versions were also made, and were so stamped for identification on the frame.

Webley New Model Army Express Revolver UK

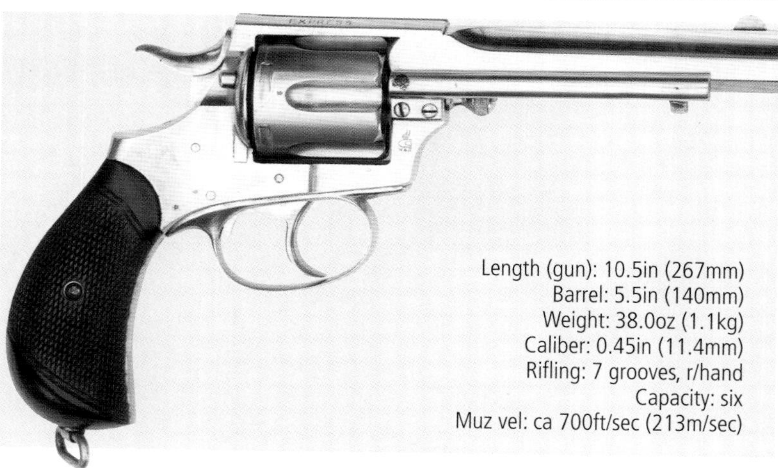

Length (gun): 10.5in (267mm)
Barrel: 5.5in (140mm)
Weight: 38.0oz (1.1kg)
Caliber: 0.45in (11.4mm)
Rifling: 7 grooves, r/hand
Capacity: six
Muz vel: ca 700ft/sec (213m/sec)

The appearance in 1877 of the new Colt double-action revolver was quickly followed by that of a new Webley revolver of very similar appearance. Like the Colt, the Webley is a solid-frame revolver, with a loading gate and a sliding ejector rod. Its barrel, which is basically octagonal but with a higher and narrower top flat, is screwed into the frame, although the joint is virtually imperceptible. It has an unusually large trigger-guard, presumably so that it could be used by a man wearing gloves. Its bird-beak butt is somewhat larger than that of the corresponding Colt, and was a good deal more comfortable to handle as a result. The arm was made in one caliber only, nominally 0.45in (11.4mm), but, like all Webley service arms of the period, it would accept cartridges of both 0.455in (11.5mm) and 0.476in (12.1mm) caliber. There was only one standard length of barrel 5.5in (140mm), as seen here – but a few models were made with 12in (305mm) barrels to special orders, and these were supplied with a detachable shoulder stock. The specimen illustrated is numbered "4506" and carries the well-known trademark of the flying bullet; the top of the frame is marked "ARMY & NAVY C.S.L." and "EXPRESS." In spite of its strong similarity to the new Colt it is, in fact, probable (according to The Webley Story by Dowell) that it was based on a prototype designed some 10 years earlier to handle the heavy 0.577in (14.6mm) pistol cartridge used in the Webley No 1 since it does not seem possible that a completely new arm could have been put into production in the time which elapsed between the appearance of the new Colt and that of the Webley.

Webley-Kaufmann Revolver UK

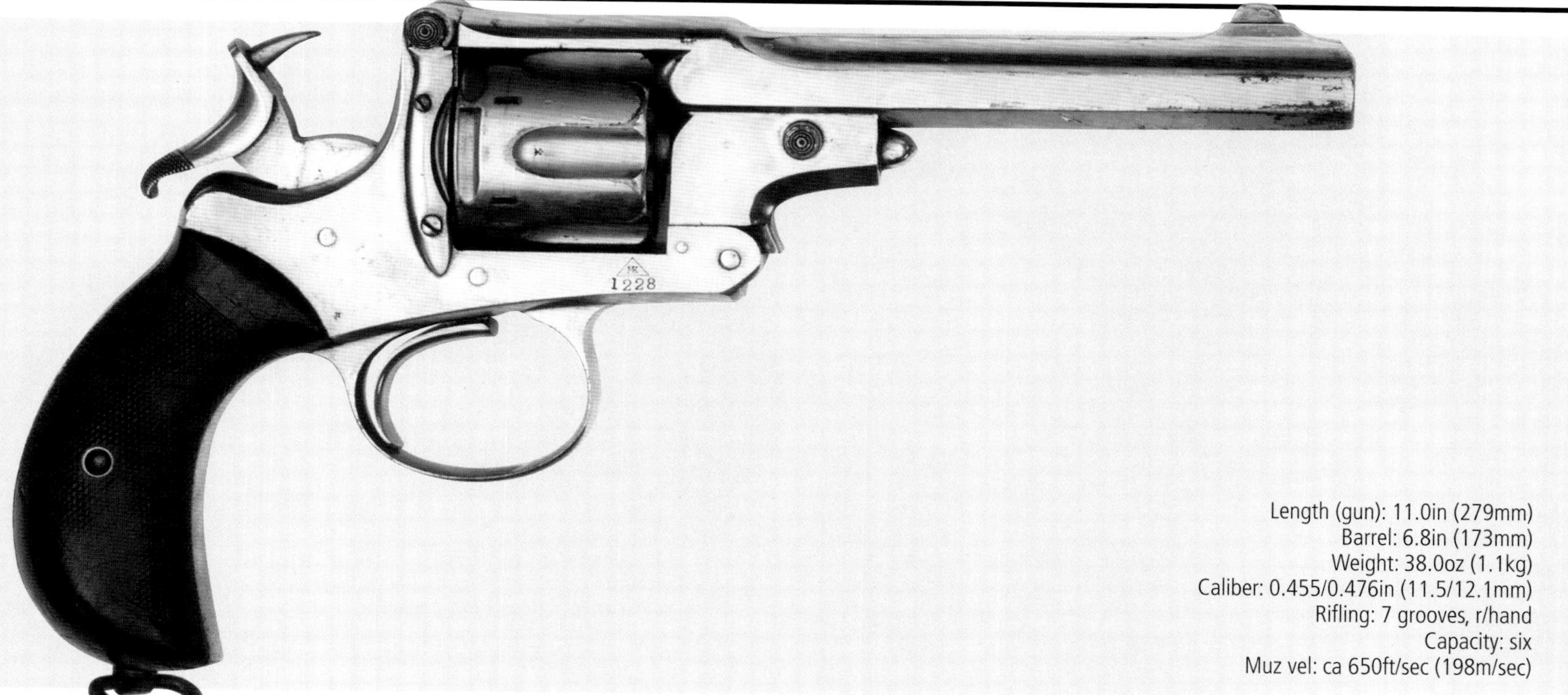

Length (gun): 11.0in (279mm)
Barrel: 6.8in (173mm)
Weight: 38.0oz (1.1kg)
Caliber: 0.455/0.476in (11.5/12.1mm)
Rifling: 7 grooves, r/hand
Capacity: six
Muz vel: ca 650ft/sec (198m/sec)

Michael Kaufmann was a very talented British inventor of firearms. His association with Webley in the period 1878-81 led to the appearance of the revolver seen here, which bears his name and which provided, in effect, the basic design for Webley's famous range of Government (Webley-Green) models, produced from 1882 onward. The Webley-Kaufmann revolver has an octagonal barrel with its top flat drawn up into a rib. It is of break-open type, and perhaps its main point of interest is the system by which it was locked. A rear extension on the top strap fits into a corresponding slot in the standing breech, and running through both is a cylindrical hole, with a diameter of about 0.16in (4mm), in which the locking bolt worked. Pressure on a lever on the left side of the body caused a spring bolt (the milled end of which is visible in the photograph) to be forced outward, thus allowing the revolver to be closed. When the lever was released, the bolt was returned inward, entering the hole in the rear extension. This held a floating bolt, which was pushed over to the left in order to engage with the far hole on the standing breech, thus providing a very strong locking device indeed. The fluted, six-chambered cylinder is fitted with the usual star extractor, which was forced out automatically when the weapon was opened. The lock is of double-action, rebounding type. The bird-beak butt has two side plates of finely checkered walnut held by a single screw, and the trigger-guard was made integrally with the frame.

WEBLEY-PRYSE 0.45IN REVOLVER — UK

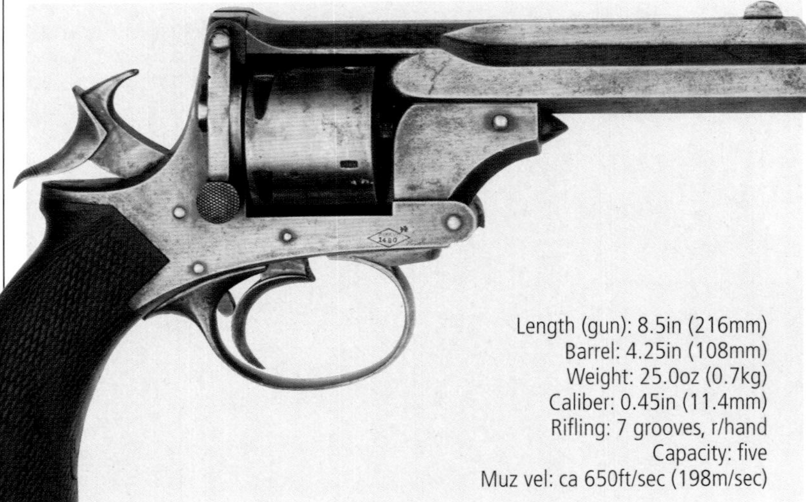

Length (gun): 8.5in (216mm)
Barrel: 4.25in (108mm)
Weight: 25.0oz (0.7kg)
Caliber: 0.45in (11.4mm)
Rifling: 7 grooves, r/hand
Capacity: five
Muz vel: ca 650ft/sec (198m/sec)

In 1876 Charles Pryse patented a new type of break-down, self-extracting revolver. The weapon was hinged at the lower front of the frame and when the barrel was pushed down to an angle of about 90 degrees a star-shaped ejector was forced automatically from the rear-end of the cylinder, throwing out the empty cartridge cases with some force. Two long register pins working in holes in the cylinder were attached to the base of the extractor. The barrel hinge was formed by two lugs on the barrel, with the extractor lever between them, and two outer lugs on the frame. The whole was held by a threaded pin. The cocking system consisted of two vertical arms, one on each side of the frame, each of which had a flat, milled stud at the bottom and a short bolt on the inner side at the top, and was hinged centrally. A rear extension of the barrel entered a slot in front of the hammer; the bolts on the arms passed through holes in the side of this slot and engaged in recesses on the extension, where they were held in place by springs. This would appear to constitute a strong and reliable locking system but considerable care was needed to ensure that the various holes and apertures for the locking pins were free from grease and dirt, because if they were not it was just possible that the gun might blow open. Pryse did not have his own production facilities and this was undertaken by a variety of licensees, starting with the well-known firm of Webley in 1877, who made this example.

WEBLEY-PRYSE REVOLVER NO 4 — UK

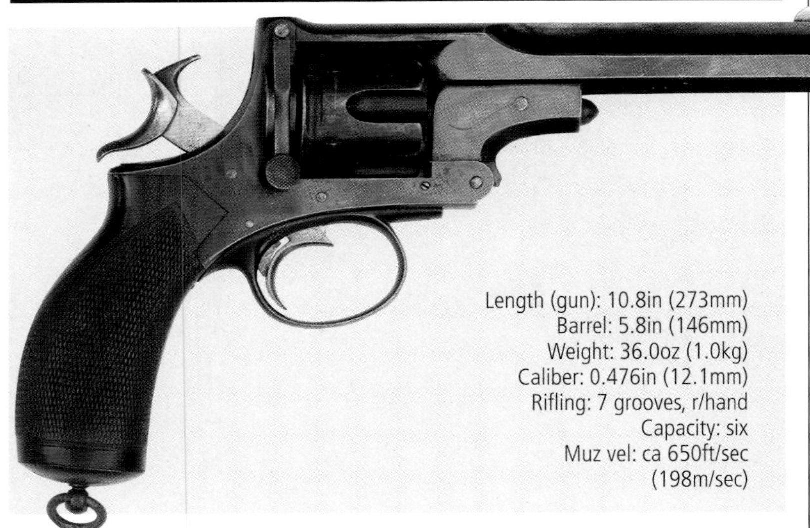

Length (gun): 10.8in (273mm)
Barrel: 5.8in (146mm)
Weight: 36.0oz (1.0kg)
Caliber: 0.476in (12.1mm)
Rifling: 7 grooves, r/hand
Capacity: six
Muz vel: ca 650ft/sec (198m/sec)

This weapon is one of the early hinged-frame, self-extracting revolvers incorporating the system patented by Charles Pryse, first put into production by P. Webley and Son in 1877. It was the first revolver to make use of a rebounding hammer; this was automatically lifted back by about 0.15in (4mm) when the trigger was released after firing, thus holding the hammer nose well clear of the base of the next cartridge. The fluted cylinder was reliably locked at all times, except when the lock mechanism was actually being operated. This was achieved by means of a double stop worked by the trigger. When there was no pressure on the trigger, the forward stop engaged one of the smaller slots; then the trigger was pressed, the cylinder rotated, and the rear part of the stop engaged in one of the long, bullet-shaped slots at the rear of the cylinder. The cylinder could be removed by unscrewing a large, milled screwhead to the left of the frame; the end of the screw may be seen immediately below the barrel in the photograph. The cylinder has a star extractor which was forced sharply outward when the revolver was opened; this was done by pressing in the milled discs on the lower ends of the locking arms (one of which is visible), thus disengaging two bolts from a rear extension of the top frame. The extractor was provided with two long register pins which fitted into holes in the cylinder. The left side of the frame of this specimen is marked "WEBLEYS NO4 .476CF." Below this inscription is the famous flying-bullet trademark and the serial number "7546."

WEBLEY-PRYSE-TYPE 0.45IN REVOLVER — UK

Length (gun): 7.5in (190mm)
Weight: 25.0oz (0.7kg)
Barrel: 3.5in (89mm)
Caliber: 0.45in (11.4mm)
Rifling: 3 grooves, r/hand
Capacity: five
Muz vel: ca 650ft/sec (198m/sec)

Charles Pryse licensed a number of gunsmiths to manufacture revolvers to his patent design and even Webley was one of these, even though it had its own designs on the market, as has already been mentioned. Other makers of Pryse-type revolvers included British makers such as Thomas Horsley and Christopher Bonehill, while copies were inevitably made by Belgian manufacturers in Liège. The arm illustrated here is marked "T.W. WATSON, 4, PALL MALL, LONDON" on the top flat of the barrel, but this is almost certainly the name of the retailer rather than that of the maker. The weapon bears the London proof marks and has the number "358" on the frame. Although of the same caliber as the Webley-Pryse shown earlier, this weapon had a much shorter barrel (3.5in/89mm compared to 4.25in/108mm) and there were differences in the trigger group and butt.

WEBLEY GOVERNMENT (WEBLEY-GREEN) REVOLVER — UK

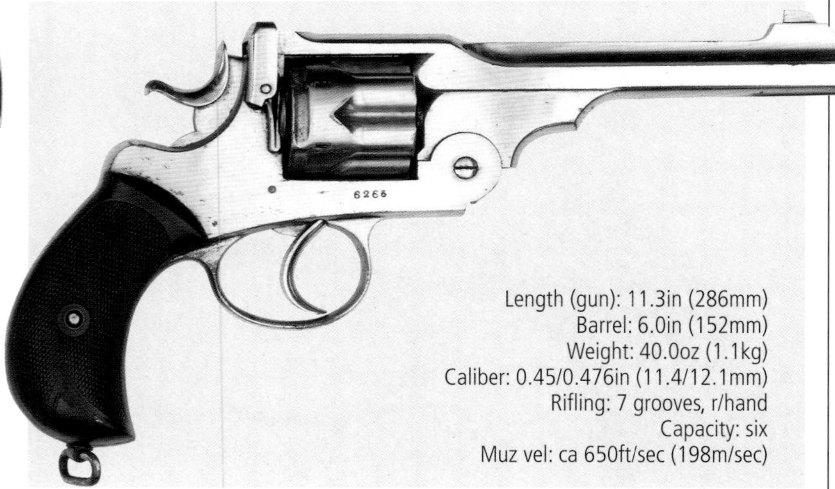

Length (gun): 11.3in (286mm)
Barrel: 6.0in (152mm)
Weight: 40.0oz (1.1kg)
Caliber: 0.45/0.476in (11.4/12.1mm)
Rifling: 7 grooves, r/hand
Capacity: six
Muz vel: ca 650ft/sec (198m/sec)

This revolver, frequently known as the "W.G.," is a development of the Webley-Kaufmann weapon (qv), and was developed in the period 1882-85. It is of the familiar break-open type, although the barrel is of slightly different section: the lower part is rounded. The six-chambered cylinder is distinctively fluted in the manner sometimes referred to as "church steeple," from the very characteristic shapes of the flutes, and it is fitted with the usual spring extractor. The system of locking is really the main point of difference between this arm and the Webley-Kaufmann. The top strap of the Webley-Green has a rear extension with a rectangular slot which fits closely over an upper projection from the standing breech. A stirrup-type catch, essentially similar to the one on the Webley-Wilkinson, fits over this whole assembly, and was activated by a lever on the left side. The design was such that, unless the catch was properly home, the nose of the hammer could not reach the cartridges; this made it not only strong but also very safe. The lock is of the usual double-action type. The bird-beak butt, which is itself on the small side for a service arm, has plates of a composition that resembles very hard rubber. The left side of the frame is marked "'WG' MODEL, '·455/476," and "WEBLEY PATENT."

Webley Mk I Service Revolver — UK

Length (gun): 8.5in (216mm)
Barrel: 4.0in (102mm)
Weight: 34.0oz (0.96kg)
Caliber: 0.455in (11.5mm)
Rifling: 7 grooves, r/hand
Capacity: six
Muz vel: ca 600ft/sec (183m/sec)

The Enfield Mark II revolver (qv) was adopted as the British service revolver in 1880. However, after further extensive trials and a good deal of practical use in the field, it was finally felt to be inadequate. Two new weapons were therefore tested: the first was a Smith & Wesson; and the second a Webley revolver of the type shown here. After exhaustive trials, it was decided in 1887 to adopt the British weapon. Since both the arms tested were of break-open type, the principal factor bearing on the decision was the relative reliability of the method of holding the weapons closed; in this respect, in particular, the Webley was considered superior. Tests found the system to be strong and absolutely safe, for if the stirrup catch was not properly fastened, only two things could happen. Either the projection on the upper part of the hammer knocked the catch safely into position, allowing the revolver to be fired; or it fouled the catch and prevented the hammer nose from reaching the cap. The Webley Mark I is a stubby, compact weapon, with a short barrel. Its bird-beak butt, of adequate size to afford a good grip, is fitted with plates of brown vulcanite and is provided with a lanyard ring. The horizontal projection visible in front of the cylinder (there is one on the left side also) is a holster guide, designed to prevent the face of the cylinder from catching on the edge of the leather holster. This arm set the style for almost all later Webley service revolvers.

Webley 0.45in Target Model Revolver — UK

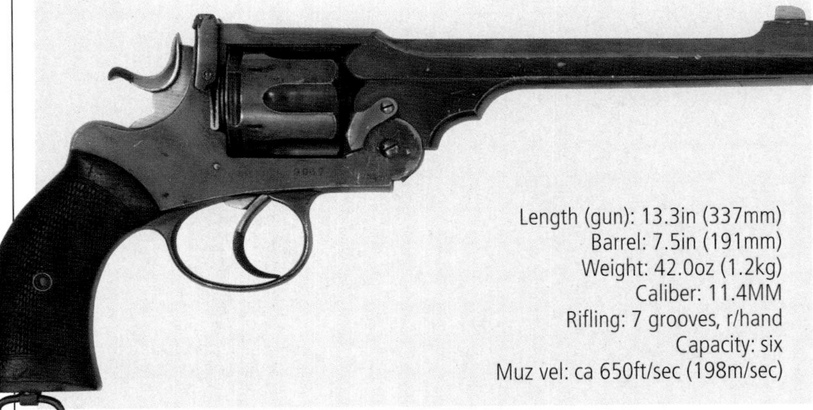

Length (gun): 13.3in (337mm)
Barrel: 7.5in (191mm)
Weight: 42.0oz (1.2kg)
Caliber: 11.4MM
Rifling: 7 grooves, r/hand
Capacity: six
Muz vel: ca 650ft/sec (198m/sec)

Most specialists regard the Webley WG Model (Webley-Government/Webley-Green (qv) as the finest production revolver ever made. The WG went through several evolutions until it was eventually replaced after World War II by the WS Model, which used the same frame and mechanism as the Mark VI Service revolver. The WG was produced in two versions: "service" for purchase by army officers; and "target." The latter dominated the pistol competition scene for several years, and it is generally agreed that it possessed one of the finest trigger actions ever made. The WG introduced the famous Webley stirrup latch, with the thumb lever on the left of the frame. When the Webley horseshoe cylinder retainer was introduced, the WG was fitted with that as well. Unlike the Government revolver, the WG had a sideplate on the left of the receiver, which permitted access to the mechanism, and also had a trigger guard that was an integral part of the receiver forging. The target version had a U-notch backsight, drift-adjustable for windage, which was laterally dovetailed into the cross-bar of the barrel latch. The foresight was a blade.

Webley Wilkinson Service Revolver — UK

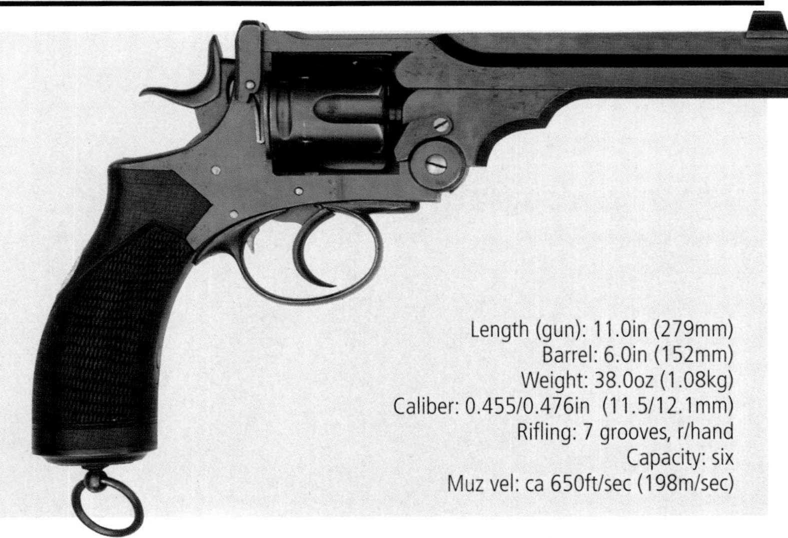

Length (gun): 11.0in (279mm)
Barrel: 6.0in (152mm)
Weight: 38.0oz (1.08kg)
Caliber: 0.455/0.476in (11.5/12.1mm)
Rifling: 7 grooves, r/hand
Capacity: six
Muz vel: ca 650ft/sec (198m/sec)

This is a service revolver of a type first produced by Webley in 1892. With one important exception: it is very similar in most ways to the earlier Webley-Pryse model (qv). It is a break-open type. Its octagonal barrel has a very high top rib – somewhat higher at the front than the rear – with a bead foresight inset into it. The backsight is a simple U on the barrel catch. This catch is the most interesting feature of the arm: a rear extension on the top strap fits over a raised part of the standing breech and is held in place by a spring top latch. This was worked by a lever on the left-hand side and it is very robust and reliable. The revolver could not be fired when it was open, for unless the latch was fully in position, the upper part of the hammer fouled it and this prevented the hammer nose from reaching the cartridge. When the revolver was opened, a star extractor came automatically into play and threw out the empty cases. The one-piece, wrap-round butt is of fine checkered walnut, with an escutcheon plate, and the weapon is particularly well finished. It was made for retail by the famous Wilkinson Sword Company of Pall Mall, London, whose name and address is on the top strap. Wilkinson found it convenient to provide officers with revolvers as well as swords and bought revolvers from Webley for this purpose. Although these arms were standard models, they are distinguished by their fine finish, in keeping with the high reputation of the firm of Wilkinson.

Webley Mk III Police and Civilian Revolver — UK

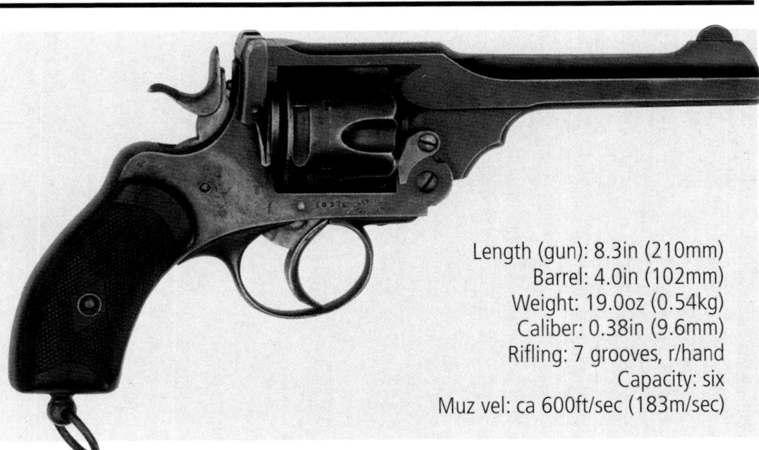

Length (gun): 8.3in (210mm)
Barrel: 4.0in (102mm)
Weight: 19.0oz (0.54kg)
Caliber: 0.38in (9.6mm)
Rifling: 7 grooves, r/hand
Capacity: six
Muz vel: ca 600ft/sec (183m/sec)

In 1896 Webley introduced a series of 0.38in (9.6mm) caliber pocket revolvers, mainly for use by plain-clothes police or civilians. The first model to appear was the Mark II; this came in two sub-types, one with a fixed hammer and the other with a flat-nosed hammer that fell on to a spring-loaded striker on the standing breech. In terms of style, both sub-types followed the general lines of the 0.455in (11.5mm) Government models, being simply scaled down for their reduced caliber. The Mark III, introduced almost immediately, differed from the Mark II chiefly in the shape of its butt and in its system of cylinder release. Like the Mark II, it had two types of hammer: the revolver illustrated has a flat-headed hammer with a separate striker. It has an octagonal barrel with a foresight; the backsight is a V-shaped notch on the barrel catch. The latter is of orthodox type, with a thumb lever on the left side of the frame; the V-spring which takes it forward may be clearly seen in the photograph. When the revolver was opened and the barrel forced down, the extractor came into action in the usual way, throwing out the cartridges or cases. The arm has a double cylinder stop: a forward stop, which worked when the hammer was down; and a rear stop, which operated when the trigger was pressed. It is a compact and handy little weapon and proved popular; its only disadvantage lay in its rather small butt. This fault was rectified in a later model, which first appeared in 1932; this had a very much larger butt and, somewhat unusually, was also fitted with a safety catch, which was positioned on the right-hand side of the frame.

WEBLEY-MARS 0.38IN PISTOL — UK

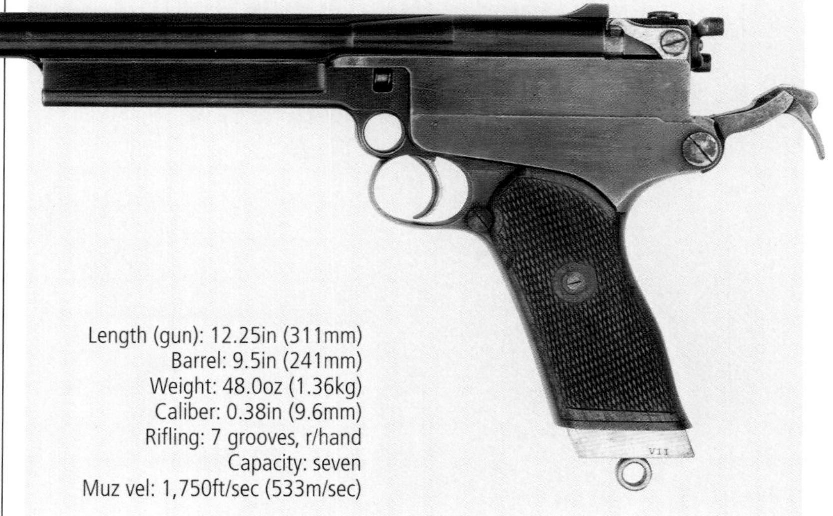

Length (gun): 12.25in (311mm)
Barrel: 9.5in (241mm)
Weight: 48.0oz (1.36kg)
Caliber: 0.38in (9.6mm)
Rifling: 7 grooves, r/hand
Capacity: seven
Muz vel: 1,750ft/sec (533m/sec)

In 1898 Hugh Gabbet-Fairfax submitted a design to the famous Birmingham firm of Webley and Scott, which was seeking a suitable design for a self-loading arm. The firm did not wish to adopt this particular model under its own name, but agreed to manufacture it for the inventor, presumably on a commission basis. The British Army tested it in the period 1901-03 but did not adopt it, partly due to the arm's heavy recoil, and partly to its persistent tendency either to fail to eject empty cases or to eject them into the firer's face. In 1902, Gabbet-Fairfax decided that the latter fault was due to defective ammunition, and promised a new batch in which this would be rectified, but the whole project had to be abandoned. The Webley-Mars was a huge arm and was designed to fire a powerful bottle-necked cartridge. Although it was extremely well made, it was mechanically complex, since the cartridge necessitated a robust system of locking the bolt to the barrel at the moment of firing. This was done by arranging for the bolt to turn so that four lugs on it engaged in recesses behind the chamber. When a shot was fired, the barrel and bolt at first recoiled together, until the latter turned and unlocked itself. The pistol was made in both 0.45in and 0.38in calibers.

WEBLEY 0.38IN MK IV REVOLVER (DAMAGED) — UK

Length (gun): 11.0in (280mm)
Barrel: see text
Weight: 36.0oz (1.0kg)
Caliber: 0.455in (11.4mm)
Rifling: 7 grooves, r/hand
Capacity: six
Muz vel: ca 650ft/sec (198m/sec)

The Webley & Scott Mark I revolver was accepted for service by the British Army in 1887 and was followed by the Marks II and III, which incorporated minor improvements. The Mark IV, however, which was officially adopted in 1899, represented a substantial improvement. It was widely used in the South African War, where it was carried by all officers, non-commissioned officers, and trumpeters of cavalry regiments, and by certain categories of artillery driver, and was also purchased by individual infantry officers; indeed, it was so popular that it earned the unofficial nickname of the "Boer War Model." It was made in four barrel lengths – 3.0in (76mm); 4.0in (102mm); 5.0in (127mm); and 6.0in (152mm). The picture shows a Mark IV with a 3.0in (76mm) barrel, which has had its trigger guard removed at some stage in its life. Of much greater significance, however, is that the weapon has suffered catastrophic damage, three of its six chambers having been blown out, while the top strap has disappeared completely. The neat way in which the outer walls of the chambers have been removed suggests that the cause was an internal explosion, almost certainly in the central chamber, which was probably under the hammer at the time.

WEBLEY AND SCOTT TARGET PISTOL — UK

Length (gun): 14.3in (362mm)
Barrel: 10.5in (267mm)
Weight: 36.0oz (1.0kg)
Caliber: 0.22in (5.6mm)
Rifling: 7 grooves, r/hand
Capacity: one
Muz vel: ca 1,100ft/sec (335m/sec)

This weapon, made in Birmingham by the well-known firm of Webley and Scott, may be taken as the British equivalent of the American "bicycle" arm. Britain is a relatively crowded country, where the use of rifled arms in or near public roads is frowned on, if not always deemed illegal. In the more spacious United States, however, the 0.22in rifle or pistol was, and still is, a very popular arm, regarded as a suitable first weapon for a boy. But it must be remembered that even in Britain there were no really stringent laws for the control of firearms until well into the 20th Century: thus, ordinary citizens were at liberty to purchase and use rifled arms, provided they were handled carefully and employed for lawful purposes. The pistol illustrated here was very much a dual-purpose weapon: when used single-handed, without the butt, it was well balanced and suitable for normal practice; while the addition of the butt at once converted it to a useful arm for small game or vermin. The barrel was hinged and could be lowered to expose the breech by pulling down on the trigger-guard. The action of opening the arm also activated the extractor, which was semi-circular and occupied half of the end of the barrel. There was an inspection plate on the left side of the frame, just below the hammer. The "rifle" butt (not shown here) was attached by pushing its rod portion through a hole in the pistol butt, where it was then held firmly in position by the pressure of a spring stud.

Webley Self-Cocking Revolver (Webley-Fosbery) UK

Length (gun): 11.5in (292mm)
Barrel: 7.5in (190mm)
Weight: 38.0oz (1.1kg)
Caliber: 0.455in (11.5mm)
Rifling: 7 grooves, r/hand
Capacity: six
Muz vel: ca 650ft/sec (198m/sec)

Colonel George Vincent Fosbery, VC, invented a unique revolver, which made use of recoil to rotate the cylinder and cock the hammer. This revolver, which was made by Webley and Scott, was first demonstrated at Bisley in 1900 and was put into production the following year. It was of service caliber and handled and loaded in exactly the same way as the standard issue revolver – but with the very important difference that after the first shot the recoil did much of the work: all the firer needed to do was apply light pressure to the trigger. The barrel and cylinder were made in such a way that they were free to recoil along guide ribs on the butt and trigger component. On the way back, the cylinder was rotated one-twelfth by the action of a stud working in the zig-zag grooves on its surface, also cocking the action; going forward, the cylinder turned a further one-twelfth, bringing the next chamber into line with the hammer. The revolver was both fast and accurate: Walter Winans, one of the finest pistol shots of all time, was able to put six shots into a 2.0in (51mm) bull at 12 paces in seven seconds, which is impressive shooting indeed. The Webley-Fosbery was, however, never really popular as a service weapon; partly because mud and dirt tended to clog the recoiling apparatus, which naturally had to be made to fine tolerances; and partly because, unless the weapon was fired with an absolutely rigid arm, the recoil was not always sufficient to ensure smooth working. A seven-chambered version in 0.38in (9.6mm) caliber was made in small numbers.

Webley and Scott 0.455in Model 1904 Pistol UK

Length (gun): 10.0in (254mm)
Barrel: 6.5in (165mm)
Weight: 48.0oz (1.4kg)
Caliber: 0.455in (11.5mm)
Rifling: 7 grooves, r/hand
Capacity: seven
Muz vel: ca 750ft/sec (229m/sec)

By the end of the 19th Century it had become clear that the self-loading pistol had a future. Much of the work of development was done in Western Europe and, initially, neither the United States nor Britain showed much interest; both countries preferred to stick to their various revolvers, which had proved to be powerful and reliable weapons. However, the new system could not be ignored completely, and as early as 1898 Webley and Scott had sought a suitable design. Apart from the Webley-Mars (qv) the firm found nothing to its liking until the model illustrated here, which first went on to the market in 1904. As may be seen, it is of the characteristically square style which was later to become a noticeable feature of all Webley and Scott pistols of this type. It fired a powerful cartridge which necessitated a locked breech. The barrel and breech block remained locked on initial recoil until a vertical bolt dropped and allowed them to separate. The V-shaped recoil spring was situated under the right butt-plate. Overall, the weapon was of rather complex design; it was perhaps too well made, and is said to have been susceptible to stoppages caused by dirt. However, it set the general style for Webley self-loaders.

Webley No 1 Mk I 0.455in Pistol UK

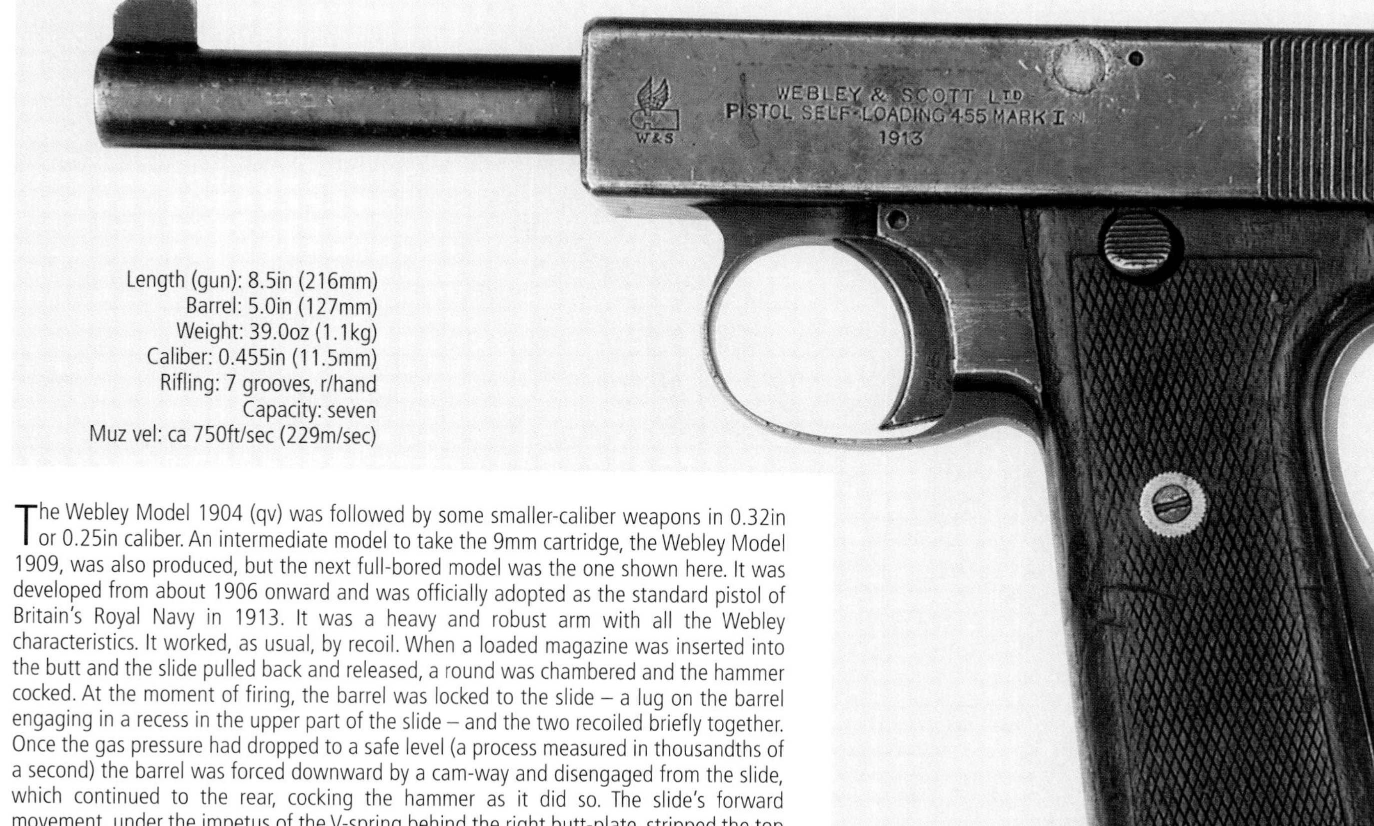

Length (gun): 8.5in (216mm)
Barrel: 5.0in (127mm)
Weight: 39.0oz (1.1kg)
Caliber: 0.455in (11.5mm)
Rifling: 7 grooves, r/hand
Capacity: seven
Muz vel: ca 750ft/sec (229m/sec)

The Webley Model 1904 (qv) was followed by some smaller-caliber weapons in 0.32in or 0.25in caliber. An intermediate model to take the 9mm cartridge, the Webley Model 1909, was also produced, but the next full-bored model was the one shown here. It was developed from about 1906 onward and was officially adopted as the standard pistol of Britain's Royal Navy in 1913. It was a heavy and robust arm with all the Webley characteristics. It worked, as usual, by recoil. When a loaded magazine was inserted into the butt and the slide pulled back and released, a round was chambered and the hammer cocked. At the moment of firing, the barrel was locked to the slide – a lug on the barrel engaging in a recess in the upper part of the slide – and the two recoiled briefly together. Once the gas pressure had dropped to a safe level (a process measured in thousandths of a second) the barrel was forced downward by a cam-way and disengaged from the slide, which continued to the rear, cocking the hammer as it did so. The slide's forward movement, under the impetus of the V-spring behind the right butt-plate, stripped the top round from the magazine and chambered it. A Mark II version, fitted with a stock was issued to the Royal Flying Corps in 1915 but was withdrawn upon the introduction of the aerial machine gun.

WEBLEY AND SCOTT 0.32IN PISTOL — UK

Length (gun): 6.3in (159mm)
Barrel: 3.5in (89mm)
Weight: 20.0oz (0.6kg)
Caliber: 0.32in (8.1mm)
Rifling: 7 grooves, r/hand
Capacity: eight
Muz vel: ca 900ft/sec (274m/sec)

Webley and Scott's earlier self-loading pistols were, in general, heavy-caliber weapons of service type, but there also appeared to be a demand for smaller and more compact pocket arms. The pistol illustrated here was patented in 1905 and was in production by the following year. It very soon proved popular; so much so, in fact, that its manufacture continued for almost 35 years. It was of simple blowback type with an external hammer; a point of interest is the fact that the recoil spring was V-shaped and was fitted to the frame inside the right butt-plate. Once the magazine was in position, all that was necessary was to pull back the slide by means of the ribbed finger-pieces, push up the safety catch, and fire. The original model had a safety on the left side of the hammer, but most of these pistols, including the one shown here, had the safety situated on the left side of the frame, where it also locked the slide. The trigger-guard was hinged at its top end and held into a socket at its lower end by the natural spring of its metal. When it was pulled clear, it was possible to strip the pistol by drawing forward the slide. Although this pistol was too small to be considered as a service arm, a good many officers owned and carried one as a secondary arm in the two World Wars. In addition, it was adopted in 1911 as the official pistol of the Metropolitan Police of London: this particular specimen was a police arm, for it is marked with a crown and the letters "MP."

WEBLEY AND SCOTT 0.25IN PISTOL — UK

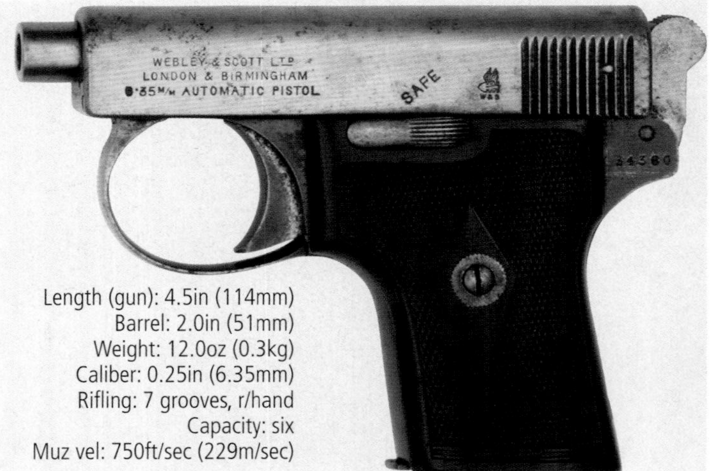

Length (gun): 4.5in (114mm)
Barrel: 2.0in (51mm)
Weight: 12.0oz (0.3kg)
Caliber: 0.25in (6.35mm)
Rifling: 7 grooves, r/hand
Capacity: six
Muz vel: 750ft/sec (229m/sec)

The Webley and Scott pistol of 0.32in caliber was closely followed by an even smaller version of the same type. Since laws for the control of firearms hardly existed in 1906, there appears to have been a very large market for pocket arms of this type. There were, however, numerous makers in Belgium, Germany, and elsewhere who were turning out such weapons at competitive prices; thus, it was necessary for the British company to produce its version as cheaply as possible. This pistol was essentially a scaled-down version of the 0.32in model. It was well and simply made. Because it was of small caliber and fired a low-powered cartridge, it was of simple blowback design. The main point of difference between this and other Webley self-loaders is that the V-spring under the grip was replaced by two coil springs in the slide, one on each side of the firing-pin. It was fitted with a safety catch and this example bears the usual Webley markings. It was strictly a pocket pistol, designed to fit into a waistcoat pocket or a lady's handbag, and lacked power and accuracy – although it would have been effective enough at close quarters. The model seen here was followed in 1909 by a hammerless version.

WEBLEY MODEL 1909 0.38IN PISTOL — UK

Length (gun): 8.0in (203mm)
Barrel: 5.0in (127mm)
Weight: 34.0oz (1.0kg)
Caliber: 0.38in (9.6mm)
Rifling: 7 grooves, r/hand
Capacity: seven
Muz vel: ca 750ft/sec (229m/sec)

In 1908, Webley began work on a pistol of international caliber, to meet the needs of civilian customers who did not require anything quite so powerful as the full-sized 0.455in cartridge used in the firm's various military models. The new weapon was on the market by 1909. It was designed principally to handle the 9mm Browning long cartridge, which had been introduced initially for the 1903 Browning pistol made by Fabrique Nationale. This round was of fair velocity and provided adequate stopping-power: it was popular in many parts of the world for civilian and police use, although it was not widely employed in the United States. The round was not sufficiently powerful to necessitate a locked breech, so it was possible for the arm to be of a simple blowback design. The first round had to be manually loaded in the usual way, but when it was fired it blew back the slide, cocked the hammer and compressed the recoil spring in the butt. The spring then drove the action forward and stripped and chambered the next cartridge. In this model, the barrel was held in position by a lug on top of the trigger-guard, which was pulled forward to strip the weapon. The earliest versions had a safety catch on the left-hand side of the frame, but later examples had a grip safety at the back of the butt, as seen in the photograph. When the safety was out, the sear was engaged, but when the butt was firmly gripped, the sear was forced into position so that the weapon could be fired. The Model 1909 was adopted by the South African Police in 1920 and production did not end until 1930.

WEBLEY 0.22IN MK III SINGLE-SHOT TARGET PISTOL — UK

Length (gun): 14.25in (362mm)
Barrel: 10.5in (267mm)
Weight: 36.0oz (1.0g)
Caliber: 0.22in (5.56mm)
Rifling: 7 grooves, r/hand
Capacity: one
Muz vel: ca 1,100ft/sec (335m/sec)

This Webley & Scott 0.22in target pistol remained in production with only the most minor changes from 1909 until 1965. The gun was of all-steel construction and was famed for the simplicity of its mechanism, which consisted of the hammer, trigger, and mainspring guide. The hammer had to be cocked for each shot and the gun was opened by pressing forward on the trigger guard, which released the barrel to tip forward, pivoting on the hinge at the front of the frame. There were some minor changes during this long production run: the original wooden grips were changed to plastic and the sights were made slightly more sophisticated, but the front end and action never changed at all. The pictures shows an early production version. In the opinion of shooters Webley showed a curious lack of ambition about this gun, never developing and offering trigger adjustments, decent sights, or choices of barrel length or weights. Indeed, very skilled shooters regarded it as on the light side and rather whippy, and many taped spare wheelweights under the barrel in an attempt to tame these characteristics. The sights were in square format, with the backsight windage and elevation adjustable by opposing screws.

Webley & Scott Single-Shot 0.22in Target Pistol — UK

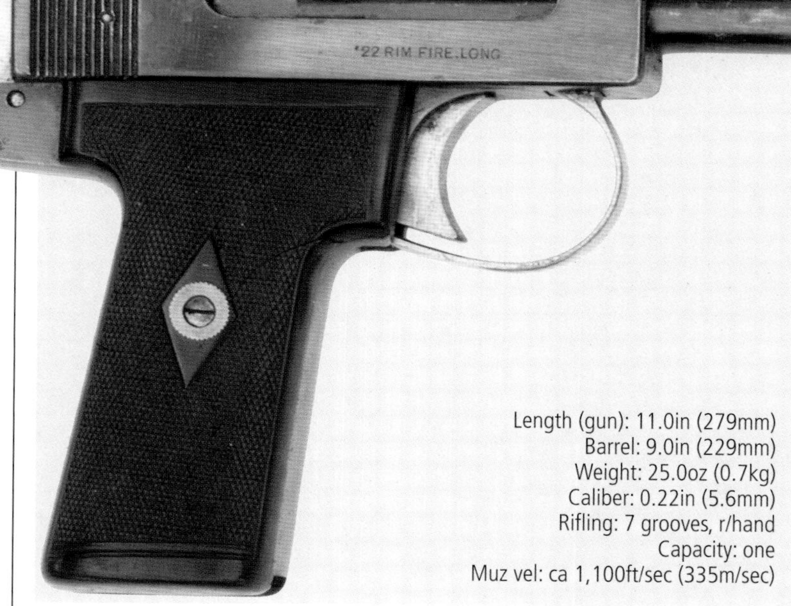

Length (gun): 11.0in (279mm)
Barrel: 9.0in (229mm)
Weight: 25.0oz (0.7kg)
Caliber: 0.22in (5.6mm)
Rifling: 7 grooves, r/hand
Capacity: one
Muz vel: ca 1,100ft/sec (335m/sec)

This somewhat unusual weapon was produced by Webley & Scott in 1911 to provide a means of cheap target practice for users of the firm's 0.32in self-loading pistol, the two weapons having a strong similarity in all but barrel length. The frame of the single-shot pistol was the same as that of the self-loader, although modified to accept a different barrel. The single-shot arm was made in two barrel lengths, 4.5in (114mm) and 9.0in (229mm); the one shown is of the latter type. In order to load the pistol, the slide was drawn back a distance of about 1.7in (44mm) with finger and thumb, thus exposing the breech; this action also cocked the hammer. A cartridge was then pushed into the chamber and, as there was no recoil system, the slide had to be pushed forward manually. The pistol was then ready to fire. After the shot had been fired, the slide was again pulled back and the case ejection. This action was performed by a flat ejector bar set on to the upper side of the barrel; at its front end was a milled slide (which is visible in the photograph, just in front of the slide). As with loading, the action had to be performed manually. At the moment of firing, the slide was held in position by a very light spring latch, situated on the bottom of the slide, which engaged in a groove in the body. There was a machined groove in the bottom of the butt where the magazine opening would normally be; this was intended for the attachment of a rifle-type butt.

Webley & Scott Mk V 0.455in Revolver — UK

The first of the Webley series of government service revolvers, the Mark I, was replaced in 1894 by a Mark II, which gave place in 1897 to a Mark III, which was chambered to take cartridges of 0.45in (11.4mm), 0.455in (11.5mm) and 0.476in (12.1mm) and had a different system of releasing the cylinder. The Mark IV which followed in 1899 is often referred to as the Boer War model. In December 1913, the Mark V was sealed as the standard government pistol, but only 20,000 were made before it was superseded in 1915 by the Mark VI. Thus, the Mark V is almost certainly the rarest of all the Webley and Scott government series. In general appearance it resembles its predecessors. It has an octagonal barrel with an integral foresight bed, the blade being inserted separately and held in place by a small screw. The locking system remains unchanged from earlier marks, as do the general details of the lock mechanism. The new system of removing the cylinder, first used on the Mark III, was retained. It consists of a cam (visible below the holster guide), which engaged a slot in the front of the cylinder. Loosening the screw allowed it to be pushed downwards: the cylinder could then be lifted clear. The butt is of the familiar bird-beak type, and this was the last mark to feature it. Most Mark Vs had 0.4in (102mm) barrels, but a few had barrels that were 2.0in (51mm) longer.

Length (gun): 11.0in (279mm)
Barrel: 6.0in (152mm)
Weight: 38.0oz (1.1kg)
Caliber: 0.455in (11.5mm)
Rifling: 7 grooves, r/hand
Capacity: six
Muz vel: ca 650ft/sec (198m/sec)

Webley & Scott Mk VI 0.455in Revolver — UK

Length (gun): 11.0in (279mm)
Barrel: 6.0in (152mm)
Weight: 37.0oz (1.1kg)
Caliber: 0.455in (11.5mm)
Rifling: 7 grooves, r/hand
Capacity: six
Muz vel: ca 650ft/sec

The famous Birmingham firm of P. Webley and Son (later Webley and Scott) had a virtual monopoly in the supply of British Government revolvers for very many years. The company's last, and probably best-known, service arm was the Webley and Scott Mk VI, seen here. It was officially introduced in 1915 and did not differ very much from its predecessors, except that the earlier bird-beak butt had been abandoned in favor of the more conventional squared-off style. It is of standard hinged-frame type, with a robust, stirrup-type, barrel catch: a tough and durable arm, and generally well suited to service use. Certainly, it stood up remarkably well to the mud and dirt inseparable from trench warfare in the period 1914-18. In the course of World War I, a short bayonet was designed for the revolver; although it was never officially adopted, it proved effective for trench raids and similar operations, and many officers bought them privately. A detachable butt, much like those available for the Mauser and Luger self-loading pistols, was also provided, but it was not widely used. This model was officially abandoned in 1932 in favor of a similar arm in 0.38in (9.6mm) caliber but many reserve officers still carried Mk VIs in 0.455in (11.5mm) caliber when they were recalled in 1939. The model was made in huge quantity, and many still exist.

Webley and Scott 0.22in Mk VI Revolver — UK

Length (gun): 11.0in (279mm)
Barrel: 6.0in (152mm)
Weight: 38.0oz (1.08kg)
Caliber: 0.22in (5.6mm)
Rifling: 7 grooves, r/hand
Capacity: six
Muz vel: ca 600ft/sec (183m/sec)

In 1915 there appeared the Webley and Scott Mark VI revolver which was made in large numbers, Webley having a contract to deliver 2,500 weekly. It was a solid and reliable arm, well suited to trench warfare. In order to improve its effectiveness as a close-quarter weapon, a bayonet was developed for it; this was never officially issued, but many were bought privately. To give individuals some preliminary practice, a small-caliber version (illustrated here) was made. It fired 0.22in (5.6mm) rimfire cartridges, allowing the revolver to be used on indoor ranges, and was economical in ammunition. As may be seen, it bears a strong resemblance to its patent arm. The main differences are its round barrel and its stepped cylinder, but its locking system, trigger-pull, and method of ejection resemble the orthodox Mark VI. There was a slightly different version, which was sometimes fitted with a shorter cylinder, the barrel then being correspondingly extended to the rear. It was a very accurate and well-balanced weapon and proved to be suitable for introductory practice for beginners; but it was not of much instructional value otherwise, because of the complete absence of recoil. And recoil, which tends to throw the muzzle more or less violently upward, is the chief difficulty for the novice user to overcome when using full-bore ammunition.

Webley 0.38in Mk IV Revolver — UK

Length (gun): 10.0in (254mm)
Barrel: 5.0in (127mm)
Weight: 27.0oz (0.8kg)
Caliber: 0.38in (9.6mm)
Rifling: 7 grooves, r/hand
Capacity: six
Muz vel: ca 700ft/sec (213m/sec)

The introduction of the Enfield No 2 Mk I revolver in 1932 marked the end of a long line of British service revolvers made by Webley and Scott, who had been virtually sole suppliers to the government since the introduction of their Mark I in 1887. However, the firm still had a great many other customers, and in 1923 it produced a Mark IV revolver in 0.38in (9.6mm) caliber to meet the demands of various military and police forces. It was, like other Webleys, a robust and reliable arm, and would chamber a variety of 0.38in (9.6mm) cartridges, thus making it suitable for worldwide use. The lead bullet originally used in the British Enfield had been abandoned in 1938 because of doubts as to whether it was, in fact, in breach of the St Petersburg convention. By the end of World War II, the supply of Enfield revolvers (many of which were, in fact, made by outside contractors) was beginning to lag: thus, in 1945, the British Government placed a large order with Webley and Scott for the Mk IV. This was not only a reliable arm, but also was so like the Enfield in handling qualities (and, indeed, in appearance; the dimensions differed only slightly) that no retraining was needed. It was, moreover, a double-action weapon, which most soldiers preferred. The Mk IV was produced with a strictly utility finish and lacked the handsome appearance of Webley's peace-time products.

Welrod 0.32in Silent Pistol — UK

Length (gun): 12.0in (305mm)
Barrel: 5.0in (127mm)
Weight: 32.0oz (0.9kg)
Caliber: 0.32in (8.1mm)
Rifling: 4 grooves, r/hand
Capacity: one
Muz vel: 700ft/sec (213m/sec)

There is, perhaps, a certain sinister fascination in the idea of being able to deliver death silently from a distance, although silent weapons have a limited value in war – there is usually so much noise in battle that one explosion more or less is hardly noticeable. Technically, it is not very difficult to silence a weapon; what is difficult is to make an effective silencer which is not so bulky as to make the weapon hopelessly clumsy in use. One requirement is to suppress the noise of the explosion; the other is to conceal what amounts to a sonic boom when the bullet breaks the sound barrier (assuming that it is of such velocity). Many pistol bullets do not exceed the speed of sound, which reduces the problem very considerably, as was the case with the cartridge fired by the Welrod pistol. The pistol's barrel was relatively short, but the outer casing in front of it was fitted with a series of self-sealing, oil-impregnated, leather washers. These closed behind the passage of the bullet and trapped the sound; but, of course, they tended to burn out after comparatively few shots. This would, naturally, have been a great disadvantage in a weapon designed for general use. However, in the case of the Welrod, the situation presumably never arose, because it was a weapon for use by special forces only.

PETER WEST "EXCELSIOR"/"SOUVERAIN" REVOLVER — UK

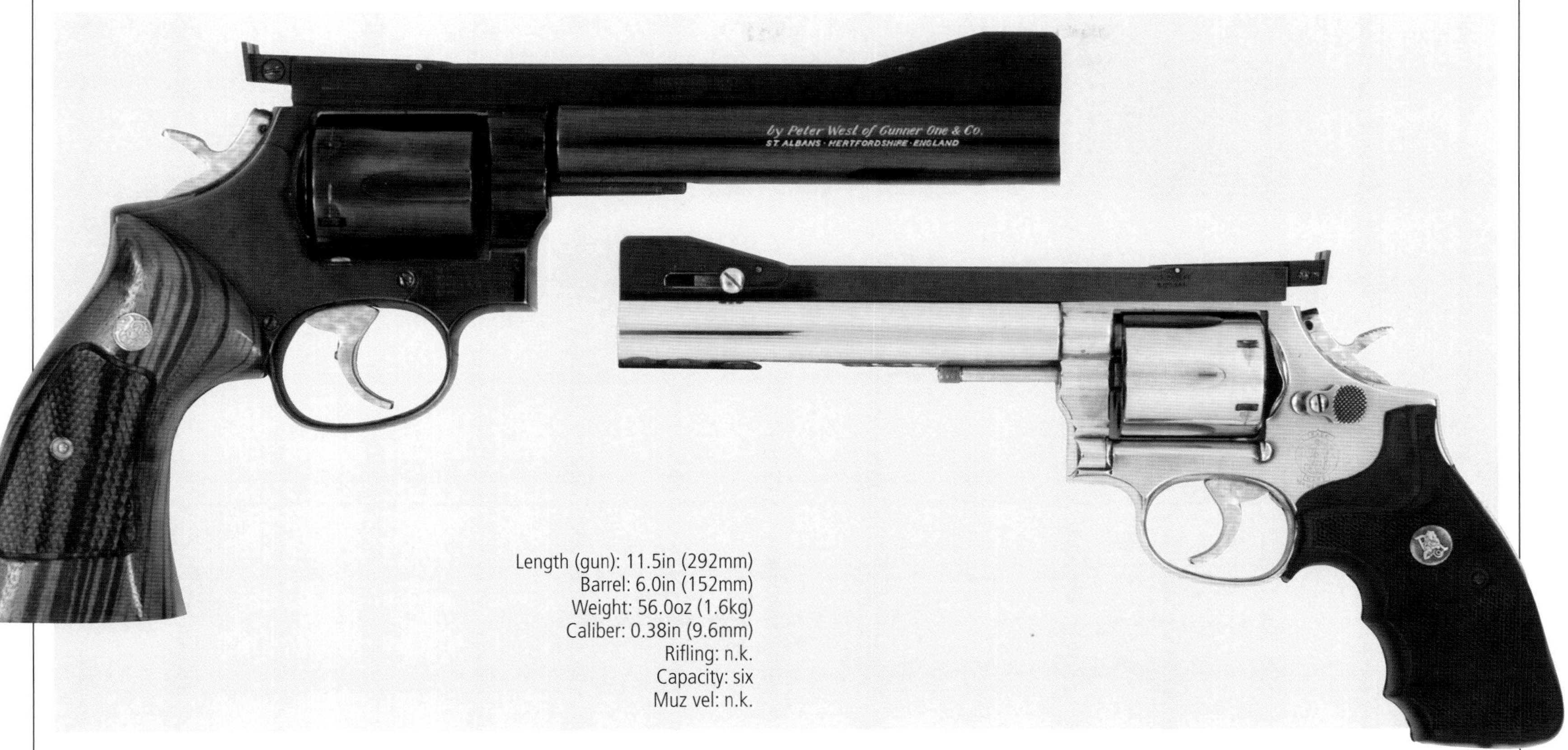

Length (gun): 11.5in (292mm)
Barrel: 6.0in (152mm)
Weight: 56.0oz (1.6kg)
Caliber: 0.38in (9.6mm)
Rifling: n.k.
Capacity: six
Muz vel: n.k.

Around 1960 United States police forces began to hold national meetings to discuss improvements on shooting techniques and this led to the idea of competitions with the intention of improving techniques. Unfortunately, the "experts" quickly became involved, rules were written, and then designers started to design handguns specifically for competition use. Like most other pistols in these police competitions, the two Peter West designs shown here are based on the Smith & Wesson Model 586/686 (qv), which was chosen because of its excellent mechanical design. This mechanism is comparatively straightforward to work on, with the crucial adjustments of cylinder timing and trigger return easy to effect, while the double engagement on double action gives a longer hammer throw, thus allowing a somewhat softer mainspring to be used. Both weapons have the Smith & Wesson frame and mechanism, coupled to a 6.0in (152mm) long Douglas barrel, which is 1.0in (25mm) wide at the muzzle. The two weapons differ slightly in their sighting arrangements and the Excelsior (see specifications) is blued with wooden grips, while the Souverain is of polished steel finish with Pachmayr grips.

WESTLEY RICHARDS REVOLVER — UK

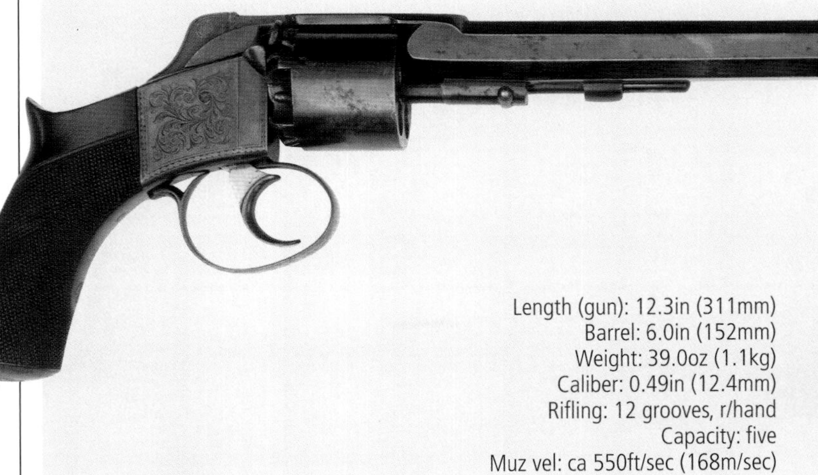

Length (gun): 12.3in (311mm)
Barrel: 6.0in (152mm)
Weight: 39.0oz (1.1kg)
Caliber: 0.49in (12.4mm)
Rifling: 12 grooves, r/hand
Capacity: five
Muz vel: ca 550ft/sec (168m/sec)

The name of Westley Richards has long been a well-respected one in British gunmaking, with a reputation for a wide variety of firearms. Westley Richards revolvers are, however, comparatively rare. This arm, which was made in about 1856, is of unusual design and construction. The barrel and top straps are a completely separate component. The barrel is held to the frame by the combination of two parts: a hook at the rear of the strap engaged in the top of the standing breech, where it was locked by means of a rotating pin, the handle of which is on the left-hand side. A sleeve below the barrel fits over the forward extension of the axis pin. This latter also has a small catch which engaged a slot in the axis pin to prevent accidental removal. The revolver has a double-action lock with a combless side-hammer. As this is positioned off-center, the nipples are necessarily angled so that the actual chamber is aligned with the bore. There is a push-in safety stud on the left-hand side. The top flat bears the inscription "WESTLEY RICHARDS 170 NEW BOND ST LONDON (PATENTEE)."

WILKINSON DOUBLE-BARREL, OVER-AND-UNDER PISTOL — UK

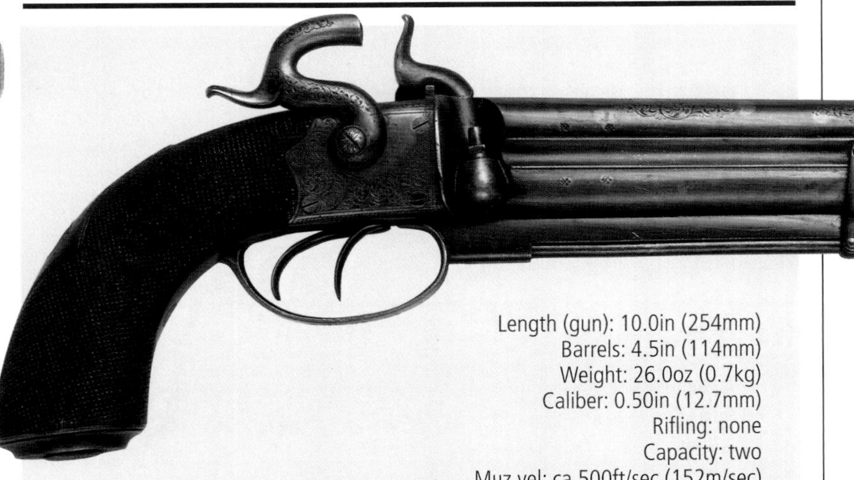

Length (gun): 10.0in (254mm)
Barrels: 4.5in (114mm)
Weight: 26.0oz (0.7kg)
Caliber: 0.50in (12.7mm)
Rifling: none
Capacity: two
Muz vel: ca 500ft/sec (152m/sec)

One of the first answers to the requirement for greater firepower was the double-barreled pistol, although the requirement for a flintlock on each side, one for each barrel, made it heavy and clumsy. Note that in the picture the left-hand barrel has been discharged, while the right-hand side is cocked. The barrels were "over-and-under" with the ramrod being retained by a swiveling stirrup to ensure that it did not fall to the ground or get lost. This weapon, made by Wilkinson of London in about 1830, for example, weighed 26.0oz (0.7kg), a hefty weight for such a small weapon. The problem would, however, soon be solved by the appearance of the revolver.

HOME-MADE REVOLVER

UK

Length (gun): 7.5in (190mm)
Barrel: 3.3in (83mm)
Weight: 25.0oz (0.71kg)
Caliber: 0.22in (5.6mm)
Rifling: none
Capacity: six
Muz vel: n.k.

This is an example of one of the most dangerous of weapons, a home-made firearm; it can only be described as a monstrosity. The manufacture of cartridges would prove a serious problem for almost anyone, but when factory-made ammunition is obtainable it is not difficult to improvize an instrument with which to fire it. Any person with basic knowledge of metalwork and access to a small workshop can do it – but, this said, it is essential to emphasize that the result is likely to be much more dangerous to the firer than to anyone else. The arm illustrated originated in Northern Ireland, although it is not known whether it was meant for serious use, or if it is simply the essay of an amateur gunsmith. It has a solid frame of heavy but crude construction. The round barrel has been bored very wide of center and it is not rifled. The cylinder has a capacity of six and its chambers are countersunk to cover the rims of the cartridges. The lump of metal below the cylinder contains a spring plunger; this engages in the circular depressions in the cylinder and thus ensures that the chamber under the hammer is aligned with the barrel. The cylinder itself must be rotated manually. As may be seen, the revolver has no trigger: the hammer is so designed that it must be drawn back by the thumb and then released, when a spring drives it forward with enough force to fire a 0.22in (5.6mm) rimfire round. This caliber was presumably chosen because such cartridges are easily obtained.

ZIP GUNS

UK

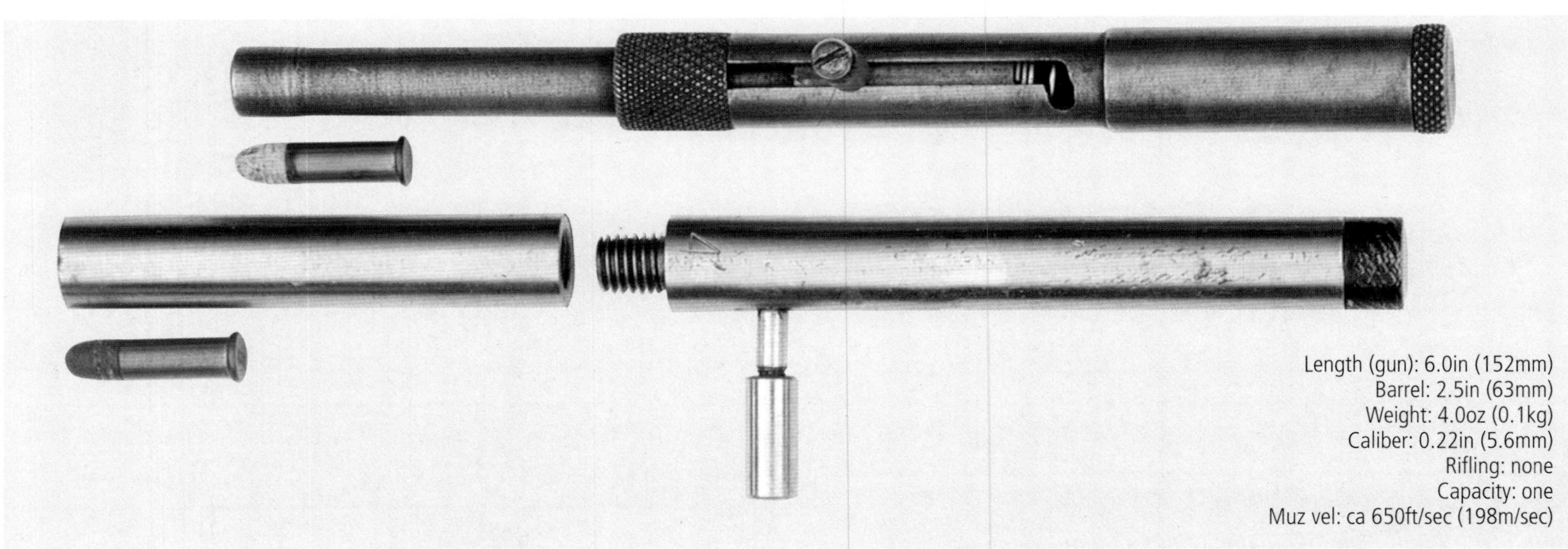

Length (gun): 6.0in (152mm)
Barrel: 2.5in (63mm)
Weight: 4.0oz (0.1kg)
Caliber: 0.22in (5.6mm)
Rifling: none
Capacity: one
Muz vel: ca 650ft/sec (198m/sec)

Home-made firearms are relatively common and it is difficult to generalize about their genesis. The really difficult thing for an amateur gunsmith is to obtain a supply of modern cartridges, but if these can be obtained, it is relatively simple for anyone with some basic skills in the use of metal-working tools to produce a device from which they may be fired. Such improvized weapons are usually of a two-piece construction, with a smooth-bored, screw-off barrel, and a simple striker mechanism in the handle. Some, however, are more sophisticated: they may be disguised as pens, torches, screwdrivers, or some other apparently harmless piece of equipment. The two specimens illustrated here originated in Northern Ireland, where they were found in about 1976. The data given apply only to the arms shown; naturally, individual weapons vary considerably.

HOME-MADE SINGLE-SHOT PISTOL

UK

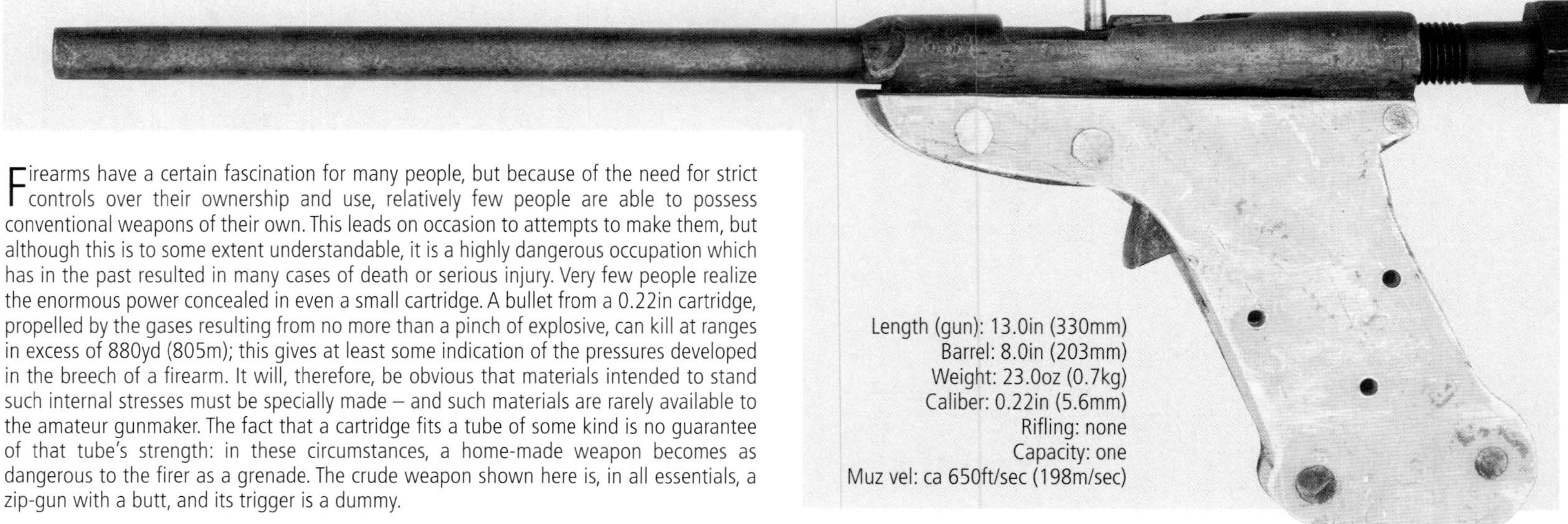

Firearms have a certain fascination for many people, but because of the need for strict controls over their ownership and use, relatively few people are able to possess conventional weapons of their own. This leads on occasion to attempts to make them, but although this is to some extent understandable, it is a highly dangerous occupation which has in the past resulted in many cases of death or serious injury. Very few people realize the enormous power concealed in even a small cartridge. A bullet from a 0.22in cartridge, propelled by the gases resulting from no more than a pinch of explosive, can kill at ranges in excess of 880yd (805m); this gives at least some indication of the pressures developed in the breech of a firearm. It will, therefore, be obvious that materials intended to stand such internal stresses must be specially made – and such materials are rarely available to the amateur gunmaker. The fact that a cartridge fits a tube of some kind is no guarantee of that tube's strength: in these circumstances, a home-made weapon becomes as dangerous to the firer as a grenade. The crude weapon shown here is, in all essentials, a zip-gun with a butt, and its trigger is a dummy.

Length (gun): 13.0in (330mm)
Barrel: 8.0in (203mm)
Weight: 23.0oz (0.7kg)
Caliber: 0.22in (5.6mm)
Rifling: none
Capacity: one
Muz vel: ca 650ft/sec (198m/sec)

Home-Made Single-Shot 0.41in Pistol — UK

In the era of muzzle-loading arms, most pistols were smooth-bored and could, of course, be used to fire either for shot or ball – although the combination of slow-burning black powder and a short barrel probably had an adverse effect on both pattern and velocity. After the introduction of the breechloader firing self-contained cartridges, however, production of such dual-purpose arms virtually ceased, and specialized types necessarily emerged. One such type was the shot pistol.The pistol illustrated was home-made, and although a good deal has already been said on the very real dangers involved in making and using home-made firearms, the point may usefully be reiterated here. It will, perhaps, surprise many readers to learn that a diminutive 0.410in cartridge of the type fired by this weapon develops appreciably higher pressures than those normally produced by the much larger 12-bore cartridge. The reason for this is that, in order to produce an effective shot pattern, the column of shot in the smaller cartridge has to be very long in relation to its diameter. Sufficient force must then be applied to the very small area at the base of this column of shot to force it from the barrel at a lethal velocity of something in the region of 1,200ft/sec (366m/sec); thus, the charge must be a comparatively large one. The weapon shown here was made with the cut-down barrel of a 0.410in shotgun, but the locking system was fundamentally weak and the metal used in it was inadequate both in weight and quality. It was probable that a few shots would have been enough to destroy it.

Length (gun): 9.0in (229mm)
Barrel: 6.0in (152mm)
Weight: 25.0oz (0.7kg)
Caliber: 0.410in (10.4mm)
Rifling: none
Capacity: one
Muz vel: ca 1,000ft/sec (305m/sec)

Cannon-Barreled Flintlock Pistol — UK

Weapons of this type took their name from the obvious resemblance of their barrels to those of the type of cannon then in use. As an alternative, they are frequently known as "Queen Anne pistols," although this suggests a date that is really a trifle early; the queen died in 1714, at a time when arms of this type were only just beginning to appear. They continued to be made thereafter until at least 1775 – and possibly very much later. The pistol seen here bears no maker's name, but it was almost certainly made in England in about 1725. Its size shows it to be a holster pistol and it was probably originally one of a pair. It is of medium quality, of the kind which would have been carried by the guard on a coach or by a mounted servant escorting his master on a journey (a very necessary precaution in the 18th Century, when footpads lurked on most highways). The pistol has no butt-cap and the butt itself is of slightly unusual shape: generally, butts of this type had more bulbous ends. It has a swan-necked cock (from which the top jaw and screw are missing), and the slight roughening on the surface of the jaw was to ensure that the flint, which was often seated in leather, was held firmly. The tail of the combined pan cover and steel (now often known as the frizzen) would bear on a characteristically shaped curved spring which governed the degree of resistance to the falling flint: it was necessary for the pan to open quickly and smoothly, while still offering enough resistance to ensure good sparks. Some weapons of this type had ramrods held in a pipe or pipes below the barrel.

Length (gun): 14.8in (375mm)
Barrel: 9.3in (235mm)
Weight: 28.0oz (0.79kg)
Caliber: 0.65in (16.5mm)
Rifling: none
Capacity: one
Muz vel: ca 450ft/sec (137m/sec)

Over-and-Under Pistol — UK

It was the advent of the percussion system in the first quarter of the 19th Century which first made it possible to produce double-barreled pistols of reasonably large calibers, without at the same time making them unacceptably bulky. Even with the use of the percussion system, however, a double-barreled, side-by-side pistol of musket bore would be about 2in (51mm) wide across the breech. Gunmakers therefore developed weapons with one barrel set above the other, which, if it did not reduce the actual bulk, at least ensured that it was better distributed, thus resulting in a somewhat more compact weapon. The pistol seen here is a good example of the type. Although of good quality, it has no maker's mark: this is rather surprising, but since it bears Birmingham proof marks it may well be one of the many pirated copies of fine arms, which were turned out in large quantity, and in widely varying quality, by a number of small Birmingham makers. The barrels, with fixed sights, are bored out of a single block of steel, with a flat top rib, complete with fore- and backsight, and concave side ribs. The lower barrel has a separate rib to accommodate the swivel ramrod, which is held securely in place by a small spring catch situated inside the end pipe, in front of the trigger-guard. The breech ends of the barrels have flash shields, the right-hand one being longer than the left because of the lowness of the nipple on the under barrel. This also necessitates the long, trunk-like (and rather ugly) nose on the right-hand hammer. The checkered butt, which is of modern shape, contains the usual cap compartment, and all the metalwork is lightly engraved.

Length (gun): 9.8in (248mm)
Barrel: 4.0in (102mm)
Weight: 30.0oz (1.9kg)
Caliber: 0.500in (12.7mm)
Rifling: none
Capacity: two
Muz vel: ca 550ft/sec (168m/sec)

TRANSITIONAL REVOLVER WITH BAYONET — UK

Length (gun): 12.0in (305mm)
Barrel: 5.8in (147mm)
Weight: 32.0oz (0.9kg)
Caliber: 0.42in (10.7mm)
Rifling: 9 grooves, r/hand
Capacity: six
Muz vel: ca 500ft/sec (152m/sec)

This interesting arm shows the lines along which the transitional revolver developed in the mid-19th Century. The revolver has a folding bayonet, part of which is just visible above the barrel. It will, however, be seen that there is a strong projection below the cylinder to which a corresponding projection below the barrel is firmly screwed, thus making a very considerable contribution to the strength and rigidity of the weapon. The frame is made of iron and the butt is of a handy size and it is in most respects a robust and serviceable arm. The exact function of arms like this cannot be defined with certainty: it was probably intended to be for self-defense; but the presence of the bayonet (although of little larger size than a pen-knife) suggests at least some degree of offensive intent. The weapon may possibly have been of the naval type often referred to as boarding pistols.

DUAL-IGNITION REVOLVER — UK

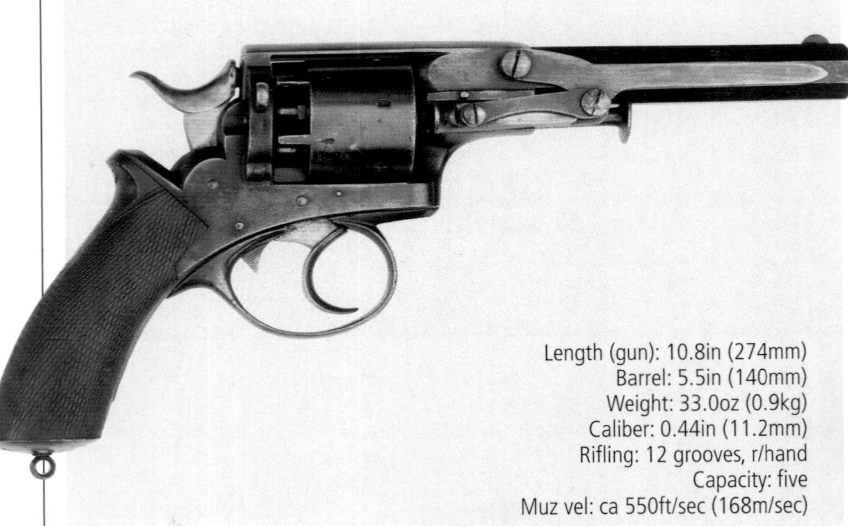

Length (gun): 10.8in (274mm)
Barrel: 5.5in (140mm)
Weight: 33.0oz (0.9kg)
Caliber: 0.44in (11.2mm)
Rifling: 12 grooves, r/hand
Capacity: five
Muz vel: ca 550ft/sec (168m/sec)

Apart from some anonymous copies of the early Smith and Wesson cartridge revolver which appeared in Britain in 1860, it is probable that cartridge arms by known makers did not appear until 1863. In the meantime, as had happened during the period of transition from flintlock to percussion arms some 30 years earlier, more conservative users preferred to stick to their well-tried percussion revolvers rather than change. There was, however, a small intermediate category of dual-ignition revolver which, thanks to a certain amount of ingenuity by the makers, could be used either as percussion or cartridge arms, simply by changing the cylinder. The revolver seen here is one such. Its origin is by no means certain. It is of Webley style and is marked "WEBLEYS PATENT," but since this inscription appears on many arms with little or no connection with the firm, it is not a reliable guide. Webley did make a dual-purpose revolver of similar type, but it had a Kerr-type rammer on the left-hand side. In fact, the arm shown is probably a hybrid from some unknown workshop. It is of robust construction and the cylinders were easily changed (the cartridge cylinder is, unfortunately, missing from this example). The rammer, the lever of which acted downward, drove a very tight ram into the chambers and was equally effective for loading bullets or ejecting cases, the latter by bearing on their front edges. It was, however, slow to operate, because of the need for absolute alignment of ram and chamber. It has a hinged loading-gate for use with centerfire cartridges. This type of arm had a short life, for the metallic cartridge was soon in universal use, rendering it obsolete.

TIP-UP REVOLVER — UK

Length (gun): 10.5in (267mm)
Barrel: 5.8in (146mm)
Weight: 35.0oz (1.0kg)
Caliber: 0.50in (12.7mm)
Rifling: 3 grooves, r/hand
Capacity: six
Muz vel: ca 600ft/sec (183m/sec)

This large and robust revolver by an unknown maker has Birmingham proof marks and bears the words "CAST STEEL" on the barrel. It is of "tip-up" type. When the milled head of an arm attached to the rear part of the trigger-guard was pushed hard over to the left, it not only locked the hammer at half-cock, so as to prevent any accidental discharge, but also unlocked the barrel catch. This allowed the barrel and cylinder to be turned over well beyond the vertical, until the top strap rested on the head of the hammer. Increased pressure on the lever forming the front half of the trigger-guard activated a pin attached to a star extractor, forcing it out from the rear of the cylinder to eject the rounds or empty cases from the chambers. When the lever was released, the extractor returned automatically to its original position and the cylinder could then be reloaded. The barrel and cylinder were then returned to the closed position and locked by means of the lever with the milled head. This action also had the effect of freeing the hammer and allowing the double-action lock mechanism to function in the normal way. It was desirable that the pistol be held horizontally on its side during this process; otherwise, there was a considerable risk that the rounds would fall out of the chambers under their own weight. Cylinder rotation in this arm was by the usual method of pawl and ratchet. Although the principle of this revolver was sound enough, it would have been too complex for a service arm. In particular, the risk of cartridges falling accidentally from the cylinder when reloading in a hurry was considerable.

Copy of Webley R.I.C. Revolver — UK

Length (gun): 8.8in (222mm)
Barrel: 4.0in (102mm)
Weight: 30.0oz (0.9kg)
Caliber: 0.45in (11.4mm)
Rifling: 7 grooves, r/hand
Capacity: five
Muz vel: ca 650ft/sec (198m/sec)

In 1867, P. Webley and Son placed on the market a new revolver, which was adopted by the Royal Irish Constabulary (R.I.C.) In 1868. It was also adopted by many other colonial military and police forces, and sold widely as a civilian arm. In fact, it was possibly the most popular arm ever made by Webley. The model went through many variations and, almost inevitably, was widely copied. As may be seen by comparison with the genuine Webley models (qv), the weapon shown is a very close copy of the original: this particular example is based on the Webley No 1 New Model of 1883. The weapon has a solid frame; the barrel (unlike that of the original Webley) is integral with it and not screwed in. The barrel is practically cylindrical, but its upper part is drawn to a rib, making it basically ovate in section, with a very slight taper towards the breech-end. The five-chambered cylinder has the half-fluting associated with later Webley models. There is the usual bottom-hinged loading gate on the right-hand side of the frame, with a deep groove to facilitate loading. The extractor pin was normally housed in the hollow cylinder axis pin, but it could be withdrawn and swiveled out to the right so as to align with the chamber opposite the loading gate.

Tip-Up Revolver — UK

Length (gun): 8.5in (216mm)
Barrel: 4.0in (102mm)
Weight: 21.0oz (0.6kg)
Caliber: 0.38in (9.6mm)
Rifling: 5 grooves, r/hand
Capacity: six
Muz vel: ca 600ft/sec (183m/sec)

This weapon is another attempt to speed up the reloading rate of a cartridge revolver. Although of good quality, it bears no maker's name; but its general style and its London proofmarks indicate that it is of British origin. It is a cartridge revolver of the "tip-up" type: upward pressure on the circular catch at the lower front of the frame allowed the barrel to be raised to the vertical. Then, the very thick ejector pin – which is, in fact, shaped with a right-angled knob like an ordinary door bolt – was first rotated as far as possible, exerting a powerful camming action on the star-shaped extractor, and then pushed sharply backwards, thus thrusting out the extractor with its empty cases. The general principle was a sound one and foreshadowed the introduction of the "tip-down" revolver with its automatic ejector. Its main weakness appears to lie in the catch, which did not engage deeply with the frame and might have opened accidentally.

Bulldog-Type Revolver — UK

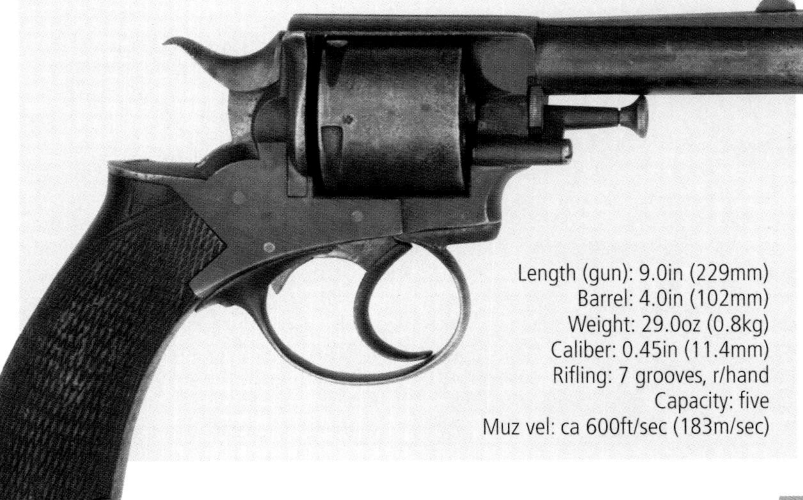

Length (gun): 9.0in (229mm)
Barrel: 4.0in (102mm)
Weight: 29.0oz (0.8kg)
Caliber: 0.45in (11.4mm)
Rifling: 7 grooves, r/hand
Capacity: five
Muz vel: ca 600ft/sec (183m/sec)

Many revolvers like the one illustrated here were purchased in the mid-19th Century for self-protection, especially against burglars and, because many of them spent their lives lying in readiness in chests or cupboards, but were rarely or never used, they survived in surprisingly large numbers. This particular specimen has the usual ovate barrel with top rib and is of solid-frame construction. The five-chambered cylinder is plain, except for slots for the cylinder stop, and bears Birmingham proof marks. The ejector is of the usual pin pattern and it was carried inside the hollow cylinder axis pin when it was not in use. In addition, it is fitted with a swivel carrier on the right front of the frame; this allowed it to be drawn out and swung over so as to come into line with the chamber aligned with the loading gate. The gate itself is hinged at the bottom and turned down sideways; the usual groove is cut in the frame beside it to facilitate the loading of cartridges into the chambers. The lock is of orthodox double-action type, with a fairly wide, milled comb on the hammer. The arm has a one-piece, wrap-over grip of checkered walnut; this is fastened to the revolver by two vertical screws, one running downward from the rear of the frame behind the hammer, and the other running upward from the butt-plate. The revolver originally had a swivel ring, but this is now missing; such rings were often provided with a short wrist-strap instead of the lanyards usually found on heavier arms of the type. The arm is marked on the top strap with the words "G. E. GIBBS 29 CORN ST, BRISTOL."

ALLEN AND THURBER PEPPERBOX USA

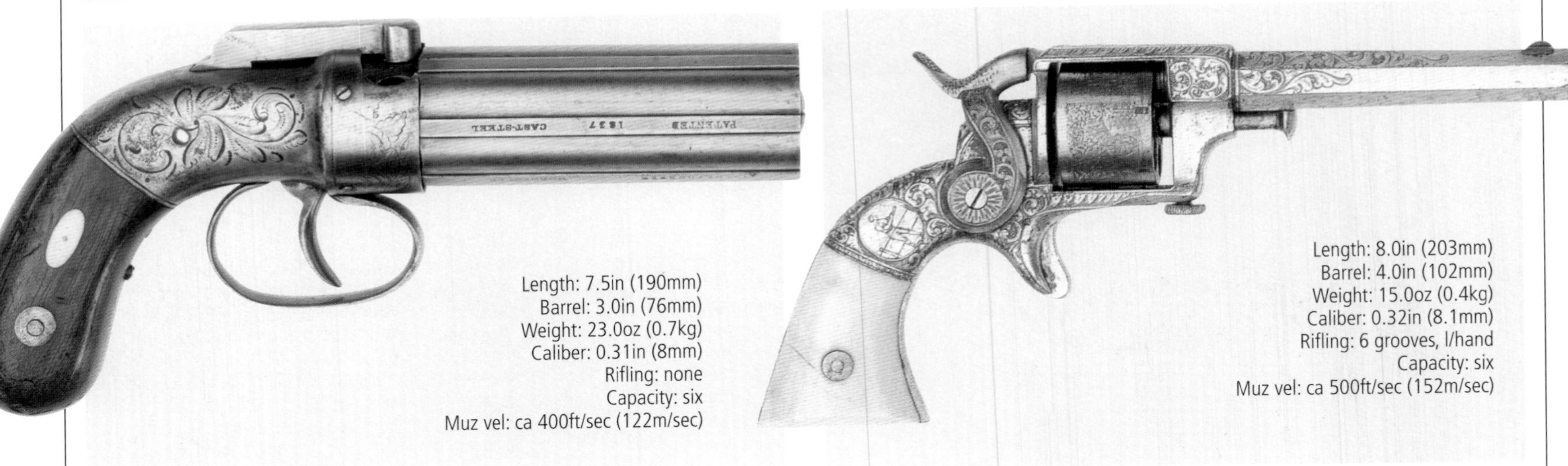

Length: 7.5in (190mm)
Barrel: 3.0in (76mm)
Weight: 23.0oz (0.7kg)
Caliber: 0.31in (8mm)
Rifling: none
Capacity: six
Muz vel: ca 400ft/sec (122m/sec)

This pistol was made in Worcester, Massachusetts, by the well-known American firm of Allen and Thurber. Ethan Allen set up in business as a gunmaker with his brother-in-law in the late 1830s and thereafter made a variety of civilian arms, including rifles. He was, however, best known for his pepperbox pistols. These were for some years by far the most popular repeating arms in the United States, until they were finally displaced by the more modern percussion revolvers of Colt and others. The weapon seen here is neat, compact and of the quality traditionally associated with the firm. Its six barrels are bored out of a single block of steel, with ribs between: two of the ribs bear the inscriptions "PATENTED 1837, CAST STEEL" and "ALLEN & THURBER WORCESTER." The subject of the patent referred to was, in fact, the double-action bar hammer mechanism. Steady pressure on the trigger caused the rear-hinged hammer (which is inscribed "ALLEN PATENT") to rise until the lifter hook disengaged, allowing it to fall and strike the cap. The action of the trigger also rotated the barrel cluster by means of a pawl and ratchet. Access to the lock mechanism was gained by removing a plate on the left-hand side of the breech. The nipples, which are set at right-angles to the barrels, are covered by a close-fitting shield; an aperture to the right of the hammer nose gave access to them for recapping. Light pressure on the trigger lifted the nose clear of the nipple and allowed the barrels to be rotated clockwise for recapping. The butt consists of a continuous metal strap made integrally with the body; both of its two wooden side plates, held by a screw, bear small, oval, escutcheon plates.

ALLEN AND WHEELOCK REVOLVER USA

Length: 8.0in (203mm)
Barrel: 4.0in (102mm)
Weight: 15.0oz (0.4kg)
Caliber: 0.32in (8.1mm)
Rifling: 6 grooves, l/hand
Capacity: six
Muz vel: ca 500ft/sec (152m/sec)

This revolver, made by Ethan Allen and Thomas P. Wheelock has a solid frame, including the butt, into which an octagonal barrel is screwed. There were no facilities either for loading the revolver or ejecting the empty cases with the cylinder in position. In order to perform these operations, it was necessary first to remove the large-headed screw below the front frame, which allowed the cylinder axis to be drawn forward and the cylinder removed. Empty cases could then be punched out by the axis pin, the chambers reloaded, if necessary, and the cylinder replaced. This made the revolver very slow to reload, but it also greatly simplified manufacture and thus made it cheap to produce. The weapon has a single-action lock with an external hammer on the right-hand side, access to the mechanism being gained by way of an oval inspection plate on the left. The trigger is of the variety known as "sheathed"; it has no trigger-guard, and this reduced its bulk and made it a suitable pocket arm. The barrel and frame are crudely engraved with a standing pugilist on the right side and a kneeling one on the left, with a further motif of boxing gloves on the inspection plate cover. The butt plates are of ivory or bone, probably the latter. The arm is cheap in overall appearance, but was probably sufficiently robust for use as an occasional pocket arm. The left-hand flat of the barrel is marked "ALLEN AND WHEELOCK, WORCESTER, MS US" and "ALLENS PAT'S SEP 7 NOV 9 1858," and the weapon is numbered 444.

ETHAN ALLEN POCKET REVOLVER USA

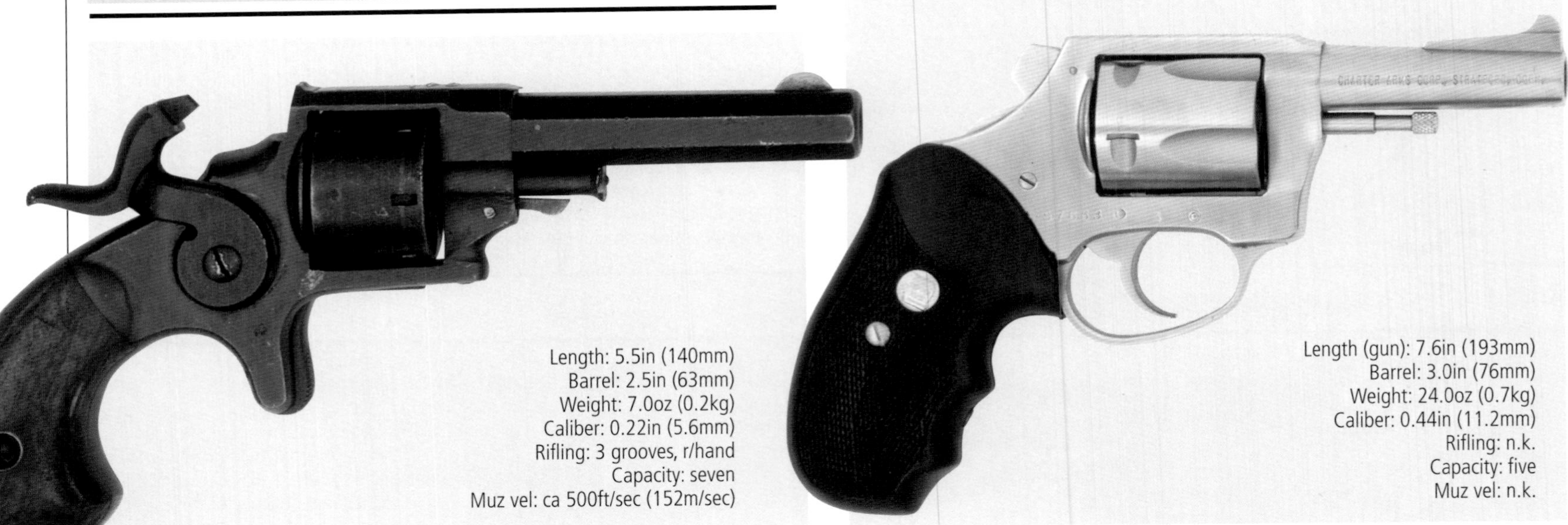

Length: 5.5in (140mm)
Barrel: 2.5in (63mm)
Weight: 7.0oz (0.2kg)
Caliber: 0.22in (5.6mm)
Rifling: 3 grooves, r/hand
Capacity: seven
Muz vel: ca 500ft/sec (152m/sec)

The perfection of the rimfire cartridge and the expiry of Smith & Wesson's patent for the bored-through cylinder in 1869 gave rise to a great increase in production of small, cheap, pocket pistols – for which there was apparently an almost insatiable demand in the United States. Ethan Allen continued to manufacture pepperbox pistols for some time, but after his death in 1871 his company switched to pistols of the type seen here. It has an octagonal steel barrel screwed into a gunmetal frame, and a seven-chambered steel cylinder to take rimfire cartridges. In order to load the weapon, it was necessary first to press up the catch under the cylinder axis pin, which would then be drawn out and the cylinder removed. The empty cases were knocked out with the axis pin; this made the weapon relatively cheap to manufacture.

CHARTER ARMS 0.44IN BULLDOG REVOLVER USA

Length (gun): 7.6in (193mm)
Barrel: 3.0in (76mm)
Weight: 24.0oz (0.7kg)
Caliber: 0.44in (11.2mm)
Rifling: n.k.
Capacity: five
Muz vel: n.k.

Practice aside, the 0.44in Special round's primary modern role is defensive and the gun most frequently selected by American users in the 1970s and 1980s was the Charter Arms Bulldog. This was introduced in 1973 and proved to be a great success, with well over half-a-million made up the mid-1980s, with production running at some 37,000 per year. It is a selective double-action weapon with an outside hammer and a solid frame (of stainless steel in the picture above) with a thumb latch on the left which releases the crane-mounted cylinder to swing out to the left for loading and unloading. There is a square concave foresight and a square notch backsight milled into the top of the receiver. The Bulldog makes an interesting comparison with the 0.44in Smith & Wesson "Horton Special" (qv).

Colt Dragoon Model 1849 Revolver — USA

Length: 13.5in (343mm)
Barrel: 7.5in (190mm)
Weight: 68.0oz (1.9kg)
Caliber: 0.44in (11.2mm)
Rifling: 7 grooves, l/hand
Capacity: six
Muz vel: ca 850ft/sec (259m/sec)

The earliest versions of the unusually heavy arm seen here were the Walker or Whitneyville-Walker models, which appeared as a result of the increased demand for arms caused by the Mexican War of 1846. These were followed by the Dragoon series, so called because the weapons were primarily used to arm cavalry of that description. This particular specimen is the Colt Dragoon Model 1849 (although it should be noted that it has the square-backed trigger-guard not often found at such a late date). It has a round barrel with a fixed foresight; the backsight is incorporated into the top of the hammer. The barrel is keyed to the very robust axis pin and is further supported by a solid lug butted to the lower frame. Below the barrel is the arm's very powerful compound rammer, which forced the bullets into the chambers so tightly that neither damp nor the flash from previous shots could enter. This weapon has been over-cleaned, but traces of the engraving showing a "Red Indian" combat scene remain on the cylinder. The trigger-guard and butt-straps are of brass, and the butt has walnut sideplates. The weapon is numbered 5818; the barrel lug bears the inscription "ADDRESS SAML COLT NEW YORK CITY." The frame is marked "PATENT US."

Colt Navy Revolver — USA

Length: 12.9in (328mm)
Barrel: 7.5in (190mm)
Weight: 39.0oz (1.1kg)
Caliber: 0.36in (9.1mm)
Rifling: 7 grooves, r/hand
Capacity: six
Muz vel: ca 700ft/sec (213m/sec)

The Navy revolver, first introduced in 1851, was in every respect a more manageable arm than the Dragoon Model 1849 and very soon became extremely popular. Colt, having begun production at his new factory, decided that the time had come to aim at exporting on a large scale. The Great Exhibition held in London in 1851 provided him with an excellent opportunity for publicity, and his very impressive display of revolvers there attracted a great deal of attention. The revolver was then little known in England, but its merits were quickly appreciated. There were, in addition, one or two excellent British-made arms of similar type on view at the Exhibition, notably the Adams revolver; but these were largely hand-made prototypes and there was little immediate chance of their being made in large numbers, whereas Colt was ready to go into production. The revolver illustrated is of broadly similar type to the Dragoon, although of course, smaller. It has an octagonal barrel with a bead foresight; the barrel is secured to the frame by means of a wedge through the very stout cylinder axis pin and is firmly braced against the lower frame. The six-chambered cylinder is plain, except for rectangular depressions for the stop, and still bears traces of engraving showing a naval engagement. The revolver has a hemispherical standing breech, in which a depression is located on the right-hand side so as to allow access to the nipples. The revolver was made in Colt's London factory, which was in operation in 1853-57, and is stamped "ADDRESS COL COLT LONDON" on the top barrel flat.

Colt 0.44in Model 1860 Army Revolver — USA

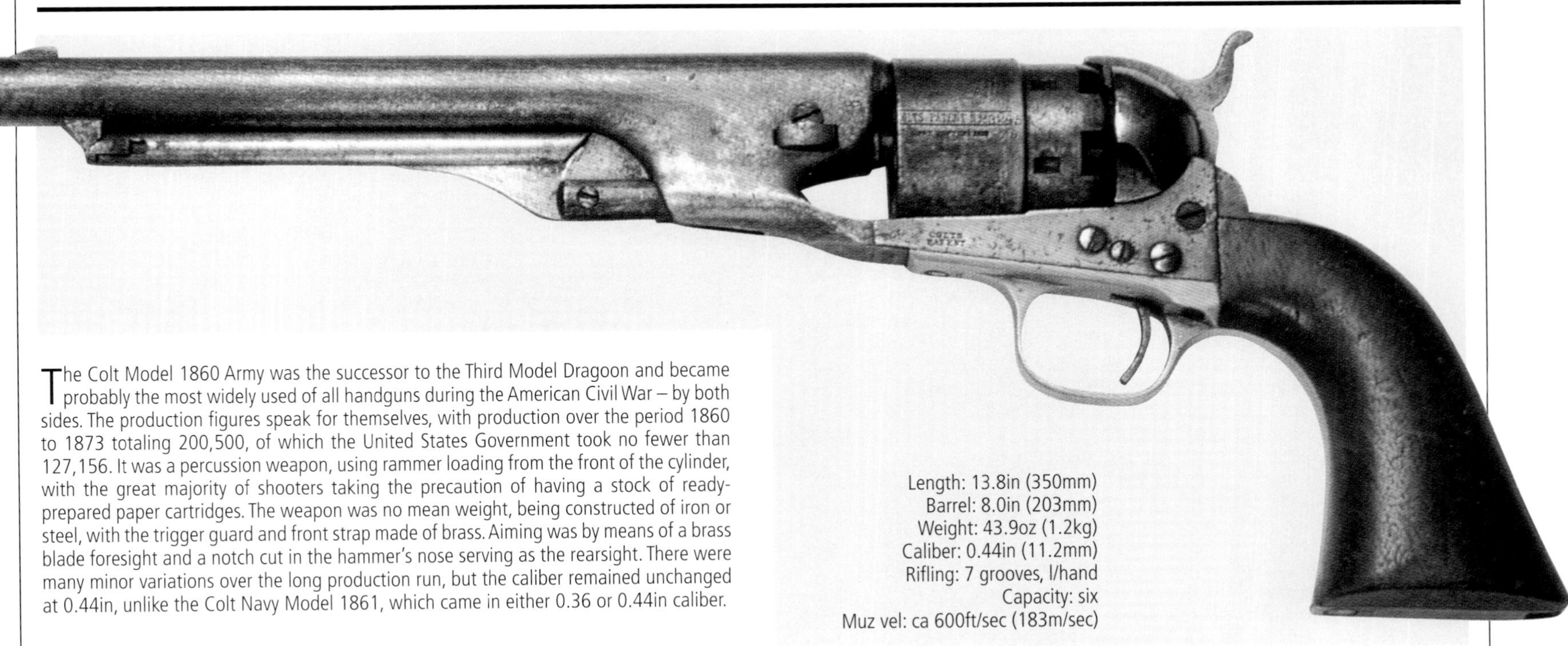

The Colt Model 1860 Army was the successor to the Third Model Dragoon and became probably the most widely used of all handguns during the American Civil War – by both sides. The production figures speak for themselves, with production over the period 1860 to 1873 totaling 200,500, of which the United States Government took no fewer than 127,156. It was a percussion weapon, using rammer loading from the front of the cylinder, with the great majority of shooters taking the precaution of having a stock of ready-prepared paper cartridges. The weapon was no mean weight, being constructed of iron or steel, with the trigger guard and front strap made of brass. Aiming was by means of a brass blade foresight and a notch cut in the hammer's nose serving as the rearsight. There were many minor variations over the long production run, but the caliber remained unchanged at 0.44in, unlike the Colt Navy Model 1861, which came in either 0.36 or 0.44in caliber.

Length: 13.8in (350mm)
Barrel: 8.0in (203mm)
Weight: 43.9oz (1.2kg)
Caliber: 0.44in (11.2mm)
Rifling: 7 grooves, l/hand
Capacity: six
Muz vel: ca 600ft/sec (183m/sec)

COLT FRONTIER/PEACEMAKER 0.44IN REVOLVER USA

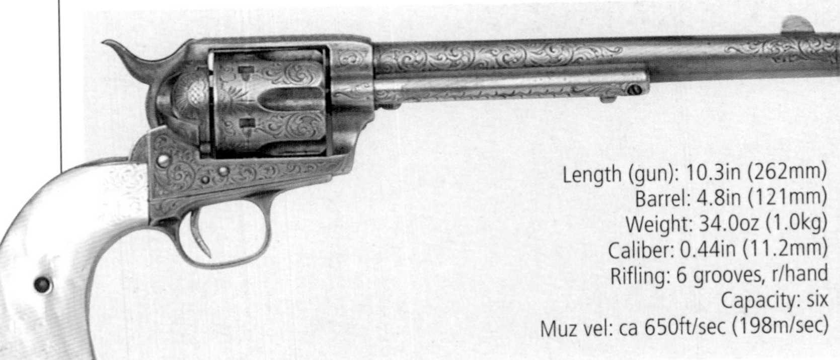

Length (gun): 10.3in (262mm)
Barrel: 4.8in (121mm)
Weight: 34.0oz (1.0kg)
Caliber: 0.44in (11.2mm)
Rifling: 6 grooves, r/hand
Capacity: six
Muz vel: ca 650ft/sec (198m/sec)

The civilian version of the Colt Single-Action Army became one of the most important and widely used handguns in the American West, where it was known either as the "Peacemaker" or, in this 0.44in-40 form, as the "Frontier." The gun had excellent balance and felt right in anyone's hand. The actual gun shown here is a presentation version of the Colt Frontier 0.44in-40 caliber, which was silver-plated and embellished by an artist named Cuno Helfricht in about 1880. It also has engraved, mother-of-pearl butt grips and is, in every way, a superior example of the gunmaker's art, but quite capable of killing someone, for all that. Most civilian models had a 4.75in (121mm) barrel, but some were much longer and the "Buntline Model" (named after the author of "Westerns" who commissioned them) had a 12.0in (305mm) barrel. The butt grips of these civilian models appeared in a variety of materials including walnut (as in the military version) but also hard rubber, ivory, and even mother-of-pearl, as shown here. The Colt Peacemaker/Frontier remained in production by Colt until 1941, by which time 357,859 had been produced in around 36 different calibers. After a gap of some 15 years Colt was persuaded to place it back in production. This was one of the best revolvers that Colt ever produced; it is certainly the most famous and is much a part of the Western legend as the Winchester rifle and the cowboy himself.

COLT HOUSE PISTOL USA

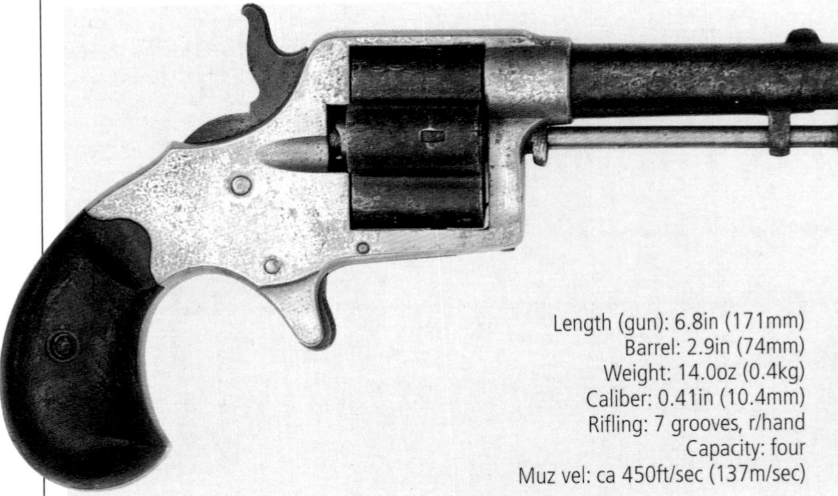

Length (gun): 6.8in (171mm)
Barrel: 2.9in (74mm)
Weight: 14.0oz (0.4kg)
Caliber: 0.41in (10.4mm)
Rifling: 7 grooves, r/hand
Capacity: four
Muz vel: ca 450ft/sec (137m/sec)

The revolver seen here, which appeared in 1871, is one of the earliest of weapons known as "house pistols." It has a solid brass frame into which a steel barrel is screwed. These barrels were made in a variety of lengths, from 1.5in (38mm) to 3.5in (89mm). Perhaps the most interesting aspect of the weapon is its four-chambered cylinder: this has a section shaped like a four-leafed clover, which gave rise to the widely used nickname of "Cloverleaf Colt." The breech-ends of the chambers are recessed to take the rims of the short, copper-cased, rimfire cartridges. The lock is of single-action type and, the comb of the hammer on the earlier models (of which this is one) was almost vertical; in later models, the comb was slanted much farther back. The hammer activated the cylinder stop, which is housed in a long slot below the frame. The trigger is of the sheathed type. There is no loading gate, but the side of the frame is grooved to facilitate loading. A flat fence on the left-hand side of the frame prevented the cartridges from slipping backwards out of their chambers. The rod below the barrel is, in fact, a forward extension of the cylinder axis pin, which is somewhat thicker than the section visible; it could be drawn forward to remove the cylinder. A retaining ring is fitted below the barrel to ensure that the pin could not be dropped. To make the weapon more compact for carriage in a pocket, the cylinder could be partially rotated so that there were two chambers on each side of the frame. When this was done, the nose of the hammer fitted into one of the small apertures situated between each chamber: this prevented the cylinder from rotating. The butt is of the type usually referred to as bird-beak.

COLT NEW LINE 0.22IN POCKET MODEL REVOLVER USA

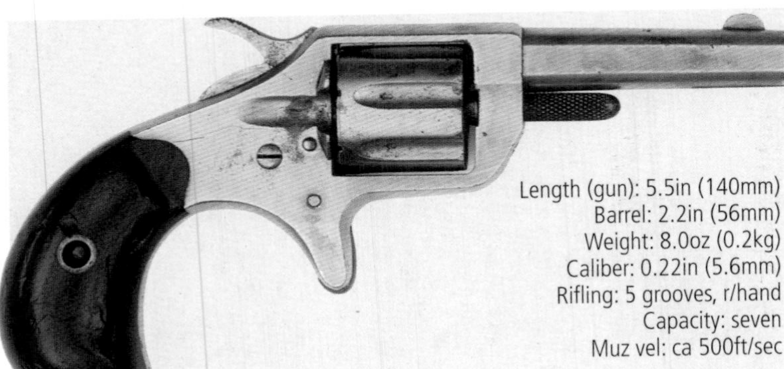

Length (gun): 5.5in (140mm)
Barrel: 2.2in (56mm)
Weight: 8.0oz (0.2kg)
Caliber: 0.22in (5.6mm)
Rifling: 5 grooves, r/hand
Capacity: seven
Muz vel: ca 500ft/sec

Although the famous Colt Company had been a leader in the production of what may fairly be described as the modern revolver, Colt's development of revolvers firing metallic cartridges was delayed by the fact that Smith & Wesson had overall rights in Rollin White's patent for bored-through cylinders. This did not expire until 1869. It is improbable that the Colt Company was much disturbed by this delay, for they had established a huge market for their percussion revolvers, and most users of such arms in remote frontier areas preferred to retain them until the new metallic cartridges were universally obtainable. Even after the Rollin White patent had expired, some time was necessary to reorganize. Thus, it was not until 1872 that the Colt New Line series of pocket revolvers went on to the market, in a variety of calibers from 0.41in (10.4mm) down to 0.22in (5.6mm). The example shown is of the smallest caliber. It has an octagonal barrel complete with foresight, screwed into a solid frame; along the top of the frame runs a long groove to act as a backsight. The cylinder, which is fluted, was rotated by means of the usual pawl and ratchet and held steady by a cylinder stop. This projected from the bottom of the standing breech and engaged slots cut into the rear of the cylinder between the chambers. The cylinder was removed by pressing a retaining spring on the right-hand side of the frame and drawing forward the axis pin, which could also be used to knock out the empty, copper, rimfire cases. There was no loading gate, but cartridges could be inserted through a small gap in the rear of the frame.

COLT NEW LINE 0.41IN POCKET REVOLVER USA

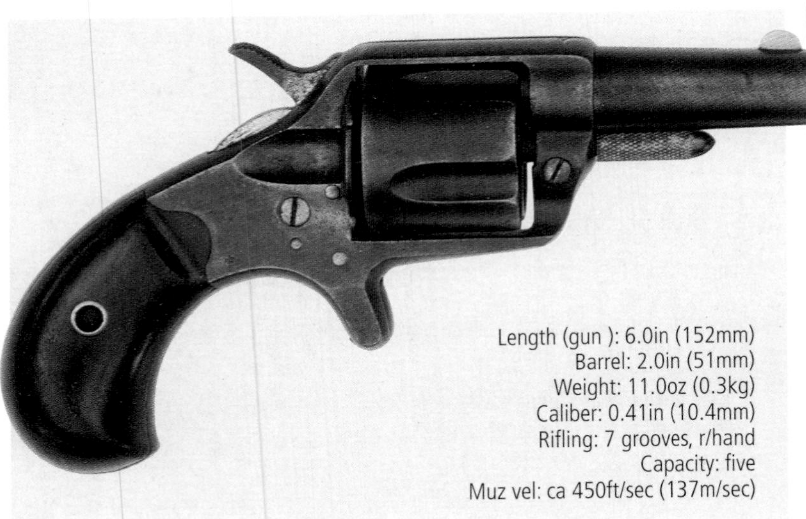

Length (gun): 6.0in (152mm)
Barrel: 2.0in (51mm)
Weight: 11.0oz (0.3kg)
Caliber: 0.41in (10.4mm)
Rifling: 7 grooves, r/hand
Capacity: five
Muz vel: ca 450ft/sec (137m/sec)

The Colt House Pistol was succeeded in 1873 by a series of New Line, single-action, pocket revolvers, one of which is seen here. These were made in a variety of calibers from 0.22in (5.6mm) to 0.41in (10.4mm), including some centerfire models, and with barrel lengths ranging from 1.5in (38mm) to 3.5in (89mm). The revolver shown is the 0.41in (10.4mm) rimfire version with a 2in (51mm) barrel. It is a compact, stream-lined weapon, admirably suited to pocket or handbag. The round barrel, which has a noticeable taper from muzzle to breech, is screwed into a solid iron frame in which is contained a half-fluted, five-chambered cylinder, without recesses for cartridge rims. The loading gate, on the right-hand side, could be opened with a thumbnail when the revolver was cocked or half-cocked. A corresponding shield is fitted on the left-hand side to retain the rounds in the chambers. Pressure on a small stud at the front of the frame, on the right-hand side, allowed the cylinder axis pin to be withdrawn: it was then used to push out the empty cases. A circular inspection plate on the left-hand side of the frame (the head of its retaining screw can be seen below the cartridge groove) gave access to the lock mechanism. The revolver has the typical bird-beak butt; the only piece of brass in its construction is to be found in the liners for the butt retaining screw. It is marked "COLT NEW LINE" on the left side of the barrel, ".41 Cal" on the lower left frame, and is inscribed with the company's name on the barrel.

Colt Single-Action Army (Artillery Model) Revolver — USA

Length (gun): 11.0in (279mm)
Barrel: 5.5in (140mm)
Weight: 35.0oz (1.0kg)
Caliber: 0.45in (11.4mm)
Rifling: 6 grooves, r/hand
Capacity: six
Muz vel: ca 650ft/sec (198m/sec)

Colt"s first venture into the rimfire field was to develop a slightly tapered cartridge which could be loaded into the front face of the cylinder and firmly seated with the orthodox percussion rammer. But this method, known as the Thuer conversion, was only temporary and as soon as possible after the expiry of the Smith & Wesson patent Colt had a revolver of its own ready to launch on the market. This weapon appeared in 1873 and is sometimes referred to as the Model 1873. It fired a brass-cased, centerfire cartridge with a copper cap in its base and was an immediate success. It was first known by the awkward title of the "New Metallic Cartridge Revolving Pistol" but later became known by the more familiar title of the "Single-Action Army Revolver." The earliest model was of 0.45in (11.4mm) caliber and fired a 235-grain (15g) lead bullet by means of 617 grains (40g) of black powder, but it was later made in a wide variety of different calibers and in several barrel lengths. The version shown here is the "Artillery Model" with a 5.5in (140mm) barrel.

Colt Single-Action Army (Cavalry Model) Revolver — USA

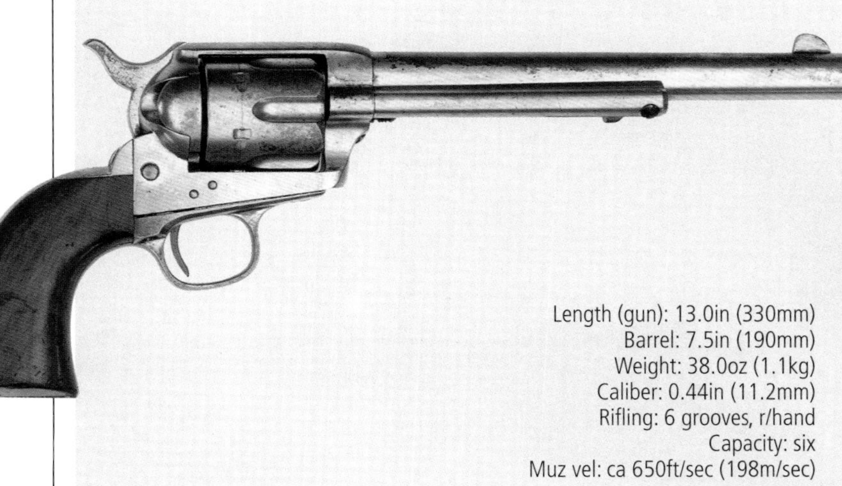

Length (gun): 13.0in (330mm)
Barrel: 7.5in (190mm)
Weight: 38.0oz (1.1kg)
Caliber: 0.44in (11.2mm)
Rifling: 6 grooves, r/hand
Capacity: six
Muz vel: ca 650ft/sec (198m/sec)

The Colt Model 1873 revolver remains the archetypal American handgun and was manufactured in many different versions and under a variety of names. To the company it was known as the Model P, but to the military it was the "Single-Action Army, Model 1873" and was issued in two barrel lengths: Cavalry Model, 7.5in (190mm); and Artillery Model, 5.5in (140mm). Both military versions were characterized by a solid frame with a top strap, a round barrel screwed into the frame, and a bored-through cylinder. There was a robust, hemispherical standing breech, with a contoured loading gate built into its right side, and ejection was by means of a rod sliding in a sleeve below and to the right of the barrel. As its official name implies, the lock was of the single-action type. The butt-plates of the Army models are almost invariably of walnut (as seen here) and the metal parts were usually plainly finished in blue or nickel, The weapon shown is of 0.44in (11.2mm) caliber (as stamped on the left of the trigger guard), which was a very popular caliber since the Winchester 1873 Model rifle was chambered for the same cartridge, making resupply much less of a problem.

Colt Deringer No.3 — USA

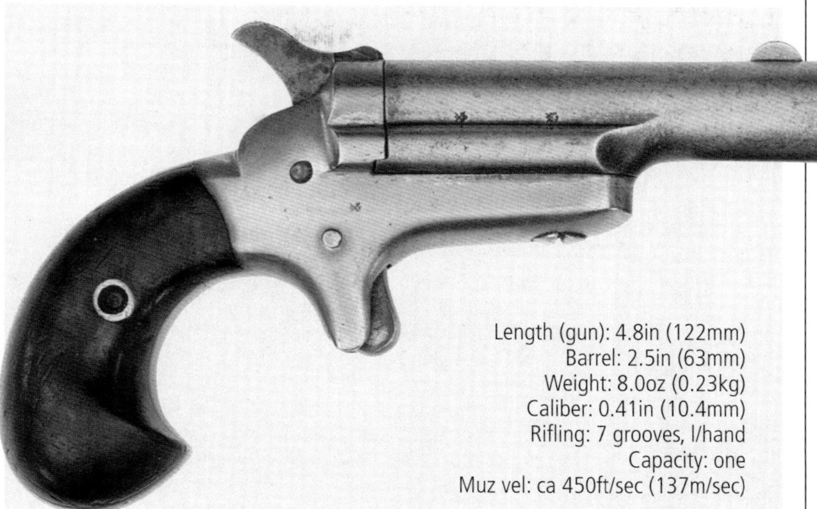

Length (gun): 4.8in (122mm)
Barrel: 2.5in (63mm)
Weight: 8.0oz (0.23kg)
Caliber: 0.41in (10.4mm)
Rifling: 7 grooves, l/hand
Capacity: one
Muz vel: ca 450ft/sec (137m/sec)

Weapons of this type take their names from Henry Deringer of Philadelphia, who specialized, from the 1830s onward, in the production of small pocket pistols of quite large caliber. These soon achieved popularity in the United States and elsewhere as small and easily concealed weapons. A pistol of this type was used to assassinate Abraham Lincoln. This brought the arm increased "fame" and led to extensive copying, until eventually the word "deringer" (sometimes spelt incorrectly – or deliberately, by copyists – as "derringer") came to denote a type rather than a trademark. Weapons of this kind were extensively carried in the United States, often as a second, concealed weapon to back up the revolver visible in a holster. They were also popular with ladies, for carriage in handbag or garter (depending on the kind of lady!). The specimen illustrated here was made by Colt in the period 1875-1912, and is classed as the company's Model No 3. It has a brass frame and bird-beak butt. To load the arm, it was necessary to put the hammer at half-cock and swing the breech out to the right in order to insert the cartridge. Then the barrel was swung back and the pistol was cocked. The empty case was ejected automatically when the breech was opened.

Colt Double-Action Army Revolver — USA

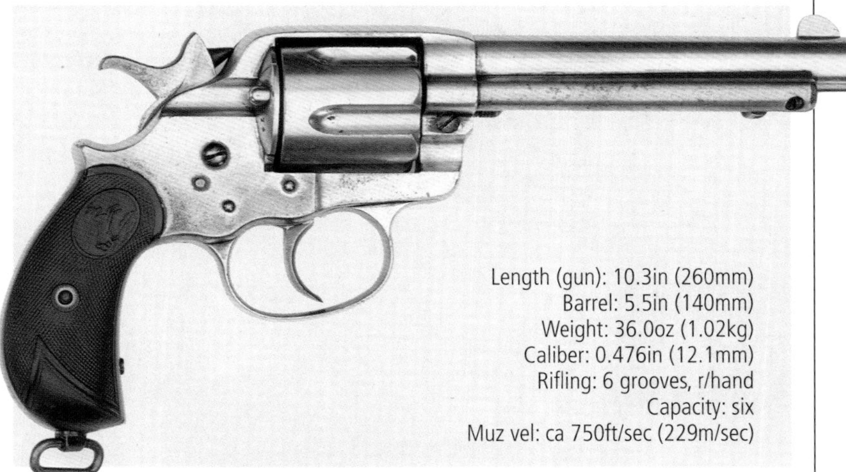

Length (gun): 10.3in (260mm)
Barrel: 5.5in (140mm)
Weight: 36.0oz (1.02kg)
Caliber: 0.476in (12.1mm)
Rifling: 6 grooves, r/hand
Capacity: six
Muz vel: ca 750ft/sec (229m/sec)

In 1877 the Colt company added a new revolver to its existing range, the Double-Action Army model illustrated here. It has the usual solid frame, with a round barrel screwed into it and an ejector rod sliding in a sleeve. The six-chambered cylinder has a loading gate, and a cartridge groove is provided on the right-hand side of the frame. The butt is of the type known as bird-beak and has a swivel for a strap or a flat lanyard. However, the most interesting aspect of the weapon is the fact that it is the first Colt revolver to have been fitted with a double-action lock in place of the popular and well-tried single-action mechanism. It is possible that the US Cavalry may have expressed a preference for such a weapon, which was faster to operate in a mêlée. The revolver was made in three major calibers – 0.32in (8.1mm); 0.38in (9.6mm); and 0.45in (11.4mm) – and in three barrel lengths: 4.75in (121mm); 5.5in (140mm); and 7.5in (190mm). The caliber of the revolver illustrated is, however, 0.476in (12.1mm), which indicates that this particular specimen was probably made for the British market – for this was the standard British service caliber at the time. This attribution is confirmed by the fact that the words "DEPOT 14 PALL MALL LONDON" have been added to the standard inscription on the barrel. This model continued to be made in the United States until 1909, but it never proved popular: it had the reputation of being both badly balanced and mechanically unreliable – remarkable and almost unprecedented allegations to be made against a Colt product.

THE COLT SINGLE-ACTION ARMY REVOLVER — USA

Few firearms are as readily identified with the gunfighter and the combats of the American West as the Colt "Single-Action Army" revolver, which was first fielded in 1872 and quickly spread from the military to civilian users. Its many names convey the ideas of frontiersmen and gunmen – "Peacemaker," "Frontier Six-Shooter," "Thumb-Buster," "Colt '45," "Hog-Leg" – among others, but, whatever name they had for it, the gun was widely used and relied upon by both men and women on both sides of the law, and by civilians and military alike. Indeed, if it seldom earned affection, it was always treated with the greatest respect.

The name "Single-Action" meant that the hammer had to be pulled rearwards to the cocked position, using the thumb or free hand, each time the weapon was to be fired, as was shown by this company demonstration plate (1) and the cut-away model (19). The first-ever Single-Action Colt to come off the production line (6) did so in 1872 and was followed by 357,858 more before production ended (temporarily) in 1942.

Various barrel lengths were available, of which the 4.75in (121mm) was the most popular (13), and the longest "normal" version was the 7.5in (191mm) (5), although an "extra-long" version with a detachable shoulder-stock became available to special order from 1876 onwards (9). Many different calibers were also available, although the most popular were 0.45in (18), followed by 0.44-40in (16). Various experimental models were also produced, such as this model with an automatic cartridge extractor (7).

Among the variables were the finish of the gun and the type of grips to be fitted. The latter depended simply on the imagination of the Colt factory and its customers. Some examples of special finishes are this gold-plated gun (10), with pearl steer-head grips and the owner's name inlaid in silver on the backstab; a second (11) which is nickel-plated and fitted with ivory grips; a third (3) with pearl handgrips; and a fourth (12), which can be identified by the carved Mexican eagles on the ivory grips as being intended for a customer "south of the border."

Several special models were produced, including this competition model (8), the Bisley (named after the premier British target ranges), which had longer curved grips and special target sights, and was popular in both the USA and the UK. This, too, came in a variety of models and finishes, including one with fixed sights and a 5.5in (140mm) barrel (4), and another with chrome-plating (2).

The Colt Single-Action was also produced to meet bulk orders by specific groups or companies. Such orders were placed by the Texas Rangers (14), Wells Fargo (15), and the Adams Express Company (17), among many others.

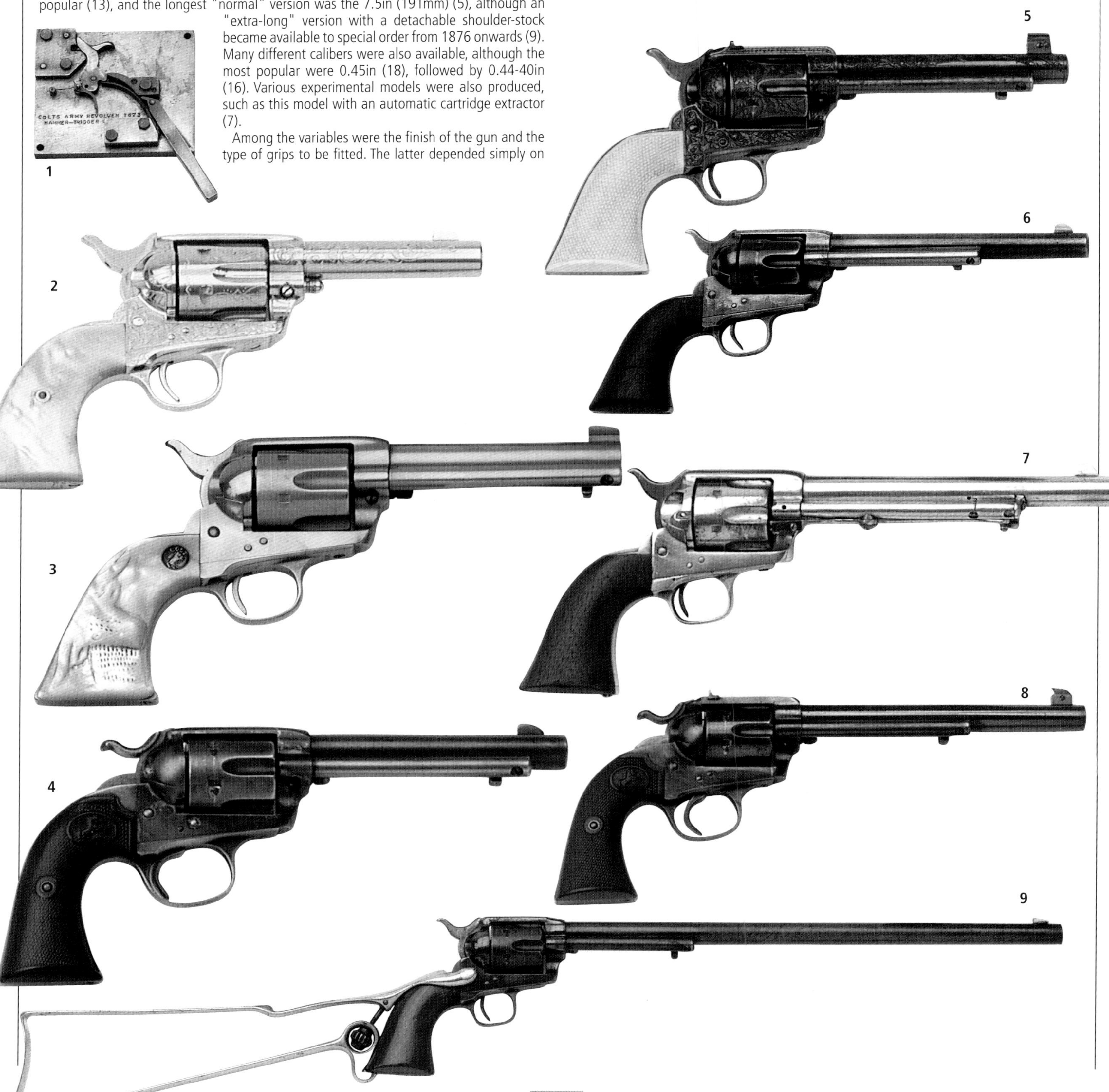

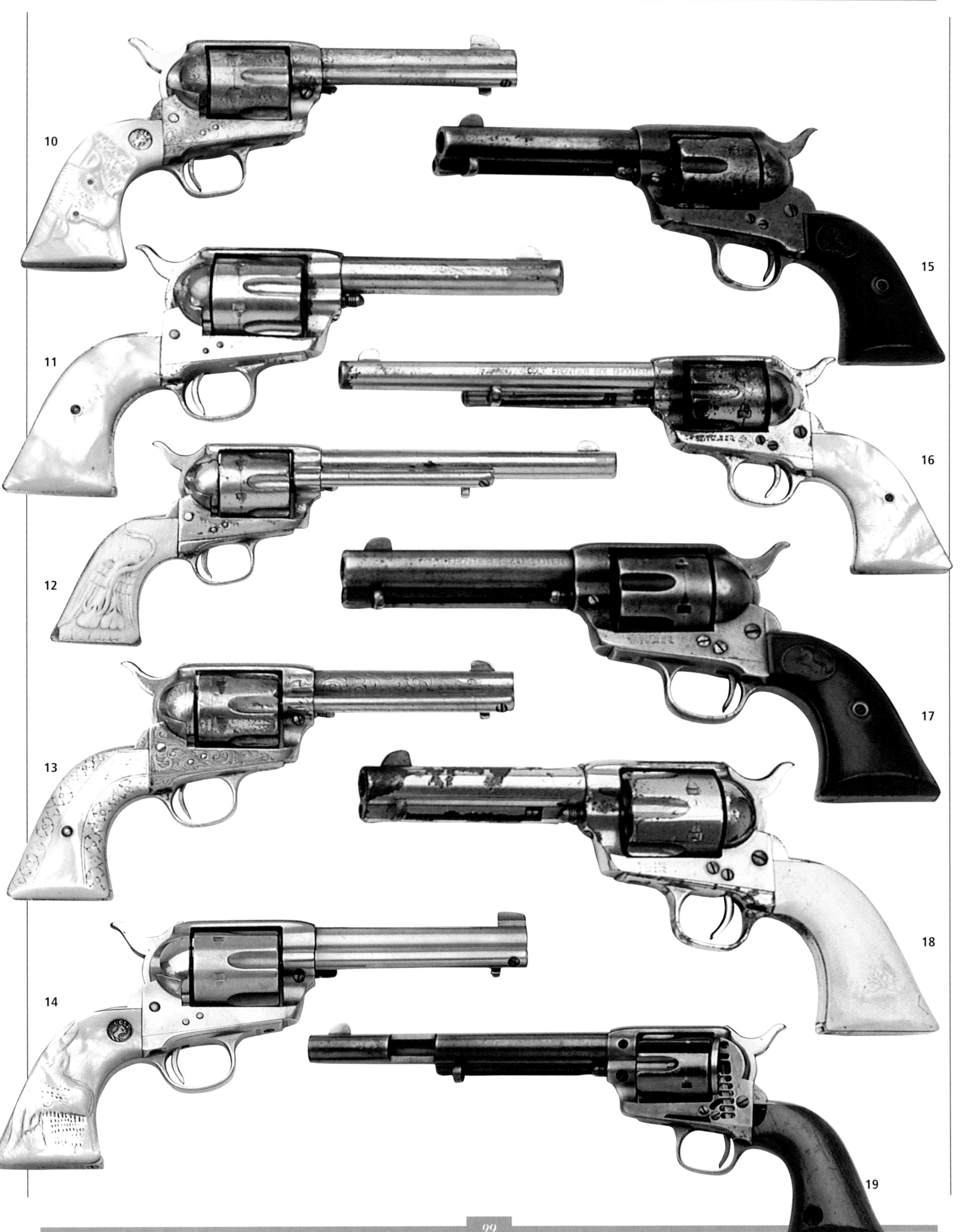
10
15
11
COLT FRONTIER SIX SHOOTER
16
12
17
13
18
14
19

DERINGER POCKET GUNS: THE PERCUSSION MODELS, 1845-1860 USA

Henry Deringer was a Philadelphia gunsmith who developed a range of small, very compact, but large-caliber pocket pistols, which were so successful that his name soon became synonymous with all such weapons, whether or not they were made by his company. (Here, all except weapons actually produced by Deringer are referred to as "deringers.") There were, in effect, two sub-types: the original percussion type which appeared in the early 1830s and continued in production and use for many years, and its much superior replacement, the cartridge-type, which appeared in 1861 and ultimately achieved much greater popularity. One of the most infamous applications for the Deringer was as an assassin's weapon, its most dramatic use in such a role being in the hand of John Wilkes Booth who assassinated President Abraham Lincoln in 1865. (It is appropriate to note here that it was in a newspaper report on this incident that the word was written "Derringer," resulting in a misspelling that has persisted down the years.) The main characteristics of the Deringer were that it was small – usually less than 6.0in (152mm) long – and of large caliber, which resulted in a short-range weapon, but one with considerable power; a few had rudimentary sights, but these were of little practical use, since ranges were usually so short that all that was necessary was for the firer to point and

shoot. The deringer was much favored as an offensive weapon by gamblers and gunfighters, and as a personal defense weapon by anyone who feared being caught unawares or at a disadvantage.

The weapons shown here include a number of genuine Deringers of varying sizes: (1) – (13), of which the 0.4in caliber (8) is the most significant, being identical to the weapon used by John Wilkes Booth to murder President Lincoln. Another maker of such small pistols was Ethan Allen, most of whose products employed an unusual bar hammer – (14), (15), and (23) – although some used a more conventional center hammer (19). A number of other identifiable products are also shown: Blunt & Symes side hammer pocket pistol (16); Bacon & Co single-shot ring trigger pocket pistol (22); Lindsay two-shot belt pistol with brass frame (21), (25); and the Massachusetts Arms Co single-shot pistol fitted with Maynard's tape primer mechanism (24). However, many deringers were not stamped with their makers' names, such anonymous weapons including: 0.28in (7mm) caliber pinfire pistol shown opened for loading (17); screw-on barrel pistol (18, seen here with barrel removed), a type which was more popular in Europe than in the USA; an English pocket pistol converted from flintlock to percussion (20); and a 0.2in caliber single-shot, breech-loading, pocket pistol (26).

DERINGER POCKET GUNS: THE RIMFIRE CARTRIDGE AND OTHER MODELS, 1860-1875 — USA

Rimfire cartridges started to become widely available in the early 1860s and "deringer-type" single- or double-barreled pistols using them were soon in great demand. Hiding places for such weapons gave rise to much ingenuity: some men, for example, used their boot tops, sleeve cuffs or waistbands, while others hid them in their hats. These pistols were also popular with ladies, of whom the well-bred tended to carry them in their handbags, while those of lesser virtue hid them in their stocking tops or even, occasionally, in a form of "crotch pouch."

The first shot from a deringer might not always have achieved the desired result, giving rise to the need for a multi-shot weapon. The double-barreled Remington model is shown in its original packing (7) and opened for loading (8). Next came three-barreled weapons, such as those made by William Marston (4) and (12), and even four-barreled "pepper-boxes," produced by Sharp & Co (1), (2), (9), (10), (11); Starr (13); and Remington-Eliot (6). Another solution to the same problem was to combine the pistol with a stabbing weapon, as in the Wesson two-shot pistol, which had a central tube housing a small

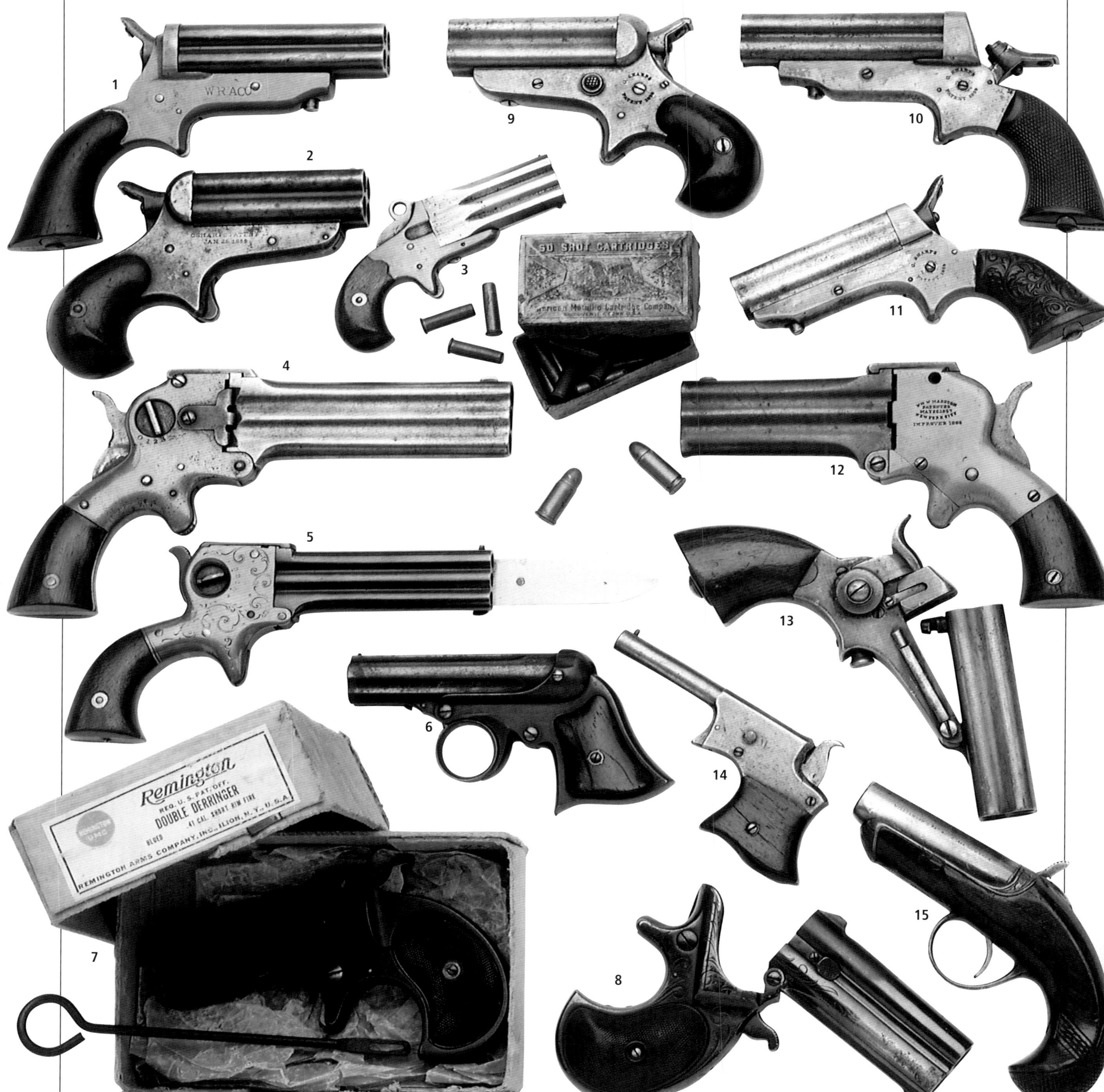

bayonet (3), while some of the Marstons not only had three barrels but also a nasty-looking bayonet attachment (5). These weapons obtained their multi-shot capability by having multiple barrels, but others sought a different method, such as the Schoop two-shot "harmonica" 0.30in rimfire pocket pistol (28), which had only a single barrel, while the American Arms Co Wheeler "roll-over" pistol (24) used two barrels which could be twisted to align the barrels with the hammer one at a time.

The great majority of deringers were, however, single-shot weapons, with Samuel Colt being one of the most prolific producers; starting with the first model (16) and the No.3 (23), and, as usual, some of these were highly decorated (18). There was also a wide range available from the numerous gunsmiths then at work around the United States, including: Dexter Smith (17); Dickinson (25); Merwin & Bray (22); Remington (14); Rupertus (19), (27); and Union Arms Co (20). Also among this group was the Hammond Bulldog 0.44in pistol (26), which was very reliable and effective, and, as a result, was particularly popular during the Civil War as a "second" weapon. Some designers sought unusual answers to the users' requirements. David Williamson, for example, modeled his rim-fire deringer (15) on Henry Deringer's original, but incorporated a percussion insert, to be used in the event that rimfire ammunition was not available. The inventor of the drilled-through cylinder, Rollin White, also produced a pocket pistol with a swiveling breech (21). The great majority of pistols whose barrels "broke" for loading/unloading had the pivot either under the barrel (as shown in (13)) or above it (as in the "tip-up" models), but the Brown Manufacturing Company's "Southerner" (29) was most unusual in having a barrel which swung out sideways.

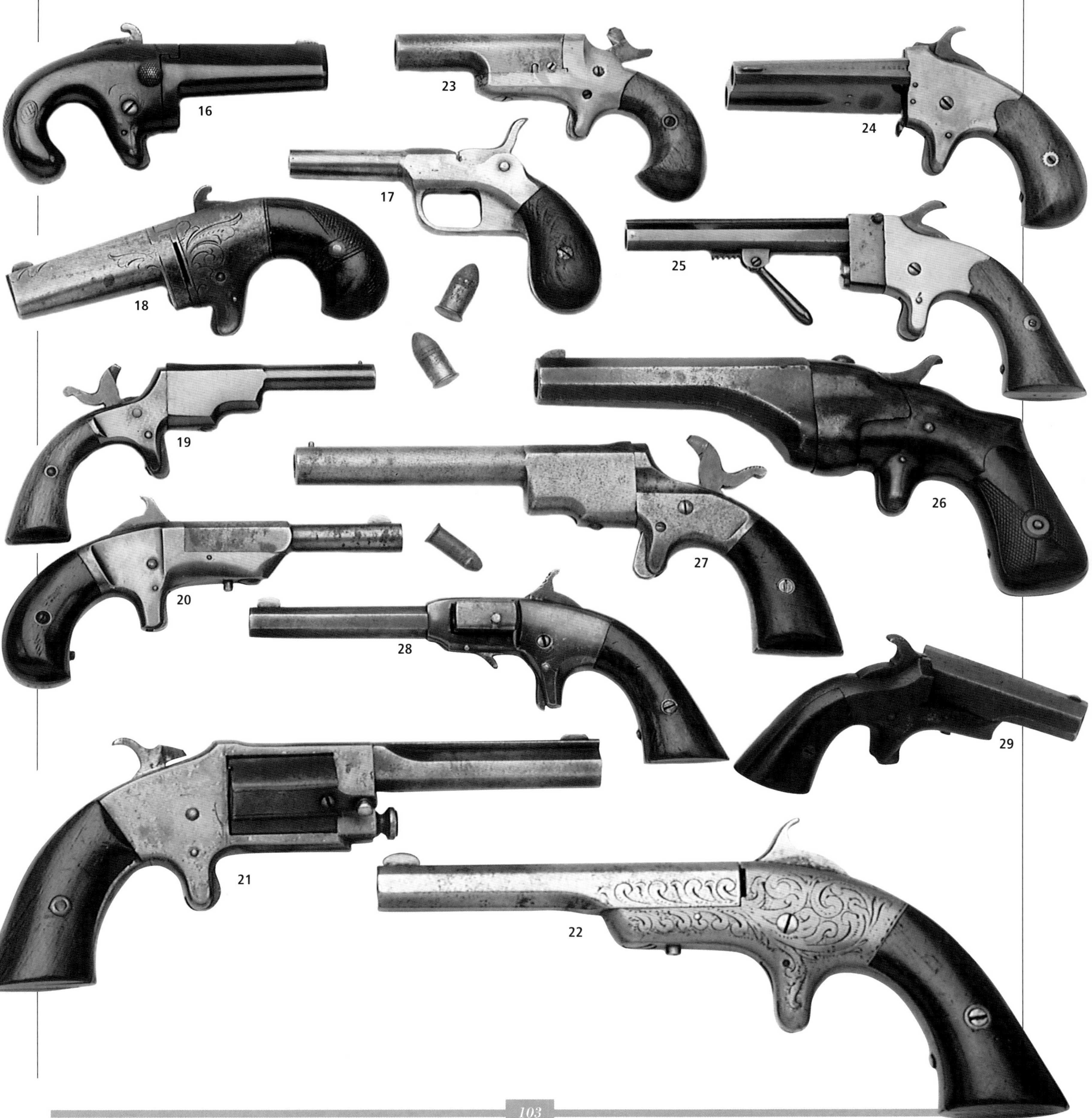

COLT DERINGERS AND POCKET PISTOLS — USA

Colt started to design deringers from about 1869 and, as usual with the company, they appeared in a wide variety of models. The line started with the "First Model" in about 1870 and the example shown here (1) is of 0.41in caliber and is engraved. It was shaped so that it could be used as iron knuckles in a fist fight, although whether this was deliberate or accidental on the part of Colt is no longer known. The next to appear was the "Second Model deringer" which remained in production from 1870-1890; the model shown here (2) fired a 0.42in rimfire cartridge. Also appearing in 1870 (and remaining in production until 1912) was the "Third Model deringer" (3) which was 4.8in (122mm) long and weighed 8.0oz (230g), firing a 0.41in round. The weapon had a brass frame, a 2.5in (63mm) long steel barrel, and a wooden "bird's-beak" butt. The weapon was opened by swinging the barrel laterally to the right, which automatically ejected the spent cartridge case.

Once the Rollin White patent held by Smith & Wesson expired in 1869, Colt was able to start manufacturing revolvers, including a compact range which started with the Open Top Pocket line. There were a basic steel version (7) and a nickel-plated version with pearl grips (8); both were 0.22in caliber and held seven rounds. A slightly heavier version, from 1880, was chambered for 0.32in rimfire (8). Nor had the increase in caliber ended, for this was followed by even larger calibers, by now restricted to five rounds: 0.38in (9) – this is an unfinished factory prototype – and then 0.41in (10).

Another line of development resulted in a slightly heavier, if more conventional weapon known as a "House Revolver," which was intended to provide self-defense against burglars and other uninvited intruders. Products here included the "Cloverleaf House Model" revolver of 1874 (5), which was the company's first solid frame weapon made to fire metallic cartridges and carried four 0.41in cartridges in a somewhat rudimentary cylinder. This was followed in 1881 by the "New House Model" (6), which fired five 0.38in centerfire rounds.

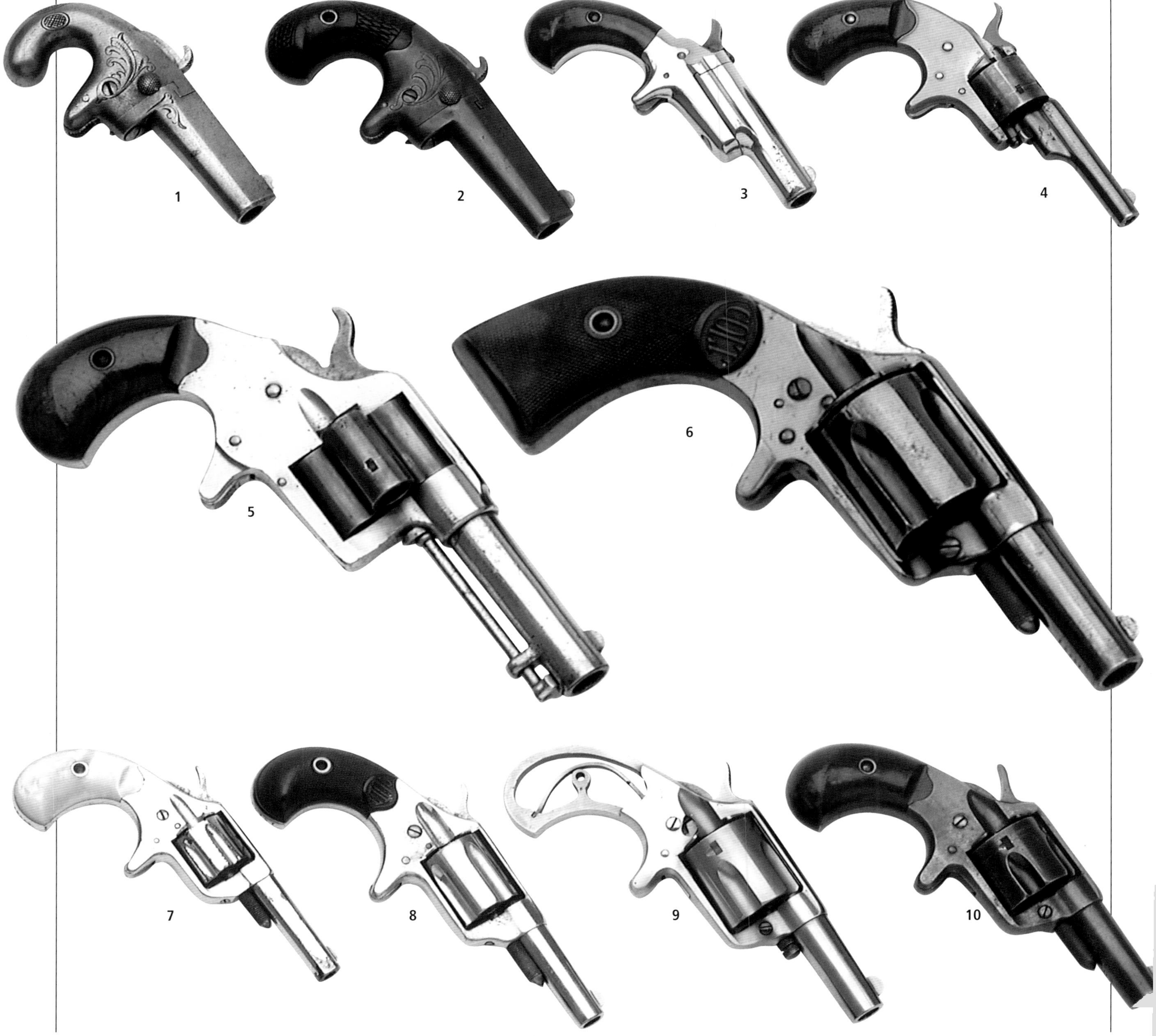

Unusual Colts — USA

A company the size of Colt produced a large number of new designs: some never got beyond the drawing board; some resulted in a prototype but stopped there; the others went into production. In addition, production models differed widely, partly as a result of options offered by the company and partly as a result of requests from customers. The standard production 1878 double-action Frontier revolver (1) has been fitted with the long 7.5in barrel, while the Model 1877 double-action Lightning revolver (4) of 0.41in caliber is in standard blued finish but has been fitted with the more expensive pearl grips. The Model 1877 double-action Lightning revolver of 0.38in caliber (5) has been heavily engraved and is fitted with ivory grips, a longer barrel, and an attached ejector rod.

Another type of weapon which is of particular interest to the historian and modern collector is one which bears its owner's name, such as this Third Model 1877 double-action Lightning revolver (0.38in caliber) (3), whose backstrap is engraved "Capt Jack Crawford," who was a well-known scout.

Two weapons which reached the prototype stage but which did not go into production were a hammerless double-action weapon of 1878 (2) and what was probably the first-ever with a swing-out cylinder, a device which Colt patented in 1884 (6). This particular design did not go into production, but five years later Colt started to sell their first models with this swing-out device, and these soon became the standard.

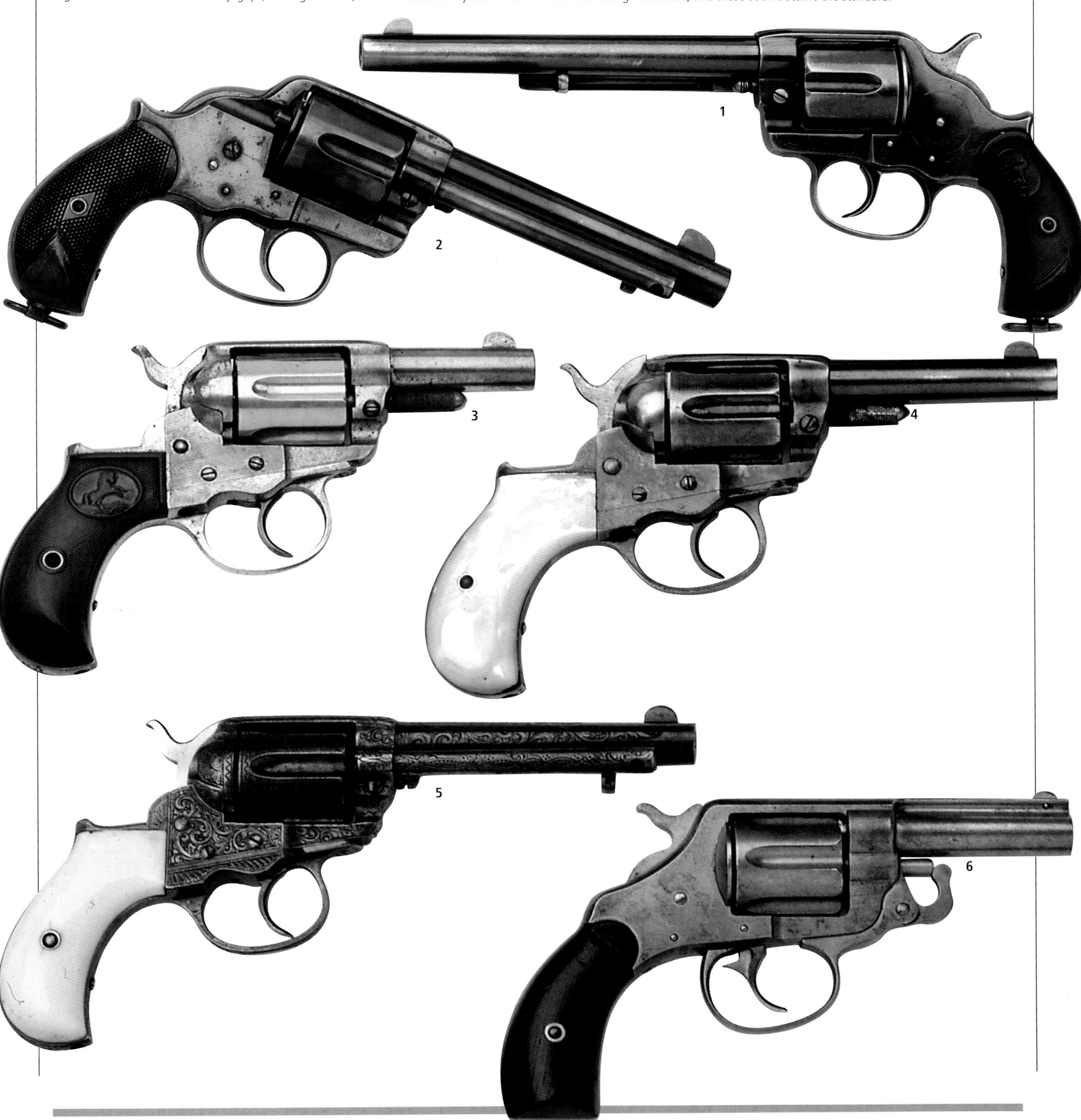

HANDGUNS USED BY THE CONFEDERATE STATES ARMY — USA

The Confederated States Army (CSA) had control of only a few of its own armaments manufacturing facilities at the start of the Civil War. It developed more during the course of the conflict, but it was always limited by lack of production equipment and skilled manpower, as well as by the scarcity of materials. As a result, the CSA had to use a mixture of whatever weapons it could find at the start of the war: new manufacture of antiquated designs and of a few new designs of its own, weapons captured from Union forces, and a small number of imports, especially from Great Britain. The few genuine examples shown here are representative of a large number of companies and models.

At the outbreak of war, the weapons immediately available included antiquated flintlock pistols like the US Government-pattern Model 1836 (1) and Model 1842 (2), and production of such weapons continued at the Virginia Manufactory, resulting in their 1st Model (3) and 2nd Model (4) pistols. Not all production was of such old designs; modern weapons came from many small gunsmiths, among whom were T.W. Cofer (8); J.H. Dance and Brothers (12); J. & F. Garrett (7); Griswold & Gurnison (9); Leech & Rigdon (10); Le Mat (1st Model (5) and 2nd Model (11)); and Wesson & Leavitt (6). Perhaps the largest single source was weapons captured from the Union Army, which covered the entire range of Northern equipment, in which Colt products inevitably featured large. These are just a few representative examples of such captured Colt equipment: Model 1848 Army (19); Model 1849 pocket revolver (13); Whitney Navy (a Colt design) (14); Model 1851 Navy (21); Model 1860 with fluted cylinder (15) and with non-fluted cylinder (20); and the Massachusetts Arms Company Adams-patent Navy revolver (22) – actually, a British design produced under license in the United States.

Yet another source was direct importation from Europe, particularly Great Britain, some examples being: Beaumont-Adams (16); Kerr (23); Tranter with single trigger (17) and with double-trigger (18); and Webley (24).

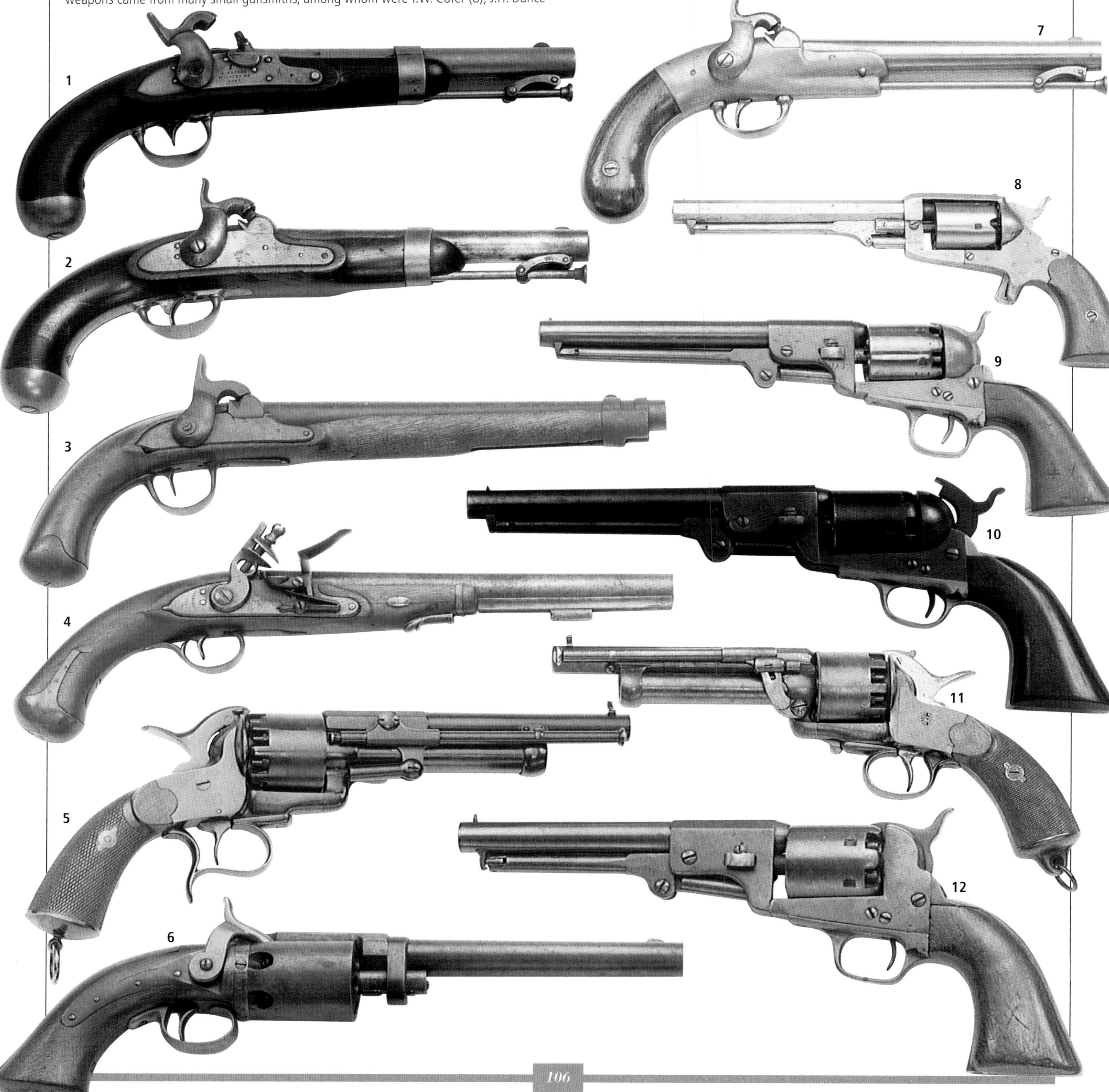

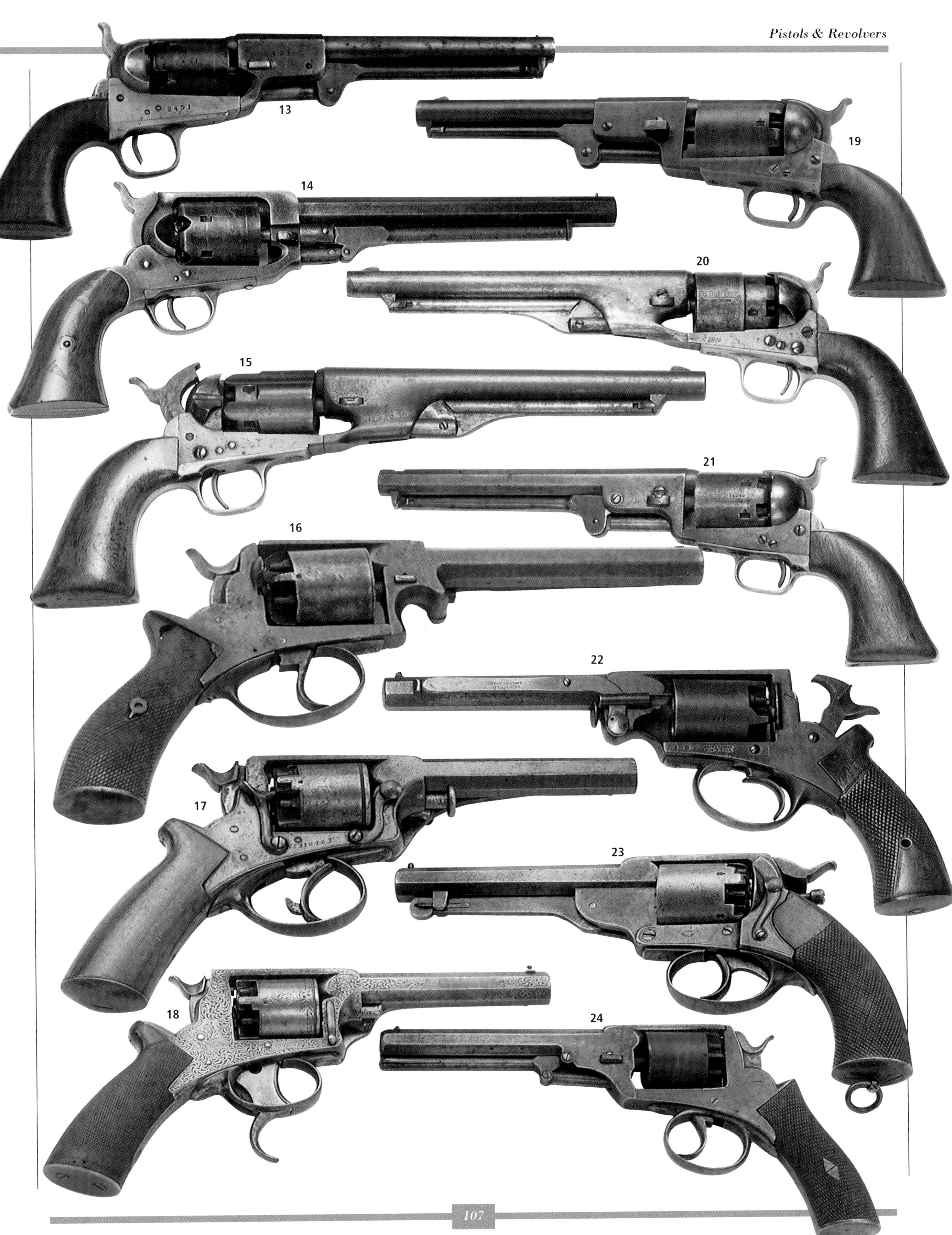
13
14
15
16
17
18
19
20
21
22
23
24

THE HANDGUNS OF THE AMERICAN WEST — USA

Seldom has one particular type of weapon become so associated with an historical era as the handgun and the American West, where a large proportion of the population carried a weapon. Many of these weapons were the products of famous names such as Colt, Remington, and Smith & Wesson. They were sold in vast numbers and, like today's automobiles, the customer was faced with a bewildering variety of models and calibers. Then, having settled on the model, there was a further variety of options, such as barrel length, metal finish, type of butt grips, and, for the wealthier, engravings. Apart from such big-name manufacturers, however, there was also a large number of much smaller gunsmiths whose names are now all but forgotten, but whose products also took part in the stirring events on "The Frontier." A small selection of the what was available is shown here.

Samuel Colt (1814-1862) never claimed to have invented the revolver, but he certainly brought it to an unprecedented state of perfection. Initially lacking his own factory, one of Colt's earliest models was produced by Eli Whitney, an example being the 2nd Model Navy Revolver (9), but then Colt was able to buy Whitney out and set up his factory at Hartford, Connecticut, where he started to produce weapons under his own name. One of the first was the "Dragoon" revolver of 1848; an example of the 3rd Model Dragoon is shown (3). Then as now, the placing of an order by the Army or Navy inevitably impressed civilian customers and among the most famous Colt products were the Model 1851 Navy revolver (shown here in 0.36in caliber) (6) and the long series for the Army. The latter included the Model 1860 Army revolver 0.44in (7), and the most famous of all, the Single-Action, which appeared in a variety of calibers, including 0.38-40 (14), and in various barrel lengths, such as the 0.45in caliber, long barrel (15), and the 0.45in caliber, short barrel (17). Later came the Model 1878 double-action Army revolver (18). Colt also produced special models for law enforcement officers, such as this Model 1862 police revolver in 0.36in caliber (8), while weapons intended for the civilian market bore dramatic and eye-catching names, such as Thunderer (16). Smaller firearms produced for self-defense included the Model 1849 pocket revolver 0.31in (4) and the Model 1855 side hammer pocket revolver 2nd series (5). Innovations not only resulted in new models, but in modifications for older models, such as this Model 1861 Navy (10), factory-modified in Colt's own works or by outside agencies, such as Reynolds-modified Model 1860 Army (11).

Other big-name players included Smith & Wesson, among whose products were the No. 2 Army 0.32in (23); and the No. 3 Single-Action Army (24) and 1st Model American Single-Action (25), both firing the 0.44in S&W round. Another Smith & Wesson weapon was the Double-Action 1st Model (26), while Remington, which was more famous for its rifles, also produced some revolvers, including the New Model Army (12).

The weapons produced by the Volcanic Company, which enjoyed a limited popularity in the 1850s, used a lever-action to load from a tubular magazine housing eight or 10 rounds, and their products such as the Navy No. 1 (1) and Navy No. 2 pistols (2) were both well-made and accurate. Volcanic was subsequently renamed, first as the New Haven Arms Company and, second as the Winchester Arms Company, after which it concentrated on the famous rifles.

Other gunsmiths were less well known, but had their own niches in the market. Such gunsmiths and their products included the Starr single-action Model 1863 Army (13); Merwin & Hulbert (Army revolver, early type with square butt (19) and bird's-head butt (20)); Forehand & Wadsworth New Model Army revolver (22); Manhattan Firearms Company pocket model 0.31in caliber (27); and the Hopkins & Allen XL No 8 Army revolver (21).

That famous men did not always use famous-name guns is borne out by the two revolvers carried by Sheriff Patrick Floyd Garrett at Fort Sumner, who on the night of July 14/15 1881 shot "Billy the Kid" with a 0.45in Colt Single-Action. Among his extensive personal armory, however, were these Merwin & Hulbert 0.38in caliber with ivory grips (29) and the Hopkins & Allen 0.32in (28), both of them inscribed with his name.

16
17
18
19
20
21
22
23
24
25
26
27
28
29
PAT F. GARRETT

Colt's Cartridge Competitors

USA

The Rollin White patent for bored-through cylinder was held by Smith & Wesson and they challenged any infringement with great vigor, but when it expired a host of new revolvers appeared on the market, of which the most successful was the Colt Single-Service Army and its civilian versions, such as the Peacemaker. The US Army Ordnance department conducted official tests, and these concluded that what the Colt lacked in manufacturing precision it more than made up for in reliability and its ability to withstand rough handling, making it an ideal weapon for military and frontier use. But Colt by no means had matters all their own way, and there were a number of serious competitors, some of which are shown here.

Smith & Wesson's success in winning an order from Russia meant that it had to devote its entire capacity for five years to meeting the order. The model that won this order was the No. 3 Model Army "Russian" (20), which used a special 0.44in cartridge specified by the Russian Army. This was later succeeded by the New Model No. 3 Russian (23), in the same 0.44in caliber, which incorporated some changes; note, for example, the absence of the finger spur in the later gun. In an effort to regain its place in the domestic market Smith & Wesson produced the No. 3 American model (21) in 0.32in caliber, which was later improved by Schofield who installed a better barrel latch (22). Then Smith & Wesson themselves upgraded the design with the 0.44in double-action 1881 Frontier revolver (24), but it never supplanted the Colt.

Remington was, of course, one of the major contenders. The original Remington Model 1863 was a percussion weapon, but various conversions to rimfire cartridges were designed, resulting in the New Model Army of 1875, various versions of which are shown

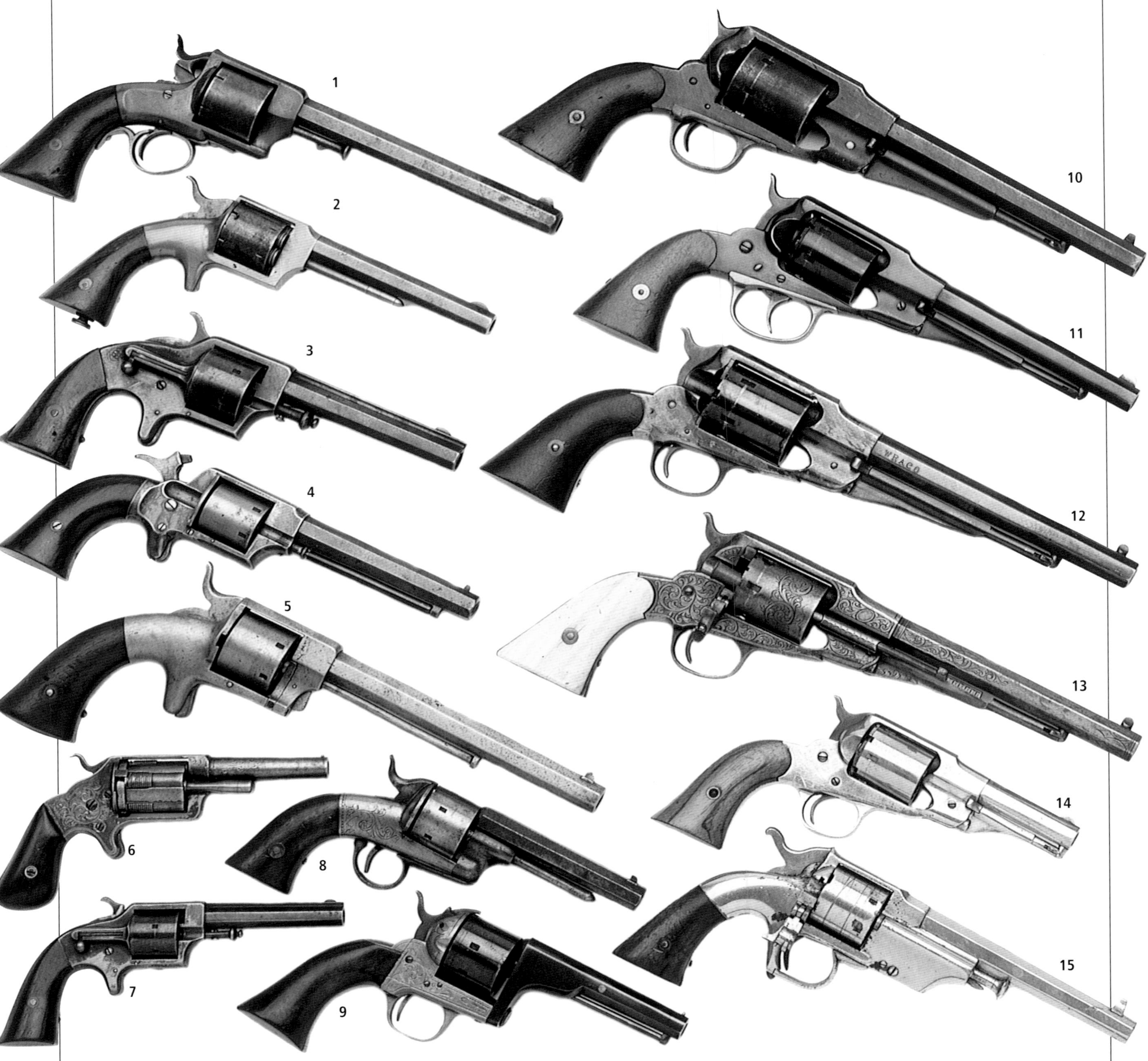

at (10), (12), and, in an elaborately engraved version, at (13). Other products on the market were the Double-Action New Model belt pistol (11), No. 2 Pocket Revolver (14), and, albeit slightly later, the Model 1890 Single-Action Army revolver (19), of which about 2,000 were made.

A company with a high reputation in the West for well-made products was Merwin & Hulbert, whose guns included the Open-top Army revolver shown here in blued (16) and nickel-plated finishes (17), which was later produced with a top strap (18).

A company which produced a number of revolver designs was Allen & Wheelock, whose "center hammer/lipfire" (15) had a notch cut into the rear of the each chamber to enable the hammer face to strike the cartridge "lips." The Bacon Company encountered the wrath of Smith & Wesson when it marketed its 0.32in rimfire pocket pistol (8) which incorporated a cylinder with bored-through cylinders; having been found guilty of infringing the copyright, the company was ordered to withdraw it. A later model (5), produced after the copyright had expired, was more successful.

Among the other companies and models challenging Colt's supremacy were: Brooklyn Firearm Company's "Slocum" pocket pistol in 0.32in rimfire (6); Eagle Arms Company's cup-primed pocket revolver (7); Merwin & Bray's pocket pistol (3); Moore's "Seven-Shooter" 0.32in rimfire pocket revolver (9); Pond's pocket/belt pistol (2); Prescott's single-action, six-shot Navy revolver in 0.38in rimfire (1); and Uhlinger's pocket revolver in 0.32in rimfire (4).

COLT NEW NAVY M1895 REVOLVER USA

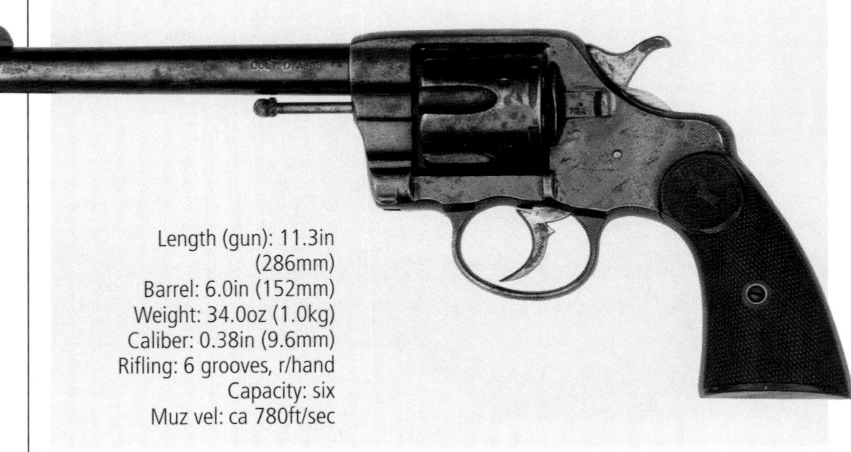

Length (gun): 11.3in (286mm)
Barrel: 6.0in (152mm)
Weight: 34.0oz (1.0kg)
Caliber: 0.38in (9.6mm)
Rifling: 6 grooves, r/hand
Capacity: six
Muz vel: ca 780ft/sec

The New Navy model was one of four new types brought out by Colt in the period 1889-97; it was adopted by the United States Navy in 1892. It was made in both 0.38in (9.6mm) and 0.41in (10.4mm) calibers, being chambered for both the normal and long cartridge in each case, and in barrel lengths of 3.0in (76mm), 4.5in (114mm) and 6.0in (152mm). The revolver illustrated here is of 0.38in (9.6mm) caliber and has a round, 6.0in (152mm) barrel with the typical Colt half-round foresight. The backsight is formed by a notch in the rear of the frame, with a shallow groove along the top strap. The six-chambered cylinder is fluted and has two separate sets of slots for the cylinder stops. When the arm was cocked, the rear stop rose; when the trigger was released, the rear stop dropped and a forward stop came up in its turn to engage the horizontal slots about 0.5in (12.7mm) from the back of the cylinder. The thumbcatch, visible in the photograph, was drawn back to allow the cylinder to swing out; the fit between the yoke and the main frame is so good that the joint is difficult to detect, although the vertical line by the hinge is visible at the bottom front of the frame. The lock is of double-action variety. The butt-plates are of some hard rubber composition and bear the trademark and the word "COLT." This particular arm, numbered "77," has no lanyard ring, although a flat one for a strap was usually fitted. The US Army adopted this revolver just after the Navy, and it was then also listed as the New Army. A variation, with a butt of different shape and with plain walnut grips, was produced for the Marine Corps in the period 1905-10.

COLT MODEL 1903 POCKET PISTOL USA

Length (gun): 6.8in (171mm)
Barrel: 3.8in (95mm)
Weight: 24.0oz (0.7kg)
Caliber: 0.32in (8.1mm)
Rifling: 6 grooves, l/hand
Capacity: eight
Muz vel: ca 900ft/sec (274m/sec)

Colt's first pocket self-loading pistol appeared in 1903, but it did not prove entirely popular and was replaced in the same year by a new weapon designed by the famous John M. Browning. This was a success – and with various modifications it remained in production for many years. The example of the Model 1903 illustrated here is of post-1911 manufacture: before that date, the barrel, which was rather thin, was held in place by a barrel-bushing which is absent from this specimen. It worked by blowback, no locking device being required for the 0.32 ACP cartridge, and had a concealed hammer. It was also the first Colt self-loading pistol to be fitted with a grip safety. Most models have vulcanite grips bearing the word "COLT" and the rearing-horse trademark, and it is not clear whether the wooden grips on the arm seen here were optional or are a private replacement. In 1926, a safety disconnecter, which separated the sear from the trigger when the magazine was removed, was incorporated into the design, but this feature is not present in the example shown here. This was an unusually handy and well-balanced pistol and well deserves its popularity.

COLT NEW SERVICE TARGET REVOLVER USA

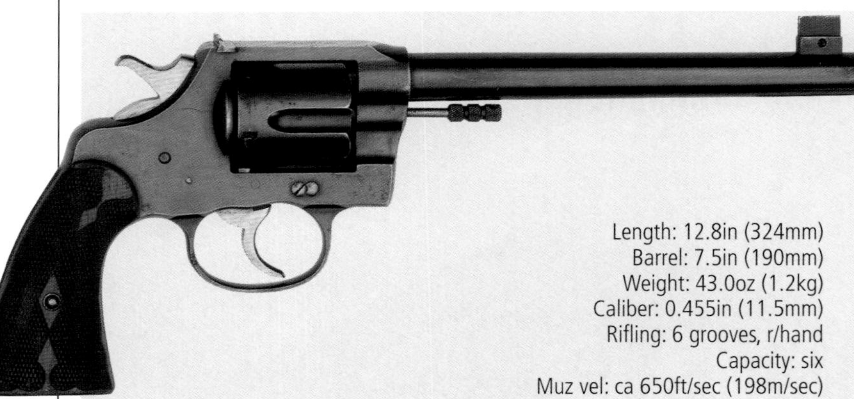

Length: 12.8in (324mm)
Barrel: 7.5in (190mm)
Weight: 43.0oz (1.2kg)
Caliber: 0.455in (11.5mm)
Rifling: 6 grooves, r/hand
Capacity: six
Muz vel: ca 650ft/sec (198m/sec)

Well before the end of the 19th Century, the great American firm of Colt had begun to manufacture solid-frame revolvers with swing-out cylinders. The firm did not, of course, abandon its earlier fixed-cylinder type, with loading gate and ejector rod; these arms retained their popularity and are, indeed, still made in large numbers as reproductions of traditional weapons. Although the new models were made in considerable variety, they were all basically built upon four frame sizes only. The last of the frames to appear was also the largest, and it is on this frame that the New Service revolver was built. It first appeared in 1897 and is still manufactured, with only minor changes to its original specification. It has been made in a variety of barrel lengths – from 4.0in (102mm) to 7.5in (190mm), the weapon illustrated here having a barrel of the latter size – and in numerous calibers. In 1900 a new service target revolver was introduced; the revolver shown here is of this type. It has a rectangular blade foresight, screwed into its bed, and a laterally-adjustable U-backsight at the rear of the frame. The hand-finished lock worked very smoothly and the trigger was checkered to prevent the finger from slipping. The butt-plates are of finely checkered walnut with a diamond pattern down the center; they are unusual in that they do not bear Colt's name or trademark. This particular weapon is chambered for the British 0.455in (11.5mm) Eley cartridge, and is so marked on the left side of the barrel at the breech end.

COLT ARMY SPECIAL, M1908 REVOLVER USA

Length (gun): 11.3in (286mm)
Barrel: 6.0in (152mm)
Weight: 35.0oz (1.0kg)
Caliber: 0.38in Special (9.6mm)
Rifling: 6 grooves, r/hand
Capacity: six
Muz vel: ca 1,000ft/sec (305m/sec)

This revolver had its origins in the New Navy double-action arm, which was first patented in 1884 and was brought out five years later, when it was almost immediately adopted by the US Navy. The Army quickly followed suit and large numbers were made. In 1904 a new version, the Officer's Model Target, was introduced. This was essentially similar to the original model, except for a slight difference in the lower front silhouette of the frame and, of course, the addition of adjustable target sights. At the same time, all the 0.38in (9.6mm) caliber weapons of the series were chambered to take the 0.38in (9.6mm) Special cartridge, firing smokeless powder. In 1908 some changes were made both to the lock mechanism and to the cylinder locking system; the latter was reduced to a single stop, instead of the front and rear alternating stops on the original arm. The revolver illustrated here is of post-1908 pattern: the different arrangement of notches on the cylinder is apparent by comparison with the original New Navy, M1895 (qv). The only other visible differences are the shape of the cylinder release catch and the style of the butt grips. After 1908, this revolver was usually known as the Army Special; then, in 1926, the type became generally classed as Official Police (a version in 0.22in/5.6mm caliber was produced in 1930). The 0.41in (10.4mm) caliber was discontinued at the same time. The 0.38in (9.6mm) Special cartridge for which the arm was re-chambered differed considerably from the 0.38in (9.6mm) Long Colt for which it was originally intended, principally in power.

Colt Model 1908 Pistol USA

Length (gun): 4.5in (114mm)
Barrel: 2.1in (53mm)
Weight: 14.0oz (0.4kg)
Caliber: 0.25in (6.35mm)
Rifling: 6 grooves, l/hand
Capacity: six
Muz vel: ca 800ft/sec (244m/sec)

Colt began to make self-loading pistols in 1900, and this weapon was a very small pocket pistol designed by John M. Browning and was originally made in Belgium, until Colt bought the patent and made it in the United States. It was of blowback type and orthodox operation; unusually for a pocket pistol, it was fitted with a grip safety in addition to a second safety catch on the frame. The pistol was so small that only the second finger could be placed around the butt – but its recoil was, of course, negligible. It has sights situated in a groove on the top of the slide.

Colt New Service Revolver, M1909 USA

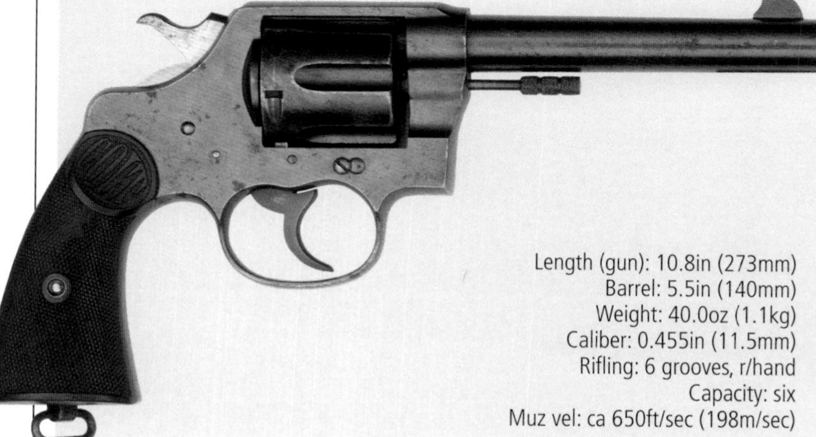

Length (gun): 10.8in (273mm)
Barrel: 5.5in (140mm)
Weight: 40.0oz (1.1kg)
Caliber: 0.455in (11.5mm)
Rifling: 6 grooves, r/hand
Capacity: six
Muz vel: ca 650ft/sec (198m/sec)

The Colt New Service revolver was one of the modern group of Colt arms designed in the last decade of the 19th Century, and it was the largest and most robust of all. It was made in six barrel lengths – 4.0in (102mm); 4.5in (114mm); 5.0in (127mm); 5.5in (140mm); 6.0in (152mm); and 7.5in (190mm) – and was used as a United States service arm from 1907 onward, until it was at last superseded by a self-loading pistol. Even after that, however, many continued to be carried privately. The specimen illustrated is of the usual solid-frame type and has as round, 5.5in (140mm) long barrel, with the standard foresight and V-backsight. Access to its six-chambered cylinder was obtained by pulling back a thumb-catch on the left side of the frame. This allowed the cylinder to be swung out sideways, to the left, on its separate yoke. Then the manual extractor could be brought into play. The butt is large, providing a comfortable grip, and has checkered plates bearing the word "COLT." The well-known trademark of the rearing horse is borne on the left side of the frame, below the hammer. The revolver was made in a variety of calibers: the one shown here is chambered for the British 0.455in (11.5mm) Eley cartridge. This arm bears the additional view marks of the Royal Small Arms Factory, Enfield, showing that it was one of the revolvers imported for use by the British Army in World War I. British proof laws were very strict, and in the absence of any system of government proof in the United States, even the finest products of that country's gunmakers had to be tested on import into Britain.

Colt New Service Revolver (Cut-Down), M1909 USA

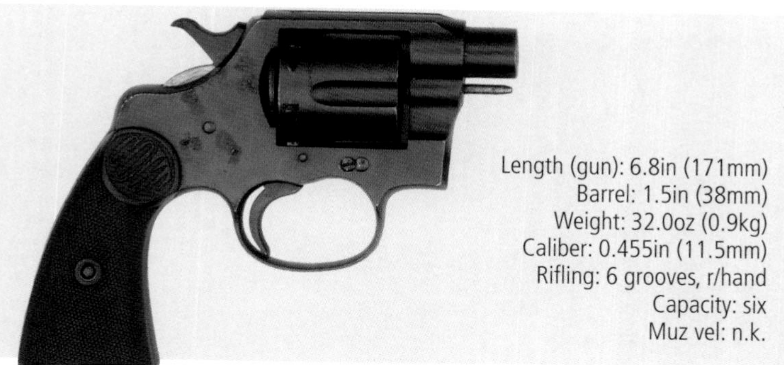

Length (gun): 6.8in (171mm)
Barrel: 1.5in (38mm)
Weight: 32.0oz (0.9kg)
Caliber: 0.455in (11.5mm)
Rifling: 6 grooves, r/hand
Capacity: six
Muz vel: n.k.

In the 1890s and early 1900s the US Army and Navy both used an excellent Colt revolver which was made either in 0.38in (9.6mm) or 0.41in (10.4mm) calibers. This had proved excellent until the Philippines campaign of 1899-1905, when it was found that the bullets did not have the necessary stopping power to deal with the fanatical Moros, who were fighting-men of savage temperament and great physical strength. It is interesting to compare the experience of the US Army in the Philippines with the lessons learnt by the British Army in somewhat similar campaigns, against Zulus, Afghans, and Dervishes, only a few years previously. The British had found that a large, lead bullet traveling relatively slowly – say at around 600ft/sec (183m/sec) – was the most effective, since it tended to expend the whole of its energy within the target, whereas a smaller but higher-velocity bullet simply went through. The weapon seen here has, obviously, been crudely shortened; it was originally a standard Colt New Service model. It is chambered for the British 0.455in (11.5mm) Eley cartridge, the word "ELEY" being just visible on the stump of the barrel. Its origins are not known, but it bears British Government proof marks and also the double-arrow condemnation mark, which suggests that it saw service (as many of this type did) in World War I. It is in a poor state, and as the cylinder is irretrievably jammed in the frame, it is impossible to ascertain its number. The reasons for which it was cut down are not known. It may have had a bulged barrel, or the truncation may have been performed simply to make the arm easier to conceal – although even in its present state it hardly qualifies as a pocket weapon by any stretch of the imagination! The reduction of the barrel to a length of only 1.5in (38mm) must have had a very serious effect on the accuracy of the weapon, except at point-blank range.

Colt Police Positive Target Revolver USA

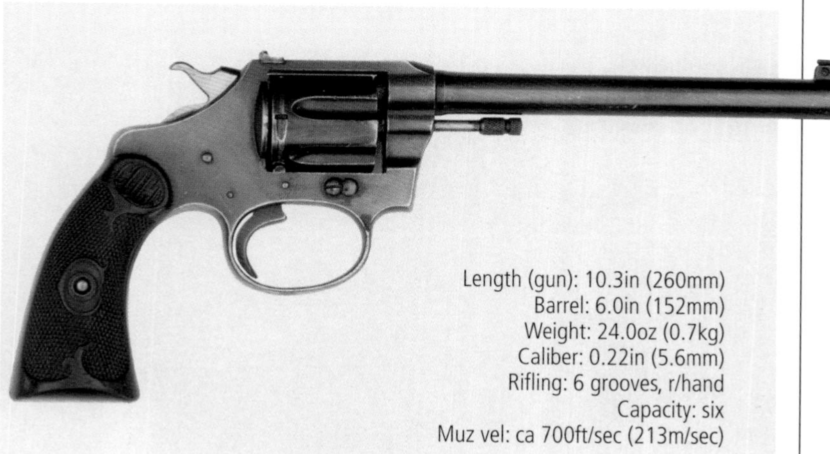

Length (gun): 10.3in (260mm)
Barrel: 6.0in (152mm)
Weight: 24.0oz (0.7kg)
Caliber: 0.22in (5.6mm)
Rifling: 6 grooves, r/hand
Capacity: six
Muz vel: ca 700ft/sec (213m/sec)

The original Police Positive revolver was produced by Colt in 1905 and was of 0.32in (8.1mm) caliber. Two years later a heavier version was produced: it was known as the Police Positive Special and was chambered for the 0.38in (9.6mm) special cartridge, which gave it ample power for most purposes. The success of these arms led to a demand for a lighter version for target shooting. In 1910 the Colt Police Positive Target revolver went into production in both 0.32in (8.1mm) and 0.22in (5.6mm) calibers. An example of the latter is seen here. The larger caliber was discontinued in 1915, but the smaller version remained in production until 1935. The arm has a round barrel with a blade-type foresight, giving a bead in the sight picture, and an adjustable U-backsight. When a catch on the left side of the frame was drawn back, the six-chambered cylinder could be swung out to the left on its hinged yoke, in order to load. The empty cases were ejected manually by means of the extractor pin. The weapon is well finished, as one would expect of a Colt product. The butt-plates are of hard rubber almost black but with a reddish tinge. The revolver was accurate and reasonably comfortable to fire, although the butt is on the short side for a user with even moderately large hands. It was frequently found that the rims of 0.22in (5.6mm) cartridges lacked strength if unsupported; in 1932, therefore, the model was changed by the addition of countersinks in the chambers, fully enclosing the rims of the cartridges and thus giving them more support.

COLT GOVERNMENT 0.45IN MODEL M1911 PISTOL — USA

Length (gun): 8.5in (216mm)
Barrel: 5.0in (127mm)
Weight: 39.0oz (1.1kg)
Caliber: 0.45in (11.4mm)
Rifling: 6 grooves, l/hand
Capacity: 7-round box magazine
Muz vel: ca 860ft/sec (262m/sec)

The Colt M1911 is one of the classic weapons of all time, having remained in front-line service with the US Armed Forces for over 80 years until replaced by the Beretta 92SB (M9) in the 1990s; indeed, many thousands are likely to remain in use well into the 21st Century. In the 1890s, there was little initial interest in the United States in self-loading pistols, but Colt, despite its success with revolvers, quickly realized the type's potential. Thus, by 1898 Colt had produced a prototype, based on the action invented by John Moses Browning, which was considered sufficiently promising to be placed in production as the Model 1900, although it achieved only limited success. The firm persevered, however, producing a series of further prototypes, all chambered for the 0.38in round, until 1905 when they completed the first for the 0.45in round. This was entered in a US Government competition in 1907 and the US Army quickly reduced the nine entries to two – the Colt and the Savage Model 1907 (qv). After further tests, the former won and was placed in production as the Model 1911. The weapon is very simple, consisting of three main parts: the receiver; the barrel; and the slide, which runs on ribs machined into the receiver. When the slide is fully forward, the barrel is locked to it by means of lugs on its upper surface which engage in slots on the slide. When the slide is forced to the rear – either manually for initial loading or by the cartridges after the first shot – the barrel moves only a very short distance before its rear end drops, disengaging it from the slide which thereafter continues to the rear and ejecting the empty cartridge case. On completion of the permitted travel it is then driven forward again, driving the top round from the magazine into the chamber.

COLT GOVERNMENT MODEL M1911 A1 PISTOL — USA

Length (gun): 8.5in (216mm)
Barrel: 5.0in (127mm)
Weight: 39.0oz (1.1kg)
Caliber: 0.45in (11.4mm)
Rifling: 6 grooves, l/hand
Capacity: 7-round box magazine
Muz vel: ca 860ft/sec (262m/sec)

The immediate success of the Colt Model 1911 led to its full-scale production throughout World War I, which resulted in a vast body of user experience. As a result, a number of relatively minor improvements were incorporated in a new production model. These changes included: a longer horn on the safety grip; the shape of the handgrip was altered slightly; the trigger was shortened and chamfered; the hammer was shortened; and arc-shaped grooves were chamfered into the frame behind the trigger. There were also some minor internal improvements. Apart from this the weapon remained essentially unchanged and no more modifications were introduced for the remainder of its very long production life. It was popular because it was good at so many things, being compact, easy to handle, reliable, robust, accurate, easy to reload, and with good stopping power. Indeed, such was the overall feeling of satisfaction with the M1911A1 that several attempts to start developing a successor were strongly resisted – not least in the United States Congress – and it was not until the mid-1980s that the US armed forces eventually managed to obtain authorization to procure a successor. Well over three million M1911s and M1911A1s were manufactured in the United States alone.

Colt M1911/1911A1 (Non-Colt Versions) USA

Length (gun): 8.5in (216mm)
Barrel: 5.0in (127mm)
Weight: 39.0oz (1.1kg)
Caliber: 0.45in (mm)
Rifling: 6 grooves, l/hand
Capacity: 7-round box magazine
Muz vel: ca 860ft/sec (262m/sec)

The Colt M1911 was so good that it was placed in immediate production for the US Army, but demand was then greatly increased by the outbreak of World War I. As a result, "the Colt" (as it has always been known) was put into license production in many other United States gun factories, as well as by companies overseas. During World War I, manufacture was undertaken in the US by Colt itself, by the civil gun manufacturer, Remington, and by the government-owned Springfield Armory. In addition, small-scale manufacture was undertaken in Canada for the Canadian Army; this was a slightly different, being chambered for the British 0.455in Webley round. The weapon was also manufactured under license in Norway as the Pistol m/1914. In 1927 the Hispano-Argentine Fabricas De Automobiles SA (generally known by its abbreviated title of HAFDASA) of Buones Aires, Argentina, started to produce a version of the M1911 designated the HAFDASA Model 1927; internally this was identical to the M1911, but there were very minor external differences. This was widely used by the Argentine armed forces and police, and a number were purchased by the British Government in 1940-41. During World War II production of the Model 1911A1 was stepped up, with lines at Colt, Ithaca, Remington, Singer, and Union Switch operating throughout the war. Foreign companies made pistols which were close copies of the M1911 and M1911A1, including the Spanish company Gabilondo (see Llama). The photographs show: HAFDASA Model 1927 (top); and Colt Remington M1911A1 (above).

Colt Offical Police Revolver USA

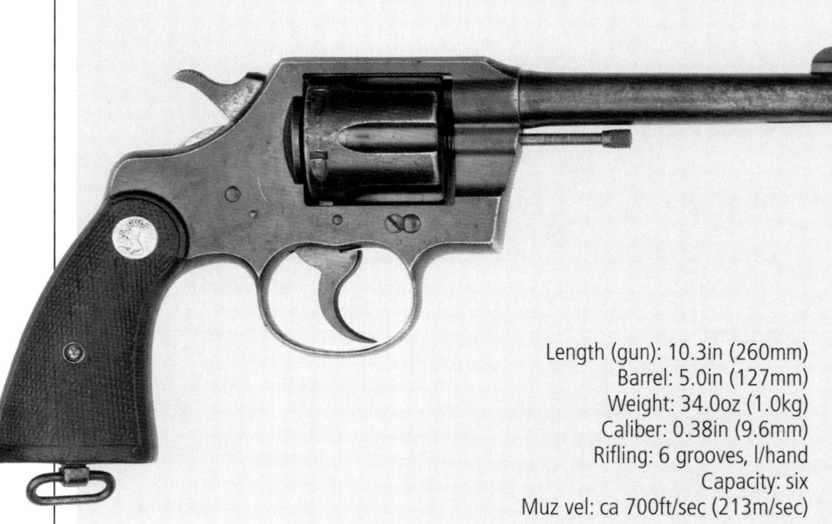

Length (gun): 10.3in (260mm)
Barrel: 5.0in (127mm)
Weight: 34.0oz (1.0kg)
Caliber: 0.38in (9.6mm)
Rifling: 6 grooves, l/hand
Capacity: six
Muz vel: ca 700ft/sec (213m/sec)

This revolver had its origins in the Colt New Navy model (qv), which first appeared in 1889. This was later re-classified as the New Army model, a slightly different version being known, later still, as the Army Special (qqv). In 1926 the name was changed once again – finally, this time – to Official Police. There was very little difference in type, the change being principally made because at that time the US police forces were markedly better customers than the US Army. The arm illustrated is of the orthodox solid-frame design, the frame being of the original 0.41in (10.4mm) caliber type. The round barrel has an integral, semi-round foresight and a square backsight notch and groove on the top strap; the upper surface of the latter is matted to reduce the shine. The cylinder swung out sideways on its own yoke when a catch on the left of the frame was pulled back; cartridges or cases could then be ejected simultaneously by pushing the pin. The lock is of rebounding, double-action type, with a separate hammer nose, and access to the mechanism was obtained by way of an irregularly-shaped inspection plate on the left-hand side of the frame. The butt-plates are of checkered walnut and bear the famous trademark of a rearing horse in white metal medallions. Large numbers of Official Police revolvers were supplied to the British Army in the course of World War II. It was made also in a 0.22in caliber version.

Colt Official Police Revolver (Damaged) USA

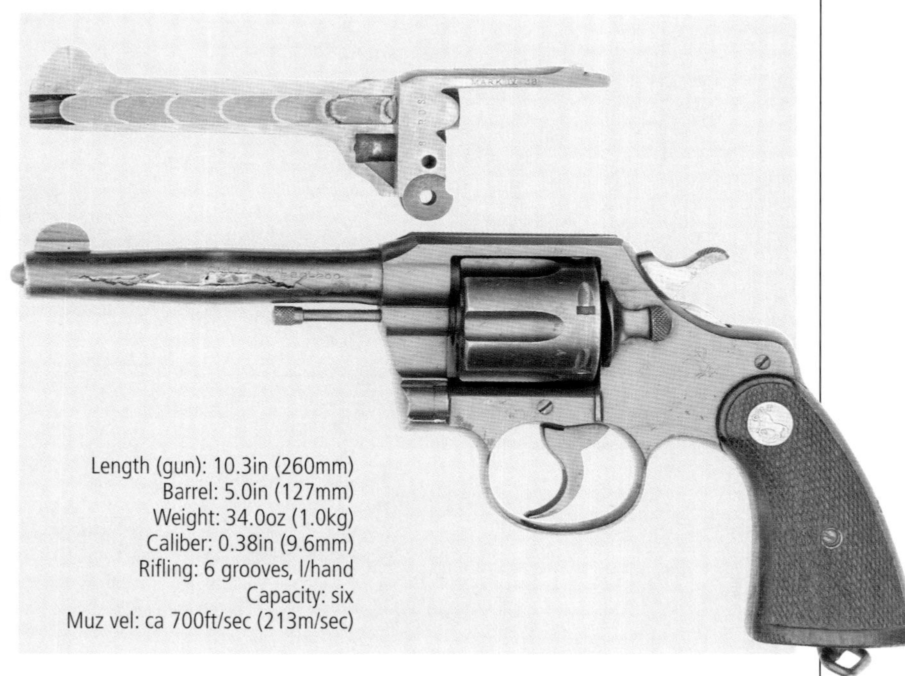

Length (gun): 10.3in (260mm)
Barrel: 5.0in (127mm)
Weight: 34.0oz (1.0kg)
Caliber: 0.38in (9.6mm)
Rifling: 6 grooves, l/hand
Capacity: six
Muz vel: ca 700ft/sec (213m/sec)

This is one of the revolvers based on the 1889 New Navy (qv) and known since 1926 as the Official Police. It was purchased by the British Government, together with thousands more, in the course of World War II, during which Colt and Smith & Wesson revolvers were almost as common in the British Army as Enfields and Webleys. The revolver shown is of orthodox solid-frame construction, with a swing-out cylinder. The damage to this particular revolver was caused by the firing of a weak cartridge, which drove its bullet only sufficiently far forward to lodge in the barrel. (Poor rounds of this kind are, of course, very rare in peacetime; but they are sometimes met with in war, when standards of inspection are less stringent. It may also happen that cartridges deteriorate through having been stored either for too long or in exceptionally bad conditions.) When a second round was fired, its bullet, traveling at normal velocity, struck the one in the barrel and pushed it forward. This probably had no effect on the barrel, partly because of the relatively low velocity of this type of 0.38in (9.6mm) cartridge and partly because of the existence of a means of escape for gas between the face of the cylinder and the barrel. The third round, also traveling normally, hit the first two and pushed them a little farther, as did the fourth – but the resistance was, of course, increasing every time: the fifth round hit the solid blockage and caused the barrel to split.

COLT 0.22IN SERVICE MODEL ACE PISTOL — USA

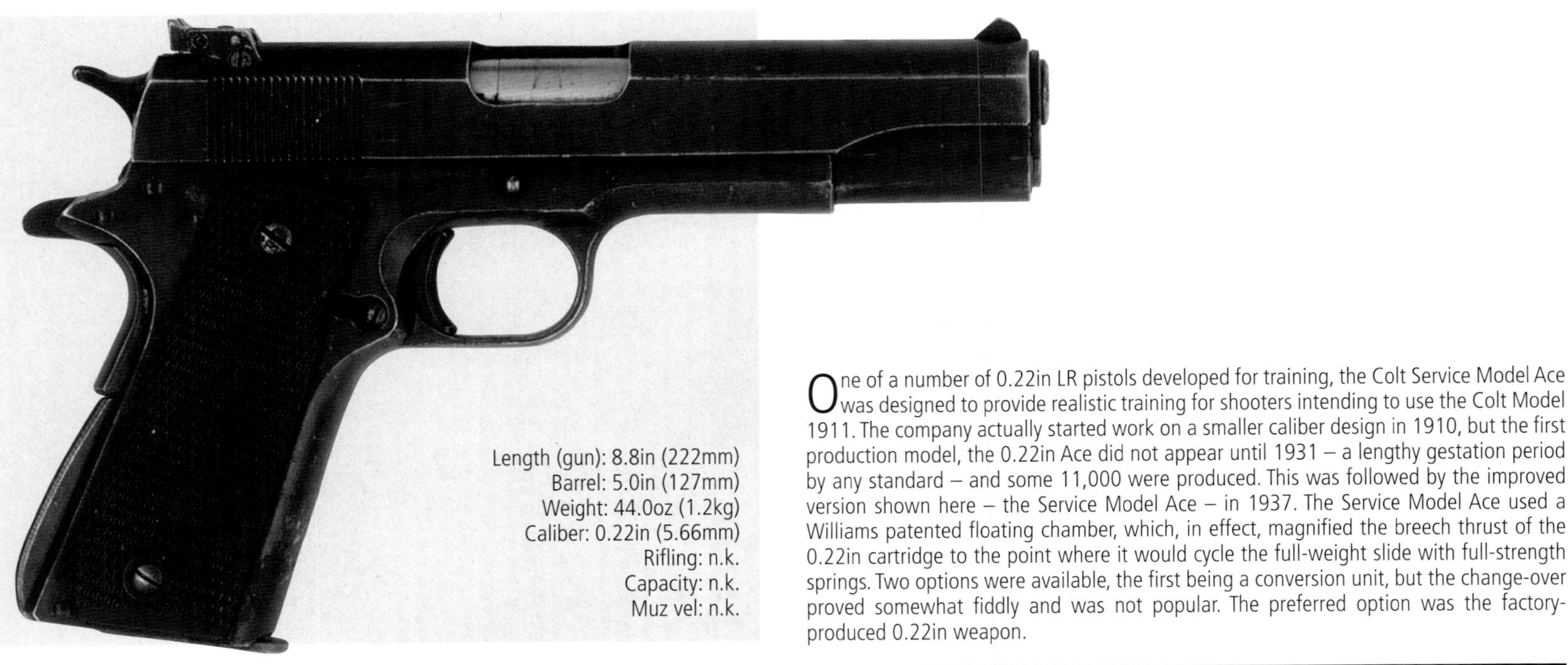

Length (gun): 8.8in (222mm)
Barrel: 5.0in (127mm)
Weight: 44.0oz (1.2kg)
Caliber: 0.22in (5.66mm)
Rifling: n.k.
Capacity: n.k.
Muz vel: n.k.

One of a number of 0.22in LR pistols developed for training, the Colt Service Model Ace was designed to provide realistic training for shooters intending to use the Colt Model 1911. The company actually started work on a smaller caliber design in 1910, but the first production model, the 0.22in Ace did not appear until 1931 – a lengthy gestation period by any standard – and some 11,000 were produced. This was followed by the improved version shown here – the Service Model Ace – in 1937. The Service Model Ace used a Williams patented floating chamber, which, in effect, magnified the breech thrust of the 0.22in cartridge to the point where it would cycle the full-weight slide with full-strength springs. Two options were available, the first being a conversion unit, but the change-over proved somewhat fiddly and was not popular. The preferred option was the factory-produced 0.22in weapon.

COLT 0.22IN TROOPER REVOLVER — USA

Length (gun): 9.3in (235mm)
Barrel: 4.0in (102mm)
Weight: 41.0oz (1.1kg)
Caliber: 0.22in (5.66mm)
Rifling: n.k.
Capacity: six
Muz vel: n.k.

As with pistols, so with revolvers, there are two options for a 0.22in weapon: to produce a conversion kit which will adapt the barrel and chamber to the smaller round, or to produce a specialist weapon. The latter is general judged to be the most satisfactory solution and the Colt Trooper is an excellent example of the breed. Firing the 0.22in Long Rifle round, this is a selective double-action weapon, with a thumb latch on the left of the frame which releases the cylinder to swing out on its yoke. The sights are square format with a large blade foresight and a backsight that is click adjustable for windage and elevation.

COLT PYTHON TARGET REVOLVER — USA

Length (gun): 11.5in (292mm)
Barrel: 6.0in (152mm)
Weight: 44.0oz (1.2kg)
Caliber: 0.57in Magnum
Rifling: n.k.
Capacity: 6
Muz vel: n.k.

The Colt Python target revolver appeared in the early 1960s, with company advertisements stating confidently that it was "the world's finest revolver." Whether that was true or not is a matter of personal opinion, but it was certainly extremely good and in its heyday – the 1960s and 1970s – its only serious competitor in revolver competitions was the Smith & Wesson Model 14K38 (qv). The Python was of all-steel construction (stainless steel was available as an option) and it came in four barrel lengths: 2.5in (63.5mm); 4.0in (102mm); 6.0in (152mm) (see specifications) and 8.0in (203mm). The Python used selective double action and a thumblatch on the left of the frame pulled rearward to release the crane-mounted cylinder, which then swung to the left. Spent cartridges were then removed by hand. There was a square ramp foresight pinned to the barrel rib while the backsight was click-adjustable for windage and elevation. The Colt was very popular and among its advantages over the Smith & Wesson competition were its muzzle heaviness and slightly greater overall weight.

Colt 0.45in Model 15 General Officers' Pistol — USA

The United States Army has a tradition of issuing personal weapons to its general officers (ie, those of the rank of brigadier-general and above) and from the 1940s to the early 1970s this was the Colt 0.38in Pocket Automatic. Production of this weapon ended in 1946 and by the late 1960s there were few remaining in stock, and as a result a requirement was issued in 1972 for a replacement, which had to be small and unobtrusive, but effective for use in emergencies. The winning design came from Rock Island Arsenal and is an M1911A1 which has been dismantled and rebuilt with all dimensions reduced, but operating in precisely the same way as the original. The slide is inscribed in italic script on the left side with the words "General Officer Model" with the abbreviation "RIA" (Rock Island Arsenal) below. On the grip the left panel has a small inlaid brass plate upon which is inscribed the holder's name and on the right grip is the badge of Rock Island Arsenal. The pistol was in production from 1972 to 1984. The barrel is somewhat shorter than that of the M1911A1, but since the same 0.45in ACP round is used, this results in the M15 generating greater flash, bang, and muzzle blast, which observers might consider to be appropriate to the rank of the users.

Length (gun): 7.9in (200mm)
Barrel: 4.2in (106mm)
Weight: 35.0oz (1.0kg)
Caliber: 0.45in (11.4mm)
Rifling: 6 grooves, l/hand
Capacity: 7-round box magazine
Muz vel: 800ft/sec (245m/sec)

Colt 0.22in New Frontier Revolver — USA

Length (gun): 9.9in (251mm)
Barrel: 4.4in (111mm)
Weight: 29.5oz (0.8)
Caliber: 0.22in (5.6mm)
Rifling: n.k.
Capacity: six
Muz vel: n.k.

Another purpose-built 0.22in revolver, this is basically a 7/8th scale model of the Single Action Army (qv), which was introduced in 1973 and given the name "New Frontier" in tribute to John F. Kennedy's campaign slogan. One difference with the original Single Action Army was that the New Frontier had an up-dated mechanism, with gate loading and rod ejection and a frame-mounted floating firing pin. Construction was of steel, with blight alloy grip straps and trigger guard. It was fitted with a ramp foresight and a click adjustable square-notch backsight. Apart from 0.22in Long Rifle, the New Frontier was also available in 0.22in Magnum, and with 6.0in (152mm) or 7.5in (191mm) barrels.

Colt Model 1873 Single Action Army Revolver (Modern Production) — USA

Length: 10.9in (274mm)
Barrel: 5.5in (140mm)
Weight: 37oz (1.0kg)
Caliber: 0.45in (11.4mm)
Rifling: 6 grooves, r/hand
Capacity: six
Muz vel: ca 650ft/sec (198m/sec)

This weapon is not, strictly speaking, a replica, since it comes from the same company, Colt, and the same production line that have always produced the genuine Colt Model 1873 Single-Action Army. Series production continued from 1873 to 1942, when it was suspended (note, not terminated) due to the United States joining World War II, by which time some 357,859 had been made. Due to public demand, production re-started in 1953 and ran on to 1982, but even after that these revolvers continue to be available as a special order item from the company. The Model 1873 was made in some 36 calibers and the modern example shown here is available in 0.357 Magnum caliber and 0.45in caliber (see specifications). This gun has been known under a variety of names: the military version, and the general name, is the "Model 1873 Single-Action Army," while in the Old West the two most widely used models were the "Peacemaker" (0.45in caliber) and the "Frontier" 0.44-40in caliber. To the company itself, however, it has always been the "Model P."

DETONICS 0.45IN COMBAT MASTER MARK 1 PISTOL USA

Length (gun): 7.0in (178mm)
Barrel: 3.4in (87mm)
Weight: 30.0oz (0.8kg)
Caliber: 0.45in
Rifling: n.k.
Capacity: 6-round box magazine
Muz vel: n.k.

In the mid-1960s Major George C. Nonte carried out a design exercise to investigate how far the Model 1911A1 could be reduced in size and weight, while still remaining capable firing a 0.45in ACP round. The Detonics Combat Master Mark I, which was introduced in 1977, draws on Nonte's experiences and is one of the smallest automatic 0.45in pistols ever built. It is of all-steel construction and is a single-action weapon with an outside hammer. It is recoil operated and the Colt/Browning-type link-unlocking barrel locks the ribs on the barrel top into corresponding recesses in the roof of the slide. It has a square post foresight and a square notch backsight which is drift-adjustable for windage. This was the first of the ultra-compact production automatics and quickly established an excellent reputation.

FOREHAND ARMS COMPANY REVOLVER USA

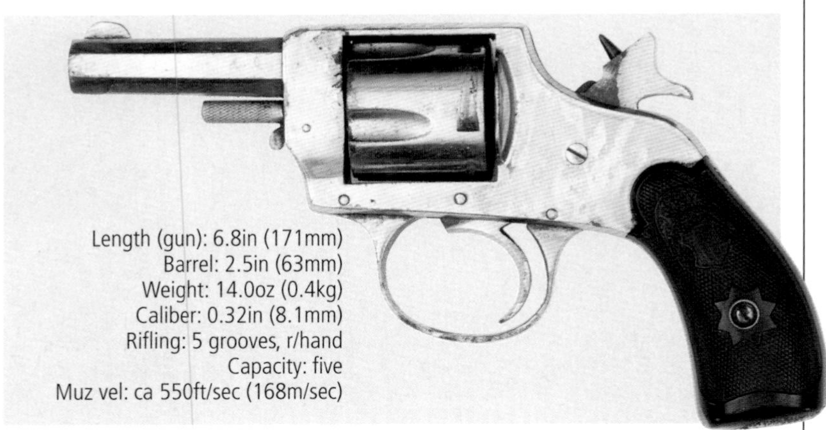

Length (gun): 6.8in (171mm)
Barrel: 2.5in (63mm)
Weight: 14.0oz (0.4kg)
Caliber: 0.32in (8.1mm)
Rifling: 5 grooves, r/hand
Capacity: five
Muz vel: ca 550ft/sec (168m/sec)

Ethan Allen, a well-known American gunmaker, died in 1871. His business then reverted to his daughters, Mrs Forehand and Mrs Wadsworth, and was run by their respective husbands. After Wadsworth left the company in 1890, it was renamed the Forehand Arms Company. In 1898, when Forehand died, the company was bought by Hopkins and Allen, another well-known firm. The arms it produced in the period 1871-98 were mainly revolvers in a variety of types and calibers for the cheaper end of the market. The arm illustrated here is inscribed with the words "FOREHAND ARMS COMPANY" on its top strap, together with the address, "WORCESTER MASS," the words "DOUBLE-ACTION," and a patent date of "JUNE 1891," the last signifying that it is of post-Wadsworth manufacture. In spite of this, however, its butt-plates, which are of black vulcanite, bear the initials "F & W" (ie, Forehand and Wadsworth); so presumably they were old stock. It is a cheap and poorly-finished arm with a solid frame and a five-chambered cylinder without a loading gate: the only provision being a gap left in the shield. In fact, it may with justice be classed as a "Suicide Special" or a "Saturday Night Special." In the summer of 1940, Britain lay under threat of imminent invasion by the German Army, and the revolver illustrated here was one of the large number of weapons sent to help.

GUIDE LAMP LIBERATOR PISTOL USA

Length (gun): 5.5in (140mm)
Barrel: 3.5in (89mm)
Weight: 16.0oz (0.5kg)
Caliber: 0.45in (11.4mm)
Rifling: none
Capacity: one
Muz vel: 800ft/sec (244m/sec)

In 1942 the United States Office of Strategic Services (OSS) asked the Guide Lamp division of General Motors, Detroit, to design a cheap, simple handgun which could be produced in large numbers. The company knew little about firearms, but it knew a great deal about the mass-production of small metal items by the most modern methods, and within about three months it had produced about one million crude pistols of the type illustrated here. This figure entailed the production of a Liberator pistol every 7.5 seconds – which was less time than it took to load the finished product, if, indeed, the term "finished" can be applied to such a device! To load the pistol it was necessary first to pull back the cocking piece and turn it anti-clockwise through 90 degrees, so as to hold it open. The breech was covered by a vertically sliding shutter with a hole for the striker, and was opened by pulling upwards on the backsight. When this was done, a 0.45in ACP cartridge was inserted, the shutter was pushed down, and the cocking piece was returned to its original position; the pistol was now ready to fire. There was, of course, no safety catch, although a pin on the upper part of the cocking piece passed through a hole in the backsight, presumably to ensure that the shutter did not open and foul the striker. Once a shot had been fired, the entire loading process had to be repeated; no extractor was fitted, so it was necessary to use a wooden rod or some similar implement to push out the fired case. Although the pistol was strictly of single-shot variety, a few extra cartridges were packed into the butt, access to them being gained through a sliding trap at the base (the catch of which is visible in the photograph). After assembly, the arm was packed into a waterproof bag, together with a sheet of comic-strip type instructions, using no words, and was air-dropped where required. At first, the pistol was classed as a "flare projector," for security reasons, but the name Liberator later came into general use.

Hammond Bulldog Pistol — USA

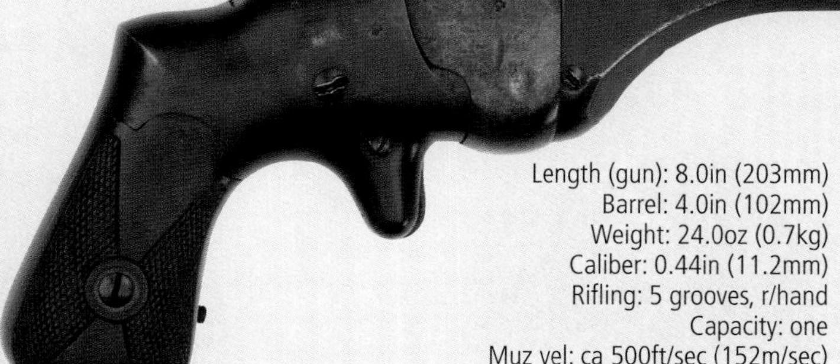

Length (gun): 8.0in (203mm)
Barrel: 4.0in (102mm)
Weight: 24.0oz (0.7kg)
Caliber: 0.44in (11.2mm)
Rifling: 5 grooves, r/hand
Capacity: one
Muz vel: ca 500ft/sec (152m/sec)

Single-shot cartridge weapons of the type broadly classed as deringers became popular during the American Civil War, when many soldiers, particularly on the Northern side, liked to carry a small, concealed pistol as a back-up gun for use in emergency. The weapon illustrated here was produced by the Connecticut Arms and Manufacturing Company, Naubuc, Conn., under a patent dated October 25 1864. It was generally known under the trade name of Hammond Bulldog. It was a solid, robust arm capable of firing a powerful cartridge. Access to the breech was gained by placing the hammer at half-cock, pressing the top stud, and then pushing the breechblock to the left. The pivot of the block was so arranged that, as the block moved, it also retracted about 0.2in (5mm), thus bringing the extractor into play.

Harrington and Richardson Defender Pocket Revolver — USA

Length (gun): 8.8in (222mm)
Barrel: 4.0in (102mm)
Weight: 23.0oz (0.7kg)
Caliber: 0.38in (9.6mm)
Rifling: 7 grooves, r/hand
Capacity: six
Muz vel: ca 625ft/sec (190m/sec)

The Harrington and Richardson Company was formed in Worcester, Massachusetts, in 1874, by Gilbert H. Harrington and William A. Richardson. Its stated intention was to produce plain, reliable revolvers at a reasonable price – and this it did with great consistency. The company's first models were, of course, solid-frame types, and most of them were pocket pistols, but the success of these caused the company to diversify. Just before the end of the 19th Century, Harrington and Richardson produced the first of their break-open "Automatic Ejector" models, which were made in a variety of calibers and barrel lengths, although they still continued to make their well-established solid-frame arms. The weapon illustrated here is of the post-World War II period. It had the trade name of "Defender." There were, in fact, several versions, with a variety of butts, calibers and barrel lengths: this one is the 0.38in (9.6mm) caliber version with a plain butt. The shape of the barrel is somewhat difficult to characterize: it is basically round, but has flattened sides and a very solid top rib, with a round foresight slotted in. The weapon was opened in the same way as a Smith & Wesson, by pushing up a T-shaped catch: this allowed the barrel to be forced downward and brought the automatic ejector into action. Although basically a pocket arm, it has a very large butt; this, although bulky, provided a very comfortable grip. The butt is of one-piece construction and is held to the weapon by a screw which passes through the back of the butt and into the tang. Overall, the revolver is of plain but robust construction.

Harrington and Richardson Revolver — USA

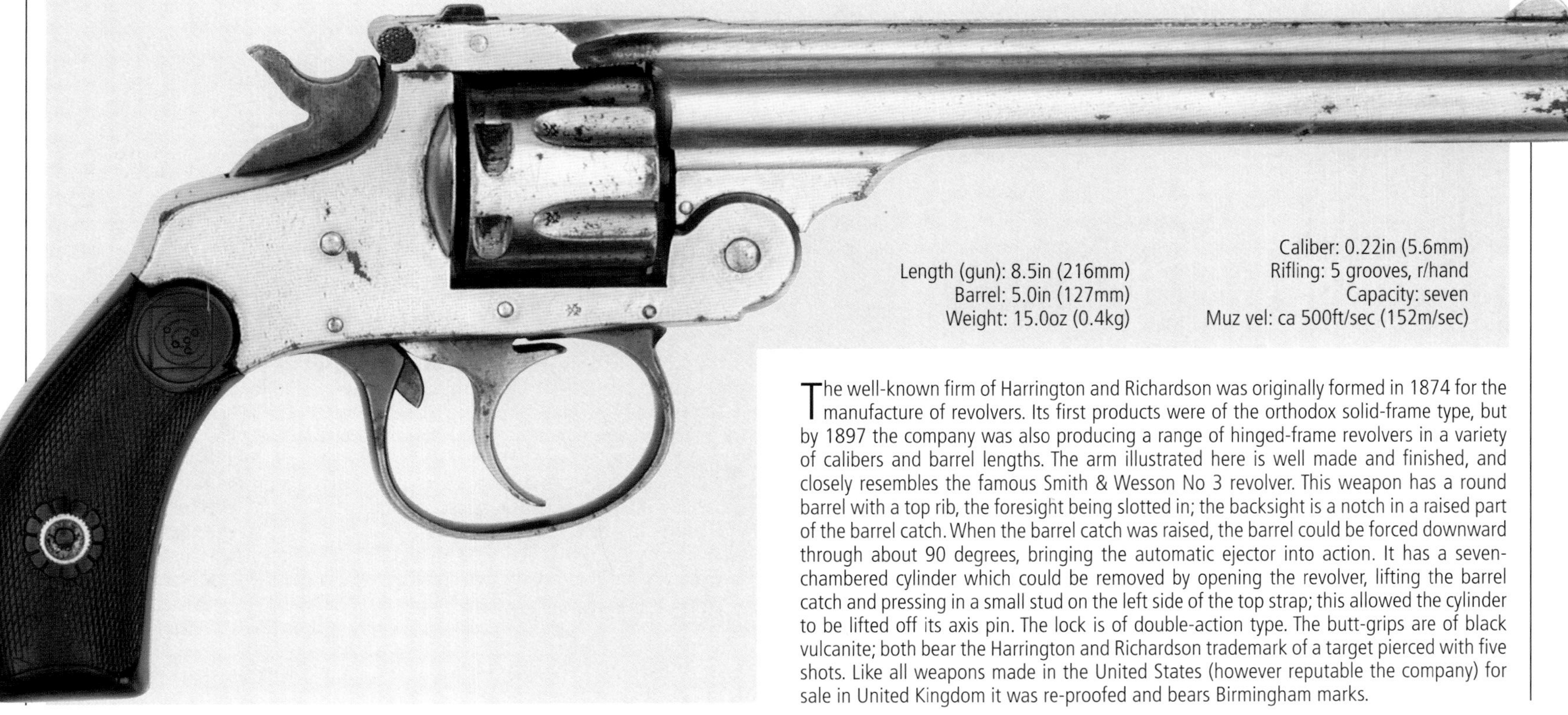

Length (gun): 8.5in (216mm)
Barrel: 5.0in (127mm)
Weight: 15.0oz (0.4kg)
Caliber: 0.22in (5.6mm)
Rifling: 5 grooves, r/hand
Capacity: seven
Muz vel: ca 500ft/sec (152m/sec)

The well-known firm of Harrington and Richardson was originally formed in 1874 for the manufacture of revolvers. Its first products were of the orthodox solid-frame type, but by 1897 the company was also producing a range of hinged-frame revolvers in a variety of calibers and barrel lengths. The arm illustrated here is well made and finished, and closely resembles the famous Smith & Wesson No 3 revolver. This weapon has a round barrel with a top rib, the foresight being slotted in; the backsight is a notch in a raised part of the barrel catch. When the barrel catch was raised, the barrel could be forced downward through about 90 degrees, bringing the automatic ejector into action. It has a seven-chambered cylinder which could be removed by opening the revolver, lifting the barrel catch and pressing in a small stud on the left side of the top strap; this allowed the cylinder to be lifted off its axis pin. The lock is of double-action type. The butt-grips are of black vulcanite; both bear the Harrington and Richardson trademark of a target pierced with five shots. Like all weapons made in the United States (however reputable the company) for sale in United Kingdom it was re-proofed and bears Birmingham marks.

Harrington and Richardson 0.25in Pistol — USA

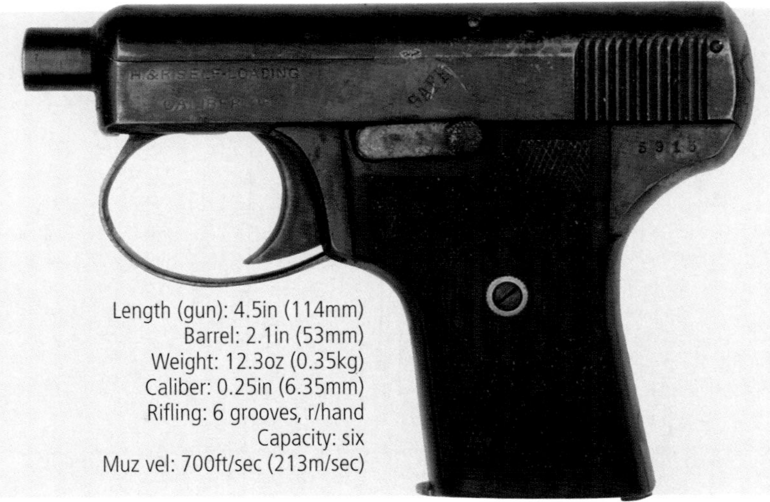

Length (gun): 4.5in (114mm)
Barrel: 2.1in (53mm)
Weight: 12.3oz (0.35kg)
Caliber: 0.25in (6.35mm)
Rifling: 6 grooves, r/hand
Capacity: six
Muz vel: 700ft/sec (213m/sec)

This particular arm was first produced by Webley and Scott in 1909 (qv) and was later made in the United States by Harrington and Richardson under agreement with the British firm. The two weapons were basically similar but the American version did have some differences. The Webley arm has a full slide with only an aperture for extraction, whereas, in the pistol seen here, the slide is partially open-topped and the rear section of the barrel is built up to conform to the general shape. Unlike its Webley prototype, however, the US version utilizes two parallel coil springs, one on each side of the firing-pin, instead of the more usual Webley V-spring under the grip. It has no sight of any kind; this is, of course, understandable, for it is a low-powered pocket arm. It did not prove popular in the United States and was not manufactured after 1914. The left side of the slide is marked "H & R Self-Loading," with the caliber. On the right are company details and patent dates.

Harrington and Richardson 0.32in Pistol — USA

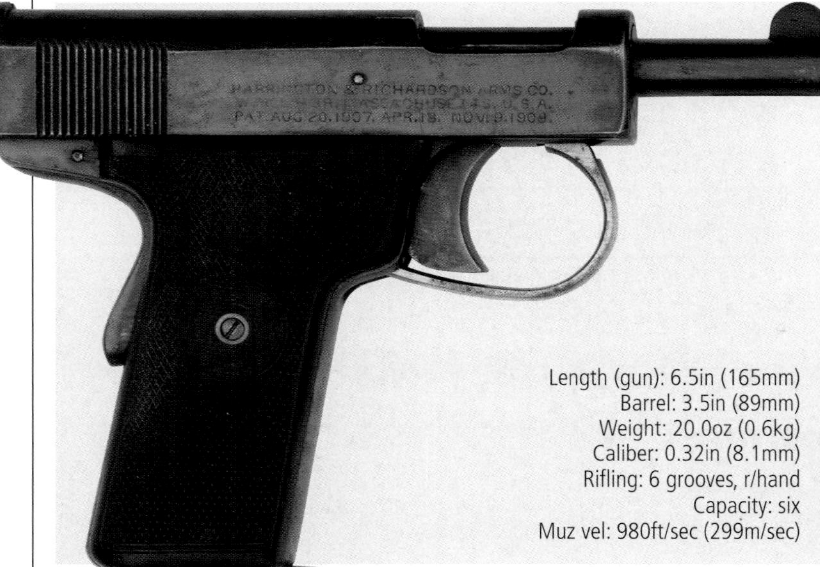

Length (gun): 6.5in (165mm)
Barrel: 3.5in (89mm)
Weight: 20.0oz (0.6kg)
Caliber: 0.32in (8.1mm)
Rifling: 6 grooves, r/hand
Capacity: six
Muz vel: 980ft/sec (299m/sec)

The firm of Harrington and Richardson was set up at Worcester, Massachusetts, in 1874 to make revolvers. It has remained in production ever since. The company does not appear to have been very interested in self-loading pistols, probably because the revolver long retained its dominance in the United States, but in 1910 it began to manufacture a small self-loader based on the Webley and Scott 0.25in Model 1909 (qv). Two or three years later, Harrington and Richardson also put into production this slightly larger self-loading model, which closely resembled the 0.32in Webley and Scott Model 1905 pistol (qv), although it was by no means an exact copy. Its principal external difference is that it lacks the characteristic hammer of the Webley pistol. The slide, too, is of different shape: it has an open top, whereas the Webley's slide has no more than an aperture of sufficient size to allow the empty cases to be ejected. A third difference is the existence on this arm of a grip safety, in addition to an orthodox safety catch. Internally, the weapon is of simple blowback design, but the recoil spring is of the coiled type, while the Webley has a V-spring under the butt plate. The right-hand side of pistol bears the name and address of the company, together with indication that it was made in accordance with patents of August 20 1907 and April 18 and November 9 1909. It is not surprising that this particular arm never achieved any real popularity in the United States, where many similar weapons were available. Even so, manufacture continued into the 1920s.

Hopkins and Allen Forehand Model 1891 Revolver — USA

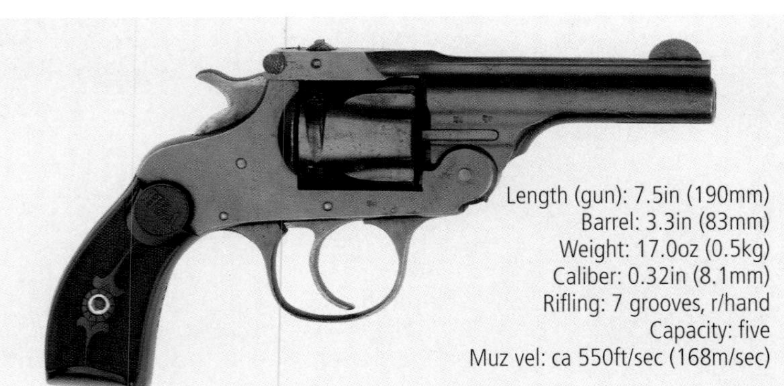

Length (gun): 7.5in (190mm)
Barrel: 3.3in (83mm)
Weight: 17.0oz (0.5kg)
Caliber: 0.32in (8.1mm)
Rifling: 7 grooves, r/hand
Capacity: five
Muz vel: ca 550ft/sec (168m/sec)

The firm of Hopkins and Allen came into existence in Norwich, Connecticut, in 1868, and manufactured a variety of arms, mainly revolvers. At the end of the 19th Century, it took over the Forehand Arms Company of Worcester, Massachusetts, on the death of its former operator, Sullivan Forehand. Soon afterwards, Hopkins and Allen began to make the so-called Forehand Model 1891, a specimen of which is illustrated here. It is a neat, compact, hinged-frame weapon, basically for pocket use. It was opened by lifting a Smith & Wesson-type T-shaped catch (one of the milled ends of the catch is visible in the photograph). When the barrel was forced downward, a star ejector was automatically brought into play and threw out the cartridges or empty cases. The five-chambered cylinder could be removed from its axis pin by pressing in the front end of the horizontal lever. The lock is of double-action type and a separate striker is built into the standing breech. The butt-plates are of a black vulcanite composition and bear the initials "H & A" in a medallion. In view of the fact that arms made in the United States bore no proof marks acceptable in Britain, all such weapons imported into the United Kingdom had to be reproofed: this particular revolver bears the marks of the Birmingham Proof House, which indicates that it was proved for black powder only.

Iver Johnson Revolver — USA

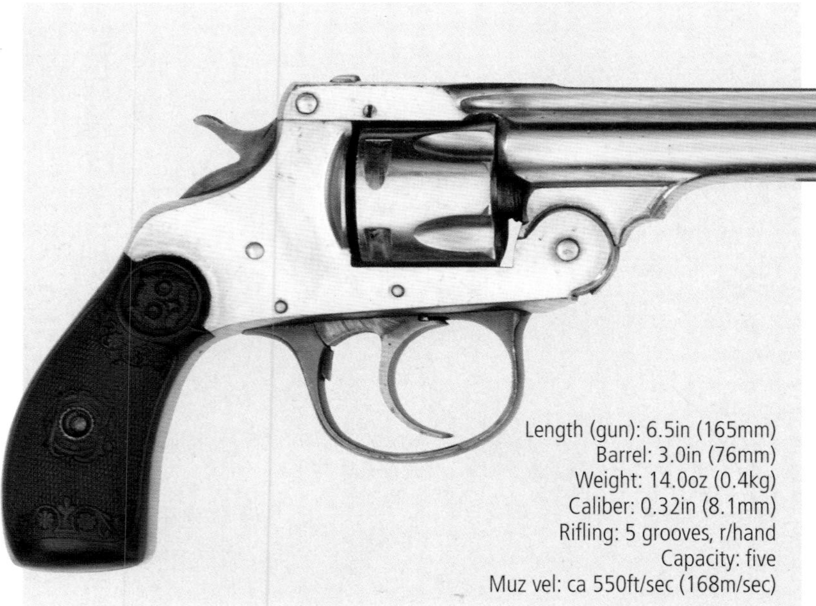

Length (gun): 6.5in (165mm)
Barrel: 3.0in (76mm)
Weight: 14.0oz (0.4kg)
Caliber: 0.32in (8.1mm)
Rifling: 5 grooves, r/hand
Capacity: five
Muz vel: ca 550ft/sec (168m/sec)

In 1871 Iver Johnson and Martin Bye set up a company to make cheap revolvers. These were mostly of pocket type and were produced under a wide variety of trade names. In 1883 Johnson bought out his partner and opened his own company in Worcester, Massachusetts, moving to Fitchburg, in the same state, in 1891. There he made revolvers of a somewhat better quality than before; although still relatively cheap, they were reasonably safe and reliable arms. The revolver seen here is of break-open pattern. It has a round barrel with a rib, the foresight being slotted in. The backsight is a notch on the top extension of the standing breech; and the standing breech itself passes through a rectangular aperture in the top frame, where it was necessary first to push up a small, milled catch on the top left side of the frame, which allowed the barrel to drop down. The action of opening the revolver also forced out the extractor at the rear of the five-chambered cylinder. The frame of the weapon is nickel-plated, the trigger-guard is blued, and the hammer and trigger are of hard rubber, with an owl's head in a circular escutcheon at the top of each. The top of the barrel is inscribed "IVER JOHNSON ARMS AND CYCLE WORKS FITCHBURG MASS USA," with a second line of patent numbers, and the number "A7924" is stamped on the bottom of the butt.

Iver Johnson Hammerless Revolver — USA

Length (gun): 7.8in (197mm)
Barrel: 3.3in (83mm)
Weight: 21.0oz (0.6kg)
Caliber: 0.32in (8.1mm)
Rifling: 7 grooves, r/hand
Capacity: six
Muz vel: ca 550ft/sec (168m/sec)

The Iver Johnson Arms Company of Worcester, Massachusetts, initially made cheap, solid-frame revolvers, but the range was gradually extended and the quality improved. In 1893, Johnson patented a weapon which he had developed with several other gunmakers: it went into production under the rather cumbersome title of the Safety Automatic Double-Action Model. This was followed in 1894 by the hammerless version, illustrated here. It was opened by lifting the T-shaped catch, which allowed two projections on the upper part of the standing breech to separate from a corresponding aperture in the top strap. Then the barrel could be pushed downward, activating a star extractor – the feature from which the word "automatic" in the revolver's title was derived. However, the most important feature of the weapon was the safety device provided for the prevention of accidental discharge. The firing-pin was mounted separately on the standing breech, so that the rear end of it was struck by the hammer. A transfer bar in the lock mechanism rose to its proper position only when the trigger had been fully and properly pulled; thus, the revolver could not be fired involuntarily by dropping or some similar mishap. This was an ingenious and reliable invention which greatly improved the company's reputation. The revolver seen here is plated, except for its trigger and guard, and has hard rubber-composition butt-plates, each with the familiar owl's-head trade mark in a medallion.

Iver Johnson Safety Automatic Double-Action Revolver — USA

Length (gun): 7.5in (190mm)
Barrel: 4.0in (102mm)
Weight: 15.0oz (0.4kg)
Caliber: 0.32in (8.1mm)
Rifling: 5 grooves, r/hand
Capacity: five
Muz vel: ca 550ft/sec (168m/sec)

The Iver Johnson arm illustrated here is a compact and well-made double-action revolver of pocket type. It was opened by lifting the top catch, which caused two parallel projections on the upper part of the standing breech to separate from two corresponding apertures on the top frame. This allowed the barrel to be pushed downward and brought the automatic extractor into play. A very interesting feature of this weapon is that it is of the type known as Safety Automatic Double-Action, a form of lock mechanism developed by Johnson and others in the 1890s and patented to the Johnson company. The firing-pin was mounted on the standing breech; its rear end was struck by the flat head of the hammer by means of a flat transfer bar, which rose into position only when the trigger was properly pulled. If the bar did not rise, the hammer was held clear of the actual pin by fouling the top of the breech. This was an ingenious and reliable system which remained in use unchanged for many years. The revolver is well finished, with blued trigger-guard and case-hardened lock mechanism, and has the usual hard rubber grips with the familiar owl's-head motif.

Le Mat Revolver — USA

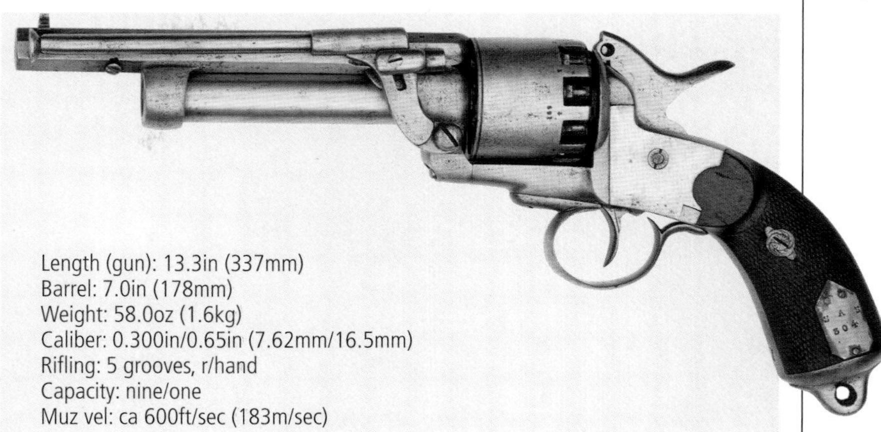

Length (gun): 13.3in (337mm)
Barrel: 7.0in (178mm)
Weight: 58.0oz (1.6kg)
Caliber: 0.300in/0.65in (7.62mm/16.5mm)
Rifling: 5 grooves, r/hand
Capacity: nine/one
Muz vel: ca 600ft/sec (183m/sec)

The Le Mat, of a type patented in the USA by Jean Alexander Le Mat in 1856, is of massive and solid construction. The frame, including the butt, is made in one piece, the lower barrel being an integral part of it. The cylinder is mounted on this lower barrel, which thus doubles as axis pin. The upper barrel is mounted on the lower one by means of a front and rear ring, the latter having an extension which locks firmly on to the lower part of the frame. The lower barrel, which is smooth-bored, is of cylindrical shape; the upper barrel, which is rifled, is octagonal and is fitted with a foresight. The weapon's rearsight was an integral part of the hammer nose, which is, unfortunately, missing in this particular specimen. The revolver is fitted with a rammer of basically similar type to that designed by Kerr and used on the Beaumont-Adams (qv) and other British revolvers. When the rammer was not in use, the lever lay along the left flat of the barrel, with its knob in a notch near the muzzle: the size of the knob, together with the natural springing of the steel, held it firmly in place. The cylinder, which bears English proofmarks, has nine chambers; the nipples, which are in prolongation of the axis, are separated by deep and solid partitions. The nipple for the lower barrel is set in a deep, cylindrical recess on top of the standing breech: when complete, the hammer had a rotatable nose which could be set to fire either the upper or the lower barrel. The lock is of single-action type, access to its mechanism being by means of an inspection plate on the left-hand side of the frame. The top flat of the barrel is inscribed "LEMAT AND GIRARDS PATENT, LONDON." The weapon was used by the Confederate Army during the Civil War.

M.B.A. 13mm Gyrojet Pistol — USA

Length: 9.2in (234mm)
Barrel: 5.0in (127mm)
Weight: 17.0oz (0.5kg)
Caliber: 0.5in (13mm)
Rifling: none
Capacity: six
Muz vel: ca 900ft/sec (274m/sec)

There have been virtually no significant developments in hand firearms for very many years and it is, therefore, arguable that these arms have reached their full development. In 1960, however, two enterprising Americans, Robert Mainhardt and Art Biehl, found this so hard to accept that they decided to attempt a breakthrough. They produced the weapon illustrated here, which although it looks at first glance very like an orthodox self-loading pistol was, in fact, a rocket-launcher! The rocket was of 13mm caliber: it was about 1.5in (38mm) long, with a solid head as the actual projectile and a tubular body containing a propellant charge. The base was closed but it had four jets to provide thrust; these were also angled to impart spin to the rocket, in order to ensure stability. Once the rocket had been loaded pressure on the trigger caused the hammer to drive it to the rear so that the cap in its base struck a fixed pin in the breech. The forward action of the rocket recocked the hammer, which lay flat so as not to impede its passage. The weapon lacked both power and accuracy and was not a success.

MASSACHUSETTS TAPE-PRIMER REVOLVER — USA

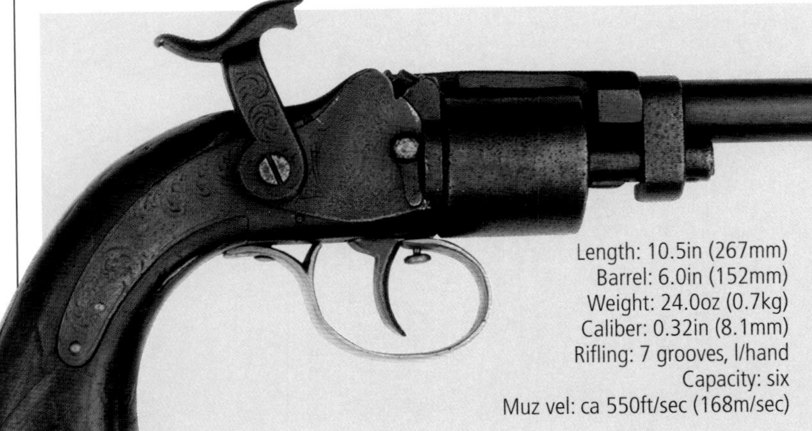

Length: 10.5in (267mm)
Barrel: 6.0in (152mm)
Weight: 24.0oz (0.7kg)
Caliber: 0.32in (8.1mm)
Rifling: 7 grooves, l/hand
Capacity: six
Muz vel: ca 550ft/sec (168m/sec)

In 1851, Colt sued the Massachusetts Arms Company for producing revolvers with mechanically rotated cylinders in contravention of a patent he had taken out earlier. The weapon illustrated is one of the modified versions of the revolvers in question, made in the interval between the court case and the expiry of Colt's patent. The barrel of this weapon, which is rifled, is attached to the top of the standing breech by a hinged strap which permitted it to be raised to an angle of about 45 degrees in order to remove the cylinder. The latter is mounted on a stout axis pin which protrudes slightly more than 1in (25.4mm) beyond the front face of the cylinder; the object of this extension was to provide a firm locking point for a hook which pivoted round the breech end of the barrel, a fitting clearly visible in the illustration. There is a small retaining spring on the end of the axis pin to prevent it being released accidentally. The lock is fitted with a tape-primer which made possible the use of a single nipple only: the flash was transmitted to the charge by means of a small hole at the rear of each chamber. When the cylinder stop pin (visible in front of the trigger) was pushed, the cylinder could be rotated manually.

MERIDEN POCKET REVOLVER — USA

Length (gun): 6.5in (165mm)
Barrel: 3.0in (76mm)
Weight: 14.0oz (0.4kg)
Caliber: 0.32in (8.1mm)
Rifling: 5 grooves, r/hand
Capacity: five
Muz vel: ca 550ft/sec (168m/sec)

Meriden may have been a subsidiary of the famous American mail-order firm of Sears Roebuck; or part of the Fyrberg; or an offshoot of the Stevens Arms and Tool Company; but the history of Meriden remains something of a mystery. The weapons produced by the firm were mostly pocket models, including some hammerless versions; and the revolver shown here can probably be classed as a typical specimen. It is of hinged-frame type with a sprung, T-shaped barrel catch (visible in the photograph), the backsight being a simple V-notch in the raised portion of the catch. It has a round barrel with a top rib of slightly peculiar section: it is wider at the top than at its junction with the barrel. Perhaps the only feature of the arm that is in any way remarkable is its somewhat unusual foresight, which has a shape reminiscent of an old-fashioned cocked-hat. The lock is of orthodox double-action type, and the butt-grips are of black vulcanite. The top flat of the barrel is marked "MERIDEN FIREARMS CO. MERIDEN CONN USA," and on the base of the butt is the number "284035" (the figure "8" being stamped upside down on this particular specimen). It is probably not too unfair to say that this weapon may with justice be classed as cheap and nasty. The workmanship is crude and the components shoddy; but as the price of these revolvers in the early 20th Century probably did not exceed a couple of dollars, these low standards are hardly to be wondered at. Such arms, sold extensively by mail order, are often classified as "Suicide Specials" in modern terms.

REMINGTON ARMY MODEL 1863 REVOLVER — USA

Length (gun): 13.8in (348mm)
Barrel: 8.0in (203mm)
Weight: 44.0oz (1.3kg)
Caliber: 0.44in (11.2mm)
Rifling: 5 grooves, r/hand
Capacity: six
Muz vel: ca 700ft/sec (213m/sec)

Eliphalet Remington was originally a blacksmith but turned to gun-making fairly early in his career. He at first specialized in military rifles and soon gained an enviable reputation for the quality of the arms he produced. By 1857, he had begun to make a few pocket revolvers to a design made by F. Beals, but it was not until the outbreak of the Civil War that he began to produce service revolvers in considerable quantity. This example is the improved Army Model of 1863; it was a fine arm in its day, perhaps its major feature being its solid frame, which gave it great rigidity. It has an octagonal barrel (the top flat inscribed "PATENTED SEP 14 1850 E REMINGTON AND SONS ILION NEW YORK USA NEW MODEL") which screws into the frame, and a plain, six-shot cylinder with rectangular slots for the stop. The axis pin could be removed by drawing it forward. The lock is of the then-customary single-action type and worked smoothly; the act of cocking the hammer also rotated the cylinder. The rammer is of orthodox type; except that its lever broadens towards the rear, presumably to prevent it from catching on the holster, and gives it a streamlined appearance. The butt-plates are of very dark walnut. The trigger-guard, which is of brass is rather small; it would not have been easy to operate the trigger while wearing gloves. This handsome, well-made service arm was used extensively by Union troops in the Civil War and remained popular afterwards.

Remington Double Deringer USA

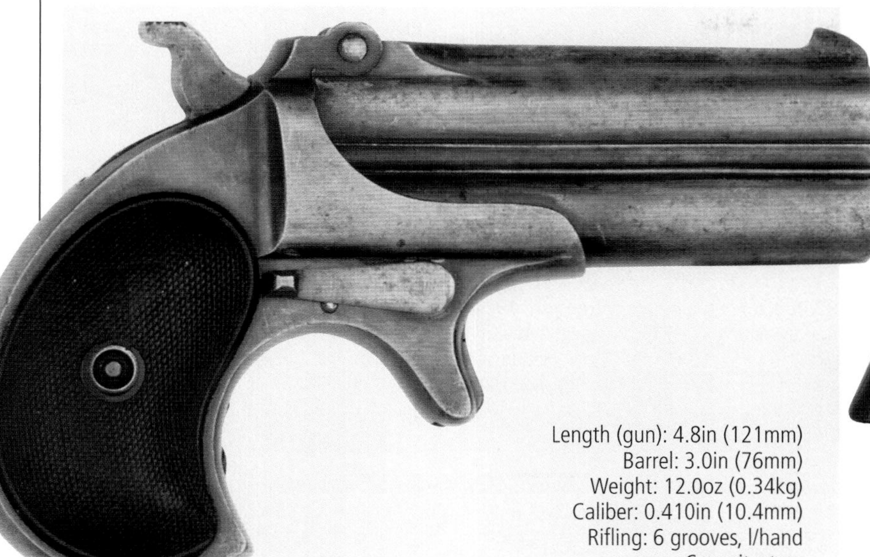

Length (gun): 4.8in (121mm)
Barrel: 3.0in (76mm)
Weight: 12.0oz (0.34kg)
Caliber: 0.410in (10.4mm)
Rifling: 6 grooves, l/hand
Capacity: two
Muz vel: ca 450ft/sec (137m/sec)

This is another of the famous deringer-type weapons designed by William H. Elliott of the Remington company. This model first appeared in about 1866 and continued to be made almost up to the outbreak of World War II. It was a neat, compact weapon which, in spite of its small size, handled surprisingly well, even though the butt could be gripped only by the second finger. To load the pistol, it was necessary first to turn the lever (visible above the trigger) until it pointed forward; then the top-hinged barrels could be raised, the cartridges inserted, and the barrels returned to their proper position and locked. The hammer was of single-action type but was, most ingeniously, equipped with a floating nose which fired the top and bottom barrels in succession. The extractor, situated on the left-hand side of the barrels, was worked by the user's thumb.

Remington Deringer USA

Length (gun): 4.8in (121mm)
Barrel: 2.4in (61mm)
Weight: 7.5oz (0.21kg)
Caliber: 0.410in (10.4mm)
Rifling: 5 grooves, r/hand
Capacity: one
Muz vel: ca 450ft/sec (137m/sec)

Many of the small pocket pistols produced by Remington were designed by William H. Elliott, who became well known for such arms. Some were of "pepperbox" design; others had fixed barrels and rotating firing pins; and yet others were of single- or double-barreled type, in which form they continued to be made until well into the 20th Century. The specimen illustrated here was the single-barreled Remington version of 1867, a simple but quite powerful arm which achieved considerable popularity. It was of very basic construction, since it had, in effect, no breechblock of any kind: the cartridge was held in position at the moment of firing by the heavy hammer. When the weapon was at full-cock, a short rimfire round of 0.41in caliber could be inserted. When the hammer fell, a small projection below it engaged in front of the sear and held the round in position to be fired by an integral striker situated on the top of the hammer face.

Remington Model 1875 Revolver USA

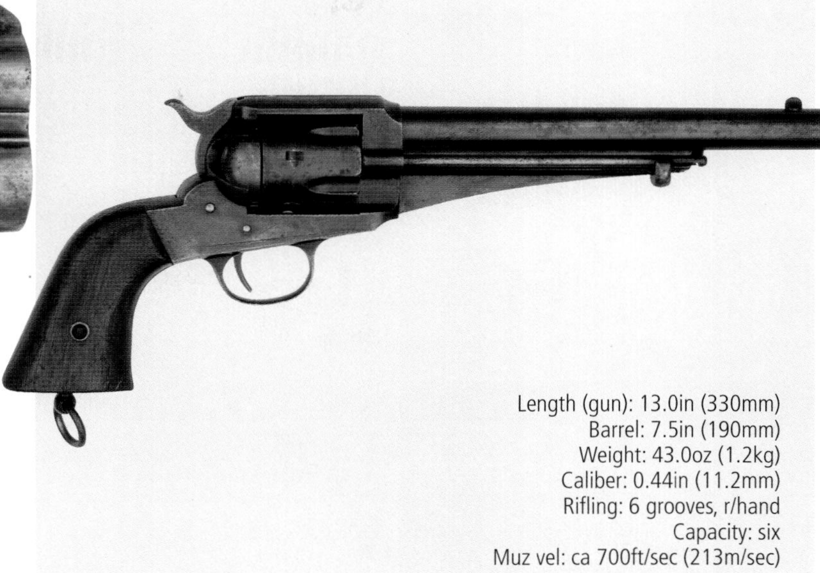

Length (gun): 13.0in (330mm)
Barrel: 7.5in (190mm)
Weight: 43.0oz (1.2kg)
Caliber: 0.44in (11.2mm)
Rifling: 6 grooves, r/hand
Capacity: six
Muz vel: ca 700ft/sec (213m/sec)

Once the Civil War was over, the great move westward increased tremendously and, as every man was to a large extent his own law, the demand for arms, particularly revolvers, remained fairly high. The first Remington cartridge revolver, which appeared in 1875, differed very little in general appearance from the firm's earlier percussion arm. The major mechanical differences were the bored-through cylinder; the loading gate; and the provision of a Colt-type ejector rod working in a sleeve. The distinctively tapered rammer handle of the earlier arm had, of course, become unnecessary; but it was replaced by a rib of similar dimensions, thus leaving the silhouette unchanged. The trigger-guard of this model is of steel and the butt is fitted with a lanyard ring. The top of the round barrel is engraved "E REMINGTON & SONS, ILION, NEW YORK, USA." Although the Western scene was largely dominated by Colt arms, the new cartridge Remingtons were excellent weapons – robust, well-made, and accurate. A new version appeared in 1891, but by then the Colt had firmly established its dominance. In 1894, Remington reverted to its first interest of long arms, a sphere in which the company still excels, as many modern rifles will bear witness.

Remington Model 51 Pistol USA

Length (gun): 6.5in (165mm)
Barrel: 3.5in (89mm)
Weight: 21.0oz (0.6kg)
Caliber: 0.38in (9.6mm)
Rifling: 7 grooves, r/hand
Capacity: seven
Muz vel: ca 900ft/sec (274m/sec)

Remington's first entry into the field of self-loading pistols occurred in 1917, when the company received a contract to manufacture Model 1911 Colts, but this contract was terminated in 1918, at the end of World War I. However, the company had plans for a self-loading pistol of its own, based on the designs of J. D. Pedersen, a well-known and well-respected figure in the world of small arms. This weapon appeared on the market in 1919 as the Model 51. It was made in two calibers – 0.38in Auto (the arm illustrated here) and, in much smaller numbers, in 0.32in. The mechanism was of the type known as delayed blowback. When the cartridge was fired, the slide and its internal breechblock recoiled briefly together; the block then stopped, allowing the slide to continue to the rear, but after a brief pause the block was released and rejoined the slide. Both then came forward under the influence of the recoil spring, which was fitted round the fixed barrel. The weapon was fitted with a grip safety (visible at the back of the butt) and also had a normal safety at the rear left end of the frame. The top of the slide was milled to reduce glare. The Remington Model 51 was an excellent weapon but, because it was expensive to produce – and thus had to be priced accordingly – it never gained the popularity it deserved.

Ruger New Model Blackhawk/Super Blackhawk Revolver — USA

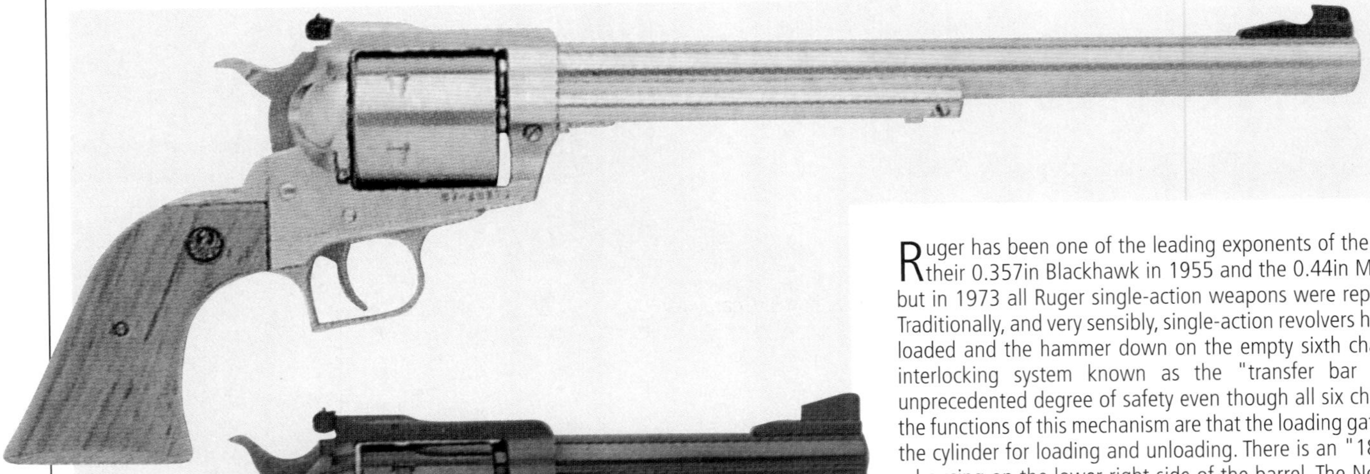

(0.44in Magnum version)
Length (gun): 13.4in (340mm)
Barrel: 7.5in (191mm)
Weight: 48.0oz (1.4kg)
Caliber: 0.44in (11.2mm)
Rifling: n.k
Capacity: six
Muz vel: n.k.

Ruger has been one of the leading exponents of the single-action revolver, introducing their 0.357in Blackhawk in 1955 and the 0.44in Magnum Super Blackhawk in 1959, but in 1973 all Ruger single-action weapons were replaced by the "New Model" range. Traditionally, and very sensibly, single-action revolvers had been carried with five chambers loaded and the hammer down on the empty sixth chamber, but Ruger designed a new interlocking system known as the "transfer bar mechanism," which ensures an unprecedented degree of safety even though all six chambers are carried loaded. Among the functions of this mechanism are that the loading gate freezes the hammer and releases the cylinder for loading and unloading. There is an "1873-pattern" sprung ejector rod in a housing on the lower right side of the barrel. The New Model Blackhawk range covers three calibers: 0.30in Carbine (one model); 0.357in Magnum (six models); and 0.45in Long Colt (seven models). These feature a variety of barrel lengths (4.6in/117mm; 5.5in/140mm; 6.5in/165mm; and 7.5in/190mm) and the usual choice of blued or stainless steel finishes. One model, the New Model Blackhawk Convertible, has two cylinders, one for 0.357in Magnum, the other for 9mm, which can be exchanged instantly by hand, without any tools or any other changes to the weapon. There are eight models in the New Model Super Blackhawk range, all in 0.44in Magnum caliber, which also come in a choice of finishes and barrel lengths, but also with a choice of cylinder and styles (fluted or unfluted) and round or square-backed trigger guards. Pictures show: above left, New Model Super Blackhawk with 10.5in (267mm) barrel, unfluted cylinder and square-backed trigger guard; and, left, the Blackhawk Convertible, which can fire either 0.357in or 9mm Parabellum simply by changing the cylinder. Specifications relate to the 0.44in Magnum version.

Ruger Bisley Revolver — USA

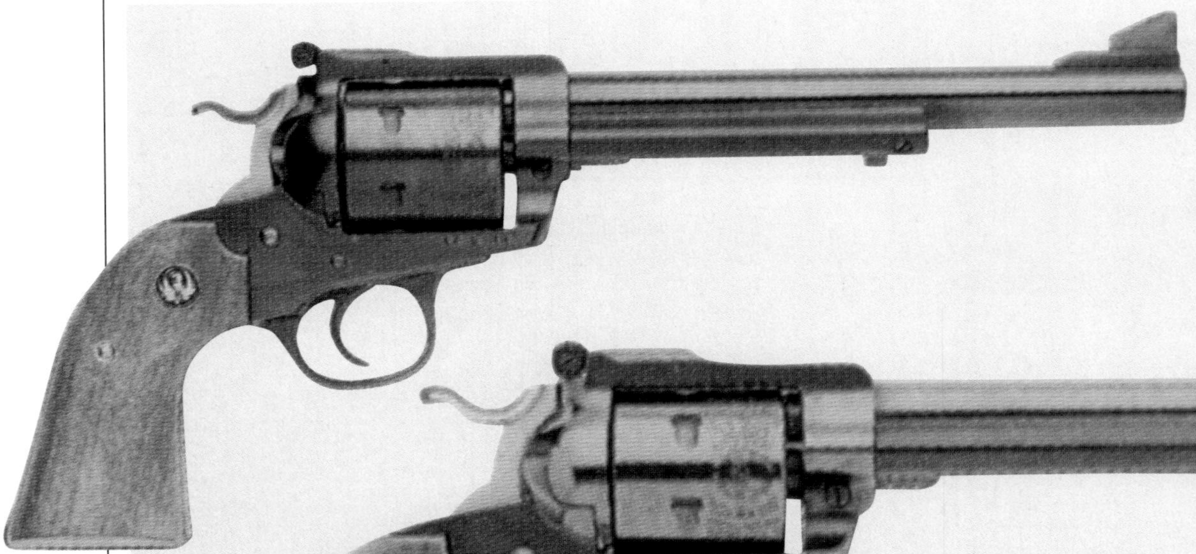

Length (gun): 13.0in (330mm)
Barrel: 7.5in (191mm)
Weight: 48oz (1.4kg)
Caliber: 0.357in Magnum
Rifling: n.k.
Capacity: six
Muz vel: n.k.

The outline of Ruger's Bisley Model, introduced in 1985, closely resembles that of Colt's 1890s Bisley model, a single-action-only weapon, designed for Edwardian-era competition shooting. The modern weapon, however, has a slightly more upright handle and a lower hammer spur, which enable the shooter to recock it using the right thumb without shifting the grip, a considerable advantage in timed competitions. It is produced in four models, chambered for 0.22in LR, 0.357in Magnum (see specifications), 0.44in Magnum, and 0.45in Long Colt. The 0.22in version has a 6.5in (165mm) barrel; the remainder have 7.5in (191mm) barrels. The Bisley has a ramp foresight and click adjustable Partridge backsight. Pictures show the 0.45in Long Colt version (above left), and 0.22in Long Rifle version (above).

Ruger Redhawk/Super Redhawk Revolver — USA

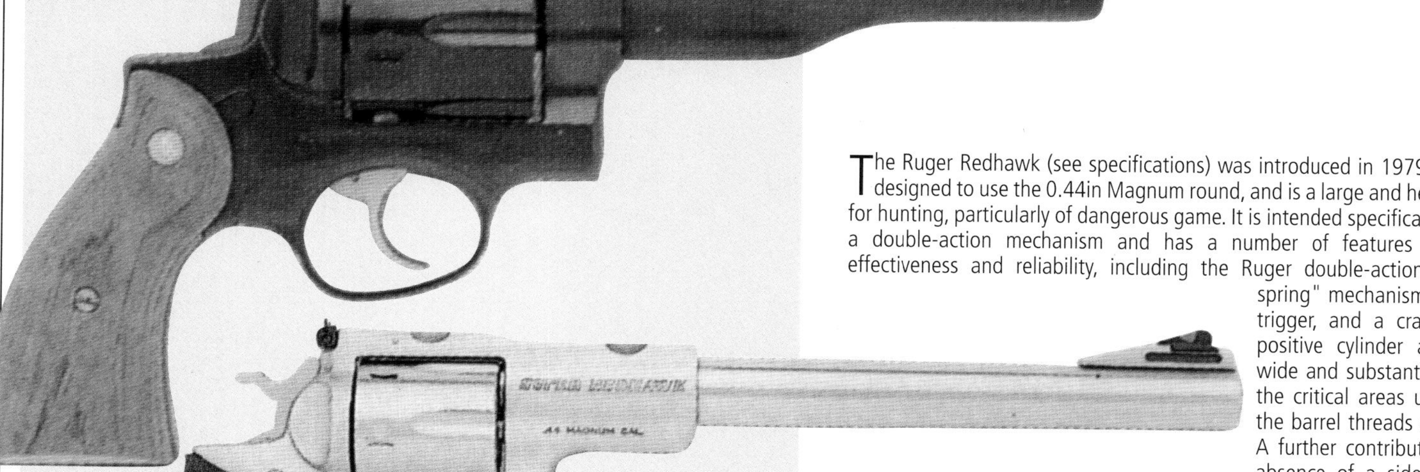

The Ruger Redhawk (see specifications) was introduced in 1979, was the first revolver designed to use the 0.44in Magnum round, and is a large and heavy handgun designed for hunting, particularly of dangerous game. It is intended specifically for those who prefer a double-action mechanism and has a number of features designed to increase effectiveness and reliability, including the Ruger double-action mechanism, "single-spring" mechanism for both hammer and trigger, and a crane-locking system for positive cylinder alignment. There is a wide and substantial extra top strap and the critical areas under and surrounding the barrel threads are particularly strong. A further contribution to strength is the absence of a sideplate, thus preserving both sidewalls intact as integral sections of the frame. The Redhawk is available with 5.5in (140mm) and 7.5in (190mm) barrels, chambered for either 0.44in Magnum or 0.45in Long Colt, and in both blued and stainless steel finishes. The Super Blackhawk is available with 7.5in (190mm) or 9.5in (241mm) barrels chambered for the 0.44in Magnum round, but the latest version with a 7.5in (190mm) barrel only is chambered for the new and very powerful 0.454in Cassul round (although it accepts the 0.45in Long Colt as well). The Super Redhawk is in stainless steel finishes only and features a new cushioned grip, made of rubber with wooden inserts and it should be mentioned that the 0.45in Magnum Super Redhawk with 9.5in (241mm) barrel weighs 3.6lb (1,644g) unloaded, no mean challenge to a shooter. The pictures show the Ruger Redhawk with blued finish, wooden grips and 5.5in (140mm) barrel (above left) and the Super Redhawk with stainless steel finish, cushioned grips and 9.5in (241mm) barrel (above).

Length (gun): 13in (330mm)
Barrel: 7.5in (190mm)
Weight: 52.5oz (1,488g)
Caliber: 0.44in (11.2mm)
Rifling: 6 grooves, r/hand
Capacity: six
Muz vel: n.k.

Ruger 0.45in "Old Army" Percussion Revolver — USA

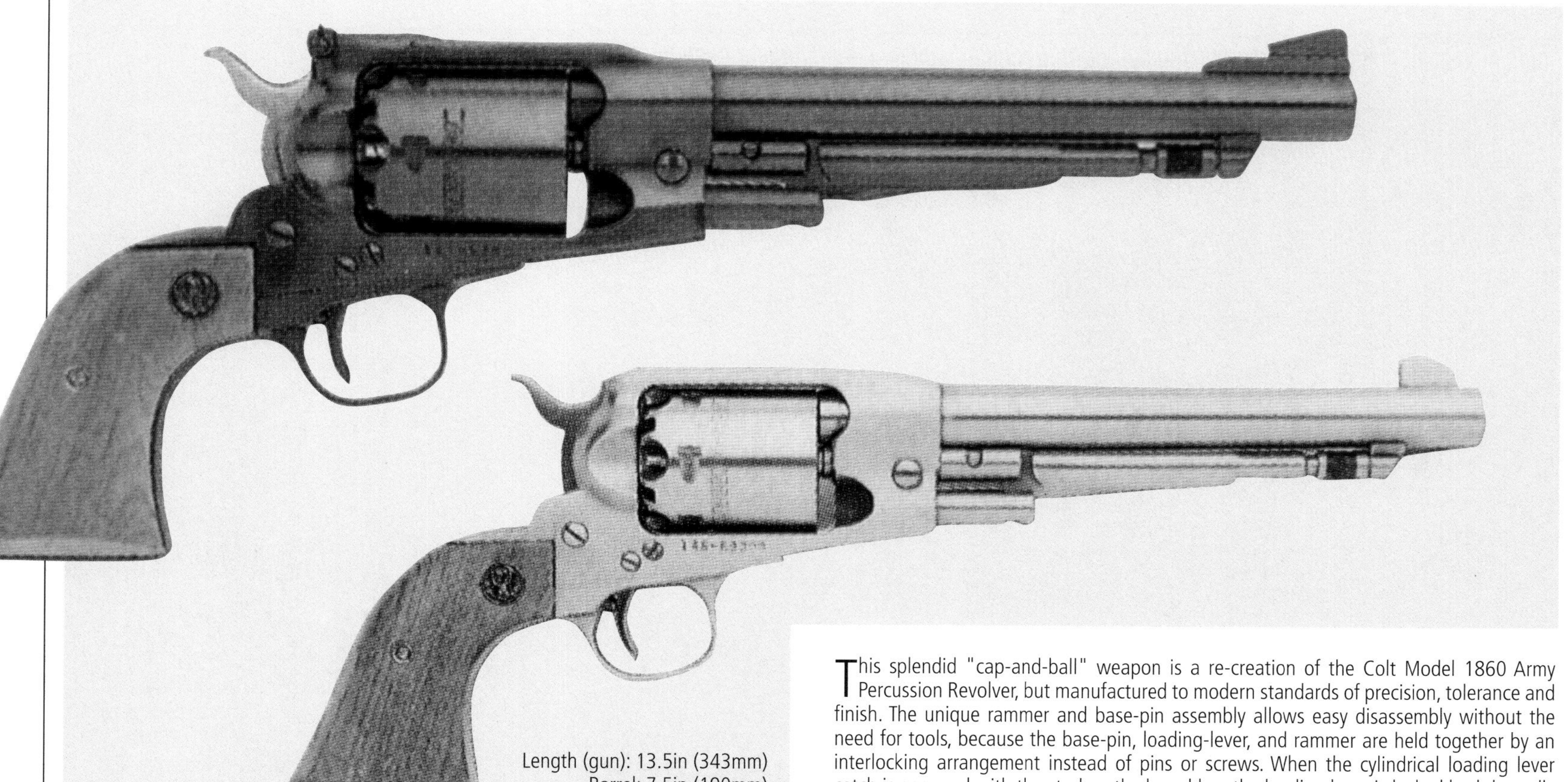

Length (gun): 13.5in (343mm)
Barrel: 7.5in (190mm)
Weight: 46.0oz (1.3kg)
Caliber: 0.45in (11.4mm)
Rifling: 6 grooves, r/hand
Capacity: six
Muz vel: n.k.

This splendid "cap-and-ball" weapon is a re-creation of the Colt Model 1860 Army Percussion Revolver, but manufactured to modern standards of precision, tolerance and finish. The unique rammer and base-pin assembly allows easy disassembly without the need for tools, because the base-pin, loading-lever, and rammer are held together by an interlocking arrangement instead of pins or screws. When the cylindrical loading lever catch is engaged with the stud on the barrel lug, the loading lever is locked both laterally and vertically, thus preventing any sideways movement. The nipples are deeply recessed to prevent cap fragments from flying to the side. There are four weapons in the series, all of 0.44in caliber: two have adjustable sights and two have fixed sights, with a choice of either blued or stainless steel finish; all have American walnut stock grips. Pictures show (above left) the blued finish, adjustable sight version; and (above) the stainless steel finish, fixed-sight version.

RUGER 0.357IN GP-100 REVOLVER — USA

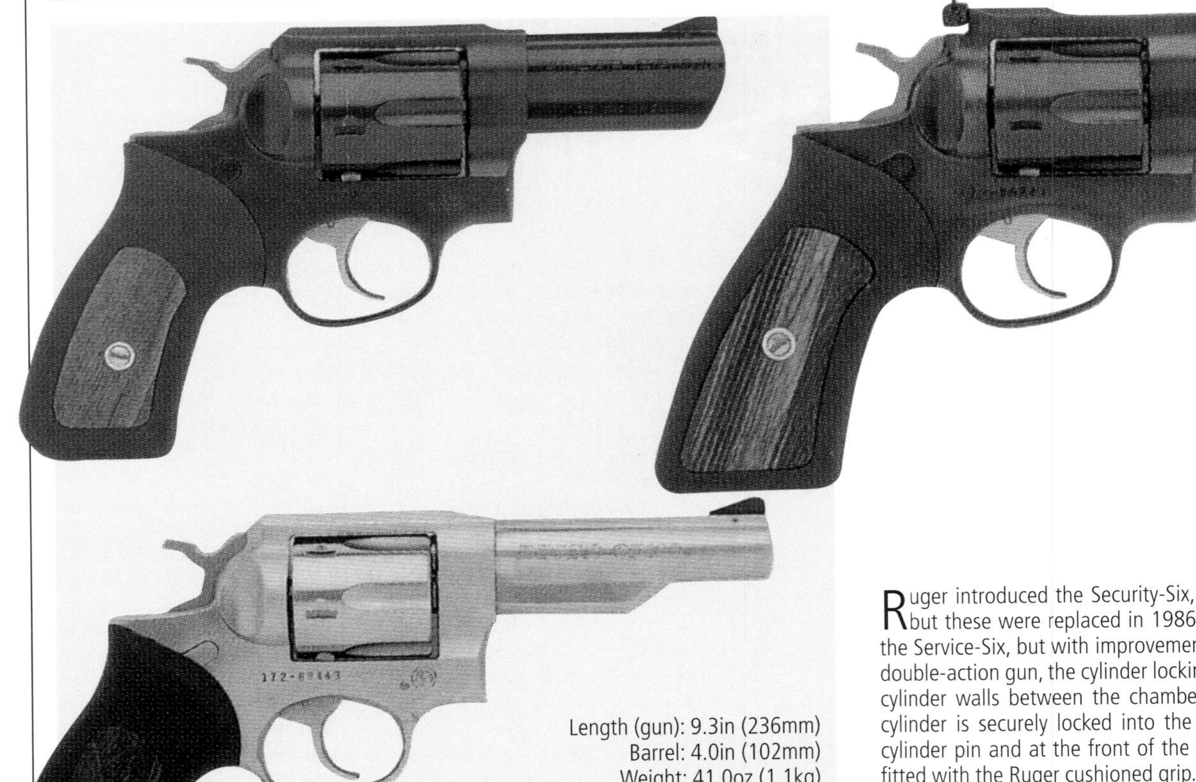

Length (gun): 9.3in (236mm)
Barrel: 4.0in (102mm)
Weight: 41.0oz (1.1kg)
Caliber: 0.357in Magnum
Rifling: 5 grooves, r/hand
Capacity: six
Muz vel: n.k.

Ruger introduced the Security-Six, Police Service-Six, and Speed-Six revolvers in 1971, but these were replaced in 1986 by the GP-100 series which has the same layout as the Service-Six, but with improvements in the mechanism and distribution of the metal. A double-action gun, the cylinder locking notches are offset and cut into the thick part of the cylinder walls between the chambers rather than over them. In the firing position the cylinder is securely locked into the frame in two places: at the rear by the traditional cylinder pin and at the front of the crane by a large, spring-loaded latch. All models are fitted with the Ruger cushioned grip. The cylinder crane locks directly to the frame, with an offset, shrouded ejection rod, which allows a thicker, stronger frame under the barrel threads. Models are available with 3.0in (76mm), 4.0in (102mm), and 6.0in (152mm) barrels and with fixed or adjustable sights. All are chambered for the 0.357in Magnum round, except for one which takes the 0.38in Special round. Pictures show: above left, 0.357in caliber, 3.0in barrel, blued finish; above right, 0.357in caliber, 6.0in barrel, stainless steel finish; and left, 0.38in Special, 4.0in barrel.

RUGER 9MM P89/0.45IN P90 PISTOLS — USA

Length (gun): 7.75in (200mm)
Barrel: 4.5in (114mm)
Weight: 32.0oz (0.9kg)
Caliber: 9mm
Rifling: 6 grooves, r/hand
Capacity: see text
Muz vel: ca 1,099ft/sec (335m/sec)

Ruger introduced its first-ever automatic pistol in the "P-Series" in 1985. This was designated P85, but was later upgraded into the P89 and P90, the models described here, which are virtually identical to each other except that the P89 (see specifications) is chambered for the NATO standard 9 x 19mm Parabellum round, while the P90 is chambered for the 0.45in ACP round, and their magazines contain 10 and 7 rounds, respectively. Most models in the series are available in three different configurations: manual safety; decock-only; and direct-action only. The first of these, the Manual Safety models, incorporate ambidextrous safety levers which, when engaged, push the firing pin forward into the slide, out of reach of the hammer, while concurrently locking the firing-pin firmly in position, at which point the hammer is decocked. The gun cannot now be fired until the safety lever is moved to the "fire" position and the trigger is pulled fully to the rear. In the Decock-only models, the hammer is decocked by depressing either of the ambidextrous decocking levers. When released the lever springs back to the "fire" position and the gun can only be fired by a double-action pull on the trigger without further contact with the decocking lever. In the Double-Action-Only models, all of which have a spurless hammer, the firing-pin is blocked from forward movement by an internal safety which prevents firing unless the trigger is completely pulled; operation is "double-action-only" for all shots. In the Ruger numbering system Decock-only models have the suffix "D," Double-Action-Only have the suffix "DAO," while Manual Safety models have no suffix. The pictures show (above right) the P89D (9mm Parabellum, blued finish, decock-only); and (above left) the P90 (0.45in ACP, blued finish, manual safety).

RUGER SP-101 REVOLVER USA

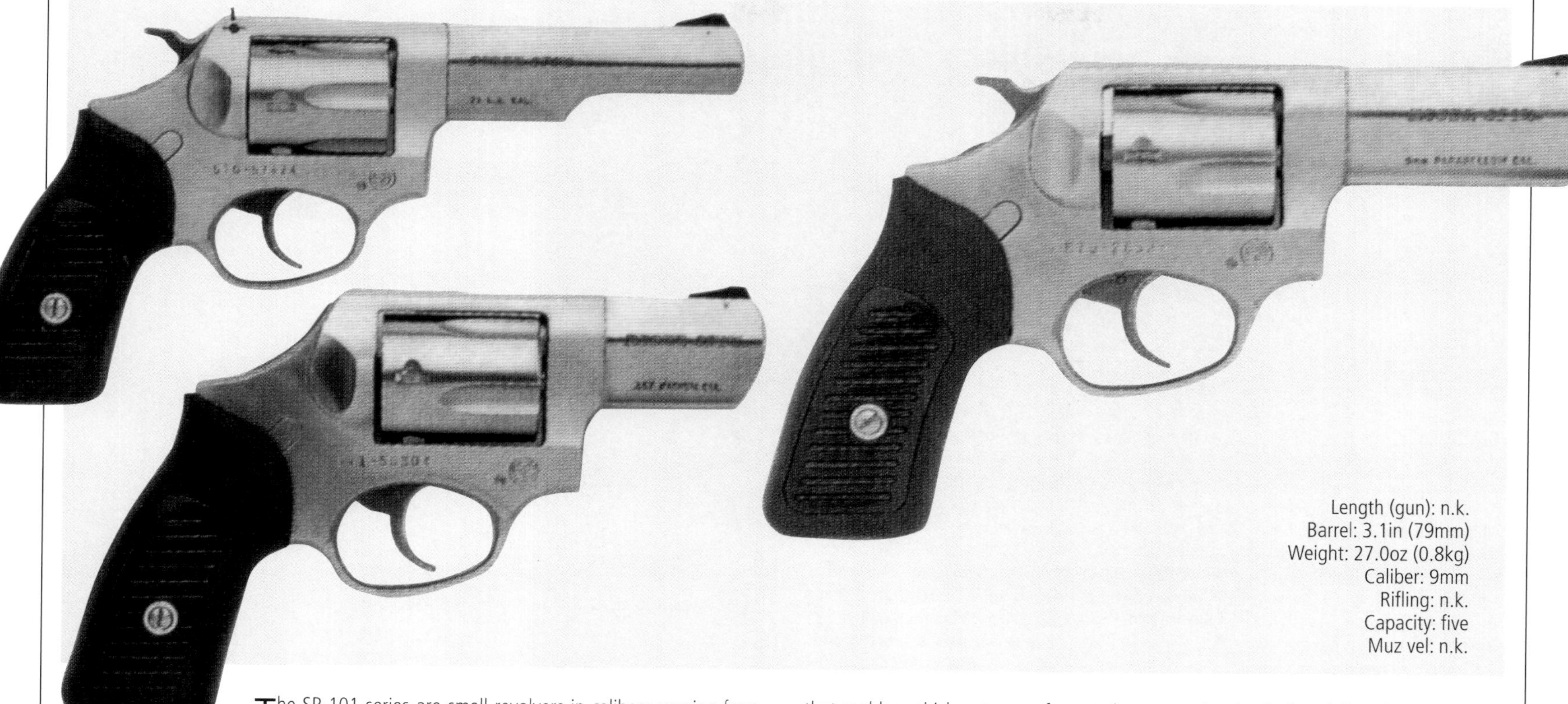

Length (gun): n.k.
Barrel: 3.1in (79mm)
Weight: 27.0oz (0.8kg)
Caliber: 9mm
Rifling: n.k.
Capacity: five
Muz vel: n.k.

The SP-101 series are small revolvers in calibers ranging from 0.22in, through 0.32in Magnum, 9mm and 0.357 Magnum to 0.38+P, with a six- or five-round cylinder depending upon the caliber. The SP-101 series are all double-action guns, with offset cylinder locking notches, which are cut into the thick part of the cylinder walls between the chambers rather than in the more customary position over them. The cylinder is securely locked into the frame in two places: at the rear, using a traditional cylinder pin and at the front by a large, spring-loaded latch. All models are fitted with a hardened rubber grip, but without wooden inserts. The cylinder crane locks directly to the frame, with an offset, shrouded ejection rod that enables a thicker, stronger frame to be mounted under the barrel threads. The hammer, trigger, and most small internal components are made of durable, corrosion-resistant stainless steel. Some models are double-action only and have a spurless hammer. Barrels are available in 2.25in (57mm), 3.1in (79mm), and 4.0in (102mm) lengths. All are finished in stainless steel. The 0.22in Long Rifle and 0.32in Magnum versions have six-round cylinders; while 9mm, 0.38+P and 0.357in Magnum have five round cylinders. Pictures show: top left, KSP-240 0.22in caliber with 4.0in barrel; above right, KSP-931 9mm with 3.1in barrel; and above left, KSP-321XL 0.357in Magnum with 2.25in barrel. Specifications are for the KSP-931 9mm version.

RUGER P93 PISTOL USA

Length (gun): 7.25in (184mm)
Barrel: 3.9in (99mm)
Weight: 31.0oz (0.9kg)
Caliber: 9mm
Rifling: 6 grooves, r/hand
Capacity: 10-round box magazine
Muz vel: ca 1,165ft/sec (355m/sec)

This is the compact model in the Ruger P-series and is produced in 9mm caliber only. It is smaller and lighter than the P89 and is available in Decock-only (D) and Double-Action-Only (DAO) versions, but not in Manual Safety. There is no equivalent model chambered for 0.45in ACP, but the P93 fires all types of 9 x 19mm ammunition including those with +P loads. The magazine holds 10 rounds and is interoperable with the magazine of the P89. The picture shows the P93D, the Decock-only version.

RUGER 9MM P94/0.40 AUTO P944 PISTOL USA

Length (gun): 7.5in (191mm)
Barrel: 4.2in (107mm)
Weight: 33.0oz (0.9kg)
Caliber: 9mm
Rifling: 6 grooves, r/hand
Capacity: 10-round box magazine
Muz vel: ca 1,165ft/sec (355m/sec)

The P94 models are sized between the P89/P90 and the compact P93. Like all other models in the P-series, the blued models in the range P94 are made from chrome-molybdenum steel, whilst the stainless steel versions are made of aircraft-quality hard-coated A356T6 aluminum alloy and Ruger's proprietary "Terhune-Anticorro" stainless steel. The grips are made of 6123 Xenoy resin, which is claimed to be virtually indestructible. The Model 94 is made in Manual Safety, Decocking-only and Double-Action-Only versions; the Manual model is made in both blued steel and stainless steel finishes, the others in stainless steel only. A second version is available, the P944, which is chambered for the 0.40 Auto round and is available in the same models as the P94. The picture shows the P94, the 9mm weapon with manual safety and stainless steel finish.

RUGER 9MM P95/0.45IN P97 PISTOLS — USA

Length (gun): 7.25in (184mm)
Barrel: 3.9in (99mm)
Weight: 27.0oz (0.8kg)
Caliber: 9mm
Rifling: 6 grooves, r/hand
Capacity: 10-round box magazine
Muz vel: ca 1,165ft/sec (355m/sec)

The latest in the Ruger P-series are the P95, chambered for the NATO standard 9 x 19mm Parabellum round (including those with +P loads), and the parallel weapon, the P97, chambered for the 0.45in ACP round. The two weapons are dimensionally identical, the only major difference, apart from the caliber, being that the magazine of the P95 holds 10 rounds while that of the P97 holds seven. They are, however, somewhat smaller than previous models in the P-range, and weigh 27.0oz (0.77kg) compared to 32.0oz (0.91kg) for the P89 and 31.0oz (0.88kg) for the P93. One of the main reasons for this reduction in weight is the use of a new compounded polymer for the frames, which incorporates a long-strand fiberglass filler. The mechanism uses the same tilting barrel system, but with a new type of lock which decelerates the fast-moving barrel and brings it to a halt without damage to the frame. The P95 (see specifications) is available in both blued and stainless steel finish and with either Decock only (D) or Double-Action Only (DAO) safety features. The P97 is currently available only in stainless steel finish, but is also available in both Decock and Double-Action Only. The pictures show (above left) the KP95DAO (9mm version, Direct-Action-Only, stainless steel finish), and (above right) the KP97D (0.45in ACP version, Decock-only, stainless steel finish).

RUGER VAQUERO REVOLVER — USA

Length (gun): 13.2in (335mm)
Barrel: 7.5in (191mm)
Weight: 41.0oz (1.1kg)
Caliber: 0.44-40in
Rifling: n.k.
Capacity: six
Muz vel: n.k.

Ruger's Vaquero is a fixed-sight version of the New Model Blackhawk (qv) and is outwardly patterned after the traditional pistols of the American West of the mid-1800s. Internally, however, it incorporates the Ruger "New Model" single-action mechanism, and is made of modern materials and produced to modern degrees of accuracy and tolerance, resulting in a weapon that is much more reliable and accurate than its predecessors. No fewer than 20 variations are marketed, including four in 0.357in Magnum, six in 0.44-40in (see specifications), four in 0.44in Magnum, and six in 0.45in Long Colt. These include the usual selections of barrel length and finishes. The Bisley-Vaquero combines the looks of the Vaquero with the Bisley-style hammer, grip frame and trigger. The pictures show (top) the 0.44-40in Vaquero with 7.5in (191mm) barrel, in high-gloss stainless steel finish; and (above) 0.44 Magnum Bisley-Vaquero with 5.5in (140mm) barrel in blued finish.

RUGER 0.22IN MARK II GOVERNMENT TARGET PISTOL — USA

Length (gun): 11.1in (282mm)
Barrel: 6.9in (175mm)
Weight: 46.0oz (1.3kg)
Caliber: 0.22in (5.56mm)
Rifling: n.k.
Capacity: 10-round box magazine
Muz vel: n.k.

The Ruger 0.22in Long Rifle target pistol was introduced in 1949 and has been developed from that original model, through the "Mark I" to the current "Mark II" design, which comprises 18 different pistols in five ranges: Standard, Target, Bull, Government (see specifications), and Competition. These ranges come in either blued or stainless steel finish, and in a variety of barrel lengths: Standard, 4.75in (121mm) or 6.0in (152mm); Target, 6.9in (175mm); Bull, 4.0in (102mm), 5.5in (140mm), 10.0in (254mm); Government and Competition, 6.9in (175mm) only. The safety positively locks to the rear, but the bolt can still be manually operated with the safety in the "on" position for added security while loading and unloading. There is a bolt stop so that the pistol locks automatically when the last cartridge has been fired (provided that the 10-round magazine is in the weapon) and the bolt stop can also be manually activated by a thumb piece on the left of the weapon to aid in loading, cleaning, and inspection. The "Target" series has added refinements for competitive target shooting, including a heavier, less-tapered barrel and competition sights, with a rear sight that is click adjustable for windage and elevation, while the front sight is a Partridge type blade (0.125in wide), undercut to prevent glare. The Government Target model is standard issue to US armed forces, and all weapons are individually targeted before leaving the factory using a patented laser sighting device and this factory-test target is enclosed with each pistol before delivery to the Government depot. Pictures show (top) Standard Model with 4.75in (121mm) barrel; (center) Government Target Model with 6.9in (175mm) barrel; and (above) Competition Model.

Ruger 0.22in New Model Super Single Six Revolver — USA

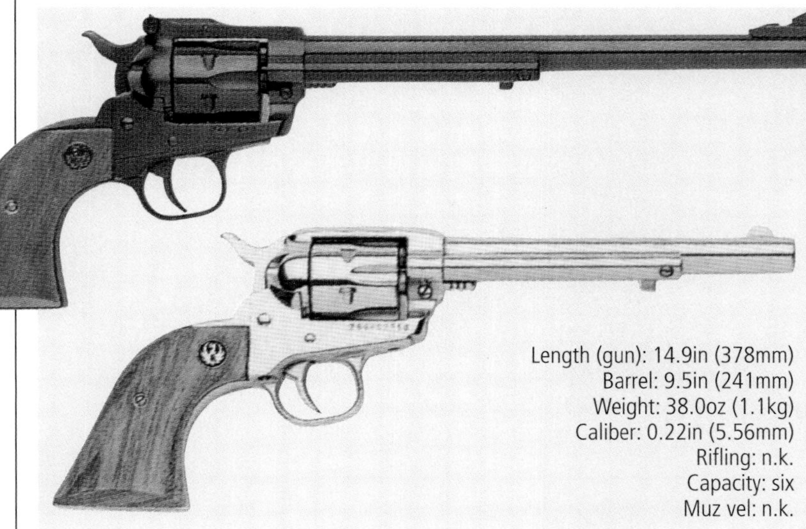

Length (gun): 14.9in (378mm)
Barrel: 9.5in (241mm)
Weight: 38.0oz (1.1kg)
Caliber: 0.22in (5.56mm)
Rifling: n.k.
Capacity: six
Muz vel: n.k.

The Ruger New Model Single-Six is a modern 0.22in caliber, single-action revolver, intended for use either for targets or on the trail. There are two types: the New Model Single-Six with fixed sights and the New Model Super Single-Six (see specifications) with ramp foresight and click adjustable rearsight. As sold, the gun has a cylinder for 0.22in Long Rifle, but an extra cylinder is also provided in Winchester Magnum Rimfire (WMR), which can be instantly interchanged without the need for tools. Pictures show (above left) New Model Super Six with 9.5in (241mm) barrel in blued finish; and (above) New Model Single-Six with 6.5in (165mm) barrel in stainless steel finish.

Savage Model 1907 Pistol — USA

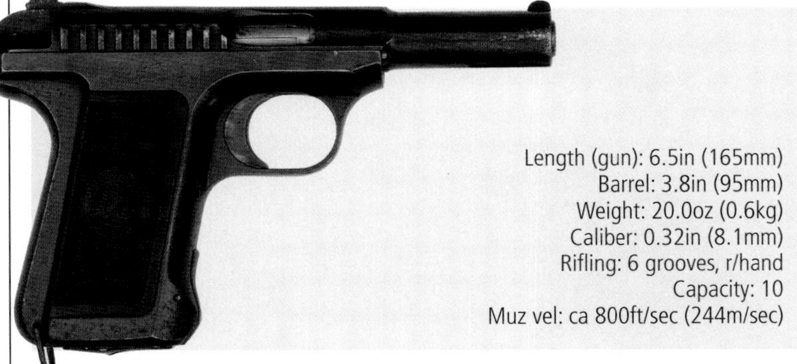

Length (gun): 6.5in (165mm)
Barrel: 3.8in (95mm)
Weight: 20.0oz (0.6kg)
Caliber: 0.32in (8.1mm)
Rifling: 6 grooves, r/hand
Capacity: 10
Muz vel: ca 800ft/sec (244m/sec)

The Savage Arms Company first produced a self-loading pistol (illustrated here) in 1907, although it is not possible to establish the identity of the weapon's inventor. The Savage Model 1907 pistol is of unusual and interesting design, and it was the subject of a great deal of controversy when it first appeared. The theory of its mechanism was as follows. The slide covered the entire top of the weapon, including the barrel proper. The pistol was loaded in the orthodox way and the slide was pulled back and released to feed the first round into the chamber. A lug on top of the barrel fitted into a curved slot on the top of the slide: when the cartridge was fired, the rearward movement of the barrel and slide was briefly checked by the cam, but the barrel overcame this by twisting slightly until the lug reached a straight stretch of groove, when the slide was again free to move to the rear. The theory of this arrangement was that the counter-rotation of the bullet in the rifling was sufficient to prevent the barrel from twisting until the bullet had actually left it; at which juncture, of course, the pressure dropped instantly. However, this theory has been disputed. The pistol had a safety catch on the left side, just below the serrated cocking piece (visible near the rear end of the slide). This weapon reached the finals of the 1907 competition for the US Army but lost to the Colt M1911.

Smith & Wesson Tip-Up Revolver — USA

When the Civil War ended in 1865 there was something of a recession in the United States. In particular, the sales of revolvers fell. Smith & Wesson therefore decided to discontinue their second issue and introduce a third issue of more attractive appearance. There was always a demand for pocket pistols in the United States, particularly, perhaps, in the more settled Eastern States where, although fewer people carried a revolver openly, many – both men and women – liked to have one handy in pocket or handbag. The new model did not differ very much mechanically from its predecessor: it had the same tip-up

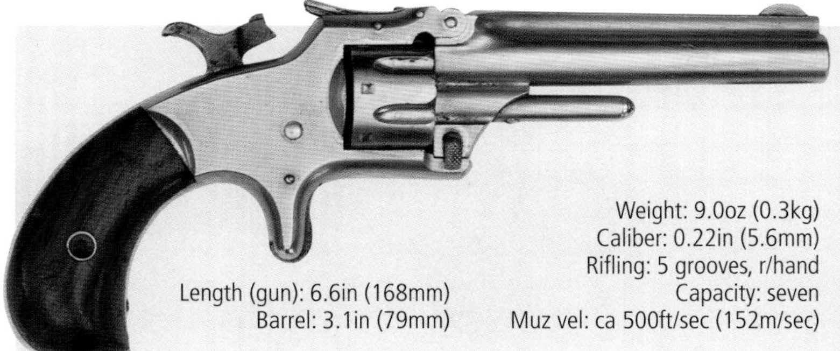

Length (gun): 6.6in (168mm)
Barrel: 3.1in (79mm)
Weight: 9.0oz (0.3kg)
Caliber: 0.22in (5.6mm)
Rifling: 5 grooves, r/hand
Capacity: seven
Muz vel: ca 500ft/sec (152m/sec)

barrel, removable cylinder and single-action lock. However, instead of having a brass frame, like the earlier model, it was made entirely of iron and the whole weapon was plated. The traditional flat-edged butt gave way to the type known as "bird-beak," with walnut side-plates held in place by a screw. The general effect was more eye-catching than previously, and after a slow start in 1868 production rose to 20,000 annually.

Smith & Wesson Tip-Up Pocket Revolver — USA

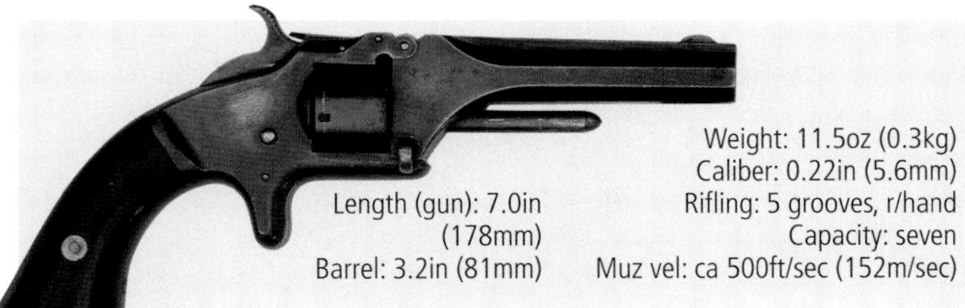

Length (gun): 7.0in (178mm)
Barrel: 3.2in (81mm)
Weight: 11.5oz (0.3kg)
Caliber: 0.22in (5.6mm)
Rifling: 5 grooves, r/hand
Capacity: seven
Muz vel: ca 500ft/sec (152m/sec)

By the mid-1850s, Smith & Wesson had designed a pocket revolver to fire rimfire cartridges and were only awaiting the expiry of Colt's patent for a revolving cylinder to put it on to the market. They also acquired Rollin White's American patent for a bored-through cylinder and agreed to pay him 25 cents thereafter for every weapon of that type made by them. The first, or Model No 1, appeared in 1857. Because the shape of its brass frame made it difficult to machine economically, a second series, of which the weapon illustrated is a specimen, was produced in 1860. The octagonal barrel is hinged at the top of the frame, just above the front of the cylinder, and opened upwards when the small catch just below the front of the cylinder was pushed up. The cylinder stop consisted of a flat spring on top of the frame. In order to load, or reload, the cylinder was removed and the empty, copper, rimfire cases were pushed out by means of the pin below the barrel. The lock is of single-action pattern and the weapon has a sheathed trigger. The frame is of brass or bronze and was originally silver-plated, although little of this refinement now remains.

Smith & Wesson 0.32in No 2 (Army) Revolver — USA

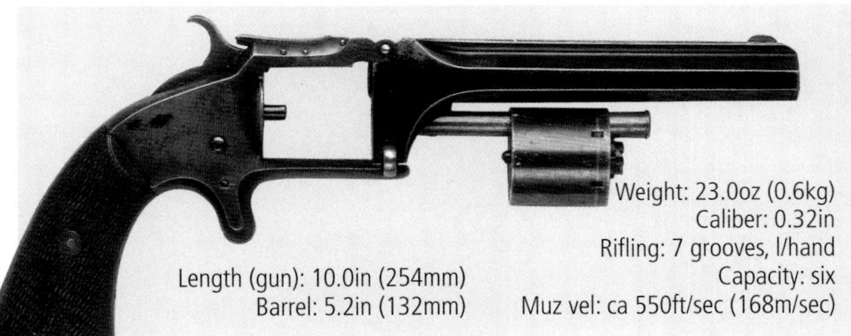

Length (gun): 10.0in (254mm)
Barrel: 5.2in (132mm)
Weight: 23.0oz (0.6kg)
Caliber: 0.32in
Rifling: 7 grooves, l/hand
Capacity: six
Muz vel: ca 550ft/sec (168m/sec)

This weapon represents a significant step on the road towards an effective revolver, from the first exponent of such a weapon: Smith & Wesson. The company had acquired the Rollin White patent for revolvers with bored-through cylinders which would accommodate self-contained metallic cartridges. In 1857 the company produced a cartridge meeting this requirement, which was made of copper with the percussion powder arranged around the internal circumference of the rim, which were thus known as "rim-fire" cartridges. Smith & Wesson's first designs using this principle were all on the lines of the No 2 revolver seen here, which appeared in 1861. There was a hinge at the top of the front plate of the frame and a catch at the foot, so that when the catch was released the octagonal barrel could be lifted up, giving rise to the generic name: "tip-up revolver." Once the barrel was out of the way the cylinder was removed from the weapon, reversed in the shooter's hand, and then each chamber was pressed in turn against the built-in spike; once all six empty cases had been ejected, the shooter reloaded, returned the cylinder to the gun, closed the barrel, and was then ready to fire again. This weapon, which was very popular with officers during the Civil War, came in three barrel lengths: 6.0in (152mm), 5.0in (127mm), and 4.0in (102mm). The picture shows the spike being used to eject a spent cartridge case.

SMITH & WESSON NEW MODEL NO 3 REVOLVER USA

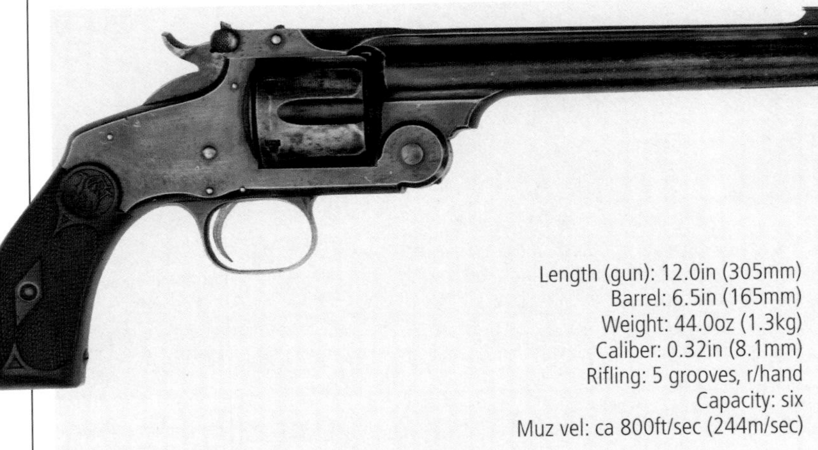

Length (gun): 12.0in (305mm)
Barrel: 6.5in (165mm)
Weight: 44.0oz (1.3kg)
Caliber: 0.32in (8.1mm)
Rifling: 5 grooves, r/hand
Capacity: six
Muz vel: ca 800ft/sec (244m/sec)

Smith & Wesson's No 3 First Model American, a bottom-hinged, break-open revolver with a system of simultaneous extraction, attracted the attention of Russia, which was then in the process of re-equipping its Army with modern weapons. By 1871 a contract had been signed for 20,000 revolvers of a type known as Model No 3, Russian 1st Model. There then appeared a second model of similar general type, but with some changes to the frame and with the addition of a finger spur below the trigger-guard. This was followed by a third model, until the order was completed in 1878. Generally similar arms were made in smaller numbers for export to various other countries during this period. The firm then turned to the home market with its New Model No 3, produced from 1878 to 1912, and later with the New Model 3 Frontier. This was intended as a rival to the Colt, but it never became popular and was replaced in its turn by a double-action version. The single-action arm illustrated here first appeared in 1887. It is of broadly similar type to its predecessors, except that the round foresight was replaced by a square-cut bead-type blade pinned into a groove on the top rib. When the milled catch in front of the hammer was pushed upward, the barrel and cylinder could be pushed sharply downward; this caused the star-shaped ejector at the rear of the cylinder to be forced outward, throwing the cartridges or cases clear of the cylinder, a system which allowed for very fast reloading. This specimen, numbered "415," is in 0.32in (8.1mm) caliber; a 0.38in (9.6mm) caliber arm came into production soon afterwards.

SMITH & WESSON NEW MODEL NO 3 REVOLVER USA

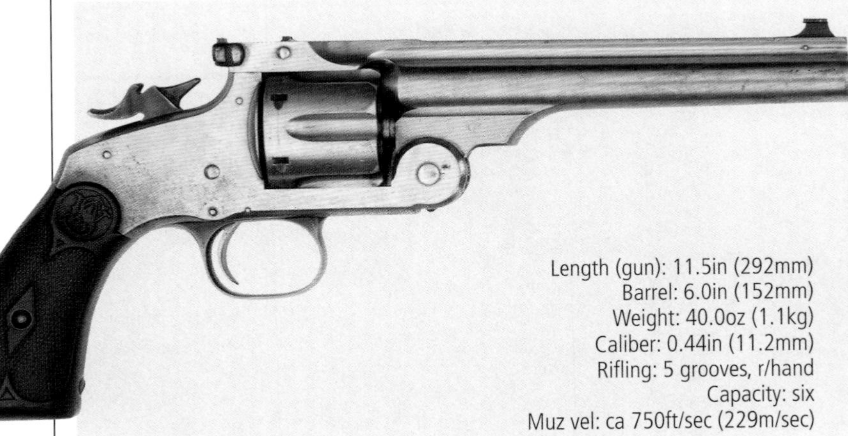

Length (gun): 11.5in (292mm)
Barrel: 6.0in (152mm)
Weight: 40.0oz (1.1kg)
Caliber: 0.44in (11.2mm)
Rifling: 5 grooves, r/hand
Capacity: six
Muz vel: ca 750ft/sec (229m/sec)

The arm illustrated here is a New Model No 3 revolver, chambered to take the 0.44in (11.2mm) Russian cartridge. It has a round, tapered barrel with a full top rib, and it is fitted with a target sight instead of the round blade usually found on service models. The revolver was opened by pushing up the milled catch visible in front of the hammer and pushing down the barrel. This automatically forced out the star-shaped ejector, which was mounted on a hexagonal rod and was activated by means of a rack and gear. The six-chambered cylinder is 1.44in (37mm) long: a few later models had cylinders with a length of 1.56in (40mm). The locking device, in itself quite adequate, is further reinforced by the provision of a notch above the hammer nose which engaged over a flange on the catch when the hammer was fully down. The lock is of single-action type with a rebounding hammer which, like the trigger and guard, is case-hardened. Although this was a very fine arm and popular with expert target shots, it never really caught on in the United States. American users preferred a more powerful cartridge than was ever considered to be a safe and practical proposition in a break-open arm. Thus, they favored solid-frame revolvers as a general rule, the only exception being contributed by small, pocket-type arms firing low-powered cartridges.

SMITH & WESSON REVOLVING RIFLE USA

Length (gun): 35.0in (889mm)
Barrel: 18.0in (457mm)
Weight: 80.0oz (2.3kg)
Caliber: 0.32in (8.1mm)
Rifling: 6 grooves, r/hand
Capacity: six
Muz vel: ca 820ft/sec (250m/sec)

This rare weapon first appeared in 1879. It is closely modeled on the No 3 revolver, but with a two-piece barrel which is screwed together about 2in (51mm) in front of the breech, although the joint is barely visible. The rifle was made in three barrel lengths: 16in (406mm), 18in (457mm), 20in (508mm). The one illustrated here is of the middle size. It has a blued foresight on the top rib and an L-shaped backsight to give two elevations. The aperture backsight, an optional extra, may be seen on the clamp which holds the rifle butt on to the pistol. The grips and fore end are of hard, mottled rubber; the grips are noticeably darker, partly because of the back escape of gases. The rifle butt, which is clamped to the revolver by means of the milled screw below the backsight pillar, is of fine-quality Circassian walnut and has a rubber butt-plate which, like those on the revolver itself, bears the Smith & Wesson monogram. This arm is an example of a variety of similar types which seek to combine the revolver and the rifle. Like most combination weapons, it was only moderately successful: it was somewhat muzzle-heavy for use as a revolver and was less accurate than a purpose-built carbine, in which loss of power between the cylinder and the barrel was avoided. It would, however, have been quite a handy arm, easy to carry below the seat of a wagon and with the advantage of being relatively easily concealed. This specimen was captured by British troops in Ireland in 1916 – the year of the Easter Rising – and would presumably have been useful in guerrilla warfare.

SMITH & WESSON MODEL 0.38IN CALIBER SAFETY REVOLVER (FIRST MODEL) USA

Length (gun): 8.0in (203mm)
Barrel: 3.3in (83mm)
Weight: 18.0oz (0.5kg)
Caliber: 0.38in (9.6mm)
Rifling: 5 grooves, r/hand
Capacity: 5
Muz vel: 745ft/sec (227m/sec)

There is a tendency to picture late 19th Century American revolvers being carried Western-style, openly in holsters on the belt, but a great many more firearms were carried covertly by townspeople and city dwellers. These were carried strictly for self-defense in what was, even at that late stage, still a fairly lawless environment and the individuals concerned had no wish to advertise the fact that they were carrying weapons. This led to a demand for a small, compact pocket revolver in which reliability and reasonable stopping power were more important than long-range accuracy. Weapons of this type were turned out by a wide variety of gunmakers and in 1887 Smith & Wesson introduced the hammerless weapon seen here, which quickly became very popular, since it had no hammer to catch in the lining of the pocket. It was also safe for the wearer, since the grip safety on the back of the butt had to be pressed before the weapon would fire. Indeed, in the last resort it could be fired through a pocket without any risk of jamming. The original weapon was in 0.38in caliber and tit was succeeded in 1902 by the second model (qv).

Smith & Wesson Military and Police First Model (cut-down) Revolver — USA

Length (gun): 8.0in (203mm)
Barrel: 3.3in (83mm)
Weight: 28.0oz (0.8kg)
Caliber: 0.38in (9.6mm)
Rifling: 7 grooves, r/hand
Capacity: six
Muz vel: ca 600ft/sec (183m/sec)

The demand in the United States was for pistols with long-range, power, and accuracy, which necessitated a very heavy charge of propellant powder in the cartridge, and it was generally believed that hinged-frame revolvers were unlikely to stand up to the strain. Although it is highly improbable that hinged-frame revolvers would have become truly dangerous in such circumstances, there was the risk that they might become loose, which would have had an adverse effect on accuracy. Smith & Wesson therefore turned to the manufacture of solid-frame revolvers of high quality at about the end of the 19th Century. This particular revolver is one of those made for the British Government during World War II, at a time when the hard-pressed British were desperately short of arms and materiel of all kinds. This arm was known variously as the British Service, the Model No 2, or the 0.38/200; the latter figure refers to the bullet weight (200 grains, 13 grams) which, by British calculations, provided much the same stopping-power as that fired from the earlier 0.455in (11.5mm) caliber Webley service arms. The lead bullet of this type had to be abandoned just before World War II because it contravened the international conventions of warfare; it was replaced by a lighter, 178-grain (11.5 gram), jacketed bullet. The weapon is of orthodox solid-frame type; but it is of interest because at some stage of its career its barrel, originally 5.0in (127mm) long, has been cut down to 3.25in (83mm) and a ramp foresight added. The work has been quite well done and it is difficult to detect at a glance, but is clear on close examination.

Smith & Wesson Single-Shot Model 91 Pistol — USA

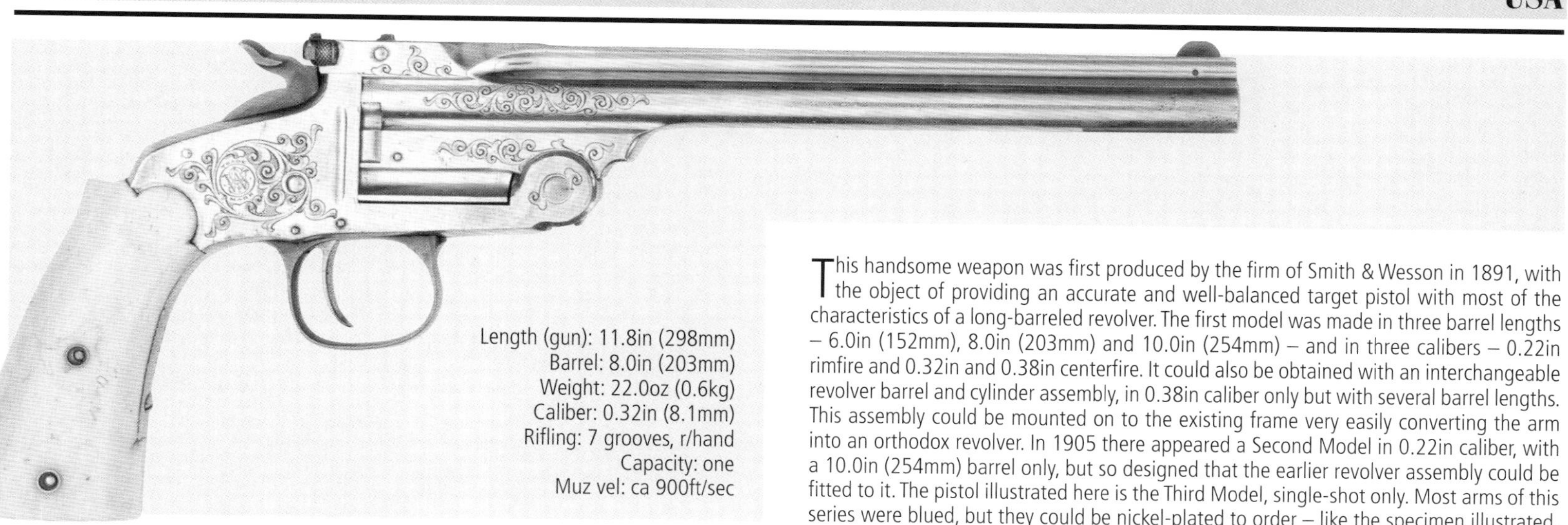

Length (gun): 11.8in (298mm)
Barrel: 8.0in (203mm)
Weight: 22.0oz (0.6kg)
Caliber: 0.32in (8.1mm)
Rifling: 7 grooves, r/hand
Capacity: one
Muz vel: ca 900ft/sec

This handsome weapon was first produced by the firm of Smith & Wesson in 1891, with the object of providing an accurate and well-balanced target pistol with most of the characteristics of a long-barreled revolver. The first model was made in three barrel lengths – 6.0in (152mm), 8.0in (203mm) and 10.0in (254mm) – and in three calibers – 0.22in rimfire and 0.32in and 0.38in centerfire. It could also be obtained with an interchangeable revolver barrel and cylinder assembly, in 0.38in caliber only but with several barrel lengths. This assembly could be mounted on to the existing frame very easily converting the arm into an orthodox revolver. In 1905 there appeared a Second Model in 0.22in caliber, with a 10.0in (254mm) barrel only, but so designed that the earlier revolver assembly could be fitted to it. The pistol illustrated here is the Third Model, single-shot only. Most arms of this series were blued, but they could be nickel-plated to order – like the specimen illustrated.

Smith & Wesson New Model Double-Action .38in Revolver — USA

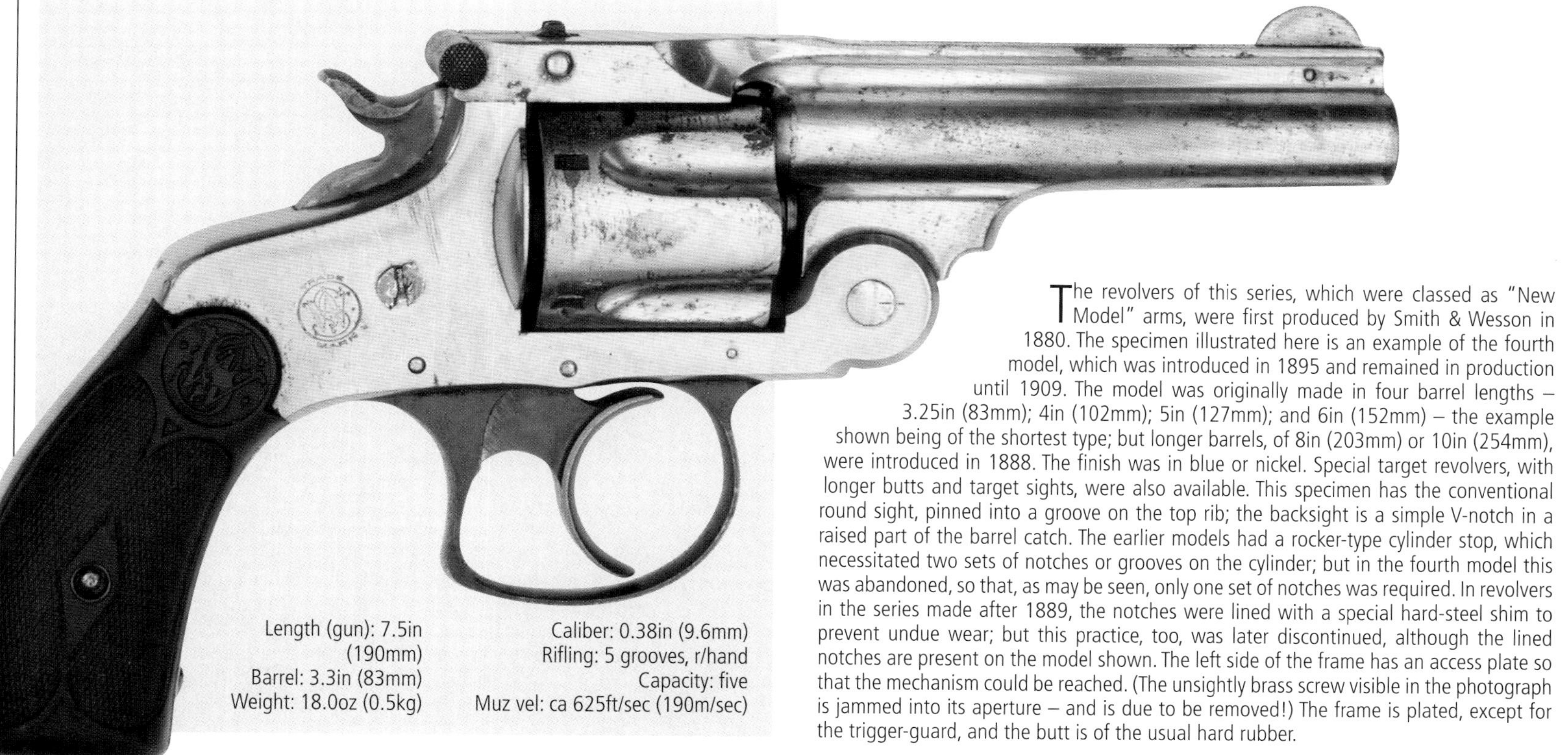

Length (gun): 7.5in (190mm)
Barrel: 3.3in (83mm)
Weight: 18.0oz (0.5kg)
Caliber: 0.38in (9.6mm)
Rifling: 5 grooves, r/hand
Capacity: five
Muz vel: ca 625ft/sec (190m/sec)

The revolvers of this series, which were classed as "New Model" arms, were first produced by Smith & Wesson in 1880. The specimen illustrated here is an example of the fourth model, which was introduced in 1895 and remained in production until 1909. The model was originally made in four barrel lengths – 3.25in (83mm); 4in (102mm); 5in (127mm); and 6in (152mm) – the example shown being of the shortest type; but longer barrels, of 8in (203mm) or 10in (254mm), were introduced in 1888. The finish was in blue or nickel. Special target revolvers, with longer butts and target sights, were also available. This specimen has the conventional round sight, pinned into a groove on the top rib; the backsight is a simple V-notch in a raised part of the barrel catch. The earlier models had a rocker-type cylinder stop, which necessitated two sets of notches or grooves on the cylinder; but in the fourth model this was abandoned, so that, as may be seen, only one set of notches was required. In revolvers in the series made after 1889, the notches were lined with a special hard-steel shim to prevent undue wear; but this practice, too, was later discontinued, although the lined notches are present on the model shown. The left side of the frame has an access plate so that the mechanism could be reached. (The unsightly brass screw visible in the photograph is jammed into its aperture – and is due to be removed!) The frame is plated, except for the trigger-guard, and the butt is of the usual hard rubber.

SMITH & WESSON NEW CENTURY REVOLVER — USA

Length (gun): 11.8in (298mm)
Barrel: 6.5in (165mm)
Weight: 38.0oz (1.08kg)
Caliber: 0.455in (11.5mm)
Rifling: 6 grooves, r/hand
Capacity: six
Muz vel: ca 650ft/sec (198m/sec)

Before the end of the 19th Century, Smith & Wesson bowed to public taste and produced a solid-frame revolver. The principle was simple and reliable: pushing forward a milled catch on the left of the frame allowed the cylinder to be swung out to the left on a separate yoke. Then, the extractor was manually operated by means of the pin, a method which was only marginally slower than a hinged-frame type. The version seen here first appeared in 1908 and was variously known as the "0.44 Hand Ejector First Model," the "New Century," the "Gold Seal," or the "Triple Lock." The latter name came from the fact that the cylinder locked not only at the rear, but also by means of one bolt into the front end of the rod and a second which emerged from the casing below it. The lock is of rebounding, double-action type and, as with all Smith & Wesson arms, worked very smoothly. The standard caliber for production arms was 0.44in (11.2mm), and it was chambered for the special cartridge, but arms in various other calibers were also made. A small number of original 0.44in (11.2mm) caliber revolvers were converted to fire the British 0.455in (11.5mm) Eley cartridge, mostly at the outbreak of World War I, but later a special version was made and sold to the British Army in some quantity. The specimen shown is one of the latter arms: it bears the serial number "1068" and also has what is apparently a British number on the bottom of the butt-strap, together with London proof marks. It is in every respect a beautiful weapon.

SMITH & WESSON MODEL 0.38IN CALIBER SAFETY REVOLVER (SECOND AND THIRD MODELS) — USA

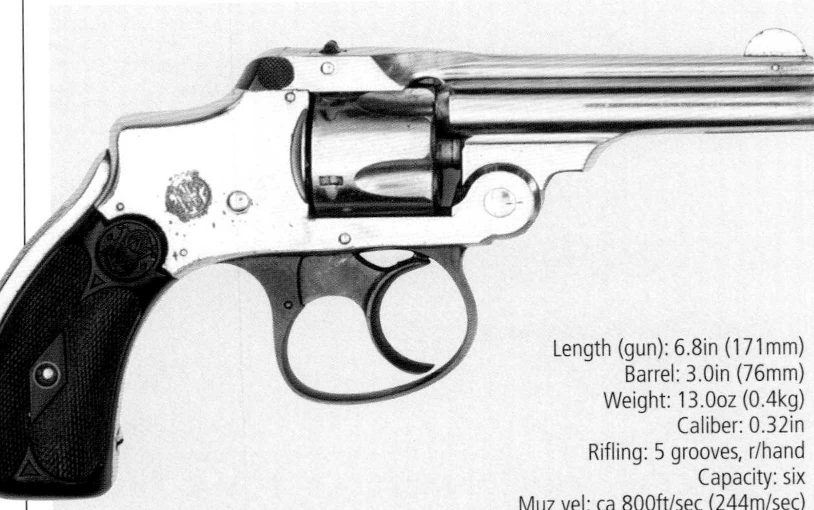

Length (gun): 6.8in (171mm)
Barrel: 3.0in (76mm)
Weight: 13.0oz (0.4kg)
Caliber: 0.32in
Rifling: 5 grooves, r/hand
Capacity: six
Muz vel: ca 800ft/sec (244m/sec)

The first model of the Smith & Wesson 0.38in caliber Safety Revolver was succeeded in 1902 by the second model, with several relatively minor variations. It was, in its turn, replaced by the third model. This third model was produced in three barrel lengths: 2.0in (51mm); 3.0in (76mm); and 3.5in (89mm). The barrel was round with a top rib and a round, blade foresight which in some cases was forged integrally with the barrel and in others was inserted into a slot and pinned. The weapon was opened by pushing up a T-shaped catch with a knurled knob on each side. This allowed the barrel to be forced down and brought the automatic ejector into play. As on the earlier model there was a grip safety, which, when the butt was properly gripped, was forced in, thus allowing the lock mechanism to function correctly, making it a very safe weapon. The stocks were of hard, black rubber and were rounded to ensure that there was no risk of snagging on the shooter's pockets. The picture shows an example of the third model whose barrel, frame and grip safety have been nickel-plated, but not the trigger, its guard and the catch. There is an inspection plate on the left side of the weapon.

SMITH & WESSON REVOLVER, M1917 — USA

Length (gun): 9.6in (244mm)
Barrel: 5.5in (140mm)
Weight: 34.0oz (1.0kg)
Caliber: 0.45in (11.4mm)
Rifling: 6 grooves, l/hand
Capacity: six
Muz vel: ca 700ft/sec (213m/sec)

The heaviest-caliber revolver normally made by Smith & Wesson was 0.44in (11.2mm), which the company considered gave better results than the 0.45in (11.4mm). It is true that the firm made various heavy-caliber arms to special order, but it was not until 1908 or 1909 that a few were put into production. These were of No 3 hinged-frame type and usually called Schofield revolvers. Various arms in 0.455in (11.5mm) caliber were made by special arrangement from 1914 onward for the British Army. When the United States entered World War I in 1917, she was not well equipped; all available weapons of suitable type had to be pressed into service. It was, however, considered essential to have uniformity of cartridge and, as the standard service pistol was then the Model 1911 Colt self-loader, a considerable number of revolvers were manufactured to take the standard 0.45in (11.4mm) ACP rimless round. The revolver illustrated here is a plain, robust arm of handsome appearance. It has the usual solid frame, with a six-chambered cylinder mounted on a separate yoke, or crane, so that it could be swung out to the left after the milled catch below the hammer had been pushed forward. When the cylinder was closed, the end of the extractor pin engaged with a spring stud in a lump below the barrel. In order to take a rimless round, the chamber contained a shoulder against which the forward edge of the case rested; this prevented the cartridge from being forced too far in. However, the star extractor would not work with rimless rounds, so the empty cases had to be pushed out with a pencil or some similar instrument. An improvement on this system was to have the cartridges in flat, half-moon clips of three, on which the extractor could grip; these were extensively used.

Smith & Wesson British Service Revolver — USA

Length (gun): 10.0in (254mm)
Barrel: 5.0in (127mm)
Weight: 29.0oz (0.8kg)
Caliber: 0.38in (9.6mm)
Rifling: 5 grooves, r/hand
Capacity: six
Muz vel: ca 650ft/sec (198m/sec)

The first weapon by Smith & Wesson made in 0.38in (9.6mm) caliber was the Military and Police First Model, which appeared in 1899 and was followed by a series with the same general title but differentiated by model number. In 1940, Smith & Wesson began production, for the British Army, of a revolver based closely on the Military and Police models the company had been making for so long. Until 1928, the official British service revolver was the Webley and Scott in 0.455in (11.5mm) caliber, but in that year a change was made to a 0.38in (9.6mm) model made at Enfield. Since the 0.38in (9.6mm) Smith & Wesson would take the new British cartridge, no difficulties were experienced in respect of ammunition. The Smith & Wesson British Service revolver, sometimes known as the "0.38/200" (from its 200 grain, 13 gram, bullet) or the Pistol No 2, was of orthodox solid-frame construction. The arm illustrated here has a round barrel with an integral half-round foresight: the backsight consists of a notch and groove on the top strap. The milled cylinder catch was pushed forward to allow the six-chambered cylinder to be swung out on its yoke. There is a projection below the barrel, with a spring-loaded stud which engaged with the end of the ejector pin when the revolver was closed. The lock is of double-action, rebounding type, and the hammer has a separate nose held by a pin (the aperture for which is visible in the photograph). The butt-plates are of checkered walnut, bearing the company's monogram in a small, silvered medallion.

Smith & Wesson Victory Model Revolver — USA

Length (gun): 8.5in (215mm)
Barrel: 4.0in (102mm)
Weight: 30.0oz (0.9kg)
Caliber: 0.38in
Rifling: 5 grooves, r/hand
Capacity: six
Muz vel: 745ft/sec (227m/sec)

This was another World War II period version of a well-established handgun, which, like the 0.38-200 for Britain, was based on the well-established Military & Police pistol. Anything fancy was removed and the result was a utilitarian weapon which was manufactured in large numbers for the US Government service, with 4.0in (101mm) versions mainly for the armed forces and 2.0in (51mm) versions mainly for civilian organizations, such as the Justice Department.

Smith & Wesson 9mm Model 39 Pistol — USA

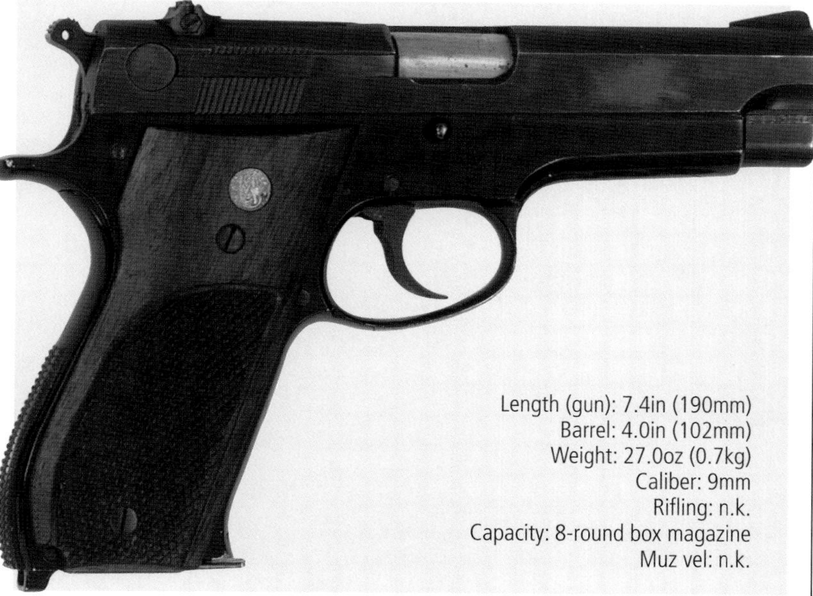

Length (gun): 7.4in (190mm)
Barrel: 4.0in (102mm)
Weight: 27.0oz (0.7kg)
Caliber: 9mm
Rifling: n.k.
Capacity: 8-round box magazine
Muz vel: n.k.

When NATO decided to standardize on the 9mm Parabellum round in 1954, Smith & Wesson quickly produced their Model 39 for possible military adoption but, although it failed in this aim, it was adopted by the Illinois State Police, which enhanced its prospects and it quickly achieved a good degree of popularity. The Model 39 has been succeeded by models with improved sights, extractors, and slide bushings, as well as large capacity magazines (Model 59) and stainless steel construction (Models 639 and 659). In later years, Smith & Wesson was the only serious American contender for the US Services pistol contract which resulted in the adoption of the Beretta 92SB (qv). The Model 39 worked on double-action for the first shot, followed by single-action for all subsequent shots. There was a square ramp foresight, and a square notch backsight, which was click adjustable for windage only.

SMITH & WESSON MODEL 29 REVOLVER — USA

Length (gun): 14.0in (356mm)
Barrel: 8.3in (210mm)
Weight: 54.0oz (1.5kg)
Caliber: 0.44in
Rifling: n.k.
Capacity: six
Muz vel: n.k.

The original 0.44in Magnum was the Smith & Wesson Model 29, which was immortalized by Clint Eastwood in the "Dirty Harry" films; it was also the revolver which made handgun hunting a recognized sport. The Model 29 was considered to be a large gun when it appeared, although it has been dwarfed by later models such as the Ruger Super Redhawk (qv). Such large revolvers are rugged and their ability to withstand an unlimited diet of top-end loads and their weight makes them reasonably comfortable to shoot, although there seems little to chose between them and a rifle. The picture shows a Model 29 with an 8.3in (210mm) barrel and wooden stock. Another version has a 4.0in (102mm) barrel and a finger-contoured synthetic stock. The Model 29 is a selective double-action weapon with an outside hammer, using hand ejection, with a crane-mounted cylinder which swings leftwards out of frame for loading and unloading. There is a square ramp foresight with a square notch backsight which is click adjustable for elevation and windage. The French Gendarmerie's special operations force – GIGN – showed considerable interest in this weapon.

SMITH & WESSON MODEL 41 PISTOL — USA

Length (gun): 9.0in (230mm)
Barrel: 5.5in (140mm)
Weight: 44.5oz (1.2kg)
Caliber: 0.22in
Rifling: n.k.
Capacity: 10-round box magazine
Muz vel: n.k.

The Model 41 was introduced in about 1957 for use in the US National Match Course competition, as well as the UIT Standard Pistol, Standard Handgun, and Ladies matches. The weapon set the fashion for rimfire target pistols with a grip angle duplicating that of the 0.45in pistol. The gun-making company High Standard soon followed suit with upright handles for their very popular and successful Supermatic Trophy and Citation models. The Model 41 has an undercut square post foresight, but its backsight attracted interest since it is mounted on a rib extending rearwards from the barrel. Henceforth slide-mounted rear sights tended to be viewed with suspicion, and High Standard soon started to mount theirs on a frame-mounted stirrup that encircled the rear of the slide, much the same system that was used by Hämmerli on their Model 208. The Model 41 is blowback-operated.

SMITH & WESSON 9MM MODEL 469 AUTOMATIC PISTOL — USA

Length (gun): 6.9in (175mm)
Barrel: 3.6in (91mm)
Weight: 27.0oz (0.7kg)
Caliber: 9mm
Rifling: n.k.
Capacity: 12-round box magazine
Muz vel: n.k.

The Model 469 appeared in the 1970s to meet requests for a smaller ("chopped") automatic pistol and was based on the 14-shot Model 459. The 469's barrel was 0.5in (12.7mm) shorter than that on the 459, while bobbing the tang and using a spurless hammer helped to achieve a reduction in overall length of about 0.8in (21mm), which was about all that could be done while still retaining a conventional recoil spring. The Model 469 used a selective double action, with no provision for "cocked-and-locked" carry and was recoil-operated with a locked breech and cam unlocking. A rib on top of the barrel locked into a mortice in the roof of the slide and the rear of the barrel then cammed downwards to unlock. There was a hammer trip safety on the left side, and the receiver was made of light alloy, all other parts of steel. The 469 accepted the 459's 14-round magazine, although its own standard magazine was a shorter one of 12-round capacity, with a Walther-type finger hook on the front. Sights were: square ramp foresight; square notch backsight adjustable for windage only.

Smith & Wesson Model 57 Revolver — USA

Length (gun): 11.4in (290mm)
Barrel: 6.0in (152mm)
Weight: 48.0oz (1.3kg)
Caliber: 0.41in
Rifling: n.k.
Capacity: six
Muz vel: n.k.

Smith & Wesson's Model 57 was fielded in 1964 to introduce the 0.41 Magnum round, and apart from the caliber was virtually identical to the Model 29 of 1957 (qv). Both weapons used Smith & Wesson's "N" frame, which dated from 1907 when it was used in the New Century revolver (qv) and it seems safe to say that by the late 1950s the design could be described as "well-proven." Sights comprised a square ramp foresight with red inset and a square notch backsight, click adjustable for both elevation and windage.

Smith & Wesson Models 586/686 Revolvers — USA

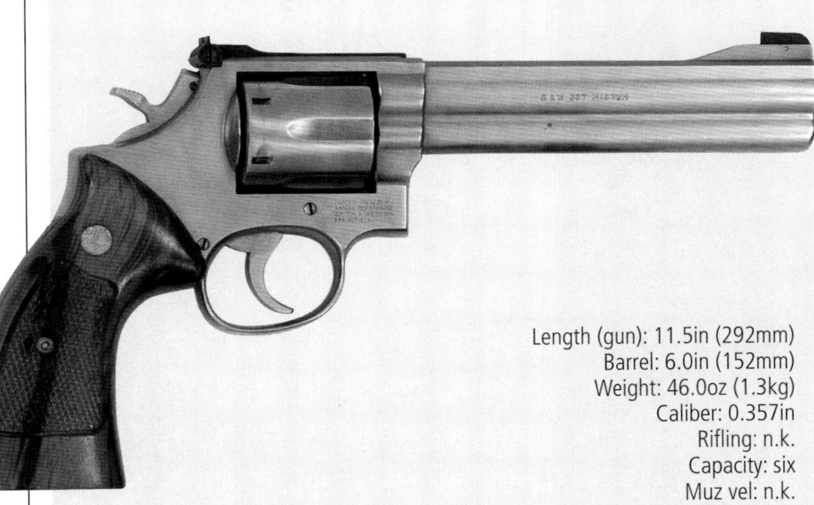

Length (gun): 11.5in (292mm)
Barrel: 6.0in (152mm)
Weight: 46.0oz (1.3kg)
Caliber: 0.357in
Rifling: n.k.
Capacity: six
Muz vel: n.k.

This revolver was produced in two guises, the blued steel Model 586 and the stainless steel Model 686, both of which were introduced in 1981, and were in direct competition with the Colt Python (qv) and Ruger GP-100 (qv). Smith & Wesson designed a new frame for these two weapons, designated the "L" frame, which was developed from the earlier "K" frame and slightly enlarged . The weapons use selective double action, with a crane-mounted cylinder that swings to the left for loading and unloading. There is a square ramp foresight with a red plastic insert, and a square notch backsight which is click adjustable for windage and elevation.

Smith & Wesson Model 64 Military & Police Revolver — USA

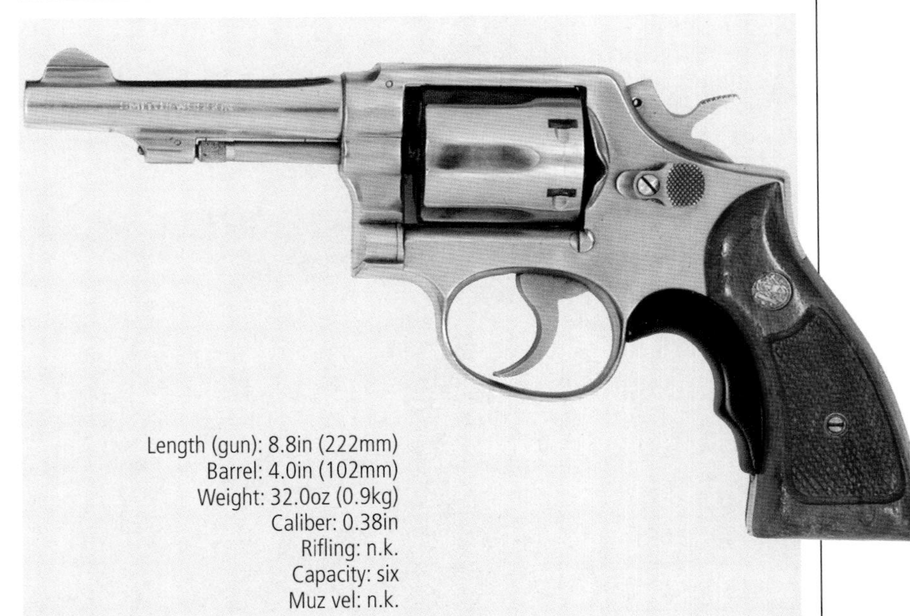

Length (gun): 8.8in (222mm)
Barrel: 4.0in (102mm)
Weight: 32.0oz (0.9kg)
Caliber: 0.38in
Rifling: n.k.
Capacity: six
Muz vel: n.k.

The Model 64 was introduced in 1981 and is the stainless steel version of the company's Model 10 Military & Police that dated from 1902 (see also Model 1). The weapon is made entirely of stainless steel, except for the hammer and trigger, which are chrome-plated. The stock grips were originally of polished walnut, but this was later replaced by a synthetic material with finger grips. There is a square ramp foresight milled into the barrel and a square notch backsight milled into the frame; neither is adjustable. The picture shows a Model 64 with a Tyler T-Grip adapter added between the stock and trigger guard, but is otherwise standard. This weapon is widely used by law enforcement agencies and other government departments.

Smith & Wesson Model 624 "Horton Special" Revolver USA

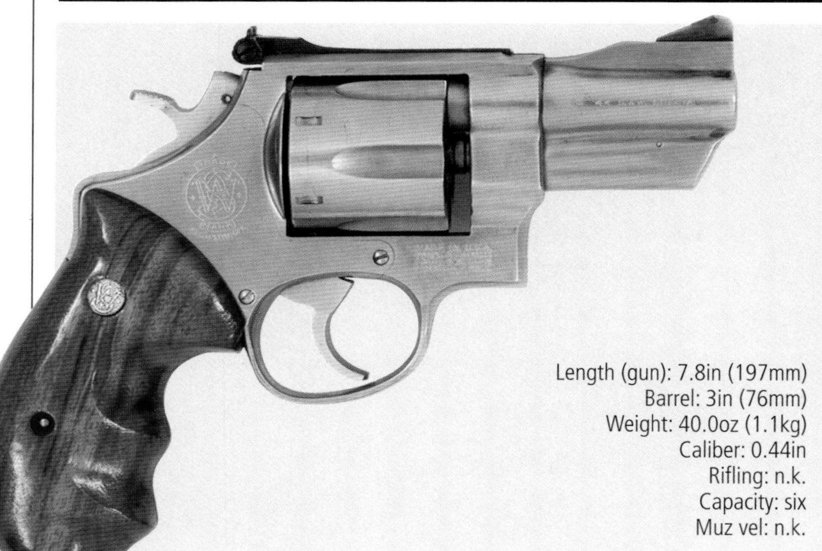

Length (gun): 7.8in (197mm)
Barrel: 3in (76mm)
Weight: 40.0oz (1.1kg)
Caliber: 0.44in
Rifling: n.k.
Capacity: six
Muz vel: n.k.

Smith & Wesson's Model 24, firing the 0.44in Special round, ended its first production run in 1958, but was re-introduced in 1983 and an initial run of 7,500 was sold-out within months. A special chrome-plated version was put into production in 1985 to meet an order from a Massachusetts gun distributor, Lew Horton, following which the weapon was known as the "Horton Special." This had a very short, 3.0in (76mm) barrel and a very smooth, chrome-plated finish, with a "birdshead" grip and deep finger grooves. The weapon has a solid frame, with hand ejection from a crane-mounted cylinder, which swings out to the left, following release by a thumb catch. Sights consisted of a square ramp foresight and a square notch backsight, click adjustable for elevation and windage. The "Horton Special" makes an interesting comparison with its contemporary, the Charter Arms Bulldog (qv), which was designed to fill the same niche in the market.

Smith & Wesson Model 14 K38 Masterpiece Revolver USA

Length (gun): 11.1in (280mm)
Barrel: 6.0in (152mm)
Weight: 36.0oz (1.1kg)
Caliber: 0.38in
Rifling: n.k.
Capacity: six
Muz vel: n.k.

The Smith & Wesson K38 was one of the most successful and popular target revolvers ever made. Part of the reason for its popularity was that it appeared just as revolver shooting was fading from the scene in National Match Course events, only to be replaced, rather by chance, by the growth of nationwide police revolver shooting competitions. Its only serious competitor was the Colt Python (qv). The K38 fired the 0.38in Special round and most models used selective double-action, although single-action versions were also available. The crane-mounted cylinder was released by a thumb-catch and then swung to the left for loading and unloading. The weapon came with two barrel sizes: 6.0in (152mm) and 8.4in (213mm). It was fitted with a square post foresight and a square notch backsight, click adjustable for elevation and windage. Production of the K38 ceased in 1982. The lower photo shows the 14-4 K38 model.

Smith & Wesson 0.45in Model 4500 Series Pistol USA

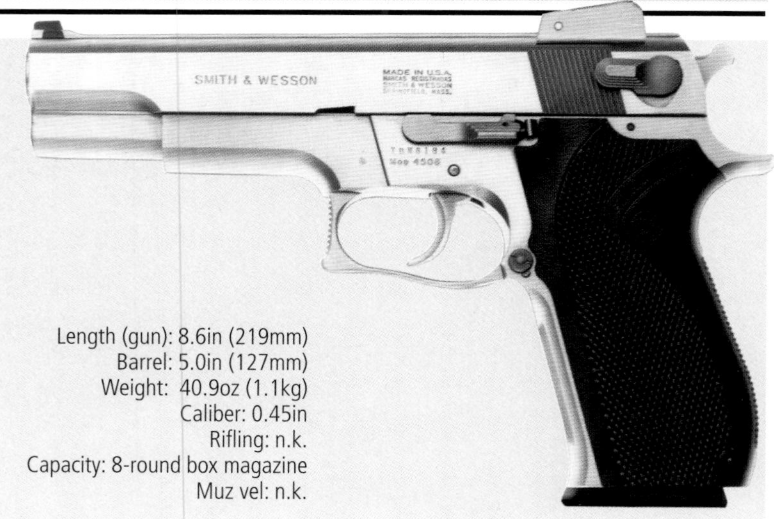

Length (gun): 8.6in (219mm)
Barrel: 5.0in (127mm)
Weight: 40.9oz (1.1kg)
Caliber: 0.45in
Rifling: n.k.
Capacity: 8-round box magazine
Muz vel: n.k.

Smith & Wesson involved US Government and law enforcement agencies in a major redesign exercise, which resulted in a completely new range of automatic pistols, known as the "Third Generation." Most of the resulting pistols fire the 9 x 19mm Parabellum round, but the heaviest in this group is the Model 4500 series which fires the 0.45in ACP round. There are currently three weapons in the series, Models 4506 (see specifications), 4566, and 4586, with the numbers, under the new Smith & Wesson system for their Third Generation pistols, giving a lot of information about the weapon. In this system, the first two digits indicate the caliber, except in 9mm where the first digit indicates the model number and the second digit (always "9") the caliber. The third digit indicates the type of weapon – eg, standard, compact, non-standard barrel length, etc – and the fourth digit the type of finish. The full system cannot be described here, but the weapons in the 4500 Series can be identified as follows. The first two digits – 45 – indicate 0.45in caliber. In the third digit: 0 = standard; 6 = non-standard barrel length; 8 = non-standard barrel length with double-action only. The fourth digit, which is 6 in all three cases, shows that they have stainless steel frames and slides. Of these, the 4506 has a 6.0in (127mm) barrel, while the 4566 and 4568 both have a 4.25in (108mm) barrel.

Starr Revolver USA

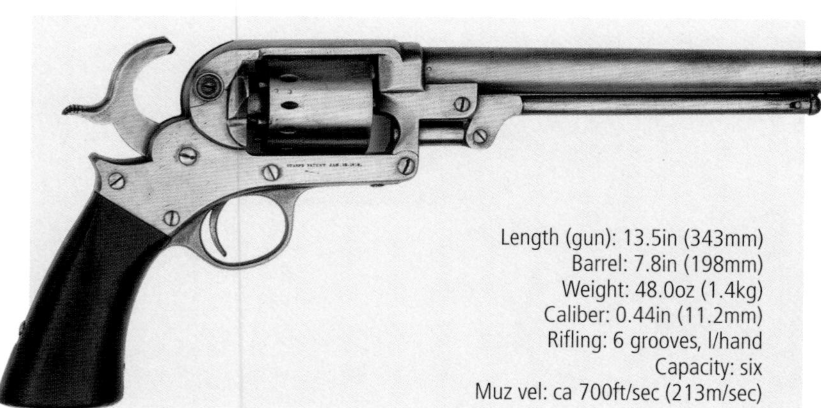

Length (gun): 13.5in (343mm)
Barrel: 7.8in (198mm)
Weight: 48.0oz (1.4kg)
Caliber: 0.44in (11.2mm)
Rifling: 6 grooves, l/hand
Capacity: six
Muz vel: ca 700ft/sec (213m/sec)

The Starr Arms Company of New York began to manufacture revolvers of the kind seen here as a result of a patent of January 15 1856. There were three types: a Navy double-action model of 0.36in (9.1mm) caliber; a double-action Army model of 0.44in (11.2mm) caliber; and a somewhat heavier 0.44in (11.2mm) caliber, single-action model, like the weapon illustrated here. Unlike the Colts of the period, the Starr has a top strap and the barrel is hinged at the front of the frame. The removal of the screw visible below the hammer nose (a task needing no tools) enabled the revolver to be broken (rather like the later Webleys) and stripped for cleaning very easily. This particular arrangement made it possible to dispense with a cylinder pin: the cylinder was mounted by means of its rear-projecting ratchet and by a forward plug fitting into recesses in the frame. The six-chambered cylinder is plain, except for 12 oval slots for the stop. These slots allowed the cylinder to be locked with a nipple on either side of the nose of the hammer, thus eliminating the chance of accidental discharge by a drop or jolt. The rammer is of the powerful type usually found on such weapons. The one-piece walnut butt is held between two tangs. All the metalwork of the pistol is of steel. It has a blade foresight, adjustable laterally; the backsight is formed by a notch on the top of the nose of the hammer. The frame is marked "STARRS PATENT JAN 15 1856" on the right hand side, and "STARR ARMS CO NEW YORK" on the left, while the cylinder is numbered "27479." The letter "C," presumably a viewer's mark, also appears on various components.

Stevens Bicycle Rifle Pistol — USA

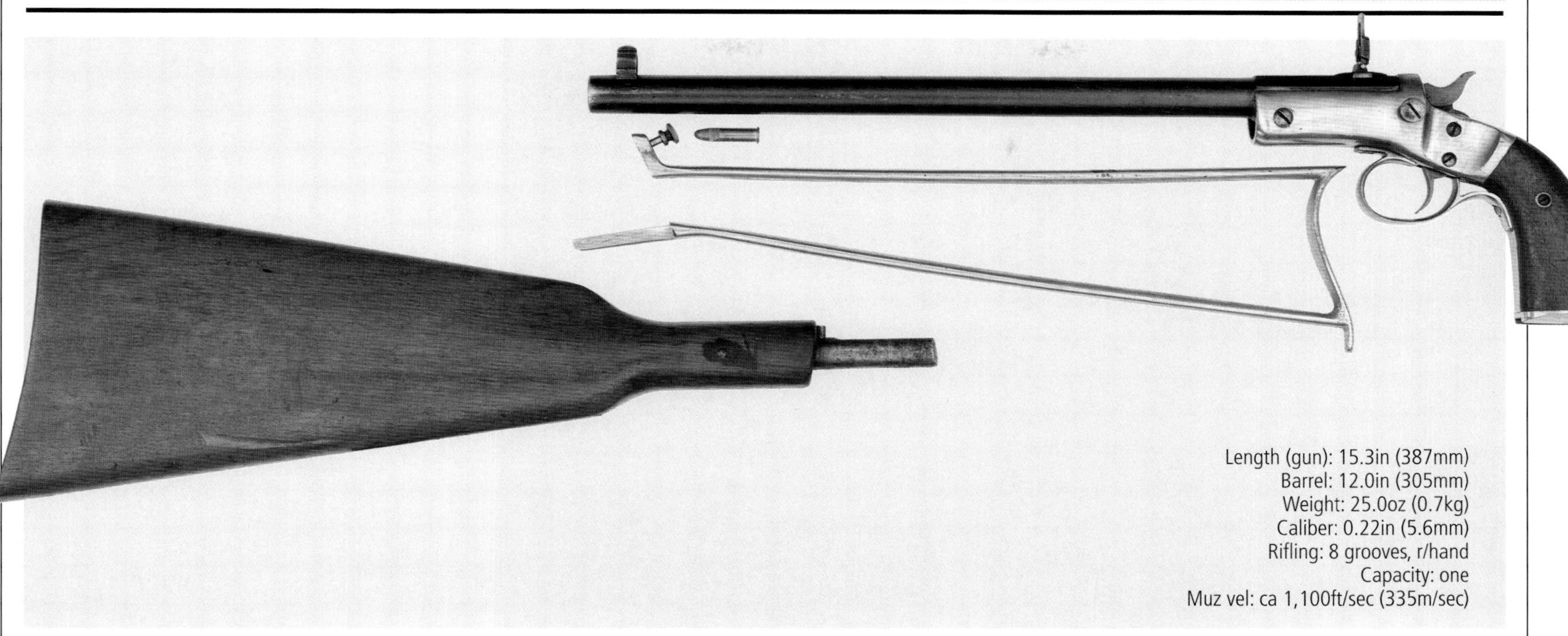

Length (gun): 15.3in (387mm)
Barrel: 12.0in (305mm)
Weight: 25.0oz (0.7kg)
Caliber: 0.22in (5.6mm)
Rifling: 8 grooves, r/hand
Capacity: one
Muz vel: ca 1,100ft/sec (335m/sec)

Weapons of this type achieved popularity in the United States towards the end of the 19th Century, when the bicycle had established itself as a cheap and popular means of transport. The arms presumably got their generic name from the ease with which they could be carried, either assembled or with the wire butt removed, attached to the crossbar of a bicycle. When small game abounded near most country roads, a small, light rifle was a convenient thing to have to hand. The barrel of this specimen was hinged: pressure on the spotted stud below the hammer allowed the barrel to drop, giving access to the breech. It was made by the Stevens Company of Chicopee Falls, Massachusetts.

Thompson/Center Contender Target Pistol — USA

Length (gun): 18.1in (460mm)
Barrel: see text
Weight: 61.0oz (1.7kg)
Caliber: 0.30in-30
Rifling: n.k.
Capacity: one
Muz vel: n.k.

This remarkable pistol was introduced by Ken Thompson and Warren Center in 1967 as a highly specialized single-shot pistol for competition use. Sales were initially poor, being confined mainly to ballistics experts who needed a test-bed. By the early 1990s, however, nearly half-a-million Contenders had been sold. It owes its popularity to a number of factors, including the extraordinary flexibility of the design in which barrels can be changed with ease. The Contender is a single-action, break-open pistol, in which forward pressure on the trigger guard spur releases the barrel to hinge down from the frame for loading and unloading. There are two types of receiver, which are dimensionally identical, but differ in that one is blued-finished, the other plated with Armalloy. There is a vast range of barrels for different calibers; barrels are either 10.0in (254mm) or 14.0in (356mm) long. A plated barrel will only fit on a plated receiver, and a blued barrel will only fit on a blued receiver. Thompson/Center themselves produce some 23 different chamberings, but other manufacturers offer even more, one as many as 70. The top photo shows the 0.357 Magnum caliber Contender with, above it, a replacement 0.45in Colt/0.410in shotshell chambering and scew-in choke type key; the bottom photo shows the 0.30-.30 Winchester caliber weapon with Armalloy finish.

Wesson & Leavitt Tape-Primer Revolver — USA

Length: 6.6in (168mm)
Barrel: 3.0in (76mm)
Weight: 10.0oz (0.3kg)
Caliber: 0.28in (7.1mm)
Rifling: 7 grooves, l/hand
Capacity: six
Muz vel: ca 500ft/sec (152m/sec)

The popularity of Colt's percussion revolvers naturally led to attempts by many manufacturers in the United States and elsewhere to circumvent the patents under which Colt's arms were made. One such manufacturer was the Massachusetts Arms Company which was sued by Colt in 1851 for contravention of his patent in respect of a mechanically revolving cylinder. Massachusetts pleaded that the revolver in question, originally designed by Wesson and Leavitt, made use of a system of bevel gears rather than a pawl and ratchet to rotate the cylinder, and that it was, therefore, not bound by the patent referred to. The court found against the company, which had to pay heavy damages to Colt and was forced to cease the manufacture of these particular arms until Colt's patent expired in 1857. The small pocket revolver seen here is one of the pistols modified so as not to contravene the patent. It has several interesting features. The rear end of the top strap, which is integral with the barrel, is hinged to the standing breech in such a way that it could be turned upwards through about 45 degrees, thus allowing the cylinder to be removed by pulling it forward off its axis pin. The length of this is such that, when the cylinder was fully home, about 1in (25.4mm) protruded beyond its front face; this extension served as a peg on which is fixed a hook attached to the breech end of the barrel by means of a collar. A single nipple is screwed into the top of the breech at such an angle that it is exactly aligned with the vent leading into the rear of each chamber. The use of only one nipple was made possible by the incorporation of a device known as a tape-primer.

RIFLES & SHOTGUNS

A "rifled" firearm is one in which the projectile is made to spin as it travels up the bore. The term "rifle," however, was originally applied to muskets to differentiate them from the earlier smoothbore weapons and is used today to designate the infantryman's personal weapon, fired from the shoulder or the hip, or, in some modern weapons, from a bipod.

As the following pages show, the rifle progressed from being a muzzle-loader to a breechloading, bolt-operated weapon, then to a semi-automatic rifle, and now to a lightweight "assault rifle." The emphasis throughout these developments has been in increasing the rate of fire, reducing the weight and making the weapons more accurate, simpler to fire, more reliable and easier to maintain. Effective range has been a relatively unimportant factor and most modern rifles have an effective range of some 300yd (275m), whereas a skilled British rifleman in World War I could use his Lee-Enfield accurately to ranges of 600yd (550m) or more.

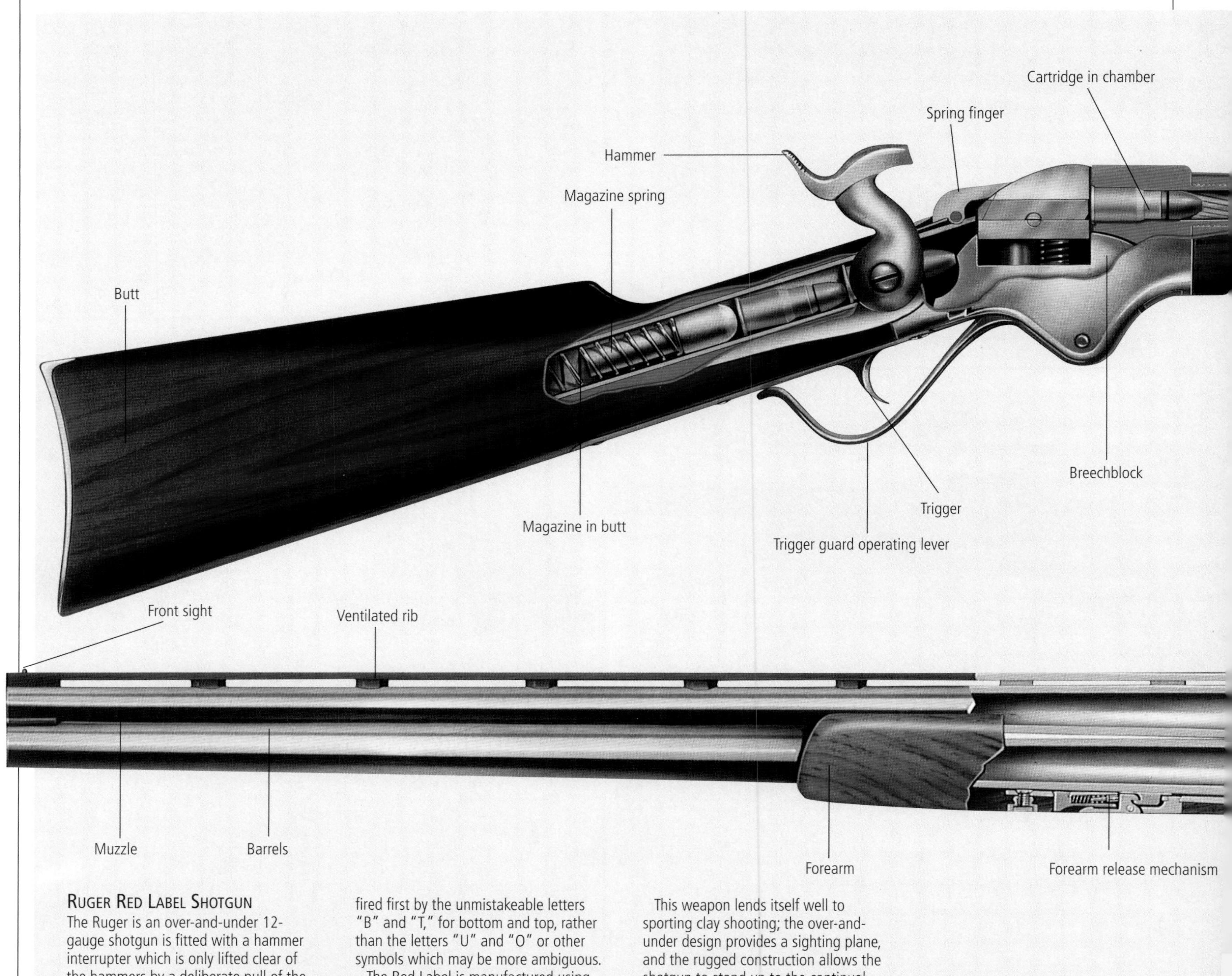

RUGER RED LABEL SHOTGUN

The Ruger is an over-and-under 12-gauge shotgun is fitted with a hammer interrupter which is only lifted clear of the hammers by a deliberate pull of the trigger, a valuable safety device similar in its effect to the intercepting safety sears found on most quality sidelock guns and some high-quality boxlocks.

The automatic safety catch incorporates the barrel selector, which pivots from one side to the other and, unlike other over-and-unders, indicates the barrel to be fired first by the unmistakeable letters "B" and "T," for bottom and top, rather than the letters "U" and "O" or other symbols which may be more ambiguous.

The Red Label is manufactured using stainless steel in the receiver, trigger, and forend iron. The stock and semi-beavertail forearm are produced from American walnut. The weapon is taken down by opening the latch and pivoting the barrels off the frame, then removing the forend. The barrels pivot on trunnions which are one piece with the frame.

This weapon lends itself well to sporting clay shooting; the over-and-under design provides a sighting plane, and the rugged construction allows the shotgun to stand up to the continual shooting of thousands of shells.

One area where national requirements have differed is in the need for a bayonet. Some armies still insist on a traditional bayonet, most of which are nowadays capable of being used as multi-purpose tools as well as for attacking the enemy, but other armies have dispensed with them altogether, considering them to be an irrelevance in the 21st Century.

Shotguns are also shoulder-fired weapons but with a larger caliber, smoothbore (unrifled) barrel, and normally fire multi-pellet shot. They are widely used by civilians for sporting purposes, but are also used by para-military and some military forces for short-range operations. They have a devastating effect at short range, and have proved most effective in clearing buildings and in jungle ambushes.

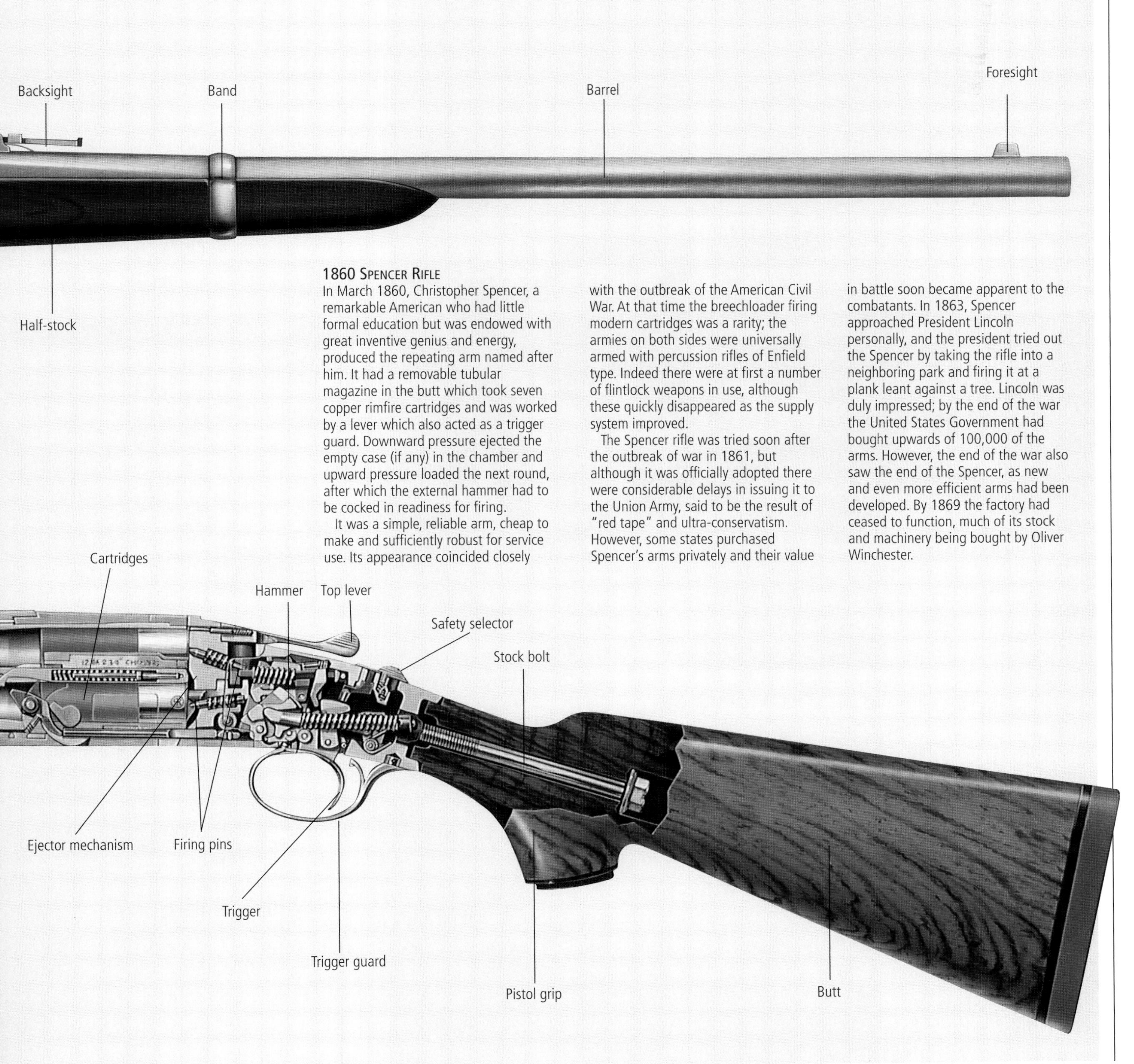

1860 Spencer Rifle

In March 1860, Christopher Spencer, a remarkable American who had little formal education but was endowed with great inventive genius and energy, produced the repeating arm named after him. It had a removable tubular magazine in the butt which took seven copper rimfire cartridges and was worked by a lever which also acted as a trigger guard. Downward pressure ejected the empty case (if any) in the chamber and upward pressure loaded the next round, after which the external hammer had to be cocked in readiness for firing.

It was a simple, reliable arm, cheap to make and sufficiently robust for service use. Its appearance coincided closely with the outbreak of the American Civil War. At that time the breechloader firing modern cartridges was a rarity; the armies on both sides were universally armed with percussion rifles of Enfield type. Indeed there were at first a number of flintlock weapons in use, although these quickly disappeared as the supply system improved.

The Spencer rifle was tried soon after the outbreak of war in 1861, but although it was officially adopted there were considerable delays in issuing it to the Union Army, said to be the result of "red tape" and ultra-conservatism. However, some states purchased Spencer's arms privately and their value in battle soon became apparent to the combatants. In 1863, Spencer approached President Lincoln personally, and the president tried out the Spencer by taking the rifle into a neighboring park and firing it at a plank leant against a tree. Lincoln was duly impressed; by the end of the war the United States Government had bought upwards of 100,000 of the arms. However, the end of the war also saw the end of the Spencer, as new and even more efficient arms had been developed. By 1869 the factory had ceased to function, much of its stock and machinery being bought by Oliver Winchester.

M1867 INFANTRY RIFLE (WERNDL) — AUSTRIA-HUNGARY

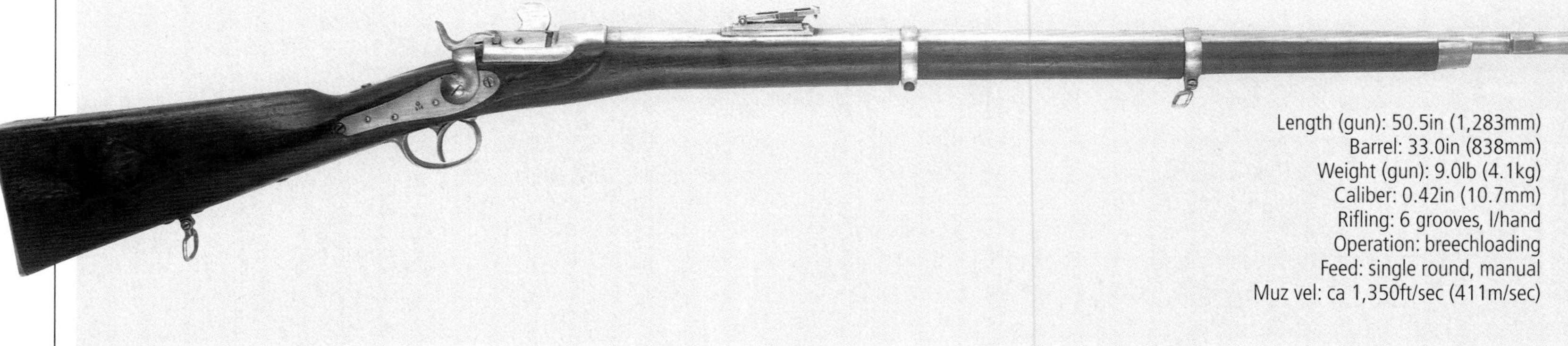

Length (gun): 50.5in (1,283mm)
Barrel: 33.0in (838mm)
Weight (gun): 9.0lb (4.1kg)
Caliber: 0.42in (10.7mm)
Rifling: 6 grooves, l/hand
Operation: breechloading
Feed: single round, manual
Muz vel: ca 1,350ft/sec (411m/sec)

Joseph Werndl founded a weapons factory at Steyr in Austria in 1834, which was taken over by his widow in 1855 and later by her son, Joseph, thus founding a business which continues to this day as the famous Steyr company. Joseph went to the United States in 1862 and was deeply impressed by the extent to which the Americans had progressed in making weapons by modern mass-production methods. On returning home he completely re-organized the factory, installing the most up-to-date and sophisticated equipment which he ordered from the United States and Great Britain. Impressed by this, the Austrian government placed the order for their new rifle with Werndl, who produced it as the M1867 Infantry Rifle, although it was more commonly known as the Werndl Rifle. This had a cylindrical breechblock mounted on a pin parallel to and just below the line of the barrel, designed so that it could move through 90 degrees. A deep semi-circular groove was cut out of one side of the block in such a way that when it was turned level with the chamber it acted as a guide way for the cartridge, this action only being possible when the action was at half-cock. The block was then turned back to the closed position by means of a protruding thumb-piece, the hammer drawn back to full cock, and the trigger pulled. The weapon was progressively developed through two major models: M1873 (improved action with a central hammer); M1877 (new cartridge, sights). As with most rifles of this period, a cavalry carbine was produced by shortening the barrel. The illustration shows the M1867 version. The Werndl Rifle was sighted to 1,750yd (1,600m), although it is doubtful that it was very accurate at such a range.

STEYR AUG 5.56MM — AUSTRIA

Length (gun): 31.1in (790mm)
Weight (gun): 7.9lb (3.6kg)
Barrel: 20.0in (508mm)
Caliber: 5.56mm
Rifling: 6 grooves, r/hand
Operation: gas
Feed: 30-round box magazine
Cyclic rate: 650rpm
Muz vel: 3,182ft/sec (970m/sec)

The A Universalgewehr (= universal army rifle) was designed in response to an Austrian Army requirement for a new assault rifle and it entered service in 1977, but even after more than 20 years' service its bullpup design and unusual shape still give it a futuristic appearance. The AUG has a solid, indestructible feel and all users report that it is very reliable and accurate. It is fitted with a Swarovski x1.5 scope mounted in the carrying handle. Barrels can be changed rapidly, locking into a machined steel ring, which is contained within the cast aluminum breech housing; the bolthead locks into the same steel ring. The gun uses a rotating bolt that recoils along two substantial guide rods, the right one housing the operating rod. Both rods impinge on recoil springs contained with the butt-stock. The use of polymers extends to the firing unit, most components of which were originally of plastic, although some of these were later replaced by metal parts. The AUG is rated as an excellent weapon, although its trigger pull of 10lb (4.5kg) seems unnecessarily heavy. The casing can be finished in black, sand or olive drab colors, while the magazine is translucent to enable the firer to see how many rounds remain unfired. Following entry into service with the Austrian Army in 1977 (where it is designated the StuG-77), the AUG has been adopted by a number of other countries, including Australia, Ireland, Morocco, New Zealand, and the Oman. Variants can be easily assembled by changing a few components, including: carbine (16.0in/407mm barrel); submachine gun (13.8in/350mm barrel); and light support weapon (bipod, heavy 24in/621 mm barrel, 40-round magazine).

LITHGOW L1A1 — AUSTRALIA

Length (gun): 45.0in (1,143mm)
Barrel: 24.4in (618mm)
Weight (gun): 9.8lb (4.5kg)
Caliber: 7.62mm
Rifling: 4 grooves, r/hand

Operation: gas-operated
Feed: 20-round box magazine
Cyclic rate: 700rpm
Muz vel: 2,756ft/sec (840m/sec)

In the early post-war years, the British developed the bullpup EM2 (qv) rifle, firing a newly developed British 0.280in round. The weapon was briefly adopted under the Atlee (Labour) government, but the next Prime Minister, Churchill (Conservative) rescinded that decision under strong US pressure and ordered that the NATO standard 7.62mm round be adopted instead. The FN FAL (qv) was the best rifle available in that chambering and that was the weapon adopted, with some modifications, by the British as the L1A1. This was a gas-operated weapon with a tipping bolt and a short-stroke piston that acted on the bolt carrier. Lock-up was against a shelf in the lower receiver. The gas regulator had six positions, so that the rifle and ammunition could be exactly matched. The recoil spring was in the butt and the folding cocking handle on the left of the gun. The axis of the bore was as low as possible without turning to a straight stock with raised sights. The latter option was rejected by FN, since they considered that it would prevent the firer making the best use of cover, which has subsequently proved to the disadvantage of "straight-line" weapons such as the M16. In the 1950s most Commonwealth countries still continued to follow the lead set by UK in military matters, so when the British adopted the FN FAL as the L1A1 the Australians and Canadians followed suit. The weapon illustrated here is the Australian Army's Lithgow L1A1, which was very similar to the British original, but with furniture made of ICI Maranyl nylon.

BROWNING A5 SELF-LOADING SHOTGUNS — BELGIUM

Length (gun): 44.5in (1,130mm)
Barrel: 24.8in(629mm)
Weight (gun): 8.6lb (3.9kg)
Caliber: 12-gauge (see text)

Rifling: none
Operation: long recoil, locked breech
Feed: tubular magazine
Muz vel: n.k.

John Browning patented his self-loading shotgun design in 1900 and he first offered production rights to the Winchester Repeating Arms Co, New Haven, Connecticut, as he had done with many of his earlier designs. This time however, he asked for a royalty arrangement, rather than a single, fixed payment, and when the American company refused to agree he approached Fabrique National in Belgium, which was only too happy agree. Production started in 1903 and the A5 became one of the classic guns of modern times, with millions being made over the following 80 years, both by FN in Belgium and from 1905 to 1948 by Remington in the United States (Model 11). The famous square-backed receiver was seen in gun shops all over the world and its long recoil action was copied by almost every rival gun-making factory. On firing, the barrel and bolt both recoiled, locked together, over the full length of the receiver. The barrel then returned forward alone, ejecting the spent shell, whereupon the bolt followed, loading a fresh shell and feeding it into the chamber. At 8.6lb (3.9kg), the A5 was heavy, but it was also very solid and reliable, and could easily be adjusted to suit different loads. It was made in almost every format: Magnum; police guns; riot guns; and barrels with or without ribs. It was also produced in 12-, 16- and 20-gauge. Indeed, between the wars and for many years after World War II, if one saw a semi-automatic shotgun at a clay-pigeon shoot, it was a safe bet that it was a Browning. It was also used by British troops during the Emergency in Malaya, who found it ideal, when loaded with buckshot, for short-range, quick-response, heavy firepower. The example illustrated is fitted with the optional Cutts Compensator.

BROWNING 125 SHOTGUN — BELGIUM

Length (gun): 45.5in (1,156mm)
Barrel: 28.0in (71.0mm)
Weight (gun): 7.7lb (3.5kg)
Caliber: 12-gauge

Rifling: none
Operation: drop-down, over-and-under
Feed: manual
Muz vel: n.k.

John Browning died in 1926, but his last design, which appeared in the early 1920s, was his first over-and-under shotgun, which, as so often happened with him, turned out to be a most influential design which had a major effect on the habits of the shooting world. Prior to Browning's design, a few famous London gun-makers had produced over-and-unders, but they had been very expensive and it was FN and Browning who made it possible for such a weapon to be manufactured at a price that many people could and did afford. By the 1930s these over-and-unders were selling in substantial numbers in both Europe and the USA and they were still in production in the 1980s, being made in Liège, Belgium, by Fabrique National (FN) and by B.C. Miroku in Japan. These guns were made both with standard barrels and with internally threaded variable chokes, a device which Browning called the "Invector" system. Variations are made for all the clay-shooting disciplines and for field use.

BROWNING SPECIAL SKEET GUN — BELGIUM

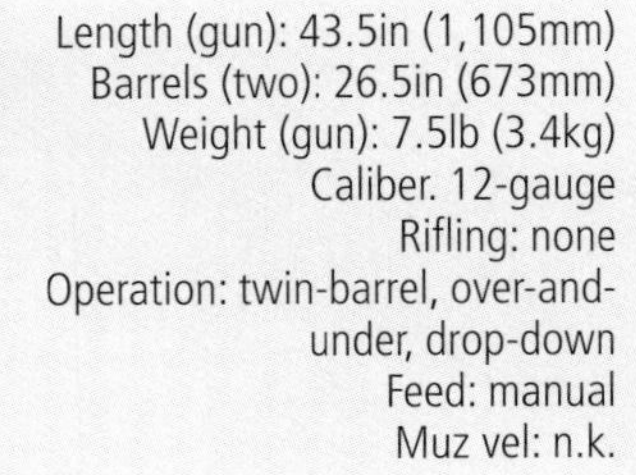

Length (gun): 43.5in (1,105mm)
Barrels (two): 26.5in (673mm)
Weight (gun): 7.5lb (3.4kg)
Caliber. 12-gauge
Rifling: none
Operation: twin-barrel, over-and-under, drop-down
Feed: manual
Muz vel: n.k.

Despite the simplicity and elegance of the side-by-side double-barreled gun, the over-and-under (also known as the "stacked-barrel") continues to be popular. This is the Special Skeet Model, which was manufactured in the 1950s and 1960s by Fabrique Nationale (FN) of Belgium, chiefly for North American customers, where it was marketed under the Browning label. The stock has a half pistol grip rather than the full pistol grip now almost universal on over-and-unders. Like all Browning skeet guns of this period, this gun has four points of choke in each barrel, so that the selection of which barrel to fire first is of little consequence. Over the 30 years or so since this gun was made, skeet guns have tended to be made with no choke at all in the barrels; in fact, even "trumpet" choking has been seen, whereby the barrels actually open out at the muzzles to give the widest possible spread to the shot pattern.

SELF-LOADING EXPERIMENTAL MODEL RIFLE — BELGIUM

Length: 44.0in (1,117mm)
Barrel: 23.25in (591mm)
Weight: 9.5lb (4.3kg)
Caliber: 7.92mm
Rifling: 4 grooves, r/hand
Operation: gas
Feed: 10-round box
Muz vel: 2,400ft/sec (730m/sec)

This weapon was designed by a M. Saive in Belgium in the 1930s as a replacement for the existing bolt-action rifles of Mauser type then in use in the Belgian Army. But when the Germans invaded Belgium in 1940 all work on the new rifle naturally stopped. The designer escaped with the plans for his new weapon which he took to Britain, where he worked on various wartime projects. A number of these new rifles were made at the Royal Small Arms Factory at Enfield late in the war, being generally known as the Self-Loading Experimental Model, often abbreviated to SLEM. They were gas-operated with a gas cylinder above the barrel, and had a bolt very similar to that of the Russian Tokarev rifle. They were general well made and full-stocked in walnut which made them very expensive weapons to produce. These prototypes, which were all made to fire the full size German 7.92mm Mauser round, were extensively tested, but although they proved to be most successful the British were then also carrying out tests on their own EM2, and so they took no further action on the Belgian rifle. When Saive returned to Belgium, however, he continued his work there and soon perfected an improved model known usually as the Model 49, after the date of its appearance. This was a time when a good many countries were looking for cheap and reliable self-loaders with which to re-arm their infantry, and the Model 49 was an immediate success, being sold to a considerable number of countries including Columbia, Venezuela, Egypt and Luxemburg. The Model 49 was manufactured in a variety of calibers. The Belgian Army also adopted it and it saw service in Korea. It subsequently developed into the highly successful FAL.

FN FAL (MODEL 50) 7.62MM RIFLE — BELGIUM

Length (gun): 41.5in (1,054mm)
Barrel: 21.0in (533mm)
Weight (gun): 9.5lb (4.3kg)
Caliber: 7.62mm
Rifling: 4 grooves, r/hand
Operation: gas
Feed: 20-round box
Muz vel: 2,800ft/sec (853m/sec)

As described in the Model 49 entry (qv), the Belgians took the design of the Self-Loading Experimental Model rifle (qv) and developed it into the Model 49, which was produced by Fabrique Nationale in some numbers for the Belgian and foreign armies. This was then developed into the Model 50, usually known as the Fusil Automatique Legere (FAL), which first appeared in 1950. The FAL was initially designed to fire the 7.92 x 57mm Mauser round (also known as the "German intermediate") but when the newly formed NATO alliance standardized on the 7.62 x 51mm round a new version of the FAL was produced chambered to this round. The 7.62mm FAL was a great success: it was gas-operated, could fire automatic or single shots as required, and was generally a robust and effective arm well suited to military needs. It was sold to a great many countries. Although it had the capability to fire bursts this led to problems of accuracy, due to the inevitable rise of the muzzle, and most countries therefore had their rifles permanently set at semi-automatic, which still allowed 20 to 30 well-aimed shots to be fired in one minute. There was also a heavy barreled version with a bipod which was adopted by some countries as a section automatic weapon. When the UK abandoned development of the EM2 (qv) it adopted a version of the FN FAL and purchased one thousand direct from FN for trials, one of which is shown here. These were then tested in the UK, Germany, Kenya, and Malaya, which led to the modified version which was produced in the UK as the L1A2 (qv).

FN FAL (Model 50) 0.280in Rifle — Belgium

Length (gun): ca 40.0in (1,016mm)
Barrel: 19.0in (483mm)
Weight (gun): ca 10.0lb (4.5kg)
Caliber: 0.280in (7mm)
Rifling: 4 grooves, r/hand
Operation: gas
Feed: 20-round box
Muz vel: n.k.

In the years following World War II the British expended a great deal of development effort on the Enfield 0.280 (7mm Mk1Z) round and two new rifles to fire it: the EM1 and EM2 (qv). When NATO was formed, the British offered this round as their candidate for the standard infantry round, but it was rejected in favor of the Belgian 7.62 x 51mm round. At some time during this period the Belgian FN factory developed a version of its new Model 50 (FAL), which is seen here. This was chambered to fire the British 0.280in round and was presumably intended as a safeguard against the possibility that the British round was selected, in which case the Belgians would have offered this weapon to third parties in competition with the British "bullpup" EM2. Note that, unlike the Model 50 (FAL), this weapon has a shorter barrel fitted with a flash suppressor and a different fore hand-grip which has grooves for the fingers and does not fully enclose the gas cylinder. It also lacks a carrying handle, and has a plainer and less angled pistol grip.

Ross Rifle — Canada

Length: 50.5in (1,283mm)
Barrel: 30.2in (765mm)
Weight: 9.9lb (4.5kg)
Caliber: 0.303in
Rifling: 4 grooves, l/hand
Operation: straight-pull
Feed: 5-round box
Muz vel: 2,600ft/sec (794m/sec)

This rifle was designed by a Canadian, Sir Charles Ross, towards the end of the 19th Century, first issues being made in 1905 to the Royal Canadian Mounted Police. The rifle was unusual in being of the "straight-pull" type in which the bolt handle was drawn straight back, the breech being unlocked by the rotation of the locking lugs by means of cams. It had a magazine capacity of five rounds which in the early models had to be loaded singly, and it proved to be an excellent target rifle. There were however, fundamental defects in its design which rendered it unsuitable as a service rifle and although a whole series of modifications were hastily made there was no significant improvement. The British School of Musketry reported unfavorably on it but in spite of this the Canadian Army went to war with it in 1914, their particular weapon being the Mark III which could be loaded by charger. Its main fault, that the bolt stop bore on one of the locking lugs causing it to burr, led to disastrous consequences, particularly in the mud of the trenches when Canadian soldiers were seen angrily kicking their rifle bolts to open them during German attacks. It was quickly replaced by the Lee-Enfield and little more was heard of it although a few were resurrected for the British Home Guard in the early years of World War II.

DIEMACO C7A1 5.56MM ASSAULT RIFLE — CANADA

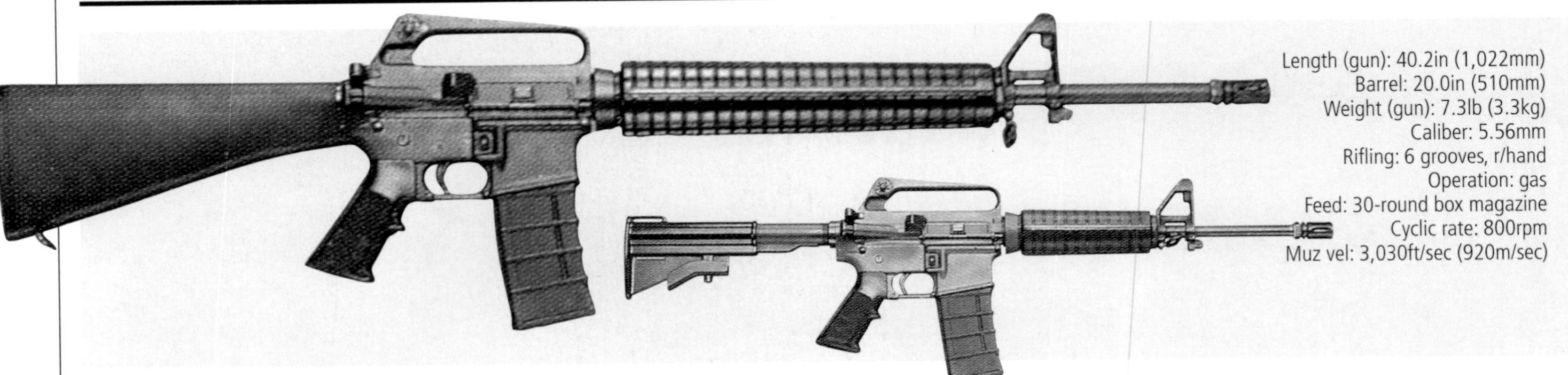

Length (gun): 40.2in (1,022mm)
Barrel: 20.0in (510mm)
Weight (gun): 7.3lb (3.3kg)
Caliber: 5.56mm
Rifling: 6 grooves, r/hand
Operation: gas
Feed: 30-round box magazine
Cyclic rate: 800rpm
Muz vel: 3,030ft/sec (920m/sec)

Canada has manufactured weapons for many years and in the 1950s and 1960s produced the C1A1, a license-built copy of the British 7.65mm L1A1 (which was, itself, derived from the Belgian FN FAL). A copy of the heavy-barreled FN rifle was also produced under license as the C2 and the virtually identical C2A1. When the Canadian armed forces adopted the NATO 5.56mm round, Diemaco commenced production of the US 5.56mm Colt M16A2. The latest series of weapons are a development of this, designated C7 Combat Rifle (top) and C8 Carbine (Lower photo). The C7 has three modes: safe, single rounds, and fully automatic; it does not have a three-round burst mode. It uses a simple, two-position rearsight situated on top of the rear of the receiver, between two prominent protectors. The barrel is cold-forged and chrome-lined and the weapon will fire either the NATO SS109 or US M193 5.56mm rounds. The C7 is used by the Canadian armed forces and the Royal Netherlands Army, and a small quantity was purchased by Denmark for its forces deployed in Bosnia. The C7A1 is an improved version with a low-mounted optical sight mounted atop the receiver rail and is used by the Dutch special forces. The C8 is a further development which is, in essence, a compact version of the C7, with a telescopic butt, butt pad, and a shorter barrel (14.6in/370mm long) and is intended for troops needing a more compact weapon, such as armored crews, engineers and signalers. A sub-type, the C8A1, which is a C8 with a telescopic sight, is used by Dutch gendarmerie. Both C8 and C8A1 share all major components with the C7.

TYPE 56 RIFLE — CHINA (PRC)

Length: 34.7in (880mm)
Barrel: 16.3in (415mm)
Weight: 9.5lb (4.3kg)
Caliber: 7.62mm intermediate
Rifling: 4 grooves, r/hand
Operation: gas
Feed: 30-round box
Cyclic rate: 600rpm
Muz vel: 2,350ft/sec (717m/sec)

The Chinese fought their war against the United Nations in Korea with a considerable mixture of outdated weapons mainly of American, Russian, or British origin, but after it was over the Russians started arming their fellow Communists with a variety of more up to date Russian arms, notably the SKS carbine, the AK-47 assault rifle, and the RPD light machine gun, all of which fired the same 7.62mm intermediate cartridge. The demand however was enormous and as soon as they were able to do so the Chinese set up their own factories to manufacture military weapons. As there was considerable urgency over the matter, the Chinese wasted no time in trying to produce new or original designs, but simply stuck as closely to the originals as their own somewhat less sophisticated manufacturing techniques allowed them. The weapon which they originally concentrated on was a locally developed version of the SKS, but this was soon relegated to a training role in favor of their Type 56 assault rifle. Mechanically this was a very close copy of the original AK-47, the principal difference being a permanently attached folding bayonet of cruciform section. Although a very old idea, the Chinese were the only country still using it in the 1960s, all others having opted for a detachable knife-type bayonet which the soldier can use as a general purpose implement. Chinese-made Type 56 rifles were extensively used in Vietnam by the Viet Cong who found them to be ideal weapons for soldiers who were mostly small and slight by Western standards; the specimen illustrated is one of the many captured there by the US Army. They are also found in large numbers in Middle East and African countries.

NORINCO 7.62MM TYPE 81 ASSAULT RIFLE — CHINA (PRC)

Length (gun): 37.6in (955mm)
Barrel: 15.8in (400mm)
Weight (gun): 7.5lb (3.4kg)
Caliber: 7.62mm
Rifling: 4 grooves, r/hand
Operation: gas
Feed: 30-round box magazine (see text)
Cyclic rate: 750rpm
Muz vel: 2,395ft/sec (730m/sec)

The People's Liberation Army (PLA) commenced indigenous rifle production with the Type 56 assault rifle, a Kalashnikov clone, and the Type 56 Carbine, which was a direct copy of the Russian Simonov SKS. The first Chinese weapon was the Type 68 Rifle, which combined features of the Simonov and Kalashnikov systems, but with the Type 81, which was intended primarily for export, Chinese designers began to strike out on their own. The Type 81 was based on the Type 68 and used the Kalashnikov receiver and stock, but there were many other modifications and inspection of the weapon shows it to be built to a particularly high standard. It has a gas-operated action, derived from that of the Type 68 and is normally fed from a 30-round box magazine, although a 75-round drum magazine can also be fitted. The Type 81 has a solid butt, while the Type 81-1 has a frame butt which folds sideways to the right, although in other respects it appears no different from the Type 81. There is also a Type 81 light machine gun, with most components being interchangeable. Maximum effective range is of the order of 435yd (400m).

Model VZ-52 Assault Rifle — Czech Republic

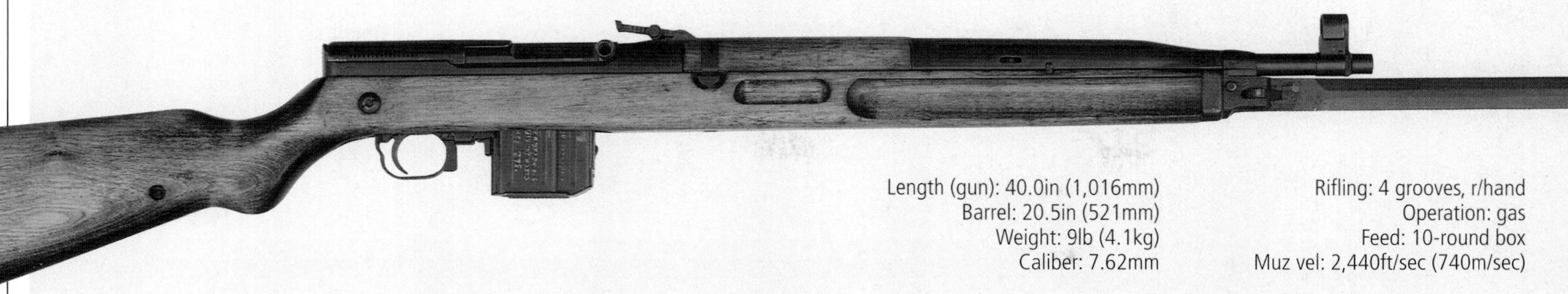

Length (gun): 40.0in (1,016mm)
Barrel: 20.5in (521mm)
Weight: 9lb (4.1kg)
Caliber: 7.62mm
Rifling: 4 grooves, r/hand
Operation: gas
Feed: 10-round box
Muz vel: 2,440ft/sec (740m/sec)

This self-loading rifle incorporated a considerable variety of ideas borrowed from earlier arms of similar type. It was originally designed to fire a 7.62 × 45mm cartridge of purely Czech design and not be interchangeable with any other. It was gas-operated, but the method adopted was unusual in that the weapon had no gas cylinder or piston, power being transmitted by a sleeve around the barrel, which was forced sharply to the rear by the pressure of the gas tapped off from the bore and taking the bolt with it. The bolt was also unusual in that it worked on the tilting principle under which the front end of the bolt dropped into a recess cut into the bottom of the body which had the effect of locking it firmly at the instant of firing. The rifle performed well with the original cartridge for which it was designed, but the Russians later compelled the Czechs to abandon that round in favor of their own less powerful 7.62 × 39mm round, which adversely affected its performance even though it helped standardization. The new modified rifle was known as the Model 52/57. The original VZ-52 was relatively heavy which reduced recoil but added to the soldier's load. It lacked any simple system of gas regulation, so that any change involved the removal of the foregrip before the gas stop could be adjusted. It was often stocked in poor quality wood of a dirty yellow color and had a generally cheap and clumsy look about it. It was fitted with a permanently attached blade bayonet which folded back along the right-hand side of the body when not in use.

VZ-58 7.62mm Assault Rifle — Czech Republic

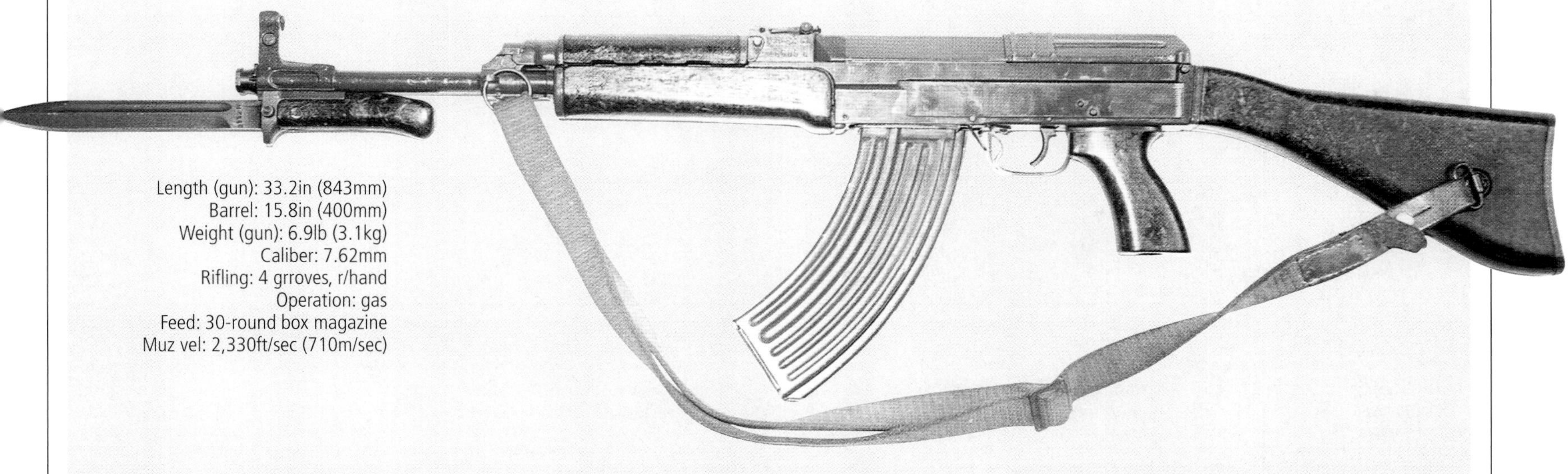

Length (gun): 33.2in (843mm)
Barrel: 15.8in (400mm)
Weight (gun): 6.9lb (3.1kg)
Caliber: 7.62mm
Rifling: 4 grroves, r/hand
Operation: gas
Feed: 30-round box magazine
Muz vel: 2,330ft/sec (710m/sec)

Another product of the Czech Republic's imaginative arms industry, the VZ-58 assault rifle appears at first glance to be based on the Kalashnikov series of rifles, but it is, in fact, a completely different weapon. Internally, it has a gas-operated tilting bolt, similar to that used in the earlier VZ-52 (qv), and no gas regulator, all the gas force being brought to bear on the piston head and the entire piston system is chrome-plated to prevent fouling. Externally, early production models were fitted with wooden furniture, but this was later replaced with plastic-impregnated wood fiber, and later still by plastic. Three versions were produced: one with a fixed butt (VZ-58P, shown in the photographs), one with a fixed butt, bipod, and special attachment for a night-sight (VZ-58Pi); and the third with a single strut, side-folding butt (VZ-58V). All versions were chambered for the 7.62 x 39mm M1943 Soviet round. The VZ-58 was used to equip the (then) Czechoslovak armed forces and a few were sold on the commercial market. Large numbers are in reserve stocks and may be sold off in due course.

CZ 2000 5.56MM WEAPONS FAMILY

CZECH REPUBLIC

Length (gun): 33.5in (850mm)
Barrel: 15.0in (382mm)
Weight (gun): 6.6lb (3.0kg)
Caliber: 5.56 x 45mm
Rifling: 6 grooves, r/hand
Operation: gas
Feed: 30-round box
Cyclic rate: 800rpm
Muz vel: 2,985ft/sec (910m/sec)

The Czech Republic's new range of infantry weapons was revealed in 1993 and was said at that time to be under development in both 5.45mm and 5.56mm versions; in the event, only the NATO 5.56 x 45mm version has been developed, clearly in anticipation of Czech membership of NATO. At the time it was unveiled, the family was known as the "Lada" system, but that name has since been dropped in favor of "CZ 2000." The system is gas operated and uses a rotating bolt, derived from that used in the Kalashnikov, which locks into the barrel at the moment of firing. The weapon fires full automatic, single rounds or three-round bursts and has a pressed steel receiver with plastic furniture, and a twin-tubed, side-folding butt (there is no solid butt version). The 30-round magazine is made of clear plastic so that the firer can see how many rounds it contains, but the US M16 magazine can also be used. The CZ 2000 Short Assault Rifle appeared in 1995 and is a lighter and shorter version; indeed, it is virtually a submachine gun. The receiver, butt, trigger group, and pistol grip are the same, but the barrel is considerably shorter (7.3in/185mm compared to 15.0in/382mm), which has resulted in a shorter gas cylinder. In addition, the slotted flash suppressor has been replaced by a more conventional coned type. The CZ 2000 series also includes a light machine gun version.

MODEL 96 FALCON 12.7MM ANTI-MATERIEL RIFLE

CZECH REPUBLIC

Length (gun): 54.3in (1,380mm)
Barrel: 36.5in (927mm)
Weight (gun, loaded): 32.9lb (14.9kg)
Caliber: 12.7mm
Rifling: 8 grooves, r/hand
Operation: bolt
Feed: 5-round box or manual
Muz vel: 2,790ft/sec (850m/sec)

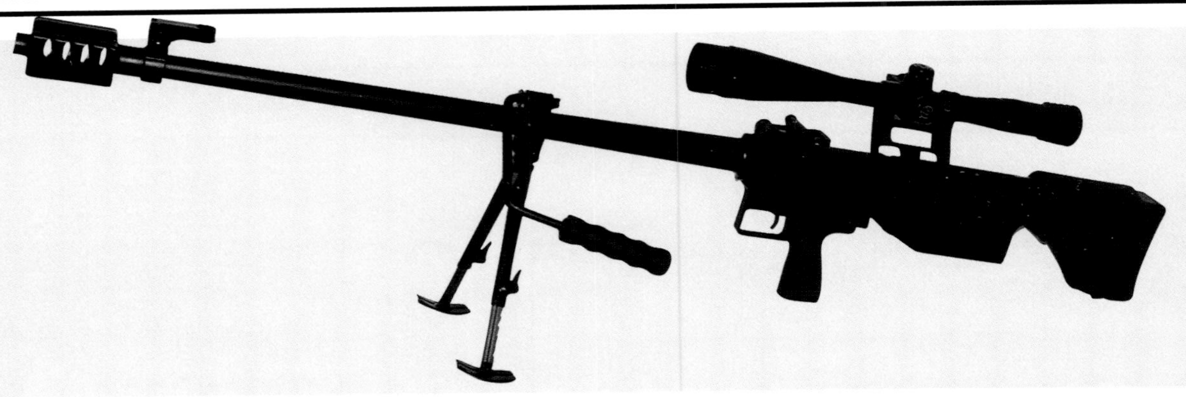

The Model 96 Falcon is one of a gradually increasing number of heavy rifles firing 12.7mm rounds, a caliber which has previously been the province of the heavy machine gun. The Model 96 was originally designated the OPV 12.7mm and was fitted with a 140.4in (1,027mm) barrel, which was capable of firing either the 12.7 x 99mm (0.50in Browning) or the 12.7 x 108mm Russian DshK rounds. This presumably proved too ambitious, since the production weapons have two barrels: one is 36.5in (927mm) long for the 12.7 x 108mm round, the other 33.0in (838mm) long for the 12.7 x 99mm round. The weapon is manually operated, using bolt action, with the prominent bolt lever projecting from the right-hand side of the weapon. The considerable recoil from the 12.7mm round is attenuated in part by a large, four-baffle muzzle-brake, the remainder by a buffer spring in the tubular, detachable butt. The barrel screws on to the receiver and is locked in position by a spring-actuated lever. There is a detachable five-round box magazine, but if the firer wishes to use manual feeding, he can insert a cover over the magazine well. Maximum effective range is claimed to be 2,187yd (2,000m) with the optical sight and 1,094yd (1,000m) at night. There is a carrying handle for moving the weapon into position, and the barrel and butt can be removed for transportation over longer distances. A 10 x 40 scope is supplied with the weapon, with a sight reticle which can be illuminated by internal batteries. Iron sights are also fitted. Specifications above relate to the 12.7 x 108mm DshK version.

SCHULTZ & LARSEN UIT FREE RIFLE

DENMARK

Length (gun): 45.0in (1,143mm)
Barrel: 28.3in (718mm)
Weight (gun): 13.9lb (6.3kg)
Caliber: 0.22in LR
Rifling: n.k.
Operation: bolt
Feed: single round, manual
Muz vel: n.k.

The Danish weapons firm, Schultz & Larsen, was established about the beginning of the 20th Century and produced some fine competition rifles. The rifle shown here was introduced in the late 1940s to meet the requirements of the UIT "Free" competitions, and remained in production, with improvements, into the 1970s. It was the outcome of the pressure of competition and the search for improvements which reached a degree of sophistication that was eventually difficult to exceed. This particular weapon, which was made in the 1960s, had working parts of all-steel construction, with wooden furniture and an aluminum buttplate assembly. Operation was by lifting the bolt handle, which unlocked the breech and cocked the striker. There was no magazine and reloading was by hand. There was a micrometer rear sight and a tunnel foresight with interchangeable elements. The Schultz & Larsen rifles never attained the popularity which their quality deserved, largely because they were designed for optimum performance with Finnish Lapua ammunition, when all the winners were using Eley Tenex. In addition, the trigger set was considered not to be of the same standard as the rest of the weapon.

Schultz & Larsen Model 68DL Rifle — Denmark

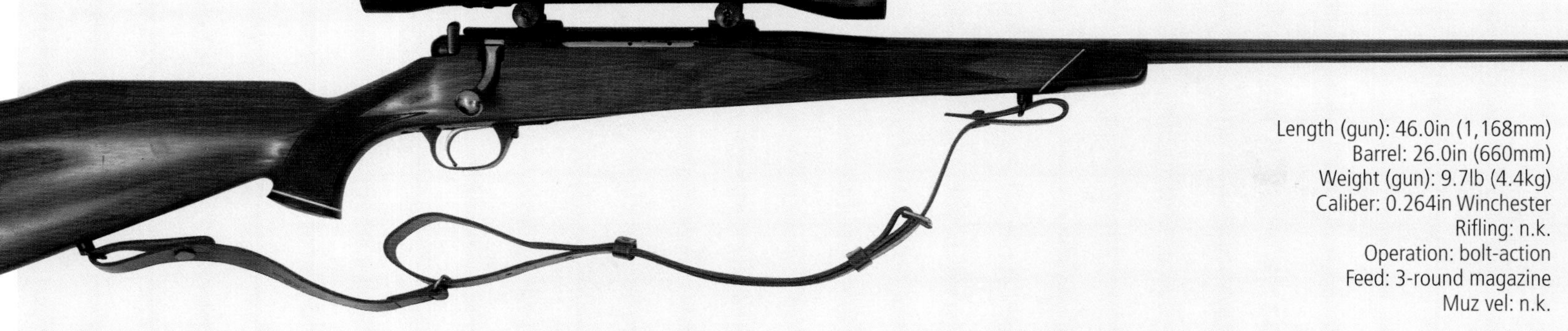

Length (gun): 46.0in (1,168mm)
Barrel: 26.0in (660mm)
Weight (gun): 9.7lb (4.4kg)
Caliber: 0.264in Winchester
Rifling: n.k.
Operation: bolt-action
Feed: 3-round magazine
Muz vel: n.k.

The Schultz & Larsen Model 68DL was an exceptionally fine weapon, but a commercial disaster. It was originally designed by the Dane, Uffe Larsen, the son of the firm's founder, in the late 1940s and was introduced in 1954 in match target and hunting versions, under the designation Model 54. A number of subsequent modifications were intended to make it more appealing to the North American market and included changing from cock-on-closing to cock-on-opening and a faster lock time. It was one of the most accurate, safest, and smoothest operating rifles ever made, combining fine metallurgy with exquisite workmanship. The key to the excellence of the design were the four equidistantly spaced locking lugs mounted just ahead of the bolt handle, which permitted an extremely stiff, enveloping receiver to guide the ground-and-lapped bolt throughout the operating stroke, eliminating the flop, slop, and binding characteristic of bolt actions. This, combined with excellent gas venting and a back deflector shield, made the weapon exceptionally strong and safe. Some 3,000 of all models were made, of which only 200-odd of the perfected Model 68DL were delivered to the United States. The gun was expensive, but not over-priced, but suffered from a prejudice against rear locking actions, and when Schultz & Larsen realized that they were actually losing $50 on every gun sold its manufacture was abruptly terminated.

Valmet M1962 Assault Rifle — Finland

Length (gun): 36.0in (914mm)
Barrel: 16.5in (419mm)
Weight: 8.0lb (3.6kg)
Caliber: 7.62mm
Rifling: 4 grooves r/hand
Operation: gas
Feed: 30-round box
Cyclic rate: 650rpm
Muz vel: 2,350ft/sec (718m/sec)

Finland has always employed a number of Russian weapons, locally made in her own factories and often better made and finished than the originals. This reliance on her neighbor stood her in good stead in 1939 when she was able to make use of large quantities of captured arms and ammunition. The first Soviet type assault rifle made by the Finns was developed in the late 1950s and appeared as the Model 1960. Mechanically it was virtually identical to the Russian AK-47 but there were many external differences. The M1960, which was made at Valmet, hence its name, had no woodwork on it, everything being made of metal and much of it plastic covered. It had a plastic forehand grip ventilated with a series of holes and a rather ugly tubular butt with a shoulder piece welded on to the end of it. This early model was unusual, in that it had no trigger guard in the accepted sense of the term, but only a vertical bar in front of the trigger to allow the weapon to be fired by a soldier wearing heavy gloves in the fierce Finnish winter. The Model 1962 illustrated was essentially similar but made increased use of pressings and riveting. It had the same curved magazine and a tangent backsight mounted on the receiver cover. The three-pronged flash hider incorporated below it a bayonet bar by which the knife-like bayonet could be fixed. It fired the Russian-type intermediate cartridge. Later models included the M1971 with solid butt and M1976 with changes incorporated to facilitate production.

Valmet M90 7.62mm Assault Rifle — Finland

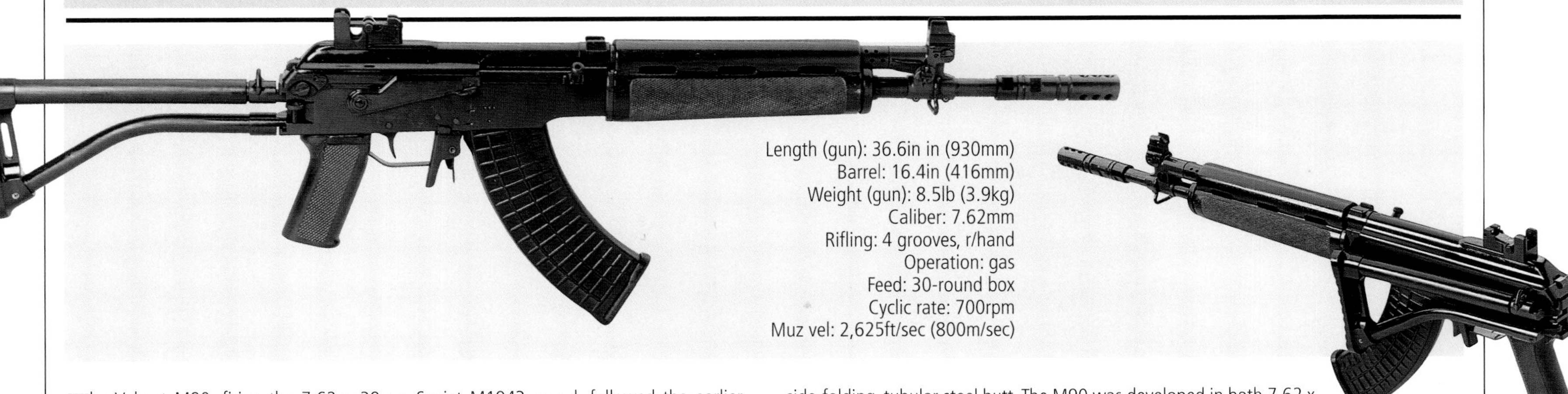

Length (gun): 36.6in in (930mm)
Barrel: 16.4in (416mm)
Weight (gun): 8.5lb (3.9kg)
Caliber: 7.62mm
Rifling: 4 grooves, r/hand
Operation: gas
Feed: 30-round box
Cyclic rate: 700rpm
Muz vel: 2,625ft/sec (800m/sec)

The Valmet M90, firing the 7.62 x 39mm Soviet M1943 round, followed the earlier Valmet M60, M62, and M70 series into service with the Finnish Army. It was designed around the basic and well-proven Kalashnikov gas-operated, rotating-bolt system, but with a much improved and lighter receiver. At the muzzle is a prominent cylindrical device, which serves as a combined flash suppressor and grenade launcher. It had a new pattern, side-folding, tubular steel butt. The M90 was developed in both 7.62 x 39mm and 5.56 x 45mm versions, but, so far as is known, only the former was ever put into production. The manufacturer, Sako, also developed a special hard core bullet for this rifle. Designated K413, it was made of special alloy steel and was intended to penetrate targets not vulnerable to the normal 7.62mm round.

THOUVENIN PILLAR-BREECH RIFLE — FRANCE

Length (gun): 49.3in (1,251mm)
Barrel: 34.0in (864mm)
Weight (gun): 9.0lb (4.1kg)
Caliber: 0.7in (17.5mm)

Rifling: 4 grooves, r/hand
Operation: percussion
Feed: muzzle-loading
Muz vel: ca 1,000ft/sec (305m/sec)

Colonel Thouvenin, a senior officer in the French Army, designed a rifle which was fitted with a "pillar-breech." In this, a small metal rod – the pillar – was inserted inside the breech so that it left precisely the necessary space for the powder charge. When the spherical ball was inserted in the muzzle and pushed down the barrel it was eventually stopped by the pillar, at which point the rifleman gave a number of firm taps on the ramrod with a mallet, which forced the ball to spread slightly, thus fitting into the rifling grooves. This rifle came into service with the French Army in 1846 and the idea was later improved by using elongated, rather than spherical bullets. In service, however, it was found that repeated explosions tended to weaken and distort the pillar, while fouling quickly built-up in the confined spaces.

MODEL 66 "CHASSEPOT" RIFLE — FRANCE

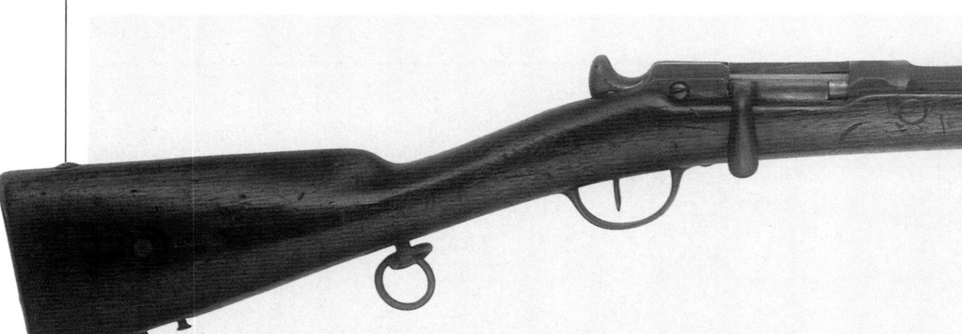

Length (gun): 51.8in (1,314mm)
Barrel: 32.8in (832mm)
Weight (gun): 8.3lb (3.7kg)
Caliber: 0.433in (11mm)

Rifling: 4 grooves, r/hand
Operation: bolt-action
Feed: single round, manual
Muz vel: ca 1,300ft/sec (396m/sec)

Intelligence on the performance of the Prussian "needle gun" (qv) in the short war against Denmark caused some alarm in the French Army and an urgent program was started to find an equivalent, French-designed weapon. This led to the Model 1866 Rifle, generally known by its designer's name of Antoine Alphonse Chassepot. This was a single-shot, bolt-action weapon, although it was not actually cocked by the bolt, it being necessary to pull the cocking-piece to the rear with thumb and forefinger before the breech could be opened. The bolt lever normally projected horizontally to the right and had to be turned upwards through 90 degrees to open it. The barrel was of 0.433in (11mm) caliber and was rifled with four deep grooves, but the bullet, unlike that of the Prussian needle gun, did not have a sabot but fitted the barrel direct. The rifle was sighted to a maximum of 1,312yd (1,200m) and was fitted with a long, heavy bayonet. One of the most surprising features of the Chassepot was its consumable cartridge, although this proved to be somewhat fragile and caused a great deal of fouling, resulting in an escape of gases rearwards, despite the fitting of a rubber obturating ring on the bolt. The picture shows the version of the Chassepot which was produced for the cavalry; it had a shorter barrel and the bolt handle turned down to lie against the rifle, rather than sticking out at right-angles as in the infantry version.

MODÈLE 1886 (LEBEL) RIFLE — FRANCE

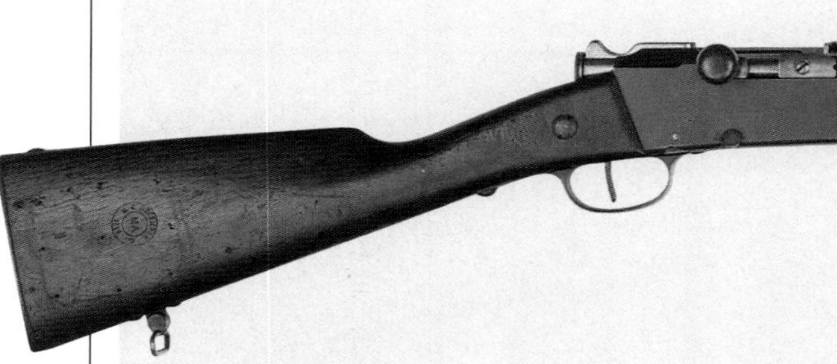

Length (gun): 51.0in (1,295mm)
Barrel: 31.5in (800mm)
Weight: 9.3lb (4.2kg)
Caliber: 8mm

Rifling: 4 grooves, r/hand
Operation: bolt-action
Feed: 8-round tubular-magazine
Muz vel: 2,350ft/sec (716m/sec)

The first breechloading rifle adopted by France was the Modèle 1866 or Chassepot, a bolt-action needle-fire weapon which was similar to the Prussian needle gun, although of superior performance, and was used by the French in the war of 1870–71. It was converted to fire a modern metallic cartridge in 1873 and replaced by the Gras, a very similar weapon, in 1874. Four years later the French Marine Infantry was rearmed with the Austrian Kropatschek rifle, and it was on this weapon that the new Modèle 1886 (Lebel) was based. It was a bolt-action rifle with a tubular magazine concealed in the woodwork below the barrel. This type of magazine incorporated a powerful coil spring at its front end, the rear end of the spring being fitted with a close fitting plug. The rifle was loaded by pushing the rounds nose first into the magazine opening below the chamber until the full capacity of eight had been reached. The contents of the magazine could if necessary be kept in reserve by a cut-off device, allowing the rifle to be used as a single-loader until a more rapid burst of fire was required. The most important feature of the Lebel was undoubtedly the fact that its cartridges were loaded with a recently developed smokeless propellant instead of the old black powder, the French being the first to make this important change. Smokeless powder had two obvious advantages, in that the firing line could be easily concealed while the target was never obscured by smoke as had often been the case with black powder. In order to get the maximum power from the cartridge, it was made bottle shaped instead of cylindrical so as to get as much propellant in as possible.

M1890 Cavalry Carbine — France

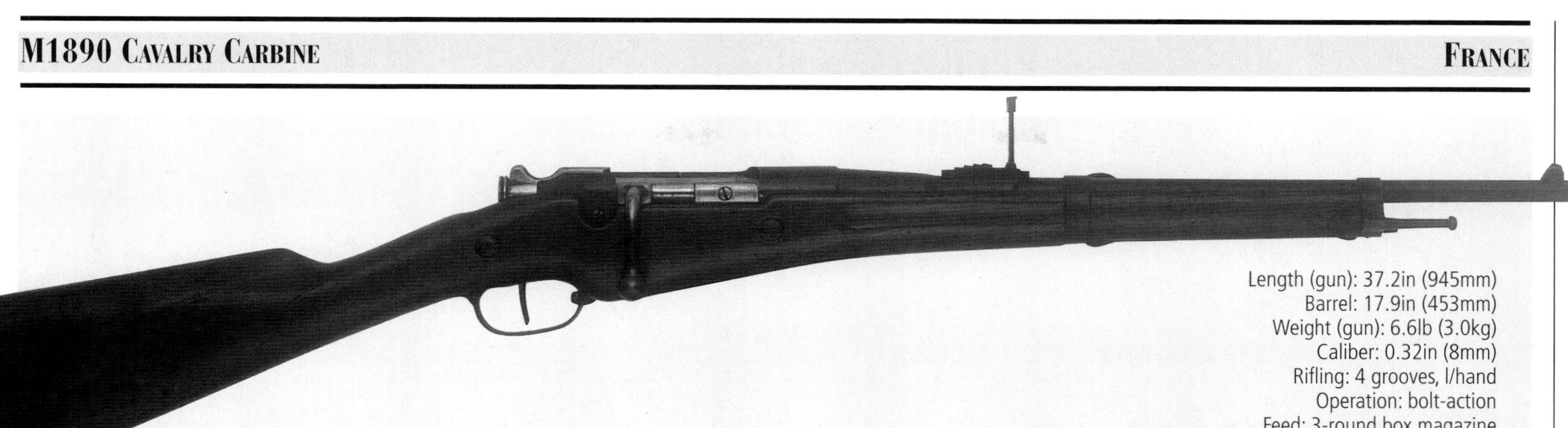

Among the major European powers, France was one of the last to convert to box magazines, sticking, instead, to the rather slow but reliable Lebel with its tube magazine. In 1890, however, the French adopted a carbine developed by Adolphe Berthier, an engineer employed on the Algerian railway. It was intended for mounted troops and had a three-round box magazine, loaded from a single charger, which was pushed out through a hole in the bottom of the magazine when the last round had been removed from it; the entire charger could also be ejected by pressing a catch inside the trigger guard. The stock of the rifle bulged downwards in front of the trigger guard to cover the magazine, giving the weapon a characteristic silhouette. The bolt was similar to that of the Lebel except that it was turned down close to the body, which was considered more convenient for cavalry use. The cartridge was the same as that used in the Lebel. As usual, there were special versions, including the M1890 Cuirassier Carbine, the M1890 Gendarmerie Carbine and the M1892 Artillery Musketoon (the French name for a carbine fitted with a bayonet). In an unusual reversal the carbine was later converted to a rifle, initially for use by colonial troops, but the M1907/15 was a World War I version of the colonial rifle which was rushed into production to replace the aged Lebel as the standard infantry rifle.

Fusil Mas 36 Rifle — France

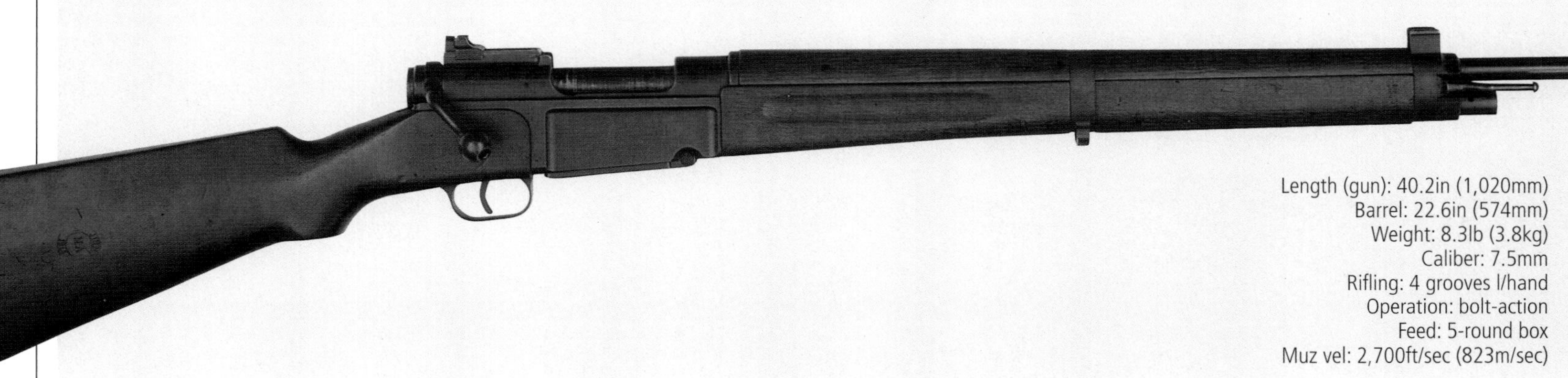

By the end of World War I it was clear to the French that they required a new rifle cartridge. The original Lebel smokeless round of 1886 had been revolutionary in its day but inevitably more modern rounds had been developed since. Its real disadvantage was its shape, since its very wide base and sharp taper made it a very difficult cartridge to use in automatic weapons. Since by 1918 these dominated the battlefield a change was necessary. In 1924 therefore a new rimless cartridge was developed, based fairly closely on the German 7.92mm round. The first priority was to develop suitable automatic weapons (which are described elsewhere in this book) but once this was complete a new rifle was also put into production. MAS 36 was a bolt-action rifle of modified Mauser type, but with the bolt designed to lock into the top of the body behind the magazine. This made it necessary to angle the bolt lever forward so as to be in reach of the firer's hand, the general effect being rather ugly. The magazine was of standard integral box type with a capacity of five rounds and there was no manual safety catch. The rifle had a cruciform bayonet carried in a tube beneath the barrel. It was fixed by withdrawing it and plugging its cylindrical handle into the mouth of the tube where it was held in place by a spring. Small numbers of a modified MAS 36 were later made for airborne troops; they had shorter barrels and folding butts and were designated the MAS 36 CR39.

Bretton Double-barrel ("Baby Bretton") Shotgun — France

This bizarre French, 12-gauge weapon is more of a "garden-gun," but is of interest because of its very unusual action and lightness. The two over-and-under barrels are unlocked by means of the large lever seen on the right of the weapon and are then slid forward, which ejects the spent cartridge cases, although not particularly forcibly. The barrels are secured to each other at the breech and with a detachable twin collar at the muzzle, which, it should be noted, is not fitted in this photograph. There are two triggers, one for each barrel, but there are no sights, not even a bead on the muzzle. The main claim to fame for the "Baby Bretton" is its extraordinary lightness – just 5.1lb (2.3kg) – although since one never gets something for nothing, this results in a rather more powerful recoil than would be found in a heavier weapon.

FA MAS 5.56MM ASSAULT RIFLE — FRANCE

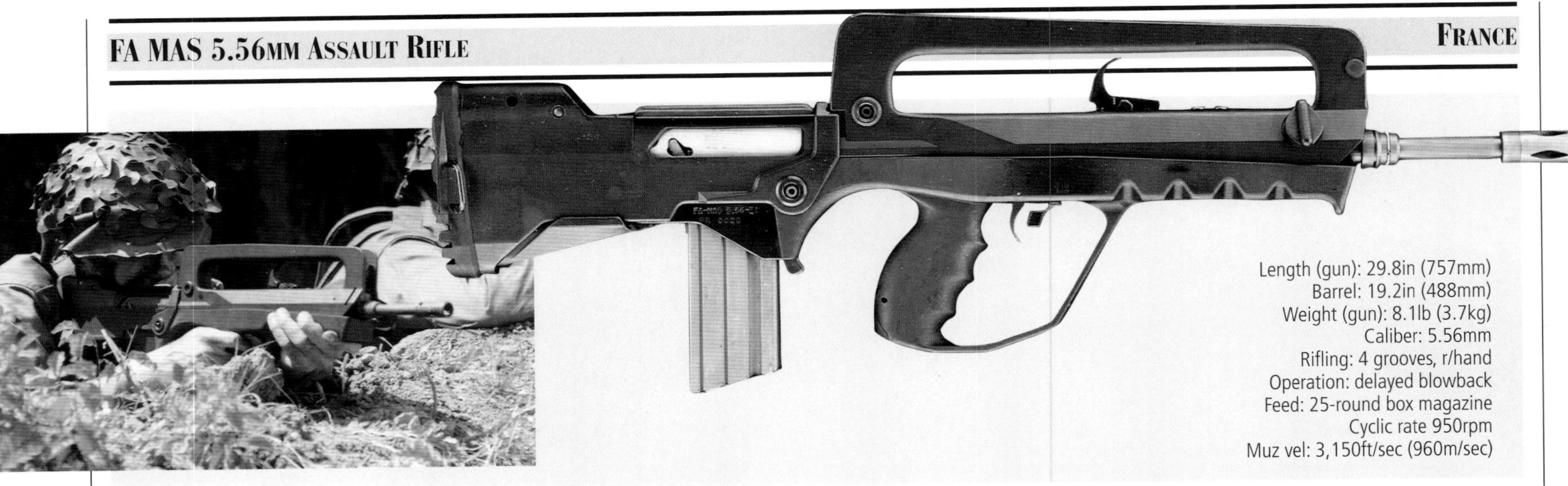

Length (gun): 29.8in (757mm)
Barrel: 19.2in (488mm)
Weight (gun): 8.1lb (3.7kg)
Caliber: 5.56mm
Rifling: 4 grooves, r/hand
Operation: delayed blowback
Feed: 25-round box magazine
Cyclic rate 950rpm
Muz vel: 3,150ft/sec (960m/sec)

The FA MAS (Fusil Automatique, Manufacture d'Armes de St Etienne) was introduced into service in 1980 and has proved to be an effective and generally well-conceived weapon for general service and special forces' use. It fires the 5.56 x 45mm French round from the closed bolt position, using a delayed blowback mechanism that was derived from the French AA-52 general-purpose machine gun. A black plastic lower handguard, pinned to the barrel and receiver, extends to the magazine well and cannot be removed. Because it has a "bullpup" configuration, the trigger mechanism and pistol grip have been mounted to the lower handguard, forward of the magazine housing. Among the features of the FA MAS are the prominent carrying handle (which also houses the sight), left- or right-side ejection, a three-round burst option, and a built-in biped, whose legs fold individually against the receiver when not in use.The G1 version is shown above right. A slightly modified version, FA MAS, is offered for export, and this has a revised trigger guard and is capable of firing the standard 5.56 x 45mm NATO round.

PRUSSIAN MODEL 1849 NEEDLE GUN — GERMANY

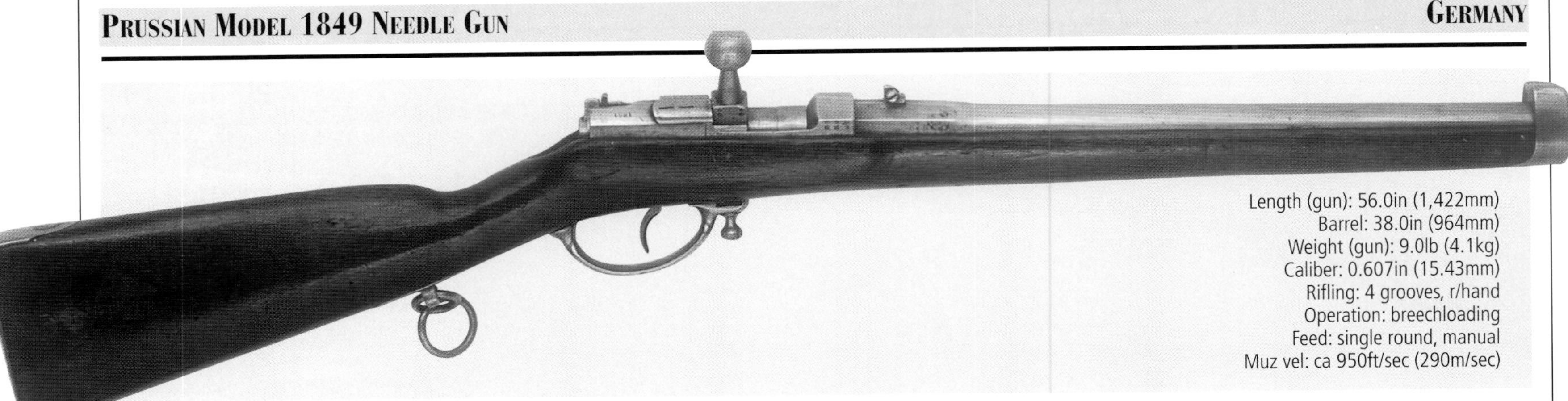

Length (gun): 56.0in (1,422mm)
Barrel: 38.0in (964mm)
Weight (gun): 9.0lb (4.1kg)
Caliber: 0.607in (15.43mm)
Rifling: 4 grooves, r/hand
Operation: breechloading
Feed: single round, manual
Muz vel: ca 950ft/sec (290m/sec)

The famous Prussian needle gun stemmed from a design produced by Johann von Dreyse in 1838, which was approved for production as the Model 1841, although it was not formally issued to the army until 1848. It was a solid weapon and its breech mechanism consisted of an enormous bolt, the lever of which stuck up at an angle of about 10 degrees from the vertical when closed. The bolt contained an inner sleeve with the firing pin and spring, which had to be drawn back by means of a thumb-piece before the breech could be opened, which was done by turning the bolt lever to the vertical and then pulling it back. Having inserted the cartridge the breech was closed and the inner sleeve pushed forward until it was caught by a spring, leaving the striker protruding from the back end.

MODEL 1888 COMMISSION RIFLE — GERMANY

Length (gun): 49.0in (1,245mm)
Barrel: 29.0in (737mm)
Weight (gun): 8.5lb (3.9kg)
Caliber: 0.317in (7.92mm)
Rifling: 4 grooves, r/hand
Operation: breechloading
Feed: 5-round box magazine
Muz vel: 2,035ft/sec (620m/sec)

The introduction of the Lebel rifle into the French Army caused the Germans to have a close look at their own infantry weapons and in 1888 they set up a Small Arms Commission to chart the way ahead. Such committees rarely produce anything useful, but this was the exception and the group designed an effective and thoroughly up-to-date weapon, which although officially designated the Model 1888, became known as the "Commission Rifle." It was part Mauser, firing the 7.92 x 57mm Mauser smokeless round, and part Mannlicher (for example, the box magazine holding five 0.317in/7.92mm rounds. The magazine protruded a short distance below the receiver, but was non-removable. Rounds were issued to the soldier in clips of five, which was inserted into the magazine from the top, but the empty clip fell through the bottom of the magazine after the fifth round had been fired. There was no wooden forward handguard, but the barrel was surrounded by a metal casing, which was claimed to dissipate the heat caused by rapid firing. There were two shortened versions: the M1888 Cavalry Carbine and the M1891 Artillery Carbine. The rifle was used by various armies and was also manufactured in Austria by Steyr. An export model for China, however, the M1907, failed to win an order, although a number were made which were later impressed into German service in 1914.

Gewehr 98 Rifle — Germany

Length (gun): 49.3in (1,250mm)
Barrel: 29.0in (740mm)
Weight: 9.0lb (4.1kg)
Caliber: 7.92mm
Rifling: 4 grooves, r/hand
Operation: bolt-action
Feed: 5-round box
Muz vel: 2,850ft/sec (870m/sec)

The Germans were the first nation to adopt a bolt-action rifle which they did as early as 1848 when their needle-gun officially came into service. Thereafter, the Germans remained constant to this original system which they developed progressively. The first rifle to fire a smokeless round was introduced in 1888 and was of 7.92mm caliber; this was followed in 1898 by the model illustrated made by Mauser. It was a strong and reliable arm with the forward locking lugs made famous by the makers, and a five-round magazine the bottom of which was flush with the stock, and although its straight bolt lever was clumsy and not well adapted to fast fire, this was a minor disadvantage which did nothing to detract from its popularity. In one form or another it was sold to a great number of different countries and there can have been few rifles produced in such large quantities. A considerable number of the earliest ones were bought by the Boers who used them with tremendous effect in their war with the British which broke out a year later, and it served the German Army well in World War I. In 1918 the Germans experimented with a 20-round magazine to prevent the constant entry of mud from the continuous reloading inseparable from the five-round magazine, but this was not a success, chiefly because a spring powerful enough to lift such a column of cartridges made manual operation difficult. The lower photo shows the K98k version with x1.5 Zielfernrohr sight.

Glaser Heeren System Rifle — Germany

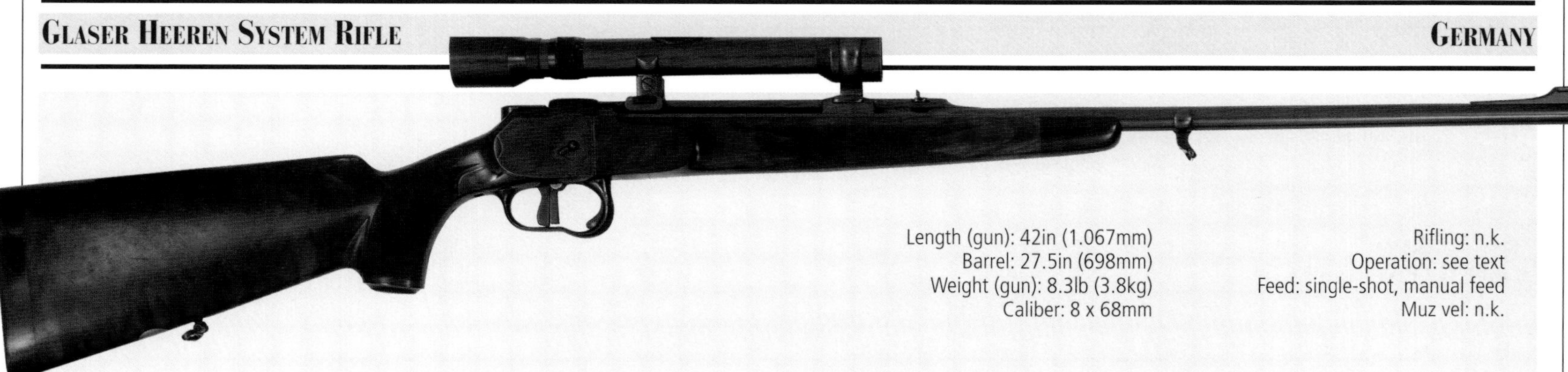

Length (gun): 42in (1.067mm)
Barrel: 27.5in (698mm)
Weight (gun): 8.3lb (3.8kg)
Caliber: 8 x 68mm
Rifling: n.k.
Operation: see text
Feed: single-shot, manual feed
Muz vel: n.k.

The Heeren action was patented in Paris and is still built by Glaser of Zurich, Switzerland, and by various small makers in Ferlach and Kufstein in Austria. The Heeren has an integral set trigger, and the trigger guard, hinged at the rear, forms the operating lever. The lever draws the breech block downwards, recocks the striker and activates the extractor. The release latch is in the bow of the guard. The Heeren is a strong, efficient and extremely compact action. It lacks the Farquarson's (qv) elegance and powerful extractor.

Mauser Tank-Gewehr Model 1918 Anti-tank Rifle — Germany

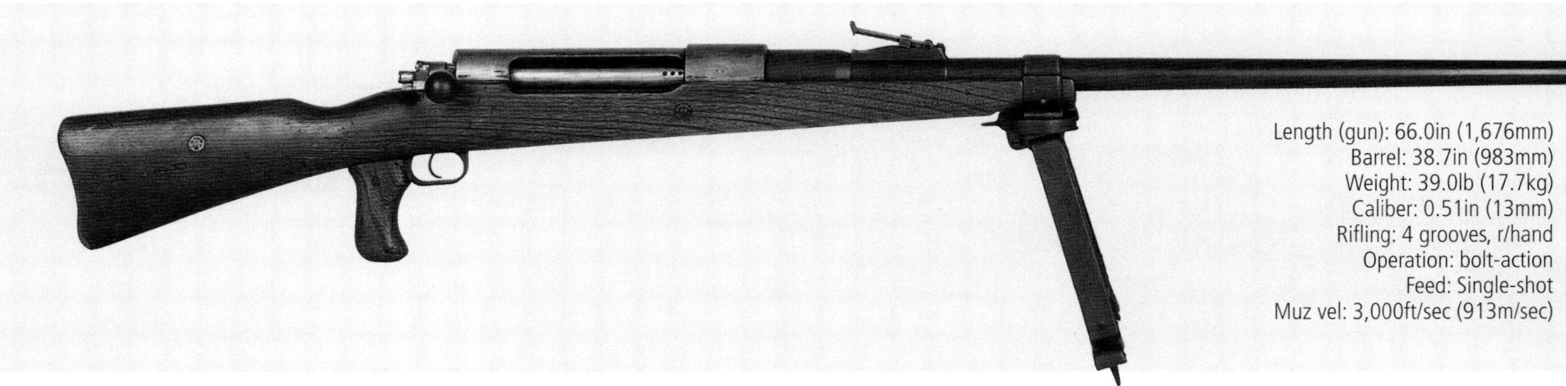

Length (gun): 66.0in (1,676mm)
Barrel: 38.7in (983mm)
Weight: 39.0lb (17.7kg)
Caliber: 0.51in (13mm)
Rifling: 4 grooves, r/hand
Operation: bolt-action
Feed: Single-shot
Muz vel: 3,000ft/sec (913m/sec)

The tank came as a complete surprise to the Germans when first used in battle in 1916. Fortunately for them the early tanks were deployed in only small numbers and for various reasons they were not used again until the spring of 1917, by when there had been time to develop counter-measures. The Germans soon found that high-velocity rifle bullets would often penetrate a tank and from here it was only a matter of time and ingenuity to produce an even more formidable answer in the shape of an anti-tank rifle. This was basically a large-scale version of the standard service rifle, designed to fire a special 0.51in (13mm) caliber round, which had itself to be invented since nothing of that size existed in the German armory. Although of normal bolt-action it was a single-shot weapon, half-stocked and with a simple bipod and an unusually long barrel, and as it was impossible to grasp it with the right hand in the normal way a pistol-grip was added. As was to be expected, this rifle had a fearsome recoil and was not universally popular with the Germans. Nevertheless there were always some hardy souls to fire it, and when grouped in well defended anti-tank localities its effect was considerable. However, it came far too late to have any seriously adverse effect on the bigger and better tanks then in production. It was the forerunner of several similar weapons and is also of particular interest in that its cartridge was closely copied by the Americans in order to provide a suitable round for the 0.50in Browning, which was just coming into production.

GEBRÜDER MERKEL DOUBLE RIFLE

GERMANY

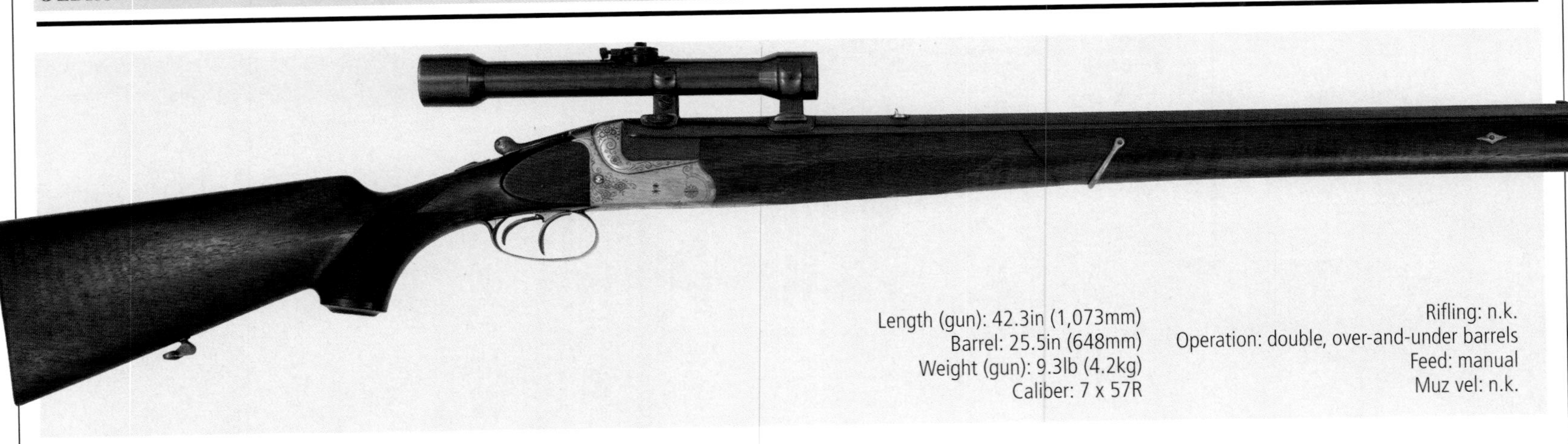

Length (gun): 42.3in (1,073mm)
Barrel: 25.5in (648mm)
Weight (gun): 9.3lb (4.2kg)
Caliber: 7 x 57R

Rifling: n.k.
Operation: double, over-and-under barrels
Feed: manual
Muz vel: n.k.

This over-and-under rifle was made by Gebrüder Merkel in the 1930s. The problem with doubles, whether side-by-side or over-and-under, lies in regulating the two barrels to shoot to the same point of impact. There is also the consideration that the two barrels will converge (if at all) only at the precise range for which they were regulated, and only with the precise load with which they were regulated. The Merkel is chambered for the 7 x 57R Normaliziert, a round specially loaded by Dynamit Nobel and guaranteed for ballistic uniformity. With loads of comparable uniformity, this rifle will pattern shots from alternate barrels into 1.5in (38mm) at 109yd (100m), and will hold excellent groups even further. The rifle is fitted with a telescopic sight made by Carl Zeiss, of Jena, Germany, a 4x scope featuring a 3-post reticle, and is fitted to the rifle by means of the integral claw mounts, clearly visible in the picture. The full-length fore-end is an unusual feature, giving the Merkel a highly distinctive appearance. It should be noted that over-and-under weapons have to hinge over a much greater arc in order that the lower barrel will clear the standing breech, and then be closed again over the same arc. Also, the top chamber is high enough over the hinge to put a great strain on the lower lock-up, which, in effect, requires an extended rib to lock into the end of the standing breech.

HALGER NO 7 RIFLE

GERMANY

Length (gun): 47.8in (1,213mm)
Barrel: 26.3in (667mm)
Weight (gun): 7.8lb (3.6kg)
Caliber: 0.244in HV Magnum

Rifling: n.k.
Operation: bolt-action
Feed: 5-round magazine
Muz vel: see text

The German rifle company named Halger was run by the famous designer Harold Gerlich and there are two theories about the derivation of the name, both suggesting that it was a combination of the first three letters of two names. One of these theories is that it took the names of the two original business partners, Halbe and Gerlich (who were brothers-in-law); the other that it was derived from Gerlich's own name, using the first three letters of the diminutive of Harold (Hal) with those of his surname. Gerlich was born in the United States of German parents and was working in London, England, when World War I broke out, so he went to Germany to enlist in the Imperial Army, but was turned down as being a "foreigner." Despite this he returned to England and in the early 1930s was working at Woolwich Arsenal. He had a fascination with ever higher muzzle velocities and designed the 0.224in HV Magnum round, with which he claimed to achieve 3,700ft/sec (1,128m/sec) and the 0.280 Magnum, for which he claimed 3,900ft/sec (1,189m/sec). As Halger only made about 150 rifles, however, and not a single loaded cartridge survives, these claims are impossible to substantiate. The rifle shown is somewhat crude, having a rough trigger, non-adjustable iron sights and no provision for mounting a scope. It was Halger's intention that it would sell in the USA for approximately $90, but the importer offered it at over $1,000 and, not surprisingly, it failed to find many buyers.

GEWEHR 41 (W) RIFLE

GERMANY

Length (gun): 44.5in (1,130mm)
Barrel: 21.5in (546mm)
Weight: 11.0lb (5.0kg)
Caliber: 7.92mm

Rifling: 4 grooves, r/hand
Operation: gas
Feed: 10-round box
Muz vel: 2,550ft/sec (776m/sec)

The Germans were among the pioneers of self-loading rifles and had a complete regiment armed with weapons of this type as early as 1901. This experiment was not followed up, principally because the rifle then used was too heavy for an individual weapon. A few weapons of this type were used in World War I, but the main pre-occupation in 1914–18 was with a great volume of fire from somewhat heavier automatic weapons, so again no progress was made. It was not therefore until the appearance of the Russian Tokarev self-loader just before World War II that any real attention was paid to the subject and by 1941 two separate models were undergoing tests. The first was the Gewehr 41 (Mauser) which incorporated a bolt similar to that of the manually operated rifle; it was never a success and was soon abandoned. The second was the Gewehr 41 (Walther), an example of which is shown here, which was a good deal more successful. It incorporated a muzzle cap which deflected part of the gases back on to an annular piston that worked a rod placed above the barrel, its return spring however being below it. This piston rod worked the bolt and the concept was reasonably satisfactory, although the arm had certain defects notably its weight and balance, together with a serious tendency to foul very badly round the muzzle cap. It was manufactured in some quantity and issued chiefly to units on the Russian Front.

Fallschirmjägergewehr 42 Rifle — Germany

Length (gun): 37.0in (940mm)
Barrel: 20.0in (508mm)
Weight: 9.9lb (4.5kg)
Caliber: 7.92mm
Rifling: 4 grooves, r/hand
Operation: gas
Feed: 20-round box
Cyclic rate: 750rpm
Muz vel: 2,500ft/sec (762m/sec)

The Fallschirmjägergewehr 42 (Paratroop Rifle, Model 1942) was one of the earliest assault rifles, being introduced in 1942. Its main disadvantage was that, although the Germans had gained some success with intermediate cartridges, this particular arm fired the full-sized 7.92 × 57mm rifle round which was really too powerful for it. In spite of this it proved to be a remarkably good weapon to the limited number of troops armed with it, most of whom were parachutists. It was capable of single rounds or bursts. When bursts were employed the FG 42 fired from an open bolt – that is, there was no round in the chamber until the bolt drove one in and fired it in the same movement; the reason for this was that the chamber tended to get sufficiently hot to fire a cartridge left in it even for a very short time. The gun was supplied with either a wooden stock or stamped metal stock (as in the photograph, which also shows a ZFG 42 telescope sight, whereas standard sights were, front, barleycorn, and, rear, aperture). It would take a bayonet and was equipped with a light bipod. Unfortunately it was expensive to make and, being something of a specialist weapon for paratroops, its use declined during the war.

Maschinenpistole MP 44 Rifle — Germany

Length (gun): 37.0in (940mm)
Barrel: 16.5in (420mm)
Weight: 11.3lb (5.1kg)
Caliber: 7.92mm
Rifling: 4 grooves, r/hand
Operation: gas
Feed: 30-round box
Cyclic rate: 500rpm
Muz vel: 2,125ft/sec (647m/sec)

The experience of World War I led the Germans to the opinion that in the future the infantryman should have a lighter weapon than the standard rifle. Work on this project started before World War II and by 1942 the Germans had developed a new 7.92 "Kurz" (short) round for which two new weapons were developed, one by Haenel, the other by Walther, both being described as machine carbines. The Haenel version was modified by Schmeisser in 1943 in the light of actual combat experience, after which it became the MP 43(H), the Walther alternative being dropped at the same time. The new weapon, which was gas-operated through a piston working in a gas cylinder above the barrel, was an immediate success and by the end of 1943 the German Army had received 14,000 of them. The long-term idea seems to have been to make the MP 43 a universal weapon at squad or section level, so doing away with rifles, submachine guns and light machine guns in favor of the new arm. Perhaps fortunately, production declined very rapidly after the first few months of 1944 and so the new concept was never realized. There were some variations to the standard type, notably an MP 43(1) which had a fixture allowing it to fire grenades, but no really significant changes. In 1944 the designation was changed to MP 44, apparently to mark the change in year since no other reason was ever offered, and by the end of the same year the weapon had been given the additional title of "Sturm-Gewehr," (Assault Rifle). It is said that the expression was coined by Hitler himself; whether this is true or not it was a very apt description and one which has been used ever since. The MP 44 had a profound effect on the development of infantry firearms and the Russians in particular were quick to see the advantages of this new type of arm, and very soon developed their own version in the shape of the AK-47.

WALTHER KK MATCH GX1 — GERMANY

The UIT Free Rifle is a very sophisticated piece of engineering, even more so than the Bench Rest rifle, since, because it is fired from the standing position, a great deal of mechanical ingenuity has gone into compensating for the lack of a solid rest. A Free Rifle is so called because it is relatively free of restriction. It must not have an optical sight, the pistol grip may not contact the sling, weight must not exceed 17.6lb (8kg), butthooks must be no longer than 6in (153mm), and the forward palm rest must not extend more than 7.9in (200mm) below the centerline of the barrel. The picture shows the Walther KK Match GX1, a top quality UIT Free Rifle, which is made of steel, with a one-piece walnut stock. It should be noted, however, that this is the bare rifle; for competition it would have a number of accessories. These would include a long armpit prong extending from the butt plate, a black elastic tape some 2in (51mm) wide along the complete length of the barrel (to break heatwaves), an antenna-like prong extending forward from the fore-end tip with adjustable weights on it, a spade-handle palm rest, and a leather sling to attach the rifle firmly to the shooter. KK in the title stands for Klein Kaliber (small caliber).

WALTHER UIT BV UNIVERSAL — GERMANY

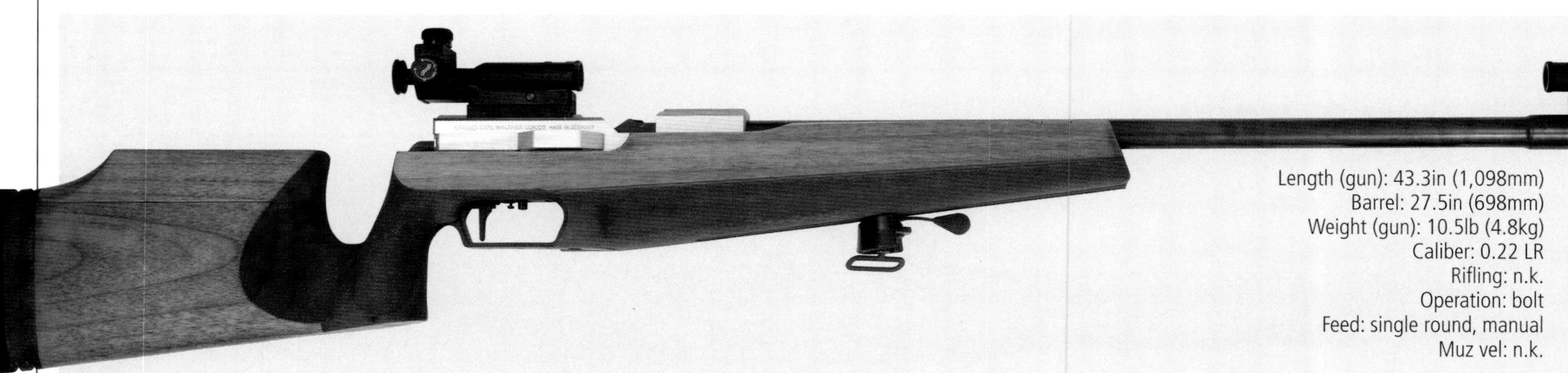

This rifle is made by the famous German firm of Walther, of Ulm an der Donau. The Standard Rifle was introduced in the 1960s in an effort to simplify the Free Rifle designs which had become somewhat outlandish. Thus, the Standard Rifle rules banned buttplate extensions, external adjustable weights, thumbhole stocks, adjustable palm-rests and cheek pieces, and forward hand rests. In addition, the maximum weight was lowered to 11lb (5kg). The weapon shown here was built to Standard Rifle configuration, although the cheek piece and buttplate are capable of considerable adjustment; once set, however, they must be locked in place for the remainder of that particular competition. In the designation, "BV" stands for Blockverschluss and "E" for the electric trigger system, which did not prove very popular.

HECKLER & KOCH HK 33 RIFLE — GERMANY

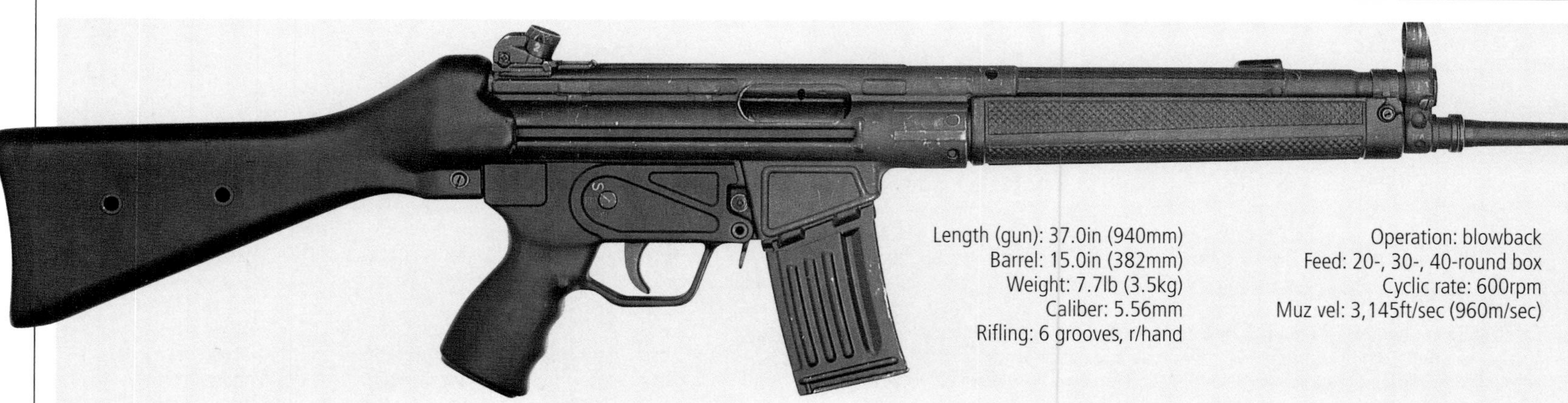

This weapon had its origins in a German rifle designed in World War II, and was largely redesigned by a number of German designers and engineers working in Spain in the late 1940s. The resulting weapon was the Spanish CETME (qv). When the German Army was reformed in the 1950s Heckler & Koch, which had been involved with CETME, developed the design to produce a rifle known as the Gewehr 3 (G3) which was adopted by the West German and many other armies. The G3 was of somewhat unusual design in that it worked not on gas but on delayed blowback. The breech was never fully locked in the strict sense of the word; it was equipped with rollers which the forward movement of the firing pin forced outwards into the recesses in the receiver. The shape of these recesses and their relationship to the rollers was such that the breech was held closed until the pressure dropped to a safe level when the rollers were forced out of the recesses. The residual gas pressure in the chamber blew the empty case backwards, taking the bolt with it and compressing the return spring which caused the cycle to be repeated. This method proved to be successful although the use of a full-sized rifle cartridge does often cause problems in a breech of this nature. The main difficulty is that the bolt comes back fairly fast, with no preliminary turning motion to start the case, and this can cause problems of extraction. The problem was dealt with by fluting the chamber and by ensuring that the quality of brass used in the case was sufficient to withstand the initial jerk without having its base torn off. The HK 33 was simply a logical development of the G3, to which it bears a strong resemblance both externally and mechanically. The chief, and important difference is that the HK 33 was designed to fire the 5.56mm round giving good performance at reasonable ranges and more accurate automatic fire than was possible with the more powerful 7.62mm cartridge.

Heckler & Koch G3 7.62mm Rifle — Germany

Length (gun): 40.2in (1,021mm)
Barrel: 17.7in (450mm)
Weight (gun): 9.7lb (4.4kg)
Caliber: 7.62mm

Rifling: 4 grooves, r/hand
Operation: delayed blowback
Feed: 20-round box magazine
Muz vel: 2,625ft/sec (800m/sec)

After World War II a group of German weapons designers set themselves up in Spain where they worked for CETME, developing a new rifle for the Spanish Army. This worked on the roller-delayed blowback system and was subsequently used as the basis for a new, German rifle for the recently re-established West German Army. This weapon, the G3, was then the basis for every German rifle design until the G36, which appeared in the mid-1990s. The G3 design (shown in bottom photo with 1.57in/40mm grenade launcher) subsequently went through a number of developments. The G3A1 was identical to the original, except that it had a folding butt, while the G3A2 introduced a free-floating barrel, and the great majority of G3s were modified to this standard. The G3A3, fielded in 1964, had a new flash suppressor and drum rear sight, while the butt and forward handgrip were made of plastic instead of wood. The G3A4 was a G3A3 with a retracting butt. Several countries undertook licensed production of the G3A3, including Turkey (G3A7) and Iran (G3A6). Other Heckler & Koch projects included the HK32A2, which was a G3A2 rechambered to take the Russian 7.62 x 39mm round, the HK32A3, which was an HK32A2 with a retracting butt, and the HK32KA1, a carbine with a short barrel and retracting butt; none of these ever went into production.

Heckler & Koch G3SG/1 7.62mm Sniper Rifle — Germany

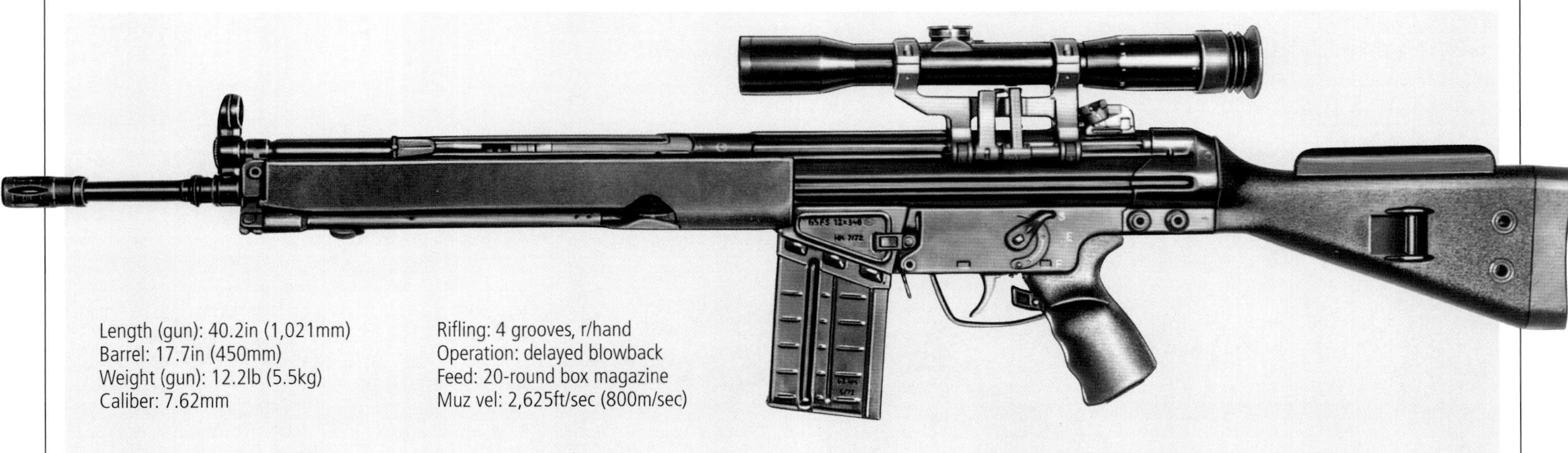

Length (gun): 40.2in (1,021mm)
Barrel: 17.7in (450mm)
Weight (gun): 12.2lb (5.5kg)
Caliber: 7.62mm

Rifling: 4 grooves, r/hand
Operation: delayed blowback
Feed: 20-round box magazine
Muz vel: 2,625ft/sec (800m/sec)

The Heckler & Koch G3 rifle (qv) replaced the FN FAL in the West German Army from 1959 onwards. The first sniper version was the G3A3ZF, introduced in 1964, which was simply a G3 with a telescopic sight. A more substantial modification came with the G3SG/1 of 1973, in which specially selected specimens of the G3A3 version were converted for use as sniper rifles. This version retains the great majority of the features of the G3, but has a new trigger, butt-stock and bipod. A standard feature of the rifle, which enhances accuracy, is the roller-delayed, blowback action, which does not require any gas to be bled off, nor does it require a piston moving backwards and forwards. Thus, since there are no attachments to the barrel, there is nothing to interfere with its harmonic variable and thus its accuracy. The G3SG/1 retains the G3's iron sights, but also has a mounting rail for a Zeiss 1.5-6x scope. There is a modified trigger which features a "set" lever behind the trigger itself, the use of which reduces the pull to 2.8lb (1.3kg). Also, the butt-stock is fitted with a detachable comb which allows for up to 1in (25.4mm) of variation for proper eye-to-scope orientation. There is also a detachable cheek rest.

BLASER "ULTIMATE" SR830 RIFLE — GERMANY

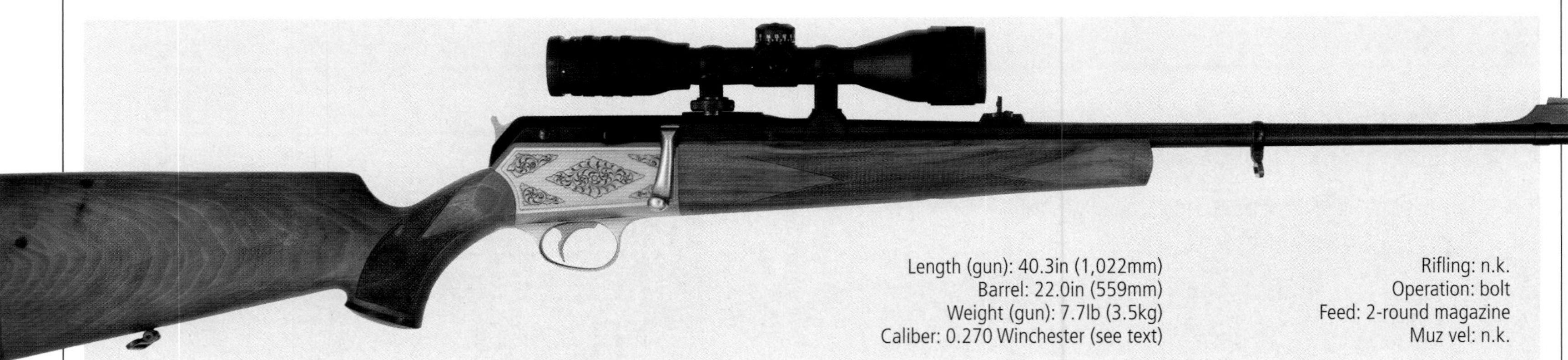

Length (gun): 40.3in (1,022mm)
Barrel: 22.0in (559mm)
Weight (gun): 7.7lb (3.5kg)
Caliber: 0.270 Winchester (see text)
Rifling: n.k.
Operation: bolt
Feed: 2-round magazine
Muz vel: n.k.

The Blaser "Ultimate" was designed by Horst Blaser of Isny, Bavaria, and entered the market in 1984. It incorporated some novel and sensible ideas in the search for a "take-down" rifle (ie, one that can be dismantled into its major components) that worked. Mauser re-entered this field some 30 years ago with their Model 66, which had no receiver in the traditional sense, but rather a set of rails that carried a bolthead mounted on a pistol-like slide. The bolthead locked into the barrel extension and all the stress of the discharge was taken there. The barrel indexed on a brass plate in the fore-end channel, which worked poorly because fore-end timber is dimensionally unstable. Recoil transfer to the stock was another problem, which took several redesigns to solve. Blaser built shrewdly on Mauser's experience, using a two-piece stock, a bolt-bearing slide mounted on an aluminum receiver, and with the barrel mounted on a forward extension of the receiver. It seems to work: the gun comes apart in a moment, the barrels interchange with a hexagonal (Allen) screw, and are said to return to zero and shoot sub-minute of angle (MoA) groups. Because the barrels are so easy to change, different calibers can also be used, with 10 being offered, ranging from 0.22-250 to 0.375 Holland & Holland Magnum. Two boltheads suit two caliber families: these are the 0.30-06 and 0.375 H&H.

HECKLER & KOCH PSG-1 7.62MM SNIPER RIFLE — GERMANY

Length (gun): 47.6in (1,208mm)
Barrel: 25.6in (650mm)
Weight (gun): 17.0lb (8.1kg)
Caliber: 7.62mm
Rifling: 4 grooves, r/hand, polygonal
Operation: delayed blowback
Feed: 5- or 20-round box magazine
Muz vel: 2,723ft/sec (830m/sec)

Like many other modern sniper rifles, the Präzisionsschutzengewehr-1 (High-precision Marksman's Rifle-1) was developed in the early 1980s to meet the renewed military and police requirement for a long-range and very accurate weapon. The PSG-1 uses Heckler & Koch's roller-locked bolt system and fires semi-automatic, single-shots only. Its design was based on that of the G3 military assault rifle (qv), but it is fitted with a polygonally bored, heavy, free-floating barrel and the trigger, fitted with an adjustable trigger shoe, is normally set to break at 3.3lb (1.5kg). A special, low-noise, bolt-closing device is fitted and the stock has an adjustable comb and butt-pad that allow fitting to individual shooters. A bipod attaches directly to the stock. The PSG-1 is normally fitted with the Hensoldt 6 x 42 scope with LED-enhanced manual reticle. The scope-mounted activator produces a helpful red dot for approximately 30 seconds, plenty of time to get off that critical shot. Windage and elevation adjustments are by moving base, six settings from 110 to 655yd (100 to 600m), and there is a fine adjustment facility to compensate for any mounting offset angle.

M1/M2 GEPARD 12.7MM ANTI-MATERIEL RIFLE — HUNGARY

Length (gun): 60.2in (1,530mm)
Barrel: 43.4in (1,100mm)
Weight (gun): 26.5lb (12.0kg)
Caliber: 12.7mm
Rifling: 8 grooves, r/hand
Operation: long-recoil, semi-automatic
Feed: 5- or 10-round box magazine
Muz vel: 2,756ft/sec (840m/sec)

The Hungarian firm, Technika, produced a series of heavy rifles in the 1980s and 1990s, with the type name Gepard. The first in the series, the Gepard M1, is a bolt-action, single-shot weapon firing the Russian 12.7 x 108mm DshK round and was described as a sniper rifle, it being claimed that any adequately-trained shot could achieve a 300mm group at 600m range. Firing an AP-T (armor-piercing - tracer) round it could penetrate 0.6in (15mm) of homogenous armor at a range of 655yd (600m), enabling it to pass through most cover in rural or urban environments. The pistol grip doubles as the bolt handle and to reload the weapon this is rotated in an anti-clockwise direction and then pulled to the rear, ejecting the spent cartridge; a new cartridge is then inserted, the bolt closed, the hammer cocked (this requires a separate action), and the weapon aimed and fired. The Gepard M1A1 is essentially the same, but includes a frame, which can be used either to carry the weapon or as a firing rest. The Gepard M2 (see specifications) was developed from the M1 and is intended for the anti-materiel role, but has an entirely different, semi-automatic action, using a positive locking, long-recoil system, which is fed from either a 5- or 10-round box magazine. The M2 has a cylindrical receiver and a cylindrical cradle which extends almost to the muzzle, together with a built-in bipod and a short butt. The M2A1 is a shortened version intended for use by airborne troops, the barrel being only 32.7in (830mm) long. The makers have said that both the M1/M1A1 and M2/M2A1 (shown in lower photo) could easily be converted to take the 12.7 x 99mm (0.50in Browning) round, but, so far as is known, this has never been implemented. A Gepard M3 (shown in upper photo), chambered for the 14.5 x 114mm Russian round, is under development.

Manton Mauser 98 — India

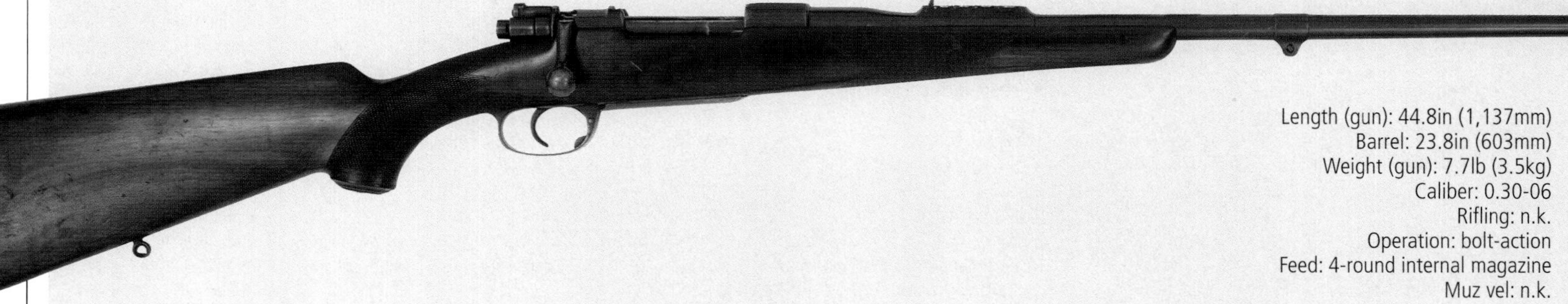

Length (gun): 44.8in (1,137mm)
Barrel: 23.8in (603mm)
Weight (gun): 7.7lb (3.5kg)
Caliber: 0.30-06
Rifling: n.k.
Operation: bolt-action
Feed: 4-round internal magazine
Muz vel: n.k.

The name of Manton is famous in shooting circles. Joseph Manton was at first apprenticed to his older brother, John, but set up his own company in 1792 and became the most celebrated gun-maker of his time. A designer of genius and a kindly man, he defined the form of the classic English shotgun, which remains essentially unchanged to this day. In his time, a Manton gun cost £73.10s, the equivalent of £2,750 (ca $4,400) at today's prices, a sum that was willingly paid by the rich sportsmen of the time. Manton's gun-making genius was not, however, matched by his business acumen; he went to debtor's prison twice and died poor. In 1825, however, he sent his son, Frederick, to Calcutta, where he founded the Indian branch of the business, which flourished under the patronage of successive British viceroys. The gun shown was made by Manton in India from parts supplied by Mauser, whose crest appears on the receiver ring. It has the standard Mauser Model 98 bolt-action, with a front-locking turnbolt and two lugs. It cocks on opening and has a clip guide on the receiver bridge.

Galil 7.62 /5.56mm ARM Assault Rifle — Israel

Length (gun): 38.6in (979mm)
Barrel: 18.1in (460mm)
Weight (gun): 9.6lb (4.4kg)
Caliber: 5.56mm
Rifling: 6 grooves, r/hand
Operation: gas
Feed: 35- or 50-round box magazine
Cyclic rate: 700rpm
Muz vel: 3,116ft/sec (950m/sec)

Israel's Galil 7.62mm assault rifle, first fielded in 1973, has a rich, battle-tested heritage. The gas and rotating bolt system used is actually that of the Russian AK-47 Kalashnikov (qv), while the firing mechanism comes from the US M1 Garand (qv), but credit for the weapon's overall design goes to an Israeli army officer, Uziel Gal. The weapon operates using a rotating bolt gas system and, with the exception of the stamped steel breech cover, the Galil is fully machined. The foregrip is wood, lined with Dural, and has ample clearance around the barrel for heat dissipation. When extended the butt-stock has a positive latching system which prevents wobble by wedging the hinge end's tapered latching lugs into corresponding slots. The ambidextrous safety switch on the left side is a small lever, but its reciprocal right side member also acts as an ejection port cover. There is a bipod, which folds and rotates into a slot ion the underside of the foregrip. The Galil ARM originally appeared in 1973 as a 7.62mm (lower photo) weapon, firing the NATO standard round, in three versions with only minor differences between them: assault rifle/light machine gun (as described above); assault rifle (basically the ARM, but minus the bipod); and the SAR (short assault rifle), which had a shorter barrel (15.8in/400mm). This series was followed by the 5.56mm weapon (see top photo and specifications), which basically was a scaled-down version of the 7.62mm weapon and came in the same three versions: assault rifle/light machine gun; assault rifle; and short assault rifle. Apart from size, the only noticeable difference between the two is that the 7.62mm weapon has a straight magazine, while in the 5.56mm the magazine is curved. There is also a sniper version of the 7.62mm rifle and a "micro" version of the 5.56mm version for special forces.

MANNLICHER-CARCANO CARBINE M1891

ITALY

Length (gun): 36.2in (920mm)
Barrel: 17.1in (444mm)
Weight: 6.6lb (3kg)
Caliber: 6.5mm
Rifling: 4 grooves, r/hand
Operation: bolt-action
Feed: 6-round magazine
Muz vel: 2,300ft/sec (701m/sec)

The Model 91 weapons were the first of a series developed for the Italian Army towards the end of the 19th Century. In spite of the word "Mannlicher" in its official title, it was primarily of Mauser design, the only feature of Mannlicher origin being the six-round clip with which the weapons were loaded. They were developed at Turin by S. Carcano, a designer at the Italian Government Arsenal; the name of General Parravicino, President of the Italian Small Arms Committee, is also associated with them. The first of the series was a full-length infantry rifle, but this was closely followed by the weapon illustrated, the Model 91 cavalry carbine which actually went into service in 1893. In those days, of course, the cavalry still rode horses and therefore needed a short, handy weapon which could be carried either slung across their backs or in a scabbard or bucket on the saddle. Most cavalry of that time deluded themselves as to the superiority of the sword and professed to regard firearms as of little importance but the pretence was wearing thin. One feature of the Model 91 carbine is its folding bayonet which indicates that even then the Italian cavalry understood that it might have to act as mounted infantry and fight on foot. One interesting feature of these early models, which were otherwise undistinguished, was that their rifling was of the type known as progressive twist, i.e. the degree of twist increased progressively towards the muzzle. This was a system originally experimented with by the English inventor, Metford, but soon abandoned as being not worth the increased difficulties of manufacture.

CEI-RIGOTTI AUTOMATIC RIFLE

ITALY

Length (gun): 39.4in (1,000mm)
Barrel: 19.0in (483mm)
Weight: 9.6lb (4.3kg)
Caliber: 6.5mm
Rifling: 4 grooves, r/hand
Operation: gas
Feed: 25-round box
Cyclic rate: up to 900rpm
Muz vel: 2,400ft/sec (730m/sec)

Captain Cei-Rigotti, an officer in the Italian Army, carried out experiments with gas-operated automatic rifles and in 1895 he demonstrated one to his Divisional Commander, the Prince of Naples. It was not until 1900 that his efforts were made public in a Roman newspaper, which included a reference to the use of mounted infantry in the war in South Africa. It was probably this which drew British attention to the new weapon and specimens were obtained and a series of tests carried out by both Army and Navy experts. The rifle worked by a short-stroke piston from the barrel to a rod connected to the bolt, this rod and the cocking handle at its rear being clearly visible in the photograph, and was designed to fire both single shots and bursts. Although some success was achieved the tests were generally unfavorable, both authorities commenting on the difficulties of ejection and the high rate of misfires. It was also reported that the bolt came so far to the rear in operation that accurate fire was impossible and some adverse comment was made on the general quality of the workmanship. One hundred years later, however, it can be seen that the rifle had great potential and many of its features have been copied.

MANNLICHER-CARCANO CARBINE MODEL M1938

ITALY

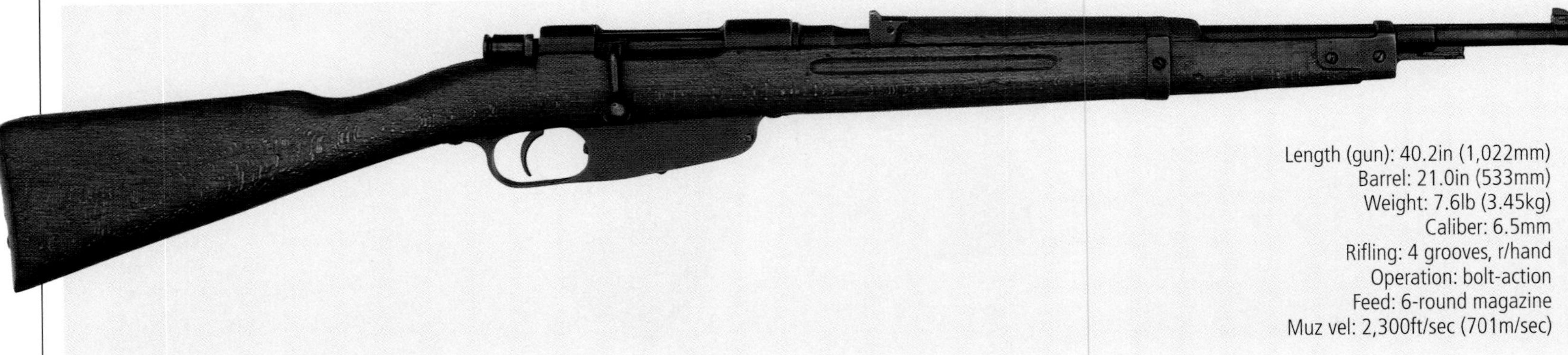

Length (gun): 40.2in (1,022mm)
Barrel: 21.0in (533mm)
Weight: 7.6lb (3.45kg)
Caliber: 6.5mm
Rifling: 4 grooves, r/hand
Operation: bolt-action
Feed: 6-round magazine
Muz vel: 2,300ft/sec (701m/sec)

In the course of their Abyssinian campaign of 1936–38 the Italians were somewhat disconcerted to find that their 6.5mm cartridge lacked stopping power. In 1938 therefore they provisionally introduced a 7.35mm round and developed a modified version of their earlier Model 91 to fire it. This new project was short-lived however because when the Italians entered World War II in 1940 they were naturally reluctant to embark at the same time on a major change of caliber, so they reverted to their 6.5mm round. There are thus two versions of the Model 1938 carbine, which except for caliber are virtually indistinguishable, the one illustrated being an example of the later reversion to the small caliber. One of its unusual features was the abandonment of the tangent backsight in favor of a fixed one, set at 328yd (300mm). This Model 1938 carbine is of considerable interest as being of the type used to assassinate President Kennedy in November 1963. The particular weapon was an item of Italian war surplus fitted with a cheap Japanese telescope and purchased by mail order for a few dollars. It seems to have been an odd choice for that dreadful deed, since the Carcano has no great reputation for accuracy and although its bolt works smoothly enough, the rate of fire would have been slowed down by the telescope. It is notoriously difficult to shoot rapidly using such a sight, particularly on a carbine with a good deal of recoil. There has, therefore, been speculation as to whether the three shots known to have been fired could have come from a single weapon of this type.

Beretta Model 303 Shotgun — Italy

Length (gun): 45.3in (1,150mm)
Barrel: 28.0in (711mm)
Weight (gun): 7.3lb (3.3kg)
Caliber: 12-gauge
Rifling: none
Operation: semi-automatic, gas-operated
Feed: 4-round tubular magazine
Muz vel: n.k.

The Beretta Model 303 is a gas-operated, self-loading shotgun, which uses the gases generated by the firing of the cartridge to drive the action. The gases are tapped off through a vent in the lower part of the barrel, whence they impinge on the head of the piston, which is connected by a rod to the action. When the gases drive the piston-rod backwards, the action is driven to the rear, ejecting the spent cartridge case on its way, and cocking the trigger. The action is then stopped by the buffer, with the return spring at maximum compression, at which point the return spring rod starts to drive the action forwards again, picking up the new cartridge and driving it into the breech. The operation is semi-automatic – that is to say, the shooter must pull the trigger to fire each round; there is no question of firing bursts! The four rounds are contained in a tubular magazine which is mounted under the barrel. The trigger and safety on the Beretta Model 303 are gold-plated, which seems a slightly unnecessary refinement. The foresight blade is coated with "day-glo," but there is no rear sight. The Beretta 303 is normally supplied in 12-gauge (as shown here), but a 20-gauge version is also available.

Fabricca Nazionale Combination Gun — Italy

Length (gun): 41.0in (1,041mm)
Barrel: 24.5in (622mm)
Weight (gun): 6.2lb (2.8kg)
Caliber: see text
Rifling: none
Operation: hinged barrel, break-open, over-and-under
Feed: manual
Muz vel: n.k.

The Fabricca Nazionale Combination Gun has two up-and-over barrels of different caliber, the upper being 0.410in gauge and the lower 0.22in LR. It is much used by trappers, farmers, ornithologists and those who might need an easily packed survival gun. The thumb lever releases the barrels to pivot downwards, while the over-sized hinge allows the gun to be folded up on itself, thus making for easy stowage. The chambering makes the gun ideal for shooting rats and most garden pests, although it may be a little light for larger species such as crows or foxes.

Kentucky Flintlock Rifle (Reproduction) — Italy

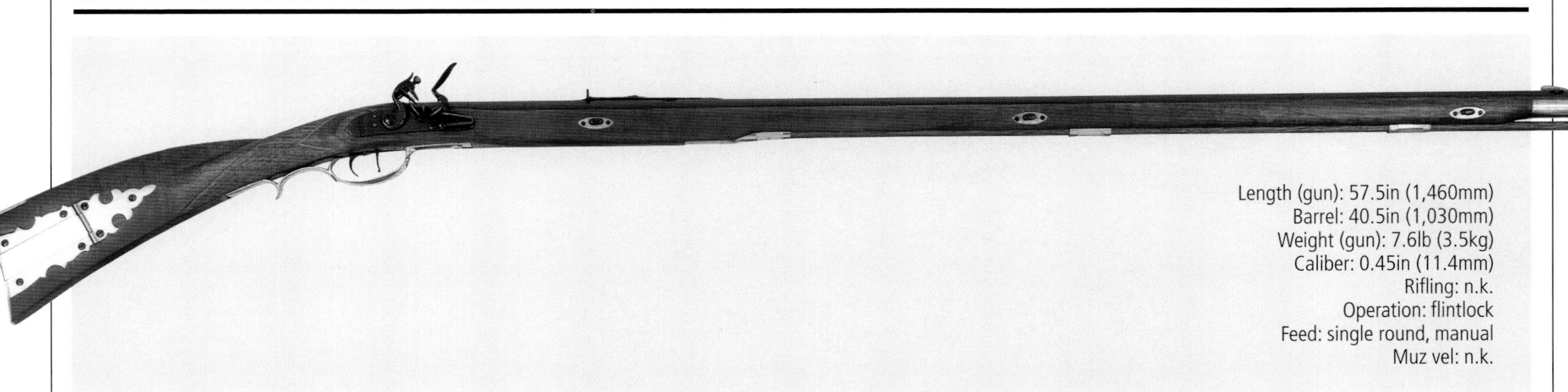

Length (gun): 57.5in (1,460mm)
Barrel: 40.5in (1,030mm)
Weight (gun): 7.6lb (3.5kg)
Caliber: 0.45in (11.4mm)
Rifling: n.k.
Operation: flintlock
Feed: single round, manual
Muz vel: n.k.

Many copies of early American firearms are made in Europe to satisfy the wants of collectors who cannot afford a rare and increasingly expensive original, although, according to experts, the quality of such reproductions varies widely. This particular example, made in Italy by the Palmetto Armory, is a replica of a type of musket having the generic title "Kentucky rifle" which, despite its name, actually originated in the New England states. Rifles of this type featured an unusually long barrel of very small bore, typically between 0.400in (10.2mm) and 0.450in (11.4mm) and were reputed to be extremely accurate, as well as economical in their use of powder and lead. Their range was, however, somewhat limited, probably of the order of 80yd (73m), although this would have been perfectly adequate for the purpose for which they were intended – shooting game for the pot at close range in the New England forests.

Beretta Special Trap Model 682 — Italy

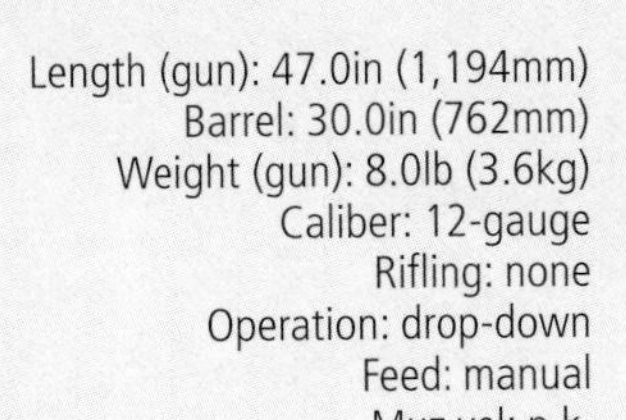

Length (gun): 47.0in (1,194mm)
Barrel: 30.0in (762mm)
Weight (gun): 8.0lb (3.6kg)
Caliber: 12-gauge
Rifling: none
Operation: drop-down
Feed: manual
Muz vel: n.k.

Trap shooting, or, as it was called in Britain, "down-the-line" shooting is the oldest form of competitive clay shooting, both in Britain and the USA. It evolved directly from the 19th Century sport of putting a live, specially bred, pigeon under an old top hat, which was then pulled away by a cord, thus releasing the bird. The gun (there was only one shooter at a time) then fired at the bird, which was either "killed" or "lost." By the 1890s the sport had spread over most of Europe and special guns were being designed and made for it. These were often known as "pigeon guns" and were generally heavier than game guns, because the shot loads allowed for trap shooting were usually 1.25oz (35.5g) and the extra weight of the gun counteracted the extra recoil produced by such loads. When the shooting of live pigeons from traps was banned in both Great Britain and the United States it gave a great boost to the sport of clay-pigeon shooting which had, in fact, begun in the 1880s. This very modern Beretta trap-shooting gun is an over-and-under weapon, specifically designed for this sport.

Beretta S04 Sporting Multi-choke Sporting Gun — Italy

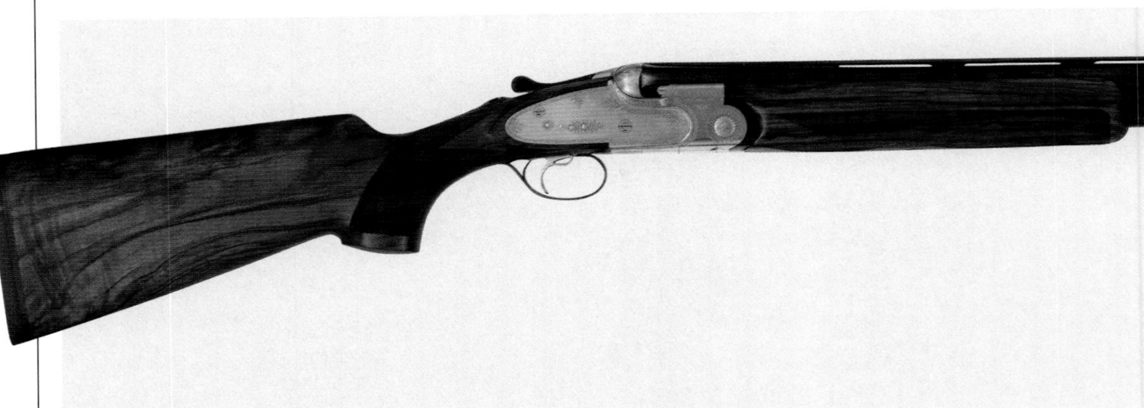

Length (gun): 46.8in (1,187mm)
Barrel: 28.0in (711mm)
Weight (gun): 7.8lb (3.5kg)
Caliber: 12-gauge
Rifling: none
Operation: over-and-under, side-lock
Feed: manual
Muz vel: n.k.

This elegant sidelock is one of the most popular models in a comparatively new breed of competition gun. Until fairly recently, the game of Sporting Clays was shot with a variety of guns, most of them skeet guns, field guns, or even trap guns from which, maybe, some of the choke had been bored out. After World War II sporting shooting began to increase and by the early 1970s such events as the British Open Sporting Championship were attracting many hundreds of entries. Gun-makers realized that what was wanted was a gun bored neither so open as a skeet gun nor as tightly choked as a trap gun. And so sporting guns such as this were born, with fixed borings of 1/4 and 1/2 choke, or 1/4 and 3/4, but at some time thereafter multi-choke models were also introduced. In this particular case, the Beretta SO4 has an internally threaded multi-choke system.

Brown Bess Flintlock Musket Reproduction — Italy

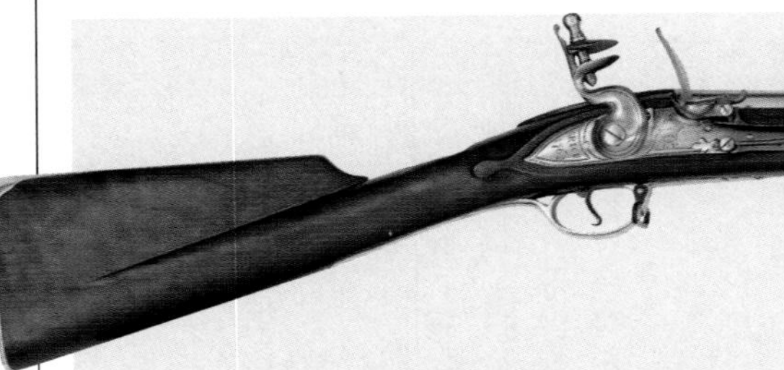

Length (gun): 58.5in (1,486mm)
Barrel: 42in (1,067mm)
Weight (gun): 9.4lb (4.3kg)
Caliber: 0.75in (19.1mm)
Rifling: none
Operation: muzzle-loading flintlock
Feed: single round, muzzle-loader
Muz vel: n.k.

This is a reproduction, made by Pedersoli of Italy, of the famous British "Brown Bess" (qv), which was the standard British infantry longarm for some 130 years. The reproduction is closely based on a model made specifically for use by the Militia by a firm named Grice in 1762, although the iron ramrod and forward ferrule have been taken from the Short Land Pattern Musket of 1768. Modern smoothbore musket competitive shooting began in 1958 with the introduction of the Brown Bess Cup, which called for the firing of 10 shots in 10 minutes at a distance of 75yd (69m). The demand for weapons for such competitions remained limited for some years, but wider interest was generated by the growth of historical battle re-enactments, which led to the formation of various display societies, such as the British "Sealed Knot," a group of enthusiasts dedicated to re-creating battles of the 17th Century English Civil War. This Brown Bess replica is, admittedly, somewhat out-of-period for that conflict but not to such an extent that the non-afficionado would notice.

Enfield Pattern 1853 Percussion Rifle (Reproduction) — Italy

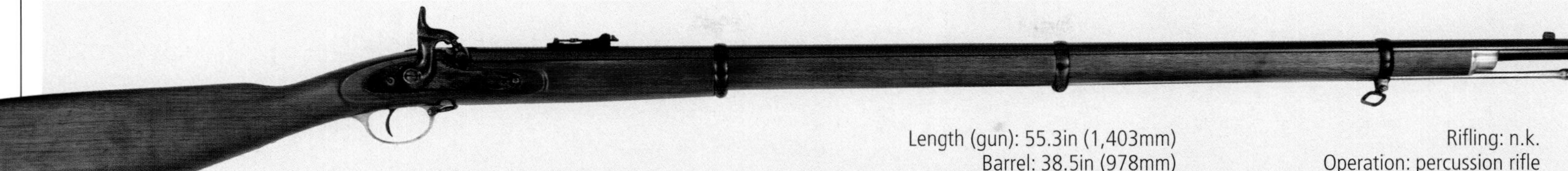

Length (gun): 55.3in (1,403mm)
Barrel: 38.5in (978mm)
Weight (gun): 9.94lb (4.5kg)
Caliber: 0.577in (14.7mm)
Rifling: n.k.
Operation: percussion rifle
Feed: single round, muzzle-loader
Muz vel: n.k.

The demand for replicas of 19th Century rifles was slow to materialize in the United Kingdom because of the comparatively easy availability of good shooting originals and also because of a lack of interest in American-style shooting. In the 1970s, however, there was perceived to be a substantial market for the Enfield series of rifles in the United States, created by the increasingly popular American Civil War re-enactment societies, who not only needed the rifles for parades and re-enactments, but also shot them competitively. The greatest original production was of the Pattern 1853 Infantry Rifle-Musket (also known as the Long Enfield and the Three-Band Enfield). The replica shown here was made in Italy for a company named Euroarms in the United States, but perhaps the most famous Enfield replicas were made by the gun-making company, Parker-Hale of Birmingham, England, who responded to the demand with a splendid series, which now usually constitute the majority of weapons to be seen at any British muzzle-loading rifle meetings.

Beretta 5.56mm AR-70 Assault Rifle — Italy

Length (gun): 37.6in (955mm)
Barrel: 17.8in (450mm)
Weight (gun): 7.6lb (3.5kg)
Caliber: 5.56mm
Rifling: 4 grooves, r/hand
Operation: gas
Feed: 30-round box magazine
Cyclic rate 650rpm
Muz vel: 3,116ft/sec (950m/sec)

Beretta started work in 1968 on a 5.56mm replacement for their in-service 7.62mm BM-59, the project being headed by the head of research and development, Vittorio Valle, and the company's general manager, P.C. Beretta. They evaluated the Stoner 63, M16A1, FN FAL, and AK-47, hoping to arrive at a blend of the best features, which would then be combined with their own innovations. The basic design was put in final form in 1970, hence the designation, Beretta Model 70. This weapon fires the 5.56 x 45mm M193 round from a closed bolt and is gas-operated, but there is no gas regulator. Since the gas port has been placed close to the muzzle end of the barrel, the system needs a relatively long (14in/355mm) piston. The trigger system is simple and clean, semi-automatic fire being obtained by the usual disconnector between the trigger and sear. Upper and lower receiver bodies are sheet metal stampings, and guide rails and ejector are welded and riveted to the upper receiver shell. The hold-open system which retains the bolt group in the rearward position after the magazine has been emptied is almost identical to that used on the M16. There are two easily interchangeable butt-stock configurations, with a high-impact rigid plastic stock with a steel buttplate being used in the AR-70 assault rifle version (see specifications), and a folding, tubular strutted stock in the SC-70 (special carbine). These weapons were used by the Italian and South African forces.

Benelli Model 121-M1 Shotgun — Italy

Length (gun): 39.8in (1,010mm)
Barrel: 20.0in (508mm)
Weight (gun): 7.2lb (3.3kg)
Caliber: 12-gauge
Rifling: none
Operation: see text
Feed: 8-round tubular magazine
Muz vel: n.k.

The Benelli Model 121 is an elegant weapon, beautifully styled and technically radical. The use of upper and lower receiver assemblies, which slide apart on disassembly, makes maintenance easy, while the locking system confuses even engineers. The lower receiver is made of aluminum, while all other parts are of steel. Basically, the Model 121 is recoil-operated but with a static barrel and the bolt is cammed out of engagement by an inertial piece. That this works is undeniable, but the cyclic speed is such as to suggest semi-blowback operation; one professional shooter is reputed to fire so rapidly that all eight spent cartridge cases are in the air at the same time. This rapid-fire capability made the Benelli the first choice in the United States for shotgun skittles matches. The modifications consist of porting, muzzle brakes, and weights, all calculated to diminish muzzle lift, allowing the gun's potential rate of fire to be deployed in a lateral sweep along the table-top. Most Benelli afficionados aver that they can deliver five shots per second if everything goes aright.

FRANCHI SPAS 12 SHOTGUN — ITALY

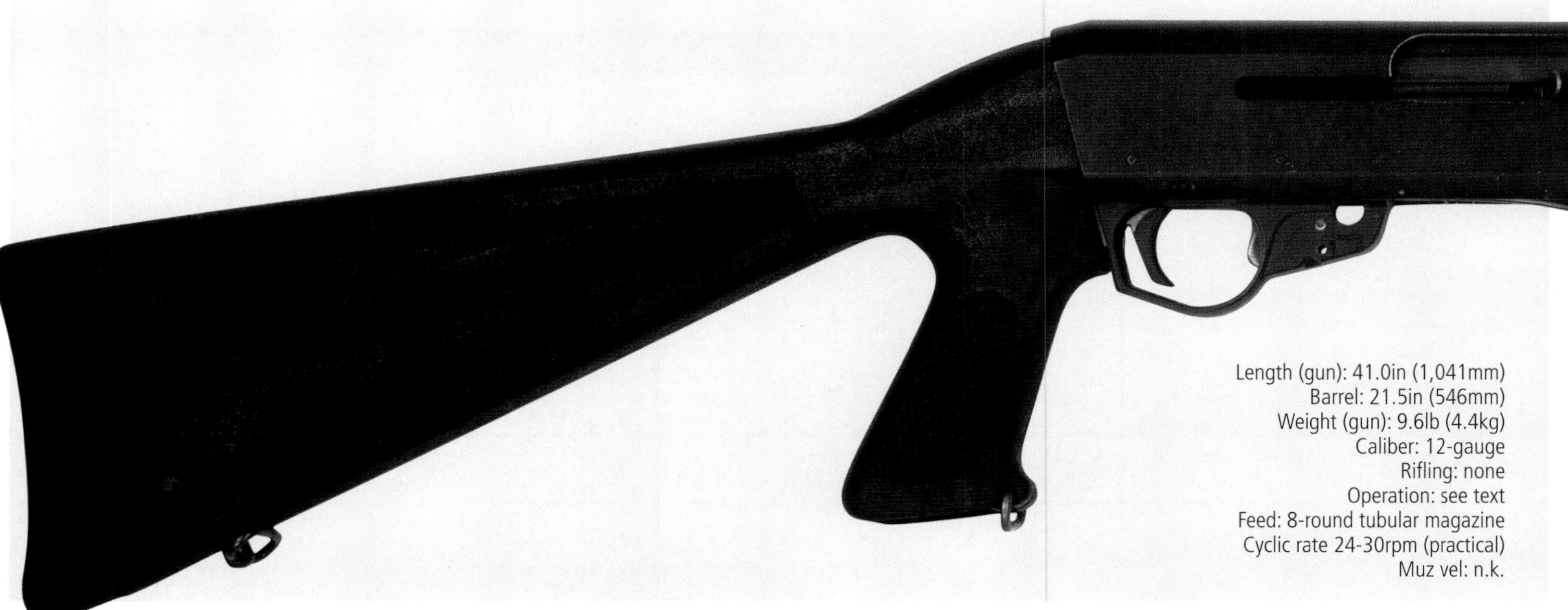

Length (gun): 41.0in (1,041mm)
Barrel: 21.5in (546mm)
Weight (gun): 9.6lb (4.4kg)
Caliber: 12-gauge
Rifling: none
Operation: see text
Feed: 8-round tubular magazine
Cyclic rate 24-30rpm (practical)
Muz vel: n.k.

The Franchi SPAS 12 (SPAS = Special Purpose Automatic Shotgun) was introduced in 1979 by the Italian company, Luigi Franchi Development, and was specifically designed for anti-riot duties. It is strictly functional in appearance. The pistol grip is an unusual feature for a shotgun, but the SPAS 12 also has a folding metal stock with a pivoting "shepherd's crook" which hooks under the forearm; holding the pistol grip, the shooter can fire the gun single-handed, either from the hip or with arm outstretched. The massive front-end derives from the fact that the SPAS 12 is a dual-function gun, being capable of operating either with pump action or as a gas-operated self-loader. An inset push-button in the fore-end can be clicked rearward, closing the gas system for manual operation. The purpose of this is to allow the gun to be used as a manual repeater with special low-pressure ammunition, which would not be sufficiently powerful to cycle it as a self-loader. Examples are gas munitions, plastic baton rounds, high explosives, and flares. A launcher can be fitted to the muzzle, enabling grenades to be fired to a range of 165yd (150m). The gun shown here has a molded Choate replacement stock, minus the hook; this solid butt is fitted when the SPAS 12 is used as a conventional civilian shotgun and it should be noted that, although it is muzzle-heavy and slow to mount, it also has the softest of 12-bore recoils and can be used by shooters who would find the recoil of any other weapon impossible.

INTERARMCO MUZZLE-LOADING SHOTGUN (REPRODUCTION) — ITALY

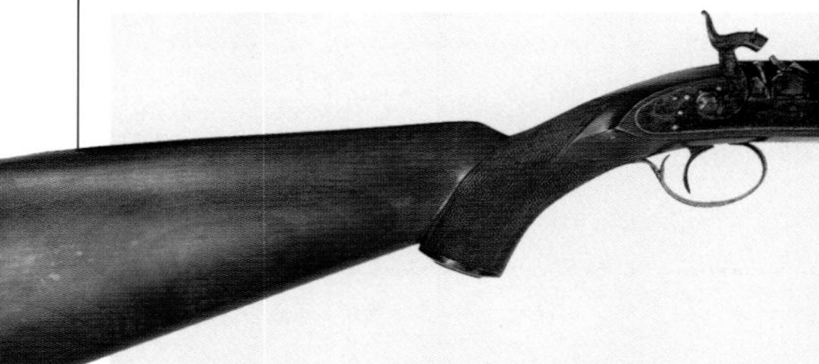

Length (gun): 51.0in (1,295mm)
Barrel: 34.5in (876mm)
Weight (gun): 7.0lb (3.2kg)
Caliber: 12-gauge
Rifling: n.k.
Operation: muzzle-loading, percussion-cap
Feed: single round, manual
Muz vel: n.k.

An original flintlock sporting gun would be too valuable to actually shoot, so there are now a number of reproductions available to enable enthusiasts to discover what such weapons felt like to use. This reproduction by the Italian company, Interarmco, is modeled on an original by the great Scottish gun maker, Alexander Henry. It is a beautifully made, single-barrel, muzzle-loading weapon, using a percussion firing system. The latter, which was a vast improvement on the flintlock system which preceded it, had only a relatively brief lifespan, from about 1836 until the first breechloaders with pin-fire, rim-fire, and center fire came onto the market in the late 1860s.

FALCO ALBERTI GARDEN GUN — ITALY

Length (gun): 40.5in (1,030mm)
Barrel: 27.6in (702mm)
Weight (gun): 2.9lb (1.3kg)
Caliber: 9mm rimfire
Rifling: none
Operation: single-action, exposed hammer
Feed: single round, manual
Muz vel: n.k.

The little 9mm Falco Alberti Bruno garden gun is basic, with little to go wrong. The 9mm rimfire shells put little strain on the mechanism and pose little in the way of public hazard, although they are quite sufficient for small vermin at close range. The spur ahead of the trigger guard presses rearwards to release the barrel, which can then fold back over the gun for ease of transport. The ludicrously long barrel is fitted solely for qualifying as a shotgun under British firearms laws, otherwise it would be about 12in (305mm) shorter. The hammer must be thumb-cocked to fire.

Beretta Special Skeet Model 682 — Italy

Length (gun): 45.3in (1,149mm)
Barrel: 28.0in (711mm)
Weight (gun): 7.8lb (3.5kg)
Caliber: 12-gauge
Rifling: none
Operation: over-and-under drop-down
Feed: single round, manual
Muz vel: n.k.

Beretta is one of the largest firearms manufacturing companies in the world and for many years claimed to be the oldest in continuous existence, dating back to 1680. Further records have, however, been discovered relating to a Bartolomeo Beretta (1490-1567), a master barrel-maker in Brescia, Italy, showing that the company is even older than the Beretta family itself, which still runs the company, had known. The Skeet Model 682 is one of several skeet models offered by the company and is an over-and-under weapon with a drop-down operation.

Beretta 5.56mm AR-70/90 Assault Rifle — Italy

Length (gun): 39.3in (998mm)
Barrel: 17.7in (450mm)
Weight (gun): 8.8lb (4.0kg)
Caliber: 5.56mm
Rifling: 6 grooves, r/hand
Operation: gas
Feed: 30-round box magazine
Cyclic rate: 625rpm
Muz vel: 3,050ft/sec (930m/sec)

The Beretta AR-70/90 is an updated version of the AR-70 (qv), which incorporates a number of significant improvements, the most important of which is that the cranked butt-stock is replaced by a new butt giving a straight-line configuration. The weapon retains the same system of gas operation with a rotating bolt, but now includes a three-round burst capability. It can accommodate any standard M16 magazine. In addition to the AR-70/90 assault rifle there are three other versions. The SC-70/90 is identical to the AR-70 apart from a twin-strut folding butt, which makes it slightly shorter in overall length, but some 0.4lb (0.2kg) heavier. The SCS-70/90 and SCP-70/90 are for use by special forces and both have a shorter (13.9in/352mm) barrel and a folding butt; they differ in that the SCS-70/90 does not have a gas-regulator and is not capable of launching grenades, while the SCP-70/90 does have a gas-regulator and can launch grenades.

MEIJI 38TH YEAR CAVALRY CARBINE — JAPAN

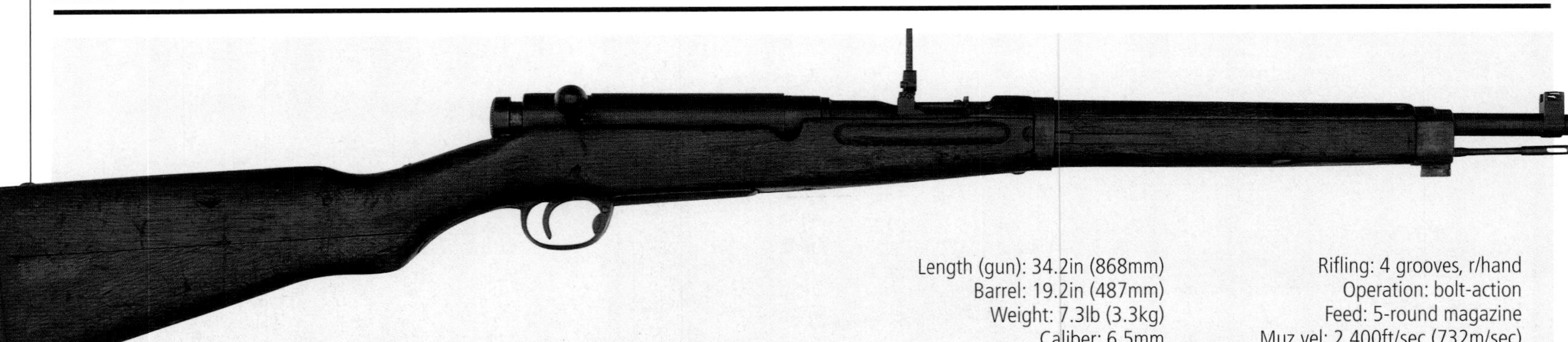

Length (gun): 34.2in (868mm)
Barrel: 19.2in (487mm)
Weight: 7.3lb (3.3kg)
Caliber: 6.5mm
Rifling: 4 grooves, r/hand
Operation: bolt-action
Feed: 5-round magazine
Muz vel: 2,400ft/sec (732m/sec)

Japan made a remarkable change from a medieval to a modern state in the second half of the 19th Century. Her first rifle was a single-shot bolt-action model of 0.43in (11mm) caliber which appeared in 1887 but which was replaced almost immediately by a rifle of smaller 0.31in (8mm) caliber with a tube magazine. Her war with China in 1894 showed some defects in her armament and a commission headed by Colonel Arisaka was appointed to investigate the whole matter and made recommendations for improvement. The result was a series of Mauser type rifles, first adopted in 1897 and often known as Arisaka rifles, but their title was the Meiji 30th Year type, having been made in the 30th year of the rule of Emperor Meiji. Rifles of this type were used in the war against Russia in 1904–5 and a number were purchased by the British in 1914 to train their new armies. The 38th Year type came into use in 1905 and was an improved version of the earlier model. It had a long life, being used in World War II. The 38th Year carbine was simply a shortened version of the rifle for use by arms other than infantry, and would take the standard bayonet. It had a metal dust cover over its bolt, similar to the one on the British Lee-Metford, but it proved very noisy in close-quarter jungle fighting. In many ways it would have been a better service weapon for the infantry than the long rifle, being much handier. Like most carbines however it suffered from fairly heavy recoil. There was a 1944 version with folding bayonet.

ARISAKA MEIJI 44 CAVALRY CARBINE (MODEL 1911) — JAPAN

Length (gun): 38.5in (978mm)
Barrel: 18.5in (470mm)
Weight (gun): 8.9lb (4.0kg)
Caliber: 6.5mm
Rifling: 6 grooves, r/hand
Operation: bolt-action
Feed: 5-round integral magazine
Muz vel: 2,250ft/sec (685m/sec)

The Meiji 44th Year Cavalry Carbine (Model 1911) was accepted for service in 1911 and actually reached the Imperial Japanese Army in 1912, replacing the Meiji 38th year Carbine (Model 1905) (qv), and remained in production until 1942. It was essentially similar to the Meiji 38, with the same bolt action, but, most unusually for a weapon intended for horsed cavalry, it was fitted with a permanently attached bayonet, which, when not in use, folded downwards and to the rear, where it was secured below the barrel. Even more surprising is that in successive modifications even longer bayonets were fitted. The picture shows the weapon with the bayonet in the folded position.

TYPE 97 20MM ANTI-TANK RIFLE — JAPAN

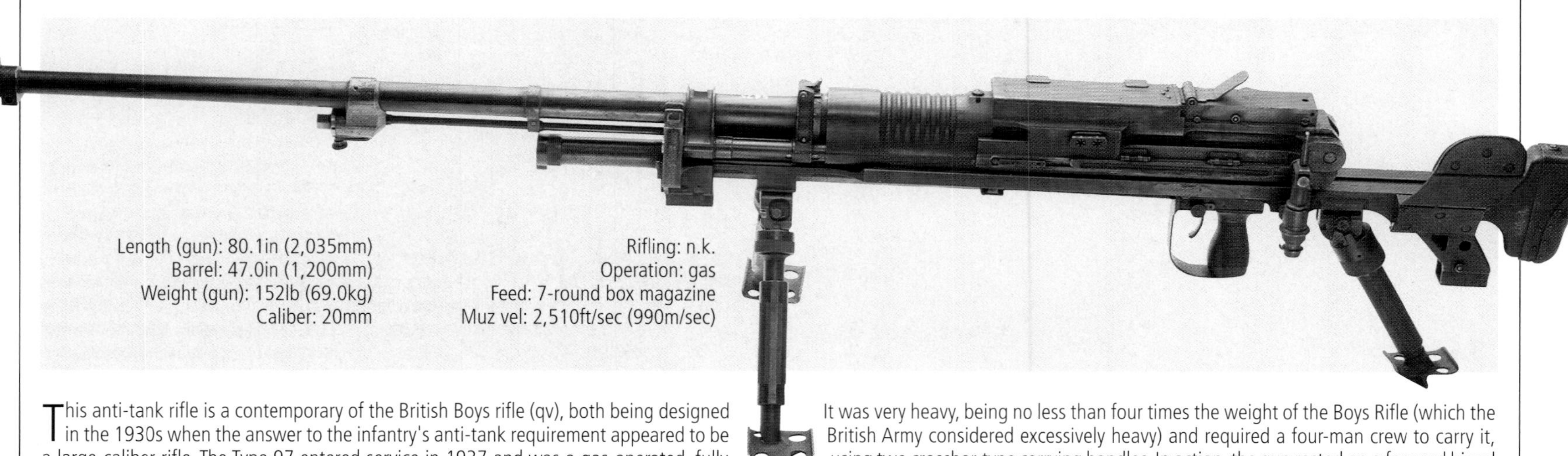

Length (gun): 80.1in (2,035mm)
Barrel: 47.0in (1,200mm)
Weight (gun): 152lb (69.0kg)
Caliber: 20mm
Rifling: n.k.
Operation: gas
Feed: 7-round box magazine
Muz vel: 2,510ft/sec (990m/sec)

This anti-tank rifle is a contemporary of the British Boys rifle (qv), both being designed in the 1930s when the answer to the infantry's anti-tank requirement appeared to be a large-caliber rifle. The Type 97 entered service in 1937 and was a gas-operated, fully automatic weapon, firing a specially developed 20 x 124mm round, which was available in armor-piercing (solid shot) and high explosive natures. The weapon fired from a closed bolt, which was unlocked by a gas-piston and then driven to the rear by blowback forces, with the entire barrel and receiver moving some 6in (150mm) along a track in the stock. It was very heavy, being no less than four times the weight of the Boys Rifle (which the British Army considered excessively heavy) and required a four-man crew to carry it, using two crossbar-type carrying handles. In action, the gun rested on a forward bipod and rear monopod, and was fired by one man. Despite the muzzle brake, the recoil must have been very heavy and the prospect of taking advantage of the fully automatic firing capability must have been daunting, even to a grimly determined Japanese soldier.

Type 99 Rifle — Japan

Length (gun): 44.0in (1,117mm)
Barrel: 25.8in (655mm)
Weight: 8.6lb (3.9kg)
Caliber: 7.7mm
Rifling: 4 grooves, r/hand
Operation: bolt-action
Feed: 5-round box
Muz vel: 2,350ft/sec (715m/sec)

Japanese experience in China in the 1930s (like that of the Italians in the same period) showed the need for a more powerful cartridge than the 0.256in (6.5mm) they then used, and after a good deal of experiment they settled in 1939 for a rifle built to fire a rimless version of their 0.303in (7.7mm) round already used in their 1932 model medium machine gun. The original intention of the Japanese had been to use a carbine, which would have been a good deal handier type of weapon in view of the small size of most of their soldiers. Carbines, however, particularly when firing powerful rounds, inevitably have increased recoil which would adversely affect any lightweight soldiers however tough and hardy they might be. As a compromise the new rifle, which was designated the Type 99, was made in two lengths, a "short" rifle in line with modern European custom and a "normal" version some 6in (152mm) longer, the one illustrated being of the shorter type. This new rifle had a rather odd attachment in the shape of a folding wire monopod (seen in top photograph) which was designed to support the rifle when fired from the prone position, but although of some theoretical advantage it can have been of little practical value due to its lack of rigidity. The backsight was also fitted with two graduated horizontal extensions to right and left, intended to be used to give a degree of lead when firing at crossing aircraft; nothing is known regarding their effectiveness. The Type 99 was not widely used in World War II.

Type 0/1/2 Parachutist Rifle — Japan

Length (gun): 45.3in (1,150mm)
Barrel: 25.4in (645mm)
Weight (gun): 8.9lb (4.1kg)
Caliber: 7.7mm
Rifling: 4 grooves, r/hand
Operation: bolt-action
Feed: 5-round integral magazine
Muz vel: 2,368ft/sec (722m/sec)

Many facets of the Japanese World War II military machine were extremely inefficient and ineffective, and it comes as no surprise that when a paratroop force was formed there were no submachine guns or similar lightweight and short weapons with which to arm them. The Type 99 rifle was far too long to be carried in an aircraft, so the first attempt was the Parachutist Rifle Type 0, which consisted of a Type 99 rifle divided into two parts, the inner end of each being fitted with an interrupted screw thread; this allowed the weapon to be carried in two parts during the flight and the subsequent jump and then reassembled immediately after landing. This was not a success and the next attempt was the Type 2, again a two-piece rifle, but this time with a wedge above the front of the receiver which had to be inserted into a receptacle above the barrel. Although trials were reasonably successful, only a few were produced, probably because by the time this weapon was available for production in late 1942 the need for parachute troops in the Japanese Army had passed. The Type 1 Parachutist Rifle was developed as a fall-back in case the Types 0 and 2 failed and was a Meiji 38th Year carbine with a folding butt; it never served with paratroop units but the few that were manufactured were pressed into service in the desperate final months of the war.

HOWA TYPE 89 5.56MM ASSAULT RIFLE — JAPAN

Length (gun): 36.1in (916mm)
Barrel: 16.5in (420mm)
Weight (gun): 7.7lb (3.5kg)
Caliber: 5.56mm
Rifling: 6 grooves, r/hand
Operation: gas
Feed: 20- or 30-round box magazine
Cyclic rate: 750rpm
Muz vel: 3020ft/sec (920m/sec)

The Japanese Ground Self Defense Force (JGSDF) realized in the late 1950s that the future rifle had to be self-loading and in the early 1960s it authorized the development of a self-loading rifle, which was undertaken by a project team which consisted of a mixture of military officers and engineers from the civilian arms firm, Howa. After considering a number of prototypes, they settled on one particular version which then entered production as the Type 64. It was a straight-line design, which was somewhat shorter than contemporary Western rifles to suit the Japanese soldiers' physique. The Type 64 was gas-operated, with a tilting breech-block, with a perforated fore guard, a built-in bipod, and a slotted flash suppressor; a bayonet could be fitted. It was capable of firing full-charge cartridges, but normally fired a specially manufactured 7.62 x 51mm with a slightly reduced charge. Some 250,00 Type 64s were manufactured, all for the JSDF, since export of military equipment is banned. The next rifle to be developed for the JSDF followed the international move to 5.56mm and was accepted for service in 1989. This weapon – the Type 89 – fires the standard NATO 5.56 x 45mm round and comes in two versions - one with a fixed butt, the other with a twin-strut, folding butt. Both versions have a folding bipod. The Type 89 uses an unusual method of operation, in which the piston head is slightly narrower than the diameter of the gas cylinder, with a full-bore collar behind it. The result is that when the gas hits the piston head it imparts an initial low momentum to the bolt-carrier (a form of "kick-start"), so that when, microseconds later, the full gas pressure moves past the piston head to the collar and the full momentum is passed to the bolt carrier, the latter is already in motion. This, it is claimed, results in a smoother motion and also reduces wear-and-tear on the working parts, thus enhancing reliability. The Type 89 has a slotted flash suppressor and is capable of accepting a bayonet. It is in service only with the JSDF.

KRAG-JÖRGENSEN RIFLE — NORWAY

One of the most interesting rifles to appear towards the end of the 19th Century was designed in Norway in the 1880s by Colonel Ole Krag, director of the Kongsberg Arsenal, assisted by Eric Jörgensen, the works superintendent. This rifle was of turn-bolt design, locking being effected by a single lug on the bolt head, which engaged in a recess behind the chamber, further support being given by a rib on the bolt, the rear end of which rested on a shoulder on the body. The magazine consisted of a sheet steel box of L-shaped section which curved under the action with a loading gate on the right-hand side of the body. The gate was hinged at the front and was held in position by a spring catch at the rear; inside the gate was a spring and a follower (platform). To load the rifle, the gate was first pushed fully open, which also caused the follower and spring to be held back under compression. The rifle was then tilted slightly to the left, five rounds (0.32in [8mm] rimmed) introduced singly into the magazine opening and then the gate closed, which also released the spring, thus pushing the rounds up, the topmost into the shorter arm of the magazine, where it was ready to be pushed into the chamber by the bolt. The Krag-Jörgensen was adopted by Denmark in 1889 and by the US Army in 1892, although the various modifications required delayed its service introduction until 1896. Norway also adopted the weapon in 1894, selecting a version similar to the US version. The picture and specifications relate to the US Army's "Model 1896 Krag Rifle." In the USA the rifle was manufactured by the Springfield Armory, who produced both infantry carbine versions as the M1896 and M1898, and yet another carbine as the M1899. There was also a special version for the Philippine Constabulary.

Length (gun): 49.0in (1,245mm)
Barrel: 30.0in (762mm)
Weight (gun): 9.35lb (4.2kg)
Caliber: 0.30in (7.62mm)
Rifling: 6 grooves, l/hand
Operation: breechloading
Feed: five rounds, integral magazine
Muz vel: 2,480ft/sec (756m/sec)

DAEWOO 5.56MM K2 ASSAULT RIFLE — ROK (SOUTH KOREA)

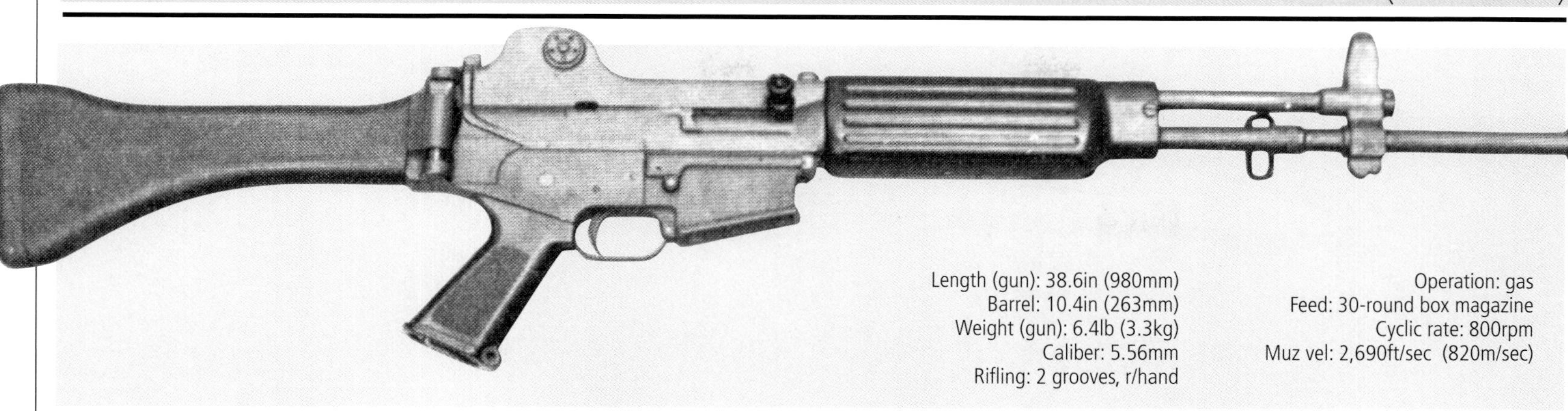

Length (gun): 38.6in (980mm)
Barrel: 10.4in (263mm)
Weight (gun): 6.4lb (3.3kg)
Caliber: 5.56mm
Rifling: 2 grooves, r/hand
Operation: gas
Feed: 30-round box magazine
Cyclic rate: 800rpm
Muz vel: 2,690ft/sec (820m/sec)

The first infantry weapon to be manufactured in South Korea was based on the US M16 5.56mm (Armalite). Designated the K1 Carbine, it was produced in the late 1970s/early 1980s in limited quantities. The next rifle, which was manufactured in large quantities, was the K2 Rifle, which appears to have been an original Korean design, but, as has happened in many other nations, incorporating ideas from foreign designs. The K1, which entered service with the RoK Army in 1987 is 5.56mm caliber and can fire either M193 or SS109 rounds. The K1 action has a long-stroke piston, similar in many respects to that used in Russian Kalashnikov rifles, and it operates a rotating bolt. The weapon is capable of full automatic, semi-automatic, and three-round burst fire, although a curious feature of the latter is that, instead of resetting when the trigger is released, as in most other actions with a burst facility, when the trigger is again pressed the cycle simply carries on from where it left off in the previous burst. The receiver, which is made from two separate aluminum forgings, appears at first sight to be similar to that of the M16, but there are, in fact, many differences. The backsight is housed between two prominent protectors and can be set to a maximum of 655yd (600m). The K2 has a solid butt which folds sideways to the right. The Daewoo K1A1 Short Carbine is based on the K2, but has a shorter barrel and uses direct gas action rather than a piston.

MOSIN-NAGANT 7.62MM MODEL 1891/30 RIFLE — RUSSIA

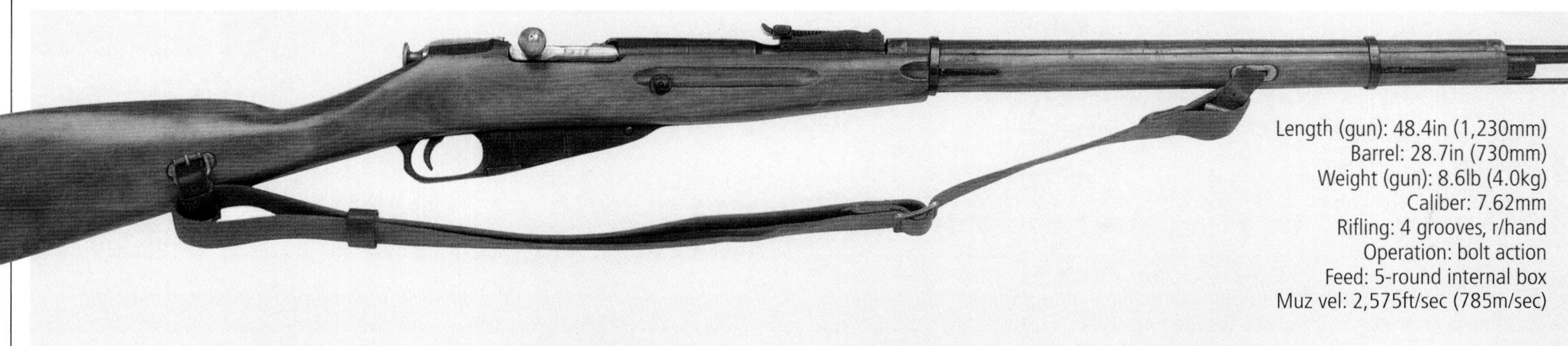

Length (gun): 48.4in (1,230mm)
Barrel: 28.7in (730mm)
Weight (gun): 8.6lb (4.0kg)
Caliber: 7.62mm
Rifling: 4 grooves, r/hand
Operation: bolt action
Feed: 5-round internal box
Muz vel: 2,575ft/sec (785m/sec)

The Mosin-Nagant Model 1891 had an exceptionally long life, first entering service with the Tsarist Army in 1891 and undergoing periodic updating until the final model, the Carbine M1944, was phased out of production in the Soviet Union in the late 1940s. The original M1891 was a straightforward bolt-action rifle with an internal five-round magazine, produced in three versions. The basic Infantry version had a 31.6in (802mm) barrel and was designed to be fired with the socket-bayonet in place, while the Dragoon and Cossack versions had a shorter (28.8in/730mm) barrel and differed from each other only in that the Dragoon version came with a bayonet while the Cossack version did not. Next came the Carbine M 1910, which had a much shorter barrel – 20.0in (510mm) – but was otherwise the same as the Dragoon version. Following the Revolution in 1917 the Mosin-Nagant remained unchanged until the appearance of the M1891/1930, in which the barrel was shortened to 28.8in (730mm), the receiver was changed from hexagonal to circular profile to ease production, and new fore- and rear-sights were fitted. As can be seen, this had a long forestock covering the whole of the barrel except for a short length at the muzzle, with a cleaning rod housing below. There was a tubular guard around the foresight and a leaf backsight. The five-round magazine was integral to the weapon and a leather carrying sling was supplied. The M1891/1930 Sniper Rifle was simply the standard infantry weapon fitted with a rudimentary telescope.

MOSIN-NAGANT CARBINE MODEL 1938 — RUSSIA

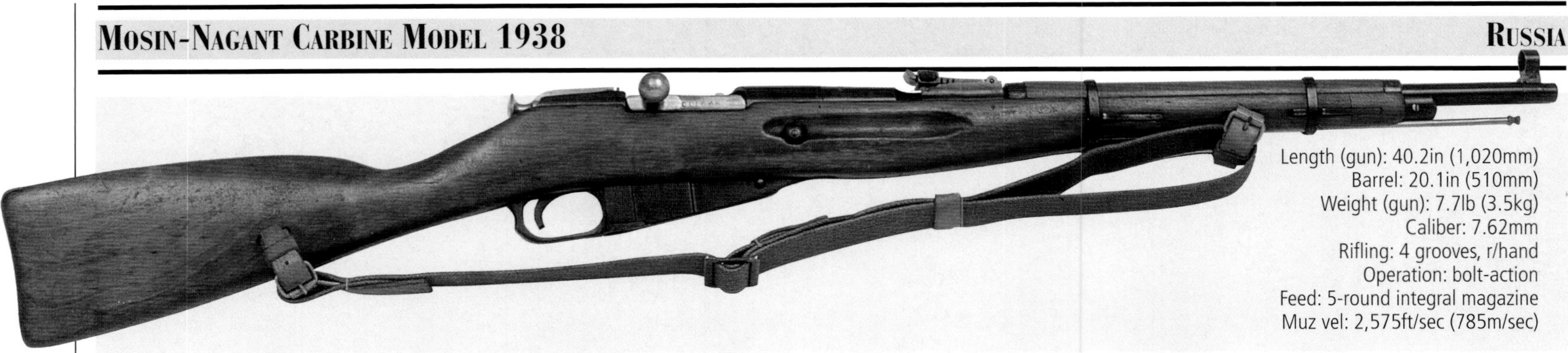

Following the Mosin-Nagant M1891/1930, described on the previous page, the next in the series was the weapon illustrated here, the Mosin-Nagant 7.62mm Carbine M1938, which was, in essence, the Carbine M1910 incorporating the same modifications as had been made to produce the M1891/1930. This weapon was specifically intended for use by front-line troops other than infantry, such as artillery, engineers, cavalry, and communications, and certain logistics troops such as supply-vehicle drivers, all of whom needed a lighter, handy weapon, basically for self-defense. As the illustration shows, this was simply a shorter, handier version of the M1819/1930. The final version was the Carbine M1934, which was simply the Carbine M1938 with a permanently attached, folding bayonet, which, it should be noted, was anchored to a block on the right-hand side of the barrel and did not fit over the muzzle.

TOKAREV 7.62MM SVT-40 RIFLE — RUSSIA

Designed by Fedor Tokarev, the self-loading SVT-40 was the outcome of a lengthy development process which started in the early 1920s. Tokarev submitted several prototypes for State trials in the 1920s, followed by the Model 1930 and the Model 1935, both of which were produced in small numbers. Tokarev finally achieved some success with his Model 1938, although, even then, he had to make many changes before full production could start. Then, when early production weapons were used in the1940 "Winter War" against Finland, yet more shortcomings were identified. When solutions had been found, the SVT Model 1940 was ordered into full production and some two million were produced. The Samozaryadnaya i avtomaticheskaya Vintovky sistemy Tokareva (SVT = semiautomatic and automatic rifle, Tokarev pattern) utilized a gas-operated system, in which locking was achieved by the tail of the breech-block dropping into a recess in the receiver. The gas cylinder was above the barrel and a long wooden stock covered about half the barrel with a further vented stock in front of that. A cleaning rod was carried in a recess under the barrel. Other versions included the SNT sniper rifle, the SKT carbine, and the AKT-40, which had a fully automatic capability only. This series was not an overwhelming success, mainly because the weapon was too complicated, making both manufacture and field stripping difficult. Added to this was the fact that production standards in Soviet factories for both rifles and ammunition were low, although this was scarcely surprising in view of the disruption caused to Soviet industry during the period 1941-45. As a result production slowed in 1943 and was phased out completely in 1944.

MOSIN-NAGANT CARBINE MODEL 1944 — RUSSIA

The first Mosin-Nagant arms were developed by Colonel Sergei Mosin of the Russian Artillery and a Belgian designer named Nagant. The 1891 model was the first of the modern small-bore bolt-action magazine rifles to be used by Russia and virtually all her later rifles of the type are based on it. The basic rifle was of fairly orthodox design and took a somewhat outmoded socket bayonet. There were several variations, chiefly in the length of the barrel. The caliber was originally measured in an old Russian unit known as a line and equivalent to 1/10in. As a result they were often known as "three-line" rifles until the metric system was introduced after the Revolution. Their sights were also calibrated in arshins, another ancient measurement based on the human pace. Many of these earlier rifles were made in other European countries, and during World War I the United States manufactured 1.5 million of them for Russia. The next major change came in 1930, although even this was little more than a general modernization of the early type. It did however lead to the production of a sniper version with a telescopic sight. The weapon illustrated was introduced towards the end of World War II and was the very last of the Mosin-Nagant series to be made. It was still very similar to its predecessors, but incorporated a permanently attached bayonet which folded back along the right side of the rifle when not in use.

7.62 SKS Carbine (Simonov)

Russia

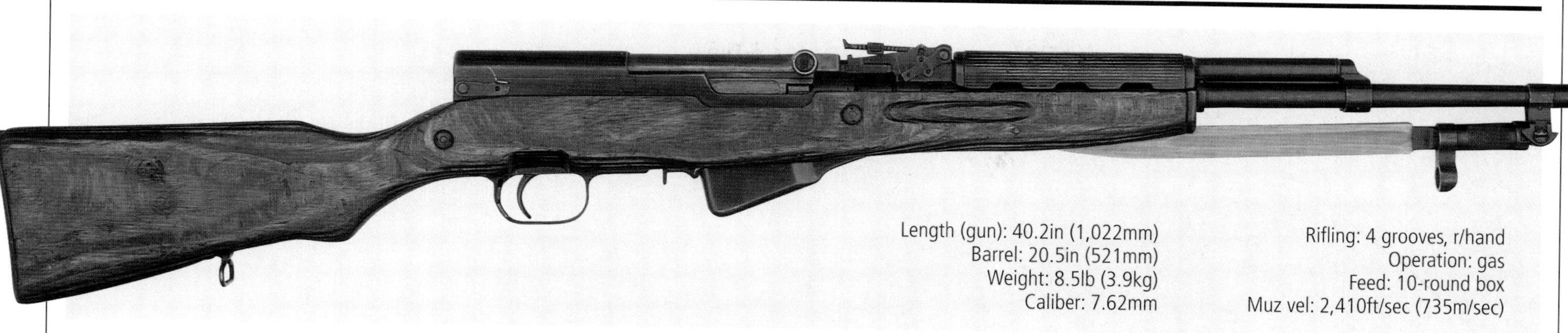

Length (gun): 40.2in (1,022mm)
Barrel: 20.5in (521mm)
Weight: 8.5lb (3.9kg)
Caliber: 7.62mm
Rifling: 4 grooves, r/hand
Operation: gas
Feed: 10-round box
Muz vel: 2,410ft/sec (735m/sec)

This was an early type of self-loader, developed and produced by Russia in the course of World War II. It was a gas-operated weapon of orthodox appearance, and was designed to fire an "intermediate" round of the type originally developed by the German Army for their MP 43/44. It had a magazine capacity of 10 rounds which could be loaded either separately or by clips, and was equipped with a folding bayonet of bladed type, which turned back under the barrel when not required. The woodwork was of laminated beech, heavily varnished. The SKS was an efficient weapon, if somewhat heavy, and the cartridge gave adequate power at the sort of ranges envisaged in modern war, which by Russian techniques were of the order of 330 or 440yd (300–400m). This was probably a perfectly practical maximum for an army well equipped with machine guns of one kind or another. The SKS was used and manufactured by many Communist bloc countries, and a number of non-Communist states, among them Egypt, were equipped with it. At one period it became very much a standard guerrilla arm, being widely used in Aden, the Yemen, Oman and elsewhere in the Middle East, but was superseded by the AK-47 in its various forms.

Kalashnikov AK-47 Assault Rifle

Russia

Length (gun): 34.7in (880mm)
Barrel: 16.3in (415mm)
Weight: 9.5lb (4.3kg)
Caliber: 7.62mm intermediate
Rifling: 4 grooves, r/hand
Operation: gas
Feed: 30-round box
Cyclic rate: 600rpm
Muz vel: 2,350ft/sec (717m/sec)

As soon as World War II was over the Russians set out to produce a weapon similar to the German MP 44 in which they were almost certainly helped by various German designers and engineers who had fallen into their hands. The designer finally responsible for the AK-47 was Mikhail Kalashnikov and his weapon was officially adopted for use in the Russian Army in 1951. It was in every way an exceptionally fine assault rifle. It worked by gas, tapped off from the barrel and impinging on a piston working in a cylinder above the barrel. This piston took with it the rotating bolt, the whole being thrust forward again by the coiled return spring at the proper time. The AK-47 is accurate and sufficiently heavy to shoot well at automatic up to the sort of ranges likely to be required in modern war, that is, about 330yd (300m) without undue vibration. It is well made and well finished, being in this respect considerably in advance of most earlier Soviet weapons. It fires an intermediate cartridge which contrary to mistakenly held beliefs is not inter-changeable with the NATO round. The bore is chromed and the weapon is easy to strip and handle. It is designed to take a knife-type bayonet and in later models the wooden butt has been replaced by a folding metal one. The AK-47 was manufactured extensively by various countries of the former Soviet Bloc. It was replaced by an improved version, the AKM, but is still an almost universal arm for subversive and terrorist groups.

AK-47 (Folding-butt) (Automatic-Kalashnikova) Rifle

Russia

Length (gun): 34.7in (880mm)
Barrel: 16.3in (415mm)
Weight: 9.5lb (4.3kg)
Caliber: 7.62mm
Rifling: 4 grooves, r/hand
Operation: gas
Feed: 30-round box
Cyclic rate: 600rpm
Muz vel: 2,350ft/sec (717m/sec)

The earliest versions of the AK-47, which came into use in the Russian Army in 1951. had wooden butts. These, like many other Soviet arms of their era, were of poor quality timber which detracted greatly from the otherwise excellent quality and finish. Soon afterwards there appeared an alternative version with a folding metal butt which could, if required, be turned forward under the weapon without affecting its use. This type was probably originally intended for use by airborne troops, but its compactness made it easily concealed and therefore an obvious weapon for guerrillas, terrorists, and similar irregular orgainzations and it now appears to be almost universally used all over the world in this role. Apart from its compactness the AK-47 has certain other obvious advantages in this respect; it is strongly made and shoots as well as an orthodox rifle to 437yd (400m) with the additional advantage of automatic fire if needed. Perhaps even more important is its general simplicity; the sort of organizations using it rarely have the time or facilities for extensive training of recruits so that something which can be taught quickly to an individual with no previous experience of firearms is useful.

DRAGUNOV 7.62MM SNIPER RIFLE (SVD)

RUSSIAN FEDERATION

Length (gun): 48.2in (1,225mm)
Barrel: 24.5in (622mm)
Weight (gun): 9.5lb (4.3kg)
Caliber: 7.62mm
Rifling: 4 grooves, r/hand
Operation: gas
Feed: 10-round box magazine
Muz vel: 2,723ft/sec (830m/sec)

Development of the SVD began in 1965 and the weapon entered service with the (then) Soviet Army in 1967. It quickly became the standard sniper rifle of most Warsaw Pact armies, as well as of allies, and it was built under license in China, Iraq, and Romania. The SVD was normally issued on a scale of one to a motorized rifle platoon, and selected riflemen received regular, centralized sniper training. The SVD is long, but largely due to its open stock it is actually lighter than previous Russian sniper rifles. Many Western sniper rifles retain a bolt mechanism, but the SVD is gas-operated, using a system similar to that of the AKM assault rifle, but modified to take a short-stroke piston in order to avoid the shift of balance inherent in log-stroke systems, which would upset a sniper's point-of-aim. The SVD has a combined flash suppressor/compensator and can mount the standard AKM bayonet. There is a cheek-pad atop the open butt-stock and it is fitted with a detachable, non-variable, 4x telescopic sight, with an extension tube to afford eye relief. Four magazines, a cleaning kit, and an extra battery and lamp for the telescopic sight are included with the weapon. It fires only in the semi-automatic mode. The SVD, shown in Afghan (left) and Russian (right) hands,was generally considered to be one of the best sniper rifles of its era.

5.45MM AK-74-SU ASSAULT RIFLE

RUSSIAN FEDERATION

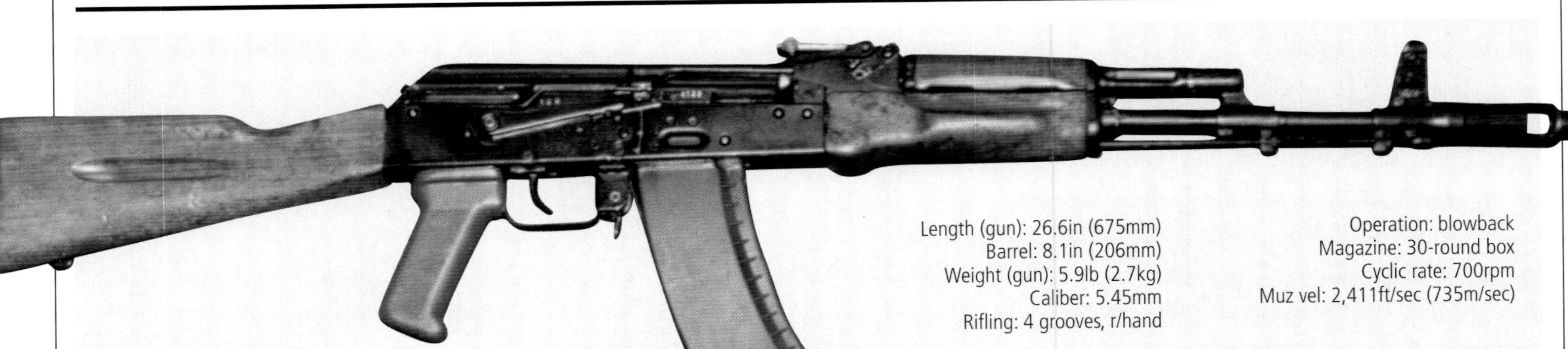

Length (gun): 26.6in (675mm)
Barrel: 8.1in (206mm)
Weight (gun): 5.9lb (2.7kg)
Caliber: 5.45mm
Rifling: 4 grooves, r/hand
Operation: blowback
Magazine: 30-round box
Cyclic rate: 700rpm
Muz vel: 2,411ft/sec (735m/sec)

The Soviet Army used the 7.62mm PPSh-41 and PPS-43, throughout World War II and for many years afterwards. It then seemed to allow the SMG as a separate type to fade out, using AK-47 or AK-74 assault rifles where other armies carried on using SMGs. In the 1970s, however, this policy seems to have been reversed, with the appearance of a totally new Soviet SMG, based on the Kalashnikov AKS-74 assault rifle (shown in photo), but considerably smaller and lighter. The barrel was only 8.1in (206mm) long and was fitted with a screw-on, cylindrical attachment at the front of which was a cone-shaped flash suppressor. Unlike the majority of SMGs the AK-74-SU fired standard, full-charge rifle ammunition, in this case the Russian 5.45 x 39.5mm. In addition, due to the shortness of the barrel, the gas was tapped off very close to the chamber which resulted in a very high pressure for such a small weapon and the muzzle attachment was an expansion chamber, designed to reduce the pressure acting on the gas piston; it also served as a flame damper. The weapon was fitted with basic iron sights, the rear sight being a basic flip-over device which was marked for 220yd (200m) and 440yd (400m), although the latter range seemed somewhat optimistic for such a weapon. The internal mechanism was identical with that of the AK-74 except that the gas piston, return spring, and spring guide rod were shorter. The weapon also had a very simple skeleton stock which folded forwards along the left side of the weapon.

BAIKAL MODEL 628 (MC-8-0) SHOTGUN

RUSSIA

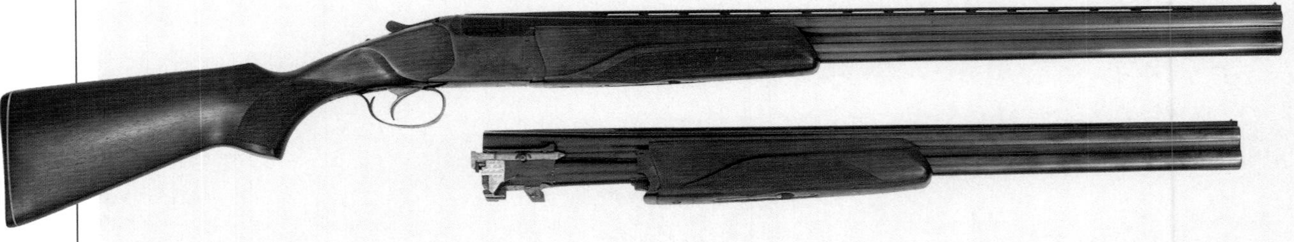

Length (gun): 43.0in (1,092mm) (with longer barrels)
Barrel: long – 28.0in (711mm); short – 26.0in (660mm)
Weight (gun): 7.0lb (3.2kg)
Caliber: 12-gauge
Rifling: none
Operation: boxlock, over-and-under
Feed: manual
Muz vel: n.k.

This gun was manufactured in the (then) Soviet Union during the Cold War and was sold in Western countries at a low price, undercutting weapons made in Europe or North America. The Model 628 was a 12-bore with two sets of boxlock, over-and-under barrels, both of which are shown here. The longer (28in/711mm) set (here shown mounted) was more tightly bored and was used for trap and wildfowling, while the shorter (26in/660mm), more open set (shown dismounted, below) served for skeets and upland game. The quality varied from one gun to another, but, in general, they were well-made and had chrome-lined barrels. They were well regarded and popular with users.

CIS 5.56mm SR-88 — Singapore

Length (gun): 38.1in (970m)
Barrel: 18.1in (459mm)
Weight (gun): 8.1lb (3.7kg)
Caliber: 5.56mm
Rifling: 6 grooves, r/hand
Operation: gas
Feed: 20- or 30-round box magazine
Cyclic rate 750rpm
Muz vel: 3,182ft/sec (970m/sec)

Like many other countries, Singapore entered the arms business by undertaking license production in the 1960s of the US 5.56mm M16, a factory being set up for this purpose by Chartered Industries of Singapore (CIS). In the early 1970s the Singapore Armed Forces (SAF) asked CIS to develop a more cost-effective rifle, which had to be simple, rugged, reliable, economical to manufacture and, at the very least, as good as the M16. This led to the SAR-80, which was produced in some numbers. Next came the SR-88, which was conventional in design, but thoroughly sensible in approach. The SR-88 is built on the straight-line principle, with barrel, bolt, recoil mechanism, and stock all in-line, dispersing the recoil straight into the firer's shoulder, minimizing barrel climb, and increasing controllability and accuracy. There are four main assemblies: upper receiver; gas piston; bolt group; and stock/lower receiver. (The removable-butt version is shown in lower photo.) There are two versions of the rifle: one has a fixed glassfiber stock, the other a folding, twin-strut stock. There is also a carbine, (top photo) which has a shorter barrel and a folding stock. A model with further improvements, designated SR-88-A, was fielded in 1990, in both rifle and carbine versions.

CIS 5.56mm SAR-21 Assault Rifle — Singapore

Length (gun): 31.7in (805mm)
Barrel: 20.0in (508mm)
Weight (gun): 8.4lb (3.8kg)
Caliber: 5.56mm
Rifling: n.k.
Operation: gas-operated, bullpup
Feed: 30-round box magazine
Cyclic rate: 650rpm
Muz vel: n.k.

The Chartered Industries of Singapore (CIS) SAR-21 assault rifle was announced in 1999 and is a 5.56mm gas-operated weapon designed on the "bullpup" principle, in which the use of metal components has been kept to a minimum with most components being made of high strength engineering plastics and composites. It consists of four main elements: barrel group, which includes the main part of the body and the carrying handle; bolt group; upper receiver group, including the trigger and magazine housing; and the lower receiver group, which includes the butt plate. The weapon has a rotating bolt, and can fire either full or semi-automatic; there is no burst capability. One unusual feature is the patented high-pressure vent hole in the chamber wall, which is designed to release high-pressure gas harmlessly into the atmosphere in the event of a chamber explosion. There is a x1.5 optical scope (x3 optional) integrated into the carrying handle with back-up iron sights on the top. In addition, there is a laser-aiming device mounted in the front plate of the body, underneath the barrel, which is powered by one AA size battery. To enhance the firer's safety there is a Kevlar plate on the butt, where the firer rests his/her cheek. The 30-round magazine is made of translucent plastic, enabling the firer to see precisely how many rounds remain.

VEKTOR 5.56MM R4/R5/R6 RIFLES — SOUTH AFRICA

Length (gun): 39.6in (1,005mm)
Barrel: 18.1in (460mm)
Weight (gun): 9.4lb (4.3kg)
Caliber: 7.62mm
Rifling: 6 grooves, r/hand
Operation: gas
Feed: 35-round box magazine
Cyclic rate: 700rpm
Muz vel: 3,215ft/sec (980m/sec)

In the 1970s and 1980s there was close co-operation in defense matters between Israel and the white-dominated regime in South Africa, one fruit of which was the 5.56mm R4 rifle (see specifications), which was, in essence, a modified version of the Israeli Galil rifle (qv). The R4 was first fielded in 1982 and replaced the Belgian FN FAL and Heckler & Koch G3 in South African service. The modifications were intended to make the weapon easier to use by the South African troops who were taller and more heavily built than the Israelis, and also to meet the more stringent demands of bush warfare. The R4 was originally fitted with a solid butt but this was later replaced by a twin-strutted stock which could be folded to the right. A detachable bipod was also issued with every weapon. The R5 (top photo) was a shorter version of the R4 (bottom photo) used by the South African Marine Corps and Air Force, while the LM4 and LM5 were identical to the R4 and R5, except that they were not capable of full automatic fire and were intended for police forces. The R6 was an even shorter version, 31.7in (805mm) overall, intended for use by airborne troops and tank/vehicle crewmen.

VEKTOR 5.56MM CR-21 ASSAULT RIFLE — SOUTH AFRICA

Length (gun): 29.9in (760mm)
Barrel: 18.1in (460mm)
Weight (gun): 8.4lb (3.8kg)
Caliber: 5.56mm
Rifling: 6 grooves, r/hand
Operation: gas, bullpup
Feed: 20- or 35-round box magazine
Cyclic rate: 700rpm
Muz vel: 3,215ft/sec (980m/sec)

Another of the current generation of "new look" assault rifles, the South African CR-21 (Combat Rifle for the 21st Century) was under development for some years before being revealed in 1997. It takes advantage of combat experience with the Vektor R4, R5, and R6 rifles (qqv), but unlike those weapons its action is designed on the "bullpup" principle, with a short butt and the magazine housing behind the trigger group. Handling and strength considerations have been optimized in the design and, as a result, it does not look at all like a traditional rifle, while extensive use of modern synthetic polymer-based materials make it very light, just 8.4lb (3.8kg) fully loaded. It is gas-operated, with a rotating bolt and has its center-of-gravity above the pistol grip, making it easy for the firer to control. The carrying grip (it is not a handle) contains the x1 reflex optical sight, made by Vektor, which is intended to be used with both eyes open and is claimed to make training easy and to improve the probability of a first-round hit in combat. The sight also includes a unique, Vektor-developed adjustment mechanism for zeroing. The CR-21 can fire both SS109 and M193 series 5.56 x 45mm ammunition and the muzzle has a pronged flash suppressor, which is claimed to virtually eliminate flash, even at night, and can also be used as a grenade launcher. Maximum effective range is about 500yd (457m).

AYA NUMBER ONE SHOTGUN — SPAIN

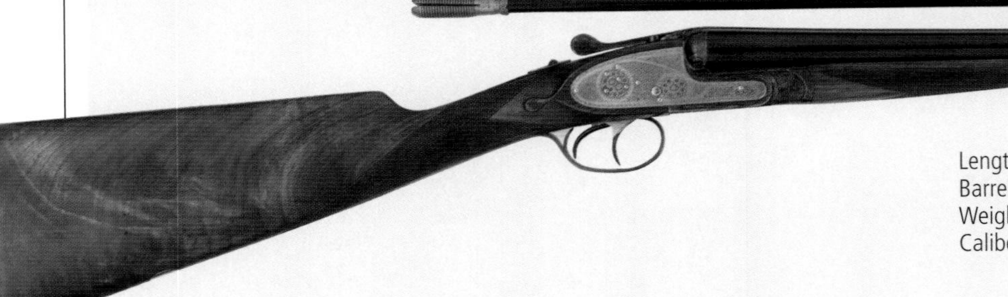

Length (gun): 44.5in (1,130mm)
Barrel: 27.0in (686mm)
Weight (gun): 6.4lb (2.9kg)
Caliber: 12-gauge
Rifling: none
Operation: break-open sidelock
Feed: manual
Muz vel: n.k.

In the 1950s a company known as Anglo-Spanish Imports of Ipswich, England, placed a contract with AyA, a Spanish gun-making company, to produce guns for the British market, which were to be virtual copies of British guns but at a fraction of the contemporary prices. Prior to this, Spanish guns exported to the United Kingdom had been designs produced for the Spanish market, rather heavy, often fitted with sling swivels, and – among the cheaper of them – roughly finished and with metal softer than it should have been. The 1950s contract saw a complete change and AyA were soon exporting a variety of guns specifically tailored to the British market, ranging from a boxlock non-ejector, through several boxlock ejectors to the gun shown here, the Number One model, double-barreled, break-open, sidelock ejector. With an assisted opening system fitted it can be made in more than one caliber if required, at a quarter of the price of the equivalent British gun. The illustration shows the excellent finish of this weapon, the two triggers, and the top opening lever.

AyA Yeoman Shotgun — Spain

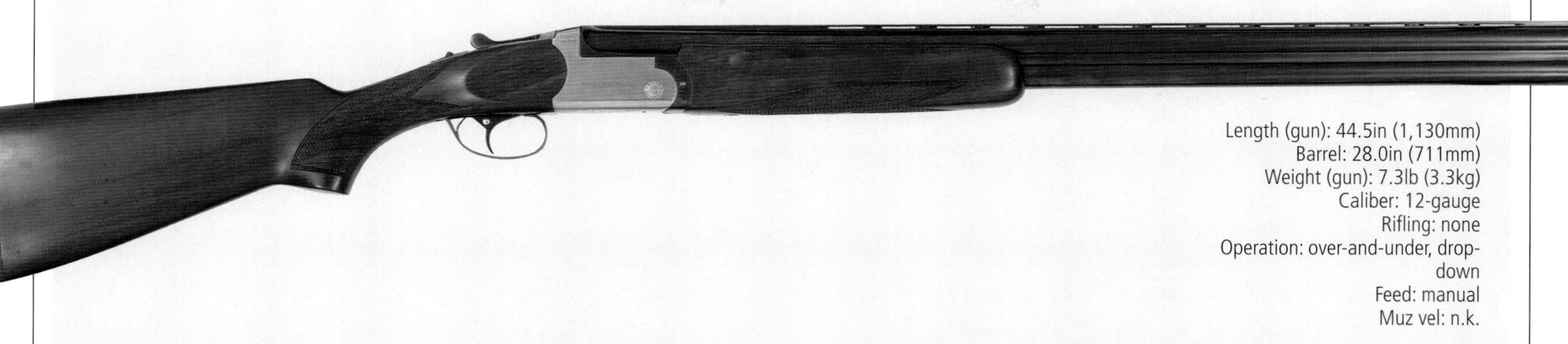

Length (gun): 44.5in (1,130mm)
Barrel: 28.0in (711mm)
Weight (gun): 7.3lb (3.3kg)
Caliber: 12-gauge
Rifling: none
Operation: over-and-under, drop-down
Feed: manual
Muz vel: n.k.

The Spanish gunmaking company, AyA, moved to a new factory in 1986 and shortly thereafter introduced this new over-and-under, 12-gauge shotgun, called the Yeoman, which was intended for the clay pigeon shooting market rather than the game shot. There were two models, one with standard barrels bored 1/2 and full chokes, and the other a multi-choke version, with three internally threaded choke tubes supplied with the gun and others available at extra cost. The selector for the selective single trigger was a button on the actual trigger rather than the more conventional device fitted to the strap. A free or non-auto safety catch was fitted as standard, but an automatic one was available at slightly extra cost.

Lanber 12-Gauge Over-and-under Sporting Shotgun — Spain

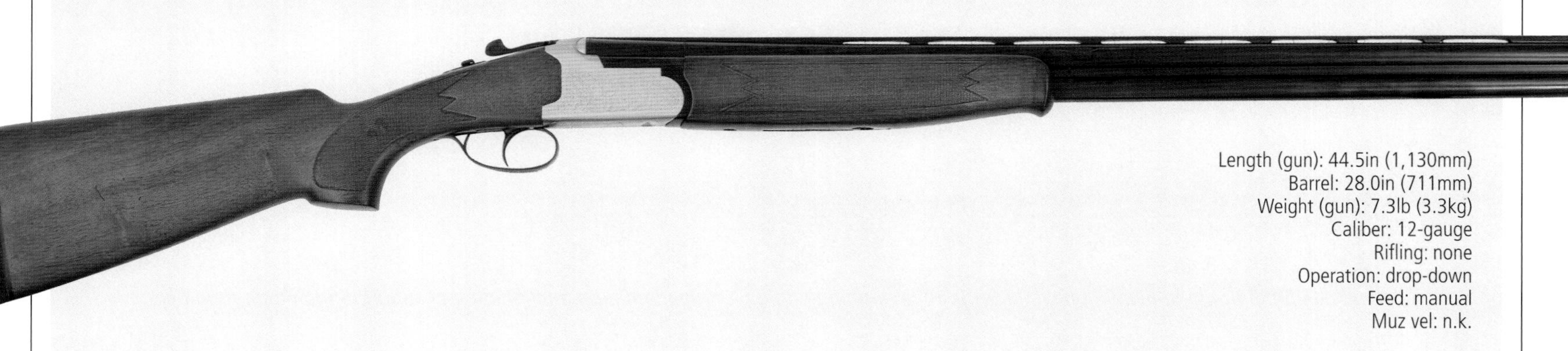

Length (gun): 44.5in (1,130mm)
Barrel: 28.0in (711mm)
Weight (gun): 7.3lb (3.3kg)
Caliber: 12-gauge
Rifling: none
Operation: drop-down
Feed: manual
Muz vel: n.k.

The ubiquitous over-and-under sporting weapon comes at all levels of sophistication from rustic to exquisite, passing through the category of "sound but unexciting" – a label that well fits this Lanber clay-pigeon target gun. Built by one of Spain's largest makers of "over-and-unders" it has the reputation of being a "good gun for the money." There are six guns in the range and one of their features is that, apart from the 3in (76mm) Magnum model, the field models have rather more open boring than some others at the inexpensive end of the market, where the half- and full-choke seems to be the norm. The multi-choke models come with five different chokes and a hefty spanner to assist in screwing or unscrewing them. The engraving, although done by machine, is at least respectable.

Hawken Percussion Rifle (Reproduction) — Spain

Length (gun): 49.0in (1,245mm)
Barrel: 32.0in (813mm)
Weight (gun): 9.3lb (4.2kg)
Caliber: 0.54in (13.7mm)
Rifling n.k.
Operation: muzzle-loading, percussion lock
Feed: single round, manual
Muz vel: n.k.

During the early 19th Century, as exploration opened up the "plains" areas of mid-Western America and the explorers started to encounter larger game, it became necessary to enhance the power of rifles by increasing both their bore and their powder charges. Among the most prolific gunsmiths of the time were the Hawken brothers of St Louis, and a new type of rifle came to have the generic name of a "Hawken" regardless of whether it was made by the brothers or not. Such weapons had larger caliber than their predecessors, which meant that the barrel was much heavier, and to compensate the overall length of the barrel had to be reduced to enable the frontiersman to handle it. The weapon shown here is a replica of a typical "Hawken Rifle" made by Ardesa of Spain.

CREEDMORE MATCH, RIGBY TYPE PERCUSSION RIFLE (REPRODUCTION) — SPAIN

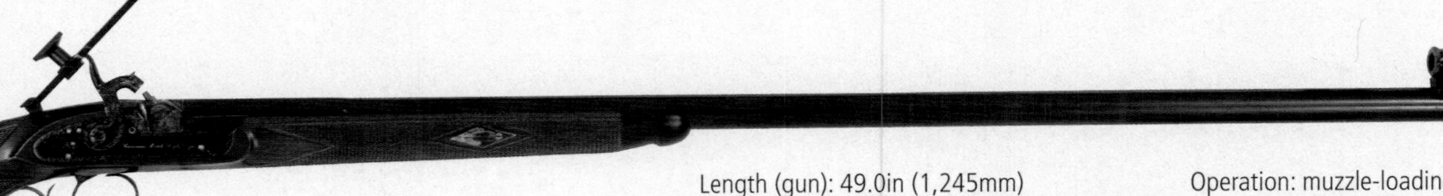

Length (gun): 49.0in (1,245mm)
Barrel: 32.5in (825mm)
Weight (gun): 8.2lb (3.7kg)
Caliber: 0.45in (11.4mm)
Rifling: n.k.
Operation: muzzle-loading, percussion cap
Feed: single round, manual
Muz vel: n.k.

The name "Creedmore" derives from a place on Long Island, New York, where a British and a United States team competed in 1877 for what was called, perhaps immodestly, the "Championship of the World," and this is a replica of the British Rigby muzzle-loader used in that event. The barrel of this example is some 4in (102mm) shorter than would normally be expected in a long-range rifle of this kind – although it is perfectly adequate for shooting at 100m (109yd), the range at which the vast majority of rifles of this type might be expected to be used. The advent on the "black powder" scene of English-style replicas, such as this, including the Enfield as well as the German Schützen rifles, marked a clear break with the American concept of the replica arm.

CETME 7.62MM MODEL 58 SELF-LOADING RIFLE — SPAIN

Length (gun): 39.4in (1,000mm)
Barrel: 17.0in (432mm)
Weight (gun): 11.4lb (5.1kg)
Caliber: 7.62mm
Rifling: 4 grooves, r/hand
Operation: see text
Feed: 20-round box magazine
Cyclic rate: 600rpm
Muz vel: 2,493ft/sec (760m/sec)

The Spanish Army's Model 58 was developed at CETME (Centro de Estudios Technicos de Materiales Especiales = Center for the Study of Technology and Special Materials) and was developed from the German World War II Mauser StG45. This rifle had reached the prototype stage in 1945, but when the war ended the design team took it to Spain to continue working on the unique roller-locked, delayed-action breech mechanism. This resulted in a self-loading rifle firing the specially developed 7.92 x 40mm CETME round, which was shorter than the 7.92 x 57mm Mauser round and fired a lighter bullet. This rifle was offered to the Federal Republic of Germany to arm the newly created Bundesheer, but, not surprisingly, the Germans required a rifle firing the standard NATO 7.62mm round, so the design was passed to Heckler & Koch who developed the G3 rifle (qv). CETME continued work in Spain, producing their own 7.62mm version, the Model 58, but although it appeared externally similar to the G3, the Spanish rifle fired the 7.62 x 51mm CETME round, which contained a reduced charge. The Model 58 used the Mauser system, but with fluted chamber walls and fired single rounds with a closed bolt and full automatic with an open bolt; it also had a flash suppressor and a bipod. In the early 1970s the Spanish General Staff adopted the full-charge NATO round, which led to the Model C, which also incorporated some minor improvements and was slightly larger, but lighter than the Model 58. When Spain followed NATO in adopting 5.56mm caliber, the Model C design was scaled down to accept the new round, the new rifle being known as the Model L, which entered service in 1988, as did a cut-down carbine. All Spanish weapons are manufactured at the State arsenal: Empresa Nacional "Santa Barbara."

M1869 VETTERLI INFANTRY RIFLE — SWITZERLAND

Length (gun): 52.0in (1,320mm)
Barrel: 33.1in (841mm)
Weight (gun): 10.3lb (4.7kg)
Caliber: 0.41in (10.4mm)
Rifling: 4 grooves, l/hand
Operation: breechloading
Feed: 12-round, tube
Muz vel: ca 1,427ft/sec (435m/sec)

The Swiss company, Vetterli, produced their breechloading rifle in two forms. In its single-round, breechloading form it was adopted by Italy as the M1870. It was manufactured by Beretta under license in four versions: M1870 Infantry Rifle with a 53.0in (1,345mm) barrel; M1870 Short Rifle with a 43.1in (1,095mm) barrel; M1870 Cavalry Carbine with an even shorter 36.8in (929mm) barrel; and the M1882 Naval Rifle, which was the M1870 with an eight-round tube magazine. It was later converted to take a four-round, Vitali box magazine, when it was designated the M1870/87 Infantry Rifle (Vetterli-Vitali), which was also produced in full length, short and cavalry versions. Somewhat surprisingly, yet another model was produced as late as 1915, when the 1870/87 conversions were re-converted, being fitted with a 6.5mm caliber barrel and a new type of clip-loaded magazine to take these rounds. The Vetterli was a bolt-action rifle with four locking lugs at the rear of the bolt, which locked into the recesses in the body. It had a somewhat unusual safety device which consisted of a small catch below the bolt lever and when this was pushed forward and the breech closed, the catch slipped backwards, pulling the striker to half-cock; full cock was restored by the simple process of raising and lowering the bolt lever. The Swiss Army, meanwhile, had taken their own tubular-magazine version into service as the M1869 and this, too, was produced in various versions, as in Italy. The picture shows the Swiss M1869.

M1889 Schmidt-Rubin Infantry Rifle — Switzerland

Length (gun): 43.0in (1,092mm)
Barrel: 23.3in (592mm)
Weight (gun): 8.0lb (3.6kg)
Caliber: 0.295in (7.5mm)
Rifling: 3 grooves, r/hand
Operation: breechloading
Feed: 12-round box magazine
Muz vel: 1,920ft/sec (585m/sec)

In Switzerland a great deal of research was carried out, much of it by Major Rubin, who, by 1886, had developed a 0.30in (7.5mm) cartridge firing a copper-jacketed bullet by means of smokeless powder, while Colonel Schmidt made a survey of breech mechanisms. This work was combined and resulted in a new rifle, officially adopted by the Swiss Army as the Model 1889. This employed a breech mechanism of the straight pull type, but on a somewhat different principle to that of Mannlicher. The bolt consisted of a long bolt cylinder, over the rear half of which was fitted a sleeve with two locking lugs on its outer surface, the operating rod being parallel to it and in its own housing. The receiver was unusually long, the rear end consisting of a complete cylinder, on the inside of which were two recesses for the locking lugs. A straight pull on the handle brought it to the rear, with its unlocking stud traveling in a slot on the locking sleeve, which was curved in such a way that the pressure of the stud caused the sleeve to rotate and unlock the locking lugs. The forward movement of the operating rod reversed the process and also cocked the striker, which was fitted with a cocking piece in the form of a ring, allowing it to be cocked without opening the breech. The magazine protruded below the level of the stock, holding two chargers of six cartridges each. The design was improved in 1896 by shortening the action and strengthening the cocking sleeve (M1888/96). A further improvement was made in 1900 when a shorter rifle (M1900) was adopted, which held only six (rather than 12) rounds. Further models were the M1911 with improvements to the bolt and barrel, and the M1931 with a redesigned action. There were also cavalry carbine versions. The picture shows the M1900 Short Rifle.

SIG 7.5mm SG-57 Rifle — Switzerland

Length (gun): 43.4in (1.102mm)
Barrel: 20.5in (520mm)
Weight (gun): 12.3lb (5.6kg)
Caliber: 7.5mm
Rifling: 4 grooves, r/hand
Operation: delayed blowback
Feed: 24-round box
Cyclic rate: 475rpm
Muz vel: 2,493ft/sec (760m/sec)

The main Swiss small-arms firm is the Schweizerische Industrie Gesellschaft (SIG = Swiss Industrial Company) of Neuhausen am Rheinfall, which has produced a number of outstanding designs, the SG-57 (Schweizerisches Gewehr = Swiss Rifle Model 1957), being one of them. Switzerland is a neutral country and its Cold War national requirements were to face potential attackers with a well-armed and well-trained militia spread over the entire country and taking full advantage of detailed local knowledge. This meant that every member kept his rifle at home and was fully prepared to use it at a moment's notice. The SG-57 was developed specifically to meet this very exacting national operational requirement and by modern standards it was very heavy for a self-loading rifle, weighing some 12.3lb (5.6kg); indeed it weighed 2.9lb/1.3kg more than the comparable British L1A1 of the same period and no less than 5.4lb (2.45kg) more than the Armalite AR18. The SG-57 was designed to be very robust, which explains part of the extra weight, but it also included an integral bipod. This bipod, together with the semi/full automatic selector lever and straight-line stock, enabled the weapon to be used for controlled burst-fire, followed up by semiautomatic. The SG-57 fired the 7.5 x 55mm Swiss M1911 round and was a delayed-blowback weapon using the roller-delayed system pioneered in the Mauser StG-45, which had been further developed in the late 1940s by German designers in Spain (see the entries for G3 and CETME Model 58 self-loading rifles). The SG-57 had a pressed steel receiver, a vented foregrip, folding bipod, wooden butt with an integral rubber butt-pad, carrying handle, and a 24-round box magazine, and was capable of launching grenades from the combined grenade-launcher/compensator. Some 600,000 were manufactured for the Swiss defense forces and a further 100,000 for the export market, the latter under the overall designation of SG-510. Individual export models were: the SG-510-1, which fired the 7.62 x 51mm (M38) NATO round; the SG-510-2, which was a slightly lighter version of the -1; the SG-510-3, which fired the Soviet 7.62 x 39mm cartridge and was slightly smaller; and the SG-510-4, which fired the NATO cartridge, but also included various minor improvements over the SG-57.

The SG-57 was developed into the SG-530 assault rifle, which was, in essence, a smaller and lighter version of the SG-57, chambered for the 5.56mm cartridge; this proved to be an excellent weapon but far too expensive and led to the SG-540 firing the 5.56mm cartridge and the SG-542 firing the 7.62mm round. The weapon illustrated here is the SG-510-4 AMT (AMT = American Match Target) and the prominent white rectangular tab above the pistol grip denotes that the full-automatic facility has been de-activated.

India Pattern Brown Bess Musket UK

Length (gun): 54.3in (1,378mm)
Barrel: 38.6in (921mm)
Weight (gun): 9.9lb 4.5(kg)
Caliber: 0.753in (19.1mm)
Rifling: none
Operation: flintlock
Feed: manual, muzzle-loading
Muz vel: n.k.

The famous "Brown Bess" was the standard British Army infantry weapon throughout the Napoleonic wars, with a maximum rate of fire, depending upon the firer's skills and the circumstances of the battle, of about four rounds per minute. Its accuracy was estimated as being capable of hitting a man-size target at 75yd (69m). The reason for the title "India Pattern" is that when the French Revolutionary Wars started in 1793 the British Army was, as was almost invariably the case, short of weapons and turned to the Honourable East India Company (HEIC) for help. The HEIC immediately handed over what muskets it had in stock in Britain, and armories throughout the country were encouraged to produce the "India Pattern Brown Bess" in as large numbers as possible. This remained the standard British infantry musket well into the 19th Century and was still being made at the start of the reign of Queen Victoria. The weapon illustrated carries the Tower Ordnance Store Keeper's Stamp dated 1800, which indicates that it was accepted for service in that year, having been made at the Tower of London in the armory operated by the Board of Ordnance, a department of the government. The butt-plate tang is marked "2 BWA" indicating that it was issued to the Bridge Ward Association of the City of London Volunteer Forces, a local defense body of the era, when an invasion by Napoleon's forces was considered a distinct possibility.

Baker Rifle UK

Length (gun): 46.0in (1,168mm)
Barrel: 30.0in (762mm)
Weight (gun): 9.1lb (4.1kg)
Caliber: 0.614in (15.6mm)
Rifling: 7 grooves, r/hand
Operation: flint
Feed: Muzzle-loading
Muz vel: ca 1,000ft/sec (305m/sec)

The Baker rifle was designed by Ezekiel Baker and submitted to the tests which were held at the Royal Arsenal, Woolwich, England in February 1800. It duly won and was ordered into production, entering service with the British Army in 1801. It was the weapon with which the specialist "rifle" regiments fought in the Peninsular War and at the Battle of Waterloo in 1815. For its day it was a light, robust, handy and well-made weapon, in which its users had great confidence. It was usually fitted with fixed sights with which targets could be engaged with reasonable accuracy up to ranges of some 200yd (183m), although marksmen might be able to achieve 300yd (274m) on a windless day. A few examples have been found with a folding rear sight. It remained in service until 1838 when it was replaced by the Brunswick rifle (qv).

Samuel Staudenmayer Target Rifle UK

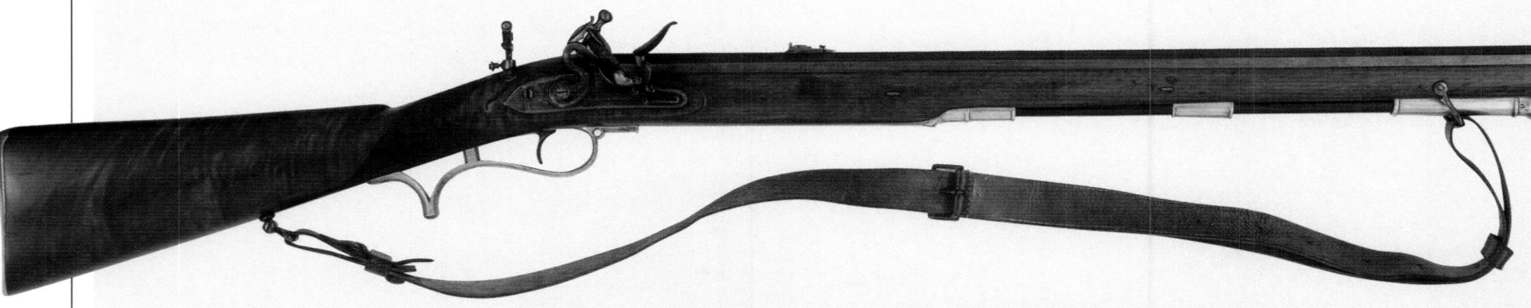

Length (gun): 45.5in (1,158mm)
Barrel: 30.0in (762mm)
Weight (gun): 8.9lb (4.0kg)
Caliber: 0.615in (15.6mm)
Rifling: n.k.
Operation: muzzle-loading, flintlock
Feed: single-round, manual
Muz vel: n.k.

This Regency-period target rifle was made by the celebrated London gunsmith, Samuel Staudenmayer, in about 1805. Its design is based on that of the contemporary service long arm, the Baker rifle, but the bore carries a faster twist and the weapon is fitted with superior sights. The barrel is made of iron and of octagonal cross-section and is stocked to the muzzle, with no provision for a bayonet. It has a walnut stock, brass mounts and a wooden ramrod. The foresight is a plain blade protected by a sun-shade. It has two backsights, the forward of which is a notched sight mounted atop the barrel, with blades for 100yd (91m), 200yd (183m) and 300yd (274m), which can be moved along two mounting grooves. The second rear sight is a tang-mounted aperture sight adjustable for both windage and elevation. Such an accurate weapon would have been used by Regency-period marksmen corps, among which were the splendidly named Duke of Cumberland's Sharpshooters; the Robin Hood Riflemen; and the Acrotomentarian Society of Riflemen.

Theophilus Richards Muzzle-loading Sporting Shotgun — UK

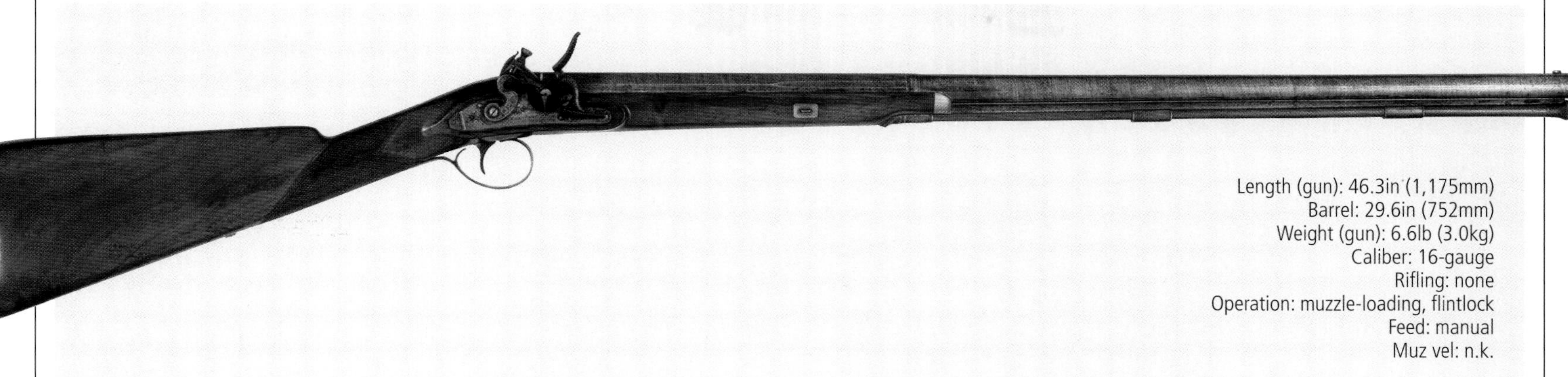

Length (gun): 46.3in (1,175mm)
Barrel: 29.6in (752mm)
Weight (gun): 6.6lb (3.0kg)
Caliber: 16-gauge
Rifling: none
Operation: muzzle-loading, flintlock
Feed: manual
Muz vel: n.k.

This single-barreled, sporting, muzzle-loading shotgun was made by the British gunsmith Theophilus Richards and has a post-1813 Birmingham proof mark, suggesting that it was probably made in 1815, the year of the Battle of Waterloo. It has a twist barrel manufactured from horse-shoe nails and stamped "Stubs twisted," being octagonal at the breech, changing to 16-sided and then, after a baluster turn, round. The stock is made from walnut and the mounts are iron. The shooter of such a weapon would have needed to carry a number of accessories with him, including powder, flask, shot flask, wads, spare flints, and a third flask for fine grain powder.

Brunswick Rifle — UK

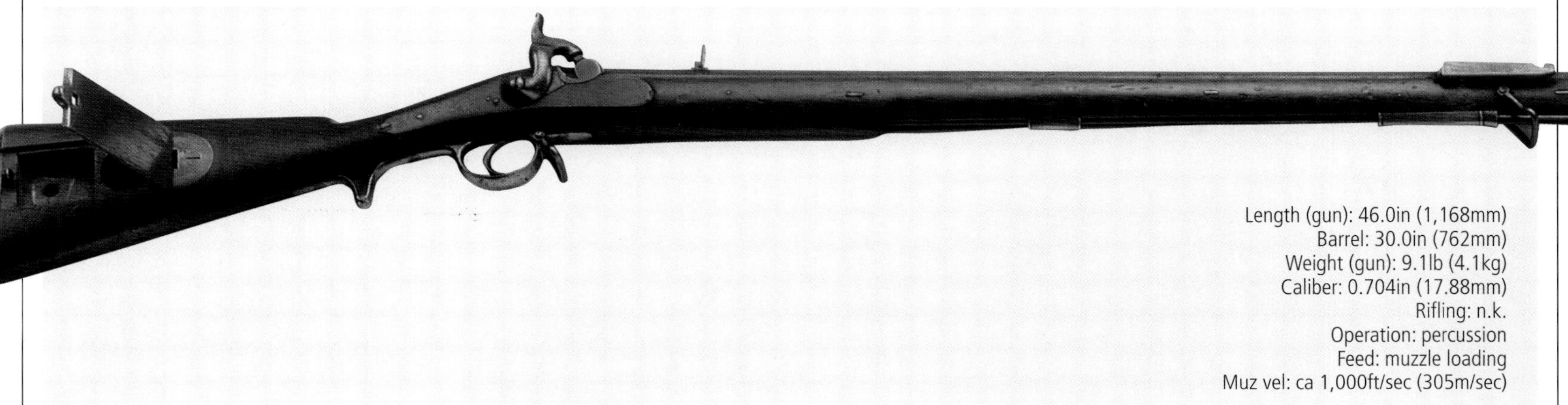

Length (gun): 46.0in (1,168mm)
Barrel: 30.0in (762mm)
Weight (gun): 9.1lb (4.1kg)
Caliber: 0.704in (17.88mm)
Rifling: n.k.
Operation: percussion
Feed: muzzle loading
Muz vel: ca 1,000ft/sec (305m/sec)

By 1835 British Army stocks of the Baker rifle had dropped to a low level and instructions were given to develop a new weapon, which emerged as a percussion lock with 11 grooves of rifling. This was found to be reasonably accurate, but with too low a muzzle velocity; it was also far too heavy. The designer (Lovell) then produced a much modified weapon, whose barrel had two deep grooves 180 degrees apart and fired a spherical ball with a belt cast around its circumference, the intention being that, when the ball was held between forefinger and thumb with the belt horizontal, the edges of the belt would then fit the grooves, which were cut away into semi-circular notches at the muzzle to facilitate loading. This weapon was accepted as the "Brunswick Rifle," but before it was put into production it was decided to increase the caliber to 0.704in (17.88mm) so that it could also take the standard musket ball. Details of tests survive to show that the Brunswick would place the majority of its shots into a 2ft (610mm) target at 200yd (183m) and just over 50percent into a 3ft (914mm) target at 300yd (274m). To facilitate shooting at longer ranges the rifle had a fixed backsight for 200yd and a folding leaf backsight for 300yd. A further version was produced as the "Heavy Brunswick" for the Royal Navy. The Brunswick was superseded in British service in the early 1850s and some ended up in North America in the Civil War, this particular example having been used by the Confederate Army.

Short Sea Service Musket — UK

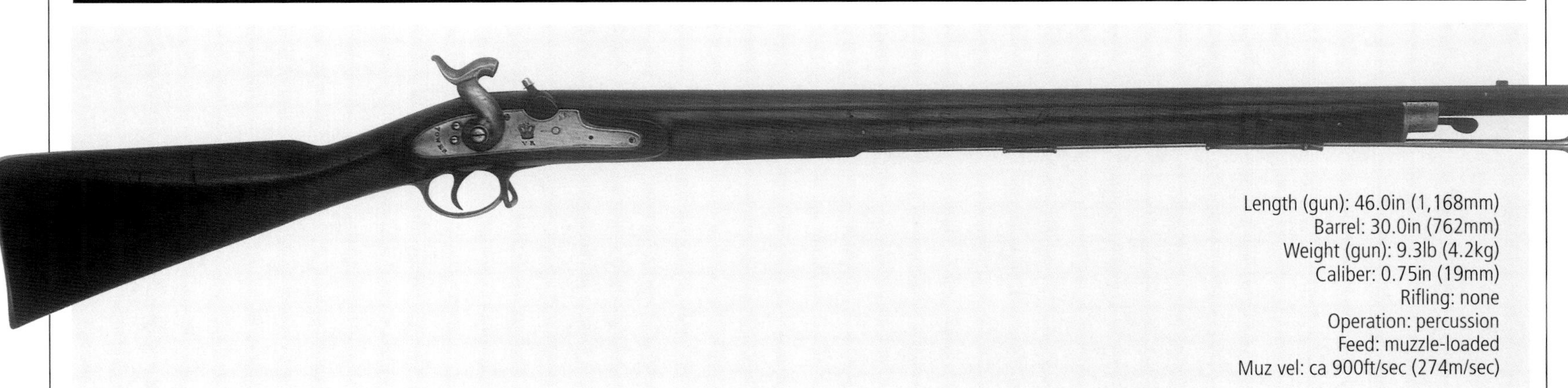

Length (gun): 46.0in (1,168mm)
Barrel: 30.0in (762mm)
Weight (gun): 9.3lb (4.2kg)
Caliber: 0.75in (19mm)
Rifling: none
Operation: percussion
Feed: muzzle-loaded
Muz vel: ca 900ft/sec (274m/sec)

The Short Sea Service Musket of the type used by the British Royal Navy was originally issued as a flintlock but was altered to percussion by means of a conversion lock, designed by George Lovell of the Royal Small Arms Factory at Enfield in 1839. The lock plate has on its upper surface the depression which once housed the pan but is now filled by the nipple lump, and the holes for the frizzen spring. Note also the Royal Crown and initials "VR" (Victoria Regina).

1853 PATTERN ENFIELD RIFLE UK

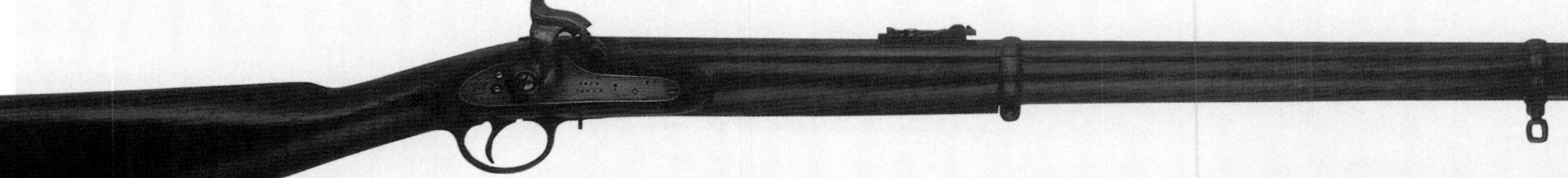

Length (gun): 55.0in (1,397mm)
Barrel: 39.0in (991mm)
Weight (gun): 8.6lb (3.9kg)
Caliber: 0.577in (14.6mm)
Rifling: 3 grooves, l/hand
Operation: percussion
Feed: muzzle-loading
Muz vel: n.k

The new British rifle introduced in 1853 was known simply as "the Enfield." It had a 39.0in (991mm) long barrel of 0.577in (14.65mm) caliber and was rifled with three grooves, which made one complete turn in 78.0in (1,982mm). It was light in comparison to other service rifles, weighing 8.6lb (3.9kg) and, for the first time, the barrel was secured to the stock by bands rather than the traditional pins (The shorter, two-band version of 1856 is shown). The backsight was a ladder, hinged at the rear and with a notch on the bridge; at rest it was set for 100yd (91.4m) and the slider could be pushed forwards to be set for 200yd (183m), 300yd (274m) and, finally, 400yd (366m). At ranges greater than 400yd the ladder was raised to the vertical and the slider set according to the range, with the firer using a second notch, which was in the slider itself. There were different bullets, but a typical round was just over 1.0in (25.4mm) in length and weighed about 530 grains. One of the Enfield rifle's claims to fame is that it was the weapon that, quite unintentionally, sparked off the Indian Mutiny. The first weapons were in the course of issue to the Indian Army in 1857 and the problem centered on the loading drill which involved the firer in holding his rifle with one hand and the cartridge in the other. He then tore open the paper cartridge with his teeth and poured the powder it contained down the barrel. Disaffected elements seized upon this and spread the story that the cartridge contained not only gunpowder but also a lubricant which was, so they claimed, a mixture of pig fat, which was anathema to the Muslims, and cow fat, which was sacred to the Hindus.

WHITWORTH RIFLE UK

Length (gun): 49.0in (1,245mm)
Barrel: 30.0in (762mm)
Weight (gun): 7.5lb (3.4kg)
Caliber: 0.45in (11.4mm)
Rifling: n.k.
Operation: percussion
Feed: muzzle loading
Muz vel: ca 1,000ft/sec (305m/sec)

Sir Joseph Whitworth was a brilliant British mechanical engineer with a considerable reputation for precision measurement, particularly for screw threads (he was the inventor of the "Standard Whitworth Gauge" (SWG). In 1854 the British government asked him to design machinery for the mass-production of service rifles, which he agreed to do, but he then went one step further and undertook the design of his own rifle as well. With the help of an experienced small arms designer and two Army officers, he produced a rifle with a caliber of 0.451in (11.45mm), somewhat smaller than other contemporary weapons, a change which was not greeted with any marked enthusiasm by British Army "experts." Whitworth's rifles proved to be exceptionally accurate, but were considered to be too well made and also suffered from such excessive fouling that they had to be cleaned regularly with a special scraper. Despite this an order was placed in 1864 and some 8,000 were delivered to the British Army. This particular example was used by the Confederate Army in the American Civil War and was even fitted with an early type of telescopic sight, suggesting that it was used by a sniper.

WEBLEY REVOLVING RIFLE UK

Length (gun): 45.5in (1,156mm)
Barrel: 27.8in (705mm)
Weight: 4.5lb (2.0kg)
Caliber: 0.500in (12.7mm)
Rifling: 18 grooves, r/hand
Capacity: five
Muz vel: ca 800ft/sec (244m/sec)

Carbines with revolving chambers were made as early as the 17th Century, mainly for use by mounted men, but the weapon illustrated was made by James Webley in 1853. It is an extension arm with very strong family resemblance to the Webley Longspur revolver (qv). It has a 27in (686mm), octagonal, rifled barrel with a foresight and one fixed and one hinged backsight; the top flat is inscribed "WILLIAM HENRY FAIRFAX BIRMINGHAM." The barrel lump is hinged to the lower part of the frame, the whole being held rigid by a wedge through the cylinder axis pin. The plain cylinder has five chambers, each serially numbered. The butt is held between two tangs, the upper inscribed "BY HER MAJESTY'S ROYAL LETTERS PATENT." The removable side-plate on the left of the frame is marked "WEBLEYS PATENT." The butt is fitted with a rectangular escutcheon plate and the whole arm is decorated with well-executed scrolls. Because no rammer was provided, the flash of firing was occasionally liable to reach the bullets in the neighboring chambers and cause a multiple discharge – a fault by no means unknown, even with Colt's rammer. In order to minimize the risk of damage, the barrel lump is grooved so that the mouths of the two chambers are not obstructed; and it was usual for the firer to hold his left hand back, round the trigger-guard.

Samuel & Charles Smith Sporting Muzzle-loading Shotgun — UK

Length (gun): 45.9in (1,165mm)
Barrel: 29.3in (743mm)
Weight (gun): 6.5lb (3.0kg)
Caliber: 12-gauge
Rifling: none
Operation: muzzle-loading, percussion cap
Feed: manual
Muz vel: n.k.

This 12-bore, double-barreled, percussion-cap game gun was made by leading London gun-makers of their time (about 1858), the brothers Samuel and Charles Smith. It consists of a pair of Damascus barrels, with a walnut stock and iron mounts. The history of this particular gun is recorded: it was one of a pair made in 1858 for the Chaworth Musters family, who lived in Nottinghamshire, England.

Converted Short Sea Service Musket — UK

Length (gun): 46.0in (1,168mm)
Barrel: 30.0in (762mm)
Weight (gun): 9.3lb (4.2kg)
Caliber: 0.76in (19.3mm)
Rifling: 3 or 4 grooves, r/hand
Operation: percussion
Feed: muzzle-loaded
Muz vel: ca 1,000ft/sec (305m/sec)

News of the success of the French Minié system with a rifled barrel and percussion firing came to the notice of the British authorities in 1850 and led to the conversion of a number of existing weapons, among them being those then used by the Royal Marines, which became the "Altered Pattern 1842 Rifle – Muskets." Once this had been seen to be successful the Admiralty authorized the conversion of most of the Sea Service muskets (qv) then in use. These converted weapons were fitted with an adjustable leaf backsight and issued to sailors when required for arming landing parties or in ship-to-ship duels.

Pattern 1861 Enfield Short Rifle — UK

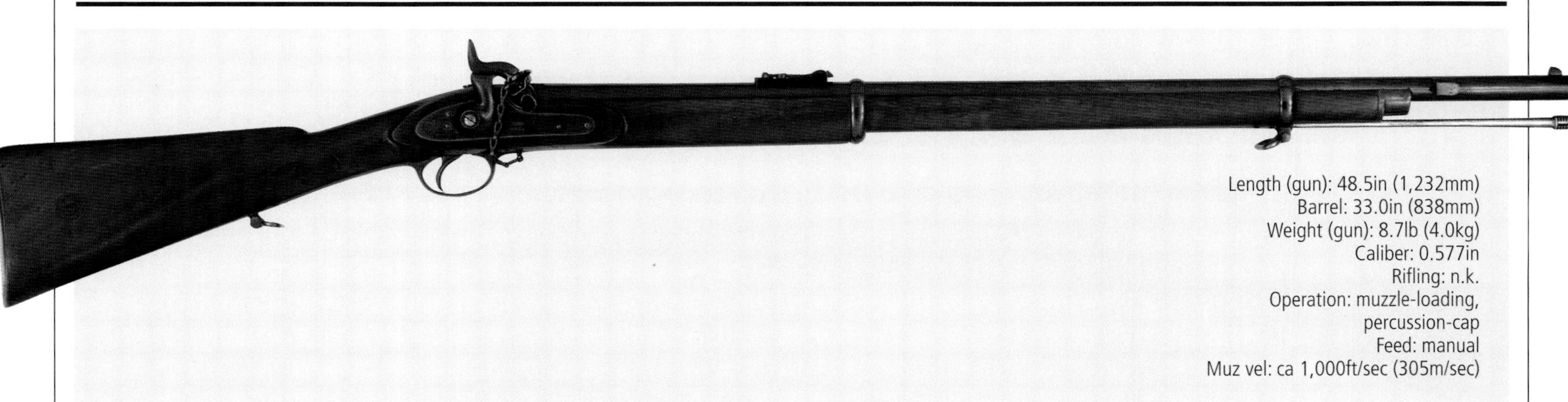

Length (gun): 48.5in (1,232mm)
Barrel: 33.0in (838mm)
Weight (gun): 8.7lb (4.0kg)
Caliber: 0.577in
Rifling: n.k.
Operation: muzzle-loading, percussion-cap
Feed: manual
Muz vel: ca 1,000ft/sec (305m/sec)

In 1859 the British Government and people became obsessed by an apparent threat of invasion by the French, since the improved railways systems and steamships made it possible to concentrate and move a large body of troops with unprecedented speed. The majority of the regular army was overseas in India and the colonies, and as a result many hundreds of volunteer rifle corps were formed. These volunteers were largely middle-class and used their own money to obtain weapons. A vast number of rifles were manufactured over a short period. Typical of these is this "Pattern 1861 Short Enfield" (also known as the "Two-Band Enfield"), which was made to government design by a private contractor, the London Armory Company. A muzzle-loader, it had an iron barrel with five-groove rifling in a 48in (1,129mm) spiral. It was fitted with a barleycorn foresight and a rear sight which was adjustable for elevation only from 100yd (91m) to 1,250yd (1,143mm). This particular rifle is known to have been used in the Ashburton Shield, one of Britain's premier shooting competitions, in 1866. (Note that this "Short Enfield" should not be confused with the "Short Magazine Lee-Enfield," which was a totally different weapon.)

GEORGE GIBBS LONG-RANGE TARGET RIFLE — UK

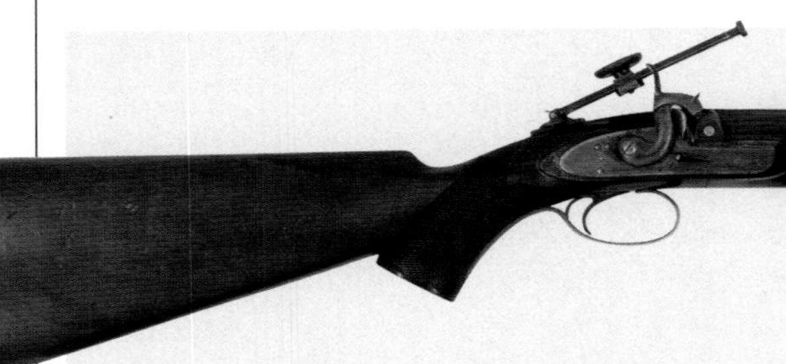

Length (gun): 51.8in (1,314mm)
Barrel: 36.0in (914mm)
Weight (gun): 9.8lb (4.5kg)
Caliber: 0.461in (11.7mm)
Rifling: n.k.
Operation: muzzle-loading, percussion-cap
Feed: manual
Muz vel: n.k.

This Metford Rifle by George Gibbs of Bristol, England, was made in about 1866 and represents the high-water marks in precision long-range shooting with muzzle-loaders and was intended for accurate shooting at ranges up to 1,000yd (914m). The rifling was Metford's pattern with shallow grooves and a gaining twist, and the barrel was fitted with a muzzle extension, designed to protect the end of the rifling when the weapon was being loaded and cleaned. The long-range backsight was mounted on a tang behind the action and had a vernier adjustment for elevation only. The variable aperture foresight was adjustable for windage and had a cross-leveling spirit-level; there was also provision for different foresight blades. The caliber of this example was 0.461in (11.7mm) and it fired a hardened cylindrical, paper-patched slug of 550 grains (6g), which was driven by 90 grains (6g) of the finest quality black powder available. In this connection it is worth noting that modern powder is not as good as the powder used for weapons such as those in the middle of the 19th Century. The gun illustrated is marked "Metford Barrel Licence Patent serial No. 45."

SNIDER RIFLE — UK

Length (gun): 48.0in (1,219mm)
Barrel: 33.0in (838mm)
Weight (gun): 8.3lb (3.7kg)
Caliber: 0.577in (14.7mm)
Rifling: 3 grooves, l/hand
Operation: breechloading
Feed: single round, manual
Muz vel: ca 1,100ft/sec (335m/sec)

By 1864 the British Army had concluded that breechloading rifles were essential and that the quickest way to re-equip the troops was to convert the existing stock rather than to develop a completely new weapon, although that, obviously, was the long-term goal. As a result, in August 1864 all leading British gun-makers were invited to submit mechanisms for converting the existing Enfield muzzle-loading rifles to breechloading and of 45 submissions the clear winner was the Snider, but it was only after lengthy tests that it was finally accepted for service in May 1866. In this weapon the breech block was hinged on the right and opened sideways to enable the firer to load a single cartridge, which he placed in the trough, pushed home and then closed the breech. He then cocked the action and, when ready, took aim and pulled the trigger, releasing the striker (which was from the original Enfield) which struck the firing pin which, in turn, hit the cap in the base of the cartridge. The main problem lay with the ammunition and a succession of rounds was developed until, finally, the Mk IX was deemed fully acceptable. Once things had got moving, large numbers of existing rifles were converted in a remarkably short space of time and the picture shows a "Rifle, Snider, Mark II**" with its breech open. This model (see specifications) was also known as the "Short Snider" in military service, although it was not as short as those specially produced for use by the Royal Irish Constabulary, which were Long Enfields, which not only had Snider actions, but also had their barrels cut down to 27in (686mm).

HILL DOUBLE 10-BORE SHOTGUN — UK

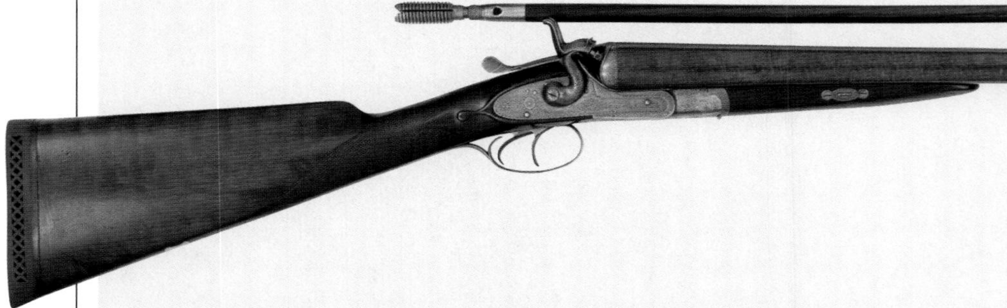

aLength (gun): 47.3in (1,200mm)
Barrel: 31.3in (794mm)
Weight (gun): 9.7lb (4.4kg)
Caliber: 10-gauge
Rifling: none
Operation: external hammer, breech loader
Feed: manual
Muz vel: n.k.

The double-trigger side-by-side Hill shotgun is a good example of an early breech loading wildfowling gun of the "black powder" era, before the appearance of inside-hammer mechanisms. It is capable of projecting 2oz (57g) of shot, somewhat more than that fired by the average modern 10-bore shotgun, which uses a nitro powder cartridge, although in the Hill's case, the firer has to load his own cartridge. The shotgun shown in the picture is in original condition, except for the butt-pad, which had to be replaced as the older one had crumbled away.

JACOB'S RIFLE — UK

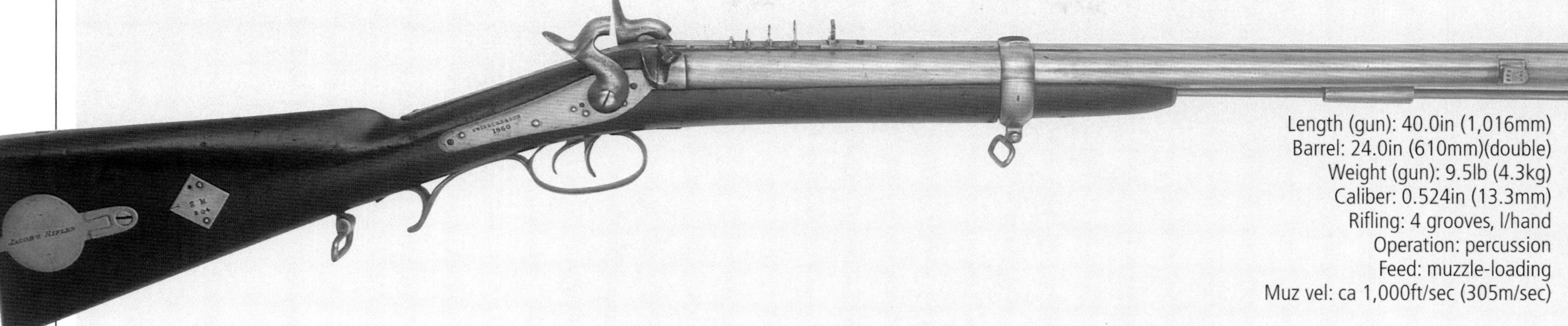

Length (gun): 40.0in (1,016mm)
Barrel: 24.0in (610mm)(double)
Weight (gun): 9.5lb (4.3kg)
Caliber: 0.524in (13.3mm)
Rifling: 4 grooves, l/hand
Operation: percussion
Feed: muzzle-loading
Muz vel: ca 1,000ft/sec (305m/sec)

The Jacob's Rifle was one of a large number of weapons designed by Brigadier-General John Jacob, a British officer who originally served in the Bombay Artillery, but later commanded a cavalry regiment, the Scinde Horse. He was a skillful engineer and imaginative designer, who also believed in thorough testing, even to the extent of having a 2,000yd (1,828m) range built outside his headquarters. His early work was devoted to improving the existing Brunswick rifle, but he then went on to design his own, one of which was this double-barreled weapon which was adopted for use by some regiments of the British Indian Army. The problem in the early 19th Century was the long time it took for an infantryman to reload his weapon, and by giving him a second barrel the Jacob's rifle did at least double the number of rounds immediately available – although it also took double the usual time to reload! The two barrels were both rifled, with four grooves to take flanged bullets and it had a variety of backsights including one 4.5in (114.3mm) high and graduated up to 2,000yd (1,828m).

MARTINI-HENRY RIFLE — UK

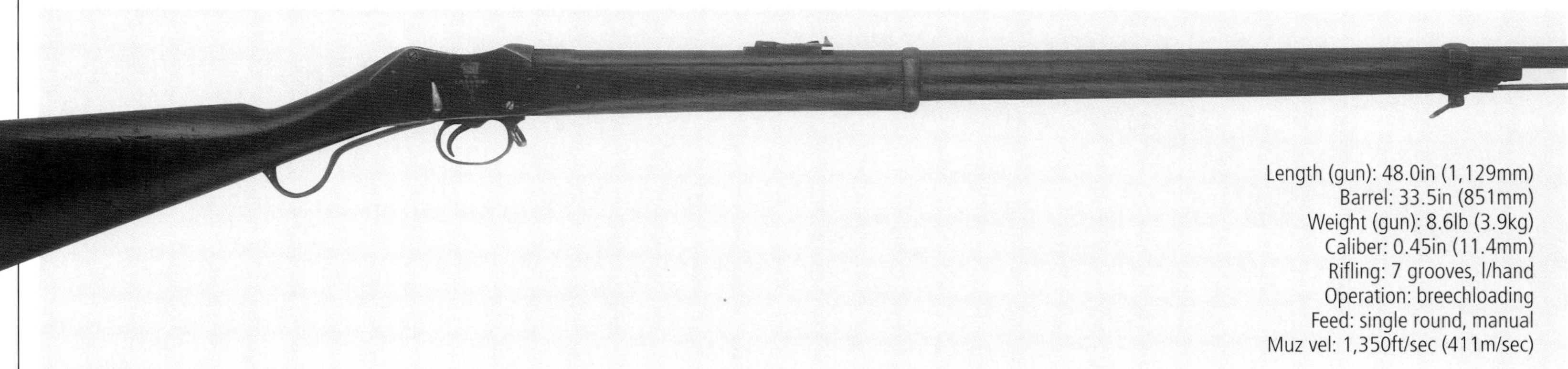

Length (gun): 48.0in (1,129mm)
Barrel: 33.5in (851mm)
Weight (gun): 8.6lb (3.9kg)
Caliber: 0.45in (11.4mm)
Rifling: 7 grooves, l/hand
Operation: breechloading
Feed: single round, manual
Muz vel: 1,350ft/sec (411m/sec)

The British Army committee which selected the Snider (qv) action for converting existing Enfield muskets then went on to look for a long-term solution, which would offer substantial improvements in both action and barrel. This led to the selection of the Martini breech and the Henry barrel. In the Martini system, the block, which had a scoop-like top, was hinged at the rear, and a smart pull on the lever caused the front end of the block to drop, thus exposing the breech, partially extracting the empty cartridge case, and cocking the striker. The firer then removed the empty cartridge case, inserted a new one, pulled the lever back against the stock, took aim, and fired. The barrel selected by the committee was designed by Alexander Henry (see Farquarson rifle). His steel Barrel was 0.45in (11.43mm) caliber and fired bullets of 0.5in (12.7mm) in diameter, with seven grooves making a left-hand turn in every 22.0in (559mm). The bullet weighed 480 grains (31.1g) and was hardened by the addition of small amounts of tin; it also had a slightly hollow base. User trials found some shortcomings in the cartridge and a new design was then developed which was bottle-shaped and fitted into an enlarged and slightly tapered chamber. Thus modified, the new weapon was accepted into service in 1871 as the "Rifle, Martini-Henry Mk1" and was developed through the Mk2 (modified trigger), Mk3 (improved backsight) and Mk4 (general improvements). There were also two shorter carbine versions: one for the cavalry, the other for the artillery. A further version was originally to have been designated the Mk5, but as it had a new 0.303in barrel designed by William Metford, it was renamed the Martini-Metford before entering service. The picture shows a standard issue Martini-Henry Mk2 rifle, manufactured in 1882.

GREENER GP SHOTGUN — UK

Length (gun): 48.5in (1232mm)
Barrel: 32.0in (813mm)
Weight (gun): 6.8lb (3.1kg)
Caliber: 12-gauge
Rifling: none
Operation: see text
Feed: manual
Muz vel: n.k.

This Greener used the rugged and reliable Martini tipping-block mechanism to produce an extremely robust sporting gun, and the "GP" in the designation is believed to have stood for "General Purpose." The manufacturer, W.W. Greener & Co, has long since gone out of business, having been bought out by the British Webley company, which was still manufacturing this gun on a small scale in the early 1990s. It is also said to be manufactured in the Philippines. The picture shows an original Greener model, with a tubular steel operating lever under the small of the butt and a large safety lever on the side of the receiver, above and to the rear of the trigger. Lowering the operating lever ejected the spent case and cocked the striker.

WILLIAM EVANS FARQUARSON ACTION RIFLE — UK

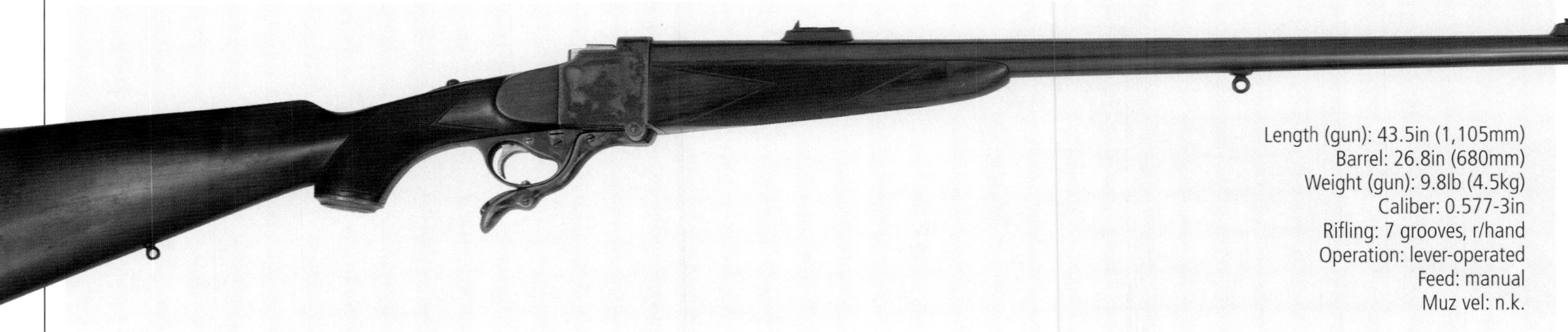

Length (gun): 43.5in (1,105mm)
Barrel: 26.8in (680mm)
Weight (gun): 9.8lb (4.5kg)
Caliber: 0.577-3in
Rifling: 7 grooves, r/hand
Operation: lever-operated
Feed: manual
Muz vel: n.k.

Farquarson, a Scotsman, was the most famous poacher of his age, a record of his exploits in this sphere eventually being published in a book. He was also a superb marksman, winning the Scottish rifle championship in 1863 and the "King of the Belgians" prize in 1869. At some time in the course of these two careers he invented the "Farquarson action" which he patented. He was immediately taken to court by his former employer, the great Edinburgh gun-maker, Alexander Henry (of Martini-Henry rifle fame), but Farquarson was supported by Sir Henry Halford and William Ellis Metford, respectively the most famous ballistician and engineer of the day, and duly won the case. The Farquarson action involved a lever under the trigger guard, which is pushed down and forward, recocking the striker and activating the ejector. The Farquarson was made under license until the patent expired, when it was marketed by Webley using actions bought in from Francotte of Italy. The weapon shown here was made by William Evans of 63 Pall Mall, London, and using a 3.0in (76mm) case and 100 grains of cordite it fired a 750-grain bullet, either full-jacketed or soft point, against heavy or dangerous game, such as buffalo, rhinoceros or elephant. It was rifled, with seven grooves in a right-hand twist, with a pillar foresight and a backsight consisting of three leaves, marked for 100, 200 and 300 yards (91, 182 and 273m), respectively.

PURDEY DOUBLE RIFLE — UK

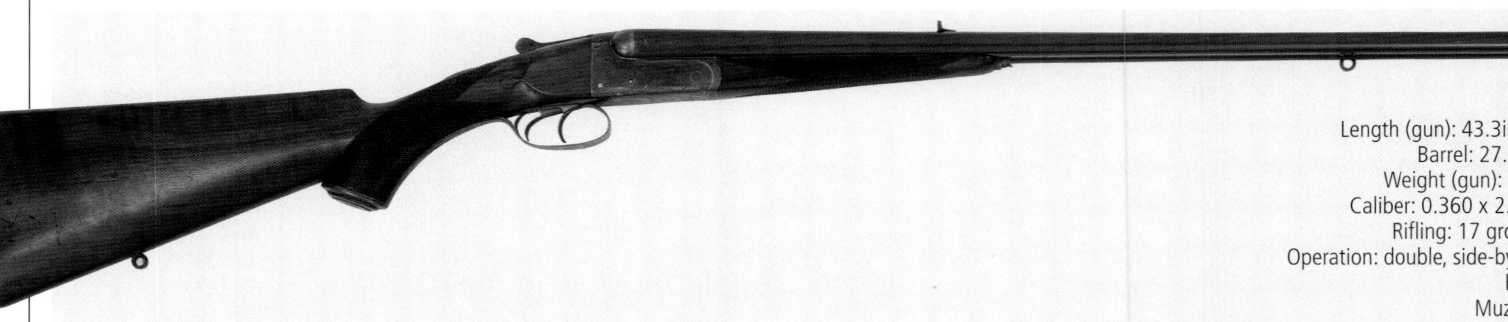

Length (gun): 43.3in (1,098mm)
Barrel: 27.1in (689mm)
Weight (gun): 7.1lb (3.2kg)
Caliber: 0.360 x 2.25in Express
Rifling: 17 grooves, r/hand
Operation: double, side-by-side barrels
Feed: manual
Muz vel: see text

This is a double-barreled, side-by-side, rifled, hammerless, boxlock made by J. Purdey & Sons of South Audley Street, London, in the 1890s. It was chambered for the 0.360 x 2.25in Express, a cartridge which threw a 190-grain bullet, often paper-patched, at about 1,700ft/sec (518m/sec), and was probably used for culling fallow deer in the parkland of some great house. In general, side-by-sides such as this are preferred to over-and-unders, such as the GebrÅder Merkel (qv), when dealing with dangerous game because of their greater reliability and speed of fire. The Purdey operates by pushing the top lever to the right, which allows the barrels to open on a hinge, recocking the internal hammers and activating the extractors. The barrels are made of steel and are rifled, with a seven-grooved right-hand twist.

VICKERS-ARMSTRONG JUBILEE MODEL RIFLE — UK

Length (gun): 44.5in (1,130mm)
Barrel: 29.0in (737mm)
Weight (gun): 9.6lb (4.3kg)
Caliber: 0.22in LR
Rifling: n.k.
Operation: lever-operated tipping breechblock
Feed: single round, manual
Muz vel: n.k.

The British heavy engineering and armaments firm of Vickers-Armstrong has involved itself only sporadically in the small arms business. It produced the Vickers-Maxim machine gun, for example, and some Luger pistols under license, but quite why they should have produced this 0.22in marksman's rifle at the beginning of the 20th Century is not clear. The "Jubilee" is a lever-operated, tipping block, single-shot rifle, whose operation bears a passing resemblance to the Martini action, and it was one of the leading target rifles of its day. The stock is one-piece, which made it easier to bed, and the receiver and barrel are one piece as well. A wing screw on the right side frees the action to drop out for cleaning or adjustment. A brass capscrew on the fore-end top houses nine interchangeable foresight elements. Ring foresights of various diameters were used at different ranges and in differing light conditions, while a post foresight was used in the so-called "Mad Minute" competitions, which involved logging as many hits as possible within 60 seconds.

Short Magazine Lee-Enfield Marks III and III* Rifles

UK

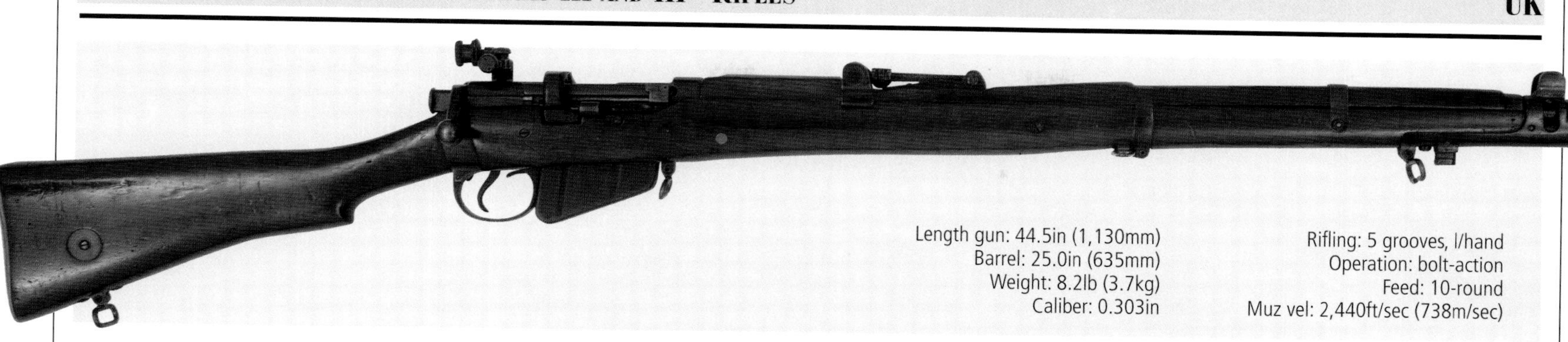

Length gun: 44.5in (1,130mm)
Barrel: 25.0in (635mm)
Weight: 8.2lb (3.7kg)
Caliber: 0.303in
Rifling: 5 grooves, l/hand
Operation: bolt-action
Feed: 10-round
Muz vel: 2,440ft/sec (738m/sec)

British experience in the South African war of 1899–1902 showed the need for a short rifle for universal use and even before the war a new weapon, the Short Magazine Lee-Enfield Mark I, had been produced and 1,000 made for trials. It was also tested operationally in the fighting against the Mad Mullah in Somaliland, and after some modification emerged as the Short Magazine Lee-Enfield (SMLE) Mark III in 1907. It was an excellent weapon and although slightly less accurate than its predecessor it had certain compensating advantages, notably its easy breech mechanism which allowed a fast rate of manipulation. The British Army had concentrated on rapid rifle fire to the stage where every soldier could fire at least 15 well-aimed shots in a minute, and the devastating effects of this were clearly seen in the first few months of World War I when the gallant German infantry suffered heavily. The Mark III was a complex weapon to make, and in 1916 various simplifications were introduced, notably the abolition of the magazine cut-off and the disappearance of the special long-range collective fire sight which was clearly unnecessary in the age of the machine gun. These changed its designation to the Mark III*, perhaps the most famous rifle in British military history. It remained an excellent weapon with an 18in (457mm) sword bayonet for close quarter work and the ability to project grenades, either rodded or from a screw-on cup.

Farquhar-Hill Rifle

UK

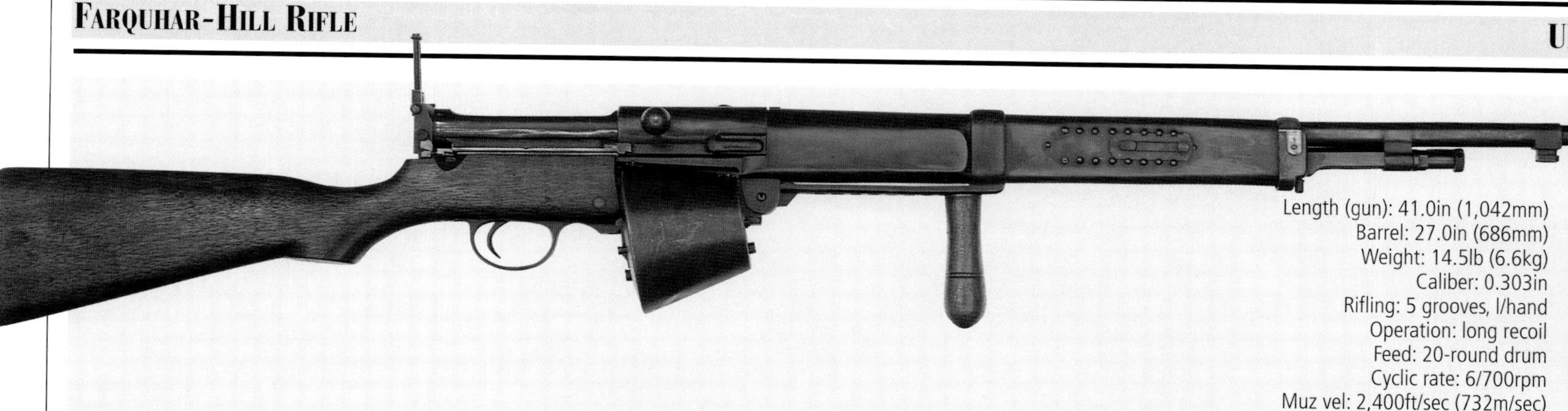

Length (gun): 41.0in (1,042mm)
Barrel: 27.0in (686mm)
Weight: 14.5lb (6.6kg)
Caliber: 0.303in
Rifling: 5 grooves, l/hand
Operation: long recoil
Feed: 20-round drum
Cyclic rate: 6/700rpm
Muz vel: 2,400ft/sec (732m/sec)

In 1908 Major Farquhar and Mr Hill produced an automatic rifle which was tested by the Automatic Rifle Committee of the British Army. The Farquhar-Hill turned out to be an extremely complex weapon. It utilized the system of long recoil, but faulty design kept the barrel and breech locked together long after the bullet had left the muzzle. The gun was rejected and nothing more was heard of it until 1917 when a second version appeared, its main difference being its unusual magazine which was in the shape of a truncated cone, powered by a clockwork spring. This version was also tested and rejected, being very liable to fouling and prone to a variety of complex stoppages. The inventors were extremely persistent and as late as 1924 they submitted the weapon illustrated. This had a similar but much smaller magazine with a capacity of 10 rounds (as compared with up to 65 in the earlier versions) but again it was unsatisfactory (still mainly because of its defective magazine) and was not therefore adopted.

Vickers Automatic Rifle (Pedersen)

UK

Length (gun): 45.0in (1,143mm)
Barrel: 24.0in (610mm)
Weight: 9lb (4.1kg)
Caliber: 0.276in
Rifling: 6 grooves, r/hand
Operation: blowback
Feed: 10-round box
Muz vel: 2,500ft/sec (762m/sec)

John Pedersen was a well-known designer of firearms in the United States, and between the world wars he designed a self-loading rifle, together with a special cartridge for it, which attracted favorable attention in America, where it was designated T2E1. This new weapon also came to the notice of Vickers who manufactured a number under license in England as the Vickers Automatic Rifle. The Pedersen was unusual in that its breech was not positively locked at the moment of discharge. Instead it made use of a hesitation-type lock, similar in principle to that of the Luger pistol but so designed that its various bearing surfaces held it closed until the chamber pressure had dropped to a safe level. The rifle was tested by the British Army in 1932, who described it as the most promising arm of its type that it had then seen. In spite of a magazine capacity of only 10 rounds it was reported to have fired 140 rounds in three minutes, a remarkable performance. Unfortunately, the breech, although safe, began to open when the chamber pressure was still quite high, which led to difficulties of extraction. In order to overcome this Pedersen had his cartridges dry waxed, which was not acceptable in a military cartridge which would have to be stored world-wide in a variety of conditions and climates. The Pedersen was not accepted, which was a pity because it was a neat, handy weapon which shot well and its cartridge was of exceptionally good performance. It might have performed well with a fluted breech, which was later designed for this type of contingency, but by that time better self-loading rifles were available. The model illustrated was made in England for test by the British Army and is the reason it is shown here rather than under "USA."

SHORT MAGAZINE LEE-ENFIELD MARK V RIFLE — UK

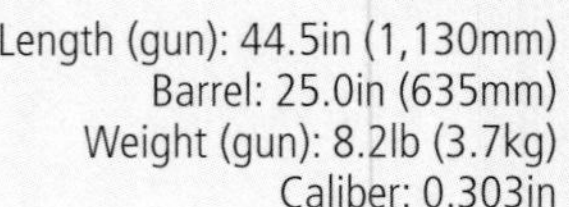

Length (gun): 44.5in (1,130mm)
Barrel: 25.0in (635mm)
Weight (gun): 8.2lb (3.7kg)
Caliber: 0.303in

Rifling: 5 grooves, l/hand
Operation: bolt-action
Feed: 10-round box magazine
Muz vel: 2,440ft/sec (738m/sec)

Soon after the end of World War I the British Army began to consider a new rifle, similar to its predecessor, but easier to make by modern mass-production methods. The first step in this direction was the new Short Magazine Lee-Enfield Mk V, which appeared in small numbers as early as 1923. Apart from an extra barrel band just in front of the forward sling swivel, the main difference was that it had an aperture backsight, rather than the "U" sight of the earlier models, experience showing that this type of sight was easier to teach to recruits. In addition, the rearsight was moved from above the barrel to a new position, much further back, on the bridge above the bolt. The sight was graduated only as far as 1,400yd (1,280m) and this, coupled with the increased distance between the fore and rear sights, reduced the margin of error and made for more accurate shooting. After trials with the Mk V it was decided that conversion of the large existing stocks of rifles would be too expensive and, although the development of a new rifle was continued (which led eventually to the Number 4 Rife [qv]), large numbers of Short Magazine Lee-Enfields remained in service well into World War II.

HOLLAND & HOLLAND 0.375IN MAGAZINE RIFLE — UK

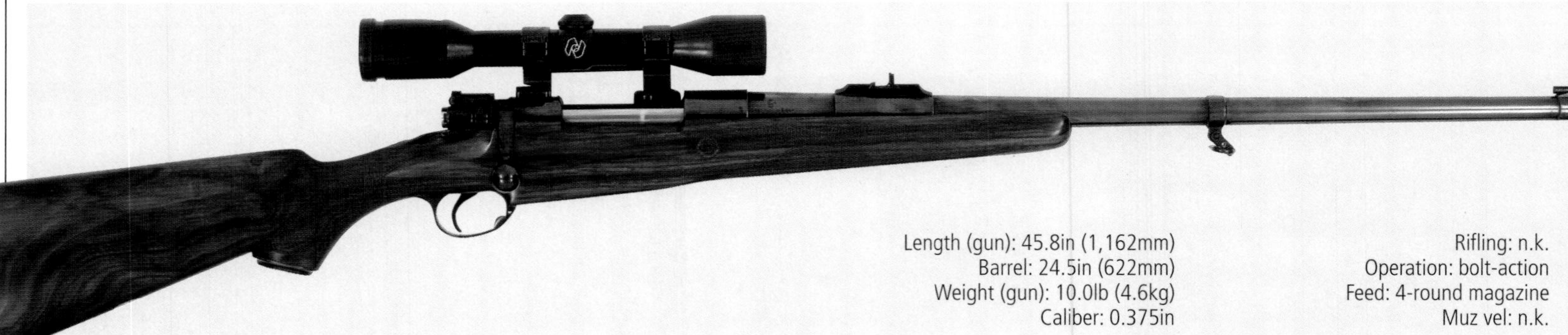

Length (gun): 45.8in (1,162mm)
Barrel: 24.5in (622mm)
Weight (gun): 10.0lb (4.6kg)
Caliber: 0.375in

Rifling: n.k.
Operation: bolt-action
Feed: 4-round magazine
Muz vel: n.k.

The British company of Holland & Holland has manufactured some of the finest rifles in use and their showroom at Bruton Street in London is a Mecca for lovers of fine firearms the world over. The firm was founded in 1835 by Harris J. Holland and took its present name in 1877. The rifle illustrated here was intended primarily for use in what used to be termed "big-game hunting," an activity that does not meet with approval today, except under closely defined and carefully monitored conditions. Holland & Holland also designed and produced their own cartridges and this rifle was designed around the company's 0.375in round, which was introduced in 1912 and which is generally considered to have been the finest "big game" round of its time. Experts of the time considered it to be ideal for shooting big bear, tiger, and lion, although it was considered to be slightly less effective against larger animals, such as elephant, rhinoceros and Cape buffalo. This weapon had a Mauser 98 turn-bolt action, with two forward lugs locking into the receiver ring. The normal sights were two leaf rear sights, which were marked "50/200yds" and "300yds", respectively (46/183m and 274m), and a gold post and folding "big bead" foresight. The weapon illustrated, however, is fitted with a Zeiss Diatal-C 4 x 32 telescopic sight.

PATTERN 1913 RIFLE — UK

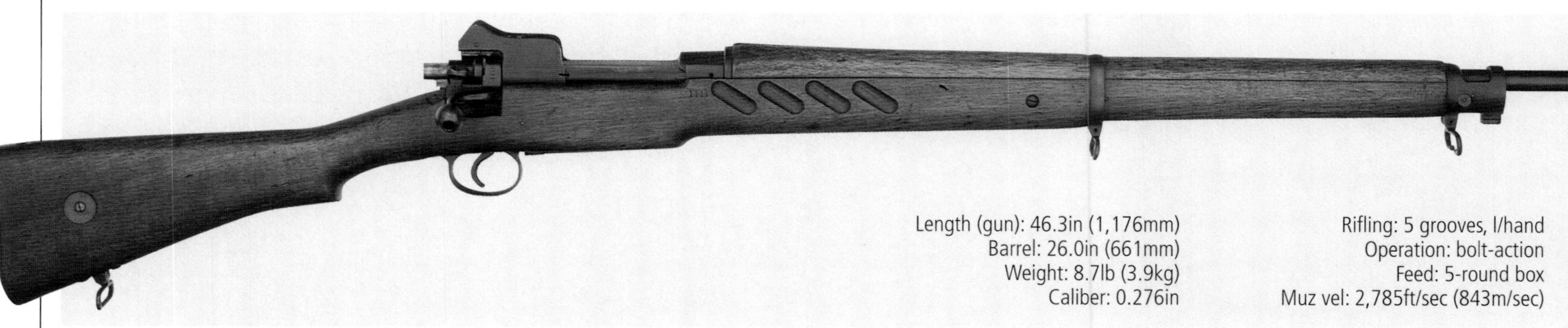

Length (gun): 46.3in (1,176mm)
Barrel: 26.0in (661mm)
Weight: 8.7lb (3.9kg)
Caliber: 0.276in

Rifling: 5 grooves, l/hand
Operation: bolt-action
Feed: 5-round box
Muz vel: 2,785ft/sec (843m/sec)

Although the Lee-Enfield series of rifle proved successful there was some prejudice against its bolt in favor of the forward-locking Mauser system, which led to the development of the new rifle shown here. Work started in 1910 and by 1912 it was in limited production for troop trials which began the next year, hence the designation of the arm. It differed from earlier Enfields in that it had a Mauser-type bolt and fired a new rimless Enfield 0.276in cartridge from an integral five-round magazine. It also had an aperture backsight protected by a somewhat bulky extension on the body above the bolt way. Although it was very accurate the Pattern 1913 was slow and clumsy to manipulate particularly for men accustomed to the Lee-Enfield; it was subject to excessive metallic fouling in the bore; it had a tremendous flash and a correspondingly loud report; worst of all, the breech heated so fast that after 15 rounds or so there was a distinct risk of the round firing as it went into the chamber, which was not conducive to good morale. The project was shelved by the outbreak of World War I, but then the rifle was converted to fire the standard British 0.303in service round, but as there were no suitable facilities for making it in the United Kingdom it was manufactured in the United States by Winchester, Eddystone, and Remington. This new rifle was designated the Pattern 1914 and in view of its accuracy it was eventually used as a sniping rifle with the addition of a telescope sight. The Pattern 1914 was also modified for use by the United States Army, but using the standard US 0.30in round. This was designated the Enfield 1917; large numbers of these were bought by Great Britain in 1940, mainly for the use of her Home Guard and the fact that they were of 0.30in caliber led to some confusion.

BSA 0.260in Model 1922 Sporting Rifle — UK

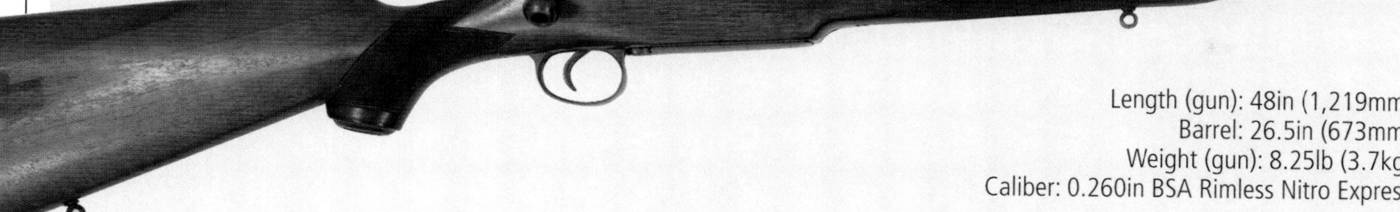

Length (gun): 48in (1,219mm)
Barrel: 26.5in (673mm)
Weight (gun): 8.25lb (3.7kg)
Caliber: 0.260in BSA Rimless Nitro Express
Rifling: n.k.
Operation: bolt-action
Feed: 5-round magazine
Muz vel: n.k.

Described elsewhere (see "Pattern 1913 Rifle") is how the British developed a 0.280in rifle prior to World War I. This became the 0.303in Pattern 1914 and was then manufactured in the USA to meet British wartime requirements. That weapon was then adapted by US manufacturers to take the 0.30-06 round and adopted by the US Army as the "Enfield M1917." By late 1918 Remington was manufacturing 4,000 such rifles per day and when production ran down to peacetime levels they not unnaturally had a vast stock of parts left over. For some reason, the British firm of BSA (Birmingham, Small Arms) decided to produce a sporting rifle based on M1917 components, which, presumably, they acquired as surplus from the USA. They also designed a new round for it – the 0.260in Rimless Nitro Express – which was a Holland & Holland 0.375in round necked down to 0.256in (6.5mm) and shortened, driving a 110 grain (7.1g) bullet at 3,100ft/sec (945m/sec), giving a level of performance which was largely wasted in a rifle, as seen here, without telescopic sights. The Model 1922 was not very popular, being very heavy and large for a sporting rifle

Number 4 Rifle — UK

Length gun: 44.5in (1,130mm)
Barrel: 25.2in (640mm)
Weight: 9.1lb (4.1kg)
Caliber: 0.303in
Rifling: 5 grooves, l/hand
Operation: bolt-action
Feed: 10-round
Muz vel: 2,440ft/sec (743m/sec)

By 1928 the British Government had developed a new service rifle, similar in general appearance and capacity to the Lee-Enfield but a good deal easier to mass-produce. This new rifle, the Number 4, was a most serviceable arm, its main difference from its predecessor being its aperture sight. It was produced from 1941 onwards mainly in Canada and the United States, although some were made in England. It underwent some modifications, mainly in the substitution of a simple two-range flip backsight for the earlier and more complex one, and some were made with two-groove rifling, but otherwise remained substantially unchanged, the main feature being perhaps the variety of bayonets made to fit it. Selected specimens were fitted with No 32 telescopic sights and detachable cheek-rests and were successfully used as sniper rifles (lower photo). It remained in service in the British regular army until 1957, but was used by cadets for many years after that. It was also popular as a target rifle.

Boys Anti-tank Rifle — UK

Length: 63.5in (1,613mm)
Barrel: 36.0in (914mm)
Weight: 36.0lb (16.3kg)
Caliber: 0.55in (13.97mm)
Rifling: 7 grooves, r/hand
Operation: bolt-action
Feed: 5-round box
Muz vel: 3,250ft/sec (990m/sec)

In October 1934 the British Army issued a requirement for a light anti-tank weapon. The officer directly concerned was a Captain Boys and for security reasons the new project was given the code-name "Stanchion." Good progress was made and tests proved encouraging, with penetration of 1in (25mm) being obtained in armor plate, so the new weapon was put into production and named after its designer. The Boys rifle was essentially a large-scale version of a service rifle firing as large a bullet with as big a charge as a reasonable man might be expected to hold, given the help of a spring absorber, a muzzle brake, and a front support. In the original weapon the muzzle brake was circular, and the front support was a monopod like an inverted T. In the second version, the one illustrated, the muzzle brake was flat with holes on each side and the monopod had been replaced by a bipod. Both models were bolt-action weapons with detachable top-mounted box magazines holding five rounds, but while the first model had a double sight for 300 and 500yd (274 and 457m) the second had a fixed sight only. The first few were in the hands of the infantry by 1937 but unfortunately tank design had advanced, and soon after the outbreak of war it was clear that the weapon was of limited use. It was also uncomfortable to fire due to its enormous recoil and by 1943 it had largely been replaced. A shortened version was briefly re-introduced for airborne troops but in the absence of a muzzle brake this recoiled even more severely than its predecessor and was soon abandoned.

NUMBER 5 0.303IN RIFLE — UK

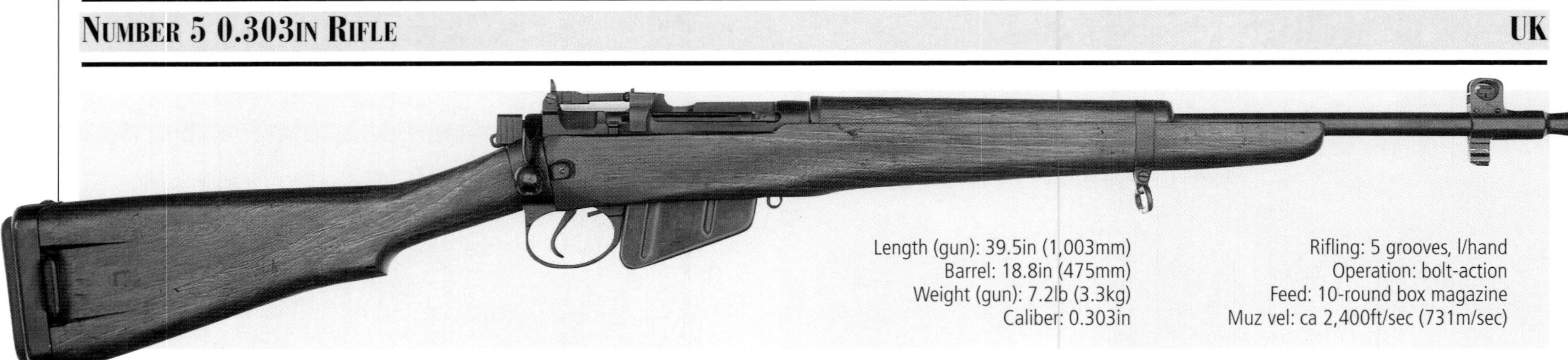

Length (gun): 39.5in (1,003mm)
Barrel: 18.8in (475mm)
Weight (gun): 7.2lb (3.3kg)
Caliber: 0.303in
Rifling: 5 grooves, l/hand
Operation: bolt-action
Feed: 10-round box magazine
Muz vel: ca 2,400ft/sec (731m/sec)

Once committed to the war against Japan in 1941, the British Empire forces took readily to jungle warfare. It was quickly found, however, that the standard infantry rifles – the Rifle Number 4 and Short Magazine Lee-Enfield (qqv) – were too long and heavy for a war which was being fought at very short ranges and in which the man who fired the first round was usually the survivor. In addition, these longer rifles easily snagged on the many obstructions in which the jungle abounded. This led to the development of the Rifle, Number 5, Mk 1, which was, in essence, a cut-down version of the Number 4, being some 5.0in (127mm) shorter and 1.9lb (0.85kg) lighter. The shorter barrel necessitated a flash suppressor, which, in turn, necessitated a new type of bayonet; in addition, the fore-end stock was cut back. The working parts were identical to those of the Number 4, but a rubber butt-pad was fitted to protect the firer's shoulder from the increased recoil, and the rear sling swivel was replaced by a different type of hook. As sometimes happens with conversions, the result was an excellent weapon, which was very popular with all those who used it in the Burma campaign during World War II and in the post-war Malayan Emergency. In the latter campaign, its replacement by the L1A1 (qv) was, for some years, treated as a definite step backwards.

EM 2 RIFLE — UK

Length (gun): 35.0in (889mm)
Barrel: 24.5in (623mm)
Weight: 7.6lb (3.42kg)
Caliber: 0.280in
Rifling: 4 grooves, r/hand
Operation: gas
Feed: 20-round box
Cyclic rate: 450rpm
Muz vel: 2,530ft/sec (772m/sec)

Soon after the end of World War II work began at the Royal Small Arms Factory, Enfield, on a new assault rifle to replace the existing bolt-action Number 4, one of its principal designers being Mr Stefan Janson. The new arm was of somewhat unconventional design with the working parts and magazine housed behind the trigger in a rearward extension of the body, which also had the buttplate attached to it. As the buttplate was in line with the axis of the barrel it was necessary to elevate the line of sight and this was done by incorporating an optical sight as part of the carrying handle. Although the sight was non-magnifying it did away with the need to focus and align front and rear sights and target. All that was necessary was to align the pointer on the target image which made it very quick to handle. It did very well on trials, its only minor disadvantage being that owing to the situation of the ejection opening on the right side above the magazine the rifle could not be fired from the left shoulder. In spite of its effectiveness NATO, and in particular the United States (which comprised the backbone of the organization), rejected it, mainly because of understandable American reluctance to change caliber at a time when they had huge stocks of the current cartridge and the almost unlimited capacity to produce more. A few EM 2s were rebarreled experimentally to take the 7.62mm round, but the rifle really needed a major re-design to do this and as time was pressing the UK reluctantly abandoned it in favor of the L1A1 (qv), a British adaptation of the Belgian FAL (qv).

L1A1 RIFLE — UK

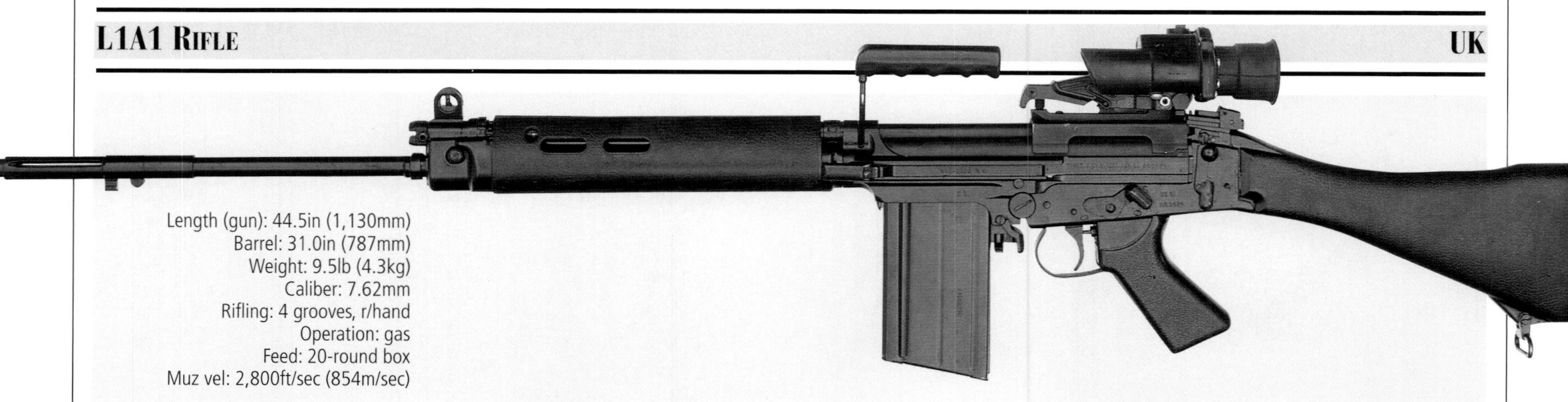

Length (gun): 44.5in (1,130mm)
Barrel: 31.0in (787mm)
Weight: 9.5lb (4.3kg)
Caliber: 7.62mm
Rifling: 4 grooves, r/hand
Operation: gas
Feed: 20-round box
Muz vel: 2,800ft/sec (854m/sec)

Once the EM 2 rifle (qv) had been rejected, the British Army decided to adopt a new self-loading rifle firing the standard NATO cartridge. After extensive tests it was decided to adopt the Belgian FN FAL (qv) rifle, which was already in use by many other countries and this, with a number of modifications, became the L1A1. The British version was a self-loader only and would not fire bursts; nor did the British Army adopt the heavy barreled version which some countries used as their squad or section light machine gun. The early rifle was modified in some respects particularly as regards the use of glass fiber instead of wood, but remained unchanged in principle. It was gas-operated, and capable of 30 or 40 well-aimed shots a minute and generally a sound and reliable weapon. Its principal disadvantage was its length. The specimen illustrated is fitted with a night sight. A variety were available varying from the simple foresight with a self-powered light source to the Trilux sight shown, which could be quickly and easily mounted. It was self-energizing and easily adjusted for intensity and was useful not only for night work but also against indistinct targets by day. It entered service in 1974, its official designation being the Sight Unit Infantry Trilux.

Thomas Wild Sidelock Ejector Shotgun

UK

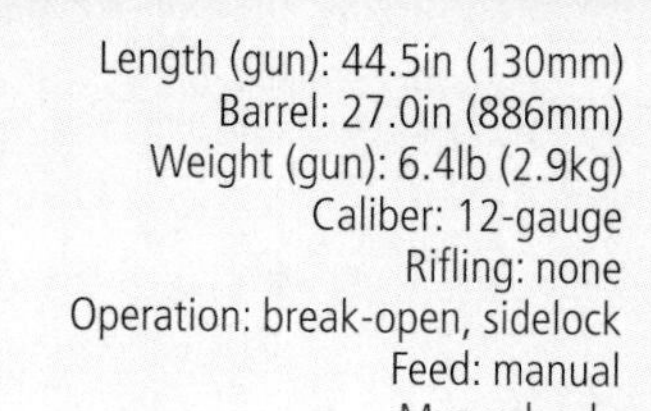

Length (gun): 44.5in (130mm)
Barrel: 27.0in (886mm)
Weight (gun): 6.4lb (2.9kg)
Caliber: 12-gauge
Rifling: none
Operation: break-open, sidelock
Feed: manual
Muz vel: n.k.

This is a good quality sporting gun by a well-known British gunsmith, and was made as one of a pair in 1955. The firm of Thomas Wild & Co operated from Whitehall Street in Birmingham, in what was once a very busy gun-making area, but which has long since succumbed to "inner city development." The double-barreled gun is light, with 2.75in (70mm) chambers and a sidelock, but is so well balanced that shooting even 1.125oz (32g) loads from it does not produce any unacceptable recoil.

Holland & Holland 0.458in Magazine Rifle

UK

Length (gun): 46.3in (1,175mm)
Barrel: 24.8in (629mm)
Weight (gun): 10.1lb (4.6kg)
Caliber: 0.458in Winchester
Rifling: n.k.
Operation: bolt-action
Feed: 3-round magazine
Muz vel: n.k.

When the American company, Winchester, decided in around 1955 to seek a slice of the then very profitable African market, the cartridge case the firm looked to was the venerable belted rimless 0.375in round. They blew this out, straight-walled it, and trimmed its length to 2.5in (63.5mm) overall, and arrived at the 0.458in, which quickly became the world standard in its category, and is the round used by this Holland & Holland rifle. Part of the reason for the popularity of this round lay in its dimensional compatibility with standard-length, bolt-action receivers, another with the excellent performance of its 510 grain (33g) bullets: one a reliable soft-nose, the other a tough, steel-jacketed solid. This combination of affordability and performance in the 0.458in round quickly overcame all competition. The action is Mauser 98 turn-bolt, with two forward lugs locking in the receiver ring. The weapon has a single-stage trigger, with rocking safety on the right of the receiver. It has a gold bead foresight with folding guard, and a two-leaf backsight marked, respectively, for 50-200yd (45-183m) and 350yd (320m).

Swing SIN 71 M5 Rifle

UK

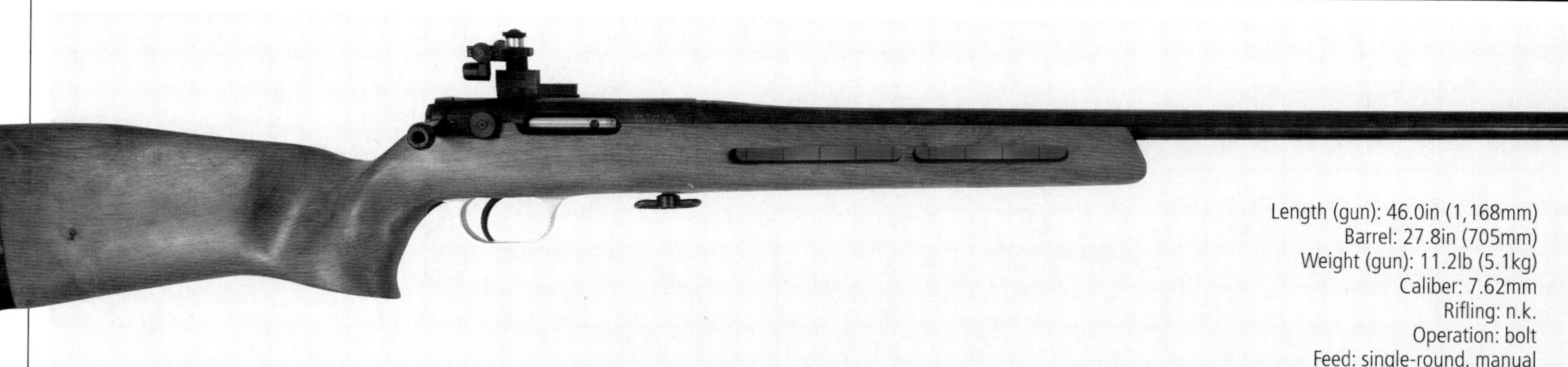

Length (gun): 46.0in (1,168mm)
Barrel: 27.8in (705mm)
Weight (gun): 11.2lb (5.1kg)
Caliber: 7.62mm
Rifling: n.k.
Operation: bolt
Feed: single-round, manual
Muz vel: n.k.

In the late 1980s most top British marksmen were using the Swing SIN 71 M5 rifle, which had been designed by George Swenson for use at longer ranges. The SIN 71 M5 has an ultra-stiff action delivering dense, round (as opposed to elliptical) groups, with a very fast lock time to minimize shooter-related departure error. The M5 has a massively rigid, round-bottomed action, with the smallest possible loading/ejection port, and with two massive recoil lugs, one at the back, underneath the bolt handle, the other just to the rear of the locking engagements. Vertical bedding bolts engage each lug. The rifle is Devcon bedded up to the bore line, and the positioning of the recoil lugs is intended to minimize torquing of the receiver within the bedding. The bolthead carries four large, equally spaced locking lugs, with a plunger-ejector. The extractor is set into the right lug and by using titanium components and a massive main spring the lock time has been reduced to 1.24 milliseconds, while retaining 100 percent reliability on military primers. The trigger unit, which is an adaptation of a Montari design of the 1930s, is adjustable down to 1.0lb (0.45kg) and is a much sought-after item in its own right, as are the Swing's micrometer sights (backsight, adjustable aperture; foresight, tunnel with interchangeable elements).. The rifle is normally fitted with 28.0in (711mm) or 30.0in (762mm) Schultz & Larsen barrels. The Swing is not a particularly easy weapon to fire, having steep camming angles and a bolt which takes some effort to operate, but it is very accurate at long ranges.

WEBLEY & SCOTT MODEL 700 SHOTGUN — UK

Length (gun): 43.0in (1,092mm)
Barrel: 26.0in (660mm)
Weight (gun): 6.3lb (2.9kg)
Caliber: 12-gauge
Rifling: none
Operation: break-open, box-lock
Feed: manual
Muz vel: n.k.

The internationally respected British firm of Webley & Scott was founded in about 1900 by the amalgamation of two leading British gunsmiths: P. Webley and W. & C. Scott. This combined company was well-known for its action, in which the forward lump of the barrels showed through the action body – a method not commonly used by other makers of box-lock guns. When production of sporting guns resumed after World War II demand quickly outstripped supply and production delays led to an increasing number of imports, particularly from Spain. In an effort to solve its problems, Webley & Scott absorbed Greener (qv) in 1966 but this failed to provide a solution, and the gunmaking business was then sold off to a group of former employees, who created a new company with the much earlier name of W. & C. Scott Ltd, although this has since been taken over by Holland & Holland (qv). By the late 1980s the Model 700 seen here (which is also known as the "Kinmount") was one of the cheapest British-made double guns still on the market.

HOLLAND & HOLLAND 0.264IN MAGAZINE RIFLE — UK

Length (gun): 46.3in (1,175mm)
Barrel: 24.5in (622mm)
Weight (gun): 9.6lb (4.4kg)
Caliber: 0.264in
Rifling: n.k.
Operation: bolt-action
Feed: 4-round magazine
Muz vel: n.k.

The 0.264in Winchester round used in this rifle is ultimately of Holland & Holland parentage, being nothing more than the 0.458in necked to 0.256in (6.5mm). The capacious case is doubtless somewhat over-bore capacity, but the ballistics are nevertheless impressive. The standard load throws a 100 grain (6.5g) bullet at 3,700ft/sec (1,128m/sec), or a 140 grain (9.1g) bullet at 3,200ft/sec (975m/sec). Excellent sectional density helps the projectile hold its velocity and deliver a very fast trajectory. With the heavier bullet, it should be suitable for most plains game. The rifle shown has a Zeiss scope, although careful inspection will reveal an array of four V-notch backsights mounted on a quarter-rib and graduated to 450yd (411m).

4.85MM INDIVIDUAL WEAPON — UK

Length (gun): 30.3in (770mm)
Barrel: 20.4in (518mm)
Weight: 8.5lb (3.9kg)
Caliber: 4.85mm
Rifling: 4 grooves, r/hand
Operation: gas
Feed: 20-round box
Cyclic rate: n.k.
Muz vel: 2,952ft/sec (900m/sec)

After NATO's rejection of the EM 2 (qv) Britain relied for many years on the L1A1 7.62mm self-loading rifle. By the early 1970s, however, it was finally clear that an assault rifle was necessary, partly for reasons of morale but also because the existing rifle was too long and bulky for modern armored warfare. The weapon finally developed bears a strong outward resemblance to the EM 2 but is small and lighter, and mechanically more advanced. It works by the normal method of gas and piston with a rotating bolt, and extensive trials proved it to be highly effective. It has an optical sight and fores either single rounds or bursts as required. Its magazine holds 20 5.56mm rounds which are just under half the weight of the NATO 7.62mm cartridge, and it can be adapted to fire grenades. There is also a heavy-barreled version which is identical in operation. This weapon has a light bipod and about 80 percent of the components are common to both weapons. A 30-round magazine is available for the grenade-firing type, although each version will take both kinds of magazine. The gun fires from a closed bolt, ie, the round is pre-positioned in the chamber ready to fire. This can in theory lead to premature discharge, when the chamber is very hot, so the weapon was successfully modified to fire bursts from an open bolt. When NATO decided to standardize on the 5.56 x 45mm SS109 cartridge, the British ceased development of their 4.85mm cartridge and produced a new weapon, based on the 4.85 IW (see 5.56mm L85A1).

Sniper Rifle L42A1 — UK

Length (gun): 42.2in (1,071mm)
Barrel: 27.5in (699mm)
Weight: 9.75lb (4.4kg)
Caliber: 7.62mm
Rifling: 4 grooves, r/hand
Operation: bolt-action
Feed: 10-round box
Muz vel: 2,750ft/sec (838m/sec)

Sniping first came into large scale use in World War I and World War II soon proved that there was still a need for it. After 1945 the British Army neglected sniping until its long experience in internal security duties round the world made it think differently. Self-loading rifles of the time were not well suited to a telescopic sight, so it therefore became necessary to look back rather than forward for a suitable weapon. It so happened that a commercial conversion of the Number 4 rifle, the Enfield Envoy, was available which had been developed for target use, principally by being rebarreled to fire the standard NATO rifle cartridge and by cutting it down to half stock. The Royal Small Arms Factory at Enfield then converted a number of specially selected Number 4s in similar fashion and fitted them with sights which are a modified version of the original No 32 telescopic sight.

Parker-Hale Model 81 Classic — UK

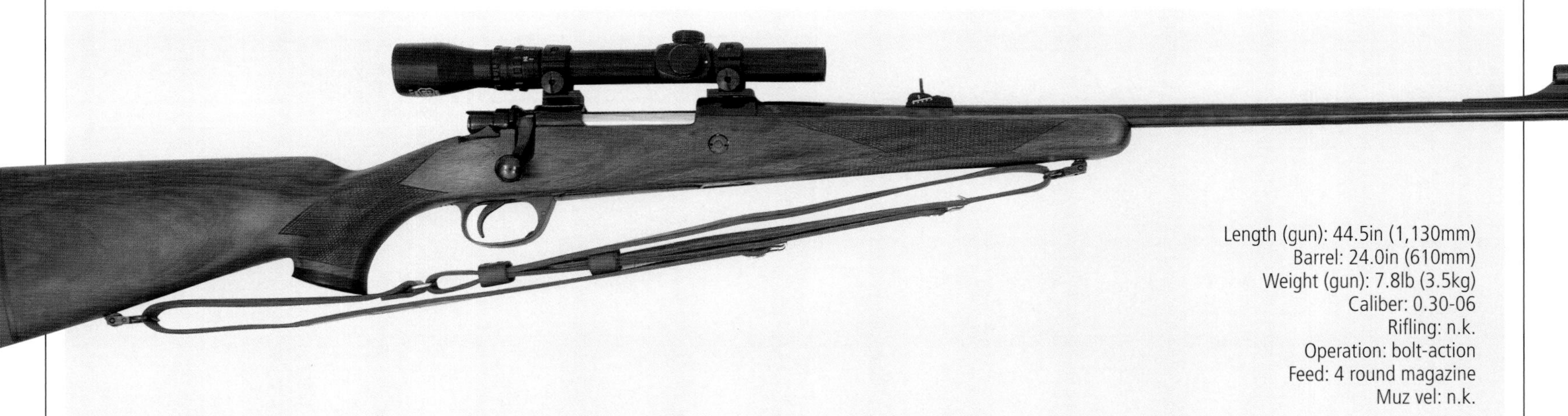

Length (gun): 44.5in (1,130mm)
Barrel: 24.0in (610mm)
Weight (gun): 7.8lb (3.5kg)
Caliber: 0.30-06
Rifling: n.k.
Operation: bolt-action
Feed: 4 round magazine
Muz vel: n.k.

The Model 81 Classic was made by Parker-Hale in Birmingham, England, using their hammer-forged barrels and a new commercial receiver made by the La Coruna arsenal in Spain, one of the modern sources of new Mauser 1898-type actions (the other being in the former Yugoslavia). The Model 81 was manufactured by Parker-Hale and then bought-in by the London firm of Rigby, who then did some additional work on it, before marketing it under their combined names. The Model 81 was rated as a fine rifle, the only noteworthy modification being a side-mounted safety, which became necessary if a scope was fitted. This picture shows such a rifle, fitted with a Pecar 1 x 4 variable, although it also carries the standard ("as supplied") gold bead foresight and Williams semi-buckhorn U-notch backsight, the latter being adjustable for windage and elevation. The Model 81 Classic was not only based on the 1898 Mauser action, but was chambered for the equally classic round: the 0.30-06 cartridge, which was introduced, as its designation indicates, in 1906.

ACCURACY INTERNATIONAL L96A1 7.62MM SNIPER RIFLE — UK

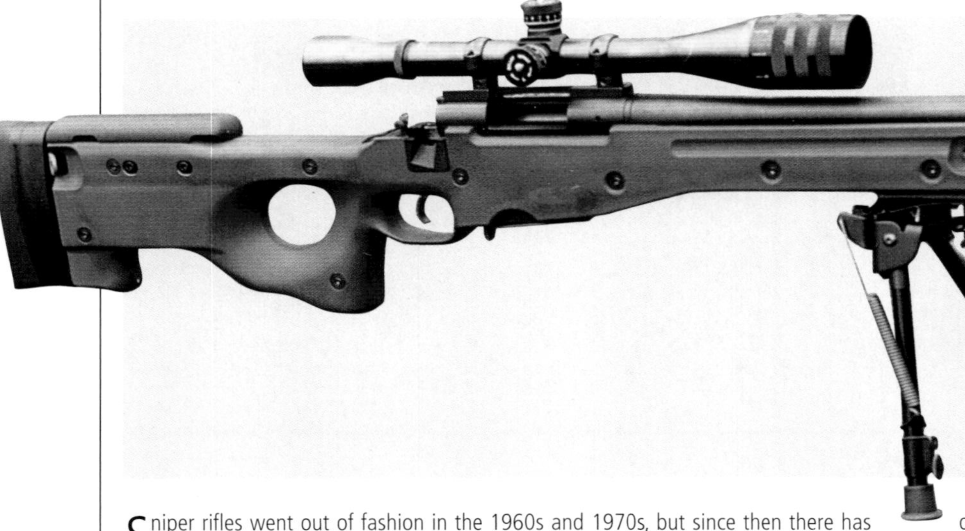

Length (gun): 47.0in (1,194mm)
Barrel: 25.8in (655mm)
Weight (gun): 14.3lb (6.5kg)
Caliber: 7.62mm
Rifling: 4 grooves, r/hand
Operation: bolt
Feed: 10-round box magazine
Muz vel: 2,788ft/sec (850m/sec)

Sniper rifles went out of fashion in the 1960s and 1970s, but since then there has been a strong resurgence, with many models becoming available. One weapon designed from the start for sniping is the Accuracy International Model PM. This was designed to meet challenging criteria: guaranteed first round accuracy; unchanging zero; a stock unaffected by environmental changes; bipod; stock and trigger adjustable to meet individual firer's requirements; telescopic sight; reliability; interoperability; and economy. The solution fixed upon by A.I. was to use a massive and very stiff integral chassis, which is impervious to environmental changes and is precisely reproducible. The barrel is made of stainless steel and has a normal accuracy life in excess of 5,000 rounds. It attaches to the action by a screw thread bedding against a locking-ring, and can be changed in approximately five minutes without stripping the rifle. The sniper can carry out all but the most major repairs on his weapon himself, three Allen keys and a screwdriver being the only tools required. All accessories mate directly to the chassis, including the stock, butt, spacers, sling swivels, trigger unit, magazine and catch, handstop and bipod. The weapon entered service with the British armed forces in 1985 as the L96A1, and also serves with a number of other armies. (The weapon above is shown without its bolt.)

ENFIELD 7.62MM L39A1 TARGET RIFLE — UK

Length (gun): 46.5in (1,180mm)
Barrel: 27.6in (700mm)
Weight (gun): 9.7lb (4.4kg)
Caliber: 7.62 x 51mm
Rifling: 4 grooves, r/hand
Operation: bolt-action
Feed: 10-round box magazine
Muz vel: ca 2,758ft/sec (841m/sec)

When the British Army adopted the 7.62mm L1A1 rifle it was discovered that, while it was sufficiently accurate for use in combat, it was not up to the standard required for competition firing. As there were many service teams wishing to take part in such competitions, it was decided (but only after very considerable discussion) to produce such a weapon by taking carefully selected 0.303in Number 4 rifles (qv) and modifying them to competition standards, firing the new 7.62 x 51mm NATO rimless round. This involved fitting a new, heavy, cold-forged, 27.6in (700mm) barrel, which, for some curious reason, was fitted with a foresight block, although it was known that no foresight blade would ever be fitted (users fitted their own commercial optical sights). The forward stock was cut back, leaving some 15in (380mm) of the barrel exposed. The receiver and bolt were modified to take the 7.62mm rimless round. The Number 4 butt was retained unchanged, apart from a new recess, which was intended to accommodate spare foresight blades (although these were never provided). The 0.303in magazine from the Number 4 rifle was normally retained, but only to provide a platform, since in competitions the rounds were loaded and spent cases removed by hand, although a 10-round 7.62mm magazine was also available; this incorporated a special lip, which served to eject the empty cases as the bolt was withdrawn.

5.56MM L85A1 INDIVIDUAL WEAPON — UK

Length (gun): 30.9in (785mm)
Barrel: 20.4in (518mm)
Weight (gun): 8.4lb (3.8kg)
Caliber: 5.56mm
Rifling: 6 grooves, r/hand
Operation: gas
Feed: 30-round box magazine
Cyclic rate: 800rpm
Muz vel: 3,084ft/sec (940m/sec)

After the demise of the 4.85mm EM2 rifle (qv) in the early 1950s, the British Army relied for many years on the Belgian 7.62mm FN FAL, which was built under license in the United Kingdom as the L1A1. When it became clear that the next NATO standard round would be smaller than the then current 7.62mm, the British produced the 4.85mm IW (qv), but this, too, had to be abandoned when NATO adopted the 5.56mm round. The work done on design of the weapon was, however, carried over into the new system, which eventually entered service in 1986 as the 5.56mm L85A1 Individual Weapon. This is a bullpup design using conventional gas operation, with a rotating bolt which engages in lugs in the rear of the breech. The design makes maximum use of stampings, pressings and spot-welding for the metal components, and of high-impact plastic elsewhere. It was designed to use an optical sight – the Sight Unit, Small Arms, Trilux (SUSAT) – which enables trainees to attain a high standard of accuracy very quickly, although this sight is fitted in weapons intended for the infantry only, and soldiers of other arms (eg, artillery, engineers, communicators, and logisticians) are issued with a weapon with iron sights. The first weapons were issued to troops in 1984 and over the first decade of service it received much criticism, some of which was undoubtedly deserved, especially concerning the fact that it cannot be fired satisfactorily by left-handers. With time, experience, and numerous minor modifications it is now a satisfactory weapon, although it has conspicuously failed to attract any export orders from major armies. A much-modified, non-automatic, bolt-operated version was developed for use by young people, as the 5.56mm Cadet Rifle L98A1, and a carbine version was also developed but never went into production.

PSG-90 7.62 Sniper Rifle — UK

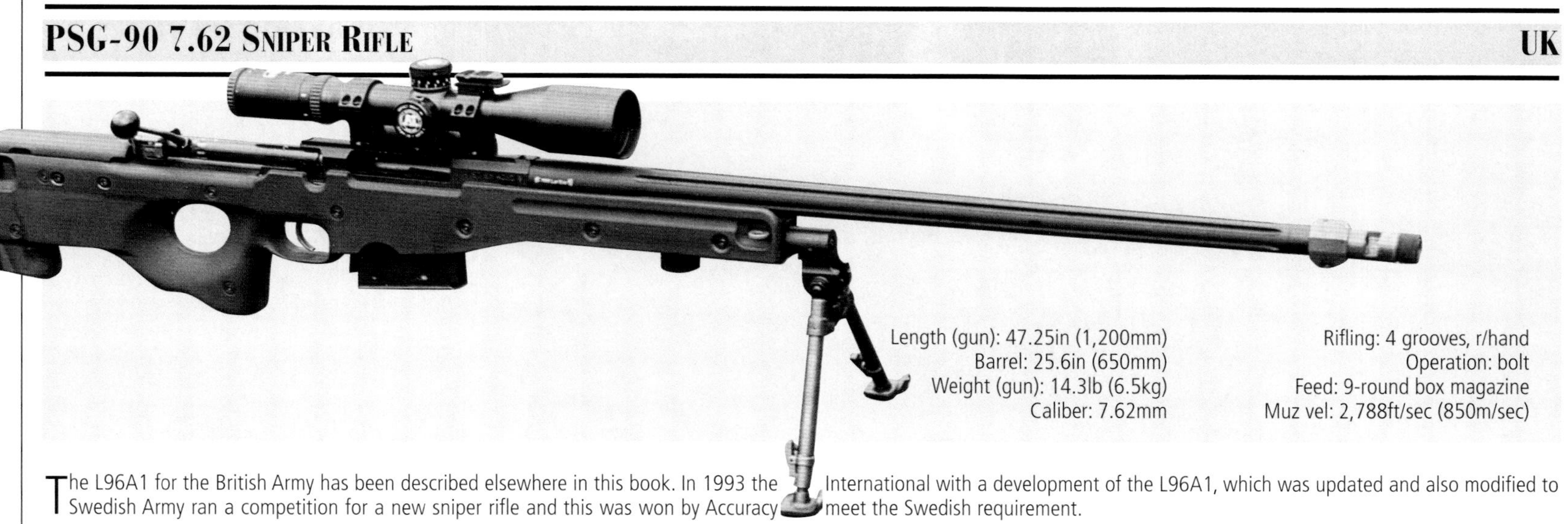

Length (gun): 47.25in (1,200mm)
Barrel: 25.6in (650mm)
Weight (gun): 14.3lb (6.5kg)
Caliber: 7.62mm

Rifling: 4 grooves, r/hand
Operation: bolt
Feed: 9-round box magazine
Muz vel: 2,788ft/sec (850m/sec)

The L96A1 for the British Army has been described elsewhere in this book. In 1993 the Swedish Army ran a competition for a new sniper rifle and this was won by Accuracy International with a development of the L96A1, which was updated and also modified to meet the Swedish requirement.

Jennings Rifle — USA

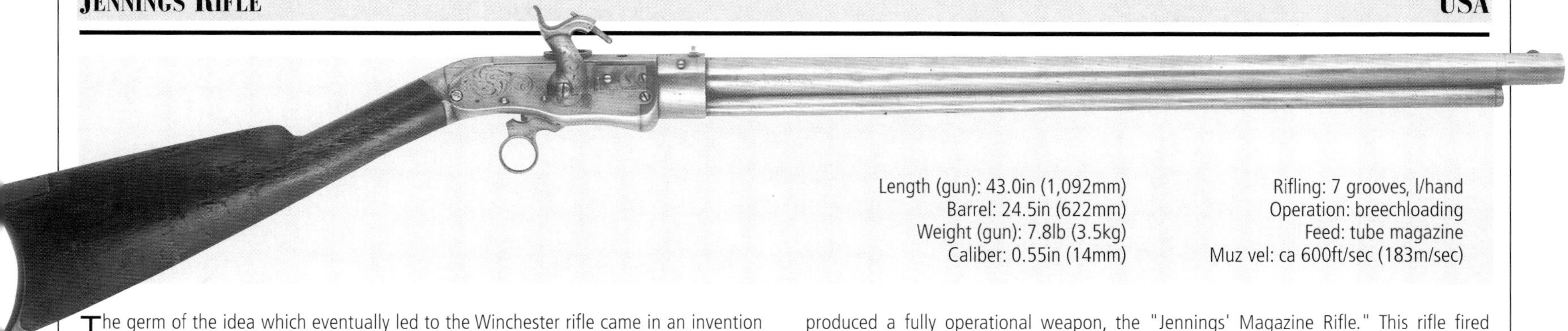

Length (gun): 43.0in (1,092mm)
Barrel: 24.5in (622mm)
Weight (gun): 7.8lb (3.5kg)
Caliber: 0.55in (14mm)

Rifling: 7 grooves, l/hand
Operation: breechloading
Feed: tube magazine
Muz vel: ca 600ft/sec (183m/sec)

The germ of the idea which eventually led to the Winchester rifle came in an invention by an obscure New Yorker, Walter Hunt, who, like so many inventors, had tremendous imagination (his inventions included a sewing-machine and a safety-pin) but little business sense. By 1848 he had invented a new type of bullet which contained its own charge of powder, the base being sealed by a thin piece of cork, pierced at the center to allow the flash of a cap to reach the contents. Soon after this he produced a firearm with a tubular magazine fitted with a coil spring which pushed the rounds steadily towards the chamber. Hunt did not have the money or business acumen to pursue this and the project passed into the hands of Lewis Jennings, a highly skilled mechanic, who, after further work, produced a fully operational weapon, the "Jennings' Magazine Rifle." This rifle fired charged bullets on Hunt's original design, ignition being by means of percussion pills held in a flat, cylindrical container just above the breech. When the ring trigger was pushed forward the rearmost round in the magazine was forced in to a scoop-shaped carrier by the magazine spring. The hammer was then cocked and the ring trigger drawn to the rear, which lifted the carrier into line with the breech, chambered the round and dropped a percussion pill into position. A final, harder pull then fired the round and the process was repeated; since there was no separate case, no extraction was required, the charge and cork being completely consumed in the explosion when the round was fired.

Spencer Repeating Rifle — USA

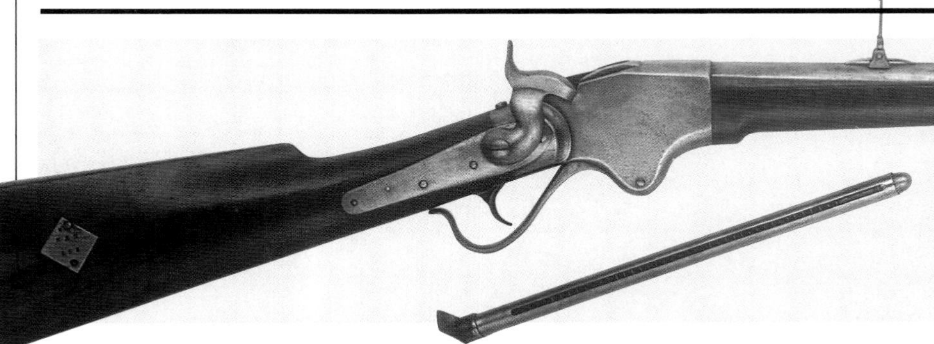

Length (gun): 43.0in (1,092mm)
Barrel: 26.0in (660mm)
Weight (gun): 9.0lb (4.1kg)
Caliber: 0.56in (14.2mm)

Rifling: 6 grooves, l/hand
Operation: breechloading
Feed: tube in butt
Muz vel: ca 1,200ft/sec (366m/sec)

Christopher Spencer (1833-1922) was, like Colt and Maxim, a man who had little formal education but was endowed with inventive genius allied to great energy, his inventions including machinery for silk mills, a steam-driven automobile and a screw-cutting machine. In March 1860 Spencer produced the repeating rifle which bears his name, which used a removable tubular magazine in the butt housing seven copper rim-fire cartridges. It was worked by a lever which also acted as a trigger guard; downward pressure ejected the empty case (if any) in the chamber and upward pressure loaded the next round, after which the external hammer had to be cocked in readiness for firing. It was a simple, reliable weapon, cheap to manufacture and sufficiently robust for service use. The Spencer Repeater was tried soon after the outbreak of the Civil War in 1861 and was officially adopted by the Union Army, but nothing much seems to have happened until Spencer managed to demonstrate the weapon to President Lincoln in 1863 and by the following year one complete division of 12,000 men had been completely equipped with the new rifle. The Spencer Repeater was also made in carbine form with a shorter barrel and a number were also converted by Springfield. A few were also produced in the immediate post-war years for sporting use. The illustration shows the carbine version with a shortened forestock; the tubular device underneath is the magazine, which was usually housed in the butt. Considerable numbers were purchased during the war but the factory went out of business in 1869 and most of its stock and machinery were purchased by Oliver Winchester.

WEAPONS OF THE AMERICAN WEST – 1 USA

The men who penetrated, settled, and eventually "won" the West needed firearms for self-protection from competitors, enemies, and wild animals, and for game-hunting in order to obtain food for survival. Weapons were thus an essential, and not an optional, part of their lives. Among the earliest of these men were the members of the Lewis and Clark expedition, which was a direct outcome of the Louisiana Purchase in 1803 and involved trekking from St Louis, Missouri, then a frontier town, to the Pacific coast and back, through country never previously explored by white men. Their weapons were rifles and muskets, some from reputable gun-makers in the United States or Great Britain, but others from anonymous gunsmiths who, either through accident or design, failed to put their names on their products. After the explorers came the hunters and trappers, who, quite literally, lived by their guns, and for whom Samuel Hawken of St Louis produced some excellent weapons. These were followed by men armed with carbines like the Spencer and the Sharp, and, above all, by the "gun that won the West" – the Winchester '73.

1. Harper's Ferry Model 1803. A 0.54in (13.7mm) caliber flintlock rifle manufactured at the government arsenal at Harper's Ferry in West Virginia. It is shown with a powder horn with turned wood plug and carved neck. Such weapons are known to have been included among those carried by members of the Lewis and Clark expedition.

2. Flintlock (ca 1820). A flintlock from an unidentified manufacturer. Brass-mounted, with plain brass patch box.

3. Kuntz air rifle. The air reservoir was contained in the hollow metal butt and the false flint cocking action actuated the release of air, firing the weapon. This type of weapon was taken on the Lewis and Clark expedition.

4. Sam Hawken rifle. Brass-mounted, half-stocked plains rifle made by Samuel Hawken, a gunsmith of St Louis, Missouri.

5. Sam Hawken rifle. An iron-mounted plains rifle, also made by Sam Hawken.

6. Winchester Model 1873 rifle. A lever-action Model 1873. Caliber, 0.45-60in.

7. Winchester Model 1873 rifle. This lever-action Model 1873 differs from the above in being 0.44-40in caliber. It is believed to have been used to "enforce the rules" in a Western gambling saloon.

8. Modified Spencer rifle. This Spencer rifle has been modified to take a 0.50in (12.7mm) caliber cartridge. Octagonal barrel and a set trigger.

9. Sharps Model 1874 carbine. A 0.45in (11.4mm) caliber carbine with heavy octagonal barrel. The branded "S" on the butt is an owner's rather than maker's mark.

10. English shotgun. A double-barreled 12-gauge shotgun, manufactured by W. & O. Scott, a firm of English gun-makers.

11. Ballard sporting rifle. A high quality, light, lever-action rifle, made by the Brown Manufacturing Company and intended for hunting game.

WEAPONS OF THE AMERICAN WEST – 2 USA

Prior to the Civil War the US Army's presence on the frontier was limited and the units were small in size and widely scattered. Their mission was to protect civilians in their area of responsibility and to look after immigrants passing through on their way westwards. Compared with those of the people they had to fight, their weapons were sophisticated and up-to-date. Their re-supply of ammunition was guaranteed and maintenance facilities were of a high standard. A selection of the arms they used up to 1871 is shown here, together with a selection of firearms used by "Indians," most of them readily identifiable by their characteristic use of brass studs as decorations, their generally well-used condition and their use of rawhide to effect all types of repair. Indians did not have any manufacturing facilities and acquired all their weapons from trading posts or by purchase from individuals, although usually only antiquated flint and percussion muzzle-loading weapons could be obtained in this way. The most modern weapons were usually acquired by capture, although these became useless once the ammunition was expended.

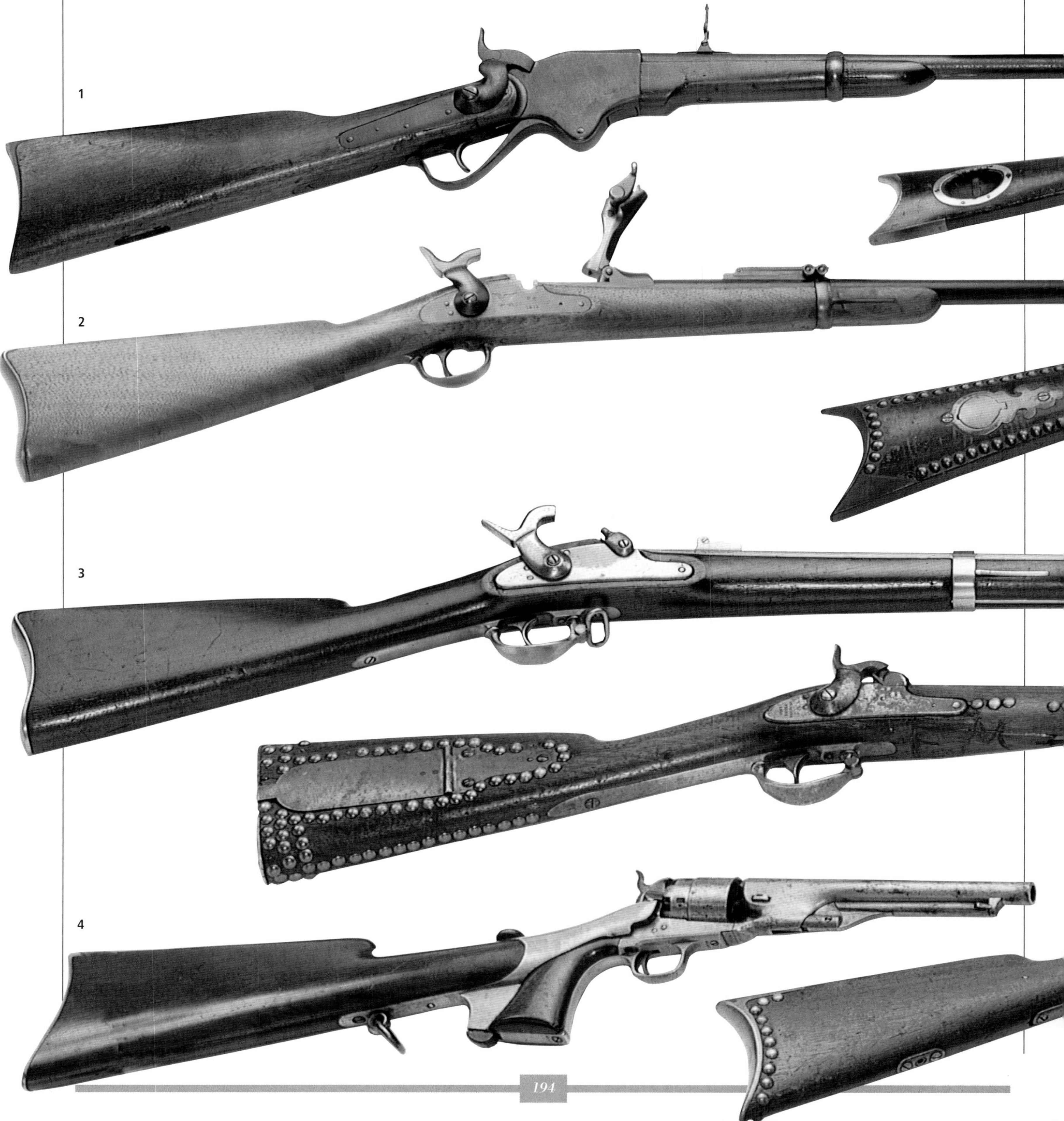

1

2

3

4

1. Spencer Model 1865 carbine. As used by the US Army, this has the standard barrel, rather than the modified barrel shown on page 193. Note the half stock, neat action and the back sight, which has been raised for long-range shooting.

2. Springfield Model 1884 carbine. Note that the "trapdoor" breech cover is raised.

3. US Army Model 1861 rifle musket. Of 0.58in caliber, made by an unidentified contractor.

4. Colt Third Model Dragoon revolver. The shoulder stock is mounted to convert it into a carbine, although the absence of any sights would have precluded any great accuracy.

5. Percussion rifle. An unmarked percussion rifle of 0.45in caliber. One of the owners has used rawhide to make repairs around the lock area and at the rear of the barrel.

6. Percussion rifle. Another of the many types of percussion rifles used by Plains Indian warriors.

7. US Army Model 1841 percussion rifle. Probably captured in a frontier engagement, it is identifiable as an "Indian" weapon by its brass stud decorations.

8. Winchester Model 1866 rifle. Probably also captured from the Army, this Winchester has added brass stud decorations.

Weapons of the American West – 3 USA

The name "Winchester" is synonymous with the "Wild West," the American frontier, and all the romance that has been attached to the subject by Hollywood film-makers and generations of writers. The company which later bore the Winchester name was originally called "Volcanic" but was later taken over by Oliver Winchester, who had earlier been involved in manufacturing shirts. The company was re-named the Winchester Repeating Arms Company in 1866 and concentrated its efforts on the design, development and production of long arms, the most popular caliber being 0.44-40, which was also the same as that used by the Colt single-action handgun. On the right-hand page below are rifles produced by less well-known companies and several of the less popular products of the larger companies, all of which played their part in the "taming of the West."

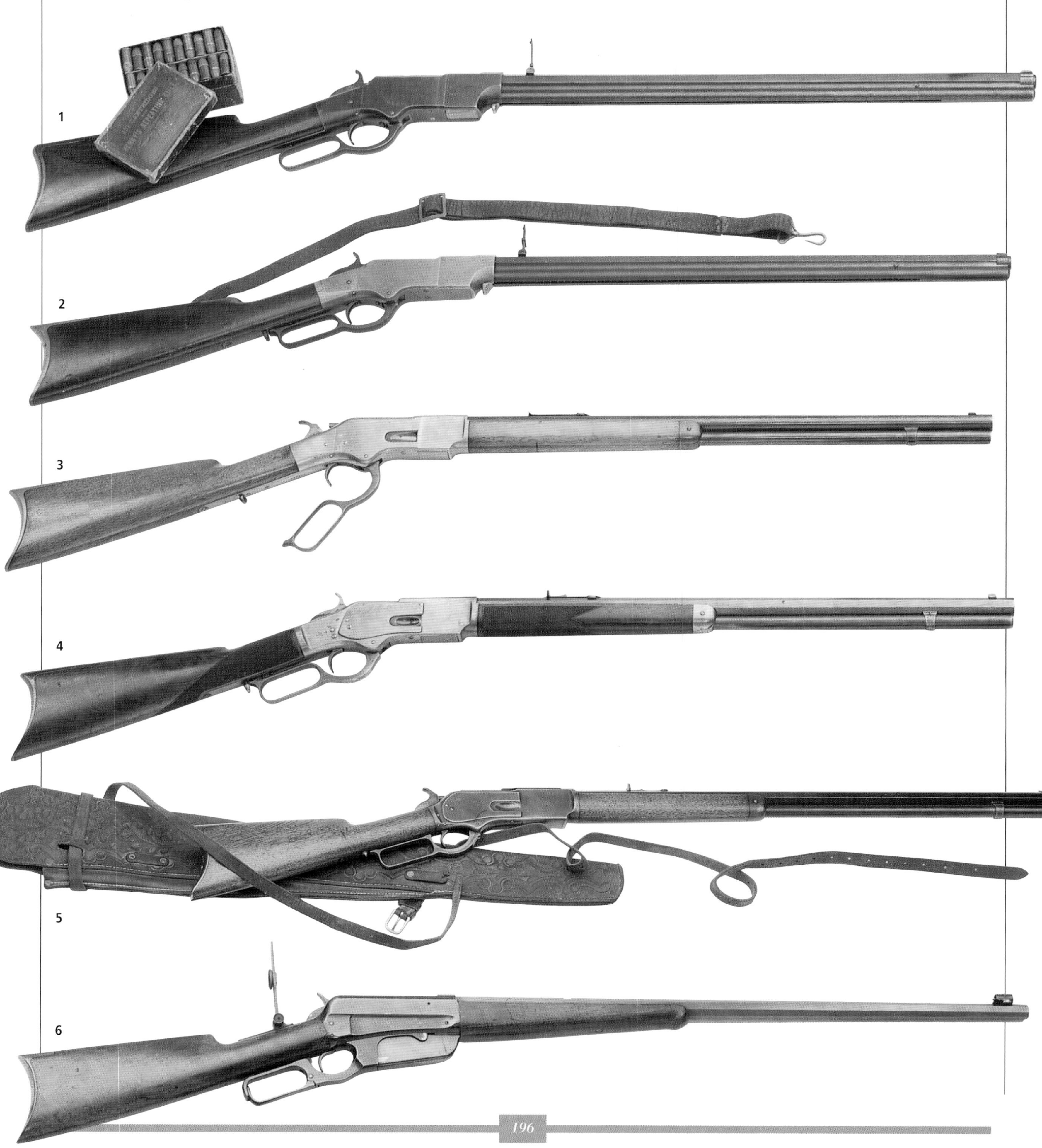

1. Henry rifle. An early iron-framed Henry lever-action, repeating rifle, with its rear sight raised for long-range firing, shown with 100-round box of cartridges.

2. Henry rifle, generally similar to the one above, but with a brass frame.

3. Winchester Model 1866 rifle. This Winchester 1866 clearly shows its development from the Henry rifles above, but with the addition of the loading gate and lever action, which transformed a good weapon into an outstanding one.

4. Winchester Model 1873 rifle with the round barrel replaced by an octagonal one. In general, this was the most popular weapon in the West, combining reliability and accuracy with a high rate of fire. A military version was sold to several overseas armies, including those of Spain and Turkey, which was similar to the civilian model, except for a longer forestock, which extended forwards almost to the muzzle.

5. Winchester Model 1876 rifle shown with leather saddle scabbard. This weapon is a development of the Model 1873, with a longer barrel.

6. Winchester Model 1895 rifle. This rifle incorporated significant changes, with the tubular magazine replaced by a box containing five rounds. Note also the tang backsight, here in the raised position. In its military version, this rifle was purchased in large quantities by Imperial Russia.

7. Colt Lightning Repeater rifle. Unlike most of the others shown in these pages, this weapon worked by slide (pump) action. Though reasonable effective this system was never as popular as the lever action, marketed by firms such as Winchester and Marlin.

8. Remington-Creedmore rifle. This particular weapon is significant because it was once owned by General George Armstrong Custer. With a 0.44-100 caliber, it is generally acknowledged to have been one of the finest weapons ever made by Remington.

9. Marlin Model 1881 rifle. This lever action rifle had a half-length magazine and an octagonal barrel. It was a serious competitor for the contemporary Winchesters, but never triumphed over its rival.

10. Colt Model 1855 rifle. This half-stock percussion sporting rifle was made between 1857 and 1864 and operated on the revolver principle, with four rounds in the revolving chamber. Such "revolver-rifles" were never entirely successful, being prone to mechanical failure, not infrequently at the worst possible moment.

11. Remington-Keane rifle. This bolt-action, magazine-fed rifle is shown with its bolt open. Note the short, vertical bolt handle and the cocking lever on the rear of the bolt. This weapon was popular with frontiersmen and was purchased by the Department of the Interior to arm "Indian police."

12. Roper revolving shotgun. This was one of many attempts to find an efficient repeating action. A 12-gauge weapon, the cylinder housed four cartridges, but overall the weapon proved to be fragile in service.

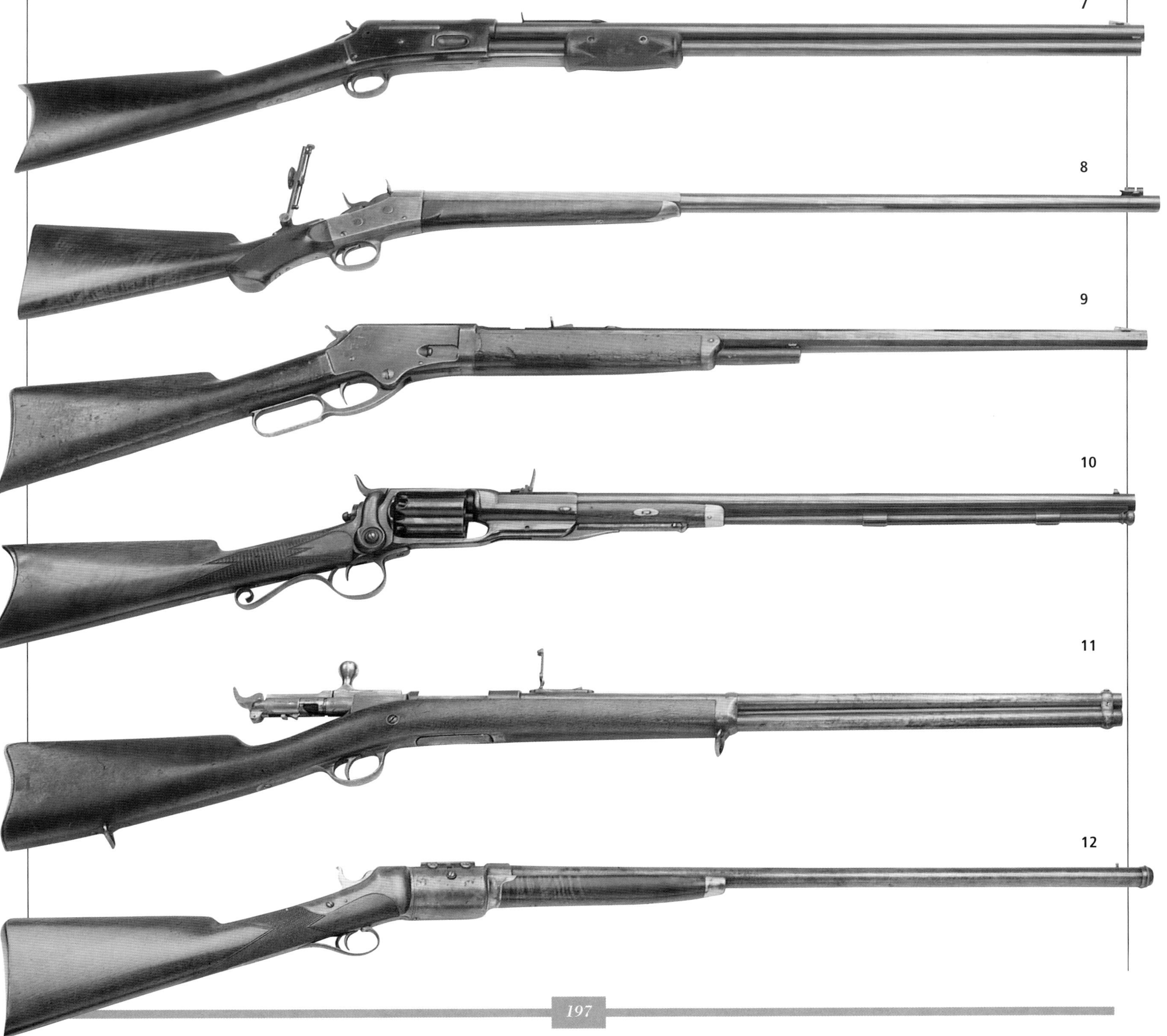

WEAPONS OF THE AMERICAN CIVIL WAR: CONFEDERACY CAVALRY WEAPONS USA

Both sides in the Civil War had large forces of cavalry who required weapons that were lighter and shorter than the infantry rifles. Their rifles needed to be fired from horseback and carried without snagging. Some such weapons were simple adaptations of infantry rifles, but a few were specifically designed for cavalry use. As in other spheres, the Confederacy was poorly provided for compared to the Union, and much use was made of weapons imported from Europe.

1

2

3

4

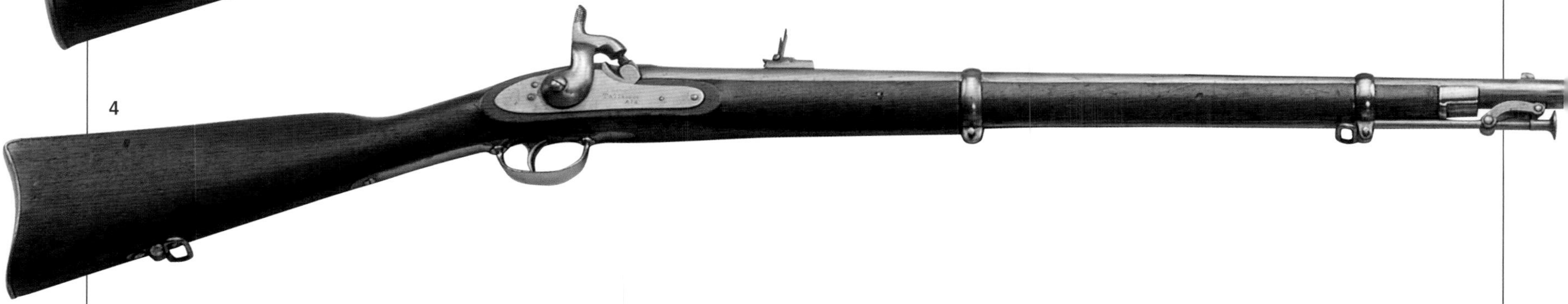

5

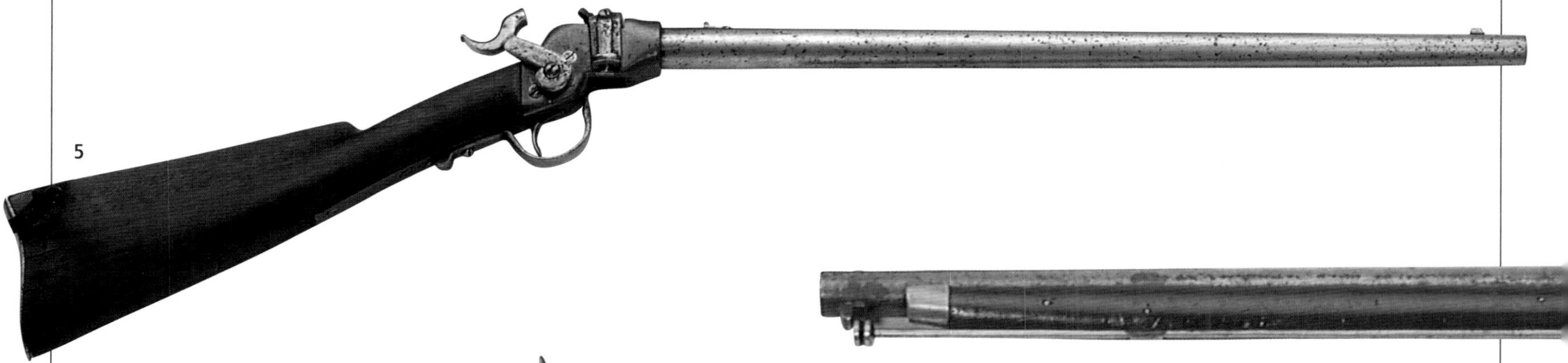

6

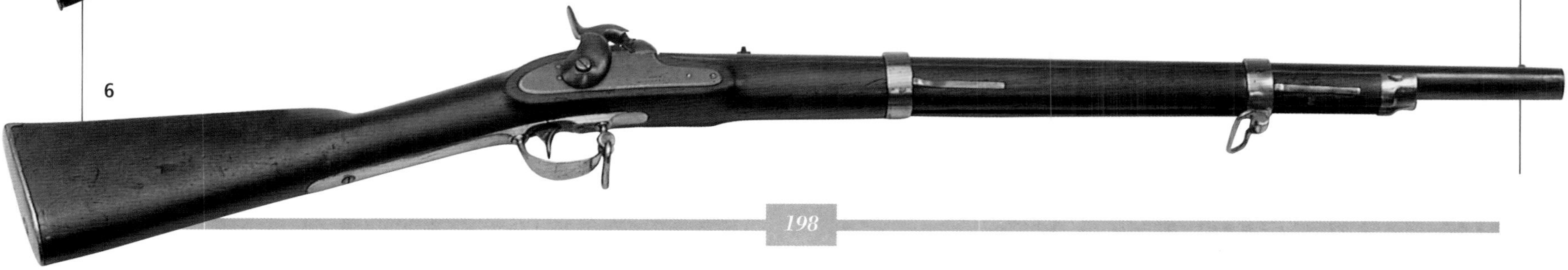

1. Dickson, Neilson & Company carbine. The ramrod is in the stowed position, but note the retaining swivel below the muzzle, which prevented it from being lost.

2. British Enfield Pattern 1853 musketoon. This is an adaptation of the standard British rifle, cut back for cavalry use.

3. J.P. Murray musketoon.

4. Talahassee carbine. Note the ramrod and retaining swivel, and the raised leaf backsight.

5. Tarpley carbine.

6. J.P. Murray carbine.

7. Terry Pattern 1860 carbine. A British design, the Terry carbine had an early form of bolt action, with the device seen here in the open position.

8. C. Chapman musketoon.

9. Bilharz, Hall & Company carbine. This rising breech carbine shows the lever depressed and the breech in its raised position for reloading.

10. Bilharz, Hall & Company carbine. This is a muzzle-loading carbine.

11. Richmond carbine. Made in the capital of the Confederacy, this carbine includes the original ramrod and carrying sling.

12. Morse carbine. Another very early breech-loader, this example has its breech open for reloading.

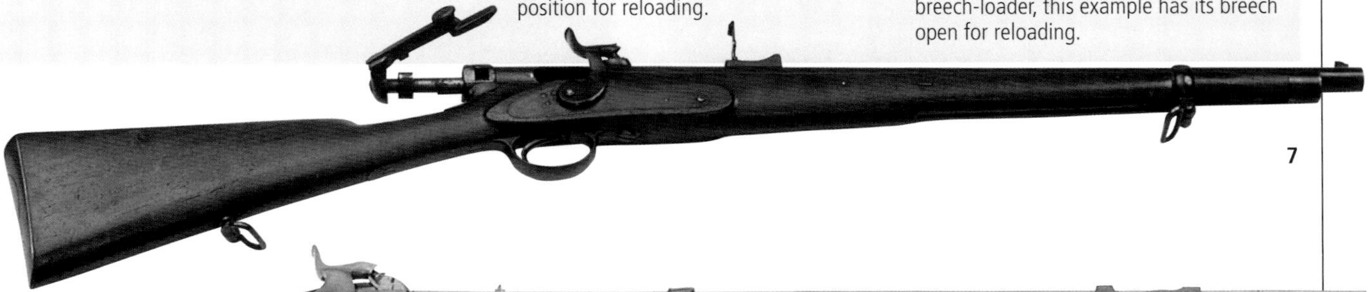

7

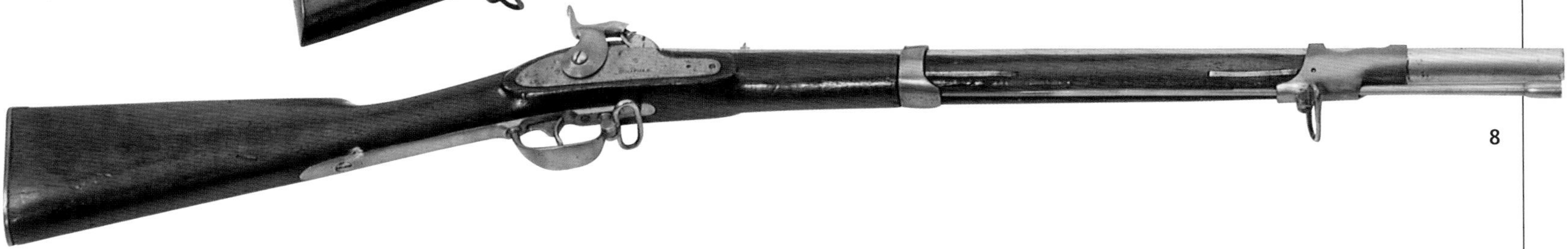

8

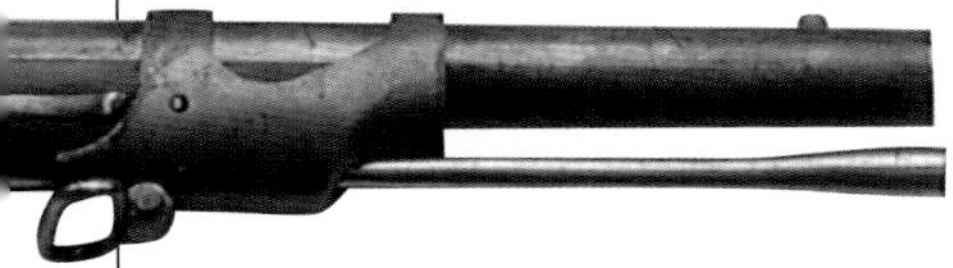

9

10

11

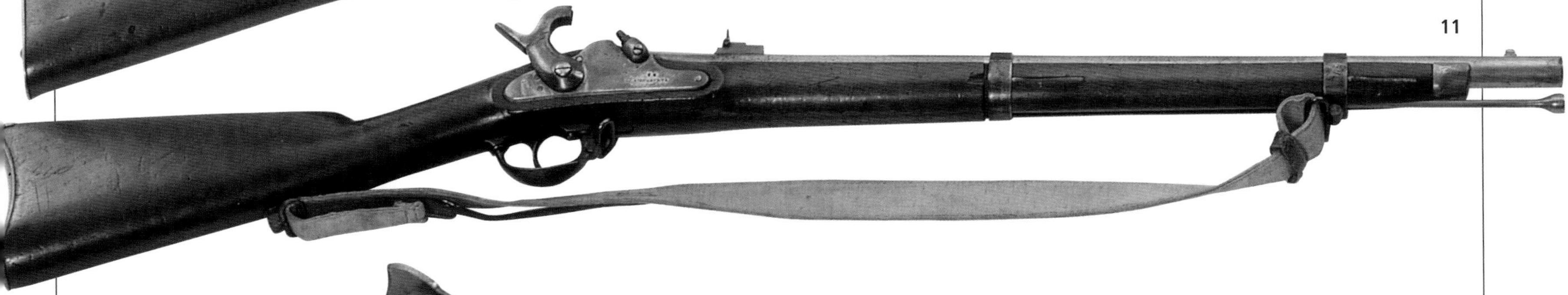

12

Weapons of the American Civil War: Confederacy Infantry Weapons USA

The Confederate States' Army (CSA) had to take its weapons from wherever it could find them, whether from abroad, from existing pre-war stocks found in Confederate territory on the outbreak of the Civil War, or from local manufacture once the war had started. Here are a miscellany of weapons from all three such sources.

1. Belgian Pattern 1842 short rifle. A number of Belgian rifles were imported for use by the CSA, where they gained a reputation for a heavy recoil (earning the nickname "mules") and shoddy workmanship.

2. Kerr's Patent rifle. This was a product of one of Britain's many small gunsmiths of the middle 19th Century, but certainly appears to be of good quality workmanship.

3. Palmetto Armory Model 1842 musket. A pre-war musket, manufactured in the United States, but used by the Confederate Army. Note the very dangerous looking bayonet, ramrod in place beneath the muzzle, and the raised leaf backsight.

4. Dickson, Nelson & Co muzzle-loader, an undistinguished and very conventional muzzle-loading design.

5. Davis, Bozeman & Co muzzle-loader.

6. Mendenhall, Jones and Gardner muzzle-loading rifle, complete with ramrod and carrying sling.

7. Richmond rifle-musket. Early type of rifled musket, with sling.

8. Fayetteville rifle, shown with CS-embossed cartridge box complete with strap; an early model muzzle-loading rifle which could also have been fitted with a bayonet.

9. Fayetteville rifle. Later model muzzle-loading rifle from Fayetteville. This does not have a bayonet fitting and has a modified rear sight.

10. Richmond rifle-musket. Later type of rifled musket from the Confederate capital's arsenal, with minor improvements as a result of combat experience.

11. Cook & Brother rifle, produced in a small gunsmith's shop.

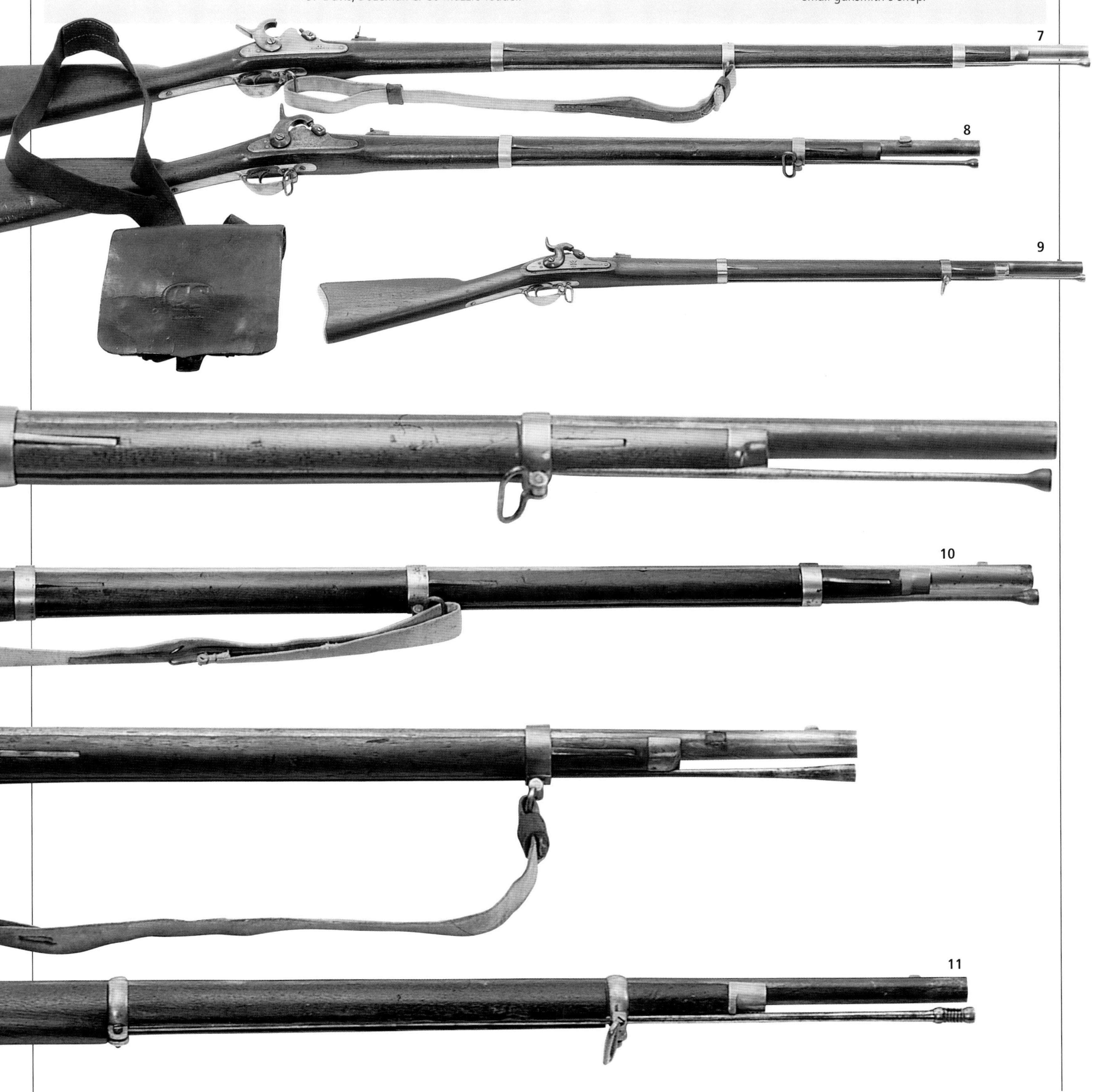

WEAPONS OF THE AMERICAN CIVIL WAR: UNITED STATES ARMY WEAPONS — USA

The US Army had the advantage over the CSA in that it had and retained control over the great majority of the pre-war arsenals and thus not only was able to maintain production, but was also able to make do with far fewer different makes of weapon. Here some representative types of cavalry carbine are shown on the left and infantry rifles on the right.

1. Starr cavalry carbine. A conventional, lever-action, breech-loading carbine.

2. Maynard 1st Model carbine. An unusual type of carbine where the lever action released a lock so that the gun could be "broken" (as shown here) to enable it to be reloaded.

3. Merril carbine. A late model Merril carbine, with the unusual breech mechanism open for reloading.

4. Joslin Model 1864 carbine.

5. Burnside 4th Model carbine. Note that the breech mechanism has been opened to show its operation.

6. Spencer carbine. On this weapon the backsight has been raised and the breech opened to show its action. Note also the spring-fed tubular magazine, which is partially withdrawn from its housing in the butt.

7. US Army Model 1816 musket. A smoothbore weapon, shown here with its bayonet in place.

8. US Army Model 1855 rifle-musket, shown with rifle-musket cartridge box with shoulder belt. The successor to the Model 1842, the Model 1855 had a rifled barrel, which necessitated proper sights (note the raised backsight).

9. US Army Model 1842 musket. The successor to the weapon shown immediately below, the Model 1842 offered little improvement in any department.

10. US Army Model 1861 rifle-musket. Again, this seems to have offered only marginal improvements over its three predecessors.

11. British Pattern 1853 rifle-musket. Although this has been shown elsewhere in this book, the British Enfield muzzle-loading rifle-musket is shown here for comparison with its two United States contemporaries, the Model 1855 and Model 1861 shown above.

12. Justice rifle-musket. US Army rifle-musket from a private contractor.

WEAPONS OF THE AMERICAN CIVIL WAR: CONFEDERATE STATES ARMY WEAPONS

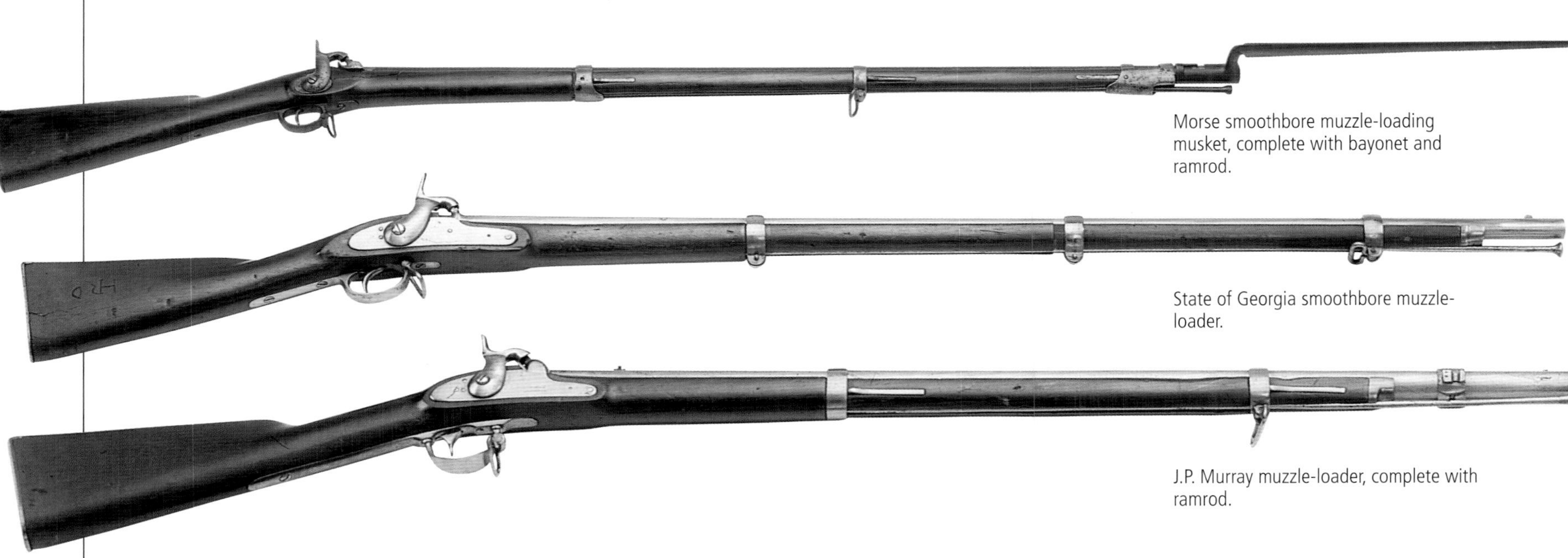

Morse smoothbore muzzle-loading musket, complete with bayonet and ramrod.

State of Georgia smoothbore muzzle-loader.

J.P. Murray muzzle-loader, complete with ramrod.

WEAPONS OF THE AMERICAN CIVIL WAR: AFTER THE BATTLE

Many tens of thousands of artIfacts of the Civil War have been found and continue to be found, even today. These six rifles were dropped on various battlefields, almost certainly as the owners were wounded or killed. The metal parts have shown remarkable endurance but the woodwork has gone forever.

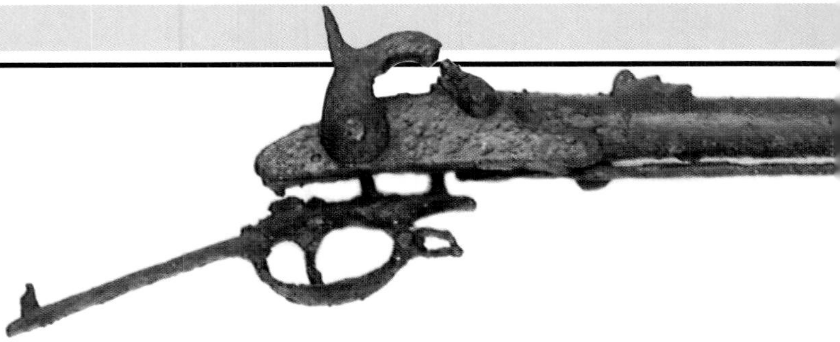

Model 1816 musket. This is many years older than the other weapons shown on this page.

Model 1842 rifle. This was found on the battlefield of Shiloh in Tennessee.

Model 1855 rifle, found at Kennesaw, Georgia.

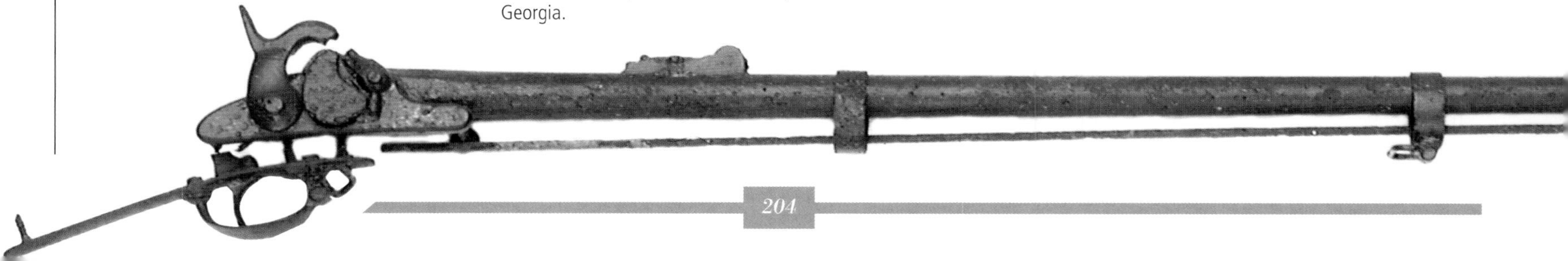

USA

Pulaski muzzle-loading rifle.

Read & Watson late design muzzle-loading rifle

H.C. Lamb muzzle-loader.

USA

Model 1861 rifle musket, found near Bethesda Church, Virginia.

Model 1841 rifle, found in the Wilderness, Virginia. Note that the muzzle is split, suggesting that the weapon may have been deliberately thrown away.

Sharps Model 1859 rifle. Note that even the backsight leaf is still preserved.

SHARPS RIFLES USA

Christian Sharps (1811-1874) produced his first breechloading single-shot rifle in the late 1840s and by the mid-1850s had established himself as one of America's premier gun-makers and even sold several thousand to the British Army for use by cavalry regiments in India. By the late 1850s the weapon was a firm favorite on the American frontier and the Model 1853 carbine was shipped in Kansas territory by the Reverend Beecher and other abolitionists in crates marked "Bibles," leading to Sharps rifles being nicknamed "Beecher Bibles." By the time of the Civil War, Sharps rifles and carbines were in great demand and Colonel Hiram Berman, chief of the celebrated "Sharpshooters," used a number of Model 1859 rifles in 0.52in (13.2mm) caliber, some with set triggers which enhanced accuracy.

Sharps dissolved his own company in the early 1860s and entered in a partnership with William Hankins, with whom he manufactured small four-barreled pistols, breechloading rifles, and carbines. The partnership was dissolved in 1866 and Sharps set up on his own again to produce small pistols and long arms. After his death the company began producing powerful rifles that bore his name, among them the celebrated 0.50in caliber buffalo rifle known as the "Big Fifty." The accuracy and stopping power of the large caliber Sharps rifles are legendary and at ranges of 1,000yd (915m) they were reckoned to be deadly. Many Sharps replicas were made from the 1970s onwards, most of them in Italy.

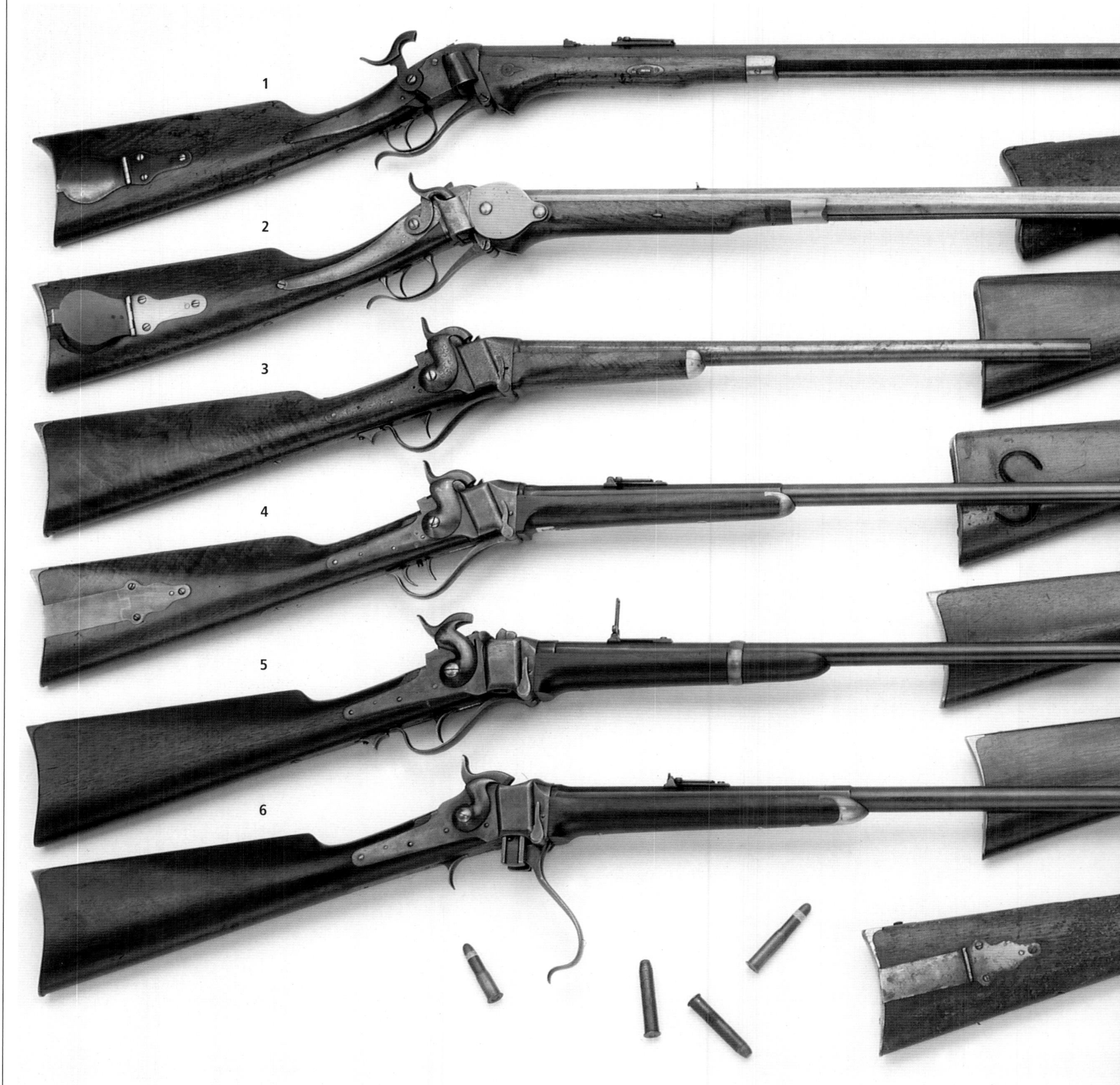

1. Sharps Model 1850 rifle complete with Maynard's tape primer.

2. Model 1849 with circular disk automatic capping device.

3. Model 1852 carbine in 0.52in caliber and slanting breech.

4. The rifle version complete with set triggers for targets and hunting.

5. 1869 carbine, produced in calibers as large as 0.60in.

6. Rifle version of the Model 1869.

7. This 1874 Sharps rifle has a repaired stock. Many rifles were prone to breakage at this point due to recoil.

8. Version of 1874 model with blade foresight.

9. A fine Sharps in "as new" condition.

10. This rifle has normal rear sights on the barrel and peep or adjustable sights on the stock.

11. Round-barreled Sharps rifle, which is uncommon.

12. New Model 1863 rifle with, above it, a box of 0.40 caliber shells 1 7/8in long, and, below it, a plains cartridge belt.

COLT LONG ARMS USA

Throughout the 19th Century a wide variety of long arms found favor in the American West, including the trappers' Hawken rifle, the buffalo hunters' Sharps, the soldiers' Springfield, and, of course, the Winchester. Prior to the Civil War, Samuel Colt had included in the company's line-up various rifles, carbines, and shotguns with revolving cylinders, but many of these were not practical until the advent of metallic cartridges after the war, following which Colt began to develop and produce more successful shoulder arms. Single-shot military rifles sold world-wide helped to keep the firm in business through hard economic times. From 1883 until just after 1900 Samuel Colt tried to compete with Winchester in the rifle market. Thus, the Burgess lever-action 0.44in-40 (11.2mm) rifle was introduced in 1883 in an effort to compete with Winchester's Models 1873 and 1876, while the first slide-action Colt Lightning rifles followed in 1884. Winchester countered with several prototype revolvers, sending a very clear message to Colt, which forced the latter to abandon the rifle market. Numbers of Westerners did, however, use Colt long arms and these became important additions to the armory of many law officers, outlaws, and performers.

1

2

3

4

1. This half-stock Colt revolving sporting rifle version of the Model 1855 is equipped with a sighting scope and has a special finish and set triggers. It was the top of the Colt company's rifle line at the time.

2. Colt Burgess, deluxe engraved, inlaid with gold, presentation inscribed from the Colt factory to William F. "Buffalo Bill" Cody in 1883, the first year his famed Wild West show traveled to the east.

3. Lightning slide-action rifle, medium frame, 0.44-40 caliber, purchased about 1898 for the San Francisco Police Department.

4. This hammerless model 1883 Colt shotgun was a presentation from Samuel Colt's son Caldwell in about 1891.

5. Lever-action 0.44 caliber Colt Burgess rifle, manufactured between 1883 and 1885. Fewer than 7,000 were made.

6. Lightning slide-action rifle, large frame, 0.40-60-260 caliber, half magazine, peep sight.

7. Lightning slide-action rifle, small frame, 0.22 caliber, made in 1890.

HENRY RIFLES USA

The Henry rifle was a derivative of the Smith & Wesson/Volcanic arms, with Henry's modified action and improved cartridge revolutionizing the concept. The latter consisted of a brass casing with the propellant in its base and a 216-grain bullet and 25 grains of powder. The Henry was fitted with a tubular magazine holding 16 rounds. The "rimfire" round proved successful and tests by the US Army's Ordnance Department were encouraging, showing that at a range of 400yd (365m) the bullet could embed itself 5.0in (127mm) in a wooden post. Despite this success, the US Government was somewhat slow in accepting the Henry rifle, but by 1863 a large number had been purchased and issued to volunteer and State troops, and the State of Kansas, in particular, took to the Henry. The only real problem lay in the price: in October 1862 the rifle was listed at US$42, while ammunition cost US$10 per thousand. Even though the dealers failed to get a good discount, however, demand was sufficient to keep the company busy. One particular weakness was the magazine spring which was exposed by a slot underneath through which dust and dirt could enter. This was cured in 1866 by placing a "gate" in the receiver, which enabled the firer to charge the magazine from the receiver rather than from the muzzle end. This invention came too late for Henry, however, and the device was instead incorporated in its successor, the Winchester Model 1866.

1. An early brass frame Henry rifle (serial no. 14).

2. Iron frame Henry rifle, levered for loading.

3. Iron frame Henry rifle (serial no. 155).

4. Early production (rounded butt) brass framed, engraved Henry rifle (serial no. 172).

5. Early production brass framed, silver plated Henry (serial no. 2115) with, above, a box of early cartridges, and, below, a box of post-Civil War cartridges, both 0.44 caliber Henry rimfire.

6. Early production brass frame, silver plated, engraved Henry rifle.

7. Early production brass frame Henry military rifle (serial no. 2928), with, below it, a four-pieve wooden cleaning rod normally stored in the butt trap.

8. Later production (crescent butt)brass frame Henry military rifle (serial no. 6734).

9. Later production silver plated Henry military rifle (serial no.7001) with leather sling.

10. Later production brass frame Henry military rifle (serial no. 9120).

11. Later production brass frame Henry military rifle (serial no. 12832) with, below it, a quartet of 0.44 caliber Henry flat nosed cartridges.

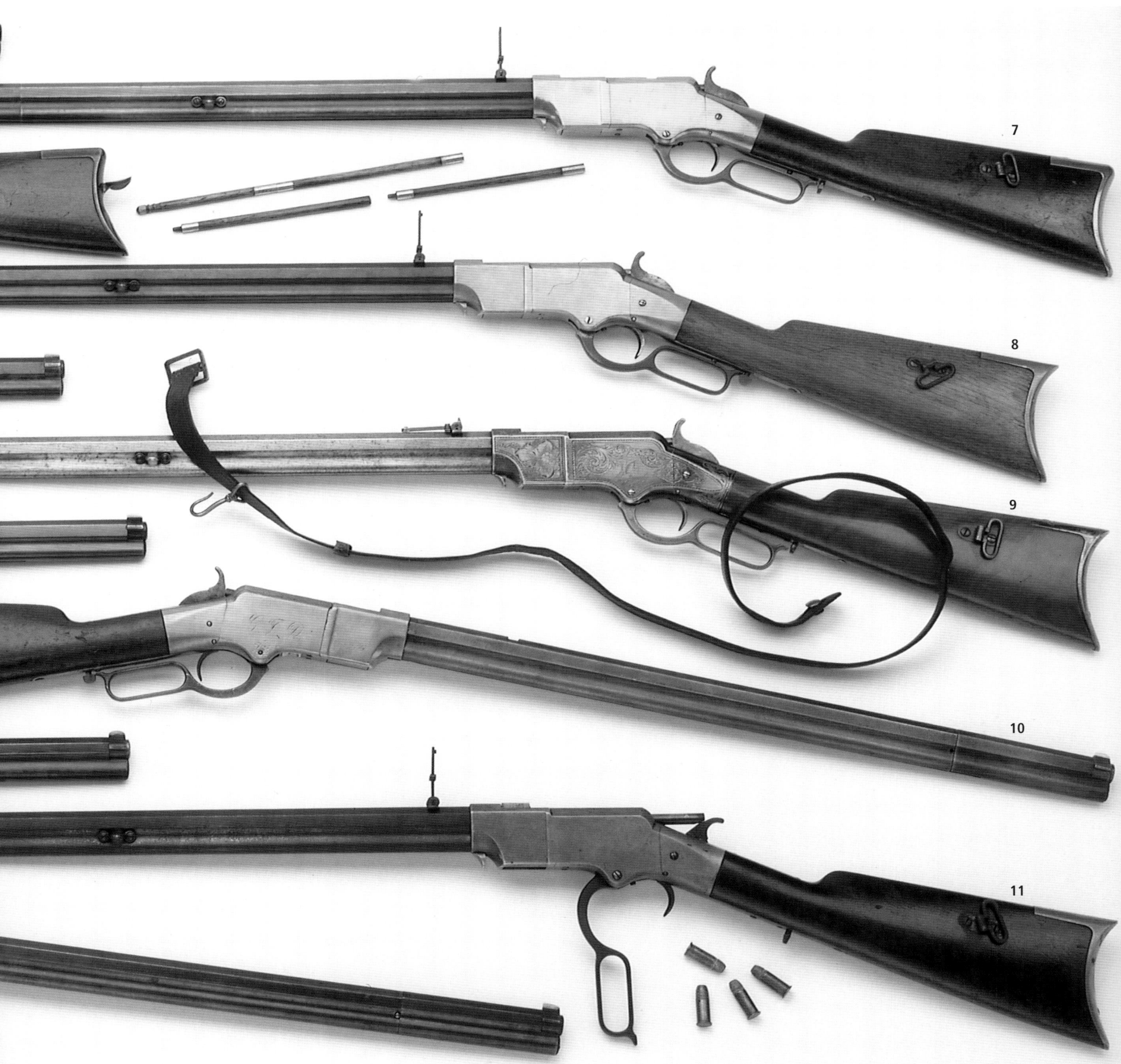

HUNTING AND BUFFALO RIFLES USA

While Sharps' weapons dominated the American hunting scene in the 1860s, by the early 1870s a number of serious competitors had appeared, seeking to break into this specialized but lucrative market, especially among those hunters who seemed determined to exterminate the West's vast herds of buffalo. Ballard, in particular, produced a number of "hunting" rifles in calibers ranging from 0.32in (8.1mm) to 0.44in (11.2mm), which met with some success. But Sharps' main competition came from Remington, whose sporting and hunting rifles, with their calibers ranging from 0.40in (10.2mm) to 0.50in (12.7mm), and their powerful cartridges, proved ideal for hunting buffalo and other big game.

No matter who the makers were, however, rifles for hunting large animals were expensive, usually between US$100 and US$300, depending upon the maker and the quality of the weapon. Further, the addition of special iron sights or even of the early telescopic sights added yet more to the hunter's outlay. Ammunition also aroused controversy, although hunters generally loaded their own most of the time and paid particular attention to the black powder they used: American powders tended to burn "hot and dry" and to cake up the bore, whereas British powders, particularly that made by Curtis & Harvey, burned "moist."

1. Maynard 0.50 caliber rifle in fitted case with reloading tools, powder flask, and cartridges. Note thesecond barrel, normally supplied in different calibers from 0.32 to 0.44 rim- or centerfire.

2. Cartridge box for the Maynard rifle.

3. Remington-Hepburn rifle with pistol grip.

4. Fine example of Frank Wesson's two-trigger rifle.

5. The outside hammer Peabody hunting rifle appeared in 0.44 to 0.45 calibers.

6. Remington Rolling Block short-range rifle in the "Light Baby Carbine" model.

7. Winchester single-shot rifle Model 1885 with a 20in round barrel.

8. Similar Winchester to that above, with 30in octagonal barrel. Both weapons have adjustable rear sights.

9. Fine Marlin-Ballard No. 2 sporting rifle in 0.38in centerfire, with "shells" for it below.

10. Sturdy breech-loader by the Brown Mfg Co.

11. Remington No. 1 Rolling Block sporting rifle. It was chambered for various calibers from 0.40 to 0.50, and was popular with hunters and plainsmen alike.

WINCHESTER RIFLES 1866-1873 USA

The legendary Winchester rifle owed its origin to the early Smith & Wesson and later Volcanic arms. But by the mid-1860s it was a much-improved weapon and the Model 1866 (called the "Yellow Boy" on account of its brass receiver) could be loaded with 15 cartridges. By far the most popular model was the standard rifle with a 24.0in (610mm) octagonal barrel, followed by the carbine, which had a somewhat shorter, 2.,0in (508mm), round barrel. Early advertisements for the Model 1866 made much of the fact that an expert shot could empty the magazine in 15 seconds, giving a remarkable, if theoretical, rate of fire of 60 shots a minute.

By the late 1860s, however, rimfire ammunition for rifles and other large arms was in decline. With the centerfire cartridge came the new and improved Winchester – the legendary Model 1873, usually known as the Winchester '73. In this model, Winchester improved the mechanism and replaced the brass lever with an iron one, while the new 0.44in-40 (10.2mm) cartridge was a great improvement, even if it failed to impress the Army's Ordnance Department because it was a pistol round and the Army wanted something much more powerful. The civilian market, on the other hand, welcomed the new cartridge and in 1878 Colt chambered some of their Peacemakers and double-action Army pistols in 0.44-l, which were marked "Frontier Six-Shooter." Despite a lack of military orders, the Model 1873 enjoyed a popularity which kept it in production until 1919.

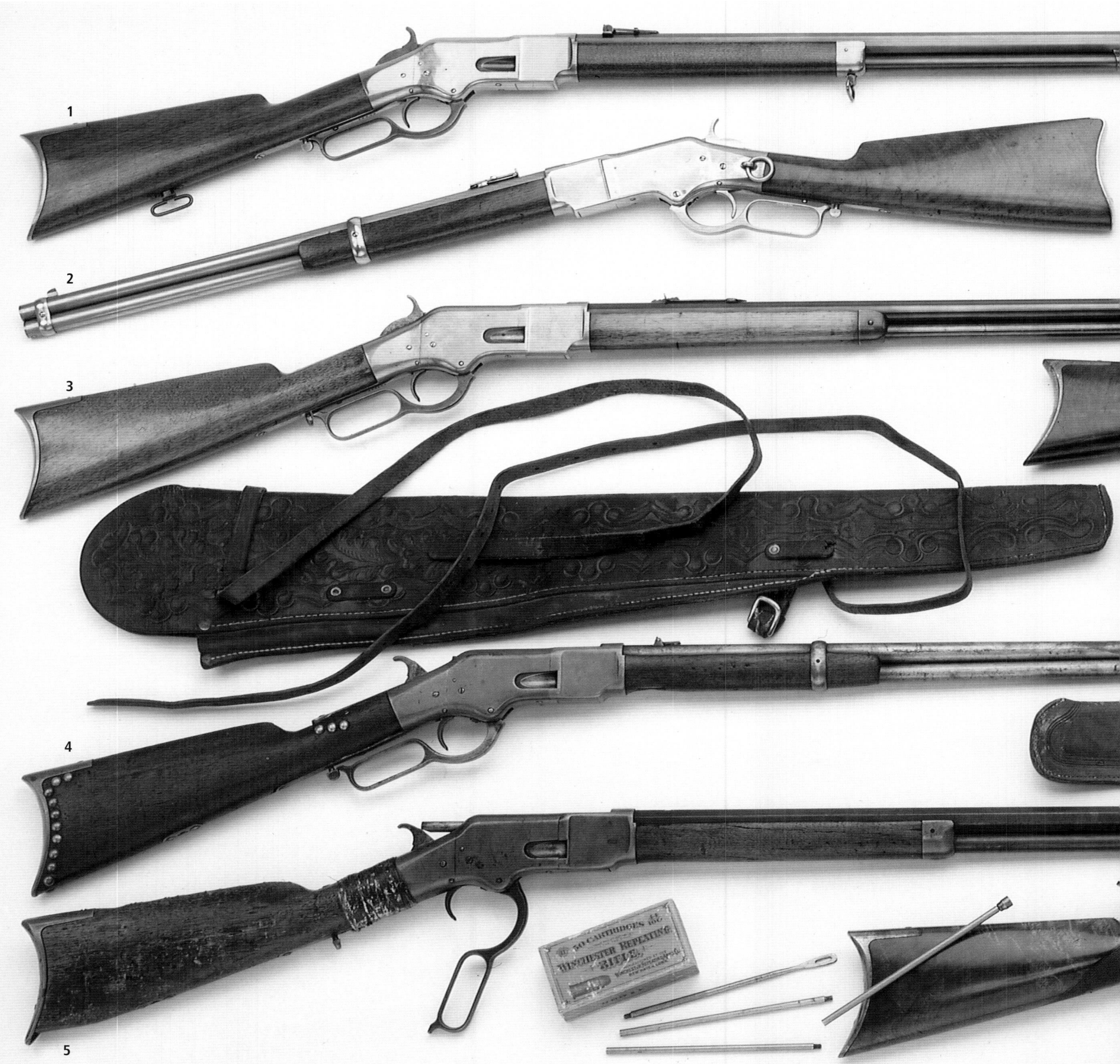

1. A fine Winchester Model 1866, 0.44 caliber, with 24in octagonal barrel and sling swivels.

2. Carbine version with a saddle ring and a round 20in barrel.

3. Some Model '66 rifles were made with round barrels on request. Below it is a fine hand-carved leather scabbard.

4. This Model 1866 was once Indian-owned – note the typical brass tack design.

5. Model 1866 with broken stock, repaired with wet rawhide strips.

6. Cocking action of the Winchester – note how the breech-pin cocks the hammer as the lever drops.

7. Typical 1973 carbine with the round barrel and saddle ring. Above it are a box of original "shells" for the '73, and two-part cleaning rod.

8. A '73 with round barrel and shortened magazine.

9. A fine '73 carbine, with below it, a typical saddle scabbard for a Winchester rifle.

10. Fine example of the Winchester '73 target rifle with additional sights set behind the hammer and, at its butt, its cleaning rod, and an original box of 50 0.44-100 rifle cartridges.

Winchester Rifles 1876-1886 USA

Faced with the rejection of the Model 1873 by the US Army because of its ammunition, Winchester produced a modified version, known as the Model 1876. This had a receiver able to accept the pressures generated by the Army's 0.45in-70 (11.4mm) cartridge which was 2.0in (50.8mm) long – almost twice the length of the standard 0.44in-40 (10.2mm) round. In fact, the Model 1876 could accept a 0.45in-75 (11.4mm) cartridge, with a bullet weight of 350 grains, which was more powerful than the government version. This rifle never achieved the fame of the '73, but it was accepted by the North-West Mounted Police and, like its predecessor, enjoyed a good reputation among frontiersmen.

John M. Browning, whose brilliant designs would later enhance Colt's reputation, completely redesigned the Winchester rifle to produce the most powerful of them all, the Model 1886. Chambered for 0.45in-90 (11.4mm), it also appeared in 0.50in-110-300 (12.7mm) Express, which proved to be a very popular caliber. The Browning-inspired Models 1877, 1892, and 1894 also met with great success. Keen-eyed movie-goers will observe that most "Winchesters" featured in "Westerns" are in fact usually either 1892 or 1894 models, rather than the '73s they are claimed to be.

Many old-time gunfighters and plainsmen carried a Winchester. The Model 1873 and the 1886, or even the Henry rifle, were used by buffalo hunters, but most hunters preferred larger calibered rifles.

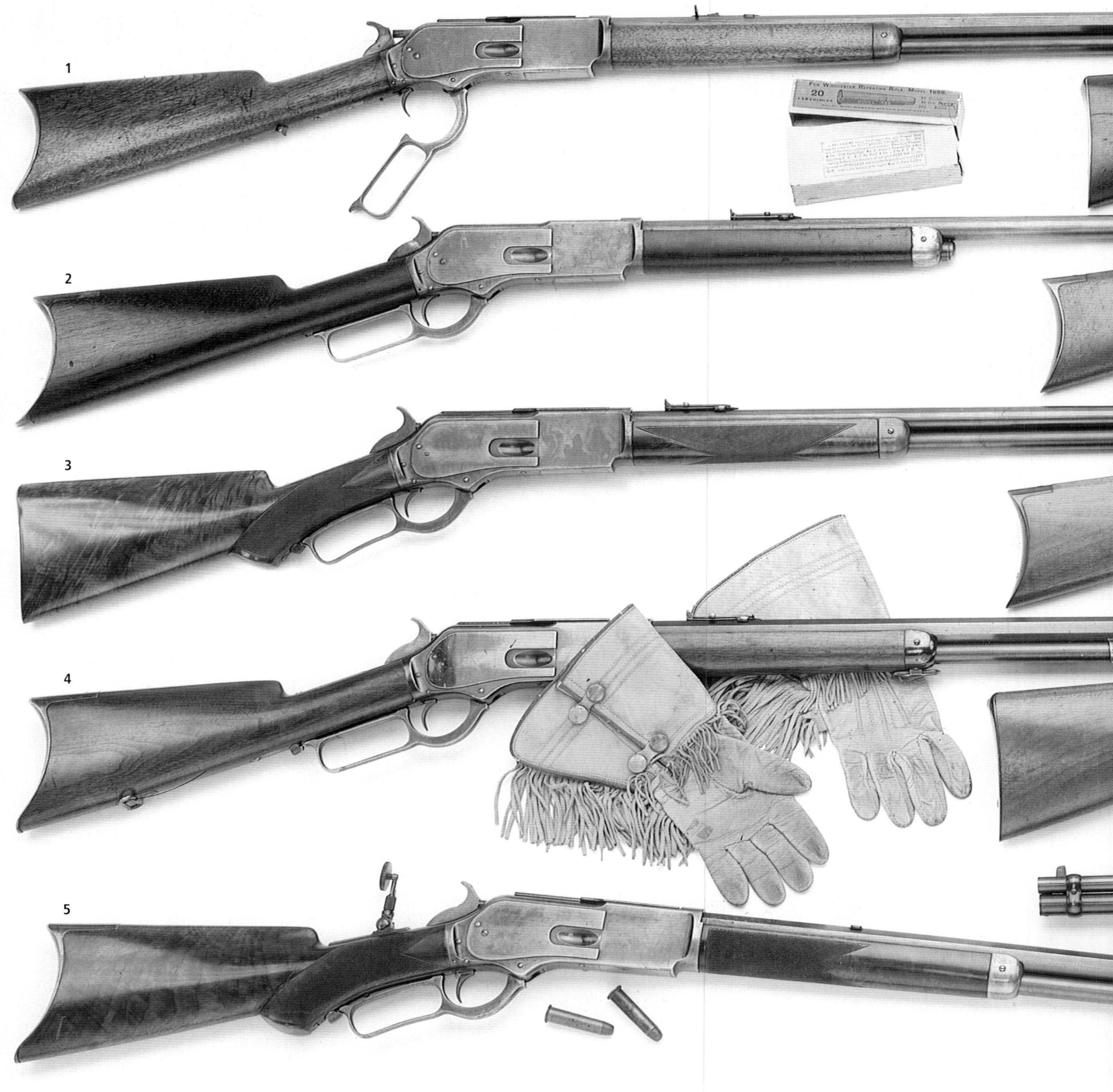

1 . Superficially similar to the Model '73, the '76 had an enlarged receiver and bigger loading-slot plate.

2. Like the '73, some Model '76s were sold with short magazines. Above the rifle is a box of cartridges for the '76.

3. Fine example of the Model 1876 carbine (serial no. 45569).

4. Fully blued '76 rifle (serial no. 40330), with a pair of ladies' buckskin gauntlets.

5. A '76 (serial no. 10018) equipped with a checkered pistol stock and target sights; below it are two 0.45-70 cartridges for the '76.

6. The Browning-designed Model 1886 rifle, a big improvement on earlier models.

7. A similar 1886 rifle, with choice wood pistol stock and target sights. Note the long "shell" case below it.

8. An "as new" carbine version of the Model 1886 (serial no. 8484).

9. The short magazine 1886 rifle (serial no. 57909) and, below it, high-powered cartridges.

10. Model 1886 carbine with a ring which allowed it to be slung over a saddle or shoulder and, above it, a silver-embossed, hand-tooled rifle scabbard for the 1886.

SPENCER RIFLES AND CARBINES — USA

In 1864, Brigadier-General James W. Ripley, Chief of the US Army's Ordnance Department, submitted a report to the Secretary of War in which he stated that the Spencer rifles and carbines were the "cheapest" and the "most efficient" of the many weapons in use by the Union forces, and that they enjoyed an excellent reputation among cavalry regiments. This seven-shot weapon, fitted with a Blakeslee quick-loader, was designed so that the ammunition was contained in a tube set into the stock. It took a matter of seconds to remove an empty tube and replace it with a fully charged one.

More than 90,000 carbines were purchased during the Civil War, and, following the conflict, the Spencer enjoyed a great reputation on the frontier. In 1865 the company introduced a 0.50in (12.7mm) caliber version, complete with magazine cut-off that enabled it to be used as a single-shot weapon, if required. Issued to various regiments, including the legendary Seventh Cavalry, the Spencer was considered to be the finest weapon of its type then available and what it lacked in magazine capacity compared with the Winchester it made up for by being easier and faster to load. In 1874 the Spencer was superseded by the Springfield Model 1873, a single-shot carbine in 0.45-70 caliber capable of firing 12 or 13 rounds a minute. At the Battle of Little Bighorn, poor ammunition and the lack of a proper means of removing jammed cases led to disaster; had Custer and his men not deliberately left their Spencers behind, the outcome of the battle might have been very different.

1. Spencer 0.36 caliber light sporting rifle (serial no. 15).

2. Spencer 0.44 caliber light carbine (serial no. 5) and, below it, a seven-round tubular magazine for Spencer rifles and carbines.

3. Spencer US Navy contract 0.36-56 caliber military rifle and, below it, four rounds of Spencer 0.56-52 caliber rimfire ammunition.

4. Spencer US Army 0.56-56 military carbine (serial no. 30670) carried at the Battle of the Little Bighorn by a Cheyenne warrior.

5. Spencer US Army Model 1865 0.56-50 caliber military carbine (serial no. 5909) and, below it, 0,56-56 Spencer rimfire cartridges.

6. Spencer 0.56-46 caliber sporting rifle (serial no. 17444).

7. Spencer 0.38 caliber prototype sporting rifle (no serial no.).

8. Spencer 0.56-50 caliber carbine (serial no. obliterated), rebarreled to a sporting rifle. Above it are a pair of typical Western saddle boxes which might have carried loose ammunition.

9. Spencer 0.56-46 caliber sporting rifle (no serial no.).

10. Spencer 0.56-56 cliber carbine (serial no. 35862), rebarreled to 0.56-50 by John Gemmer of St Louis under S. Hawken's stamp.

BURGESS-WHITNEY RIFLES — USA

Andrew Burgess, a prolific inventor, took out patents in 1873 and 1875 on a lever action for rifles, parts of which included features patented by G.W. Morse in 1856. Burgess then contracted with Eli Whitney, Jr (whose company had made Sam Colt's Walker pistols back in 1847) to produce a magazine lever-action rifle based on these patents, which would compete with the Winchester. The venture was not a success and in the mid-1880s Burgess turned to Samuel Colt, who then manufactured an improved version of the lever-action rifle, but, according to tradition, Winchester threatened to start producing revolvers unless Colt ceased production of the Burgess. Whatever the reason, production suddenly stopped! Whitney, however, went on to produce other lever-action weapons, notably the Whitney-Kennedy series, on of which was owned by "Billy the Kid."

The Whitney range of lever-action rifles was designed for frontier or sporting rather than military use, and an estimated 20,000 were made, Like the Winchester arms, the carbine version had a 20.0in (508mm) barrel, while the rifle had a 24.0in (610mm) barrel. The company also produced several bolt-action models intended for military use, but none was ever ordered into production by the Ordnance Department. There were, however, reports that a number of these military rifles later found favor among Central and South American armies. In 1886, the company introduced another lever-action rifle, based on William Scharf's patent, which looked uncannily like the Winchester Model 1873. But it was too late to save their dwindling finances and in 1888 Whitney sold out to Winchester.

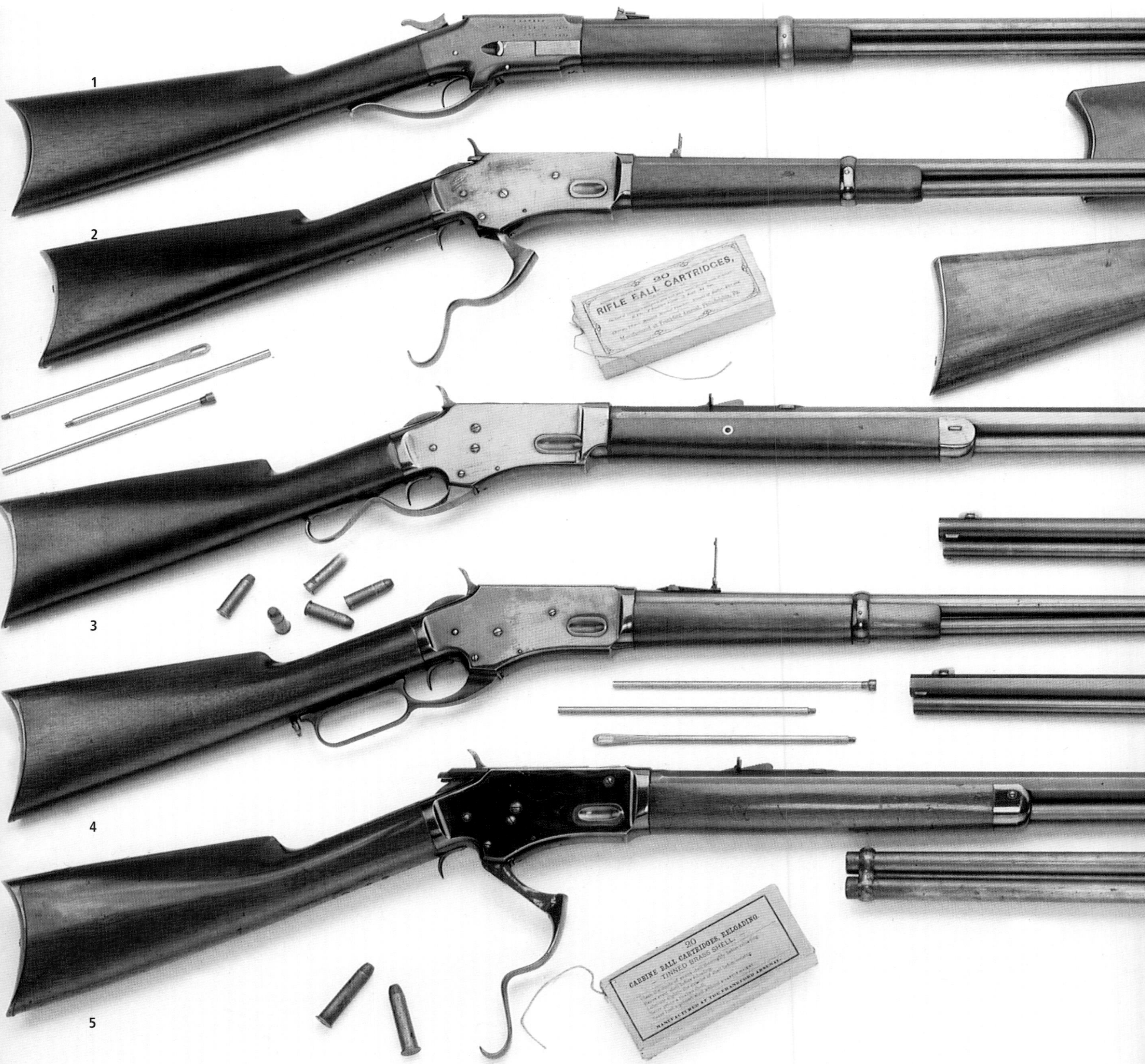

1. Whitney-Burgess carbine in 0.40 caliber.

2. Whitney-Kennedy lever-action carbine showing the "S" lever on early models and, below it, its three-part cleaning rod, and a box of 0.45 caliber rifle cartridges.

3. A Whitney-Burgess-Morse lever-action rifle in 0.44 caliber with, below it, cartridges for it (called "shells" out West).

4. Whitney-Kennedy carbine fitted with a full loop lever and, below it, a cleaning rod for it .

5. Whitney-Kennedy rifle in 0.40-60 caliber and, below it, cartridges for it.

6. Whitney-Scharf lever-action hunting rifle. It was sold in 0.32-20, 0.38-40, and 0.44-40 calibers. Below it are hunting cartridges.

7. Another version of the sporting rifle and, below it, a box of government cartridges, and a fine example of a typical Stetson-type broad-rimmed hat.

8. Colt-Burgess lever-action rifle, with cleaning rods below it.

9. Colt Lightning slide-operated rifle. Colt produced a number of variants of this rifle.

10. Remington-Keene magazine bolt-action rifle in 0.45-79 caliber.

WINCHESTER MODEL 1866 RIFLE — USA

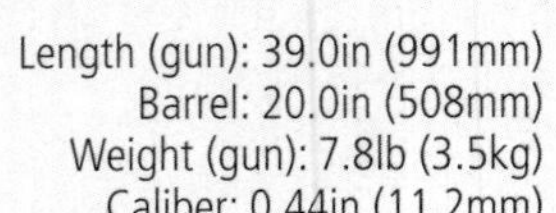

Length (gun): 39.0in (991mm)
Barrel: 20.0in (508mm)
Weight (gun): 7.8lb (3.5kg)
Caliber: 0.44in (11.2mm)
Rifling: 5 grooves, l/hand
Operation: breechloading
Feed: 16-round tubular magazine
Muz vel: ca 1,125ft/sec (343m/sec)

The patent which had originated with Hunt (qv) and passed on to Jennings (qv) then passed to a group of New York businessmen, among them a shirt manufacturer named Oliver Winchester, who put it into production as the "Volcanic Rifle." This venture was not a success, however, and when the company collapsed in 1857 its assets (including the patents) were bought by Winchester, who brought in a skilled and experienced weapons engineer, Benjamin Tyler, who quickly analyzed the problems and designed and developed a new, self-contained, much more powerful and very reliable 0.44in (11mm) cartridge. Henry also refined the design of the Volcanic rifle, which held 16 of the new rounds in a tubular magazine beneath the barrel. The new weapon, dubbed the "Henry repeater," was introduced in 1862, just after the beginning of the Civil War, and large numbers were bought, mainly by individual soldiers. By 1866 Winchester was able to reorganize the company, which became the Winchester Repeating Arms Company, with himself as president. One more development was then incorporated in the form of a loading gate on the right-hand side of the rifle, enabling rounds to be fed quickly and easily into the magazine, nose first, and the deservedly famous Winchester Rifle, with its distinctive brass receiver (which gave rise to the nickname "Yellow-boy") was complete. The original Model 1866 remained in production until 1898, but improvements were incorporated, resulting in further versions, including the Model 1873, known as the "gun that won the West." A 0.38in (9.65mm) round was introduced in 1880, followed by a much more powerful 0.45in (11.2mm) round in 1886.

US ARMY MODEL 1866 RIFLE (SPRINGFIELD-ALLIN CONVERSION) — USA

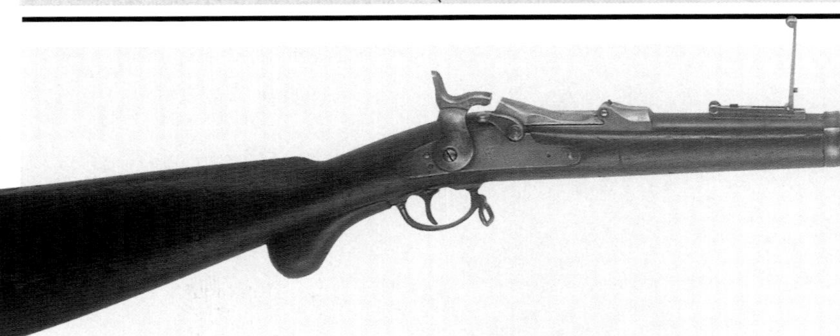

Length (gun): 51.0in (1.295mm)
Barrel: 32.5in (825mm)
Weight (gun): 8.3lb (3.7kg)
Caliber: 0.45in (11.4mm)
Rifling: 6 grooves, l/hand
Operation: breechloading
Feed: single round, manual
Muz vel: ca 1,350ft/sec (411m/sec)

The Springfield-Allin conversion, so called from the factory at which the work was carried out under the general supervision of Erskine Allin, the Master Armorer, was of fairly standard type. There was a trough leading into the breech which was closed by a front-hinged block containing a striker, the end of which was so positioned that it could be struck by the original percussion hammer. To load, it was necessary to place the hammer at half-cock, release a spring catch on the right-hand side, and raise the block until it was inclined forward at an angle of about 45 degrees; this action also worked the extractor. When the cartridge was in the breech the block was pulled back into position and the trigger pressed in the usual way. The nose of the hammer fitted exactly into a recess around the end of the striker, which effectively locked the block at the moment of firing. This rifle, with only minor modifications, remained in service until replaced by the Krag-Jörgensen magazine rifle (qv) and as late as 1898 United States Volunteer units were in action in the Spanish-American War still armed with these Springfields. The action of raising and lowering the block earned these weapons the nickname of the "Trapdoor Springfield."

REMINGTON RIFLE — USA

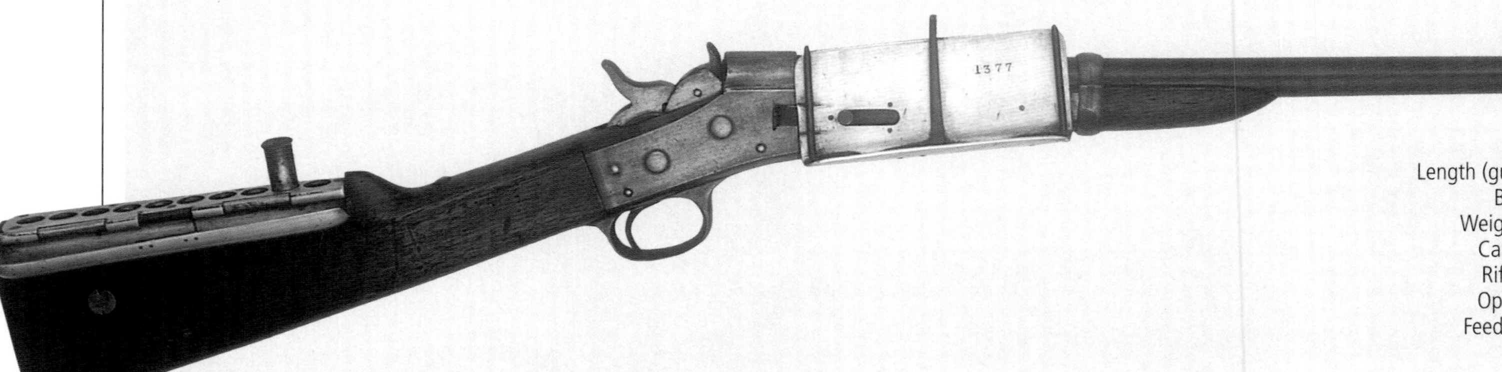

Length (gun): 50.5in (1,283mm)
Barrel: 35.0in (889mm)
Weight (gun): 9.3lb (4.2kg)
Caliber: 0.45in (11.4mm)
Rifling: 5 grooves, l/hand
Operation: breechloading
Feed: single round, manual

An American named Leonard Geiger patented a rifle mechanism in 1863, but when he was subsequently employed by Remington that company's name was applied to the resulting weapon. An order was placed by the US Army during the Civil War but the war ended before any deliveries had been made and, despite its success elsewhere, the Remington rifle was never adopted by the US Army. After some improvements had been made, it was exhibited at the Paris Imperial Exposition in 1867 where it won a silver medal, which attracted a number of overseas orders. The French bought a quantity for use as an interim weapon, but other countries ordered it as a permanent choice, including: Argentina (1879); Denmark (1867); Egypt (1870); Norway (1868); Spain (1869); and Sweden (1868). In the Remington action the breast of the hammer and the rear of the block were so designed that the former wedged so closely behind the latter that together they made an absolutely rigid support for the cartridge, a support strengthened even more by the fact that the nose of the hammer also engaged in a recess at the rear of the striker. The Remington Rifle was normally sighted to 1,000yd (914m), although some had sights for 1,400yd (1,280m). The weapon shown here was made for the Royal Danish Army and has a protective cover over the breech.

SHARPS CARBINE — USA

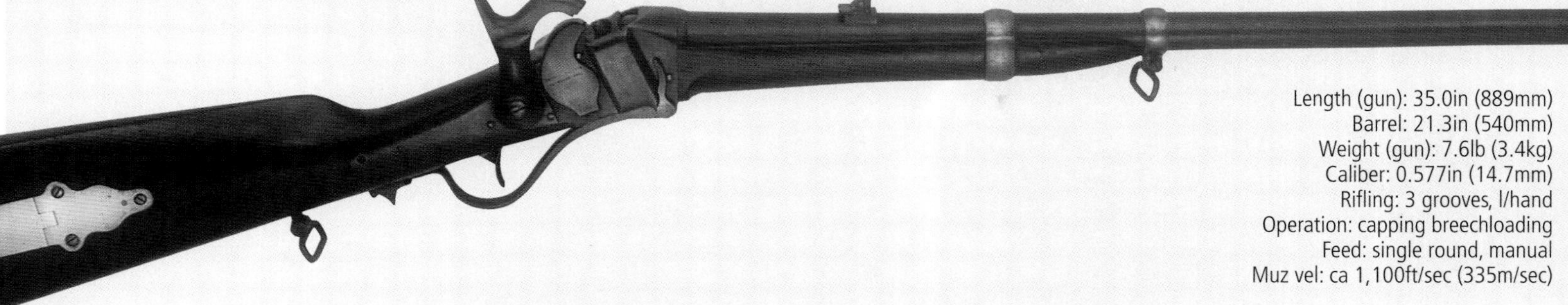

Length (gun): 35.0in (889mm)
Barrel: 21.3in (540mm)
Weight (gun): 7.6lb (3.4kg)
Caliber: 0.577in (14.7mm)
Rifling: 3 grooves, l/hand
Operation: capping breechloading
Feed: single round, manual
Muz vel: ca 1,100ft/sec (335m/sec)

The Sharps carbine was one of a number of weapons which saw service in the mid-19th Century known as "capping breech loaders." In these weapons a made-up cartridge of powder and bullet were wrapped in some combustible material, loaded into the breech, and then fired by a separate percussion cap, as in a muzzle-loader. In the American Sharps, the breech mechanism was a vertical sliding block working in grooves in the receiver by means of a lever, which also acted as a trigger guard. This system leaked some gas, but had the advantage of a dual system of ignition; it took the ordinary percussion cap and was also fitted with a tape primer. This took rolls of caps, rather like those used today in children's pistols, a fresh one being pushed over the nipple when the hammer was cocked, which meant that a mounted soldier did not have to fumble with relatively small caps when he had to prime. Over the years some 1,000 Sharps carbines were ordered and some British cavalry regiments used them in India towards the end of the Mutiny. Although generally reliable, British troops in India found that the tape became soggy in damp weather and brittle in the heat.

GREEN'S CARBINE — USA

Length (gun): 34.0in (837mm)
Barrel: 18.0in (457mm)
Weight (gun): 7.5lb (3.4kg)
Caliber: 0.55in (14mm)
Rifling: 3 grooves, l/hand
Operation: capping breechloading
Feed: single round, manual
Muz vel: ca 1,000ft/sec (305m/sec)

Like Sharps carbine (qv), Green's carbine was an American-designed capping breechloader, and in many ways one of the best. In this case the barrel was undocked from the breech by pressure on the forward trigger; it was then given an anti-clockwise twist, pushed forward and then swung out sideways for reloading. The reverse procedure then locked the barrel back in position and as the barrel was pulled back into position it pushed the cartridge onto a spike in the standing breech which tore the cartridge cover so that the flash could reach the powder. It was gas-tight and had a tape primer on a wheel, like the Sharps. Unfortunately, because of ignition difficulties the cartridge had to be made in very thin material which made it too flimsy for military use.

WINCHESTER 0.22IN SINGLE-SHOT MUSKET — USA

Length (gun): 43.8in (1,111mm)
Barrel: 28.0in (711mm)
Weight (gun): 8.4lb (3.8kg)
Caliber: 0.22 LR
Rifling: n.k.
Operation: lever-operated, tipping block
Feed: single round, manual
Muz vel: n.k.

Naming this weapon a "musket" is slightly misleading, since it is not a muzzle-loading, non-rifled weapon, as the name would normally imply. Instead, the name, which was given in the late 1880s, derived from what was considered to be the military-style woodwork and general appearance of the weapon. This was one of a number of "miniature" (ie, 0.22in) weapons which appeared in the United States towards the end of the 19th Century in response to a popular movement for the widespread training of civilians in the shooting arts. Indeed, the National Rifle Association of America had been lobbying to have shooting with such weapons included in all school curriculums. This weapon, of which some 109,327 were manufactured in 28 years of production, was made of either steel or iron, with wooden furniture, and in a wide variety of calibers.

MARLIN MODEL 39A RIFLE — USA

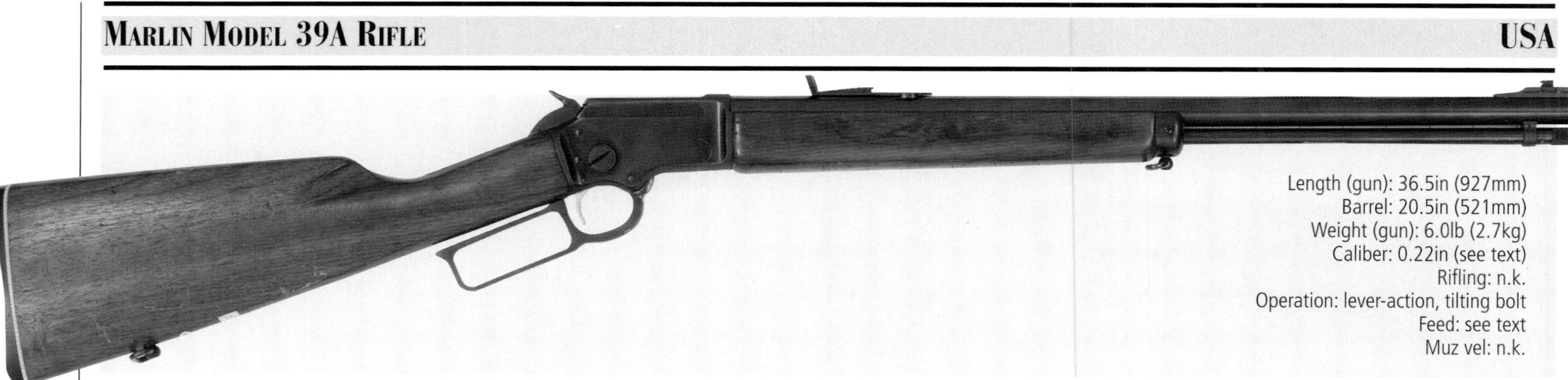

Length (gun): 36.5in (927mm)
Barrel: 20.5in (521mm)
Weight (gun): 6.0lb (2.7kg)
Caliber: 0.22in (see text)
Rifling: n.k.
Operation: lever-action, tilting bolt
Feed: see text
Muz vel: n.k.

The 0.22in Marlin Model 39A was introduced in 1891 and has been in continuous production ever since; in fact, like its near contemporary, the Savage (qv), it is a well-loved classic. The Model 39A was innovative in the 1890s being the first rifle with a front-loading, tubular magazine, which can take 26 0.22 Short or 19 Long/Long Rifle rounds. The nose of the lever locks the bolt, while pulling the lever down and forwards drives the bolt to the rear, over-riding and cocking the hammer, extracting and ejecting the spent case, and raising the cartridge lever, which elevates a new round from the magazine. Then, as the lever is closed, the new round is chambered ready for firing. There is a bead foresight with an open-notch backsight, which has a notched elevation ladder, drift adjustable for windage. There is a large screw on the right of the receiver, which allows disassembly into two parts for easier transport.

LEE MODEL 1895 (US NAVY) RIFLE — USA

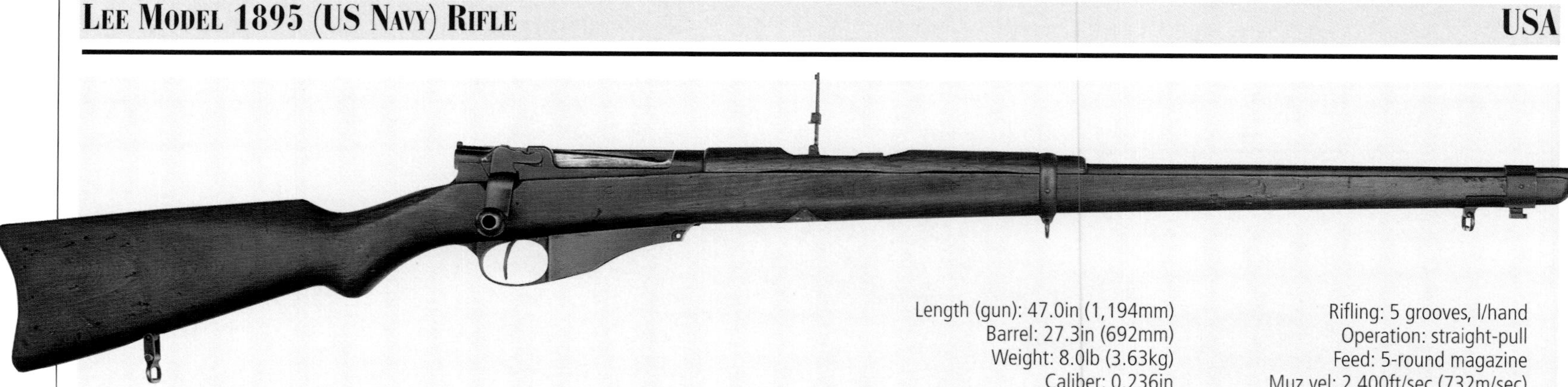

Length (gun): 47.0in (1,194mm)
Barrel: 27.3in (692mm)
Weight: 8.0lb (3.63kg)
Caliber: 0.236in
Rifling: 5 grooves, l/hand
Operation: straight-pull
Feed: 5-round magazine
Muz vel: 2,400ft/sec (732m/sec)

This rifle is probably better known as the Lee straight-pull which indicates both its inventor and its mechanism. James Lee, a Scot by birth but educated in Canada, eventually became a citizen of the United States where all his experimental work was done. He is probably best known for his box magazine for bolt-action rifles; it was widely adopted and his name appears on a long series of British service rifles. Towards the end of the 19th Century he invented a rifle which in 1895 was adopted by the United States Navy who placed an order for 10,000 of them. The rifle was unusual in that it incorporated a "straight-pull" breech in which direct backward pressure on the lever caused the breech to rise slightly, opening as it did so. No manual turning was required; locking worked by an arrangement of cams on the bolt. It was of unusually small caliber and had a magazine capacity of five rounds; it was also the first United States service rifle ever to be loaded by means of a charger. Unfortunately, straight-pull rifles have no real advantage over the more orthodox turn-bolt types, but they do have several disadvantages, chief of which are their complex structure and the fact that their operation, perhaps surprisingly, is more tiring than that of normal types. The US Navy disliked it very much and it soon disappeared from the service. A sporting version was also made but this also proved unpopular and the model was soon withdrawn, some 18,300 of the 20,000 produced never seeing daylight.

SAVAGE MODEL 99A RIFLE — USA

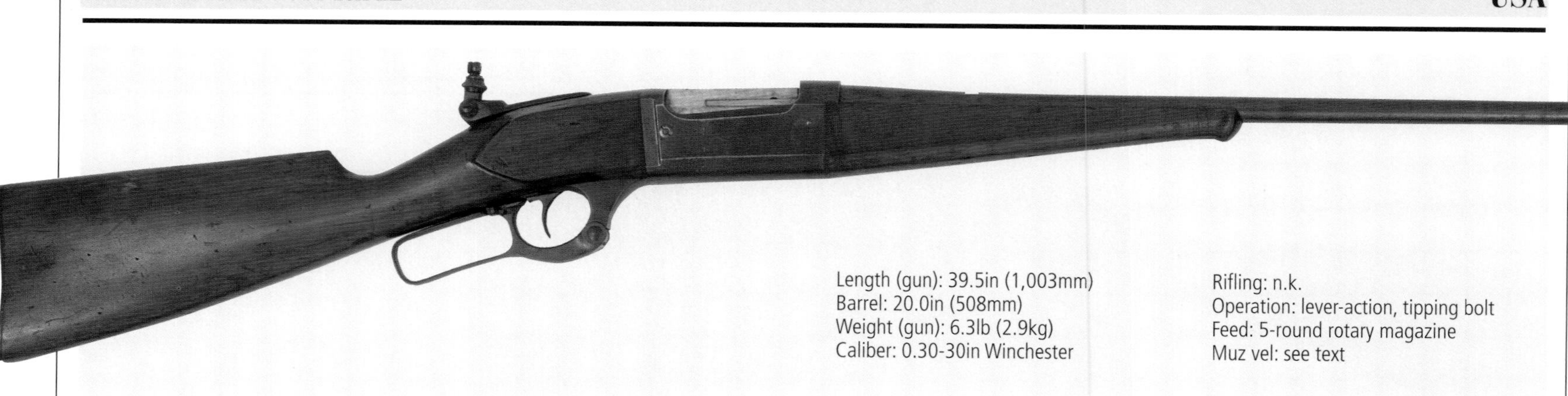

Length (gun): 39.5in (1,003mm)
Barrel: 20.0in (508mm)
Weight (gun): 6.3lb (2.9kg)
Caliber: 0.30-30in Winchester
Rifling: n.k.
Operation: lever-action, tipping bolt
Feed: 5-round rotary magazine
Muz vel: see text

Lever-action rifles remained popular in the United States for a long time after Europe had switched to bolt-actions, one of the main reasons being that they were capable of accurate and rapid fire, a skilled firer being able to loose off some 15 shots in a minute. This was a particularly important factor in a country where large areas, particularly the West, were lawless and there was a need for a weapon for both hunting and self-defense. The Savage was introduced in 1895 and improved in 1899 (hence the designation) and over one-and-a-half million have been subsequently produced. For the first 15 or so years the '99 was chambered for the usual run of low-pressure, lever-action cartridges: 0.30-30, 0.25-35 and 0.32-40, but the breakthrough came in 1915 with the introduction of the 0.250-300, which put this rifle in a class of its own. Charles Newton designed the 0.250 on a cut-down 0.30-40 Krag case as a useful deer-hunting cartridge. Then Harvey Donaldson, another leading ballistic experimenter, suggested basing it on the 0.30-06 instead, while Arthur Savage cut the bullet weight from 100 to 87 grains, enabling him to launch the first commercially loaded American cartridge with a muzzle velocity in excess of 3,000ft/sec (914m/sec), hence the cartridge's designation. Thus, the lever-action Savage remains popular to this day, although it is now generally chambered for the 0.243 and 0.308 Winchester rounds.

Springfield Rifle Model 1903 — USA

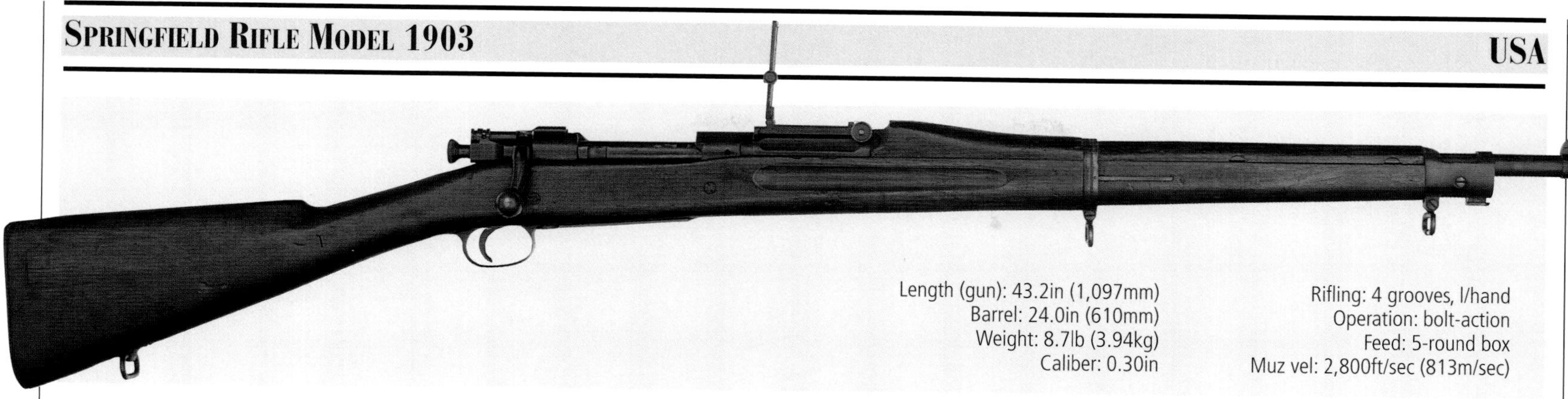

Length (gun): 43.2in (1,097mm)
Barrel: 24.0in (610mm)
Weight: 8.7lb (3.94kg)
Caliber: 0.30in
Rifling: 4 grooves, l/hand
Operation: bolt-action
Feed: 5-round box
Muz vel: 2,800ft/sec (813m/sec)

Soon after the introduction of the Krag-Jörgensen rifle into the United States Army in 1894 the authorities began to examine the idea of yet another rifle, this time on the Mauser principle, and 5,000 infantry models with 30in (762mm) barrels were ordered in 1901. Before they were made however the United States Army decided that the time had come for a short universal rifle, and had the barrels reduced to 24in (610mm). In this they were probably influenced by their experience in Cuba and also by the lessons of the Anglo-Boer War which caused the British Army to reach a similar conclusion. The new rifle, commonly known as the Springfield after its place of manufacture, had a Mauser-type bolt and a five-round magazine with a cut-off, and after some basic modifications, notably the introduction of a lighter, pointed bullet, in place of the earlier round-nosed variety, it was brought into general issue by 1906. It proved to be a very popular rifle, its chief disadvantage, a minor one, being its small magazine capacity, and it remained in use for many years. In this time it underwent various modifications, notably one to allow it to be converted to an automatic weapon by the addition of the Pedersen device of 1918 and another which added a pistol grip to the stock in 1929. There was also a target variety, equipped with a Weaver telescopic sight, which was used successfully as the sniping rifle in World War II, together with a variety of other sporting variations, many of which are still in use. The picture shows the original production M1903. (See also M1903A3 and Springfield Armory M1A.)

Garand Rifle 0.30in Cal M1 — USA

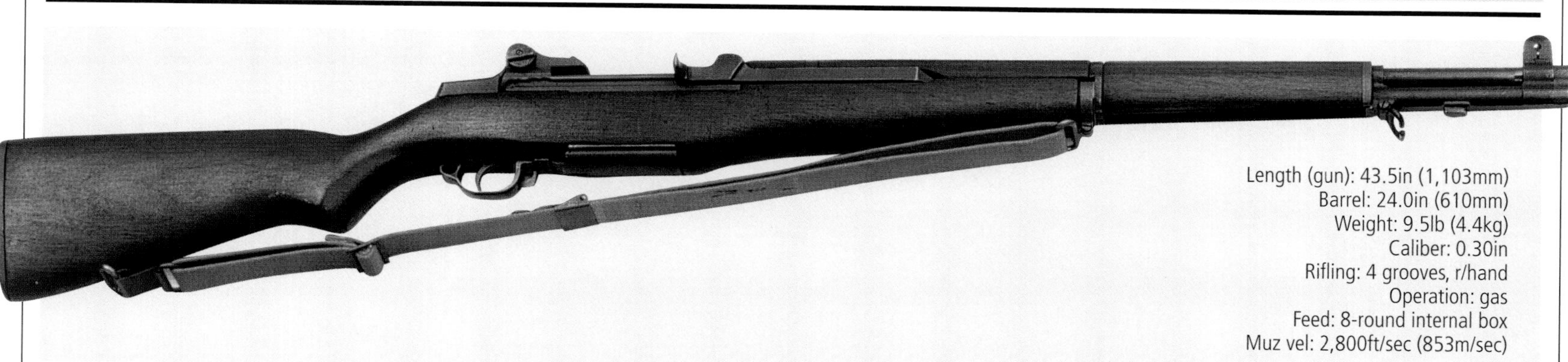

Length (gun): 43.5in (1,103mm)
Barrel: 24.0in (610mm)
Weight: 9.5lb (4.4kg)
Caliber: 0.30in
Rifling: 4 grooves, r/hand
Operation: gas
Feed: 8-round internal box
Muz vel: 2,800ft/sec (853m/sec)

This rifle, commonly known as the Garand, was the first self-loader ever to be adopted by any army as a standard weapon. A whole series of similar rifles were exhaustively tested before it was finally selected in 1936. It was a good weapon, robust (and therefore heavy) but simple and reliable. It was operated by gas and piston. The eight-round magazine had to be loaded by a special charger holding the cartridges in two staggered rows of four each. When the last round had been fired the empty clip was automatically ejected and the bolt remained open as an indication to the firer that reloading was necessary. The Garand was the standard rifle of the US Army in World War II, and was the only self-loader generally used. They were made mainly by the Springfield Armory and the Winchester Repeating Arms Company, although smaller numbers were also produced by other American arms companies and after the war a quantity were made by the Italian firm of Beretta. When manufacture finally ceased in the middle of 1950s an astonishing total of some five and a half million had been produced. There were several variations to the Garand in its long history, including a National Match model and three sniper rifles but none differed from the prototype.

US Carbine 0.30in Caliber M1 — USA

Length (gun): 35.7in (905mm)
Barrel: 18.0in (458mm)
Weight: 5.5lb (25kg)
Caliber: 0.30in
Rifling: 4 grooves, r/hand
Operation: gas
Feed: 15-/30-round box
Muz vel: 1,950ft/sec (585m/sec)

Just before World War II the US Army decided that it needed a new light weapon, intermediate between the pistol and the rifle, as a convenient arm for officers and non-commissioned officers at rifle company level and as a secondary weapon for mortarmen, drivers, and similar categories for whom the service rifle would have been awkward. By the end of 1941 the Army had settled for the M1 carbine and it had gone into large-scale production. The M1 was a short, light, self-loading rifle, and although its caliber was the same as that of the service rifle it fired a different, pistol-type cartridge, so that there was no question of inter-changeability between the two. The M1 carbine was an odd weapon to have been produced so late, since in a very real sense it looked back towards the arms of the stocked Luger or Mauser pistol-type, rather than forward to the submachine gun, which at the time of the introduction of the new carbine had amply demonstrated that it had an important part to play in modern warfare. At that period the United States submachine gun was however still the Thompson, heavy and expensive to produce, and these considerations probably justified the introduction of a new category of arm.

US CARBINE 0.30IN CALIBER M1A1 — USA

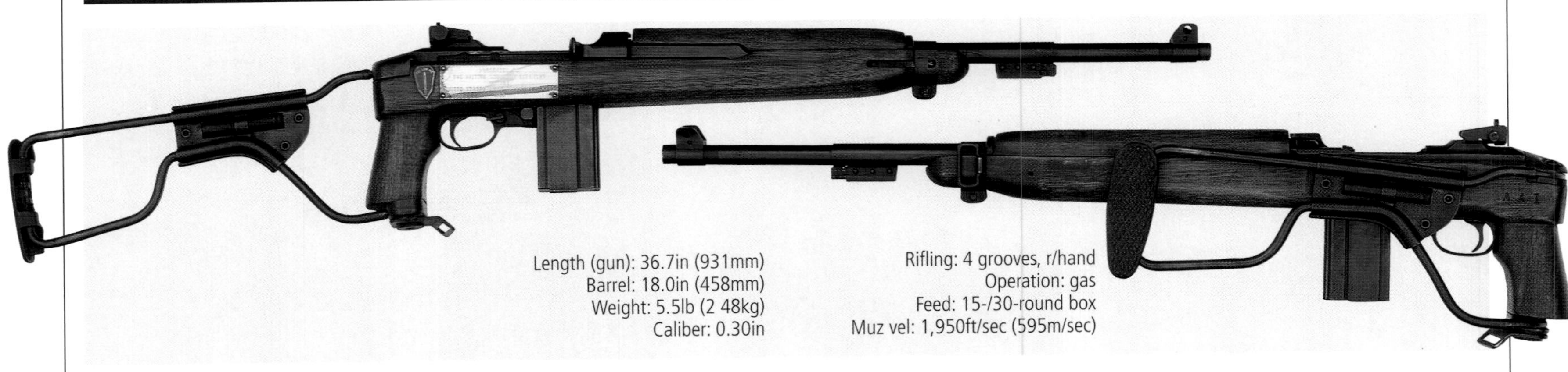

Length (gun): 36.7in (931mm)
Barrel: 18.0in (458mm)
Weight: 5.5lb (2 48kg)
Caliber: 0.30in
Rifling: 4 grooves, r/hand
Operation: gas
Feed: 15-/30-round box
Muz vel: 1,950ft/sec (595m/sec)

The general details regarding the history and introduction of the 0.30 caliber have already been described in the text for the original weapon of the series. There were however a number of variations, notably the M1A1, which, although the same basic weapon as the M1, was equipped with a folding stock, the central bracing plate of which carried an oil bottle. This skeleton stock was pivoted on a pistol grip so that the carbine could be fired if necessary with the stock folded, which made it a convenient weapon for parachute and airborne forces. The true gun enthusiast may feel that this spoils the general lines of the weapon as compared with its prototype and this is to some extent true. The modification however was made at a time when practical considerations were important. The M1 carbine in its various forms was the commonest weapon produced by the United States, the total production reaching the astonishing figure of just over seven million. They were light, handy weapons which in spite of some lack of stopping power fulfilled an obvious need. At one stage a selective fire version was produced which in effect converted the carbine into a submachine gun and there was also a version designed to take various types of night sight, no conventional sights being fitted. The two versions were known respectively as M2 and M3.

SPRINGFIELD M1903A3 RIFLE — USA

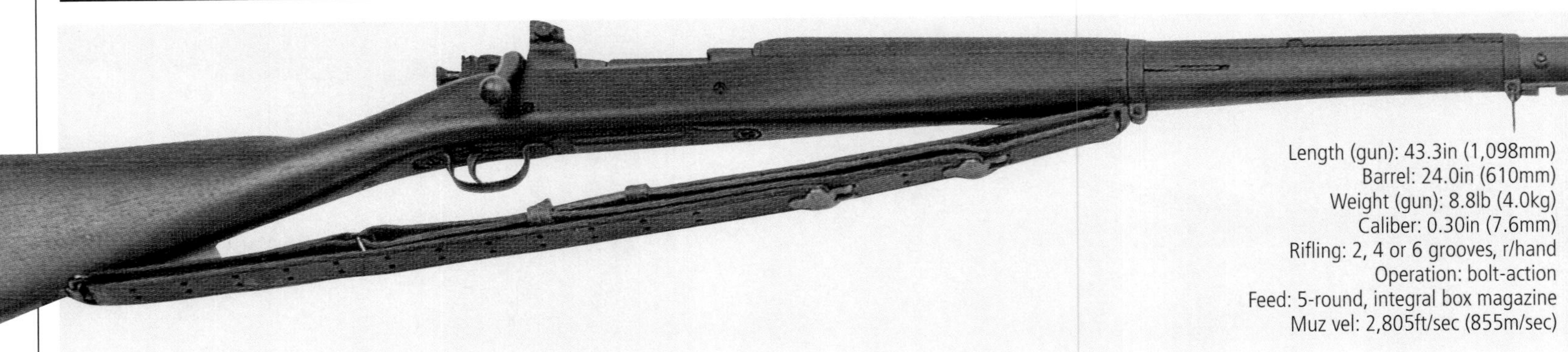

Length (gun): 43.3in (1,098mm)
Barrel: 24.0in (610mm)
Weight (gun): 8.8lb (4.0kg)
Caliber: 0.30in (7.6mm)
Rifling: 2, 4 or 6 grooves, r/hand
Operation: bolt-action
Feed: 5-round, integral box magazine
Muz vel: 2,805ft/sec (855m/sec)

The Springfield M1903 remained in service throughout World War I and was given a very minor facelift in 1929 by fitting a different type of butt stock, becoming the M1903A1. With the outbreak of World War II, however, there was a requirement for infantry rifles in vast numbers and the M1903 was re-engineered to make it more suitable for mass production in the quantities now required. Among the changes were the substitution of sheet-metal stampings wherever feasible, but the most obvious external changes were the removal of the leaf backsight on top of the barrel and its replacement by an aperture sight atop the receiver bridge, and the deletion of the grasping groove for the fingers on the forestock. The new sight, which was adjustable for windage, was graduated up to 800yd (732m). About 950,000 of these weapons were produced between 1942 and 1944, when production switched to the Garand rifle (qv). The M1903A4 was an M1903A3 modified for use as a sniper rifle by the addition of a permanently mounted optical x2.5 telescope. In the mid-1950s a further batch of some 850 M1903A3s were produced for use in National Match championships as the Springfield Armory M1A (qv).

REMINGTON 870 WINGMASTER SLIDE-ACTION SHOTGUN — USA

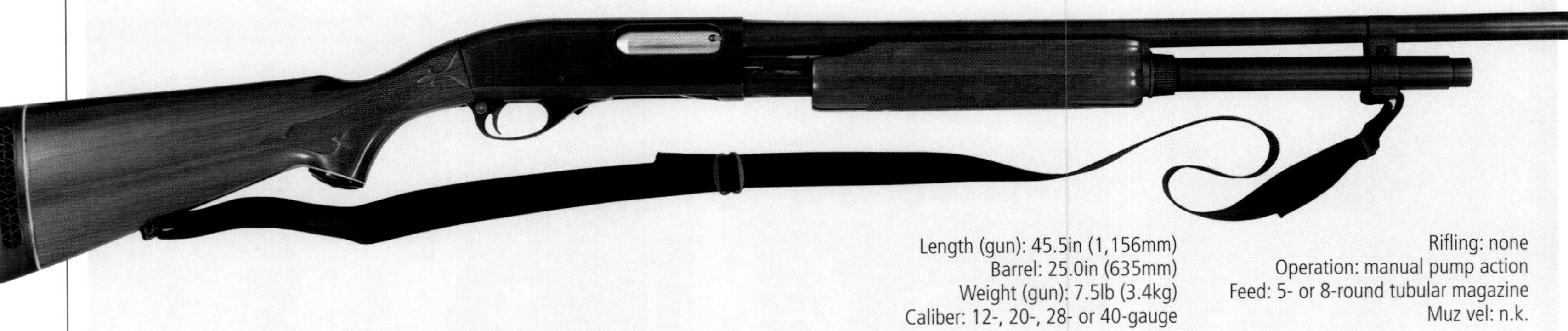

Length (gun): 45.5in (1,156mm)
Barrel: 25.0in (635mm)
Weight (gun): 7.5lb (3.4kg)
Caliber: 12-, 20-, 28- or 40-gauge
Rifling: none
Operation: manual pump action
Feed: 5- or 8-round tubular magazine
Muz vel: n.k.

The Remington 870 was introduced in 1950, since when over four million have been made. It is produced in a wide variety of models, with barrel lengths varying from 18in (457mm) in the Police Model to 30in (762mm) for 3in (76mm) Magnum cartridges, and in four gauges: 12-, 20-, 28-, and 40-gauge. Normal magazine capacity is five rounds, but an extension giving eight-round capacity is also available. It has a strong and positive action, with double action bars, and all except the Police and Special-Purpose models are fitted with walnut stocks and fore ends. One shortcoming in earlier models occurred when cartridges not pushed fully into the magazine might slip and cause a stoppage, but this was rectified in later versions. Other later modifications included fitting the "Rem" internally threaded choke system, and recoil pads on the 12- and 20-gauge models.

Armalite AR15 (M16) Rifle — USA

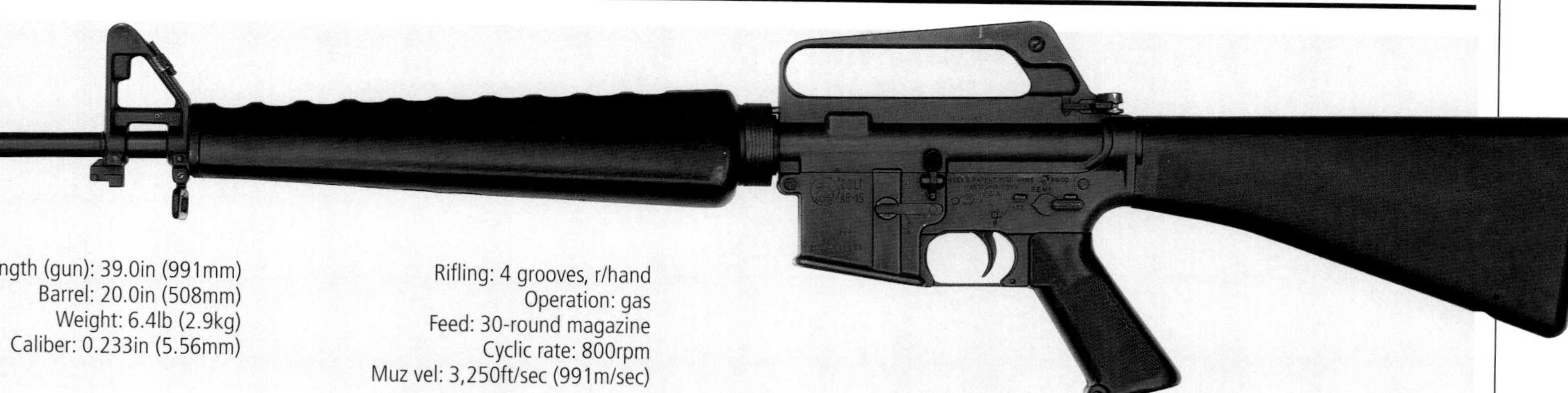

Length (gun): 39.0in (991mm)
Barrel: 20.0in (508mm)
Weight: 6.4lb (2.9kg)
Caliber: 0.233in (5.56mm)

Rifling: 4 grooves, r/hand
Operation: gas
Feed: 30-round magazine
Cyclic rate: 800rpm
Muz vel: 3,250ft/sec (991m/sec)

The prototype for this weapon was the AR-10 which first went into production in 1955. It was a very advanced arm employing plastic and aluminum wherever possible but it proved too light to fire the powerful NATO 7.62mm cartridge for which it was designed, and manufacture ceased in 1962. It was soon followed by the small caliber high-velocity AR-15, designed by Eugene Stoner and made under license by the Colt company from July, 1959 onwards. This new weapon soon became popular. It was a good jungle rifle and, being light and easy to handle by small men, it soon found favor in various countries in the Far East. It was quickly adopted by the United States after their intervention in Vietnam, and, as the M16, is now their standard rifle (except in NATO). It has no piston, the gases simply passing through a tube and striking directly on to the bolt, which is efficient but means that the weapon needs careful and regular cleaning. It was used by the British Army in small numbers in Borneo.

Springfield Armory 7.62mm M1A Rifle — USA

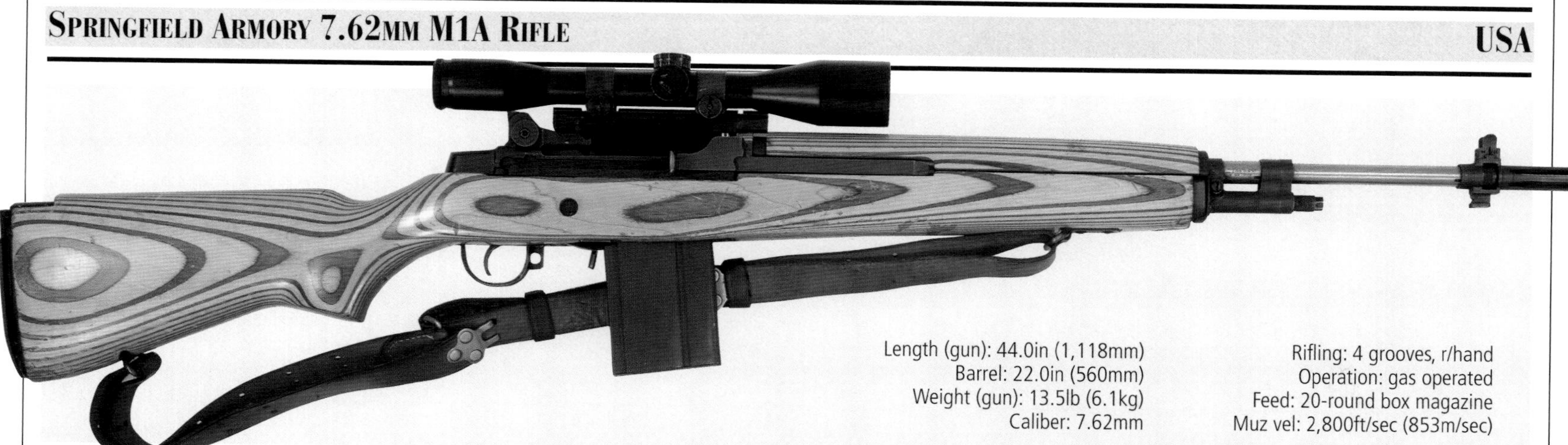

Length (gun): 44.0in (1,118mm)
Barrel: 22.0in (560mm)
Weight (gun): 13.5lb (6.1kg)
Caliber: 7.62mm

Rifling: 4 grooves, r/hand
Operation: gas operated
Feed: 20-round box magazine
Muz vel: 2,800ft/sec (853m/sec)

When the Springfield Armory was closed, the name itself was sold to an Illinois based light engineering firm, which saw a golden opportunity on the civil market for the M14 rifle (qv). This weapon, which had been the ultimate development of the Garand series, had been produced in only small numbers for the US Army when production was halted and switched to the 5.56mm M16 (AR15 Armalite). The new company, however, placed the M14 rifle back in production for the civilian market under the company designation, M1A, and this has proved to be a superb and very popular target performer.

7.62mm M14 Rifle — USA

Length (gun): 44.0in (1,117mm)
Barrel: 22.0in (558mm)
Weight: 8.6lb (3.9kg)
Caliber: 7.62mm
Rifling: 4 grooves, r/hand
Operation: gas
Feed: 20-round box
Cyclic rate: 750rpm
Muz vel: 2,800ft/sec (853m/sec)

Before the end of World War II the US Army was working on the concept of a selective fire weapon of assault rifle type. By 1953, NATO having settled on a common cartridge, good progress had been made, and although most European countries opted for Belgian-type weapons the United States settled for the M14. This was a logical development of the Garand. A number of important improvements were made, notably the abolition of the awkward eight-round clip and the substitution of a pre-filled detachable box magazine holding 20 rounds. The new rifle was capable of firing single shots or bursts, and although most were issued permanently set for semi-automatic fire only, a number were fitted with light bipods with a view to being used as squad or section light automatics. They were however only marginally suitable for this role because sustained fire caused them to overheat and there was no provision for changing barrels. A heavy barreled version was contemplated but never produced, but there was also an excellent sniper version. Some 1,500,000 M14s were made in all.

ITHACA 37 SHOTGUN — USA

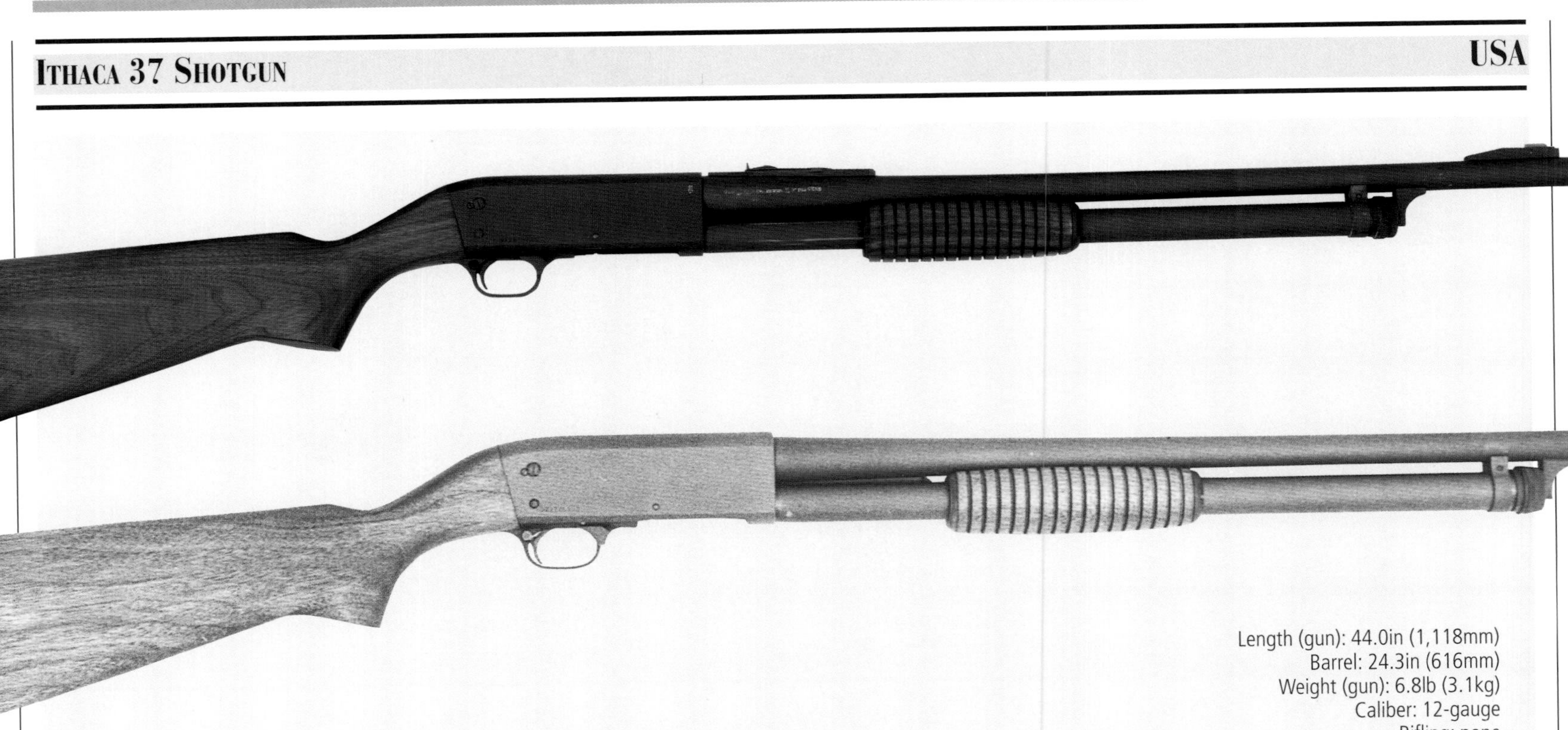

Length (gun): 44.0in (1,118mm)
Barrel: 24.3in (616mm)
Weight (gun): 6.8lb (3.1kg)
Caliber: 12-gauge
Rifling: none
Operation: slide-action, repeater shotgun
Feed: 8-round tubular magazine
Muz vel: n.k.

The Ithaca 37 was a very robust, reliable, and easy-to-handle pump gun, which was used by sportsmen and, in certain circumstances, by police and special forces. The Ithaca Gun Company of Ithaca, New York, was founded in 1880 and proceeded to produce almost every type of shotgun and, during World War II, a variety of military weapons for the US Government. However, they are best known for their trap guns and slide (pump-action) shotguns. In 1911 they produced a single-barreled gun designed specially for trap shooting and it was succeeded in 1922 by a new model which remained in production for many years. In 1937 Ithaca introduced this slide-action gun, the Model 37 Featherlight, which has become a classic. Unlike other weapons in its field, it used bottom ejection for spent cartridges, which had four benefits: it gave protection in rain and snow; in the event of a burst cartridge the debris was ejected downwards; the gun could be used with equal ease by either right- or left-handed shooters; and the shorter receiver resulted in a lighter weapon. It was, in fact, over 1.0lb (0.45kg) lighter than any competitor. The Model 37 was made in 12-, 16-, and 20-gauge and in many formats, including the "Deerslayer" hunting gun, seen here at top. Another version, the "Stakeout" police shotgun, had a pistol grip, no stock, and a shorter barrel with a magazine holding just four rounds.

WINCHESTER 8500 SPECIAL TRAP SHOTGUN — USA

Length (gun): 50.8in (1,290mm)
Barrel: 30.0in (762mm)
Weight (gun): 8.3lb (3.8kg)
Caliber: 12-gauge
Rifling: none
Operation: standard
Feed: manual
Muz vel: n.k.

At the other end of the target shooting spectrum from the French "Baby Bretton" (qv) is this Winchester 8500 Special Trap, which is of quite distinctive appearance, with a plain black action, high trap rib, and ventilated mid-rib. An unusual feature is that the bottom barrel is "ported" – in other words, it has a series of small round holes running along the barrel for some 4.0in (102mm) to the rear from a point around 3.0in (76mm) from the muzzle. The theory behind this is that the gases, or some portion of them, are vented through these ports before they leave the muzzle, thus helping to reduce muzzle "flip" and assisting in keeping the gun on target for the second shot. The method has been used before, mainly by means of venting right at the end of the barrels, but "porting" is claimed to be more effective and less noisy.

HARRINGTON & RICHARDSON TOPPER SINGLE-BARRELED SHOTGUN — USA

The most basic form of working gun is the break-open, single-shot weapon with simple accessories such as sling, recoil-pad and iron sights. Pump actions and other types of repeater give much greater firepower, but at a very considerable increase in price. As a result, the single shot was an integral element of every American small farm, being regarded as almost as much of a tool as an axe or a spade. One reason for the cheapness of these weapons was that they could be made almost entirely by machine and the Harrington & Richardson gun shown here is typical of the breed. Such guns were also very widely used In Britain by small farmers and smallholders for pest control and for a long time, particularly in the wars before World War I, between the two wars, and from 1945 to the early 1980s, American guns such as this were popular in Britain, because of their simplicity, efficiency, and cheapness. From the early 1980s, however, even cheaper imports from Spain and Italy stole the market.

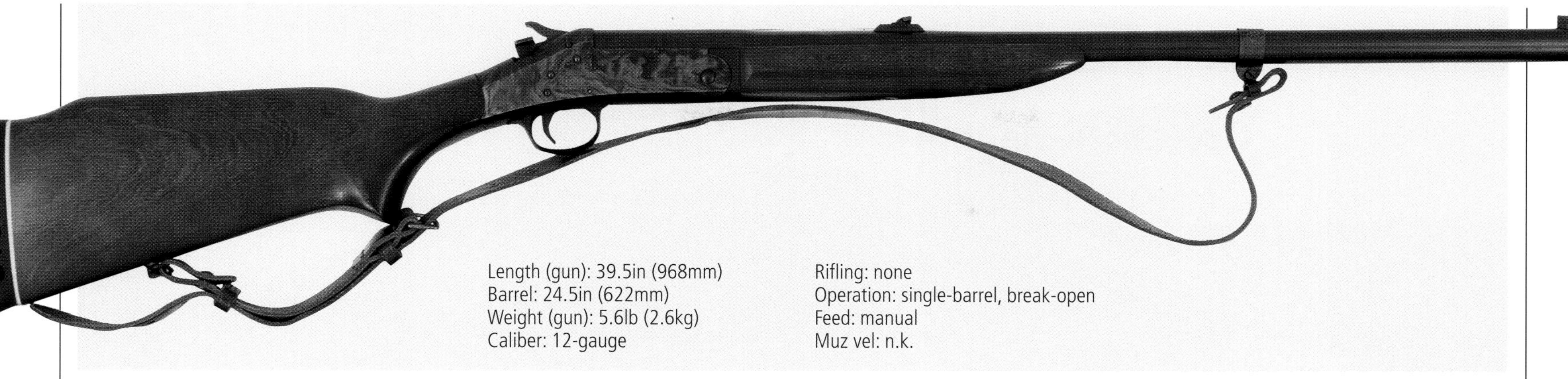

Length (gun): 39.5in (968mm)
Barrel: 24.5in (622mm)
Weight (gun): 5.6lb (2.6kg)
Caliber: 12-gauge
Rifling: none
Operation: single-barrel, break-open
Feed: manual
Muz vel: n.k.

Armalite AR18 — USA

Length (gun): 37.0in (940mm)
Barrel: 10.1in (257mm)
Weight (gun): 6.9lb (3.2kg)
Caliber: 5.56mm
Rifling: 6 grooves, r/hand
Operation: gas operated
Feed: 20-, 30-, 40-round box magazine
Cyclic rate: 800rpm
Muz vel: 3,280ft/sec (1,000m/sec)

The Armalite AR18 was designed by Arthur Miller, following the departure of Eugene Stoner and the AR-15/M16 (qv) design to Colt. The AR18 was intended to be a cheaper alternative to the AR15, and, in particular, it was meant to be suitable for production in Third World countries which might lack the sophisticated tooling necessary to deal with the forged aluminum receiver of the AR15. It used a seven-lugged rotating bolt locking into the breech end of the barrel, with a short-stroke piston driving the bolt-carrier rearwards. Twin recoil springs, running on guides through the upper part of the carrier on each side, gave a well-supported, straight-line return from recoil, permitting a rigid, folding butt-stock to be fitted. Construction was all steel, with extensive use being made of sheet steel pressings for the upper and power receiver bodies, and for a number of external and internal parts; all furniture was plastic. The AR18 (which was also known as the AR-180) was manufactured in small numbers by Armalite Inc of California; Howa Machinery of Japan; and Sterling Armament of Dagenham, England. The picture shows one of the examples produced by Sterling (the AR180 with extended magazine).

Mossberg 500ATP Shotgun — USA

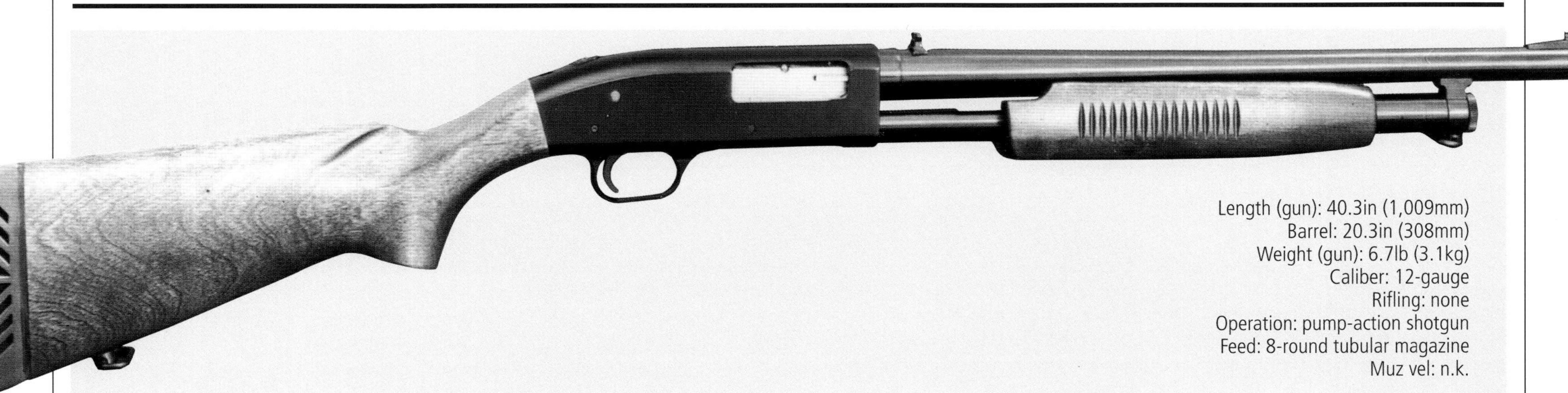

Length (gun): 40.3in (1,009mm)
Barrel: 20.3in (308mm)
Weight (gun): 6.7lb (3.1kg)
Caliber: 12-gauge
Rifling: none
Operation: pump-action shotgun
Feed: 8-round tubular magazine
Muz vel: n.k.

The basic series of Mossberg 500 sporting shotguns were specially modified for police and military use, and these are described in some circles as "re-loadable Claymores." There are two main types – the six- and eight-shot models – and the latter is generally used by military forces. Its design is such as to ensure maximum reliability in use and has an aluminum receiver for good balance and light weight. The cylinder-bored barrel is proof-tested to full Magnum loads, provides optimum dispersion patterns, and permits firing of a variety of ammunition. The shotgun has two extractors and the slide mechanism has twin guide bars which help prevent twisting or jamming during rapid operation. A later modification was the creation of a muzzle brake by cutting slots in the upper surface, thus allowing gas to escape upwards and exerting a downward force which prevented the muzzle from lifting during firing. The ATP-8 version has no butt-stock and a pistol grip is added, resulting in an extremely compact weapon, which can be stowed more easily inside a vehicle.

REMINGTON 40XB BR RIFLE — USA

Length (gun): 38.0in (965mm)
Barrel: 20.0in (508mm)
Weight (gun): 10.5lb (4.8kg)
Caliber: 0.222 Remington
Rifling: n.k.
Operation: bolt-action
Feed: single round, manual
Muz vel: n.k.

"Bench Rest" shooting is devoted to the elimination of skill and as many variables as possible, and the promotion of accuracy and consistency. In modern bench rest shooting the activity is split into three categories. Varmint involves 0.22 center-fire cartridges and is split into "light" using a weapon weighing less than 10.5lb (4.8kg), and "heavy varmint," less than 13.5lb (6.12kg). The third category, "sporting," requires a minimum bullet diameter of 0.243in (6mm). The Remington Model 40XB BR in 0.222in Remington caliber dominated the sport for a decade starting in 1969. It offered "out-of-the-box" accuracy of 0.4MOA and used the 0.222 cartridge with a 0.378in (9.6mm) head diameter and 1.7in (43mm) length, which is generally regarded as the most accurate factory cartridge ever produced. A slightly lengthened version with the shoulder moved forward was adopted by the US armed forces, and subsequently by NATO, as the standard service round, the 5.56 x 45mm NATO round. The 40XB BR as shown typifies the "light varminter" of the 1970s with a short, massive, free-floating stainless steel barrel, glass-bedded action, and walnut stock with a broad flat fore-end to lie steadier on the sandbags. The telescope is a x20 Remington-Unertl with adjustments in the back mount.

REMINGTON MODEL 1100 SHOTGUN — USA

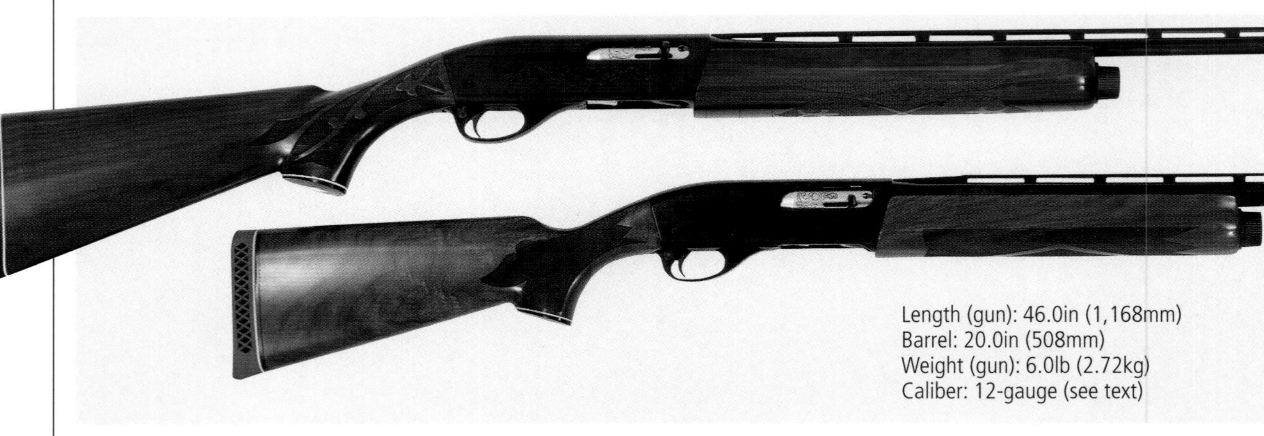

Length (gun): 46.0in (1,168mm)
Barrel: 20.0in (508mm)
Weight (gun): 6.0lb (2.72kg)
Caliber: 12-gauge (see text)
Rifling: none
Operation: self-loading
Feed: 3-round tubular magazine
Muz vel: n.k.

The Remington 1100 was introduced in the mid-1960s and quickly established itself as one of the most popular sporting guns of all time, with some three million built up to 1987 and many more since. The Model 1100 was designed by Robert P. Kelly assisted by a team of Remington engineers and was distinguished by its piston, which surrounded the magazine tube and which was impaled on two rather long and narrow gas ports. By design, this had a "metering" effect which delivered a reasonably uniform impulse over a wide range of cartridge pressures, thus ensuring functional (without adjustment) reliability whatever the load used. Capitalizing on a good thing, Remington offered the Model 1100 in four gauges: 12-, 20- 0.28- and 0.410-, and in a host of formats, guises and configurations, including: goose guns; quail guns; skeet guns; trap guns; deer guns; riot guns; youth guns; and many more. There were also straight-grip stocks, folding stocks, Monte Carlo stocks, and mirror-image actions for left-handers. The guns shown here are: 0.410-gauge skeet gun (see specifications), (top) and wildfowler (bottom) which has a longer 30in (762mm) full-choked barrel chambered for 3in (76.2mm) shells. The current (2000) model is the Remington Model 11-87, which, again, exists in a large number of permutations. Typical is the Model 11-87LC "Premier" 12-gauge, which is marketed with 26in (660mm), 28in (711mm), or 30in (762mm) vent-rib barrels, all of them with the interchangeable Remington Choke system and full tubes, and there is also a 28in barrel version for left-handed firers. The major versions of the Model 11-87 LC 12-gauge are: overall length, 50.5in (1,283mm), 48.4in (1,227mm), and 46.0in (1,168mm); barrel length, 30.0in (762mm), 28.0in (711mm), and 26.0in (660mm); and average weight, 7.9lb (3.6kg), 7.8lb (3.5kg), and 7.6lb (3.4kg).

RUGER RED LABEL SHOTGUN — USA

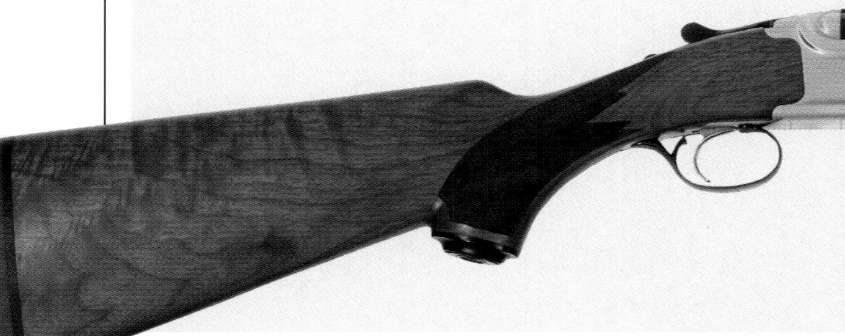

Length (gun): 43.0in (1,092mm)
Barrel: 26.0in (660mm)
Weight (gun): 7.5lb (3.4kg)
Caliber: 12-gauge
Rifling: none
Operation: over-and-under, drop-down
Feed: manual
Muz vel: n.k.

Rivaling the traditional Browning for popularity in the USA is Ruger's elegant Red Label, introduced in the 1980s, which was the firm's first shotgun, but still bore the hallmarks of this famous gun inventor and his team. Sturm, Ruger produced rifles for many years but this first shotgun was an over-and-under 20-bore, which was followed some years later by a 12-bore. Both guns come in several barrel lengths and degrees of choke boring, with the actions being offered in both blued and stainless steel finisher. There are no visible screws or pins on the actions which, although devoid of any engraving, still manage to look very handsome. Both the 20-bore and 12-bore are available in two barrel lengths: 26.0in (660mm) and 28.0in (711mm), and two Field choke borings, plus a skeet gun, and are chambered for 3.0in (76mm) cartridges. The guns are fitted with a hammer interrupter which is only lifted clear of the hammers by a deliberate pull of the trigger, a valuable safety device similar in its effect to the intercepting safety sears found on most quality sidelock guns and some high-quality boxlocks. The automatic safety catch incorporates the barrel selector, which pivots from one side to the other and, unlike any other over-and-under, indicates the barrel to be fired first by the unmistakable letters "B" and "T" for bottom and top, rather than the letters "U" and "O" or other symbols, which may be more ambiguous.

Remington 40XB Rangemaster Target Rifle — USA

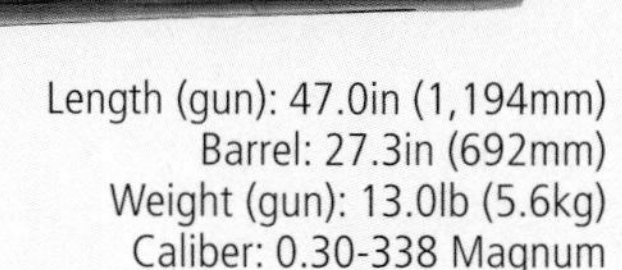

Length (gun): 47.0in (1,194mm)
Barrel: 27.3in (692mm)
Weight (gun): 13.0lb (5.6kg)
Caliber: 0.30-338 Magnum
Rifling: n.k.
Operation: bolt-action
Feed: single round, manual
Muz vel: n.k.

The Model 40XB is built in Remington's "Custom Shop" on Model 700 receivers taken from the production line before the magazine opening is cut. They are then lathe-turned to very tight standards of concentricity and fitted with special barrels, with barrel and receiver being trued square and adjusted for minimum headspace. The bolt lugs are lapped for full bearing contact, and most of these guns carry Remington's 2oz (57g) trigger. They come with three five-round test targets, with guaranteed accuracy of a minute of angle (1MOA) or less. In 0.222 or 0.223, Remington guarantee 0.45in (11mm) groups, and in 7.62mm, 0.75in (19mm) groups at 100yd (91m). The illustration shows a Remington Model 40X in 0.30-338 – a 0.38 Winchester Magnum necked to 0.30cal, since the 0.338 itself is a necked-down 0.458. The cartridge is short for its power, which permits a relatively beefier, stiffer receiver than a 0.300 Winchester Magnum, with much less vibration on discharge, and more sheer in the barrel and action. Such weapons are fired from a bench rest at longer ranges, although extended firing with one of these weapons can become punishing due to the recoil, and most long-range bench-resters have taken to placing a sandbag or lead-shot bag between the buttplate and their shoulder as a form of physical protection against the recoil forces. At shorter ranges the rifle is fired with the fore-end resting across a saddle-shaped leather sandbag on a heavy, cast-iron pedestal.

Hart Model 2 — USA

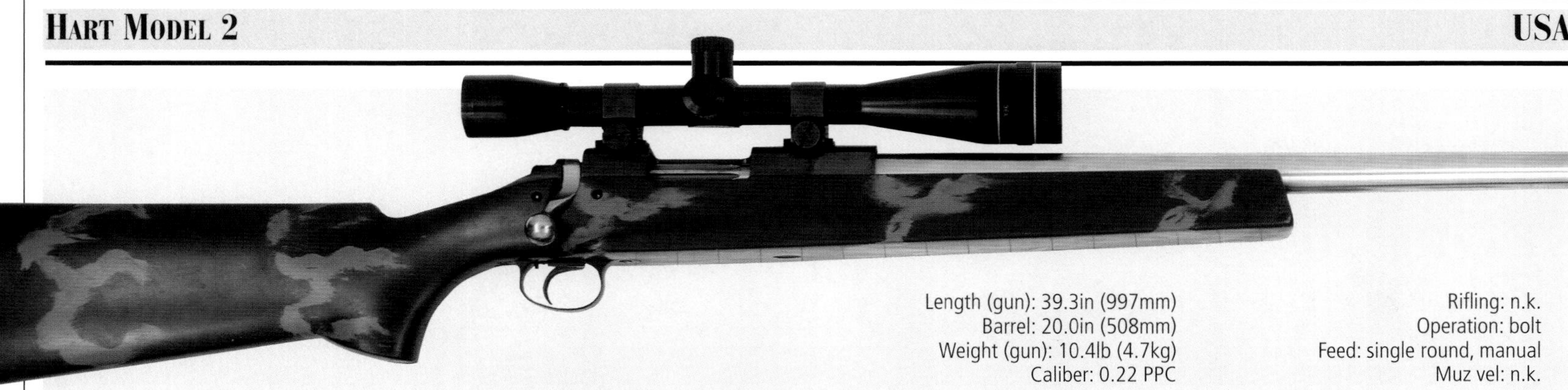

Length (gun): 39.3in (997mm)
Barrel: 20.0in (508mm)
Weight (gun): 10.4lb (4.7kg)
Caliber: 0.22 PPC
Rifling: n.k.
Operation: bolt
Feed: single round, manual
Muz vel: n.k.

The successor to the Remington 40XB BR as top rifle was the Model 2, built by Robert Hart of Pennsylvania. This used a fluted bolt (to save weight) and a massive action, with thick receiver walls and a receiver ring nearly twice the length of that on the Remington. The barrel unscrewed by hand, but all the engagements of barrel, bolt, and receiver were machined to be absolutely true. Operation is by bolt-action, with the bolt handle lifted to unlock the breech and cock the striker. Each round must be placed in the breech by hand, as there is no magazine. The Hart is chambered for the 0.22 PPC, the initials being taken from the surnames of the designers, Pindell and Palmisano, together with "C" for cartridge. This was derived from a necked-down 7.62 x 39mm Soviet case and was based on computer calculations concerning the most efficient combustion chamber configuration for a given projectile. The 6mm PPC, based on the same case, is often used at 300yd (274m) range, or, if the wind should rise, at 100 or 200yd (91 or 182m) as well.

Barrett 0.50in Model 82A1 "Light Fifty" — USA

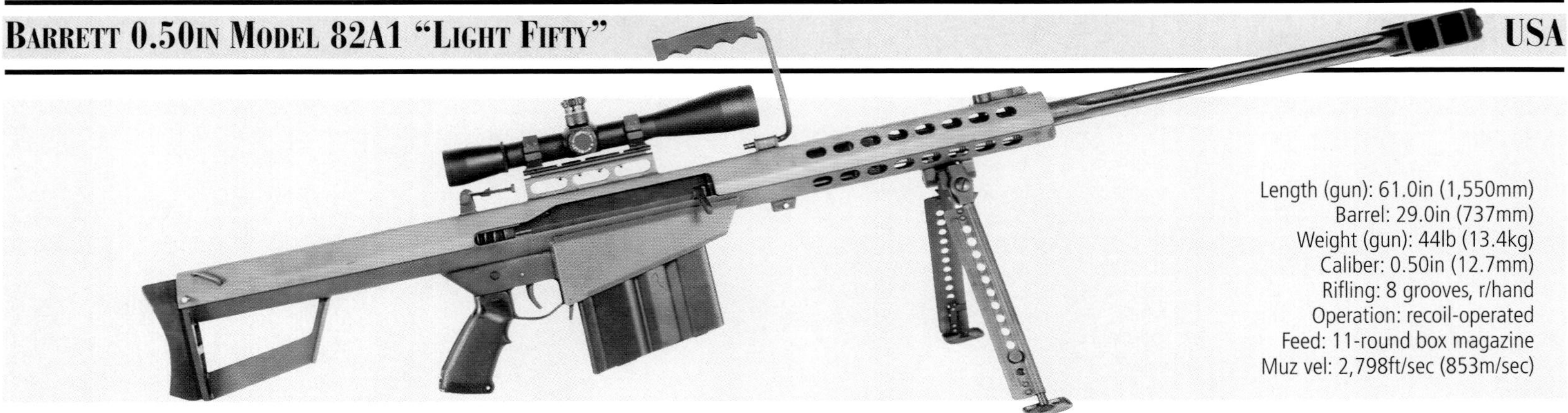

Length (gun): 61.0in (1,550mm)
Barrel: 29.0in (737mm)
Weight (gun): 44lb (13.4kg)
Caliber: 0.50in (12.7mm)
Rifling: 8 grooves, r/hand
Operation: recoil-operated
Feed: 11-round box magazine
Muz vel: 2,798ft/sec (853m/sec)

Introduced in 1983, the Barrett "Light Fifty" fires the 0.50in Browning (12.7 x 99mm) round and was intended for use as a high-power, long-range sniper weapon. The "Light Fifty" operates on the short-recoil principle, with a substantial amount of energy being imparted by the cartridge to the bolt-face and both barrel and bolt-carrier start to travel to the rear. Once the bolt-carrier disengages from the barrel, the latter is moved forward again by a spring, while the bolt-carrier extracts and ejects the spent cartridge case and then loads a new round. The M82A1 (see specifications) has both iron sights and a x10 optical sight. It is normally fired from the built-in bipod, but can also use the standard US Army M60 tripod. Maximum effective range is 1,970yd (1,800m) and in the early 1990s there were reports in the British Press that the Provisional IRA forces in Northern Ireland included a sniping team armed with one of these awesome sniper rifles. The next version, the M82A2, which was introduced in 1992, involved some major redesign, although the basic mechanism remained unchanged, but the major components were moved around to change it into a bullpup configuration. This involved placing the shoulder rest beneath the butt, immediately behind the magazine housing, allowing the rear end of the receiver to pass over the firer's shoulder in a manner similar to a recoilless rocket launcher. The pistol grip/trigger group was moved forward of the magazine housing, while a reversed pistol grip served as the forward handgrip. There was no built-in bipod, as in the M82A1, and the weapon could be fired without one. The overall result is a slightly smaller, lighter, and simpler version of the M82A1: length, 55.5in (1,410mm); weight 29.0lb (12.2kg).

Submachine Guns

A submachine gun (SMG) is a close-range, automatic weapon, firing pistol cartridges (eg, 9mm Parabellum), and is compact, easy to carry, and light enough to be fired from either the shoulder or the hip. The first true SMG was the curious, Italian-designed, double-barreled, 9mm Villar-Perosa, introduced in 1915, but the first to be produced in significant quantities was the German Bergmann air-cooled, 9mm MP18, designed by Hugo Schmeisser, which had a wooden rifle stock and a simple, blow-back action. Development thereafter was rapid and one of the most famous to appear in the 1920s was the Thompson 0.45in SMG, its reputation being enhanced by its association with Chicago-style gangsters.

New techniques, such as stamping and spot-welding, enabled SMGs to be simplified, to the extent that the British Sten, designed to be produced in vast numbers during World War II, cost then not much more than a postage stamp does today. Others, such as the US M3A1 0.45in "Burp" gun, German 9mm MP40 ("Schmeisser"), and Soviet 7.62mm PPSh-41 were in the same category.

At the beginning of the 21st Century SMGs are becoming ever smaller and lighter, some being no more than an automatic pistol with a rudimentary stock.

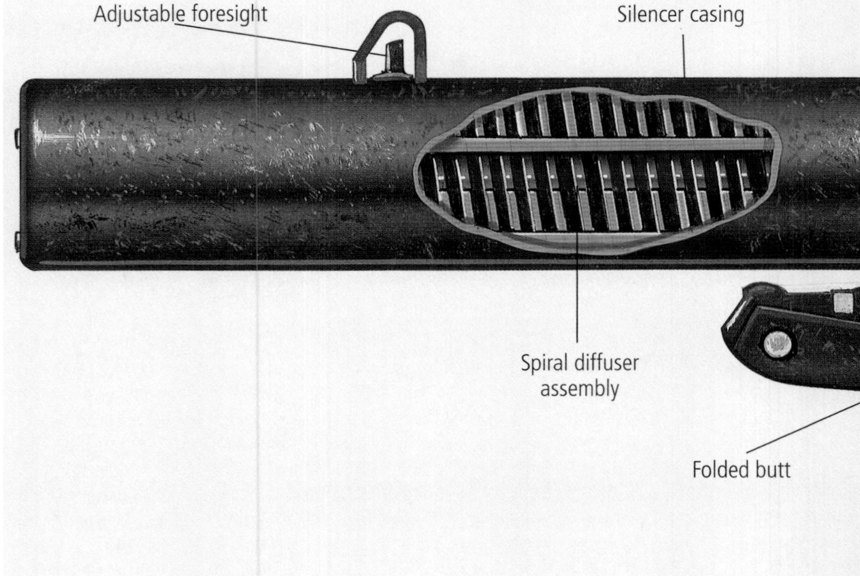

Sterling L34A1 Submachine Gun (Silenced)

Sterling L34A1 Submachine Gun (Silenced)

The L34A1 is the silenced version of the British Sterling SMG adopted in 1954, which is itself the successor to the Sten gun which was used widely during World War II and since. The Sterling has a normal blowback mechanism, but is unusual in having a ribbed bolt which cuts away dirt and fouling as it accumulates and forces it out of the receiver. In the L34A1 the barrel jacket is covered by a silncer casing, with front and rear supports. The barrel has 72 radial holes drilled through it, which permits propellant gas to escape, thus reducing the muzzle velocity of the bullet. The barrel has a metal wrap and diffuser tube; the extension tube goes beyond the silencer casing and barrel. A spiral diffuser beyond the barrel is a series of discs, which has a hole through the center that allows passage of the round. Gas follows the round closely and is deflected back by the end cap; it mingles with the gases coming forward – with the result that the gas velocity leaving the weapon is low.

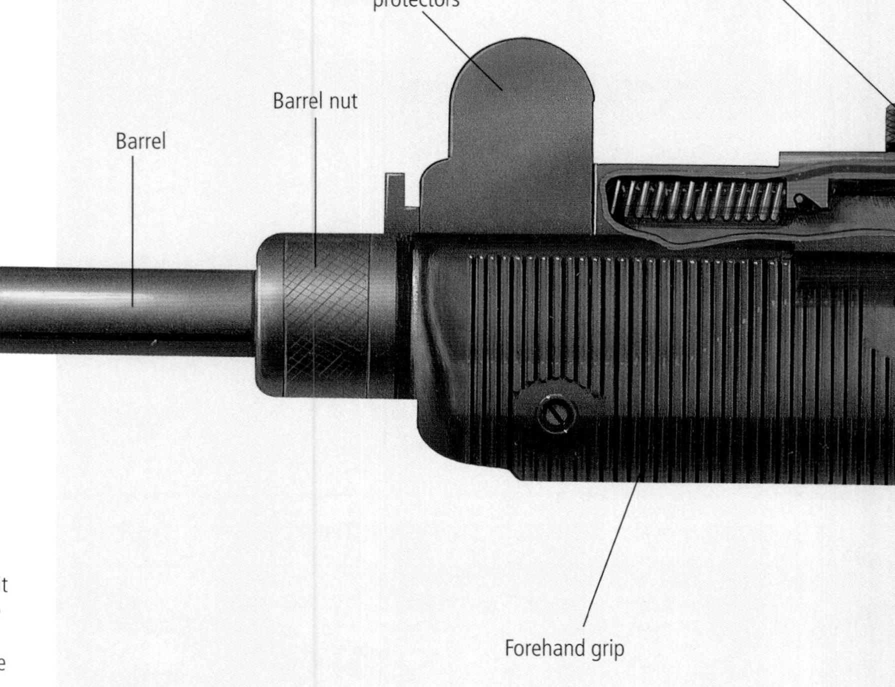

Uzi Submachine Gun

Uzi Submachine Gun

Designed by Uziel Gal and based on post-World War II Czechoslovakian 9mm Models 23 and 25, the Uzi was developed to fill the Israeli requirement to arm her defense forces with reliable, home-produced guns following the establishment of the state of Israel in 1948. It is now probably the most widely used submachine gun in the Western world, in service with, in addition to Israeli forces, Belgium, Germany, Iran, the Netherlands, Thailand, Venezuela, and other countries, as well as a plethora of para-military forces and terrorist groups. A Mini-Uzi has been developed, smaller, lighter, and having different firing characteristics.

It is of simple blowback design. The bolt is cocked by drawing it to the rear. The sear rotates up to engage and hold it open. A coil spring is used to tension the sear; pulling the trigger to the rear allows the sear to move down and rotate out of engagement with the bolt. The bolt's own coil spring drives it forward, stripping a cartridge from the magazine, chambering it and firing it as the striker in the bolt face impacts the primer. The momentum generated by the exploding cartridge then drives the bolt to the rear, extracting and ejecting the fired case – until it comes up against the bolt stop. Its spring then drives it forward again in a repeat cycle. Current Uzis are fitted with a grip safety, which blocks the trigger unless depressed.

Expanded metal wrap
Cocking handle
Backsight
Return spring locking mechanism
Return spring
Diffuser tube
Trigger guard
Trigger
Trigger assembly
Pistol grip
Backsight protectors
Sling swivel
Chamber
Sear
Guide rod
Ejector
Bolt
Return spring
Trigger
Trigger guard
Magazine platform
Magazine spring
Grip safety
Magazine catch
Butt (folded)
Magazine

OWEN MACHINE CARBINE — AUSTRALIA

Length (gun): 32.0in (813mm)
Barrel: 9.8in (250mm)
Weight: 9.4lb (4.2kg)
Caliber: 9mm
Rifling: 7 grooves, r/hand
Operation: blowback
Feed: 32-round box
Cyclic rate: 700rpm
Muz vel: 1,375ft/sec (420m/sec)

When Japan entered World War II Australia found herself in a precarious position. Most of her small army was engaged in the Middle East and her vast and sparsely inhabited country presented a most attractive target to a warlike race seeking living room. Although there was a well established arms factory in existence at Lithgow, Australia was not then a very industrialized country, but she began to produce arms as a matter of hard necessity. One of her first efforts was an Australian Sten, known, perhaps inevitably, as the Austen, but although by no means a bad weapon it was never popular with the Australian Army. The first locally designed submachine gun was the work of Lieutenant E. Owen, of the Australian Army, which was adopted in November 1941 and put into production immediately. It was a well made weapon, if a little on the heavy side, and was an immediate success with the soldiers. It was of fairly orthodox design and its point-of-balance was immediately above the pistol grip which allowed it to be fired one-handed if necessary. The magazine was vertically above the gun and although this involved offset sights the idea was popular because it helped when moving through thick cover. Some early weapons had cooling fins on the barrel but this was found unnecessary and discontinued. All were camouflaged after 1943. A later, prototype version (Mark 2) was fitted with a different method of attaching the butt, and a bayonet lug above the muzzle compensator to receive a special tubular-haft bayonet. Overall weight was also reduced to 7.6lb (3.5kg).

AUSTEN — AUSTRALIA

Length (gun): 33.3in (845mm)
Barrel: 7.8in (198mm)
Weight (gun): 8.66lb (3.97kg)
Caliber: 9mm
Rifling: 6 grooves, r/hand
Operation: blowback
Magazine: 32-round box
Cyclic rate: 500rpm
Muz vel: 1,200ft/sec (366m/sec)

This efficient and effective weapon owed its design to a combination of the best features of the British Sten gun (qv) and the German Erma MP40 (qv), which had been encountered and admired by Australian troops in the Middle East. Some 25-30,000 were produced in Australia from 1943 to 1946, the name Austen being a combination of "Australia" and "Sten." Mechanically, the Austen took the telescopic mainspring housing and bolt from the MP40 and married them to the Sten, but with some further Australian refinements, including a forward grip and a folding butt. The Mark II differed in having a two-piece cast aluminum receiver and overall weight was reduced to 8.5lb (3.86kg).. Despite being manufactured in Australia, the Austen was never as popular with Australian troops as the Owen (qv).

F1 Submachine gun — Australia

Length (gun): 28.1in (925mm)
Barrel: 8.0in (203mm)
Weight: 7.2lb (3.3kg)
Caliber: 9mm
Rifling: 6 grooves, r/hand
Operation: blowback
Feed: 34-round box
Cyclic rate: 600rpm
Muz vel: 1,200ft/sec (365m/sec)

The Owen gun (qv) remained in service until 1962, but in spite of its excellent reputation, it had certain drawbacks, principally its weight, its somewhat high cyclic rate of fire, and the fact that due to the exigencies of wartime manufacture many of its components were not interchangeable which made maintenance difficult. The Australian Army canvassed the views of battle-experienced soldiers to what an ideal submachine gun should be, giving them ample information on which to base any specifications for a new weapon. The first gun to be based on these ideas was similar in many ways to the Owen, but much lighter and with its magazine in the pistol grip. This model was not a success and was not developed. However, in 1959 and 1960 two further models were produced; these were known provisionally as the X1 and X2, and after minor modifications became the weapon illustrated, the F1. It was based largely on the originally specification and was light in weight and with a much lower cyclic rate than its predecessor. It retained the top magazine of the Owen which was universally popular, although it required offset sights. The backsight was a shaped metal flap which folded forward over the receiver when not required. The cocking handle, on the left of the body, had a cover attached to it to keep dirt out of the cocking slot. Although the cocking handle was normally non-reciprocating, the F1 incorporated a device by which it could be made to engage the bolt. This meant that if the mechanism became jammed with dirt the bolt could be worked backwards and forwards by means of the handle in order to loosen it. The pistol grip was a standard rifle component.

Steyr Solothurn S100 — Austria/Germany/Switzerland

Length (gun): 33.5in (850mm)
Barrel: 7.8in (199mm)
Weight: 8.6lb (3.9kg)
Caliber: 9mm
Rifling: 6 grooves, r/hand
Operation: blowback
Feed: 32-round box
Cyclic rate: 500rpm
Muz vel: 1,375ft/sec (417m/sec)

By the early 1920s various German designers had resumed work on several new small arms projects, amongst them being Louis Stange of the firm of Rheinmetall. German arms production was seriously restricted in the years following World War I by the Treaty of Versailles, so in 1929 Rheinmetall acquired the Swiss firm of Solothurn to enable it to make and sell arms legally. One of the first projects was the S100 which had been destroyed by Rheinmetall, and through Solothurn they sub-contracted actual production to the Austrian firm of Steyr which started work in 1929. The origins of the weapon are thus to some extent international. The S100 was of orthodox mechanism but extremely well made, the machining, milling and general finish being of an unusually high standard which must have made it expensive to produce. A light tripod mount was also designed but never produced commercially. Most of the production models were also fitted with an unusual device in the shape of a built-in magazine filler. The magazine housing had a slot on top with recesses to take the Mauser pistol type clip, and a magazine locking device underneath. In 1934 two of these guns, one the normal version and one with the longer barrel, were bought and tested by the British government but although it was well reported on no further action was taken. The gun was widely sold. At least four South American countries bought it in considerable quantities and it was also adopted by Austria for her army and her police, the gun in this case being modified to fire the more powerful Mauser cartridge, and manufactured in Austria.

Steyr 9mm MPi-69 and -81 — Austria

The Austrian arms manufacturer, Steyr-Mannlicher, started production of the MPi-69 (MPi = Machine Pistole) (machine pistol or submachine gun) in 1969 and this was superseded by a later and slightly modified version, MPi-81, in 1981; production ended in 1993. It was of straightforward but rugged design and consisted of a square-sectioned body with, beneath it, a trigger group and a pistol grip containing the housing for either a 25-round or 32-round box magazine. On top were conventional iron fore and rear sights. The barrel could be easily changed and there were two lengths, the standard barrel being 10.2in (260mm) long. A second and considerably longer barrel was available for longer range or more accurate use and was used in conjunction with an optical sight. The longer barrel was fitted with a flash suppressor and required a different, heavier bolt. The MPi-69 had a unique cocking system in which the forward end of the sling was attached to the cocking lever and the weapon was cocked by the firer gripping the sling, holding it at 90 degrees to the weapon and pulling it to the rear. The principle change in the MPi-81 was replacing this arrangement by a conventional cocking handle, with the forward end of the sling being attached to a swivel anchored to the front of the weapon in the usual way. The MPi-81 also had an increased rate of fire: 700 rounds per minute compared to 550. Both MPi-69 and MPi-81 had a sliding, steel wire butt and three position safety, enabling the firer to select safe, single rounds, or full automatic.

Length (gun): 26.4in (670mm)
Barrel: 10.2in (260mm)
Weight (gun): 6.9lb (3.1kg)
Caliber: 9mm
Rifling: 6 grooves, r/hand
Operation: blowback
Magazine: 25- or 32-round box
Cyclic rate: 550rpm
Muz vel: 1,250ft/sec (381m/sec)

STEYR AUG 9MM PARA — AUSTRIA

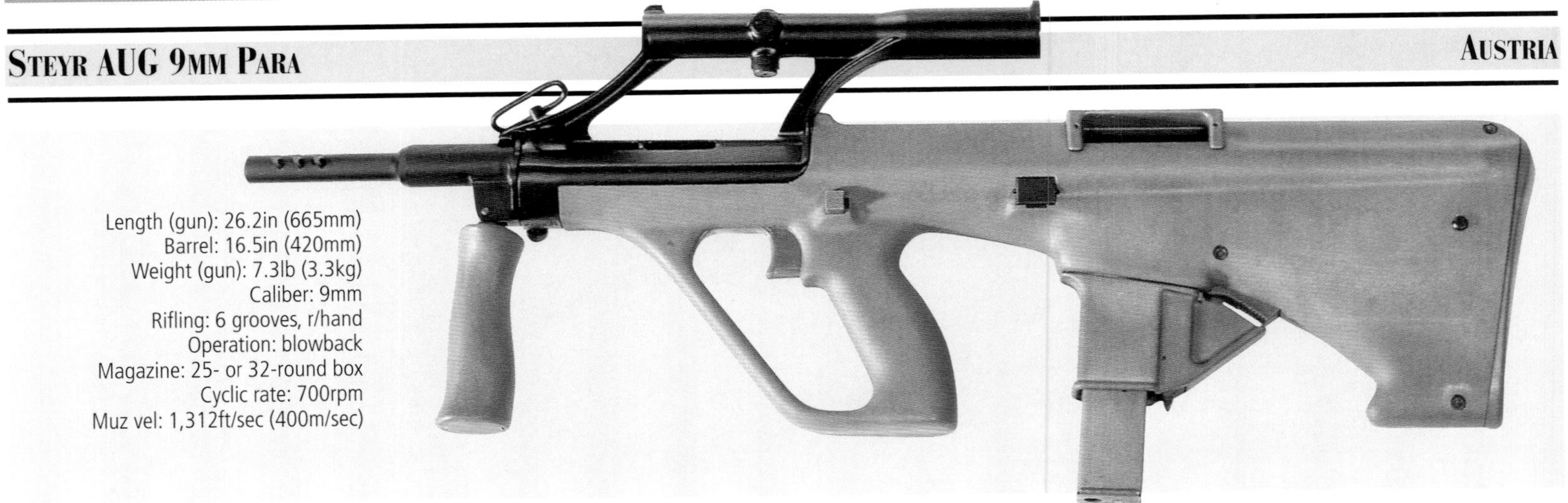

Length (gun): 26.2in (665mm)
Barrel: 16.5in (420mm)
Weight (gun): 7.3lb (3.3kg)
Caliber: 9mm
Rifling: 6 grooves, r/hand
Operation: blowback
Magazine: 25- or 32-round box
Cyclic rate: 700rpm
Muz vel: 1,312ft/sec (400m/sec)

Steyr-Mannlicher produces the AUG assault rifle (qv) and this weapon, introduced in 1986, is the submachine gun model in that range. Externally they appear very similar and many elements are common to both weapons, including the bullpup layout, plastic casing, canted carrying handle with inbuilt x1.5 optical sight, forward handgrip, and pistol grip with handguard. But, although it bears an outward resemblance to the assault rifle, the submachine gun has substantial differences internally. It fires the 9 x 19mm Parabellum round rather than the rifle's 5.56mm and the barrel is shorter: 16.5in (420mm) compared to 20.0in (508mm). The method of operation is also different in that the submachine gun version has a new bolt and operates by blowback from a closed bolt. The magazine housing is fitted with an adapter enabling it to accommodate the new magazine holding 9mm rounds. The submachine gun's barrel can be fitted with a screw-on silencer.

STEYR 9MM TACTICAL MACHINE PISTOL (TMP) — AUSTRIA

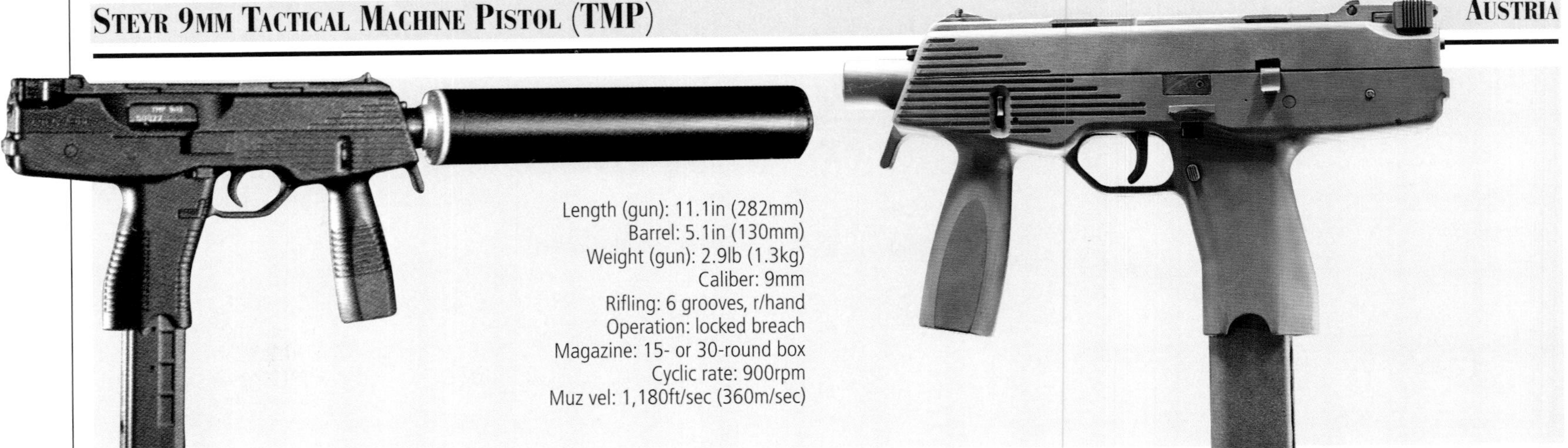

Length (gun): 11.1in (282mm)
Barrel: 5.1in (130mm)
Weight (gun): 2.9lb (1.3kg)
Caliber: 9mm
Rifling: 6 grooves, r/hand
Operation: locked breach
Magazine: 15- or 30-round box
Cyclic rate: 900rpm
Muz vel: 1,180ft/sec (360m/sec)

The TMP is another of those weapons which do not fit neatly into any one category, its small size and lack of a butt-stock suggesting a pistol, while its full automatic firing and forward handgrip are more akin to a submachine gun, and it is treated as such here. The receiver is made from a synthetic material and incorporates a rail along the top for an optical sight, if required. Internally, there is a guide-rail for the bolt, and the operating system consists of a locking breech and a rotating barrel. There is no butt stock, enabling the cocking handle to be mounted at the foot of the back-plate, the weapon being cocked by pulling it straight to the rear. The barrel is threaded to accommodate a cylindrical sound suppressor (left), which is longer than the weapon itself.

FN 5.7MM P-90 — BELGIUM

Length (gun): 19.7in (500mm)
Barrel: 10.4in (263mm)
Weight (gun): 5.5lb (2.5kg)
Caliber: 5.7mm
Rifling: 8 grooves, r/hand
Operation: blowback, closed-bolt
Magazine: 50-round box
Cyclic rate: 900rpm
Muz vel: 2,345ft/sec (715m/sec)

The futuristic-looking FN P-90 was designed as a self-defense weapon for use by support and technical troops whose primary function is not direct combat using rifles or machine guns. There are many such troops on a modern battlefield, including: headquarters personnel; engineers; gunners; communicators; army aviators; and logistics troops. The P-90 is a submachine gun which has been re-designed from basic principles and incorporates a host of new and imaginative ideas. The shape of the weapon is based on extensive ergonomic research and care has been taken to ensure that the weapon can be used with equal ease by left- or right-handed firers, while its smooth contours ensure that it will not snag on the firer's clothing or equipment. The magazine, made of clear plastic, is positioned along the top of the receiver and contains 50 rounds which, in a unique arrangement, lie in two rows across the line of the weapon. These are pushed forward by a spring and as they arrive at the end of the magazine they are, first, fed into a single row and, secondly, rotated through 90 degrees, thus aligning them with the chamber, into which they are then fed. The carrying handle incorporates a tritium-illuminated sight, but there are also conventional iron sights on the top of the receiver. A totally new round was designed by FN for use in this weapon: the 5.7 x 28mm. This is lead-free and causes extensive wounds to humans, since it is designed not only to transfer the maximum energy to the target, but also to "tumble" inside the target. Two versions are also available for special forces, and they include a number of optional accessories, including a silencer.

Uru 9mm Model 2 — Brazil

Length (gun): 26.4in (671mm)
Barrel: 6.9in (175mm)
Weight (gun): 6.6lb (3.0kg)
Caliber: 9mm
Rifling: 6 grooves, r/hand
Operation: blowback
Magazine: 30-round box
Cyclic rate: 750rpm
Muz vel: 1,276ft/sec (390m/sec)

The Uru Model 2 was developed from the Model 1, which was designed in 1974 and placed in production by a company called Mekanika in 1977 to meet orders placed by Brazil's Army and police forces. All design and production rights to the weapon were acquired by the FAU Guns division of Bilbao SA in 1988, who developed the weapon into the Model 2. The Model 2 has a cylindrical body; the forward end is drilled with vents for cooling the barrel and the rear end is closed with a cap, which can be replaced by a butt stock, either solid or a single-strut tubular steel assembly, if required. Beneath the tubular assembly is a box-like feature which includes the magazine housing (which also serves as the forward hand grip), the trigger and pistol grip (which incorporates a grip safety), and the change lever, which can be set to safe, semi-automatic, or full automatic. A silencer can be screwed onto the muzzle. Other versions include one firing the 0.38 ACP round, and a carbine with a wooden stock, which is also available in either 9mm Parabellum or 0.38 ACP versions.

SAF 9 — Chile

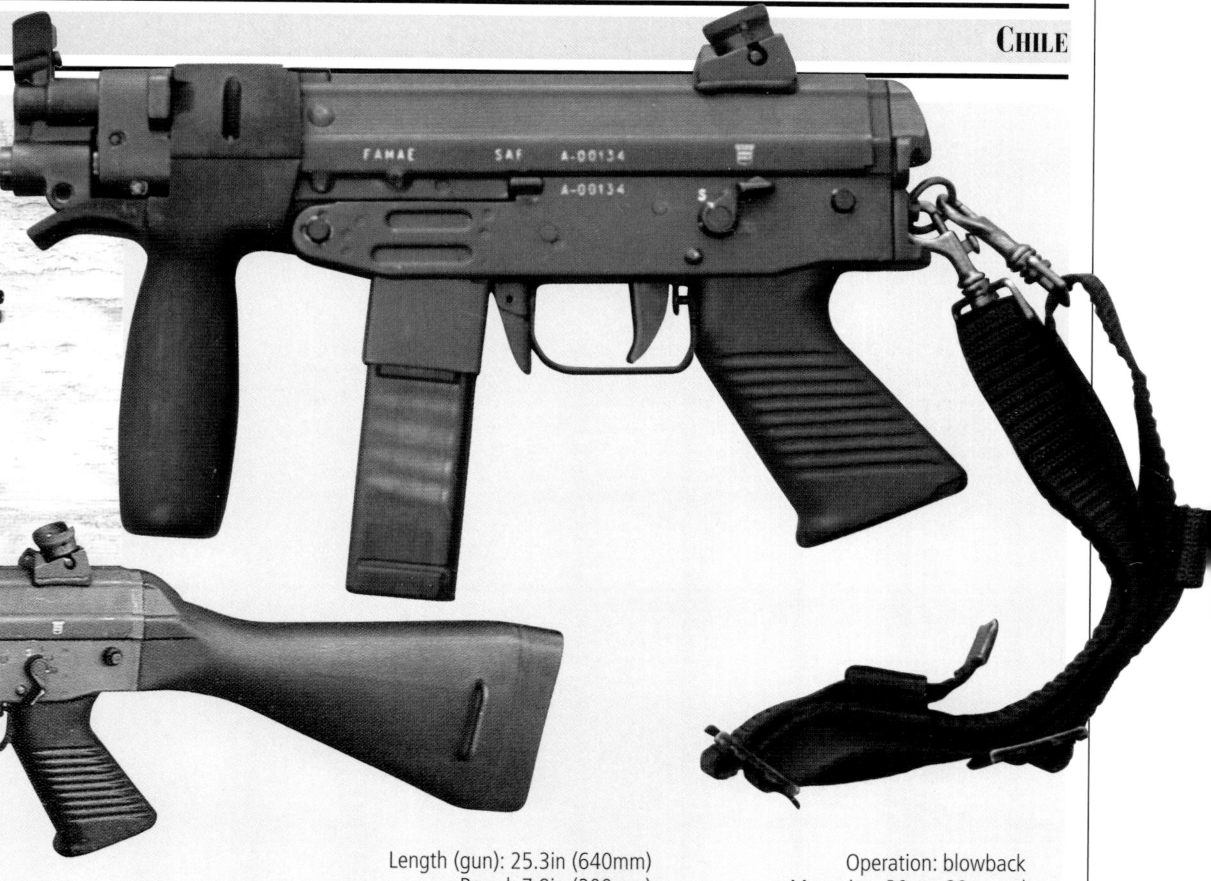

Length (gun): 25.3in (640mm)
Barrel: 7.9in (200mm)
Weight (gun): 5.9lb (2.7kg)
Caliber: 9mm
Rifling: 6 grooves, r/hand
Operation: blowback
Magazine: 30- or 20-round
Cyclic rate: 1,200rpm
Muz vel: 1,280ft/sec (390m/sec)

The Swiss SIG 540 is manufactured under license in Chile by Fabricas y Maestranzas del Ejercito (FAMAE) at Santiago, Chile, and that company has developed a new submachine gun, the SAF 9mm, which uses a large number of features from the SIG 540. The weapon works by blowback, both barrel and chamber are chrome-plated, and, unlike the SIG 540, it has a three-round burst capability. There are three basic models: standard, with fixed or folding stock; silenced, with fixed (lower left) or folding (top left) stocks; and the Mini-SAF (top right), which is intended for concealed carriage. The Mini-SAF has the same basic mechanism as the larger weapon, but with a very short barrel (4.5in/115mm), a forward handgrip, and no butt stock. It takes the standard 30-round, translucent magazine but there is also a 20-round version for maximum compactness. Both magazines have slots and studs to enable them to be connected back-to-back, thus effectively doubling the capacity. The Mini-SAF is in service with the Chilean armed forces and police, but, as far as is known, has not been exported.

TYPE 50 — CHINA

Length (gun): 33.8in (858mm)
Barrel: 10.8in (273mm)
Weight: 8.0lb (3.6kg)
Caliber: 7.62mm
Rifling: 4 grooves, r/hand
Operation: blowback
Feed: 35-round box
Cyclic rate: 900rpm
Muz vel: 1,400ft/sec (472m/sec)

Like many of the weapons used by Communist China, their submachine gun Type 50 had its origins in a weapon first produced by the Soviet Union, in this case the PPSh 41. As with most other combatant nations the Russians soon saw the need for mass production and the new gun was largely made of heavy gauge stampings, welded, pinned and brazed as necessary. The gun was of normal blowback mechanism and had the interior of the barrel chromed, a fairly common Soviet device. One of its distinctive features was that the front end of the perforated barrel casing sloped steeply backward from top to bottom, thus acting as a compensator to keep the muzzle down. In spite of its high cyclic rate of fire the gun was reasonably accurate and could be fired in single rounds if required. The earliest versions had a tangent backsight but this was soon replaced by a simpler flip sight. The Chinese Communists received many of these guns in and after 1949 and started their own large scale manufacture of them in 1949 or 1950. Their version was essentially similar to its Russian counterpart, but had a somewhat lighter stock. It was also designed to take a curved box magazine though it could also fire the 71-round drum which was the standard magazine on the original Russian model. All Chinese versions had the two-range flip sight. The first locally-made weapons were crude in the extreme and gave the impression of having been made by apprentice blacksmiths (as perhaps they were), but they worked, which was the first and only requirement of the Chinese. The Type 50 was used extensively by the Chinese in the Korean War, and by the Viet Minh against the French in Indo-China in the 1950s.

TYPE 54 — CHINA

Length (gun): 32.3in (819mm)
Barrel: 10.0in (254mm)
Weight: 7.5lb (3.4kg)
Caliber: 7.62mm
Rifling: 4 grooves, r/hand
Operation: blowback
Feed: 35-round box
Cyclic rate: 700rpm
Muz vel: 1,600ft/sec (488m/sec)

The origins of this particular weapon are unusual, since it was designed by A. Sudarev at Leningrad in 1942 when the city was under siege by the Germans. The new gun, originally known as the PPS 42, was designed and made in the city itself, so that weapons coming off the production line were in action in a matter of hours. The gun was made of stampings, using any suitable grade of metal, and was held together by rivetings, welding, and pinning. Nevertheless it was not only cheap but it turned out to be effective. It worked on the usual simple blowback system and would only fire automatic; perhaps its oddest feature was its semi-circular compensator, which helped to keep the muzzle down but increased blast considerably. This was followed by the PPS 43, also modified and improved by Sudarev. Its most unusual feature was that it had no separate ejector in the normal sense of the word. The bolt moved backwards and forwards along a guide rod which was of such a length that, as the bolt came back with the empty case, the end of the rod caught it a sharp blow and knocked it clear. After the Chinese Revolution of 1949, the Soviet Union naturally supplied its new ally with a considerable quantity of arms including large numbers of the PPS 43, and by 1953 the Chinese had begun large-scale manufacture of these weapons, virtually unchanged in appearance from the Russian prototypes. The only way in which it could be distinguished was by the fact that the plastic pistol grips often bore a large letter K, although other designs, including a diamond, have also been found.

NORINCO 7.62MM TYPE 64/TYPE 85 (SILENCED) — CHINA

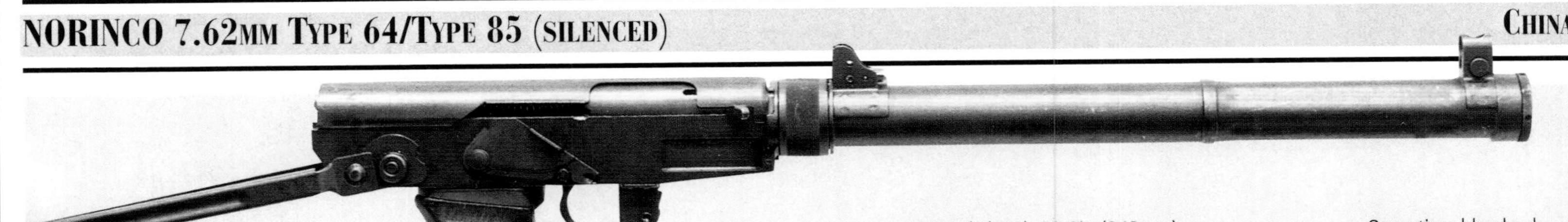

Length (gun): 33.2in (843mm)
Barrel: 9.6in (244mm)
Weight (gun): 7.5lb (3.5kg)
Caliber: 7.62mm
Rifling: 4 grooves, r/hand
Operation: blowback
Magazine: 30-round box
Cyclic rate: 1,000rpm
Muz vel: 960ft/sec (298m/sec)

Few operational silenced weapons are designed as such, starting life instead as normal weapons and then having the noise suppressor added later. The Chinese NORINCO (Northern Industries Corporation) Type 64, however, was designed for silent operation from the start. It uses the Chinese Type 51 7.62 x 25mm pistol round (a Chinese-manufactured version of the Soviet Tokarev round) in a weapon which incorporated a number of features taken from weapons already produced in China. Thus, the bolt mechanism comes from the Type 43 (Chinese-manufactured Soviet PPS43) while the trigger group comes from Czechoslovakian ZB VZ/26 7.92mm machine gun, which was produced under license in China in the 1930s as the Type 26. The weapon operates by blowback and takes a curved, 30-round box magazine. The Maxim-type noise suppressor is 14.4in (365mm) long and screws on to the weapon. The outer third of the barrel is perforated with 36 holes, allowing a proportion of the gas to escape. On leaving the barrel the round passes through a stack of disc-shaped baffles, which have a 9mm diameter hole in their centers and which are held in place by two long rods. The suppressor was fairly efficient for its time, but later models are superior.

NORINCO Type 79/Type 85 7.62mm — China

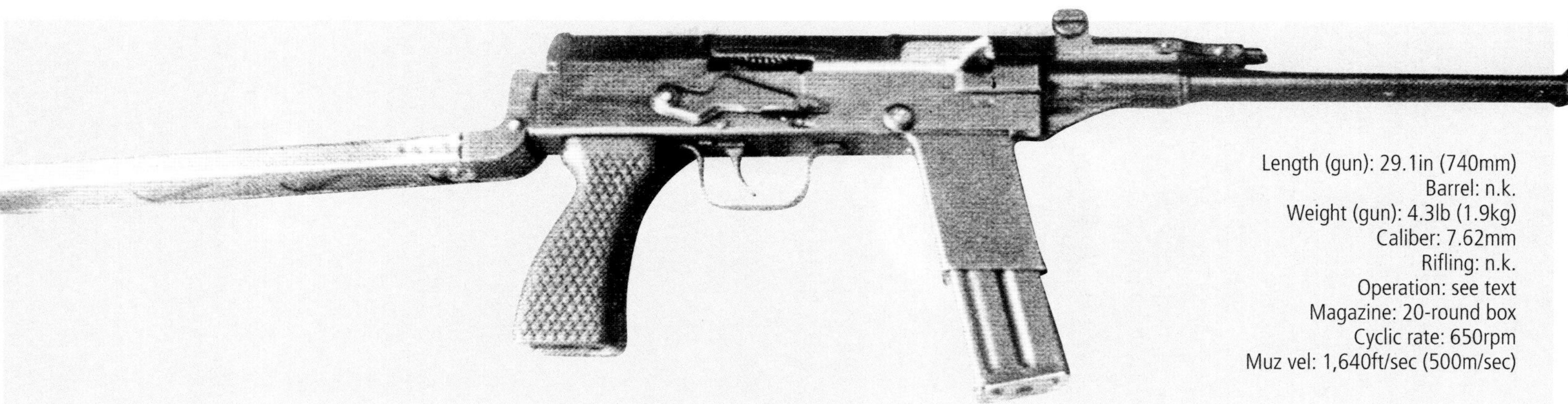

Length (gun): 29.1in (740mm)
Barrel: n.k.
Weight (gun): 4.3lb (1.9kg)
Caliber: 7.62mm
Rifling: n.k.
Operation: see text
Magazine: 20-round box
Cyclic rate: 650rpm
Muz vel: 1,640ft/sec (500m/sec)

The Chinese designers employed an unusual mechanism in the Type 79 (see specifications) in which a tappet above the barrel was activated by the projectile gases to drive rearwards a short-stroke piston which was attached to the bolt carrier. Because of the short distances traveled the components are smaller and lighter than usual, resulting in a very light weapon, weighing (with an empty magazine) just 4.33lb (1.9kg). The Type 79 uses the Chinese Type 51 7.62 x 25mm pistol round. The weapon has a folding butt, although the strut is box-shaped, rather than the more usual tube. Despite the apparent advantages of the Type 79, a much modified version appeared as the Type 85, using a straightforward blowback operation, with a cylindrical receiver. The Type 85 has the same folding butt as the Type 79 and uses the same 30-round box magazine. The Type 85 normally fires the Type 51 7.62 x 25mm pistol round, but it can also fire the lighter and slower Chinese Type 64 7.65 x 17mm rimless round.

CZ-23, CZ-24, CZ-25, CZ-26 9mm/7.62mm — Czechoslovakia

CZ-23

CZ-24

CZ-26

CZ-25

Length (gun): 27.0in (68mm)
Barrel: 11.2in (284mm)
Weight (gun): 6.8lb (3.1kg)
Caliber: 9mm
Rifling: 4 grooves, r/hand
Operation: blowback
Magazine: 24- or 40-round box
Cyclic rate: 600rpm
Muz vel: 1,250ft/sec (380m/sec)

This series of four weapons began with the CZ-23 (see top photo and specifications), which appeared in 1948 and continued until the CZ-26. The CZ-23 entered service in 1951 and the CZ-25 (bottom left) in 1952, both firing the 9mm Parabellum round, which was available in vast quantities in the early post-World War II years. The two weapons differed only in that the CZ-23 had a wooden stock, while the CZ-25 had no stock. Following the formation of the Warsaw Pact in 1955, however, came standardization, which meant in essence that all the other members adopted Soviet standards and weapons. One result was the replacement of the 9mm round by the Soviet Tokarev 7.62 x 25mm pistol round, which led to two new Czech submachine guns chambered for the new round: the CZ-24, which replaced the CZ-23, and the CZ-26, which replaced the CZ-25. The adoption of the new round meant that the CZ-24 and -26 were slightly heavier (7.25lb/3.3kg), and had a higher muzzle velocity (1,800ft/sec [550m/sec]); they were also provided with a 32-round box magazine. These weapons were all used by the Czech Army until the mid-1960s, and were also exported, especially those firing the Soviet round.

VZ61 (THE SKORPION) — CZECH REPUBLIC

Length (gun, folded): 10.0in (271mm)
Barrel: 4.5in (114mm)
Weight: 2.9lb (1.31kg)
Caliber: 7.65mm
Rifling: 6 grooves, r/hand
Operation: blowback
Feed: 10/20-round box
Cyclic rate: 700 rpm
Muz vel: 970ft/sec (294m/sec)

This was a good example of the rather small number of true machine pistols, its general dimensions being comparable to those of the Mauser pistol model 1896. It was therefore of relatively limited use as a military weapon, except possibly for tank crews, motor cyclists, and similar categories for whom a compact secondary weapon was more important than performance. Its small caliber also reduced its stopping power although of course the use of automatic fire helped considerably in this respect. There was also a bigger version, made only in limited quantities, which fired a 9mm round and was in consequence a good deal heavier although similar in essence. The Skorpion worked on the normal blowback system. Very light automatic weapons often have the disadvantage that their cyclic rate of fire is unacceptably high, but in this weapon the problem was largely overcome by the use of a type of buffer device in the butt. It had a light wire butt for use from the shoulder; this could be folded forward when not required without affecting the working of the weapon. Although the size and capacity of the Skorpion reduced its military efficiency, it was an excellent weapon for police or other forms of internal security work since it was inconspicuous and easily concealed. Its low muzzle velocity also made it relatively easy to silence. The VZ61 was sold to many African countries. Other versions fired the 9mm short round (VZ63), 9mm Mokarov (VZ65); or 9mm Parabellum (VZ68).

ZK 383 — CZECH REPUBLIC

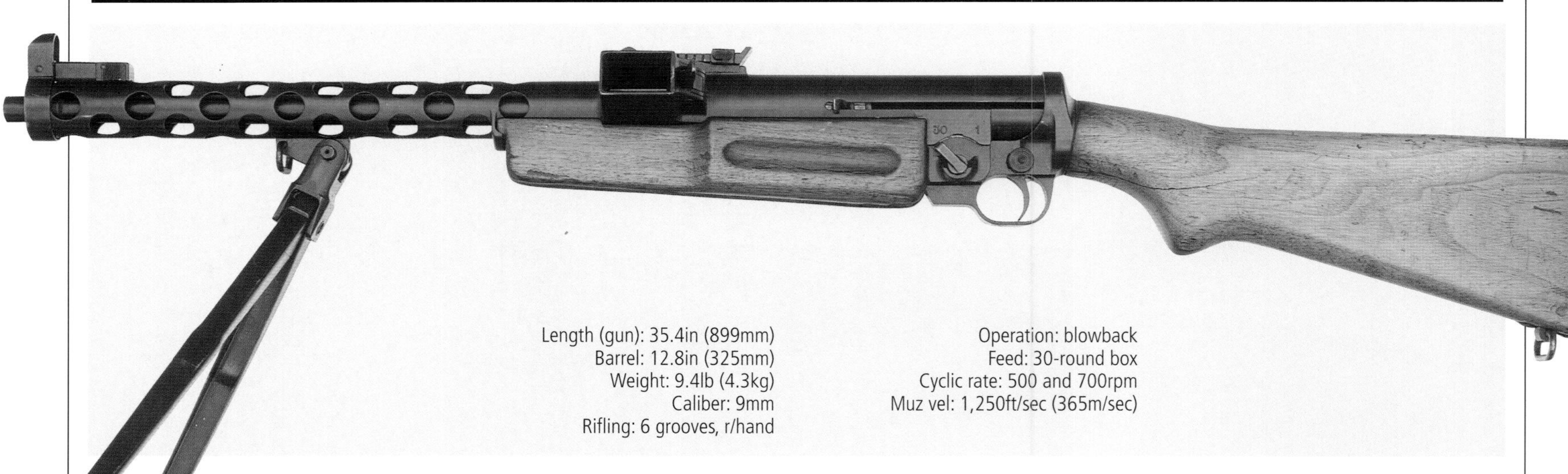

Length (gun): 35.4in (899mm)
Barrel: 12.8in (325mm)
Weight: 9.4lb (4.3kg)
Caliber: 9mm
Rifling: 6 grooves, r/hand
Operation: blowback
Feed: 30-round box
Cyclic rate: 500 and 700rpm
Muz vel: 1,250ft/sec (365m/sec)

This weapon, which was designed by the Koucky brothers at Brno, first appeared in 1933 and was still in production three years after the end of World War II. It was a most sophisticated and very well made weapon, manufactured of precision castings of excellent finish, and cannot have been cheap to produce. It is of particular interest in having a dual rate of fire, achieved by removing a weight on the bolt, which increased its rate of functioning. There was also a quick release barrel. The ZK 383 fired either single rounds or automatic as required, the change lever above the trigger being pushed back or forward as necessary. The stud behind it was the push-in safety. The pierced barrel casing carried the foresight and a well made tangent backsight. Another unusual feature was the folding bipod, which when not required for use was turned backward into a recess in the woodwork. This bipod made a considerable improvement in the accuracy of the gun, but even so it is likely that the maximum setting of 800yd (800m) was optimistic. This was the standard submachine gun used by the Bulgarian Army during and after World War II. The Germans continued to manufacture it after they had over-run Czechoslovakia and it was used by their SS troops. A modified version was also produced for police use, which had no bipod and no tangent sight. Some models took a bayonet.

Madsen Model 50 — Denmark

The first submachine gun made in Denmark was the Finnish Suomi, made under license by the Danish Madsen Industrial Syndicate in 1940. Production continued throughout the war, the gun being used by the Danes, Germans and Finns. The first weapon of the present series was the Model 1946, and the Danes, profiting from wartime advances in mass production, made sure that it was designed to take advantage of these improved techniques. The main body, including the pistol grip, is made from two side pieces, hinged together at the rear, so that the weapon can be easily opened for repair, cleaning or inspection. It does, however, have the disadvantage that springs are liable to fall out unless care is taken. The Madsen works on the normal blowback system and will fire single rounds or bursts as required. One of its unusual features is a grip safety behind the magazine housing which (with the magazine itself) acts as a forward handgrip. Unless this safety is in the gun will not function, which makes it impossible to fire it one-handed. The tubular metal stock is on a pivot and folds on to the right side of the weapon. The Model 50, the gun illustrated, is similar to the Model 46, the main difference being the milled knob cocking handle which replaced the flat plate of the earlier model. The curved magazine actually belongs to the later model. When the new model was demonstrated in 1950 many countries showed great interest but few orders were placed. British authorities were sufficiently impressed to recommend that the Model 50 should be considered in the search for a new weapon to replace the Sten gun (qv). It was extensively tested against other arms and was actually recommended for adoption by non-fighting troops if the new British EN2 rifle made a submachine gun unnecessary for the infantry. In the event the new rifle was not adopted and the Sterling (qv) was taken into general use. The Madsen submachine gun is also produced in Brazil as IMBEL.

Suomi Model 1931 — Finland

The first of this series bearing the name Suomi (the native word for Finland) was developed from 1922 onwards making it one of the earliest submachine guns to appear. It was designed by the well-known Finnish designer Johannes Lahti, and the first completed models appeared in 1926. They were effective but very complex weapons, designed to fire the 7.62mm Parabellum cartridge from a magazine with such a pronounced curve that three of them placed end to end formed a complete circle. This gun was produced in only very small numbers and is chiefly of interest because it was the first of a series. The model illustrated was also designed by Lahti, but although it retained some of the features of the Model 26, so many changes were made that it was virtually a new weapon. Although patents were not finally granted until 1932 the gun was in use by the Finnish Army in the previous year, hence its final designation of Model 31. At the end of 1939 the Russians, having failed to persuade the Finns to make some territorial adjustments to enhance Soviet security, invaded Finland. Thje Finns fought bravely and made good use of the Suomi. It worked by normal blowback system and had no fewer than four different magazines, a single 20-round box, a double 50-round box, and two drums, one of 40-round capacity and one of 71. It was very well made of good steel, heavily machined and milled and unusually well finished. The end product was therefore an exceptionally reliable and robust weapon and although it was very heavy by modern standards (with the bigger drum magazine it weighed over 15lb/6.8kg) this at least had the merit of reducing recoil and vibration and thus increasing its accuracy, for which it was very well known. It was made under license in Sweden, Denmark, and Switzerland, and apart from Finland was also used by Sweden, Switzerland, Norway, and Poland. The Suomi was still used in many units of the Finnish Army as late as the 1980s, although by then thed surviving weapons had been modified to take a modern 36-round box magazine of improved pattern.

MAT49 — FRANCE

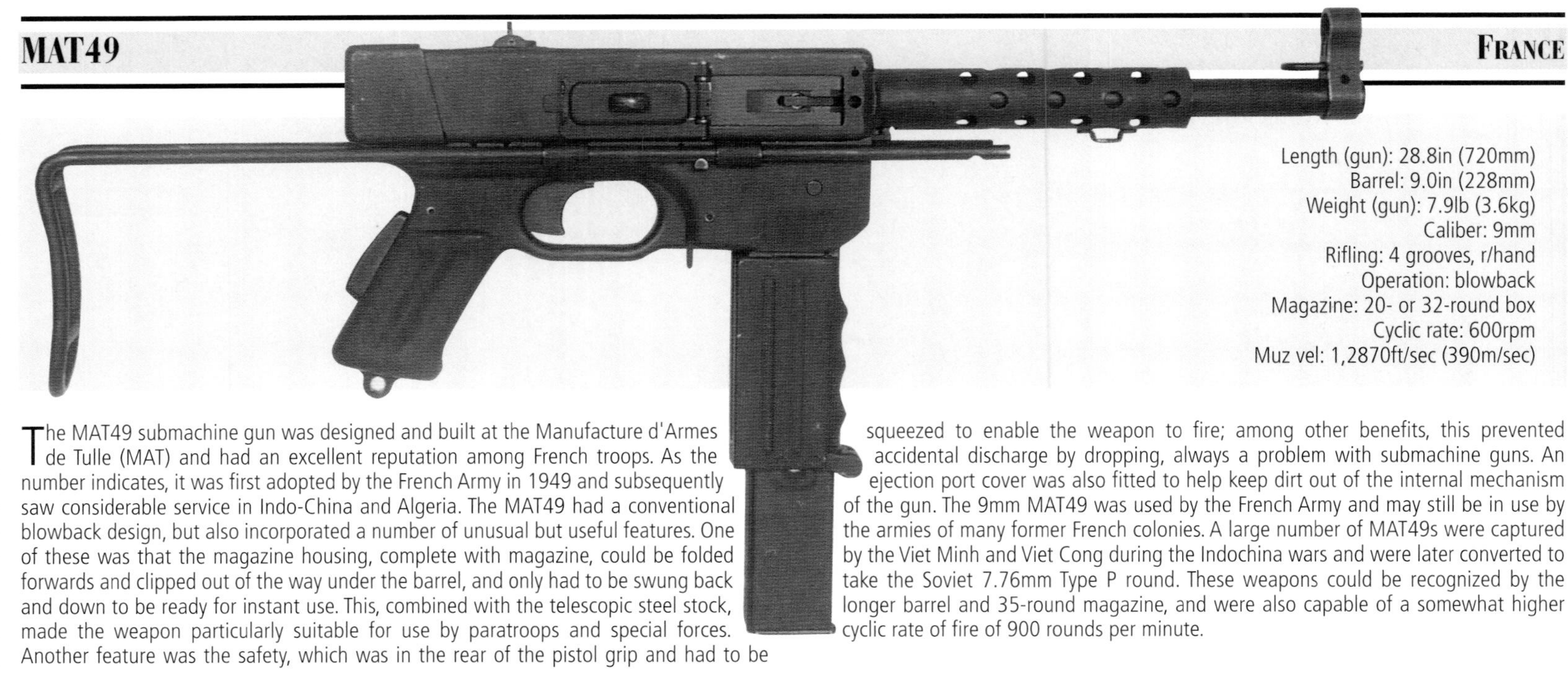

Length (gun): 28.8in (720mm)
Barrel: 9.0in (228mm)
Weight (gun): 7.9lb (3.6kg)
Caliber: 9mm
Rifling: 4 grooves, r/hand
Operation: blowback
Magazine: 20- or 32-round box
Cyclic rate: 600rpm
Muz vel: 1,2870ft/sec (390m/sec)

The MAT49 submachine gun was designed and built at the Manufacture d'Armes de Tulle (MAT) and had an excellent reputation among French troops. As the number indicates, it was first adopted by the French Army in 1949 and subsequently saw considerable service in Indo-China and Algeria. The MAT49 had a conventional blowback design, but also incorporated a number of unusual but useful features. One of these was that the magazine housing, complete with magazine, could be folded forwards and clipped out of the way under the barrel, and only had to be swung back and down to be ready for instant use. This, combined with the telescopic steel stock, made the weapon particularly suitable for use by paratroops and special forces. Another feature was the safety, which was in the rear of the pistol grip and had to be squeezed to enable the weapon to fire; among other benefits, this prevented accidental discharge by dropping, always a problem with submachine guns. An ejection port cover was also fitted to help keep dirt out of the internal mechanism of the gun. The 9mm MAT49 was used by the French Army and may still be in use by the armies of many former French colonies. A large number of MAT49s were captured by the Viet Minh and Viet Cong during the Indochina wars and were later converted to take the Soviet 7.76mm Type P round. These weapons could be recognized by the longer barrel and 35-round magazine, and were also capable of a somewhat higher cyclic rate of fire of 900 rounds per minute.

BERGMANN MP 18.I — GERMANY

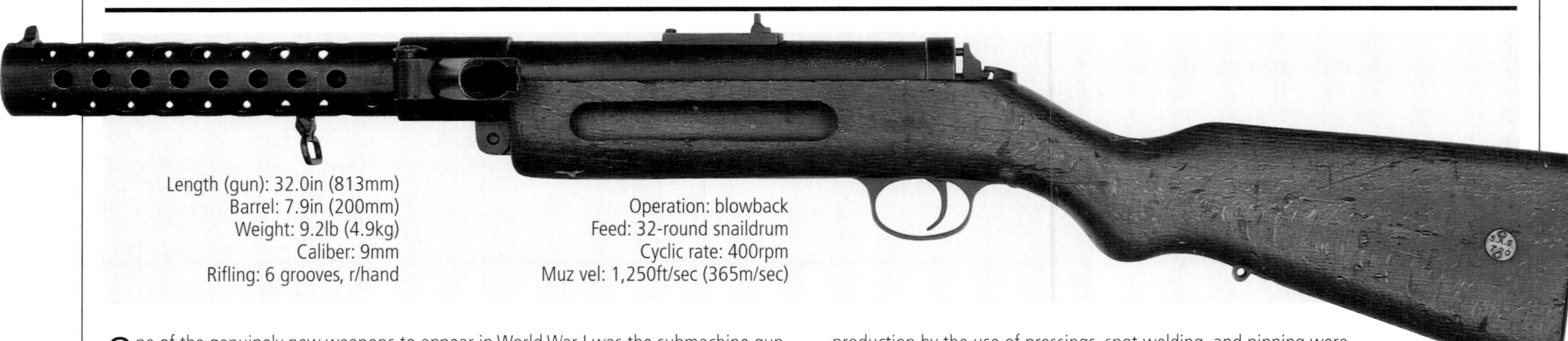

Length (gun): 32.0in (813mm)
Barrel: 7.9in (200mm)
Weight: 9.2lb (4.9kg)
Caliber: 9mm
Rifling: 6 grooves, r/hand
Operation: blowback
Feed: 32-round snaildrum
Cyclic rate: 400rpm
Muz vel: 1,250ft/sec (365m/sec)

One of the genuinely new weapons to appear in World War I was the submachine gun. Once trench warfare had become the norm, the Germans began to arm a proportion of their infantry with stocked pistols of the Mauser and Luger type (both of which are dealt with elsewhere in this book), and it was a short step to the introduction of a somewhat heavier version with the capacity to fire bursts. Work on a prototype weapon started in 1916 at the Bergmann factory, the designer being Hugo Schmeisser, the famous son of an almost equally famous father, and by the early months of 1918 it was in limited production. The Germans, always realists, appreciated that at that late stage of the war, when their manufacturing capacity was fully extended, any new weapon would have to be simple to make and the MP 18.I fulfilled that requirement. The techniques of mass production by the use of pressings, spot welding, and pinning were, however, hardly developed so that "simple" is a relative term when compared with, say, the Sten gun of a quarter of a century later. The Bergmann was machined, and although elaborate milling had necessarily been abandoned, its general finish was relatively good. Its weakest component was its magazine, which was a of a type originally developed for the Luger pistol, and which was too complex and liable to stoppage to be fully reliable. The Germans proposed to have six guns per company; each was to have a number two to carry ammunition, and there were to be three hand carts in addition, which presupposed a type of barrage fire, but the weapon came too late. Its main interest is therefore its influence on future design, which was very significant.

BERGMANN MP 28.II — GERMANY

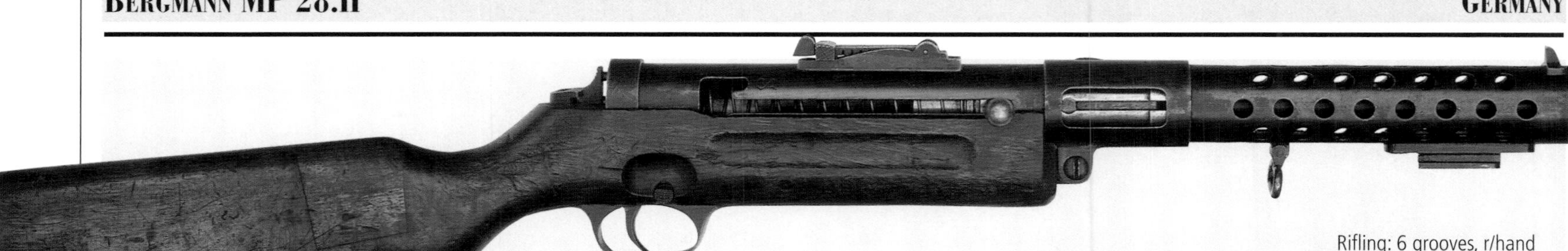

Length (gun): 32.0in (812mm)
Barrel: 7.8in (199mm)
Weight: 8.8lb (4kg)
Caliber: 9mm
Rifling: 6 grooves, r/hand
Operation: blowback
Feed: 20/30/50-round box
Cyclic rate: 500rpm
Muz vel: 1,250ft/sec (365m/sec)

A modified MP 18.1 appeared in 1928 as the MP 28.II, the II denoting two minor modifications to the prototype. The new gun had some interesting features, chief of which was its ability to fire either bursts or single shots using a circular stud above the trigger, which had to be pushed in from the right for automatic, and from the left for single shots. The gun also incorporated an elaborate tangent backsight graduated by hundreds up to 1,094yd (1,000m), which must have been far outside any practical service range. It was equipped with straight box magazines, but the magazine housing was so designed that it would if necessary accept the old snaildrum type. These various improvements did not change its general appearance very materially so that it still resembled the old MP 18. The Bergmann MP 28.II was produced in Germany by the Haenel-Weapon Factory at Suhl, but as there were still some restrictions on domestic production of military firearms a great many more were produced under Schmeisser license by a Belgian company in Herstal, and it was adopted by the Belgian Army in small numbers in 1934. The Bergmann soon established a reputation for reliability and was purchased in South America and by the Portuguese who used it as a police weapon. Although it was mainly manufactured in 9mm Parabellum, it also appeared in 9mm Bergmann, 7.65mm Parabellum, 7.63mm, and even for the American 0.45in cartridge. It seems probable that its main use was in the Spanish Civil War of 1936-39, where its robustness made it an ideal weapon for the militias.

Maschinenpistole MP 40 (Schmeisser) — Germany

Length (gun): 32.8in (833mm)
Barrel: 9.9in (251mm)
Weight: 8.9lb (4.0kg)
Caliber: 9mm
Rifling: 6 grooves, r/hand
Operation: blowback
Feed: 32-round box
Cyclic rate: 500rpm
Muz vel: 1,250ft/sec (365m/sec)

In 1938 the German Army ordered the Erma factory to design and produce a reliable and easily manufactured submachine gun, mainly for use by armored and airborne troops. This was quickly achieved, and in the same year the new weapon had been issued as the MP 38, the first weapon of its type to be adopted by the German Army since 1918. This MP 38 was the first arm of its type ever to be made entirely from metal and plastic, with no woodwork of any kind. Gone was the heavy butt and carefully machined body, and in their place had come a folding tubular metal stock and a receiver of steel tube, slotted to reduce weight. The MP 38, although an excellent weapon, was relatively slow and expensive to produce and this led to the gun illustrated, the MP 40, which although of similar appearance to its predecessor made more extensive use of pressing, spot-welding, and brazing. Perhaps its most important change was the introduction of a safety device, it having been found (like the Sten) that a moderately severe jolt was sometimes enough to bounce the bolt back and fire a round. A number of the earlier 1938 models were also modified in this way as a result of active service experience. Most of the later MP 40s were made with horizontal ribs on the magazine housing. Only a few, like the one illustrated, were made without them. A later model was fitted with a double side-by-side magazine in a sliding housing. Known as the "Schmeisser," the gun became one of the most famous weapons of World War II, some even being used by Allied soldiers in preference to their own submachine guns. Over 1,000,000 had been produced by 1945.

Heckler & Koch MP5 — Germany

Length (gun): 26.0in (660mm)
Barrel: 8.9in (225mm)
Weight (gun): 5.6lb (2.6kg)
Caliber: 9mm
Rifling: 6 grooves, r/hand
Operation: delayed blowback
Magazine: 15- or 30-round box
Cyclic rate: 800rpm
Muz vel: 1,312ft/sec (400m/sec)

The Heckler and Koch MP5 is used by most of the world's elite forces, including such prestigious units as the German GSG 9 and the British SAS and Metropolitan Police. This submachine gun uses the same roller-delayed blowback operating principle as the G3 rifle and features good handling qualities as well as interchangeability of most parts with other weapons in the H&K range. The MP can fire semi-automatic, fully automatic or in three, four or five round bursts. In the latter mode the effect is achieved by a small ratchet counting mechanism which interacts with the sear. Each time the bolt cycles to the rear the ratchet advances one notch until the third, fourth or fifth cycle allows re-engagement of the sear. Firing also ceases the instant the trigger is released, regardless of how many rounds have been fired in the current burst. The actual number of rounds in each burst is pre-set in the factory, and cannot be altered by the firer. H&K uses metal stampings and welded sub-group parts. The receiver is constructed of stamped sheet steel in 19 operations (several combined) and is attached to the polygonal rifled barrel by a trunnion which is spot-welded to the receiver and pinned to the barrel. The trigger-housing, butt-stock and fore-end are fabricated from high-impact plastic. The specifications above refer to the MP5A3. There is a variety of specialized versions. MP5K has a shorter barrel with a vertical foregrip underneath, and the butt is replaced by a simple cap. MP5SD is a series of silenced weapons: MP5SD1 has no stock; MP5SD2 has a fixed stock; and MP5SD3 has a retractable stock. The photo at left shows tyhe MP5SD, with silencer and special laser sight which enables the firer to lay a laser beam on the target.

Uzi, Mini-Uzi, and Micro-Uzi — Israel

Length (gun): 25.2in (640mm)
Barrel: 10.2in (260mm)
Weight: 7.7lb (3.5kg)
Caliber: 9mm
Rifling: 4 grooves, r/hand
Operation: blowback
Feed: 25/32/40-round box
Cyclic rate: 600rpm
Muz vel: 1,280ft/sec (390m/sec)

At midnight on May 14 1948 the British mandate over Palestine ceased, and the Jewish state of Israel was declared. On the very next day the new state was invaded by its Arab neighbors, and there followed nearly eight months of war, at the end of which Israel had not only defended her own territory successfully but had also occupied some of that belonging to her attackers. In spite of her success however it was clear that she needed a reliable weapon which she could make from her own resources in sufficient numbers to arm the bulk of her population if necessary, and by 1950 Major Uziel Gal of the Israeli Army had designed the weapon illustrated. Production started almost immediately and still continues to date. The Uzi works on the normal blowback principle and is made from heavy pressings in conjunction with certain heat-resistant plastics. The rear end of the barrel extends backward into the body and the front of the bolt is hollowed out so as to wrap round this rear projection. The magazine fits into the pistol grip which affords it firm support and also keeps the point-of-balance above it, so that the gun can if necessary be fired one-handed like a pistol. It fires single rounds or bursts as required. Most of the early UzIs had a short wooden butt 8in (203mm) long, but a very few were made longer. Later models have a folding metal stock and other versions include the Mini-Uzi (1981), (as illustrated) and Micro-Uzi (1982). The Uzi is also manufactured in Croatia as the ER09 and the Mini-Uzi as the Mini ERO9.

TZ 45 — Italy

Length (gun): 33.5in (851mm)
Barrel: 9.0in (229mm)
Weight: 7.2lb (3.3kg)
Caliber: 9mm
Rifling: 6 grooves, r/hand
Operation: blowback
Feed: 20/40-round box
Cyclic rate: 550rpm
Muz vel: 1,250ft/sec (365m/sec)

The TZ 45 was designed by the Giandoso brothers as a wartime expedient and first went into limited production in 1945. This new gun, which worked on the normal blowback system, was very crudely made and finished, partly of roughly machined parts and partly of stampings. One of the interesting features of this gun is that it incorporated a grip safety; this consisted of an L-shaped lever just behind the magazine housing (which also acted as a forward handgrip). Firm pressure on the vertical part of the lever (clearly visible in the photograph) caused the horizontal arm to be depressed sufficiently to withdraw an upper stud from the bolt way, thus allowing the working parts to function. This device, which was similar to the one employed on some models of the Danish Madsen submachine gun (qv), was a useful one, but it did of course prevent the weapon being used single-handed. The TZ 45 had a retractable stock, made of light tubing; when pushed in the front ends engaged in holes in a plate below the barrel about 6in (153mm) from the muzzle. There were parallel slots cut into the top of the barrel at the muzzle end which acted as a crude but moderately effective compensator. Although it was an adequate weapon the TZ 45 came too late in the war to be of much use and only about 6,000 were made. These were chiefly used by Italian troops on internal security duties including the rounding up of the armed deserters of half-a-dozen nationalities. After the war the gun was offered commercially on the world market, but only the Burmese showed interest, a number being locally made there in the early 1950s under the title BA 52.

Beretta Modello 38A — Italy

Length (gun): 37.3in (946mm)
Barrel: 12.4in (315mm)
Weight: 9.3lb (5.0kg)
Caliber: 9mm
Rifling: 6 grooves, r/hand
Operation: blowback
Feed: 10/20/40-round box
Cyclic rate: 600rpm
Muz vel: 1,378ft/sec (420m/sec)

The Northern Italian firm of Beretta had a deservedly high reputation for its submachine guns, most of which were designed by Tullio Marengoni. The Modello 38A has good claims to be regarded as his most successful submachine gun. It had its origins in a self-loading carbine first produced in small numbers for police use in 1935, but which by 1938 had been discharged into a true submachine gun. It was well machined and finished which made it expensive to produce, but which resulted in a most reliable and accurate arm. It functioned by normal blowback and had a separate firing pin, again a somewhat unusual refinement. Its forward trigger was for single shots, the other for bursts. The first model can be distinguished by the elongated slots in its jacket, by its compensator, which consisted of a single large hole in the top of the muzzle with a bar across it, and a folding, knife-type bayonet. Not many of these were produced before the elongated cooling slots were replaced by round holes, which thereafter remained standard. The third version, seen here, had a new compensator consisting of four separate cuts across the muzzle, but no bayonet. This version remained in production for the remainder of the war, being used by both the Italian and the German armies; captured specimens were popular with Allied soldiers. The Beretta Modello 38A was also used by a number of other countries, notably Romania and Argentina.

BERETTA MODELLO 38/42 — ITALY

Length (gun): 31.5in (800mm)
Barrel: 8.4in (216mm)
Weight: 7.2lb (3.3kg)
Caliber: 9mm
Rifling: 6 grooves, r/hand
Operation: blowback
Feed: 20/40-round box
Cyclic rate: 550rpm
Muz vel: 1,250ft/sec (381m/sec)

The Beretta Modello 38/42, designed by Marengoni, came into full production in 1942 and was for all practical purposes a utility version of the earlier Modello 38, although it also incorporated a number of features from another submachine gun, the Modello 1, which had been designed for airborne forces on the lines of the German MP 40, but which had never gone into production. The whole weapon had been simplified for mass-production, but in spite of this was an efficient and popular gun. As far as external appearances were concerned there were a number of differences. The rifle-type stock was cut short at the magazine housing, and the adjustable rearsight disappeared, as did the perforated jacket which had been such a notable feature of many Beretta guns. The barrel had deep parallel fluting along its whole length, to assist the dissipation of heat in the absence of the jacket, while the compensator was reduced to two cuts instead of the previous four. The general appearance of the gun (the Type II of which is shown in lower photo) was utilitarian as compared with its predecessors, stampings and welding having been used wherever possible, although the finish was surprisingly good and the whole weapon strong and serviceable. Later productions had plain barrels instead of the distinctive fluted ones and were sometimes referred to as the Modello 38/44. There was a later variation still, in which the weight and dimensions of the bolt were reduced; this led in turn to a somewhat shorter return spring and rod, which did not protrude beyond the rear of the receiver as in the earlier models. The Beretta 38/42 was widely used by the Italians and Germans and after the war a number of the 38/44 Model were sold to various countries including Syria and Pakistan.

BERETTA 9MM MODEL 12 — ITALY

Length (gun): 26.0in (660mm)
Barrel: 7.9in (3.4kg)
Weight (gun): 6.6lb (3.0kg)
Caliber: 9mm
Rifling: 6 grooves, r/hand
Operation: blowback
Magazine: 20-, 32- or 40-round box
Cyclic rate: 550rpm
Muz vel: 1,250ft/sec (380m/sec)

The world famous Beretta company has produced a long series of submachine guns since fielding a modified version of the Villar Perosa in 1918. A series of prototypes, designated Models 6 through 11, were designed and tested in the early and mid-1950s resulting in the definitive Model 12, which entered service with the Italian Army in 1959. It was widely exported and although production in Italy ended in 1980 the Model 12 remained in license production in Brazil and Indonesia for many years thereafter. The Model 12 uses a conventional blowback operation and is of all-metal construction, except for the optional wooden butt. The gun is fabricated from sheet metal stampings, which are spot-welded to form the tubular receiver, the combined trigger housing and pistol grip, and the rectangular magazine housing. The breechblock is the wrap-around type, with a fixed firing-pin, and there is a separate forward handgrip. There are two safety systems, with a grip safety located on the front of the pistol grip, which must be depressed before the action can be cocked, but a button safety then controls safe, semi-automatic or automatic fire. The normal stock consists of a metal tube and a metal butt plate, which can be folded to the right. Alternatively, a detachable wooden stock can be used. The Model 12S (the S2 version is shown in bottom photo) was introduced in 1983, is very similar to the earlier weapon, but with an altered safety system, different sights, and a somewhat improved overall finish.

SITES SPECTRE 9MM M-4 — ITALY

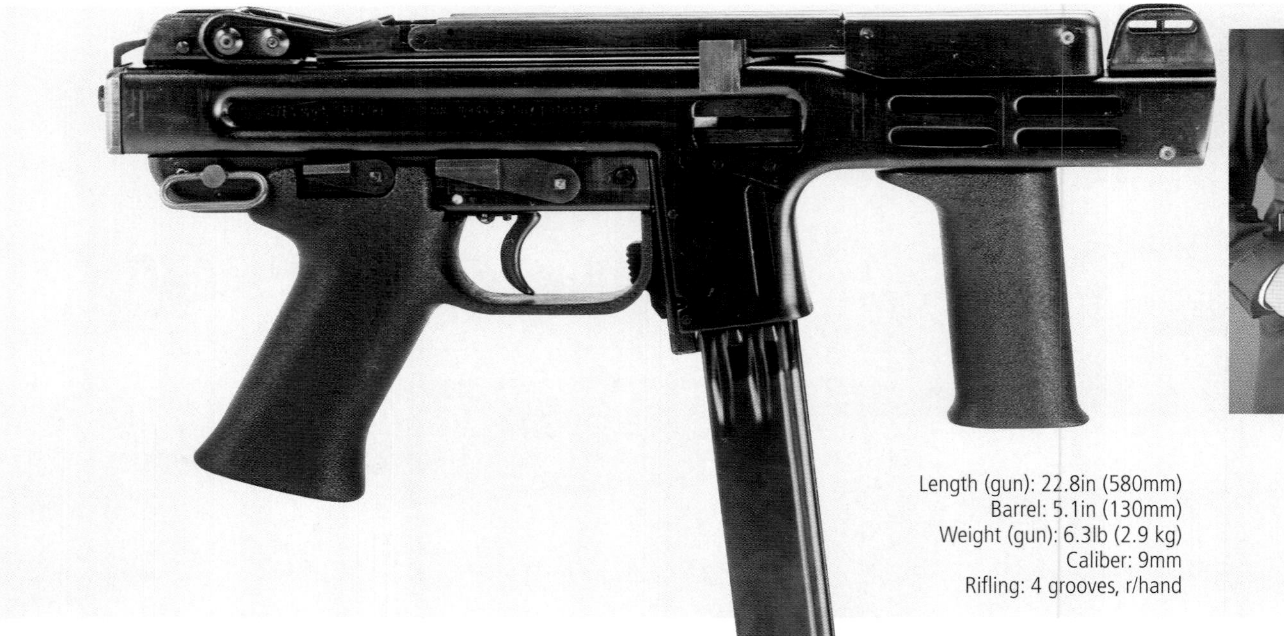

Length (gun): 22.8in (580mm)
Barrel: 5.1in (130mm)
Weight (gun): 6.3lb (2.9 kg)
Caliber: 9mm
Rifling: 4 grooves, r/hand

Operation: blowback
Magazine: 30- or 50-round
Cyclic rate: 850rpm
Muz vel: 1,312ft/sec (400m/sec)

The Spectre M-4, which was first announced in 1983, is made by the SITES company of Turin. It uses a blowback system, but fires from a closed bolt, by means of an unusual double-acting trigger. In this the gun is cocked as normal, which allows the bolt to move forward, driving a round into the chamber, but leaving the hammer to the rear. There is a decocking lever and if this is now pressed the hammer moves forward until it is held a short distance behind the bolt. When it is necessary to fire the weapon, the firer pulls the trigger, whereupon the hammer goes forward to strike the rear of the firing pin, which fires the first round, and firing then proceeds as normal. The purpose of this arrangement is to overcome the problem inherent in the closed-bolt system of having to cock the weapon before firing and to enable the weapon to be carried safely with "one round up the spout" and then brought immediately into action. Another feature of the Spectre is that the bolt and the interior of the receiver are so designed that as the bolt travels forwards it forces air ahead of it and around the barrel, thus cooling it. The magazine is thicker than normal since it accommodates 50 rounds in four vertical rows. There are three variants of the Spectre: the Model C is a carbine firing single rounds only; the Model P is a pistol (qv); and the Model PCC is for police use and can be chambered for either the 9mm Parabellum or the 0.45in ACP rounds. As of late 1999 the Spectre was reported to be in production, although the names of the customers had not been announced.

8MM TYPE 100/40 AND TYPE 100/44 — JAPAN

Length (gun): 35.0in (890mm)
Barrel: 9.0in (228mm)
Weight (gun): 8.4lb (3.8kg)
Caliber: 8mm
Rifling: 6 grooves, r/hand

Operation: blowback
Magazine: 30-round box
Cyclic rate: 450rpm
Muz vel: 1,100ft/sec (335m/sec)

The Imperial Japanese Army was very slow to adopt the submachine gun. The Type 100, introduced in 1940, was the first to enter service, just in time for the opening campaigns of World War II, although, in the event, it proved to be less than satisfactory. It had a tubular receiver and a perforated jacket around the barrel, which was fitted with a muzzle compensator. One attribute sought in most submachine gun designs was lightness, but the woodwork on the Type 100 included not only the stock but also an extensive fore-end, which made a major contribution to the overall weight (unloaded) of 8.4lb (3.8kg). It was an Army requirement, based on Japanese tradition, that as many weapons as possible be fitted with bayonets, so the Type 100/40 (see specifications) had a long bayonet bar under the barrel. The Type 100/40 fired the 8 x 21mm Nambu round, with 30 rounds carried in a forward-curving, box magazine. There were two versions: one with a fixed stock made at Kokura State Arsenals, the other (in top photo) with a folding stock, which was manufactured at Nagoya. The Type 100-40 proved unsatisfactory for a variety of reasons, including frequent stoppages and being too complicated to manufacture, while combat experience showed that the bayonet was of very limited value. As a result, a modified version entered service in 1944, known as the Type 100/44 (bottom photo), which was simpler to produce due to the substitution, wherever possible, of machining by welding, and the removal of the bayonet bar. The cyclic firing rate was also increased to 800rpm.

8mm Type 11 — Japan

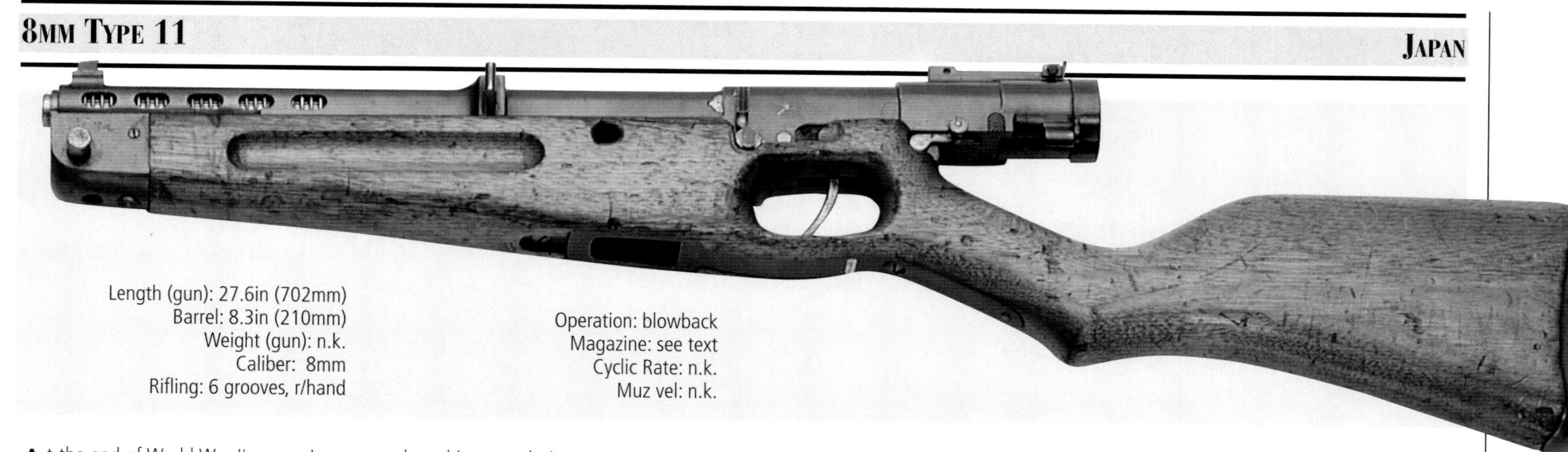

Length (gun): 27.6in (702mm)
Barrel: 8.3in (210mm)
Weight (gun): n.k.
Caliber: 8mm
Rifling: 6 grooves, r/hand
Operation: blowback
Magazine: see text
Cyclic Rate: n.k.
Muz vel: n.k.

At the end of World War II a new Japanese submachine gun design was just entering service, the Type 11. It was one of the most unusual-looking submachine guns ever made. The wooden furniture of the Type 10 was retained, albeit somewhat shorter, but with the working parts sitting along the top, as shown in the picture. The weapon was of bullpup configuration with the box magazine (missing in the example shown) inserted from beneath the weapon. The return spring fitted around the barrel and the trigger was inset so that the stock provided the guard. There was a fixed foresight but the backsight was mounted on a ramp, suggesting a somewhat optimistic assessment of the weapon's accuracy at longer ranges.

Glauberyt PM-84 — Poland

Length (gun): 22.6in (575mm)
Barrel: 7.3in (185mm)
Weight (gun): 4.6lb (2.1kg)
Caliber: 9mm
Rifling: 6 grooves, r/hand
Operation: blowback
Magazine: 15- or 25-round box
Cyclic rate: 600rpm

The first known Polish submachine gun was the Blyskawicza, which was manufactured clandestinely by the Polish resistance in 1943-44. Its design was based on the British Sten MkII (qv) but with minor changes to suit the local, and very limited, production capabilities. The current series of submachine guns are manufactured by Zaklady Metalowe Lucznik, at Radom. The first was the PM-63 (also designated the Wz-63), fielded in 1963 and now phased out of production in Poland, although it may still be in production in China. This weapon was notable for its unusual reciprocating receiver and was chambered for the Soviet 9 x 18mm Makarov, which was the standard Warsaw Pact round. The PM-84 is an updated version of the PM-63, in which the major change is that the bolt and other moving elements are now housed inside the receiver, so that there are no external reciprocating parts. The butt strut is hinged just behind the pistol grip and folds down and forwards until it clips below the receiver, with the butt plate acting as the forward handgrip. The pistol grip acts as the housing for 15- or 25-round box magazines. With the butt folded, the pistol grip is at the point-of-balance, enabling single rounds to be fired with one hand, although for automatic it would be usual to hold the forward handgrip. Like the PM-63, the PM-84 Glauberyt is chambered for the 9 x 18mm Makarov round and this version is widely used in the Polish forces. A new version, PM-84P, appeared in 1985 for the export market. It is chambered for the 9mm Parabellum round, the weapon being slightly heavier at 4.75lb (2.2kg). The latest version is the PM-98, which is an updated version of the PM-84P and is slightly larger still, weighing 5.1lb (2.3kg).

INDEP 9mm Lusa A2 — Portugal

Length (gun): 23.0in (585mm)
Barrel: 6.3in (160mm)
Weight (gun): 6.2lb (2.9kg)
Caliber: 9mm
Rifling: 6 grooves, r/hand
Operation: blowback
Magazine: 30-round box
Cyclic rate: 900rpm
Muz vel: 1,280ft/sec (390m/sec)

The first submachine gun to be manufactured in Portugal was the M-948, the design of which included a mixture of features of the US M3A1, the German MP-40 and a number of local parts. It fired the 9mm Parabellum round. This was followed by an improved M-976, but in 1986 a totally new weapon was introduced, the Lusa A1. This was a blowback weapon, firing 9 x 19mm Parabellum ammunition, the receiver having a figure-of-eight cross-section, with the overhung bolt in the top cylinder, while the lower cylinder contained the trigger group and the feed mechanism, with the barrel at the fore-end. The telescopic stock retracted along the waist between the upper and lower cylinder and the magazine housing acted as the forward handgrip. Firing modes were fully automatic, single rounds, and three-round bursts. There were two versions: one with a plain, detachable barrel, the other with a fixed barrel surrounded by a vented cooling jacket. The Lusa A2 (see specifications) appeared in 1994 and is an improved version of the A1. Among the changes are a stronger butt and a detachable barrel, which comes in two versions: one a normal barrel, the other a long cylindrical silencer, which incorporates a special barrel. The A2 also has a mounting for a laser aiming device.

RATMIL 9MM — ROMANIA

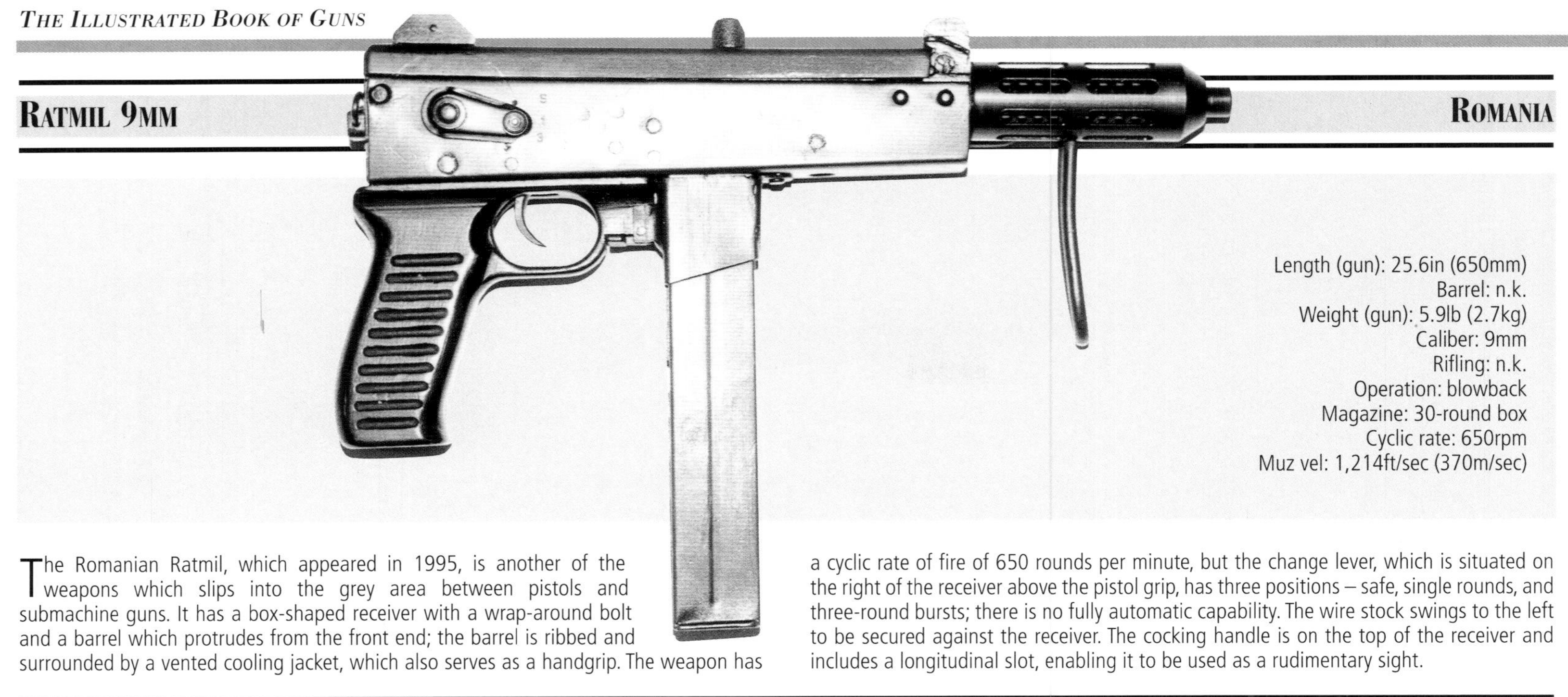

Length (gun): 25.6in (650mm)
Barrel: n.k.
Weight (gun): 5.9lb (2.7kg)
Caliber: 9mm
Rifling: n.k.
Operation: blowback
Magazine: 30-round box
Cyclic rate: 650rpm
Muz vel: 1,214ft/sec (370m/sec)

The Romanian Ratmil, which appeared in 1995, is another of the weapons which slips into the grey area between pistols and submachine guns. It has a box-shaped receiver with a wrap-around bolt and a barrel which protrudes from the front end; the barrel is ribbed and surrounded by a vented cooling jacket, which also serves as a handgrip. The weapon has a cyclic rate of fire of 650 rounds per minute, but the change lever, which is situated on the right of the receiver above the pistol grip, has three positions – safe, single rounds, and three-round bursts; there is no fully automatic capability. The wire stock swings to the left to be secured against the receiver. The cocking handle is on the top of the receiver and includes a longitudinal slot, enabling it to be used as a rudimentary sight.

PPD 34/38 — RUSSIA

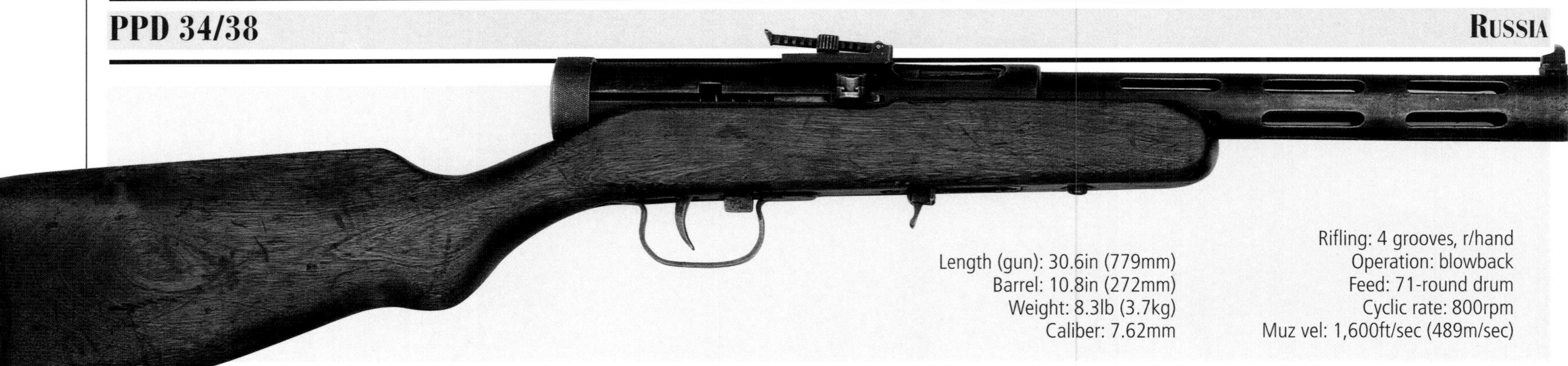

Length (gun): 30.6in (779mm)
Barrel: 10.8in (272mm)
Weight: 8.3lb (3.7kg)
Caliber: 7.62mm
Rifling: 4 grooves, r/hand
Operation: blowback
Feed: 71-round drum
Cyclic rate: 800rpm
Muz vel: 1,600ft/sec (489m/sec)

This weapon was designed by Vasily Degtyaryev, the well-known Russian expert on automatic weapons, and the D in the title in his initial, the PP standing for Pistolet-Pulemyot, the Russian term for a submachine gun. It initially appeared in 1934 and may be regarded as the first really successful weapon of its type to be used in the Soviet Army. It was based fairly closely on the German MP 28.II, and coming before the days of mass-production was reasonably well made and finished by the standards of Russian industry as it then was. The PPD worked by normal blowback on the open bolt principle, single rounds or bursts being obtained by the use of a selector in front of the trigger. Both bore and chamber were chromed to prevent undue wear. The cartridges were fed from a near-vertical drum with an unusual extension piece which fitted into the bottom of the receiver; this drum, which was worked by clockwork, was very similar mechanically to that of the Finnish Suomi (qv), and held 71 rounds. This gave the soldier using it a good reserve of fire without having to reload, but made the gun heavy. As drum magazines are susceptible to dirt, there were probably also problems over stoppages; there was in fact also a curved box magazine but this was very rarely used. One or two minor variations to the original model were made, the most obvious being the reduction in the number of jacket slots from rows of eight small ones to three larger ones. Although the gun was technically replaced by the PPD 40 in 1940 it was used in the Finnish campaign of World War II and probably also saw later service elsewhere.

PPSh 41 — RUSSIA

Length (gun): 33.1in (841mm)
Barrel: 10.6in (269mm)
Weight: 8.0lb (3.6kg)
Caliber: 7.62mm
Rifling: 4 grooves, r/hand
Operation: blowback
Feed: 71-round drum/35-round box
Cyclic rate: 900rpm
Muz vel: 1,600ft/sec (489m/sec)

The PPSh 41 was put into limited production in 1941 and after stringent testing by the Soviet Army was finally approved early in 1942, after which production was on a vast scale. It was designed by Georgii Shpagin, another well-known Russian expert, which is denoted by his initial in the official designation. The PPSh was an early and successful example of the application of mass-production techniques to the manufacture of firearms. As far as possible it was made from sheet metal stampings, welding and riveting being used wherever feasible, and although it retained the wooden butt it was a sturdy and reliable arm. It worked on the usual blowback system with a buffer at the rear end of the receiver to reduce vibrations and had a selector lever in front of the trigger to give single rounds or burst as required. As its cyclic rate of fire was high and would have tended to make the muzzle rise when firing bursts, the front of the barrel jacket was sloped backwards to act as a compensator. Feed was either by a 71-round drum, basically similar to that of the earlier PPD series but not interchangeable with them, or by a 35-round box. To reduce wear and help cleaning, the bore and chamber of these guns were all chromed. There were two models of this gun; the first (illustrated) had a complicated tangent backsight, while the second had a two aperture flip sight. The Soviet armies greatly favored the submachine gun and on occasions whole battalions were armed with it, so it is not surprising that the total numbers manufactured should have exceeded five million. It was also widely copied by other Communist countries, and the Chinese in particular copied it as their Type 50 and must themselves have produced it in vast numbers.

5.45mm AK-74-SU — Russia

Length (gun): 26.6in (675mm)
Barrel: 8.1in (206mm).
Weight (gun): 5.9lb (2.7kg)
Caliber: 5.45mm
Rifling: 4 grooves, r/hand
Operation: gas
Magazine: 30-round box
Cyclic rate: 700rpm
Muz vel: 2,411ft/sec (735m/sec)

The Soviet Army used the 7.62mm PPSh 41 and PPS 43 throughout World War II and for many years afterwards. It then seemed to allow the SMG as a separate type to fade out, using AK-47 or AK-74 assault rifles where other armies carried on using SMGs. In the 1970s, however, this policy seems to have been reversed, with the appearance of a totally new Soviet SMG, based on the Kalashnikov AKS-74 assault rifle, but considerably smaller and lighter. The barrel was only 8.1in (206mm) long and was fitted with a screw-on, cylindrical attachment at the front of which was a cone-shaped flash suppressor. Unlike the majority of SMGs the AK-74-SU fired standard, full-charge rifle ammunition, in this case the Russian 5.45 x 39.5mm. In addition, due to the shortness of the barrel, the gas was tapped off very close to the chamber which resulted in a very high pressure for such a small weapon, and the muzzle attachment was an expansion chamber, designed to reduce the pressure acting on the gas piston; it also served as a flame damper. The weapon was fitted with basic iron sights, the rear sight being a basic flip-over device which was marked for 220yd (200m) and 440yd (400m), although the latter range seemed somewhat optimistic for such a weapon. The internal mechanism was identical to that of the AK-74 except that the gas piston, return spring, and spring guide rod were shorter. The gun also had a very simple skeleton stock which folded forwards along the left side of the weapon.

Bison 9mm — Russian Federation

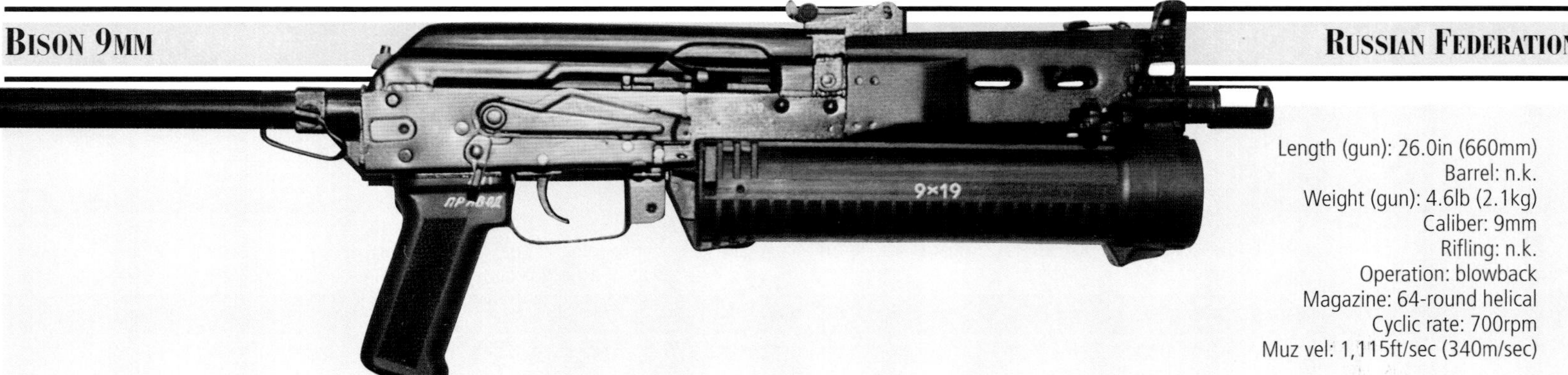

Length (gun): 26.0in (660mm)
Barrel: n.k.
Weight (gun): 4.6lb (2.1kg)
Caliber: 9mm
Rifling: n.k.
Operation: blowback
Magazine: 64-round helical
Cyclic rate: 700rpm
Muz vel: 1,115ft/sec (340m/sec)

The Bison submachine gun was designed by a team led by Viktor Kalashnikov, the son of the much respected weapons designer, Captain Mikhail Kalashnikov, who was responsible for weapons such as the AK-47 and AK-74. With such a heritage, it is not surprising that the Bison uses many well-proven Kalashnikov components to produce a weapon with many interesting features. It operates on the blowback principle, and the left-folding, twin-strut buttstock, trigger mechanism, receiver cover, and magazine catch all come straight from other Kalashnikov designs. The barrel protrudes a considerable distance from the front of the receiver and is completely surrounded by a forestock, which has three horizontal cooling slots in each side. The most unusual feature is the totally new type of magazine, which is helical in shape and is secured under the forestock with its rear-end engaged in the magazine feed and held in place by a Kalashnikov magazine catch. The magazine holds 64 rounds and while the prototype was made from pressed steel, production versions will be made of translucent plastic. The first prototype (Bison 1) fires either 9 x 18mm Makarov pistol rounds or the newer and more powerful 9 x 18mm "Special." Bison 2 fires the newer "Special" round only as does the Bison 3, but the latter also has a different style folding butt. The weapon is ready for production, but as of late 1999 no orders had been announced.

OTS-02 (Kiparis) 9mm — Russian Federation

Length (gun): 23.2in (590mm)
Barrel: n.k.
Weight (gun): 3.5lb (1.6kg)
Caliber: 9mm
Rifling: n.k.
Operation: blowback
Magazine: 20- or 30-round box
Cyclic rate: 900rpm
Muz vel: 1,100ft/sec (335m/sec)

The OTs-02 9mm submachine gun, also known as Kiparis (cypress tree) has been developed in Kazakhstan, one of the republics of the Russian Federation. The weapon works on the standard blowback principle and fires the standard Russian 9 x 18mm Makarov round. The change lever is to the left of the trigger group and has three positions: safe, single rounds, and fully automatic. The receiver is made from pressed steel and the twin-strut butt folds upwards and over the top of the receiver, with the butt plate straddling the barrel. A laser-aiming device can be fitted, which sits below the barrel and also serves as a forward handgrip. The weapon is intended primarily for use by police and other internal security troops.

MECHEM BXP 9MM — SOUTH AFRICA

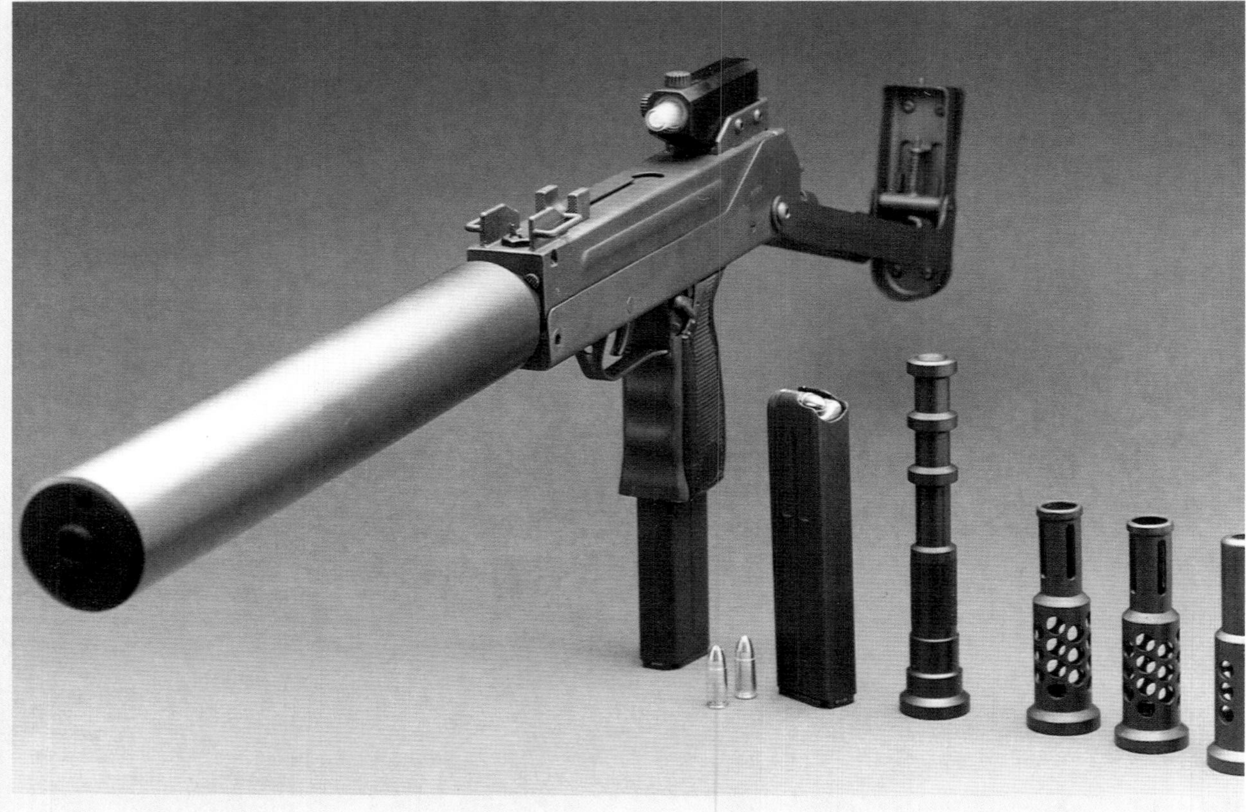

Length (gun): 23.9in (607mm)
Barrel: 8.2in (208mm)
Weight (gun): 5.8lb (2.7kg)
Caliber: 9mm
Rifling: 6 grooves, r/hand
Operation: blowback
Magazine: 22- or 32-round box
Cyclic rate: 800rpm
Muz vel: 1,250ft/sec (380m/sec)

The BXP 9mm submachine gun, which entered service in 1984, is one of a number of weapons developed in South Africa during the period when that country was subjected to an international arms embargo, while concurrently involved in a series of conflicts in the southern part of the continent. The BXP has a short, box-shaped receiver and a very short barrel with a screw-on flash suppressor, which can be removed and replaced by a large, cylindrical noise suppressor. In its normal mode the barrel is fitted with a short, vented jacket. One very unusual feature for a submachine gun is that the BXP can be fitted with a grenade-launcher attachment for use in anti-riot situations to project CS and other types of grenade. The twin-strut butt folds down and forwards, with the butt plate swivelling to lie under the receiver and act as a fore-grip. The BXP is used by the South African armed forces and police, and has also been exported to a number of other countries.

STAR 9MM MODEL Z-70 — SPAIN

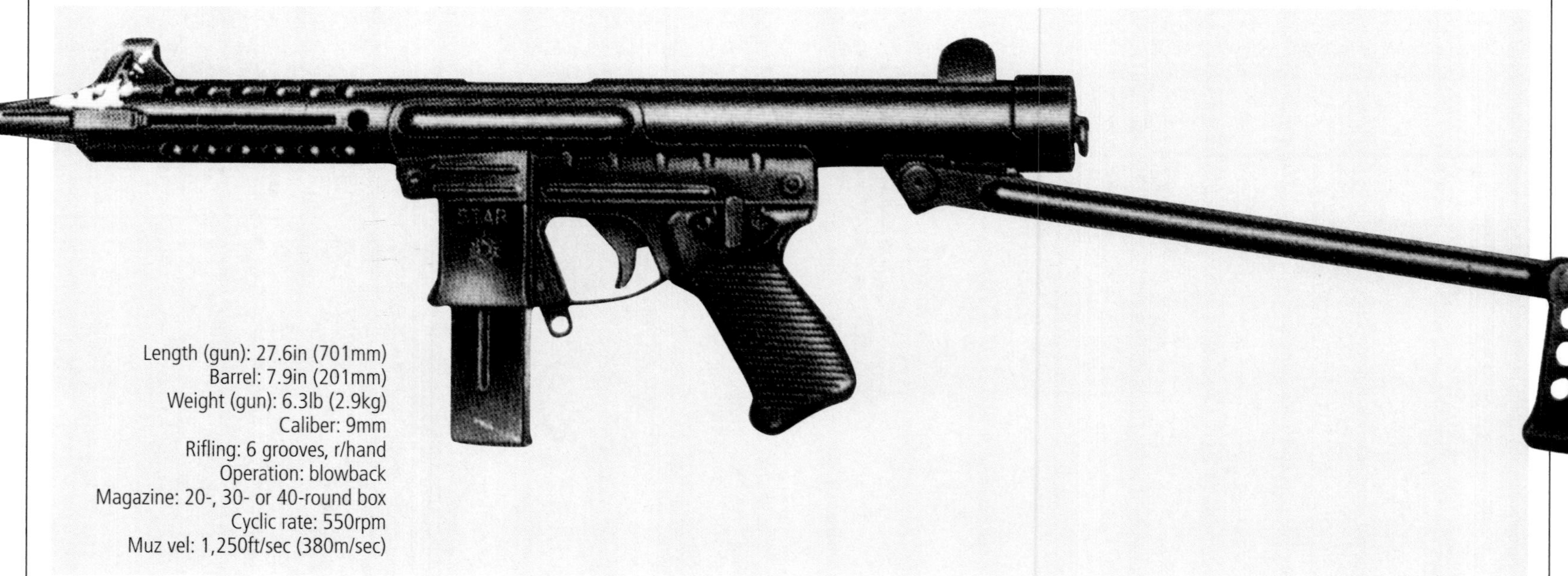

Length (gun): 27.6in (701mm)
Barrel: 7.9in (201mm)
Weight (gun): 6.3lb (2.9kg)
Caliber: 9mm
Rifling: 6 grooves, r/hand
Operation: blowback
Magazine: 20-, 30- or 40-round box
Cyclic rate: 550rpm
Muz vel: 1,250ft/sec (380m/sec)

Star Bonifacio Echeverria, of Eibar, has produced a series of submachine guns dating back to the SI-35, which was introduced in 1935. Most have been the company's own design apart from the Z-45 of 1944, which was loosely based on the German MP-40. The Z-62 of 1960 was, once again, a company design, with two models produced, one firing 9 x 19mm Parabellum, the other 9 x 23mm Largo rounds. However, the Z-62 appears to have had some problems with the trigger group and the Star Model Z-70/B was brought into service in 1971 to overcome this. The Z-70/B has a cylindrical receiver, with a perforated barrel jacket, similar to that on the British Sterling (qv), but with the muzzle protruding several inches. The butt has two parallel steel struts with a centrally pivoted plate at the end; it folds down and forwards. Beneath the receiver are the magazine housing and the trigger group. In the Z-62 the trigger was solid and two pressures were used for single shot or automatic, but in the Z-70/B there is a more conventional change lever and a stand-alone trigger. The Z-70/B was used by the Spanish armed forces and police, but has been superseded by the Z-84. Most Z-70/Bs take the 9 x 19mm Parabellum round, but some take the 9 x 23mm Largo round.

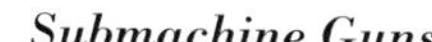

Star 9mm Model Z-84 — Spain

Length (gun): 24.2in (615mm)
Barrel: 8.5in (215mm)
Weight (gun): 6.6lb (3.0kg)
Caliber: 9mm
Rifling: n.k.
Operation: blowback
Magazine: 25- or 30-round box
Cyclic rate: 600rpm
Muz vel: 1,312ft/sec (400m/sec)

The Star Z-84 is a totally new design, which was first seen in public in 1984. It has a box-shaped receiver with the muzzle protruding a short distance from the barrel nut at the front. At the rear is a twin-strut butt, similar to that on the Z-70B, which folds down and forwards when not required. Beneath the receiver is the pistol grip, which contains the magazine housing and which is at the point-of-balance to ensure good control when firing, even when single-handed. One unusual feature is that the ejection slot is on the top of the receiver. Particular care has been taken to ensure that no dust or dirt can be admitted to the working parts and that, even it is, the weapon will continue to operate efficiently.

Carl Gustav Model 45 — Sweden

Length (gun): 31.8in (808mm)
Barrel: 8.0in (203mm)
Weight: 7.6lb (3.5kg)
Caliber: 9mm
Rifling: 6 grooves, r/hand
Operation: blowback
Feed: 36/50-round box
Cyclic rate: 600rpm
Muz vel: 1,210ft/sec (369m/sec)

Sweden did not adopt a submachine gun until 1937, when she began to manufacture a slightly modified form of the Finnish Suomi, which was made under license by the Carl Gustav factory. This was replaced soon afterwards by a second version of the same gun, which had a shorter barrel, a very large trigger guard, which could accommodate gloved fingers in winter, and a much straighter stock than the original Finnish gun; this gun was made by the firm of Husqvarna. In the course of World War II Sweden, although neutral, increased her army considerably to defend herself if necessary and this led to the realization that she had no simple submachine gun for mass-production. She set out to rectify this but the result, the Model 1945, was not in fact put into production until after the war. The Model 1945 was made of stampings from heavy gauge steel, riveted or welded as necessary, and within the limits imposed by these methods was a sound and reliable weapon. Mechanically it bore a strong resemblance to the British Sten gun, but had a rectangular stock of tubular metal which could be folded forward on the right of the gun without in any way interfering with its working. Although it was designed for firing on automatic only, single rounds could be fired by anyone with a reasonably sensitive trigger finger. It fired a special high velocity cartridge, and the original model used the old Suomi 50-round magazine. Later versions fired a new 36-round type but as large stocks of the older magazines, which were not interchangeable, remained, the new gun had an easily detached magazine housing which could be replaced by one of the older type if required.

Rexim-Favor — Switzerland

Length (gun): 32.0in (813mm)
Barrel: 10.8in (273mm)
Weight: 7.0lb (3.2kg)
Caliber: 9mm
Rifling: 5 grooves, r/hand
Operation: see text
Feed: 20-round box
Cyclic rate: 600rpm
Muz vel: 1,300ft/sec (396m/sec)

The Rexim submachine gun appeared in 1953, designed by the Rexim Small Arms Company of Geneva, Switzerland. It was at one time known as the Favor submachine gun, and is believed to have been made under contract by the Spanish Arsenal at Corunna. Attempts were made in the 1950s to sell the Rexim in the Middle East, but there is no record of any substantial deals being made, principally because the gun was considered too complicated, never a good recommendation for a submachine gun in which simplicity is almost the most important factor. The chief interest of the Rexim was that it fired from a closed bolt, that is, the round was fed into the chamber by the action of the cocking handle and remained there until pressure on the trigger allowed the firing pin to go forward. Motive power was provided by two coiled springs, one working inside the other with an intermediate hollow hammer, and looking exactly like an old-fashioned three-draw telescope. When the trigger was pressed the depression of the sear released the hammer which went forward under the force of the large outer spring, struck the firing pin, and fired the round. Normal blowback then followed and the cycle continued. The gun was well made, chiefly of pressings, but with a superior finish. It had a quick release barrel, in which the withdrawal of the small catch under the milled nut allowed the nut to be unscrewed and the barrel pulled out forward. In the model illustrated the butt had a separate pistol grip, presumably designed as a rear handgrip when using the short spring bayonet permanently attached to the muzzle. The magazine was identical to that of the German MP 40.

STEN MARK 1 — UK

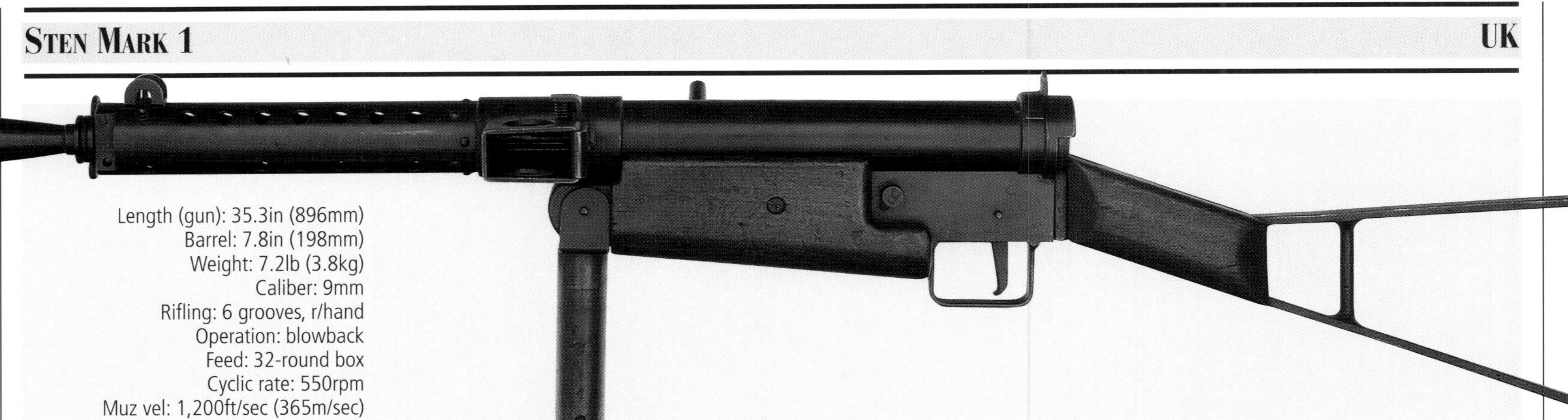

Length (gun): 35.3in (896mm)
Barrel: 7.8in (198mm)
Weight: 7.2lb (3.8kg)
Caliber: 9mm
Rifling: 6 grooves, r/hand
Operation: blowback
Feed: 32-round box
Cyclic rate: 550rpm
Muz vel: 1,200ft/sec (365m/sec)

By mid-1941 large numbers of submachine guns were being sent to Great Britain from the United States. Great Britain and the Commonwealth were, however, engaged in raising and equipping new armies and in addition there were urgent demands for supplies and replacements for North and East Africa where British and Colonial troops were operating against the Italians. There was an urgent requirement for a simple, home-produced submachine gun, and by the middle of 1941 a weapon had been designed, and was in limited production and undergoing user trials. This was the famous Sten, which took its name from the initial letters of the surnames of the two people mostly closely concerned with its development, Major Shepherd and Mr Turpin, allied to the first two letters of Enfield, the location of the Royal Small Arms factory where it was first produced. As soon as the few inevitable weaknesses revealed by the trials had been rectified the Sten gun went into large-scale production and in its various forms was to provide an invaluable source of additional automatic fire power to the British forces. The Sten worked on a simple blowback system using a heavy bolt with a coiled return spring, but in spite of its simple concept the first models made were still relatively elaborate, with a cone-shaped flash hider and a rather crude forward pistol grip which could be folded up underneath the barrel when not in use. It could fire either single shots or bursts, the change lever being a circular stud above the trigger. It also had some woodwork at the fore-end and as a bracer at the small of the butt.

LANCHESTER MARK I — UK

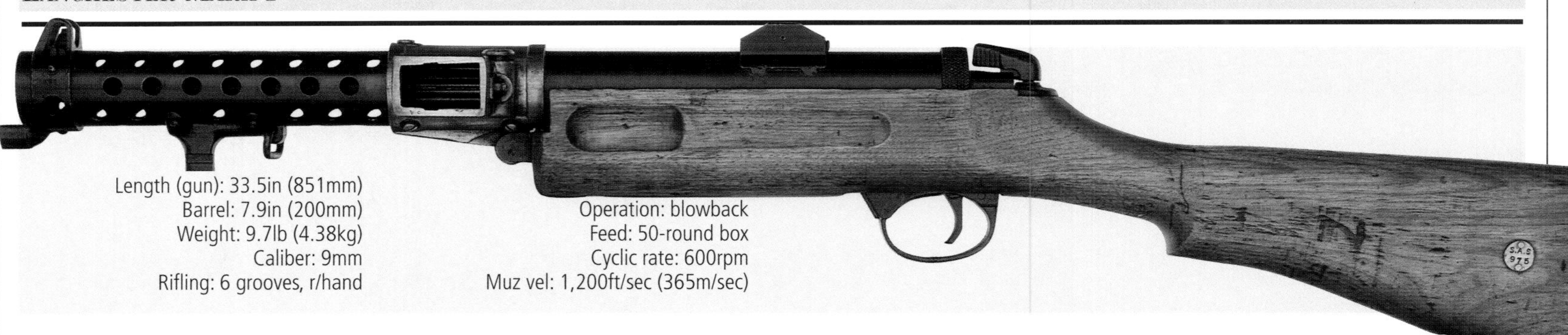

Length (gun): 33.5in (851mm)
Barrel: 7.9in (200mm)
Weight: 9.7lb (4.38kg)
Caliber: 9mm
Rifling: 6 grooves, r/hand
Operation: blowback
Feed: 50-round box
Cyclic rate: 600rpm
Muz vel: 1,200ft/sec (365m/sec)

In June 1940 there was a very real risk that the advancing German Army would invade the British Isles, and there was a grave shortage of weapons to meet them with. There was, therefore, an urgent need for submachine guns, but although large numbers had been ordered from the United States there was no British model available. Arrangements were therefore hastily made to copy the German MP 28 which was known to be reliable, and a British version was designed by George Lanchester of the Sterling Armament Company, after whom the completed weapon was named. The new weapon was intended for the Royal Air Force and the Royal Navy, but in the event most of them went to the latter. The Lanchester, which bore an obvious resemblance to the MP 28, was a robust and reliable gun; British industry had not then been converted totally to a war footing so that the machining and finish of the weapon was of a very high quality, with a rifle type walnut stock (complete with brass buttplate), and a brass magazine housing. It was also fitted with a standard boss to allow the ordinary Lee Enfield bayonet to be fixed if necessary. It had a simple blowback mechanism and could fire either single rounds or automatic as required. It functioned well with most of the standard makes of 9mm rimless cartridge with the exception of the one for the Beretta. There was also a later Mark I which fired automatic only. The Lanchester saw little real service except with the occasional boat or landing party, but it remained in service with the Royal Navy for a long time. Many years after the war most HM ships carried racks of them chained for security, though rarely used.

STEN MARK 2 — UK

Length (gun): 30.0in (762mm)
Barrel: 7.8in (197mm)
Weight: 6.7lb (3.0kg)
Caliber: 9mm
Rifling: 6/2 grooves, r/hand
Operation: blowback
Feed: 32-round box
Cyclic rate: 550rpm
Muz vel: 1,200ft/sec (365m/sec)

The Mark 2, was the first of a long series of changes in the general design of the Sten gun. It was basically a somewhat stripped-down version of the Mark 1, the intention being to simplify manufacturing processes wherever possible. By this time Great Britain was fighting very literally for her existence and had therefore reached the conclusion that appearance was much less important than effectiveness. This resulted in the Sten gun Mark 2, the ugliest, nastiest weapon ever used by the British Army. It looked cheap because it was cheap, with its great unfiled blobs of crude welding metal, its general appearance of scrap-iron, and its tendency to fall to pieces if dropped on to a hard surface. Nevertheless it not only worked but managed to incorporate one or two improvements over the Mark 1, notably by attaching the magazine housing to a rotatable sleeve, held by a spring, so that in bad conditions it could be turned upwards through 90 degrees, thus acting as a dust cover for the ejection opening. The British Army was accustomed to its high quality Short Magazine Lee Enfield rifles and handsomely finished Bren light machineguns and joked about their tin Tommy-gun but they got good value out of it. One of the most persistent weaknesses of the wartime Sten gun was in the poor quality of its magazine, although in the circumstances of hasty construction with inferior metal this is not altogether to be wondered at. In particular the lips were very susceptible to damage, which had a serious effect on the feed and led to endless stoppages. It was also found that dirt tended to clog the magazine, and although careful attention to cleanliness helped in this respect the problem was never really solved. Despite these drawbacks, the Mark 2 was an important weapon.

Sten Mark 2 (Canadian Pattern) — UK

Length (gun): 30.0in (762mm)
Barrel: 7.8in (197mm)
Weight: 6.7lb (3kg)
Caliber: 9mm
Rifling: 2 or 5 grooves, r/hand
Operation: blowback
Feed: 32-round box
Cyclic rate: 550rpm
Muz vel: 1,200ft/sec (365m/sec)

British and Colonial forces had an insatiable appetite for Sten guns. Over 100,000 of the earlier Marks had been produced by early 1942 and there was still no slackening of the demand. Apart from the inevitable loss and damage in action, more troops were being raised and trained, and as the prospect of an Allied invasion of North West Europe drew closer the need for submachine guns continued to increase. There was also an increasing demand for light, easily concealed automatic weapons for the various Resistance movements in German-occupied Europe. Much help was given by Canada, and the weapon illustrated is an example of the type made there at the famous Long Branch factory. Although made to similar specifications to the British Mark 2 it was of somewhat better finish, with a more robust skeleton butt. It also had a bayonet and examples of this are now very rare. This type was first used in action on the ill-fated Dieppe raid of August 19 1942.

De Lisle Silent Carbine — UK

Length (gun): 35.0in (889mm)
Barrel: 9.0in (228mm)
Weight: 7.0lb (3.18kg)
Caliber: 0.45in
Rifling: 7 grooves, l/hand
Operation: Bolt feed
Feed: 10-round magazine
Muz vel: ca 1,200ft/sec (366m/sec)

The de Lisle carbine was originally produced in small numbers during World War II, when special forces required some unorthodox weapons. The de Lisle was a conversion of the standard Short Magazine Lee-Enfield rifle (qv) altered to fire a rimless pistol cartridge. This involved shortening the bolt and a corresponding rearward extension to the chamber. The new short barrel of .45in caliber was screwed into this, and a new magazine opening fitted below. The rest of the weapon consisted of a sheet metal tube 15in (381mm) long and 1.75in (44mm) in diameter, which housed the silencer. This was the most interesting aspect of the arm, and the casing of the weapon illustrated at top has been cut away to show its interior, which consisted of ten metal discs. Each disc had a central hole just over 0.5in (12.7mm) in diameter with a smaller hole on each side, and each was cut along one radius. The pieces on each side of the cut were then pulled apart, so that when the discs were strung along two parallel rods one on each side of the barrel 0.75in (19mm) apart and with stops between, they formed a continuous Archimede screw. The front end of the casing was closed by a circular plug with a hole for the bullet to leave by, and two small screw sockets to hold the front ends of the silencer rods. The bullet never exceeded the speed of sound, so there was no "sonic boom," and this system worked remarkably well, the sound of the discharge being quite inaudible a short distance away. The carbine shot accurately to about 300yd (274m) which indicates the extra power given to a pistol cartridge by a relatively long barrel and a locked breech. There are minor variations in surviving specimens of the carbine. Many had the standard walnut rifle butt, but others had light folding metal stocks, combined with a wooden pistol grip (bottom). Some also had cooling holes in the casing below the backsight, others not. The de Lisle was mainly used in the eradication of sentries who could not be disposed of in any other way, and proved very effective. Although not an automatic, this seems a suitable place for a weapon that is in a category of its own.

STEN MARK 6(S) — UK

Length (silenced): 35.8in (908mm)
Barrel: 7.8in (198mm)
Weight: 9.8lb (4.45kg)
Caliber: 9mm
Rifling: 6 grooves, r/hand
Operation: blowback
Feed: 32-round box
Cyclic rate: 550rpm
Muz vel: ca 1,000ft/sec (305m/sec)

The Mark 2 Sten probably marked the lowest point in the gun's history, and thereafter quality began to improve. Practically all components were still made in small factories and workshops with no previous connection with the manufacture of firearms, but, perhaps due to experience, the general finish was markedly better than in the early days. There was a Mark 3 (similar in appearance to the Mark 2) which was made in huge numbers and this was followed by a Mark 4, which never went into full scale production. This in turn was followed by probably the best Sten of all, the Mark 5, which was to see service from 1944 until well into the 1950s. Although very similar to its predecessors it was of more robust construction with a wooden butt (some with brass buttplates) and pistol grip, and provision was made for it to take the standard bayonet. Experiments had been conducted earlier with a silenced Mark 6 Sten and in 1944 it was decided that a weapon of this type was again required. The standard Mark 2 silencer was thus fitted to the Mark 5, which was then re-designated Mark 6(S). The muzzle velocity of the Mark 5 bullet was in excess of the speed of sound which posed a number of problems in connection with the "sonic boom" effect, but by drilling gas escape holes in the barrel the velocity was brought down to the required figure. The silencer tended to heat rapidly so a canvas hand guard was laced over it. It was not considered advisable to fire bursts through the silencer except in emergencies. The Mark 6 Sten was used mainly by airborne forces and Resistance fighters in World War II, and as late as 1953.

BSA EXPERIMENTAL 1949 — UK

Length (gun): 27.9in (697mm)
Barrel: 8.0in (203mm)
Weight: 6.5lb (2.9kg)
Caliber: 9mm
Rifling: 6 grooves, r/hand
Operation: blowback
Feed: 32-round box
Cyclic rate: 600rpm
Muz vel: 1,200ft/sec (365m/sec)

Even before World War II ended a new British General Staff specification had been issued for a post-war submachine gun. This laid down that it should weigh a maximum of 6lb (2.7kg) without magazine, fire at not more than 600 rounds per minute, have a magazine capacity of 30–60 rounds, and take the No 5 rifle bayonet. Various tests were arranged between 1947 and 1952 for which a number of weapons were entered, among them the Birmingham Small Arms Company's weapon of the type illustrated. It was of conventional blowback mechanism, but was unusual in having no cocking handle, that function being performed by a flat rod attached to the plastic covered fore-end grip. When the grip was twisted and pushed forward the rod went too, its rear end engaging the bolt which was then in the forward position. As the grip was pulled back the rod forced the bolt back also until it was caught by the sear, at which stage it disengaged from the rod. The gun also had another unusual feature in that the magazine housing could be released and swung forward on a hinge without removing the magazine, which was thought to facilitate the clearing of stoppages. It was fitted with a sturdy folding stock which did not interfere with the firing of the gun when forward, and its change lever was situated above the left-hand pistol grip. The first model took a straight magazine, later ones being curved, and as a result of a change in specification it was modified to take a bayonet. The gun was not finally accepted for service and specimens of it are now quite rare.

MCEM 2 — UK

Length (gun): 23.5in (598mm)
Barrel: 8.5in (216mm)
Weight: 6.0lb (2.7kg)
Caliber: 9mm
Rifling: 6 grooves, r/hand
Operation: blowback
Feed: 18-round box
Cyclic rate: 1,000rpm
Muz vel: 1,200ft/sec (365m/sec)

Among the post-war designs to replace the Sten gun were the Military Carbine Experimental Model (MCEM) series produced at Enfield. The first in the series (MCEM 1) was the work of H. J. Turpin who had been instrumental in designing the original Sten gun. The weapon illustrated, the MCEM 2, was the work of another designer, a Polish officer named Lieutenant Podsenkowsky, and it was a very unusual weapon. It was under 15in (380mm) long and its magazine fitted into the pistol grip; it was also well balanced which meant that it could be fired one-handed like an automatic pistol. The bolt was of advanced design and consisted of a half cylinder 8.5in (216mm) long with the striker at the rear, so that at the instant of firing almost the whole of the barrel was in fact inside it. There was a slot above the muzzle into which the firer placed his finger to draw the bolt back to cock it, and the gun had a wire-framed canvas holster which could also be used as a butt. It fired at a cyclic rate of one thousand rounds per minute which made it very hard to control and which may have led to its rejection.

Sterling L2A1/L2A3 — UK

Length (gun): 28.0in (800mm)
Barrel: 7.8in (198mm)
Weight: 6.0lb (2.8kg)
Caliber: 9mm
Rifling: 6 grooves, r/hand
Operation: blowback
Feed: 32-round box
Cyclic rate: 550rpm
Muz vel: 1,200ft/sec (365m/sec)

This gun was designed by George Patchett and was at first known as the Patchett submachine gun. It was originally patented in 1942 and by the end of the war a small number had been made by the Sterling Engineering Company, which had earlier been involved in the production of the Lanchester. A few of these early guns were used by British airborne troops towards the end of the war and their reports on them were encouraging. In the course of the search for a replacement for the Sten this gun was tested against various others in 1947; none was accepted as a result of this first trial because all were considered to need modification. By the time of the next trial in 1951 the Patchett, as it was still then called, was clearly the best gun of those available, and in September 1953 it was finally accepted for service in the British Army. Its official title was the SMG L2A1, but from the date of its introduction it was commonly known as the Sterling. The gun, which was well made and finished, was of normal blowback mechanism but was unusual in having a ribbed bolt which cut away dirt and fouling as it accumulated and forced it out of the receiver. This allowed the gun to function well under the most adverse conditions. The gun underwent a good many modifications after its initial introduction, notably in the addition of foresight protectors, varying shapes of muzzle and butt, and on one light version a spring-loaded bayonet. Some of the earlier models also took a straight magazine. The final production version was the L2A3, which was also produced (in a slightly modified form) in Canada as the C1 9mm submachine gun.

L34A1 Sterling Silenced SMG — UK

Length (gun): 34.6in (864mm)
Barrel: 7.9in (198mm)
Weight (gun): 8.0lb (3.6kg)
Caliber: 9mm
Rifling: 6 grooves, r/hand
Operation: blowback
Magazine: 34-round box
Cyclic rate: 550rpm
Muz vel: 1,020ft/sec (310m/sec)

The L34A1, which entered service in 1966, was the silenced version of the British L2A3 Sterling, with which it shared many components. The silenced weapon was, however, almost 2lb (1kg) heavier and considerably longer, due to the large silencing device fitted around and beyond the barrel. The barrel itself was the same length as on the unsilenced version, but had 72 radial holes drilled in its walls to allow the propellant gases to escape, thus reducing the muzzle velocity of the bullet. Beyond the end of the barrel there was a spiral diffuser, which consisted of a series of discs, each with a hole in the center through which the bullet passed. Propellant gas followed the round but was deflected back by the end cap to mingle with the advancing gases, thus ensuring that the gases leaving the barrel did so at a low velocity. The silenced Sterling was very effective and was used by the British and other armies, principally by special forces, although some also got into the hands of various terrorist groups. Most silenced weapons require special rounds, but the L34A1 was unusual in firing standard 9mm Parabellum ammunition.

Parker-Hale Personal Defense Weapon (PDW) — UK

Length (gun) (stock extended): 22.0in (560mm)
Weight (gun) (pistol configuration): 4.75lb (2.1kg)
Barrel: 4.0in (108mm) (see text)
Caliber: 9mm
Rifling: see text
Operation: blowback
Magazine: 12-/20-/32-round boxes
Cyclic rate: 400rpm
Muz vel: 1,155ft/sec (352m/sec)

The British firm of Parker-Hale has been known for many years as a provider of high-quality target rifles, so it came as something of a surprise in 1999, when the company announced the introduction of its totally new Personal Defense Weapon (PDW). This is primarily intended for use by military, paramilitary and police counter-terrorist teams, but obviously has many other applications, and is clearly targeted at the market currently dominated by the Heckler & Koch MP5. In the PDW, the rate of fire has been deliberately restricted to some 400 rounds per minute, which, in conjunction with other so far undisclosed measures, prevent the "climb" which detracts from the accuracy of virtually all other submachine guns. The PDW can be fitted with a variety of barrels, which simply screw on to the front of the receiver. The standard barrel is 4.0in (108mm) long with barrel twist of 1 turn in 10, but there are also 6.0in (152mm), 10.0in (254mm), 12in (305mm), and 14in (356mm) versions. All except the 4.0in and 6in barrels are fitted with a cylindrical heat shroud and can also accept a bipod, enabling the weapon to be used as a light machinegun. A noise-suppressed barrel is also available. Iron ring sights are fitted as standard, but a Picatinny Arsenal rail on top of the receiver accepts a wide variety of sights, while a flashlight, red dot or laser designator can be fitted beneath the barrel. Effective range is claimed to be 164yd (150m). Firing rate is set at 400 rounds per minute and the weapon can be fired in single rounds, or two- or three-round bursts, using finger control. There is no separate mode selector and full automatic is not available. The PDW fires standard 9 x 19mm Parabellum ammunition and three sizes of magazine are available, housing 12, 20 or 32 rounds, respectively. The magazine is housed inside the forward handgrip.

THOMPSON M1928AI — USA

Length (gun): 33.8in (857mm)
Barrel: 10.5in (267mm)
Weight: 10.8lb (4.9kg)
Caliber: 0.45in
Rifling: 6 grooves, r/hand
Operation: blowback
Feed: 50-round drum/20-round box
Cyclic rate: 800rpm
Muz vel: 920ft/sec (281m/sec)

The Thompson ("Tommy") gun was developed in the course of World War I by Colonel J. T. Thompson but came too late to be used in action. Very few people wanted submachine guns after the war had ended so that the Auto-Ordnance Corporation which made them found it very difficult to keep going, particularly in the depression of the 1930s. Good advertising and publicity helped, however, and there was a small but steady sale to law enforcement agencies and also, regrettably but unavoidably, to criminals of various types. A surprising variety of models of the Thompson were made, almost all in 0.45in caliber and one or two as automatic rifles rather than submachine guns. A few were even made in England by the Birmingham Small Arms Company. The weapon illustrated is the M1928A1, which with minor changes was the last peacetime version. The gun worked by the usual blowback system, but somewhat unusually it had a delay device to prevent the bolt from opening until the barrel pressure had dropped. Two squared grooves were cut into the sides of the bolt at an angle of 45 degrees, the lower ends being nearer the face of the bolt, and an H-shaped bridge fitted into these. When the bolt was fully home the bottom ends of the H-piece engaged in recesses in the receiver. When the cartridge fired, the pressure was enough to cause it to rise, thus allowing the bolt to go back after a brief delay. This was hardly necessary in terms of safety but had the useful effect of slowing the cyclic rate which assisted accurate firing. The gun took either a 50-round drum or a 20-round box magazine.

THOMPSON M1A1 — USA

Length (gun): 32.0in (813mm)
Barrel: 10.5in (267mm)
Weight: 10.5lb (4.7kg)
Caliber: 0.45in
Rifling: 6 grooves, r/hand
Operation: blowback
Feed: 20/30-round box
Cyclic rate: 700rpm
Muz vel: 920ft/sec (281m/sec)

The real breakthrough for the Thompson submachine gun came in 1938 when it was adopted by the United States Army. It was somewhat out of date and there were better weapons in existence but the Thompson was available and therefore accepted. Then the war came and the demand rose instantly. Apart from the domestic needs of the United States the main external purchaser was Great Britain which was glad to buy as many as could be provided in 1940. As with most other pre-war weapons the Thompson had been relatively luxuriously made, and to speed up production some simplification became essential. The first result was the M1, the main mechanical difference being the abolition of the H-piece and the substitution of a heavier bolt to compensate for it. The main external differences were the absence of the compensator on the muzzle, the substitution of a straight forehand for the forward pistol grip (although this had been optional on the Model 28), the removal of the rather complex backsight, and its replacement by a simple flip. The new gun would not take the 50-round drum, but as this had never been very reliable in dirty conditions it was no loss. A new 30-round box magazine was introduced and the earlier 20-round magazine would also fit the new model. There was yet another simplification, the incorporation of a fixed firing pin on the face of the bolt; this resulted in the M1A1 which is the weapon illustrated. Although the basic design was almost a quarter of a century old by then, the Thompson gave excellent service in 1939-45, for even if it was heavy to carry it was reliable, and its bullets had very considerable stopping power.

SMITH & WESSON LIGHT RIFLE MODEL 1940 — USA

This weapon, which is believed to have been invented by a designer named Edward Pomeroy, was made in small numbers just before the outbreak of World War II by the famous American firm of Smith & Wesson. One of them was tested at the United States Army Proving Grounds at the end of the same year but was rejected, partly because it fired a 9mm round whereas the American Army favored 0.45in and partly because it was only semi-automatic. Smith & Wesson were advised to convert it to a full automatic weapon in the larger caliber and re-submit it, but there is no record that they did so. It is said that a few of the original prototypes were made to fire automatic, which marginally justifies its inclusion here as a submachine gun, but if so they were never tested, probably because Smith & Wesson had enough war work on their hands at the time. A slightly modified version of the type illustrated (on next page, top) was in fact re-issued in 1940, when Great Britain, desperate for arms, bought the whole batch of 2,000 for the Royal Navy, all the tools and gauges being forwarded with the order. The main thing that strikes one about this weapon is its quality; the bolt and barrel were made of chrome nickel steel, the remainder of the metalwork being of manganese steel, and the machining, blueing, and general finishing are fully up to the peacetime standards expected of such a famous firm. It worked on the usual blowback system and fired from the open bolt position. One of its unusual features was that the back of the very wide magazine housing contained an ejector tube down which the empty cases passed after firing. In view of the small numbers made, specimens of this gun are very rare and much sought after. Official records of it are scarce and its history obscure.

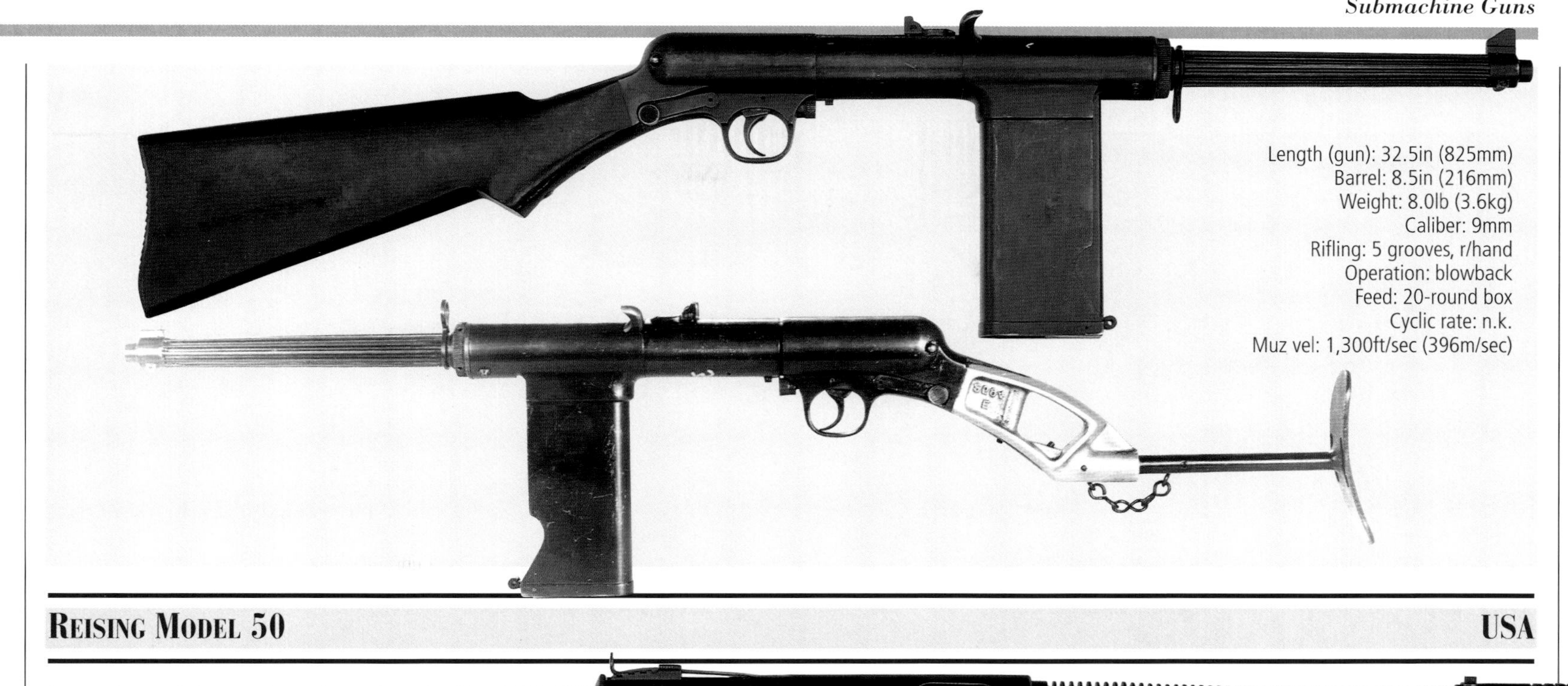

Reising Model 50 — USA

Eugene Reising produced the weapon named after him in 1938. After incorporating some improvements he patented it in 1940 and the well-known United States arms firm of Harrington and Richardson began the manufacture at the end of the next year. After several tests had led to minor improvements it was accepted for service by the United States Marine Corps and was first used in action on Guadalcanal where it proved to be a complete failure, jamming so frequently that the exasperated Marines, who were fighting desperately, threw it away in disgust and resorted to more reliable weapons. The problems were due principally to the complexity of the mechanism and its susceptibility to dirt. Most unusually, and quite unnecessarily, the gun fired with the breech locked, this being achieved by the action of a ramp which raised the rear of the bolt into a recess in the top of the receiver after the moment of firing. This would have been quite acceptable if there had been some self-clearing device, but the bolt recess soon filled with dirt, particularly in hot, dry climates, rendering the weapon useless. The Reising had no cocking handle, this action being achieved by means of a finger catch at the bottom of the stock a few inches in front of the magazine. It is believed that the British Purchasing Commission bought a small number for Canada and the Soviet Union but neither country has left any opinion on record. In spite of its complexity the gun had good points and would probably have performed well in a reasonably temperate climate, perhaps as a weapon for police or other internal security forces.

United Defense Model 42 — USA

The United States Defense Supply Corporation was a US Government corporation which was formed in 1941 to supply weapons to the various Allied nations involved in World War II. The first weapon it submitted for trial was a rather odd one with interchangeable barrels, one of 9mm and the other of 0.45in, the barrel not actually being used for its proper function, being screwed to the back of the receiver to act as a butt. This gun was a failure and never went into production. The UDM42, (illustrated) was designed in about 1938 by a Carl Swebilius and was manufactured by the Marlin Firearms Company. The Model 42 was of normal blowback operation with a separate firing pin inside the bolt, and after one or two modifications it performed particularly well, being accurate, easy to handle, and almost impervious to dirt. The original models were of 0.45in caliber and took a 20-round box magazine, but the production models were all of 9mm and were fitted with double back-to-back magazines, with a total capacity of 40 rounds. The gun was one of the best produced in the United States at that period. It was of the pre-war style of manufacture, made of machined steel and well finished, but its main problem was that it came at a time when the United States was already well-equipped with submachine guns. Simplified wartime versions of the Thompson were available and the mass-produced M3 gun was in an advanced stated of preparation. Once the M3 became available guns of pre-war quality and finish largely disappeared from the scene; a sad end for an excellent gun.

M3A1 — USA

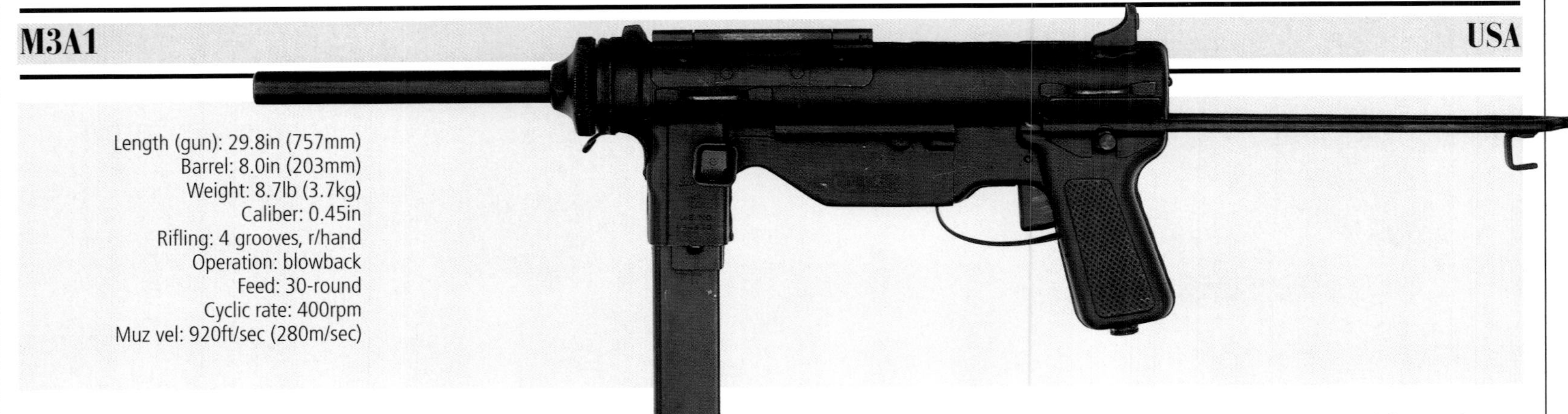

Length (gun): 29.8in (757mm)
Barrel: 8.0in (203mm)
Weight: 8.7lb (3.7kg)
Caliber: 0.45in
Rifling: 4 grooves, r/hand
Operation: blowback
Feed: 30-round
Cyclic rate: 400rpm
Muz vel: 920ft/sec (280m/sec)

In 1941 the Small Arms Development Branch of the United States Army Ordnance Corps set out to produce a weapon which could be mass-produced by modern methods, and once the basic design had been established a very detailed study of the methods used to manufacture the successful British Sten gun was also made, and development work went ahead so quickly that prototypes had been successfully tested well before the end of 1942. The new weapon was accepted as standard under the designation of M3. The new gun was a very utilitarian looking arm, made as far as possible from stampings and with practically no machining except for the barrel and bolt. It worked by blowback and had no provision for firing single rounds, but as its cyclic rate was low this was acceptable. Its stock was of retractable wire and the caliber was 0.45in although conversion to 9mm was not difficult. It bore a strong resemblance to a garage mechanic's grease gun, from which it derived its famous nickname. Large-scale use revealed some defects in the gun, and further successful attempts to simply it were initiated, resulting in the M3A1 (illustrated). It worked, as before, by blowback but had no handle, instead, the firer inserted a finger into a slot in the receiver, by which the bolt could be withdrawn. The bolt had an integral firing pin, worked on guide rods which saved complicated finishing of the inside of the receiver and which gave smooth functioning with little interruption from dirt. An oil container was built into the pistol grip and a small bracket added to the rear of the retractable butt acted as a magazine filler. It used a box magazine which was not altogether reliable in dirty or dusty conditions until the addition of an easily removed plastic cover eliminated this defect. By the end of 1944 the new gun officially replaced the Thompson as the standard submachine gun of the United States Army. Early in 1945 a simple flash hider, held in place by a wing nut, was added, and some were fitted with silencers.

INGRAM MODELS 10 AND 11 — USA

Length (gun): 10.5in (267mm)
Barrel: 5.75in (146mm)
Weight: 6.4lb (2.8kg)
Caliber: 0.45in
Rifling: 5 grooves, r/hand
Operation: blowback
Feed: 30-round box
Cyclic rate: 1,100rpm
Muz vel: 900ft/sec (275m/sec)

Gordon Ingram's first submachine gun design, the M5, never got beyond a single model. He then worked on a new model for two years, producing his Model 6 in 1949, which came in two types, one in 0.38in caliber, which looked superficially like a Thompson, and another in 0.45in caliber; both sold reasonably well, partly to police departments and partly to South American countries. Ingram persevered and by 1959 had produced Models 7, 8 and 9, all of which were sufficiently successful to encourage him to continue. In 1970 he began to design weapons entirely different from his earlier ones and two Models, Numbers 10 and 11, soon appeared. These were virtually identical except for size, the Number 10 being designed for a 0.45in cartridge and the smaller Number 11 being designed for a 0.38in cartridge. The general appearance of these new weapons was similar in a general way to the early Webley automatic pistols; they worked on blowback but had wrap-around bolts which made it possible to keep the weapon short, and improved control at full automatic fire. The cocking handle, which was on the top, was equally convenient for right- or left-handed firers; it had a slot cut in the center of it so as not to interfere with the line of sight. The magazine fitted into the pistol grip and the gun had a simple retractable butt. The whole thing was made of stampings with the exception of the barrel; even the bolt being made of sheet metal and filled with lead. The Models 10 and 11 were both fitted with suppressors which reduced the sound very considerably. Approximately 16,000 M10s were produced between 1964 and the mid-1980s, but only a few M11s were ever sold.

5.56MM COLT COMMANDO — USA

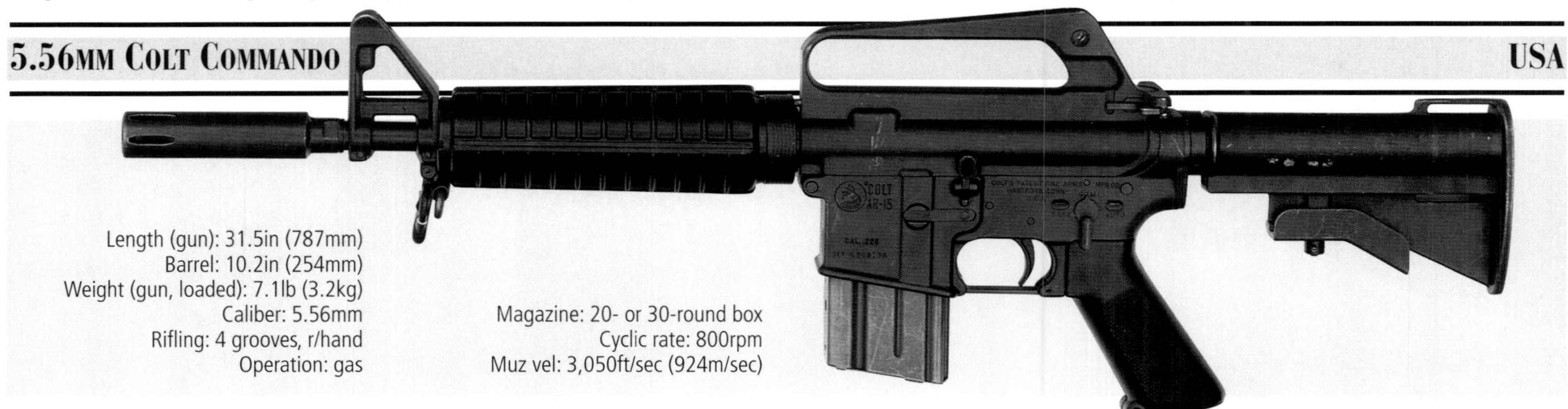

Length (gun): 31.5in (787mm)
Barrel: 10.2in (254mm)
Weight (gun, loaded): 7.1lb (3.2kg)
Caliber: 5.56mm
Rifling: 4 grooves, r/hand
Operation: gas
Magazine: 20- or 30-round box
Cyclic rate: 800rpm
Muz vel: 3,050ft/sec (924m/sec)

The Colt Commando is one of those weapons which do not fit neatly into any one particular category and is variously described as an assault rifle or carbine and submachine gun, but here it is being treated as a submachine gun. The weapon was, in fact, a shorter and handier version of the M16 rifle (qv) and was intended for use in the Vietnam War as a close-quarter survival weapon. Mechanically, it was identical to the M16 but with a much shorter barrel, which reduced the muzzle velocity slightly and also reduced its accuracy at longer ranges. The short barrel also caused considerable muzzle flash which had to be overcome by a 4in (100mm) flash suppressor, which could be unscrewed, if necessary. The Colt Commando had a telescopic butt which could be extended when it was necessary to fire the weapon from the shoulder. It featured selective fire and a holding-open device, and was actuated by the same direct gas action as the M16. In spite of the limitations on range, the weapon proved useful in Indochina and although it had been designed as a survival weapon it fitted the submachine gun role so well that it was later issued to the US Special Operations Forces and was also used in small numbers by the British SAS.

Ruger MP-9 9mm — USA

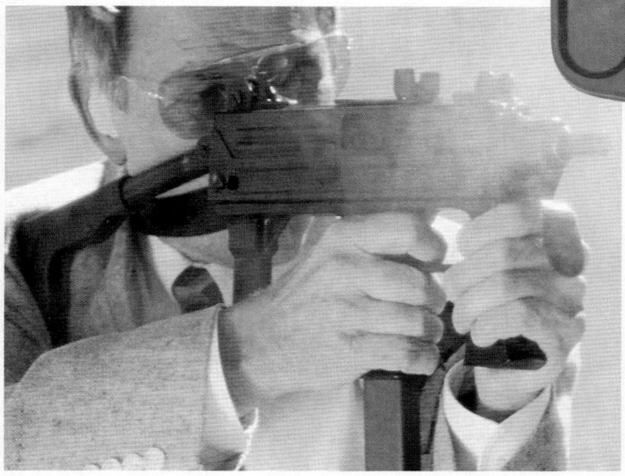

Length (gun): 21.9in (556mm)
Barrel: 6.8in (173mm)
Weight (gun): 6.6lb (3.0kg)
Caliber: 9mm
Rifling: 6 grooves, r/hand
Operation: blowback
Magazine: 32-round box
Cyclic rate: 600rpm
Muz vel: 1,148ft/sec (350m/sec)

The Ruger MP-9 is, in effect, an updated and improved Uzi (qv). The design work was carried out by Uzi Gal in the mid-1980s and was then passed to the Ruger company for final touches and production, which started in 1994. Unlike the Uzi, the MP-9 fires from a closed bolt. The upper part of the receiver is made of polished and treated steel alloy, while the lower part is fabricated from glass fiber reinforced synthetic material. The chrome/molybdenum steel barrel is detachable and can be fitted with a noise suppressor. The folding butt telescopes and then folds downwards to combine with the frame behind the pistol grip/magazine housing. The MP-9 is in production, but the identity of the customers has not been revealed.

La France 0.45in M16K — USA

Length (gun): 26.6in (676mm)
Barrel: 7.2in (184mm)
Weight (gun): 8.5lb (3.9kg)
Caliber: 0.45in
Rifling: 6 grooves, r/hand
Operation: blowback
Magazine: 30-round box
Cyclic rate: 625rpm
Muz vel: 853ft/sec (260m/sec)

Designed by the La France company of San Diego, California, the M16K submachine gun is based on the M16 rifle (qv) but is chambered to take the 0.45in ACP round. It is intended for special operations forces' missions and the 0.45in round was selected for its superior stopping power and better range than the 9mm Parabellum, which is used in most submachine guns. The weapon operates on the blowback principle, firing from a closed bolt. There is a solid, non-folding butt, which, as in the M16, gives a straight-through configuration in order to ensure good fire control, especially when firing automatic. The only part of the barrel protruding from the cylindrical forward casing is the screw-on flash suppressor, but a silencer is under development which would use the same mount. The carrying handle incorporates the rear sight and there is a prominent foresight, the rear leg of which is used for the forward clip of the sling.

LIGHT MACHINE GUNS

Although heavy and medium machine guns proved extremely valuable in World War I, they were large and heavy items of equipment, and required a tripod which made them difficult to conceal in the forward areas. As a result, inventors started to design lighter automatic weapons, which could be carried by one man and fired from cover, mounted on a bipod, used the same round as the infantry they supported, and which used air-cooling rather than the cumbersome water-cooling of HMGs.

The result was the light machine gun (LMG), of which the earliest types appeared in World War I, prime examples being the British Lewis Gun and the French Chauchat M1915. The search for a satisfactory weapon continued in the inter-war years, with the United States adopting the 0.30in Browning Automatic Rifle (BAR) and the British the outstanding Czech-designed 0.303in Bren gun, both of which saw wide-scale service in World War II, together with the excellent Soviet 7.62mm RPD. In the postwar era armies required ever-lighter and more compact LMGs, preferably simple modifications of the standard infantry assault rifle fitted with a bipod.

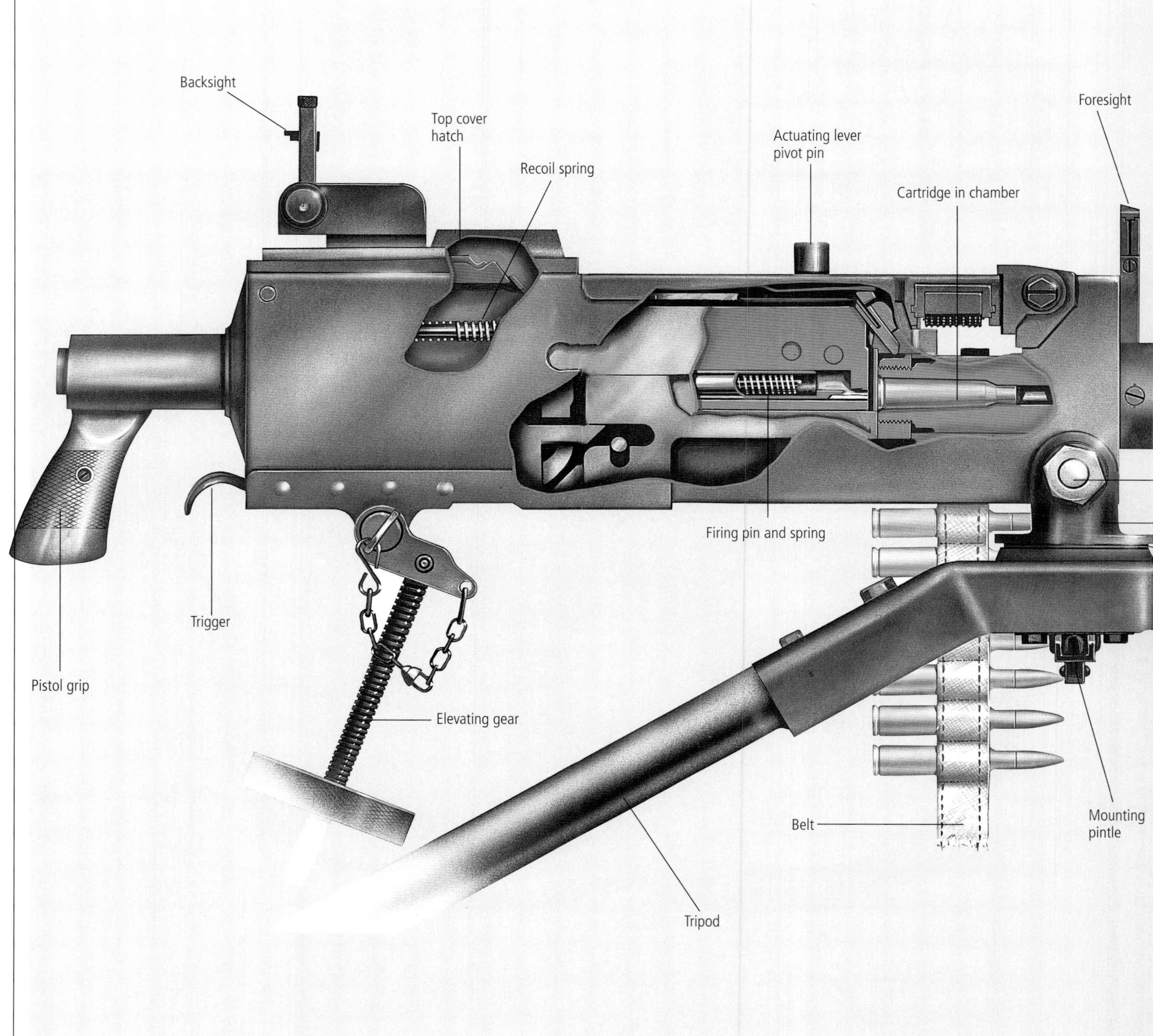

Browning 0.30in M1919A4 Light Machine gun

One of the most successful machine guns ever produced, the Browning 0.30in M1919A4 is recoil-operated and usually employed as a light machine gun, although it could also be employed in the heavy/medium role (as seen here). The method of operation enabled the mechanical elements to be housed in a neat, box-like structure and there was no requirement for a gas-tube along the barrel. The M1919A4 entered service with the United States Army in 1934 and remains in large-scale use with many armies at the start of the 21st Century. It was developed from the air-cooled 0.30in M1919 tank machine gun, although many elements of its design dated back to the water-cooled weapon first produced in 1910. The 24in (610mm) barrel is surrounded by a slotted jacket, which provides all the necessary cooling. The gun is not light, weighing 31lb (14kg), while the tripod, which is required for the sustained fire role, weighs 14lb (6.4kg). The M1919A4 has a pistol grip with the horizontal trigger mounted on the back-plate, but another version, the M1919A6, which appeared during World War II, was fitted with a butt, a bipod and a carrying handle, thus enabling it to be used as a light machine gun by an infantry squad. The M1919A4 fires the Springfield 0.30-06 round, which is normally supplied in a 250-round cloth belt; firing rate is 500 rounds per minute.

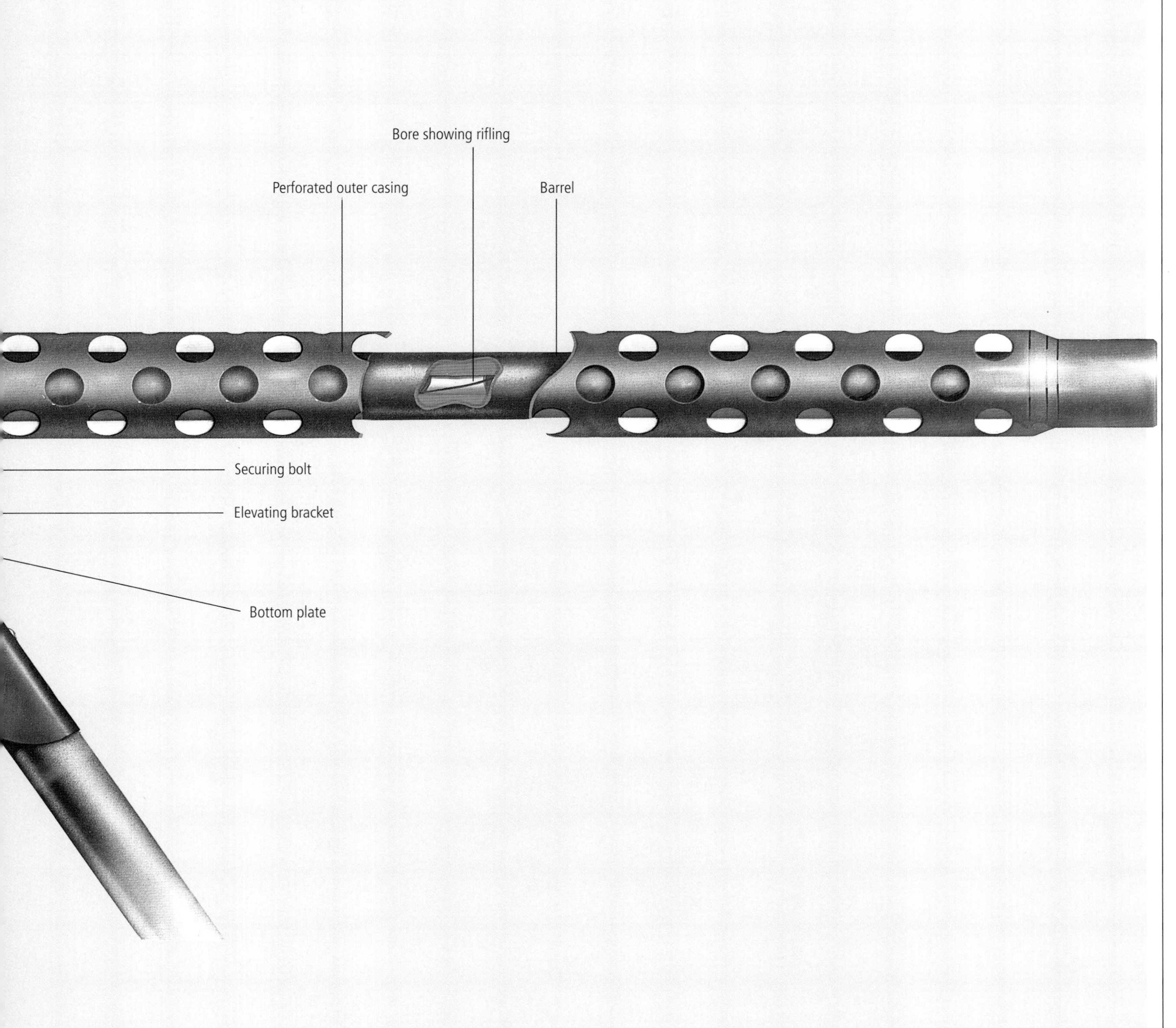

FN 5.56MM MINIMI — BELGIUM

Length (gun): 40.9in (1,040mm)
Barrel: 18.4in (466mm)
Weight (gun): 15.2lb (6.8kg)
Caliber: 5.56mm
Rifling: 6 grooves, r/hand
Operation: gas piston
Feed: magazine or belt
Cyclic rate: 850rpm
Muz vel: 3,000ft/sec (915m/sec)

The 5.56mm Minimi is one of a long line of successes for the Belgian weapons company, Fabrique Nationale (FN). Development started in the early 1960s and the weapon was originally designed around the 5.56 x 45mm M193 round, but this later changed to the 5.56 x 45mm SS109 round. Prototypes appeared in the early 1970s but long development work was not translated into production until the early 1980s. The Minimi uses gas operation and a rotating bolt which is locked into place by a patented FN system. The weapon is belt-fed, with the belt normally housed in a large, lightweight, 200-round plastic box, which is secured underneath, immediately in front of the trigger. The Minimi Para is designed for use by paratroops and features a shorter barrel (13.7in/347mm) long and a telescopic butt. A Minimi Mark 2 has been developed, which incorporates a number of minor improvements (such as a folding cocking handle) which are intended to make it easier to handle without changing its major features and without any loss in interchangeability of components. The weapon has been adopted many armed forces, including those of Australia, Belgium, Canada, France, Indonesia, Italy, New Zealand, Sri Lanka, Sweden, and the United Arab Emirates. Production takes place in Australia (as Type 89 Minimi) and the USA (as M249 SAW). The Minimi is normally fired from its integral bipod, but a tripod is also available for use in the sustained fire role.

NORINCO 7.62MM TYPE 67-2C — CHINA (PRC)

Length (gun): 49in (1,254mm)
Barrel: 23.9in (606mm)
Weight (gun): 36.4lb (16.5kg)
Weight (tripod): 12.3lb (5.6kg)
Caliber: 7.62mm
Rifling: 4 grooves, r/hand
Operation: gas
Feed: belt
Cyclic rate: 650 rpm
Muz vel: 2,755ft/sec (840m/sec)

The weapons used by the People's Republic of China in the 1940s and 1950s were mostly Russian, although there were many others, particularly of US origin, which had been captured from the Nationalists. The Type 67 was the first Chinese-designed LMG and incorporates a number of features from other weapons which were in PRC service at the time, such as the feed mechanism from the Maxim (Chinese Type 24), the gas regulator from the RPD (Type 56), and the piston and flash suppressor from the Czech ZB 26 (Type 26). The result was a thoroughly practical and very reliable weapon which has subsequently seen a lot of service with the People's Liberation Army (PLA); some were also supplied to North Vietnam during the 1970s. The original Type 67 was fired from a bipod but a new version appeared in the late 1980s – Type 67-2C – which can be fired from a specially designed tripod and used in the sustained fire role. The new weapon also includes a number of other improvements including a barrel made from a new type of steel alloy. As with all Chinese infantry weapons, the Type 67 and Type 67-2C are also intended for use in the anti-aircraft role.

NORINCO 7.62MM TYPE 74 — CHINA (PRC)

Length (gun): 43.6in (1.107mm)
Barrel: 20.8in (528mm)
Weight (gun): 14.1lb (6.4kg)
Caliber: 7.62mm
Rifling: 4 grooves, r/hand
Operation: gas
Feed: drum magazine
Cyclic rate: 750rpm
Muz vel: 2,410ft/sec (735m/sec)

The Type 74 is intended to be used as a section/squad LMG and entered service in the mid-1970s. The weapon is gas-operated, using a piston mounted above the barrel, with a four-position gas regulator. The barrel is 20.8in (528mm) long and is fitted with a ZB-type flash suppressor; the barrel is chrome-plated, as is the chamber. The Type 74 (upper photo) is fed from a vertically mounted 101-round drum magazine, which is attached below the weapon, and the magazine from the Type 56 rifle (qv) can also be used. Newer types of Chinese LMGs are the Type 80, a copy of the Russian PK (qv) and the Type 81 (lower photo), a 7.62mm weapon, apparently intended primarily for export.

ZB 26 and ZGB vz30 Series — Czech Republic

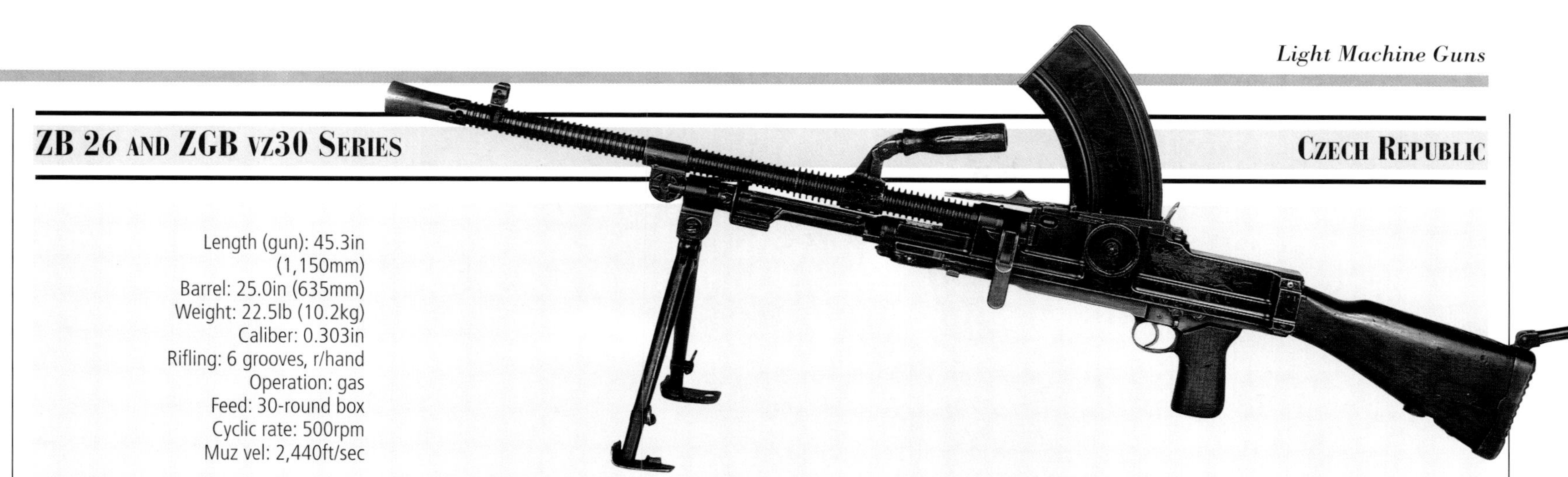

Length (gun): 45.3in (1,150mm)
Barrel: 25.0in (635mm)
Weight: 22.5lb (10.2kg)
Caliber: 0.303in
Rifling: 6 grooves, r/hand
Operation: gas
Feed: 30-round box
Cyclic rate: 500rpm
Muz vel: 2,440ft/sec

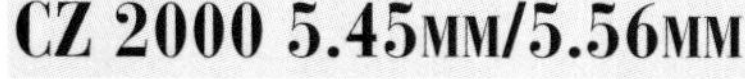

In 1932 the British Army held a series of trials to select a new light machine gun to replace the Lewis. A late entry and the surprise winner was the ZB 26 from Czechoslovakia. The Czechoslovakian factory was located at Brno, and adopted the initials ZB for its international dealings. It had come into existence in 1923 and within a year had begun experiments with a prototype automatic, designed by individual Vaclac Holek, a designer of genius. Having started in the ZB works as an ordinary workman he had risen rapidly, and the Czechoslovakian Army's request for a new light automatic gave him his chance; his team included his brother Emmanuel and two expatriate Poles, Marek and Podrabsky. The gun produced was gas operated, with a piston working to a tilting breechblock, an easily removed barrel, and a vertical box magazine, and was chambered for the rimless 7.92mm German round. After exhaustive tests it was very clear to the British that they had found a potential winner. Some modifications were of course necessary, principally to enable the gun to fire the British 0.303in rimmed round, and this became the ZGB vz30 series (including vz33 with reduced rate of fire). The barrel finning was also dispensed with, but otherwise there were no fundamental changes. The weapon illustrated is one of the final modified models made in Czechoslovakia. Once accepted, the British Government decided that it should be made at Enfield. The body of the new gun, which was cut from solid metal, required 270 operations to complete it, involving 550 gauges accurate to one two-thousandth of an inch, which gives some idea of the complexity of the undertaking. The new gun entered British service in 1938 and was one of the finest infantry weapons used in World War II.

CZ 2000 5.45mm/5.56mm — Czech Republic

Length (gun): 41.3in (1,050mm)
Barrel: 22.7in (577mm)
Weight (gun): 9.1lb (4.1kg)
Caliber: 5.45mm
Rifling: 6 grooves, r/hand
Operation: gas
Feed: magazine
Cyclic rate: 800rpm
Muz vel: 3,150ft/sec (960m/sec)

This LMG is one of three elements of the CZ 2000 weapons system, of which the other members are an assault rifle and a carbine (qv). The LMG is essentially similar to the rifle, but with a heavy barrel and bipod to suit it for the support weapon role. It was originally known as the "Lada" but this name has since been dropped. The CZ 2000 LMG has three modes of fire, controlled by a lever moved by the firer's right thumb: fully automatic; three-round bursts; and single-round semi-automatic. There is a skeleton stock, formed by two tubular steel struts and a base plate, which folds sideways to the right. The CZ 2000 LMG can be fed from either a 30-round curved box, as used in the CZ 2000 assault rifle, or a 75-round drum magazine. The fore and rear sights are fitted with luminous blades for use in adverse conditions, and both optical and night sights can be mounted. The three weapons in the CZ 2000 system can be chambered to take either the Russian 5.45mm round or the NATO 5.56mm round, and although the latter round must be the long-term choice it seems that simple economics will force the Czech armed forces to retain the 5.45mm caliber for several years to come. A limited number of 5.45mm CZ 2000 weapons have, therefore, been produced for the Czech armed forces and the design has also been offered to countries still using the Russian round, such as North Korea.

Madsen 1902 — Denmark

This gun was often known as the Madsen after a Danish Minister of War, while the British called it the Rexer. The weapon had an unusual mechanism in which the basic breech mechanism consisted of a rectangular steel frame sliding on ribs in the main body of the gun. Inside this steel frame there was a breechblock, pivoted at the rear so that it worked in the vertical plane with three positions, locked, dropped, or raised, this vertical movement being controlled by a curved feed arm attached to the left hand side of the box. The gun was of the long recoil type in which barrel and breech both recoiled sufficiently far for the next cartridge to be stripped from the magazine and fed into the chamber. When the first round, which had of course to be located manually by a lever, was fired, the barrel and breech mechanism recoiled together. In the course of this movement the feed arm caused the front of the breechblock to rise, allowing the empty case to be extracted and ejected underneath it. When the rearward action was complete a return spring took over, forcing the mechanism forward; during this stage the next round was stripped from the magazine and carried forward on top of the breechblock which acted as a feed tray. At the proper time the feed arm depressed the front of the block so that the chamber was exposed and forced the cartridge in, after which the block rose to the locked position and the round was fired. The Madsen was tested by many armies between 1903 and 1917 but was not adopted in any numbers.

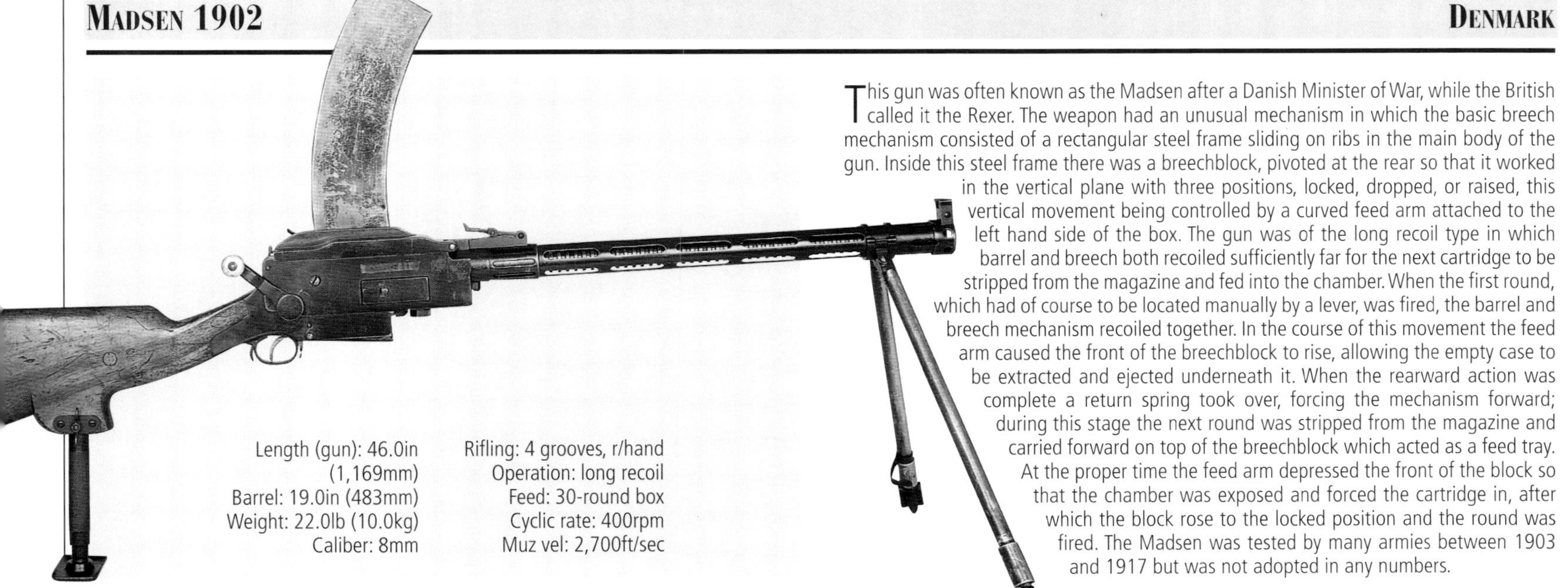

Length (gun): 46.0in (1,169mm)
Barrel: 19.0in (483mm)
Weight: 22.0lb (10.0kg)
Caliber: 8mm
Rifling: 4 grooves, r/hand
Operation: long recoil
Feed: 30-round box
Cyclic rate: 400rpm
Muz vel: 2,700ft/sec

CHAUCHAT MODÈLE 1915 (CSRG)

FRANCE

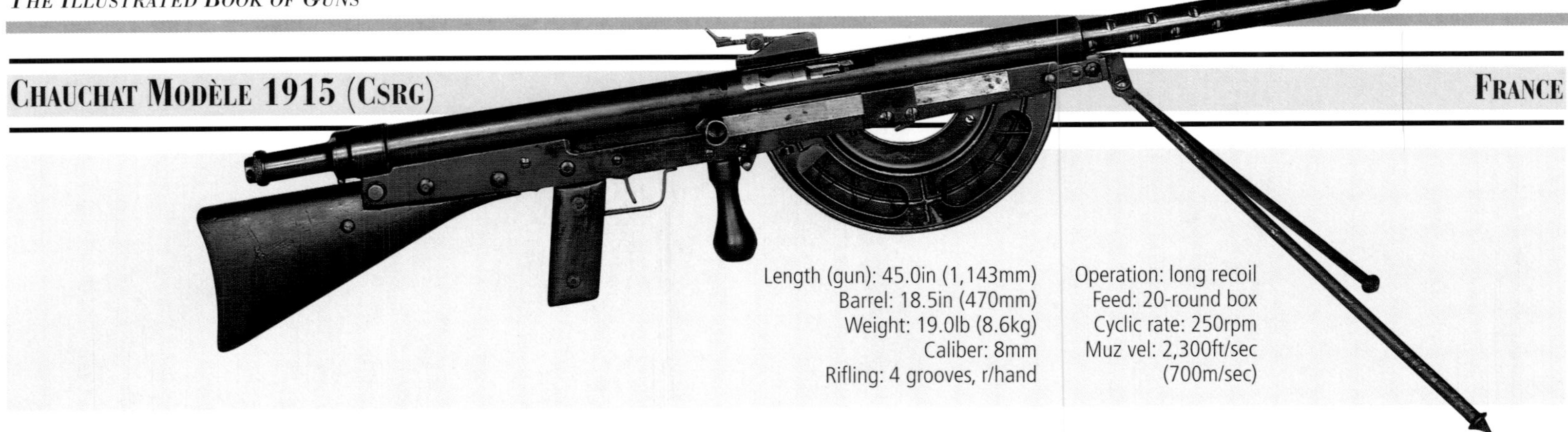

Length (gun): 45.0in (1,143mm)
Barrel: 18.5in (470mm)
Weight: 19.0lb (8.6kg)
Caliber: 8mm
Rifling: 4 grooves, r/hand
Operation: long recoil
Feed: 20-round box
Cyclic rate: 250rpm
Muz vel: 2,300ft/sec (700m/sec)

The Chauchat was rushed into production in 1914. Much of it was constructed of ordinary commercial tubing never intended for the strains inherent in an automatic weapon firing a full-sized rifle cartridge, and even locking lugs and similar essentials were stamped, pressed, and screwed and generally botched together. As can be seen from the photograph the pistol grip was rough wood and the forehand grip no more than a crudely shaped tool handle. When the gun was fired (assuming that it did fire which was by no means always the case) the barrel and bolt recoiled together, the bolt being locked to the barrel by locking lugs. This action continued for the whole of the backward phase when the bolt was turned and unlocked allowing the barrel to go forward. The bolt then followed it, taking a round with it, chambering it, and firing it. The long recoil necessarily caused a great deal of vibration making it virtually impossible to hold the weapon steady on a target when firing automatic. Another feature of the Chauchat was its semi-circular magazine, which was made necessary by the fact that the standard 8mm Lebel rifle cartridge had a very wide base. The front end of the magazine was engaged first and then the rear end pulled upwards until it was engaged and held by the magazine catch. The first round then had to be loaded manually by means of the cocking handle. When US forces arrived in France in 1918 they were equipped with the Chauchat (which they called the "Shoshos") and they also found it totally unsatisfactory.

CHÂTELLERAULT MODÈLE 1924-9

FRANCE

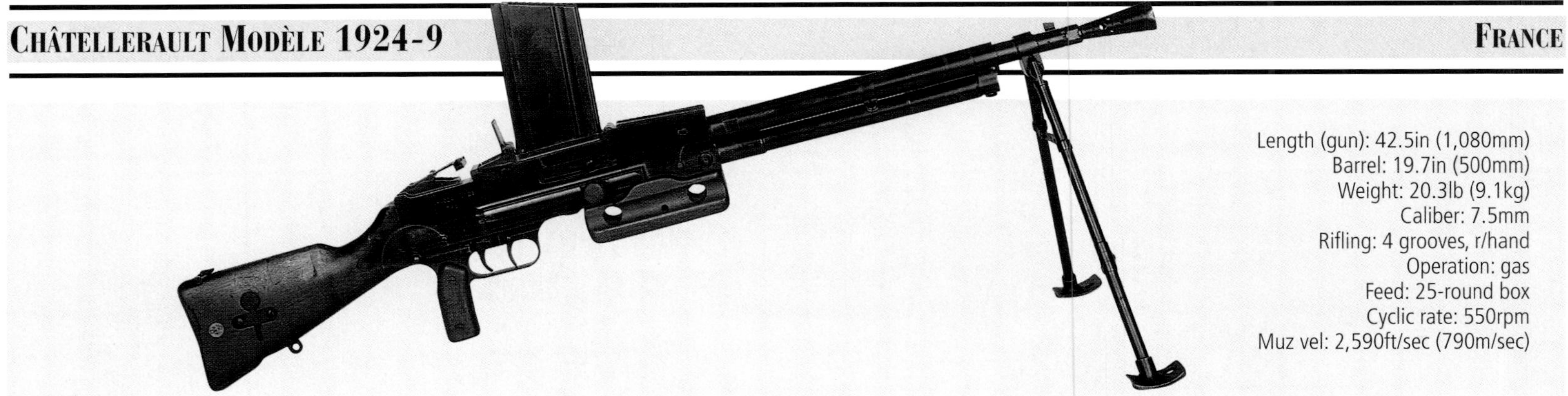

Length (gun): 42.5in (1,080mm)
Barrel: 19.7in (500mm)
Weight: 20.3lb (9.1kg)
Caliber: 7.5mm
Rifling: 4 grooves, r/hand
Operation: gas
Feed: 25-round box
Cyclic rate: 550rpm
Muz vel: 2,590ft/sec (790m/sec)

The 1924 Model Châtellerault light machine gun was of orthodox appearance and action, being a gas- and piston-operated arm with a mechanism very similar to that of the Browning Automatic Rifle. It had two triggers, the forward one for automatic fire, together with a selector which had to be previously set for the type of fire required. It was fitted with a gas regulator which could be used in conjunction with an adjustable buffer to allow the firer to vary his cyclic rate, but perhaps most important of all it was designed to fire the new 7.5mm rimless round, similar in type and general performance to the German 7.92mm cartridge. There was a further modification in 1928 when the round was shortened slightly, after which the gun functioned with great efficiency. It was also simple to use and teach, an important matter for a country which relied on fairly short-term conscription for the great bulk of its armed forces. In order to increase the firepower of the infantry garrisons in the Maginot Line, the French made modifications to their Modèle 1924-9 which resulted in the Modèle 31. This was fundamentally the same weapon, but instead of the usual box magazine it was fitted with a huge side-mounted drum, similar to that of the Lewis gun in general principle but designed to hold no fewer than 150 cartridges. This gun had a pistol grip only and was designed to fire from a loophole on a swivel mounting, and in order to allow a long burst without overheating the French devised a system under which a small jet of cold water was squirted into the barrel between the extraction of the empty case and the loading of the next round into the chamber.

MAS AA-52 7.5/7.62MM

FRANCE

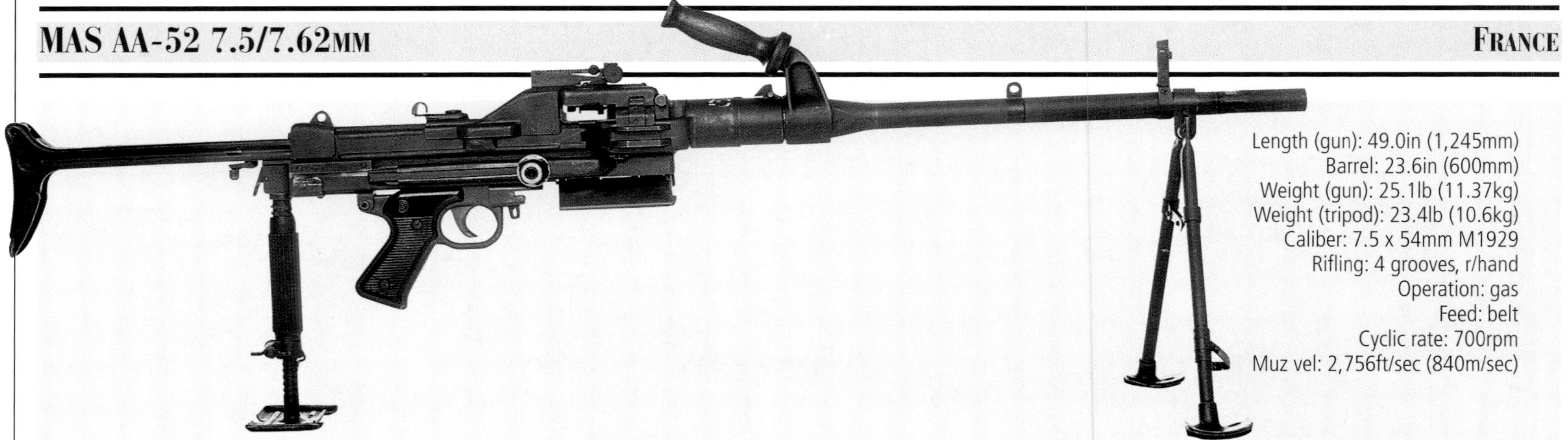

Length (gun): 49.0in (1,245mm)
Barrel: 23.6in (600mm)
Weight (gun): 25.1lb (11.37kg)
Weight (tripod): 23.4lb (10.6kg)
Caliber: 7.5 x 54mm M1929
Rifling: 4 grooves, r/hand
Operation: gas
Feed: belt
Cyclic rate: 700rpm
Muz vel: 2,756ft/sec (840m/sec)

The Arme Automatique Transformable Modèle 52 (general purpose machine gun) was first fielded in 1952 and three models were eventually produced. Specifications here are for the AA-52 Heavy Barrel version. The original AAT-52 was designed to fire the somewhat elderly French 7.5 x 54mm M1929 round but when NATO standardized on the 7.62 x 51mm NATO cartridge the majority of in-service guns were converted to take the new round, in which guise they were designated AA-7.62 F1. Both 7.5mm and 7.62mm versions were available in two version. The general support version had a light barrel and bipod, although the latter could be supplemented by a rear-mounted monopod which enabled the weapon to be fired on fixed lines. The second version had a heavier barrel and the US M2 tripod which enabled it to be used in the sustained fire role. The gun was air-cooled and operated using delayed blowback with a two-piece bolt; the chamber was fluted, with a number of lengthwise grooves to enable the gas to aid smooth extraction. The 7.62mm version can use either a French or the NATO M13 belts, although one unusual feature is that when the gun is carried with a belt in place it must be cocked. Apart from being used in the ground role with a bipod or tripod, the the 7.62mm F1 could also be mounted in a vehicle turret, when the butt stock was removed and the weapon fired electrically. The 7.5mm version was used in large numbers by the French Army, although the 7.62mm F1 version replaced it in the 1960s and 1970s, when any unconverted guns were withdrawn from service. Both 7.5mm and 7.62mm versions were exported in large numbers.

Light Maxim MG08/15 — Germany

Length (gun): 55.0in (1,398mm)
Barrel: 24.0in (610mm)
Weight: 39.0lb (17.7kg)
Caliber: 7.92mm
Rifling: 4 grooves, r/hand
Operation: recoil
Feed: 250-round box
Cyclic rate: 400rpm
Muz vel: 2,900ft/sec (885m/sec)

The Lewis came as a surprise to the Germans in 1914 but they soon had an answer to it in the shape of the Maschinengewehr 08/15, generally known as the "Light Maxim." The new gun was water-cooled like its larger counterpart, but whereas the 08 Maxim had a pump which actually kept the water moving, and so helped it to dissipate its heat, the light model had a plain but effective water jacket. It fired a 50-round belt, which avoided any major redesign of the original mechanism, and was equipped with a belt box which fitted on to the right-hand side of the gun and allowed it to be moved rapidly. As this gun was so similar to the 08 Model it posed few manufacturing problems and was produced in large numbers in a very short period. It was an effective weapon and soon became as popular with the German infantry as the Lewis gun was with those on the British side. Light Maxims were used in German Zepellin airships with the bulky and heavy water jacket replaced by a simple ventilated casing, as the movement of airships through the air was in itself a sufficient means of cooling for automatic guns. After the airships had been discontinued a version of this air-cooled Maxim was issued to the German Army under the designation 08/18. It was not a success and was presumably used only because by 1918, the year of its issue, the Germans were so short of matériel of all kinds that they could not afford to waste anything. When used on the ground this air-cooled version overheated so rapidly that it was of very limited use.

Heckler & Koch 7.62mm HK11 — Germany

Length (gun): 40.2in (1,020mm)
Barrel: 17.7in (450mm)
Weight (gun): 15.0lb (6.8kg)
Caliber: 7.62mm
Rifling: 4 grooves, r/hand
Operation: delayed blowback
Feed: box or drum
Cyclic rate: 850rpm
Muz vel: 2,560ft/sec (780m/sec)

The German company of Heckler & Koch is one of the most successful of all modern weapons manufacturers and, among many other projects, developed a series of light machine guns firing the NATO standard 7.62mm cartridge. This series has consisted of two parallel developments, one belt-fed, the other magazine-fed. The first in the 7.62mm magazine-fed series was the HK11 (see specifications), which could accept either the G3 20-round box or a 50-round drum magazine. Internally, it used the normal H&K delayed blowback system with a two-part breech-block and roller delays, which is the same as that used in the HK21 series of belt-fed machine guns and the G3 rifle. The next model in the series was the HK11A1 which did away with the 50-round drum magazine option, depending instead solely upon the 20-round box magazine. Next to appear was the HK11E which had the same internal improvements as the HK21E (qv), including a three-round burst capability, a drum rear sight, and a forward hand grip midway under the barrel. The HK11E also had a new trigger and trigger guard, which enabled the gun to be fired while wearing heavy Arctic gloves, and a device to ensure that the bolt closes more quietly.

Heckler & Koch 7.62mm HK21 and HK23 — Germany

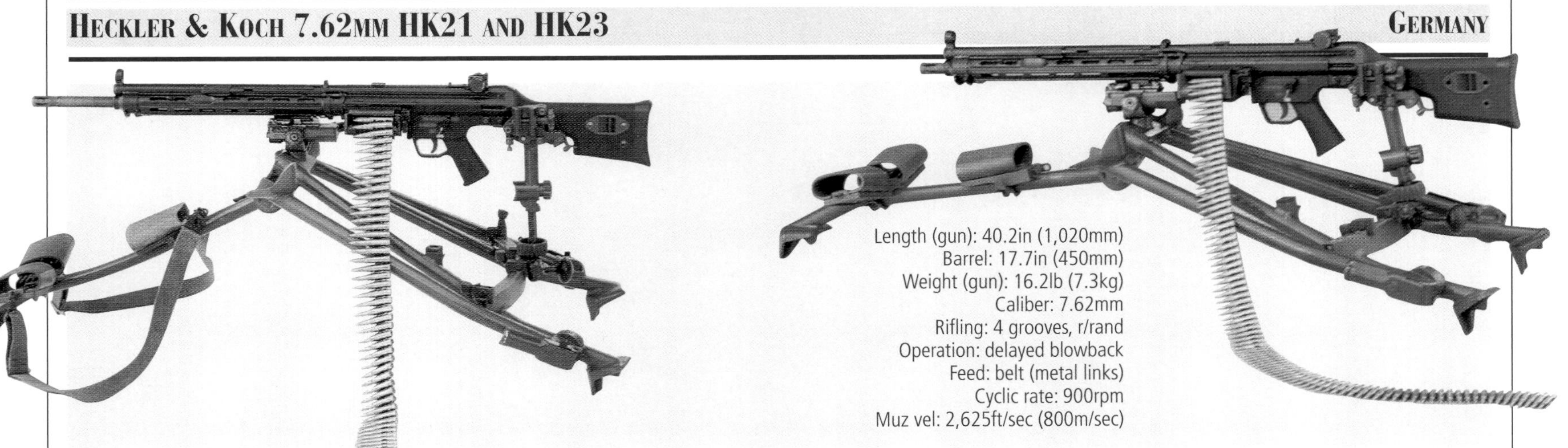

Length (gun): 40.2in (1,020mm)
Barrel: 17.7in (450mm)
Weight (gun): 16.2lb (7.3kg)
Caliber: 7.62mm
Rifling: 4 grooves, r/rand
Operation: delayed blowback
Feed: belt (metal links)
Cyclic rate: 900rpm
Muz vel: 2,625ft/sec (800m/sec)

The HK21 (specifications are for basic model) was the second version of the H&K machine guns using the NATO 7.62 x 51mm cartridge. The gun was designed to be belt fed, but an adapter could also be fitted to enable box or drum magazines to be used. The weapon could use most of the belt systems found within NATO, including the M13 (US), and DM1 and DM60 (German).

Internally, it used the normal H&K delayed blowback system with a two-part breech-block and roller delays, together with a fluted chamber to ensure efficient extraction, which is the same as that used in the HK21 series of belt-fed machine guns and the G3 rifle. Firing was controlled by a two-position lever for either single rounds or full automatic. Other rounds, such as the 7.62 x 39mm or 5.56 x 45mm, could be fired by changing the barrel, feed plate, and bolt. The HK21A1 was generally similar to the HK21 except that it lacked the magazine and 7.62 x 39mm options, and had an improved belt-feed mechanism. The final gun in the series was the HK21E (left photo) which had a longer receiver; longer barrel (26.4in/560mm compared to 17.7in/450mm); new forward handgrip; a three-round burst capability; and a new trigger enabling the firer to use Arctic gloves. The HK21 series were used by many armies and were produced in Germany (all models); Greece (HK21A) and Portugal (HK21). The HK23E (right photo) was generally similar to the HK21E except that it fired 5.56 x 45mm cartridge, while the HK73 was a variant of the HK23E using a linkless belt-feed system.

HECKLER & KOCH G36 — GERMANY

Length (gun): 39.0in (990mm)
Barrel: 18.9in (480mm)
Weight (gun): 7.7lb (3.5kg)
Caliber: 5.56mm
Rifling: 6 grooves, r/hand
Operation: gas
Feed: magazine
Cyclic rate: 750rpm
Muz vel: 3,020ft/sec (920m/sec)

Following the modern trend, the G36 is the light support weapon (LSW) version of the Heckler & Koch G36 rifle and is identical in most respects to that weapon. The differences lie in optimizing it for the support role (ie, in giving sustained automatic fire) with a different barrel, which has the same dimensions but is of thicker construction, particularly at the chamber end. It is also permanently fitted with a bipod, which is optional in the rifle. Like the assault rifle version, the LSW has a large carrying handle with a built-in x3 optical sight; a folding, skeleton butt; and a muzzle compensator/flash suppressor. It is magazine-fed, using a 30-round box. There is also a G36E export version, which differs mainly in having a less powerful x1.5 optical sight.

INSAS 5.56MM — INDIA

Length (gun): 41.3in (1,050mm)
Barrel: 21.1in (535mm)
Weight (gun): 13.5lb (6.1kg)
Caliber: 5.56mm
Rifling: 4 grooves, r/hand
Operation: gas piston
Feed: magazine
Cyclic rate: 650rpm
Muz vel: 3,130ft/sec (954m/sec)

The Indian weapons industry dates back several centuries and the modern industry is healthy, primarily because it has the benefit of a large domestic market, consisting of the huge regular forces and large and diverse paramilitary forces. The INSAS (Indian Small Arms System), which was revealed in 1993, is a family of weapons, with two basic models: an assault rifle (qv) and an LMG. All these weapons fire a 5.56 x 45mm cartridge, but it is important to note that although this is based on the Belgian SS-109 it is not to the NATO standard. The INSAS family appears to share a number of features with other weapons which have been manufactured in India and mechanically the operation appears to resemble that of the Kalashnikov family, while the solid butt resembles that used on the Bren gun. As with other families of weapons, the INSAS LMG has a different barrel from the assault rifle, and this is not only of heavier construction, but is longer (21.1in/535mm compared to 18.3in/464mm) but, in this case, is also chrome-plated. It also gives a greater range. The LMG has a bipod (based on that used by the Indian-produced Bren gun) and has a special 30-round magazine, although the 22-round rifle magazine can also be used; both types of magazine are made of clear plastic. As with the assault rifle, the LMG is available in fixed and folding butt versions, while the INSAS Para LMG also has a shorter barrel (20.1in/510mm), although this is still longer than the rifle barrel. The LMG fire selector can be used for either single rounds or full automatic, but there is no three-round burst capability as in the assault rifle.

IMI 5.56MM NEGEV — ISRAEL

Length (gun): 40.2in (1,020mm)
Barrel: 18.1in (460mm)
Weight (gun): 16.5lb (750kg)
Caliber: 5.56mm
Rifling: 6 grooves, r/hand
Operation: gas-piston
Feed: magazine or belt
Cyclic rate: 1,000rpm
Muz vel: 3,280ft/sec (1,000m/sec)

The Israeli Army used the Galil (qv) family of small arms from the 1960s onwards, in which the light machine gun version (ARM) differed only minimally from the assault rifle. The Negev, however, which was announced in 1990, was designed from the start as a multi-purpose light machine gun and is not an adaptation of an assault rifle; somewhat perversely, however, and as described below, it can be adapted to enable it to be used as an assault rifle. The Negev is gas-operated, fires from an open-bolt, and employs a rotating bolt that locks into a barrel extension. It is normally fed by magazines, but an adapter enables it to fire 200-round belts. A bipod with finned legs is fitted as standard. The Assault Negev is an assault rifle version, which has the same internal mechanisms, but has a shorter barrel, forward handgrip and folding butt, while the bipod is not fitted. This brings overall length with butt folded down to 25.6in (650mm), while the total weight is reduced to 15.4lb (7.0kg), enabling the weapon to be used as an assault rifle. All weapons in the Negev series can be used to launch grenades and all have a three-position gas regulator, which can be adjusted to launch grenades or to fire at either 850rpm or 950 rpm.

BREDA MODELLO 30

ITALY

Length (gun): 48.5in (1,232mm)
Barrel: 20.5in (520mm)
Weight: 22.7lb (10.3kg)
Caliber: 6.5mm
Rifling: 4 grooves, r/hand
Operation: blowback
Feed: 20-round box
Cyclic rate: 500rpm
Muz vel: 2,063ft/sec (618m/sec)

In 1930 the Breda company took over all the armament work previously carried out by the Fiat factory, and in the same year they produced their new Modello 30. This was a light machine gun weighing under 23lb (10.4kg) and fired from a bipod by means of a normal rifle-type butt, pistol grip, and trigger. Mechanically it was somewhat similar to the earlier Revelli gun, since it worked on a combination of gas and recoil. When the round was fired the barrel recoiled for about 0.5in (12.7mm) and then stopped; this allowed the breech to unlock, and once this had happened the working parts were able to move further backwards, partly due to the recoil and partly due to the residual gas pressure in the barrel. On striking the buffer the compressed recoil spring thrust them forward again, allowing the bolt to strip a round from the magazine, chamber it, lock itself to the barrel, and allow the firing pin to function. The gun would fire automatic only. The use of direct blowback led to the continued use of an oiler to lubricate the rounds as they went into the chamber. The feed system consisted of a box magazine on the right side but hinged to the gun at its front corner so that by releasing a catch the whole magazine could be pivoted forwards until it was parallel with the barrel for rebacking. The best that can be said about the Modello 30 is that it was adequate, but no more. It was the standard light machine gun of the Italian Army in Abyssinia and in its campaigns in North and East Africa during World War II. When the Italian Army briefly introduced a larger round of 7.35mm caliber as a result of its experience against the Abyssinians in the 1930s, a number of Modello 30s were converted to fire it.

BERETTA AS70/90

ITALY

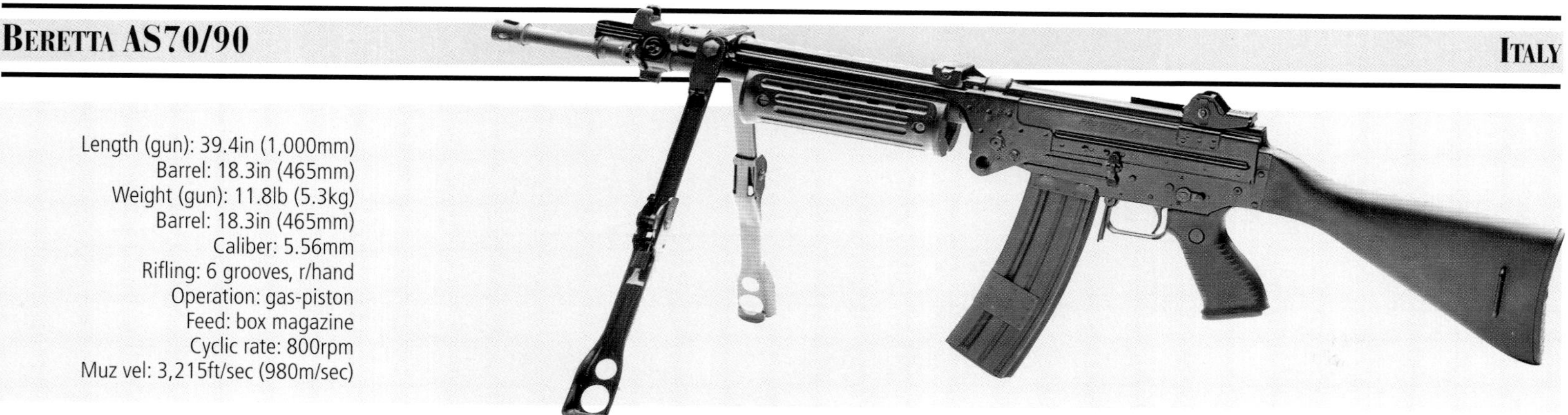

Length (gun): 39.4in (1,000mm)
Barrel: 18.3in (465mm)
Weight (gun): 11.8lb (5.3kg)
Barrel: 18.3in (465mm)
Caliber: 5.56mm
Rifling: 6 grooves, r/hand
Operation: gas-piston
Feed: box magazine
Cyclic rate: 800rpm
Muz vel: 3,215ft/sec (980m/sec)

The first major Italian post-war light machine gun was a locally produced version of the German MG3, designated the MG42/59, which fired the NATO standard 7.62 x 51mm round. Following the adoption of the NATO standard 5.56 x 45mm round the Italian Army has adopted the Belgian Minimi (qv), but despite this Beretta has designed a series of light machine guns for the new caliber, although, as far as is known, none of these has yet been put in full production. First was the AR70/78, which was designed around the US M193 5.56 x 45mm round, and was, in essence, a heavy barrel version of the AR70 assault rifle. This design was then adapted to produce the AR70/84, which took the 5.56 x 45mm NATO round, and also incorporated some other modifications such as the deletion of the rapid-change barrel facility. Next in the series was this weapon, the AS70/90, which is the light machine gun version of the AR70/90 assault rifle (qv), with a heavy barrel and various other modifications. Feed is from a 30-round box magazine and the AS70/90 can also fire grenades, but from a different launcher to that used on the AR70/90. There is a large, fixed carrying handle, which can accommodate optical sights, if required, although normally metal sights are used. The butt has a large slot to enable the firer to get a good grip with his/her disengaged hand.

TYPE 11 (NAMBU)

JAPAN

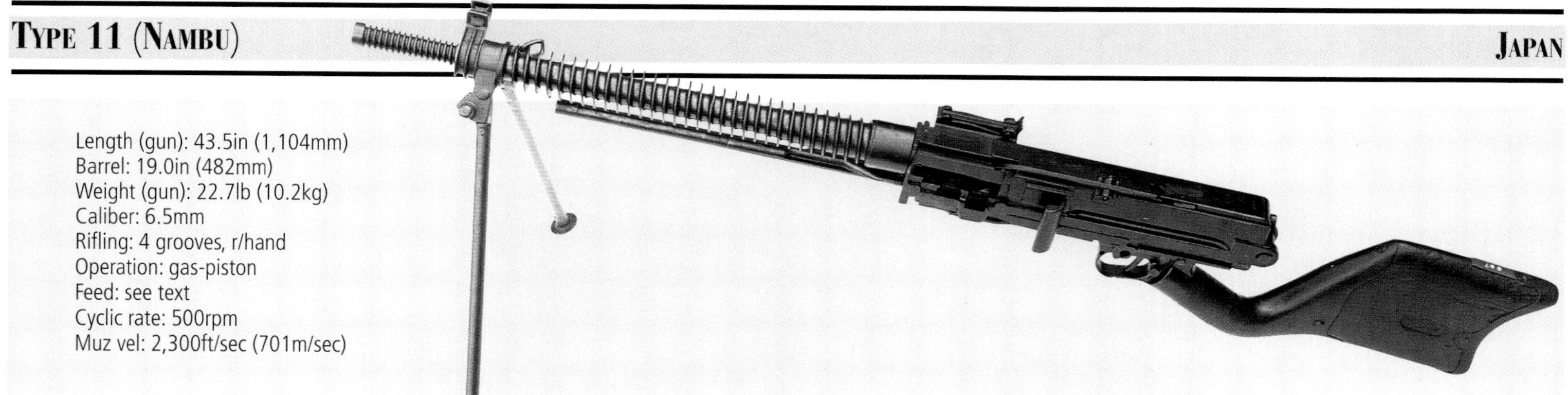

Length (gun): 43.5in (1,104mm)
Barrel: 19.0in (482mm)
Weight (gun): 22.7lb (10.2kg)
Caliber: 6.5mm
Rifling: 4 grooves, r/hand
Operation: gas-piston
Feed: see text
Cyclic rate: 500rpm
Muz vel: 2,300ft/sec (701m/sec)

The Japanese Army was the first in the world fully to appreciate the potential of automatic weapons on the battlefield, as they demonstrated during their many successes against the Russians in the Russo-Japanese War of 1904/5. Such successes were, however, achieved using foreign weapons and it was not until 1922 that the first indigenously designed light machine gun appeared. This was officially known as the Type 11, but is also often referred to as the "Nambu" after the army general who was responsible for small arms development at the time. The Type 11 was an air-cooled, gas-operated gun with a finned barrel, but one of its oddities was the feed system, in which, instead of magazines or belts, it used a large hopper on the left-hand side of the gun, which contained six five-round chargers of the type normally used by the infantryman to load his rifle. The six chargers were held down by a strong spring-loaded arm and on the backward action of the gun a sliding ratchet drew the rounds into the gun, discarding the clip as it did so. The theory behind this arrangement was that any infantryman could contribute loaded chargers to the hopper, thus overcoming the need for belts or magazines. But experience showed that the hopper accumulated mud and dust, which it then pushed through the mechanism causing very heavy wear. This was overcome by introducing a less powerful round, but this meant that the infantryman now had to carry two different types of round, one for his rifle and one for the machine gun, thus getting away from the original intention of the system. The Type 91 was a version of the Type 11 for use in tanks.

TYPE 91 6.5MM — JAPAN

Length (gun): 42.0in (1,066mm)
Barrel: 19.2in (488mm)
Weight (gun): 24.4lb (11.0kg)
Caliber: 6.50mm
Rifling: 4 grooves, r/hand
Operation: gas-piston
Capacity: 50-round hopper
Muz vel: 2,300ft/sec (701m/sec)

The Type 91 light machine gun was fielded in 1931 and was a tank version of the Type 11 infantry LMG. It used the same type of hopper-feeding system, but in a larger size, taking 50 rounds in clips. This seems to have been a somewhat pointless exercise, since the ability to accept infantrymen's clipped ammunition simply did not exist in a tank, while the restricted space in a turret made refilling the hopper a complicated task. Then, in a curious reversal, most of these Type 91s were removed from tanks and returned to the infantry, who mounted a rather inelegant cranked butt stock, bipod, and x1.5 telescopic sight (shown in the top photo of weapon without its wooden stock). The Type 91 fired the 6.5 x 51SR Arisaka round, and was rather heavy for an LMG, weighing 24.4lb (11.0kg) compared to 22lb (9.9kg) for the British Bren.

TYPE 96 — JAPAN

Length (gun): 41.5in (1,054mm)
Barrel: 21.7in (553mm)
Weight: 20.0lb (9.1kg)
Caliber: 6.5mm
Rifling: 4 grooves, r/hand
Operation: gas
Feed: 30-round box
Cyclic rate: 550rpm
Muz vel: 2,400ft/sec (732m/sec)

The Type 96 was introduced in 1936 as a replacement for Type 11. At this time the Japanese were engaged in more or less continuous warfare with their ancient enemies the Chinese, and as usually happens extensive practical experience led to a number of improvements being incorporated in the new gun. It was still of basic Hotchkiss design, to which the Japanese usually remained faithful, one of the principal differences from its predecessor being the abolition of the inefficient system of charger loading by hopper and the substitution of a more orthodox top-mounted box magazine. It still fired the rather unsatisfactory 6.5mm cartridge but the oil pump was situated in the magazine loader and thus completely divorced from the gun itself, which was a considerable improvement. The gun also had a quick system for changing barrels which did something to help its capacity for sustained fire without overheating. It had a carrying handle and a distinctive one-piece butt and pistol grip combined, and would take the standard infantry bayonet, although this was largely to demonstrate the offensive spirit, since a 20lb (9.1kg) gun makes a poor basis for a thrusting weapon, particularly for the Japanese who although strong and wiry tend to be of small physique. Perhaps its oddest feature was the frequent incorporation of a low-powered telescopic sight, which is not usually considered to be of great value on an automatic weapon.. The cartridge used was still the reduced charge pattern used in the previous gun, which must have continued to cause complications over resupply of ammunition.

TYPE 99 — JAPAN

Length (gun): 46.5in (1,181mm)
Barrel: 23.6in (600mm)
Weight (gun): 23.0lb (10.4kg)
Caliber: 7.7mm rimless
Rifling: 4 grooves, r/hand
Operation: gas
Feed: magazine (30 rounds)
Cyclic rate: 850rpm
Muz vel: 2,350ft/s (715m/sec)

Japanese experience fighting the Chinese in Manchuria in 1936 highlighted a number of problems with the newly-introduced Type 96 light machine gun and work began in 1937 to produce a new weapon based on the Type 96 but without the need for lubricating the cartridges. This resulted in the Type 99 which fired a new and better round, the 7.7mm Arisaka rimless round, which was fed from an overhead magazine containing 30 rounds. There was also a new method of adjusting the headspace and this, together with the new round, did away with the need for lubrication. The Type 99 had finned barrel and a bipod, but also had a monopod under the butt, which, at least in theory, could be used in conjunction with the bipod to enable the weapon to be fired on fixed lines, although in practice vibration soon shook it off target. Like the Type 96, the Type 99 could be fitted with a bayonet, in line with the Japanese Army's very aggressive tactics, which required light machine gunners to accompany the riflemen in a charge, firing a complete magazine as they did so, and finishing by using the bayonet on any surviving enemy. Large numbers of Type 99s were abandoned by the Japanese following their defeat in 1945 and were left all over South-East Asia. The Chinese Army collected many of these and modified them to take the standard Russian-pattern 7.62mm round. The bottom photo shows the break-down of parts for paratroop use.

DAEWOO 5.56MM K3 LMG — ROK (SOUTH KOREA)

Length (gun): 40.6in (1,030mm)
Barrel: 21.0in (533mm)
Weight (gun): 15.1lb (6.9kg)
Caliber: 5.56mm
Rifling: 6 grooves, r/hand
Operation: gas-piston
Feed: belt or magazine
Cyclic rate: 850rpm
Muz vel: 3,000ft/sec (915m/sec)

The weapons industry in South Korea expanded with great speed from the 1970s onwards and the K3 was the first indigenously designed light machine gun, being designed to fire the NATO 5.56 x 45mm M193 and SS109 rounds, and outwardly at least it bears a resemblance to the Belgian FN Minimi. The weapon fires on full automatic only and can be fired either from the integral bipod or from an M122 tripod. The gas regulator can be adjusted between three positions, giving rates of fire between 700 and 1,000 rounds per minute. Feed is from either a 200-round, metal link belt or a 30-round box magazine mounted on the left of the gun.

DEGTYAREV PAKHONTNYI (DP) — RUSSIA

Length (gun): 50.3in (1,290mm)
Barrel: 23.8in (605mm)
Weight: 20.5lb (9.3kg)
Caliber: 7.62m
Rifling: 4 grooves, r/hand
Operation: gas
Feed: 47-round box
Cyclic rate: 500rpm
Muz vel: 2,730ft/sec (849m/sec)

This gun was put into limited production in 1926 and after two years of exhaustive trials was adopted for service by the Soviet Army; its full title was Ruchnoi Pulemyot Degtyaryeva Pakhotnyi which literally translated means "Automatic Weapon, Degtyaryev, Infantry," but is abbreviated to DP. The original gun was of simple construction and contained only 65 parts, having been designed for manufacture and assembly by semi-skilled labor. The gun had some defects, principally in its very large bearing surfaces which caused undue friction in action; its susceptibility to dirt; and overheating. The earliest guns had finned barrels to help dissipate the heat, but this problem was never fully overcome except by restricting the rate of fire. The gun was used extensively in the Spanish Civil War (1936–39) as a result of which certain improvements eliminated its worst faults. The gun worked by tapped-off gas impinging on a piston and driving it to the rear, taking with it the bolt, which was then forced forward again by the action of the compressed return spring. The feed system was reasonably efficient, with a large flat single-deck drum, although its very size and thinness naturally made it susceptible to damage. Unlike the drum on the British Lewis gun, the Degtyaryev magazine was not driven by the action of the gun, but by an integral clockwork mechanism in the magazine itself. he magazine capacity was originally 49, but this was found to be excessive, and it was necessary to reduce it by two. The modified guns (of which the one illustrated is an example) had removable barrels, and the mainspring was placed in its own sleeve below the receiver and which suffered from the effects of heat. The gun worked on the open bolt system and fired automatic only. The weapon gave good service in World War II and was used in Korea and Vietnam.

RUCHNOI PULEMYOT DEGTYARYEV (RDP) — RUSSIA

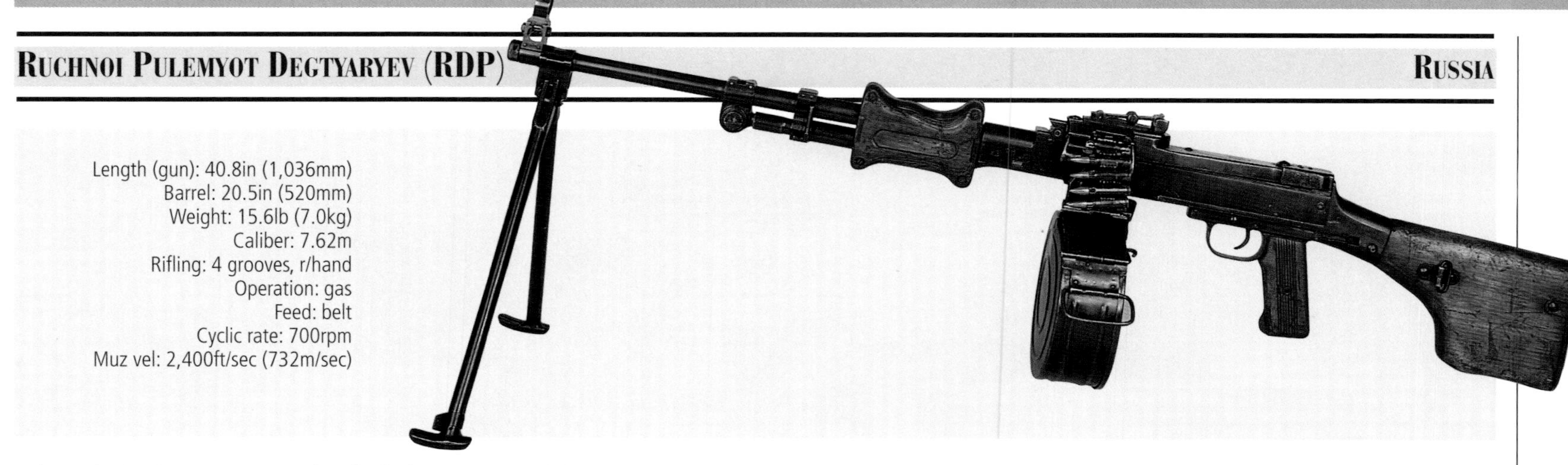

Length (gun): 40.8in (1,036mm)
Barrel: 20.5in (520mm)
Weight: 15.6lb (7.0kg)
Caliber: 7.62m
Rifling: 4 grooves, r/hand
Operation: gas
Feed: belt
Cyclic rate: 700rpm
Muz vel: 2,400ft/sec (732m/sec)

The Ruchnoi Pulemyot Degtyaryev (RPD)'s chief merits were its lightness and simplicity of working. Like its predecessor from Degtyaryev, it was gas-operated, with the bolt locked by means of hinged lugs, which were normally retained flush with the body of the bolt, but which were forced outwards into recesses in the receiver so as to lock the breech at the instant of firing. The gun was belt fed, each belt holding 50 rounds. Belts could easily be connected to each other or could be coiled tightly and fitted into a sheet metal drum (see picture). The gun was fitted with a rotatable gas regulator, had a fixed barrel, and would fire only automatic, overheating being avoided by the gunner ensuring that he did not exceed 100 rounds a minute. The first model had a reciprocating cocking handle which worked backwards and forwards with the piston, the latter having a hollow head which fitted over the gas spigot. The second model revised the piston head arrangements and added protectors for the backsights, while the third model finally incorporated a folding, non-reciprocating handle and a much needed dust cover over the ejector opening. It was not, however, until the fourth model that any significant change was made; the power of the gun had always been marginal as regards its capacity to move a fairly heavy belt, so the size of the piston was significantly increased in an effort to improve this. The RPD was produced in vast numbers throughout the Cold War and is still used in many smaller countries and by guerrillas. It was produced in China as the Type 56.

RUCHNOI PULEMYOT KALASHNIKOVA (RPK) — RUSSIA

Length (gun): 40.5in (1,029mm)
Barrel: 23.3in (592mm)
Weight: 11.0lb (5.0kg)
Caliber: 7.62m
Rifling: 4 grooves, r/hand
Operation: gas
Feed: 30 or 40-round box or 70-round drum
Cyclic rate: 600rpm
Muz vel: 2,410ft/sec (735m/sec)

As will be seen from the photograph this weapon is essentially similar in general appearance to the AK47 assault rifle, from which it was in fact developed by the original inventor, the prolific and highly successful designer Kalashnikov. Its principal external differences are its very characteristic club butt and its appreciably longer and heavier barrel. It is equipped with a bipod, fitted well forward and designed to be folded back and held by a clip when not required as a support. The weapon is gas-operated; when the first, manually loaded round is fired part of the gases pass through a vent in the barrel and thence into the cylinder visible above it, where they strike and force back the piston. The initial rearward action of the piston causes the bolt locking lugs to rotate anti-clockwise, thus allowing the breech to open, after which the bolt continues to the rear with the piston compressing the return spring as it does so. The power of the gas having been exhausted, the return spring takes over and drives the mechanism forward, and during this phase the bolt strips a round from the magazine and forces it into the chamber. It then stops, but the piston continues sufficiently to cause the locking lugs to engage with the locking shoulders after which the striker is free to fire the round and the cycle continues. There is a change lever on the right hand side of the receiver above the trigger. The RPK takes the same 30-round magazine as the rifle or a drum holding 75 rounds.

CIS 5.56MM ULTIMAX 100 — SINGAPORE

Length (gun): 40.3in (1,024mm)
Barrel: 20.0in (508mm)
Weight (gun): 10.8lb (4.9kg)
Caliber: 5.56mm
Rifling: 6 grooves, r/hand
Operation: gas-piston
Feed: 20/30-round boxes; 100 round drum
Cyclic rate: 500rpm
Muz vel: 3,182ft/sec (970m/sec)

The Ultimax 100 was fielded in 1982 and is in service with the Singapore Armed Forces and several other armies, including at least one in Europe. Entirely of Singaporean design, the Ultimax 100 has a rotating bolt, uses the open bolt position, and fires automatic only, at a rate which can be varied between 400 and 600 rounds per minute by use of the three-position gas regulator. Feed is from either 20- or 30-round box magazines or a clockwork-powered 100-round drum. The bipod is positively locked in either up or down positions and allows 30-degree movement without adjusting the feet. The barrel is designed for quick changes and two models are available, the normal barrel being 20.0in (508mm) long, but this can be replaced by a short "Para" barrel 12.9in (330mm) long for use by special forces or in tight spaces. The weapon can also be fired without the butt, if necessary, and is fitted (unusually for an LMG) with a forward pistol grip.The Markj III version is shown in the photo at left.

Vektor 7.62mm SS-77 GPMG/5.56mm Mini-SS — South Africa

Length (gun): 45.5in (1,155mm)
Barrel: 21.7in (550mm)
Weight (gun): 21.2lb (9.6kg)
Caliber: 7.62mm
Rifling: 4 grooves, r/hand
Operation: gas piston
Feed: belt (metal link)
Cyclic rate: 750rpm
Muz vel: 2,756ft/sec (840m/sec)

The South African company, Vektor, has produced a series of weapons designs, all of them based on some 30 years of combat experience by the South African Army in various campaigns in southern Africa. Most of them were also produced to overcome the effects of the international arms embargo which was imposed prior to the end of apartheid. The Vektor SS-77 general-purpose machine gun was one of these weapons and was designed around the NATO 7.62mm round; it entered service in 1985. The SS-77 was not fitted with a gas regulator, which meant that the cyclic rate could not be varied, but eased the maintenance requirements. The 7.62mm SS-77 could be converted into the Mini-SS (pictured) to take the new NATO standard 5.56mm round by means of a relatively simple kit. This consisted of a gas piston; feed cover; 5.56mm barrel, which was chrome-plated and included a new style flash suppressor; and a new integral bipod. The total weight of these new components was no more than 8.1lb (3.7kg). A folding butt was optional. Both weapons could be fired from their bipod or from a tripod for use in the sustained fire role.

Santa Barbara 5.56mm Ameli — Spain

Length (gun): 38.2in (970mm)
Barrel: 15.8in (400mm)
Weight (gun): 11.4lb (5.2kg)
Caliber: 5.56mm
Rifling: 6 grooves, r/hand
Operation: gas
Feed: magazine or belt
Cyclic rate: 900rpm
Muz vel: 2,870ft/sec (875m/sec)

The Spanish Ameli light machine gun is produced by the Santa Barbara company, which is named after the patron saint of artillerymen. The Ameli, which appeared in 1981, was designed around the NATO 5.56 x 45mm round and uses a delayed blowback system with a two-part bolt, similar to that used in all Spanish automatic weapons for many years. Feed is by magazines holding either 100 or 200 rounds or by a disintegrating metal link belt. Unusually among modern light machine guns, the Ameli has a slotted barrel jacket, which incorporates the foresight and carrying handle and flash suppressor.

Lewis Machine Gun — UK

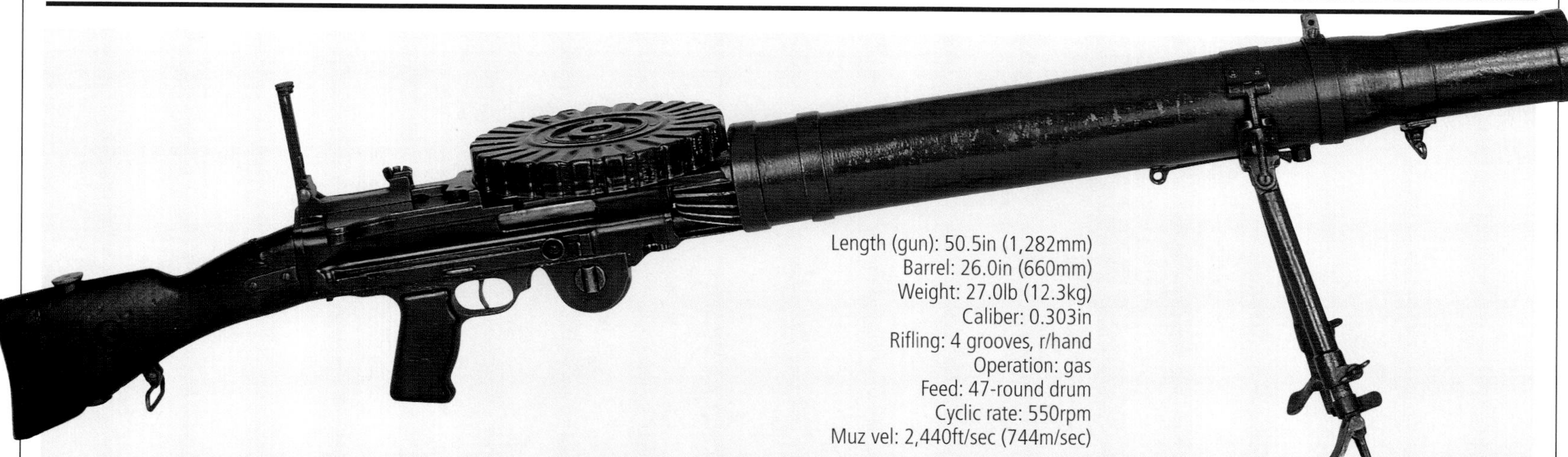

Length (gun): 50.5in (1,282mm)
Barrel: 26.0in (660mm)
Weight: 27.0lb (12.3kg)
Caliber: 0.303in
Rifling: 4 grooves, r/hand
Operation: gas
Feed: 47-round drum
Cyclic rate: 550rpm
Muz vel: 2,440ft/sec (744m/sec)

Colonel Isaac Newton Lewis of the US Coast Artillery offered his gun to the US Army but it was rejected in 1912 and he set up a factory in Belgium. This was overrun in 1914 and the business was handed over to the British Small Arms Company. The principle on which the gun worked was simple. Gases were tapped off from the barrel to drive back a piston, which took the bolt with it, extracting and ejecting the empty case. A stud on top of the bolt also activated a feed arm which took the next round from the double-layer, circular magazine on top of the gun, the mechanism being equipped with two stop pawls which ensured that the magazine rotated the correct amount only. During this backward movement a rack on the underside of the piston engaged a pinion which wound a clock-type spring which took over, driving the working parts forward and chambering and firing the round. The bolt was of the turning variety with lugs which locked into recesses in the barrel extension. In order to keep the barrel cool it was surrounded by radial fins, the ends of which are visible in the illustration, these being surrounded in turn by a light outer-casing to keep the whole thing clean. The gun was designed to fire automatic only, but a good gunner with a sensitive trigger finger could often fire single rounds, while "double tapping" (firing two rounds at a time) was very simple. The Lewis was also used as an aircraft weapon, being flexibly mounted and with a different sight system clamped on, and fired by the observer.

HOTCHKISS MARK 1 — UK

Length (gun): 46.7in (1,187mm)
Barrel: 23.5in (597mm)
Weight: 27.6lb (12.2kg)
Caliber: 0.303in
Rifling: 4 grooves, r/hand
Operation: gas
Feed: 30-round strip
Cyclic rate: 500rpm
Muz vel: 2,440ft/sec (744m/sec)

In 1915 the British cavalry needed a light machine gun and selected the French Benet-Mercie which was put into production as the Hotchkiss Machine Gun Mark 1. It was of course manufactured to take the British 0.303in cartridge. The Mark 1 operated in the usual way by the action of gas tapped off from the bore and striking a piston to which the breechblock was attached. The forward action of the mechanism under the impulse of the return spring caused the bolt to turn and lock into a fitting, forming part of the barrel extension and known by its French term of fermeture nut. The cocking handle was a long rod, and its rear end, which was basically similar in appearance to a rifle bolt, can be seen just above the pistol grip in the photograph. It was pulled back to its full extent (almost 6in/152mm) to cock and then forced forward again. When it was fully home it could then be turned to the right until a line on it coincided with either A, R, or S on the receiver which gave automatic fire, rounds only, or safe as required. It was considered best to use both hands to cock the gun. The Hotchkiss gun was also a tank gun. It remained in service with cavalry units until World War II and the fixed guns were not discarded until 1946.

BEARDMORE-FARQUHAR EXPERIMENTAL — UK

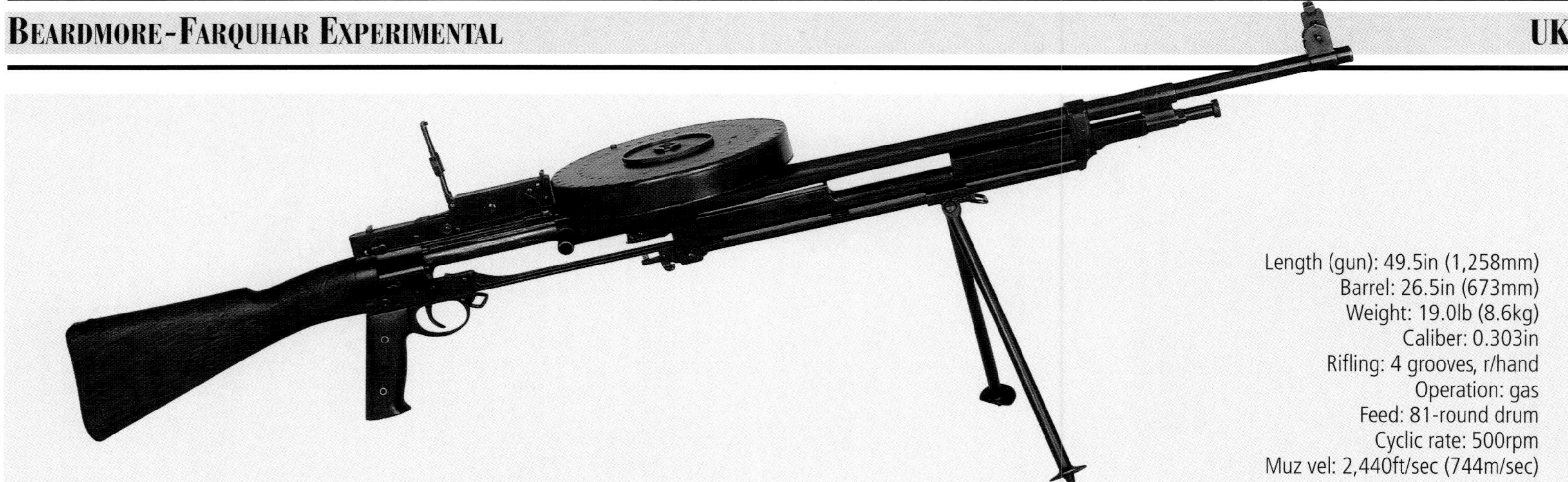

Length (gun): 49.5in (1,258mm)
Barrel: 26.5in (673mm)
Weight: 19.0lb (8.6kg)
Caliber: 0.303in
Rifling: 4 grooves, r/hand
Operation: gas
Feed: 81-round drum
Cyclic rate: 500rpm
Muz vel: 2,440ft/sec (744m/sec)

The Beardmore-Farquhar Experimental light machine gun of 1923 was based on a most unusual mixture of gas and spring operation. Virtually all orthodox gas-operated light machine guns have a piston which is driven back by the pressure of gas tapped off the bore near the muzzle, taking the breechblock with it, and which is then driven forward by the energy stored in the return spring which it has compressed on its rearward travel. The Beardmore was unusual in that the piston was not directly connected to the bolt. Instead of an operating rod, there was a coil spring and when the piston moved back it compressed this spring. The other end bore against the bolt and this bolt was so designed that the pressure of the gas helped to keep it locked. When the pressure had dropped to a safe level the piston spring overcame the bolt locking and the usual reciprocating motion began. When the bolt reached the buffer it tripped the piston sear and the return spring could then force bolt and piston forward again to repeat the cycle. The usual feed action took place on the forward stroke, but another peculiarity was that the return spring was stretched, and not compressed as on all other guns. One consequence of this was a smooth action with much less likelihood of stoppages and extraction problems. But it also had a much slower rate of fire than its rivals. This weapon was officially tested in late 1922, but while it had some good features its overall performance was poor and it was not developed further.

Vickers-Berthier

UK

Length (gun): 46.5in (1,181mm)
Barrel: 23.9in (607mm)
Weight: 20.8lb (9.4kg)
Caliber: 0.303in
Rifling: 5 grooves, r/hand
Operation: gas
Feed: 30-round box
Cyclic rate: 500rpm
Muz vel: 2,440ft/sec (744m/sec)

This gun was designed by a French officer, Lieutenant André Berthier, in 1908 but failed to win any orders. In the early 1920s the British firm of Vickers bought the manufacturing rights for Berthier guns and began to make a modified version of the 1908 model. A few small countries purchased the gun and this just about allowed Vickers to keep their factory going. The British Government was at that time considering the adoption of a new machine gun and in 1925 Vickers demonstrated the gun to the Small Arms Committee and, apart from some minor points, it was reported as being efficient and referred to as a serious rival to the Browning Automatic Rifle which was also being considered at the time. Two more guns, complete with spare barrels and accessories were bought and at the end of this series of tests the Vickers-Berthier came out best. A new entry, the Czech ZB, was second, with the Danish Madsen third and the BAR in fourth place. Next year there were further tests, the stated need being for a gun which could fire 1,500 rounds in 15 minutes and 5,000 in 30, and the general opinion was that the Vickers-Berthier could be improved to this standard. In 1933 one of the prospective customers, the Indian Army, became impatient and settled unilaterally on the Vickers-Berthier Mark 3 as a replacement for the Lewis gun, but the British Army was more cautious and decided to go on with the testing. In 1934 the final endurance trials were held and the Czech gun began to demonstrate its unmistakable superiority. Had it not been for the sudden appearance of the ZB gun, the Vickers-Berthier might well have been adopted as the standard British gun.

Bren

UK

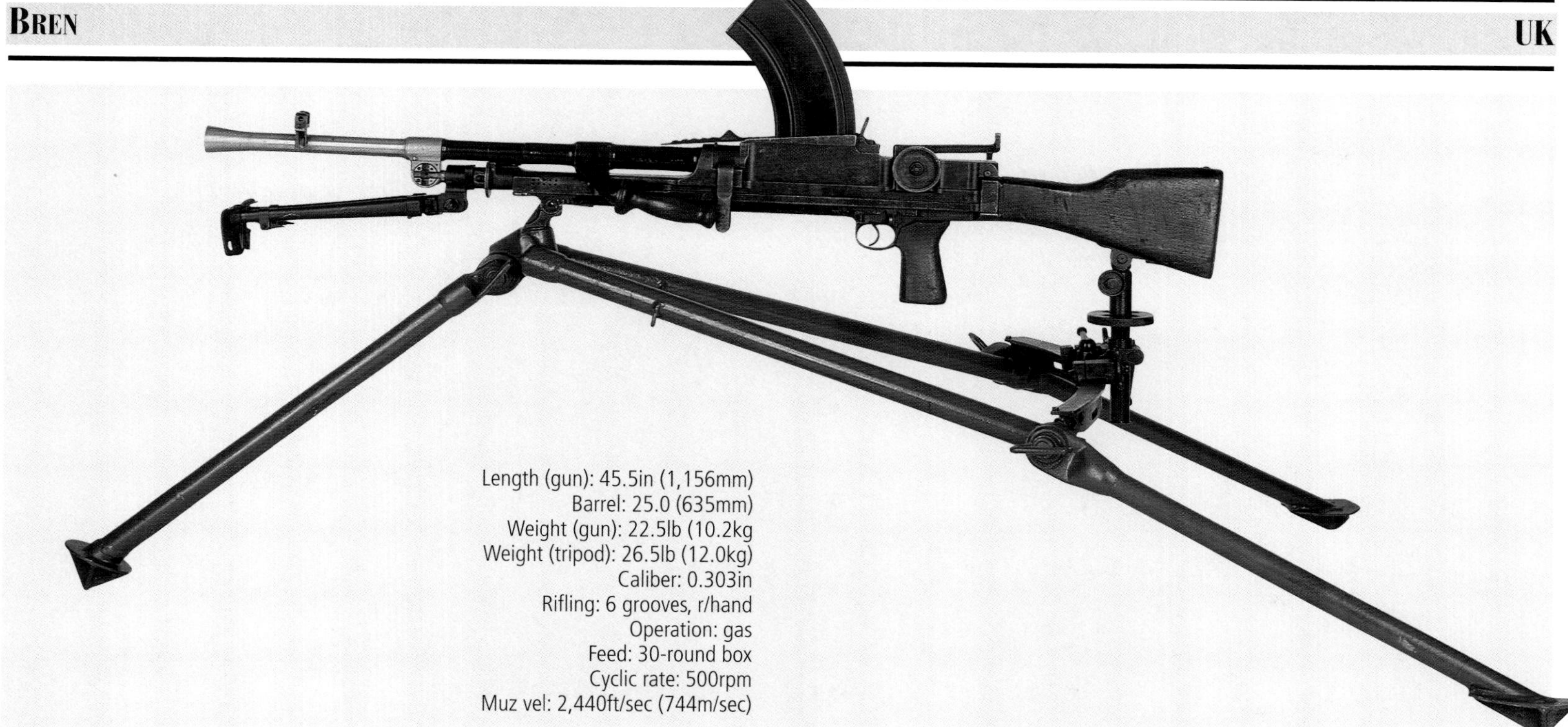

Length (gun): 45.5in (1,156mm)
Barrel: 25.0 (635mm)
Weight (gun): 22.5lb (10.2kg
Weight (tripod): 26.5lb (12.0kg)
Caliber: 0.303in
Rifling: 6 grooves, r/hand
Operation: gas
Feed: 30-round box
Cyclic rate: 500rpm
Muz vel: 2,440ft/sec (744m/sec)

The Bren gun was developed from the Czechoslovakian ZB 26 in the mid-1930s and its basic mechanism was similar to that of its Czech prototype. It was designed for either single rounds or bursts, this being controlled by a change lever, the trigger pull being noticeably longer for single rounds than for automatic fire. There was a rather elaborate backsight with a drum and a pivoted lever carrying the aperture, and because the magazine was top-mounted the sights were offset to the left. Each gun had a spare-parts wallet containing a combination tool and small replacement parts, and a holdall containing cleaning kit and the second barrel which could be put on to the gun in two or three seconds. Although the magazine capacity was nominally 30 it was soon found that this was too many, and the total was reduced to 28, but even then meant that rimmed cartridges magazines had to be loaded carefully and the commonest stoppage on the gun, fortunately easy to clear, was caused by careless loading. As shown in the picture the Bren could be mounted on a tripod for firing on a fixed line. The Bren proved to be a most reliable and efficient gun and all who used it had great confidence in it. When Great Britain adopted the standard 7.62mm NATO round a number of the later marks of Bren were converted to fire it. Designated L4A1 to L4A6, these are readily recognizable by the absence of the cone-shaped flash hider and the straight magazine, the latter being made necessary by the rimless NATO round.

BESAL MK 2 — UK

The Bren gun, adopted by the British in the 1930s, was a precision instrument with a complicated production process. Thought was therefore given to a gun based on the Bren but requiring much simpler production processes. The individual who finally produced the answer was H. Faulkener, chief designer for the famous Birmingham Small Arms Company, who abandoned all thought of milling and machining and turned, instead, to pressings, pinnings, spot welding, and a variety of other inelegant but effective means of speeding up manufacturing processes. The body was made entirely of pressings, riveted and spot welded with a non-adjustable bipod fitted over a sleeve at the forward end. The barrel, although robust and well rifled, was roughly finished externally, with a handle, a simple tubular flash hider, and a foresight on a bracket. The gas passed to the piston through a simple flanged gas regulator which could be turned by the point of a bullet and was held in place by a pin suspended by a link chain from the foresight block. The piston held the return spring; as the piston blew back, the end of the return spring frame was held firmly by a vertical pin, the milled head of which can be seen below the breech, thus allowing the spring to be compressed. The backsight consisted of an L-shaped flip for 300 and 500 yards (275 and 457m). There were two Marks which differed in their method of cocking. In addition, the Mark 1 had a skeleton butt and the Mark 2 (seen here) had a solid butt. In the event, the BESAL did not go into production.

GPMG L7A1 AND L7A2 — UK/BELGIUM

The British carried out a series of trials in the late 1950s to find a new machine gun firing the newly adopted NATO standard 7.62mm round. The winner was the Belgian FN MAG (Mitrailleur á Gaz). The first guns used by the British Army were made in Belgium, but later they were made at the Royal Small Arms Factory at Enfield. This involved certain modifications to conform with British manufacturing processes but there were no fundamental changes made to the gun, which remained substantially as it had been in its original state. The British-made gun is designated the L7A1, but is generally referred to as the GPMG. The new gun, like many original FN products, owes a great deal to the patents of the American John M. Browning, an American and one of the most prolific and most successful designers in the field of firearms that the world has ever seen. It is gas-operated with a bolt locking system similar to the original Browning Automatic Rifle of 1917, its feed mechanism being virtually identical to that the German MG42, as is its trigger. The original idea was to have two different barrels for the gun, a plain steel one for the light role and a heavy barrel with a special liner for the sustained fire role, but the latter was abandoned. Other versions include: L8A1 (co-axial gun in tanks); L37A1 (for use in vehicles or on the ground); and L2OA1 (for use in helicopters). The L7A2 model (in photographs) has modified trigger and feed mechanisms, fitting of a belt box to the left side, and other minor changes.

Browning Automatic Rifle 1918A2 — USA

Length (gun): 48.0in (1,220mm)
Barrel: 24.0in (610mm)
Weight: 19.5lb (8.9kg)
Caliber: 0.30in
Rifling: 4 grooves, r/hand
Operation: gas
Feed: 20-round box
Cyclic rate: 350 or 600rpm
Muz vel: 2,800ft/sec (855m/sec)

John M. Browning demonstrated his "Automatic Rifle" in February 1917. This new weapon weighed just under 16lb (7.25kg) and was correctly described as a rifle, since its general appearance and handling qualities allowed it to be used in that role; indeed, the first models had no bipods. Strictly speaking it would probably be described in modern terminology as a squad automatic weapon. Much of Browning's original work on the automatic rifle, which was of normal gas and piston operation, had been done at the Colt factory, but Winchester also gave a good deal of assistance later. Manufacture started early in 1918, the final total production being in excess of 50,000. The BAR was received with great enthusiasm by the Allies, none of whom had a weapon of quite the same type, and they were ordered in large numbers, France alone asking for 15,000. Model 1918A, like the original, was able to fire bursts or single rounds as required, and also had a bipod. The next change came in 1940 with the introduction of yet another variation, the Model 1918A2, which had a light bipod attached to the tubular flash hider. One interesting variation on this model was the fact that, although it would fire bursts only, it incorporated a selector which would allow two cyclic rates, the higher being some 600 and the lower being 350 rounds per minute. The BAR was used by many countries and was made in Belgium as the Herstal. A number were sold to Great Britain in 1940 and were used to arm the Home Guard, where they gave good service but caused some problems over caliber. The BAR Model 1922 was used by the US Cavalry and had a heavier, finned barrel, a bipod, and a butt rest; it fired automatic only.

Browning Model 1919A4 — USA

Length (gun): 41.0in (1,041mm)
Barrel: 24.0in (610mm)
Weight (gun): 31.0lb (14.0kg)
Weight (tripod): 14.0lb (6.4kg)
Caliber: 0.30in
Rifling: 4 grooves, r/hand
Operation: recoil
Feed: belt
Cyclic rate: 500rpm
Muz vel: 2,800ft/sec (854m/sec)

The Browning Model 1919A2 was developed for the US Cavalry and from it was developed the Model 1919A4, a sort of general purpose light machine gun which, with minor changes in mounts, could be used in tanks and armored cars, as a multiple anti-aircraft gun, and in a ground role. The mechanism of this gun was substantially similar to that of the Model 1917 water-cooled Browning, working by the recoil power of the barrel which in a brief rearward thrust unlocked the breechblock and sent it to the rear, extracting the case as it did so. The force of the compressed return spring provided the motive power for the forward action in which a new round was stripped from the belt, chambered, and fired. It had a heavy barrel enclosed in a light perforated outer casing. Feed was by means of a woven fabric belt holding 150 rounds with brass tags at each end to facilitate loading. At normal operating temperatures the gun maintained an actual rate of fire of 60 rounds per minute for up to 30 minutes without any serious problems of overheating. The weapon had a single pistol-type grip, very similar in shape and appearance to that of the Colt revolver, and its trigger, which had no guard, protruded almost horizontally from the rear of the receiver. When used in the ground role the gun was mounted on the standard M2 tripod. The gun was simple to handle and reliable in use, the few stoppages to which it was liable being easy to deal with. The lower photo shows the improved model, M1919A6, with rifle-type butt and pistol grip, and flash hider.

CRANSTON & JOHNSON MODEL 1941 — USA

Length (gun): 42.3in (1,074mm)
Barrel: 22.0in (558mm)
Weight (gun): 14.3lb (6.5kg)
Caliber: 0.30in
Rifling: 4-grooves, r/hand
Operation: recoil
Feed: box magazine
Cyclic rate: 600rpm
Muz vel: 2,800ft/sec (853m/s)

The M1941 was developed from a rifle design by former US Marine Corps Captain Melvin Johnson and was manufactured in limited numbers by the Cranston Arms Company, Rhode Island. Prototypes appeared in the late-1930s and the first order came from the Dutch East Indies Army, although no deliveries were made prior to the Dutch defeat in 1941. Samples were then offered for US Army tests and a limited number were procured for field trials in 1942, equipping one Marine battalion in the Pacific and the First Special Service Force (1SSF) in Italy, total orders amounting to about 650 weapons. Johnson had prepared his designs in close collaboration with World War I veterans, his basic idea being for a rifle capable of rapid aimed fire (it was often used as a sniper weapon in the Pacific at ranges up to 1,000yd/915m), but which could switch to automatic fire when the need arose. The M1941 was noted for its simplicity, ease of handling, accuracy and reliability, and was light for a machine gun: 14.3lb (6.5kg) empty and 15.9lb (7.2kg) with sling and loaded magazine. One unusual feature was that in single-round mode it used a closed bolt, which locked before firing, but in automatic it used an open bolt. It had a quick detachable barrel. It was also designed for ease of manufacture, being produced using conventional lathes and milling machine s. The Mannlicher-type box magazine was on the left side of the weapon and a unique feature was that reloading could be achieved using rifle chargers from the right-hand side without removing the magazine. The automatic firing rate could be adjusted by altering the tension in the buffer spring, with a theoretical maximum of 900rpm. The Johnson appeared in two versions, which differed only in minor details: M1941 had a bipod and a wooden butt (as shown in the photographs, the upper one with bipod folded under); M1944 had a monopod made of light tubing while the butt was fabricated from two parallel pieces of tubing closed by a butt plate. The Johnson machine gun appears to have been a good weapon but as it appeared just after the US Army had decided on the BAR it stood little chance of adoption.

M60 — USA

Length (gun): 43.8in (1,111mm)
Barrel: 25.5in (647mm)
Weight: 23.0lb (10.4kg)
Caliber: 7.62mm
Rifling: 4 grooves, r/hand
Operation: gas
Feed: belt
Cyclic rate: 600rpm
Muz vel: 2,800ft/sec (853m/sec)

The US Army based the design of its first post-war LMG on the best features of the German MG 42 and assault rifle FG 42. The resulting M60 relied largely on stampings, rubber, and plastics, and had a somewhat fussy, cluttered look about it, and it had some unfortunately characteristics. In the first place there was no gas regulator; i.e., the supply of gas was fixed, and outside the control of the firer, and under certain conditions the gun either stopped, or less usually, ran-away. A "run-away" is where the working parts go back far enough to feed, chamber and fire another round, but not far enough to be engaged by the sear so that even when the finger is removed from the trigger the gun goes on firing. This is a disconcerting business, by no means confined to the M60, which could be overcome only by holding on to the belt, and preventing it feeding. The M60 had no system under which single shots could be fired, but with its slow rate it was possible for a good gunner to fire single rounds simply by quick trigger release. No barrel handle was fitted, and as the barrel might well have reached a temperature of 500° Centigrade, great care had to be taken in changing it. An asbestos mitten was issued with each gun but was lost easily in action, in which case any handy piece of rag had to be used instead. One of the best features of the gun was that its barrels were chromium plated and had stellite liners for the first 6in (152mm) from the chamber. The sights on the gun were adequate although the system of zeroing was not. A belt box was supplied when the gun was being used on the move, and a simple, robust tripod was available for the sustained fire role. The M60 was used extensively in Vietnam and partly because of practical experience there it was improved considerably and the resulting weapon issued as the M60E1.

Stoner 5.56mm

USA

Length (gun): see text
Barrel: 21.7in (550mm)
Weight (gun): 10.4lb (4.7kg)
Caliber: 5.45mm
Rifling: 6 grooves, r/hand
Operation: gas
Feed: belt
Cyclic rate: 700rpm
Muz vel: 3,270ft/sec (990m/sec)

Eugene Stoner was responsible for a number of revolutionary weapons in the latter half of the 20th Century, the most famous being the Armalite rifle, which saw world-wide service as the M16. He also, however, designed numerous other weapons, including light machine guns. The Stoner 63 was manufactured by Cadillac-Gage and a later design was prepared for production by ARES. This latter weapon has subsequently been updated to produce the weapon now known as the Stoner 5.56mm LMG. The Stoner LMG is remarkably light, the bare weapon weighing 10.4lb (4.7kg), while it weighs only 16.1lb (7.3kg) loaded with a 200-round belt, which is fed from a 200-round box attached to the left side of the weapon. There are two barrels: one is 21.7in (551mm) long, but the other (shown in lower photograph) is much shorter, 15.6in (397mm), and with this barrel and the detachable butt stock removed overall length is 26in (660mm). The forward grip can be positioned either vertically downwards or at 90 degrees to the left to suit the firer's requirements. Iron sights are standard but there is a mounting on top of the receiver for optical or night sights.

M249 Squad Automatic Weapon (SAW)

USA

Length (gun): 40.9in (1,040mm)
Barrel: 20.6in (523mm)
Weight (gun): 15.1lb (6.9kg)
Caliber: 5.56mm
Rifling: 6 grooves, r/hand
Operation: gas
Feed: metal link or magazine
Cyclic rate: 750rpm
Muz vel: 3,000ft/sec (915m/sec)

The M249 SAW is a development of the Belgian Fabrique Nationale (FN) "Minimi" for the US Army and Marine Corps. Original orders were met from the FN factory but a production line was subsequently established in the USA. The US Army's concept for a Squad Automatic Weapon (SAW) was formulated in the 1960s when a requirement was established for a weapon which would have greater range than the M16 Armalite but would be lighter and easier to handle than the 7.62mm M60 LMG. The weapon selected to meet this requirement was the FN Minimi but with certain minor changes to meet US military and to suit US manufacturing processes, the main external differences being in the shape of the butt and the handguard. The M249 is very smooth in operation and displays an exceptional degree of reliability. Fully combat ready, with a magazine of 200 rounds, bipod, sling, and cleaning kit, the M249 weighs 22lb (9.97kg), which is still 1lb (0.4kg) less than an empty M60! The Minimi can accept either magazine- or belt-fed ammunition without any modification. It is normally fired using the built-in bipod, but a tripod is also available. The FN company also markets a "Para" model with a sliding stock and shorter barrel; it is a little lighter than the standard weapon but is shorter and easier to handle in confined spaces.

Heavy Machine Guns

The search for an automatic weapon which would enable one gunner to emulate the fire of 20 or more riflemen started as early as the 17th Century and took many years to come to fruition. Early attempts centered upon either revolving chambers, as in the Puckle, or multiple revolving barrels, as in the Gatling, but it was the American, Hiram Maxim, who appreciated in the early 1880s that the recoil generated by one cartridge could be used to load the next, and the machine gun was born.

World War I saw machine guns established as one of the most effective weapons on the battlefield and they were manufactured in vast numbers and fired countless millions of bullets. They continued in large-scale use throughout World War II and the campaigns that followed (for example, Korea, Vietnam), although over the past 30 years the tendency has been for ever-lighter and more compact machine guns. One brilliant design, however, the United States' 0.50in M2HB Browning, is still in service after 70 years of use. It is such an effective weapon that it seems set to continue in use for many years to come. Another is the German MG 42, which was developed early in Word War II and is still in service, with various improvements, as the MG3A1.

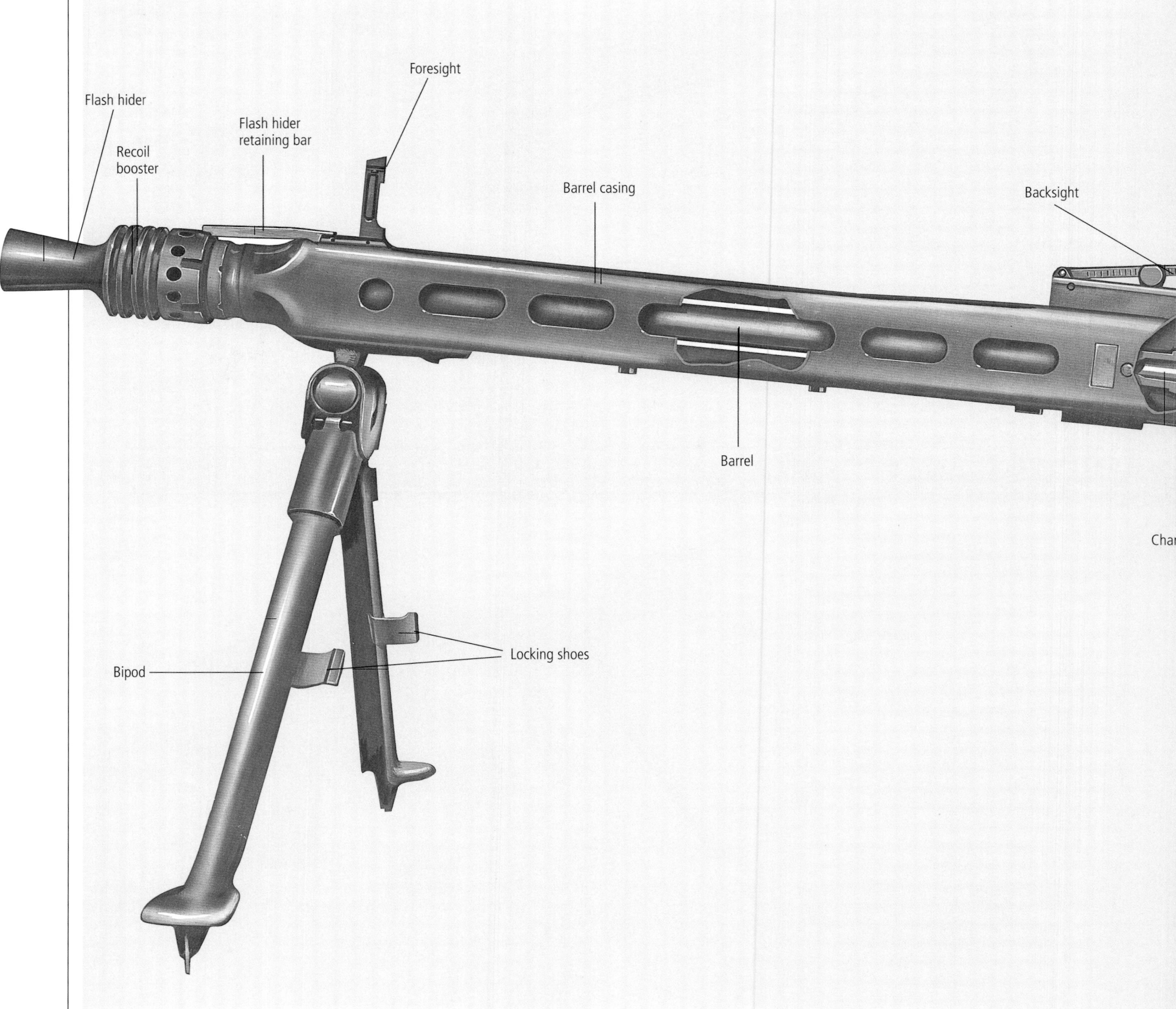

Mauser MG 42 Machine Gun

One of the most feared weapons of World War II, the Mauser Maschinengewehr Model 1942 (MG 42) became the German Army's standard machine gun in the latter part of the war and, in various guises, is still in service with many armies today. It was developed from the MG 34 but was designed to be easier to manufacture, lighter, and to have enhanced performance. Thus, compared to MG 34, the MG 42 had slightly lower muzzle velocity (2,480ft/sec [755m/sec] compared to 2,7800ft/sec [820m/sec]) but it had virtually double the rate of fire (1,200 compared to 650 rounds per minute), giving rise to the characteristic sound which was likened by Allied soldiers to the noise of tearing cloth. The MG 42 was recoil operated, used a roller-locked bolt, and weighed 25.3lb (11.5kg), rather more than the contemporary British Bren Mk 3 which weighed 19.3lb (8.8kg). The MG 42 could also be employed by an infantry squad as a light machine gun, using a bipod (as seen here) or as a medium/heavy machine gun, using a large and complicated tripod, which weighed 42.3lb (19.2kg).

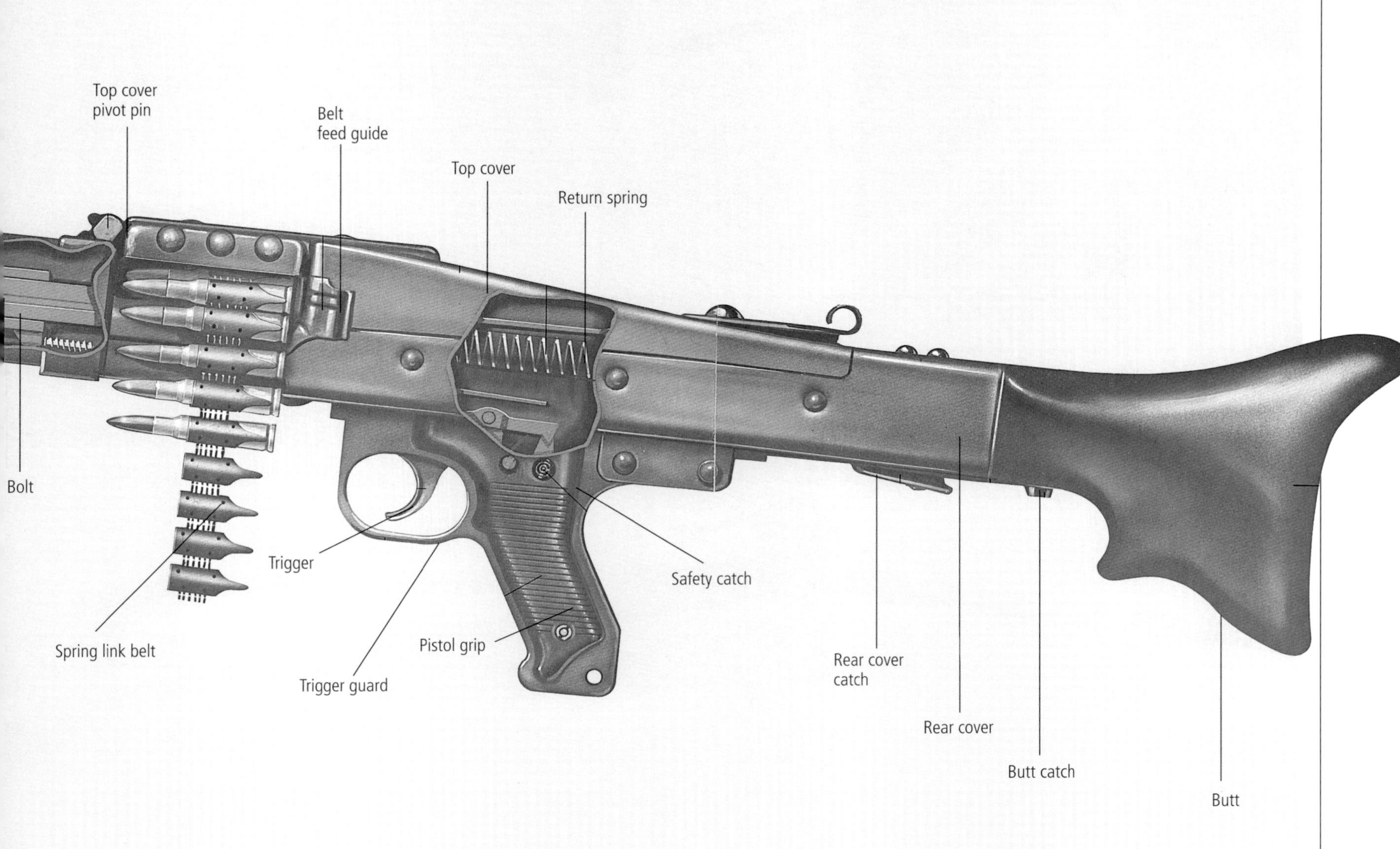

SCHWARZLOSE MASCHINEGEWEHR MODELL 05 — AUSTRIA-HUNGARY

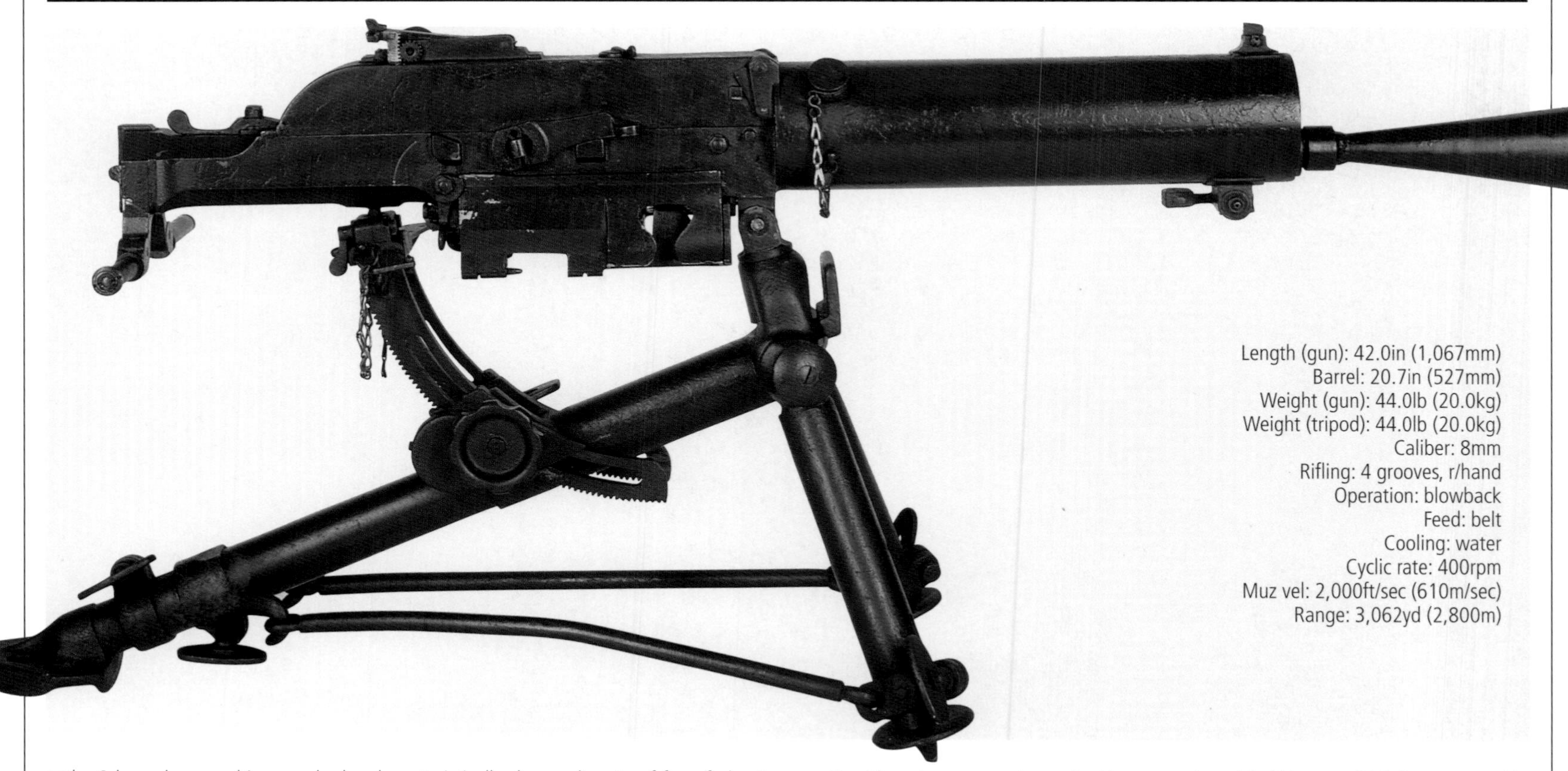

Length (gun): 42.0in (1,067mm)
Barrel: 20.7in (527mm)
Weight (gun): 44.0lb (20.0kg)
Weight (tripod): 44.0lb (20.0kg)
Caliber: 8mm
Rifling: 4 grooves, r/hand
Operation: blowback
Feed: belt
Cooling: water
Cyclic rate: 400rpm
Muz vel: 2,000ft/sec (610m/sec)
Range: 3,062yd (2,800m)

The Schwarzlose machine gun had a characteristically slow cyclic rate of fire of about four hundred rounds per minute. The system of lubricating the cartridge case in order to assist its extraction, although quite widely used in those days, was in many ways an undesirable one, since it was always liable to lead to difficulties in service, particularly in very dry or dusty countries. After some further work Schwarzlose finally succeeded in actually eliminating this feature from his machine gun. This he did by increasing the weight of the breechblock and the strength of the spring, and also by increasing the various mechanical disadvantages working against the bolt during the initial stages of its rearward action. These improvements resulted in a second model of his gun which first appeared in 1912. The new Schwarzlose had proved to be a reliable weapon from the beginning, when two of the early models fired 35,000 rounds each with minimal stoppages and no apparent loss of accuracy. It was also simple to fire and maintain and was soon in service with the Austro-Hungarian Army where it was used with considerable success. The Austrians calculated the fire of a single well-handled gun as being equivalent to that of 80 riflemen. The weapon is now officially obsolete but there may be a few still in use in remote areas of the globe.

NORINCO 12.7MM TYPE 85 — CHINA (PRC)

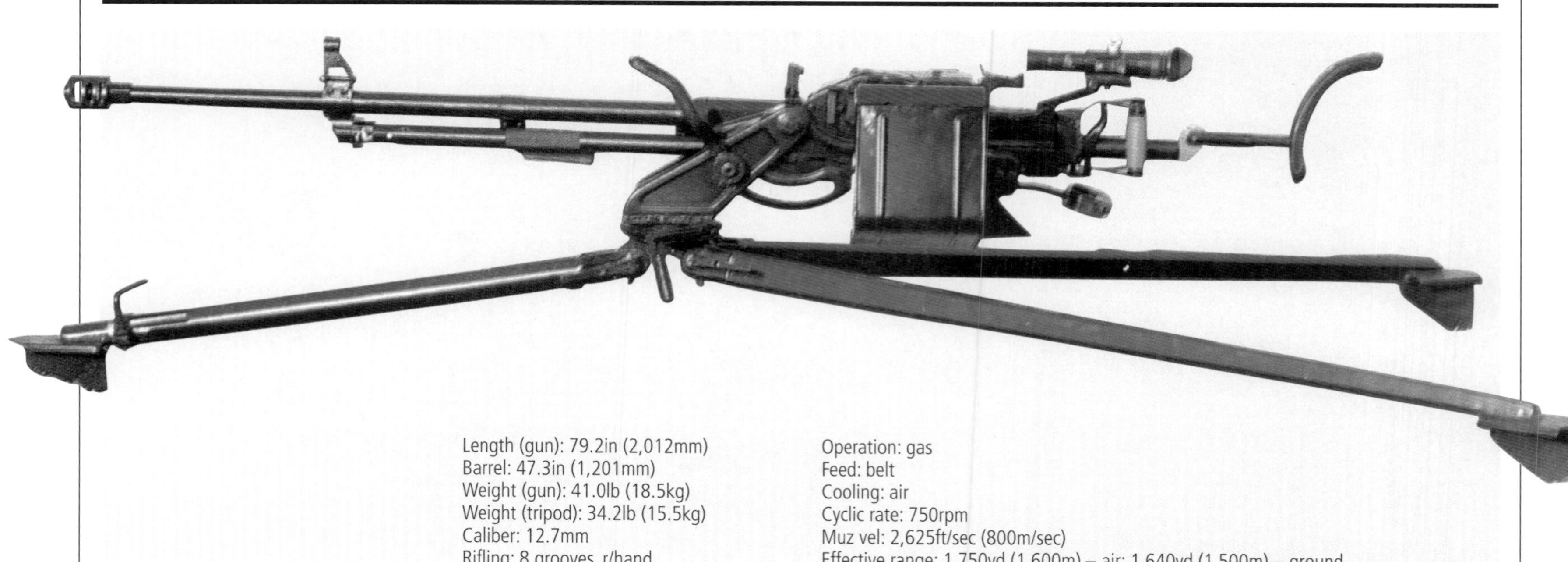

Length (gun): 79.2in (2,012mm)
Barrel: 47.3in (1,201mm)
Weight (gun): 41.0lb (18.5kg)
Weight (tripod): 34.2lb (15.5kg)
Caliber: 12.7mm
Rifling: 8 grooves, r/hand
Operation: gas
Feed: belt
Cooling: air
Cyclic rate: 750rpm
Muz vel: 2,625ft/sec (800m/sec)
Effective range: 1,750yd (1,600m) – air; 1,640yd (1,500m) – ground.

The Chinese Red Army has long placed a strong emphasis on machine guns, particularly heavy types of 12.7mm or 14.5mm caliber, for use in both ground and air defense roles. An early model was the Type 54, which was a direct copy of the Russian DShk produced under license. Two more recent models are, however, Chinese designs. The first was the 12.7mm Type 77, which used an unusual direct-action gas tube, similar in concept to that used in the United States' M16 rifle, which delivered the gas through a tube under the barrel to the forward face of the bolt-carrier, thus driving it to the rear. The most recent weapon is the 12.7mm Type 85, seen here, which is very light, the bare gun weighing only 41lb (18.5kg). The Type 85 uses a new design of tripod, which enables the weapon to be used either as an anti-aircraft weapon or in the ground role, and in the latter case it is especially low. All Chinese 12.7mm machine guns fire the NORINCO Type 54 ammunition, which is available in a variety of types, including armor-piercing discarding sabot (APDS) with tungsten-carbide core for use against lightly armored vehicles such as armored personnel carriers. The Type 85 is belt-fed with the ammunition carried in a metal box on the left side of the weapon. An optical sight is mounted above the spade grips.

Saint-Etienne Modèle 1907

France

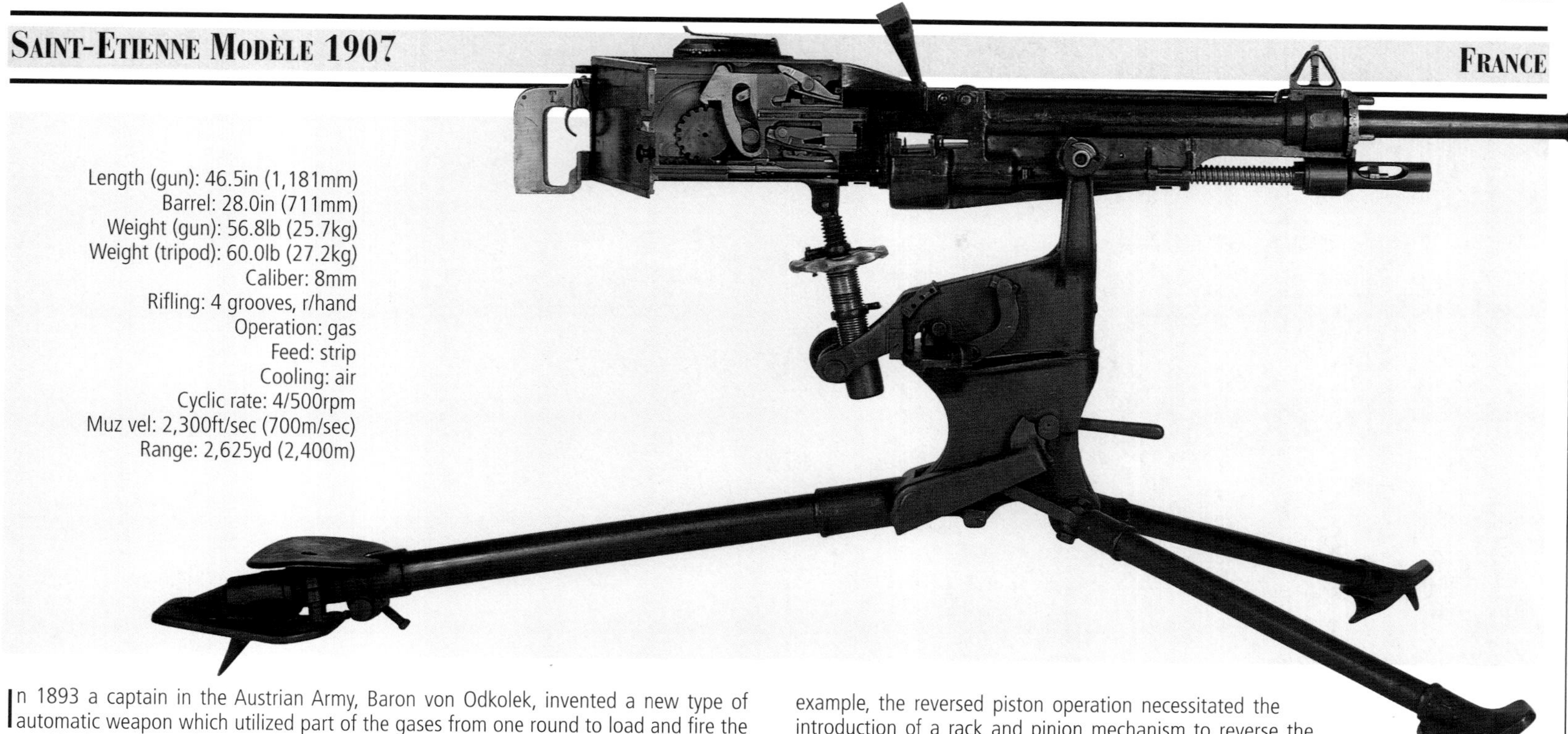

Length (gun): 46.5in (1,181mm)
Barrel: 28.0in (711mm)
Weight (gun): 56.8lb (25.7kg)
Weight (tripod): 60.0lb (27.2kg)
Caliber: 8mm
Rifling: 4 grooves, r/hand
Operation: gas
Feed: strip
Cooling: air
Cyclic rate: 4/500rpm
Muz vel: 2,300ft/sec (700m/sec)
Range: 2,625yd (2,400m)

In 1893 a captain in the Austrian Army, Baron von Odkolek, invented a new type of automatic weapon which utilized part of the gases from one round to load and fire the next. Having no manufacturing facilities of his own he turned to the French gun-making firm of Hotchkiss which showed great interest, not only in the completed weapon which they rightly decided was of quite impracticable design, but in one of its components, the system of tapping gases from the barrel to activate the piston. After many years' work, they produced the weapon illustrated. Although basically of Hotchkiss type, the piston was blown forward instead of backward to activate a mechanism of astonishing complexity. For example, the reversed piston operation necessitated the introduction of a rack and pinion mechanism to reverse the motion again. The mainspring, which was coiled on a steel rod, was largely exposed below the massive brass receiver so as to keep it cool, and the gun was fed by 30-round strips of standard Lebel rifle cartridges. The gun shown is mounted on a 1914 pattern tripod; this was interchangeable with the 1907 pattern, the main obvious difference being the very large brass wheel which was essentially used for clamping the elevating gear in the earlier model.

Hotchkiss Modèle 1914

France

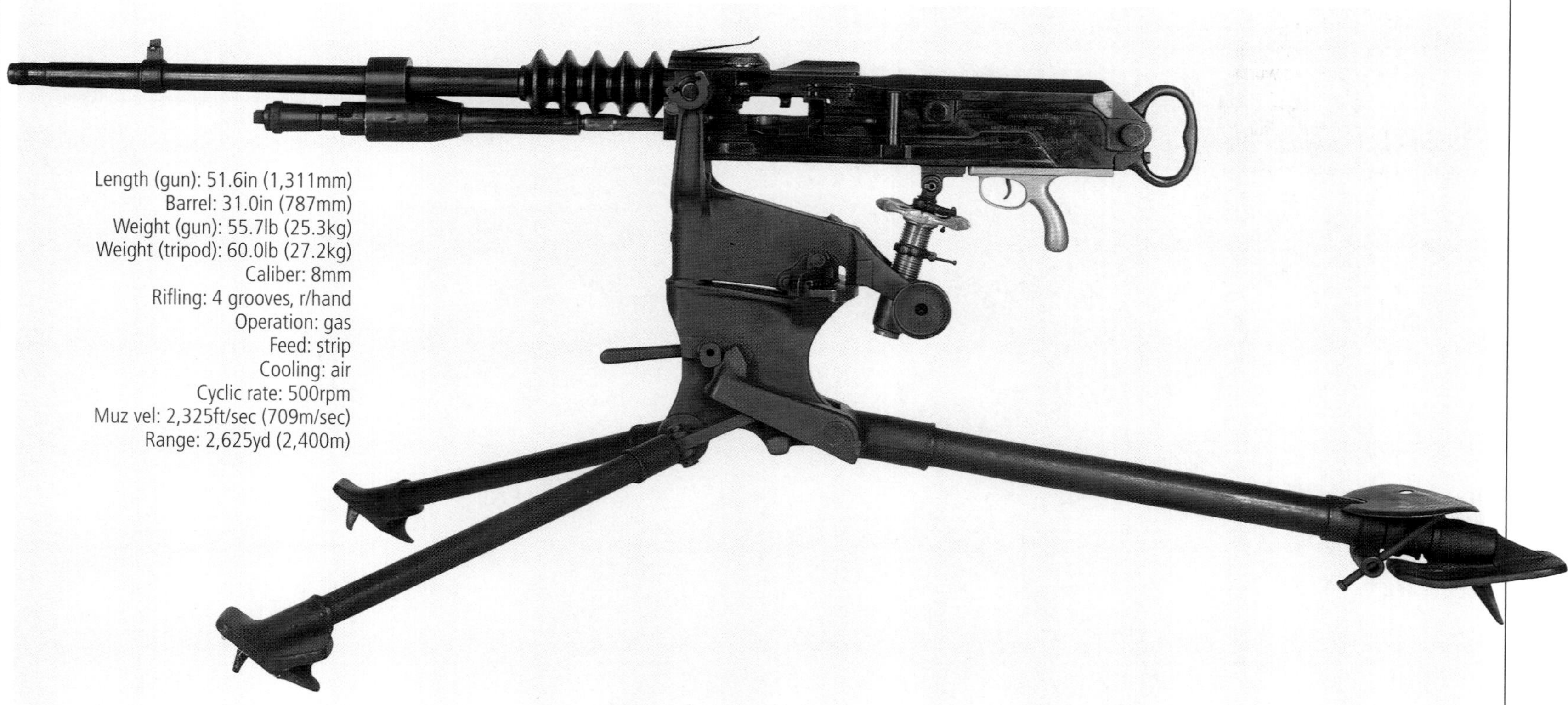

Length (gun): 51.6in (1,311mm)
Barrel: 31.0in (787mm)
Weight (gun): 55.7lb (25.3kg)
Weight (tripod): 60.0lb (27.2kg)
Caliber: 8mm
Rifling: 4 grooves, r/hand
Operation: gas
Feed: strip
Cooling: air
Cyclic rate: 500rpm
Muz vel: 2,325ft/sec (709m/sec)
Range: 2,625yd (2,400m)

In the early 1900s most machine guns were equipped with waterjackets which were efficient but bulky. As the water had to be constantly replaced they posed something of a military problem in areas where water was difficult to procure. The Hotchkiss answer was to encircle the breech end of the barrel with five solid metal discs which increased the radiating surface by more than 10 times its original area. The general shape of these discs, which were about 3.15in (80mm) in diameter, can be seen in the photograph. They helped make the gun an extremely serviceable weapon. In 1900 a United States Army board tested one to compare its performance with a water-cooled gun. The trial was very rigorous and it was found that the Hotchkiss had performed remarkably well. In the Russo-Japanese War (1904–5) the Russians used a water-cooled belt-fed Maxim while the Japanese used a Hotchkiss and both were quite capable of standing up to the demands of modern warfare. In 1914 the French Army found itself in serious difficulties over its relative lack of automatic weapons, which trench warfare quickly showed to be required in vast numbers. Fortunately the reliable Hotchkiss was readily available and manufacture soon started in huge quantities. The earliest models went to reserve units, the regular Army being then largely equipped with the Saint-Etienne 07, but once the Hotchkiss guns began to appear in large numbers they quickly demonstrated their superiority and the French Army clamored for more and more of them. In 1916 two Hotchkiss guns remained in almost continuous action for 10 days during which they fired the astonishing total of over 150,000 rounds without anything worse than brief and easily cleared stoppages. When the US Army arrived in France in 1918 12 of its divisions were therefore equipped with the Modèle 1914 Hotchkiss.

MAXIM MG08 — GERMANY

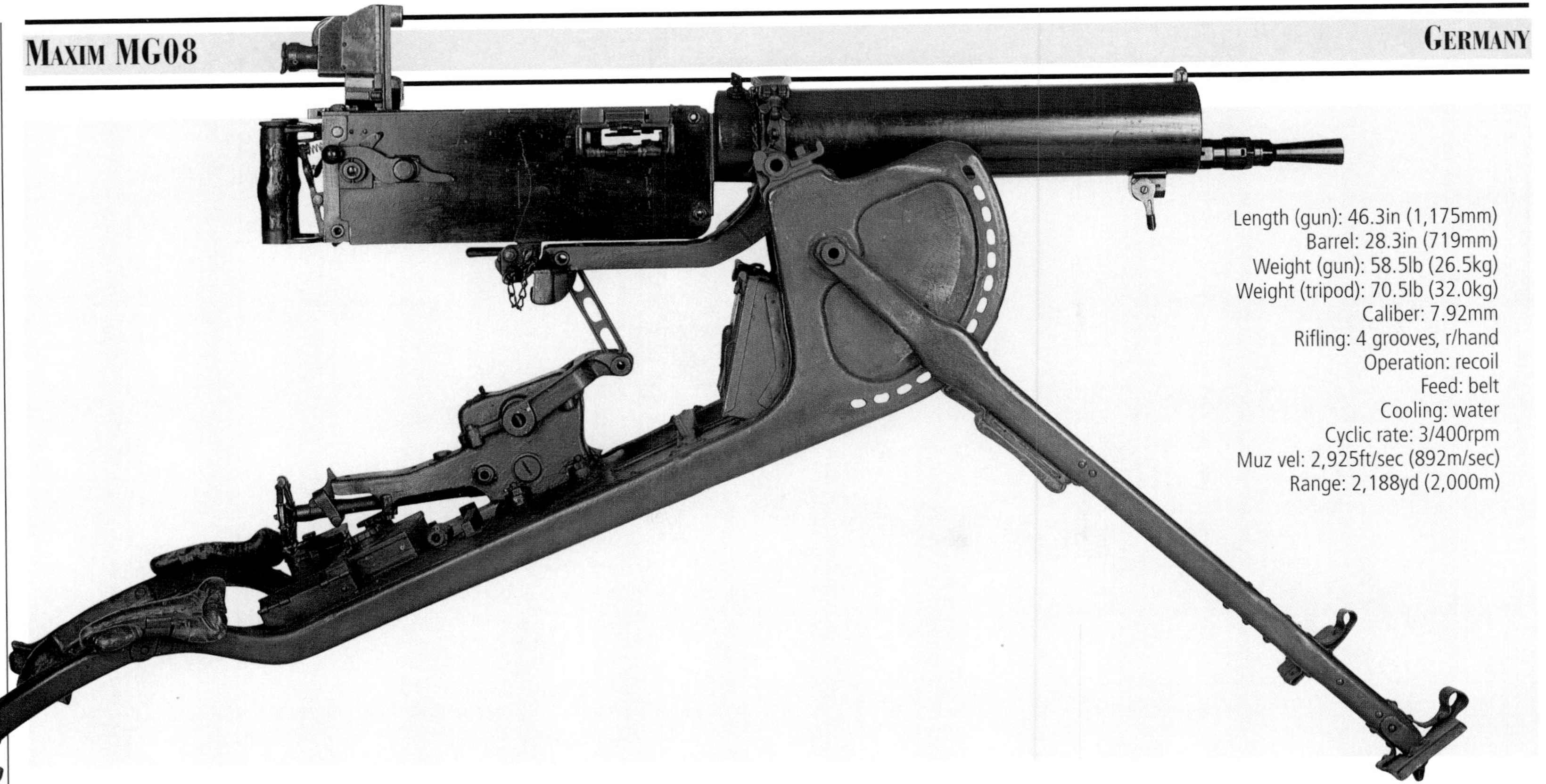

Length (gun): 46.3in (1,175mm)
Barrel: 28.3in (719mm)
Weight (gun): 58.5lb (26.5kg)
Weight (tripod): 70.5lb (32.0kg)
Caliber: 7.92mm
Rifling: 4 grooves, r/hand
Operation: recoil
Feed: belt
Cooling: water
Cyclic rate: 3/400rpm
Muz vel: 2,925ft/sec (892m/sec)
Range: 2,188yd (2,000m)

The Germans, like the British, used machine guns in their colonial wars, but again like the British the German Army had little regard for them as a serious weapon. But the Kaiser watched a demonstration of one of Hiram Maxim's new guns and according to the inventor at once said, "That is the gun – there is no other," and in 1899 a number of Maxim batteries, each of four guns, were tried out at the Imperial maneuvers. Following its success in the Russo-Japanese War, a heavy Maxim gun was developed at the great factory at Spandau and came into service in 1908. The gun itself was of normal Maxim pattern but its mount was distinctly new, for instead of either a wheeled artillery-type carriage or a tripod it had a solid heavy mount based on a sledge. As can be seen from the photograph it was necessary only to elevate the gun and swing the forward legs over it to have it ready to drag along. When the legs were down they could readily be adjusted so that the firers could sit, kneel, or lie down according to the type of cover available. By the end of 1908 every German regiment of three battalions had its own six-gun battery. The guns were carried on light horsedrawn carts and the detachments, usually of four men each, marched, extra vehicles being of course provided for ammunition. The German battery was under the direct hand of the Regimental Commander and similar batteries were provided for the cavalry but these were more mobile, the wagons having four horses instead of two and the detachments being mounted on horses. A modified sledge mount was also introduced at this time which reduced the total weight significantly and allowed the individual guns to be manhandled if necessary, either by carrying or dragging. By the outbreak of war in 1914 the German Army probably had 12 or 13 thousand of the guns in actual service.

MACHINENGEWEHR MG34 — GERMANY

Length (gun): 48.0in (1,220mm)
Barrel: 24.8in (628mm)
Weight (gun): 26.7lb (12.1kg)
Weight (tripod): 42.3lb (19.2kg)
Caliber: 7.92mm
Rifling: 4 grooves, r/hand
Operation: short recoil
Feed: belt or saddle drum
Cooling: air
Cyclic rate: 8-900rpm
Muz vel: 2,480ft/sec (756m/sec)
Range: 2,188yd (2,000m)

The MG34 was designed by Louis Stange, who worked for the firm of Rheinmetall, and Mauser at once set to work to produce the first truly modern machine gun ever to be placed in the hands of the German Army. The new weapon, which appeared in 1934 and which was thus allotted the year of its appearance in its designation, was a remarkable achievement in many respects. It worked by the somewhat unusual combination of recoil and gas; when the round was fired the barrel recoiled, additional thrust being given to this by some of the gases which were trapped in a muzzle cone and deflected backwards. The actual recoil of the barrel was short, just enough in fact for the bolthead to be rotated through 90 degrees and unlocked when the pressure was low enough for this to happen safely. This rearward movement of the bolt continued after that of the barrel had stopped, until the return spring was fully compressed, when the forward action started. This involved the forward movement of the bolt which fed the next cartridge from the belt into the chamber, locked itself, and fired the round. This new gun had many excellent features including a quick means of changing the barrel, easy stripping, and the use of high impact plastics, and unusually it had no change lever. There was simply a two-part trigger which fired single rounds or automatic according to whether the upper or lower part was pressed. The MG34 would fire either a belt, sometimes coiled inside a drum for transport, or a double saddle drum. The upper photo shows the bipod folded under the barrel.

Machinengewehr MG42 — Germany

Length (gun): 48.0in (1,220mm)
Barrel: 21.0in (533mm)
Weight (gun): 25.5lb (11.6kg)
Weight (tripod): 42.3lb (19.2kg)
Caliber: 7.92mm
Rifling: 4 grooves, r/hand
Operation: recoil/gas
Feed: belt
Cooling: air
Cyclic rate: 1,100/1,200rpm
Muz vel: 2,480ft/sec (756m/sec)
Range: 2,188yd (2,000m)

Early in World War II the Germans established a requirement for a gun which would be effective and could be mass-produced without undue strain on their dwindling resources. Once the basic design of the weapon had been established the whole thing was placed in the hands of Dr Grunow, a well-known German industrialist whose particular forte was mass-production by metal stampings, riveting, spot welding and brazing, and any other method not requiring complicated equipment or specialized techniques which called for the use of skilled manpower. The result, based on long experience, high industrial skills, and a great deal of active service experience, was the MG42, one of the finest weapons to come out of World War II. It resembled the MG34, and made use of the same principles of short recoil assisted by gas pressure from a muzzle booster, perhaps its main difference being the way in which the bolt locked. The MG34 had made use of a rotating bolt with an interrupted thread which locked into the barrel extension, but the new gun used a system originally patented by Edward Stecke, a Polish citizen, in which the bolt head carried two small rollers which were held close to the bolt until it was ready to lock when they were forced outwards into grooves in the barrel extension. The firing pin could not move forward between them until they were fully into their grooves which ensured that the bolt was locked at the moment of firing. Once recoil started the rollers hit a cam path which forced them inwards out of their recesses, thus unlocking the bolt and allowing the cycle to continue. The gun fired 50-round belts of the standard 7.92mm cartridge using a new and effective feed system which has since been widely copied. The lightness of the MG42, combined with its particular system of operation, led to a very high rate of fire of about 1,200 rounds a minute which produced a considerable degree of vibration that had some adverse effect on accuracy. The muzzle brake was ingeniously designed to help stabilize the weapon but the problem was never fully overcome. The gun in the upper photo is rare, having special periscope optics, stock and trigger group, allowing the gunner to operate the weapon from a concealed position.

Breda Modello 37 — Italy

Length (gun): 50.0in (1,270mm)
Barrel: 25.0in (635mm)
Weight (gun): 42.9lb (19.9kg)
Weight (tripod): 41.5lb (18.8kg)
Caliber: 8mm
Rifling: 4 grooves, r/hand
Operation: gas
Feed: strip
Cooling: air
Cyclic rate: 450rpm
Muz vel: 2,600ft/sec (793m/sec)
Range: 3,280yd (3,000m)

In 1931 Breda produced a 13.2mm caliber gun which proved to be a sound design and the firm then scaled it down to fire the 8mm Modello 35 cartridge. The mechanism was simple, using a piston worked by gases tapped off the bore. The piston also activated the breechblock which was locked in the firing position by the action of a ramp on the piston which lifted the end of the block into a recess on the top of the body. The gun fired automatic only and it was possible to control its cyclic rate by the use of a gas regulator through which the gases passed on their way to the piston head, which was interchangeable. The need to keep the gas port in its proper place in relation to the gas regulator made it impossible to increase or decrease the headspace, which was therefore somewhat larger than necessary. This naturally gave rise to the risk of ruptured cases, due to the direct lack of support by the breechblock, but Breda overcame this by the familiar method of oiling each case as it entered the chamber by means of a pump. This allowed the case to "float" in the chamber and set back firmly against the block before the pressure got too high. This system of lubricating cartridges was widely used and it is possible that Breda got the idea from the Schwarzlose which they had received in large numbers from the Austrians after the end of World War I. It is not, however, altogether satisfactory and can sometimes cause trouble in hot and dusty climates, although the Italians appeared not to have suffered unduly from this defect in their African campaigns. The gun was air-cooled, and its heavy barrel of 9.7lb (4.4kg) allowed a satisfactory degree of sustained fire without overheating.

TAISHO 14 (TYPE 3), TYPE 92 (LEWIS COPY), AND AIR-COOLED TYPE (1941) — JAPAN

This weapon, also known as the Type 3 (photo, right), was based closely on the French Hotchkiss but used the Japanese 6.5mm round, a poor round of only moderate power, and not well adapted to machine guns because the relative lack of taper of its case caused problems of extraction. The Japanese also had difficulties in adjusting their head space, that is the distance between the base of the round and the face of the bolt. This is very important because if it is too small the breech will not always close, whereas if it is too great the cartridge blows back unsupported and is liable to rupture. The Japanese solved the problem by oiling each round as it was fed into the chamber. This allowed the round to slip back easily and be supported by the face of the bolt before the pressure reached it maximum. In view of the propensity of the earlier Hotchkiss to overheat, the Japanese increased the number of cooling rings so that they extended along the full length of the barrel. As mobility was an important feature in Japanese machine gun tactics, the tripod legs had sockets on them into which carrying handles could be inserted. In 1932 the gun was modified to take the more powerful 7.7mm cartridge, but apart from the barrel and the breech it is almost identical to the earlier version, the chief difference being the abolition of the old spade-grips in favor of a double pistol type. Strangely enough the new version still incorporated a cartridge oiler. This new gun, known as the Type 92 (photo center right), was Japan's standard medium machine gun of World War II. It fired a rather heavy 30-round strip, and due presumably to the inertia of this dead weight, the gun fired its first few rounds rather hesitantly before picking up speed. It was a characteristic sound which made the presence of the gun very easily identified in action. The photo at left shows the Type 92 (Aircraft), a 1932 copy of the Lewis gun (qv) in 7.7mm caliber, shown in anti-aircraft configuration with its 47-round drum magazine in position and a spare drum beneath the weapon. The photo at bottom right is of an air-cooled Type (1941) machine gun, also of 7.7mm caliber, with spade-grips and flash suppressor. Above the barrel are stripper ammunition clips of 7.7mm, complete in their original cardboard packing boxes.

Length (gun): 45.5in (1,155mm)
Barrel: 29.0in (737mm)
Weight (gun): 62.0lb (28.1kg)
Weight (tripod): 60.0lb (27.3kg)
Caliber: 6.5mm
Rifling: 4 grooves, r/hand
Operation: gas
Feed: 30-round strip
Cooling: air
Cyclic rate: 450rpm
Muz vel: 2,400ft/sec (732m/sec)
Range: 2,406yd (2,200m)

DEGTYAREV DSHK-38 12.7MM — RUSSIA

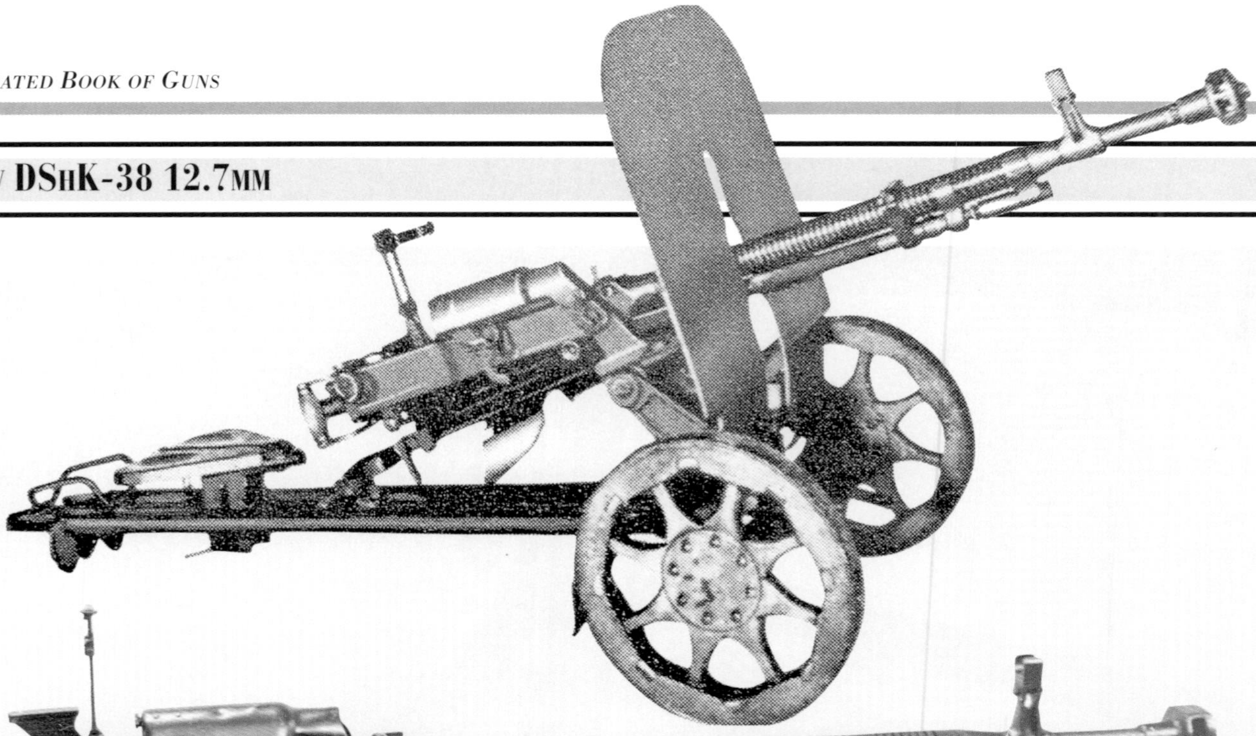

Length (gun): 62.3in (1,582mm)
Barrel: 39.4in (1,000m)
Weight (gun): 73.3lb (33.33kg)
Weight (tripod): n.k.
Caliber: 12.7mm
Rifling: 8 grooves, r/hand
Operation: gas
Feed: belt
Cooling: air
Cyclic rate: 575rpm
Muz vel: 2,805ft/sec (855m/sec)
Max range: n.k.

Designed by Vasily Degtyarev, the Degtyarev-Shpagin DShK-38 12.7mm heavy machine gun entered service in time to be used in vast numbers during World War II and has remained in wide-scale use ever since. The infantry version was normally mounted on a two-wheel chassis, which increased total weight to 368lb (167kg) and the trail legs could be opened out to form a tall tripod for use in the anti-aircraft role. A modified version – DShK-38/46 (lower photo, also known as DShK-M) – appeared after the war and incorporated numerous minor improvements. The most important change was replacing the original rotary ammunition feed system, which was mounted above the receiver, with a much simpler and more reliable lever system. There was also a new and slightly longer barrel and the new weapon was some 5lb (2.3kg) heavier than its predecessor. In the Cold War period the DShK-38/46 was widely used as an air defense weapon in armored fighting vehicles, particularly in all tanks from the T-54 to the T-72, as well as in armored cars and armored personnel carriers. In the earlier turreted installations the commander had to expose his head and upper torso through the hatch in order to fire the weapon but later tanks featured a full remote control facility, which enabled the gun to be fired from under armored cover. The DShK-M was produced in Russia, Czechoslovakia and China, and was supplied to virtually all pro-Soviet armies during the Cold War. It was also supplied to a number of guerrilla movements. The DShK-M was widely used by North Vietnamese and Viet Cong forces during the Vietnam war, where it was known to US forces as the "51-caliber."

GORYUNOV SGM — RUSSIA

The Goryunov SGM entered service in 1942. It was belt-fed and gas-operated, and of simple, robust construction. When the first round was fired a part of the gases passed through a gas port in the barrel and struck the piston which was forced to the rear, taking the slide with it. The first brief movement of the slide unlocked the bolt and allowed the whole to go to the rear, compressing the return spring as it did so. In the course of this rearward action a pair of claws drew the next cartridge from the belt whence it was forced into a cartridge guide in readiness for the bolt to feed it into the chamber on its forward travel. This somewhat complex arrangement was made necessary by the fact that the gun fired a rimmed cartridge which could not therefore be thrust straight forward from the belt, but this action appeared to be efficient. As the bolt approached its forward position, a cam forced it slightly to the right, where it engaged in a recess in the body and was thus locked before the round was fired. This was effective but meant that the face of the bolt had to be recessed at an angle so that it gave proper support to the base of the cartridge. Cooling was achieved by the use of a very heavy barrel with a chromed bore. This barrel could be changed very quickly and therefore allowed the gun to fire almost continuously for long periods without undue overheating. Although a number had been made by 1945 the old Maxim remained in service until the end of the war. The gun illustrated is the modernized version of the Goryunov and has some mechanical improvements. It is, however, fundamentally the same gun, its chief distinguishing feature being the distinctive longitudinal flanging of the barrel to assist cooling.

Length (gun): 44.1in (1,120mm)
Barrel: 28.3in (719mm)
Weight (gun): 29.8lb (13.5kg)
Weight (mount): 50.9lb (23.1kg)
Caliber: 7.72mm
Rifling: 4 grooves, r/hand
Operation: gas
Feed: belt
Cooling: air
Cyclic rate: 650rpm
Muz vel: 2,700ft/sec (823m/sec)
Range: 2,187yd (2,000m)

KPV 14.5mm — Russia

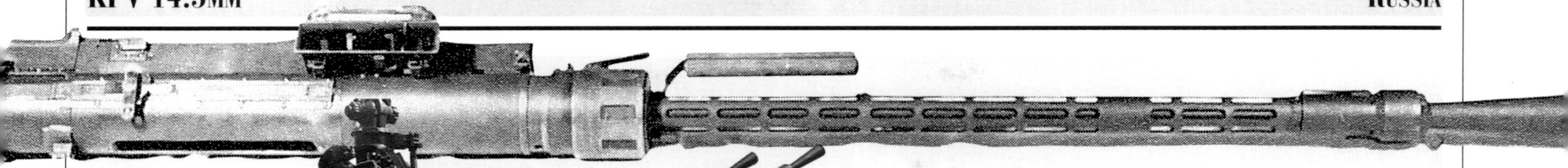

Length (gun): 79.0in (2,006mm)
Barrel: 53.0in (1,346mm)
Weight (gun): 108.2lb (49.1kg)
Caliber: 14.5mm
Rifling: 4 grooves, r/hand
Operation: recoil
Feed: metal link belt
Cooling: air
Cyclic rate: 600rpm
Muz vel: 3,280ft/sec (1,000m/sec)
Max range: 8,750yd (8,000m)

One of the largest caliber true machine guns ever to enter service, the 14.5mm KPV heavy machine gun was designed by Vladimirov and first appeared towards the end of World War II. The KPV was the only weapon ever to use the 14.5 x 114mm Soviet round, which was available in armor-piercing (AP), armor-piercing incendiary (API), and high explosive (HE) versions. The weapon was recoil-operated, with a rotating bolt and an air-cooled, quick-change barrel mounted in a perforated jacket. The mechanism was very simple, with no adjustments for the headspace or timing. The KPV was employed in two principle modes: as a trailer-mounted anti-aircraft weapon, and as a tank-, armored personnel carrier-, or armor car-mounted, dual-purpose (ie, anti-ground/anti-air) weapon. The ground version was mounted on a two-wheeled chassis with either one (ZPU-1) or two (ZPU-2) guns, or on a four-wheeled chassis with a quadruple gun installation (ZPU-4). The latter was widely considered to be a most effective weapon system, since the 14.5mm round had a much heavier "punch" than smaller caliber weapons, the weapon itself was much easier to hide than heavier systems, such as the tracked ZSU-23-4, and the quad installation had a very high rate of fire. In particular, the ZU-series was widely used by the North Vietnamese and Viet Cong, where they were regarded with great respect by US pilots. A new version of this weapon has been developed in Poland. Designated the Pirat, this comprises KPVT, normally used as a coaxial machine gun in tanks, mounted on a newly developed tripod.

NSV 12.7mm — Russia

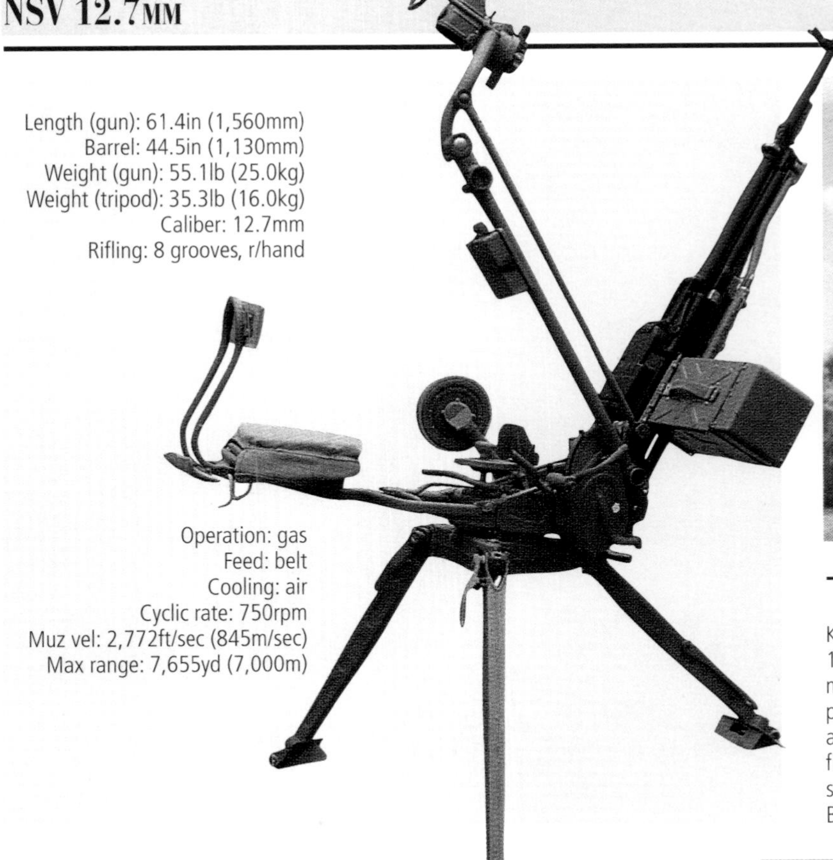

Length (gun): 61.4in (1,560mm)
Barrel: 44.5in (1,130mm)
Weight (gun): 55.1lb (25.0kg)
Weight (tripod): 35.3lb (16.0kg)
Caliber: 12.7mm
Rifling: 8 grooves, r/hand
Operation: gas
Feed: belt
Cooling: air
Cyclic rate: 750rpm
Muz vel: 2,772ft/sec (845m/sec)
Max range: 7,655yd (7,000m)

The NSV used the standard 12.7 x 108mm Russian round and entered service in about 1971. It was basically a scaled-up version of the PKM light machine gun, using the Kalashnikov action,which resulted in a smaller and much lighter weapon than previous 12.7mm weapons and which was also much more reliable. As with other Russian heavy machine guns, it was employed either as a ground weapon, mounted on a tripod, or as a pintle-mounted air defense weapon on tank turrets. It was a gas-operated weapon, using a three-piece bolt with locking lugs, and a quick-change, air-cooled barrel, which was fitted with a carrying handle and a flash hider. The weapon was fitted with either a twin spade grip or a hollow butt. It was manufactured in Russia, and also under license in Bulgaria, Poland, and Yugoslavia.

CIS 0.50IN — SINGAPORE

Length (gun): 66.0in (1,676mm)
Barrel: 45.0in (1,143mm)
Weight (gun): 66.2lb (30.0kg)
Weight (tripod): 51.0lb (23.0kg)
Caliber: 0.50in (12.7mm)
Rifling: 8 grooves, r/hand
Operation: gas
Feed: belt
Cooling: air
Cyclic rate: 600rpm
Muz vel: 2,920ft/sec (890m/sec)
Maximum range: 7,440yd (6,800m)

The State of Singapore has developed an efficient and internationally respected weapons industry from scratch in a little over 20 years. In the early 1980s Singaporean market research identified a continuing requirement for a heavy machine gun and also established that, despite its many merits, the US Browning M2(HB) suffers from some long-standing limitations, including complexity and heavy production costs. The Singaporeans therefore set out to do better and have succeeded. The Chartered Industries of Singapore (CIS) 0.50in MG is simple in design and consists of just 210 separate components in five assemblies: receiver body; feed mechanism; trigger module; barrel group; and bolt-carrier group. The weapon has a rotating bolt and the ammunition feed system uses disintegrating belts which can be fed in from either side. The 0.50in MG fires normal Browning 12.7 x 99mm ammunition, but can also fire the Saboted Light Armor Penetrating (SLAP) round, which was specially developed by CIS.

NORDENFELT MULTI-BARREL VOLLEYGUN — SWEDEN

Length (gun): 41.5in (1,054mm)
Barrels: 28.5in (724mm)
Weight (gun): Two 93.0lb (42.2kg)
Caliber: 0.577in
Rifling: 5 grooves, r/hand
Operation: mechanical
Feed: 27-round, gravity
Cooling: air
Cyclic rate: 300rpm
Muz vel: ca 1,350ft/sec (411m/sec)
Range: n.k.

Although known as "Nordenfelts" after the international arms tycoon, these guns were designed by a Swedish engineer, Palmcrantz, and produced in England in 1898 by the Maxim-Nordenfelt company. Various models with between two and 12 barrels and from 0.303in (7.69mm) to over 1in (25.4mm) were marketed but the principle was identical, with all barrels being loaded simultaneously and then fired in rapid succession. The gunner operated a lever, which on the forward stroke carried the required number of cartridges from an overhead hopper to the breechblock, which then chambered the rounds. A block containing the firing pins then moved in, lined up with the cartridge caps, and as the handle reached the end of the forward stroke, tripped the firing pins in rapid succession. The operator then pulled the handle to the rear extracting the empty cases and restarting the sequence. One effect of firing the barrels in succession was to spread the recoil over a short period of time, thus reducing the vibration in the system. The Nordenfelts had the first-ever armor-piercing round with a hard steel core, and another unusual facility in models with five or more barrels was an "automatic scattering gear." This enabled each barrel to be adjusted manually so that at a range of 300yd (275m) there would be a spread of some 3ft (0.9m) between rounds, which was calculated to cover up to 10 men advancing in line. At 500yd (457m) or more, it was believed that natural dispersion achieved the same effect. Nordenfelts were adopted by England in 1878, being used by both Army and Navy in five and three-barreled versions, and in both 0.45in and 0.303in calibers. These guns were somewhat clumsy in design, but Nordenfelt was a brilliant salesman and managed to get it adopted by a number of European countries. However, it was effective and the twelve-barreled gun, for example, could fire about 4,000 rounds per minute.

Puckle Repeating Gun — UK

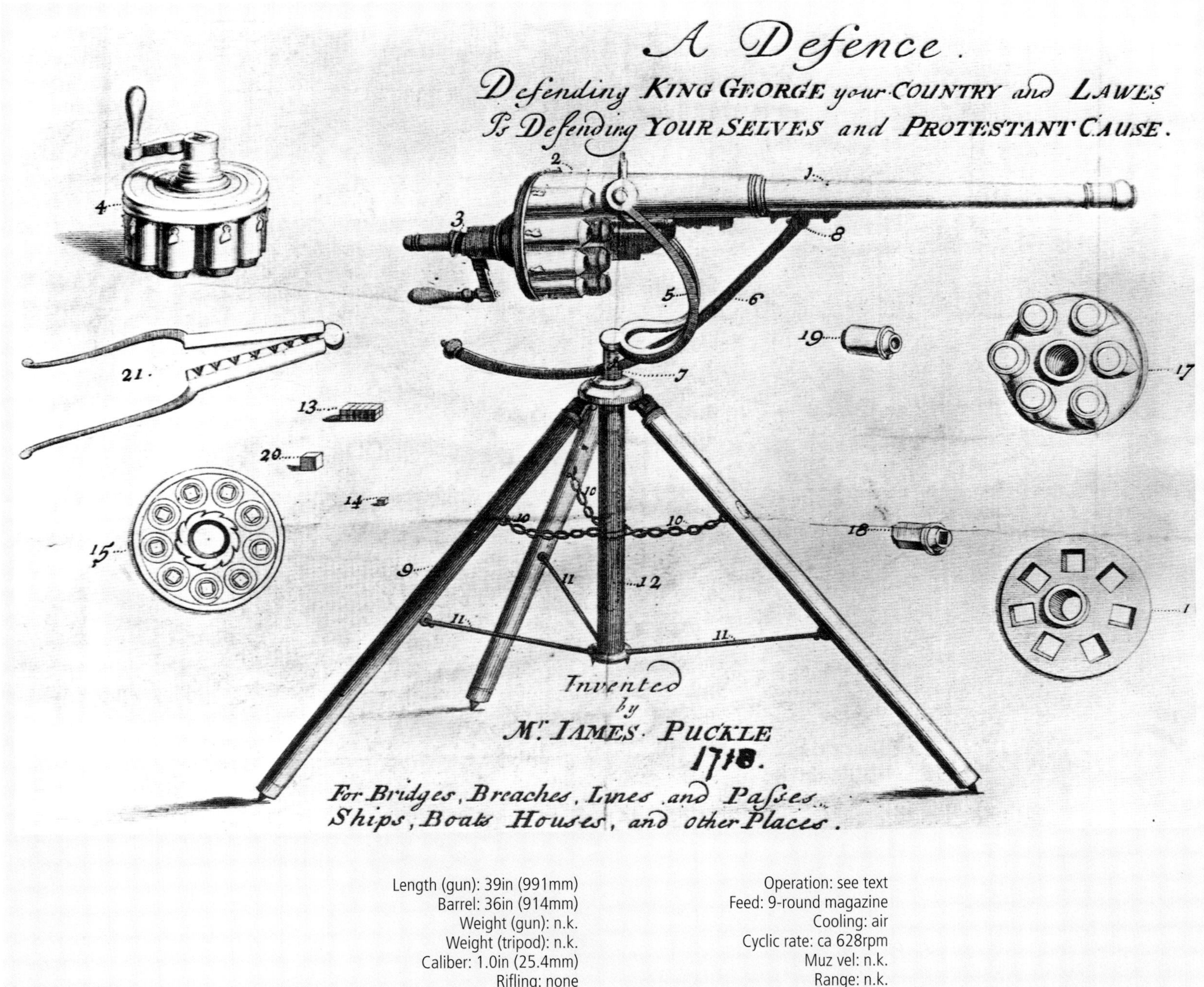

Length (gun): 39in (991mm)
Barrel: 36in (914mm)
Weight (gun): n.k.
Weight (tripod): n.k.
Caliber: 1.0in (25.4mm)
Rifling: none

Operation: see text
Feed: 9-round magazine
Cooling: air
Cyclic rate: ca 628rpm
Muz vel: n.k.
Range: n.k.

The Puckle gun fully merits inclusion as one of the earliest known machine guns. This most unusual weapon was invented by James Puckle, an Englishman, in 1718. At that time a particular problem in naval engagements was to repel boarders, which required a weapon producing a large volume of fire over a relatively short range. The existing weapon was the naval blunderbuss, which certainly propelled a large volume of metal in the general direction of the approaching enemy ship, but was extremely inaccurate, had a very short range and was also very inefficient, since much of its load was scattered at random, with little or no effect on the enemy. The Puckle gun was intended to answer this problem by producing a large volume of fire, but which was much more effective because each round could be aimed. The gun consisted of a single, long, brass barrel, fed by a 9-round, circular magazine which was rotated by a handle. On loading the magazine, the first round was aligned with the barrel, then fired by means of the flintlock, whereupon the magazine was rotated until the next round was aligned, the flintlock was re-cocked, and the second round was fired, and so on. The rate of fire cannot have been high but would certainly have been better than that of a blunderbuss. A note on the drawing above indicates that the machine could be made to discharge grenades as well as bullets. The gun was mounted on a well-designed tripod with metal stays, which gave a firm base, while the cradle allowed the gun to be both elevated and traversed. All this shows that James Puckle had not only a strong imagination, but also that he was a skilled engineer who could translate his ideas into practice, which makes one further feature of the gun rather more difficult to understand. This was that Puckle decided that round bullets were only for use against Christians, and that for engagements against Muslims (for example, in the Mediterranean) square bullets would have to be used! Quite why a man who had the intelligence and imagination to design such an innovative weapon should then come to such and extraordinary and perverse conclusion is not recorded. The Puckle gun certainly worked but was never adopted by either the British Navy or Army.

GARDNER MACHINE GUN, 2-BARREL, 0.45IN — UK

An American, William Gardner, designed a series of mechanically cranked guns between 1874 and 1900. He originally worked for Pratt & Whitney, but although his designs were tested by both the US Army and Navy they failed to attract significant orders, mainly because the Army was already committed to the Gatling. Gardner then moved to England where several of his designs were adopted. The main Gardner design consisted of two barrels placed parallel to each other, 1.25in (32mm) apart; in earlier versions these were supported at both ends, but in later versions were secured at the barrel end only. These were housed inside a bronze casing, through which cooling water could be passed. Each barrel was activated (load, fire, extract) in turn, with a cam system so ordered that one bolt was withdrawn as the other was pushed in. There was a two-man crew, one aiming and cranking the gun, while the second was responsible for the ammunition feed system, ensuring that the rounds fed correctly and topping up the hopper. The Gardner was adopted by the British Royal Navy in 1880 and later also by the British Army, being manufactured for both at the Royal Small Arms Factory at Enfield and used, also by both, in various colonial campaigns. The Gardner gun also continued to be produced by Pratt & Whitney, who sold small numbers of the twin-barreled version to the US Army and a single-barreled version to the US Navy. The original design had two barrels, but once he had moved to England Gardner produced a more ambitious weapon, with five barrels which were mounted side-by-side in a cradle (1882), but this did not enter service.

Length (gun): 47.0in (1,193mm)
Barrels: 30.0in (762mm)
Weight (gun): 218.0lb (98.9kg)
Caliber: 0.45in
Operation: mechanical
Feed: see text
Cooling: air
Cyclic rate: up to 250rpm
Muz vel: n.k.
Max range: 2,000yd (1,830m)

MAXIM GUN — UK

Hiram Maxim (photo, left), born in Maine, USA, moved to England in the 1880s where he designed, built (largely it seems with his own hands), tested, and patented a true automatic gun in which the recoil of the first manually loaded round was used to fire the next. The principle was that the barrel recoiled a short distance before unlocking the breechblock from it and allowing that to continue backwards under the momentum given to it, extending a strong fuzee spring as it did so, and also drawing a cartridge from the belt. When the bolt had reached its most rearward position the extended fuzee spring drew it forward again, so that it chambered and fired the cartridge, after which the process was repeated as long as the trigger was pressed and there were cartridges in the belt. The actual cyclic rate of fire was about 600 rounds per minute, the cartridges being of 0.45in Boxer type loaded with black powder, and the barrel got so hot that it was necessary to surround it with a brass water-jacket. The gun itself was mounted on a rather long tubular metal tripod with a canvas seat for the firer. It was fitted with elevating and traversing gear and was sighted to 1,000 yards (914m). The British Army used the rifle-caliber gun of the type illustrated (mounted on a light two-wheel artillery type carriage instead of the tripod) in its various colonial wars where it proved remarkably effective in breaking up mass attacks of Dervishes and the like. It was best sited on a flank, and because an enormous cloud of grey smoke resulted from its high rate of fire with black powder it was very desirable to position the weapon to take advantage of a good breeze to disperse it.

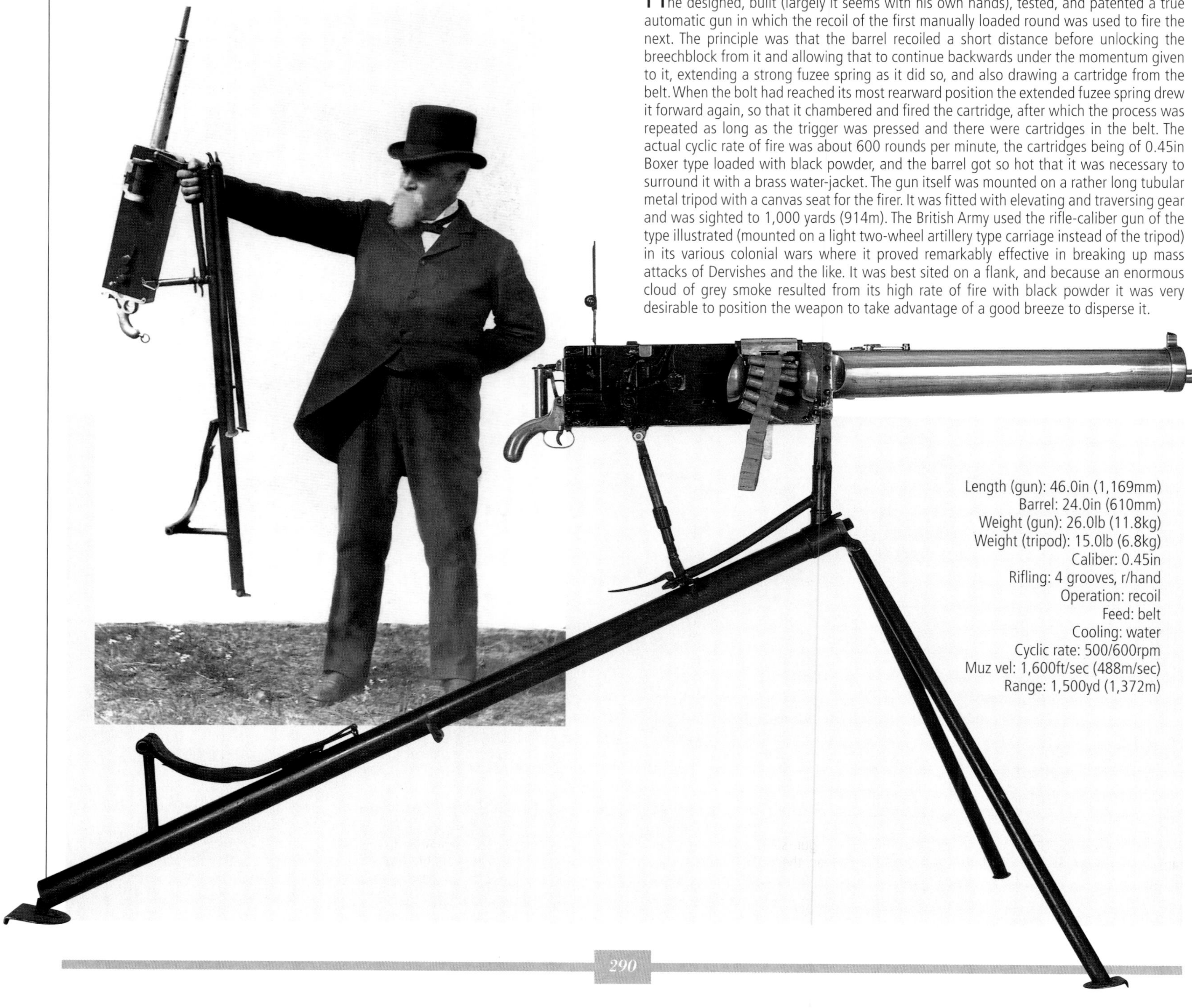

Length (gun): 46.0in (1,169mm)
Barrel: 24.0in (610mm)
Weight (gun): 26.0lb (11.8kg)
Weight (tripod): 15.0lb (6.8kg)
Caliber: 0.45in
Rifling: 4 grooves, r/hand
Operation: recoil
Feed: belt
Cooling: water
Cyclic rate: 500/600rpm
Muz vel: 1,600ft/sec (488m/sec)
Range: 1,500yd (1,372m)

0.303in Vickers-Maxim UK

Length (gun): 42.5in (1,079mm)
Barrel: 26.5in (673mm)
Weight (gun): 60.0lb (27.2kg)
Length (mounting): 75.0in (1,905mm)
Weight (mounting): 178.0lb (80.7kg)
Caliber: 0.303in
Rifling: 4 grooves, r/hand
Operation: recoil
Feed: belt
Cooling: water
Cyclic rate: ca 550rpm
Muz vel: 2,440ft/sec (744m/sec)
Range: 2,900yd (2,652m)

The British Army changed to a new, smokeless propellant, cordite, in 1891 and soon found that the greater heat and pressures necessitated a new type of rifling, so all rifles and machine guns were changed. This change was particularly beneficial to the Vickers-Maxim because, apart from the better range and flatter trajectory, the more powerful propellant naturally increased the recoil and thus the amount of power required to ensure a smooth operation. The new rifle-caliber cordite cartridge gun soon showed its fearful capacity, particularly in the Sudan in 1898. At Omdurman the huge Dervish armies, charging with the most reckless bravery across flat, open desert, sustained hideous casualties in their fruitless attempts to reach the British firing line. The weapon proved somewhat less useful in South Africa but it was in the peculiar conditions of the trench warfare of 1914–18 that it was finally recognized as an indispensable arm for modern warfare. The weapon illustrated has been specially selected because of its "parapet" carriage in which the two horn-shaped projections at the front could be raised and hooked into the top of a wall or earth parapet so that the gun, mounted on a sleeve which could be slipped up and down the central pole as required, could be raised to fire over the defenses with a reasonably wide arc of traverse. The flat circular plate at the rear of the central pole was simply a foot to give the third point of support to the triangle. It had two holes in it of about 1in (25.4mm) diameter so that it could be held rigidly in place by pegs if necessary.

VICKERS 0.303IN

UK

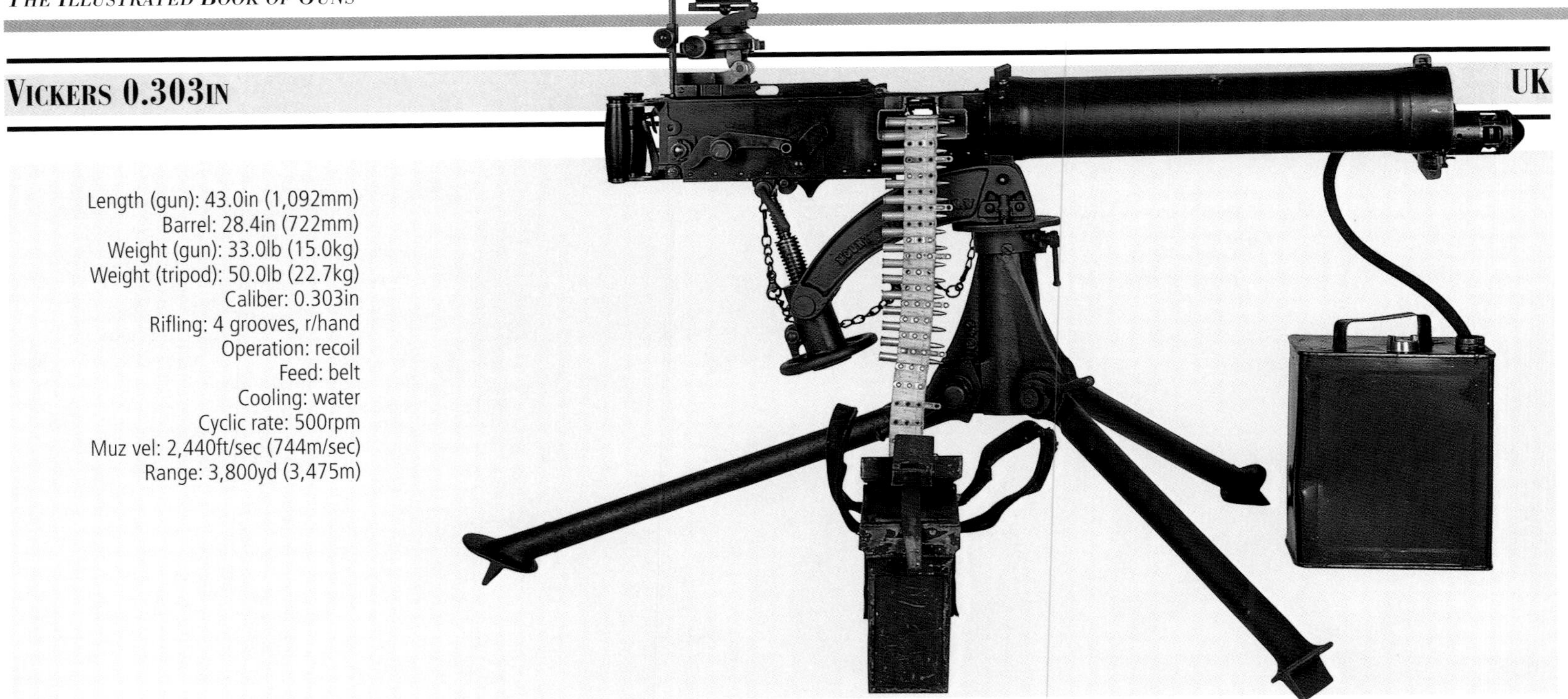

Length (gun): 43.0in (1,092mm)
Barrel: 28.4in (722mm)
Weight (gun): 33.0lb (15.0kg)
Weight (tripod): 50.0lb (22.7kg)
Caliber: 0.303in
Rifling: 4 grooves, r/hand
Operation: recoil
Feed: belt
Cooling: water
Cyclic rate: 500rpm
Muz vel: 2,440ft/sec (744m/sec)
Range: 3,800yd (3,475m)

Mechanically, the Vickers was similar to the earlier Maxim, the rear impulse being produced by recoil supplemented by the action of a muzzle attachment which deflected some of the gas. This thrust the lock backwards taking with it a round from the belt and extending the fuzee spring which was situated in an elongated box on the left-hand side of the gun. The fuzee spring then took over and forced the bolt forward and so the cycle was repeated. The gun had a remarkable capacity for sustained fire but this led to obvious problems of wear. A barrel would last for about 10,000 rounds at 200 rounds a minute, after which the rifling would have been worn away to the stage where the bullet ceased to be spun effectively by it and so lost accuracy very quickly. The barrel could be changed very quickly and as spares were carried this was not a serious problem. The gun was, of course, water-cooled with a jacket capacity of about 7 pints (4 liters). This began to boil after 3,000 rounds of steady fire, about 200 a minute, and thereafter evaporated steadily at the rate of one or two pints for each thousand rounds fired depending on the rate of fire and the climatic conditions at the time. The gun was fitted with a condenser tube leading into an old-fashioned one-gallon petrol can, and if some water was put into the can first and the steam passed through it, a considerable amount of the water lost could be used again, which was an important factor in desert conditions where water was scarce. There were various models of Vickers gun, none very different from the rest. Some water jackets were fluted and some plain, but this does not necessarily indicate a different mark of gun.

BESA

UK

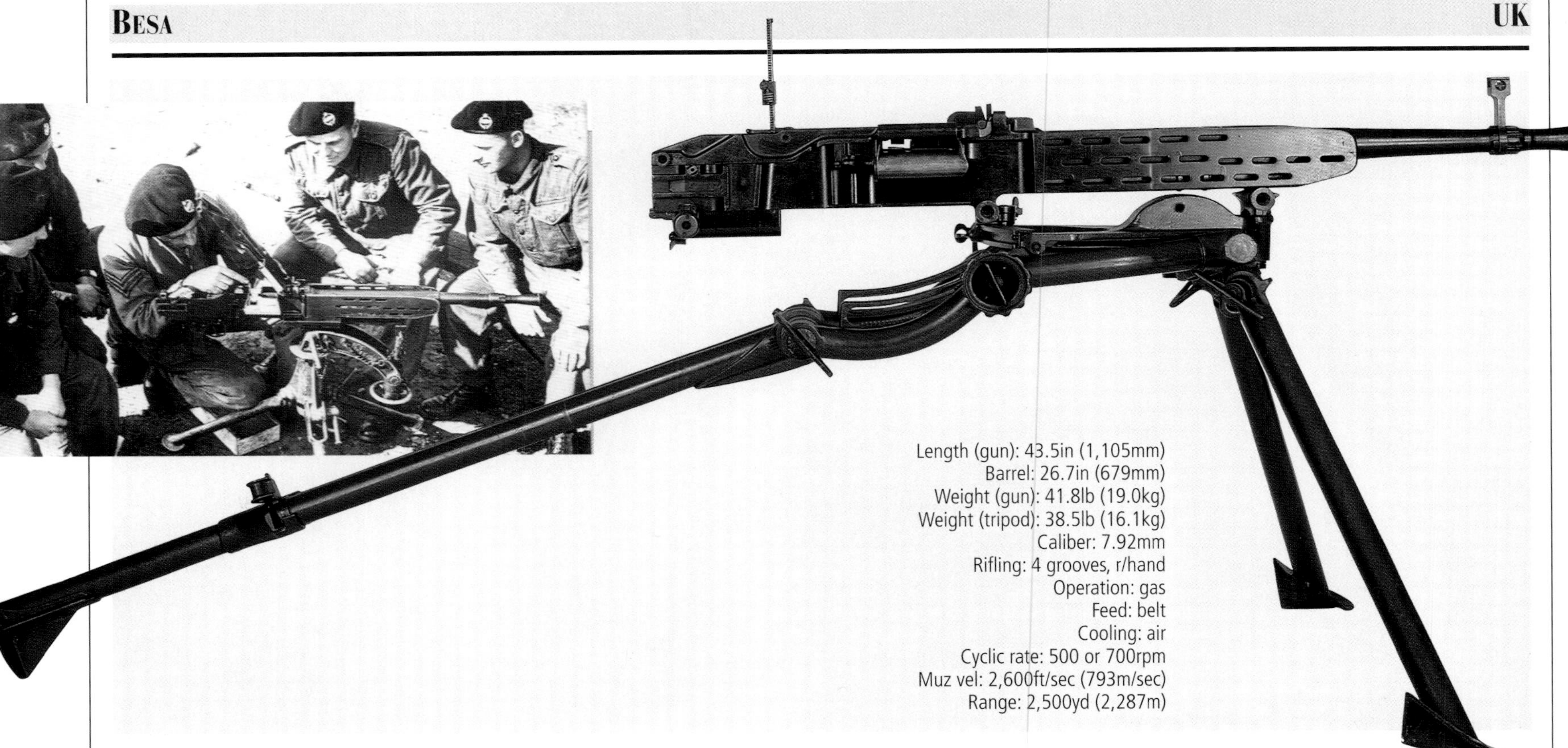

Length (gun): 43.5in (1,105mm)
Barrel: 26.7in (679mm)
Weight (gun): 41.8lb (19.0kg)
Weight (tripod): 38.5lb (16.1kg)
Caliber: 7.92mm
Rifling: 4 grooves, r/hand
Operation: gas
Feed: belt
Cooling: air
Cyclic rate: 500 or 700rpm
Muz vel: 2,600ft/sec (793m/sec)
Range: 2,500yd (2,287m)

The Czech-designed ZB 53 was strictly speaking gas-operated, but the barrel also moved back under the force of the recoil, the timing being so arranged that the cartridge was fed into the chamber and fired as the barrel went forward. This, of course, meant that the backward force of the recoil had first to arrest, and then reverse, the forward movement, which had the effect not only of diminishing the next recoil considerably but also reducing various stresses and strains on the weapon generally. The guns had very heavy barrels, some finned, which allowed for sustained fire, and the earlier models also had the means to vary their cyclic rate of fire from 450 to 850 rounds per minute. All reports indicated that the gun was a success; indeed, it was so reliable that in 1937 there was a possibility that it would replace the Vickers gun in the ground role. The reason it did not do so was due to the fact that it fired the 7.92mm rimless round and could not be modified to handle the rimmed 0.303in British cartridge. The weapon illustrated is something of a mystery, since although it is an obvious ZB 53 is bears no markings of any kind. It seems probable that it is one of the early prototypes sent from Czechoslovakia to England for testing, mounted on the standard Czech Model 45 tripod, which offers a rigid platform. In 1936 the Birmingham Small Arms Company came to an arrangement with ZB under which they were allowed to manufacture the No 53 gun, under the name "Besa," from the initial letters of Brno and Enfield and the last two of BSA. There was a larger version, also for tanks, which was produced in 0.59in (15mm) caliber.

VANDENBURGH VOLLEY GUN — USA

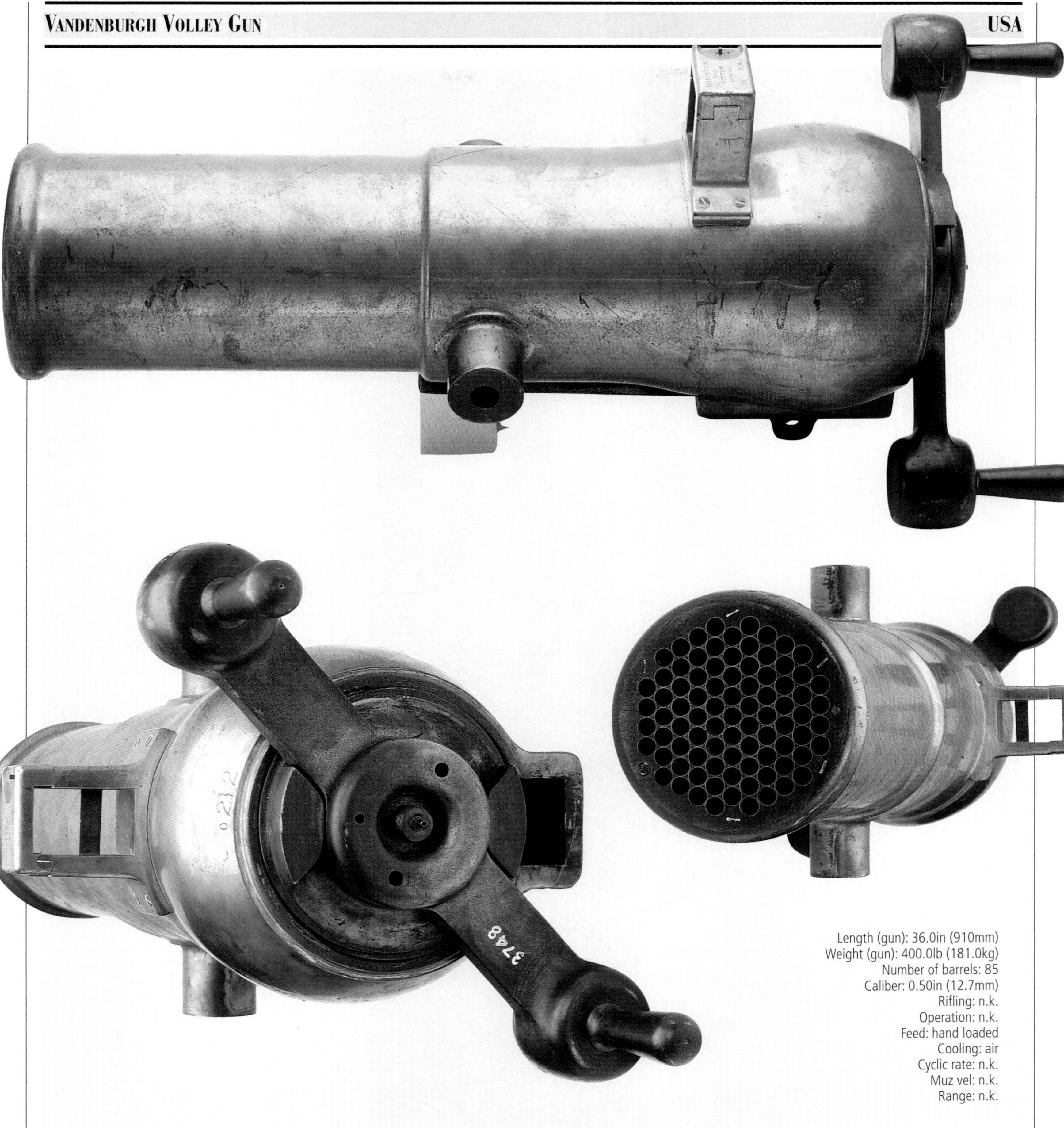

Length (gun): 36.0in (910mm)
Weight (gun): 400.0lb (181.0kg)
Number of barrels: 85
Caliber: 0.50in (12.7mm)
Rifling: n.k.
Operation: n.k.
Feed: hand loaded
Cooling: air
Cyclic rate: n.k.
Muz vel: n.k.
Range: n.k.

Although not strictly speaking a machine gun, this weapon deserves mention as one of the steps taken in the middle of the 19th Century on the way towards a fully automatic weapon. The Volley Gun"s history was convoluted, to say the least, since it was designed and developed in 1860 by a Northerner, General Origen Vandenburgh of the New York State Militia. Having failed to find a manufacturer in his home country, the gun was produced in small numbers by a British gunsmith, Robinson and Cottam of London, but when it failed to find a market in Europe, Vandenburgh sold it to the Confederate Army (even though he was a Northerner!). The weapon consisted of a cast brass barrel containing 85 individual 0.50in (12.7mm) rifled barrels, each of which had to be individually loaded by hand. The screw breech was then closed and secured using the large handles, which made an airtight seal with the firing chamber. A single percussion cap in the center of the breech fired all rounds simultaneously. The weapon would have had a devastating effect upon densely packed infantry at close quarters, but would have taken a long time to reload. The square device above the breech is a sight and the trunnions show that the weapon must have rested on a simple artillery mount, in the same manner as the contemporary Gatling (qv). This particular example was captured by Union cavalry near Salisbury, North Carolina, in April 1865 and is now exhibited in the museum at the United States Military Academy, West Point.

Gatling, 0.45in, Model 1875 — USA

Length (gun): 59.4in (1,360mm)
Barrels: 31.9in (812mm)
Weight (with carriage): 444.0lb (201.4kg)
Number of barrels: 6
Caliber: 0.45in (11.43mm)
Rifling: 7 grooves, r/hand
Operation: mechanical
Feed: various (see text)
Cooling: air
Cyclic rate: 800rpm
Muz vel: n.k.
Range: n.k.

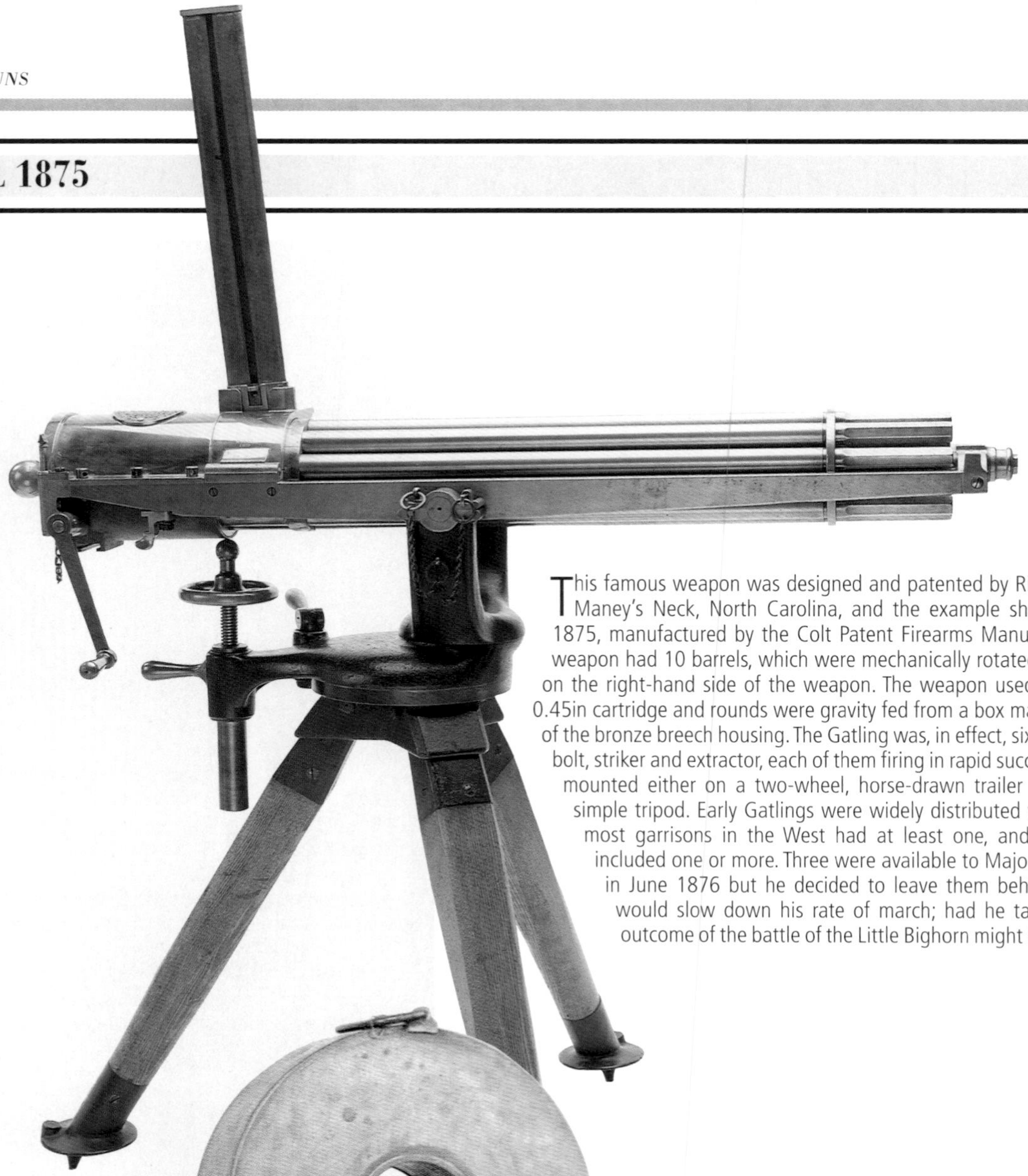

This famous weapon was designed and patented by Richard Jordan Gatling of Maney's Neck, North Carolina, and the example shown here is the Model 1875, manufactured by the Colt Patent Firearms Manufacturing Company. The weapon had 10 barrels, which were mechanically rotated and fired using a lever on the right-hand side of the weapon. The weapon used the US Army standard 0.45in cartridge and rounds were gravity fed from a box magazine mounted on top of the bronze breech housing. The Gatling was, in effect, six rifles, each with its own bolt, striker and extractor, each of them firing in rapid succession. The weapon was mounted either on a two-wheel, horse-drawn trailer or (as seen here) on a simple tripod. Early Gatlings were widely distributed within the US Army and most garrisons in the West had at least one, and most field expeditions included one or more. Three were available to Major-General George Custer in June 1876 but he decided to leave them behind as he felt that they would slow down his rate of march; had he taken them with him the outcome of the battle of the Little Bighorn might have been very different.

Gatling, 0.45in, Model 1883 — USA

Length (gun): 42.5in (1,080mm)
Barrel: 24in (610mm)
Weight (gun): 260.0lb (118.0kg)
Number of barrels: 10
Caliber: 0.45in (11.4mm)
Rifling: n.k.
Operation: mechanical
Feed: circular magazine
Cooling: air
Cyclic rate: ca 200rpm
Muz vel: n.k.
Range: n.k.

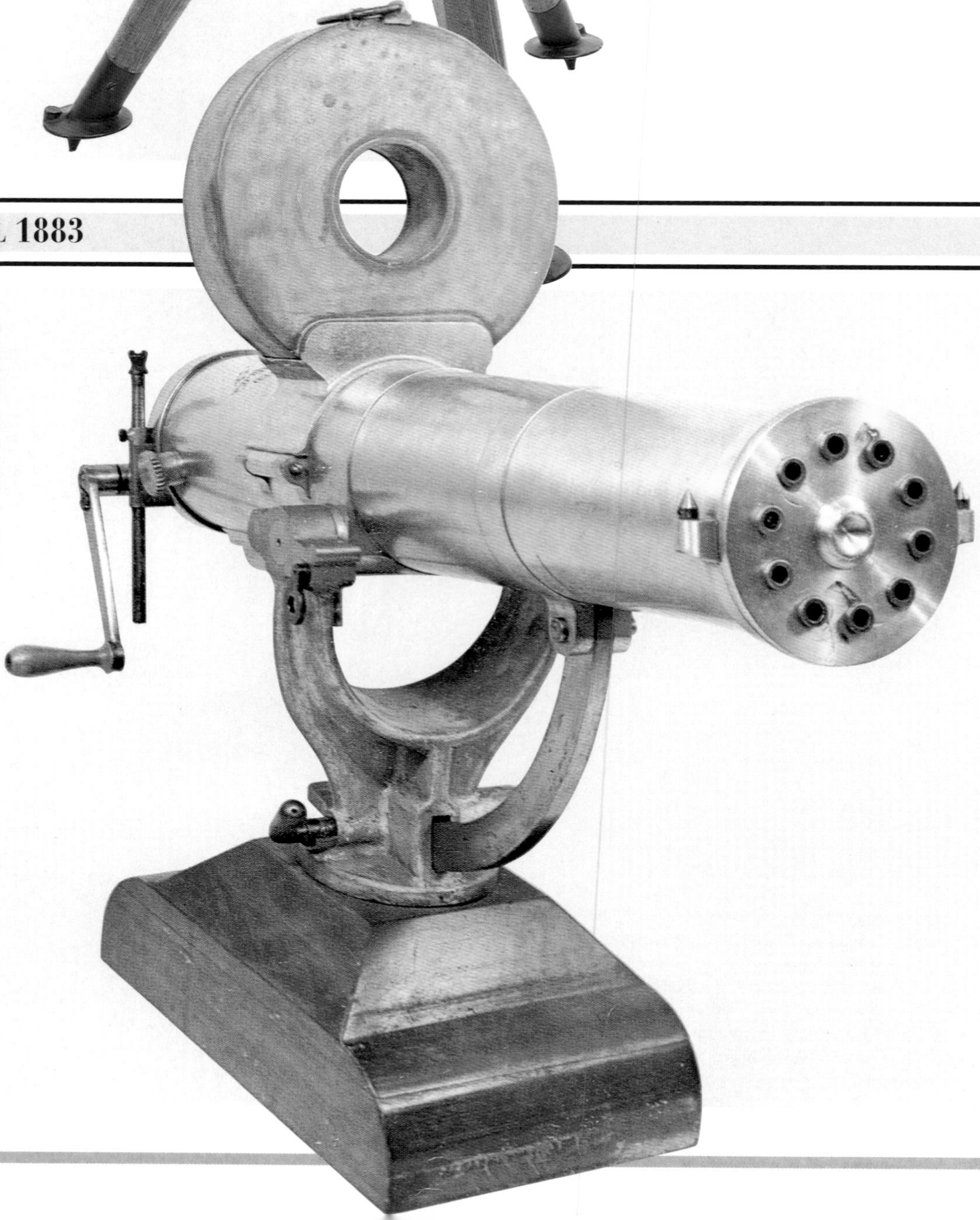

Gatling and Colt produced several improved versions of the Gatling machine gun, that shown here being the Model 1883, which had 10 barrels enclosed in a brass casing. These barrels were fed by a circular Accles patent magazine placed centrally above the gun, which meant, as can be seen from the picture, that the sights were displaced to the right. As with the earlier model, the weapon rested in an artillery-type trunnion mounting and was lockable in elevation. Gatlings were regularly used by late-Victorian armies against unsophisticated enemies; for example, by the US Army in the American West and by European armies in their many colonial wars in Africa and Asia. In such engagements, the employment of Gatlings could be crucial. They also found naval use, where they were mounted in the fighting tops and intended for use in sweeping the decks of enemy ships or repelling boarders, although the rapidly increasing range of ships' main guns meant that this diminished rapidly in importance. Gatlings could also, however, be used in close-range naval engagements against torpedo-boats, for which 0.65in (16.5mm) and even 1in (25mm) Gatlings were developed. Ship-mounted Gatlings were also used against land artillery crews serving open batteries. All Gatling guns suffered from two basic problems. First, their black-powder cartridges generated a dense cloud of smoke, which hampered visibility, often at a critical moment. This led to a demand for smokeless powder, which was quickly met. The other was that the nature of the mechanics required a steady and even turning of the handle, but, not surprisingly, the firer could become excited in action, turn the crank too fast and cause a jam, which, almost by definition, would happen at precisely the wrong moment.

Colt-Browning Model 1895/1904/1917 — USA

Length (gun): 40.8in (1,035mm)
Barrel: 28.0in (712mm)
Weight (gun): 35.0lb (15.9kg)
Weight (tripod): 61.3lb (27.8kg)
Caliber: 0.30in
Rifling: 4 grooves, r/hand
Operation: gas
Feed: belt
Cooling: air
Cyclic rate: 480rpm
Muz vel: 2,800ft/sec (855m/sec)
Range: 2,000yd (1,829m)

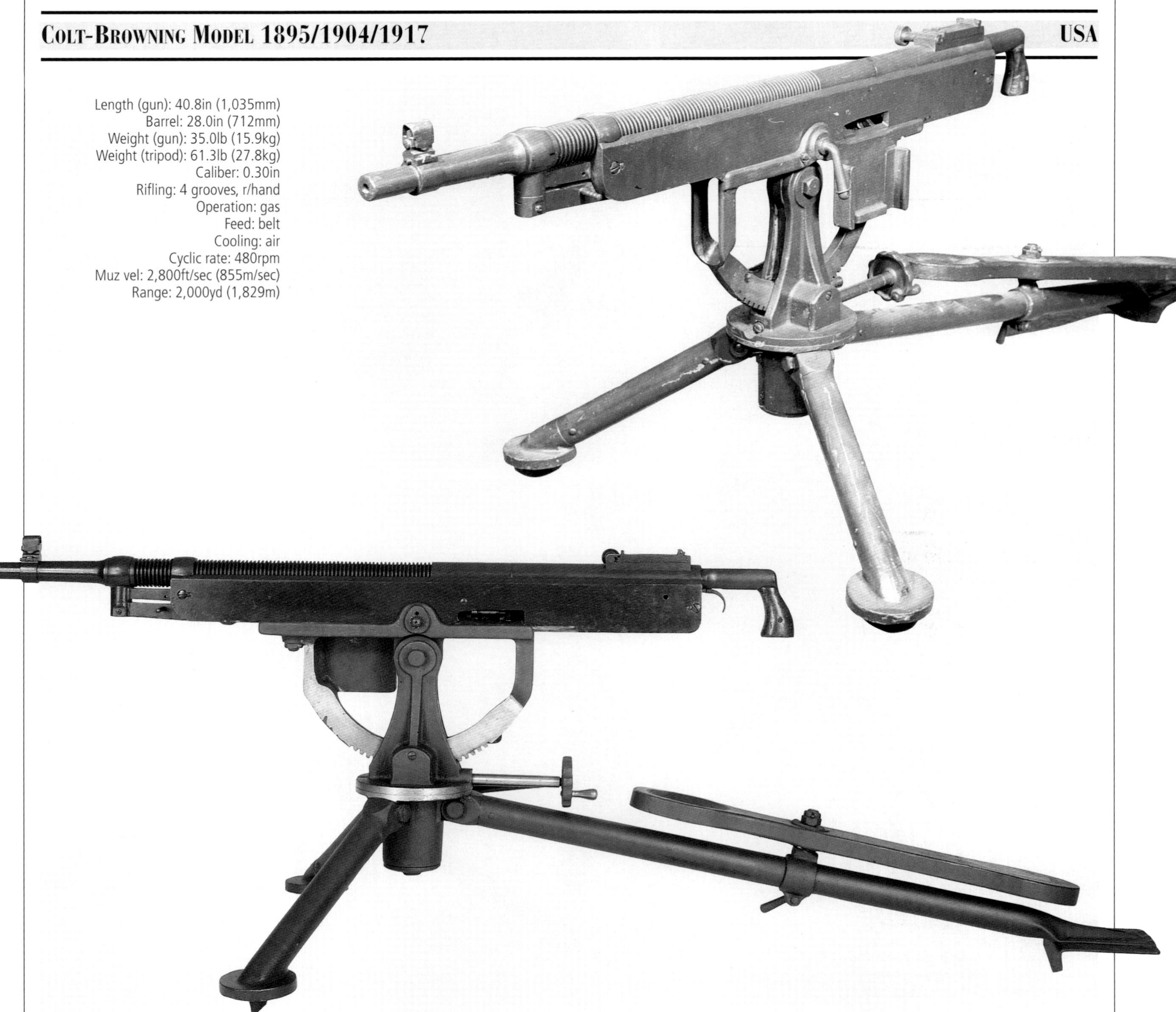

Invented by John M. Browning and produced by Colt, this gun was adopted by the US Navy in 1893 and by 1898 the whole Navy was equipped with them. The general style of the Colt gun is clear from the photographs. It worked by gas but in a somewhat unusual way in that the piston, which was below the barrel, was hinged at the rear. The gas port was situated in the bottom of the bore and when the gas passed through it struck the front end of the piston and blew it downwards through 90 degrees. A lever from this piston then activated the working parts. The gun was belt fed, had a single handle of Colt revolver type, and was mounted on an adjustable tripod. It had no cooling system beyond a heavy barrel, which limited the number of rounds it could fire without over-heating. The Navy used the Colt gun in the Spanish-American war at a time when the Army still had manually operated Gatlings which led the Army to investigate the possibility of adopting it, but it was finally decided that it was too complex for land service. In the meantime some modifications were made, and the eventual result, the Model 1904, was bought by a number of other countries. It so happened that when the United States entered World War I in 1917 its Army had no modern machine guns. A new model, the 1917 (Army), was ordered in considerable quantities, about 1,500 being supplied before the end of the war. One serious defect was that it could not be used in the prone position because the 10in (254mm) piston used to hit the ground if the gun was too low. This tendency inevitably led the United States infantrymen to nickname it the "potato digger," a name by which it is often recognized by people otherwise quite ignorant of its official designation.

BROWNING MODEL 1917 USA

Length (gun): 38.5in (978mm)
Barrel: 24.0in (610mm)
Weight (gun): 32.6lb (15.0kg)
Weight (tripod): 53.0lb (24.0kg)
Caliber: 0.30in
Rifling: 4 grooves, r/hand
Operation: recoil
Feed: belt
Cooling: water
Cyclic rate: 5/600rpm
Muz vel: 2,800ft/sec (855m/sec)
Range: 2,800yd (2,560m)

The outstanding feature of the Browning M1917 was its mechanical simplicity which not only helped mass-production but also made it relatively easy to teach to the hastily raised American troops. When the trigger was pressed (the first round having been loaded manually by means of a cocking handle which duplicated the action of the recoil) and the round fired, the barrel and breechblock recoiled together, for just over half an inch until pressure had dropped to a safe level and the barrel and breechblock unlocked, the barrel stopping, while the block continued backwards under its initial impetus. During this time the empty case was extracted from the breech and ejected from the gun, and a fresh cartridge drawn from the belt. When this backward phase was complete the return spring drove the working parts forward again, chambering the cartridge, locking the block to the barrel, and firing the round, and this cycle could continue as long as the trigger was pressed and there were rounds in the belt. The Browning gun was made in considerable variety, including air-cooled models for use in tanks and aircraft for which water-cooled weapons were clearly unsuitable, but there were no fundamental changes made mechanically. The final modification before the outbreak of World War II resulted in the Model 1917A1 (lower photos – ground-mounted left, and anti-aircraft mount right) which was introduced in 1936. World War II was the first real combat test of the Browning gun since its introduction and, as was to be expected, it turned out to be an excellent weapon. It also saw much service in Korea, and was not replaced until the early 1960s when the new M60 entered service.

Browning 0.50in Caliber M2HB USA

Length (gun): 65.0in (1,651mm)
Barrel: 45.0in 1,143mm)
Weight (gun): 84.0lb (38.1kg)
Weight (tripod): 44.0lb (19.09g)
Caliber: 0.50in
Rifling: 8 grooves, r/hand
Operation: recoil
Feed: belt
Cooling: air
Cyclic rate: 500rpm
Muz vel: 2,930ft/sec (894m/sec)
Range: 2,600yd (2,378m)

John Browning's M2 first appeared in 1933 and was intended principally for use on multiple anti-aircraft mounts but there was a version for use as a tank turret gun and yet another for use on a ground mount. It worked on the usual Browning system of short recoil. When the cartridge was fired the barrel and breechblock, securely locked together, recoiled for just under an inch when the barrel was stopped by means of an oil buffer. At this stage the pressure had dropped sufficiently for the breechblock to unlock and continue to the rear under the initial impetus given to it by the barrel, extracting and ejecting the empty case and extracting the next live round from the belt. Once the rearward action had stopped the compressed return spring then took over and drove the working parts sharply forward, chambering the round, locking the breechblock, and firing the cartridge, after which the cycle continued as long as the trigger was pressed and there were rounds in the belt. The gun would fire automatic only, although some were equipped with bolt latches to allow single rounds to be fired if necessary. Although this gun functioned well enough mechanically it showed an unfortunate tendency to overheat, so that 70 or 80 rounds was about the maximum which could be fired continuously without a considerable pause for allowing the barrel to cool. This was of course quite unacceptable so a heavy barreled version (M2HB) was adopted, the weapon illustrated being one of these. The extra metal in the barrel made a considerable difference and this new gun was most effective, being extensively used by the United States and many other countries in the course of World War II and all subsequent campaigns up to the present day. The upper photo shows a Belgian FN version with quick-change barrel, and the lower photo shows the MsHB mounted on a Land Rover Defender Combat Vehicle

GLOSSARY

ACP round: Automatic Colt Pistol, a type of ammunition.
Action: The mechanism of a firearm involved in presenting the cartridge for firing and in ejecting the spent case and introducing a fresh cartridge.
Aperture sights: A type of iron sights in which the backsight takes the form of a small hole or aperture; also called a "peep sight."
Automatic: A firearm which continues firing for as long as the trigger remains depressed or until the magazine or belt containing extra ammunition runs empty. A machine gun.
Automatic ejection: A system predominantly used on breakopen revolvers on which, as the barrel is tipped down, the ejector is automatically activated to clear the chambers. See "Hand ejection" and Rod ejection."
Automatic revolver: A rare type of revolver, of which the Webley Fosbery and the Union are the best known examples, that uses the recoil energy of cartridge discharge to rotate the cylinder and cock the hammer for each succeeding shot.
Backstrap: The rear of the two gripstraps on a handgun, which lies under the heel of the hand when a firing grip is taken.
Ball: A military term for standard, full jacketed ammunition.
Ballistics: The science of cartridge discharge and the bullet's flight.
Barrel: A cylindrical part of a firearm through the bore of which the shot is fired. The barrel serves the purposes of imparting direction and velocity to the projectile or projectiles.
Battery: The disposition of parts of a firearm when the breech is locked up, ready for firing.
Bedding: The manner in which the barreled action of a rifle is fitted to the stock.
Birdshot: Shotgun pellets of comparatively small diameter, meant to be used on birds in flight and on small game such as rabbit and squirrel. See "Buckshot."
Black powder: See "Gunpowder."
Blowback: Also called "unlocked breech." Said of a self-loading or automatic firearm whose breechblock and barrel are not mechanically locked together when in battery or at the moment of firing. Used in comparatively low-powered weapons, in which the inertia of the breechblock, and casewall adhesion against the chamber, are sufficient to retard opening until breech pressures have fallen to a safe level.
Bolt: A form of breechblock, usually cylindrical in cross-section, that operates on a prolongation of the bore axis, and is withdrawn over a distance greater than the length of the cartridge, to expose the chamber. Lends itself well to magazine feeding. On a revolver, the cylinder stop.
Bolt action: A firearm that uses a mobile breechblock acting along a linear extension of the bore axis, and hand operated either on a pull-push basis, or on a turnbolt basis.
Bore: The caliber of a shotgun. See "Gauge." The interior of a gun barrel.
Bore diameter: The diameter of the inside of the barrel after boring but before rifling. The land diameter.
Bottle necked: Said of a cartridge whose projectile diameter is substantially less than the body diameter of the case. Such a case affords adequate power capacity and is necked down as required to grip the projectile.
Boxlock: A firearm – normally a double-barreled shotgun or rifle – on which the firing mechanisms are housed in recesses in the rear of the receiver. See "Sidelock."
Breech plug: A threaded plug, often incorporating the tang, that closes the breech end of the barrel of most muzzleloading firearms.
Breechblock: The part that seals the rear of the chamber and supports the casehead when the cartridge is fired. Breechloading firearms are classified according to the type of employed, and the mechanical means of locking it into place for firing and displacing it for reloading.
Breechloader: A firearm which is loaded from the rear. The firing chamber will normally be machined into the rear end of the barrel, but may be (as, for example, is the case with revolvers) a separate piece aligned with the barrel for firing.
Buckshot: A term for the larger sizes of shotgun pellets, useful against fox and feral dogs, and in an anti-personnel role, but not usually humane on deer.
Bullpup: A shoulder gun in which the receiver is located well back in the stock, so much so that the cheek is alongside the breech on firing.
Burst fire: Said of a firearm the mechanism of which is fitted with a ratchet escapement device that permits a predetermined number of shots (usually three) to be fired each time the trigger is pressed. See "Selective fire."
Buttstock or **Butt:** That portion of the stock that enables the firearm to be braced against the shoulder and cheek for firing.
Caliber: The diameter, nominal diameter, or designation of a bore, projectile or cartridge, normally expressed in hundredths of an inch or thousandths of an inch, or in millimeters, although shotgun caliber is usually expressed in a system based on fractions of a pound (e.g., 12 bore).
Cannelure: A circumferential groove or indentation round a bullet or cartridge case.
Capping breechloader: A type of early breechloader circa 1860, which was fired by a standard percussion cap which was placed on an external nipple or chimney after the breech had been closed.
Carbine: A small rifle, shorter, lighter, and handier than a full size rifle.
Cartridge: A round of ammunition consisting, in modern times, of case, primer, powder, and projectile (either single or multiple). In previous times the cartridge (from the French "cartouche") consisted of the powder and ball in a paper packet, with the percussion cap or priming powder separate.
Case: The metallic body of a cartridge, made usually of brass but sometimes of steel, aluminum or plastic.
Centerfire: A cartridge in which the primer or primer assembly is seated in a pocket or recess in the center of the base of the case. A firearm which uses centerfire cartridges.
Chamber: The part of a firearm that contains the cartridge when it is fired.
Charger: A device, normally of pressed metal, which holds a group of cartridges for easy and virtually simultaneous loading into the magazine of a firearm.
Choke: A barely discernible construction near the muzzle of a shotgun that has the function and effect of regulating pattern density, as measured by the percentage of pellets that would normally be contained in a 30in (762mm) circle at 400yd (366m). Choke classifications are: cylinder bore (40 percent), improved cylinder (50 percent), quarter choke (55 percent), half choke (60 percent), three-quarter choke (65 percent), full choke (70 percent).
Clip: A device, normally of pressed steel, which holds a group of cartridges and which is inserted into the magazine, along with the cartridges it contains, in order to reload the gun.
Cock: A pivoted piece, normally spring activated, that loads the match, pyrites or flint on a matchlock, wheellock or flintlock mechanism; often called the "dog" in Mediterranean countries.
Crane: The pivoting member on which the cylinder is mounted on a revolver, the cylinder of which swings out for loading. Also called the "yoke."
Crown: The form of the muzzle where the bore emerges, normally chamfered or recessed.
Cylinder stop: On a revolver, the part, normally spring activated and housed in the floor of the frame, which engages in the cylinder stop notch (also called "bolt cut") arresting the cylinder's rotation and locking it so that the chamber to be fired is locked in alignment with the barrel.
Delayed blowback: Also called "retarded blowback" and "hesitation locked." Said of a self-loading or automatic firearm whose breechblock and barrel are not positively locked together, but which incorporates a mechanism which causes the breechblock to operate against an initial mechanical disadvantage, thus delaying its opening.
Double-action: A revolver or pistol on which a long pull-through on the trigger will rock the hammer back against the mainspring and release it at the top of its travel to fire the shot. On a revolver, subsequent shots may be fired the same way; on a pistol, the slide will normally cock the hammer after the first shot so that subsequent shots are taken with just a light pressure on the trigger.
Ejector: A part whose function is to throw a spent case clear of the gun.
Ejector star: On a revolver, the collective ejector, operating through the cylinder axis which, when activated, clears all chambers at once. The ratchet is normally machined as part of the ejector star.
Elevation: Vertical disparity in a bullet's flight, due to errors in range estimation or what have you. See "Windage."
Extractor: A part, normally hook- or crescent-shaped, which withdraws a spent case from the chamber.
Face: The front surface of the standing breech on a breakopen shotgun – the surface that supports the base of the cartridge. A worn gun with looseness or space at the breech is said to be "off the face."
Falling block: An action type in which the breechblock, usually lever operated, moves vertically (or nearly so) in internal receiver mortises. A very strong, compact, and usually elegant action.
Firearm: A lethal, barreled weapon which uses the pressure of combustion-generated gases to propel a projectile or group of projectiles.
Firing pin: In a hammer-fired gun, that part which physically impacts the primer to detonate it. NB, a striker-fired gun does not have a firing pin. See "Striker."
Flash hider: A device, usually consisting of linear slots or prongs, fitted to the muzzles of some firearms, designed to break up and minimize flash.
Flintlock: A system widely used in the 17th-19th Centuries in which ignition is achieved by striking a flint against an upright steel face called the frizzen. The resultant sparks ignite the priming powder in the pan, which burn through the touch hole to ignite the main charge in the barrel.
Fore-end: The portion of a gun or rifle stock located ahead of the receiver, which is normally gripped by the left hand.
Frame: The receiver of a revolver or pistol.
Freebore: The distance between the front of the bearing surface of the chambered bullet and the beginning of the rifling. Zero freebore gives best accuracy.
Frizzen: The vertical iron face of a flintlock gun against which the flint strikes to produce sparks. Usually formed as a vertical extension of the pan cover.
Front locking: Said of a bolt-action gun which has locking lugs on the front of the bolt which engage in corresponding mortises either in front of the receiver or in the rear of the barrel, or in an intermediate sleeve or collar between the two, and immediately behind the chamber.
Frontstrap: The forward of the two gripstraps on a handgun, that falls underneath the fingers when a firing grip is taken.
Gas-operated: Said of a self-loading or automatic firearm which uses combustion gases, tapped via a port along the barrel, to impulse a piston that cycles the action. Gas-operated systems are classified as long stroke, short stroke or direct delivery.
Gas-retarded: Said of a firearm if gas bled from the bore is used not to cycle the action but to delay its opening by acting to hold the breech closed. See "Delayed blowback."
Gauge: The caliber of a shotgun, usually expressed in fractions of a pound. British: "bore" as in "12 bore," "20 bore," etc. The bore diameter of a 12 gauge gun would correspond to the diameter of a spherical lead ball weighing 0.5lb (0.23kg).
Grain: An avoirdupois unit of measurement used for expressing the weight of cartridge components. There are 7,000 grains to the pound; one grain = 0.002285 ounce or 64.79891 milligrams.
Groove: The spiral cut produced by a rifling cutter.
Gunpowder: Also called black powder, the standard propellant for firearms from their introduction in the early 14th Century until the late 19th Century when black powder was quickly superseded by smokeless powder.
Hammer: The part, powered by the mainspring, that is driven round its axis of rotation, and drives the firing pin into the base of the chambered cartridge. The firing pin may or may not be part of the hammer. See "Firing pin" and "Striker."
Hammer spur: The thumbpiece on the top rear of the hammer that enables it to be drawn to full cock.
Hammerless: Said of a firearm, particularly a shotgun, without visible, external hammers. Most such guns are in fact hammer fired, but use internal hammers.
Hand ejection: A system most often used on swingout cylinder revolvers, in which the ejector rod is pushed rearward by hand in order to clear the chambers. See "Automatic ejection" and "Rod ejection."
Handgun: A firearm intended to be aimed and fired in the hand or hands, without being braced against the shoulder and cheek. A catch-all term for any pistol or revolver.
Hangfire: A cartridge which discharges after a delay. Dangerous.
Headspace: The distance between the face of the breechblock in battery and the point at which the cartridge case abuts against the chamber, normally the front surface of the rim, belt, shoulder or mouth.
Heeled bullet: An early type of revolver bullet which had a reduced diameter heel which seated in the mouth of the cartridge case.
Hinged frame: A breakopen gun, that hinges open for loading or disassembly.
Hollow point: A bullet with a hollow in the nose, designed to mushroom on impact.
Iron sights: A sighting system consisting normally of a foresight and backsight not containing glass or reflective elements, magnifying or not.
Jacket: The skin or covering of a composite bullet, usually made of copper, gilding metal, cupro-nickel or mild steel. The core, inside the jacket, is normally of a lead alloy. The jacket is hard enough to hold rifling at velocities that would strip a lead bullet.
Lands: The upstanding ridges of metal left between the grooves when a barrel is rifled. The lands bite into the bullet, causing it to spin in flight, thus imparting gyrostatic stability and preventing it from tumbling end over end.
LC: Long Colt, a type of ammunition.
Lever action: A firearm that uses a breechblock that is operated by a downward rotational action on a sidelever or underlever.
Lock: The ignition mechanism of a firearm, e.g. matchlock, wheellock, flintlock, miquelet lock, percussion lock, sidelock, boxlock, back action lock, etc.
Locked breech: Self-loading or automatic

firearm whose breechblock and barrel are mechanically locked together when in battery and at the moment of firing.
Lockplate: The flat metal plate on which the mechanism or lock of early firearms is mounted.
Long recoil: A recoil operated firearm in which the barrel and breechblock are locked together for the full distance of travel, after which the barrel returns forward while the breechblock is retained rearward. When the barrel has fully returned, the breechblock is released to fly forward, chambering a fresh cartridge in the process.
Long stroke: Said of a gas-operated firearm if the piston is attached to the bolt and accompanies it during the full length of the operating cycle.
LR: Long Rifle, a designation of the most popular variety of 0.22in rimfire cartridge, universally used in pistols as well as rifles.
Machine carbine: A submachine gun.
Machine pistol: European continental parlance, a submachine gun, sometimes applied to a pistol, with or without buttstock attachment, capable of fully automatic fire.
Magazine: The part of a firearm containing the reserve ammunition supply, and out of which cartridges are mechanically fed to the chamber for firing.
Magnum: A term borrowed from the vintner's trade to designate a cartridge that is notably powerful.
Mainspring: The spring, in a firearm, which powers the hammer or striker.
Matchlock: An early ignition system in which a smouldering "match" – usually a nitrate-soaked cord – was applied directly to the priming powder in the flashpan to ignite it to burn through the touch hole and ignite the main charge.
Mauser type: Said of a bolt-action rifle containing many of the design elements of the Model 1898 Mauser, notably twin forward locking lugs, an integral double column magazine, and often a collar-mounted external extractor and fixed ejector.
Misfire: A cartridge which fails to discharge.
Musket: A smoothbore military shoulder gun intended to fire a single projectile, normally a round ball of nearly bore diameter.
Muzzle brake: A device fitted to or machined into the muzzle of a firearm and intended to reduce recoil and muzzle flip by redirecting the combustion gases.
Muzzle-loader: A firearm that loads from the front end: the end of the barrel (muzzle) or, in the case of revolvers, the front of the cylinder.
Muzzle velocity: The speed of the bullet, measured in feet per second or meters per second, a short distance from the muzzle.
Neck: The constricted forward section of a bottle-necked cartridge case – the portion that grips the bullet.
Neck (v): To alter the diameter of the neck of a cartridge case so as to change its caliber. Thus, the 0.25-06 is the 0.30-06 necked down to 0.25in caliber, while the 0.35in Whelen is the 0.30-06 necked out to 0.35in caliber.
Needle-fire: A transitional ignition type in which the firing pin took the form of a "needle" which was driven forward through the base of the cartridge, through the powder charge, until it impacted the primer, which was affixed to the base of the bullet.
Ogive: The curved portion of a bullet between the bearing surface and the tip.
Open frame: Said of a revolver frame which has no topstrap.
Open sights: A sighting system consisting of a post or bead foresight and a notch, V or groove backsight.
Over-and-under: A double-barreled gun on which the two barrels are mounted one above the other.
Pepperbox: A type of early percussion revolver with a barrel cluster rather like a long cylinder (but with no single, separate barrel) and with a bar type hammer striking from above. Normally double-action only. Popular during the early and mid-19th Century.
Pinfire: A metallic cartridge in which the primer is normally contained, cup upward, in a base wad and which is discharged by the blow of the hammer, falling at 90 degrees to the axis of the cartridge, which drives a protruding pin into the primer. A gun which takes cartridges of this type.
Pistol: A handgun. In normal usage, the term "pistol" refers to any handgun except revolvers, and includes self-loaders, manual repeaters, single-shots, double- or multi-barreled pistols, and freak types such as belt buckle pistols, cutlass pistols, and so forth.
Pitch: Also called twist. The rate at which rifling turns, measured in calibers, inches or centimeters. A typical pitch would be one turn in 14 inches (35.56cm).
Port pressure: In a gas-operated firearm, the peak pressure over the gas port; determines port diameter.
Primer: The part of the cartridge that ignites the propellant powder. In a metallic cartridge, the primer is part of the assembly, but earlier ignition systems used various types of separate and external primers. A modern primer consists essentially of the cup, anvil, and pellet, the latter usually a lead styphnate based compound, although mercury fulminate was previously used.
Primer pocket: The counterbore in the center of the base of a centerfire cartridge in which the primer assembly is seated.
Proof: The testing of forearms for their ability to withstand safely the pressure of cartridge discharge.
Proof mark: A mark or symbol stamped or engraved on a firearm to indicate that it has successfully been proof tested.
Pump-action: A firearm that employs a breechblock that is operated by linear manual pressure, normally on a mobile fore-end, although variants with mobile pistol grips or handgrips exist.
Ramrod: A rod, normally of wood or iron, used for loading a muzzle-loading firearm, and normally stored in a groove underneath the barrel.
Rear locking: Said of a bolt-action gun on which the locking lugs are toward the rear of the bolt and which lock into the receiver behind the magazine well.
Receiver: The principal structural component of a firearm. The buttstock is attached to the back of the receiver, the barrel, and fore-end to the front, and the action operates within it. Called the "frame" on a revolver or pistol.
Recoil lug: A lug or face, normally on the underside or rear of a receiver that transfers the forces of recoil from the barrel/receiver group to the stock.
Recoil-operated: Said of a self-loading or automatic firearm operated by mobile components – the barrel and breechblock – which recoil rearward in reaction to the projectile, which is being propelled forward. See "Short recoil" and "Long recoil."
Repeater: A firearm containing reserve ammunition which may be discharged, shot after shot, until the reserve is exhausted, as opposed to a single-shot firearm, for which the reserve ammunition is normally carried in a belt, pocket or pouch worn by the shooter.
Revolver: A repeating handgun that carries its cartridges in a cylinder that is drilled linearly with chambers that are disposed round a common central axis. Each chamber contains a cartridge, and is rotated into alignment with the barrel for firing. See "Pistol," "Cylinder," and "Chamber."
Rifle: A shoulder gun intended to fire a solid or composite projectile of bore diameter, and having a rifled barrel designed to impart a spin to the projectile. See "Musket," "Shotgun," and "Carbine."
Rifling: A series of spiral grooves cut or formed into the interior of a barrel. The upstanding ridges of metal between the grooves are termed lands.
Rimfire: A metallic cartridge in which the priming compound is deposited centrifugally in the hollow rim of the case round its entire circumference. The firing pin crushes the rim against the rear face of the barrel, which serves as an anvil for the purpose.
Rimless: Said of a cartridge of which the base diameter and body diameter are the same. Such a case will normally have an extraction groove machined round it, yielding a "rim" of body diameter.
Rod ejection: A system primarily used on solid frame revolvers, in which ejection is accomplished by rotating the cylinder so that each chamber in turn aligns with the ejector rod mounted under the barrel, and with the loading gate, out through which the spent case may be pushed.
Round: A unit of ammunition consisting of the primer, case, propellant, and bullet. A cartridge.
Safety: A mechanical device intended to prevent accidental discharge; may be either manually operated at will, such as a thumblever or crossbolt, or an automatic safety such as a firing pin block or magazine disconnector, or indeed something between the two, such as a grip safety.
Sear: The piece – either part of the trigger or an intermediate piece – that holds the hammer or striker at full cock, Pressure on the trigger causes the sear to release the hammer or striker to fly forward and fire the shot.
Selective fire: Said of a firearm capable of either semi- or full automatic fire, or semi-automatic or burst fire, or all three. Most selective fire weapons have a selector switch or lever; some have separate triggers for each mode while others fire semi-auto on short pulls and automatic on a long pull of the same trigger.
Self-loader: A firearm which harnesses the energy of cartridge discharge to extract and eject the spent case and to load a fresh cartridge into the chamber. Also called semi-automatic or, sometimes, automatic.
Semi-automatic: Self-loader.
Short recoil: A recoil-operated firearm in which the barrel and breechblock are locked together through a short distance of travel, whereupon the two are uncoupled, the barrel is arrested, and the breechblock continues rearward, extracting the spent case from the chamber. Most self-loading pistols are of short recoil operation. See "Recoil-operated" and "Long recoil."
Short stroke: Said of a gas-operated firearm if the piston operates over only a short distance and impulses the bolt and bolt carrier rearward. Also called "tappet-operated."
Shot: A pellet of a shotgun cartridge; alternatively, all of the pellets or the pattern of the pellets from a shotgun cartridge. The effect or the noise or the incident of a cartridge being fired. The person who shoots.
Shotgun: A smoothbore shoulder gun intended for the most part to fire shells containing a number of small round pellets, the size of which varies according to the application.
Shoulder gun: A firearm meant to be fired supported by the shoulder and cheek, as opposed to a handgun. A catch-all term for any rifle, shotgun or combination gun.
Side-by-side: A double-barreled gun on which the two barrels are mounted one beside the other, i.e., in a horizontal plane.
Sidelock: A firearm – normally a double-barreled shotgun or rifle – on which the lockwork is mounted on detachable lockplates which are mortised into the stock on either side, just to the rear of the receiver.
Silencer: A sound moderator.
Single-action: A revolver or pistol on which the hammer must be cocked before the first shot may be fired. On single-action revolvers, the hammer must be drawn to full cock for each shot; on pistols, the slide will automatically recock the hammer for the second and subsequent shots. See "Double-action."
Small arm: A firearm capable of being carried and used by one man, as opposed to crew-served weapons.
Smokeless powder: A form of nitrocellulose-based propellant which replaced gunpowder in small arms cartridges at the end of the 19th Century. Smokeless powder is classified as single-based or double-based depending on whether the nitrocellulose is used with a nitroglycerine additive.
Smoothbore: A firearm, such as a musket or shotgun, which is not rifled. A shotgun.
Snaphaunce: An early type of flintlock in which the frizzen and the pan were separate parts.
Solid frame: Said of a revolver on which the frame window is broached through a solid piece; i.e., the construction is neither breakopen nor open-framed. Most swing-out cylinder revolvers have solid frames.
Sound moderator: A device attached to the muzzle of a firearm, and sometimes sleeving the barrel and parts of the breech as well, intended to attenuate the noise of cartridge discharge by containing the expanding gases until they have slowed to subsonic levels.
Speedloader: A device that carries revolver cartridges in circular pattern, enabling a revolver to be reloaded in a single gesture.
Standing breech: The receiver face that supports the casehead when the chambered cartridge is fired in certain types of firearm, notably revolvers and breakopen shotguns and rifles.
Stock: The part of a firearm that facilitates its being held for firing, notably the butt, fore-end, pistol grip, handguard, etc.
Striker: In a gun that does not have a hammer, the part that impacts the primer to detonate it. A striker is itself powered by the mainspring, and operates linearly; a hammer operate rotationally. See "Firing pin" and ""Hammer."
Submachine gun: A fully automatic or selective fire weapon of pistol caliber.
Tipping block: An action type in which the breechblock, usually lever-operated, is hinged at the back and tips down at the front to expose the chamber.
Tipping bolt: Said of a bolt type breechblock which tips to lock. Normally a square face on the rear underside of the bolt will lock against a corresponding face on the receiver.
Topstrap: Part of a revolver frame extending over the top of the cylinder and connecting the top of the standing breech with the forward portion of the frame into which the barrel is screwed.
Trajectory: The arc described by a projectile from the muzzle to its point of impact.
Transitional revolver: An early type of percussion revolver with a pepperbox action but with a single, rifled barrel.
Trigger: A part which, when pressed, releases the hammer or striker to fire the gun.
Trigger bar: On a self-loading pistol, or any other firearm in which the trigger is at some distance from the sear, an intermediate piece connecting the two parts.
Twist: The rate at which rifling causes the bullet to rotate. See "Pitch."
WCF: Winchester Center Fire; a type of ammunition.
Web: The wall of brass between the casehead and the combustion chamber or case body.
Wheellock: An early ignition system in which a serrated steel wheel was spun against iron pyrites contained in a clamp in order to generate sparks to ignite the priming charge.
Windage: The lateral deflection in a bullet's flight, due to wind drift, the earth's rotation, sighting error or whatever. See "Elevation."
Yoke: See "Crane."

INDEX

1
2
3
4
6
7
8
11
12
13